SEA SWEPT

NORA ROBERTS

JOVE
New York

A JOVE BOOK
Published by Berkley
An imprint of Penguin Random House LLC
penguinrandomhouse.com

Copyright © 1998 by Nora Roberts
Excerpt from *Naked in Death* by J. D. Robb copyright © 1995 by Nora Roberts
Penguin Random House supports copyright. Copyright fuels creativity, encourages
diverse voices, promotes free speech, and creates a vibrant culture. Thank you for buying
an authorized edition of this book and for complying with copyright laws by not
reproducing, scanning, or distributing any part of it in any form without permission.
You are supporting writers and allowing Penguin Random House to continue to
publish books for every reader.

A JOVE BOOK, BERKLEY, and the BERKLEY & B colophon
are registered trademarks of Penguin Random House LLC.

ISBN: 9780515121841

Jove mass-market edition / January 1998
Berkley trade paperback edition / May 2013

Printed in the United States of America
52 54 56 58 60 61 59 57 55 53

Cover design and photo composition by Rita Frangie

Welcome to Nora Roberts's captivating saga about the lives and loves of a family on the windswept shores of the Chesapeake Bay.

Cameron, Ethan, Phillip, and Seth are four brothers bound by the love of the extraordinary couple who raised them. Now grown and living on their own, the oldest Quinns must return home to honor their father's last request. . . .

A champion boat racer, Cameron Quinn traveled the world spending his winnings on champagne and women. But when his dying father calls him home to care for Seth, a troubled young boy not unlike Cameron once was, his life changes overnight.

After years of independence, Cameron has to learn to live with his brothers again, while he struggles with cooking, cleaning, and caring for a difficult boy. In the end, a social worker will decide Seth's fate, and as tough as she is beautiful, she has the power to bring the Quinns together—or tear them apart. . . .

"A book that just drips with guyness. . . . *Sea Swept* proves that Nora Roberts is very good at writing true-to-life male characters."
—All About Romance

Don't miss the other books
in the Chesapeake Bay Saga

RISING TIDES
INNER HARBOR
CHESAPEAKE BLUE

Turn the page for a complete list of titles by
Nora Roberts and J. D. Robb from Berkley. . . .

Nora Roberts

HOT ICE
SACRED SINS
BRAZEN VIRTUE
SWEET REVENGE
PUBLIC SECRETS
GENUINE LIES
CARNAL INNOCENCE
HONEST ILLUSIONS
DIVINE EVIL
PRIVATE SCANDALS
HIDDEN RICHES
TRUE BETRAYALS
MONTANA SKY
SANCTUARY
HOMEPORT
THE REEF
RIVER'S END
CAROLINA MOON
THE VILLA
MIDNIGHT BAYOU
THREE FATES
BIRTHRIGHT
NORTHERN LIGHTS
BLUE SMOKE
ANGELS FALL
HIGH NOON
TRIBUTE
BLACK HILLS
THE SEARCH
CHASING FIRE
THE WITNESS
WHISKEY BEACH
THE COLLECTOR
TONIGHT AND ALWAYS
THE LIAR
THE OBSESSION

Series

eBooks by Nora Roberts

Nora Roberts & J. D. Robb

REMEMBER WHEN

J. D. Robb

For Mary Blayney
of the warm and generous heart

PROLOGUE

PROLOGUE

CAMERON QUINN WASN'T quite drunk. He could get there if he put his mind to it, but at the moment he preferred the nice comfortable buzz of the nearly there. He liked to think it was just the two-steps-short-of-sloppy state that was holding his luck steady.

He believed absolutely in the ebb and flow of luck, and right now his was flowing fast and hot. Just the day before, he'd raced his hydrofoil to victory in the world championship, edging out the competition by the point of the bow and breaking the standing record for time and speed.

He had the glory, and the hefty purse, and he'd taken both over to Monte Carlo to see how they held up.

They held up just dandy.

A few hands of baccarat, a couple of rolls of the dice, the turn of a card, and his wallet weighed heavier. Between the paparazzi and a reporter from *Sports Illustrated*, the glory showed no signs of dimming either.

Fortune continued to smile—no, make that leer, Cameron thought—by turning him toward that little jewel in the Med at the same time that popular magazine was wrapping its swimsuit-edition shoot.

1

And the leggiest of those long-stemmed gifts from God had turned her high-summer blue eyes on him, tipped her full, pouty lips up in an invitational smile a blind man could have spotted, and opted to stay on a few days longer.

And she'd made it clear that with very little effort, he could get a whole lot luckier.

Champagne, generous casinos, mindless, no-strings sex. Yes indeed, Cameron mused, luck was definitely being his kind of lady.

When they stepped out of the casino into the balmy March night, one of the ubiquitous paparazzi leaped out, snapping frantically. The woman pouted—it was, after all, her trademark look—but gave her endless mane of ribbon-straight silvery-blond hair an artful toss and shifted her killer body expertly. Her red-is-the-color-of-sin dress, barely thicker than a coat of paint, made an abrupt halt just south of the Gates of Paradise.

Cameron just grinned.

"They're such pests," she said with a hint of a lisp or a French accent. Cameron was never sure which. She sighed, testing the strength of that thin silk, and let Cameron guide her down the moon-dappled street. "Every place I look is a camera. I'm so weary of being viewed as an object for the pleasure of men."

Oh, yeah, right, he mused. And because he figured the pair of them were as shallow as a dry creek after a drought, he laughed and turned her into his arms. "Why don't we give him something to splash on page one, sugar?"

He brought his mouth down to hers. The taste of her tickled his hormones, engaged his imagination, and made him grateful their hotel was only two blocks away.

She skimmed her fingers up into his hair. She liked a man with plenty of hair, and his was full and thick and as dark as the night around them. His body was hard, all tough muscle and lean, disciplined lines. She was very choosy about the body of a potential lover, and his more than met her strict requirements.

His hands were just a bit rougher than she liked. Not

the pressure or movement of them—that was lovely—but the texture. They were a working man's hands, but she was willing to overlook their lack of class because of their skill.

His face was intriguing. Not pretty. She would never be coupled, much less allow herself to be photographed, with a man prettier than she. There was a toughness about his face, a hardness that had to do with more than tanned skin tight over bones. It was in the eyes, she thought as she laughed lightly and wiggled free. They were gray, more the color of flint than smoke, and they held secrets.

She enjoyed a man with secrets, as none of them were able to keep them from her for long.

"You're a bad boy, Cameron." The accent was on the last syllable. She tapped a finger against his mouth, a mouth that held no softness whatsoever.

"So I've always been told—" He had to think for a moment as her name skimmed along the edges of his memory. "Martine."

"Maybe, tonight, I'll let you be bad."

"I'm counting on it, sweetie." He turned toward the hotel, slanted a glance over. At six feet, she was nearly eye to eye with him. "My suite or yours?"

"Yours." She all but purred it. "Perhaps if you order up another bottle of champagne, I'll let you try to seduce me."

Cameron cocked an eyebrow, asked for his key at the desk. "I'll need a bottle of Cristal, two glasses, and one red rose," he told the clerk while keeping his eyes on Martine. "Right away."

"Yes, Monsieur Quinn, I'll take care of it."

"A rose." She fluttered at him as they walked to the elevator. "How romantic."

"Oh, did you want one too?" Her puzzled smile warned him humor wasn't going to be her strong point. So they'd forget the laughs and conversation, he decided, and shoot straight for the bottom line.

The minute the elevator doors closed them in, he pulled

her against him and met that sulky mouth with his own. He was hungry. He'd been too busy, too focused on his boat, too angled in on the race to take any time for recreation. He wanted soft skin, fragrant skin, curves, generous curves. A woman, any woman, as long as she was willing, experienced, and knew the boundary lines.

That made Martine perfect.

She let out a moan that wasn't altogether feigned for his benefit, then arched her throat for his nipping teeth. "You go fast."

He slid his hand down the silk, up again. "That's how I make my living. Going fast. Every time. Every way."

Still holding her, he circled out of the elevator, down the corridor to his rooms. Her heart was rapping hard against his, her breath catching, and her hands . . . well, he figured she knew just what she was doing with them.

So much for seduction.

He unlocked the door, shoved it open, then closed it by bracing Martine against it. He pushed the two string-width straps off her shoulders and with his eyes on hers helped himself to those magnificent breasts.

He decided her plastic surgeon deserved a medal.

"You want slow?"

Yes, the texture of his hands was rough, but God, exciting. She brought one mile-long leg up, wrapped it around his waist. He had to give her full marks for a sense of balance. "I want now."

"Good. Me too." He reached up under her excuse for a skirt and ripped away the whisper of lace beneath. Her eyes went wide, her breath thickened.

"Animal. Beast." And she fastened her teeth in his throat.

Even as he reached for his fly, the knock sounded discreetly on the door behind her head. Every ounce of blood had drained out of his head to below his belt. "Christ, service can't be that good here. Leave it outside," he demanded and prepared to take the magnificent Martine against the door.

"Monsieur Quinn, I beg your pardon. A fax just came for you. It was marked urgent."

"Tell him to go away." Martine wrapped a hand around him like a clamp. "Tell him to go to hell and fuck me."

"Hold on. I mean," he continued, unwrapping her fingers before his eyes could cross. "Wait just a minute." He shifted her behind the door, took a second to be sure he was zipped, then opened it.

"I'm sorry to disturb—"

"No problem. Thanks." Cameron dug in his pocket for a bill, didn't bother to check the denomination, and traded it for the envelope. Before the clerk could babble over the amount of the tip, Cameron shut the door in his face.

Martine gave that famous head toss again. "You're more interested in a silly fax than me. Than this." With an expert hand, she tugged the dress down, wiggling free of it like a snake shedding skin.

Cameron decided whatever she'd paid for that body, it had been worth every penny. "No, believe me, baby, I'm not. This'll just take a second." He ripped the envelope open before he could give in to the urge to ball it up, toss it over his shoulder, and dive headlong into all that female glory.

Then he read the message and his world, his life, his heart stopped.

"Oh, Jesus. Goddamn." All the wine cheerfully consumed throughout the evening swam giddily in his head, churned in his stomach, turned his knees to water. He had to lean back against the door to steady himself before reading it again.

Cam, damn it, why haven't you returned a call? We've been trying to reach you for hours. Dad's in the hospital. It's bad, as bad as it gets. No time for details. We're losing him fast. Hurry. Phillip.

Cameron lifted a hand—one that had held the wheel of dozens of boats, planes, cars that raced, one that could show a woman shuddery glimpses of heaven. And the hand shook as he dragged it through his hair.

"I have to go home."

"You are home." Martine decided to give him another chance and stepped forward to rub her body over his.

"No, I have to go." He nudged her aside and headed for the phone. "You have to go. I need to make some calls."

"You think you can tell me to go?"

"Sorry. Rain check." His mind just wouldn't engage. Absently he pulled bills out of his pocket with one hand, picked up the phone with the other. "Cab fare," he said, forgetting she was booked in the same hotel.

"Pig!" Naked and furious, she launched herself at him. If he had been steady, he'd have dodged the blow. But the slap connected, and the quick swipe. His ears rang, his cheek stung, and his patience snapped.

Cameron simply locked his arms around her, revolted when she took that as a sexual overture, and carted her to the door. He took the time to scoop up her dress, then tossed both the woman and the silk into the hall.

Her shriek rattled the teeth in his head as he threw the bolt. "I'll kill you. You pig! You bastard! I'll kill you for this. Who do you think you are? You're nothing! Nothing!"

He left Martine screaming and pounding at the door and went into the bedroom to throw a few necessities into a bag.

It looked like luck had just taken the nastiest of turns.

ONE

             CAM CALLED IN MARK-
ers, pulled strings, begged favors, and threw money in a
dozen directions. Hooking transportation from Monaco to
Maryland's Eastern Shore at one o'clock in the morning
wasn't an easy matter.

He drove to Nice, bulleting down the winding coastal
highway to a small airstrip where a friend had agreed to
fly him to Paris—for the nominal fee of a thousand American dollars. In Paris he chartered a plane, for half again
the going rate, and spent the hours over the Atlantic in a
blur of fatigue and gnawing fear.

He arrived at Washington Dulles Airport in Virginia at
just after six A.M. eastern standard time. The rental car was
waiting, so he began the drive to the Chesapeake Bay in
the dark chill of predawn.

By the time he hit the bridge crossing the bay, the sun
was up and bright, sparkling off the water, glinting off
boats already out for the day's catch. Cam had spent a
good part of his life sailing on the bay, on the rivers and
inlets of this part of the world. The man he was racing to
see had shown him much more than port and starboard.

7

Whatever he had, whatever he'd done that he could take pride in, he owed to Raymond Quinn.

He'd been thirteen and racing toward hell when Ray and Stella Quinn had plucked him out of the system. His juvenile record was already a textbook study of the roots of the career criminal.

Robbery, breaking and entering, underage drinking, truancy, assault, vandalism, malicious mischief. He'd done as he'd pleased and even then had often enjoyed long runs of luck where he hadn't been caught. But the luckiest moment of his life had been being caught.

Thirteen years old, skinny as a rail and still wearing the bruises from the last beating his father had administered. They'd been out of beer. What was a father to do?

On that hot summer night with the blood still drying on his face, Cam had promised himself he was never going back to that run-down trailer, to that life, to the man the system kept tossing him back to. He was going somewhere, anywhere. Maybe California, maybe Mexico.

His dreams had been big even if his vision, courtesy of a blackened eye, was blurry. He had fifty-six dollars and some loose change, the clothes on his back, and a piss-poor attitude. What he needed, he decided, was transportation.

He copped a ride in the cargo car of a train heading out of Baltimore. He didn't know where it was going and didn't care as long as it was away. Huddled in the dark, his body weeping at every bump, he promised himself he'd kill or he'd die before he went back.

When he crept off the train, he smelled water and fish, and he wished to God he'd thought to grab some food somewhere. His stomach was screamingly empty. Dizzy and disoriented, he began to walk.

There wasn't much there. A two-bit little town that had rolled up its streets for the night. Boats bumping at sagging docks. If his mind had been clear, he might have considered breaking into one of the shops that lined the waterfront, but it didn't occur to him until he had passed through town and found himself skirting a marsh.

The marsh's shadows and sounds gave him the willies. The sun was beginning to break through the eastern sky, turning those muddy flats and that high, wet grass gold. A huge white bird rose up, making Cam's heart skip. He'd never seen a heron before, and he thought it looked like something out of a book, a made-up one.

But the wings flashed, and the bird soared. For reasons he couldn't name, he followed it along the edge of the marsh until it disappeared into thick trees.

He lost track of how far and what direction, but instinct told him to keep to a narrow country road where he could easily tuck himself into the high grass or behind a tree if a black-and-white cruised by.

He badly wanted to find shelter, somewhere he could curl up and sleep, sleep away the pangs of hunger and the greasy nausea. As the sun rose higher, the air grew thick with heat. His shirt stuck to his back; his feet began to weep.

He saw the car first, a glossy white 'Vette, all power and grace, sitting like a grand prize in the misty light of dawn. There was a pickup beside it, rusted, rugged and ridiculously rural beside the arrogant sophistication of the car.

Cam crouched down behind a lushly blooming hydrangea and studied it. Lusted after it.

The son of a bitch would get him to Mexico, all right, and anywhere else he wanted to go. Shit, the way a machine like that would move, he'd be halfway there before anybody knew it was gone.

He shifted, blinked hard to clear his wavering vision, and stared at the house. It always amazed him that people lived so neatly. In tidy houses with painted shutters, flowers and trimmed bushes in the yard. Rockers on the front porch, screens on the windows. The house seemed huge to him, a modern white palace with soft blue trim.

They'd be rich, he decided, as resentment ground in his

stomach along with hunger. They could afford fancy houses and fancy cars and fancy lives. And a part of him, a part nurtured by a man who lived on hate and Budweiser, wanted to destroy, to beat all the bushes flat, to break all the shiny windows and gouge the pretty painted wood to splinters.

He wanted to hurt them somehow for having everything while he had nothing. But as he rose, the bitter fury wavered into sick dizziness. He clamped down on it, clenching his teeth until they, too, ached, but his head cleared.

Let the rich bastards sleep, he thought. He'd just relieve them of the hot car. Wasn't even locked, he noted and snorted at their ignorance as he eased the door open. One of the more useful skills his father had passed on to him was how to hot-wire a car quickly and quietly. Such a skill came in very handy when a man made the best part of his living selling stolen cars to chop shops.

Cam leaned in, shimmied under the wheel, and got to work.

"It takes balls to steal a man's car right out of his own driveway."

Before Cam could react, even so much as swear, a hand hooked into the back of his jeans and hauled him up and out. He swung out, and his bunched fist seemed to bounce off rock.

He got his first look at the Mighty Quinn. The man was huge, at least six-five and built like the offensive line of the Baltimore Colts. His face was weathered and wide, with a thick shock of blond hair that glinted with silver surrounding it. His eyes were piercingly blue and hotly annoyed.

Then they narrowed.

It didn't take much to hold the boy in place. He couldn't have weighed a hundred pounds, Quinn thought, if he'd fished the kid out of the bay. His face was filthy and badly battered. One eye was nearly swollen shut, while the other, dark slate gray, held a bitterness no child should feel.

There was blood dried on the mouth that managed to sneer despite it.

Pity and anger stirred in him, but he kept his grip firm. This rabbit, he knew, would run.

"Looks like you came out on the wrong end of the tussle, son."

"Get your fucking hands off me. I wasn't doing nothing."

Ray merely lifted a brow. "You were in my wife's new car at just past seven on a Saturday morning."

"I was just looking for some loose change. What's the big fucking deal?"

"You don't want to get in the habit of overusing the word 'fuck' as an adjective. You'll miss the vast variety of its uses."

The mildly tutorial tone was well over Cam's head. "Look, Jack, I was just hoping for a couple bucks in quarters. You wouldn't miss it."

"No, but Stella would have dearly missed this car if you'd finished hot-wiring it. And my name isn't Jack. It's Ray. Now, the way I figure it you've got a couple of choices. Let's outline number one: I haul your sorry butt into the house and call the cops. How do you feel about doing the next few years in a juvenile facility for bad-asses?"

Whatever color Cam had left in his face drained away. His empty stomach heaved, his palms suddenly covered in sweat. He couldn't stand a cage. Was sure he would die in a cage. "I said I wasn't stealing the goddamn car. It's a four-speed. How the hell am I supposed to drive a four-speed?"

"Oh, I have a feeling you'd manage just fine." Ray puffed out his cheeks, considered, blew out air. "Now, choice number two—"

"Ray! What are you doing out there with that boy?"

Ray glanced toward the porch, where a woman with wild red hair and a ratty blue robe stood with her hands on her hips.

"Just discussing some life choices. He was stealing your car."

"Well, for heaven's sake!"

"Somebody beat the crap out of him. Recently, I'd say."

"Well." Stella Quinn's sigh could be heard clearly across the dewy green lawn. "Bring him in and I'll take a look at him. Hell of a way to start the morning. Hell of a way. No, you get inside there, idiot dog. Fine one you are, never one bark when my car's being stolen."

"My wife, Stella." Ray's smile spread and glowed. "She just gave you choice number two. Hungry?"

The voice was buzzing in Cam's head. A dog was barking in high, delighted yips from miles and miles away. Birds sang shrilly and much too close by. His skin went brutally hot, then brutally cold. And he went blind.

"Steady there, son. I'll get you."

He fell into the oily black and never heard Ray's quiet oath.

When he woke, he was lying on a firm mattress in a room where the breeze ruffled the sheer curtains and carried in the scent of flowers and water. Humiliation and panic rose up in him. Even as he tried to sit up, hands held him down.

"Just lie still a minute."

He saw the long, thin face of the woman who leaned over him, poking, prodding. There were thousands of gold freckles over it, which for some reason he found fascinating. Her eyes were dark green and frowning. Her mouth was set in a thin, serious line. She'd scraped back her hair, and she smelled faintly of dusting powder.

Cam realized abruptly that he'd been stripped down to his tattered Jockeys. The humiliation and panic exploded.

"Get the hell away from me." His voice came out in a croak of terror, infuriating him.

"Relax now. Relax. I'm a doctor. Look at me." Stella leaned her face closer. "Look at me now. Tell me your name."

His heart thundered in his chest. "John."

"Smith, I imagine," she said dryly. "Well, if you have the presence of mind to lie, you're not doing too badly." She shined a light in his eyes, grunted. "I'd say you've got yourself a mild concussion. How many times have you passed out since you were beat up?"

"That was the first." He felt himself coloring under her unblinking stare and struggled not to squirm. "I think. I'm not sure. I have to go."

"Yes, you do. To the hospital."

"No." Terror gave him the strength to grab her arm before she could rise. If he ended up in the hospital, there would be questions. With questions came cops. With cops came the social workers. And somehow, before it was over, he'd end up back in that trailer that stank of stale beer and piss with a man who found his greatest relief in pounding on a boy half his size.

"I'm not going to any hospital. I'm not. Just give me my clothes. I've got some money. I'll pay you for the trouble. I have to go."

She sighed again. "Tell me your name. Your real one."

"Cam. Cameron."

"Cam, who did this to you?"

"I don't—"

"Don't lie to me," she snapped.

And he couldn't. His fear was too huge, and his head was starting to throb so fiercely he could barely stop the whimper. "My father."

"Why?"

"Because he likes to."

Stella pressed her fingers against her eyes, then lowered her hands and looked out of the window. She could see the water, blue as summer, the trees, thick with leaves, and the sky, cloudless and lovely. And in such a fine world, she thought, there were parents who beat their children because they liked to. Because they could. Because they were there.

"All right, we'll take this one step at a time. You've been dizzy, experienced blurred vision."

Cautious, Cam nodded. "Maybe some. But I haven't eaten in a while."

"Ray's down taking care of that. Better in the kitchen than me. Your ribs are bruised, but they're not broken. The eye's the worst of it," she murmured, touching a gentle finger to the swelling. "We can treat that here. We'll clean you up and doctor you and see how you do. I am a doctor," she told him again, and smiled as her hand, blissfully cool, smoothed his hair back. "A pediatrician."

"That's a kid doctor."

"You still qualify, tough guy. If I don't like how you do, you're going in for X-rays." She reached into her bag for antiseptic. "This is going to sting a little."

He winced, sucked in his breath as she began to treat his face. "Why are you doing this?"

She couldn't stop herself. With her free hand she brushed back a messy shock of his dark hair. "Because I like to."

THEY'D KEPT HIM. IT HAD been as simple as that, Cam thought now. Or so it had seemed to him at the time. He hadn't realized until years later how much work, effort, and money they'd invested in first fostering, then adopting him. They'd given him their home, their name, and everything worthwhile in his life.

They'd lost Stella nearly eight years ago to a cancer that had snuck into her body and eaten away at it. Some of the light had gone out of that house on the outskirts of the little water town of St. Christopher's, and out of Ray, out of Cam, and out of the two other lost boys they'd made their own.

Cam had gone racing—anything, anywhere. Now he

was racing home to the only man he'd ever considered his father.

He'd been to this hospital countless times. When his mother had been on staff, and then when she'd been in treatment for the thing that killed her.

He walked in now, punchy and panicked, and asked for Raymond Quinn at the admission's desk.

"He's in Intensive Care. Family only."

"I'm his son." Cameron turned away and headed for the elevator. He didn't have to be told what floor. He knew too well.

He saw Phillip the moment the doors opened onto ICU. "How bad?"

Phillip handed over one of the two cups of coffee he held. His face was pale with fatigue, his normally well-groomed tawny hair tousled by his hands. His long, some-what angelic face was roughened by stubble, and his eyes, a pale golden brown, shadowed with exhaustion.

"I wasn't sure you'd make it. It's bad, Cam. Christ, I've got to sit down a minute."

He stepped into a small waiting area, and dropped into a chair. The can of Coke in the pocket of his tailored suit clunked. For a moment he stared blindly at the morning show running brightly on the TV screen.

"What happened?" Cam demanded. "Where is he? What do the doctors say?"

"He was heading home from Baltimore. At least Ethan thinks he'd gone to Baltimore. For something. He hit a telephone pole. Dead on." He pressed the heel of his hand to his heart because it ached every time he pictured it. "They say maybe he had a heart attack or a stroke and lost control, but they're not sure yet. He was driving fast. Too fast."

He had to close his eyes because his stomach kept trying to jump into his throat. "Too fast," he repeated. "It took them nearly an hour to cut him out of the wreck. Nearly an hour. The paramedics said he was conscious on and off. It was just a couple miles from here."

He remembered the Coke in his pocket, opened the can, and drank. He kept trying to block the image out of his head, to concentrate on the now, and the what happened next. "They got ahold of Ethan pretty quick," Phillip continued. "When he got here Dad was in surgery. He's in a coma now." He looked up, met his brother's eyes. "They don't expect him to come out of it."

"That's bullshit. He's strong as an ox."

"They said . . ." Phillip closed his eyes again. His head felt empty, and he had to search for every thought. "Massive trauma. Brain damage. Internal injuries. He's on life support. The surgeon . . . he . . . Dad's a registered organ donor."

"Fuck that." Cam's voice was low and furious.

"Do you think I want to consider it?" Phillip rose now, a tall, rangy man in a wrinkled thousand-dollar suit. "They said it's a matter of hours at most. The machines are keeping him breathing. Goddamn it, Cam, you know how Mom and Dad talked about this when she got sick. No extreme measures. They made living wills, and we're ignoring his because . . . because we can't stand not to."

"You want to pull the plug?" Cam reached out, grabbed Phillip by the lapels. "You want to pull the goddamn plug on him?"

Weary and sick at heart, Phillip shook his head. "I'd rather cut my hand off. I don't want to lose him any more than you do. You'd better see for yourself."

He turned, led the way down the corridor, where the scent was hopelessness not quite masked by antiseptics. They moved through double doors, past a nurse's station, past small glass-fronted rooms where machines beeped and hope hung stubbornly on.

Ethan was sitting in a chair by the bed when they walked in. His big, calloused hand was through the guard and covering Ray's. His tall, wiry body was bent over, as if he'd been talking to the unconscious man in the bed beside him. He stood up slowly and, with eyes bruised from lack of sleep, studied Cam.

"So, you decided to put in an appearance. Strike up the band."

"I got here as soon as I could." He didn't want to admit it, didn't want to believe it. The man, the old, terrifyingly frail man, lying in the narrow bed, was his father. Ray Quinn was huge, strong, invincible. But the man with his father's face was shrunken, pale and still as death.

"Dad." He moved to the side of the bed, leaned down close. "It's Cam. I'm here." He waited, somehow sure it would take only that for his father's eyes to open, to wink slyly.

But there was no movement, and no sound except the monotonous beep of the machines.

"I want to talk to his doctor."

"Garcia." Ethan scrubbed his hands over his face, back into his sun-bleached hair. "The brain cutter Mom used to call Magic Hands. The nurse'll page him."

Cam straightened, and for the first time he noticed the boy curled up asleep in a chair in the corner. "Who's the kid?"

"The latest of Ray Quinn's lost boys." Ethan managed a small smile. Normally it would have softened his serious face, warmed the patient blue eyes. "He told you about him. Seth. Dad took him on about three months ago." He started to say more but caught Phillip's warning look and shrugged. "We'll get into that later."

Phillip stood at the foot of the bed, rocking back and forth on his heels. "So how was Monte Carlo?" At Cam's blank stare, he shrugged his shoulder. It was a gesture all three of them used in lieu of words. "The nurse said that we should talk to him, to each other. That maybe he can . . . They don't know for sure."

"It was fine." Cam sat and mirrored Ethan by reaching for Ray's hand through the bed guard. Because the hand was limp and lifeless, he held it gently and willed it to squeeze his own. "I won a bundle in the casinos and had a very hot French model in my suite when your fax came through." He shifted, spoke directly to Ray. "You should have seen her. She was incredible. Legs up to her ears, gorgeous man-made breasts.''

''Did she have a face?'' Ethan asked dryly.

''One that went just fine with the body. I tell you, she was a killer. And when I said I had to leave, she got just a little bitchy.'' He tapped his face where the scratches scored his cheek. ''I had to toss her out of the room into the hall before she tore me to ribbons. But I did remember to toss her dress out after her.''

''She was naked?'' Phillip wanted to know.

''As a jay.''

Phillip grinned, then had his first laugh in nearly twenty hours. ''God, leave it to you.'' He laid his hand over Ray's foot, needing the connection. ''He'll love that story.''

IN THE CORNER, SETH pretended to be asleep. He'd heard Cam come in. He knew who he was. Ray had talked about Cameron a lot. He had two thick scrapbooks filled to busting with clippings and articles and photos of his races and exploits.

He didn't look so tough and important now, Seth decided. The guy looked sick and pale and hollow-eyed. He'd make up his own mind about what he thought of Cameron Quinn.

He liked Ethan well enough. Though the man'd work your butt raw if you went out oystering or clamming with him. He didn't preach all the time, and he'd never once delivered a blow or a backhand even when Seth had made mistakes. And he fit Seth's ten-year-old view of a sailor pretty well.

Rugged, tanned, thick curling hair with streaks of blond in the brown, hard muscles, salty talk. Yeah, Seth liked him well enough.

He didn't mind Phillip. He was usually all pressed and polished. Seth figured the guy must have six million ties, though he couldn't imagine why a man would want even one. But Phillip had some sort of fancy job in a fancy office in Baltimore. Advertising. Coming up with slick ideas to sell things to people who probably didn't need them anyway.

Seth figured it was a pretty cool way to run a con.

Now Cam. He was the one who went for the flash, who lived on the edge and took the risks. No, he didn't look so tough, he didn't look like such a badass.

Then Cam turned his head, and his eyes locked onto Seth's. Held there, unblinking and direct until Seth felt his stomach quiver. To escape, he simply closed his eyes and imagined himself back at the house by the water, throwing sticks for the clumsy puppy Ray called Foolish.

Knowing the boy was awake and aware of his gaze, Cam continued to study him. Good-looking kid, he decided, with a mop of sandy hair and a body that was just starting to go gangly. If he grew into his feet, he'd be a tall one before he was finished sprouting. He had a kiss-my-ass chin, Cam observed, and a sulky mouth. In the pretense of sleep, he managed to look harmless as a puppy and just about as cute.

But the eyes . . . Cam had recognized that edge in them, that animal wariness. He'd seen it often enough in the mirror. He hadn't been able to make out the color, but they'd been dark. Blue or brown, he imagined.

"Shouldn't we park the kid somewhere else?"

Ethan glanced over. "He's fine here. Nobody to leave him with anyhow. On his own he'd just look for trouble."

Cam shrugged, looked away, and forgot him. "I want to talk to Garcia. They've got to have test results, or something. He drives like a pro, so if he had a heart attack or a stroke . . ." His voice trailed off—it was simply too much to contemplate. "We need to know. Standing around here isn't helping."

"You need to do something," Ethan said, his soft voice a sign of suppressed temper, "you go on and do it. Being here counts." He stared at his brother across Ray's unconscious form. "It's always what counted."

"Some of us didn't want to dredge for oysters or spend our lives checking crab pots," Cam shot back. "They gave us a life and expected us to do what we wanted with it."

"So you did what you wanted."

"We all did," Phillip put in. "If something was wrong with Dad the last few months, Ethan, you should have told us."

"How the hell was I supposed to know?" But he had known something, just hadn't been able to put his finger on it. And had let it slide. That ate at him now as he sat listening to the machines that kept his father breathing.

"Because you were there," Cam told him.

"Yeah, I was there. And you weren't—not for years."

"And if I'd stayed on St. Chris he wouldn't have run into a damn telephone pole? Christ." Cam dragged his hands through his hair. "That makes sense."

"If you'd been around. If either of you had, he wouldn't have tried to do so much on his own. Every time I turned around he was up on a damn ladder, or pushing a wheelbarrow, or painting his boat. And he's still teaching three days a week at the college, tutoring, grading papers. He's almost seventy, for Christ's sake."

"He's only sixty-seven." Phillip felt a hard, ice-edged chill claw through him. "And he's always been healthy as a team of horses."

"Not lately he hasn't. He's been losing weight and looking tired and worn-out. You saw it for yourself."

"All right, all right." Phillip scrubbed his hands over his face, felt the scrape of a day's growth of beard. "So maybe he should have been slowing down a little. Taking on the kid was probably too much, but there wasn't any talking him out of it."

"Always squabbling."

The voice, weak and slurred, caused all three men to jolt to attention.

"Dad." Ethan leaned forward first, his heart fluttering in his chest.

"I'll get the doctor."

"No. Stay," Ray mumbled before Phillip could rush out of the room. It was a hideous effort, this coming back, even for a moment. And Ray understood he had moments only. Already his mind and body seemed separate things, though he could feel the pressure of hands on his hands, hear the sound of his sons' voices, and the fear and anger in them.

He was tired, oh, God, so tired. And he wanted Stella. But before he left, he had one last duty.

"Here." The lids seemed to weigh several pounds apiece, but he forced his eyes to open, struggled to focus. His sons, he thought, three wonderful gifts of fate. He'd done his best by them, tried to show them how to become men. Now he needed them for one more. Needed them to stay a unit without him and tend the child.

"The boy." Even the words had weight. It made him wince to push them from mind to lips. "The boy's mine. Yours now. Keep the boy, whatever happens, you see to him. Cam. You'll understand him best." The big hand, once so strong and vital, tried desperately to squeeze. "Your word on it."

"We'll take care of him." At that moment, Cam would have promised to drag down the moon and stars. "We'll take care of him until you're on your feet again."

"Ethan." Ray sucked in another breath that wheezed through the respirator. "He'll need your patience, your heart. You're a fine waterman because of them."

"Don't worry about Seth. We'll look after him."

"Phillip."

"Right here." He moved closer, bending low. "We're all right here."

"Such good brains. You'll figure how to make it all work. Don't let the boy go. You're brothers. Remember you're brothers. So proud of you. All of you. Quinns." He smiled a little, and stopped fighting. "You have to let me go now."

"I'm getting the doctor." Panicked, Phillip rushed out

of the room while Cam and Ethan tried to will their father back to consciousness.

No one noticed the boy who stayed curled in the chair, his eyes squeezed tightly shut against hot tears.

TWO

They came alone and in crowds to wake and to bury Ray Quinn. He'd been more than a resident of the dot on the map known as St. Christopher's. He'd been teacher and friend and confidant. In years when the oyster crop was lean, he'd helped organize fund-raisers or had suddenly found dozens of odd jobs that needed to be done to tide the watermen over a hard winter.

If a student was struggling, Ray found a way to carve out an extra hour for a one-on-one. His literature classes at the university had always been filled, and it was rare for one to forget Professor Quinn.

He'd believed in community, and that belief had been both strong and supple in deed. He had realized that most vital of humanities. He had touched lives.

And he had raised three boys that no one had wanted into men.

They had left his gravesite buried in flowers and tears. So when the whispering and wondering began, it was most often hushed quickly. Few wanted to hear any gossip that reflected poorly on Ray Quinn. Or so they said, even as their ears twitched to catch the murmurs.

Sexual scandals, adultery, illegitimate child. Suicide.

Ridiculous. Impossible. Most said so and meant it. But others leaned a bit closer to catch every whisper, knit their brows, and passed the rumor from lip to ear.

Cam heard none of the whispers. His grief was so huge, so monstrous, he could barely hear his own black thoughts. When his mother had died, he'd handled it. He'd been prepared for it, had watched her suffer and had prayed for it to end. But this loss had been too quick, too arbitrary, and there was no cancer to blame for it.

There were too many people in the house, people who wanted to offer sympathy or share memories. He didn't want their memories, couldn't face them until he'd dealt with his own.

He sat alone on the dock that he'd helped Ray repair a dozen times over the years. Beside him was the pretty twenty-four-foot sloop they'd all sailed in countless times. Cam remembered the rig Ray had had that first summer—a little Sunfish, an aluminum catboat that had looked about as big as a cork to Cam.

And how patiently Ray had taught him how to sail, how to handle the rigging, how to tack. The thrill, Cam thought now, of the first time Ray had let him handle the tiller.

It had been a life-altering experience for a boy who'd grown up on hard streets—salty air in his face, wind snapping the white canvas, the speed and freedom of gliding over water. But most of all, it had been the trust. Here, Ray had said, see what you can do with her.

Maybe it had been that one moment, on that hazy afternoon when the leaves were so full and green and the sun already a white-hot ball behind the mist, that had turned the boy toward the man he was now.

And Ray had done it with a grin.

He heard the footsteps on the dock but didn't turn. He continued to look out over the water as Phillip stood beside him.

''Most everybody's gone.''

''Good.''

Phillip slipped his hands into his pockets. "They came for Dad. He'd have appreciated it."

"Yeah." Tired, Cam pressed his fingers to his eyes, let them drop. "He would have. I ran out of things to say and ways to say them."

"Yeah." Though he made his living with clever words, Phillip understood exactly. He took a moment to enjoy the silence. The breeze off the water had a bit of a bite, and that was a relief after the crowded house, overheated with bodies. "Grace is cleaning up in the kitchen. Seth's giving her a hand. I think he's got a case on her."

"She looks good." Cam struggled to shift his mind to someone else. Anything else. "Hard to imagine her with a kid of her own. She's divorced, right?"

"A year or two ago. He took off right before little Aubrey was born." Phillip blew out a breath between his teeth. "We've got some things to deal with, Cam."

Cam recognized the tone, and the tone meant it was time for business. Resentment bubbled up instantly. "I was thinking of taking a sail. There's a good wind today."

"You can sail later."

Cam turned his head, face bland. "I can sail now."

"There's a rumor going around that Dad committed suicide."

Cam's face went blank, then filled with red-hot rage. "What the fuck is this?" he demanded as he shot to his feet.

There, Phillip thought with dark satisfaction, that got your attention. "There's some speculation that he aimed for the pole."

"That's just pure bullshit. Who the hell's saying that?"

"It's going around—and some of it's rooting. It has to do with Seth."

"What has to do with Seth?" Cam began to pace, long, furious strides up and down the narrow dock. "What, do they think he was crazy for taking the kid on? Hell, he was crazy for taking any of us on, but what does that have to do with an accident?"

"There's some talk brewing that Seth is his son. By blood."

That stopped Cam dead in his tracks. "Mom couldn't have kids."

"I know that."

Fury pounded in his chest, a hammer on steel. "You're saying that he cheated on her? That he went off with some other woman and got a kid? Jesus Christ, Phil."

"I'm not saying it."

Cam stepped closer until they were face to face. "What the hell are you saying?"

"I'm telling you what I heard," Phillip said evenly, "so we can deal with it."

"If you had any balls you'd have decked whoever said it in their lying mouth."

"Like you want to deck me now. Is that your way of handling it? Just beat on it until it goes away?" With his own temper bubbling, Phillip shoved Cam back an inch. "He was my father too, goddamn it. You were the first, but you weren't the only."

"Then why the hell weren't you standing up for him instead of listening to that garbage? Afraid to get your hands dirty? Ruin your manicure? If you weren't such a damn pussy, you'd have—"

Phillip's fist shot out, caught Cam neatly on the jaw. There was enough force behind the punch to snap Cam's head back, send him staggering for a foot or two. But he regained his balance quickly enough. With eyes dark and eager, he nodded. "Well, then, come on."

Hot blood roaring in his head, Phillip started to strip off his jacket. Attack came swiftly, quietly and from behind. He barely had time to curse before he was sailing off the dock and into the water.

Phillip surfaced, spat, and shoved the wet hair out of his eyes. "Son of a bitch. You son of a bitch."

Ethan had his thumbs tucked in his front pockets now and studied his brother as Phillip treaded water. "Cool off," he suggested mildly.

"This suit is Hugo Boss," Phillip managed as he kicked toward the dock.

"That don't mean shit to me." Ethan glanced over at Cam. "Mean anything to you?"

"Means he's going to have a hell of a dry-cleaning bill."

"You, too," Ethan said and shoved Cam off the dock. "This isn't the time or place to go punching each other. So when the pair of you haul your butts out and dry off, we'll talk this through. I sent Seth on with Grace for a while."

Eyes narrowed, Cam skimmed his hair back with his fingers. "So you're in charge all of a sudden."

"Looks to me like I'm the only one who kept his head above water." With this, Ethan turned and sauntered back toward the house.

Together Cam and Phillip gripped the edge of the dock. They exchanged one long, hard look before Cam sighed. "We'll throw him in later," he said.

Accepting the apology, Phillip nodded. He pulled himself up on the dock and sat, dragging off his ruined silk tie. "I loved him too. As much as you did. As much as anyone could."

"Yeah." Cam yanked off his shoes. "I can't stand it." It was a hard admission from a man who'd chosen to live on the edge. "I didn't want to be there today. I didn't want to stand there and watch them put him in the ground."

"You were there. That's all that would have mattered to him."

Cam peeled off his socks, his tie, his jacket, felt the chill of early spring. "Who told you about—who said those things about Dad?"

"Grace. She's been hearing talk and thought it best that we knew what was being said. She told Ethan and me this morning. And she cried." Phillip lifted a brow. "Still think I should have decked her?"

Cam heaved his ruined shoes onto the lawn. "I want to know who started this, and why."

"Have you looked at Seth, Cam?"

The wind was getting into his bones. That was why he suddenly wanted to shudder. "Sure I looked at him." Cam turned, headed for the house.

"Take a closer look," Phillip murmured.

WHEN CAM WALKED INTO the kitchen twenty minutes later, warm and dry in a sweater and jeans, Ethan had coffee hot and whiskey ready.

It was a big, family-style kitchen with a long wooden table in the center. The white countertops showed a bit of age, the wear and tear of use. There'd been talk a few years back of replacing the aging stove. Then Stella had gotten sick, and that had been the end of that.

There was a big, shallow bowl on the table that Ethan had made in his junior year in high school wood shop. It had sat there since the day he'd brought it home, and was often filled with letters and notes and household flotsam rather than the fruit it had been designed for. Three wide, curtainless windows ranged along the back wall, opening the room up to the yard and the water beyond it.

The cabinet doors were glass-fronted, and the dishes inside plain white stoneware, meticulously arranged. As would be, Cam thought, the contents of all the drawers. Stella had insisted on that. When she wanted a spoon, by God, she didn't want to search for one.

But the refrigerator was covered with photos and newspaper clippings, notes, postcards, children's drawings, all haphazardly affixed with multicolored magnets.

It gave his heart a hitch to step into that room and know his parents wouldn't ever again be there.

"Coffee's strong," Ethan commented. "So's the whiskey. Take your choice."

"I'll have both." Cam poured a mug, added a shot of

Johnnie Walker to the coffee, then sat. "You want to take
a swing at me, too?"

"I did. May again." Ethan decided he wanted his whiskey alone and neat. And poured a double. "Don't much
feel like it now." He stood by the window, looking out,
the untouched whiskey in his hand. "Maybe I still think
you should have been here more the last few years. Maybe
you couldn't be. It doesn't seem to matter now."

"I'm not a waterman, Ethan. I do what I'm good at.
That's what they expected."

"Yeah." He couldn't imagine the need to run from the
place that was home, and sanctuary. And love. But there
was no point in questioning it, or in holding on to resent-
ments. Or, he admitted, casting blame. "The place needs
some work."

"I noticed."

"I should have made more time to come around and see
to things. You always figure there's going to be plenty of
time to go around, then there's not. The back steps are
rotting out, need replacing. I kept meaning to." He turned
as Phillip came into the room. "Grace has to work tonight,
so she can't keep Seth occupied for more than a couple
hours. You lay it out, Phil. It'll take me too long."

"All right." Phillip poured coffee, left the whiskey
alone. Rather than sit, he leaned back against the counter.
"It seems a woman came to see Dad a few months back.
She went to the college, caused a little trouble that nobody
paid much attention to at the time."

"What kind of trouble?"

"Caused a scene in his office, a lot of shouting and
crying on her part. Then she went to see the dean and tried
to file sexual molestation charges against Dad."

"That's a crock."

"The dean apparently thought so, too." Phillip poured
a second cup of coffee and this time brought it to the table.
"She claimed Dad had harassed and molested her while
she was a student. But there was no record of her ever
being a student at the college. Then she said she'd just

been auditing his class because she couldn't afford full tuition. But nobody could verify that either. Dad's rep stood up to it, and it seemed to go away.''

"He was pretty shaken," Ethan put in. "He wouldn't talk to me about it. Wouldn't talk to anybody. Then he went away for about a week. Told me he was going down to Florida to do some fishing. He came back with Seth.''

"You're trying to tell me people think the kid's his? For Christ's sake, that he had something going on with this bimbo who waits, what, ten, twelve years to complain about it?''

"Nobody thought too much of it then," Phillip put in. "He had a history of bringing strays home. But then there was the money.''

"What money?''

"He wrote checks, one for ten thousand dollars, another for five, and another for ten over the last three months. All to Gloria DeLauter. Somebody at the bank noticed and mumbled to somebody else, because Gloria DeLauter was the name of the woman who'd tried to hang him up on the sexual misconduct charges.''

"Why the hell didn't somebody tell me what was going on around here?''

"I didn't find out about the money until a few weeks ago.'' Ethan stared down into his whiskey, then decided it would do him more good inside than out. He downed it, hissed once. "When I asked him about it, he just told me the boy was what was important. Not to worry. As soon as everything was settled he'd explain. He asked me for some time, and he looked so . . . defenseless. You don't know what it was like, seeing him scared and old and fragile. You didn't see him, you weren't here to see him. So I waited." Whiskey and guilt paired with resentment and grief to burn a hole inside him. "And I was wrong.''

Shaken, Cam pushed back from the table. "You think he was paying blackmail. That he diddled some student a dozen years ago and knocked her up? And now he was paying so she'd keep quiet. So she'd hand over the kid for him to raise?''

''I'm telling you what was, and what I know.'' Ethan's voice was even, his eyes steady. ''Not what I think.''

''I don't know what I think,'' Phillip said quietly. ''But I know Seth's got his eyes. You only have to look at him, Cam.''

''No way he fucked with a student. And no way he cheated on Mom.''

''I don't want to believe it.'' Phillip set down his mug. ''But he was human. He could have made a mistake.'' One of them had to be realistic, and he decided he was elected. ''If he did, I'm not going to condemn him for it. What we have to do is figure out how to do what he asked. We have to find a way to keep Seth. I can find out if he started adoption proceedings. They couldn't be final yet. We're going to need a lawyer.''

''I want to find out more about this Gloria DeLauter.'' Deliberately, Cam unclenched his fists before he could use them on something, or someone. ''I want to know who the hell she is. Where the hell she is.''

''Up to you.'' Phillip shrugged his shoulders. ''Personally, I don't want to get near her.''

''What's this suicide crap?''

Phillip and Ethan exchanged a look, then Ethan rose and walked to a kitchen drawer. He pulled it open, took out a large sealed bag. It hurt him to hold it, and he saw by the way Cam's eyes darkened that Cam recognized the worn green enameled shamrock key ring as their father's.

''This is what was inside the car after the accident.'' He opened it, took out an envelope. The white paper was stained with dried blood. ''I guess somebody—one of the cops, the tow truck operator, maybe one of the paramedics—looked inside and read the letter, and they didn't trouble to keep it to themselves. It's from her.'' Ethan tapped out the letter, held it out to Cam. ''DeLauter. The postmark's Baltimore.''

''He was coming back from Baltimore.'' With dread,

Cam unfolded the letter. The handwriting was a large, loopy scrawl.

Quinn, I'm tired of playing nickel and dime. You want the kid so bad, then it's time to pay for him. Meet me where you picked him up. We'll make it Monday morning. The block's pretty quiet then. Eleven o'clock. Bring a hundred and fifty thousand, in cash. Cash money, Quinn, and no discounts. You don't come through with every penny, I'm taking the kid back. Remember, I can pull the plug on the adoption any time I want. A hundred and fifty grand's a pretty good bargain for a good-looking boy like Seth. Bring the money and I'm gone. You've got my word on it.
Gloria

"She was selling him," Cam murmured. "Like he was a—" He stopped himself, looked up sharply at Ethan as he remembered. Ethan had once been sold as well, by his own mother, to men who preferred young boys. "I'm sorry, Ethan."

"I live with it," he said simply. "Mom and Dad made sure I could. She's not going to get Seth back. Whatever it takes, she won't get her hands on him."

"We don't know if he paid her?"

"He emptied his bank account here," Phillip put in. "From what I can tell—and I haven't gone over his papers in detail yet—he closed out his regular savings, cashed in his CDs. He only had a day to get the cash. That would have come to about a hundred thousand. I don't know if he had fifty more—if he had time to liquidate it if he did."

"She wouldn't have gone away. He'd have known that." Cam put the letter down, wiped his hands on his jeans as if to clean them. "So people are whispering that he killed himself in what—shame, panic, despair? He wouldn't have left the kid alone."

"He didn't." Ethan moved to the coffeepot. "He left him with us."

"How the hell are we supposed to keep him?" Cam sat again. "Who's going to let us adopt anybody?"

"We'll find a way." Ethan poured coffee, added enough

sugar to make Phillip wince in reaction. "He's ours now."

"What the hell are we going to do with him?"

"Put him in school, put a roof over his head, food in his belly, and try to give him something of what we were given." He brought the pot over, topped off Cam's coffee. "You got an argument?"

"Couple dozen, but none of them get past the fact that we gave our word."

"We agree on that, anyway." Frowning, Phillip drummed his fingers on the table. "But we've left out one pretty vital point. None of us knows what Seth's going to have to say about it. He might not want to stay here. He might not want to stay with us."

"You're just looking to complicate things, as usual," Cam complained. "Why wouldn't he?"

"Because he doesn't know you, he barely knows me." Phillip lifted his cup and gestured. "The only one he's spent any time with is Ethan."

"Didn't spend all that much with me," Ethan admitted. "I took him out on the boat a few times. He's got a quick mind, good hands. Doesn't have much to say for himself, but when he does, he's got a mouth on him. He's spent some time with Grace. She doesn't seem to mind him."

"Dad wanted him to stay," Cam stated with a shrug. "He stays." He glanced over at the sound of a horn tooting three quick beeps.

"That'll be Grace dropping him back off on her way to Shiney's Pub."

"Shiney's?" Cam's brows shot up. "What's she doing down at Shiney's?"

"Making a living, I expect," Ethan returned.

"Oh, yeah." A slow grin spread. "Does he still have his waitresses dress in those little skirts with the bows on the butt and the black fishnet stockings?"

"He does," Phillip said with a long, wistful sigh. "He does indeed."

"Grace would fill out one of those outfits pretty well, I'd imagine."

"She does." Phillip smiled. "She does indeed."

"Maybe I'll just mosey down to Shiney's later."

"Grace isn't one of your French models." Ethan pushed back from the table, took his mug and his annoyance to the sink. "Back off."

"Whoa." Behind Ethan's back, Cam wiggled his brows at Phillip. "Backing off, bro. Didn't know you had your eye aimed in that particular direction."

"I don't. She's a mother, for Christ's sake."

"I had a really fine time with the mother of two in Cancun last winter," Cam remembered. "Her ex was swimming in oil—olive oil—and all she got in the divorce settlement was a Mexican villa, a couple of cars, some trinkets, art, and two million. I spent a memorable week consoling her. And the kids were cute—from a distance. With their nanny."

"You're such a humanitarian, Cam," Phillip told him.

"Don't I know it."

They heard the front door slam and looked at each other. "Well, who talks to him?" Phillip wanted to know.

"I'm no good at that kind of stuff." Ethan was already edging toward the back door. "And I've got to go feed my dog."

"Coward," Cam muttered as the door shut at Ethan's back.

"You bet. Me, too." Phillip was up and moving. "You get first crack. I've got those papers to go through."

"Wait just a damn minute—"

But Phillip was gone, and cheerfully telling Seth that Cameron wanted to talk to him. When Seth came to the kitchen door, the puppy scrambling at his heels, he saw Cam scowling as he poured more whiskey in his coffee.

Seth stuck his hands in his pockets and lifted his chin. He didn't want to be there, didn't want to talk to anybody. At Grace's he'd been able to just sit on her little stoop, be alone with his thoughts. Even when she'd come out for a little while and sat beside him with Aubrey on her knee, she'd let him be.

Because she understood he'd wanted to be quiet.

Now he had to deal with the man. He wasn't afraid of big hands and hard eyes. Wouldn't—couldn't—let himself be afraid. He wouldn't care that they were going to kick him loose, toss him back like one of the runt fish Ethan pulled out of the bay.

He could take care of himself. He wasn't worried.

His heart scrambled in his chest like a mouse in a cage.

"What?" The single word was ripe with defiance and challenge. Seth stood, his legs locked, and waited for a reaction.

Cam only continued to frown and sip his doctored coffee. With one hand, he absently stroked the puppy, who was trying valiantly to climb into his lap. He saw a scrawny boy wearing jeans still stiff and obviously new, a screw-you sneer, and Ray Quinn's eyes. "Sit down."

"I can stand."

"I didn't ask you what you could do, I told you to sit down."

On cue, Foolish obediently plopped his fat butt on the floor and grinned. But boy and man stared at each other. The boy gave way first. It was the quick jerk of the shoulders that had Cam setting his mug down with a click. It was a Quinn gesture, through and through. Cam took a moment to settle, tried to gather his thoughts. But they remained scattered and elusive. What the hell was he supposed to say to the boy?

"You get anything to eat?"

Seth watched him warily from under girlishly thick lashes. "Yeah, there's stuff."

"Ah, Ray, did he talk to you about . . . things. Plans for you?"

The shoulders jerked again. "I don't know."

"He was working on adopting you, making it legal. You knew about that."

"He's dead."

"Yeah." Cam picked up his coffee again, let the pain roll through. "He's dead."

"I'm going to Florida," Seth burst out as the idea slammed into his mind.

Cam sipped coffee, angled his head as if mildly interested. "Oh, yeah?"

"I got some money. I figured I'd leave in the morning, catch a bus south. You can't stop me."

"Sure I can." More comfortable now, Cam leaned back in his chair. "I'm bigger than you. What do you plan to do in Florida?"

"I can get work. I can do lots of things."

"Pick some pockets, sleep on the beach."

"Maybe."

Cam nodded. That had been his plan when his destination had been Mexico. For the first time he thought he might be able to connect with the boy after all. "I guess you can't drive yet."

"I could if I had to."

"Harder to boost a car these days unless you've got some experience. And you need to be mobile to keep ahead of the cops. Florida's a bad idea."

"That's where I'm going." Seth set his jaw.

"No, it isn't."

"You're not sending me back." Seth lurched up from the chair, his thin frame vibrating with fear and rage. The sudden move and shout sent the puppy racing fearfully from the room. "You got no hold over me, you can't make me go back."

"Back where?"

"To her. I'll go right now. I'll get my stuff and I'm gone. And if you think you can stop me, you're full of shit."

Cam recognized the stance—braced for a blow but ready to fight back. "She knock you around?"

"That's none of your fucking business."

"Ray made it my fucking business. You head for the door," he added as Seth shifted to the balls of his feet, "I'll just haul you back." Cam only sighed when Seth made his dash.

Even as he caught him three feet before the front door, he had to give Seth credit for speed. And when he caught the boy around the waist, took the backhanded fist on his already tender jaw, he gave him credit for strength.

"Get your goddamn hands off me, you son of a bitch. I'll kill you if you touch me."

Grimly, Cam dragged Seth into the living room, pushed him into a chair, and held him there with their faces close. If it had just been anger he saw in the boy's eyes, or defiance, he wouldn't have cared. But what he saw was raw terror.

"You got balls, kid. Now try to develop some brains to go with them. If I want sex, I want a woman. Understand me?"

He couldn't speak. All he'd known when that hard, muscled arm had wrapped around him was that this time he wouldn't be able to escape. This time he wouldn't be able to fight free and run.

"There's nobody here who's going to touch you like that. Ever." Without realizing it, Cam had gentled his voice. His eyes remained dark, but the hardness was gone. "If I lay hands on you, the worst it means is I might try to knock some sense into you. You got that?"

"I don't want you to touch me," Seth managed. His breath was gone. Panic sweat slicked his skin like oil. "I don't like being touched."

"Okay, fine. You sit where I put you." Cam eased back, then pulled over a footstool and sat. Since Foolish was now shivering in terror, Cam plucked him up and dumped him in Seth's lap. "We got a problem," Cam began, and prayed for inspiration on how to handle it. "I can't watch you twenty-four hours a day. And if I could, I'm damned if I would. You take off for Florida, I'm going to have to go find you and haul you back. That's really going to piss me off."

Because the dog was there, Seth stroked him, gaining comfort while giving it. "What do you care where I go?"

"I can't say I do. But Ray did. So you're going to have to stay."

"Stay?" It was an option Seth had never considered. Certainly hadn't allowed himself to believe. "Here? When you sell the house—"

"Who's selling the house?"

"I—" Seth broke off, decided he was saying too much. "People figured you would."

"People figured wrong. Nobody's selling this house." It surprised Cam just how firm his feelings were on that particular point. "I don't know how we're going to manage it yet. I'm still working on that. But in the meantime, you'd better get this into your head. You're staying put." Which meant, Cam realized with a jolt, so was he.

It appeared his luck was still running bad.

"We're stuck with each other, kid, for the next little while."

THREE

CAM FIGURED THIS HAD to be the weirdest week of his life. He should have been in Italy, prepping for the motocross he'd planned to treat himself to. Most of his clothes and his boat were in Monte Carlo, his car was in Nice, his motorcycle in Rome.

And he was in St. Chris, baby-sitting a ten-year-old with a bad attitude. He hoped to Christ the kid was in school where he belonged. They'd had a battle royal over that little item that morning. But then, they were at war over most everything.

Kitchen duty, curfews, laundry, television picks. Cam shook his head as he pried off the rotting treads on the back steps. He'd swear the boy would square up for a bout if you said good morning.

And maybe he wasn't doing a fabulous job as guardian, but damn it, he was doing his best. He had the tension headache to prove it. And mostly, he was on his own. Phillip had promised weekends, and that was something. But it also left five hideous days between. Ethan made a point of coming by and staying a few hours every evening after he pulled in the day's catch.

But that left the days.

Cam would have traded his immortal soul for a week in
Martinique. Hot sand and hotter women. Cold beer and no
hassles. Instead he was doing laundry, learning the mysteries of microwave cooking, and trying to keep tabs on a
boy who seemed hell-bent on making life miserable.

"You were the same way."

"Hell I was. I wouldn't have lived to see twelve if I'd
been that big an idiot."

"Most of that first year Stella and I used to lie in bed
at night and wonder if you'd still be here in the morning."

"At least there were two of you. And . . ."

Cam's hand went limp on the hammer. His fingers simply gave way until it thudded on the ground beside him.
There in the old, creaking rocker on the back porch sat
Ray Quinn. His face was wide and smiling, his hair a tousled white mane that grew long and full. He wore his favored gray fishing pants, a faded gray T-shirt with a red
crab across the chest. His feet were bare.

"Dad?" Cam's head spun once, sickly, then his heart
burst with joy. He leaped to his feet.

"You didn't think I'd leave you fumbling through this
alone, did you?"

"But—" Cam shut his eyes. He was hallucinating, he
realized. It was stress and fatigue, grief tossed in.

"I always tried to teach you that life's full of surprises
and miracles. I wanted you to open your mind not just to
possibilities, Cam, but to impossibilities."

"Ghosts? God!"

"Why not?" The idea seemed to cheer Ray immensely
as he let loose with one of his deep, rumbling laughs.
"Read your literature, son. It's full of them."

"Can't be," Cam mumbled to himself.

"I'm sitting right here, so it looks like it can. I left too
many things unfinished around here. It's up to you and
your brothers now, but who says I can't give you a little
help now and again?"

"Help. Yeah, I'm going to need some serious help.
Starting with a psychiatrist." Before his legs gave out on

him, Cam picked his way through the broken stairs and
sat down on the edge of the porch.

"You're not crazy, Cam, just confused."

Cam took a steadying breath and turned his head to
study the man who lazily rocked in the old wooden chair.
The Mighty Quinn, he thought while the air whooshed out
of his lungs. He looked solid and real. He looked, Cam
decided, there.

"If you're really here, tell me about the boy. Is he
yours?"

"He's yours now. Yours and Ethan's and Phillip's."

"That's not enough."

"Of course it is. I'm counting on each of you. Ethan
takes things as they come and makes the best of them.
Phillip wraps his mind around details and ties them up.
You push at everything until it works your way. The boy
needs all three of you. Seth's what's important. You're all
what's important."

"I don't know what to do with him," Cam said impatiently. "I don't know what to do with myself."

"Figure out one, you'll figure out the other."

"Damn it, tell me what happened. Tell me what's going
on."

"That's not why I'm here. I can't tell you if I've seen
Elvis either." Ray grinned when Cam let out a short, help-
less laugh. "I believe in you, Cam. Don't give up on Seth.
Don't give up on yourself."

"I don't know how to do this."

"Fix the steps," Ray said with a wink. "It's a start."

"The hell with the steps," Cam began, but he was
alone again with the sound of singing birds and gently
lapping water. "Losing my mind," he murmured, rubbing an unsteady hand over his face. "Losing my goddamn mind."

And rising, he went back to fix the steps.

•   •   •

ANNA SPINELLI HAD THE radio blasting. Aretha Franklin was wailing out of her million-dollar pipes, demanding respect. Anna was wailing along with her, deliriously thrilled with her spanking-new car.

She'd worked her butt off, budgeted and juggled funds to afford the down payment and the monthly installments. And as far as she was concerned it would be worth every carton of yogurt she ate rather than a real meal.

Despite the chilly spring air, she'd have preferred to have the top down as she sped along the country roads. But it wouldn't have looked professional to arrive wind-blown. Above all else, it was essential to appear and be-have in a professional manner.

She'd chosen a plain and proper navy suit and white blouse for this home visit. What she wore under it was nobody's business but her own. Her affection for silk strained her ever beleaguered budget, but life was for liv-ing, after all.

She'd fought her long, curling black hair into a tidy bun at the nape of her neck. She thought it made her look a bit more mature and dignified. Too often when she wore her hair down she was dismissed as a hot number rather than a serious-minded social worker.

Her skin was pale gold, thanks to her Italian heritage. Her eyes, big and dark and almond-shaped. Her mouth was full, with a ripe bottom lip. The bones in her face were strong and prominent, her nose long and straight. She wore little makeup during business hours, wary of drawing the wrong kind of attention.

She was twenty-eight years old, devoted to her work, satisfied with the single life, and pleased that she'd been able to settle in the pretty town of Princess Anne.

She'd had enough of the city.

As she drove between long, flat fields of row crops with the scent of water a hint on the breeze through her window, she dreamed of one day moving to such a place. Country lanes and tractors. A view of the bay and boats.

She'd need to save up, to plan, but one day she hoped
to manage to buy a little house outside of town. The commute wouldn't be so hard, not when driving was one of
her greatest personal pleasures.

The CD player shifted, the Queen of Soul to Beethoven.
Anna began to hum the "Ode to Joy."

She was glad the Quinn case had been assigned to her.
It was so interesting. She only wished she'd had the chance
to meet Raymond and Stella Quinn. It would take very
special people to adopt three half-grown and troubled boys
and make it work.

But they were gone, and now Seth DeLauter was her
concern. Obviously the adoption proceedings couldn't go
forward. Three single men—one living in Baltimore, one
in St. Chris, and the other wherever he chose to at the
moment. Well, Anna mused, it didn't appear to be the best
environment for the child. In any case, it was doubtful they
would want guardianship.

So Seth DeLauter would be absorbed back into the system. Anna intended to do her best by him.

When she spotted the house through the greening leaves,
she stopped the car. Deliberately she turned the radio down
to a dignified volume, then checked her face and hair in
the rearview mirror. Shifting back into first, she drove the
last few yards at a leisurely pace and turned slowly into
the drive.

Her first thought was that it was a pretty house in a
lovely setting. So quiet and peaceful, she mused. It could
have used a fresh coat of paint, and the yard needed tending, but the slight air of disrepair only added to the hom-
iness.

A boy would be happy here, she thought. Anyone
would. It was a shame he'd have to be taken away from
it. She sighed a little, knowing too well that fate had its
whims. Taking her briefcase, she got out of the car.

She hitched her jacket to make certain it fell in line. She
wore it a bit loose, so it wouldn't showcase distracting
curves. She started toward the front door, noting that the

perennial beds flanking the steps were beginning to pop.

She really needed to learn more about flowers; she made a mental note to check out a few gardening books from the library.

She heard the hammering and hesitated, then in her practical low heels cut across the lawn toward the back of the house.

He was kneeling on the ground when she caught sight of him. A black T-shirt tucked into snug and faded denim. From a purely female outlook, it was impossible not to react and approve of him. Muscles—the long and lean sort—rippled as he pounded a nail into wood with enough anger, Anna mused, enough force, to send vibrations of both into the air to simmer.

Phillip Quinn? she wondered. The advertising executive. Highly doubtful.

Cameron Quinn, the globe-trotting risk-taker? Hardly.

So.this must be Ethan, the waterman. She fixed a polite smile on her face and started forward. "Mr. Quinn."

His head came up. With the hammer still gripped in his hand, he turned until she saw his face. Oh, yes, the anger was there, she realized, full-blown and lethal. And the face itself was more compelling and certainly tougher than she'd been prepared for.

Some Native American blood, perhaps, she decided, would account for those sharp bones and bronzed skin. His hair was a true black, untidy and long enough to fall over his collar. His eyes were anything but friendly, the color of bitter storms.

On a personal level, she found the package outrageously sexy. On a professional one, she knew the look of an alley brawler when she saw one, and decided on the spot that whichever Quinn this was, he was a man to be careful with.

He took his time studying her. His first thought was that legs like that deserved a better showcase than a drab navy skirt and ugly black shoes. His second was that when a woman had eyes that big, that brown, that beautiful, she probably got whatever she wanted without saying a word.

He set the hammer down and rose. "I'm Quinn."

"I'm Anna Spinelli." She kept the smile in place as she walked forward, hand extended. "Which Quinn are you?"

"Cameron." He'd expected a soft hand because of the eyes, because of the husky purr of her voice, but it was firm. "What can I do for you?"

"I'm Seth DeLauter's caseworker."

His interest evaporated, and his spine stiffened. "Seth's in school."

"I'd hope so. I'd like to speak with you about the situation, Mr. Quinn."

"My brother Phillip's handling the legal details."

She arched a brow, determined to keep the small polite smile in place. "Is he here?"

"No."

"Well, then, if I could have a few moments of your time. I assume you're living here, at least temporarily."

"So what?"

She didn't bother to sigh. Too many people saw a social worker as the enemy. She'd done so once herself. "My concern is Seth, Mr. Quinn. Now we can discuss this, or I can simply move forward with the procedure for his removal from this home and into approved foster care."

"It'd be a mistake to try that, Miz Spinelli. Seth isn't going anywhere."

Her back went up at the way he drawled out her name. "Seth DeLauter is a minor. The private adoption your father was implementing wasn't finalized, and there is some question about its validity. At this point, Mr. Quinn, you have no legal connection to him."

"You don't want me to tell you what you can do with your legal connection, do you, Miz Spinelli?" With some satisfaction he watched those big, dark eyes flash. "I didn't think so. I can resist. Seth's my brother." The saying of it left him shaken. With a jerk of his shoulder, he turned. "I need a beer."

She stood for a moment after the screen door slammed.

When it came to her work, she simply didn't permit herself to lose her temper. She breathed in, breathed out three times before climbing the half-repaired steps and going into the house.

"Mr. Quinn—"

"Still here?" He twisted the top off a Harp. "Want a beer?"

"No. Mr. Quinn—"

"I don't like social workers."

"You're joking." She allowed herself to flutter her lashes at him. "I never would have guessed."

His lips twitched before he lifted the bottle to them. "Nothing personal."

"Of course not. I don't like rude, arrogant men. That's nothing personal either. Now, are you ready to discuss Seth's welfare, or should I simply come back with the proper paperwork and the cops?"

She would, Cam decided after another study. She might have been given a face suitable for painting, but she wasn't a pushover. "You try that, and the kid's going to bolt. You'd pick him up sooner or later, and he'd end up in juvie—then he'd end up in a cell. Your system isn't going to help him, Miz Spinelli."

"But you can?"

"Maybe." He frowned into his beer. "My father would have." When he looked up again, there were emotions storming in his eyes that pulled at her. "Do you believe in the sanctity of a deathbed promise?"

"Yes," she said before she could stop herself.

"The day my father died I promised him—we promised him—that we'd keep Seth with us. Nothing and no one is going to make me break my word. Not you, not your system, not a dozen cops."

The situation here wasn't what she'd expected to find. So she would reevaluate. "I'd like to sit down," Anna said after a moment.

"Go ahead."

She pulled out a chair at the table. There were dishes in

the sink, she noted, and the faint smell of whatever had
been burnt for dinner the night before. But to her that only
meant someone was trying to feed a young boy. "Do you
intend to apply for legal guardianship?"

"We—"

"You, Mr. Quinn," she interrupted. "I'm asking you if
that is your intention." She waited, watching the doubts
and resistance sweep over his face.

"Then I guess it is. Yeah." God help them all, he
thought. "If that's what it takes."

"Do you intend to live in this house, with Seth, on a
permanent basis?"

"Permanent?" It was perhaps the only truly frightening
word in his life. "Now I have to sit down." He did so,
then pinched the bridge of his nose between his thumb and
forefinger to relieve some of the pressure. "Christ. How
about we use 'for the foreseeable future' instead of 'permanent'?"

She folded her hands on the edge of the table. She didn't
doubt his sincerity, would have applauded him for his intentions. But . . . "You have no idea what you're thinking
of taking on."

"You're wrong. I do, and it scares the hell out of me."

She nodded, considering the answer a point in his favor.
"What makes you think you would be a better guardian
for a ten-year-old boy, a boy I believe you've known for
less than two weeks, than a screened and approved foster
home?"

"Because I understand him. I've been him—or part of
him. And because this is where he belongs."

"Let me lay out some of the bigger obstacles to what
you're planning. You're a single man with no permanent
address and without a steady income."

"I've got a house right here. I've got money."

"Whose name is the house in, Mr. Quinn?" She only
nodded when his brows knit. "I imagine you have no
idea."

"Phillip will."

"Good for Phillip. And I'm sure you have some money, Mr. Quinn, but I'm speaking of steady employment. Going around the world racing various forms of transportation isn't stable employment."

"It pays just fine."

"Have you considered the risk to life and limb of your chosen lifestyle when you propose to take on a responsibility like this? Believe me, the court will. What if something happens to you when you're trying to break land and speed records?"

"I know what I'm doing. Besides, there are three of us."

"Only one of you lives in this house where Seth will live."

"So?"

"And the one who does isn't a respected college professor with the experience of raising three sons."

"That doesn't mean I can't handle it."

"No, Mr. Quinn," she said patiently, "but it is a major obstacle to legal guardianship."

"What if we all did?"

"Excuse me?"

"What if we all lived here? What if my brothers moved in?" What a damn mess, Cam thought, but he kept going. "What if I got a . . ." Now he had to take a deep swallow of beer, knowing the word would stick in his throat. "A job," he managed.

She stared at him. "You'd be willing to change your life so dramatically?"

"Ray and Stella Quinn changed my life."

Her face softened, making Cam blink in surprise as her generous mouth curved in a smile, as her eyes seemed to go darker and deeper. When her hand reached out, closed lightly over his, he stared down at it, surprised by a quick jolt of what was surely pure lust.

"When I was driving here, I was wishing I could have met them. I thought they must have been remarkable people. Now I'm sure of it." Then she drew back. "I'll need to speak with Seth, and with your brothers. What time does Seth get home from school?''

"What time?" Cam glanced at the kitchen clock without a clue. "It's sort of . . . flexible."

"You'll want to do better than that if this gets as far as a formal home study. I'll go by the school and see him. Your brother Ethan.'' She rose. "Would I find him at home?''

"Not at this time of day. He'll be bringing in his catch before five.''

She glanced at her watch, gauged her time. "All right, and I'll contact your other brother in Baltimore.'' From her briefcase she took a neat leather notebook. "Now, can you give me names and addresses of some neighbors. People who know you and Seth and who would stand for your character. The good side of your character, that is.''

"I could probably come up with a few.''

"That's a start. I'll do some research here, Mr. Quinn. If it's in Seth's best interest to remain in your home, under your care, I'll do everything I can to help you.'' She angled her head. "If I reach the opinion that it's in his best interest to be taken out of your home, and out of your care, then I'll fight you tooth and nail to make that happen.''

Cam rose as well. "Then I guess we understand each other.''

"Not by a long shot. But you've got to start somewhere.''

THE MINUTE SHE WAS out of the house, Cam was on the phone. By the time he'd been passed through a secretary and an assistant and reached Phillip, his temper had spilled over.

"There was a goddamn social worker here.''

"I told you to expect that.''

"No, you didn't.''

"Yes, I did. You don't listen. I've got a friend of mine—a lawyer—working on the guardianship. Seth's mother took a hike; as far as we can tell, she's not in Baltimore."

"I don't give a damn where the mother is. The social worker was making noises about taking Seth."

"The lawyer's putting through a temporary guardianship. It takes time, Cam."

"We may not have time." He shut his eyes, tried to think past the anger. "Or maybe I bought us some. Who owns the house now?"

"We do. Dad left it—well, everything—to the three of us."

"Fine, good. Because you're about to change locations. You're going to need to pack up those designer suits of yours, pal, and get your butt down here. We're going to be living together again."

"Like hell."

"And I've got to get a goddamn job. I'm going to expect you by seven tonight. Bring dinner. I'm sick to death of cooking."

It gave him some satisfaction to hang up on Phillip's vigorous cursing.

ANNA FOUND SETH SULlen and smart-mouthed and snotty. And liked him immediately. The principal had given her permission to take him out of class and use a corner of the empty cafeteria as a makeshift office.

"It would be easier if you'd tell me what you think and feel, and what you want."

"Why should you give a damn?"

"They pay me to."

Seth shrugged and continued to draw patterns on the table with his finger. "I think you should mind your own business, I feel bored, and I want you to go away."

"Well, that's enough about me," Anna said and had the pleasure of seeing Seth struggle to suppress a smile. "Let's talk about you. Are you happy living with Mr. Quinn?"

"It's a cool house."

"Yes, I liked it. What about Mr. Quinn?"

"He thinks he knows everything. Thinks he's a BFD because he's been all over the world. He sure as hell can't cook, let me tell you."

She left her pen on the table and folded her hands over her notebook. He was much too thin, she thought. "Do you go hungry?"

"He ends up going to get pizza or burgers. Pitiful. I mean what's it take to work a microwave?"

"Maybe you should do the cooking."

"Like he'd ask me. The other night he blows up the potatoes. Forgets to poke holes in them, you know, and bam!" Seth forgot to sneer, laughing out loud instead. "What a mess! He swore a streak then, man, oh, man."

"So the kitchen isn't his area of expertise." But, Anna decided, he was trying.

"You're telling me. He's better off when he's going around hammering things or fiddling with that cool-ass car. Did you see that 'Vette? Cam said it was his mom's and she had it for like ever. Drives like a rocket, too. Ray kept it in the garage. Guess he didn't want to get it out."

"Do you miss him? Ray?"

The shoulder shrugged again, and Seth's gaze dropped. "He was cool. But he was old and when you get old you die. That's the way it is."

"What about Ethan and Phillip?"

"They're okay. I like going out on the boats. If I didn't have school, I could work for Ethan. He said I pulled my weight."

"Do you want to stay with them, Seth?"

"I got no place to go, do I?"

"There's always a choice, and I'm here to help you find the one that works best for you. If you know where your mother is—"

"I don't know." His voice rose, his head snapped up. His eyes darkened to nearly navy against a pale face. "And I don't want to know. You try to send me back there, you'll never find me."

"Did she hurt you?" Anna waited a beat, then nodded when he only stared at her. "All right, we'll leave that alone for now. There are couples and families who are willing and able to take children into their home, to care for them, to give them a good life."

"They don't want me, do they?" The tears wanted to come. He'd be damned if he'd let them. Instead his eyes went hot and burning dry. "He said I could stay, but it was a lie. Just another fucking lie."

"No." She grabbed Seth's hand before he could leap up. "No, they do want you. As a matter of fact, Mr. Quinn—Cameron—was very angry with me for suggesting you should go into another home. I'm only trying to find out what you want. And I think you just told me. If living with the Quinns is what you want, and what's best for you, I want to help you to get that."

"Ray said I could stay. He said I'd never have to go back. He promised."

"If I can, I'll try to help him keep that promise."

FOUR

SINCE THERE SEEMED TO be nothing cold to drink in the house but beer, carbonated soft drinks, and some suspicious-looking milk, Ethan put the kettle on to boil. He'd brew up some tea, ice it, and enjoy a tall glass out on the porch while evening moseyed in.

He was in hour fourteen of his day and ready to relax.

Which wasn't going to be easy, he decided while he hunted up tea bags and overheard Cam and Seth holding some new pissing match in the living room. He figured they must enjoy sniping at each other or they wouldn't spend so much time at it.

For himself, he wanted a quiet hour, a decent meal, then one of the two cigars he allowed himself per day. The way things sounded, he didn't think the quiet hour was going to make the agenda.

As he dumped tea bags in the boiling water, he heard feet stomping up the stairs, followed by the bullet-sharp sound of a slamming door.

"The kid's driving me bat-shit," Cam complained as he stalked into the kitchen. "You can't say boo to him without him squaring up for a fight."

"Mm-hmm."

"Argumentative, smart-mouthed, troublemaker." Feeling grossly put upon, Cam snagged a beer from the fridge.

"Must be like looking in a mirror."

"Like hell."

"Don't know what I was thinking of. You're such a peaceable soul." Moving at his own relaxed pace, Ethan bent down to search out an old glass pitcher. "Let's see, you were just about fourteen when I came along. First thing you did was pick a fight so you'd have the excuse to bloody my nose."

For the first time in hours, Cam felt a grin spread. "That was just a welcome-to-the-family tap. Besides, you gave me a hell of a black eye as a thank-you."

"There was that. Kid's too smart to try to punch you," Ethan continued and began to dump generous scoops of sugar into the pitcher. "So he razzes you instead. He sure as hell's got your attention, doesn't he?"

It was irritating because it was true. "You got him pegged so neatly, why don't you take him on?"

"Because I'm on the water every morning at dawn. Kid like that needs supervision." That, Ethan thought, was his story and he'd stick to it through all the tortures of hell. "Of the three of us, you're the only one not working."

"I'm going to have to fix that," Cam muttered.

"Oh, yeah?" With a mild snort, Ethan finished making the tea. "That'll be the day."

"The day's coming up fast. Social worker was here today."

Ethan grunted, let the implications turn over in his mind. "What'd she want?"

"To check us out. She's going to be talking to you, too. And Phillip. Already talked to Seth—which is what I was trying to diplomatically ask him about when he started foaming at the mouth again."

Cam frowned now, thinking more of Anna Spinelli of the great legs and tidy briefcase than of Seth. "If we don't pass, she's going to work on pulling him."

"He isn't going anywhere."

"That's what I said." He dragged his hand through his hair again, which for some reason reminded him he'd meant to get a haircut. In Rome. Seth wasn't the only one not going anywhere. "But, bro, we're about to make some serious adjustments around here."

"Things are fine as they are." Ethan filled a glass with ice and poured tea over it so that it crackled.

"Easy for you to say." Cam stepped out on the porch, let the screen door slap shut behind him. He walked to the rail, watched Ethan's sleek Chesapeake Bay retriever, Simon, play tag and tumble with the fat puppy. Upstairs, Seth had obviously decided to seek revenge by turning his radio up to earsplitting. Screaming headbanger rock blasted through the windows.

Cam's jaw twitched. He'd be damned if he'd tell the kid to turn it down. Too clichéd, too terrifyingly adult a response. He sipped his beer, struggled to loosen the knots in his shoulders, and concentrated on the way the lowering sun tossed white diamonds onto the water.

The wind was coming up so that the marsh grass waved like a field of Kansas wheat. The drake of a pair of ducks that had set up house where the water bent at the edge of the trees flew by quacking.

Lucy, I'm home, was all Cam could think, and it nearly made him smile again.

Under the roar of music he heard the gentle rhythmic creak of the rocker. Beer fountained from the lip of the bottle when he whirled. Ethan stopped rocking and stared at him.

"What?" he demanded. "Christ, Cam, you look like you've seen a ghost."

"Nothing." Cam swiped a hand over his face, then carefully lowered himself to the porch so he could lean back against the post. "Nothing," he repeated, but set the beer aside. "I'm a little edgy."

"Usually are if you stay in one place more than a week."

"Don't climb up my back, Ethan."

"Just a comment." And because Cam looked exhausted and pale, Ethan reached in the breast pocket of his shirt, took out two cigars. It wouldn't hurt to change his smoke-after-dinner routine. "Cigar?"

Cam sighed. "Yeah, why not?" Rather than move, he let Ethan light the first and pass it to him. Leaning back again, he blew a few lazy smoke rings. When the music shut off abruptly, he felt he'd achieved a small personal victory.

For the next ten minutes, there wasn't a sound but the lap of water, the call of birds, and the talk of the breeze. The sun dropped lower, turning the western sky into a soft, rosy haze that bled into the water and blurred the horizon. Shadows deepened.

It was like Ethan, Cam mused, to ask no questions. To sit in silence and wait. To understand the need for quiet. He'd nearly forgotten that admirable trait of his brother's. And maybe, Cam admitted, he'd nearly forgotten how much he loved the brother Ray and Stella had given him.

But even remembering, he wasn't sure what to do about it.

"See you fixed the steps," Ethan commented when he judged Cam was relaxing again.

"Yeah. The place could use a coat of paint, too."

"We'll have to get to that."

They were going to have to get to a lot of things, Cam thought. But the quiet creak of the rocker kept taking his mind back to that afternoon. "Have you ever had a dream while you were wide awake?" He could ask because it was Ethan, and Ethan would think and consider.

After setting the nearly empty glass on the porch beside the rocker, Ethan studied his cigar. "Well . . . I guess I have. The mind likes to wander when you let it."

It could have been that, Cam told himself. His mind had wandered—maybe even gotten lost for a bit. That could have been why he'd thought he saw his father rocking on the porch. The conversation? Wishful thinking, he decided. That was all.

"Remember how Dad used to bring his fiddle out here? Hot summer nights he'd sit where you're sitting and play for hours. He had such big hands."

"He could sure make that fiddle sing."

"You picked it up pretty well."

Ethan shrugged, puffed lazily on his cigar. "Some."

"You ought to take it. He'd have wanted you to have it."

Ethan shifted his quiet eyes, locked them on Cam's. Neither spoke for a moment, nor had to. "I guess I will, but not right yet. I'm not ready."

"Yeah." Cam blew out smoke again.

"You still got the guitar they gave you that Christmas?"

"I left it here. Didn't want it banging around with me." Cam looked at his fingers, flexed them as though he were about to lay them on the strings. "Guess I haven't played in more than a year."

"Maybe we should try Seth on some instrument. Mom used to swear playing a tune pumped out the aggression." He turned his head as the dogs began to bark and race around the side of the house. "Expecting somebody?"

"Phillip."

Ethan's brows lifted. "Thought he wasn't coming down till Friday."

"Let's just call this a family emergency." Cam tapped out the stub of the cigar before he rose. "I hope to Christ he brought some decent food and none of that fancy pea pod crap he likes to eat."

Phillip strode into the kitchen balancing a large bag on top of a jumbo bucket of chicken and shooting out waves of irritation. He dumped the food on the table, skimmed a hand through his hair, and scowled at his brothers.

"I'm here," he snapped as they came through the back door. "What's the damn problem?"

"We're hungry," Cam said easily, and peeling the top from the bucket, he grabbed a drumstick. "You got dirt on your 'I'm an executive' pants there, Phil.''

''Goddamn it.'' Furious now, Phillip brushed impatiently at the pawprints on his slacks. ''When are you going to teach that idiot dog not to jump on people?''

''You cart around fried chicken, dog's going to see if he can get a piece. Makes him smart if you ask me.'' Unoffended, Ethan went to a cupboard for plates.

''You get fries?'' Cam poked in the bag, snagged one. ''Cold. Somebody better nuke these. If I do it they'll blow up or disintegrate.''

''I'll do it. Get something to dish up that cole slaw.''

Phillip took a breath, then one more. The drive down from Baltimore was long, and the traffic had been ugly. ''When you two girls have finished playing house, maybe you'll tell me why I broke a date with a very hot-looking CPA—the third date by the way, which was dinner at her place with the definite possibility of sex afterward—and instead just spent a couple hours in miserable traffic to deliver a fucking bucket of chicken to a couple of boobs.''

''First off, I'm tired of cooking.'' Cam heaped cole slaw on his plate and took a biscuit. ''And even more tired of tossing out what I've cooked because even the pup—who drinks out of the toilet with regularity—won't touch it. But that's only the surface.''

He took another hefty bite of chicken as he walked to the doorway and shouted for Seth. ''The kid needs to be here. We're all in this.''

''Fine. Great.'' Phillip dropped into a chair, tugged at his tie.

''No use sulking because your accountant isn't going to be running your figures tonight, pal.'' Ethan offered him a friendly smile and a plate.

''Tax season's heating up.'' With a sigh, Phillip scooped out slaw. ''I'll be lucky to get a warm look from her until after April fifteenth. And I was so close.''

''None of us is likely to be getting much action for the next little while.'' Cam jerked a head as Seth's feet pounded down the stairs. "The patter of little feet plays hell with the sex life."

Cam tucked away the urge for another beer and settled on iced tea as Seth stepped into the kitchen. The boy scanned the room, his nose twitching at the scent of spicy chicken, but he didn't dive into the bucket as he would have liked to.

"What's the deal?" he demanded and tucked his hands in his pockets while his stomach yearned.

"Family meeting," Cam announced. "With food. Sit." He took a chair himself as Ethan put the freshly buzzed fries on the table. "Sit," Cam repeated when Seth stayed where he was. "If you're not hungry you can just listen."

"I could eat." Seth sauntered over to the table, slid into a chair. "It's got to be better than the crud you've been trying to pass off as food."

"You know," Ethan said in his mild drawl before Cam could snarl, "seems to me I'd be grateful if somebody tried to put together a hot meal for me from time to time. Even if it was crud." With his eyes on Seth, Ethan tipped down the bucket, contemplated his choices. "Especially if that somebody was doing the best he could."

Because it was Ethan, Seth flushed, squirmed, then shrugged as he plucked out a fat breast. "Nobody asked him to cook."

"All the more reason. Might work better if you took turns."

"He doesn't think I can do anything." Seth sneered over at Cam. "So I don't."

"You know, it's tempting to toss this little fish back into the pond." Cam dumped salt on his fries and struggled to hold onto a simmering temper. "I could be in Aruba this time tomorrow."

"So go." Seth's eyes flashed up, full of anger and defiance. "Go wherever the hell you want as long as it's out of my face. I don't need you."

"Smart-mouthed little brat. I've had it." Cam had a long reach and used it now to shoot a hand across the table and pluck Seth out of his chair. Even as Phillip opened his mouth to protest, Ethan shook his head.

"You think I've enjoyed spending the last two weeks baby-sitting some snot-nosed monster with a piss-poor attitude? I've put my life on hold to deal with you."

"Big deal." Seth had turned sheet-white and was ready for the blow he was sure would come. But he wouldn't back down. "All you do is run around collecting trophies and screwing women. Go back where you came from and keep doing it. I don't give a shit."

Cam watched the edges of his own vision turn red. Fury and frustration hissed in his blood like a snake primed to strike.

He saw his father's hands at the end of his arms. Not Ray's, but the man who had used those hands on him with such casual violence throughout his childhood. Before he did something unforgivable, he dropped Seth back into his chair. His voice was quiet now, and the room vibrated with his control.

"If you think I'm staying for you, you're wrong. I'm staying for Ray. Have you got any idea where the system will toss you if one of us decides you're not worth the trouble?"

Foster homes, Seth thought. Strangers. Or worse, *her*. Because his legs were trembling badly, he locked his feet around the legs of his chair. "You don't care what they do with me."

"That's just one more thing you're wrong about," Cam said evenly. "You don't want to be grateful, fine. I don't want your goddamn gratitude. But you'll start showing some respect, and you'll start showing it now. It's not just me who's going to be hounding your sorry ass, pal. It's the three of us."

Cam sat down again, waited for his composure to solidify. "The social worker who was here today—Spinelli, Anna Spinelli—has some concerns about the environment."

"What's wrong with the environment?" Ethan wanted

to know. The nasty little altercation had cleared the air, he decided. Now they could get to the details. "It's a good, solid house, a nice area. School's good, crime's low."

"I got the impression *I'm* the environment. At the moment, I'm the only one here, supervising things."

"The three of us will go down as guardians," Phillip pointed out. He poured a glass of iced tea and set it casually next to the hand Seth had fisted on the table. He imagined the boy's throat would be burning dry right about now. "I checked with the lawyer after you called. The preliminary paperwork should go through by the end of the week. There'll be a probationary period—regular home studies and meetings, evaluations. But unless there's a serious objection, it doesn't look like a problem."

"Spinelli's a problem." Cam refused to let the altercation spoil his appetite and reached for more chicken. "Classic do-gooder. Great legs, serious mind. I know she talked to the kid, but he's not inclined to share their conversation, so I'll share mine. She had doubts about my qualifications as guardian. Single man, no steady means of employment, no permanent residence."

"There are three of us." Phillip frowned and poked at his slaw. A trickle of guilt was working through, and he didn't care for it.

"Which I pointed out. Miz Spinelli of the gorgeous Italian eyes countered with the sad fact that I happen to be the only one of the three of us actually living here with the kid. And it was tactfully implied that of the three of us I'm the least likely candidate for guardian. So I tossed out the idea of all of us living here."

"What do you mean living here?" Phillip dropped his fork. "I work in Baltimore. I've got a condo. How the hell am I supposed to live here and work there?"

"That'll be a problem," Cam agreed. "Bigger one will be how you'll fit all your clothes into that closet in your old room."

While Phillip tried to choke out a response, Ethan tapped a finger on the edge of the table. He thought of his small, and to him perfect, house. The quiet and solitude of it. And he saw the way Seth stared down at his plate with dark, baffled eyes. "How long you figure it would take?"

"I don't know." Cam dragged both hands back through his hair. "Six months, maybe a year."

"A year." All Phillip could do was close his eyes. "Jesus."

"You talk to the lawyer about it," Cam suggested. "See what's what. But we present a united front to Social Services or they're going to pull him. And I've got to find work."

"Work." Phillip's misery dissolved in a grin. "You? Doing what? There aren't any racetracks in St. Chris. And the Chesapeake, God bless her, sure ain't the Med."

"I'll find something. Steady doesn't mean fancy. I'm not looking at something I'll need an Armani suit for."

He was wrong, Cam realized. This damn business *was* going to spoil his appetite. "The way I figure it, Spinelli's going to be back tomorrow, the next day at the latest. We have to hammer this out, and it has to look like we know what the hell we're doing."

"I'll take my vacation time early." Phillip bid farewell to the two weeks he'd planned to spend in the Caribbean. "That buys us a couple of weeks. I can work with the lawyer, deal with the social worker."

"I'll deal with her." Cam smiled a little. "I liked the looks of her, and I ought to get some perks out of this. Of course, all this depends on what the kid said to her today."

"I told her I wanted to stay," Seth mumbled. Tears were raw in his stomach. The food sat untouched on his plate. "Ray said I could. He said I could stay here. He said he'd fix it so I could."

"And we're what's left of him." Cam waited until Seth lifted his gaze. "So we'll fix it."

•　•　•　•

LATER, WHEN THE MOON was up and the dark water was slashed by its luminous white beam, Phillip stood on the dock. The air was cold now, the damp wind carrying the raw edge of the winter that fought not to yield to spring.

It suited his mood.

There was a war raging inside him between conscience and ambition. In two short weeks, the life he had planned out, plotted meticulously, and implemented with deliberation and simple hard work had shattered.

Now, still numb with grief for his father, he was being asked to transplant himself, to compromise those careful plans.

He'd been thirteen when Ray and Stella Quinn took him in. Most of those years he'd spent on the street, dodging the system. He was an accomplished thief, an enthusiastic brawler who used drugs and liquor to dull the ugliness. The projects of Baltimore were his turf, and when a drive-by shooting left him bleeding on those streets, he was prepared to die. To simply end it.

Indeed, the life he'd led up to the point when he wound up in a gutter choked with garbage ended that night. He lived, and for reasons he never understood, the Quinns wanted him. They opened a thousand fascinating doors for him. And no matter how often, how defiantly he tried to slam them shut again, they didn't allow it.

They gave him choices, and hope, and a family. They offered him a chance for an education that had saved his soul. He used what they'd given him to make himself into the man he was. He studied and worked, and he buried that miserable boy deep.

His position at Innovations, the top advertising firm in the metropolitan area, was solid. No one doubted that Phillip Quinn was on the fast track to the top. And no one who knew the man who wore the elegant tailored suits, who could order a meal in perfect French and always knew the proper wine, would have believed he had once bartered his body for the price of a dime bag.

He had pride in that, perhaps too much pride, but he considered it his testament to the Quinns.

There was enough of that selfish, self-serving boy still inside him to rebel at the thought of giving up one inch of it. But there was too much of the man Ray and Stella had molded to consider doing otherwise.

Somehow he had to find the compromise.

He turned, looked back at the house. The upstairs was dark. Seth was in bed by now, Phillip mused. He didn't have a clue how he felt about the boy. He recognized him, understood him, and he supposed resented just a bit those parts of himself he saw in young Seth DeLauter.

Was he Ray Quinn's son?

There, Phillip thought as his teeth clenched—more resentment at even the possibility of it. Had the man he'd all but worshiped for more than half his life really fallen off his pedestal, succumbed to temptation, betrayed wife and family?

And if he had, how could he have turned his back on his own blood? How could this man who had made strangers his own ignore for more than a decade a son who'd come from his own body?

We've got enough problems, Phillip reminded himself. The first was to keep a promise. To keep the boy.

He walked back, using the back porch light to guide him. Cam sat on the steps, Ethan in the rocker.

"I'll go back into Baltimore in the morning," Phillip announced. "I'll see what the lawyer can firm up. You said the social worker was named Spinelli?"

"Yeah." Cam nursed a cup of black coffee. "Anna Spinelli."

"She'd be county, probably out of Princess Anne. I'll pass that on." Details, he thought. He'd concentrate on the facts. "The way I see it, we're going to have to come off as three model citizens. I already pass." Phillip smiled thinly. "The two of you are going to have to work on your act."

"I told Spinelli I'd get a job." Even the thought of it disgusted Cam.

"I'd hold off on that a while." This came from Ethan, who rocked quietly in the shadows. "I got an idea. I want to think on it a while more. Seems to me," he went on, "that with Phil and me around, both of us working, you could be running the house."

"Oh, Jesus" was all Cam could manage.

"It goes like this." Ethan paused, rocked, continued. "You'd be what they'd call primary caregiver. You're available if the school calls with a problem, if Seth gets sick or whatever."

"Makes sense," Phillip agreed and, feeling better, he grinned at Cam. "You're Mommy."

"Fuck you."

"That's no way for Mommy to talk."

"If you think I'm going to be stuck washing your dirty socks and swabbing the toilet, you wasted that fine education you're so proud of."

"Just temporarily," Ethan said, though he enjoyed the image of his brother wearing an apron and hunting up cobwebs with a feather duster. "We'll work out shifts. Seth ought to have some regular chores too. We always did. But it's going to fall to you for the next few days anyway, while Phillip figures out how we handle the legal end and I see how I can juggle my time."

"I've got business of my own to deal with." The coffee was beginning to burn a hole in his gut, but Cam drank it down anyway. "My stuff's scattered all over Europe."

"Well, Seth's in school all day, isn't he?" Absently Ethan reached down to stroke the dog snoring beside his chair.

"Fine. Great." Cam gave up. "You," he said, pointing at Phillip, "bring some groceries back with you. We're out of damn near everything. And Ethan can throw whatever you bring in together into a meal. Everybody makes their own bed, goddamn it. I'm not a maid."

"What about breakfast?" Phillip said dryly. "You're

not going to send your men off in the morning without a hot meal, are you?''

Cam eyed him balefully. ''You're enjoying this, aren't you?''

''Might as well.'' He sat on the steps beside Cam, leaned back on his elbows. ''Somebody ought to talk to Seth about cleaning up his language.''

''Oh, yeah.'' Cam merely snorted. ''That'll work.''

''He swears that way in front of the neighbors, the social worker, his teachers, it's going to give a bad impression. How's his schoolwork anyway?''

''How the hell should I know?''

''Now, Mother—'' Phillip grunted, then laughed when Cam's elbow jabbed his ribs.

''Keep it up and you're going to end up with another ruined suit, ace.''

''Let me change and we can go a couple rounds. Or better yet . . .'' Phillip arched a brow, slid his gaze over toward Ethan, then back to Cam.

Approving the plan, Cam scratched his chin, set down his empty cup. They shot off the steps in tandem, so fast that Ethan barely had a chance to blink.

His fist shot out, was blocked, and he was hauled out of the chair by armpits and ankles, cursing all the way. Simon leaped up to bark delightedly and raced circles around the men who hauled his struggling master off the porch.

Inside the kitchen, the pup wiggled madly and yipped in answer. To keep him close, Seth pulled off a chunk of the chicken he'd come down to forage and dropped it on the floor. While Foolish gobbled, Seth watched in puzzled amazement as the silhouettes headed for the dock.

He'd come down to fill his empty belly. He was used to moving quietly. He'd stuffed his mouth with chicken and listened to the men talk.

They acted like they were going to let him stay. Even when they didn't know he was there to hear, they talked as if it was a simple fact. At least for now, he decided, until they forgot they'd made a promise, or no longer cared.

He knew promises didn't mean squat.

Except Ray's. He'd believed Ray. But then he'd gone and died and ruined everything. Still, every night he spent in this house, between clean sheets with the puppy curled beside him, was an escape. Whenever they decided to ditch him, he'd be ready to run.

Because he'd die before he went back to where he'd been before Ray Quinn.

The pup was nosing at the door, drawn by the sound of laughter and barking and the shouts. Seth fed him more chicken to distract him.

He wanted to go out too, to run across the lawn and join in that laughter, that fun . . . that family. But he knew he wouldn't be welcome. They'd stop and they'd stare at him as if they wondered where the hell he'd come from and what the hell they were supposed to do about it.

Then they'd tell him to get back to bed.

Oh, God, he wanted to stay. He just wanted to be here. Seth pressed his face against the screen, yearning with all his heart to belong.

When he heard Ethan's long, laughing oath, the loud splash that followed it, and the roars of male satisfaction that came next, he grinned.

And he stayed there, grinning even as a tear escaped and trickled unnoticed down his cheek.

FIVE

ANNA GOT IN TO WORK early. Odds were her supervisor would already be at her desk. You could always count on Marilou Johnston to be at her desk or within hailing distance.

Marilou was a woman Anna both admired and respected. When she needed advice, there was no one whose opinion she valued more.

When she poked her head around the open office door, Anna smiled a little. As expected, Marilou was there, buried behind the files and paperwork on her cluttered desk. She was a small woman, barely topping five feet. She wore her hair close-cropped for convenience as much as style. Her face was smooth, like polished ebony, and the expression on it could remain composed even during the worst crises.

A calm center was how Anna often thought of Marilou. Though how she could be calm when her life was filled with a demanding career, two teenage boys, and a house that Anna had seen for herself was constantly crowded with people was beyond her.

Anna often thought she wanted to be Marilou Johnston when she grew up.

"Got a minute?"

"Sure do." Marilou's voice was quick and lively, ripe with that Southern Shore accent that caught words between a drawl and a twang. She waved Anna to a chair with one hand and fiddled with the round gold ball in her left ear. "The Quinn-DeLauter case?"

"Right the first time. There were a couple of faxes waiting for me yesterday from the Quinns' lawyer. A Baltimore firm."

"What did our Baltimore lawyer have to say?"

"The gist of it is they're pursuing guardianship. He'll be pushing through a petition to the court. They're very serious about keeping Seth DeLauter in their home and under their care."

"And?"

"It's an unusual situation, Marilou. Up 'til now I've only spoken with one of the brothers. The one who lived in Europe until recently."

"Cameron? Impressions?"

"He certainly makes one." And because Marilou was also a friend, Anna allowed herself a grin and a roll of her eyes. "A treat to look at. I came across him when he was repairing the back porch steps. I can't say he looked like a happy man, but he was certainly a determined one. There's a lot of anger there, and a lot of grief. What impressed me the most—"

"Other than his looks?"

"Other than his looks," Anna agreed with a chuckle, "was the fact that he never questioned keeping Seth. It was simply fact. He called Seth his brother. He meant it. I'm not sure he knows exactly how he feels about it, but he meant it."

She went on, while Marilou listened without comment, detailing the conversation, Cam's willingness to change his life, and his lifestyle, his concerns that Seth would bolt if he were taken out of the home.

"And," she continued, "after speaking with Seth, I tend to agree with him."

"You think the boy's a runner?"

"When I suggested foster care, he became angry, resentful. And afraid. If he feels threatened, he'll run." She thought of all the children who ended up on the mean streets of inner cities, homeless, desperate. She thought of what they did to survive. And she thought of how many didn't survive at all.

It was her job to keep this one child, this one boy, safe.

"He wants to stay there, Marilou. Maybe he needs to. His feelings about his mother are very strong, and very negative. I suspect abuse, but he's not ready to discuss it. At least not with me."

"Is there any word on the mother's whereabouts?"

"No. We have no idea where she is, or what she'll do. She signed papers allowing Ray Quinn to begin adoption proceedings, but he died before they were finalized. If she comes back and wants her son . . ." Anna shook her head. "The Quinns would have a fight on their hands."

"You sound as though you'd be in their corner."

"I'm in Seth's," Anna said firmly. "And I'm going to stay there. I spoke with his teachers." She pulled out a file as she spoke. "I have my report on that. I'm going back today to speak with some of the neighbors, and hopefully to meet with all three of the Quinns. It may be possible to stop the temporary guardianship until I complete the initial study, but I'm inclined against it. That boy needs stability. He needs to feel wanted. And even if the Quinns only want him because of a promise, it's more than he's had before, I believe."

Marilou took the file, set it aside. "I assigned this case to you because you don't look just at the surface. And I sent you in cold because I wanted your take. Now I'll tell you what I know about the Quinns."

"You know them?"

"Anna, I was born and raised on the Shore." She smiled, beautifully. It was a simple fact, but one she had great pride in. "Ray Quinn was one of my professors at college. I admired him tremendously. When I had my two boys, Stella Quinn was their pediatrician until we moved to Princess Anne. We adored her.''

''When I was driving out there yesterday I kept wishing I'd had the chance to meet them.''

''They were exceptional people,'' Marilou said simply. ''Ordinary, even simple in some ways. And exceptional. Here's a case in point,'' she added, leaning back in her chair. ''I graduated from college sixteen years ago. The three Quinns were teenagers. You heard stories now and again. Maybe they were a little wild, and people wondered why Ray and Stella had taken on half-grown men with bad tendencies. I was pregnant with Johnny, my first, working my butt off to get my degree, and help my husband, Ben, pay the rent. He was working two jobs. We wanted a better life for ourselves, and we sure as hell wanted one for the baby I was carrying.''

She paused, turned the double picture frame on her desk to a closer angle so that she could see her two young men smile out at her. ''I wondered too. Figured they were crazy, or just playing at being Samaritans. Professor Quinn called me into his office one day. I'd missed a couple of classes. Had the worst case of morning sickness known to woman.''

It still made her grimace. ''I swear I don't understand how some women reminisce over that kind of thing. In any case, I thought he was going to recommend me dropping his class, which meant losing the credits toward my degree. With me an inch away—an inch away and I would be the first in my family with a college degree. I was ready to fight. Instead, he wanted to know what he could do to help. I was speechless.''

She smiled, remembering, then beamed over at Anna. ''You know how impersonal college can be—the huge lectures where a student is just one more face in the crowd. But he'd noticed me. And he'd taken the time to find out something about my situation. I burst into tears. Hormones,'' she said with a wry grin. ''Well, he patted my hand, gave me some tissues, and let me cry it out. I was on a scholarship, and if my grades dropped or I blew a class, I could lose it. I only had one more semester. He said for me not to worry, we'd work it all out, and I was going to get my degree. He started talking, about this and that, to calm me down. He was telling me some story about teaching his son to drive. Made me laugh. It wasn't until later, I realized he hadn't been talking about one of the boys he'd taken in. Because that's not what they were to him. They were his.''

A sucker for a happy ending, Anna sighed. ''And you got your degree.''

''He made sure I did. I owe him for that. Which is why I didn't tell you about this until you'd formed some impressions of your own. As for the three Quinns, I don't really know them. I've seen them at two funerals. Saw Seth DeLauter with them at Professor Quinn's. For personal reasons I'd like to see them have a chance to be a family. But . . .'' She laid her hands palm to palm. ''The best interest of the boy comes before that—and the structure of the system. You're thorough, Anna, and you believe in structure and in the system. Professor Quinn would have wanted what's best for Seth, and to repay an old debt, I gave him you.''

Anna blew out a long breath. ''No pressure, huh?''

''Pressure's all we've got around here.'' As if on cue, her phone began to ring. ''And the clock's running.''

Anna rose. ''I'd better get to work, then. Looks like I'll be in the field most of today.''

IT WAS NEARLY ONE P.M. when Anna pulled up in the Quinns' drive. She'd managed to conduct interviews with three of the five names Cam had given her the day before, and she hoped to expand on that before too much more time passed.

Her call to Phillip Quinn's office in Baltimore had given her the information that he was on leave for the next two weeks. She was hoping she would find him here and be able to file an impression of another Quinn.

But it was the pup who greeted her. He barked ferociously even as he backed rapidly away from her. Anna watched with amusement as he peed on himself in terror. With a laugh, she crouched down, held out a hand.

"Come on, cutie, I won't hurt you. Aren't you sweet, aren't you pretty?" She kept murmuring to him until he bellied over to sniff her hand, then rolled over in ecstasy as she scratched him.

"For all you know, he's got fleas and rabies."

Anna glanced up and saw Cam in the front doorway. "For all I know, so do you."

With a snort of a laugh and his hands tucked in his pockets, he came out on the porch. It was a brown suit today, he noted. For the life of him he couldn't figure why she'd pick such a dull color. "I guess you're willing to risk it, since you're back. Didn't expect you so soon."

"A boy's welfare is at stake, Mr. Quinn. I don't believe in taking my time under the circumstances."

Obviously charmed by her voice, the puppy leaped up and bathed her face. The giggle escaped before she could stop it—a sound that made Cam raise his eyebrows—and defending herself from the puppy's eager tongue, she rose. Tugged down her jacket. And her dignity.

"May I come in?"

"Why not?" This time he waited for her, even opened the door and let her go in ahead of him.

She saw a large and fairly tidy living area. The furniture showed some wear but appeared comfortable and colorful. The spinet in the corner caught her eye. "Do you play?"

"Not really." Without realizing it, Cam ran a hand over the wood. He didn't notice that his fingers left streaks in the dust. "My mother did, and Phillip's got an ear for it."

"I tried to reach your brother Phillip at his office this morning."

"He's out buying groceries." Because he was pleased to have won that battle, Cam smiled a little. "He's going to be living here . . . for the foreseeable future. Ethan, too.''

"You work fast."

"A boy's welfare is at stake," he said, echoing her.

Anna nodded. At a distant rumble of thunder, she glanced outside, frowned. The light was dimming, and the wind beginning to kick. "I'd like to discuss Seth with you." She shifted her briefcase, glanced at a chair.

"Is this going to take long?"

"I couldn't say."

"Then let's do it in the kitchen. I want coffee."

"Fine."

She followed him, using the time to study the house. It was just neat enough to make her wonder if Cam had been expecting her. They passed a den where the dust was layered over tables, the couch was covered with newspapers, and shoes littered the floor.

Missed that, didn't you? she thought with a smirk. But she found it endearing.

Then she heard his quick and vicious oath and nearly jumped out of her practical shoes.

"Goddamn it. Shit. What the hell is this? What next? Jesus Christ." He was already sloshing through the water and suds flowing over the kitchen floor to slap at the dishwasher.

Anna stepped back to avoid the flood. "I'd turn that off if I were you."

"Yeah, yeah, yeah. Now I've got to take the bitch apart." He dragged the door open. An ocean of snowy-white suds spewed out.

Anna bit the inside of her cheek, cleared her throat. "Ah, what kind of soap did you use?"

"Dish soap." Vibrating with frustration, he yanked a bucket out from under the sink.

"Dish*washer* soap or dish-washing soap?"

"What the hell's the difference?" Furious, he started to bail. Outside, the rain began to fall in hard, driving sheets.

"This." Keeping her face admirably sober, she gestured

to the river running over the floor. "This is the difference. If you use the liquid for hand-washing dishes in a dishwasher, this is the inevitable result."

He straightened, the bucket in his hand, and a look of such pained irritation on his face, she couldn't hold back the laugh. "Sorry, sorry. Look, turn around."

"Why?"

"Because I'm not willing to ruin my shoes or my hose. So turn around while I take them off and I'll give you a hand."

"Yeah." Pathetically grateful, he turned his back, and even did his best not to imagine her peeling off her stockings. His best wasn't quite good enough, but it was the effort that counted. "Ethan handled most of the kitchen chores when we were growing up. I did my share, but it doesn't seem to have stuck with me."

"You seem to be out of your element." She tucked her hose neatly in her shoes, set them aside. "Get me a mop. I'll swab, you get the coffee."

He opened a long, narrow closet and handed her a string mop. "I appreciate it."

Her legs, he noted as he sloshed over for mugs, didn't need hose. They were a pale and fascinating gold in color, and smooth as silk. When she bent over, he ran his tongue over his teeth. He'd had no idea a woman with a mop would be quite so . . . attractive.

It's so amazingly pleasant, he realized, to be here, with the rain drumming, the wind howling, and a pretty, barefoot woman keeping him kitchen company. "You seem to be in your element," he commented, then grinned when she turned her head and eyed him balefully. "I'm not saying it's woman's work. My mother would have skinned me for the thought. I'm just saying you seem to know what you're doing."

As she'd worked her way through college cleaning houses, she knew very well. "I can handle a mop, Mr. Quinn."

"Since you're mopping my kitchen floor, you ought to make it Cam."

"About Seth—"

"Yeah, about Seth. Do you mind if I sit down?"

"Go ahead." She caught herself before she began to hum. The mindless chore, the rain, the isolation were just a tad too relaxing. "I'm sure you know I spoke with him yesterday."

"Yeah, and I know he told you he wanted to stay here."

"He did, and it's in my report. I also spoke with his teachers. How much do you know about his schoolwork?"

Cam shifted. "I haven't had a lot of time to get into that yet."

"Mmm-hmm. When he was first enrolled, he had some trouble with the other students. Fistfights. He broke one boy's nose."

Good for him, Cam thought with a surprising tug of pride, but he did his best to look disapproving. "Who started it?"

"That's not the point. However, your father handled the situation. At this point I'm told that Seth keeps mostly to himself. He doesn't participate in class, which is another problem. He rarely turns in his homework assignments, and those he does bother to turn in are most often sloppily done."

Cam felt a new headache begin to brew. "So the kid's not a scholar—"

"On the contrary." Anna straightened up, leaned on the mop. "If he participated even marginally in class, and if his assignments were done and turned in on time, he would be a straight A student. He's a solid B student as it is."

"So what's the problem?"

Anna closed her eyes a moment. "The problem is that Seth's IQ and evaluation tests are incredibly high. The child is brilliant."

Though he had his doubts about that, Cam nodded. "So, that's a good thing. And he's getting decent grades and staying out of trouble."

"Okay." She would try this a different way. "Suppose you were in a Formula One race—"

"Been there," he said with wistful reminiscence. "Done that."

"Right, and you had the finest, fastest, hottest car in the field."

"Yeah." He sighed. "I did."

"But you never tested its full capabilities, you never went full-out, you never punched it on the turns or popped it into fifth and poured down the straights."

His brow lifted. "You follow racing?"

"No, but I drive a car."

"Nice car, too. What have you had it up to?"

Eighty-eight, she thought with secret glee, but she would never admit it. "I consider a car transportation," she said, lying primly. "Not a toy."

"No reason it can't be both. Why don't I take you out in the 'Vette? Now that's a fine mode of entertaining transportation."

While she would have loved to indulge in the fantasy of sliding behind the wheel of that sleek white bullet, she had a point to make. "Try to stick with the analogy here. You're racing a superior machine. If you didn't drive that car the way it was meant to be driven, you'd be wasting its potential, and maybe you'd still finish in the money, but you wouldn't win."

He got her point, but couldn't help grinning. "I usually won."

Anna shook her head. "Seth," she said with admirable patience. "We're talking about Seth. He's socially stunted, and he defies authority consistently. He's regularly given in-school suspension. He needs supervision here at home when it comes to this area of his life. You're going to have to take an active roll in his schoolwork and his behavior."

"Seems to me a kid gets B's he ought to be left the hell alone." But he held up a hand before she could speak. "Potential. I had potential drummed into my head by the best. We'll work on it."

"Good." She went back to mopping. "I had communications from your lawyer in regard to the guardianship. It's likely you'll be granted that, at least temporarily. But you can expect regular spot checks from Social Services."

"Meaning you."

"Meaning me."

Cam paused a moment. "Do you do windows?"

She couldn't help it, she laughed as she dumped sudsy water into the sink. "I've also talked to some of your neighbors and will talk to more." She turned back. "From this point on, your life's an open book for me."

He rose, took the mop, and to please himself stood just an inch closer than was polite. "You let me know when you get to a chapter that interests you, on a personal level."

Her heart gave two hard knocks against her ribs. A dangerous man, she thought, on a personal level. "I don't have time for much fiction."

She started to step back, but he took her hand. "I like you, Miz Spinelli. I haven't figured out why, but I do."

"That should make our association simpler."

"Wrong." He skimmed his thumb over the back of her hand. "It's going to make it complicated. But I don't mind complications. And it's about time my luck started back on an upswing. You like Italian food?"

"With a name like Spinelli?"

He grinned. "Right. I could use a quiet meal in a decent restaurant with a pretty woman. How about tonight?"

"I don't see any reason why you shouldn't have a quiet meal in a decent restaurant with a pretty woman tonight." Deliberately, she eased her hand free. "But if you're asking me for a date, the answer's no. First, it wouldn't be smart; second, I'm booked."

"Damn it, Cam, didn't you hear me honking?"

Anna turned and saw a soaking wet and bitterly angry man cart two heaping bags of groceries into the room. He was tall, bronzed, and very nearly beautiful. And spitting mad.

Phillip shook the hair out of his eyes and focused on
Anna. The shift of expression was quick and smooth—
from snarling to charming in the space of a single heartbeat.

"Hello. Sorry." He dumped the bags on the table and
smiled at her. "Didn't know Cam had company." He
spied the bucket, the mop held between them, and leaped
to the wrong conclusion. "I didn't know he was going to
hire domestic help. But thank God." Phillip grabbed her
hand, kissed it. "I already adore you."

"My brother Phillip," Cam said dryly. "This is Anna
Spinelli, with Social Services. You can take your Ferragamo out of your mouth now, Phil."

The charm didn't shift or fade. "Ms. Spinelli. It's nice
to meet you. Our lawyer's been in touch, I believe."

"Yes, he has. Mr. Quinn tells me you'll be living here
now."

"I told you to call me Cam." He walked to the stove
to top off his coffee. "It's going to be confusing if you're
calling all of us Mr. Quinn." Cam heard the rattle at the
back door and got out another mug. "Especially now," he
said as the door burst open and let in a dripping dog and
man.

"Christ, this bitch blew in fast." Even as Ethan dragged
off his slicker, the dog set his feet and shook furiously.
Anna only winced as water sprayed her suit. "Barely
smelled her before—"

He spotted Anna and automatically pulled off his soaked
cap, then scooped a hand through his damp, curling hair.
Seeing woman, bucket, mop, he thought guiltily about his
muddy boots. "Ma'am."

"My other brother, Ethan." Cam handed Ethan a steaming cup of coffee. "This is the social worker your dog's
just sprayed water and dog hair all over."

"Sorry. Simon, go sit."

"It's all right," Cam went on. "Foolish already slobbered all over her, and Phillip just got finished hitting on
her."

Anna smiled blandly. "I thought you were hitting on me."

"I asked you to dinner," Cam corrected. "If I'd been hitting on you, I wouldn't have been subtle." Cam sipped his coffee. "Well, now you know all the players."

She felt outnumbered, and more than a little unprofessional standing there in the dimly lit kitchen in her bare feet, facing three big and outrageously handsome men. In defense, she pulled out every scrap of dignity and reached for a chair.

"Gentlemen, shall we sit down? This seems to be an ideal time to discuss how you plan to care for Seth." She angled her head at Cam. "For the foreseeable future."

"WELL," PHILLIP SAID AN hour later. "I think we pulled that off."

Cam stood at the front door, watching the neat little sports car drive away in the thinning rain. "She's got our number," Cam muttered. "She doesn't miss a trick."

"I liked her." Ethan stretched out in the big wing chair and let the puppy climb into his lap. "Get your mind out of the sewer, Cam," he suggested when Cam snickered. "I mean I liked her. She's smart, and she's professional, but she's not cold. Seems like a woman who cares."

"And she's got great legs," Phillip added. "But regardless of all that, she's going to note down every time we screw up. Right now, I figure we've got the upper hand. We've got the kid, and he wants to stay. His mother's run off to God knows where and isn't making any noises—at the moment. But if pretty Anna Spinelli talks to too many people around St. Chris, she's going to start hearing the rumors."

He dipped his hands in his pockets and started to pace. "I don't know if they're going to count against us or not."

"They're just rumors," Ethan said.

"Yeah, but they're ugly. We've got a good shot at keeping Seth because of Dad's reputation. That reputation gets smeared, and we'll have battles to fight on several fronts."

"Anyone tries to smear Dad's rep, they're going to get more than a fight."

Phillip turned to Cam. "That's just what we have to avoid. If we start going around kicking ass, it's only going to make things worse."

"So you be the diplomat." Cam shrugged and sat on the arm of the sofa. "I'll kick ass."

"I'd say we're better off dealing with what is than what might be." Thoughtfully, Ethan stroked the puppy. "I've been thinking about the situation. It's going to be rough for Phillip to live here and commute back and forth to Baltimore. Sooner rather than later, Cam's going to get fed up with playing house."

"Sooner's already here."

"I was thinking we could pay Grace to do some of the housework. Maybe a couple days a week."

"Now that's an idea I can get behind one hundred percent." Cam dropped onto the sofa.

"Trouble with that is it leaves you with nothing much to do. The idea is for the three of us to be here, share responsibility for Seth. That's what the lawyer says, that's what the social worker says."

"I said I'd find work."

"What are you going to do?" Phillip asked. "Pump gas? Shuck oysters? You'd put up with that for a couple of days."

Cam leaned forward. "I can stick. Can you? Odds are, after the first week of commuting, you'll be calling from Baltimore with excuses about why you can't make it back. Why don't you stay here and try pumping gas or shucking oysters for a while?"

The argument was inevitable. In minutes they were both up and nose to nose. It took several attempts before Ethan's voice got through. Cam stepped back and with a puzzled frown turned. "What?"

"I said I think we ought to try building boats."

"Building boats?" Cam shook his head. "For what?"

"For business." Ethan took out a cigar, but ran it through his fingers rather than lighting it. His mother hadn't allowed smoking in the house. "We got a lot of tourists coming down this way in the last few years. And a lot more people moving down to get out of the city. They like to rent boats. They like to own boats. Last year I built one in my spare time for this guy out of D.C. Little fourteen-foot skiff. Called me a couple months ago to see if I'd be interested in building him another one. Wants a bigger boat, with a sleep cabin and galley."

Ethan tucked the cigar back in his pocket. "I've been thinking on it. It'd take me months to do it alone, in my spare time."

"You want us to help you build a boat?" Phillip pressed his fingers to his eyes.

"Not one boat. I'm talking about going into business."

"I'm in business," Phillip muttered. "I'm in advertising."

"And we'd be needing somebody who knew about that kind of thing if we were starting a business. Boat building's got a history in this area, but nobody's doing it anymore on St. Chris."

Phillip sat. "Did it occur to you that there might be a reason for that?"

"Yeah, it occurred to me. And I thought about it, and I figure it's because nobody's taking the chance. I'm talking wooden boats. Sailing vessels. A specialty. And we already got one client."

Cam rubbed his chin. "Hell, Ethan, I haven't done that kind of work seriously since we built your skipjack. That's been—Jesus—almost ten years."

"And she's holding, isn't she? So we did a good job with her. It's a gamble," he added, knowing that single word was the way to Cam's heart.

"We've got money for start-up costs," Cam murmured, warming up to the idea.

"How do you know?" Phillip demanded. "You don't

have a clue how much money you need for start-up costs.''

''You'll figure it out.'' A roll of the dice, Cam thought. He liked nothing better. ''Christ knows, I'd rather be swinging a hammer than a damn vacuum hose. I'm in.''

''Just like that?'' Phillip threw up his hands. ''Without a thought to overhead, profit and loss, licenses, taxes, insurance. Where the hell are you going to set up shop? How're you going to run the business end?''

''That's not my problem,'' Cam said with a grin. ''That would be yours.''

''I have a job. In Baltimore.''

''I had a life,'' Cam said simply, ''in Europe.''

Phillip paced away, back, away again. Trapped, was all he could think. ''I'll do what I can to get things started. This could be a huge mistake, and it's going to cost a lot of money. And you'd both better consider that the social worker might take a dim view of us starting a risky business at this point. I'm not giving up my job. At least that's one steady income.''

''I'll talk to her about it,'' Cam decided on impulse. ''See how she reacts. You'll talk to Grace about pitching in around the house?'' he asked Ethan.

''Yeah, I'll go down to the pub and run it by her.''

''Fine. That leaves you to deal with Seth tonight.'' He smiled thinly at Phillip. ''Make sure he does his homework.''

''Oh, God.''

''Now that that's settled,'' Cam eased back, ''who's cooking dinner?''

SIX

TRACKING DOWN ANNA
Spinelli was the perfect excuse to escape the post-dinner
chaos at home. It meant the dishes were someone else's
problem—and that he couldn't be pulled into the homework argument that had just begun to heat up between
Phillip and Seth.

In fact, as far as Cam was concerned, a rainy evening
drive to Princess Anne was high entertainment. And that
was pretty pitiful for a man who'd grown accustomed to
jetting from Paris to Rome.

He tried not to think about it.

He'd arranged to have his hydrofoil stored, his clothes
packed up and sent. He had yet to have his car shipped
over, though. It was just a bit too permanent a commitment. But between the time spent repairing steps and doing
laundry, he'd entertained himself by tuning up and tinker-
ing with his mother's prized 'Vette.

It gave him a great deal of pleasure to drive it—so much
that he accepted the speeding ticket he collected just outside of Princess Anne without complaint.

The town wasn't the hive of activity it had been during
the eighteenth and nineteenth centuries when tobacco had

been king and wealth poured into the area. But it was pretty enough, Cam supposed, with the old homes restored and preserved, the streets clean and quiet. Now that tourism was becoming the newest deity for the Shore, the charm and grace of historic towns were a huge economic draw.

Anna's apartment was less than half a mile from the offices of Social Services. Easy walking distance to work, to the courts. Shopping was convenient. He imagined she'd chosen the old Victorian house for those reasons as well as for the ambience.

The building was tucked behind big trees, their branches now hazed with new leaves. The walkway was cracked but flanked by daffodils that were ready to pop out with sunny yellow. Steps led to a covered veranda. The plaque beside the door stated that the house was on the historic register.

The door itself was unlocked and led Cam into a hallway. The wood floor was a bit worn, but someone had troubled to polish it to a dull gleam. The mail slots on the wall were brass, again polished, and indicated that the building had been converted to four apartments. A. Spinelli occupied 2B.

Cam trooped up the creaking stairs to the second floor. The hallway was more narrow here, the lights dimmer. The only sound he heard was the muffled echo of what sounded like a riotous sitcom from the television of 2A.

He knocked on Anna's door and waited. Then he knocked again, tucked his hands in his pockets, and scowled. He'd expected her to be home. He'd never considered otherwise. It was nearly nine o'clock, a weeknight, and she was a civil servant.

She should have been quietly at home, reading a book or filling out forms and reports. That was how practical career women spent their evenings—though he hoped eventually to show her a more entertaining way to pass the time.

Probably at some women's club meeting, he decided, annoyed with her. He searched the pockets of his black leather bomber jacket for a scrap of paper and was about to disturb 2A in hopes of borrowing something to write on and with when he heard the quick, rhythmic click that an experienced man recognized as a woman's high heels against wood.

He glanced down the hall, pleased that his luck had changed.

He barely noticed that his jaw dropped.

The woman who walked toward him was built like a man's darkest fantasy. And she was generous enough to showcase that killer body in a snug electric-blue dress scooped low at the breasts and cut high on the thighs. It left nothing—and everything to a male's imagination.

The click of heels on wood was courtesy of ice pick heels in the same shocking color, which turned her legs into endless fascination.

Her hair, dewy with rain, curled madly to her shoulders, a thick ebony mane that brought images of gypsies and campfire sex to mind. Her mouth was red and wet, her eyes huge and dark. The scent of her reached him ten seconds before she did and delivered a breathtaking punch straight to the loins.

She said nothing, only narrowed those amazing eyes, cocked one glorious hip, and waited.

"Well." He had to work on getting his breath back. "I guess you've never heard the one about hiding your light under a bushel."

"I've heard it." She was furious to find him on her doorstep, furious that she was without her professional armor. And even more furious that he'd been on her mind throughout the evening a great deal more than her date. "What do you want, Mr. Quinn?"

Now he grinned, fast and sharp as a wolf baring fangs. "That's a loaded question at the moment, Miz Spinelli."

"Don't be ordinary, Quinn. You've avoided that so far."

"I promise you, I don't have a single ordinary thought in my mind." Unable to resist, he reached out to toy with the ends of her hair. "Where ya been, Anna?"

"Look, it's well after business hours, and my personal life isn't—" She broke off, struggled not to curse or moan as the door across the hall opened.

"You're back from your date, Anna."

"Yes, Mrs. Hardelman."

The woman of about seventy was wrapped in a pink chenille robe and peered over the glasses perched on her nose. Heat and canned laughter poured out into the hall. She beamed at Cam, the smile lighting her pleasant face. "Oh, he's much better-looking than the last one."

"Thanks." Cam stepped over and smiled back. "Does she have a lot of them?"

"Oh, they come and they go." Mrs. Hardelman chuckled and fluffed at her thin white hair. "She never keeps them."

Cam leaned companionably on the doorjamb, enjoying the sounds of frustration Anna made behind him. "Guess she hasn't found one worth keeping yet. She sure is pretty."

"And such a nice girl. She picks up things at the market for us if Sister and I aren't feeling up to going out. Always offers to drive us to church on Sunday. And when my Petie died, Anna took care of the burial herself."

Mrs. Hardelman looked over at Anna with such affection and sweetness, Anna could only sigh. "You're missing your show, Mrs. Hardelman."

"Oh, yes." She glanced back into the apartment, where the television blasted. "I do love my comedies. You come back now," she told Cam and gently closed the door.

And because Anna was perfectly aware that her neighbor wouldn't be able to resist peeping through the security hole hoping to catch a romantic good-night kiss, she dug out her keys.

"You might as well come in since you're here."

"Thanks." He crossed the hall, waiting while she unlocked her door. "You buried your neighbor's husband."

"Her parakeet," Anna corrected. "Petie was a bird. She

and her sister have both been widows for about twenty years. And all I did was get a shoe box and dig a hole out back next to a rosebush.''

He brushed a hand over her hair again as she pushed the door open. ''It meant something to her.''

''Watch your hands, Quinn,'' she warned and flicked on the lights.

To indicate that he was willing to oblige, he held them out, then tucked them into his pockets while he studied the room. Soft, deep cushions, bright, bold colors. He decided the choices meant she had a deep-rooted sensual side.

He liked to think that.

The room was spacious, and she'd furnished it sparingly. The sofa was big and plush enough for sleeping, but there was only a wide upholstered chair and two tables to keep it company.

Yet she'd covered the walls with art. Prints, posters, pen-and-ink sketches. They were of places rather than people, and many of the scenes he recognized. The narrow streets of Rome, the wild cliffs of western Ireland, the classy little cafes of Paris.

''I've been here.'' He tapped the frame of the Paris cafe.

''How nice for you.'' She said it dryly, trying not to resent the fact that her pictures were the only way she could afford to travel. For now. ''Now, what are you doing here?''

''I wanted to talk to you about—'' He made the mistake of turning, looking at her again. She was obviously a very annoyed woman, but it only added to her appeal. Her eyes and mouth were sulky, her body braced in challenge. ''Christ, you're a looker, Anna. I was attracted to you before—I imagine you caught that—but . . . who knew?''

She didn't want to be flattered. She certainly didn't want her heartbeat to pick up speed and lose its steady rhythm. But it was difficult to control either reaction when a man like Cameron Quinn was standing there looking at her as if he'd like to start nibbling at any single part of her body and keep going till he'd devoured it all.

She took a careful breath. "You wanted to talk to me about . . . ?" she prompted.

"The kid, stuff. How about some coffee? That's civilized, right?" He decided to test them both by walking to her. "I figure you expect me to act civilized. I'm willing to give it a shot."

She brooded a moment, then pivoted on those sexy blue heels. Cam appreciated the rear view, rolled his eyes toward heaven, then followed her to the spotless counter that separated living room and kitchen. He leaned on it, pleased that the location gave him a perfect view of her legs.

Then he heard the electric rumble and caught the amazing scent of fresh coffee. "You grind your own beans?"

"If you're going to make coffee, you might as well make good coffee."

"Yeah." He closed his eyes to better appreciate the aroma. "Oh, yeah. Do I have to marry you to get you to make my coffee every day, or can we just live together?"

She looked over her shoulder, lifted her brows at his wide, winning grin, then got back to the task at hand.

"I bet you've used that look to shut men down with enormous success. But me, I like it. So where were you tonight?"

"I had a date."

He moved around the counter. The kitchen area was small, no more than a narrow passageway. He liked being close enough so that her scent mixed with the smell of coffee. "Early evening," he commented.

"It was going to be." She felt the hair on the back of her neck prickle. He was too damn close. Instinctively she employed her usual method with men who crowded her space. She rammed her elbow into his gut.

"Practiced move," he murmured and, rubbing his stomach, backed off an inch. "Do you ever have to use it in your social worker mode?"

"Rarely. How do you want your coffee?"

"Strong and black."

She set it to brew, turned around, and bumped solidly into him. Her radar, she decided as his hands came up to take her arms, had definitely been off. Or, she was forced to admit, she'd ignored it because she'd wondered how they might fit.

Well, now she knew.

He deliberately kept his eyes on her face, didn't let them dip down to the small gold cross nestled between her breasts. He wasn't particularly devout, but he was afraid he would go to hell for having lascivious thoughts about the framework for a religious symbol.

Besides, he liked her face.

"Quinn," she said with a long, irritated sigh. "Back off."

"You dropped the *Mister* Quinn. Does that mean we're pals?"

Because he smiled when he said it, and because he did step back, she found herself chuckling. "Jury's still out."

"I like the way you smell, Anna. Lusty, provocative. Challenging. Of course, I like the way Miz Spinelli smells, too. Quiet and practical and subtle."

"All right . . . Cam." She turned, took out two pretty, deep cups from the cupboard. "Let's stop dancing and agree that we're attracted to each other."

"I was hoping once we agreed to that we'd start dancing."

"Wrong." She tossed her hair back and poured coffee. "I'm Seth's caseworker. You're proposing to be his guardian. It would be incredibly unwise for either of us to act on a physical attraction."

He picked up the cup, leaned back against the counter. "I don't know about you, but I love doing stuff that's unwise. Especially if it feels good." He brought the cup to his lips, then smiled slowly. "And I bet acting on that physical attraction would feel damn good."

"It's fortunate that I happen to be very wise." With a mirroring smile, she leaned back on the opposite counter.

"Now, you wanted to discuss Seth—and stuff, as I believe you put it."

Seth, the rest of his brothers, and the situation had gone completely out of his mind. He supposed he'd used it as an excuse to see her. That was something to consider later. "I have to admit, coming into Princess Anne to talk to you was a great reason to escape. I was about to get stuck with dish duty, and Phil and the kid were already into round one on the homework issue."

"I'm glad someone's dealing with his schoolwork. And why don't you ever refer to Seth by his name?"

"I do. Sure I do."

"No, not as a rule." She cocked her head. "Is that a habit of yours, Cameron, to avoid the personal contact of names with people you don't intend to have an important or permanent relationship with?"

Her point, he was forced to admit, but he lifted a brow. "I use your name."

He saw her blink, heard her sigh, then she waved the issue away. "What about Seth?"

"It's not about him, directly. Except I figure we're starting to divvy things up more evenhandedly. Phil's the best to keep on him—keep on Seth," he corrected with emphasis, "about school because for some reason Phil actually liked school. And we decided to get somebody to come in and deal with most of the housework a couple of days a week."

She still had a picture of him standing in a puddle of suds with a look of baffled fury on his face. Her lips wanted badly to twitch into a smile. "You'll be happier."

"I hope never to see another vacuum cleaner bag. Ever had one rip on you?" He shuddered deliberately and made her laugh. "Anyhow, Ethan had this brainstorm. I'm at loose ends, Phillip needs something to occupy him if he's going to be staying here—though he figures on commuting to Baltimore for now. So we're going into business."

"Into business? What kind of business?"

"Boat building."

She lowered her cup. "You're going to build boats?"

"I've built plenty—so has Ethan. And actually, though Phil went over to the suit-and-tie life, he's done some himself. The three of us worked on the skipjack that Ethan still sails."

"That's fine for recreation, for personal use, for a hobby. But to consider starting a business, a risky one, at the very time when you're trying to take on a minor dependent . . ."

"He won't go hungry. For Christ's sake, Ethan holds his own on the bay, and Phil's got that desk job in Baltimore. I could get busywork, but what's the point?"

"I'm only pointing out that a venture of this nature would consume a great deal of money and time, particularly during the first months. Stability—"

"Isn't every damn thing." Annoyed, he set his coffee down and began to pace. "Shouldn't the kid learn there's more to life than nine-to-fiving it? That there can be choices, that you can take a chance? How good is it for him if I'm stuck in that house dusting furniture and hating every goddamn minute of it? Ethan's already got one client, and if Ethan brought this up you can believe he's weighed it from every angle. Nobody thinks things through as much as he does."

"And since you felt you wanted to discuss this with me, I'm simply trying to do the same. Weigh it from every angle."

"And you think it would be better if I went out and got some nice, stable, time-clock job that brings in a nice, stable, time-clock paycheck every week." He stopped in front of her. "Is that the kind of man who appeals to you? The kind who reports in at nine five days a week, who takes you out to dinner on a rainy night and lets you get away at a reasonable hour without even trying to convince you to take off what there is of that dress?"

She took a minute, reminding herself it wouldn't solve anything if both of them lost the battle with temper. "What appeals to me, what I wear, and how I choose to spend my evenings aren't the issues here. As Seth's caseworker, I'm concerned that his home life be as stable and happy as possible.''

"Why should me building boats make him unhappy?"

"My question regarding this idea of yours is whether your attention will be taken away from him and turned toward this new business. A business that you would, I imagine, find exciting, challenging, and interesting, at least for a time."

His eyes narrowed. "You just don't think I can stick, do you?"

"That's yet to be proved. But I do think you'll try. What worries me is that you're not trying for Seth, you're trying for your father. For your parents. I don't think that's a count against you, Cam," she said more gently. "But it's not a point in Seth's favor."

How the hell did you argue with a woman who insisted on dotting every *i*? he wondered. "So you think he's better off with strangers?"

"No, I think he's better off with you and your brothers." She smiled, satisfied that she had shut him up for the moment. "And that's what went into my report. This idea of starting a boat-building business is something new to think about, and I hope none of you intends to rush into it."

"Do you sail?"

"No, I've never tried it. Why?"

"I'd never been on a boat in my life until Ray Quinn took me out."

Because he remembered how those eyes of hers could warm with compassion, he decided to tell her how it had been for him. "I was scared to death, but too tough to admit it. I'd only been with them a few days, never figured I'd stay. He took me out on this little Sunfish he had back then. Told me the air would do me good."

All he had to do was think, and the image of that morning came clear as sunlight in his head. "My father was a big man. The Mighty Quinn. Built like a bull. I knew that little boat was going to tip over, and I'd probably drown, but he had a way of getting you to do things.''

Love, Anna thought. It was pure and simple love in his voice. It attracted her, she admitted, every bit as much as that toughly handsome face. "Could you swim?"

"No—but I still hated it that he made me wear a PFD. Personal flotation device," he explained. "Life jacket. Figured it was for sissies."

"You'd rather have drowned?"

"Hell, no, but I had to make him think so. Anyway, I sat in the stern, my stomach clutched. I was wearing these sunglasses my mother—Stella," he corrected, for she'd been Stella then—"had dug up somewhere because my eye was pretty banged up and the sunlight hurt."

He'd been beaten, abused, neglected, she remembered, when the Quinns had found him. Her heart went out to the little boy. "You must have been terrified."

"Down to the bone, but I'd have choked on my tongue before I'd have admitted it. He must have known that," Cam said quietly. "He always knew what was in my head. It was hot, and the humidity was up so that every time you took a breath it was like swallowing water. He said it would be cooler when we moved out of the gut and onto the river, but I didn't believe him. I figured we'd just sit there and fry. The boat didn't even have a motor. Christ, he laughed when I said that. He told me we had something better than a motor."

He'd forgotten his coffee, and even the point of the story drifted away in the memory. "We headed out across the water, slow and easy at first, the boat rocked when we turned into the bend, and I figured that was it. Game over. This heron came out of the trees. I'd seen it once before. At least I like to think it was the same one. It winged right over the boat, wings spread to trap the air. And then we caught the wind and that little sail filled. We started to fly. He turned around and grinned at me. I didn't even know I was grinning back until I split my lip open again. I'd never felt like that before in my life. Not once."

Without thinking, he lifted his hand and tucked her hair behind her ear. "Not once in my life."

"It changed you." She knew that single moments, both simple and dramatic, could alter courses forever.

"It started to. A boat on the water, and people who were giving me a chance. It wasn't much more complicated than that. It doesn't have to be that much more complicated here. We'll have the kid swing the hammer, put some sweat and effort into building a boat. If it's going to be a Quinn operation, that includes him."

Her smile came quickly, fully, and to his surprise, she patted him on the cheek. "That last part said it all. It's a gamble. I'm not sure if it's the time or the place for one, but . . . it should be interesting to watch."

"Is that what you're going to do?" He eased forward, nudging her back against the counter. "Watch me?"

"I don't intend to take my eyes off you—on a professional level—until I'm assured that you and your brothers provide Seth with the proper home and guardianship."

"Fair enough." He moved in just a little closer, just a fraction till two well-toned bodies brushed. "And how about on a personal level?"

She weakened enough to let her gaze skim down, linger. His mouth was definitely tempting—dangerous and very close. "Keeping my eyes on you on a personal level isn't a hardship. A mistake, maybe—but not a hardship."

"I always figure if you're going to make a mistake . . ." He put his hands on the counter, caging her. "Make it a big one. What do you say, Anna?" He dipped his head a little lower, hovered.

She tried to think, to consider the consequences. But there were times when needs, desire, and lust simply overpowered logic. "Hell," she muttered and, cupping her hand at the back of his neck, dragged his mouth down on hers.

It was exactly as she wanted. Hungry and fierce and mindless. His mouth was hot, and it was hard, and it was almost heathen as he crushed down to devour hers. She gave in to it, gave all to it, a moment's madness where body ruled mind and blood roared over reason.

And the thrill snapped through her like a whip, sharp, painful, and with a quick, shocking burn.

"Christ." His breath was gone, his mind was reeling. Reflexively, his hands dug into the counter before he jerked them away and filled them with her.

Whatever he'd expected, whatever he'd imagined didn't come close to the volcano that had so suddenly erupted in his arms. He dragged a hand through her hair, the wild, curling mass of it, fisted it there, then plundered as if his life depended on it.

"Can't," she managed, but her arms wound around him, banded around him until it seemed his heart wasn't merely thundering against hers but inside hers. Her moan was a rumble of desperate, delirious pleasure that sounded in her throat exactly where his teeth nipped, then scraped, then dug greedily into flesh.

The counter bit into her back, her fingers bit into his hips as she dragged him closer. Oh, God, she wanted contact, friction, more. She found his mouth with hers again, plunged blindly into the next kiss.

Just one more, she promised herself, meeting, matching his reckless demand.

Her scent seduced his senses. Her name was a murmur on his lips, a whisper in his mind. Her body was a glorious banquet melded to his. No woman had ever filled him so quickly, so completely, so utterly to the exclusion of all else.

"Let me." It was a plea, and he'd never in his life begged for a woman. "For God's sake, Anna, let me have you." His hands ran up her legs, those endless thighs. "Now."

She wanted. It would be so easy to take, and be taken. But easy, she knew, was rarely right.

"No. Not now." Regret smothered her even as she lifted her hands to frame his face. For a moment longer, her mouth stayed on his. "Not yet. Not like this."

Her eyes were dark, clouded. He knew enough of a woman's pleasures and his own skills to believe he could make them go blind. "It's perfect like this."

"The timing's wrong, the circumstances. Wait." Someone had to move, she decided. To break that contact. She sidestepped, let out a shaky breath. She closed her eyes, lifted a hand to hold him off. "Well," she managed after another moment, "that was insane."

He took the hand she'd raised, brought it to his lips and nipped his teeth into her forefinger. "Who needs sanity?"

"I do." She nearly managed a genuine smile as she tugged her hand free. "Not that I don't regret that deeply at this moment, but I do need it. Wow." She drew in another long breath, pushed her hands up through her hair. "Cameron. You're every bit as potent as I expected."

"I haven't even started."

The smile widened. "I bet. I just bet." She eased back a little more, picked up her rapidly cooling coffee. "I don't know as that episode's going to make either one of us sleep easier tonight, but it was bound to happen." She angled her head when his eyes narrowed. "What?"

"Most women, especially in your position, would make excuses."

"For what?" She lifted a shoulder and promised herself her system would level again eventually. "That was as much my doing as yours. I wondered what it might be like to get my hands on you from the first time I saw you."

Cam decided he might never be the same again. "I think I'm crazy about you."

"No, you're not." She laughed and handed him his coffee. "You're intrigued, you're attracted, you've got a good healthy case of lust, but those are entirely different matters. And you don't even know me."

"I want to." He let out a short laugh. "And that's a big surprise to me. I don't usually care one way or the other."

"I'm flattered. I'm not sure if that's a tribute to your charm or my own stupidity, but I'm flattered. But—"

"Damn, I knew that was coming."

"But," she repeated and set her cup in the sink. "Seth is my priority. He has to be." The warmth that was both compassion and understanding came into her eyes, and it touched something in him that was buried under that healthy lust. "And he should be yours. I hope I'm around if and when that happens."

"I'm doing everything I can think of."

"I know you are. And you're doing more than most would." She touched his arm briefly, then moved away. "I have a feeling you've got more inside you yet. But . . ."

"There it is again."

"You'd better go now."

He wanted to stay, even if it was just to stand there and talk to her, to be. "I haven't finished my coffee."

"It's cold. And it's getting late." She glanced toward the window where raindrops ran like tears. "And the rain makes me wonder about things I shouldn't be wondering about."

He winced. "I don't suppose you said that to make me suffer."

"Sure I did." She laughed again and moved to the door, opened it wide to make her point. "If I'm going to, why shouldn't you?"

"Oh, I like you, Anna Spinelli. You're a woman after my own heart."

"You're not interested in a woman going for your heart," she said as he crossed the room. "You want one who's after your body."

"See, we're getting to know each other already."

"Good night." She didn't evade when he pulled her in for another kiss as he walked out the door. Evading would have been a pretense, and she wasn't one to delude herself.

So she met the kiss with teasing heat and honest enthusiasm. Then she shut the door in his face.

And then she leaned back against it weakly.

Potent? That wasn't the half of it. Her pulse was likely to stay on overdrive for hours. Maybe days.

She wished she didn't feel so damn happy about it.

SEVEN

Cam was scowling at a basket full of pink socks and Jockey shorts when the phone rang. He knew damn well the socks and underwear had been white—or close to it—when he'd dumped them in the machine. Now they were Easter-egg pink.

Maybe they just looked that way because they were wet.

He pulled them out to stuff them in the dryer, saw the red sock hiding among the pink. And bared his teeth.

Phillip, he vowed, was a dead man.

"Fuck it." He dumped them inside, slapped the dryer on what he hoped was broil and went to answer the phone.

He remembered, just in time, to turn down the little portable TV tucked in the corner of the counter. It wasn't as if he was actually watching it, it certainly wasn't that he was paying any attention at all to the passion and betrayals of the late-morning soap opera.

He'd just switched it on for the noise.

"Quinn. What?"

"Hey, Cam. Took some doing to track you down, hoss. Tod Bardette here."

Cam reached into an open bag of Oreos on the counter and took out a handful. "How's it going, Tod?"

"Well, I have to tell you it's going pretty damn good. I've been spending some time anchored off the Great Barrier Reef."

"Nice spot," Cam muttered over a cookie. Then his brows shot up as an impossibly gorgeous woman tumbled into bed with a ridiculously handsome man on the tiny screen across the kitchen.

Maybe there was something to this daytime TV after all.

"It'll do. Heard you kicked ass in the Med a few weeks ago."

A few weeks? Cam thought while he munched on a second cookie. Surely it had been a few years ago that he'd flown across the finish line in his hydrofoil. Blue water, speed, cheering crowds, and money to burn.

Now he was lucky if he found enough milk in the fridge to wash down a stale Oreo.

"Yeah, that's what I heard too."

Tod gave a rich chuckle. "Well, the offer to buy that toy from you still holds. But I got another proposition coming at you."

Tod Bardette always had another proposition coming at you. He was the rich son of a rich father from East Texas who used the world as his playground. And he was boat happy. He raced them, sponsored races, bought and sold them. And collected wives, trophies, and his share of the purse with smooth regularity.

Cam had always felt Tod's luck had run hot since conception. Since it never hurt to listen—and the bedroom scene had just been displaced by a commercial featuring a giant toilet brush, he switched off the set.

"I'm always ready to hear one."

"I'm setting up a crew for La Coupe Internationale."

"The One-Ton Cup?" Cam felt his juices begin to flow, and he lost all interest in cookies and milk. The international race was a giant in the sailing world. Five legs, he thought, the final one an ocean race of three hundred grueling miles.

"You got it. You know the Aussies took the cup last

year, so it's being held down here in Australia. I want to whip their butts, and I've got a honey of a boat. She's fast, hoss. With the right crew she'll bring the cup back to the U S of A. I need a skipper. I want the best. I want you. How soon can you get Down Under?''

Give me five minutes. That's what he wanted to say. He could have a bag packed in one, hop a plane and be on his way. For men who raced, it was one of life's golden opportunities. Even as he opened his mouth, his gaze landed on the rocker outside the kitchen window.

So he closed his eyes, listened resentfully to the hum of the pink socks drying in the utility room behind him.

''I have to pass, Tod. I can't get away now.''

''Lookie here, I'm willing to give you some time to put your affairs—pun intended,'' he said with a snorting laugh, ''in order. Take a couple weeks. If you've got another offer, I'll beat it.''

''I can't do it. I've got—'' Laundry to do? A kid to raise? Damn if he was going to humiliate himself with that piece of information. ''My brothers and I started a business,'' he said on impulse. ''I've got a commitment here.''

''A business.'' This time Tod's laugh was long and delighted. ''You? Don't pull my leg so hard, it hurts.''

Now Cam's eyes narrowed. He didn't doubt Tod Bardette of East Texas would be joined by others of his friends and acquaintances in laughing at the idea of Cameron Quinn, businessman.

''We're building boats,'' he said between his teeth. ''Here on the Eastern Shore. Wooden boats. Custom jobs,'' he added, determined to play it to the hilt. ''One of a kinds. In six months, you'll be paying me top dollar to design and build you a boat by Quinn. Since we're old friends, I'll try to squeeze you in.''

''Boats.'' The interest in Tod's voice picked up. ''Well now, you know how to sail them, guess maybe you'd know how to build them.''

''There's no maybe about it.''

''That's an interesting enterprise, but come on, Cam,

you're not a businessman. You're not going to stay stuck on some pretty little bay in Maryland eating crabs and nailing planks. You know I'll make this race worth your while. Money, fame and fortune.'' And he chuckled. ''After we win, you can go back and put a couple of little sloops together.''

He could handle it, Cam promised himself. He could handle the insults, the frustration of not being able to pack and go as he chose. What he wouldn't do was give Bardette the satisfaction of knowing he was ruffled. ''You're going to have to find another skipper. But if you want to buy a boat, give me a call.''

''If you actually get one finished, give me a call.'' A sigh came through the receiver. ''You're missing the chance of a lifetime here. You change your mind in the next couple hours, get in touch. But I need to nail down my crew this week. Talk to you.''

And Cam was listening to a dial tone.

He didn't hurl the receiver through the window. He wanted to, considered it, then figured he'd be the one sweeping up the glass, so what would be the point?

So he hung up the phone, with careful deliberation. He even took a deep breath. And if whatever he'd put in the washing machine hadn't chosen that moment to spin out of balance and send the machine hopping, he wouldn't have slammed his fist into the wall.

''I thought for a minute there you were going to pull it off.''

He whirled, and saw his father sitting at the kitchen table, chuckling. ''Oh, God, this caps it.''

''Why don't you get some ice for your knuckles?''

''It's all right.'' Cam glanced down at them. A couple of scrapes. And the sharp pain was a good hold on reality. ''I thought about this, Dad. Really thought about it. I just don't believe you're here.''

Ray continued to smile. ''You're here, Cam. That's what matters. It was tough turning down a race like that. I'm grateful to you. I'm proud of you.''

"Bardette said he had a honey of a boat. With his money behind it . . ." Cam pressed his hands on the counter and stared out the window toward the quiet water. "I could win that bastard. I captained a crew to second in the Little America's Cup five years ago, and I took the Chicago-Mackinac last year."

"You're a fine sailor, Cam."

"Yeah." He curled his fingers into fists. "What the hell am I doing here? If this keeps up I'm going to get hooked on soap operas. I'll start thinking Lilac and Lance are not only real people but close personal friends. I'll start obsessing that my whites aren't white enough. I'll clip coupons and collect recipes and go the rest of the way out of my fucking mind."

"I'm surprised at you, thinking of tending a home in those terms." Ray's voice was sharp now, with disappointment around the edges. "Making a home, caring for family is important work. The most important work there is."

"It's not my work."

"It seems it is now. I'm sorry for that."

Cam turned back. If you were going to have a conversation with a hallucination, you might as well look at it. "For what? For dying on me?"

"Well, that was pretty inconvenient all around."

He would have laughed, the comment and the ironic tone were so typically Ray Quinn. But he had to get out what was nibbling at his mind. "Some people are saying you aimed for the pole."

Ray's smile faded, and his eyes turned sober and sad. "Do you believe that?"

"No." Cam let out a breath. "No, I don't believe that."

"Life's a gift. It doesn't always fit comfortably, but it's precious. I wouldn't have hurt you and your brothers by throwing mine away."

"I know that," Cam murmured. "It helps to hear you say it, but I know that."

"Maybe I could have stopped things. Maybe I could have done things differently." He sighed and turned the gold wedding band around and around on his finger. "But I didn't. It's up to you now, you and Ethan and Phillip. There was a reason the three of you came to me and Stella. A reason the three of you came together. I always believed that. Now I know it."

"And what about the kid?"

"Seth's place is here. He needs you. He's in trouble right now, and he needs you to remember what it was like to be where he is."

"What do you mean, he's in trouble?"

Ray smiled a little. "Answer the phone," he suggested seconds before it rang.

And then he was gone.

"I've got to start getting more sleep," Cam decided, then yanked the receiver off the hook. "Yeah, yeah."

"Hello? Mr. Quinn?"

"Right. This is Cameron Quinn."

"Mr. Quinn, this is Abigail Moorefield, vice principal of St. Christopher Middle School."

Cam felt his stomach sink to his toes. "Uh-huh."

"I'm afraid there's been some trouble here. I have Seth DeLauter in my office."

"What kind of trouble?"

"Seth was in a fight with another student. He's being suspended. Mr. Quinn, I'd appreciate it if you could come to my office so matters can be explained to you and you can take Seth home."

"Great. Wonderful." At his wits' end, Cam dragged a hand through his hair. "On my way."

The school hadn't changed much, Cam noted, since he'd done time there. The first morning he'd passed through those heavy front doors, Stella Quinn had all but dragged him.

He was nearly eighteen years older now, and no more enthusiastic.

The floors were faded linoleum, the light bright from wide windows. And the smell was of contraband candy and kid sweat.

Cam jammed his hands in his pockets and headed for the administration offices. He knew the way. After all he'd beaten a path to those offices countless times during his stay at St. Chris Middle.

It wasn't the same old eagle-eyed secretary manning the desk in the outer room. This one was younger, perkier, and beamed smiles all over him. "May I help you?" she asked in a bouncing voice.

"I'm here to post bail for Seth DeLauter."

She blinked at that, and her smile turned puzzled. "I beg your pardon?"

"Cameron Quinn to see the VP."

"Oh, you mean Mrs. Moorefield. Yes, she's expecting you. Second door down the little hallway there. On the right." Her phone rang and she plucked it up. "Good morning," she sang, "St. Christopher's Middle School. This is Kathy speaking."

Cam decided he preferred the battle-ax who had guarded the offices in his day to this terminally pert newcomer. Even as he started toward the door, his back went up, his jaw set—and his palms went damp.

Some things, he supposed, never changed.

Mrs. Moorefield was sitting behind her desk, calmly entering data into a computer. Cam thought her fingers moved efficiently. And the movement suited her. She was neat and trim, probably early fifties. Her hair was short and sleek and light brown, her face composed and quietly attractive.

Her gold wedding band caught the light as her fingers moved over the keys. The only other jewelry she wore were simple gold shells at her ears.

Across the room, Seth was slumped in a chair, staring up at the ceiling. Trying to look bored, Cam assumed, but coming off as sulky. Kid needed a haircut, he realized and wondered who was supposed to deal with that. He was wearing jeans frayed to strings at the cuffs, a jersey two sizes too big, and incredibly dirty high-tops.

It looked perfectly normal to Cam.

He rapped on the doorjamb. Both the vice principal and Seth glanced over, with two dramatically different expressions. Mrs. Moorefield smiled in polite welcome. Seth sneered.

"Mr. Quinn."

"Yeah." Then he remembered he was supposed to be here as a responsible guardian. "I hope we can straighten this out, Mrs. Moorefield." He stuck his own polite smile into place as he stepped to her desk and offered a hand.

"I appreciate your coming in so quickly. When we have to take regrettable disciplinary action such as this against a student, we want the parents or responsible parties to have the opportunity to understand the situation. Please, Mr. Quinn, sit down."

"What is the situation?" Cam took his seat and found he didn't like it any more than he used to.

"I'm afraid Seth physically attacked another student this morning between classes. The other boy is being treated by the school nurse, and his parents have been informed."

Cam lifted a brow. "So where are they?"

"Both of Robert's parents are at work at the moment. But in any case—"

"Why?"

Her smile returned, small, attentive, questioning. "Why, Mr. Quinn?"

"Why did Seth slug Robert?"

Mrs. Moorefield sighed. "I understand you've only recently taken over as Seth's guardian, so you may not be aware that this isn't the first time he's fought with other students."

"I know about it. I'm asking about this incident."

"Very well." She folded her hands. "According to Robert, Seth demanded that Robert give him a dollar, and when Robert refused to pay him, Seth attacked him. At this point," she added, shifting her gaze to Seth, "Seth has neither confirmed nor denied. School policy requires that students be suspended for three days as a disciplinary action when involved in a fight on school premises."

"Okay." Cam rose, but when Seth started to get up, he pointed a finger. "Stay," he ordered, then crouched until they were eye to eye. "You try to shake this kid down?"

Seth jerked a shoulder. "That's what he says."

"You slugged him."

"Yeah, I slugged him. Went for the nose," he added with a thin smile, and shoved at the straw-colored hair that flopped into his eyes. "It hurts more."

"Why'd you do it?"

"Maybe I didn't like his fat face."

With his patience as frayed as Seth's jeans, Cam gripped Seth by the shoulders. When Seth winced and hissed in a breath, alarm bells went off. Before Seth could evade him, Cam tugged the arm of the oversized jersey down. Nasty little bruises—knuckle rappers, Cam would have called them—ran from Seth's shoulder to his elbow.

"Get off me." His face heated with shame, Seth squirmed, but Cam merely shifted him. Scrapes were scored high on Seth's back, red and raw.

"Hold still." Cam moved his grip and laid his hands on the arms of the chair. His eyes stayed on Seth. "You tell me what went down. And don't even think about lying to me."

"I don't want to talk about it."

"I didn't ask you what you wanted. I'm telling you to spill it. Or," he said, lowering his voice so only Seth could hear, "are you going to let that punk get away clean?"

Seth opened his mouth, closed it again. He had to set his jaw so it wouldn't wobble. "He was pissed off. We had this history test the other day and I aced it. An idiot could've gotten an ace, but he's less than an idiot and he flunked. So he kept hassling me, dogged me down the hall, jabbing at me. I walked away because I'm sick to death of ISS."

"Of what?"

Seth rolled his eyes. "In-School Suspension. It's boring. I didn't want to do more time, so I walked. But he kept jabbing and calling me names. Egghead, teacher's pet, and all that shit. Didn't let it bother me. But then he shoved me back against the lockers and he said I was just a son of a whore and everybody knew it, so I decked him.''

Shamed and sick, he jerked a defiant shoulder. "So I get a three-day vacation. Big deal.''

Cam nodded and rose. When he turned around his eyes were nearly black with fury. "You're not suspending this kid for defending himself against an ignorant bully. And if you try, I'll go over your head to the Board of Education.''

Shocked to the core, Seth stared up at Cam. Nobody had ever stood up for him. He'd never expected anyone to stand up for him.

"Mr. Quinn—''

"Nobody calls my brother a son of a whore, Mrs. Moorefield. And if you don't have a school policy against vicious name-calling and harassment, you damn well should. So I'm telling you, you better take another look at this situation. And you better rethink just who gets suspended here. *And* you can tell little Robert's parents that if they don't want their kid crying over a bloody nose, they better teach him some manners.''

She took a moment before speaking. She'd been teaching and counseling children for nearly thirty years. What she saw on Seth's face at that moment was hope, stunned and wary, but hope nonetheless. It was a look she didn't want to extinguish.

"Mr. Quinn, you can be certain that I will investigate this matter further. I wasn't aware that Seth had been injured. If you'd like to take him down to the nurse while I speak with Robert and . . . others—''

"I can take care of him.''

"As you wish. I'll hold the suspension in abeyance until I've satisfied myself with the facts.''

"You do that, Mrs. Moorefield. But I'm satisfied with the facts. Now I'm taking Seth home for the rest of the day. He's had enough.''

"I agree with you.''

The child hadn't looked shaken when he'd come into her office, she thought. He'd looked cocky. He hadn't looked shaken when she'd told him to sit down and called his home. He'd looked belligerent.

But he looked shaken now, finally, with his eyes wide and stunned and his hands gripping the arms of the chair. The thin, hard shield he'd kept tight around him, a shield neither she nor any of his teachers had been able to so much as scratch, appeared to be deeply dented.

Now, she decided, they would see what they could do for him.

"If you will bring Seth into school in the morning and meet with me here, we'll resolve the matter."

"We'll be here. Let's go," he said to Seth and headed out.

As they walked down the hall toward the front doors, their footsteps echoed hollowly. Cam glanced down, noted that Seth was staring at his shoes.

"Still gives me the creeps," he said.

Seth shoved at the door. "What?"

"The way it sounds when you take the long walk to the VP's office."

Seth snorted, hunched his shoulders and kept walking. His stomach felt as if a thousand butterflies had gone to war inside it.

The American flag on the pole near the parking lot snapped in the wind. From an open window behind them, the pathetically off-key sounds of a mid-morning music class clamored. The elementary school was separated from the middle by a narrow swatch of grass and a few sad-looking evergreen bushes.

Across the small outdoor track stood the brown brick of the high school. It seemed smaller now, Cam noted, almost quaint, and not at all like the prison he'd once imagined it to be.

He remembered leaning lazily against the hood of his first secondhand car in the parking lot and watching girls. Walking through those noisy hallways from class to class, and watching girls. Sitting in the butt-numbing chairs during brain-numbing classes. And watching girls.

The fact that his high school experience came back to him in a parade of varying female forms made him almost sentimental.

Then a bell rang shrilly, and the noise level through the open windows behind him erupted. Sentiment dried up quickly. Thank God, was all he could think, that chapter of his life was over.

But it wasn't over for the kid, he remembered. And since he was here, he could try to help him through it. They opened opposite doors of the 'Vette, and Cam paused, waited for their eyes to meet. "So, do you figure you broke the asshole's nose?"

A glimmer of a smile worked around Seth's mouth. "Maybe."

"Good." Cam got in, slammed the door. "Going for the nose is fine, but if you don't want a lot of blood messing things up, go for the belly. A good, solid short arm punch to the gut won't leave as much evidence."

Seth considered the advice. "I wanted to see him bleed."

"Well, you make your choices in life. Pretty good day for a sail," he decided as he started the engine. "Might as well."

"I guess." Seth picked at the knee of his jeans. Someone had stood up for him, was all his confused mind could think. Had believed him, defended him and taken his part. His arm hurt, his shoulders ached, but someone had taken his part. "Thanks," he muttered.

"No problem. You mess with one Quinn, you mess with them all." He glanced over as he drove out of the lot and saw Seth staring at him. "That's how it shakes down. Anyway, let's get some burgers or something to take on the boat."

"Yeah, I could eat." Seth swiped a hand under his nose. "Got a dollar?"

When Cam laughed and punched the accelerator it was one of the best moments of Seth's life.

T HE WIND WAS OUT OF the southwest and steady so that the marsh grasses waved lazily. The sky was clear and cheerfully blue, the perfect frame for the heron that rose up, out of the waving grass over the glinting water, then down like a flashing white kite to catch an early lunch.

On impulse, Cam had tossed some fishing gear into the boat. With any luck they'd have fried fish for dinner.

Seth already knew more about sailing than Cam had expected. He shouldn't have been surprised by it, he realized. Anna had said the boy had a quick mind, and Ethan would have taught him well, and patiently.

When he saw how easily Seth handled the lines, he trusted him to trim the jib. The sails caught the wind, and Cam found speed.

God, he had missed it. The rush, the power, the control. It poured through him, clearing his mind of worries, obligations, disappointments, even grief. Water below and sky above, and his hands on the helm coaxing the wind, daring it, tricking it into giving more.

Behind him, Seth grinned and caught himself just before he yelled out in delight. He'd never gone so fast. With Ray it had been slow and steady, with Ethan work and wonder. But this was a wild, free ride, rising and falling with the waves, shooting like a long white bullet to anywhere.

The wind nearly took his cap, so he turned the bill backward so the breeze wouldn't catch it and flip it away.

They skimmed across the shoreline, passed the waterfront docks that were the hub of St. Chris before they finally slowed. An old skipjack no longer in use was docked there, a symbol to the waterman's way of life.

The men and women who harvested the bay brought

their day's catch there. Flounder and sea trout and rockfish at this time of year, and . . .

"What's the date?" Cam demanded as he glanced over his shoulder.

"Like the thirty-first." Seth shoved up his wraparound sunglasses and stared at the dock. He was hoping for a glimpse of Grace. He wanted to wave to someone he knew.

"Crab season starts tomorrow. Hot damn. Guarantee you tomorrow Ethan brings home a bushel of beauties. We'll eat like kings. You like crabs, right?"

"I dunno."

"What do you mean you don't know?" Cam popped the top of a Coke and guzzled. "Haven't you had crab before?"

"No."

"You'd better prepare your mouth for a treat, then, kid, because you'll have it tomorrow."

Mirroring Cam's move, Seth reached for a soft drink himself. "Nothing you cook's a treat."

It was said with a grin and received with one. "I can do crab just fine. Nothing to it. Boiling water, lots of spices, then you pop those snapping bastards into the pot—"

"Alive?"

"It's the only way."

"That's sick."

Cam merely shifted his stance. "They aren't alive for long. Then they're dinner. Add a six-pack of beer and you got a feast. Another few weeks, and we're talking soft-shell blues. You plop 'em between a couple pieces of bread and bite in."

This time Seth actually felt his stomach roll. "Not me."

"Too squeamish?"

"Too civilized."

"Shit. Sometimes on Saturday in the summer Mom and Dad used to bring us down to the docks. We'd get us some soft-shell crab sandwiches, a tub of peanut oil fries, and watch the tourists try to figure out what to eat. Laughed our asses off.''

The memory made him suddenly sad, and he tried to shake off the mood. ''Sometimes we sailed down like this. Or we'd cruise down to the river and fish. Mom wasn't much on fishing, so she'd swim, then she'd head to shore and sit on the bank and read.''

''Why didn't she just stay home?''

''She liked to sail,'' Cam said softly. ''And she liked being there.''

''Ray said she got sick.''

''Yeah, she got sick.'' Cam blew out a breath. She had been the only woman he'd ever loved, the only woman he'd ever lost. The missing of her could still creep up and cut him off at the knees.

''Come about,'' he ordered. ''Let's head down the Annemessex and see if anything's biting.''

It didn't occur to either of them that the three hours they spent on the water was the most peaceful interlude either had experienced in weeks.

And when they returned home with six fat striped bass in the cooler, they were for the first time in total harmony.

''Know how to clean them?'' Cam asked.

''Maybe.'' Ray had taught him, but Seth was no fool. ''I caught four of the six, that ought to mean you clean them.''

''That's the beauty of being boss,'' Cam began, then stopped dead when he saw sheets snapping on the ancient clothesline. He hadn't seen anything hanging out on the line since his mother had gotten sick. For a moment he was afraid he was having another hallucination, and his mouth went dry.

Then the back door opened, and Grace Monroe stepped out on the porch.

''Hey, Grace!''

It was the first time Cam had heard Seth's voice raised in happiness and pure boyish pleasure. It surprised him enough to make him look over sharply, then nearly drop the cooler on his foot as Seth let go of his end and dashed forward.

"Hey, there." She had a warm voice that contrasted with cool looks. She was tall and slim, with long limbs she'd once dreamed of using as a dancer.

But Grace had learned to put most of her dreams aside.

Her hair was boyishly short, and that was for convenience. She didn't have the time or energy to worry about style. It was a dark, honey blond that was often streaked with paler color during the summer. Her eyes were a quiet green and all too often had shadows dogging them.

But her smile was pure and sunny and never failed to light up her face, or to set the dimple just beside her mouth winking.

A pretty woman, Cam thought, with the face of a pixie and the voice of a siren. It amazed him that men weren't throwing themselves at her feet.

The boy all but did, Cam noted, surprised when Seth just about ran into her open arms. He hugged and was hugged—this prickly kid who didn't like to be touched. Then he flushed and stepped back and began to play with the puppy, who'd followed Grace out of the house.

"Afternoon, Cam." Grace shielded her eyes from the sun with the flat of her hand. "Ethan came by the pub last night and said y'all could use a hand around here."

"You're taking over the housework."

"Well, I can give you three hours two days a week until—"

She got no farther, for Cam dumped the cooler, took the steps three at a time, and grabbed her into a loud, enthusiastic kiss. It set Seth's teeth on edge to see it, even as Grace stuttered and laughed.

"That's nice," she managed, "but you're still going to have to pay me."

"Name your price. I adore you." He snatched her hands and planted more kisses there. "My life for you."

"I can see I'm going to be appreciated around here—

and needed. I've got those pink socks soaking in some diluted bleach. Might do the trick.''

"The red sock was Phil's. He's responsible. I mean, what reasonable guy even owns a pair of red socks?"

"We'll talk more about sorting laundry—and checking pockets. Someone's little black book went through the last cycle."

"Shit." He caught her arched-brow look down at the boy and cleared his throat. "Sorry. I guess it was mine."

"I made some lemonade, and I was going to put a casserole together, but it looks like you may have caught your supper."

"Tonight's, but we could do with a casserole too."

"Okay. Ethan wasn't really clear about what you'd need or want done. Maybe we should go over things."

"Darling, you do whatever you think we need, and it'll be more than we can ever repay."

She'd already seen that for herself. Pink underwear, she mused, dust an inch thick on one table and unidentified substances sticking to another. And the stove? God only knew when it had last been cleaned.

It was good to be needed, she thought. Good to know just what had to be done. "We'll take it as it goes, then. I may have to bring the baby along sometimes. Julie minds her at night when I'm working at the pub, but I can't always find somebody to take her otherwise. She's a good girl."

"I can help you watch her," Seth offered. "I get home from school at three-thirty."

"Since when?" Cam wanted to know, and Seth shrugged.

"When I don't have ISS."

"Aubrey loves playing with you. I've got another hour here today," she said because she was a woman constantly forced to budget time. "So I'll make up that casserole and put it in the freezer. All you have to do is heat it up when you want it. I'll leave you a list of cleaning supplies you're low on, or I can pick them up for you if you like."

"Pick them up for us?" Cam could have knelt at her feet. "Want a raise?"

She laughed and started back inside. "Seth, you see that that pup stays out of the fish guts. He'll smell for a week otherwise."

"Okay, sure. I'll be finished in a few minutes and I'll be in." He stood up, then stepped off the porch so Grace wouldn't hear him through the door. Manfully, he sized up Cam. "You're not going to start poking at her, are you?"

"Poking at her?" He was blank for a moment, then shook his head. "For God's sake." Hefting the ice chest, he started around the side of the house to the fish-cleaning table. "I've known Grace half my life, and I don't poke at every woman I see."

"Okay, then."

It was the boy's tone that made Cam run his tongue around his teeth as he set the cooler down. Possessive, proprietary, and satisfied. "So . . . you got your eye on her yourself, huh?"

Seth colored a little, opened the drawer for the fish scaler. "I just look out for her, that's all."

"She sure is pretty," Cam said lightly and had the pleasure of seeing Seth's eyes flash with jealousy. "But as it happens I'm poking at another woman right now, and it gets sticky if you try that with more than one at a time. And this particular female is going to take a lot of convincing."

EIGHT

He DECIDED TO GET
started on poking at Anna. Since she was on his mind,
Cam left Seth to deal with the last couple of fish on his
own and wandered inside. He made appreciative noises at
whatever Grace was putting together over at the stove, then
wandered upstairs.

He'd have a little more privacy on the phone in his
room. And Anna's business card was in his pocket.

At the door to his room, he stopped and could have wept
with gratitude. Since his bed was freshly made, the plain
green spread professionally smoothed, the pillows plumped,
he knew some of the sheets hanging out on the line were
his.

Tonight he would sleep on fresh, clean sheets he hadn't
even had to launder. It made the prospect of sleeping alone
a little more tolerable.

The surface of his old oak dresser wasn't just dust-free.
It gleamed. The bookshelves that still held most of his
trophies and some of his favorite novels had been tidied,
and the overstuffed chair he'd taken to using as a catchall
was now empty. He hadn't a clue where she'd put his

things, but he imagined he'd find them in their logical place.

He supposed he'd gotten spoiled living in hotels over the last few years, but it did his heart good to walk into his bedroom and not see a half a dozen testy little chores waiting for attention.

Things were looking up, so he plopped down on the bed, stretched out, and reached for the phone.

"Anna Spinelli." Her voice was low, professionally neutral. He closed his eyes to better fantasize how she looked. He liked the idea of imagining her behind some bureaucratic desk wearing that tight little blue number she'd had on the night before.

"Miz Spinelli. How do you feel about crabs?"

"Ah . . ."

"Let me rephrase that." He scooted down until he was nearly flat and realized he could be asleep in five minutes without really trying. "How do you feel about eating steamed crabs?"

"I feel favorable."

"Good. How about tomorrow night?"

"Cameron—"

"Here," he specified. "At the house. The house that's never empty. Tomorrow's the first day of crab season. Ethan'll bring home a bushel. We'll cook them up. You can see how the Quinns—what would you call it?—relate, interact. See how Seth's getting along—acclimating to this particular home environment."

"That's very good."

"Hey, I've dealt with social workers before. Of course, never one who wore blue high heels, but . . ."

"I was off the clock," she reminded him. "However, I think dinner might be a workable idea. What time?"

"Six-thirty or thereabouts." He heard the flap of papers and found himself slightly annoyed that she was checking her calendar.

"All right, I can do that. Six-thirty."

She sounded entirely too much like a social worker

making an appointment to suit him. "You alone in there?"

"In my office? Yes, at the moment. Why?"

"Just wondering. I've been wondering about you on and off all day. Why don't you let me come into town and get you tomorrow, then I could drive you home. We could stop and—I'd say climb into the backseat, but the 'Vette doesn't have one. Still, I think we could manage."

"I'm sure we could. Which is why I'll drive myself down."

"I'm going to have to get my hands on you again."

"I don't doubt that's going to happen. Eventually. In the meantime—"

"I want you."

"I know."

Because her voice had thickened and didn't sound quite so prim, he smiled. "Why don't I tell you just what I'd like to do to you? I can go step by step. You can even take notes in your little book for future reference."

"I . . . think we'd better postpone that. Though I may be interested in discussing it at another time. I'm afraid I have an appointment in a few minutes. I'll see you and your family tomorrow evening."

"Give me ten minutes alone with you, Anna." He whispered it. "Ten minutes to touch you."

"I—we can try for that time frame tomorrow. I have to go. Good-bye."

" 'Bye." Pleased that he'd rattled her, he slid the phone back on the hook and let himself drift off into a well-deserved nap.

HE WAS AWAKENED JUST over an hour later by the slamming of the front door and Phillip's raised and furious voice.

"Home, sweet home," Cam muttered and rolled out of bed. He stumbled to the door and down the hall to the steps. He was a lousy napper, and whenever he indulged he woke up groggy, irritable, and in desperate need of coffee.

By the time he got downstairs, Phillip was in the kitchen uncorking a bottle of wine. "Where the hell is everybody?" Phillip demanded.

"I dunno. Get out of my way." Rubbing one hand over his face, Cam poured the dregs of the pot into a mug, stuck the mug in the microwave, and punched numbers at random.

"I've been informed by the insurance company that they're holding the claim until such time as an investigation is complete."

Cam stared at the microwave, willing those endless two minutes to pass so he could gulp caffeine. His bleary brain took in insurance, claim, investigation, and couldn't correlate the terms. "Huh?"

"Pull yourself together, damn it." Phillip gave him an impatient shove. "They won't process Dad's policy because they suspect suicide."

"That's bullshit. He told me he didn't kill himself."

"Oh, really?" Sick and furious, Phillip still managed to raise an ironic eyebrow. "Did you have this conversation with him before or after he died?"

Cam caught himself, but very nearly flushed. Instead he cursed again and yanked open the microwave door. "I mean, there's no way he would have, and they're just stalling because they don't want to pay off."

"The point is, they're not paying off at this time. Their investigator's been talking to people, and some of those people were apparently delighted to tell him the seamier details of the situation. And they know about the letter from Seth's mother—the payments Dad made to her."

"So." He sipped coffee, scalded the roof of his mouth, and swore. "Hell with it. Let them keep their fucking blood money."

"It's not as simple as that. Number one is if they don't pay, it goes down that Dad committed suicide. Is that what you want?"

"No." Cam pinched the bridge of his nose to try to relieve some of the pressure that was building. He'd lived most of his life without headaches, and now it seemed he was plagued with them.

"Which means we'd have to accept their conclusions, or we'd have to take them to court to prove he didn't, and it'd be one hell of a public mess." Struggling to calm himself, Phillip sipped his wine. "Either way it smears his name. I think we're going to have to find this woman— Gloria DeLauter—after all. We have to clear this up."

"What makes you think finding her and talking to her is going to clear this up?"

"We have to get the truth out of her."

"How, through torture?" Not that it didn't have its appeal. "Besides, the kid's scared of her," Cam added. "She comes around, she could screw up the guardianship."

"And if she doesn't come around we might never know the truth, all of the truth." He needed to know it, Phillip thought, so he could begin to accept it.

"Here's the truth as I see it." Cam slammed his mug down. "This woman was looking for an easy mark and figured she'd found one. Dad fell for the kid, wanted to help him. So he went to bat for him, just the way he did for us, and she kept hitting him up for more. I figure he was upset coming home that day, worried, distracted. He was driving too fast, misjudged, lost control, whatever. That's all there is to it."

"Life's not as simple as you live it, Cam. You don't just start in one spot, then finish in the other as fast as you can. Curves and detours and roadblocks. You better start thinking about them."

"Why? That's all you ever think about, and it seems to me we've ended up in exactly the same place."

Phillip let out a sigh. It was hard to argue with that, so he decided a second glass of wine was in order. "Whatever you think, we've got a mess on our hands and we're going to have to deal with it. Where's Seth?"

"I don't know where he is. Around."

"Christ, Cam, around where? You're supposed to keep an eye on him."

"I've had my eye on him all damn day. He's around." He walked to the back door, scanned the yard, scowled when he didn't see Seth. "Probably around front, or taking a walk or something. I'm not keeping the kid on a leash."

"This time of day he should be doing his homework. You've only got to watch out for him on your own a couple of hours after school."

"It didn't work out that way today. There was a little holiday from school."

"He hooked? You let him hook when we've got Social Services sniffing around?"

"No, he didn't hook." Disgusted, Cam turned back. "Some little jerk at school kept razzing him, poked bruises all over him and called him a son of a whore."

Phillip's stance shifted immediately, from mild annoyance to righteous fury. His gilt eyes glittered, his mouth thinned. "What little jerk? Who the hell is he?"

"Some fat-faced kid named Robert. Seth slugged him, and they said they were going to suspend him for it."

"Hell they are. Who the hell's principal now, some Nazi?"

Cam had to smile. When push came to shove, you could always count on Phillip. "She didn't seem to be. After I went down and we got the whole story out of Seth, she shifted ground some. I'm taking him back in tomorrow for another little conference."

Now Phillip grinned, wide and wicked. "You? Cameron Kick-Ass Quinn is going in for a parent conference at the middle school. Oh, to be a fly on the wall!"

"You won't have to be, because you're coming too."

Phillip swallowed wine hastily before he choked. "What do you mean, I'm coming?"

"And so's Ethan," Cam decided on the spot. "We're all going. United front. Yeah, that's just the way it's going to be."

"I've got an appointment—"

"Break it. There's the kid." He spotted Seth coming out of the woods with Foolish beside him. "He's just been fooling around with the dog. Ethan ought to be along any minute, and I'm tagging him for this deal."

Phillip scowled into his wine. "I hate it when you're right. We all go."

"It should be a fun morning." Satisfied, Cam gave Phillip a friendly punch on the arm. "We're the big guys this time. And when we win this little battle with authority, we can celebrate tomorrow night—with a bushel of crabs."

Phillip's mood lightened. "April Fool's Day. Crab season opens. Oh, yeah."

"We got fresh fish tonight—I caught it, you cook it. I want a shower." Cam rolled his shoulders. "Miz Spinelli's coming to dinner tomorrow."

"Uh-huh, well, you—what?" Phillip whirled as Cam started out of the room. "You asked the social worker to dinner? Here?"

"That's right. Told you I like her looks."

Phillip could only close his eyes. "For God's sake, you're hitting on the social worker."

"She's hitting on me, too." Cam flashed a grin. "I like it."

"Cam, not to put down your warped idea of romance, but use your head. We've got this problem with the insurance company. And we've got a problem with Seth at school. How's that's going to play to Social Services?"

"We don't tell them about the first, and we give them the straight story on the second. I think that's going to go over just fine with Miz Spinelli. She's going to love it that the three of us went in to stand for Seth."

Phillip opened his mouth, reconsidered, and nodded. "You're right. That's good." Then as new thoughts began to play, he angled his head. "Maybe you could use your . . . influence on her to get her to move this case study along, get the system out of our hair."

Cam said nothing for a moment, surprised at how angry even the suggestion of it made him. So his voice was quiet.

"I'm not using anything on her, and it's going to stay that way. One situation has nothing to do with the other. That's staying that way too."

When Cam strode off, Phillip pursed his lips. Well, he thought, wasn't that interesting?

A S   ETHAN   GUIDED   HIS boat toward the dock, he spotted Seth in the yard. Beside Ethan, Simon gave a high, happy bark. Ethan ruffled his fur. "Yeah, fella, almost home now."

While he worked the sails, Ethan watched the boy toss sticks for the pup. There had always been a dog in this yard to chase sticks or balls, to wrestle in the grass with. He remembered Dumbo, the sweet-faced retriever he'd fallen madly in love with when he'd come to the Quinns.

He'd been the first dog to play with, to be comforted by, in Ethan's life. From Dumbo he'd learned the meaning of unconditional love, had certainly trusted the dog long before he'd trusted Ray and Stella Quinn or the boys who would become his brothers.

He imagined Seth felt much the same. You could always depend on your dog.

When he'd come here all those years ago, damaged in body and soul, he had no hope that his life would really change. Promises, reassurances, decent meals and decent people meant nothing to him. So he'd considered ending that life.

The water had drawn him even then. He imagined himself walking out into it, drifting out until it was over his head. He didn't know how to swim then, so it would have been simple. Just sinking down and down and down until there was nothing.

But the night he'd slipped out to do it, the dog had come with him. Licking his hand, pressing that warm, furry body against his legs. And Dumbo had brought him a stick, tail wagging, big brown eyes hopeful. The first time, Ethan threw the stick high and far and in fury. But Dumbo chased it happily and brought it back. Tail wagging.

He threw it again, then again, then dozens of times. Then he simply sat down on the grass, and in the moonlight cried his heart out, clutching the dog like a lifeline.

The need to end it had passed.

A dog, Ethan thought now as he rubbed a hand over Simon's head, could be a glorious thing.

He saw Seth turn, catch sight of the boat. There was the briefest of hesitations, then the boy lifted a hand in greeting and with the pup raced to the dock.

"Secure the lines, mate."

"Aye, aye." Seth handled the lines Ethan tossed out competently enough, slipping the loop over the post. "Cam said how you'd be bringing crabs tomorrow."

"Did he?" Ethan smiled a little, pushed back his fielder's cap. Thick brown hair tickled the collar of his work-stained shirt. "Go on, boy," he murmured to the dog, who was sitting, vibrating in place as he waited for the command to abandon ship. With a celebrational bark, Simon leaped into the water and swam to shore. "As it turns out, he's right. Winter wasn't too hard and the water's warming up. We'll pull in plenty. Should be a good day."

Leaning over the side, he pulled up a crab pot that dangled from the dock. "No winter hair."

"Hair, why would there be hair in an old chicken wire box?"

"Pot. It's a crab pot. If I pulled this up and it was hairy—full of blond seaweed—it'd mean the water was too cold yet for crabs. Seen them that way, nearly into May, if there's been a bad winter. That kind of spring, it's hard to make a living on the water."

"But not this spring, because the water's warm enough for crabs."

"Seems to be. You can bait this pot later—chicken necks or fish parts do the job fine—and in the morning we may just find us a couple of crabs sulking inside. They fall for it every time.''

Seth knelt down, wanting a closer look. ''That's pretty stupid. They look like big ugly bugs, so I guess they're bug-dumb.''

''Just more hungry than smart, I'd say.''

''And Cam says you boil them alive. No way I'm eating those.''

''Suit yourself. Me, I figure on going through about two dozen come tomorrow night.'' He let the pot slip back into the water, then leaped expertly from boat to dock.

''Grace was here. She cleaned the house and stuff.''

''Yeah?'' He imagined the house would smell lightly of lemon. Grace's house always did.

''Cam kissed her, right on the mouth.''

Ethan stopped walking, looked down at Seth's face. ''What?''

''Smackaroo. It made her laugh. It was like a joke, I guess.''

''Like a joke, sure.'' He shrugged and ignored the hard, sick ball in his gut. None of his business who Grace kissed. Nothing to do with him. But he found his jaw clenched when Cam, hair dripping, stepped out on the back porch.

''How's the crab business looking?''

''It'll do,'' Ethan said shortly.

Cam lifted his brows at the tone. ''What, did one crawl out of the pot early and up your butt?''

''I want a shower and a beer.'' Ethan moved past him and into the house.

''Woman's coming for dinner tomorrow.''

That stopped Ethan again, and he turned, keeping the screen door between them. ''Who?''

''Anna Spinelli.''

''Shit,'' was Ethan's only comment as he walked away.

''Why's she coming? What does she want?'' Panic rose up inside Seth like a fountain and spewed out in his voice before he could stop it.

''She's coming because I asked her, and she wants a

crab dinner.'' Cam tucked his thumbs in his pockets, rocked back on his heels. Why the hell was he the one who always had to handle this white-faced fear? ''I figure she wants to see if all we do around here is fart and scratch and spit. We can probably hold off on that for one evening. You gotta remember to put the toilet seat down, though. Women really hate when you don't. They make it a social and political statement if you leave it up. Go figure.''

Some of the tension eased out of Seth's face. ''So, she's just, like, coming to see if we're slobs. And Grace cleaned everything up and you're not cooking, so it's mostly okay.''

''It'll be more than mostly if you watch that foul mouth of yours.''

''Yours is just as foul.''

''Yeah, but you're shorter than I am. And I don't intend to ask you to pass the fucking potatoes in front of her.''

Seth snorted at that, and his rock-hard shoulders relaxed. ''Are you going to tell her about that shit in school today?''

Cam blew out a breath. ''Practice finding an alternate word for 'shit,' just for tomorrow night. Yeah, I'm going to tell her what happened in school. And I'm telling her that Phil and Ethan and I went in with you tomorrow to deal with it.''

This time all Seth could do was blink. ''All of you? You're all going?''

''That's right. Like I said, you mess with one Quinn, you mess with them all.''

It shocked and appalled and terrified them both when tears sprang to Seth's eyes. They swam there for a moment, blurring that deep, bright blue. Instantly both of them stuck their hands in their pockets and turned away.

''I have to do . . . something,'' Cam said, groping. ''You go . . . wash your hands or whatever. We'll be eating pretty soon.''

Just as he worked up the nerve to turn, intending to lay a hand on Seth's shoulder, to say something that would undoubtedly make them both feel like idiots, the boy darted inside and rushed through the kitchen.

Cam pressed his fingers to his eyes, massaged his temples, dropped his arms. ''Jesus, I've got to get back to a race where I know what I'm doing.'' He took a step toward the door, then shook his head and walked quickly away from it. He didn't want to go inside with all that emotion, all that need, swirling in the air.

God, what he wanted was his freedom back, to wake up and find it had all been a dream. Better, to wake up in some huge, anonymous hotel bed in some exotic city with a hot, naked woman beside him.

But when he tried to picture it, the bed was the same one he slept in now, and the woman was Anna.

As a substitute it wasn't such a bad deal, but . . . it didn't make the rest of it go away. He glanced up at the windows of the second floor as he walked around the house. The kid was up there, pulling himself together. And he was out here, trying to do the same thing.

The look the kid had shot him, Cam thought, just before things got sloppy. It had stirred up his gut. He'd have sworn he'd seen trust there, and a pathetic, almost desperate gratitude that both humbled and terrified him.

What the hell was he going to do with it? And when things settled down and he could pick up his own life again . . . That had to happen, he assured himself. Had to. He couldn't stay in charge like this. Couldn't be expected to live like this forever. He had places to go, races to run, risks to take.

Once they had everything under control, once they did what needed to be done for the kid and got this business Ethan wanted established, he'd be free to come and go as he pleased again.

A few more months, he decided, maybe a year, then he was out of here. No one could possibly expect more from him.

Not even himself.

NINE

VICE PRINCIPAL MOORE-
field studied the three men who stood like a well-mortared
wall in her office. The outward appearance would never
indicate they were brothers. One wore a trim gray suit and
perfectly knotted tie, another a black shirt and jeans, and
the third faded khakis and a wrinkled denim work shirt.

But she could see that at the moment they were as united
as triplets in the womb.

"I realize you have busy schedules. I appreciate all of
you coming in this morning."

"We want to get this straightened out, Mrs. Moorefield." Phillip kept a mild, negotiating smile on his face.
"Seth needs to be in school."

"I agree. After Seth's statement yesterday, I did some
checking. It does appear as though Robert instigated the
incident. There does seem to be some question over the
motivation. The matter of the petty extortion—"

Cam held up a hand. "Seth, did you tell this Robert
character to give you a dollar?"

"Nah." Seth tucked his thumbs in his front pockets, as
he'd seen Cam do. "I don't need his money. I don't even
talk to him unless he gets in my face."

131

Cam looked back at Mrs. Moorefield. "Seth says he aced that test and Robert flunked. Is that right?"

The vice principal folded her hands on her desk. "Yes. The test papers were handed back yesterday just before the end of class, and Seth received the highest grade. Now—"

"Seems to me," Ethan interrupted in a quiet voice, "that Seth told you straight, then. Excuse me, ma'am, but if the other boy lied about some of it, could be he's lying about all of it. Seth says the boy came after him, and he did. He said it was about this test, so I figure it is."

"I've considered that, and I tend to agree with you, Mr. Quinn. I've spoken with Robert's mother. She's no happier than you are about this incident, or about the fact that both boys are to be suspended."

"You're not suspending Seth." Cam planted his feet. "Not over this—not without a fight."

"I understand how you feel. However, blows were exchanged. Physical violence can't be permitted here."

"I'd agree with you, Mrs. Moorefield, under most circumstances." Phillip laid a hand on Cam's arm to prevent him from stepping forward. "However, Seth was being physically and verbally attacked. He defended himself. There should have been a teacher monitoring the hallway during the change of classes. He should have been able to depend on an adult, on the system to protect him. Why didn't one come forward to do so?"

Moorefield puffed out her cheeks, blew out a breath. "That's a reasonable question, Mr. Quinn. I won't start weeping to you about budget cuts, but it's impossible, with a staff of our size, to monitor all the children at all times."

"I sympathize with your problem, but Seth shouldn't have to pay for it."

"There's been a rough time recently," Ethan put in. "I don't figure that kicking the boy out of school for a couple days is going to help him any. Education's supposed to be more than learning—leastways that's how we were taught. It's supposed to help build your character and help teach you how to get on in the world. If it tells you that you get booted for doing what you had to, for standing up for yourself, then something's wrong with the system.''

''You punish him the same way you punish the boy who started it,'' Cam said, ''you're telling him there's not much difference between right and wrong. That's not the kind of school I want my brother in.''

Moorefield steepled her hands, looked over the tips of her fingers at the three men, then down at Seth. ''Your evaluation tests were excellent, and your grades are well above average. However, your teachers say you rarely turn in homework assignments and even more rarely participate in class discussion.''

''We're dealing with the homework.'' Cam gave Seth a subtle nudge. ''Right?''

''Yeah, I guess. I don't see why—''

''You don't have to see.'' Cam cut him off with one lowering glance. ''You just have to do it. We can't sit in the classroom with him and make him open his mouth, but he'll turn in his homework.''

''I imagine he will,'' she murmured. ''This is what I'll agree to do. Seth, because I believe you, you won't be suspended. But you will go on a thirty-day probation. If there are no more disruptive incidents, and your teachers report that you have improved your at-home-assignment record— we'll put this matter aside. However, your first homework assignment comes now and from me. You have one week to write a five-hundred-word essay on the violence in our society and the need for peaceful resolutions to problems.''

''Oh, man—''

''Shut up,'' Cam ordered mildly. ''That's fair,'' he said to Mrs. Moorefield. ''We appreciate it.''

''THAT WASN'T SO BAD.'' Phillip stepped back into the sunlight and rolled his shoulders.

"Speak for yourself." Ethan snugged his cap back on his head. "I was sweating bullets. I don't want to have to do that again in this lifetime. Drop me off at the waterfront. I can get a ride out to the boat. Jim's working her, and he ought to have pulled in a nice mess of crabs by now."

"Just make sure you bring us home our share." Cam piled into Phillip's shiny navy blue Land Rover. "And don't forget we've got company coming."

"Not going to forget," Ethan mumbled. "Principals in the morning, social workers in the evening. Christ Jesus. Every time you turn around, you have to talk to somebody."

"I intend to keep Miz Spinelli occupied."

Ethan turned around to look at Cam. "You just can't leave females alone, can you?"

"What would be the point? They're here."

Ethan only sighed. "Somebody better pick up more beer."

CAM VOLUNTEERED TO get the beer late that afternoon. It wasn't altruism. He didn't think he could stand listening to Phillip another five minutes. Going to the market was the best way to get out of the house and away from the tension while Phillip drafted and perfected a letter to the insurance company on his snazzy little laptop computer.

"Get some salad stuff while you're out," Phillip shouted, causing Cam to turn back and poke his head in the kitchen where Phillip was typing away at the table.

"What do you mean, salad stuff?"

"Field greens—for God's sake, don't come back here with a head of iceberg and a couple of tasteless hothouse tomatoes. I made up a nice vinaigrette the other day, but there's not a damn thing around here to put it on. Get some plum tomatoes if they look decent."

"What the hell do we need all that for?"

Phillip sighed and stopped typing. "First, because we want to live long and healthy lives, and second because you invited a woman to dinner—a woman who's going to look at how we deal with Seth's nutritional needs."

"Then you go to the goddamn store."

"Fine. You write this goddamn letter."

He'd rather be burned alive. "Field greens, for sweet Christ's sake."

"And get some sourdough bread. And we're nearly out of milk. Since I'm going to be bringing my juicer the next time I get back to Baltimore, pick up some fresh fruit, some carrots, zucchini. I'll just make a list."

"Hold it, hold it." Cam felt the controls slipping out of his hands and struggled to shift his grip. "I'm just going for beer."

"Whole wheat bagels," Phillip muttered, busily writing.

THIRTY MINUTES LATER, Cam found himself pondering the produce section of the grocery store. What the hell was the difference between green leaf and romaine lettuce, and why should he care? In defense, he began loading the cart at random.

Since that worked for him, he did the same thing through the aisles. By the time he reached checkout, he had two carts, overflowing with cans, boxes, bottles, and bags.

"My goodness, you must be having a party."

"Big appetites," he told the checkout clerk, and after a quick search of his brain pegged her. "How's it going, Mrs. Wilson?"

"Oh, fair enough." She ran items expertly over the belt and scanner and into bags, her quick, red-tipped fingers moving like lightning. "Too pretty a day to be stuck inside here, I can tell you that. I get off in an hour and I'm going out chicken-necking with my grandson."

"We're counting on having crab for dinner ourselves.

Probably should have bought some chicken necks for the pot off our dock.''

"Ethan'll keep you supplied, I imagine. I'm awful sorry about Ray," she added. "Didn't really get to tell you so after the funeral. We're sure going to miss him. He used to come in here once or twice a week after Stella passed, buy himself a pile of those microwave meals. I'd tell him, 'Ray, you got to do better for yourself than that. A man needs a good slab of meat now and then.' But it's a hard thing cooking for one when you're used to family.''

"Yeah." It was all Cam could say. He'd been family, and he hadn't been there.

"Always had some story to tell about one of you boys. Showed me pictures and things from foreign newspapers on you. Racing here, racing there. And I'd say, 'Ray, how do you know if the boy won or not when it's written in I-talian or Fran-say?' We'd just laugh.''

She checked the weight on a bag of apples, keyed them in. "How's that young boy? What's his name, now? Sam?''

"Seth," Cam murmured. "He's fine.''

"Good-looking boy. I said to Mr. Wilson when Ray brought him home, 'That's Ray Quinn for you, always keeping his door open.' Don't know how a man of his age expected to handle a boy like that, but if anybody could, Ray Quinn could. He and Stella handled the three of you.''

Because she smiled and winked, he smiled back. "They did. We tried to give them plenty to handle.''

"I expect they loved every minute of it. And I expect the boy, Seth, was company for Ray after y'all grew up and lit out. I want you to know I don't hold with what some people are saying. No, I don't.''

Her mouth thinned as she rang up three jumbo boxes of cold cereal. With a cluck of her tongue and a shake of her head, she continued. "I tell them straight to their face if they do that nasty gossiping in my hearing that if they had a Christian bone in their body, they'd mind their tongues.''

Her eyes glittered with fury and loyalty. "Don't you pay

any mind to that talk, Cameron, no mind at all. Why the idea that Ray would have had truck with that woman, that the boy was his by blood. Not one decent mind's going to believe that, or that he'd run into that pole on purpose. Makes me just sick to hear it.''

It was making Cam sick now. He wished to God he'd never come in the store. "Some people believe lies, Mrs. Wilson. Some people would rather believe them.''

"That they do." She nodded her head twice, sharply. "And even if they don't, they like to spread them around. I want you to know that Mr. Wilson and me considered Ray and Stella good friends and good people. Anybody says something I don't like about them around me's going to get their ears boxed.''

He had to smile. "As I remember, you were good at that.''

She laughed now, a kind of happy hoot. "Boxed yours that time you came sniffing too close to my Caroline. Don't think I didn't know what you were after, boy.''

"Caroline was the prettiest girl in tenth grade.''

"She's still a picture. It's her boy I'm going chicken-necking with. He'll be four this summer. And she's carrying her second into the sixth month now. Time does go right by.''

It seemed it did, Cam thought when he was back at home and hauling bags of groceries into the house. He knew Mrs. Wilson had meant everything she'd said for the best, but she had certainly managed to depress him.

If someone who'd been a staunch friend of his parents was being told such filthy lies, they were spreading more quickly, and more thickly, than he'd imagined. How long could they be ignored before denials had to be given and a stand taken?

Now he was afraid they would have no choice but to take Phillip's advice and find Seth's mother.

The kid was going to hate that, Cam knew. And what would happen to the trust he'd seen swimming in Seth's eyes?

"Guess you want a hand with that stuff." Phillip stepped into the kitchen. "I was on the phone. The lawyer. Temporary guardianship's a lock. There's step one anyway."

"Great." He started to relay the conversation in the grocery store, then decided to let it ride for the night. Goddamn it, they'd won two battles that day. He wasn't going to see the rest of the evening spoiled by wagging tongues.

"More out in the car," he told Phillip.

"More what?"

"Bags."

"More?" Phillip stared at the half dozen loaded brown bags. "Jesus, Cam, I didn't have more than twenty items on that list."

"So I added to it." He pulled a box out, tossed it on the counter. "Nobody's going to go hungry around here for a while."

"You bought Twinkies? *Twinkies?* Are you one of the people who believe that white stuff inside them is one of the four major food groups?"

"The kid'll probably go for them."

"Sure he will. You can pay his next dentist bill."

His temper dangerously close to the edge, Cam whirled around. "Look, pal, he who goes to the store buys what he damn well pleases. That's a new rule around here. Now do you want to get that stuff out of the car or let it fucking rot?"

Phillip only lifted a brow. "Since shopping for food puts you in such a cheery mood, I'll take that little chore from now on. And we'd better start a household fund to draw from for day-to-day incidentals."

"Fine." Cam waved him away. "You do that."

When Phillip walked out, Cam began to stuff boxes and cans wherever they fit. He would let somebody else worry about organizing. In fact, he'd let anybody else worry about it. He was done for a while.

He started out, and when he hit the front door saw that Seth had arrived home. Phillip was passing him bags, and the two of them were talking as if they hadn't a care in the world.

So, he'd go out the back, he decided, let the two of them handle things for a couple of hours. As he turned, the puppy yipped at him, then squatted and peed on the rug.

"I suppose you expect me to clean that up." When Foolish wagged his tail and let his tongue loll, all Cam could do was close his eyes.

"I still say the essay's a raw deal," Seth complained as he walked into the house. "That kind of stuff's crap. And I don't see why—"

"You'll do it." Cam pulled the bag out of Seth's arms. "And I don't want to hear any bitching about it. You can get started right after you clean up the mess your dog just made on the rug."

"My dog? He's not mine."

"He is now, and you better make sure he's housebroken all the way or he stays outside."

He stalked off toward the kitchen, with Phillip, who was trying desperately not to laugh, following.

Seth stood where he was, staring down at Foolish. "Dumb dog," he murmured, and when he crouched down, the puppy launched himself into Seth's arms, where he was welcomed with a fierce hug. "You're my dog now."

ANNA TOLD HERSELF SHE would and could be perfectly professional for the evening. She'd cleared the informal visit with Marilou, just to keep it official. And the truth was, she wanted to see Seth again. Every bit as much as she wanted to see Cam.

Different reasons, certainly, and perhaps different parts of her, but she wanted to see them both. She could handle both sides of her heart, and her mind. She'd always been able to separate areas of her life and conduct them all in a satisfactory manner.

This situation wouldn't be any different.

Verdi soared out of her speakers, wild and passionate. She rolled her window up just enough that the breeze didn't disturb her hair. She hoped the Quinns would allow her a few moments alone with Seth, so she could judge for herself, without influence, how he was feeling.

She hoped she could steal a few moments alone with Cam, so she could judge for herself how she was feeling.

Itchy, she admitted. Needy.

But it wasn't always necessary, or possible to act on feelings, however strong they might be. If, after seeing him again, she felt it best for all concerned to take a large step back, she would do so.

She had no doubt the man had an iron will. But so did Anna Spinelli. She would match herself against Cameron Quinn in that respect any day. And she could win.

Even as she reassured herself of that one single fact, Anna pulled her spiffy little car into the drive.

And Cam walked out onto the porch.

They stayed where they were for just a moment, eyeing each other. When he came off the porch and onto the walk, that hard body tucked into snug black, that dark hair unruly, those smoky eyes unreadable, her heart took one helpless spin and landed with a thud.

She wanted that tough-looking mouth on her, those rough-palmed hands on her. She wanted that all-male body pinning hers to a mattress, moving with the speed that was so much a part of his life. It was idiotic to deny it.

But she'd handle him, Anna promised herself. She only hoped she could handle herself.

She stepped out, wearing a prim, boxy suit the color of a bird's nest. Her hair was pulled up and back and ruthlessly controlled. Her unpainted lips curved in a polite, somewhat distant smile, and she carried her briefcase.

For reasons that baffled him, Cam had precisely the same reaction he'd had when she'd clipped down her hallway on stiletto heels that rainy night. Instant and raging lust.

When he started toward her, she angled her head, just a

little, just enough to send the warning signal. The hands-off sign was clear as a shout.

But he leaned forward a bit when he reached her, sniffed at her hair. "You did that on purpose."

"Did what on purpose?"

"Wore the don't-touch suit and the sex goddess perfume at the same time just to drive me crazy."

"Listen to the suit, Quinn. Dream about the perfume." She started past him, then looked down coolly when his hand clamped over her arm. "You're not listening."

"I like to play games as much as the next guy, Anna." He tugged until she turned and they were again face to face. "But you may have picked a bad time for this one."

There was something in his eyes, she realized, something along with desire, annoyance. And because she recognized it as unhappiness, she softened. "Has something happened? What's wrong?"

"What's right?" he tossed back.

She put a hand over the one still clamped to her arm and squeezed lightly. "Rough day?"

"Yes. No. Hell." Giving up, he let her go and leaned back on the hood of her car. It was a testimony to her compassion that she was able to stifle a wince. She'd just had it washed and waxed. "There was this thing at school this morning."

"Thing?"

"You'll probably get some official report or something about it, so I want to give you our side personally."

"Uh-oh, sides. Well, let's hear it."

So he told her, found himself heating up again when he got to the point where he'd seen the bruises on Seth's arm, and ended up pushing himself off the car and stalking around it as he finished the story of how it had been resolved.

"You did very well," Anna murmured, nearly laughing when he stopped and stared at her suspiciously. "Of course hitting the other boy wasn't the answer, but—"

"I think it was a damn good answer."

"I realize that, and we'll just let it go for now. My point is, you did the responsible and the supportive thing. You went down, you listened, you convinced Seth to tell you the truth, and then you stood up for him. I doubt he was expecting you to."

"Why shouldn't I—why wouldn't I? He was right."

"Believe me, not everyone goes to bat for their children."

"He's not my kid. He's my brother."

"Not everyone goes to bat for his brother," she corrected. "The three of you going in this morning was exactly right, and again unfortunately more than everyone would do. It's a corner turned for all of you, and I suspect you understand that. Is that what's upset you?"

"No, that's piddly. Other things, doesn't matter." He could hardly tell her about the investigation into his father's death or the village gossip over it at this precarious point. Nor did he think it would count in their favor if he confessed he was feeling trapped and dreaming of escape.

"How's Seth taking it?"

"He's cool with it." Cam shrugged a shoulder. "We went sailing yesterday, did some fishing. Blew off the day."

She smiled again, and this time her heart was in it. "I'd hoped I'd be around to see it happening. You're starting to fall for him."

"What are you talking about?"

"You're starting to care about him. Personally. He's beginning to be more than an obligation, a promise to be kept. He matters to you."

"I said I'd take care of him. That's what I'm doing."

"He matters to you," she repeated. "That's what's worrying you, Cam. What happens if you start caring too much. And how do you stop it from happening."

He looked at her, the way the sun dropped down in the sky at her back, the way her eyes stayed warm and dark on his. Maybe he was worrying, he admitted, and not just about his shifting feelings for Seth. "I finish what I start,

Anna. And I don't walk away from my family. Looks like the kid qualifies there. But I'm a selfish son of a bitch. Ask anybody.''

"Some things I prefer to find out for myself. Now am I getting a crab dinner or not?''

"Ethan ought to have the pot going by now.'' He moved forward as if to lead her inside. Then, judging the moment when she relaxed, he yanked her into his arms and caught her up in a hot, heart-hammering kiss.

"See, that was for me,'' he murmured when they were both breathless and quivering. "Want it, take it. I warned you I was selfish.''

Anna eased back, calmly adjusted her now rumpled jacket, ran a hand over her hair to assure herself it was in place. "Sorry, but I'm afraid I enjoyed that every bit as much as you did. So it doesn't qualify as a selfish act.''

He laughed even as his pulse scrambled. "Let me try it again. I can pull it off this time.''

"I'll take a rain check. I want my dinner.'' With that, she sauntered up the steps, knocked briefly, and slipped into the house.

Cam just stood where he was, grinning. This was a woman, he thought, who was going to make this episode of his life a memorable one.

By the time Cam made his way inside and to the kitchen, Anna was already chatting with Phillip and accepting a glass of wine.

"You drink beer with crabs,'' Cam told her and got one out of the fridge for himself.

"I don't seem to be eating any at the moment. And Phillip assures me this is a very nice wine.'' She sipped, considered, and smiled. "He's absolutely right.''

"It's one of my favorite whites.'' Since she'd approved, Phillip topped off her glass. "Smooth, buttery, and not overpowering.''

"Phil's a wine snob.'' Cam twisted off the top and lifted the bottle of Harp to his lips. "But we let him live here anyway.''

"And how is that working out?" She wondered if they realized how male the house seemed. Tidy as a pin, yes, but without even a whiff of female. "It must be odd adjusting to the three of you in the same household again."

"Well, we haven't killed each other." Cam bared his teeth in a smile at his brother. "Yet."

With a laugh she walked to the window. "And where is Seth?"

"He's with Ethan," Phillip told her. "They're doing the crabs around at the pit."

"The pit?"

"Around the side." Cam took her hand and tugged her toward the door. "Mom wouldn't let us cook crab in the house. She might have been a doctor, but she could be squeamish. Didn't like to watch." He drew her off the porch and down the steps as he spoke. "Dad had this brick pit around the side of the house. Fell down my first summer. He didn't know much about laying bricks. But we rebuilt it."

When they stepped around the corner, she saw Ethan and Seth standing by a huge kettle over an open fire in a lopsided brick-sided pit. Smoke billowed, and from a big steel barrel on the ground came the scraping and clattering of claws.

Anna looked from barrel to kettle and back again. "You know what, I think I can be a bit squeamish myself."

She stepped back, turned to the view of the water. She didn't even mind that Cam laughed at her, especially when she heard Seth's voice raised in desperate excitement.

"Are you dumping them in now? Oh, man, shit, that is so *gross*."

"I told him to watch his mouth tonight, but he doesn't know you're here yet."

She only shook her head. "He sounds very normal." She winced a little when she heard a clatter and Seth's wild exclamation of delight and disgust. "And I'd think what's happening around the corner is just barbaric enough to thrill him." Her hand lifted quickly, protectively, to her hair when she felt a tug.

"I like it down." Cam tossed the pin he'd pulled out aside.

"I want it up," she said mildly and began to walk toward the water.

"I bet we're going to knock heads about all kinds of things." He sipped his beer and sent her a sidelong look as they walked. "Ought to keep it all interesting."

"I doubt either of us will be bored. Seth comes first, Cam. I mean that." She paused, listened to the musical lap of water against the hull of the boats, the sloping shoreline. Topping one of the markers was a huge nest. Buoys bobbed in the tide.

"I can help him, and it's unlikely we'll always agree on what's right for him. It'll be essential to keep that issue completely separate when we end up in bed."

He was grateful he hadn't taken another sip from the bottle. No doubt in his mind he'd have choked on it. "I can do that."

She lifted her head as an egret soared by, and wondered if the nest belonged to her. "When I'm certain I can, we'll use my bed. My apartment's more private than your house."

He rubbed a hand over his stomach in a futile attempt to calm himself. "Lady, you're right up front, aren't you?"

"What's the point in being otherwise? We're grown-ups, unattached." She shot him a look—a flick of the lashes, an arch of a brow. "But if you're the type who'd prefer me to pretend reluctance until seduction, sorry."

"No, I'm all right with it this way." If he didn't overheat and explode in the meantime. "No games, no pretenses, no promises. . . . Where the hell do you come from?" he finished, fascinated.

"Pittsburgh," she said easily and started back toward the house.

"That's not what I meant."

"I know. But if you intend to sleep with me, you should have some interest in the basic facts. No games, no pretenses, no promises. That's fine. But I don't have sex with strangers."

He put a hand on her arm before she wandered too close to the house. He wanted another moment alone. "Okay, what are the basic facts?"

"I'm twenty-eight, single, of Italian descent. My mother . . . died when I was twelve and I was raised primarily by my grandparents."

"In Pittsburgh."

"That's right. They're wonderful—old-fashioned, energetic, loving. I can make a terrific red sauce from scratch—the recipe's been passed down in my family for generations. I moved to D.C. right after college, worked there and did some graduate studies. But Washington didn't suit me."

"Too political?"

"Yes, and too urban. I was looking for something a little different, so I ended up down here."

Cam glanced around the quiet yard, the quiet water. "It's different from D.C., all right."

"I like it. I also like horror novels, sappy movies, and any kind of music except jazz. I read magazines from back to front and don't know why, and though I'm comfortable with all sorts of people, I don't particularly like large social functions."

She stopped, considered. They would see, she decided, how much more he'd want to find out. "I think that's enough for now, and my glass is nearly empty."

"You're nothing like my first impression of you."

"No? I think you're exactly like mine of you."

"Do you speak Italian?"

"Fluently."

He leaned forward and murmured a highly charged and sexually explicit suggestion in her ear. Some women might have slapped his face, others might have giggled, some certainly would have blushed. Anna merely made a humming sound in her throat.

"Your accent's mediocre, but your imagination is exceptional." She gave his arm a light pat. "Be sure to ask me again—some other time."

"Damn right I will," Cam muttered, and watched her smile in an easy, open manner at Seth as he came barreling around the corner of the house.

"Hello, Seth."

He skidded to a halt. That wary and distant look came into his eyes. His shoulders hunched. "Yeah, hi. Ethan says we can eat anytime."

"Good, I'm starved." Though she knew he was braced against her, she kept walking toward him. "I hear you went sailing yesterday."

Seth's gaze slid by her, locked accusingly on Cam's. "Yeah. So?"

"I've never been." She said it quickly, sensing that Cam's indrawn breath was the signal for a sharp reminder of manners. "Cam offered to let me tag along with you sometime."

"It's his boat." Then catching the dark scowl on Cam's face, Seth shrugged. "Sure, that'd be cool. I'm supposed to go get a ton of newspaper to spread on the porch. That's the way you eat crabs."

"Right." Before he could dash off, she bent down and whispered in his ear. "Good thing for us Cam didn't cook them."

That got a snicker out of him and a quick, fleeting grin before he turned and ran inside.

TEN

SHE WASN'T SO BAD. FOR
a social worker. Seth came to this thoughtful conclusion
about Anna after he'd retreated to his room, ostensibly to
work on his anti-violence essay. He was drawing pictures
instead, quick little sketches of faces. He had a stupid week
to write the stupid thing, didn't he? Wouldn't take more
than a couple of hours once he got down to doing it. Which
was a raw deal all around, but better than letting fat-faced
Robert get him suspended.

He could still close his eyes and bring up the image of
all three of the Quinns standing in the principal's office.
All three of them standing beside him and facing down
the all-powerful Moorefield. It was so . . . cool, he decided
and began to doodle the moment in his notebook.

There . . . there was Phillip in his fancy suit with his hair
just right and his kind of narrow face. He looked like one
of the magazine ads, Seth thought, the ones that sold stuff
only rich guys could buy.

Next he sketched in Ethan, all serious-faced, Seth
mused, his hair a little shaggy even though Seth remembered how he'd combed it just before they'd gone into the
school. He looked exactly like what he was. The kind of

guy who made his living and lived his life outdoors.

And there was Cam, rough and tough with that light of mean in his eyes. Thumbs hooked in the front pockets of his jeans. Yeah, that was it, Seth decided. He most always stood like that when he was ticked off. Even in the rough sketch he came across as someone who'd done most everything and planned to do a whole lot more.

Last he sketched in himself, trying to see what others would see. His shoulders were too thin and bony, he thought with some disappointment. But they wouldn't always be. His face was too thin for his eyes, but it would fill out too. One day he'd be taller, and stronger, and he wouldn't look like such a puny kid.

But he'd kept his head up, hadn't he? He hadn't been afraid of anything. And he didn't look like he'd just wandered into the picture. He looked—almost—like he belonged there.

Mess with one Quinn, mess with them all. That's what Cam had said—and he must have meant it. But he wasn't a Quinn, Seth thought, frowning as he held up the sketch to study details. Or maybe he was, he just didn't know. It hadn't mattered to him if Ray Quinn had been his father like some people said. All that had mattered was that he was away from *her*.

It hadn't mattered who his father was. Still didn't, he assured himself. He just didn't give a rat's ass. All he wanted was to stay here, right here.

Nobody had used the back of their hand or their fists on him for months now. Nobody got blitzed out on drugs and laid around so long and so still he thought they were dead. Secretly hoped they were. No flabby guys with sweaty hands tried to grope him.

He wasn't even going to think about that.

Eating crabs had been pretty cool, too. Good and messy, he remembered with a grin. You got to eat them with your hands. The social worker didn't act all prim and girly about it either. She just took off her jacket and rolled up her sleeves. It didn't seem like she was watching to see if he burped or scratched his butt or anything.

She'd laughed a lot, he remembered. He wasn't used to women laughing a lot when they weren't coked up. And that was a different kind of laughing, Seth knew. Miss Spinelli's wasn't wild and hard and desperate. It was low and, well, smooth, he supposed.

Nobody'd told him he couldn't have more, either. Man, he'd bet he ate a hundred of those ugly suckers. He didn't even mind eating the salad, though he pretended he did.

He hadn't had that gnawing, sick feeling in his stomach that was desperate hunger for a long time now, so long he might have forgotten the sensation. But he hadn't forgotten. He hadn't forgotten anything.

He'd worried some that the social worker would want to pull him back in, but she seemed pretty okay to him. And he saw her sneaking little bits of crab and bread to Foolish, so she couldn't be all bad.

But he'd have liked her better if she was a waitress or something like Grace.

When the light knock sounded on his door, Seth slapped the notebook closed on his sketches and quickly opened another, where the first dozen words of his five-hundred-word essay were scrawled.

"Yeah?"

Anna poked her head in. "Hi. Can I come in a minute?"

It was weird being asked, and he wondered if she would just turn around and go if he said no. But he shrugged. "I guess."

"I have to leave soon," she began, taking a quick survey of the room. A twin bed, inexpertly made, a sturdy dresser and desk, a wall of shelves that held a few books, a portable stereo that looked very new, and a pair of binoculars that didn't. There were white miniblinds at the windows and a pale-green paint on the walls.

It needed junk, she thought. A boy's junk. Ancient broken toys, posters tacked to the walls. But the puppy snoring in the corner was a very good start.

"This is nice." She wandered to the window. "You've got a good view, water and trees. You get to watch the birds. I bought a book on local waterfowl when I moved here from D.C. so I could figure out what was what. It must be nice to see egrets every day."

"I guess."

"I like it here. It's hard not to, huh?"

He shrugged his shoulders, took the cautious route. "It's okay. I got no problems with it."

She turned, glanced down at his notebook. "The dreaded essay?"

"I started it." Defensively, he pulled the notebook closer—and knocked the other one to the floor. Before he could snatch it up, Anna crouched to pick it up herself.

"Oh, look at this!" It had fallen open to a sketch of the puppy, just his face, straight on, and she thought the artist had captured that sweet and silly expression perfectly. "Did you sketch this?"

"It's no big deal. I'm working on the damn essay, aren't I?"

She might have sighed over his response, but she was too charmed by the sketch. "It's wonderful. It looks just like him." Her fingers itched to turn the pages, to see who else Seth might have drawn. But she resisted and set the notebook down. "I can't draw a decent stick man."

"It's nothing. Just fooling around."

"Well, if you don't want it, maybe I could have it?"

He thought it might be a trick. After all, she had her jacket back on, was carrying her briefcase. She looked like Social Services again rather than the woman who'd rolled up her sleeves and laughed over steamed crabs. "What for?"

"I can't have pets in my apartment. Just as well," she added. "It wouldn't be fair to keep one closed in all day while I'm at work, but . . ." Then she smiled and glanced over at the sleeping puppy. "I really like dogs. When I can afford a house and a yard, I'm going to have a couple of them. But until then, I have to play with other people's pets."

It seemed odd to him. In Seth's mind adults ruled— often with an iron hand. Did what they wanted when they wanted. "Why don't you just move someplace else?"

"The place I've got is close to work, the rent's reasonable." She looked toward the window again, to the stretch of land and water. Both were deep with shadows as night moved in. "It has to do until I can manage to get the house and yard." She wandered to the window, drawn to that quiet view. The first star winked to life in the eastern sky. She nearly made a wish. "Somewhere near the water. Like this. Anyway . . ."

She turned back and sat on the side of the bed facing him. "I just wanted to come up before I left, see if there's anything you wanted to talk about, or any questions you wanted to ask me."

"No. Nothing."

"Okay." She hadn't really expected him to talk to her freely. Yet. "Maybe you'd like to know what I see here, what I think." She took his shoulder jerk as assent. "I see a houseful of guys who are trying to figure out how to live with each other and make it work. Four very different men who are bumping up against each other. And I think they're going to make some mistakes, and most certainly irritate each other and disagree. But I also think they'll work it out—eventually. Because they all want to," she added with an easy smile. "In their own ways they all want the same thing."

She rose and took a card out of her briefcase. "You can call me whenever you want. I put my home number on the back. I don't see any reason for me to come back—in an official capacity—for a while. But I may come back for a puppy fix. Good luck with the essay."

When she started for the door, Seth went with impulse and tore the sketch of Foolish out of his notebook. "You can have this if you want."

"Really?" She took the page, beamed at it. "God, he's

cute. Thanks.'' He jerked back when she bent to kiss his cheek, but she brushed her lips across it lightly, then straightened. She stepped back, ordering herself to keep an emotional distance. "Say good night to Foolish for me."

Anna slipped the sketch in her briefcase as she walked downstairs. Phillip was noodling at the piano, his fingers carelessly picking out some bluesy number. It was another skill she envied. It was a constant disappointment to her that she had no talent.

Ethan was nowhere to be seen, and Cam was restlessly pacing the living room.

She thought that might be a very typical overview of all three men. Phillip elegantly whiling away the time, Ethan off on some solitary pursuit. And Cam working off excess energy.

With the boy up in his room, drawing his pictures and thinking his thoughts.

Cam glanced up, and when their eyes locked, the ball of heat slammed into her gut.

"Gentlemen, thank you for a wonderful meal."

Phillip rose and held out a hand to take hers. "We have to thank you. It's been too long since we had a beautiful woman to dinner. I hope you'll come back."

Oh, he's a smooth one, she decided. "I'd like that. Tell Ethan he's a genius with a crab. Good night, Cam."

"I'll walk you out."

She'd counted on it. "First thing," she said when they stepped outside. "From what I can see, Seth's welfare is being seen to. He has proper supervision, a good home, support with his school life. He could certainly use some new shoes, but I don't imagine there's a boy of ten who couldn't."

"Shoes? What's wrong with his shoes?"

"Regardless," she said, turning to him when they reached her car. "All of you still have adjustments to make, and there's no doubt he's a very troubled child. I suspect he was abused, physically and perhaps sexually."

"I figured that out for myself," Cam said shortly. "It won't happen here."

"I know that." She laid a hand on his arm. "If I had a single doubt in that area he wouldn't be here. Cam, he needs professional counseling. You all do."

"Counseling? That's crap. We don't need to pour our guts out to some underpaid county shrink."

"Many underpaid county shrinks are very good at their job," she said dryly. "Since I have a degree in psychology myself, I could be considered an underpaid county shrink, and I'm good at mine."

"Fine. You're talking to him, you're talking to me. We've been counseled."

"Don't be difficult." Her voice was deliberately mild because she knew it would spark a flash of annoyance in his eyes. It was only fair, she thought, as he'd annoyed her.

"I'm not being difficult. I've cooperated with you from the get-go."

More or less, she mused, and continuing to be fair, admitted it was more than she'd expected. "You've made a solid start here, but a professional counselor will help all of you get beneath the surface and deal with the root of the problems."

"We don't have any problems."

She hadn't expected such hard-line resistance to such a basic step, but realized she should have. "Of course you do. Seth's afraid to be touched."

"He's not afraid to let Grace touch him."

"Grace?" Anna pursed her lips in thought. "Grace Monroe, from the list you gave me?"

"Yeah, she's doing the housework now, and the kid's nuts about her. Might even have a little crush."

"That's good, that's healthy. But it's only a start. When a child's been abused, it leaves scars."

What the hell were they talking about this for? he thought impatiently. Why were they talking about shrinks and digging at old wounds when all he'd wanted was a few minutes of easy flirtation with a pretty woman?

"My old man beat the hell out of me. So what? I survived." He hated remembering it, hated standing in the shadow of the house that had been his sanctuary and remembering. "The kid's mother knocked him around. Well, she's not going to get the chance to do it again. That chapter's closed."

"It's never closed," Anna said patiently. "Whatever new chapter you start always has some basis in the one that came before. I'm recommending counseling to you now, and I'm going to recommend it in my report."

"Go ahead." He couldn't explain why it infuriated him even to think about it. He only knew he'd be damned if he would ask himself or any of his brothers to open those long-locked doors again. "You recommend whatever you want. Doesn't mean we have to do it."

"You have to do what's best for Seth."

"How the hell do you know what's best?"

"It's my job," she said coolly now, because her blood was starting to boil.

"Your job? You got a college degree and a bunch of forms. We're the ones who lived it, who are living it. You haven't been there. You don't know anything about it, what it's like to get your face smashed in and not be able to stop it. To have some bureaucratic jerk from the county who doesn't know dick decide what happens to your life."

Didn't know? She thought of the dark, deserted road, the terror. The pain and the screams. Can't be personal, she reminded herself, though her stomach clutched and fluttered. "Your opinion of my profession has been crystal-clear since our first meeting."

"That's right, but I cooperated. I filled you in, and all of us took steps to make this work." His thumbs went into his front pockets in a gesture Seth would have recognized. "It's never quite enough, though. There's always something else."

"If there weren't something else," she returned, "you wouldn't be so angry."

"Of course I'm angry. We've been working our butts off here. I just turned down the biggest race of my career. I've got a kid on my hands who looks at me one minute as if I'm the enemy and the next as if I'm his salvation. Jesus Christ."

"And it's harder to be his salvation than his enemy."

Bull's-eye, he thought with growing resentment. How the hell did she know so much? "I'm telling you, the best thing for the kid, for all of us, is to be left alone. He needs shoes, I'll get him goddamn shoes."

"And what are you going to do about the fact that he's afraid to be touched, even in the most casual way, by you or your brothers? Are you going to buy his fear away?"

"He'll get over it." Cam was dug in now and refused to allow her to pry him out.

"Get over it?" A sudden fury had her almost stuttering out the words. Then they poured out in a hot stream that made the flash of pain in her eyes all the more poignant. "Because you want him to? Because you tell him to? Do you know what it's like to live with that kind of terror? That kind of shame? To have it bottled up inside you and have little drops of that poison spill out even when someone you love wants to hold you?"

She ripped open her car door, tossed her briefcase in. "I do. I know exactly." He grabbed her arm before she could get into the car. "Get your hand off me."

"Wait a minute."

"I said get your hand off me."

Because she was trembling, he did. Somewhere during the argument she'd gone from being professionally irritated to being personally enraged. He hadn't seen the shift.

"Anna, I'm not going to let you get behind the wheel of this car when you're this churned up. I lost someone I cared about recently, and I'm not going to let it happen again."

"I'm fine." Though she bit off the words, she followed them up by a long, steadying breath. "I'm perfectly capable of driving home. If you want to discuss the possibility of counseling rationally, you can call my office for an appointment.''

"Why don't we take a walk? Both of us can cool off.''

"I'm perfectly cool.'' She slipped into her car, nearly slammed the door on his fingers. "You might take one, though, right off the dock.''

He cursed when she drove away. Briefly considered chasing her down, pulling her out of the car and demanding that they finish the damn stupid argument. His next thought was to stalk back into the house and forget it. Forget her.

But he remembered the wounded look that had come into her eyes, the way her voice had sounded when she'd said she knew what it was like to be afraid, to be ashamed.

Someone had hurt her, he realized. And at that moment everything else faded to the background.

ANNA SLAMMED THE door of her apartment, yanked off her shoes, and heaved them across the room. Her temper was not the type that flashed and boiled, then cooled. It was a simmering thing that bubbled and brewed, then spewed over.

The drive home hadn't calmed her down at all; it had merely given her rising emotions enough time to reach a peak.

She tossed her briefcase on the sofa, stripped off her suit jacket, and threw it on top. Ignorant, hardheaded, narrow-minded man. She fisted her hands and rapped them against her own temples. What had made her think she could get through to him? What had made her think she wanted to?

When she heard the knock on her door, she bared her teeth. She expected her across-the-hall neighbor wanted to exchange some little bit of news or gossip.

She wasn't in the mood.

Determined to ignore it until she could be civilized, she began yanking pins out of her hair.

The knock came again, louder now. "Come on, Anna. Open the damn door."

Now she could only stare as shock and fury made her ears ring. The man had followed her home? He'd had the *nerve* to come all the way to her door and expect to be welcomed inside?

He probably thought she'd be so consumed with lust that she'd jump him and have wild sex on the living room floor. Well, he was in for a surprise of his own.

She strode to the door, yanked it open. "You son of a bitch."

Cam took one look at her flushed and furious face, the wild, tumbling hair, the eyes that sparkled with vengeance, and decided it was undoubtedly perverse to find that arousing.

But what could he do about it?

He glanced down at her clenched fist. "Go ahead," he invited. "But if you belt me you'll have to write a five-hundred-word essay on violence in our society."

She made a low, threatening sound in her throat and tried to slam the door in his face. He was quick enough to slap a hand on it, strong enough to put his weight against it and hold it open. "I wanted to make sure you got home all right," he began as they struggled with the door. "And since I was in the neighborhood, I thought I should come up."

"I want you to go away. Very far away. In fact, I want you to go all the way to hell."

"I get that, but before I take the trip, give me five minutes."

"I've already given you what I now consider entirely too much of my time."

"So what's five more minutes?" To settle it, he braced the door open with one hand—which she found infuriating—and stepped inside.

"If it wasn't for Seth, I'd call the cops right now and have your butt tossed in jail."

He nodded. He'd dealt with his share of furious women and knew there was a time to be careful. "Yeah, I get that too. Listen—"

"I don't have to listen to you." Using the flat of her hand, she shoved him hard in the chest. "You're insulting and you're hardheaded and you're *wrong*, so I don't have to listen to you."

"I'm not wrong," he tossed back. "*You're* wrong. I know—"

"Every damn thing," she interrupted. "You drop in from bouncing around all over the world playing hotshot daredevil, and suddenly you know everything about what's best for a ten-year-old boy you've known barely a month."

"I was not playing at being a hotshot daredevil. I was making a career out of it!" He erupted, his purpose of conciliation and peacemaking shattering to bits. "A goddamn good one. And I do know what's best for the kid. I'm the one who's been there day and night. You spend a couple of hours with him and figure you got a better handle on it. That's just bullshit."

"It's my job to have a handle on it."

"Then you should know that every situation is different. Maybe it works for some people to spill their guts to a stranger and have their dreams analyzed." He'd worked it out carefully, logically on the way over. He was determined to be absolutely reasonable. "Nothing wrong with that, if it's what does it for you. But you can't rubberstamp this. You have to look at the circumstances and the personalities here and, you know, make adjustments."

She couldn't get her breathing under control, so she finally stopped trying. "I don't rubber-stamp the people I'm chosen to help. I study and I evaluate, and goddamn you, I care. I am not some bureaucratic jerk who doesn't know dick. I'm a trained caseworker with over six years' experience, and I got that training and that experience because I know exactly what it's like to be on the other side, to be hurt and scared and alone and helpless. And no one whose case is assigned to me is just a name on a form.''

Her voice broke, shocking her to silence. Quickly she stepped back, pressing one hand to her mouth, holding the other up to signal him away. She felt it rising inside her, knew she wouldn't be able to stop it. ''Get out,'' she managed. ''Get out of here now.''

''Don't do that.'' Panic closed his throat as the first hot tears spilled down her cheeks. Furious women he understood and could deal with. The ones who wept destroyed him. ''Time out. Foul. Jesus, don't do that.''

''Just leave me alone.'' She turned away, thinking only of escape, but he wrapped his arms around her, buried his face in her hair.

''I'm sorry, I'm sorry, I'm sorry.'' He'd have apologized for anything, everything, if only to put them back on even ground. ''I was wrong. I was out of line, whatever you said. Don't cry, baby.'' He turned her around, holding her close. He pressed his lips to her forehead, her temple. His hands stroked her hair, her back.

Then his mouth was on hers, gently at first, to comfort and soothe while he continued to murmur mindless pleas and promises. But her arms lifted, wrapped around his neck, her body pressed into his, and her lips parted, heated.

The change happened quickly and he was lost in her, drowning in her. The hand that had stroked gently through her hair now tangled in it, fisted as the kiss rushed toward searing.

Take me away, was all she could think. Don't let me reason, don't let me think. Just take me. She wanted his hands on her, his mouth on her, she wanted to feel her muscles quiver with need under his fingers. With that strong, half-wild taste of his filling her, she could let everything go.

She trembled against him, shuddered in his arms, and the sound she made against his desperate mouth might have been a whimper. He jerked back as if he'd been stung, and though his hands weren't completely steady he kept them on her arms, and kept her at arm's length.

"That wasn't—" He had to stop, give himself a minute. His mind was mush and was unlikely to clear if she continued to look at him with those dark, damp eyes that were clouded with passion. "I don't believe I'm going to say this, but this isn't a good idea." He ran his hands up and down her arms as he struggled to hold on to control. "You're upset, probably not thinking . . ." He could still taste her, and the flavor on his tongue had outrageous hunger stirring in his belly. "Christ, I need a drink."

Annoyed with both of them, she swiped the back of her hand over her cheek to dry it. "I'll make coffee."

"I wasn't talking about coffee."

"I know, but if we're going to be sensible, let's stick with coffee."

She stepped into the kitchen area and kept herself busy with the homey process of grinding beans and brewing. Every nerve in her body was on edge. Every need she'd ever had or imagined having was brutally aroused.

"If we'd finished that, Anna, you might have thought I used the situation."

She nodded, continued to fix coffee. "Or I would have wondered if I had. Either way, bad idea. It's important to me never to mix sex and guilt." She looked at him then, quietly, levelly. "It's vital to me."

And he knew. Knowing, he suffered both helpless rage and helpless pity. "Christ, Anna. When?"

"When I was twelve."

"I'm sorry." It made him sick, in his gut, in his heart. "I'm sorry," he said again, inadequately. "You don't have to talk about it."

"That's where we disagree. Talking about it is finally what saved me." And he would listen, she thought. And he would know her. "My mother and I had gone to Philadelphia for the day. I wanted to see the Liberty Bell because we were studying about the Revolutionary War in school. We had this clunker of a car. We drove over, saw the sights. We ate ice cream and bought souvenirs."

"Anna—"

Her head whipped up, a direct challenge. "Are you afraid to hear it?"

"Maybe." He raked a hand through his hair. Maybe he was afraid to hear it, afraid of what it would change between them. Another roll of the dice, he thought, then looked at her, waiting patiently. And he understood he needed to know. "Go ahead."

Turning, she chose cups from the cabinet. "It was just the two of us. It always had been. She'd gotten pregnant when she was sixteen and would never say who the father was. Having me complicated her life enormously and must have brought her a great deal of shame and hardship. My grandparents were very religious, very old school." Anna laughed a little. "Very Italian. They didn't cut my mother out of their lives, but my sense was that it made her uncomfortable to have more than a peripheral part in them. So we had an apartment about a quarter the size of this one."

She brought the pot to the counter, poured the rich, dark coffee. "It was in April, on a Saturday. She'd taken off work so we could go. We had the best day, and we stayed later than we'd planned because we were having fun. I was half asleep on the ride back, and she must have made a wrong turn. I know we got lost, but she just joked about it. The car broke down. Smoke started pouring out from under the hood. She pulled over to the side and we got out. Just started giggling. What a mess, what a fix."

He knew what was coming, and it sickened him. "Maybe you should sit down."

"No, I'm all right. She thought it was the radiator needing water," Anna continued. Her eyes unfocused as she looked back. She could remember how warm it had been, how quiet, and how the moon had drifted in and out of smoky-looking clouds. "We were going to hike back to the closest house and see if we could get some help. A car came along, stopped. There were two men inside, and one of them leaned out and asked us if we had a problem."

She lifted her coffee, sipped. Her hands were steady now. She could say it all again and live through it all again. "I remember the way her hand squeezed mine, clamped down so hard it hurt. I realized later that she was afraid. They were drunk. She said something about just walking down to her brother's house, that we were fine, but they got out of the car. She pushed me behind her. When the first one grabbed her, she yelled at me to run. But I couldn't. I couldn't move. He was laughing and pawing at her, and she was fighting him. And when he dragged her off the road and pushed her down, I ran up and tried to pull him off. But of course I couldn't, and the other man yanked me off and tore my shirt."

A defenseless woman and a helpless child. Cam's hands fisted at his sides as both rage and impotence coursed through him. He wanted to go back to that night, that deserted road, and use them viciously.

"He kept laughing," Anna said quietly. "I saw his face very clearly for a moment or two. Like it was frozen in front of my eyes. I kept hearing my mother screaming, begging them not to hurt me. He was raping her, I could hear him raping her, but she kept begging them to leave me alone. And she must have seen that that wasn't going to happen, and she fought harder. I could hear the man hitting her, yelling at her to shut up. It didn't seem real, even when he was raping me it didn't seem like it could be real. Just an awful dream that went on and on and on.

"When they were finished, they stumbled back to their car and drove away. They just left us there. My mother was unconscious. He'd beaten her badly. I didn't know what to do. They said I went into shock, but I don't remember anything until I was in the hospital. My mother never regained consciousness. She was in a coma for two days, then she died."

"Anna, I don't know what to say to you. What can be said to you."

"I didn't tell you for your sympathy," she said. "She was twenty-seven, a year younger than I am now. It was a long time ago, but you don't forget. It never goes away completely. And I remember everything that happened that night, everything I did afterward—after I went to live with my grandparents. I did everything I could to hurt them, to hurt myself. That was my way of dealing with what had happened to me. I refused counseling,'' she told him coolly. "I wasn't going to talk to some thin-faced, dried-up shrink. Instead I picked fights, looked for trouble, found it. I had indiscriminate sex, used drugs, ran away from home, and butted up against the social workers and the system.''

She picked up the jacket she'd stripped off earlier and folded it neatly now. "I hated everyone, myself most of all. I was the one who had wanted to go to Philadelphia. I was the reason we were there. If I hadn't been with her, she would have gotten away.''

"No.'' He wanted to touch her but was afraid to. Not because she seemed fragile—she didn't. She seemed impossibly strong. "No, you weren't to blame for any of it.''

"I felt the blame. And the more I felt it, the more I struck out at everyone and everything around me.''

"Sometimes it's all you can do,'' he murmured. "Fight back, run wild, until you get it all out.''

"Sometimes there's nothing to fight, and nowhere to run. For three years I used what had happened that night to do whatever I chose.'' She looked at Cam again with a quick, ironic lift and fall of brow. "I didn't choose well. I thought I was a pretty tough cookie when I ended up in juvie. But my caseworker was tougher. She pushed and she prodded and she hounded me. Because she refused to give up on me, she got through. And because my grandparents refused to give up on me, I got through.''

Carefully, she laid the jacket back over the arm of the sofa. "It could have been different. I could have stayed just one more failed statistic in the system. But I didn't.''

He thought it was amazing that she had turned a horror into such strength. She was amazing for choosing work that would have to remind her daily of what had ripped her life apart. "And you decided to pay it back. To go into the kind of work that had turned you around."

"I knew I could help. And yes, I owed a debt, the same way you feel you owe one. I survived," she said, looking him dead in the eyes again, "but survival isn't enough. It wasn't enough for me, or for you. And it won't be enough for Seth."

"One thing at a time," he murmured. "I want to know if they caught the bastards."

"No." She'd long ago learned to accept and to live with that. "It was weeks before I was coherent enough to make a statement. They never caught them. The system doesn't always work, but I've learned, and I believe, it does its best."

"I've never thought so, and this doesn't change my mind." He started to reach out, hesitated, then tucked his hand into his pocket. "I'm sorry I hurt you. That I said things that made you remember."

"It's always there," she told him. "You cope and you put it aside for long periods of time. It comes back now and again, because it never really goes away."

"Did you have counseling?"

"Eventually, yes. I—" She broke off, sighed. "All right, I'm not saying counseling works miracles, Cam. I'm telling you it can be helpful, it can be healing. I needed it, and when I was finally ready to use that help, I was better."

"Let's do this." He did touch her now, just laid a hand over hers on the counter. "We'll leave it as an option. Let's see how things go . . . all around."

"See how things go." She sighed, too tired to argue. Her head ached, and her body felt hollowed out and fragile. "I agree with that, but I'll still recommend counseling in my report."

"Don't forget the shoes," he said dryly and was vastly relieved when she laughed.

"I won't have to mention them, because I know you'll have him at the store by the weekend."

"We could call it a compromise. I seem to be getting better at them lately."

"Then you must have been incredibly obstinate before."

"I think the word my parents used was 'bullheaded.'"

"It's comforting to be understood." She looked down at the hand covering hers. "If you asked to stay, I couldn't say no."

"I want to stay. I want you. But I can't ask tonight. Bad timing all around."

She understood how some men felt about a woman who'd been sexually attacked. Her stomach seized into hard knots. But it was best to know. "Is it because I was raped?"

He wouldn't let it be. He refused to allow what had happened to her affect what would happen between them. "It's because you couldn't say no tonight and tomorrow you might be sorry you didn't."

Surprised, she looked up at him again. "You're never quite what I expect you to be."

He wasn't quite what he expected either, not lately. "This thing here. Whatever it is, isn't quite what I expected it to be. How about a Saturday night date?"

"I have a date Saturday." Her lips curved slowly. The knots in her stomach had loosened. She hadn't even been aware of it. "But I'll break it."

"Seven o'clock." He leaned across the counter, kissed her, lingered over it, kissed her again. "I'm going to want to finish this."

"So am I."

"Well." He heaved a sigh and started for the door while he was sure he could. "That's going to make the drive home easier."

He paused, turned around to look at her. "You said you survived, Anna, but you didn't. You triumphed. Everything about you is a testament to courage and strength." When she stared at him, obviously stunned, he smiled a little. "You didn't get either from a social worker or a counselor. They just helped you figure out how to use it. I figure you got it from your mother. She must have been a hell of a woman.''

"She was," Anna murmured, near tears again.

"So are you." Cam closed the door quietly behind him.

He decided he would take his time driving home. He had a lot to think about.

ELEVEN

PRETTY SATURDAY MORN-
ings in the spring were not meant to be spent indoors or
on crowded streets. To Ethan they were meant to be spent
on the water. The idea of shopping—actually shopping—
was very close to terrifying.

"Don't see why we all have to do this."

Because he'd gotten to the Jeep first, Cam rode in front.
He turned his head to spare Ethan a glance. "Because
we're all in this. The old Claremont barn's for rent, right?
We need a place if we're going to build boats. We have
to make the deal."

"Insanity," was all Phillip had to say as he turned down
Market Street in St. Chris.

"Can't go into business if you don't have a place of
business," Cam returned. He found that single fact inar-
guably logical. "So we take a look at it, make the deal
with Claremont, and get started."

"Licenses, taxes, materials. Orders, for God's sake,"
Phillip began. "Tools, advertising, phone lines, fax lines,
bookkeeping."

"So take care of it." Cam shrugged carelessly. "Soon

169

as we sign the lease and get the kid his shoes, you can do whatever comes next.''

"*I* can do it?'' Phillip complained at the same time Seth muttered he didn't need any damn shoes.

"Ethan got our first order, I found out about the building. You take care of the paperwork. And you're getting the damn shoes,'' he told Seth.

"I don't know how come you're the boss of everybody.''

Cam could only manage a short, grim laugh. "Me either.''

The Claremont building wasn't really a barn, but it was as big as one. In the mid-1700s it had been a tobacco warehouse. After the Revolutionary War, the British ships no longer sailed to St. Chris carrying their wide variety of goods. Businesses that had boomed went bankrupt.

The revival in the late 1800s grew directly from the bay. With improved methods of canning and packing the national market for oysters opened up and St. Chris once again prospered. And the old tobacco warehouse was refitted as a packinghouse.

Then the oyster beds played out, and the building became a glorified storage shed. Over the last fifty years it had been empty as often as it was filled.

From the outside it was unpretentious. Sun- and weather-faded brick, thumb-size holes in the mortar. A sagging old roof that was desperately in need of reshingling. What windows it could boast were small and stingy. Most were broken, all were filthy.

"Oh, yeah, this looks promising.'' Already disgusted, Phillip parked in the pitted lot at the side of the building.

"We need space,'' Cam reminded him. "It doesn't have to be pretty.''

"Good thing, because this doesn't come close to pretty.''

A bit more interested now, Ethan climbed out. He walked up to the closest window, used the bandanna from his back pocket to rub off most of the grime so he could peer through. "It's a good space. Got cargo doors at the back, a dock. Needs a little work."

"A little?" Phillip stared in over Ethan's shoulder. "Floor's rotting out. It's got to be infested with vermin. Probably termites and rodents."

"Probably be a good idea to mention that to Claremont," Ethan decided. "Keep the rent down." Hearing the tinkle of glass breaking, he saw that Cam had just put his elbow through an already cracked window. "Guess we're going inside."

"Breaking and entering." Phillip only shook his head. "That's a good start."

Cam flipped the pathetic lock on the window and shoved it up. "It was already broken. Give me a minute." He boosted himself inside, disappeared.

"Cool," Seth decided, and before a word could be spoken he climbed inside too.

"Nice example we're setting for him." Phillip ran a hand over his face and wished fervently he'd never given up smoking.

"Well, think of it this way. You could have picked the locks. But you didn't."

"Right. Listen, Ethan, we've got to think about this. There's no reason why you can't—we can't—build that first boat at your place. Once we start renting buildings, filing for tax numbers, we're committed."

"What's the worst that can happen? We waste some time and some money. I figure I've got enough of both." He heard the mix of Cam's and Seth's laughter echoing inside. "And maybe we'll have some fun while we're at it."

He started around to the front door, knowing Phillip would grumble but follow.

"I saw a rat," Seth said in pure delight when Cam shoved the front door open. "It was awesome."

"Rats." Phillip studied the dim space grimly before stepping inside. "Lovely."

"We'll have to get us a couple of she-cats," Ethan decided. "They're meaner than toms."

He looked up, scanning the high ceiling. Water damage showed clearly in the open rafters. There was a loft, but the steps leading up to it were broken. Rot, and very likely rats, had eaten at the scarred wood floor.

It would require a great deal of cleaning out and repair, but the space was generous. He began to allow himself to dream.

The smell of wood under the saw, the tang of tongue oil, the slap of hammer on nail, the glint of brass, the squeak of rigging. He could already see the way the sun would slant in through new, clean windows onto the skeleton of a sloop.

"Throw up some walls, I guess, for an office," Cam was saying. Seth dashed here and there, exploring and exclaiming. "We'll have to draw up plans or something."

"This place is a heap," Phillip pointed out.

"Yeah, so it'll come cheap. We put a couple thousand into fixing it up—"

"Better to have it bulldozed and start over."

"Phil, try to control that wild optimism." Cam turned to Ethan. "What do you think?"

"It'll do."

"It'll do what?" Phillip threw up his hands. "Fall down around our ears?" At that moment a spider—which Phillip estimated to be about the size of a Chihuahua—crawled over the toe of his shoe. "Get me a gun," he muttered.

Cam only laughed and slapped him on the back. "Let's go see Claremont."

STUART CLAREMONT WAS a little man with hard eyes and a dissatisfied mouth. The little chunks of St. Christopher that he owned were most often left to fall into disrepair. If his tenants complained loudly enough, he occasionally, and grudgingly, tinkered with plumbing or heat or patched a roof.

But he believed in saving his pennies for a rainy day. In Claremont's mind, it never rained quite hard enough to part with a cent.

Still, his house on Oyster Shell Lane was a showplace. As anyone in St. Chris could tell you, his wife, Nancy, could nag the ears off a turnip. And she ruled that roost.

The wall-to-wall carpet was thick and soft, the walls prettily papered. Fussy curtains were ruthlessly coordinated with fussy upholstery. Magazines lay in military lines over a gleaming cherry wood coffee table that matched gleaming cherry wood end tables that matched gleaming cherry wood occasional tables.

Nothing was out of place in the Claremont house. Each room looked like a picture from a magazine. Like the picture, Cam mused, and not at all like life.

"So, you're interested in the barn." With a stretched-out grin that hid his teeth, Claremont ushered them all into his den. It was decorated in English baronial style. The dark paneling was accented with hunting prints. There were deep-cushioned leather chairs in a port wine shade, a desk with brass fittings, and a brick fireplace converted to gas.

The big-screen television seemed both out of place and typical.

"Mildly," Phillip told him. It had been agreed on the drive over that Phillip would handle the negotiations. "We've just started to look around for space."

"Terrific old place." Claremont sat down behind his desk and gestured them to chairs. "Lots of history."

"I'm sure, but we're not interested in history in this case. There seems to be a lot of rot."

"A bit." Claremont waved that away with one short-fingered hand. "You live round here, what can you expect? You boys thinking of starting some business or other?"

"We're considering it. We're in the talking-about-it stages."

"Uh-huh." Claremont didn't think so, or the three of them wouldn't be sitting on the other side of his desk. As he considered just how much rent he could pry out of them for what he considered an irritating weight around his neck, he looked at Seth. "Well, we'll talk about it, then. Maybe the boy here wants to go outside."

"No, he doesn't," Cam said without a smile. "We're all talking about it."

"If that's the way you want it." So, Claremont thought, that's the way it was. He could hardly wait to tell Nancy. Why, he'd had a good, close-up look at the kid now, and a half-blind idiot could see Ray Quinn in those eyes. Saint Ray, he thought sourly. It looked like the mighty had fallen, yes sir. And he was going to enjoy letting people know what was what.

"I'm looking for a five-year lease," he told Phillip, correctly judging who would be handling the business end.

"We're looking for one year at this point, with an option for seven. Of course, we'd expect certain repairs to be completed before we took occupancy."

"Repairs." Claremont leaned back in his chair. "Hah. That place is solid as a rock."

"And we'd require termite inspection and treatment. Regular maintenance would, of course, be our responsibility."

"Ain't no damn bugs in that place."

"Well, then." Phillip smiled easily. "You'd only have to arrange for the inspection. What are you asking for in rent?"

Because he was annoyed, and because he'd always despised Ray Quinn, Claremont bumped up his figure. "Two thousand a month."

"Two—" Before Cam could choke out his pithy opinion, Phillip rose.

"No point in wasting your time, then. We appreciate you seeing us."

"Hold it, hold it." Claremont chuckled, fought off the little tug of panic at having a deal slip through his grasping fingers so quickly. "Didn't say that wasn't negotiable. After all, I knew your daddy . . ." He aimed that tight-lipped smile directly at Seth. "Knew him more than twenty-five years. I wouldn't feel right if I didn't give his . . . boys a little break."

"Fine." Phillip settled down again, resisted rubbing his hands together. He forgot all his objections to the overall plan in his delight in the art of the deal. "Let's negotiate."

"WHAT THE HELL HAVE I done?" Thirty minutes later, Phillip sat in his Jeep, methodically rapping his head against the steering wheel.

"A damn good job, I'd say." Ethan patted him on the shoulder. He'd reached the Jeep ahead of Cam this time and had taken winner's point in the front seat. "Cut his opening price in half, got him to agree to paying for most of the repairs if we do them ourselves, and confused him enough to have him go for the what-was-it—rent control clause if we take the seven-year option."

"The place is a dump. We're going to pay twelve thousand dollars a year—not including utilities and maintenance—for a pit."

"Yeah, but now it's our pit." Pleased, Cam stretched out his legs—or tried. "Pull that seat up some, Ethan, I'm jammed back here."

"Nope. Maybe you should drop me back by the place. I can start figuring things, and I can get a lift home later."

"We're going shopping," Cam reminded him.

"I don't need any damn shoes," Seth said again, but in reflex rather than annoyance.

"You're getting damn shoes, and you're getting a damn haircut while we're at it, and we're all going to the damn mall."

"I'd rather get hit with a brick than go to the mall on

a Saturday.'' Ethan hunched down in his seat, pulled the brim of his cap low over his eyes. He couldn't bear to think about it.

"When you start working in that death trap," Phillip told him, "you'll likely be hit with a ton of them."

"If I have to get a haircut, everybody's getting one."

Cam glanced briefly at Seth's mutinous face. "You think this is a democracy? Shit. Grab some reality, kid. You're ten."

"You could use one." Phillip met Cam's eyes in the rearview mirror as he drove north out of St. Chris. "Your hair's longer than his."

"Shut up, Phil. Ethan, goddamn it, pull your seat up."

"I hate the mall." In defiance, Ethan stretched his own legs out and tipped the back of his seat down a notch. "It's full of people. Pete the barber's still got his place on Market Street."

"Yeah, and everybody who walks out of it looks like Beaver Cleaver." Frustrated, Cam gave the back of Ethan's seat a solid kick.

"Keep your feet off my upholstery," Phillip warned. "Or you'll walk to the damn mall."

"Tell him to give me some room."

"If I have to get shoes, I get to pick them out. You don't have any say in it."

"If I'm paying for the shoes, you'll wear what I tell you and like it."

"I'll buy the stinking shoes myself. I got twenty dollars."

Cam snorted out a laugh. "Try to get a grip on that reality again, pal. You can't buy decent socks for twenty these days."

"You can if you don't have to have some fancy designer label on them," Ethan tossed in. "This ain't Paris."

"You haven't bought decent shoes in ten years," Cam threw back. "And if you don't pull up that frigging seat, I'm going to—"

"Cut it out!" Phillip exploded. "Cut it out right now

or I swear I'm going to pull over and knock your heads together. Oh, my God.'' He took one hand off the wheel to drag it down his face. "I sound like Mom. Forget it. Just forget it. Kill each other. I'll dump the bodies in the mall parking lot and drive to Mexico. I'll learn how to weave mats and sell them on the beach at Cozumel. It'll be quiet, it'll be peaceful. I'll change my name to Raoul, and no one will know I was ever related to a bunch of fools.''

Seth scratched his belly and turned to Cam. "Does he always talk like that?"

"Yeah, mostly. Sometimes he's going to be Pierre and live in a garret in Paris, but it's the same thing."

"Weird," was Seth's only comment. He pulled a piece of bubble gum out of his pocket, unwrapped it, and popped it into his mouth. Getting new shoes was turning into an adventure.

IT WOULD HAVE STOPPED at shoes if Cam hadn't noticed that the seat of Seth's jeans was nearly worn through. Not that he thought that was a big deal, he assured himself. But it was probably best, since they were there anyway, to pick up a couple of pairs of jeans.

He had no doubt that if Seth hadn't bitched so much about trying on jeans, he himself wouldn't have felt compelled to push on to shirts, to shorts, to a windbreaker. And somehow they'd ended up with three ball caps, an Orioles sweatshirt, and a glow-in-the-dark Frisbee.

When he tried to think back to exactly where he'd taken that first wrong turn, it all became a blur of clothes racks, complaining voices, and cash registers churning.

The dogs greeted them with wild and desperate enthusiasm the minute they pulled into the drive. This would have been endearing but for the fact that the pair of them reeked of dead fish.

With much cursing and shoving and threats, the humans escaped into the house, shutting the dogs with their hurt feelings outside. The phone was ringing.

"Somebody get that," Cam pleaded. "Seth, take this junk upstairs, then go give those stinking dogs a bath."

"Both of them?" The thought thrilled him, but he thought it best to complain. "How come I have to do it?"

"Because I said so." Oh, he hated falling back on something that lame, and that adult. "The hose is around back. God, I want a beer."

But because he lacked the energy even for that, he dropped into the closest chair and stared glassy-eyed at nothing. If he had to face that mall again in this life, he promised himself, he would just shoot himself in the head and be done with it.

"That was Anna," Phillip told him as he wandered back into the living room.

"Anna? Saturday night." He couldn't stop the groan. "I need a transfusion."

"She said to tell you she'd take care of dinner."

"Good, fine. I've got to pull myself together. The kid's yours and Ethan's for tonight."

"He's Ethan's," Phillip corrected. "I've got a date myself." But he sank into a chair and closed his eyes. "It's not even five o'clock and all I want to do is crawl into bed and oblivion. How do people do this?"

"He's got enough clothes to last him a year. If we only have to do it once a year, how bad can it be?"

Phillip opened one eye. "He's got spring and summer clothes. What happens when fall gets here? Sweaters, coats, boots. And he's bound to outgrow every damn thing we bought today."

"We can't allow that to happen. There must be a pill or something we can give him. And maybe he's got a coat already."

"He came pretty much with the clothes on his back. Dad didn't get a package deal this time either."

"Okay, we'll think about that later. Lots later." Cam

pressed his fingers to his eyes. "You saw the way Claremont looked at him, didn't you? That nasty little gleam in his beady little eyes."

"I saw it. He'll talk, and he'll say what he wants to say. Nothing we can do about it."

"You think the kid knows anything, one way or the other?"

"I don't know what Seth knows. I can't get a handle on him. But I'm going to look into investigators on Monday. Check on tracking down the mother."

"Asking for trouble."

"We've already got trouble. The only way to deal with it is to gather information. If it turns out that Seth's a Quinn by blood, then we deal with that."

"Dad wouldn't have hurt Mom that way. Marriage wasn't just a thing to them. It was *the* thing. And they were solid."

"If he'd slipped, he'd have told her." That Phillip firmly believed. "And they'd have worked it out. That part of their lives wasn't our business, and it wouldn't be our business now but for Seth."

"He wouldn't have slipped," Cam murmured, determined to believe it. "I'll tell you one thing I got from them. You get married, you make that promise, that's it. I figure that's why the three of us are still on the single side of life."

"Maybe. But we can't ignore the talk, the suspicions. And if the insurance company balks on paying off Dad's policy, it's going to put all four of us in a bind. Especially since we just signed a lease for that hellhole."

"We'll be okay. Luck's starting to move in our direction."

"Oh?" Phil asked as Cam rose. "How do you figure that?"

"Because I'm about to spend the evening with one of the sexiest women on the planet. And I intend to get very lucky." He glanced back as he started up the stairs. "Don't wait up, bro."

When he stepped into his bedroom, Cam heard the commotion from the backyard. He walked to the window and looked down on Seth and the dogs. Simon was sitting stoically while Seth soaped him down. Foolish raced in mad circles, barking in excitement and terror at the hose that was pouring out water where it had been carelessly tossed on the grass.

Of course, the kid was wearing his brand-new shoes, which were now soaking wet and muddy. He was laughing like a loon.

He hadn't known the boy could laugh like that, Cam realized as he kept watching. He hadn't known he could look like that, unreservedly happy and young and silly.

Simon stood up, gave a long, violent shake that sent water and soap flying. Backing up, Seth slipped in the wet grass and tumbled onto his back. He continued to howl with laughter as both dogs pounced on him. They wrestled over the water and mud and soap until the three of them were soaked and filthy.

Upstairs Cam just stood watching with a mile-wide grin on his face.

THE IMAGE POPPED IN his head when he headed down the hallway to Anna's apartment. He wanted to be able to tell her about it over dinner. He wanted to share it—and he thought it would certainly soften her every bit as much as a quiet meal in a candlelit restaurant.

The roses he'd picked up on the way weren't going to hurt either. He sniffed them himself. If he was any judge of the female mind and heart, he'd bet his full stake that Anna Spinelli had a weak spot for yellow roses.

Before he could knock on Anna's door, the door across the hall swung open. "Hello, there, you must be the new boyfriend."

"Hi, Mrs. Hardelman. We met a few days ago."

"No, we didn't. You met Sister."

"Oh." He smiled cautiously. She looked exactly like the woman who had popped out of that door before, even down to the pink chenille robe. "Well . . . how's it going?"

"You brought her flowers. She'll like that. My beaux used to bring me flowers, and my Henry, God rest his soul, brought me lilacs every May. You think lilacs next month, young man, if Anna lets you keep coming around. Most of them she scoots along, but maybe she'll keep you."

"Yeah." He managed to smile even as his heart stopped at the words "keep you." "Maybe." On impulse he pulled one of the roses out and gave it to her with a neat little flourish.

"Oh!" A girlish blush rose pink on her wrinkled face. "Oh, my goodness." Her eyes gleamed with pleasure as she sniffed it. "How lovely. How sweet. Why, if I were forty years younger, I'd fight Anna for you." She winked flirtatiously. "And I'd win."

"No contest." He flashed her a return wink and a grin. "Ah, say hi to . . . Sister."

"You have a nice time tonight. You go dancing," she added as she shut the door.

"Good idea." And chuckling to himself, Cam knocked.

When she answered, looking sexy enough to gobble up in three quick bites, he decided the dance should begin immediately. He snatched her up, whirled her around to the throbbing, elemental beat of classic Bruce Springsteen and the E Street Band. Then he dipped her as she laughed and stumbled.

"Well, hello." Enjoying the quick dizziness, she chuckled. "Let me up. You've got me off balance."

"That's just where I want you. Off balance." He lowered his mouth to hers in a molten kiss that melted every bone in her body. With her head spinning, she clutched at his shoulders.

"Door's still open," she managed and flailed out with a hand to slam it shut.

"Good thinking." He brought her up slowly, inch by inch, his mouth still nibbling busily on hers. "Your neighbor said I should take you dancing."

"Oh." She was surprised steam wasn't pumping out of her pores. "Is that what that was?"

"That was just a sample." He caught her bottom lip between his teeth, tugged, released. "Wanna tango, Anna?"

"I think we'd better sit this one out." But she pressed a hand to her heart to hold it in place as she eased out of his arms. "You brought me flowers." She buried her face in them as she took them from him. "Figured I was a sucker for rosebuds, did you?"

"Yeah."

"You're right." She laughed over the blooms. "I'll put them in water. You can pour us some wine. I've got it breathing on the counter. Glasses are right there."

"Okay. I—" He looked over, saw a shiny pot steaming on the stove, a platter of antipasto on the counter. "What's all this?"

"Dinner." She crouched down at a kitchen cupboard to locate a vase. "Didn't Phillip give you my message?"

"I thought when you told him you'd take care of it, you meant you had someplace you wanted to go and you'd make the reservations." He plucked a stuffed mushroom off the platter, sampled it, and sighed in pure sensory delight. "I didn't think you'd be cooking for me."

"I like to cook," she said easily as she filled a pale pink vase with water. "And I wanted to be alone with you."

He swallowed quickly. "Hard to argue with that. What are we having?"

"Linguini, with the famous Spinelli family red sauce."

She turned to take the glass of Merlot he'd poured for her. Her face was just a little flushed from the kitchen heat. The dress she'd chosen was the color of ripe peaches and molded her curves like a lover's hands. Her hair was down and curling madly, and her lips were painted nearly the same color as the wine she sipped.

Cam decided if they were to have more than a three-second conversation before he grabbed her again, he'd better stay on the opposite side of the counter.

"It smells incredible."

"It tastes better."

Her pulse was hammering everywhere at once. The way he'd looked at her, just that one long, intense, and measuring stare before he smiled, had brought out her need, a low and nagging ache of need, throbbing incessantly. On an impulse she reached back and turned the flame under the pot off. Keeping her eyes on Cam's, she walked around the counter.

"So do I," she told him. She set her glass aside, then took his, placed it on the counter. She shook her hair back, tipped her face up to his, smiled slowly. "Try me."

TWELVE

HIS BLOOD WAS ALREADY
pounding, a hard, primal beat, as he took a step forward.
He looked into her eyes, wanting to see every shift and
flicker of emotion. "I'm going to want to do more than
try. So be sure."

Sometimes, she thought, you had to go with your instincts, with your cravings. At that moment hers, all of
hers, centered on him. "You wouldn't be here tonight if I
wasn't."

With a slow curving of lips, she reached up and twined
his hair around her finger. She could handle him. She was
sure of it.

He put his hands on her hips. This was no pencil-slim
model with a body like a boy, but a woman. And he
wanted her. He smiled back. He could handle her. He was
sure of it. "You like to gamble, Anna?"

"Now and then."

"Let's roll the dice."

He brought her against him in one hard jerk, one that
made her breath catch and release an instant before his
mouth was on hers. The kiss was quickly desperate,
quickly ravenous, tongues tangling, teeth nipping. The lit-

tle feral purrs that sounded in her throat went straight to
his head like hot whiskey.

She tugged his shirt free of his waistband, then her
hands shot under. Flesh and muscle, she needed to feel it.
With a hum of pleasure she kneaded and scraped and
stroked until that flesh seemed to burn under her fingers,
and those muscles hardened like iron.

She wanted those muscles, that strength pitted against
her own.

He fumbled at the back of her dress, searching for a
zipper, and she laughed breathlessly with her mouth at his
throat. "It doesn't have a zipper." She closed her teeth
over his jaw and didn't bother to be gentle. "You have
to . . . peel it off."

"Jesus." He tugged the snug, stretchy material off her
shoulder and replaced it with teeth as the craving for the
taste of flesh, her flesh, overwhelmed him.

They circled like dancers, though their pace outdis-
tanced the dreamy strains of the Chopin prelude that had
replaced the Boss. He toed off his shoes. She rushed open
the buttons of his shirt. His head was swimming as they
bumped into the bedroom door. She laughed again, but the
sound slipped toward a moan when he yanked the dress
down to her waist, when those eyes of smoked steel
streaked down, when he lowered his head and began to
devour the flesh above the black lace edge of her bra.

His tongue slid under, teasing and tasting until her knees
were loose and her head full of flashing lights and colors.
She'd known he could do this to her, take her to that tee-
tering edge of reason and insanity. She'd wanted him to.
More, she'd wanted to take him there with her.

The wanting was huge, ruthlessly keen, recklessly primitive. And for now, for both of them, it was all that mattered.

Murmuring mindlessly, she dragged off his shirt and
dug her nails into the hard ridge of his shoulders. His chest
was broad and firm, the flesh hot and smooth under her
roaming hands. There were scars, under the shoulder,

along the ribs. The body, she thought, of a risk-taker, of a man who played to win.

With a quick and expert flick of his fingers, he opened the front hook and let her breasts fill his greedy hands. She was magnificent. Golden skin and lush curves. He thought her body almost impossibly perfect. Yet it was erotically real, soft and firm and smooth and fragrant. He wanted to bury himself in her, but when she tugged at the button of his slacks, he shook his head.

"Uh-uh. I want you in bed." He brought her hands up until they circled his neck, brought his mouth down until the kiss was savage and stunning. "I want you under me, over me, wrapped around me."

She kicked off one shoe, balancing herself as they swayed toward the bed. "I want you inside me." Kicked off the other as they tumbled to the mattress.

She rolled over him first, straddling him. The light was nearly gone. Only a pale wash from the setting sun slipped through the windows. Shadows shifted. Her lips were hungry, restless, racing over his face, his throat. Though she had wanted men before, now there was a ferocious and primal greed sweeping through her that she'd never experienced. She would take him, was all she could think, take what she wanted and ease this almost unbearable need.

When she arched back and her upper body was silhouetted in that fragile light, the breath clogged in his lungs. He wanted with an urgency he couldn't remember feeling for anything or anyone else. The desire to take, to possess, to own, surged violently in his already raging blood.

He reared up, gripping her hair in one hand, yanking her head back to expose that long column of throat to his mouth. He could have anything with her. Would have everything.

He was rougher than he meant to be as he pushed her back on the bed. His breath was already heaving as he locked his hands with hers. Her eyes were dark and gleaming—the kind of eyes, he thought, for a man to drown in.

Her hair a tangled mass of black silk against the deep bronze of the spread. The scent of her was more than a provocative invitation. It was a smoldering demand.

Take me, it seemed to say. If you dare.

"I could eat you alive," he murmured and once more crushed his mouth to hers.

He held her down, knowing that if she wrestled free it would be over too soon. Fast, God, yes, he wanted fast, but he didn't want it to end. He thought he could live his life right here in this bed with Anna's quivering body under his.

Her hands flexed under his, her body arched when he drew the tip of her breast into his mouth. He could feel her heartbeat stumble as he used teeth, tongue, lips to taste, to pleasure them both.

When he'd filled himself on her, fed himself on her, he released her hands to touch, and be touched.

They rolled over the bed, groping, tugging at the clothes that remained between them. Their breath was quick and labored, punctuated by half gasps and low moans that spoke of turbulent thrills and dark delights. Sensation slid over sensation, building trembling layers toward delirium. She shuddered under his hands, nearly wept, as each new lash of pleasure whipped through her, each sharp and separate.

She fought to bring him the same barbed and edgy ache.

His hand closed over her, and she was hot and wet and ready. Her body arched, her nails bit into his back as her system exploded to peak.

Then they went mad.

She would remember only a battle for more. And more. Still more. Wild animal sex, a craving to mate. Seeking hands slid off damp flesh, hungry mouth sought hungry mouth. She came again, and her cry of release was a half sob of both triumph and helplessness.

The light was gone, but he could still see her. The glint of those dark eyes, the generous shape of that beautiful mouth. The blood roared in his head, in his heart, in his loins. He could think only *now* and drove himself hard and deep inside her.

His vision grayed, his mind reeled. They remained poised for a shivering moment, joined, mated. He wasn't even aware that his hands sought hers, that their fingers locked into fists.

Then they began to move, a race now full of speed and urgency. There was the good, healthy sound of damp flesh slapping against damp flesh. Their gazes met and held. He watched her eyes go blind and opaque as she crested, he heard the moan tear from her lips an instant before he closed his over hers to swallow the sound.

Her hips pumped like pistons, urging him on, driving him closer to his own jagged brink. He hammered himself into her, holding onto the edge by his fingertips. Watching her, watching her while the need for release clawed viciously at his gut. Then her body went taut, a drawn bow of shock and pleasure.

It was her scream he swallowed as he let himself fall.

HE COULDN'T POSSIBLY move. Cam was certain that if someone held a gun to his head at that moment, he would simply lie there and take the bullet. At least he'd die a satisfied man.

He couldn't think of a better place to be than stretched out over Anna's curvy body, with his face buried in her hair. And if he stayed there long enough, he might get his second wind.

The music had changed again. When his mind cleared enough for him to tune in to it, he recognized Paul Simon's clever twists of lyrics and melody. He nearly drifted off as he was invited to call the singer Al.

"If you fall asleep on top of me, I'm going to have to hurt you."

He drummed up the energy to smile. "I'm not going to sleep. I'm thinking about making love to you again."

"Oh." She stroked her hands down his back to his hips. "Are you?"

"Yeah. Just give me a couple of minutes."

"I'd be glad to. If I could breathe."

"Oh." Lazily he propped himself on his elbows and looked down at her. "Sorry."

She only grinned. "No, you're not. You're smug. But so am I, so that's okay."

"It was great sex."

"It was great sex," she agreed. "Now I'm going to finish dinner. We'll need fuel if we're going to try that again."

Both delighted and baffled, he shook his head. "You're a fascinating woman, Anna. No games, no pretenses. Looking the way you do, you could have men jumping through hoops."

She gave him a little shove so she could wiggle free. "What makes you think I haven't? You're exactly where I wanted you, aren't you?" Smiling, she rose and walked naked to the closet.

"That's a hell of a body you've got there, Miz Spinelli."

She glanced over her shoulder as she wrapped herself in a short red robe. "Same to you, Quinn."

She headed out to the kitchen, humming to herself as she turned the heat back on under the sauce, filled a pot with water for the pasta. Lord, it was lovely, she thought, to feel so loose, so limber, so liberated. However reckless it might be for her to take Cameron Quinn as a lover, the results were worth every risk.

He'd made her aware of every inch of her body, and every inch of his. He made her feel painfully alive. And best of all, she mused as she took out the bread she wanted to toast lightly, he seemed to understand her.

It was one thing to be wanted by a man, to be satisfied by a man. But it warmed her heart to be liked by the man who desired her.

She turned and picked up her wine just as Cam came

out of the bedroom. He'd pulled on his slacks but hadn't bothered to hook them. Anna sipped slowly while she studied him over the rim of her glass. Broad shoulders, hard chest, the waist that tapered to narrow hips and long legs. Oh, yes, he had a terrific body.

And for now it was all hers.

She lifted a pepper from the tray and held it up to his lips.

"It's got bite," Cam said as the heat filled his mouth.

"Um-hmm. I like . . . bite." She picked up his wine and handed it to him. "Hungry?"

"As a matter of fact."

"It won't be long." And because she recognized the look in his eye, she slipped around the counter to stir her sauce. "The water's nearly on the boil."

"You know what they say about a watched pot," he began and started around the counter after her. It was the sketch on the refrigerator that distracted him from his half-formed plan to wrestle her to the kitchen floor. "Hey, that looks just like Foolish."

"It is Foolish. Seth drew it."

"Get out!" He hooked a thumb in his pocket as he took a closer study. "Really? It's damn good, isn't it? I didn't know the kid could draw."

"You would, if you spent more time with him."

"I spend time with him every day," Cam muttered. "He doesn't tell me dick." Cam didn't know where the vague annoyance had come from, but he didn't care for it. "How'd you get this out of him?"

"I asked," she said simply, and slid linguini into the boiling water.

Cam shifted on his feet. "Look, I'm doing the best I can with the kid."

"I didn't say you weren't. I just think you'll do better— with a little more practice and a little more effort."

She pushed her hair back. She hadn't meant to get into this. Her relationship with Cam was supposed to have two separate compartments, without their contents getting mixed up together. "You're doing a good job. I mean that. But you've got a long way to go, Cam, in gaining his trust, his affection. Giving your own. He's an obligation you're fulfilling, and that's admirable. But he's also a young boy. He needs love. You have feelings for him. I've seen them." She smiled over at him. "You just don't know what to do with them yet."

Cam scowled at the sketch. "So now I'm supposed to talk to him about drawing dogs?"

Anna sighed, then turned to frame Cam's face in her hands. "Just talk to him. You're a good man with a good heart. The rest will come."

Annoyed again, he gripped her wrists. He couldn't have said why the quiet understanding in her voice, the amused compassion in her eyes made him nervous. "I'm not a good man." His grip tightened just enough to make her eyes narrow. "I'm selfish, impatient. I go for the thrills because that's what suits me. Paying your debts doesn't have anything to do with having a good heart. I'm a son of a bitch, and I like it that way."

She merely arched a brow. "It's always wise to know yourself."

He felt a little flutter of panic in his throat and ignored it. "I'll probably hurt you before we're done."

Anna tilted her head. "Maybe I'll hurt you first. Willing to risk it?"

He didn't know whether to laugh or swear and ended up pulling her into his arms for a smoldering kiss. "Let's eat in bed."

"That was the plan," she told him.

THE PASTA WAS COLD BY the time they got to it, but that didn't stop them from eating ravenously.

They sat cross-legged on her bed, knees bumping, and ate in the glow of the half dozen candles she'd lighted.

Cam shoveled in linguini and closed his eyes in pure sensory pleasure. "Goddamn, this is good."

Anna wound pasta expertly around her fork and bit. "You should taste my lasagna."

"I'm counting on it." Relaxed and lazy, he broke a piece of the crusty bread she'd put into a wicker basket and handed half to her.

Her bedroom, he'd noted, was different from the rest of the apartment. Here she hadn't gone for the practical, for the streamlined. The bed itself was a wide pool covered in soft rose sheets and a slick satin duvet in rich bronze. The headboard was a romantic arch of wrought iron, curvy and frivolous and plumped now with a dozen fat, colorful pillows.

The dresser he pegged as an antique, a heavy old piece of mahogany refinished to a rosy gleam. It was covered with pretty little bottles and bowls and a silver-backed brush. The mirror over it was a long oval.

There was a mahogany lady's vanity with a skirted stool and glinting brass handles. For some reason he'd always found that particular type of furniture incredibly sexy.

A copper urn was filled with tall, fussy flowers, the walls were crowded with art, and the windows framed in the same rich bronze as the spread.

This, he thought idly, was Anna's room. The rest of the apartment was still Miz Spinelli's. The practical and the sensual. Both suited her.

He reached over the side of the bed to the floor, where he'd put the bottle of wine. He topped off her glass.

"Trying to get me drunk?"

He flashed a grin at her. Her hair was tangled, the robe loose enough to have one shoulder curving free. Her big dark eyes seemed to laugh at both of them. "Don't have to—but it might be interesting anyway."

She smiled, shrugged and drank. "Why don't you tell me about your day?"

"Today?" He gave a mock shudder. "Nightmare time."

"Really." She twirled more pasta, fed it to him. "Details."

"Shopping. Shoes. Hideous." When she laughed, he felt the smile split his face. God, she had a great laugh. "I made Ethan and Phillip go with me. No way I was facing that alone. We had to practically handcuff the kid to get him to go. You'd think I was fitting him for a straitjacket instead of new high-tops."

"Too many men don't appreciate the joys, challenges, and nuances of shopping."

"Next time, you go. Anyway, I had my eye on this building on the waterfront. We checked it out before we headed to the mall. It'll do the job."

"What job?"

"The business. Boat building."

Anna set her fork down. "You're serious about that."

"Dead serious. The place'll do. It needs some work, but the rent's in line—especially since we're strong-arming the landlord into paying for most of the basic repairs."

"You want to build boats."

"It'll get me out of the house, keep me off the streets." When she didn't smile back, he shrugged his shoulder. "Yeah, I think I could get into it. For now, anyway. We'll do this one for the client Ethan's already got lined up, see how it goes from there."

"I take it you signed a lease."

"That's right. Why putz around?"

"Some might say caution, consideration, details."

"I leave the caution and consideration to Ethan, the details to Phillip. If it doesn't work, all we've lost is a few bucks and a little time."

Odd how that prickly temper suited him, she mused. It went so well with those dark, damn-it-all looks. "And if it does work," she added. "Have you thought of that?"

"What do you mean?"

"If it works, you'll have taken on another commitment. It's getting to be a habit." She laughed now, at the expression of annoyance and surprise on his face. "It's going to be fun to ask you how you feel about all this in six months or so.'' She leaned forward and kissed him lightly. ''How about some dessert?''

The nagging worry the word ''commitment'' had brought on faded back as her lips rubbed over his. ''Whatcha got?''

''Cannoli,'' she told him as she set their plates on the floor.

''Sounds good.''

''Or—'' Watching him, she unbelted her robe, let it slide off her shoulders. ''Me.''

''Sounds better,'' he said and let her pull him to her.

It WAS JUST AFTER THREE when Seth heard the car pull into the drive. He'd been asleep but having dreams. Bad ones, where he was back in one of those smelly rooms where the walls were stained and thinner than his drawing paper, and every sound carried through them.

Sex noises—grunts and groans and creaking mattresses—his mother's nasty laugh when she was coked up. It made him sweat, having those dreams. Sometimes she would come in to where he was trying to find comfort and sleep on the musty sofa. If her mood was good, she would laugh and give him smothering hugs, waking him out of a fitful sleep into the smells and sounds of the world she'd dragged him into.

If her mood was bad, she would curse and slap and often end up sitting on the floor crying wildly.

Either way made for one more miserable night.

But worse, hundreds of times worse, was when one of the men she'd taken to bed slipped out, crept across the cramped room, and touched him.

It hadn't happened often, and waking up screaming and swinging drove them off. But the fear lived inside him like a red-hot demon. He'd learned to sleep on the floor behind the sofa whenever she had a man around.

But this time Seth hadn't waked from nightmare to worse. He fought his way out of the sweaty dream and found himself on clean sheets, with a snoring puppy curled beside him.

He cried a little, because he was alone and there was no one to see. Then he snuggled closer to Foolish, comforted by the soft fur and steady heartbeat. The sound of the car coming in stopped him from drifting back to sleep.

His first thought was *cops!* They'd come to get him, to haul him away. Then he told himself, even as his heart jumped up to pound in his throat, that he was being a baby. Still, he crept out of bed, padded silently to the window to look.

He had a hiding place picked out if one was needed.

It was the 'Vette. Seth told himself he'd have recognized the sound of its engine if he hadn't been half asleep. He saw Cam get out, heard the soft, cheerful whistling.

Been out poking at some woman, Seth decided with a sneer. Grown-ups were so predictable. When he remembered that Cam was supposed to have dinner with the social worker that night, his eyes went wide, his jaw dropped.

Man, oh, man, he thought. Cam was bouncing on Miss Spinelli. That was so . . . weird. So weird, he realized he didn't know how he felt about it. One thing for sure, he realized as Cam whistled his way to the door—Cam felt just fine and dandy about it.

When he heard the front door close, he snuck to his own bedroom door. He wanted to get a quick peek, but at the sound of feet coming up the stairs he dived back into bed. Just in case.

The puppy whimpered, began to stir, and Seth slammed his eyes shut as the door opened.

When the footsteps came slowly, quietly toward the bed, his heart began to pound in his chest. What would he do? he thought in a sick panic. God, what could he do? Foolish's tail began to thump on the bed as Seth cringed and waited for the worst.

"Guess you think this is a pretty good deal, lazing around half the day, getting your belly filled, having a nice soft bed at night," Cam murmured.

His voice was slightly slurred from lack of sleep, but to Seth it sounded like drugs or liquor. He struggled to keep his breathing slow and steady while his heartbeat pounded like a jackhammer against his ribs, in his head.

"Yeah, you fell into roses, didn't you? And didn't have to do a thing to earn it. Goofy-looking dog." Seth nearly blinked, realizing Cam was speaking to Foolish and not him. "It'll be his problem, won't it, when you're grown and take up more of the bed than he does."

Cautious, Seth slitted his eyes open just enough so he could see through his lashes. He saw Cam's hand come down, give Foolish a quick, careless stroke. Then the tangled sheets and blanket came up, smoothed over his shoulders. That same hand gave Seth's head a quick and careless stroke.

When the door closed again, Seth waited thirty full seconds before daring to open his eyes. He looked straight into Foolish's face. The pup seemed to be grinning at him as though they'd gotten away with something. Grinning back, Seth draped an arm around the pup's pudgy body.

"I guess it is a pretty good deal, huh, boy?" he whispered.

In agreement, Foolish licked Seth's face, then yawning hugely, settled down to sleep again.

This time, when Seth dropped off to sleep, there were no sweaty dreams to haunt him.

THIRTEEN

"You're awfully damn happy these days."

Cam acknowledged Phillip's pithy comment with a shrug and kept on whistling while he worked. They were making decent progress on what Cam jokingly thought of as their shipyard. It was hard, sweaty, filthy work.

And every time Cam compared it to laundry detail, he praised God.

Though what windows weren't broken were open wide, the air still carried a vague chemical scent. At Phillip's insistence they'd bought a batch of insect bombs and blasted the place with killing fog. When it cleared, the death toll was heavy. It took nearly a half a day just to clear out the corpses.

Replacement windows were slated to be delivered that day. Claremont had bitched bitterly about the expense—despite the deal he got on them because his brother-in-law managed the lumber company in Cambridge and had sold them to him at cost. He'd been only slightly mollified that the Quinns would rip out the old windows and install the new ones, saving him from hiring laborers.

If the fact that the improvements to the building would

spike the potential resale value pleased him, he kept that small delight to himself.

They'd pried or punched out rotted boards and hauled them outside to a steadily growing pile of discards. The metal banister of the stairs leading up to the overhead loft was rusted through, so they yanked it out. Claremont was able to finesse the proper permits, so they were tossing up a couple of walls to close in what would be a bathroom.

Because Cam considered this kind of work a hobby, one he enjoyed, and he came home most nights to a clean house and had a pretty woman willing to tango with him whenever time and circumstances permitted, he figured he had a right to be happy.

Hell, the kid had even been doing his homework—most of the time. He had turned in the much-despised essay and was halfway through his probation without incident.

Cam figured his luck had been running hot and strong for the past couple of weeks.

As far as Phillip was concerned, it had been the worst two weeks of his life. He had barely spent any time in his apartment, had lost his favorite pair of Magli loafers to the gnawing puppy teeth of Foolish, hadn't seen the inside of a single four-star restaurant, and hadn't so much as sniffed a woman.

Unless he counted Mrs. Wilson at the supermarket, and he damn well didn't.

Instead, he was handling and juggling and bouncing details that no one else so much as thought about, getting blisters on his hands swinging a hammer, and spending his evenings wondering what had happened to life as he'd known it.

The fact that he knew Cam was getting regular sex fried the hell out of him.

When the board he lifted gifted him with a fat splinter in the thumb, he swore ripely. "Why the hell didn't we hire carpenters?"

"Because, as keeper of our magic funds, you pointed out it's cheaper this way. And Claremont gave us the first

month's rent free if we did it ourselves.'' Cam took the
board himself, placed it, and began to hammer in the next
stud. ''You said it was a good deal.''

Gritting his teeth, he yanked out the splinter, sucked on
his aching thumb. ''I was insane at the time.''

Phillip stepped back, hands on his hips above his tool
belt, and surveyed the area. It was filthy. Dirt, sawdust,
piles of refuse, stacks of lumber, sheets of plastic. This
was not his life, he thought again, as the sound of Cam's
hammer thudded in time with the gritty rock beat of Bob
Seger that pumped out of the radio.

''I must have been insane. This place is a dump.''

''Yep.''

''Setting up this idiotic business is going to devour our
capital.''

''No doubt about it.''

''We'll go under in six months.''

''Could be.''

Phillip scowled and reached down for the jug of iced
tea. ''You don't give a good damn.''

''If it bombs, it bombs.'' Cam tucked his hammer back
in his belt, took out his measuring tape. ''We're no worse
off. But if it makes it, if it just bumps along for a while,
we'll have what we need.''

''Which is?''

Cam picked up the next board, eyeballed it along its
length, then set it over the sawhorses. ''A business—which
Ethan can run after the dust settles. He gets himself a couple of part-timers—off-season watermen—he builds three
or four boats a year to keep it afloat.''

He paused long enough to mark the board, run the saw.
Dust flew and the noise was awesome. Cam set the power
saw aside, hefted the board into place. ''I'll give him a
hand now and then, you'll keep track of the money end.
But it ought to give us room to move some. I can get in
a few races a year, you can get back to bilking the consumer with jazzy ads.'' He pulled out his hammer. ''Everybody's happy.''

Phillip cocked his head, scratched his chin. "You've been thinking."

"That's right."

"When do you figure this slide back to normality's going to happen?"

Cam swiped at the sweat on his forehead with the back of his hand. "The faster we get this place up and running, the faster we get the first boat done."

"Which explains why you've been busting your ass, and mine. Then what?"

"I've got enough contacts to line up a second job, even a third." He thought of Tod Bardette—the bastard—even now priming a crew for the One-Ton Cup. Yeah, he could finesse Bardette into a boat by Quinn. And there were others, plenty of others, who would pay and pay well. "I figure my main contribution to this enterprise is contacts. Six months," he said. "We can handle six months."

"I'm going back to work Monday," Phillip told him, braced for a fight. "I've got to. I'm flexing time so I'll only be in Baltimore Monday through Thursday. It's the best I can do."

Cam considered. "Okay. I don't have a problem with that. But you'll be busting ass on weekends."

For six months, Phillip thought. More or less. Then he hissed out a breath. "One factor you haven't worked into your plan. Seth."

"What about him? He'll be here. He's got a place to live. I'm going to use the house as a base."

"And when you're off breaking records and female hearts in Monte Carlo?"

Cam scowled and rapped the hammer harder than necessary on the head of the nail. "He doesn't want to be in my damn pocket all the time. You guys'll be around when I'm not. The kid's going to be taken care of."

"And if the mother comes back? They haven't been able to find her. Nothing. I'd feel better if we knew where she is and what she's up to."

"I'm not thinking about her. She's out of the picture."

Has to be, Cam insisted, remembering the look of pasty-faced terror on Seth's face. "She's not going to mess with us."

"I'd like to know where she is," Phillip said again. "And what the hell she was to Dad."

CAM PUT IT OUT OF HIS mind. His way of handling loose ends was to knot them up together and forget about them. The immediate problem, as he saw it, was getting the building in shape, ordering equipment, tools, supplies. If the business was a means to an end, it had to begin.

Every day he worked on the building was one day closer to escape. Every dollar he poured into supplies and equipment was an investment in the future. His future.

He was keeping his promise, he told himself. His way.

With the sun beating down on his back and a faded blue bandanna tied around his head, he ripped broken shingles off the roof. Ethan and Phillip were working behind him, replacing shingles. Seth appeared to be having a fine time winging the discarded ones from roof to ground, and a satisfying pile was forming below.

It was a cool place to be as far as Seth was concerned. Up on the roof with the sun beating down and the occasional gull flying by. You could see just about everything from up here. The town, with its straight streets and square yards. The old trees popping up out of the grass. The flowers were okay, too. From up here they were just blobs and dots of color. Someone was mowing, and the sound carried up to him like a distant hum.

He could see the waterfront, with the boats at dock or cruising along the water. A couple of kids were sailing a little skiff with blue sails, and because he envied them, he looked away toward the docks.

There were people, shopping or strolling or eating lunch at one of the outdoor tables with umbrellas. Tourists were watching the show the crab pickers put on. He liked to sneer at the tourists; when he did, he didn't envy the boys in their neat little boat quite so much.

He wished he had the binoculars Ray had given him so he could see even farther. He wished he could sit up here sometime with his sketchbook.

Everything looked so . . . clean from up here. The sky and water both so blue, the grass and leaves so green. You could smell the water if you took a good sniff—and maybe that was hot dogs grilling.

The scent made his stomach growl with hunger. He shifted a little and looked at Cam out of the corner of his eye. Man, he wished he had muscles like that. With muscles like that you could do anything and nobody could stop you. If a guy had muscles like that he would never have to be afraid of anything, anyone, ever in his whole life.

Testing his own biceps with his finger, he was far from satisfied. He thought maybe if he got to use tools, he could harden them up.

"You said I could pull some of them off," Seth reminded him.

"Later."

"You said later before."

"I'm saying it again." It was hot, nasty, tedious work, and Cam wanted it over as much as he wanted to breathe. He'd already sweated through his T-shirt and pulled it off. His back gleamed damp and his throat was desert-dry. He pried off another square and watched Seth send it soaring. "You throwing them in the same place?"

"That's what you said to do."

He eyed the boy. Seth's hair stuck out from under an Orioles fielder's cap that Cam had ended up buying him when they went to a game the week before. Now that he thought of it, Cam didn't think he'd seen the kid without the cap since he got it.

The ball game had been an impulse, he thought now, just one of those things. But it had given him a sharp tug to see the way Seth's eyes had gone huge at the sight of

Camden Yards. How he'd sat there, a hot dog clutched and forgotten in his hand as he watched every movement on the field.

And it had made Cam laugh when Seth's serious and firm opinion had been "it looks like shit on TV compared to this."

He watched Seth send another shingle flying and wondered if he should teach the kid how to field a ball. Instantly, the fact that he had had the thought irritated him. "You're not looking where you're throwing them."

"I know where they're going. If you don't like how I do it, you can throw them down yourself. You said I could pull some off."

Not worth it, Cam told himself. Not worth the effort to argue. "Fine, you want to rip shingles off the damn roof. Here, look, see how I'm doing this? You use the claw of the hammer and—"

"I've been watching you for an hour. It doesn't take brains to rip off shingles."

"Fine," Cam said between his teeth. "You do it." He shoved the hammer into Seth's eager hand. "I'm going down. I need a drink."

Cam went nimbly down the ladder, trying to assure himself that all ten-year-old boys were snotty assholes. And the more shingles the kid ripped free, the fewer there would be for him to do himself. If he survived the day, he had another Saturday night date with Anna. He wanted to make the most of it.

Now there was a woman, he thought as he grabbed the jug of ice water and glugged some down. Damn near the perfect woman. Though it occasionally gave him an uneasy feeling in the gut to think of her that way, it was tough to find the flaws.

Beautiful, smart, sexy. That great laugh she let loose so often. Those gorgeous, warm, understanding eyes. The wild spirit of adventure tucked into the practical public servant suits.

And she could cook.

He chuckled to himself and pulled out another bandanna to mop his face.

Why, if he was the settling-down type, he would snatch her right up. Get a ring on her finger, say the I-do's, and tuck her into his house—his bed—on a permanent basis.

Hot meals, hot sex.

Conversation. Laughter. Slow smiles to wake you up in the morning. Shared looks that said more than dozens of words.

When he caught himself staring into space, the jug dangling from his fingers and a stupid grin on his face, he shook himself hard. Let out a long breath.

The sun had baked his brain, he decided. Permanent wasn't his style. Never had been. And marriage—the word made him shudder—was for other people.

Thank God Anna wasn't looking for any more than he was. A nice, easy, no strings, no frills relationship suited them both.

To ensure that his mind didn't go hot again, he dumped frigid water over his head. Six months, he promised himself as he started back outside. Six months and he would start easing himself back into his own world. Competition, speed, glittery parties, and women who were only looking for a fast ride.

When the thought of it fell flat, when the image of it all left him hollow inside, he swore. It was what he wanted, goddamn it. What he knew. Where he belonged. He wasn't cut out to spend his life building boats for other people to sail, raising a kid and worrying about matching socks.

Sure, maybe he'd teach the kid how to field a grounder or a pop fly, but that was no big deal. Maybe Anna Spinelli was firmly hooked in his brain, but that didn't have to be a big deal either.

He needed room, he needed freedom.

He needed to race.

His thoughts were boiling as he stepped outside. The aluminum extension ladder nearly crashed on top of him.

His hot oath and the muffled scream overhead sounded as one.

When he looked up, his heart simply stopped beating.

Seth dangled from his fingertips from the broken frame of a window twenty feet above. In the space of a trio of heartbeats, Cam saw the pattern on the bottom of the new high-tops, the dangling laces, the droopy socks. Before he could draw the first breath, both Ethan and Phillip were leaning over the roof and struggling to reach Seth.

"You hold on," Ethan shouted. "Hear me?"

"Can't." Panic made Seth's voice thin, and very, very young. "Slipping."

"We can't reach him from here." Phillip's voice was deadly calm, but his eyes as they stared down at Cam's were bright with fear. "Put the ladder up. Quick."

He made the decision in seconds, though it seemed like the rest of his life. Cam gauged the time it would take to haul the ladder into place, to climb up or climb down to where Seth hung. Too long, was all he could think, and he moved to stand directly under Seth.

"You let go, Seth. Just let go. I'll catch you."

"No. I can't." His fingers were raw and bleeding and nearly gave way as he shook his head fiercely. Panic skittered up his spine like hungry mice. "You won't."

"Yes, you can. I will. Close your eyes and just let go. I'm here." Cam planted his legs apart and ignored his own trembling heart. "I'm right here."

"I'm scared."

"Me, too. Let go. Do it!" he said so sharply that Seth's fingers released on instinct.

It seemed as though he fell forever, endlessly. Sweat poured down Cam's face. Air refused to come into Seth's lungs. Though his eyes stung from sun and salt, Cam never took them off the boy. His arms were there, braced and ready as Seth tumbled into them.

Cam heard the explosion of breath, his, Seth's, he didn't know which as they both fell heavily. Cam used his body to cushion the boy, took the hard ground on his bare back.

But in an instant, he was up on his knees. He spun Seth around and plastered the boy against him.

"Christ! Oh, Christ!"

"Is he all right?" Ethan shouted from above.

"Yeah. I don't know. Are you okay?"

"I think. Yeah." He was shaking badly, his teeth chattering, and when Cam loosened his hold enough to look into his face he saw deathly pale skin and huge, glassy eyes. He sat down on the ground, pulled Seth into his lap, and pushed the boy's head between his knees.

"Just shaken up," he called to his brothers.

"Nice catch." Phillip sat back on the roof, rubbed his hands over his clammy face, and figured his heart rate would get back to normal in another year or two. "Jesus, Ethan, what was I thinking of, sending that kid down for water?"

"Not your fault." Hoping to steady both of them, Ethan squeezed Phillip's shoulder. "Nobody's fault. He's okay. We're okay." He looked down again, intended to tell Cam to get the ladder. But what he saw was the man holding on to the boy, his cheek pressed to the top of the boy's hair.

The ladder could wait.

"Just breathe," Cam ordered. "Just take it slow. You got the wind knocked out of you, that's all."

"I'm okay." But he kept his eyes closed, terrified that he would throw up now and totally humiliate himself. His fingers were burning, but he was afraid to look. When it finally sank in that he was being held, and held close, it wasn't sick panic, it wasn't shuddering disgust that raced through him.

It was gratitude, and a sweet, almost desperate relief.

Cam closed his eyes as well. And it was a mistake. He saw Seth falling again, falling and falling, but this time he wasn't quick enough, or strong enough. He wasn't there at all.

Fear bent under fury. He whirled Seth around until their faces were close and shook him. "What the hell were you doing? What were you thinking of? You idiot, you could have broken your neck.''

"I was just—" His voice hitched, mortifying him. "I was only—I didn't know. My shoe was untied. I must've stepped wrong. I only . . ."

But the rest of the words were muffled against Cam's hard, sweaty chest as he was pulled close again. He could feel the rapid beat of Cam's heart, hear it thunder under his ear. And he closed his eyes again. And slowly, testingly, his arms crept around to hold.

"It's all right," Cam murmured, ordering himself to calm down. "Wasn't your fault. You scared the shit out of me."

His hands were trembling, Cam realized. He was making a fool of himself. Deliberately, he pulled Seth back and grinned. "So, how was the ride?"

Seth managed a weak smile. "I guess it was pretty cool."

"Death-defying." Because they were both feeling awkward, they eased back slowly, warily. "Good thing you're puny yet. You had any weight on you, you might have knocked me out cold."

"Shit," Seth said, because he couldn't think of anything else.

"Messed up your hands some." Cam frowned consideringly at the bloody, torn fingertips. "Guess we better get the rest of the crew down and fix you up."

"It's nothing." It hurt like fire.

"No use having you bleed to death." Because his hands still weren't quite steady, Cam made quick work of lifting the ladder into place. "Go on in and get the first aid kit," he ordered. "Looks like Phil was on the mark when he made us buy the damn thing. We might as well use it on you."

After he watched Seth go inside, out of sight, Cam simply lowered his brow to the side of the ladder. His stomach continued to jump, and a headache he hadn't been aware

of until that instant roared through his temples like a
freight train.

"You okay?" Ethan put a hand on Cam's shoulder the
minute he was on the ground.

"I've got no spit. My spit's dried clean up. Never been
so fucking scared."

"That makes three of us." Phillip glanced around. Because his knees were still wobbly, he sat on one of the
rungs of the ladder. "How bad are his hands? Does he
need a doctor?"

"Fingers are ripped up some. It's not too bad." At the
sound of a car pulling into the loose-gravel lot, he turned
to see who it was. And his jittery stomach sank. "Oh,
perfect. Sexy social worker at three o'clock."

"What's she doing here?" Ethan pulled his cap down
lower on his head. He hated having women around when
he was sweaty.

"I don't know. We have a date tonight, but not until
seven. She's going to have some damn female thing to say
about us having the kid up there in the first place."

"So we won't tell her," Phillip murmured even as he
shot Anna a charming, welcoming smile. "Well, this
brightens the day. Nothing better than to see a beautiful
woman after a tough morning's work."

"Gentlemen." She only smiled when Phillip took her
hand and brought it to his lips. Amusement rippled through
her. Three men, three brothers, three reactions. Phillip's
polished welcome, Ethan's vaguely embarrassed nod, and
Cam's irritated scowl.

And there was no doubt each and every one of them
looked outrageously male and appealing in sweat and tool
belts.

"I hope you don't mind. I wanted to see the building,
and I did come bearing gifts. There's a picnic hamper in
my car—men food," she added. "For anyone who'd like
a lunch break."

"That was nice of you. Appreciate it." Ethan shifted
his feet. "I'll go fetch it out of your car."

"Thanks." She surveyed the building, tipped down her round-lensed wire-rimmed sunglasses, studied it again. All she could think was that she was glad she'd dressed casually for this impromptu visit, in roomy jeans and a T-shirt. There was no way to go in there, she imagined, and come out clean. "So this is it."

"The start of our empire," Phillip began, having just figured out that he could take her on a tour around the outside and give Cam enough time to clean Seth up—and shut him up—when the boy came out.

The color was back in his face—which was filthy with sweat, dirt, and the blood that he'd smeared on his cheeks from his fingers. His white Just Do It T-shirt was in the same condition. He carried the first aid kit like a banner.

Alarm shot into Anna's eyes. She was rushing toward Seth, taking him gently by the shoulders before either Cam or Phillip could think of a reasonable story. "Oh, honey, you're hurt. What happened?"

"Nothing," Cam began. "He just—"

"I fell off the roof," Seth piped up. He'd calmed down while he was inside and had gone from being weak-kneed to wildly proud.

"Fell off the—" Shocked to numbness, Anna instinctively began to check for broken bones. Seth stiffened, then squirmed, but she continued grimly until she was satisfied. "My God. What are you doing walking around?" She turned her head long enough to aim a furious glare at Cam. "Have you called an ambulance?"

"He doesn't need a damn ambulance. It's just like a woman to fall to pieces."

"Fall to pieces." Keeping a protective hand on Seth's shoulder, she whirled on them. "Fall to pieces! The three of you are standing around here like a herd of baboons. The child could have internal injuries. He's bleeding."

"Just my fingers." Seth held them out, admiring them. Man, was he going to be the hot topic in school come Monday! "I slipped off the ladder coming down, but I caught myself on the window frame up there." He pointed it out helpfully, while Anna's head spun from the height. "And Cam told me to let go and he'd catch me, and I did and he did."

"Damn kid won't say two words half the time," Cam muttered to Phillip. "The other half he won't shut the hell up. He's fine," he said, lifting his voice. "Just knocked the wind out of him."

She didn't bother to respond, only sent him one long, fulminating look before turning back to smile at Seth. "Why don't I take a look at your hands, honey? We'll clean them up and see if you need stitches." She lifted her chin, but the shaded glasses didn't quite conceal the heat in her eyes. "Then I'd like to speak with you, Cameron."

"I bet you would," he mumbled as she led Seth toward her car.

Seth found he didn't mind being babied a bit. It was a new experience to have a woman fuss over a little blood. Her hands were gentle, her voice soothing. And if his fingers throbbed and stung, it was a small price to pay for what now seemed a glorious adventure.

"It was a long way down," he told her.

"Yes, I know." Thinking of it only made the ball of anger in her stomach harden. "You must have been terrified."

"I was only scared for a minute." He bit the inside of his cheek so he wouldn't whimper as she carefully bandaged his wounds. "Some kids would've screamed like a girl and wet their pants."

He wasn't sure if he'd screamed or not—that part was a blur—but he'd checked his jeans and knew he was okay there. "And Cam, he was pissed off. You'd think I kicked the damn ladder out from under me on purpose."

Her head came up. "He yelled at you?"

He started to expand on that, but there was something about her eyes that made it hard to tell an out-and-out lie. "For a minute. Mostly he just got goofy about it. You'd think I'd had my arm whacked off the way he was carrying on, patting on me and stuff."

He shrugged, but remembered the warm glow in his gut at being held close, safe, tight. "Some guys, you know? They can't take a little blood."

Her smile softened, and she reached up to brush his hair back. "Yeah, I know. Well, you're in pretty good shape for a guy who likes to dive off roofs. Don't do it again, okay?"

"Once was enough."

"Glad to hear it. There's fried chicken in the hamper— unless they've eaten it all."

"Yeah. Man, I could eat a dozen pieces." He started to race off, then felt a tug on his conscience. It was another rare sensation, and it caused him to turn back and meet her eyes. "Cam said he'd catch me, and he did. He was cool."

Then he ran toward the building, shouting for Ethan to save him some damn chicken.

Anna only sighed. She sat there on the side of the passenger seat while she put the first aid kit back in order. When the shadow fell across her, she continued to tidy up. She could smell him, sweat, man, the faint undertones of the soap from his morning shower. She knew his scent so well now—and the way it would mix with her own—that she could have picked him out of a roomful of men had she been handcuffed and blindfolded.

And though it was certainly true that she'd been curious about the building, it was really only a handy excuse to drive over from Princess Anne to see him.

"I don't suppose there's any point in me telling you that boys Seth's age shouldn't be going up and down extension ladders unsupervised."

"I don't suppose there is."

"Or that boys his age are careless, often awkward, and clumsy."

"He's not clumsy," Cam said with some heat. "He's agile as a monkey. Of course," he added with a sneer in his voice, "the rest of us are baboons, so that fits."

She closed the first aid kit, rose, and handed it to him.

"Apparently," she agreed. "However, accidents happen, no matter how careful you are, no matter how hard you try to prevent them. That's why they're accidents."

She looked at his face. The irritation was still there, she noted—with her, with circumstances. And oh, that underlying anger that never seemed to fade completely away was very, very close to the surface.

"So," she said softly, "how many years of your life did that little event shave off?"

He let out a breath. "A couple of decades. But the kid handled himself."

He turned a little, to look back toward the building. It was then that Anna saw the smears of blood on his back. Smears, she realized after her heart's first leap, that had come from Seth's hands. The boy had been held, she thought. And the boy had held on.

Cam turned back, caught her smiling. "What?"

"Nothing. Well, since I'm here, and you're all eating my food, I think I'm entitled to a tour."

"How much of this business are you going to have to put in one of your reports?"

"I'm not on the clock," she told him, more sharply than she intended. "I thought I was coming to pay a visit to friends."

"I didn't mean it that way, Anna."

"Really?" She stepped around the car door and slammed it shut at her back. Damn it, she had come to see him, to be with him, not to fit in an unannounced home visit. "What I will put in my next report, unless I see something to the contrary, is that it's my opinion that Seth is bonding with his guardians and they with him. I'll make sure you get a copy. I'll take a rain check on the tour. You can get the hamper back to me at your convenience."

She thought it was a great exit as exits went, striding around the car while she tossed off her lines. Her temper was flaring but just under control. Then he grabbed her as she reached for the car door and spoiled it.

She whirled around swinging, but her fist slid off his

damp chest and ruined the impact. "Hands off."

"Where are you going? Just hold it a minute."

"I don't have to hold anything, and I don't want you holding me." She shoved at him with both hands. "God, you're filthy!"

"If you'd just be still and listen—"

"To what? You don't think I get it? You don't think I've clued in to what you saw, what you thought when I pulled up. 'Oh, hell, here comes the social worker? Close ranks, boys.' " She jerked back. "Well, fuck you."

He could have denied it, could have taken the I-don't-know-what-you're-talking-about approach and done an expert job of it. But her eyes had the same effect on him as they'd had on Seth. They wouldn't let his tongue wrap itself around a decent lie.

"Okay, you're right. It was knee-jerk."

"At least you have the decency to be honest." The depth of the hurt infuriated her as much as it surprised her.

"I don't know what you're so frosted about."

"Don't you?" She tossed back her hair. "Then I'll tell you. I looked at you and saw a man who also happens to be my lover. You looked at me and saw a symbol of a system you don't trust or respect. Now that that's cleared up, get out of my way."

"I'm sorry." He dragged the bandanna off because his head was splitting. "You're right again, and I'm sorry."

"So am I." She started to open the car door.

"Will you give me a damn minute here?" Instead of reaching for her again, he dragged his hands through his hair. It wasn't the impatient tone that stopped her, but the weariness of the gesture.

"All right." She let go of the door handle. "You've got a minute."

He didn't think there was another woman on the planet he'd explained himself to more than the one watching him now with a faint frown. "We were all a little shaken up right then. The timing couldn't have been worse. Goddamn it, my hands were still shaking."

He hated to admit that—hated it. To gather some control, he turned away, paced off, paced back. "I was in a wreck once. About three years ago. Grand Prix. Hit the chute, misjudged, went into a hell of a spin. The car was breaking apart around me. The worst fear is invisible fire. Vapors catching hold. I had this flash of myself burned to a crisp. Just for an instant, but it was vivid."

He balled the bandanna up in his hand, then pulled it out smooth. "I'm telling you, Anna, I swear to you, standing under that kid and watching his shoelaces dangle was worse. Hell of a lot worse."

How could she hold on to her anger? And why couldn't he see that he had such a huge well of love to give if he would only let himself dip into it freely? He'd said that he would probably hurt her, but she hadn't known it would come so soon, or from this direction.

She hadn't been looking in the right direction. She hadn't known she was falling in love with him.

"I can't do this," she said, half to herself, and wrapped her hands around her arms to warm them. The chill penetrated, even though she stood in streaming sun. How many steps had she taken toward love, she wondered, and how many could she take back to save herself? "I don't know what I was thinking of. Being involved with you on a personal level only complicates our mutual interest in the child."

"Don't back off from me, Anna." He experienced another level of fear now, one he'd never felt before. "So we take a few wrong steps. We get the balance back. We're good together."

"We're good in bed," she said and blinked when she saw what might have been hurt flash in his eyes.

"Only?"

"No," she said slowly as he stepped toward her, "not only. But—"

"I've got something for you inside me, Anna." He forgot his hands were grimy and laid them on her shoulders. "I haven't used it up yet. This thing with you, it's one of the first times I haven't wanted to rush to the finish line.''

They would still get there, she realized. She would have to be prepared for him to reach that line, and cross it, ahead of her. ''Don't mix up who I am and what I am,'' she told him quietly. ''You have to be honest with me, or the rest of it means nothing.''

''I've been more up front with you than I've ever been with a woman before. And I know who you are.''

''All right.'' She laid a hand on his cheek when he bent to kiss her. ''We'll see what happens next.''

FOURTEEN

IT WAS A GOOD SPRING afternoon. Balmy air, fine wind, and just enough cloud cover to filter the sun and keep it from baking your flesh down to your bones. When Ethan guided his workboat into dock, the waterfront was busy with tourists who'd come to see the watermen work and the busy fingers of the crab pickers fly.

He had reached his quota early, which suited him fine. The water tanks under the faded striped awning of his boat were crawling with annoyed crabs that would find their way into the pot by nightfall. He would turn in his catch and leave his mate to diddle with the engine. It was running just a tad rough. He planned to take himself over to the building to see how the plumbing was coming.

He was itching to have it done, and Ethan Quinn wasn't a man who itched for much—at least, he didn't allow himself to think he did. But the boat building enterprise was a little private dream that he'd nurtured for some time now. He thought it was about ripe.

Simon let out one sharp, happy woof as the boat bumped the pilings. Even as Ethan prepared to secure the lines, there were hands reaching for them. Hands he recognized before he lifted his gaze to the face. Long, pretty hands that wore no rings or polish.

"I've got it, Ethan."

He looked up and smiled at Grace. "Appreciate it. What're you doing on the docks midday?"

"Picking crabs. Betsy was feeling off this morning, so they were short a pair of hands. My mother wanted Aubrey for a couple of hours anyway."

"You ought to take some time for yourself, Grace."

"Oh . . ." She secured the lines expertly, then straightened to run a hand through her short cap of hair. "One of these days. Did y'all finish up that ham casserole I made the other day?"

"Fought over the last bite. It was great. Thanks." Now that he'd about run out of easy conversation and was standing on the dock beside her, he didn't know what to do with his hands. To compensate, he scratched Simon's head. "We pulled in a nice catch today."

"So I see." But her smile didn't reach her eyes, and she was gnawing on her lip. A sure sign, Ethan thought, that what was on Grace's mind was trouble.

"Is there a problem?"

"I hate to take up your time when you're busy, Ethan." Her eyes scanned the docks. "Could you walk with me a minute?"

"Sure. I could use something cold. Jim, you handle things from here all right?"

"You got it, Cap'n."

With the dog trotting between them, Ethan tucked his hands in his pockets. He nodded when a familiar voice called out a greeting, barely noticed the quick fingers of the crab pickers, who put on quite a show while they worked. He noticed the smells because he was so fond of them—water, fish, salt in the air. And the subtle notes of Grace's soap and shampoo.

"Ethan, I don't want to cause you or your family any grief."

"You couldn't, Grace."

"You may already know. It just bothers me so much. I just hate it so much." Her voice lowered, sizzling with a temper that Ethan knew was rare. He saw that her face was set, her mouth grim, and he decided to forgo that cold drink and lead her farther away from the docks.

"You better tell me, get it off your mind."

"And put it on yours," she said with a sigh. She hated to do it. Ethan was always there if you had trouble or needed a shoulder. Once she'd wished he would offer her more than a shoulder . . . but she'd learned to accept the way things were.

"It's best that you know," she said, half to herself. "You can't deal with things unless you know. There's an investigator for the insurance company talking to people, asking questions about your father, about Seth too."

Ethan laid a hand on her arm briefly. They were far enough away from the docks, from the storefronts and the jangle of traffic. He'd thought they were done with that. "What kind of questions?"

"About your daddy's state of mind the last few weeks before his accident. About him bringing Seth home. He came to see me this morning, first thing. I thought it was better to talk to him than not." She looked at Ethan, relieved when he nodded. "I told him Ray Quinn was one of the finest men I've ever known—and gave him a piece of my mind about going around trying to pick up nasty gossip."

Because Ethan smiled at that, her lips curved. "Well, he made me so mad. Claims he's only doing his job, and his manner's mild as skim milk. But it bothered me, especially when he asked if I knew anything about Seth's mother or where he'd come from. I told him I didn't and that it didn't matter. Seth was where he was supposed to be, and that was that. I hope I did the right thing."

"You did just fine."

Her eyes were the color of stormy seas now, as emotions churned through her. "Ethan, I know it'll hurt if some people talk, if some of them say things they've got no business saying. It doesn't mean anything,'' she continued and took his hands in hers. "Not to anyone who knows your family.''

"We'll get through it." He gave her hands a quick squeeze, then didn't know if he should hold on to them or let go. "I'm glad you told me.'' He let go. But he kept looking at her face, looked so long that the color began to rise in her cheeks. "You're not getting enough sleep,'' he said. "Your eyes are tired.''

"Oh.'' Embarrassed, annoyed, she brushed her fingertips under them. Why was it the man only seemed to notice if something was wrong with her? "Aubrey was a little fussy last night. I've got to get back,'' she said quickly and gave the patient Simon a quick rub. "I'll be by the house tomorrow to clean.''

She hurried off, thinking hopelessly that a man who only noticed when you looked tired or troubled would never pay you any mind as a woman.

But Ethan watched her walk away and thought she was too damn pretty to work herself like a mule.

THE INSPECTOR'S NAME was Mackensie, and he was making the rounds. So far, his notes contained descriptions of a man who was a saint with a halo as wide and bright as the sun. A selfless Samaritan of a man who not only loved his neighbors but cheerfully bore their burdens, who had with his faithful wife beside him saved large chunks of humanity and kept the world safe for democracy.

His other notations termed Raymond Quinn a pompous, interfering, holier-than-thou despot, who collected bad young boys like other men collected stamps and used them to provide him with slave labor, an ego balm, and possibly prurient sexual favors.

Though Mackensie had to admit the latter was more interesting, that view had come from only a scattered few.

Being a man of details and caution, he realized that the truth probably lay somewhere in between the saint and the sinner.

His purpose wasn't to canonize or condemn one Raymond Quinn, policy number 005-678-LQ2. It was simply to gather facts, and those facts would determine whether the claim against that policy would be paid or disputed.

Either way, Mackensie got paid for his time and his efforts.

He'd stopped off and grabbed a sandwich at a little grease spot called Bay Side Eats. He had a weakness for grease, bad coffee, and waitresses with names like Lulubelle.

It was why, at age fifty-eight, he was twenty pounds overweight—twenty-five if he didn't tip the scale a few notches back from zero before he stepped on it—had a chronic case of indigestion, and was twice divorced.

He was also balding and had bunions, and an eyetooth that ached like a bitch in heat. Mackensie knew he was no physical prize, but he knew his job, had thirty-two years with True Life Insurance, and kept records as clean as a nun's heart.

He pulled his Ford Taurus into the pitted gravel lot beside the building. His last contact, a little worm named Claremont, had given him directions. He would find Cameron Quinn there, Claremont had told him with a tight-lipped smile.

Mackensie had disliked the man after five minutes in his company. The inspector had worked with people long enough to recognize greed, envy, and simple malice even when they were layered over with charm. Claremont didn't have any layers that Mackensie had noticed. He was all smarm.

He belched up a memory of the dill pickle relish he'd indulged in at lunch, shook his head, and thumbed out his hourly dose of Zantac. There was a pickup truck in the lot, an aging sedan, and a spiffy classic Corvette.

Mackensie liked the looks of the 'Vette, though he

wouldn't have gotten behind the wheel of one of those death traps for love or money. No, indeed. But he admired it anyway as he hauled himself out of his car.

He could admire the looks of the man as well, he mused, when a pair of them stepped out of the building. Not the older one with the red-checked shirt and clip-on tie. Paper pusher, he decided—he was good at recognizing types.

The younger one was too lean, too hungry, too sharp-eyed to spend much time pushing papers. If he didn't work with his hands, Mackensie thought, he could. And he looked like a man who knew what he wanted—and found a way to make it so.

If this was Cameron Quinn, Mackensie decided that Ray Quinn had had his hands full while he was alive.

Cam spotted Mackensie when he walked the plumbing inspector out. He was feeling pretty good about the progress. He figured it would take another week to complete the bathroom, but he and Ethan could do without that little convenience that much longer.

He wanted to get started, and since the wiring was done and that, too, had passed inspection, there was no need to wait.

He tagged Mackensie as some sort of paper jockey. Jiggling his memory, he tried to recall if he had another appointment set up, but he didn't think so. Selling something, he imagined, as Mackensie and the inspector passed each other.

The man had a briefcase, Cam noted wearily. When people carried a briefcase it meant there was something inside they wanted to take out.

"You'd be Mr. Quinn," Mackensie said, his voice affable, his eyes measuring.

"I would."

"I'm Mackensie, True Life Insurance."

"We've got insurance." Or he was nearly sure they did. "My brother Phillip handles those kinds of details." Then it clicked, and Cam's stance shifted from relaxed to on guard. "True Life?"

"That's the one. I'm an investigator for the company. We need to clear up some questions before your claim on your father's policy can be settled."

"He's dead," Cam said flatly. "Isn't that the question, Mackensie?"

"I'm sorry for your loss."

"I imagine the insurance company's sorry it has to shell out. As far as I'm concerned, my father paid in to that policy in good faith. The trick is you have to die to win. He died."

It was warm in the sun, and the pastrami on rye with spicy mustard wasn't settling well. Mackensie blew out a breath. "There's some question about the accident."

"Car meets telephone pole. Telephone pole wins. Trust me, I do a lot of driving."

Mackensie nodded. Under other circumstances he might have appreciated Cam's no-bullshit tone. "You'd be aware that the policy has a suicide clause."

"My father didn't commit suicide, Mackensie. And since you weren't in the car with him at the time, it's going to be tough for you to prove otherwise."

"Your father was under a great deal of stress, emotional upheaval."

Cam snorted. "My father raised three badasses and taught a bunch of snot-nosed college kids. He had a great deal of stress and emotional upheaval all his life."

"And he'd taken on a fourth."

"That's right." Cam tucked his thumbs in his front pockets, and his stance became a silent challenge. "That doesn't have anything to do with you or your company."

"As it bears on the circumstances of your father's accident. There's a question of possible blackmail, and certainly a threat to his reputation. I have a copy of the letter found in his car at the scene."

When Mackensie opened his briefcase, Cam took a step forward. "I've seen the letter. All it means is there's a woman out there with the maternal instincts of a rabid alley cat. You try to say that Ray Quinn smashed into that pole because he was afraid of some two-bit bitch, I'll bury your insurance company.''

Fury he thought he'd already passed through sprang back, full-blown and fang-sharp. ''I don't give a good goddamn about the money. We can make our own money. True Life wants to welsh on the deal, that's my brother's area—and the lawyer's. But you or anybody else messes with my father's rep, you'll deal with me.''

The man was a good twenty-five years younger, Mackensie calculated, tough as a brick and mad as a starving wolf. He decided it would be best all round if he changed tactics. ''Mr. Quinn, I have no interest or desire to smear your father's reputation. True Life's a good company, I've worked for them most of my life.'' He tried a winning smile. ''This is just routine.''

''I don't like your routine.''

''I can understand that. The gray area here is the accident itself. The medical reports confirm that your father was in good physical shape. There's no evidence of a heart attack, a stroke, any physical reason that would have caused him to lose control of his car. A single-car accident, an empty stretch of road on a dry, clear day. The accident-reconstruction expert's findings were inconclusive.''

''That's your problem.'' Cam spotted Seth walking down the road from the direction of school. And there, he thought, is mine. ''I can't help you with it. But I can tell you that my father faced his problems, square on. He never took the easy way. I've got work to do.'' Leaving it at that, Cam turned away and walked toward Seth.

Mackensie rubbed eyes that were tearing up from the sunlight. Quinn might have thought he'd added nothing to the report, but he was wrong. If nothing else, Mackensie could be sure the Quinns would fight for their claim to the bitter end. If not for the money, for the memory.

''Who's that guy?'' Seth asked as he watched Mackensie head back to his car.

''Some insurance quack.'' Cam nodded down the street

where two boys loitered a half a block away. "Who're those guys?"

Seth gave a careless glance over his shoulder, followed it with a shrug. "I don't know. Just kids from school. They're nobody."

"They hassling you?"

"Nah. Are we going up on the roof?"

"Roof's done," Cam murmured and watched with some amusement as the two boys wandered closer, trying and failing to look disinterested. "Hey, you kids."

"What're you doing?" Seth hissed, mortified.

"Relax. Come on over here," Cam ordered as both boys froze like statues.

"What the hell are you calling them over for? They're just jerks from school."

"I could use some jerk labor," Cam said mildly. It had also occurred to him that Seth could use some companions of his own age. He waited while Seth squirmed and the two boys held a fast, whispering consultation. It ended with the taller of the two squaring his shoulders and swaggering down the road on his battered Nikes.

"We weren't doing anything," the boy said, his tone of defiance slightly spoiled by a lisp from a missing tooth.

"I could see that. You want to do something?"

The boy slid his eyes to the younger kid, then over to Seth, then cautiously up to Cam's face. "Maybe."

"You got a name?"

"Sure. I'm Danny. This is my kid brother, Will. I turned eleven last week. He's only nine."

"I'll be ten in ten months," Will stated and rapped his brother in the ribs with his elbow.

"He still goes to elementary," Danny put in with a sneer, which he generously shared with Seth. "Baby school."

"I'm not a baby."

As Will's fist was already clenched and lifted, Cam took hold of it, then lightly squeezed his upper arm. "Seems strong enough to me."

"I'm plenty strong," Will told him, then grinned with the charm of an angelic host.

"We'll see about that. See all this crap piled up around here? Old shingles, tar paper, trash?" Cam surveyed the area himself. "You see that Dumpster over there? The crap goes in the Dumpster, you get five bucks."

"Each?" Danny piped up, his hazel eyes glinting in a freckled face.

"Don't make me laugh, kid. But you'll get a two-dollar bonus if you do it without me having to come out and break up any fights." He jerked a thumb at Seth. "He's in charge."

The minute Cam left them alone, Danny turned to Seth. They sized each other up in narrow-eyed silence. "I saw you punch Robert."

Seth shifted his balance evenly. It would be two against one, he calculated, but he was prepared to fight. "So what?"

"It was cool," was all Danny said and began to pick up torn shingles.

Will grinned happily up into Seth's face. "Robert is a big, fat fart, and Danny said when you socked him he bled and bled."

Seth found himself grinning back. "Like a stuck pig."

"Oink, oink," Will said, delighted. "We can buy ice cream with the money up at Crawford's."

"Yeah . . . maybe." Seth started to gather up trash, with Will cheerfully dogging his heels.

ANNA WASN'T HAVING A good day. She'd started out the morning running her last pair of hose before she even got out her front door. She was out of bagels, and yogurt, and, she admitted, almost every damn thing, because she'd been spending too much time with Cam or thinking about Cam to keep to her usual marketing routine.

When she stopped off to mail a letter to her grandparents, she chipped a nail on the mailbox. Her phone was already ringing when she walked into her office at eight-thirty, and the hysterical woman on the other end was demanding to know why she had yet to receive her medical card.

She calmed the woman down, assured her she would see to the matter personally. Then, simply because she was there, the switchboard passed through a whining old man who insisted his neighbors were child abusers because they allowed their offspring to watch television every night of the week.

"Television," he told her, "is the tool of the Communist left. Nothing but sex and murder, sex and murder, and subliminal messages. I read all about them."

"I'm going to look into this, Mr. Bigby," she promised and opened her top drawer, where she kept her aspirin.

"You'd better. I tried the cops, but they don't do nothing. Those kids're doomed. Going to need to deprogram them."

"Thank you for bringing this to our attention."

"My duty as an American."

"You bet," Anna muttered after he'd hung up.

Knowing that she was due in family court at two that afternoon, she booted up her computer, intending to call up the file to review her reports and notes. When the message flashed across her screen that her program had committed an illegal act, she didn't bother to scream. She simply sat back, closed her eyes, and accepted that it was going to be a lousy day.

It got worse.

She knew her testimony in court was key. The Higgins case file had come across her desk nearly a year ago. The three children, ages eight, six, and four, had all been physically and emotionally abused. The wife, barely twenty-five, was a textbook case of the battered spouse. She'd left her husband countless times over the years, but she always went back.

Six months before, Anna had worked hard and long to get her and her children into a shelter. The woman had stayed less than thirty-six hours before changing her mind. Though Anna's heart ached for her, it had come down to the welfare of the children.

Their pinched faces, the bruises, the fear—and worse, the dull acceptance in their eyes—tormented her. They were in foster care with a couple who was generous enough and strong enough to take all of them. And seeing those foster parents flanking the three damaged boys, she vowed she would do everything in her power to keep them there.

"Counseling was recommended in January of last year when this case first came to my attention," Anna stated from the witness stand. "Both family and individual. The recommendation was not taken. Nor was it taken in May of that same year when Mrs. Higgins was hospitalized with a dislocated jaw and other injuries, or in September when Michael Higgins, the eldest boy, suffered a broken hand. In November of that year Mrs. Higgins and her two oldest sons were all treated in ER for various injuries. I was notified and assisted Mrs. Higgins and her children in securing a place in a women's shelter. She did not remain there two full days."

"You've been caseworker of record on this matter for more than a year." The lawyer stood in front of her, knowing from experience it wasn't necessary to guide her testimony.

"Yes, more than a year." And she felt the failure keenly.

"What is the current status?"

"On February sixth of this year, a police unit responding to the call from a neighbor found Mr. Higgins under the influence of alcohol. Mrs. Higgins was reported as hysterical and required medical treatment for facial bruises and lacerations. Curtis, the youngest child, had a broken arm. Mr. Higgins was taken into custody. At that time, as I was the caseworker of record, I was notified."

"Did you see Mrs. Higgins and the children on that day?" the lawyer asked her.

"Yes. I drove to the hospital. I spoke with Mrs. Higgins. She claimed that Curtis had fallen down the stairs. Due to the nature of his injuries, and the history of the case, I didn't believe her. The attending physician in ER shared my opinion. The children were taken into foster care, where they have remained since that date."

She continued to answer questions about the status of the case file and the children themselves. Once, she drew a smile out of the middle boy when she spoke of the T-ball team he'd been able to join.

Then Anna prepared herself for the irritation and tedium of cross-examination.

"Are you aware that Mr. Higgins has voluntarily entered an alcohol rehabilitation program?"

Anna spared one glance at the Higginses' pro bono lawyer, then looked directly into the father's eyes. "I'm aware that over the past year, Mr. Higgins has claimed to have entered a rehabilitation program no less than three times."

She saw the hate and fury darken his face. *Let him hate me*, she thought. She'd be damned if he would lay hands on those children again. "I'm aware that he's never completed a program."

"Alcoholism is a disease, Ms. Spinelli. Mr. Higgins is now seeking treatment for his illness. You would agree that Mrs. Higgins has been a victim of her husband's illness?"

"I would agree that she has suffered both physically and emotionally at his hands."

"And can you possibly believe that she should suffer further, lose her children and they her? Can you possibly believe that the court should take these three little boys away from their mother?"

The choice, Anna thought, was hers. The man who beat her and terrorized their children, or the health and safety of those children. "I believe she will suffer further, until

she makes the decision to change her circumstances. And
it's my professional opinion that Mrs. Higgins is incapable
of caring for herself, much less her children, at this time.''

"Both Mr. and Mrs. Higgins now have steady employment,'' the lawyer continued. ''Mrs. Higgins has stated,
under oath, that she and her husband are reconciled and
continuing to work on their marital difficulties. Separating
the family will, as she stated, only cause emotional pain
for all involved.''

"I know she believes that.'' Her steady look at Mrs.
Higgins was compassionate, but her voice was firm. ''I
believe that there are three children whose welfare and
safety are at stake. I'm aware of the medical reports, the
psychiatric reports, the police reports. In the past fifteen
months, these three children have been treated in the emergency room a combined total of eleven times.''

She looked at the lawyer now, wondering how he could
stand in a court of law and fight for what was surely the
destruction of three young boys. ''I'm aware that a four-
year-old boy's arm was snapped like a twig. I strongly
recommend that these children remain in licensed and su-
pervised foster care to ensure their physical and emotional
safety.''

"No charges have been filed against Mr. Higgins.''

"No, no charges have been filed.'' Anna shifted her
gaze to the mother, let it rest on that tired face. ''That's
just another crime,'' she murmured.

When she was finished, Anna passed by the Higginses
without a glance. But behind the rail, little Curtis reached
out for her hand. ''Do you have a lollipop?'' he whispered,
making her smile.

She made a habit of carrying them for him. He had a
weakness for cherry Tootsie Roll Pops. ''Maybe I do. Let's
see.''

She was reaching into her purse when the explosion
came from behind her. ''Get your hands off what's mine,
you bitch.''

As she started to turn, Higgins hit her full force, knocking her sprawling and sending Curtis to the floor with her in a heap of screams and wails. Her head rang like church bells and stars dazzled her eyes. She could hear screams and curses as she managed to push herself up to her hands and knees.

Her cheek ached fiercely where it had connected with the seat of a wooden chair. Her palms sang from skidding on the tile floor. And damn it, the new hose she had bought to replace the ones she'd run were torn at the knees.

"Hold still," Marilou ordered. She was crouched in Anna's office, grimly doctoring the scrapes.

"I'm all right." Indeed, the injuries were minor. "It was worth it. That little demonstration in open court ensures that he won't get near those kids for quite a while."

"You worry me, Anna." Marilou looked up with those dark, gleaming eyes. "I'd almost think you enjoyed being tackled by that two-hundred-pound putz."

"I enjoyed the results. Ouch, Marilou." She blew out a breath as her supervisor rose to examine the bruise on Anna's cheek. "I enjoyed filing charges for assault, and most of all I enjoyed seeing those kids go home with their foster family."

"A good day's work?" With a shake of her head, Marilou stepped back. "It worries me, too, that you let yourself get too close."

"You can't help from a distance. So much of what we do is just paperwork, Marilou. Forms and procedures. But every now and again you get to do something—even if it's only getting tackled by a two-hundred-pound putz. And it's worth it."

"If you care too much, you end up with more than a couple of bruises and a skinned knee."

"If you don't care enough, you should find another line of work."

Marilou blew out a breath. It was difficult to argue when she felt exactly the same way. "Go home, Anna."

"I've got another hour on the clock."

"Go home. Consider it combat pay."

"Since you put it that way. I could use the hour. I don't have anything in the house to eat. If you hear any more on—" She broke off and looked up at the knock on her doorjamb. Her eyes widened. "Cameron."

"Miz Spinelli, I wonder if you have a minute to—" His smile of greeting transformed into a snarl. The light in his eyes turned hot and sharp as a flaming sword. "What the hell happened to you?" He was in the room like a shot, filling it, nearly barreling over Marilou to get to Anna. "Who the hell hit you?"

"No one, exactly, I was—"

Instead of giving her a chance to finish, he whirled on Marilou. Torn between fascination and amusement, Marilou backed up a step and held her hands up, palms out. "Not me, champ. I only browbeat my staff. Never lay a finger on them."

"There was a ruckus in court, that's all." Struggling to be brisk and professional despite her bare legs and feet, Anna rose. "Marilou, this is Cameron Quinn. Cameron, Marilou Johnston, my supervisor."

"It's a pleasure to meet you, even under the circumstances." Marilou held out a hand. "I was a student of your father's a million years ago. I quite simply adored him."

"Yeah, thanks. Who hit you?" he demanded again of Anna.

"Someone who is even now on the wrong side of a locked cell." Quickly, Anna worked her bare feet back into her low-heeled pumps. "Marilou, I'm going to take you up on the hour off." Her only thought now was to get Cam out, away from Marilou's curious and all-too-observant eyes. "Cameron, if you need to speak with me about Seth, you could give me a ride home." She slipped on her dove-gray jacket, smoothed it into place. "It's not far. I'll buy you a cup of coffee."

"Fine. Sure." When he caught her chin in his hand, a tug-of-war of pleasure and alarm raged inside her. "We'll talk."

"I'll see you tomorrow, Marilou."

"Oh, yes." Marilou smiled easily while Anna hurriedly gathered her briefcase. "We'll talk, too."

FIFTEEN

ANNA KEPT HER MOUTH firmly shut until they were out of the building and safely alone in the parking lot. "Cam, for God's sake."

"For God's sake, what?"

"This is where I work." She stopped at his car, turned to face him. "Where I work, remember? You can't come storming into my office like an outraged lover."

He took her chin in hand again, leaned his face close. "I *am* an outraged lover, and I want the name of the son of a bitch who put his hands on you."

She wouldn't allow herself to be thrilled by the violence sparking around him. It would be, she reminded herself as her stomach gave a delicious little hop, completely unprofessional.

"The person in question is being dealt with by the proper authorities. And you're not allowed to be a lover, outraged or otherwise, during business hours."

"Yeah? Try and stop me," he challenged and leading with his temper, crushed his mouth to hers.

She wiggled for a moment. Anyone could peek out an office window and see. The kiss was too hot, too heady for a daylight embrace in an office parking lot.

The kiss was also too hot, too heady to resist. She gave in to it, to him, to herself, and wrapped her arms around him. "Will you cut it out?" she said against his mouth.

"No."

"Okay, then, let's take this indoors."

"Good idea." With his mouth still on hers, he reached back to open the car door.

"I can't get in until you let me go."

"Good point." He released her, then surprised her by gently, tenderly brushing his lips over the bruise on her cheek. "Does it hurt?"

Her heart was still flopping. "Maybe a little." She got inside, deliberately reaching for her seat belt, keeping her moves efficient and casual.

"What happened?" he asked as he slid in beside her.

"Abusive father of three, wife beater, didn't care for my testimony in family court today. He shoved me. I had my back turned or he'd have gotten a hard knee to the groin, but as it was I was off balance. Did a nosedive—which would have been embarrassing but for the fact that he's now in lockup and the kids are with their foster family."

"And the wife?"

"I can't help her." Anna let her aching head fall back. "You have to pick your battles."

He said nothing to that. He'd been thinking the same thing. It was why he'd decided to dump three kids on Ethan and come to see her. He'd made up his mind to tell her about the insurance investigation, the speculations about Seth's connection to his father, the search that Phillip had instigated for Seth's mother.

He'd decided to tell her everything, to ask her advice, to get her take. Now he found himself wondering if that was the wisest course—for her, for him, for Seth.

It would wait, he told himself, and rationalized his postponement: she'd had a rough time, needed a little attention.

"So, do you get knocked around much in your line of work?"

"Hmm? No." She laughed a little as he pulled up in

front of her building. "Now and again somebody takes a swing or throws something at you, but mostly it's just verbal abuse."

"Fun job."

"It has its moments." She took his hand, walked alongside him. "Did you know that television is the tool of the Communist left?"

"I hadn't heard that."

"I'm here to tell you." She used her key to check her mail slot, gathered letters and bills and a fashion magazine. "*Sesame Street* is just a front."

"I always suspected that big yellow bird."

"Nah, he's just a shill. The frog's the mastermind." She put her finger to her lips as they approached her door. They snuck in together like kids hooking school. "I just didn't want to have the sisters fussing over me."

"Mind if I do?"

"That depends on your definition of fussing."

"We'll start here." He slipped his arms around her waist, touched his lips to hers.

"I suppose I could tolerate that." She helped him deepen the kiss. "What are you doing here, Cam?"

"I had a lot on my mind." His lips brushed over the bruise again, then lower, to her jawline. "You, mostly. I wanted to see you, be with you, talk to you. Make love to you."

Her lips curved against his. "All at the same time."

"Why not? I did have this thought about taking you out to dinner . . . but now I'm thinking maybe we could order pizza."

"Perfect." She said it with a sigh. "Why don't you pour us some wine, and I'll change?"

"There's this other thing." He worked his way over to her ear. "Something I've been wanting to do. I've been wondering what it would be like to get Miz Spinelli out of one of her dedicated-public-servant suits."

"Have you?"

"Since the first time I saw you."

She smiled wickedly. "Now's your chance."

"I was hoping you'd say that." He brought his mouth back to hers, hungrier now, more possessive. This time her sigh caught on a trembling gasp as he jerked her jacket off her shoulders and trapped her arms. "I'm wanting the hell out of you. Day and night."

Her voice was throaty now, dark with need. "I guess that makes it handy, since I want the hell out of you too."

"It doesn't scare you?"

"Nothing about you and me scares me."

"And what if I said I want you to let me do anything I want to you? Everything?"

Her heart fluttered to her throat, but her eyes stayed steady. "I'd say who's stopping you?"

With desire dark and dangerous in his eyes, he skimmed his gaze down, then back to her face. "I wonder what Miz Spinelli wears under these prim little blouses."

"I don't think a man like you is going to let a few buttons keep him from finding out."

"You're right." He shifted his hands from her jacket to the crisply pressed cotton of her blouse. And ripped. He watched her eyes go wide and shocked. And aroused. "If you want me to stop, I will. I won't do anything you don't want."

He'd torn her blouse. And it had thrilled her. He waited, watching, for her to say stop or go. And it thrilled her even more. She understood she hadn't been completely truthful when she'd told him nothing about them scared her. She was afraid of what might be happening to her heart.

But here, in physical love, she knew she could match him.

"I want everything. All."

His blood leaped. Still, he kept his touch light, teasing, running the back of his hand above the slick white material of her demi-cut bra. "Miz Spinelli." He drawled it while his fingers slipped beneath the polished satin to rub against her stiffened nipple. "How much can you take?"

His light tugs had heat spiraling through her system.

Already the air was thick. "I think we're about to find out."

Slowly, his eyes on her face, he backed her against the wall. "Let's start here. Brace yourself," he murmured, and his hand shot under her skirt and tore aside the lacy swatch she wore beneath. Her breath exploded out, and she nearly laughed. Then he plunged his fingers into her, lancing that hard, rough shock of pleasure through her unprepared system. The orgasm ripped through her, emptying her mind, stealing her breath. When her knees gave way, he simply held her against the wall.

"Take more." He was desperate to watch her take more, to see the shocked excitement capture her face, to see those gorgeous eyes go wild and blind.

She gripped his shoulders for balance. With her head tipped back he could see the pulse in her throat beat madly and was compelled to taste just there. She moaned against him, moved against him, her breath hitching when he yanked the jacket and what was left of her blouse away.

She was helpless, staggered. The assault on her senses left her limbs shuddering and her heart hammering. She said his name, tried to, but it caught on a gasp as he spun her around. Her damp palms pressed to the wall.

He tore at the button of her skirt. She felt it give way, shivering as the material slid over her hips and pooled at her feet. His hands were on her breasts, molding, sliding from satin to flesh and back again. Then he tore that as well, and she gloried in the sound of the delicate material rending.

His teeth nipped into her shoulder. And his hands—oh, his hands were everywhere, driving her toward madness, then beyond. Rough palms against smooth skin, clever fingers pressing, sliding.

The breath that had torn ragged through her lips began to slow. Pleasure was thick, and midnight dark. She felt herself slipping into some erotic half-world where there was only sensation.

Slick, stunning, and sinful.

The wall was smooth and cool; his hands were not. The contrasts were unbearably arousing.

When he spun her around again, her eyes were dazzled by the sunlight. He was still fully dressed and she was naked. She found it exquisitely erotic, and could say nothing as he slowly lifted her arms above her head, bracketed her wrists with one hand.

Watching her, he combed his hand roughly through her hair to scatter pins. "I want more." He could barely speak. "Tell me you want more."

"Yes, I want more."

He pressed his body to hers, soft cotton, rough denim against damp flesh. And the kiss he took from her left her mind spinning.

Then his mouth went to work on her quivering body.

He wanted all the tastes of her, the dark honey of her mouth, the damp silk of her breasts. There was the creamy taste of her belly, the polished satin of her thighs.

Then the heat, the furnace flood of it as he licked his way between them.

Everything. All, was all he could think. Then more.

Her hands gripped his hair, pressing his face closer as she climbed to peak. It was her cry, the half scream, that broke the final link on his control. It had to be now.

He freed himself, then pressed against her. "I need to fill you." He panted the words out. "I want you to watch me when I do."

He drove into her where they stood, and their twin groans tangled in the air.

Afterward, he carried her to bed, lay down beside her. She curled up against him like a child, a gesture he found surprisingly sweet. He watched her sleep, thirty minutes, then a hour. He couldn't stop touching her—a hand through her hair, fingertips over the bruise on her face, a stroke over the curve of her shoulder.

Had he said he had something inside of him for her? He began to worry just what that something might be. He'd never felt compelled to stay with a woman after sex.

Had never felt the need to just look at her while she slept, or to touch only for the sake of touching and not to arouse.

He wondered what odd and slippery level they'd reached.

Then she stirred, sighed, and her eyes fluttered open and focused on him. When she smiled, his heart quite simply turned over in his chest.

"Hi. Did I fall asleep?"

"Looked like it to me." He searched for some glib remark, something light and frivolous, but all he could find to say was her name. "Anna." And he lowered his mouth to hers. Tenderly, softly, lovingly.

The sleep had cleared from her eyes when he drew away, but he couldn't read them. She breathed in once, slowly, then out again. "What was that?"

"Damned if I know." Both of them eased back cautiously. "I think we'd better order that pizza."

Relief and disappointment warred inside her. Anna put all her effort into supporting the relief. "Good idea. The number's right next to the kitchen phone. If you don't mind calling it in, I'd like to grab a quick shower, get some clothes on."

"All right." With casual intimacy he stroked a hand over her hip. "What do you want on it?"

"All I can get." She waited while he laughed and was pleased that he rolled out of bed first. She needed another minute.

"I'll pour the wine."

"Terrific." The minute she was alone, she turned her face into the pillow and let out a muffled scream of frustration. Steps back? she thought, furious with herself. Where did she get the idiotic idea she could take a few steps back? She was over her head in love with him.

My fault, she reminded herself, my problem. Sitting up, she pressed a hand to her traitorous heart. And my little secret, she decided.

• • •

SHE FELT BETTER WHEN she was dressed and had a light shield of makeup in place. She'd given herself a good talking-to in the shower. Maybe she was in love with him. It didn't have to be a bad thing. People fell in and out of love all the time, and the wise ones, the steady ones, enjoyed the ride.

She could be wise and steady.

She certainly wasn't looking for happily ever after, a white knight, a Prince Charming. Anna had outgrown fairy tales long ago, and all of her innocence had cemented into reality on the side of a deserted road at the age of twelve.

She'd learned to make herself happy because for too many years following the rape it had seemed she was helpless to do anything but make herself and everyone near her miserable.

She'd survived the worst. There was no doubt she could survive a slightly dented heart.

In any case, she'd never been in love before—she had skirted around it, breezed over it, wriggled under it, but had never before run headlong into it. It could be a marvelous adventure, certainly a learning experience.

And any woman who found herself a lover like Cameron Quinn had plenty of blessings to count.

So she was smiling when she came into the living room and found Cam, sipping wine, staring at the cover of her latest fashion magazine. He'd put music on. Eric Clapton was pleading with Laylah.

When she came up behind him and pecked a kiss on the back of his neck, she didn't expect his jolt of surprise.

It was guilt, plain and simple, and he hated it. He nearly bobbled the wine and had to fight to keep his face composed.

The pouty face on the cover of the magazine in his hand was a certain long-stemmed French model named Martine.

"Didn't mean to startle you." She raised an eyebrow as she looked at the magazine in his hands. "Absorbed with this summer's new pastels, were you?"

"Just passing the time. Pizza should be along in a minute.'' He started to set the magazine down, wanted sincerely to bury it under the sofa cushions, but she was nipping it out of his hand.

''I used to hate her.''

His throat was uncomfortably dry. ''Huh?''

''Well, not Martine the Magnificent exactly. Models like her. Slim and blond and perfect. I was always too round and too brunette. This,'' she added, giving her wet, curling hair a tug, ''made me insane as a teenager. I tried everything imaginable to straighten it.''

''I love your hair.'' He wished she'd turn the damn magazine facedown. ''You're twice as beautiful as she is. There's no comparison.''

Her smile came quick and warm around the edges. ''That's very sweet.''

''I mean it.'' He said it almost desperately—but thought it best not to add that he'd seen both of them naked and knew what he was talking about.

''Very sweet. Still, I wanted so badly to be slim and blond and hipless.''

''You're real.'' He couldn't stop himself. He took the magazine and tossed it over his shoulder. ''She's not.''

''That's one way to put it.'' Enjoying herself, she cocked her head. ''Seems to me you race-around-the-world types usually go for the supermodels—they look so good draped over a man's arm.''

''I barely know her.''

''Who?''

Jesus, he was losing it. ''Anybody. There's the pizza,'' he said with great relief. ''Your wine's on the counter. I'll get the food.''

''Fine.'' Without a clue as to what was suddenly making him so edgy, she wandered to the kitchen for her drink.

Cam saw that the magazine had fallen faceup so it appeared that Martine was aiming those killer blue eyes right at him. It brought back the memory of a scored cheek and a spitting female. He cast a wary glance at Anna. It wasn't an experience he cared to repeat.

As he paid the delivery boy, Anna took the wine out to her tiny balcony. "It's a nice evening. Let's eat out here."

She had a couple of chairs and a small folding table set out. Pink geraniums and white impatiens sprang cheerfully out of clay pots.

"If I ever manage to save enough for a house, I want a porch. A big one. Like you have." She went back in for plates and napkins. "And a garden. One of these days I'm going to learn something about flowers."

"A house, garden, porches." More comfortable out in the air, he settled down. "I pictured you as a town girl."

"I always have been. I'm not sure suburbia would suit me. Fences with neighbors just over them. Too much like apartment living, I'd think, without the privacy and convenience." She slid a loaded slice of pizza onto her plate. "But I'd like to give home owning a shot—somewhere in the country. Eventually. The problem is, I can't seem to stick to a budget."

"You?" He helped himself. "Miz Spinelli seems so practical."

"She tries. My grandparents were very frugal, had to be. I was raised to watch my pennies." She took a bite and drew in a deep, appreciative breath before speaking over a mouthful of cheese and sauce. "Mostly I watch them roll away."

"What's your weakness?"

"Primarily?" She sighed. "Clothes."

He looked over his shoulder, through the door to her clothes, heaped in a tattered pile on the floor. "I think I owe you a blouse . . . and a skirt, not to mention the underwear."

She laughed lustily. "I suppose you do." She stretched out, comfortable in pale-blue leggings and an oversized white T-shirt. "This was such a hideous day. I'm glad you came by and changed it."

"Why don't you come home with me?"

"What?"

Where the hell had that come from? he wondered. The

thought hadn't even been in his mind when the words popped out of his mouth. But it must have been, somewhere. "For the weekend," he added. "Spend this weekend at the house."

She brought her pizza back to her lips, bit in carefully. "I don't think that would be wise. There's an impressionable young boy in your home."

"He knows what the hell's going on," he began, then caught the look—the Miz Spinelli look—in her eye. "Okay, I'll sleep on the sofa downstairs. You can lock the bedroom door."

Her lips quirked. "Where do you keep the key?"

"This weekend I'll be keeping it in my pocket. But my point is," he continued when she laughed, "you can have the bedroom. On a professional level it'll give you some time with the kid. He's coming along, Anna. And I want to take you sailing."

"I'll come over Saturday and we can go sailing."

"Come Friday night." He took her hand, brought her knuckles to his lips. "Stay till Sunday."

"I'll think about it," she murmured and drew her hand away. Romantic gestures were going to undo her. "And I think if you're going to have a houseguest, you should check with your brothers. They might not care to have a woman underfoot for a weekend."

"They love women. Especially women who cook."

"Ah, so now I'm supposed to cook."

"Maybe just one little pot of linguini. Or a dish of lasagna."

She smiled and took another slice of pizza. "I'll think about it," she said again. "Now tell me about Seth."

"He made a couple of buddies today."

"Really? Terrific."

Her eyes lit with such pleasure and interest, he couldn't help himself. "Yeah, I had them all up on the roof, practiced catching them as they fell off."

Her mouth fell open, then shut again on a scowl. "Very funny, Quinn."

"Gotcha. A kid from Seth's class and his kid brother. I bought them for five bucks as slave labor. Then they wheedled an invite out to the house for dinner, so I stuck Ethan with them."

She rolled her eyes. "You left Ethan alone with three young boys?"

"He can handle it. I did for a couple of hours this afternoon." And, he recalled, it hadn't been so bad. "All he has to do is feed them and make sure they don't kill each other. Their mother's picking them up at seven-thirty. Sandy McLean—well, Sandy Miller now. I went to school with her."

He shook his head, amazed and baffled. "Two kids and a minivan. Never would've figured that for Sandy."

"People change," she murmured, surprised at how much she envied Sandy Miller and her minivan. "Or they weren't precisely what we imagined them to be in the first place."

"I guess. Her kids are pistols."

Because he said it with such easy good humor, she smiled again. "Well, now I see why you popped up at my office. You wanted to escape the madness."

"Yeah, but mostly I just wanted to rip your clothes off." He took another slice himself. "I did both."

And, he thought, as he sipped his wine and watched the sun go down with Anna beside him, he felt damn good about it.

SIXTEEN

DRAWING WASN'T ETH-
an's strong point. With the other boats he'd built, he'd
worked off very rough sketches and detailed measurements. For the first boat for this client, he'd fashioned a
lofting platform and had found working from it was easier
and more precise.

The skiff he'd built and sold had been a basic model,
with a few tweaks of his own added. He'd been able to
see the completed project in his mind easily enough and
had no trouble envisioning side or interior views.

But he understood that the beginnings of a business required all the forms Phillip had told him to sign and
needed something more formal, more professional. They
would want to develop a reputation for skill and quality
quickly if they expected to stay afloat.

So he'd spent countless hours in the evenings at his desk
struggling over the blueprints and drawings of their first
job.

When he unrolled his completed sketches on the kitchen
table, he was both pleased and proud of his work. ''This,''
he said, holding down the top corners, ''is what I had in
mind.''

Cam looked over Ethan's shoulder, sipped the beer he'd just opened, grunted. "I guess that's supposed to be a boat."

Insulted but not particularly surprised by the comment, Ethan scowled. "I'd like to see you do better, Rembrandt."

Cam shrugged, sat. Upon closer, more neutral study, he admitted he couldn't. But that didn't make the drawing of the sloop look any more like a boat. "I guess it doesn't matter much, as long as we don't show your art project to the client." He pushed the sketch aside and got down to the blueprints. Here, Ethan's thoughtful precision and patience showed through. "Okay, now we're talking. You want to go with smooth-lap construction."

"It's expensive," Ethan began, "but it's got advantages. He'll have a strong, fast boat when we're finished."

"I've been in on a few," Cam murmured. "You've got to be good at it."

"We'll be good at it."

Cam had to grin. "Yeah."

"The thing is . . ." As a matter of pride, Ethan nudged the sketch of the completed boat back over. "It takes skill and precision to smooth-lap a boat. Anybody who knows boats recognizes that. This guy, he's a Sunday sailor, doesn't know more than basic port and starboard—he's just got money. But he hangs with people who know boats."

"And so we use him to build a rep," Cam finished. "Good thinking." He studied the figures, the drawings, the views. It would be a honey, he mused. All they had to do was build it. "We could build a lift model."

"We could."

Building a lift model was an old and respected stage of boat building. Boards of equal thickness would be pegged together and shaped to the desired hull form. Then the model could be taken apart so that the shape of the mold frames could be determined. Then the builders would trace

the shape of the planks, or lifts, in their proper relation to
one another.

"We could start the lofting," Cam mused.

"I figured we could start work on that tonight and continue tomorrow."

That meant drawing the full-sized shape of the hull on
a platform in the shop. It would be detailed, showing the
mold sections—and those sections would be tested by
drawing in the longitudinal curves, waterlines.

"Yeah, why wait?" Cam glanced up as Seth wandered
in to raid the refrigerator. "Though it would be better if
we had somebody who could draw worth diddly," he said
casually and pretended not to notice Seth's sudden interest.

"As long as we have the measurements, and the work's
first class, it doesn't matter." Defending his work, Ethan
smoothed a hand over his rendition of the boat.

"Just be nicer if we could show the client something
jazzy." Cam lifted a shoulder. "Phillip would call it marketing."

"I don't care what Phillip would call it." The stubborn
line began to form between Ethan's eyebrows, a sure sign
that he was about to dig in his heels. "The client's satisfied
with my other work, and he's not going to be critiquing a
drawing. He wants a damn boat, not a picture for his
wall."

"I was just thinking . . ." Cam let it hang as Ethan,
obviously irritated, rose to get his own beer. "Lots of
times in the boatyards I've known, people come around,
hang out. They like to watch boats being built—especially
the people who don't know squat about boat building but
think they do. You could pick up customers that way."

"So?" Ethan popped the top and drank. "I don't care
if people want to watch us rabbeting laps." He did, of
course, but he didn't expect it would come to that.

"It'd be interesting, I was thinking, if we had good
framed sketches on the walls. Boats we've built."

"We haven't built any damn boats yet."

"Your skipjack," Cam pointed out. "The workboat.

The one you already did for our first client. And I put in a lot of time on a two-masted schooner up in Maine a few years ago, and a snazzy little skiff in Bristol.''

Ethan sipped again, considering. ''Maybe it would look good, but I'm not voting to hire some artist to paint pictures. We've got an equipment list to work out, and Phil's got to finish fiddling with the contract for *this* boat.''

''Just a thought.'' Cam turned. Seth was still standing in front of the wide-open refrigerator. ''Want a menu, kid?''

Seth jolted, then grabbed the first thing that came to hand. The carton of blueberry yogurt wasn't what he'd had in mind for a snack, but he was too embarrassed to put it back. Stuck with what he considered Phillip's health crap, he got out a spoon.

''I got stuff to do,'' he muttered and hurried out.

''Ten bucks says he feeds that to the dog,'' Cam said lightly and wondered how long it would take Seth to start drawing boats.

H E   H A D   A   DETAILED AND somewhat romantic sketch of Ethan's skipjack done by morning. He didn't need Phillip's presence in the kitchen to remind him it was Friday. The day before freedom. Ethan was already gone, sailing out to check crab pots and rebait. Though Seth had tried to plot how to catch all three of them together, he simply hadn't been able to figure out how to delay Ethan's dawn departure. But two out of three, he thought as he passed the table where Cam was brooding silently over his morning coffee, wasn't bad.

It took at least two cups of coffee before any man in the Quinn household communicated with more than grunts. Seth was already used to that, so he said nothing as he set down his backpack. He had his sketchbook, with his finger wedged between the pages. He dropped it on the table as if it didn't matter to him in the least, then, with his heart skipping, rummaged through the cupboards for cereal.

Cam saw the sketch immediately. Smiling into his coffee, he said nothing. He was considering the toast he'd managed to burn when Seth came to the table with a box and a bowl. "That damn toaster's defective."

"You turned it up to high again," Phillip told him and finished beating his egg-white-and-chive omelette.

"I don't think so. How many eggs are you scrambling there?"

"I'm not scrambling any." Phillip slid the eggs into the omelette pan he'd brought from his own kitchen. "Make your own."

Jeez, was the guy blind or what? Seth wondered. He poured milk on his cereal and gently nudged the sketchbook an inch closer to Cam.

"It wouldn't kill you to add a couple more while you're doing it." Cam broke off a piece of the charcoaled toast. He had almost learned to like it that way. "I made the coffee."

"The sludge," Phillip corrected. "Let's not get delusions of grandeur."

Cam sighed lustily, then rose to get a bowl. He picked up the cereal box that sat beside Seth's open sketchbook. He could all but hear the boy grind his teeth as he sat back down and poured. "Probably going to have company this weekend."

Phillip concentrated on browning the omelette to perfection. "Who?"

"Anna." Cam slopped milk into his bowl. "I'm going to take her sailing, and I think I've got her talked into cooking dinner."

All the guy could think about was girls and filling his gut, Seth decided in disgust. He used his elbow to shove the sketch pad closer. Cam never glanced up from his cereal bowl.

When he saw Phillip slide the omelette from pan to plate, he judged it time to make his move. Seth's face was a study in agonized fury. "What's this?" Cam said absently, cocking his head to view the sketch that was by now all but under his nose.

Seth nearly rolled his eyes. It was about damn time. "Nothing," he muttered, and gleefully kept eating.

"Looks like Ethan's boat." Cam picked up his coffee, glanced at Phillip. "Doesn't it?"

Phillip stood, sampling the first bite of his breakfast, approving it. "Yeah. It's a good drawing." Curious, he looked at Seth. "You do it?"

"I was just fooling around." The flush of pride was creeping up his neck and leaving his stomach jittery.

"I work with guys who can't draw this well." Phillip gave Seth an absent pat on the shoulder. "Nice work."

"No big deal," Seth said with a shrug as the thrill burst through him.

"Funny, Ethan and I were just talking about using sketches of boats in the boatyard. You know, Phil, like advertising our work."

Phillip settled down to his eggs, but lifted a brow in both surprise and approval. "You thought of that? Color me amazed. Good idea." He studied the sketch more closely as he worked it through. "Frame it rough, keep the edges of the sketch raw. It should look working-man, not fancy."

Cam made a sound in his throat, as if he were mulling it over. "One sketch won't make much of a statement." He frowned at Seth. "I guess you couldn't do a few more, like of Ethan's workboat? Or if I got some pictures of a couple of the boats I've worked on?"

"I dunno." Seth fought to keep the excitement out of his voice. He nearly succeeded in keeping his eyes bored when they met Cam's, but little lights of pleasure danced in them. "Maybe."

It didn't take Phillip long to clue in. Catching the drift, he reached for his coffee and nodded. "Could make a nice statement. Clients who came in would see different boats we've done. It'd be good to have a drawing of the one you're starting on."

Cam snorted. "Ethan's got a pathetic sketch. Looks like a kindergarten project. Don't know what can be done about it." Then he looked at Seth, narrowed his eyes. "Maybe you can take a look at it."

Seth felt laughter bubble up in his throat and gamely swallowed it. "I suppose."

"Great. You got about ninety seconds to make the bus, kid, or you're walking to school."

"Shit." Seth scrambled up, grabbed his backpack, and took off in a flurry of pounding sneakers.

When the front door slammed, Phillip sat back. "Nice work, Cam."

"I have my moments."

"Every now and again. How'd you know the kid could draw?"

"He gave Anna a picture he'd done of the pup."

"Hmm. So what's the deal with her?"

"Deal?" Cam went back to his pitiful toast and tried not to envy Phillip his eggs.

"Spending the weekend, sailing, cooking dinner. Haven't seen you sniffing around any other woman since she came on the scene." Phillip grinned into his coffee. "Sounds serious. Almost . . . domestic."

"Get a grip." Cam's stomach took an uncomfortable little lurch. "We're just enjoying each other."

"I don't know. She looks like the picket-fence type to me."

Cam snorted. "Career woman. She's smart, she's ambitious, and she's not looking for complications." She wanted a house in the country, Cam remembered, near the water, with a yard where she could plant flowers.

"Women always look for complications," Phillip said positively. "Better watch your step."

"I know where I'm going, and how to get there."

"That's what they all say."

•   •   •

ANNA WAS DOING HER best not to look for, or find, complications. It was one of the reasons she'd decided against seeing Cameron on Friday night. She made work her excuse and compromised by telling him she'd be at his house bright and early Saturday morning for a sail. When he wheedled, she weakened and promised to make lasagna.

The part of her that gained so much pleasure from watching others eat what she'd prepared herself came from her grandmother. Anna believed that was something to be proud of.

Though she didn't commit to spending the night, they both realized it was understood.

She took the evening for herself, changing out of her suit and into baggy sweats. She put some of her favorite music on, nestling Billie Holiday between Verdi and Cream. She poured a glass of good red wine and watched the sun set.

It was time, she knew, long past time, to do some clear thinking, some objective analyzing. She'd known Cameron Quinn only a matter of weeks, yet she'd allowed herself to become more involved with him than with any other man who'd touched her life.

This level of involvement hadn't been in her plans. She usually planned so well. Steps she took, both professionally and personally, were always carefully thought out. She knew that was a protective action, one she had decided upon coolly and at an early age. If she thought about where each step was leading or could lead, held back on impulse, and depended on intellect, it was much harder to make a mistake.

She felt she'd made too many mistakes years before. If she had continued along the path she blindly raced down after losing her innocence and her mother, she would have been doomed.

She'd had to learn not to blame herself for the things she had done during that dark part of her life, not to wallow in guilt for the hurt she'd caused the people who loved her. Guilt was a negative emotion. Anna preferred positive actions, results, direction.

What she had chosen and accomplished had been for her grandparents, for her mother, and for that terrified child curled on the side of a dark road.

It had taken time, a long healing time, before it came to her that while she'd lost her mother, her grandparents had lost their only child. A daughter they loved. Despite their grief, they opened their home to Anna; despite her destructive actions, their hearts never faltered.

Eventually she learned to accept the loss, the horrors she'd experienced. More, she learned to accept that everything she had done for the two years following that night was the result of a wounded soul. She was fortunate to have people love her enough to help her heal.

When she found her way again, she promised herself that she would never be reckless again.

Impulse was saved for foolish things. Spending sprees, long, fast drives to nowhere. It had become so important to her that she remain basically practical, motivated, and rational that she had buried that reckless bent of her heart. Now, she thought, it was that same heart that had led her to this.

Loving Cameron Quinn was ridiculously reckless. And she knew it was going to cost her.

But her emotions were her own responsibility, she decided. That was something she had learned the hard way. She would handle them, and she would survive them.

But it was just so odd, she admitted, and leaned against the open patio door to catch the early-evening breeze. She'd always believed that if she ever experienced love, she would be aware of every stage of it. She'd hoped to enjoy it—the gradual slide she'd imagined, the mutual awareness of deepening feelings.

But there had been no gradual slide, no gentle fall with Cam. It was one fast, hard tumble. One moment, she felt attraction, interest, enjoyment. Then it seemed she no more than blinked before she was headlong in love.

She imagined it would scare him to death—as he was racing for the hills. The image made her laugh a little. They were well matched there, she decided. She would like to do some fast running in the opposite direction herself. She'd been prepared for an affair but far from ready for a love affair.

So analyze, she ordered herself. What was it about him that made the difference? His looks? On a little hum of pleasure, she closed her eyes. There was little doubt that's what had gained her attention initially. What woman wouldn't look twice, then look again at those dangerous, dark looks? The restless steel-colored eyes, the firm mouth that was equally appealing in a grin or a snarl. His body was the perfect female fantasy of tough muscle, rough hands, and lean lines.

Naturally she'd been attracted. And his quick mind had intrigued her. So had his arrogance, she admitted—though it was a lowering thought. But it was his heart that had changed everything. Oh, she hadn't expected that generous heart—recklessly generous. He had so much to give and was so unaware of it.

He thought himself selfish, hard-bitten, even cold. And she imagined he could be. But where it counted most, he was warm and giving. She didn't think he was fully aware of how much he was offering Seth or how their relationship was changing.

She sincerely doubted he fully understood that he loved the boy. And Anna realized it was that blind spot in Cam to his own goodness that had undone her.

She supposed, when it came down to it, falling in love with him had actually been sensible.

Staying in love with him would be disastrous. She would have to work on that.

The phone rang, distracting her. Carrying her wine, she walked back in and picked up the portable on the coffee table. "Hello."

"Miz Spinelli. Working?"

She couldn't stop the smile. "Working something out,

yes.'' An aria soared out of her stereo as she sat down, propped her feet on the coffee table. ''You?''

''Ethan and I have a little something we'll fiddle with tonight yet. Then I'm not even going to think about work until Monday.''

He had a portable phone himself and had wandered outside, where he might find some privacy. It was Seth's turn to do the dinner dishes, and he heard another plate hit the floor with a crash. ''They're calling for fair weather tomorrow.''

''Are they? That's handy.''

''You could still drive up tonight.''

It was tempting, but she'd already given in to too many impulses where he was concerned. ''I'll be there early enough in the morning.''

''I don't suppose you have a bikini. A red one.''

She tucked her tongue in her cheek. ''No, I don't . . . mine's blue.''

He waited a beat. ''Don't forget to pack.''

''If I pack—if I stay—I keep the key to the bedroom door.''

''You're so strict.'' He watched an egret sail over the water and into a nest atop a marker. Making for home, he thought, settling in.

''Just cautious, Quinn. And very smart. How's the building coming?''

''Along,'' he murmured. He liked hearing her voice, feeling the moist air move, watching the evening slide gentle as a kiss over water and trees. ''I'll show you when you're here.''

He wanted to show her Seth's sketch. He'd framed it himself that afternoon and wanted to share it with . . . someone who mattered. ''We'll probably get started on the first boat next week.''

''Really? That quick?''

''Why wait? It's time to put our money down and see how the dice fall. I've been feeling lucky lately.'' From the house behind him he heard the puppy bark madly, followed by Simon's deeper tones. Then Phillip's voice, raised in a half shout, half laugh and echoed by the rarely heard sound of Seth's giggle.

It made him turn, stare at the house. The back door opened, and the two canine forms bulleted out, tumbling over each other as they reached the steps. And there, framed in the doorway with the kitchen light washing through, was the boy, grinning.

Whatever pulled at Cam's heart pulled hard. For a moment, just one wild moment, he thought he heard the creak of the porch rocker and his father's low chuckle.

"Jesus, it's weird," he murmured.

The connection began to waver and crackle as he walked. "What?"

"Everything." He found himself gripping the phone tighter, yearning for her with a wild, almost desperate desire. "You should be here. I miss you."

"I can't hear you."

He realized he'd been stepping away from the house, a kind of knee-jerk denial of the sensation of being drawn in.

Coming home. Settling in.

With a shake of his head, he walked back until the connection cleared, and thanked God for the vagaries of technology. "I said . . . what are you wearing?"

She laughed softly, looked down at her baggy, practical sweats. "Why, nothing much," she purred, and both of them fell into the ease of phone flirting with various sensations of relief.

A SHORT TIME LATER, Cam set the phone on the porch steps and wandered down to the dock. Water lapped gently against the hull of the boat. Night birds were stirring, and the deep two-toned call of an owl in the woods beyond led the chorus. The sea was ink-dark under the fragile light of a thumbnail moon.

There was work to do. He knew Ethan would be waiting
for him. But he needed to sit there by the water for a
moment. To sit in the quiet while stars winked on and the
owl called endlessly, patiently, for its mate.

He didn't jump when he saw the movement beside him.
He was getting used to it. He couldn't count the times he'd
sat on this same dock under this same sky with his father.
It occurred to him that it was probably a little different to
sit here with his father's ghost, but what the hell. Nothing
about his life was the same as it once had been.

"I knew you were here," Cam said quietly.

"I like to keep an eye on things." Ray, dressed in fisherman's pants and a short-sleeved sweatshirt that Cam remembered had once been bright blue, dangled a line in the
water. "Been a while since I did any night fishing."

Cameron decided that if Ray pulled up a wriggling catfish, it would most likely send him over the thin edge of
sanity. "How close an eye?" he asked, thinking of Anna
and just what the two of them did in the dark.

Ray chuckled. "I always respected my boys' privacy,
Cam. Don't you worry about that. She sure is a looker,"
he said lightly. "She tries to cover it up when she's working, but a man with a good eye can see through it. You
always had a good eye for the ladies."

"How about you?" Cam hated himself for asking. It
was such a peaceful night, such a perfect one. But he never
knew how long these visitations—hallucinations, whatever
they were—would last. He had to ask. "How was your
eye for the ladies, Dad?"

"Sharp enough—landed on your mother, didn't it?"
And Ray sighed. "I never touched another woman after I
made my vows to Stella, Cam. I looked, I appreciated, I
enjoyed, but I never touched."

"You have to tell me about Seth."

"I can't. It's not the way it has to be. You did a good
thing by the boy, making him a part of the business you're
starting by using his drawings. He needs to feel that he's
a part of things. I wish I'd had more time with him, with

all of you. But that's not the way it has to be either.''

"Dad—"

"You know what I miss, Cam? The silliest things. Watching the three of you argue over something. There were times when your mother and I thought you'd bicker us crazy, but I miss that now. And early-morning fishing when the sun just starts to burn off the mist over the water. I miss teaching. I miss seeing that look on a student's face when something you say, just one thing, clicks and opens the mind. I miss pretty girls in summer dresses and lying in bed at three o'clock in the morning listening to rain on the roof.''

Then he turned his head and smiled. His eyes were as bright and brilliantly blue as the sweatshirt had once been. "You should appreciate those things while you have them, but you never do. Not all the way. Too busy living. Now and again, you should try to stop to appreciate the little things. They'll build up if you do.''

"I've got a little more on my mind than rain on the roof right now.''

"I know. You've got a mess on your hands, but you're sorting it. You've still got to figure out what you want, and what you need, and what's inside you. You've got more in there than you think.''

"I want answers. I need answers.''

"You'll find them," Ray said complacently. "When you slow down.''

"Tell me this. Do Ethan and Phillip know you're . . . here?''

"They will." Ray smiled again. "When it's time for it. It should be a nice day for sailing tomorrow. Enjoy the little things," he said and faded away.

SEVENTEEN

He was watching for her. Cam figured it was just one more first in his life. He'd never watched and waited for a woman that he could recall. Even as a teenager, they had come to him. Calling on the phone, wandering by the house, loitering near his locker at school. He supposed he'd gotten used to it. Spoiled by it.

He had never faced the typical male terror of asking for that first date. He'd been asked out when he was fifteen by the luscious Allyson Brentt. An older woman of sixteen. She even picked him up at his front door in her daddy's '72 Chevy Impala. He wasn't sure how he felt about being driven around by a girl. Until Allyson had parked on Blue Crab Drive and suggested they make use of the backseat.

He didn't mind that a bit.

Losing his virginity to pretty, fast-handed Allyson at fifteen was a sweaty and delightful experience. And Cam had never looked back.

He liked women, liked everything about them—even the annoying parts. It was what made them female, and he figured men got the best part of the deal. They got to look, they got to touch and smell. And unless they were complete morons, they could usually wriggle out of those soft arms and move on to the next ones without too much trouble.

He'd never been a moron.

But he watched for Anna, and waited for her. And wondered what it was about her that made him not quite so anxious to wriggle.

Maybe it was the lack of pressure, he mused as he wandered away from the dock toward the side of the house to listen for her car. Again. It could be the very lack of any expectations. She was joyfully sexual, and she didn't seem to expect a lot of romantic trappings. She'd come from a painful childhood, yet she'd gotten past the damage and made herself into something strong and whole.

He admired that.

The way she could, and did, play up or play down her looks fascinated him. That duality kept him wondering who she would be. And yet both parts of her fit so smoothly together, a man could barely see the seam.

The more he thought about her, the more he wanted her.

"What're you doing?"

He nearly jumped out of his skin when Seth came up behind him. He'd been staring at the road, all but willing Anna to pull into the drive. Now he jammed his hands in his pockets, mortified.

"Nothing, just walking around."

"You weren't walking," Seth pointed out.

"Because I'd stopped. Now I'm walking again. See?"

Seth rolled his eyes at Cam's back, then caught up with him. "What am I supposed to do?"

Cam feigned intense interest in the candy-red tulips sunning themselves along the edge of the house. "About what?"

"Stuff. Ethan's out on the workboat and Phillip's closed up in the office doing computer stuff."

"So?" He leaned down to tug up a weed—at least he

thought it was a weed. Where the hell was she? "Where are those kids you've been hanging with?"

"They had to go to the store and have lunch with their grandmother." Seth sneered on principle. "I don't have anything to do. It's boring."

"Well, go . . . clean your room or something."

"Come on."

"Jesus, what am I, your social director? Is the TV broken?"

"Nothing on Saturday mornings but kid shit."

"You *are* a kid," Cam pointed out and heard the sound of an approaching car with vast relief. "Teach that brain-dead dog of yours some tricks."

"He's not brain-dead." Instantly insulted, Seth turned and whistled for the pup. "Watch." Foolish raced up, carrying what appeared to be a can of beer in his mouth.

"Yeah, chewing on aluminum. That's brilliant. Look, I don't—" But Cam broke off when Seth snapped a finger, pointed, and Foolish plopped his butt on the ground.

"He does it on voice command, too," Seth said matter-of-factly as he rubbed Foolish's head in reward. "But I've got him responding to hand signals." He held a hand out, and Foolish gamely lifted a paw.

"That's pretty good." Pride and surprise mixed in his voice. "How long did it take you to teach him that?"

"Just a couple hours here and there."

All three watched as Anna pulled into the drive. Foolish was the first to rush to greet her.

"He doesn't do real good with Stay yet," Seth confided. "But we haven't worked on it long."

He didn't do real good with Down, either. The minute Anna stepped out of the car Foolish was leaping and yipping, his tongue lashing out joyfully to lick everywhere.

Cam figured the dog had the right idea. He'd have liked to jump on her and start licking himself. She wore jeans that were faded to a soft, pale blue and a lipstick-red top tucked into the waistband. It was a simple outfit that borrowed from the practical and the siren.

And made Cam's mouth water.

"She looks different with her hair down," Seth commented.

"Yeah." He wanted his hands on it, on her. And that was that.

She was crouched down, purring at the puppy, who had flopped adoringly on his back to have his belly rubbed. Her head came up, and even with the shaded glasses, Cam could see her eyes widen in awareness, then shift warningly to the child who walked behind him.

Ignoring the signal, he hauled her to her feet, gave her one good yank that made her stumble over the pup and against him, and closed his mouth over her sputtering protest.

It was like being swallowed by the sun, was all she could think. The heat was huge and had reached flash point before she could draw the first breath. Need, restless and greedy, pumped out of him and slammed into her at alarming speed. The wild drumming of a woodpecker hunting breakfast echoed through the still air and matched the frantic beat of her heart. All she could do was hold on until he'd devoured enough of what he wanted from her to satisfy him.

When he eased her back, those clever lips curved—a smug look she was sure she would resent when her head settled back on her shoulders again. "Morning, Anna."

"Good morning." She cleared her throat, stepped back, and made herself look over at Seth. He appeared to be more bored than shocked, so she worked up a smile for him. "Good morning, Seth."

"Yeah, hi."

"Your dog's growing into his feet." Because she needed the distraction, she looked down at Foolish and held out a hand. He planted his rump and lifted a paw, charming her. "Oh, aren't you smart?" She crouched again, shook his paw, tugged his ears. "What else can you do?"

"We're working on a couple of things." Foolish had

just run through his entire repertoire, but Seth didn't want
to say so.

"You make a good team. I've got some groceries in the
car," she said casually. "Makings for dinner. Give me a
hand?"

"Yeah, all right." He shot a resentful look at Cam.
"I've got nothing else to do."

"We're going sailing, aren't we?" She said it brightly,
amused when she saw Cam's mouth fall open and Seth
look at her with sharp, interested eyes.

"Am I going?"

"Of course." She turned, opened the car door, then
handed him a bag. "As soon as we put this stuff away. I
hope I'm a quick learner. I know next to nothing about
boats."

Cheered, Seth settled bags on each hip. "Nothing to it.
But you should have a hat." With this, he carted his bags
toward the house.

"I was figuring on it being just you and me," Cam told
her. And he'd had a nice fantasy going about slipping into
some quiet bend of the river and making rocky love to her
in the bottom of the boat.

"Were you?" She took out a small overnight bag,
pushed it into his hands. "I'm sure it'll be great fun with
the three of us."

She closed her car door, patted Cam's cheek, then sauntered into the house behind Seth.

I T TURNED OUT TO BE
the four of them. Seth insisted on taking Foolish, and with
Anna backing him all the way, they outvoted Cam.

It was tough to stay annoyed when his crew was so
damn cheerful. Foolish sat on a bench, wearing an ancient
doggie life jacket that had belonged to one of Ray and
Stella's numerous dogs, and barked happily at waves and
birds.

Seth, already munching on one of the sandwiches from the cooler, dutifully explained to Anna the mystery of the rigging.

She looked so damned cute, Cam thought, with one of his old and battered Orioles caps on her head, watching studiously as Seth identified each line.

He maneuvered through the channels, motoring between markers at an easy speed, working through what the locals called Little Neck River into Tangier Sound and toward the bay.

There was a light chop, and Cam glanced back to see how Anna would weather it. She was kneeling in the stern, leaning over the rail, but he saw with a grin that it wasn't because of a queasy stomach. Her smile was huge, her finger pointing eagerly as she caught sight of the clumps of trees and spreading marshes of Smith Island.

He called for Seth to hoist sail.

It was a moment Anna would never forget. City life hadn't prepared her for the sounds, the motion, the sight of white sails rising, snapping in the wind, then filling with it.

For a moment the boat seemed to fly, with the wind slapping her cheeks and filling the canvas to bursting. Water churned in their wake and she tasted salt.

She wanted to watch everything at once, the waves rising from blue-green water, the sea of white canvas above, the stretches and bumps of land. And the man and boy who worked so smoothly, so competently, with barely a word passing between them.

They sailed past what Seth identified as a crab shanty. It was no more than a fragile shack of beaten and weathered gray wood stilted out of the water and attached to a rickety dock. The orange floats that marked the crab pots dotted the surface. She watched a workboat rocking in the tide as a waterman—a picture in his faded pants, battered cap, and white boots—hauled up a chicken wire cage.

He paused in his work long enough to touch the brim

of his cap in greeting before tossing two snapping crabs into his water tank.

Life on the water, Anna thought and watched the work-boat putt toward the next float.

"That's Little Donnie," Seth told her. "Ethan says they call him that even though he's grown up because his father's Big Donnie. Weird."

Anna laughed. It had looked to her as if Little Donnie was pushing two hundred pounds. "I guess that's the way it is when you live in a small community. It must be wonderful to live and work on the water that way."

Seth lifted a shoulder. "It's okay. But I'd rather just sail."

When she lifted her face to the wind, she decided he had a point. Just sail—fast and free, with the boat rising and falling, the gulls wheeling overhead. Cam looked so natural at the wheel, she thought, with his long legs planted apart to accommodate the roll of the boat, his hands firm, his dark hair flying. When he turned his head, was it any wonder her heart jumped? When he held out a hand, was it any wonder she rose and walked cautiously over the unfamiliar deck to take it.

"Want the wheel?"

Desperately. "Better not," she said, trying to be practical. "I don't know what I'm doing."

"I do." He tugged her in front of him, put his hands over hers. "That's Pocomoke," he told her, nodding toward a narrow channel. "If you want to slow down, we can head that way, dodge some crab pots."

The wind slapped playfully at her face. She watched a gull swoop toward the surface of the water, skim it, then rise up calling in that sharp cry that sounded like a laughing scream. The hell with practicalities. "I don't want to slow down."

She heard him laugh above her ear. "Atta girl."

"Where are we heading? What are we doing?"

"Heading south, southwest. Sailing to the luff," he told her. "On the edge of the wind."

"On the edge? It feels like we're in the middle of it. I didn't know we could go so fast. It's wonderful."

"Good. Hold on a minute."

To her shock, he stepped back and called to Seth to help him make some adjustments to the sails. As her hands white-knuckled on the wheel, she heard them laughing. She heard the creak of the masts, the shiver of the canvas as it turned. If anything, she thought the boat picked up speed. She tried to relax. After all, there was nothing but water ahead of them.

She could see to the right—starboard, she corrected herself—a small motorboat cruising out of one of the many rivers and channels. Too far away, she judged, for any traffic jams or accidents.

Just as she had herself convinced she could do the job without incident, the boat tilted. She muffled a scream and nearly whipped the wheel in the opposite direction of the tilt, but Cam's hands closed over hers again and held it steady.

"We're going over!"

"Nah. We're heeled in nicely. More speed."

Her heart stayed in her throat. "You left me at the wheel."

"Sails needed trimming. The kid knows how to work the sheets. Ethan's taught him a lot, and he catches on quick. He's a damn good sailor."

"But you left me at the wheel," she repeated.

"You did fine." He brushed an absent kiss on the top of her head. "That's Tangier Island up ahead. We'll go around it, then head north. There's some quiet spots on the Little Choptank. We'll hit there about lunchtime."

They didn't appear to be capsizing, she thought with a steadying breath. And since she hadn't run them aground, she relaxed enough to lean back against him.

She planted her feet apart, as Cam did, and let her body balance with the motion of the boat. Her newest ambition was to have a little sloop, skiff, whatever it was called, when she finally got that house on the water.

She would have the Quinn brothers build it for her, she decided, dreaming. "If I had a boat, I'd do this every chance I got."

"We'll have to teach you the basics. Before long we'll have you trapezing."

"What? Swinging from the mast in a spangled leotard?"

The image had its appeal. "Not quite. You use a rig—a trapeze—and you hang out over the water."

"For fun?"

"Well, I like it," he said with a laugh. "It's for speed, balancing power."

"Hanging out over the water," she mused, glancing to port. "I might like it too."

H E LET HER WORK THE jib, under Seth's watchful eye. She liked the feel of the line in her hand and knowing she was in charge—more or less—of the billowing white sheet. They rounded the little sandy spit of Tangier Island, and she was treated to the quick maneuvering of tacking, jibbing, the teamwork necessary to maintain speed while changing course.

Cam had stripped down to denim cutoffs, and his skin gleamed with sun and sweat and water. If her hands ached a little from the unfamiliar work, she didn't complain. Instead she got a foolish thrill when Cam told her she was a pretty good crew.

They had lunch on Hudson Creek off the Little Choptank River, near a broken-down wharf with only the birds and the lap of water for company. The sun was bright in a clear blue sky, and the temperature had soared into the eighties to give a hint of the summer that was still weeks away.

To the accompaniment of music on the radio, they took a cooling swim. Foolish paddled joyfully while Seth dived beneath the mirrorlike surface and swam like a wild dolphin.

"He's having the time of his life," Anna murmured. A layer of the sulky, defiant, angry boy she'd first interviewed was being washed away. She wondered if he knew it.

"Then I guess I can't be too annoyed that you insisted on his coming along."

She smiled. She'd bundled her hair on top of her head in a vain attempt to keep it dry. With the way Seth and the puppy were splashing, nothing was dry. "You don't really mind. And you'd never have had that smooth of a sail without him on board."

"True enough, but there's something to be said for a rough sail." He parted the water in front of him, then slid his arms around her.

Anna gripped his shoulders in automatic defense. "No dunking."

"Would I do anything that predictable?" His eyes were smoky with laughter. "Especially when this is more fun." He tilted his head and kissed her.

Their lips were wet and slippery, and Anna's pulse thrummed at the sensation of his mouth sliding over hers, then capturing, then taking. The cool water seemed to grow warmer as their legs tangled. She was weightless, sighing as she floated into the kiss.

Then she was underwater.

She surfaced sputtering, shaking wet hair out of her eyes. The first thing she heard was Seth's laughter. The first thing she saw was Cam's grin.

"It was irresistible," he claimed, then swallowed water himself as she flipped onto her stomach and kicked it into his face.

"You're next," she warned Seth, who was so stunned at the idea of an adult playing with him that she caught him easily and wrestled him under.

He struggled, spat out water, swallowed more when he laughed. "Hey, I didn't do anything."

"You laughed. Besides, as I see it, you guys work as a team. It was probably your idea."

"No way." He wiggled free, then got the bright idea to dive and pull her under the surface by the ankle.

It was a pitched battle, and when they were exhausted, they agreed to call it a draw. It was only then that they noticed Cam was no longer in the water but sitting comfortably on the side of the boat eating a sandwich.

"What are you doing up there?" Anna called out while she pushed her sopping-wet hair back.

"Watching the show." He washed the ham and cheese down with Pepsi. "A couple of goons."

"Goons?" She slid her eyes toward Seth, and in tacit agreement the foes became a unit. "I only see one goon around here, how about you?"

"Just one," he agreed as they swam slowly toward the boat.

Any idiot could have seen what they had in mind. Cam nearly lifted his legs out of reach, then he decided what the hell and let them pull him back into the water with an impressive splash.

It would be hours before it occurred to Seth that Anna and Cam had both had their hands on him. And he hadn't been scared at all.

AFTER THE BOAT WAS docked, the sails dropped, the decks swabbed, Anna rolled up her metaphorical sleeves and got to work in the kitchen. It was her mission to give the Quinn men a meal they wouldn't soon forget. She might have been a novice sailor, but here she was an expert.

"It smells like glory," Phillip told her when he wandered in.

"It'll taste better." She built the layers of her lasagna with an artist's flair. "Old family recipe."

"They're the best," he agreed. "We've got my father's

secret waffle batter recipe. I'll have to whip you up some in the morning.''

"I'd like that." She glanced up to smile at him and noted what she thought was worry in his eyes. "Everything all right?"

"Sure. Just some leftover tangles from work." It had nothing to do with work, but with the latest report from the private investigator he'd hired. Seth's mother had been spotted in Norfolk—and that was entirely too close. "Need any help in here?"

"Everything's under control." She finished off her casserole with a thin layer of mozzarella before popping it in the oven. "You might want to try the wine."

Absently Phillip picked up the bottle breathing on the counter. And instantly his interest was piqued. "Nebbiolo, the best of the Italian reds."

"I think so, and I can promise my lasagna's a match for it."

Phillip grinned as he poured two glasses. His eyes were a golden brown that for some reason made Anna think of archangels. "Anna, my love, why don't you toss Cam over and run away with me?"

"Because I'd hunt you both down and kill you," Cam stated as he stepped into the kitchen. "Back off from my woman, bro, before I hurt you." Though it was said lightly, Cam wasn't entirely sure he was joking. And he wasn't entirely pleased to feel the hot little spurt of jealousy.

He wasn't the jealous type.

"He doesn't know a Barolo from a Chianti," Phillip told her as he got down another glass. "You're better off with me."

"Goodness," she said in a passable imitation of their below-the-Mason-Dixon-line drawl, "I just love being fought over by strong men. And here comes one more," she added as Ethan stepped through the back door. "You want to duel for me too, Ethan?"

He blinked and scratched his head. Women confused

him, but he was pretty sure there was a joke coming on. "Did you make whatever's cooking in there?"

"With my own little hands," she assured him.

"I'll go get my gun."

When she laughed, he shot her a quick smile, then ducked out of the room to shower off the day's work.

"Jesus, Ethan nearly flirted with a woman." Amazed, Phillip lifted his glass in a toast. "We're going to have to keep you around, Anna."

"If someone will set the table while I put the salad together, I might hang around long enough to let you sample my cannoli."

Cam and Phillip eyed each other. "Whose turn is it?" Cam demanded.

"Not mine. It must be yours."

"No way. I did it yesterday." They studied each other another moment, then both turned to the door and yelled for Seth.

Anna only shook her head. Younger brothers, she supposed, were meant to be abused in such matters.

She knew the meal was a success when Seth gobbled up a third helping. He'd lost that alley-cat boniness, she noted. And the pallor. Perhaps his eyes were still occasionally wary, peeking out under his lashes as if searching for the blow that he'd learned too young to expect. But more often, Anna thought, there was humor in his eyes. He was a bright boy who was discovering how to be amused by people.

His language was rough, and she didn't expect there would be a great deal of improvement in it as long as he lived in a household of men. Though she did see that Cam booted him lightly under the table now and again when he swore too often.

They were making it work. She'd had strong doubts in the beginning that three grown men, well set in their ways, would find a way of adjusting, of making room. And especially of opening their hearts to a boy who had been thrust upon them.

But they were making it work. When she wrote her report on the Quinn case the following week, she was going to state that Seth DeLauter was home, exactly where he belonged.

It would take time for the guardianship to move from temporary to permanent, but she would add her weight. Nothing warmed her heart quite so deeply as seeing the way Seth looked over at Cam after another under-the-table kick and grinned exactly like a ten-year-old boy caught sinning.

He would make a terrific father, she thought. Just rough enough around the edges to make it fun. He'd be the type to cart a child around on his shoulders, to wrestle in the yard. She could almost see it—the handsome dark-haired little boy, the pretty rosy-cheeked girl.

"You're in the wrong business," Phillip told her as he pushed back from the table and considered loosening his belt.

She blinked, caught daydreaming, and very nearly flushed. "I am?"

"You should own a restaurant. Any time you want to shift gears in that direction, I'll be the first in line to invest." He rose, intending to make use of his cappuccino maker to complement her dessert, and answered the phone on the first ring.

At the sound of the husky female voice with a sexy Italian accent, he raised his eyebrows. "He's right here." Phillip ran his tongue over his teeth and held out the phone to Cam. "It's for you, pal."

Cam took the phone, and after one purring sentence in his ear, almost placed the voice. "Hi, sugar," he said, searching for a name. *"Come va?"*

Because he did indeed love his brother, Phillip tried his best to distract Anna. "I just picked up this machine about six months ago," he told her, holding her chair so she would rise—and perhaps move out of earshot. "It's a beaut."

"Really?" She wasn't the least bit interested in the

working of some fancy coffee machine. Not when she'd
heard just how smoothly Cam had greeted his obviously
female caller. When she heard him laugh, her teeth went
on edge.

It didn't occur to Cam to muffle his voice or censor the
content. He'd finally put a name with the voice—Sophia
of the curvy body and bedroom eyes—and was chatting
lightly about mutual acquaintances. She liked racing—all
manner of racing—and was a hot, sleek bullet in bed.

"No, I had to take a pass on the rest of the season this
year," he told her. "I don't know when I'll get back to
Rome. You'll be the first, *bella*," he answered when she
asked if he would call her when he did. "Sure, I remember—the little trattoria near the Trevi Fountain. Absolutely."

He leaned back against the counter. Her voice brought
back memories. Not of her particularly, as he could barely
get a clear image of her face in his head. But of Rome
itself, the busy, narrow streets, the smells, the sounds, the
rush.

The races.

"What?" Her question about his Porsche jerked him
back to the present time and place. "Yeah, I've got it
garaged in Nice until . . ."

He trailed off, his thoughts scattering as she asked him
if he would consider selling it. She had a friend, she told
him. Carlo. He remembered Carlo, didn't he? Carlo wondered if Cam would be interested in selling the car, since
he was staying so long in the States.

"I haven't thought about it." Sell the car? A little lance
of panic stabbed him. It would be like admitting he wasn't
going back. Not just to Europe but to his life.

She was speaking quickly, persuasively, her Italian and
English mixing and confusing him. He had her number,
si? And could call her anytime. She would tell Carlo he
was thinking about it. They were all missing Cam. Rome
was so *noioso* without him. She had heard he had said no
to a big race in Australia and was afraid it must be a

woman holding him. Had he finally fallen for a woman?

"Yes, no—" His head was spinning. "It's complicated, sweetie. But I'll be in touch." Then she made him laugh one more time when she whispered a suggestion on how they might spend his first night back in Rome. "I'll be sure to keep that in mind. Darling, how could I forget? Yeah. *Ciao*."

Phillip was busily foaming milk and trying with the air of a desperate man to engage Anna in conversation about types of coffee beans. Ethan, with the instinct of a survivor, had already deserted the kitchen. And Seth simply sat, crumbling a heel of garlic bread for Foolish, who hid under the table.

Oblivious, Cam raised a suspicious eyebrow at the cappuccino machine. "I'll stick with regular coffee," he began and smiled when Anna walked up to him. "I remember your cannoli from—" And the air whooshed out of his lungs as she plowed a fist into his gut. Before he could suck it back in, she strode past him and outside with a slap of the screen door.

"What?" Rubbing his stomach, Cam goggled at Phillip. "Jesus, what did you say to her?"

"You're such a jerk," Phillip muttered and deftly poured the first cup.

"She looked really pissed," Seth commented and sniffed the air. "Can I try some of that junk you're making?"

"Sure." Phillip made up a latte, heavy on the milk, while Cam headed outside.

Cam caught up to Anna on the dock, where she stood fuming, her arms folded over her chest. "What the hell was that for?"

"Oh, I don't know, Cam. For the hell of it." She whirled around to face him, her eyes blazing in the starlight. "Women are peculiar creatures. They get annoyed when the man they're supposed to be with flirts over the phone, right in their damn face, with some Italian bimbo."

The light dawned, but to his credit he barely winced. "Come on, sugar—"

He broke off, unsure whether he was amused or frightened when she lifted a fist. "Don't you call me sugar. You use my name. Do you think I'm an idiot? Sugar, sweetie, honey pie—that's what you say when you can't even remember the name of the woman who's underneath you in bed."

"Wait a damn minute."

"No, *you* wait a damn minute. Do you have any idea how *insulting* it is to stand there and hear you make a date to meet your Italian squeeze in Rome when my lasagna's barely settled in your stomach?"

Worse, she thought, much, much worse, he'd done it seconds after she'd been building foolish castles in the air of him with children. Their children. Oh, it was mortifying. Infuriating.

"I wasn't making a date," he began, then paused, fascinated, while a stream of impressive Italian curses poured out of her mouth. "You didn't learn those from your grandparents." When she bared her teeth and hissed, he couldn't stop the smile. "You're jealous."

"It's not a matter of jealousy. It's a matter of courtesy." She tossed her head and tried to calm down. She was only embarrassing herself more with the outburst, she realized. But by damn, she wasn't finished yet. "You're a free agent, Cameron, and so am I. No pretenses, no promises, fine. But I won't tolerate you having phone sex while I'm standing in the same room."

"It wasn't phone sex, it was a conversation."

"The little trattoria by the Trevi Fountain?" she said, coolly now. "How could I forget? You'll be the first? You want to have some Italian *zucchero*, Cam, that's your business. But don't you ever do it in my face again."

She took a breath, then held up a hand before he could speak. "I'm sorry I hit you."

He gauged her mood. Ruffled, but calming. "No, you're not."

"Okay, I'm not. You deserved it."

"It didn't mean anything, Anna."

Yes, she thought wearily, it did. To her it meant a great deal. And that was her own fault, her own small disaster. "It was rude."

"Manners never were my strong point. I'm not interested in her. I can't even remember her face."

Anna angled her head. "Do you honestly think a statement like that goes to your credit?"

What the hell did she want him to say? he wondered with a quick, impatient hiss of breath. Sometimes, he supposed, the truth was best. "It's your face, Anna, that I can't get out of my mind."

She sighed. "Now you're trying to distract me."

"Is it working?"

"Maybe." Her emotions, she reminded herself, her problem. "Let's just agree that even casual relationships have lines that shouldn't be crossed."

He wasn't sure "casual" was the word to describe what was between them. But at the moment whatever made her happy suited him. "Okay. Starting now you're the only Italian bimbo I flirt with." Her bland, unsmiling stare made him grin. "It was terrific lasagna. None of my other bimbos could cook."

She slid her gaze to the water, back to his face. Then cocked her head consideringly. Cam was pretty sure he saw the beginnings of humor in her eyes. "We'd both end up in there," he told her. "But I don't mind if you don't."

"I suppose, all in all, I'd rather stay dry." She glanced toward the house when music slipped through the windows and into the air. "Who plays the violin?"

"That's Ethan." It was a quick and lively jig, one of their parents' favorites. The piano joined in, made him smile. "And that's Phillip."

"What do you play?"

"A little guitar."

"I'd like to hear." In a gesture of peace, she held out

a hand. He took it, drawing her closer, taking her fingers to his lips.

"You're the one I want, Anna. You're the one I think of."

For now, she thought, and let him slide her into his arms. Now was all that had to matter.

EIGHTEEN

ANNA WASN'T SURE HOW she felt about seeing Cam frown in concentration as he tuned up a battered old Gibson guitar. It was a piece of him she hadn't counted on.

It surprised her, pleased her, to see how smoothly, how easily the three men had slid into a song. Strong voices, she mused, quick and clever fingers. Teamwork once again. And unbroken family ties.

Without a doubt there had been many evenings such as this in their lives. She could imagine the three of them, years younger, melding their tunes, with the two people who had given them the music, and the purpose, and the family, sitting in the room with them.

She took that image, and the music, upstairs with her when she finally went to bed. To Cam's bed.

Reminding herself there was a child in the house, she locked the door—in case Cam came tiptoeing up from his makeshift bed on the sofa downstairs. And she told herself she wouldn't unlock it if he came tapping. No matter how sexy he'd looked strumming that old guitar to life.

Most of the tunes had been old Irish ballads and pub songs that she'd been unfamiliar with. She found them sad and heart-wrenching even when the tune beneath the words was lively. They mixed in some rock, and sneered at Seth when he suggested they play something from this century.

It had been sweet, Anna thought as she undressed. They would never think of it that way, and would likely be horrified that anyone else did. But sweet was how she'd seen it. Four males—four brothers—not of the blood but of the heart. It was easy to see how well they understood each other, and how they had come to just not accept the child but to include him.

When Seth commented that violins were for girls and wusses, Ethan merely smiled and went into a hot lick designed to capture Seth's interest and imagination. And Ethan's dry comment—*let's see a wuss do that*—earned a shrug and a grin from Seth.

When Seth had fallen asleep, they'd just left him there, sprawled on the rug with the puppy's head pillowed on his butt. Another belonging, in Anna's mind.

She slipped into her nightshirt and picked up her hairbrush. This house was an easy place to feel belonging. Big, simple rooms, lived-in furniture, noisy plumbing. She caught a few female touches that hadn't been there before. A gleam to the furniture, the odd vase of spring flowers. Compliments of the housekeeper, Anna imagined, which probably went largely unnoticed by the occupants.

If it were her house, she wouldn't change much, she decided, dreaming again as she ran the brush through her hair. Maybe spruce up some of the colors, add a bit of dash here and there with thick throw pillows and splashier flowers. She would definitely want to expand the gardens. She'd been doing some reading on perennials—what worked best in sun, what thrived in shade. There was a nice spot where the trees began to take over from the yard. She thought lily of the valley, some hostas, and periwinkles would do well there and add some interest.

Wouldn't it be lovely, she reflected, to while away a Saturday morning, digging in the earth, crowding pretty bedding plants together, planning the flow of colors and textures and heights?

And to watch them grow and spread and bloom, year after year.

A movement outside the window caught her eye in the mirror. Her heart sprang into her throat as she saw the shadow move behind the dark glass. As the window crept up, she turned slowly, holding the brush like a weapon.

And Cam stepped over the sill. "Hi." He had enjoyed watching her brush her hair, hated to see her stop. "Brought you something."

He held out a clutch of wild violets, which she tried to eye suspiciously. "Just how did you get up here?"

"Climbed." He stepped forward, she stepped back.

"Climbed what?"

"Up the side of the house mostly. Used to be able to shimmy up and down the gutter, but I weighed less then." He came closer, she moved back.

"That was clever of you. What if you'd fallen?"

He'd climbed sheer rock faces in Montana, Mexico, and France, but he smiled winningly at her concern. "You'd have felt sorry for me?"

"I don't think so." Since he had maneuvered his way to arm's length, she reached out and snatched the slightly crushed flowers. "Thanks for the violets. Good night."

Interesting, he decided. Her voice and her expression were prim despite the fact that she was standing there in nothing more than a long white T-shirt. For some reason he found the plain and practical cotton ridiculously sexy. It appeared he was finally going to get the chance to seduce her.

"I couldn't sleep." He reached over, hit the light switch, and left only the small bedside lamp burning warm and gold.

"You didn't try very long," she said, flicking the switch back on again.

"Seemed like hours." He lifted a hand to trace a finger lightly up her arm from wrist to elbow. Her skin was dusky, golden against the pure white of the nightshirt. "All I could think about was you. Beautiful Anna," he said softly, "with the Italian eyes."

Her toes seemed to curl in response to that skimming finger, which moved now to trace her jawline. Her heart was fluttering. No, it was her stomach. No, it was everything. "Cam, there's a young boy in the house."

"Who's dead asleep." His fingers dipped to her throat, tested the rapid pulse beating there. "Snoring on the living room rug."

"You should have carried him up to bed."

"Why?"

"Because . . ." There had to be a good reason, but how was she supposed to think clearly when he was looking at her, those flint-gray eyes so focused, so intense on her face? "You planned this," she said weakly.

"Not exactly. I thought I would have to talk you into going for a walk in the woods after the house quieted down. And then I would make love to you outside." He took her hand, turned it palm up, and pressed his lips to the center. "In the starlight. But rain's coming in."

"Rain?" She glanced toward the window and saw the curtains billowing in the freshening wind. When she looked back he was closer, and his arms were around her, those broad-palmed, clever hands stroking up her back.

"And I want you in bed. My bed." He tipped his head to nibble kisses along her jaw, then just under it where the skin was soft as water. "I want you, Anna. Day and night."

"Tomorrow," she began.

"Tonight. Tomorrow." And the word "always" was on the edge of his mind when his mouth found hers.

She made a small sound that might have been distress when his tongue slipped through her parted lips to deepen the kiss. It went deeper, still deeper until she had no choice but to let herself sink. The pretty little flowers drifted to the floor as her fingers went limp.

He had kissed her like this only once before, with such

unspeakable tenderness that it stripped her soul bare. If she could have formed words, she would have babbled out her love for him. But her knees were jelly, her heart lost, and words were beyond her.

He barely touched her, just those hands light on her back while his mouth drank from hers—and destroyed her.

"It's not a race this time." He heard himself murmur the words but wasn't sure if he spoke to himself or to her. All he knew was he wanted slow, painfully slow, endlessly slow, so that he could savor every moment, every move, every moan.

He reached out, dimmed the lights. "I want this spot," he whispered and let his mouth journey along the fragile skin just under her jaw again. "And this one." To the slender column of her throat, where her scent was warm and smoky.

When he stepped back and tugged his shirt over his head, she took a breath. She would get her feet back under her, she thought, and offer back some of what he was giving her. She reached for him, rose on her toes until their eyes and mouths lined up.

But he kissed her temples, her brow, her eyes when they fluttered closed. "I love looking at you," he told her. He took the hem of her nightshirt in his fingers and lifted it, inch by inch. "All of you. Even when you're not around, I have a picture of you in my head."

When her nightshirt was pooled on the floor, he kept his eyes on her face, lifted her into his arms. Felt her tremble.

And he knew, in one breath-stealing flash, that he had never wanted another woman the way he wanted Anna. This time when he laid her on the bed, it was he who sank mindlessly into the kiss.

He didn't have to order his hands to be gentle, to go slowly. He didn't have to hold back an urge to plunder. Not when she sighed so softly under his touch, not when she moved so fluidly beneath his hands, not when she gave so completely before he could ask.

He explored her with a kind of wonder, as if it were the first time. The first woman, the first need. Somehow it was new, this longing to linger. To sip instead of gulp. To glide instead of race. When her hands roamed over him, his skin quivered and warmed.

Neither of them heard the first soft patters of rain or the low, poignant moan of the wind.

She rose to peak on one long, shimmering wave. Floated down again breathing out his name.

Pleasure was liquid, soft as morning dew, wide as a dark sea. She could feel it sliding through her, shifting, spreading, taking her up on another high, curving crest where only he existed.

She pressed her mouth to his throat, his shoulder, would have absorbed him into her skin if she'd known a way. No one had ever taken her away so completely. And when she framed his face, brought his mouth to hers and poured all she was into the kiss, she knew he was with her. Absolutely hers.

When he filled her, it was only one more link. She opened, took him, and gave. They moved together slowly, breath tangling, gazes locked. Moved together silkily, rhythms matched to draw out every ounce of pleasure.

It built, dizzying and dazzling so that her lips curved even as her eyes swam. "Kiss me," she demanded on one last, trembling breath.

So their mouths met, clung, as that last sweeping wave swamped them.

He didn't speak, didn't dare, when her hands slid limply from his back to the bed. He felt as if he'd tumbled off a cliff and fallen hard on his heart. Now his heart was swollen, exposed. And it was hers.

If this was love, it scared the hell out of him.

But he couldn't move, couldn't let her go. She felt so good, so right beneath him. His body was weak, sated, and his mind close to empty. It was only his heart that trembled and pumped.

He would worry about it later.

Saying nothing, nothing at all, he shifted, drew her close, possessively close, to his side, and let the rain lull him to sleep.

A NNA AWOKE WITH THE sun shooting into her eyes and was stunned to find herself wrapped up in Cam. His arms had a good strong hold on her, and hers were snug around him. Their legs were tangled, with her right hooked over his hip like an anchor.

If her mind had been clear it might have occurred to her that while they both assumed their affair was casual, even sophisticated, in sleep they'd both known better.

She slid her leg down, hoping to unknot their limbs, but he only shifted and anchored hers more firmly.

"Cam." She whispered it, feeling foolish and guilty, and when she received no response, wriggled and spoke more firmly. "Cameron, wake up."

He grunted, snuggled closer, and muttered something into her hair.

She sighed and, deciding she had no choice, lifted the leg that was caught between his until her knee pressed firmly against his crotch. Then she gave it a quick nudge.

That got his eyes open.

"Whoa! What?"

"Wake up."

"I'm awake." And his just-open eyes were all but crossed. "Would you mind moving your . . ." When the pressure eased off, he let out the breath he'd been holding. "Thanks."

"You've got to go." She was back to whispering. "You shouldn't have stayed in here all night."

"Why not?" he whispered back. "It's my bed."

"You know what I'm talking about," she hissed. "One of your brothers could get up any minute."

He exerted himself to lift his head a couple of inches and peer at the clock on the opposite nightstand. "It's after seven. Ethan's already up, has probably emptied his first crab pot. And why are we whispering?''

''Because you're not supposed to be here.''

''I live here.'' A sleepy smile moved over his face. ''Damn, you're pretty when you're all rumpled and embarrassed. I guess I have to have you again.''

''Stop it.'' She nearly giggled, until his hand snuck around to cup her breast. ''Not now.''

''We're here now, naked and everything. And you're all soft and warm.'' He nuzzled his way to her neck.

''Don't you start.''

''Too late. I'm already into the first lap.''

And indeed when he shifted, she understood that the starting gun had already sounded. He was inside her in one easy move, and it was so smooth, so natural, so lovely, she could only sigh.

''No moaning,'' he said with a chuckle at her ear. ''You'll wake up my brothers.''

She snorted out a laugh and, caught between amusement and arousal, shoved and rolled until she straddled him. He looked sleepy, and dangerous, and exciting. A little breathless, she braced her hands on either side of his head. She bent down and sucked his bottom lip into her mouth.

''Okay, smart guy, let's see who moans first.''

And arching back, she began to ride.

Afterward, they decided it was a tie.

SHE MADE HIM CLIMB OUT the window, which he claimed was ridiculous. But it made her feel a little less decadent. The house was quiet when she came downstairs, freshly showered and comfortable in olive-drab cotton slacks and a camp shirt. Seth was still sleeping on the rug. Foolish stood guard on the floor.

At the sight of Anna, the pup scrambled up, whining pitifully as he followed her into the kitchen. She assumed it was either an empty stomach or a full bladder. When she opened the back door, he shot out like a bullet and proved it was the latter by peeing copiously on an azalea just struggling into bloom.

Birds were singing with full, joyful throats. Dew sparkled on the grass—and the grass needed mowing. There was still a light mist on the water, but it was burning off quickly, like blown smoke, and through it she could see little diamond sparks of sunlight on calm water.

The air was fresh from the night's rain, and the leaves seemed greener, fuller than they had only a day before.

She built a little fantasy that included steaming coffee and a walk down to the dock. By the time she'd taken the first step toward brewing the coffee, Cam came in through the hallway door.

He hadn't shaved, she noted, and found that the stubble of beard suited her image of a lazy Sunday morning in the country. He lifted a brow.

She got two mugs out of the cupboard, then lifted hers. "Good morning, Cameron."

"Good morning, Anna." Deciding to play along, he walked over and gave her a chaste kiss. "How did you sleep?"

"Very well, and you?"

"Like a log." He wound a lock of her hair around his finger. "It wasn't too quiet for you?"

"Quiet?"

"City girl, country silence."

"Oh. No, I liked it. In fact, I don't think I've ever slept better."

They were grinning at each other when Seth stumbled in, rubbing his eyes. "Have we got anything to eat?"

Cam kept his gaze locked on Anna's. "Phillip ran his mouth about making waffles. Go wake him up."

"Waffles? Cool." He ran off, his bare feet slapping on the wood floor.

"Phillip's not going to appreciate that," Anna commented.

"He's the one who started the waffle rumor."

"I could make them."

"You made dinner. We take turns around here. To avoid chaos. And the shedding of blood." A loud and nasty thud sounded over their heads and made Cam grin. "Why don't we pour that coffee and take a walk out of the line of fire?"

"I was thinking the same thing."

On impulse, he grabbed a fishing pole. "Hold this." A hunt through the fridge netted him a small round of Phillip's Brie.

"I thought we were having waffles."

"We are. This is bait." He tucked the cheese in his pocket and picked up his coffee.

"You use Brie for bait?"

"You use what's handy. A fish is going to bite, it'll bite on damn near anything." He handed her a mug of coffee. "Let's see what we can catch."

"I don't know how to fish," she said as they headed out.

"Nothing to it. You drown a worm—or in this case some fancy cheese—and see what happens."

"Then why do guys go off with all that expensive, complicated gear and those funny hats?"

"Just trappings. We're not talking dry fly-fishing here. We're just dropping a line. If we can't pull up a couple of cats by the time Phillip's got waffles on the table, I've really lost my touch."

"Cats?" For one stunning moment, she was absolutely horrified. "You don't use cats as bait."

He blinked at her, saw that she was perfectly serious, then roared with laughter. "Sure we do. You catch 'em by the tail, skin their bellies, and drop them in." He took pity on her only because she went deathly pale. But it didn't stop him from laughing. "Cat*fish*, honey. We're going to bring up some catfish before breakfast."

"Very funny." She sniffed and started walking again. "Catfish are really ugly. I've seen pictures."

"You're telling me you've never eaten catfish?"

"Why in the world would I?" A little miffed, she sat on the side of the dock, feet dangling, and cupped her mug in both hands.

"Fry them fresh and fry them right, and you've never tasted better. Toss in some hush puppies, a couple ears of sweet corn, and you've got yourself a feast."

She eyed him as he settled beside her and began to bait his hook with Brie. His chin was stubbled, his hair untidy, his feet bare. "Fried catfish and hush puppies? This from the reckless Cameron Quinn, the man who races through the waters, roads, and the hearts of Europe. I don't think your little pastry from Rome would recognize you."

He grimaced and dropped his line in the water. "We're not going to get into that again, are we?"

"No." She laughed and leaned over to kiss his cheek. "I almost don't recognize you myself. But I kind of like it."

He handed her the pole. "You don't exactly look like the sober and dedicated public servant yourself this morning, Miz Spinelli."

"I take Sundays off. What do I do if I catch a fish?"

"Reel it in."

"How?"

"We'll worry about that when it happens." He leaned over to pull up the crab pot tied to the near piling. The two annoyed-looking jimmies inside made him grin. "At least we won't starve tonight."

The snapping claws had Anna lifting her feet slightly higher above the water. But she was content to sit there, sipping coffee, watching the morning bloom. When Mama Duck and her six fuzzy babies swam by, she had what Cam considered a typical city girl reaction.

"Oh, look! Look, baby ducks. Aren't they cute?"

"We get a nest down there in the bend near the edge of the woods most every year." And because she was looking so dreamy-eyed, he couldn't resist. "Makes for good hunting over the winter."

"Hunting what?" she murmured, charmed and already imagining what it would be like to hold one of those puffy ducklings in her hand. Then her eyes popped wide, horrified. "You shoot the little ducks?"

"Well, they're bigger by then." He had never shot a duck or anything else in his life. "You can sit right here and drop a couple before breakfast."

"You should be ashamed."

"Your city's showing."

"I'd call it my humanity. If they were my ducks, no one would shoot them." His quick grin had her narrowing her eyes. "You were just trying to get a rise out of me."

"It worked. You look so cute when you're outraged." He kissed her cheek to mollify her. "My mother's heart was too soft to allow hunting. Fishing never bothered her. She said that was more of an even match. And she hated guns."

"What was she like?"

"She was . . . steady," he decided. "It was hard to rock her. Once you did, she had a kick-ass temper, but it was tough to get it going. She loved her work, loved the kids. She had a lot of soft spots. She'd cry at movies or over books, and she couldn't even watch when we cleaned fish. But when there was trouble, she was a rock."

He'd taken Anna's hand without realizing it, lacing their fingers. "When I came here I was beat up pretty bad. She fixed me up. I kept thinking I'd take off as soon as I was steady on my feet again. I kept telling myself these people were a couple of assholes. I could rob them blind and take off anytime I wanted. I was going to Mexico."

"But you didn't take off," Anna said quietly.

"I fell in love with her. It was the day I got back from my first sail with Dad. This world had opened up for me. I was a little scared of it, but there it was. He went inside to grade some papers, I think. I was making bitching noises about having to wear that stupid life jacket, and just general bullshit. She took me by the hand and pulled me right into the water. She said then I'd better learn to swim. And she taught me. I fell in love with her about ten feet out from this dock. You couldn't have dragged me away from here.''

Moved, Anna lifted their joined hands to her cheek. ''I wish I'd had the chance to meet her. To meet both of them.''

He shifted, suddenly realizing that he had told her a story he'd never shared with anyone. And he remembered the way he'd sat here the night before, talking to his father. ''Do you, ah, believe that people come back?''

''From?''

''You know, ghosts, spirits, *Twilight Zone* stuff?''

''I don't not believe it,'' she said after a moment. ''After my mother died, there were times when I could smell her perfume. Just out of the blue, out of the air, this scent that was so . . . her. Maybe it was real, maybe it was my imagination, but it helped me. That's what counts, I suppose.''

''Yeah, but—''

''Oh!'' She nearly dropped the pole when she felt the tug. ''Something's on here! Take it!''

''Uh-uh. You caught it.'' He decided the distraction was for the best. Another minute or two, he might have made a total fool of himself and told her everything. He reached over to steady the pole. ''Reel it in some, then let it play out. That's it. No, don't jerk, just slow and steady.''

''It feels big.'' Her heart was thudding between her ears. ''Really big.''

''They always do. You got it now, just keep bringing it in.'' He rose to get the net that always hung over the edge of the dock. ''Bring her up, up and out.''

Anna leaned back, eyes half shut. They popped wide when the fish came flashing and wriggling out of the water and into the sunlight. ''Oh, my God.''

''Don't drop the pole, for God's sake.'' Shaking with laughter, Cam gripped her shoulder before she could pitch herself into the water. Leaning forward, he netted the flopping catfish. ''Nice one.''

''What do I do? What do I do now?''

Expertly Cam freed fish from hook, then to her horror handed her the full net. "Hang on to it."

"Don't leave me with this thing." She took one squinting look, saw whiskers and fishy eyes—and shut her own. "Cam, come back here and take this ugly thing."

He set the widemouthed pail he'd just filled with water on the dock, took the net, and flopped the catch into it. "City girl."

She let out a long breath of relief. "Maybe." She peeped into the pail. "Ugh. Throw it back. It's hideous."

"Not on your life. It's a four-pounder easy."

When she refused to take the pole a second time, he sacrificed the rest of his brother's Brie and settled down to catch the rest of that night's supper himself.

THE RECEPTION THAT HER morning's work received from Seth changed her attitude. Impressing a small boy by catching an indisputably ugly and possibly gourmand fish was a new kind of triumph. By the time she was driving with Cam to the boatyard, she'd decided one of her next projects would be to read up on the art of fishing.

"I think, with the proper bait, I could catch something much more attractive than a catfish."

"Want to go dig up some night crawlers next weekend?"

She tipped down her sunglasses. "Are those what they sound like?"

"You bet."

She tipped them back up. "I don't think so. I think I'd prefer using those pretty feathers and whatnot." She glanced at him again. "So, do you know your father's secret waffle recipe?"

"Nope. He didn't trust me with it. He figured out pretty fast that I was a disaster in the kitchen."

"What kind of bribe would work best on Phillip?"

"You couldn't worm it out of him with a Hermes tie. It only gets passed down to a Quinn."

They'd see about that, she decided, and tapped her fingers on her knee. She continued tapping them when he pulled into the lot beside the old brick building. She wasn't sure what reaction he expected from her. As far as she could see, there was little change here. The trash had been picked up, the broken windows replaced, but the building still looked ancient and deserted.

"You cleaned up." It seemed like a safe response, and it appeared to satisfy him as they got out of opposite doors of the car.

"The dock's going to need some work," he commented. "Phillip ought to be able to handle it." He took out keys, as shiny as the new lock on the front door. "I guess we need a sign or something," he said half to himself as he unlocked the dead bolts. When he opened the door, Anna caught the scent of sawdust, mustiness, and stale coffee. But the polite smile she'd fixed on her face widened in surprise as she stepped inside.

He flicked on lights and made her blink. They were brilliant overhead, hanging from the rafters and unshaded. The newly repaired floor had been swept clean—or nearly so. Bare drywall angled out on the near side to form a partition. The stairs had been replaced, the banister of plain wood oiled. The loft overhead still looked dangerous, but she began to see the potential.

She saw pulleys and wenches, enormous power tools with wicked teeth, a metal chest with many drawers that she assumed held baffling tools. New steel locks glinted on the wide doors leading to the dock.

"This is wonderful, Cam. You do work fast."

"Speed's my business." He said it lightly, but it pleased him to see that she was genuinely impressed.

"You had to work like dogs to get this much done." Though she wanted to see everything, it was the huge platform in the center of the building that pulled her forward.

Drawn on it in dark pencil or chalk were curves and lines and angles.

"I don't understand this." Fascinated, she circled around it. "Is this supposed to be a boat?"

"It is a boat. The boat. It's lofting. You draw the hull, full size. The mold section, transverse forms. Then you test them out by sketching in some longitudinal curves—like the sheer. Some of the waterlines."

He was on his knees on the platform as he spoke, using his hands to show her. And still leaving her in the dark.

But it didn't matter whether she understood the technique he described or not. She understood him. He might not realize it yet, but he had fallen in love with this place, and with the work he would do here.

"We need to add the bow lines, and the diagonals. We may want to use this design again, and this is the only way to reproduce it with real accuracy. It's a damn good design. I'm going to want to add in the structural details, full size. The more detail, the better."

He looked up and saw her smiling at him, swinging her sunglasses by the earpiece. "Sorry. You don't know what the hell I'm talking about."

"I think it's wonderful. I mean it. You're building more than boats here."

Faintly embarrassed, he got to his feet. "Boats is the idea." He jumped nimbly off the platform. "Come take a look at these."

He caught her hand, led her to the opposite walls. There were two framed sketches now, one of Ethan's beloved skipjack and the other of the boat yet to be built.

"Seth did them." The pride in his voice was just there. He didn't even notice it. "He's the only one of us who can really draw worth a damn. Phil's adequate, but the kid is just great. He's doing Ethan's workboat next, then the sloop. I've got to get some pictures of a couple of boats I worked on so he can copy them. We'll hang them all in here—and add drawings of the others we build. Kind of like a gallery. A trademark."

There were tears in her eyes when she turned and wrapped her arms around him. Her fierce grip surprised him, but he returned it.

"More than boats," she murmured, then drew back to frame his face in her hands. "It's wonderful," she said again and pulled his mouth down to hers.

The kiss swarmed through him, swamped him, staggered him. Everything about her, about them, spun around in his heart. Questions, dozens of them, buzzed like bees in his head. And the answer, the single answer to all of them, was nearly within his reach.

He said her name, just once, then drew her unsteadily away. He had to look at her, really look, but nothing about him seemed quite on balance.

"Anna," he said again. "Wait a minute."

Before he could get a firm grip on the answer, before he could get his feet back under him again, the door creaked open, letting in sunlight.

"Excuse me, folks," Mackensie said pleasantly. "I saw the car out front."

NINETEEN

CAM'S FIRST REACTION was pure annoyance. Something was happening here, something monumental, and he didn't want any interruptions.

"We're not open for business, Mackensie." He kept his grip on Anna's arms firm and turned his back to the man he considered no more than a paper-pushing pest.

"Didn't think you were." With his voice still mild and friendly, Mackensie wandered in. In his line of work he rarely received a warm welcome. "Door was unlocked. Well, this is going to be quite a place."

He was a Harry Homemaker at heart, and the sight of all those spanking-new power tools stirred the juices. "Got yourself some top-grade equipment here."

"You want a boat, come back tomorrow and we'll talk."

"I get seasick," Mackensie confessed with a quick grimace. "Can't even stand on a dock without getting queasy."

"That's tough. Go away."

"But I sure do admire the looks of boats. Can't say I ever gave much thought to what went into building them.

That's some band saw over there. Must've set you back some."

This time Cam did turn, the fury in his eyes as dangerous as a cocked gun. "It's my business how I spend my money."

Baffled by the exchange, Anna laid a hand on Cam's arm. She wasn't surprised that he was being rude—she'd seen him be rude before—but the snap and hiss of his anger over what appeared to be no more than a nuisance puzzled her.

If this is the way he intends to treat potential clients, she thought, he might as well close the doors now.

Before she could think of the proper calming words, Cam shook her off. "What the hell do you want now?"

"Just a couple of questions." He nodded politely to Anna. "Ma'am. Larry Mackensie, claim investigator for True Life Insurance."

In the dark, Anna automatically accepted the hand he held out. "Mr. Mackensie. I'm Anna Spinelli."

Mackensie did a quick flip through his mental file. It took only a moment for him to tag her as Seth DeLauter's caseworker. As she had come on the scene after the death of the insured, he'd had no need to contact her, but she was in his records. And the cozy little scene he'd walked in on told him she was pretty tight with at least one of the Quinns. He wasn't sure if or how that little bit of information would apply, but he would just make a note of it.

"Pleased to meet you."

"If you two have business to discuss," Anna began, "I'll just wait outside."

"I don't have anything to discuss with him, now or later. Go file your report, Mackensie. We're done."

"Just about. I figured you'd like to know I'll be heading back to the home office. Got a lot of mixed results on my interviews, Mr. Quinn. Not much of what you'd call hard facts, though." He glanced toward the band saw again, wished fleetingly he could afford one like it. "There's the letter that was found in your father's car—that goes to state of mind. Single-car accident, driver a physically fit man, no traces of alcohol or drugs.'' He lifted his shoulders. ''Then there's the fact that the insured increased his policy and added a beneficiary shortly before the accident. The company looks hard at that kind of thing.''

''You go ahead and look.'' Cam's voice had lowered, like the warning growl of an attack dog. ''But not here. Not in my place.''

''Just letting you know how things stand. Starting a new business,'' Mackensie said conversationally, ''takes a good chunk of capital. You been planning this for long?''

Cam sprang quickly, had Mackensie by the lapels and up on the toes of his shiny, lace-up shoes. ''You son of a bitch.''

''Cam, stop it!'' The order was quick and sharp, and Anna punctuated it by stepping forward and shoving a hand on each man's chest. She thought it was like moving between a wolf and a bull, but she held her ground. ''Mr. Mackensie, I think you'd better go now.''

''On my way.'' His voice was steady enough, despite the cold sweat that had pooled at the base of his neck and was even now dripping down his spine. ''It's just details, Mr. Quinn. The company pays me to gather the details.''

But it didn't pay him, he reminded himself as he walked outside where he could gulp in air, to be beaten to a pulp by a furious beneficiary.

''Bastard, fucking bastard.'' Cam desperately wanted to hit something, anything, but there was too much empty air. ''Does he really think my father plowed into a telephone pole so I could start building boats? I should have decked him. Goddamn it. First they say he did it because he couldn't face the scandal, now it's because he wanted us to have a pile of money. The hell with their dead money. They didn't know him. They don't know any of us.''

Anna let him rant, let him prowl around the building looking for something to damage. Her heart was frozen in her chest. Suicide was suspected, she thought numbly. An investigation was in place.

And Cam had known, must have known all along.

"That was a claim investigator from the company who holds your father's life insurance policy?"

"That was a fucking moron." Cam whirled, more oaths stinging his tongue. Then he saw her face—set and entirely too cool. "It's nothing. Just a hassle. Let's get out of here."

"It's suspected that your father committed suicide."

"He didn't kill himself."

She held up a hand. She had to keep the hurt buried for now and lead with the practical. "You've spoken with Mackensie before. And I assume you—your lawyer at any rate—has been in contact with the insurance company about this matter for some time."

"Phillip's handling it."

"You knew, but you didn't tell me."

"It has nothing to do with you."

No, she realized, it wasn't possible to keep all the hurt buried. "I see." That was personal, she reminded herself. She would deal with that later. "And as to how it affects Seth?"

Fury sprang up again, clawed at his throat. "He doesn't know anything about it."

"If you actually believe that, you're deluding yourself. Gossip runs thick in small towns, close communities. And young boys hear a great deal."

It was the caseworker now, Cam thought with rising resentment. She might as well be carrying her briefcase and wearing one of her dumpy suits. "Gossip's all it is. It doesn't matter."

"On the contrary, gossip can be very damaging. You'd be wiser to be open with him, to be honest. Though that seems to be difficult for you."

"Don't twist this around on me, Anna. It's goddamn insurance. It's nothing."

"It's your father," she corrected. "His reputation. I don't imagine there's much that means more to you." She drew a deep breath. "But as you said, it's nothing to do with me on a personal level. I think we're finished here.''

"Wait a minute." He stepped in front of her, blocking her exit. He had the sinking feeling that if she walked, she meant to walk a lot farther than his car.

"Why? So you can explain? It's family business? I'm not family. You're absolutely right." It amazed her that her voice was so calm, so detached, so utterly reasonable when she was boiling inside. "And I imagine you felt it best to hold the matter back from Seth's caseworker. Much wiser to show her only the positive angles, lock up any negatives."

"My father didn't kill himself. I don't have to defend him to you, or anyone."

"No, you don't. And I'd never ask you to." She stepped around him and started for the door. He caught her before she reached it, but she'd expected that and turned calmly. "There's no point in arguing, Cam, when essentially we agree."

"There's no point in you being pissed off," he shot back. "We're handling the insurance company. We're handling the gossip about Seth being his love child, for Christ's sake."

"What?" Stunned, she pressed a hand to her head. "There's speculation that Seth is your father's illegitimate son?"

"It's nothing but bull and small minds," Cam replied.

"My God, have you considered, even for a moment, what it could do to Seth to hear that kind of talk? Have you considered, even for a moment, that this was something I needed to know in order to evaluate, in order to help Seth properly?"

His thumbs went into his pockets. "Yeah, I considered it—and I didn't tell you. Because we're handling it. We're talking about my father here."

"We're also talking about a minor child in your care."

"He is in my care," Cam said evenly. "And that's the point. I'm doing what I thought was best all around. I didn't tell you about the insurance thing or about the gossip because they're both lies.''

"Perhaps they are, but by not telling me, you lied."

"I wasn't going to go around feeding anybody this crap that the kid was my father's bastard."

She nodded slowly. "Well, take it from some other man's bastard, it doesn't make Seth less of a person."

"I didn't mean it like that," he began and reached out for her. But she stepped away. "Don't do that." He exploded with it and grabbed her arms. "Don't back off from me. For Christ's sake, Anna, my life has turned inside out in the past couple of months, and I don't know how long it's going to be before I can turn it back around. I've got the kid to worry about, the business, you. Mackensie's coming around, people are speculating about my father's morals over the fresh fruit at the supermarket, Seth's bitch of a mother's down in Norfolk—''

"Wait." She didn't move away this time, she yanked away. "Seth's mother has contacted you?"

"No. No." Jesus, his brain was on fire. "We hired a detective to track her down. Phillip figured we'd be better off knowing where she is, what she's up to."

"I see." Her heart broke in two halves, one for the woman, one for the professional. Both sides bled. "And she's in Norfolk, but you didn't bother to tell me that either."

"No, I didn't tell you." He'd backed himself into this corner, Cam realized. And there was no way out. "We only know she was there a couple of days ago."

"Social Services would expect to be notified of this information."

He kept his eyes on hers, nodded slowly. "I guess they just were. My mistake."

There was a line between them now, she realized, very thick and very darkly drawn. "Obviously you don't think very much of me—or of yourself, for that matter. Let me explain something to you. However I may be feeling about you on a personal level at this moment, it's my professional opinion that you and your brothers are the right guardians for Seth.''

"Okay, so—''

"I will have to take this information I've just learned into consideration,'' she continued. "It will have to be documented.''

"All that's going to do is screw things up for the kid.'' He hated the fact that his stomach clenched at the thought. Hated the idea that he might see that look of white-faced fear on Seth's face again. "I'm not going to let some sick gossip mess things up for him.''

"Well, on that we can agree.'' She'd gotten her wish on one level, Anna realized. She'd been around to see how much Seth would come to matter to him. Just long enough, she thought hollowly.

"It's my professional opinion that Seth is well cared for both physically and emotionally.'' Her voice was brisk now, professional. "He's happy and is beginning to feel secure. Added to that is the fact that he loves you, and you love him, though neither one of you may fully realize it. I still believe counseling would benefit all of you, and that, too, will go into my report and recommendation when the court rules on permanent guardianship. As I told you from the beginning, my concern—my primary concern—is the best welfare of the child.''

She was solidly behind them, Cam realized. And would have been no matter what he'd told her. Or hadn't told her. Guilt struck him a sharp, backhanded blow.

"I was never less than honest with you,'' she said before he could speak.

"Damn it, Anna—''

"I'm not through,'' she said coolly. "I have no doubt that you'll see Seth is well settled, and that this new business is secure before—as you put it—you turn your life back around. Which I assume means picking up your racing career in Europe. You'll have to find a way to juggle your needs, but that's not my concern. But there may come a time when the guardianship is contested, if indeed Seth's mother makes her way back here. At that time, the case file will be reevaluated. If he remains happy and well cared for under your guardianship, I'll do whatever I can to see to it that he remains with you. I'm on his side, which appears to put me on yours. That's all.''

Shame layered onto guilt, with a sprinkling of relief between. ''Anna, I know how much you've done. I'm grateful.''

She shook her head when he lifted a hand. ''I'm not feeling very friendly toward you at the moment. I don't want to be touched.''

''Fine. I won't touch you. Let's find somewhere to sit down and talk the rest of this out.''

''I thought we just had.''

''Now you're being stubborn.''

''No, now I'm being realistic. You slept with me, but you didn't trust me. The fact that I was honest with you and you weren't with me is my problem. The fact that I went to bed with a man who saw me as an enjoyment on one hand and an obstacle on the other is my mistake.''

''That's not the way it was.'' His temper began to rise again, pumped by a slick panic. ''That's not the way it is.''

''It's the way I see it. Now I need to take some time and see how I feel about that. I'd appreciate it if you'd drive me back to my car.''

She turned and walked away.

HE PREFERRED FIRE TO ice, but he couldn't break through the frigid shield she'd wrapped around her temper. It scared him, a sensation that he didn't appreciate. She was perfectly polite, even friendly, to Seth and Phillip when she returned to the house to gather her things.

She was perfectly polite to Cam—so polite that he imagined he would feel the chill of it for days.

He told himself it didn't matter. She'd get over it. She was just in a snit because he hadn't bared his soul, shared all the intimate details of his life with her. It was a woman thing.

After all, women had invented the cold shoulder just to make men feel like slugs.

He would give her a couple of days, he decided. Let her stew. Let her come to her senses. Then he would take her flowers.

"She's ticked off at you," Seth commented as Cam stood by the front door staring out.

"What do you know?"

"She's ticked off," Seth repeated, entertaining himself with his sketchbook while sitting cross-legged on the front porch. "She didn't let you kiss her good-bye, and you're all the time locking lips."

"Shut up."

"What'd you do?"

"I didn't do anything." Cam kicked the door open and stomped out. "She's just being female."

"You did something." Seth eyed him owlishly. "She's not a jerk."

"She'll get over it." Cam dropped down into the rocker. He wasn't going to worry about it. He never worried about women.

He LOST HIS APPETITE. How was he supposed to eat fried fish without remembering how he and Anna had sat on the dock that morning?

He couldn't sleep. How was he supposed to sleep in his own bed without remembering how they'd made love on those same sheets?

He couldn't concentrate on work. How was he supposed to detail diagonals without remembering how she'd beamed at him when he showed her the lofting platform?

By mid-morning, he gave up and drove to Princess

Anne. But he didn't take her flowers. Now *he* was ticked off.

He strode through the reception area, straight back into her office. Then fumed when he found it empty. Typical, was all he could think. His luck had turned all bad.

"Mr. Quinn." Marilou stood in the doorway, her hands folded. "Is there something I can do for you?"

"I'm looking for Anna—Ms. Spinelli."

"I'm sorry, she's not available."

"I'll wait."

"It'll be a long one. She won't be in until next week."

"Next week?" His narrowed eyes reminded Marilou of steel sharpened to the killing point. "What do you mean, she won't be in?"

"Ms. Spinelli is taking the week off." And Marilou figured the reason for it was even now boring holes through her with furious gray eyes. She'd thought the same when Anna had dropped off her report that morning and requested the time. "I'm familiar with the case file, if there's something I can do."

"No, it's personal. Where did she go?"

"I can't give you that information, Mr. Quinn, but you're free to leave a message, either a written one or one on her voice mail. Of course, if she checks in, I'll be happy to tell her you'd like to speak with her."

"Yeah, thanks."

He couldn't get out fast enough. She was probably in her apartment, he decided as he hopped back in his car. Sulking. So he would let her yell at him, get it all out of her system. Then he'd nudge her along to bed so they could put this ridiculous little episode behind them.

He ignored the nerves dancing in his stomach as he walked down the hall to her apartment. He knocked briskly, then tucked his hands into his pockets. He knocked louder, banged his fist on the door.

"Damn it, Anna. Open up. This is stupid. I saw your car out front."

The door behind him creaked open. One of the sisters

peered out. The jingling sound of a morning game show filled the hallway. "She not in there, Anna's Young Man."

"Her car's out front," he said.

"She took a cab."

He bit back an oath, pasted on a charming smile, and walked across the hall. "Where to?"

"To the train station—or maybe it was the airport." She beamed up at him. Really, he was such a handsome boy. "She said she'd be gone for a few days. She promised to call to make sure Sister and I were getting on. Such a sweet girl, thinking of us when she's on vacation."

"Vacation to . . ."

"Did she say?" The woman bit her lip and her eyes unfocused in thought. "I don't think she mentioned it. She was in an awful hurry, but she stopped by just the same so we wouldn't be worried. She's such a considerate girl."

"Yeah." The sweet, considerate girl had left him high and dry.

S HE'D HAD NO BUSINESS flying to Pittsburgh; the airfare had eaten a large hole in her budget. But she'd wanted to get there. Had needed to get there. The minute she walked into her grandparents' cramped row house, half her burden lifted.

"Anna Louisa!" Theresa Spinelli was a tiny, slim woman with steel-gray hair ruthlessly waved, a face that fell into dozens of comfortable wrinkles, and a smile as wide as the Mediterranean Sea. Anna had to bend low to be clasped and kissed. "Al, Al, our bambina's home."

"It's good to be home, Nana."

Alberto Spinelli hurried to the door. He was a foot taller than his wife's tidy five-three, with a broad chest and a spare tire that pressed cozily against Anna as they embraced. His hair was thin and white, his eyes dark and merry behind his thick glasses.

He all but carried her into the living room, where they could begin to fuss over her in earnest.

They spoke rapidly, and in a mix of Italian and English. Food was the first order of business. Theresa always thought her baby was starving. After they'd plied her with minestrone, and fresh bread and an enormous cube of tiramisu, Theresa was almost satisfied that her chick wouldn't perish of malnutrition.

"Now." Al sat back, puffing to life one of his thick cigars. "You'll tell us why you're here."

"Do I need a reason to come home?" Struggling to relax fully, Anna stretched out in one of a pair of ancient wing chairs. It had been recovered, she knew, countless times. Just now it was in a gay striped pattern, but the cushion still gave way beneath her butt like butter.

"You called three days ago. You didn't say you were coming home."

"It was an impulse. I've been swamped at work, up to my ears. I'm tired and wanted a break. I wanted to come home and eat Nana's cooking for a while."

It was true enough, if not the whole truth. She didn't think it would be wise to tell her doting grandparents that she'd walked into an affair, eyes wide open, and ended up with her heart broken.

"You work too hard," Theresa said. "Al, don't I tell you the girl works too hard?"

"She likes to work hard. She likes to use her brain. It's a good brain. Me, I've got a good brain, too, and I say she's not here just to eat your manicotti."

"Are we having manicotti for dinner?" Anna beamed, knowing it wouldn't distract them for long. They'd seen her through the worst, stuck by her when she'd done her best to hurt them, and herself. And they knew her.

"I started the sauce the minute you called to say you were coming. Al, don't nag the girl."

"I'm not nagging, I'm asking."

Theresa rolled her eyes. "If you have such a good brain in that big head of yours, you'd know it's a boy that sent

her running home. Is he Italian?'' Theresa demanded, fixing Anna with those bright bird eyes.

And she had to laugh. God, it was good to be home. ''I
have no idea, but he loves my red sauce.''

''Then he's got good taste. Why don't you bring him
home, let us get a look at him?''

''Because we're having some problems, and I need to
work them out.''

''Work them out?'' Theresa waved a hand. ''How do
you work them out when you're here and he's not? Is he
good-looking?''

''Gorgeous.''

''Does he have work?'' Al wanted to know.

''He's starting his own business—with his brothers.''

''Good, he knows family.'' Theresa nodded, pleased.
''You bring him next time, we'll see for ourselves.''

''All right,'' she said because it was easier to agree than
to explain. ''I'm going to go unpack.''

''He's hurt her heart,'' Theresa murmured when Anna
left the room.

Al reached over and patted her hand. ''It's a strong
heart.''

ANNA TOOK HER TIME,
hanging her clothes in the closet, folding them into the
drawers of the old dresser she'd used as a child. The room
was so much the same. The wallpaper had faded a bit. She
remembered that her grandfather had hung it himself, to
brighten the room when she'd come to live with them.

And she'd hated the pretty roses on the wall because
they looked so fresh and alive, and everything inside her
was dead.

But the roses were still there, a little older but still there.
As were her grandparents. She sat on the bed, hearing the
familiar creak of springs.

The familiar, the comforting, the secure.

That, she admitted, was what she wanted. Home, children, routine—with the surprises that family always provided thrown in. To some, she supposed, it would have sounded ordinary. At one time, she had told herself the same thing.

But she knew better now. Home, marriage, family. There was nothing ordinary there. The three elements formed a unit that was unique and precious.

She wanted, needed that, for herself.

Maybe she had been playing games after all. Maybe she hadn't been completely honest. Not with Cam, and not with herself. She hadn't tried to trap him into her dreams, but underneath it all, hadn't she begun to hope he'd share them? She'd maintained a front of casual, no-strings sex, but her heart had been reckless enough to yearn for more.

Maybe she deserved to have it broken.

The hell she did, she thought, springing up. She'd been making it enough, she'd accepted the limitations of their relationship. And still, he hadn't trusted her. That she wouldn't tolerate.

Damned if she'd take the blame for this, she decided, and stalking to the streaked mirror over her dresser, she began to freshen her makeup.

She would have what she wanted one day. A strong man who loved her, respected her, *and* trusted her. She would have a man who saw her as a partner, not as the enemy. She'd have that home in the country near the water, and children of her own, and a goddamn stupid dog if she wanted. She would have it all.

It just wouldn't be with Cameron Quinn.

If anything, she should thank him for opening her eyes, not only to the flaws in their so-called relationship but to her own needs and desires.

She would rather choke.

TWENTY

A WEEK COULD BE A
long time, Cam discovered. Particularly when you had a
great deal stuck in your craw that you couldn't spit out.

It helped that he'd been able to pick fights with both
Phillip and Ethan. But it wasn't quite the same as having
a showdown with Anna.

It helped, too, that beginning work on the hull of the
boat took so much of his time and concentration. He
couldn't afford to think about her when he was planking.

He thought of her anyway.

He'd had a few bad moments imagining her running
around on some Caribbean beach—in that little bikini—
and having some overmuscled, overtanned type rubbing
sunscreen on her back and buying her mai tais.

Then he'd told himself that she'd gone off somewhere
to lick her imaginary wounds and was probably in some
hotel room, drapes drawn, sniffing into a hankie.

But that image didn't make him feel any better.

When he got home from a full Saturday at the boatyard,
he was ready for a beer. Maybe two. He and Ethan headed
straight for the refrigerator and had already popped tops
when Phillip came in.

"Seth isn't with you?"

"Over at Danny's." Cam guzzled from the bottle to wash the sawdust out of his throat. "Sandy's dropping him off later."

"Good." Phillip got a beer for himself. "Sit down."

"What?"

"I got a letter from the insurance company this morning." Phillip pulled out a chair. "The gist is, they're stalling. They used a bunch of legal terms, cited clauses, but the upshot is they're casting doubt on cause of death and are continuing to investigate."

"Fuck that. Cheapscate bastards just don't want to shell out." Annoyed, Cam kicked out a chair—and wished with all his heart it had been Mackensie.

"I talked to our lawyer," Phil continued, grimacing. "He may start rethinking our friendship if I keep calling him on weekends. He says we have some choices. We can sit tight, let the insurance company continue its investigation, or we can file suit against them for nonpayment of claim."

"Let them keep their fucking money, I don't want it anyway."

"No." Ethan spoke quietly in the echo of Cam's outburst. He continued to brood into his beer, shaking his head. "It's not right. Dad paid the premiums, year after year. He added to the policy for Seth. It's not right that they don't pay. And if they don't pay, it's going to go down somewhere that he killed himself. That's not right either. They've been doing all the pushing up to now," he added and raised his somber eyes. "Let's push back."

"If it ends up going to court," Phillip warned him, "it could get messy."

"So we turn away from a fight because it could get messy?" For the first time, amusement flickered over Ethan's face. "Well, fuck that."

"Cam?"

Cam sipped again. "I've been wanting a good fight for a while. I guess this is it."

"Then we're agreed. We'll have the papers drawn up next week, and we'll go after their asses." Revved and ready, Phillip lifted his bottle. "Here's to a good fight."

"Here's to winning," Cam corrected.

"I'm for that. It's going to cost us some," Phillip added. "Filing fees, legal fees. Most of the capital we've pooled is sunk into the business." He blew out a breath. "I guess we need another pool."

With less regret than he'd expected, Cam thought of his beloved Porsche waiting patiently for him in Nice. Just a car, he told himself. Just a damn car. "I can get my hands on some fresh cash. It'll take a couple of days."

"I can sell my house." Ethan shrugged his shoulders. "I've had some people asking about it, and it's just sitting there."

"No." The thought of it twisted in Cam's gut. "You're not selling your house. Rent it out. We'll get through this."

"I've got some stocks." Phillip sighed and waved good-bye to a chunk of his growing portfolio. "I'll tell my broker to cash them in. We'll open a joint account next week—the Quinn Legal Defense Fund."

The three of them managed weak smiles.

"The kid ought to know," Ethan said after a moment. "If we're going to take this to the wall, he ought to know what's going on."

Cam looked up in time to see both of his brothers' eyes focus on him. "Oh, come on. Why does it have to be me?"

"You're the oldest." Phillip grinned at him. "Besides, it'll take your mind off Anna."

"I'm not brooding about her—or any woman."

"Been edgy and broody all week," Ethan mumbled. "Making me nuts."

"Who asked you? We had a little disagreement, that's all. I'm giving her time to simmer down."

"Seems to me she'd simmered down to frozen the last

time I saw her.'' Phillip examined his beer. ''That was a week ago.''

''It's my business how I handle a woman.''

''Sure is. But let me know when you're done with her, will you? She's—''

Phillip broke off when Cam all but leaped over the table and grabbed him by the throat. Beer bottles flew and shattered on the floor.

Resigned, Ethan raked his hand through his hair, scattering drops of spilled beer. Cam and Phillip were on the floor, pounding hell out of each other. He got himself a fresh beer before filling a pitcher with cold water.

His work boots crunched over broken glass, which he kicked out of the way in hopes that he wouldn't have to run anybody to the hospital for stitches. With malice toward neither, he emptied the pitcher on both his brothers.

It got their attention.

Phillip's lip was split, Cam's ribs throbbed, and both of them were bleeding from rolling around on broken glass. Drenched and panting, they eyed each other warily. Gingerly, Phillip wiped a knuckle over his bloody lip.

''Sorry. Bad joke. I didn't know things were serious between you.''

''I never said they were serious.''

Phillip laughed, then winced as his lip wept. ''Brother, did you ever. I guess I never figured you'd be the first of us to fall in love with a woman.''

The stomach that Phillip's fists had abused jittered wildly. ''Who said I'm in love with her?''

''You didn't punch me in the face because you're in like.'' He looked down at his pleated slacks. ''Shit. Do you know how hard it is to get bloodstains out of a cotton blend?'' He rose, held out a hand to Cam. ''She's a terrific lady,'' he said as he hauled Cam to his feet. ''Hope you work it out.''

''I don't have to work out anything,'' Cam said desperately. ''You're way off here.''

''If you say so. I'm going to get cleaned up.''

He headed out, limping only a little.

"I ain't mopping the damn floor," Ethan stated, "because your glands got in an uproar."

"He started it," Cam muttered, not caring how ridiculous it sounded.

"No, I figure you did, with whatever you did to piss Anna off." Ethan opened the broom closet, took out a mop, and tossed it to Cam. "Now I guess you got to clean it up."

He slipped out the back door.

"The two of you think you know so goddamn much." Furious, he kicked a chair over on his way to fetch a bucket. "I ought to know what's going on in my own life. Insanity, that's what. I should be in Australia, prepping for the race of my life, that's where I should be."

He dragged the mop through water, beer, glass, and blood, muttering to himself. "Australia's just where I'd be if I had any sense left. Damn woman's complicating things. Better off just cutting loose there."

He kicked over another chair because it felt good, then shook shards of glass from the mop into the bucket.

"Who had a fight?" Seth wanted to know.

Cam turned and narrowed his eyes at the boy standing in the doorway. "I kicked Phillip's ass."

"What for?"

"Because I wanted to."

With a nod, Seth walked around the puddle and got a Pepsi out of the fridge. "If you kicked his ass, how come you're bleeding?"

"Maybe I like to bleed." He finished mopping up while the boy stood watching him. "What's your problem?" Cam demanded.

"I got no problem."

Cam shoved the bucket aside with his foot. The least Phillip could do was empty it somewhere. He went to the sink and bad-temperedly picked glass out of his arm. Then he got out the whiskey, righted a chair, and sat down with the bottle and a glass.

He saw Seth's eyes slide over the bottle and away. Deliberately Cam poured two fingers of Johnnie Walker into a glass. "Not everybody who drinks gets drunk," he said. "Not everybody who gets drunk—as I may decide to do—knocks kids around."

"Don't know why anybody drinks that shit anyway."

Cam knocked back the whiskey. "Because we're weak, and stupid, and it feels good at the time."

"Are you going to Australia?"

Cam poured another shot. "Doesn't look like it."

"I don't care if you go. I don't care where the hell you go." The underlying fury in the boy's voice surprised them both. Flushing, Seth turned and raced out the door.

Well, hell, Cam thought and shoved the whiskey aside. He pushed away from the table and hit the door as Seth streaked across the yard to the woods.

"Hold it!" When that didn't slow the boy down, Cam put some mean into it. "Goddamn it, I said hold it!"

This time Seth skidded to a halt. When he turned around, they stared at each other across the expanse of grass, temper and nerves vibrating from them in all but visible waves.

"Get your butt back over here. Now."

He came, fists clenched, chin jutting out. They both knew he had nowhere to run. "I don't need you."

"Oh, the hell you don't. I ought to kick your ass for being stupid. Everybody says you've got some genius brain in there, but if you ask me you're dumb as dirt. Now sit down. There," he added, jabbing a finger at the steps. "And if you don't do what I tell you when I tell you, I might just kick your ass after all."

"You don't scare me," Seth said, but he sat.

"I scare you white, and that gives me the hammer." Cam sat as well, watched the puppy come crawling toward them on his belly. And I scare little dogs too, he thought in disgust. "I'm not going anywhere," he began.

"I said I don't care."

"Fine, but I'm telling you anyway. I figured I would,

once everything settled down. I told myself I would. I guess I needed to. Never figured on coming back here to stay."

"Then why don't you go?"

Cam gave him a halfhearted boot on the top of his head with the heel of one hand. "Why don't you shut up until I say what I have to say?"

The painless smack and impatient order were more comforting to Seth than a thousand promises.

"I've been coming to the fact that I've been running long enough. I liked what I was doing while I was doing it, but I guess I'm pretty well finished with it. It looks like I've got a place here, and a business here, maybe a woman here," he murmured, thinking of Anna.

"So you're staying to work and poke at a girl."

"Those are damn good reasons for hanging in one place. Then there's you." Cam leaned back on the upper steps, bracing with his elbows. "I can't say I cared much for you when I first came back. There's that crappy attitude of yours, and you're ugly, but you kind of grow on a guy."

Immensely cheered, Seth snickered. "You're uglier."

"I'm bigger, I'm entitled. So I guess I'll hang around to see if you get any prettier as time goes on."

"I didn't really want you to go," Seth said under his breath after a long moment. It was the closest he could get to speaking his heart.

"I know." Cam sighed. "Now that we've got that settled, we've got this other thing. Nothing to worry about, it's just some legal bullshit. Phil and the lawyer'll handle most of it, but there might be some talk. You shouldn't pay any attention to it if you hear it."

"What kind of talk?"

"Some people—some idiots—think Dad aimed for that pole. Killed himself."

"Yeah, and now this asshole from the insurance company's asking questions."

Cam hissed out a breath. He knew he should probably

tell the kid not to call adults assholes, but there were bigger issues here. "You knew that?"

"Sure, it goes around. He talked to Danny and Will's mother. Danny said she gave him an earful. She didn't like some guy coming around asking questions about Ray. That butthead Chuck up at the Dairy Queen told the detective guy that Ray was screwing around with his students, then had a crisis of conscience and killed himself."

"Crisis of conscience." Jesus, where did the kid come up with this stuff? "Chuck Kimball? He always was a butthead. Word is he got caught cheating on a lit exam and got booted out of college. And it seems to me Phillip beat the crap out of him once. Can't remember why, though."

"He's got a face like a carp."

Cam laughed. "Yeah, I guess he does. Dad—Ray— never touched a student, Seth."

"He was square with me." And that counted for everything. "My mother . . ."

"Go ahead," Cam prompted.

"She told me he was my father. But another time she said this other guy was, and once when she was really loaded she said my old man was some guy named Keith Richards."

Cam couldn't help it, the laugh just popped out. "Jesus, now she's hitting on the Stones?"

"Who?"

"I'll see to your music education later."

"I don't know if Ray was my father." Seth looked up. "She's a liar, so I don't go with anything she said, but he took me. I know he gave her money, a lot of it. I don't know if he'd have told me if he was. He said there were things we had to talk about, but he had stuff to work out first. I know you don't want him to be."

It couldn't matter, Cam realized. Not anymore. "Do you want him to be?"

"He was decent," the boy said so simply that Cam

draped an arm around his shoulders. And Seth leaned against him.

"Yeah, he was."

EVERYTHING HAD CHAN- ged. Everything was different. And he was desperate to tell her. Cam knew his life had turned on its axis yet again. And somehow he'd ended up exactly where he needed to be.

The only thing missing was Anna.

He took a chance and drove to her apartment. It was Saturday night, he thought. She was due back at work on Monday. She was a practical woman and would want to take Sunday to catch up, sort her laundry, answer her mail. Whatever.

If she wasn't home, he was going to by God sit on her doorstep until she got there.

But when she answered his knock and stood there looking so fresh, so gorgeous, he was caught off balance.

Anna, on the other hand, had prepared for this meeting all week. She knew exactly how she would handle it. "Cam, this is a surprise. You just caught me."

"Caught you?" he said stupidly.

"Yes, but I've got a few minutes. Would you like to come in?"

"Yeah, I—where the hell have you been?"

She lifted her brows. "Excuse me?"

"You took off, out of the blue."

"I wouldn't say that. I arranged leave from work, checked in with my neighbors, had my plants watered while I was gone. I was hardly abducted by aliens, I simply took a few days of personal time. Do you want some coffee?"

"No." Okay, he thought, she was going to keep playing it cool. He could do that. "I want to talk to you."

"That's good, because I want to talk to you, too. How's Seth?"

"He's fine. Really. We got a lot of things ironed out. Just today—"

"What have you done to your arm?"

Impatient, he glanced down at the raw nicks and scrapes. "Nothing. It's nothing. Listen, Anna—"

"Why don't you sit down? I'd really like to apologize if I was hard on you last weekend."

"Apologize?" Well, that was more like it. Willing to be forgiving, he sat on the sofa. "Why don't we just forget it? I've got a lot to tell you."

"I'd really like to clear this up." Smiling pleasantly, she sat across from him. "I suppose we were both in a difficult position. A great deal of that was my fault. Becoming involved with you was a calculated risk. But I was attracted and didn't weigh the potential problems as carefully as I should have. Obviously something like last weekend's disagreement was bound to happen. And as we both have Seth's interests at heart, and will continue to, I would hate for us to be at odds."

"Good, then we won't." He reached for her hand, but she evaded his gesture and merely patted his.

"Now that that's settled, you really have to excuse me. I hate to rush you along, Cam, but I have a date."

"A what?"

"A date." She glanced at the watch on her wrist. "Shortly, as it happens, and I have to change."

Very slowly he got to his feet. "You have a date? Tonight? What the hell is that supposed to mean?"

"What it generally does." She blinked twice, as if confused, then let her eyes fill with apology. "Oh, I'm sorry. I thought we both understood that we'd ended the . . . well, the more personal aspect of our relationship. I assumed it was clear that it wasn't working out for either of us."

It felt as though someone had blown past his guard and rammed an iron fist into his solar plexus. "Look, if you're still pissed off—"

"Do I look pissed off?" she asked coolly.

"No." He stared at her, shaking his head while his

stomach did a quick pitch and roll. "No, you don't. You're dumping me."

"Don't be melodramatic. We're simply ending an affair that both of us entered freely and without promises or expectations. It was good while it lasted, really good. I'd hate to spoil that. Now as far as our professional relationship goes, I've told you that I'll do all I can to support your permanent guardianship of Seth. However, I do expect you to be more forthcoming with information from now on. I'll also be happy to consult with you or advise you on any area of that guardianship. You and your brothers are doing a marvelous job with him."

He waited, certain there would be more. "That's it?"

"I can't think of anything else—and I am a little pressed for time."

"You're pressed for time." She'd just stabbed him dead center of the heart, and she was pressed for time. "That's too damn bad, because I'm not finished."

"I'm sorry if your ego's bruised."

"Yeah, my ego's bruised. I got a lot of bruises right now. How the hell can you stand there and brush me off after what we had together?"

"We had great sex. I'm not denying it. We're just not going to have it any longer."

"Sex?" He grabbed her arms and shook her, and had the small satisfaction of seeing a flash of anger heat through the chill in her eyes. "That's all it was for you?"

"That's what it was for both of us." It wasn't going the way she'd planned. She'd expected him to be angry and storm out. Or to be relieved that she'd backed away first and walk away whistling. But he wasn't supposed to confront her like this. "Let go of me."

"The hell I will. I've been half crazy for you to get back. You turned my life upside down, and I'll be damned if you'll just stroll away because you're through with me."

"We're through with each other. I don't want you anymore, and it's your bad luck I said it first. Now take your hands off me."

He released her as if her skin had burned his palms. There'd been a hitch in her voice, a suspicious one. "What makes you think I'd have said it at all?"

"We don't want the same things. We were going nowhere, and I'm not going to keep heading there, no matter how I feel about you."

"How do you feel about me?"

"Tired of you!" she shouted. "Tired of me, tired of us. Sick and tired of telling myself fun and games could be enough. Well, it's not. Not nearly, and I want you out."

He felt the temper and panic that had gripped him ease back into delight. "You're in love with me, aren't you?"

He'd never seen a woman go from simmer to boil so fast. And seeing it, he wondered why it had taken him so long to realize he adored her. She whirled, grabbed a lamp, and hurled it.

He gave her credit for aim and gave thanks that he was light on his feet, as the base whistled by his head before it crashed into the wall.

"You arrogant, conceited, cold-blooded son of a bitch." She grabbed a vase now, a new one she'd bought on the way home to cheer herself up. She let it fly.

"Jesus, Anna." It was admiration, pure and simple, that burst through him as he was forced to catch the vase before it smashed into his face. "You must be nuts about me."

"I despise you." She looked frantically for something else to throw at him and snagged a bowl of fruit off the kitchen counter. The fruit went first. Apples. "Loathe you." Pears. "Hate you." Bananas. "I can't believe I ever let you touch me." Then the bowl. But she was more clever this time, feinted first, then heaved in the direction of his dodge.

The stoneware caught him just above the ear and had stars spinning in front of his eyes.

"Okay, game over." He made a dive for her, caught her around the waist. His already abused body suffered from kicks and punches, but he hauled her to the couch

and held her down. "Get ahold of yourself before you kill
me."

"I want to kill you," she said between gritted teeth.

"Believe me, I get the picture."

"You don't get anything." She bucked under him and
sent his system into a tangled mess of lust and laughter.
Sensing both, she reared up and bit him, hard.

"Ouch. Goddamn it. Okay, that's it." He dragged her
up and threw her over his shoulder. "You still packed?
Tells me she's got a damn date. Like hell she does. Tells
me we're finished. What bullshit." He marched her into
the bedroom, saw her bag on the bed, and grabbed it.

"What are you doing? Put me down. Put that down."

"I'm not letting loose of either until we're in Vegas."

"Vegas? Las Vegas?" She thudded both fists on his
back. "I'm not going anywhere with you, much less Vegas."

"That's exactly where we're going. It's the quickest
place to get married, and I'm in a hurry."

"And how the hell do you expect to get me on a plane
when I'm screaming my lungs out? I'll have you in jail in
five minutes flat."

At his wits' end because she was inflicting considerable
damage, he dumped her at the front door and held her
arms. "We're getting married, and that's the end of it."

"You can just—" Her body sagged, and her head
reeled. "Married?" The word finally pierced her temper.
"You don't want to get married."

"Believe me, I've been rethinking the idea since you
beaned me with the fruit bowl. Now, are you going to
come along reasonably, or do I have to sedate you?"

"Please let me go."

"Anna." He lowered his brow to hers. "Don't ask me
to do that, because I don't think I can live without you.
Take a chance, roll the dice. Come with me."

"You're angry and you're hurt," she said shakily.
"And you think rushing off to Vegas to have some wild,
plastic-coated instant marriage is going to fix everything."

He framed her face, gently now. Tears were shimmering in her eyes, and he knew he'd be on his knees if she let them spill over. "You can't tell me you don't love me. I won't believe you."

"Oh, I'm in love with you, Cam, but I'll survive it. There are things I need. I had to be honest with myself and admit that. You broke my heart."

"I know." He pressed his lips to her forehead. "I know I did. I was shortsighted, I was selfish, I was stupid. And damn it, I was scared. Of me, of you, of everything that was going on around me. I messed it up, and now you don't want to give me another chance."

"It's not a matter of chances. It's a matter of being practical enough to admit that we want different things."

"I finally figured out today what it is I want. Tell me what you want."

"I want a home."

He had one for her, he thought.

"I want marriage."

Hadn't he just asked her?

"I want children."

"How many?"

Her tears dried up, and she shoved at him. "It isn't a joke."

"I'm not joking. I was thinking two with an option for three." His mouth quirked at the look of blank-eyed shock on her face. "There, now *you're* getting scared because you're beginning to realize I'm serious."

"You—you're going back to Rome, or wherever, as soon as you can."

"*We* can go to Rome, or wherever, on our honeymoon. We're not taking the kid. I draw the line there. I might like to get in a couple of races from time to time. Just to keep my hand in. But basically I'm in the boat building business. Of course, it might go belly-up. Then you'd be stuck with a househusband who really hates housework."

She wanted to press her fingers to her temples, but he still had her by the arms. "I can't think."

"Good. Just listen. You cut a hole in me when you left, Anna. I wouldn't admit it, but it was there. Big and empty."

He rested his brow on hers for a moment. "You know what I did today? I worked on building a boat. And it felt good. I came home, the only home I've ever had, and it felt right. Had a family meeting and decided that we'd take on the insurance company and do what's right for our father. By the way, I've been talking to him."

She couldn't stop staring at him, even though her head was reeling. "What? Who?"

"My father. Had some conversations with him—three of them—since he died. He looks good."

Her breath was clogged right at the base of her throat. "Cam."

"Yeah, yeah," he said with a quick grin. "I need counseling. We can talk about that later—didn't mean to get off the track. I was telling you what I did today, right?"

Very slowly she nodded. "Yes."

"Okay, after the meeting, Phil made some smart remark, so I punched him, and we beat on each other for a bit. That felt good too. Then I talked to Seth about the things I should have talked to him about before, and I listened to him the way I should have listened before, then we just sat for a while. That felt good, Anna, and it felt right."

Her lips curved. "I'm glad."

"There's more. I knew when I was sitting there that that was where I wanted to be, needed to be. Only one thing was missing, and that was you. So I came to find you and take you back." He pressed his lips gently to her forehead. "To take you home, Anna."

"I think I want to sit down."

"No, I want your knees weak when I tell you I love you. Are you ready?"

"Oh, God."

"I've been real careful never to tell a woman I loved her—except my mother. I didn't tell her often enough.

Take a chance on me, Anna, and I'll tell you as often as you can stand hearing it.''

She hitched in a breath. "I'm not getting married in Vegas.''

"Spoilsport.'' He watched her lips bow up before he closed his over them. And the taste of her soothed every ache in his body and soul. "God, I missed you. Don't go away again.''

"It brought you to your senses.'' She wrapped her arms tight around him. And it felt good, she thought giddily. It felt right. "Oh, Cam, I want to hear it, right now.''

"I love you. It feels so damn perfect loving you. I can't believe I wasted so much time.''

"Less than three months,'' she reminded him.

"Too much time. But we'll make it up.''

"I want you to take me home,'' she murmured. "After.''

He eased back, cocked his head. "After what?'' Then he made her laugh by lifting her into his arms.

He picked his way through the wreckage, kicked a very sad-looking banana out of the way. "You know, I can't figure out why I used to think marriage would be boring.''

"Ours won't be.'' She kissed his bruised head. It was still bleeding a little. "Promise.''

Can't get enough of Nora Roberts?
Try the #1 *New York Times* bestselling
In Death series, by Nora Roberts
writing as J. D. Robb.

Turn the page to see where it all began . . .

NAKED IN DEATH

SHE WOKE IN THE DARK. Through the slats on the window shades, the first murky hint of dawn slipped, slanting shadowy bars over the bed. It was like waking in a cell.

For a moment she simply lay there, shuddering, imprisoned, while the dream faded. After ten years on the force, Eve still had dreams.

Six hours before, she'd killed a man, had watched death creep into his eyes. It wasn't the first time she'd exercised maximum force, or dreamed. She'd learned to accept the action and the consequences.

But it was the child that haunted her. The child she hadn't been in time to save. The child whose screams had echoed in the dreams with her own.

All the blood, Eve thought, scrubbing sweat from her face with her hands. Such a small little girl to have had so much blood in her. And she knew it was vital that she push it aside.

333

Standard departmental procedure meant that she would spend the morning in Testing. Any officer whose discharge of weapon resulted in termination of life was required to undergo emotional and psychiatric clearance before resuming duty. Eve considered the tests a mild pain in the ass.

She would beat them, as she'd beaten them before.

When she rose, the overheads went automatically to low setting, lighting her way into the bath. She winced once at her reflection. Her eyes were swollen from lack of sleep, her skin nearly as pale as the corpses she'd delegated to the ME.

Rather than dwell on it, she stepped into the shower, yawning.

"Give me one oh one degrees, full force," she said and shifted so that the shower spray hit her straight in the face.

She let it steam, lathered listlessly while she played through the events of the night before. She wasn't due in Testing until nine, and would use the next three hours to settle and let the dream fade away completely.

Small doubts and little regrets were often detected and could mean a second and more intense round with the machines and the owl-eyed technicians who ran them.

Eve didn't intend to be off the streets longer than twenty-four hours.

After pulling on a robe, she walked into the kitchen and programmed her AutoChef for coffee, black; toast, light. Through her window she could hear the heavy hum of air traffic carrying early commuters to offices, late ones home. She'd chosen the apartment years before because it was in a heavy ground and air pattern, and she liked the noise and crowds. On another yawn, she glanced out the window, followed the rattling journey of an aging airbus hauling laborers not fortunate enough to work in the city or by home 'links.

She brought the *New York Times* up on her monitor and scanned the headlines while the faux caffeine bolstered her system. The AutoChef had burned her toast again, but she ate it anyway, with a vague thought of springing for a replacement unit.

She was frowning over an article on a mass recall of droid cocker spaniels when her telelink blipped. Eve shifted to communications and watched her commanding officer flash onto the screen.

"Commander."

"Lieutenant." He gave her a brisk nod, noted the still-wet hair and sleepy eyes. "Incident at Twenty-seven West Broadway, eighteenth floor. You're primary."

Eve lifted a brow. "I'm on Testing. Subject terminated at twenty-two thirty-five."

"We have override," he said, without inflection. "Pick up your shield and weapon on the way to the incident. Code Five, Lieutenant."

"Yes, sir." His face flashed off even as she pushed back from the screen. Code Five meant she would report directly to her commander, and there would be no unsealed interdepartmental reports and no cooperation with the press.

In essence, it meant she was on her own.

BROADWAY WAS NOISY and crowded, a party that rowdy guests never left. Street, pedestrian, and sky traffic were miserable, choking the air with bodies and vehicles. In her old days in uniform she remembered it as a hot spot for wrecks and crushed tourists who were too busy gaping at the show to get out of the way.

Even at this hour steam was rising from the stationary and portable food stands that offered everything from rice noodles to soy dogs for the teeming crowds. She had to swerve to avoid an eager merchant on his smoking Glida-Grill, and took his flipped middle finger as a matter of course.

Eve double-parked and, skirting a man who smelled worse than his bottle of brew, stepped onto the sidewalk. She scanned the building first, fifty floors of gleaming metal that knifed into the sky from a hilt of concrete. She was propositioned twice before she reached the door.

Since this five-block area of West Broadway was affectionately termed Prostitute's Walk, she wasn't surprised. She flashed her badge for the uniform guarding the entrance.

"Lieutenant Dallas."

"Yes, sir." He skimmed his official CompuSeal over the door to keep out the curious, then led the way to the bank of elevators. "Eighteenth floor," he said when the doors swished shut behind them.

"Fill me in, Officer." Eve switched on her recorder and waited.

"I wasn't first on the scene, Lieutenant. Whatever happened upstairs is being kept upstairs. There's a badge inside waiting for you. We have a homicide, and a Code Five in number eighteen-oh-three."

"Who called it in?"

"I don't have that information."

He stayed where he was when the elevator opened. Eve stepped out and was alone in a narrow hallway. Security cameras tilted down at her, and her feet were almost soundless on the worn nap of the carpet as she approached 1803. Ignoring the hand plate, she announced herself, holding her badge up to eye level for the peep cam until the door opened.

"Dallas."

"Feeney." She smiled, pleased to see a familiar face. Ryan Feeney was an old friend and former partner who'd traded the street for a desk and a top-level position in the Electronics Detection Division. "So, they're sending computer pluckers these days."

"They wanted brass, and the best." His lips curved in his wide, rumpled face, but his eyes remained sober. He was a small, stubby man with small, stubby hands and rust-colored hair. "You look beat."

"Rough night."

"So I heard." He offered her one of the sugared nuts from the bag he habitually carried, studying her, and measuring if she was up to what was waiting in the bedroom beyond.

She was young for her rank, barely thirty, with wide brown eyes that had never had a chance to be naive. Her doe-brown hair was cropped short, for convenience rather than style, but suited her triangular face with its razor-edge cheekbones and slight dent in the chin.

She was tall, rangy, with a tendency to look thin, but Feeney knew there were solid muscles beneath the leather jacket. But Eve had more—there was also a brain, and a heart.

"This one's going to be touchy, Dallas."

"I picked that up already. Who's the victim?"

"Sharon DeBlass, granddaughter of Senator DeBlass."

Neither meant anything to her. "Politics isn't my forte, Feeney."

"The gentleman from Virginia, extreme right, old money. The granddaughter took a sharp left a few years back, moved to New York and became a licensed companion."

"She was a hooker." Dallas glanced around the apartment. It was furnished in obsessive modern—glass and thin chrome, signed holograms on the walls, recessed bar in bold red. The wide mood screen behind the bar bled with mixing and merging shapes and colors in cool pastels.

Neat as a virgin, Eve mused, and cold as a whore. "No surprise, given her choice of real estate."

"Politics makes it delicate. Victim was twenty-four, Caucasian female. She bought it in bed."

Eve only lifted a brow. "Seems poetic, since she'd been bought there. How'd she die?"

"That's the next problem. I want you to see for yourself."

As they crossed the room, each took out a slim container, sprayed their hands front and back to seal in oils and fingerprints. At the doorway, Eve sprayed the bottom of her boots to slicken them so that she would pick up no fibers, stray hairs, or skin.

Eve was already wary. Under normal circumstances there would have been two other investigators on a homicide scene, with recorders for sound and pictures. Forensics would have been waiting with their usual snarly impatience to sweep the scene.

The fact that only Feeney had been assigned with her meant that there were a lot of eggshells to be walked over.

"Security cameras in the lobby, elevator, and hallways," Eve commented.

"I've already tagged the discs." Feeney opened the bedroom door and let her enter first.

It wasn't pretty. Death rarely was a peaceful, religious experience to Eve's mind. It was the nasty end, indifferent to saint and sinner. But this was shocking, like a stage deliberately set to offend.

The bed was huge, slicked with what appeared to be genuine satin sheets the color of ripe peaches. Small, soft-focused spotlights were trained on its center where the naked woman was cupped in the gentle dip of the floating mattress.

The mattress moved with obscenely graceful undulations to the rhythm of programmed music slipping through the headboard.

She was beautiful still, a cameo face with a tumbling waterfall of flaming red hair, emerald eyes that stared glassily at the mirrored ceiling, long, milk-white limbs that called to mind visions of *Swan Lake* as the motion of the bed gently rocked them.

They weren't artistically arranged now, but spread lewdly so that the dead woman formed a final X dead-center of the bed.

There was a hole in her forehead, one in her chest, another horribly gaping between the open thighs. Blood had splattered on the glossy sheets, pooled, dripped, and stained.

There were splashes of it on the lacquered walls, like lethal paintings scrawled by an evil child.

So much blood was a rare thing, and she had seen much too much of it the night before to take the scene as calmly as she would have preferred.

She had to swallow once, hard, and force herself to block out the image of a small child.

"You got the scene on record?"

"Yep."

"Then turn that damn thing off." She let out a breath after Feeney located the controls that silenced the music. The bed flowed to stillness. "The wounds," Eve murmured, stepping closer to examine them. "Too neat for a knife. Too messy for a laser." A flash came to her—old training films, old videos, old viciousness.

"Christ, Feeney, these look like bullet wounds."

Feeney reached into his pocket and drew out a sealed bag. "Whoever did it left a souvenir." He passed the bag to Eve. "An antique like this has to go for eight, ten thousand for a legal collection, twice that on the black market."

Fascinated, Eve turned the sealed revolver over in her hand. "It's heavy," she said half to herself. "Bulky."

"Thirty-eight caliber," he told her. "First one I've seen outside of a museum. This one's a Smith and Wesson, Model Ten, blue steel." He looked at it with some affection. "Real classic piece, used to be standard police issue until the latter part of the twentieth. They stopped making them in about twenty-two, twenty-three, when the gun ban was passed."

"You're the history buff." Which explained why he was with her. "Looks new." She sniffed through the bag, caught the scent of oil and burning. "Somebody took good care of this. Steel fired into flesh," she mused as she passed the bag back to Feeney. "Ugly way to die, and the first I've seen it in my ten years with the department."

"Second for me. About fifteen years ago, Lower East Side, party got out of hand. Guy shot five people with a twenty-two before he realized it wasn't a toy. Hell of a mess."

"Fun and games," Eve murmured. "We'll scan the collectors, see how many we can locate who own one like this. Somebody might have reported a robbery."

"Might have."

"It's more likely it came through the black market." Eve glanced back at the body. "If she's been in the business for a few years, she'd have discs, records of her clients, her trick books." She frowned. "With Code Five, I'll have to do the door-to-door myself. Not a simple sex crime," she said with a sigh. "Whoever did it set it up. The antique weapon, the wounds themselves, almost ruler-straight down the body, the lights, the pose. Who called it in, Feeney?"

"The killer." He waited until her eyes came back to him. "From right here. Called the station. See how the bedside unit's aimed at her face? That's what came in. Video, no audio."

"He's into showmanship." Eve let out a breath. "Clever bastard, arrogant, cocky. He had sex with her first. I'd bet my badge on it. Then he gets up and does it." She lifted her arm, aiming, lowering it as she counted off, "One, two, three."

"That's cold," murmured Feeney.

"He's cold. He smooths down the sheets after. See how neat they are? He arranges her, spreads her open so nobody can have any doubts as to how she made her living. He does it carefully, practically measuring, so that she's perfectly aligned. Center of the bed, arms and legs equally apart. Doesn't turn off the bed 'cause it's part of the show. He leaves the gun because he wants us to know right away he's no ordinary man. He's got an ego. He doesn't want to waste time letting the body be discovered eventually. He wants it now. That instant gratification."

"She was licensed for men and women," Feeney pointed out, but Eve shook her head.

"It's not a woman. A woman wouldn't have left her looking both beautiful and obscene. No, I don't think it's a woman. Let's see what we can find. Have you gone into her computer yet?"

"No. It's your case, Dallas. I'm only authorized to assist."

"See if you can access her client files." Eve went to the dresser and began to carefully search drawers.

Expensive taste, Eve reflected. There were several items of real silk, the kind no simulation could match. The bottle of scent on the dresser was exclusive, and smelled, after a quick sniff, like expensive sex.

The contents of the drawers were meticulously ordered, lingerie folded precisely, sweaters arranged according to color and material. The closet was the same.

Obviously the victim had a love affair with clothes and a taste for the best and took scrupulous care of what she owned.

And she'd died naked.

"Kept good records," Feeney called out. "It's all here. Her client list, appointments—including her required monthly health exam and her weekly trip to the beauty salon. She used the Trident Clinic for the first and Paradise for the second."

"Both top-of-the-line. I've got a friend who saved for a year so she could have one day for the works at Paradise. Takes all kinds."

"My wife's sister went for it for her twenty-fifth anniversary. Cost damn near as much as my kid's wedding. Hello, we've got her personal address book."

"Good. Copy all of it, will you, Feeney?" At his low whistle, she looked over her shoulder, glimpsed the small gold-edged palm computer in his hand. "What?"

"We've got a lot of high-powered names in here. Politics, entertainment, money, money, money. Interesting, our girl has Roarke's private number."

"Roarke who?"

"Just Roarke, as far as I know. Big money there. Kind of guy that touches shit and turns it into gold bricks. You've got to start reading more than the sports page, Dallas."

"Hey, I read the headlines. Did you hear about the cocker spaniel recall?"

"Roarke's always big news," Feeney said patiently. "He's got one of the finest art collections in the world. Arts and antiques," he continued, noting when Eve clicked in and turned to him. "He's a licensed gun collector. Rumor is he knows how to use them."

"I'll pay him a visit."

"You'll be lucky to get within a mile of him."

"I'm feeling lucky." Eve crossed over to the body to slip her hands under the sheets.

"The man's got powerful friends, Dallas. You can't afford to so much as whisper he's linked to this until you've got something solid."

"Feeney, you know it's a mistake to tell me that." But even as she started to smile, her fingers brushed against something between cold flesh and bloody sheets. "There's something under her." Carefully, Eve lifted the shoulder, eased her fingers over.

"Paper," she murmured. "Sealed." With her protected thumb, she wiped at a smear of blood until she could read the protected sheet.

ONE OF SIX

"It looks hand-printed," she said to Feeney and held it out. "Our boy's more than clever, more than arrogant. And he isn't finished."

Welcome to Nora Roberts's captivating saga about the lives and loves of a family on the windswept shores of the Chesapeake Bay.

Cameron, Ethan, Phillip, and Seth are four brothers bound by the love of the extraordinary couple who raised them. Now grown and living on their own, the oldest Quinns must return home to honor their father's last request. . . .

Phillip Quinn has done everything to make his life seem perfect. With his career on the fast track and a condo overlooking the Inner Harbor, his life on the street is firmly in the past. But one look at Seth and he's reminded of the boy he once was.

Seth's future as a Quinn seems assured—until a stranger arrives in town. Sybill claims to be researching the town of St. Christopher's for her new book, but her true objects of study are the Quinns. Her cool reserve intrigues Phillip. He is determined to uncover her motives, but Sybill is holding a secret that has the power to threaten the life the brothers have made for Seth. A secret that could tear the family apart—forever. . . .

"With bright dialogue and lots of heart, Roberts provides a safe harbor for Phillip . . . and for her many fans."
—*Publishers Weekly*

Don't miss the other books in the Chesapeake Bay Saga

SEA SWEPT
RISING TIDES
CHESAPEAKE BLUE

Turn the page for a complete list of titles by Nora Roberts and J. D. Robb from Berkley. . . .

Nora Roberts

HOT ICE
SACRED SINS
BRAZEN VIRTUE
SWEET REVENGE
PUBLIC SECRETS
GENUINE LIES
CARNAL INNOCENCE
HONEST ILLUSIONS
DIVINE EVIL
PRIVATE SCANDALS
HIDDEN RICHES
TRUE BETRAYALS
MONTANA SKY
SANCTUARY
HOMEPORT
THE REEF
RIVER'S END
CAROLINA MOON
THE VILLA
MIDNIGHT BAYOU
THREE FATES
BIRTHRIGHT
NORTHERN LIGHTS
BLUE SMOKE
ANGELS FALL
HIGH NOON
TRIBUTE
BLACK HILLS
THE SEARCH
CHASING FIRE
THE WITNESS
WHISKEY BEACH
THE COLLECTOR
TONIGHT AND ALWAYS
THE LIAR
THE OBSESSION

Series

Ebooks by Nora Roberts

Cordina's Royal Family
AFFAIRE ROYALE
COMMAND PERFORMANCE
THE PLAYBOY PRINCE
CORDINA'S CROWN JEWEL

The Donovan Legacy
CAPTIVATED
ENTRANCED
CHARMED
ENCHANTED

The O'Hurleys
THE LAST HONEST WOMAN
DANCE TO THE PIPER
SKIN DEEP
WITHOUT A TRACE

Night Tales
NIGHT SHIFT
NIGHT SHADOW
NIGHTSHADE
NIGHT SMOKE
NIGHT SHIELD

The MacGregors
PLAYING THE ODDS
TEMPTING FATE
ALL THE POSSIBILITIES
ONE MAN'S ART
FOR NOW, FOREVER
REBELLION/IN FROM THE COLD
THE MACGREGOR BRIDES
THE WINNING HAND
THE MACGREGOR GROOMS
THE PERFECT NEIGHBOR

The Calhouns
COURTING CATHERINE
A MAN FOR AMANDA
FOR THE LOVE OF LILAH
SUZANNA'S SURRENDER
MEGAN'S MATE

Irish Legacy
IRISH THOROUGHBRED
IRISH ROSE
IRISH REBEL

LOVING JACK
BEST LAID PLANS
LAWLESS

BLITHE IMAGES
SONG OF THE WEST
SEARCH FOR LOVE
ISLAND OF FLOWERS
THE HEART'S VICTORY
FROM THIS DAY
HER MOTHER'S KEEPER
ONCE MORE WITH FEELING
REFLECTIONS
DANCE OF DREAMS
UNTAMED
THIS MAGIC MOMENT
ENDINGS AND BEGINNINGS
STORM WARNING
SULLIVAN'S WOMAN
FIRST IMPRESSIONS
A MATTER OF CHOICE

LESS OF A STRANGER
THE LAW IS A LADY
RULES OF THE GAME
OPPOSITES ATTRACT
THE RIGHT PATH
PARTNERS
BOUNDARY LINES
DUAL IMAGE
TEMPTATION
LOCAL HERO
THE NAME OF THE GAME
GABRIEL'S ANGEL
THE WELCOMING
TIME WAS
TIMES CHANGE
SUMMER LOVE
HOLIDAY WISHES

Anthologies

FROM THE HEART
A LITTLE MAGIC
A LITTLE FATE

MOON SHADOWS
(with Jill Gregory, Ruth Ryan Langan, and Marianne Willman)

The Once Upon Series
(with Jill Gregory, Ruth Ryan Langan, and Marianne Willman)

ONCE UPON A CASTLE	ONCE UPON A ROSE
ONCE UPON A STAR	ONCE UPON A KISS
ONCE UPON A DREAM	ONCE UPON A MIDNIGHT

SILENT NIGHT
(with Susan Plunkett, Dee Holmes, and Claire Cross)

OUT OF THIS WORLD
(with Laurell K. Hamilton, Susan Krinard, and Maggie Shayne)

BUMP IN THE NIGHT
(with Mary Blayney, Ruth Ryan Langan, and Mary Kay McComas)

DEAD OF NIGHT
(with Mary Blayney, Ruth Ryan Langan, and Mary Kay McComas)

THREE IN DEATH

SUITE 606
(with Mary Blayney, Ruth Ryan Langan, and Mary Kay McComas)

IN DEATH

THE LOST
(with Patricia Gaffney, Mary Blayney, and Ruth Ryan Langan)

THE OTHER SIDE
(with Mary Blayney, Patricia Gaffney, Ruth Ryan Langan, and Mary Kay McComas)

TIME OF DEATH

THE UNQUIET
(with Mary Blayney, Patricia Gaffney, Ruth Ryan Langan, and Mary Kay McComas)

MIRROR, MIRROR
(with Mary Blayney, Elaine Fox, Mary Kay McComas, and R. C. Ryan)

DOWN THE RABBIT HOLE
(with Mary Blayney, Elaine Fox, Mary Kay McComas, and R. C. Ryan)

Also available . . .

THE OFFICIAL NORA ROBERTS COMPANION
(edited by Denise Little and Laura Hayden)

INNER HARBOR

NORA ROBERTS

JOVE
New York

A JOVE BOOK
Published by Berkley
An imprint of Penguin Random House LLC
penguinrandomhouse.com

Copyright © 1999 by Nora Roberts
Excerpt from *Naked in Death* by J. D. Robb copyright © 1995 by Nora Roberts
Penguin Random House supports copyright. Copyright fuels creativity, encourages
diverse voices, promotes free speech, and creates a vibrant culture. Thank you for buying
an authorized edition of this book and for complying with copyright laws by not
reproducing, scanning, or distributing any part of it in any form without permission.
You are supporting writers and allowing Penguin Random House to continue to
publish books for every reader.

A JOVE BOOK, BERKLEY, and the BERKLEY & B colophon
are registered trademarks of Penguin Random House LLC.

ISBN: 9780515124217

Jove mass-market edition / January 1999
Berkley trade paperback edition / July 2013

Printed in the United States of America
43 45 47 49 51 52 50 48 46 44

Cover design and photo composition by Rita Frangie

For Elaine and Beth, such devoted sisters—
even if they won't wear blue organdy and sing

PROLOGUE

PHILLIP QUINN DIED AT THE age of thirteen. Since the overworked and underpaid staff at the Baltimore City Hospital emergency room zapped him back in less than ninety seconds, he wasn't dead very long.

As far as he was concerned, it was plenty long enough.

What had killed him, briefly, were two .25-caliber bullets pumped out of a Saturday night special shoved through the open window of a stolen Toyota Celica. The finger on the trigger had belonged to a close personal friend—or as near to a close personal friend as a thirteen-year-old thief could claim on Baltimore's bad streets.

The bullets missed his heart. Not by much, but in later years Phillip considered it just far enough.

That heart, young and strong, though sadly jaded, continued to beat as he lay there, pouring blood over the used condoms and crack vials in the stinking gutter on the corner of Fayette and Paca.

The pain was obscene, like sharp, burning icicles stabbing into his chest. But that grinning pain refused to take him under, into the release of unconsciousness. He lay awake and aware,

1

hearing the screams of other victims or bystanders, the squeal of brakes, the revving of engines, and his own ragged and rapid breaths.

He'd just fenced a small haul of electronics that he'd stolen from a third-story walk-up less than four blocks away. He had two hundred fifty dollars in his pocket and had swaggered down to score a dime bag to help him get through the night. Since he'd just been sprung from ninety days in juvie for another B and E that hadn't gone quite so smoothly, he'd been out of the loop. And out of cash.

Now it appeared he was out of luck.

Later, he would remember thinking, Shit, oh, shit, this *hurts*! But he couldn't seem to wrap his mind around another thought. He'd gotten in the way. He knew that. The bullets hadn't been meant for him in particular. He'd caught a glimpse of the gang colors in that frozen three seconds before the gun had fired. His own colors, when he bothered to associate himself with one of the gangs that roamed the streets and alleys of the city.

If he hadn't just popped out of the system, he wouldn't have been on that corner at that moment. He would have been told to stay clear, and he wouldn't now be sprawled out, pumping blood and staring into the dirty mouth of the gutter.

Lights flashed—blue, red, white. The scream of sirens pierced through human screams. Cops. Even through the slick haze of pain his instinct was to run. In his mind he sprang up, young, agile, street-smart, and melted into the shadows. But even the effort of the thought had cold sweat sliding down his face.

He felt a hand on his shoulder, and fingers probed until they reached the thready pulse in his throat.

This one's breathing. Get the paramedics over here.

Someone turned him over. The pain was unspeakable, but he couldn't release the scream that ripped through his head. He saw faces swimming over him, the hard eyes of a cop, the grim ones of the medical technician. Red, blue, and white lights burned his eyes. Someone wept in high, keening sobs.

Hang in there, kid.

Why? He wanted to ask why. It hurt to be there. He was never going to escape as he'd once promised himself he would. What was left of his life was running red into the gutter. What had come before was only ugliness. What was now was only pain.

What was the damn point?

HE WENT AWAY FOR A WHILE, sinking down below the pain, where the world was a dark and dingy red. From somewhere outside his world came the shriek of the sirens, the pressure on his chest, the speeding motion of the ambulance.

Then lights again, bright white to sear his closed lids. And he was flying while voices shouted on all sides of him.

Bullet wounds, chest. BP's eighty over fifty and falling, pulse thready and rapid. In and out. Pupils are good.

Type and cross-match. We need pictures. On three. One, two, three.

His body seemed to jerk, up then down. He no longer cared. Even the dingy red was going gray. A tube was pushing its way down his throat and he didn't bother to try to cough it out. He barely felt it. Barely felt anything and thanked God for it.

BP's dropping. We're losing him.

I've been lost a long time, he thought.

With vague interest he watched them, half a dozen green-suited people in a small room where a tall blond boy lay on a table. Blood was everywhere. His blood, he realized. He was on that table with his chest torn open. He looked down at himself with detached sympathy. No more pain now, and the quiet sense of relief nearly made him smile.

He floated higher, until the scene below took on a pearly sheen and the sounds were nothing but echoes.

Then the pain tore through him, an abrupt shock that made the body on the table jerk, that sucked him back. His struggle to pull away was brief and fruitless. He was inside again, feeling again, lost again.

The next thing he knew, he was riding in a drug-hazed blur. Someone was snoring. The room was dark and the bed narrow and hard. A backwash of light filtered through a pane of glass that was spotted with fingerprints. Machines beeped and sucked monotonously. Wanting only to escape the sounds, he rolled back under.

He was in and out for two days. He was very lucky. That's what they told him. There was a pretty nurse with tired eyes and a doctor with graying hair and thin lips. He wasn't ready to believe them, not when he was too weak to lift his head, not when the hideous pain swarmed back into him every two hours like clockwork.

When the two cops came in he was awake, and the pain was smothered under a few layers of morphine. He made them out to be cops at a glance. His instincts weren't so dulled that he didn't recognize the walk, the shoes, the eyes. He didn't need the identification they flashed at him.

"Gotta smoke?" Phillip asked it of everyone who passed through. He had a low-grade desperation for nicotine even though he doubted he could manage to suck on a cigarette.

"You're too young to smoke." The first cop pasted on an avuncular smile and stationed himself on one side of the bed. The Good Cop, Phillip thought wearily.

"I'm getting older every minute."

"You're lucky to be alive." The second cop kept his face hard as he pulled out a notebook.

And the Bad Cop, Phillip decided. He was nearly amused.

"That's what they keep telling me. So, what the hell happened?"

"You tell us." Bad Cop poised his pencil over a page of his book.

"I got the shit shot out of me."

"What were you doing on the street?"

"I think I was going home." He'd already decided how to play it, and he let his eyes close. "I can't remember exactly. I'd been . . . at the movies?" He made it a question, opening his eyes. He could see Bad Cop wasn't going to buy it, but what could they do?

"What movie did you see? Who were you with?"

"Look, I don't know. It's all messed up. One minute I was walking, the next I was lying facedown."

"Just tell us what you remember." Good Cop laid a hand on Phillip's shoulder. "Take your time."

"It happened fast. I heard shots—it must have been shots. Somebody was screaming, and it was like something exploded in my chest." That much was pretty close to the truth.

"Did you see a car? Did you see the shooter?"

Both were etched like acid on steel in his brain. "I think I saw a car—dark color. A flash."

"You belong to the Flames."

Phillip shifted his gaze to Bad Cop. "I hang with them sometimes."

"Three of the bodies we scraped off the street were members of the Tribe. They weren't as lucky as you. The Flames and the Tribe have a lot of bad blood between them."

"So I've heard."

"You took two bullets, Phil." Good Cop settled his face into concerned lines. "Another inch either way, you'd have been dead before you hit the pavement. You look like a smart kid. A smart kid doesn't fool himself into believing he needs to be loyal to assholes."

"I didn't see anything." It wasn't loyalty. It was survival. If he rolled over, he was dead.

"You had over two hundred in your wallet."

Phillip shrugged, regretting it as the movement stirred up the ghosts of pain. "Yeah? Well, maybe I can pay my bill here at the Hilton."

"Don't smart-mouth me, you little punk." Bad Cop leaned over the bed. "I see your kind every fucking day. You're not out of the system twenty hours before you end up bleeding into the gutter."

Phillip didn't flinch. "Is getting shot a violation of my parole?"

"Where'd you get the money?"

"I don't remember."

"You were down in Drug City to score."

"Did you find any drugs on me?"

"Maybe we did. You wouldn't remember, would you?"

Good one, Phillip mused. "I could sure as hell use some now."

"Ease off a little." Good Cop shifted his feet. "Look, son, you cooperate and we'll play square with you. You've been in and out of the system enough to know how it works."

"If the system worked I wouldn't be here, would I? You can't do anything to me that hasn't been done. For Christ's sake, if I'd known something was going down I wouldn't have been there."

The sudden disturbance out in the hall took the cops' attention away. Phillip merely closed his eyes. He recognized the voice raised in bitter fury.

Stoned, was his first and last thought. And when she stumbled into the room, he opened his eyes and saw that he'd been right on target.

She'd dressed up for the visit, he noted. Her yellow hair was teased and sprayed into submission, and she'd put on full makeup. Under it, she might have been a pretty woman, but the mask was hard and tough. Her body was good, it was what kept her in business. Strippers who moonlight as hookers need a good package. She'd peeled on a halter and jeans, and she clicked her way over to the bed on three-inch heels.

"Who the hell do you think's gonna pay for this? You're nothing but trouble."

"Hi, Ma, nice to see you, too."

"Don't you sass me. I got cops coming to the door 'cause of you. I'm sick of it." She flashed a look at the men on either side of the bed. Like her son, she recognized cops. "He's almost fourteen years old. I'm done with him. He ain't coming back on me this time. I ain't having cops and social workers breathing down my neck anymore."

She shrugged off the nurse who hustled in to grab her arm, then leaned over the bed. "Why the hell didn't you just die?"

"I don't know," Phillip said calmly. "I tried."

"You've never been any good." She hissed at Good Cop when he pulled her back. "Never been any damn good. Don't you come around looking for a place to stay when you get out of here," she shouted as she was dragged out of the room. "I'm done with you."

Phillip waited, listening to her swearing, shouting, demanding papers to sign to get him out of her life. Then he looked up at Bad Cop. "You think you can scare me? I live with that. Nothing's worse than living with that."

Two days later, strangers came into the room. The man was huge, with blue eyes bright in a wide face. The woman had wild red hair escaping from a messy knot at the nape of her neck and a face full of freckles. The woman took his chart from the foot of the bed, scanned it, then tapped it against her palm.

"Hello, Phillip. I'm Dr. Stella Quinn. This is my husband, Ray."

"Yeah, so?"

Ray pulled a chair up to the side of the bed and sat down with a sigh of pleasure. He angled his head, studied Phillip briefly. "You've got yourself into a hell of a mess here, haven't you? Want to get out of it?"

ONE

PHILLIP LOOSENED THE WINDsor knot in his Fendi tie. It was a long commute from Baltimore to Maryland's Eastern Shore, and he'd programmed his CD player with that in mind. He started out mellow with a little Tom Petty and the Heartbreakers.

Thursday-evening traffic was as bad as predicted, made worse by the sluggish rain and the rubberneckers who couldn't resist a long, fascinated goggle at the three-car accident on the Baltimore Beltway.

By the time he was heading south on Route 50, even the hot licks of vintage Stones couldn't completely lift his mood.

He'd brought work with him and somehow had to eke out time for the Myerstone Tire account over the weekend. They wanted a whole new look for this advertising campaign. Happy tires make happy drivers, Phillip thought, drumming his fingers on the wheel to the rhythm of Keith Richards's outlaw guitar.

Which was a crock, he decided. Nobody was happy driving in rainy rush-hour traffic, no matter what rubber covered their wheels.

But he'd come up with something that would make the consumers think that riding on Myerstones would make them happy, safe, and sexy. It was his job, and he was good at it.

Good enough to juggle four major accounts, supervise the status of six lesser ones, and never appear to break a sweat within the slick corridors of Innovations, the well-heeled advertising firm where he worked. The firm that demanded style, exuberance, and creativity from its executives.

They didn't pay to see him sweat.

Alone, however, was a different matter.

He knew he'd been burning not a candle but a torch at both ends for months. With one hard slap of fate he'd gone from living for Phillip Quinn to wondering what had happened to his cheerfully upwardly mobile urban lifestyle.

His father's death six months before had turned his life upside down. The life that Ray and Stella Quinn had righted seventeen years ago. They'd walked into that dreary hospital room and offered him a chance and a choice. He'd taken the chance because he'd been smart enough to understand that he had no choice.

Going back on the streets wasn't as appealing as it had been before his chest had been ripped open by bullets. Living with his mother was no longer an option, not even if she changed her mind and let him buy his way back into the cramped apartment on Baltimore's Block. Social Services was taking a hard look at the situation, and he knew he'd be dumped into the system the minute he was back on his feet.

He had no intention of going back into the system, or back with his mother, or back to the gutter, for that matter. He'd already decided that. He felt that all he needed was a little time to work out a plan.

At the moment that time was buffered by some very fine drugs that he hadn't had to buy or steal. But he didn't figure that little benefit was going to last forever.

With the Demerol sliding through his system, he gave the

Quinns a canny once-over and dismissed them as a couple of weirdo do-gooders. That was fine with him. They wanted to be Samaritans, give him a place to hang out until he was back to a hundred percent, good for them. Good for him.

They told him they had a house on the Eastern Shore, which for an inner-city kid was the other end of the world. But he figured a change of scene couldn't hurt. They had two sons about his age. Phillip decided he wouldn't have to worry about a couple of wimps that the do-gooders had raised.

They told him they had rules, and education was a priority. School didn't bother him any. He breezed his way through when he decided to go.

No drugs. Stella said that in a cool voice that made Phillip reevaluate her as he put on his most angelic expression and said a polite *No, ma'am.* He had no doubt that when he wanted a hit, he'd be able to find a source, even in some bumfuck town on the Bay.

Then Stella leaned over the bed, her eyes shrewd, her mouth smiling thinly.

You have a face that belongs on a Renaissance painting. But that doesn't make you less of a thief, a hoodlum, and a liar. We'll help you if you want to be helped. But don't treat us like imbeciles.

And Ray laughed his big, booming laugh. He squeezed Stella's shoulder and Phillip's at the same time. It would be, Phillip remembered he'd said, a rare treat to watch the two of them butt heads for the next little while.

They came back several times over the next two weeks. Phillip talked with them and with the social worker, who'd been much easier to con than the Quinns.

In the end they took him home from the hospital, to the pretty white house by the water. He met their sons, assessed the situation. When he learned that the other boys, Cameron and Ethan, had been taken in much as he had been, he was certain they were all lunatics.

He figured on biding his time. For a doctor and a college professor they hadn't collected an abundance of easily stolen or fenced valuables. But he scoped out what there was.

Instead of stealing from them, he fell in love with them. He took their name and spent the next ten years in the house by the water.

Then Stella had died, and part of his world dropped away. She had become the mother he'd never believed existed. Steady, strong, loving, and shrewd. He grieved for her, that first true loss of his life. He buried part of that grief in work, pushing his way through college, toward a goal of success and a sheen of sophistication—and an entry-level position at Innovations.

He didn't intend to remain on the bottom rung for long.

Taking the position at Innovations in Baltimore was a small personal triumph. He was going back to the city of his misery, but he was going back as a man of taste. No one seeing the man in the tailored suit would suspect that he'd once been a petty thief, a sometime drug dealer, and an occasional prostitute.

Everything he'd gained over the last seventeen years could be traced back to that moment when Ray and Stella Quinn had walked into his hospital room.

Then Ray had died suddenly, leaving shadows that had yet to be washed with the light. The man Phillip had loved as completely as a son could love a father had lost his life on a quiet stretch of road in the middle of the day when his car had met a telephone pole at high speed.

There was another hospital room. This time it was the Mighty Quinn lying broken in the bed with machines gasping. Phillip, along with his brothers, had made a promise to watch out for and to keep the last of Ray Quinn's strays, another lost boy.

But this boy had secrets, and he looked at you with Ray's eyes.

The talk around the waterfront and the neighborhoods of the little town of St. Christopher's on Maryland's Eastern Shore hinted of adultery, of suicide, of scandal. In the six months since the whispers had started, Phillip felt that he and his brothers had gotten no closer to finding the truth. Who was Seth DeLauter and what had he been to Raymond Quinn?

Another stray? Another half-grown boy drowning in a vicious sea of neglect and violence who so desperately needed a lifeline? Or was he more? A Quinn by blood as well as by circumstance?

All Phillip could be sure of was that ten-year-old Seth was his brother as much as Cam and Ethan were his brothers. Each of them had been snatched out of a nightmare and given a chance to change their lives.

With Seth, Ray and Stella weren't there to keep that choice open.

There was a part of Phillip, a part that had lived inside a young, careless thief, that resented even the possibility that Seth could be Ray's son by blood, a son conceived in adultery and abandoned in shame. It would be a betrayal of everything the Quinns had taught him, everything they had shown him by living their lives as they had.

He detested himself for considering it, for knowing that now and then he studied Seth with cool, appraising eyes and wondered if the boy's existence was the reason Ray Quinn was dead.

Whenever that nasty thought crept into his mind, Phillip shifted his concentration to Gloria DeLauter. Seth's mother was the woman who had accused Professor Raymond Quinn of sexual harassment. She claimed it had happened years before, while she was a student at the university. But there was no record of her ever attending classes there.

The same woman had sold her ten-year-old son to Ray as if he'd been a package of meat. The same woman, Phillip was certain, that Ray had been to Baltimore to see before he had driven home—and driven himself to his death.

She'd taken off. Women like Gloria were skilled in skipping out of harm's way. Weeks ago, she'd sent the Quinns a not-so-subtle blackmail letter: If you want to keep the kid, I need more. Phillip's jaw clenched when he remembered the naked fear on Seth's face when he'd learned of it.

She wasn't going to get her hands on the boy, he told himself. She was going to discover that the Quinn brothers were a tougher mark than one softhearted old man.

Not just the Quinn brothers now, either, he thought as he turned off onto the rural county road that would lead him home. He thought of family as he drove fast down a road flanked by fields of soybeans, of peas, of corn grown taller than a man. Now that Cam and Ethan were married, Seth had two determined women to stand with him as well.

Married. Phillip shook his head in amused wonder. Who would have thought it? Cam had hitched himself to the sexy social worker, and Ethan was married to sweet-eyed Grace. And had become an instant father, Phillip mused, to angel-faced Aubrey.

Well, good for them. In fact, he had to admit that Anna Spinelli and Grace Monroe were tailor-made for his brothers. It would only add to their strength as a family when it came time for the hearing on permanent guardianship of Seth. And marriage certainly appeared to suit them. Even if the word itself gave him the willies.

For himself, Phillip much preferred the single life and all its benefits. Not that he'd had much time to avail himself of all those benefits in the past few months. Weekends in St. Chris, supervising homework assignments, pounding a hull together for the fledgling Boats by Quinn, dealing with the books for the new business, hauling groceries—all of which had somehow become his domain—cramped a man's style.

He'd promised his father on his deathbed that he would take care of Seth. With his brothers he'd made a pact to move back to the Shore, to share the guardianship and the responsibilities. For Phillip that pact meant splitting his time between Baltimore and St. Chris, and his energies between maintaining his career—and his income—and tending to a new and often problematic brother and a new business.

It was all a risk. Raising a ten-year-old wasn't without headaches and fumbling mistakes under the best of circumstances, he imagined. Seth DeLauter, raised by a part-time hooker, full-time junkie, and amateur extortionist, had hardly come through the best of circumstances.

Getting a boatbuilding enterprise off the ground was a series of irksome details and backbreaking labor. Yet somehow it was working, and if he discounted the ridiculous demands on his time and energy, it was working fairly well.

Not so long ago his weekends had been spent in the company of any number of attractive, interesting women, having dinner at some new hot spot, an evening at the theater or a concert, and if the chemistry was right, a quiet Sunday brunch in bed.

He'd get back to that, Phillip promised himself. Once all the details were in place, he would have his life back again. But, as his father would have said, for the next little while . . .

He turned into the drive. The rain had stopped, leaving a light sheen of wet on the leaves and grass. Twilight was creeping in. He could see the light in the living room window glowing in a soft and steady welcome. Some of the summer flowers that Anna had babied along were hanging on, and early fall blooms shimmered in the shadows. He could hear the puppy barking, though at nine months Foolish had grown too big and sleek to be considered a puppy anymore.

It was Anna's night to cook, he remembered. Thank God. It meant a real meal would be served at the Quinns'. He rolled his shoulders, thought about pouring himself a glass of wine, then watched Foolish dash around the side of the house in pursuit of a mangy yellow tennis ball.

The sight of Phillip getting out of his car obviously distracted the dog from the game. He skidded to a halt and set up a din of wild, terrified barking.

"Idiot." But he grinned as he pulled his briefcase out of the Jeep.

At the familiar voice, the barking turned into mad joy. Foolish bounded up with a delighted look in his eyes and wet, muddy paws. "No jumping!" Phillip yelled, using his briefcase like a shield. "I mean it. Sit!"

Foolish quivered, but dropped his rump on the ground and lifted a paw. His tongue lolled, his eyes gleamed. "That's a good dog." Gingerly Phillip shook the filthy paw and scratched the dog's silky ears.

"Hey." Seth wandered into the front yard. His jeans were grubby from wrestling with the dog, his baseball cap was askew so that straw-straight blond hair spiked out of it. The smile, Phillip noted, came much more quickly and easily than it had a few months before. But there was a gap in it.

"Hey." Phillip butted a finger on the bill of the cap. "Lose something?"

"Huh?"

Phillip tapped a finger against his own straight, white teeth.

"Oh, yeah." With a typical Quinn shrug, Seth grinned, pushing his tongue into the gap. His face was fuller than it had been six months before, and his eyes less wary. "It was loose. Had to give it a yank a couple of days ago. Bled like a son of a bitch."

Phillip didn't bother to sigh over Seth's language. Some things, he determined, weren't going to be his problem. "So, did the Tooth Fairy bring you anything?"

"Get real."

"Hey, if you didn't squeeze a buck out of Cam, you're no brother of mine."

"I got two bucks out of it. One from Cam and one from Ethan."

Laughing, Phillip swung an arm over Seth's shoulders and headed toward the house. "Well, you're not getting one out of me, pal. I'm on to you. How was the first full week of school?"

"Boring." Though it hadn't been, Seth admitted silently. It had been exciting. All the new junk Anna had taken him shopping for. Sharp pencils, blank notebooks, pens full of ink. He'd refused the *X-Files* lunch box she'd wanted to get him. Only a dork carried a lunch box in middle school. But it had been really cool and tough to sneer at.

He had cool clothes and bitching sneakers. And best of all, for the first time in his life, he was in the same place, the same school, with the same people he'd left behind in June.

"Homework?" Phillip asked, raising his eyebrows as he opened the front door.

Seth rolled his eyes. "Man, don't you ever think about anything else?"

"Kid, I live for homework. Especially when it's yours." Foolish burst through the door ahead of Phillip, nearly knocking him down with enthusiasm. "You've still got some work to do on that dog." But the mild annoyance faded instantly. He could smell Anna's red sauce simmering, like ambrosia on the air. "God bless us, every one," he murmured.

"Manicotti," Seth informed him.

"Yeah? I've got a Chianti I've been saving just for this moment." He tossed his briefcase aside. "We'll hit the books after dinner."

He found his sister-in-law in the kitchen, filling pasta tubes with cheese. The sleeves of the crisp white shirt she'd worn to the office were rolled up, and a white butcher's apron covered her navy skirt. She'd taken off her heels and tapped a bare foot to the beat of the aria she was humming. *Carmen*, Phillip recognized. Her wonderful mass of curling black hair was still pinned up.

With a wink at Seth, Phillip came up behind her, caught

her around the waist, and pressed a noisy kiss onto the top of her head. "Run away with me. We'll change our names. You can be Sophia and I'll be Carlo. Let me take you to paradise where you can cook for me and me alone. None of these peasants appreciate you like I do."

"Let me just finish this tube, Carlo, and I'll go pack." She turned her head, her dark Italian eyes laughing. "Dinner in thirty minutes."

"I'll open the wine."

"Don't we have anything to eat now?" Seth wanted to know.

"There's antipasto in the fridge," she told him. "Go ahead and get it out."

"It's just vegetables and junk," Seth complained when he pulled out the platter.

"Yep."

"Jeez."

"Wash the dog off your hands before you start on that."

"Dog spit's cleaner than people spit," Seth informed her. "I read how if you get bit by another guy it's worse than getting bit by a dog."

"I'm thrilled to have that fascinating tidbit of information. Wash the dog spit off your hands anyway."

"Man." Disgusted, Seth clomped out, with Foolish slinking after him.

Phillip chose the wine from the small supply he kept in the pantry. Fine wines were one of his passions, and his palate was extremely discriminating. His apartment in Baltimore boasted an extensive and carefully chosen selection, which he kept in a closet he'd remodeled specifically for that purpose.

At the Shore, his beloved bottles of Bordeaux and Burgundy kept company with Rice Krispies and boxes of Jell-O Instant Pudding.

He'd learned to live with it.

"So how was your week?" he asked Anna.

"Busy. Whoever said women can have everything should be shot. Handling a career and a family is grueling." Then she looked up with a brilliant smile. "I'm loving it."

"It shows." He drew the cork expertly, sniffed it and approved, then set the bottle on the counter to breathe. "Where's Cam?"

"Should be on his way home from the boatyard. He and Ethan wanted to put in an extra hour. The first Boat by Quinn is finished. The owner's coming in tomorrow. It's finished, Phillip." Her smile flashed, brilliant and glowing with pride. "At dock, seaworthy and just gorgeous."

He felt a little tug of disappointment that he hadn't been in on the last day. "We should be having champagne."

Anna lifted a brow as she studied the label on the wine. "A bottle of Folonari, Ruffino?"

He considered one of Anna's finest traits to be her appreciation for good wine. "Seventy-five," he said with a broad grin.

"You won't hear any complaints from me. Congratulations, Mr. Quinn, on your first boat."

"It's not my deal. I just handle the details and pass for slave labor."

"Of course it's your deal. Details are necessary, and neither Cam nor Ethan could handle them with the finesse you do."

"I think the word they use, is 'nagging.' "

"They need to be nagged. You should be proud of what the three of you have accomplished in the last few months. Not just the new business, but the family. Each one of you has given up something that's important to you for Seth. And each one of you has gotten something important back."

"I never expected the kid to matter so much." While Anna smothered the filled tubes with sauce, Phillip opened a cupboard for wineglasses. "I still have moments when the whole thing pisses me off."

"That's only natural, Phillip."

"Doesn't make me feel any better about it." He shrugged his shoulders in dismissal, then poured two glasses. "But most of the time, I look at him and think he's a pretty good deal for a kid brother."

Anna grated cheese over the casserole. Out of the corner of her eye she watched Phillip lift his glass, appreciate the bouquet. He was beautiful to look at, she mused. Physically, he was as close to male perfection as she could imagine. Bronze hair, thick and full, eyes more gold than brown. His face was long, narrow, thoughtful. Both sensual and angelic. His tall, trim build seemed to have been fashioned for Italian suits. But since she'd seen him stripped to the waist in faded Levi's she knew there was nothing soft about him.

Sophisticated, tough, erudite, shrewd. An interesting man, she mused.

She slipped the casserole into the oven, then turned to pick up her wine. Smiling at him, she tapped her glass on his. "You're a pretty good deal too, Phillip, for a big brother."

She leaned in to kiss him lightly as Cam walked in.

"Get your mouth off my wife."

Phillip merely smiled and slid an arm around Anna's waist. "She put hers on me. She likes me."

"She likes me better." To prove it, Cam hooked a hand in the tie of Anna's apron, spun her around, and pulled her into his arms to kiss her brainless. He grinned, nipped her bottom lip and patted her butt companionably. "Don'cha, sugar?"

Her head was still spinning. "Probably." She blew out a breath. "All things considered." But she wiggled free. "You're filthy."

"Just came in to grab a beer to take into the shower." Long and lean, dark and dangerous, he prowled over to the fridge. "And kiss my wife," he added with a smug look at Phillip. "Go get your own woman."

"Who has time?" Phillip said mournfully.

• • •

AFTER DINNER, AND AN
hour spent slaving over long division, battles of the Revolutionary War, and sixth-grade vocabulary, Phillip settled down
in his room with his laptop and his files.

It was the same room he'd been given when Ray and Stella
Quinn had brought him home. The walls had been a pale green
then. Sometime during his sixteenth year he'd gotten a wild
hair and painted them magenta. God knew why. He remembered that his mother—for Stella had become his mother by
then—had taken one look and warned him he'd have terminal
indigestion.

He thought it was sexy. For about three months. Then he'd
gone with a stark white for a while, accented with moody
black-framed, black-and-white photographs.

Always looking for ambience, Phillip thought now, amused
at himself. He'd circled back to that soft green right before he
moved to Baltimore.

They'd been right all along, he supposed. His parents had
usually been right.

They'd given him this room, in this house, in this place.
He hadn't made it easy for them. The first three months were
a battle of wills. He smuggled in drugs, picked fights, stole
liquor, and stumbled in drunk at dawn.

It was clear to him now that he'd been testing them, daring
them to kick him out. Toss him back. Go ahead, he'd thought.
You can't handle me.

But they did. They had not only handled him, they had
made him.

I wonder, Phillip, his father had said, *why you want to
waste a good mind and a good body. Why you want to let the
bastards win.*

Phillip, who was suffering from the raw gut and bursting

head of a drug and alcohol hangover, didn't give a good damn.

Ray took him out on the boat, telling him that a good sail would clear his head. Sick as a dog, Phillip leaned over the rail, throwing up the remnants of the poisons he'd pumped into his system the night before.

He'd just turned fourteen.

Ray anchored the boat in a narrow gut. He held Phillip's head, wiped his face, then offered him a cold can of ginger ale.

"Sit down."

He didn't so much sit as collapse. His hands shook, his stomach shuddered at the first sip from the can. Ray sat across from him, his big hands on his knees, his silvering hair flowing in the light breeze. And those eyes, those brilliant blue eyes, level and considering.

"You've had a couple of months now to get your bearings around here. Stella says you've come around physically. You're strong, and healthy enough—though you aren't going to stay that way if you keep this up."

He pursed his lips, said nothing for a long moment. There was a heron in the tall grass, still as a painting. The air was bright and chill with late fall, the trees bare of leaves so that the hard blue sky spread overhead. Wind ruffled the grass and skimmed fingers over the water.

The man sat, apparently content with the silence and the scene. The boy slouched, pale of face and hard of eye.

"We can play this a lot of ways, Phil," Ray said at length. "We can be hard-asses. We can put you on a short leash, watch you every minute and bust your balls every time you screw up. Which is most of the time."

Considering, Ray picked up a fishing rod, absently baited it with a marshmallow. "Or we could all just say that this little experiment's a bust and you can go back into the system."

Phillip's stomach churned, making him swallow to hold

down what he didn't quite recognize as fear. "I don't need you. I don't need anybody."

"Yeah, you do." Ray said it mildly as he dropped the line into the water. Ripples spread, endlessly. "You go back into the system, you'll stay there. Couple of years down the road, it won't be juvie anymore. You'll end up in a cell with the bad guys, the kind of guys who are going to take a real liking to that pretty face of yours. Some seven-foot con with hands like smoked hams is going to grab you in the showers one fine day and make you his bride."

Phillip yearned desperately for a cigarette. The image conjured by Ray's word made fresh sweat pop out on his forehead. "I can take care of myself."

"Son, they'll pass you around like canapés, and you know it. You talk a good game and you fight a good fight, but some things are inevitable. Up to this point your life has pretty much sucked. You're not responsible for that. But you are responsible for what happens from here on."

He fell into silence again, clamping the pole between his knees before reaching for a cold can of Pepsi. Taking his time, Ray popped the top, tipped the can back, and guzzled.

"Stella and I thought we saw something in you," he continued. "We still do," he added, looking at Phillip again. "But until you do, we're not going to get anywhere."

"What do you care?" Phillip tossed back miserably.

"Hard to say at the moment. Maybe you're not worth it. Maybe you'll just end up back on the streets hustling marks and turning tricks anyway."

For three months he'd had a decent bed, regular meals, and all the books he could read—one of his secret loves—at his disposal. At the thought of losing it his throat filled again, but he only shrugged. "I'll get by."

"If all you want to do is get by, that's your choice. Here you can have a home, a family. You can have a life and make something out of it. Or you can go on the way you are."

Ray reached over to Phillip quickly, and the boy braced himself for the blow, clenched his fists to return it. But Ray only pulled Phillip's shirt up to expose the livid scars on his chest. "You can go back to that," he said quietly.

Phillip looked into Ray's eyes. He saw compassion and hope. And he saw himself mirrored back, bleeding in a dirty gutter on a street where life was worth less than a dime bag.

Sick, tired, terrified, Phillip dropped his head into his hands. "What's the point?"

"You're the point, son." Ray ran his hand over Phillip's hair. "You're the point."

Things hadn't changed overnight, Phillip thought now. But they had begun to change. His parents had made him believe in himself, despite himself. It had become a point of pride for him to do well in school, to learn, to remake himself into Phillip Quinn.

He figured he'd done a good job of it. He'd coated that street kid with a sheen of class. He had a slick career, a well-appointed condo with a killer view of the Inner Harbor, and a wardrobe that suited both.

It seemed that he'd come full circle, spending his weekends back in this room with its green walls and sturdy furniture, with its windows that overlooked the trees and the marsh.

But this time, Seth was the point.

TWO

P HILLIP STOOD ON THE FORE-
deck of the yet-to-be-christened *Neptune's Lady*. He'd personally sweated out nearly two thousand man-hours to take her
from design to finished sloop. Her decks were gleaming teak,
her bright work glinted in the yellow September sun.

Belowdecks her cabin was a woodworker's pride, Cam's
for the most part, Phillip mused. Glossy cabinets were fashioned of natural wood, hand-fitted and custom-designed with
sleeping room for four close friends.

She was sound, he thought, and she was beautiful. Aesthetically charming, with her fluid hull, glossy decks, and long
waterline. Ethan's early decision to use the smooth-lap method
of planking had added hours to the labor but had produced a
gem.

The podiatrist from D.C. was going to pay handsomely for
every inch of her.

"Well . . . ?" Ethan, hands in the pockets of his faded
jeans, eyes squinting comfortably against the sun, left it an
open-ended question.

Phillip ran a hand over the satin finish of the gunwale, an

area he'd spent many sweaty hours sanding and finishing. "She deserves a less clichéd name."

"The owner's got more money than imagination. She takes the wind." Ethan's lips curved into one of his slow, serious smiles. "Good Christ, she goes, Phil. When Cam and I tested her out, I wasn't sure he was going to bring her back in. Wasn't sure I wanted him to."

Phillip rubbed a thumb over his chin. "I've got a friend in Baltimore who paints. Most of the stuff he does is strictly commercial, for hotels and restaurants. But he does terrific stuff on the side. Every time he sells one, he bitches about it. Hates to let a canvas go. I didn't really understand how he felt until now."

"And she's our first."

"But not our last." Phillip hadn't expected to feel so attached. The boatbuilding business hadn't been his idea, or his choice. He liked to think his brothers had dragged him into it. He'd told them it was insane, ridiculous, doomed to fail.

Then, of course, he'd jumped in and negotiated for the rental of the building, applied for licenses, ordered the necessary utilities. During the construction of what was about to become *Neptune's Lady,* he'd dug splinters out of his fingers, nursed burns from hot creosote, soaked muscles that wept after hours of lifting planks. And had not suffered in silence.

But with this tangible result of long months of labor swaying gracefully under his feet, he had to admit it was all worth it.

Now they were about to start all over again.

"You and Cam made some headway this week on the next project."

"We want to have the hull ready to turn the end of October." Ethan took out a bandanna and methodically polished Phillip's fingerprints off the gunwale. "If we're going to keep to that killer schedule you worked up. Got a little bit more to do on this one, though.''

"This one?" Eyes narrowed, Phillip tipped down his Wayfarers. "Damn it, Ethan, you said she was ready to go. The owner's coming in to take her. I was about to go in and work up the last of the papers on her.''

"Just one little detail. Have to wait for Cam.''

"What little detail?" Impatient, Phillip checked his watch. "The client's due here any minute.''

"Won't take long." Ethan nodded toward the cargo doors of the building. "Here's Cam now.''

"She's too good for this yahoo," Cam called out as he came down the narrow dock with a battery-operated drill. "I'm telling you we should get the wives and kids and sail her off to Bimini ourselves.''

"She's good enough for the final draw he's going to give us today. Once he gives me that certified check, he's the captain." Phillip waited until Cam stepped nimbly aboard. "When I get to Bimini I don't want to see either of you.''

"He's just jealous because we've got women," Cam told Ethan. "Here." He shoved the drill into Phillip's hand.

"What the hell am I supposed to do with this?''

"Finish her." Grinning, Cam pulled a brass cleat out of his back pocket. "We saved the last piece for you.''

"Yeah?" Absurdly touched, Phillip took the cleat, watched it wink in the sun.

"We started her together," Ethan pointed out. "Seemed only right. It goes on the starboard.''

Phillip took the screws Cam handed him and bent over the markings on the rail. "I figured we should celebrate after." The drill whirled in his hands. "I thought about a bottle of Dom," he said, raising his voice over the noise, "but figured it'd be wasted on the two of you. So I've got three Harps chilling down in the cooler.''

They would go well, he thought, with the little surprise he was having delivered later that afternoon.

IT WAS NEARLY NOON BEfore the client had finished fussing over every inch of his new boat. Ethan had been elected to take the man out for a shakedown sail before they loaded the sloop onto its new trailer. From the dock, Phillip watched the butter-yellow sails—the client's choice—fill with the wind.

Ethan was right, he thought. She moved.

The sloop skimmed toward the waterfront, heeled in like a dream. He imagined the late-summer tourists would stop to watch, point out the pretty boat to each other. There was, he thought, no better advertising than a quality product.

"He'll run her aground the first time he sails her on his own," Cam said from behind him.

"Sure. But he'll have fun." He gave Cam a slap on the shoulder. "I'll just go write up that bill of sale."

The old brick building they rented and had modified for the boatyard didn't boast many amenities. The lion's share was a vast open space with fluorescent lights hanging from the rafters. The windows were small and always seemed to be coated with dust.

Power tools, lumber, equipment, gallons of epoxy and varnish and bottom paint were set up where they could be easily reached. The lofting platform was currently occupied by the bare skeleton of the hull for the custom-designed sport's fisher that was their second job.

The walls were pitted brick and unfinished Sheetrock. Up a steep flight of iron stairs was a cramped, windowless room that served as the office.

Despite its size and location, Phillip had it meticulously organized. The metal desk might have been a flea market special, but it was scrubbed clean. On its surface was a Month-at-a-Glance calendar, his old laptop computer, a wire in/out box, a two-line phone/answering machine and a Lucite holder for pens and pencils.

Crowded in with the desk were two file cabinets, a personal copier, and a plain-paper fax.

He settled in his chair and booted up the computer. The blinking light on the phone caught his eye. When he punched it for messages, he found two hang-ups and dismissed them.

Within moments, he'd brought up the program he'd customized for the business, and found himself grinning at the logo for Boats by Quinn.

They might be flying by the seat of their pants, he mused as he plugged in the data for the sale, but it didn't have to look that way. He'd justified the high-grade paper as an advertising expense. Desktop publishing was second nature to him. Creating stationery, receipts, bills was simple enough— he simply insisted that they have class.

He shot the job to the printer just as the phone rang.

"Boats by Quinn."

There was a hesitation, then the sound of throat clearing. "Sorry, wrong number." The voice was muffled and female and quickly gone.

"No problem, sweetheart," Phillip said to the dial tone as he plucked the printed bill of sale from the machine.

"THERE GOES A HAPPY MAN," Cam commented an hour later when the three of them watched their client drive off with the trailered sloop.

"We're happier." Phillip took the check out of his pocket and held it out. "Factoring in equipment, labor, overhead, supplies . . ." He folded the check in half again. "Well, we cleared enough to get by."

"Try to control your enthusiasm," Cam muttered. "You got a check for five figures in your hot little hand. Let's crack open those beers."

"The bulk of the profits have to go right back into the business," Phillip warned as they started inside. "Once the cold weather hits, our utility bill's going to go through the roof." He glanced up at the soaring ceiling. "Literally. And we've got quarterly taxes due next week."

Cam twisted the top off a bottle and pushed it at his brother. "Shut up, Phil."

"However," Phillip continued, ignoring him, "this is a fine moment in Quinn history." He lifted his beer, tapped the bottle to both Cam's and Ethan's. "To our foot doctor, the first of many happy clients. May he sail clean and heal many bunions."

"May he tell all his friends to call Boats by Quinn," Cam added.

"May he sail in Annapolis and keep out of my part of the Bay," Ethan finished with a shake of his head.

"Who's springing for lunch?" Cam wanted to know. "I'm starving."

"Grace made sandwiches," Ethan told him. "They're out in my cooler."

"God bless her."

"Might want to put off lunch just a bit." Phillip heard the sound of tires on gravel. "I think what I've been waiting for just got here." He strolled out, pleased to see the delivery truck.

The driver leaned out the window, worked a wad of gum into his cheek. "Quinn?"

"That's right."

"What'd you buy now?" Cam frowned at the truck, wondering how much of that brand-new check was flying away.

"Something we need. He's going to need a hand with it."

"You got that right." The driver huffed as he climbed out

of the cab. "Took three of us to load her up. Son of a bitch weighs two hundred pounds if it weighs an ounce."

He hauled open the back doors. It lay on the bed on top of a padded cloth. It was easily ten feet long, six high, and three inches thick. Carved in simple block letters into treated oak were the words BOATS BY QUINN. A detailed image of a wooden skiff in full sail rode the top corner.

Lining the bottom corner were the names Cameron, Ethan, Phillip, and Seth Quinn.

"That's a damn fine sign," Ethan managed when he could find the words.

"I took one of Seth's sketches for the skiff. The same one we use for the logo on the letterhead. Put the design together on the computer at work." Phillip reached in to run a thumb along the side of the oak. "The sign company did a pretty good job of reproducing it."

"It's great." Cam rested his hand on Phillip's shoulder. "One of the details we've been missing. Christ, the kid's going to flip when he sees it."

"I put us down the way we came along. Works out alphabetical and chronological. I wanted to keep it clean and simple." He stepped back, his hands sliding into his pockets in an unconscious mirroring of his brothers' stances. "I thought this fit the building and what we're doing in it."

"It's good." Ethan nodded. "It's right."

The driver shoved at his gum again. "Well, you guys gonna admire it all day, or you want to get this heavy bastard out of the truck?"

THEY MADE A PICTURE, SHE thought. Three exceptional specimens of the male species engaged in manual labor on a warm afternoon in early September. The building certainly suited them. It was rough, the old brick faded and pitted, the grounds around it scrabbly—more weeds than grass.

Three different looks as well. One of the men was dark, with his hair long enough to pull back in a short ponytail. His jeans were black, fading to gray. There was something vaguely European about his style. She decided he would be Cameron Quinn, the one who'd made a name for himself on the racing circuit.

The second wore scuffed work boots that looked ancient. His sun-streaked hair tumbled out of a blue-billed ball cap. He moved fluidly and lifted his end of the sign with no visible effort. He would be Ethan Quinn, the waterman.

Which meant the third man was Phillip Quinn, the advertising executive, who worked at the top firm in Baltimore. He looked gilded, she thought. Wayfarers and Levi's, she mused. Bronzed hair that must be a joy to his stylist. A long, trim body that must see regular workouts at the health club.

Interesting. Physically they bore no resemblance to each other and through her research she knew they shared a name but not blood. Yet there was something in the body language, in the way they moved as a team, that indicated they were brothers.

She intended simply to pass by, to give the building where they based their business a quick look and evaluation. Though she'd known that at least one of them would be there, since he'd answered the phone, she hadn't expected to see them outside, as a group, to have this opportunity to study them.

She was a woman who appreciated the unexpected.

Nerves shimmered in her stomach. Out of habit, she took three slow breaths and rolled her shoulders to relax them. Casual, she reminded herself. There was nothing to be uneasy about. After all, she had the advantage here. She knew them, and they didn't know her.

It was typical behavior, she decided as she crossed the street. A person strolling along and seeing three men working

to hang an impressive new sign would display curiosity and
interest. Particularly a small-town tourist, which was, for this
purpose, what she was. She was also a single female, and they
were three very attractive men. A mild flirtation would be
typical as well.

Still, when she reached the front of the building, she stood
back. It seemed to be difficult and precarious work. The sign
was bolted to thick black chains and wrapped in rope. They'd
worked out a pulley system, with the ad exec on the roof
guiding and his brothers on the ground hauling. Encourage-
ment, curses, and directions were issued with equal enthusiasm.

There were certainly a lot of muscles rippling, she observed
with a lift of her brow.

"Your end, Cam. Give me another inch. Goddamn."
Grunting, Phillip dropped onto his belly and squirmed out far
enough that she held her breath and waited for gravity to do
its work.

But he managed to balance himself and snag the chain. She
could see his mouth working as he fought to loop the heavy
link around a thick hook, but she couldn't hear what he was
saying. She thought that might be for the best.

"Got it. Hold it steady," he ordered, rising to tightwalk his
way across the eaves to the other end. The sun struck his hair,
gleamed over his skin. She caught herself goggling. This, she
thought, was a prime example of sheer male beauty.

Then he was bellying over the edge again, grabbing for the
chain, hauling it into place. And swearing ripely. When he
rose, he scowled at the long tear down the front of his shirt
where she supposed it had caught on something on the roof.

"I just bought this sucker."

"It was real pretty, too," Cam called up.

"Kiss my ass," Phillip suggested and tugged the shirt off
to use it to mop sweat off his face.

Oh, well, now, she thought, appreciating the view on a

purely personal level. The young American god, she decided. Designed to make females drool.

He hooked the ruined shirt in his back pocket, started for the ladder. And that's when he spotted her. She couldn't see his eyes, but she could tell by the momentary pause, the angle of the head, that he was looking at her. The evaluation would be instinctive, she knew. Male sees female, studies, considers, decides.

He'd seen her all right and, as he started down the ladder, was already considering. And hoping for a closer look. "We've got company," Phillip murmured, and Cam glanced over his shoulder.

"Hmmm. Very nice."

"Been there ten minutes." Ethan dusted his hands on his hips. "Watching the show."

Phillip stepped off the ladder, turned and smiled. "So," he called out to her, "how's it look?"

Curtain up, she thought and started forward. "Very impressive. I hope you don't mind the audience. I couldn't resist."

"Not at all. It's a big day for the Quinns." He held out a hand. "I'm Phillip."

"I'm Sybill. And you build boats."

"That's what the sign says."

"Fascinating. I'm spending some time in the area. I hadn't expected to stumble across boatbuilders. What sort of boats do you build?"

"Wooden sailing vessels."

"Really?" She turned her easy smile toward his brothers. "And you're partners?"

"Cam." He returned the smile, jerked a thumb. "My brother Ethan."

"Nice to meet you. Cameron," she began, shifting her gaze to read from the sign. "Ethan, Phillip." Her heartbeat accelerated, but she kept the polite smile in place. "Where's Seth?"

"In school," Phillip told her.

"Oh, college?"

"Middle. He's ten."

"I see." There were scars on his chest, she saw now. Old and shiny and riding dangerously close to his heart. "You have a very impressive sign, Boats by Quinn. I'd love to drop by sometime and see you and your brothers at work."

"Anytime. How long are you staying in St. Chris?"

"Depends. It was nice to meet you all." Time to retreat, she decided. Her throat was dry, her pulse unsteady. "Good luck with your boats."

"Drop by tomorrow," Phillip suggested as she walked away. "Catch all four Quinns at work."

She shot a look over her shoulder that she hoped revealed nothing more than amused interest. "I might just do that."

Seth, she thought, careful now to keep her eyes straight ahead. He'd just given her the open door to see Seth the following day.

Cam gave a quiet and male hum. "I gotta say, there's a woman who knows how to walk."

"Yes, indeed." Phillip hooked his hands in his pockets and enjoyed the view. Slim hips and slender legs in breezy maize-colored slacks, a snug little shirt the color of limes tucked into a narrow waist. A sleek and swinging fall of mink-colored hair just skimming strong shoulders.

And the face had been just as attractive. A classic oval with peaches-and-cream skin, a mobile and shapely mouth tinted with a soft, soft pink. Sexy eyebrows, he mused, dark and well arched. He hadn't been able to see the eyes under them, not through the trendy wire-framed sunglasses. They might be dark to match the hair, or light for contrast.

And that smooth contralto voice had set the whole package off nicely.

"You guys going to stand there watching that woman's butt all day?" Ethan wanted to know.

"Yeah, like you didn't notice it." Cam snorted.

"I noticed. I'm just not making a career out of it. Aren't we going to get anything done around here?"

"In a minute," Phillip murmured, smiling to himself when she turned the corner and disappeared. "Sybill. I sure hope you hang around St. Chris for a while."

SHE DIDN'T KNOW HOW LONG she would stay. Her time was her own. She could work where she chose, and for now she'd chosen this little water town on Maryland's southern Eastern Shore. Nearly all of her life had been spent in cities, initially because her parents had preferred them and then because she had.

New York, Boston, Chicago, Paris, London, Milan. She understood the urban landscape and its inhabitants. The fact was, Dr. Sybill Griffin had made a career out of the study of urban life. She'd gathered degrees in anthropology, sociology, and psychology along the way. Four years at Harvard, postgraduate work at Oxford, a doctorate from Columbia.

She'd thrived in academia, and now, six months before her thirtieth birthday, she could write her own ticket. Which was precisely what she'd chosen to do for a living. Write.

Her first book, *Urban Landscape*, had been well received, earned her critical acclaim and a modest income. But her second, *Familiar Strangers*, had rocketed onto the national lists, had taken her into the whirlwind of book tours, lectures, talk shows. Now that PBS was producing a documentary series based on her observations and theories of city life and customs, she was much more than financially secure. She was independent.

Her publisher had been open to her idea of a book on the dynamics and traditions of small towns. Initially, she'd considered it merely a cover, an excuse to travel to St. Christopher's, to spend time there on personal business.

But then she'd begun to think it through. It would make an interesting study. After all, she was a trained observer and skilled at documenting those observations.

Work might save her nerves in any case, she considered, pacing her pretty little hotel suite. Certainly it would be easier and more productive to approach this entire trip as a kind of project. She needed time, objectivity, and access to the subjects involved.

Thanks to convenient circumstance, it appeared she had all three now.

She stepped out onto the two-foot slab that the hotel loftily called a terrace. It offered a stunning view of the Chesapeake Bay and intriguing glimpses of life on the waterfront. Already she'd watched workboats chug into dock and unload tanks of the blue crabs the area was famous for. She'd watched the crab pickers at work, the sweep of gulls, the flight of egrets, but she had yet to wander into any of the little shops.

She wasn't in St. Chris for souvenirs.

Perhaps she would drag a table near the window and work with that view. When the breeze was right she could catch snippets of voices, a slower, more fluid dialect than she heard on the streets of New York, where she'd based herself for the last few years.

Not quite Southern, she thought, such as you would hear in Atlanta or Mobile or Charleston, but a long way from the clipped tones and hard consonants of the North.

On some sunny afternoons she could sit on one of the little iron benches that dotted the waterfront and watch the little world that had formed here out of water and fish and human sweat.

She would see how a small community of people like this, based on the Bay and tourists, interacted. What traditions, what habits, what clichés ran through them. Styles, she mused, of dress, of movements, of speech. Inhabitants so rarely realized how they conformed to unspoken rules of behavior dictated by place.

Rules, rules, rules. They existed everywhere. Sybill believed in them absolutely.

What rules did the Quinns live by? she wondered. What type of glue had fashioned them into a family? They would, of course, have their own codes, their own short-speak, with a pecking order and a reward and discipline standard.

Where and how would Seth fit into it?

Finding out, discreetly, was a priority.

There was no reason for the Quinns to know who she was, to suspect her connection. It would be better for all parties if no one knew. Otherwise, they could very well attempt, and possibly succeed in blocking her from Seth altogether. He'd been with them for months now. She couldn't be sure what he'd been told, what spin they might have put on the circumstances.

She needed to observe, to study, to consider, and to judge. Then she would act. She would not be pressured, she ordered herself. She would not be made to feel guilty or responsible. She would take her time.

After their meeting that afternoon, she thought it would be ridiculously simple to get to know the Quinns. All she had to do was wander into that big brick building and show an interest in the process of creating a wooden sailboat.

Phillip Quinn would be her entrée. He'd displayed all the typical behavioral patterns of early-stage attraction. It wouldn't be a hardship to take advantage of that. Since he only spent a few days a week in St. Chris, there was little danger of taking a casual flirtation into serious territory.

Wrangling an invitation to his home here wouldn't present a problem. She needed to see where and how Seth was living, who was in charge of his welfare.

Was he happy?

Gloria had said they'd stolen her son. That they'd used their influence and their money to snatch him away.

But Gloria was a liar. Sybill squeezed her eyes shut, struggling to be calm, to be objective, not to be hurt. Yes, Gloria was a liar, she thought again. A user. But she was also Seth's mother.

Going to the desk, Sybill opened her Filofax and slid the photograph out. A little boy with straw-colored hair and bright blue eyes smiled out at her. She'd taken the picture herself, the first and only time she'd seen Seth.

He must have been four, she thought now. Phillip had said he was ten now, and Sybill remembered it had been six years since Gloria showed up on her doorstep in New York with her son in tow.

She'd been desperate, of course. Broke, furious, weepy, begging. There'd been no choice but to take her in, not with the child staring up with those huge, haunted eyes. Sybill hadn't known anything about children. She'd never been around them. Perhaps that was why she'd fallen for Seth so quickly and so hard.

And when she'd come home three weeks later and found them gone, along with all the cash in the house, her jewelry, and her prized collection of Daum china, she'd been devastated.

She should have expected it, she told herself now. It had been classic Gloria behavior. But she'd believed, had needed to believe, that they could finally connect. That the child would make a difference. That she could help.

Well, this time, she thought as she tucked the photo away again, she would be more careful, less emotional. She knew that Gloria was telling at least part of the truth this time. Whatever she did from this point on would depend on her own judgment.

She would begin to judge when she saw her nephew again.

Sitting, she turned on her laptop and began to write her initial notes.

The Quinn brothers appear to have an easy, male-pattern relationship. From my single observation I would suspect they work together well. It will take additional study to determine what function each provides in this business partnership, and in their familial relations.

Both Cameron and Ethan Quinn are newly married. It will be necessary to meet their wives to understand the dynamics of this family. Logically one of them will represent the mother figure. Since Cameron's wife, Anna Spinelli Quinn, has a full-time career, one would suspect that Grace Monroe Quinn fulfills this function. However, it's a mistake to generalize such matters and this will require personal observations.

I found it telling that the business sign the Quinns hung this afternoon contained Seth's name, but as a Quinn. I can't say if this disposal of his legal name is for their benefit or his.

The boy must certainly be aware that the Quinns are filing for custody. I can't say as yet whether he has received any of the letters Gloria has written him. Perhaps the Quinns have disposed of them. Though I sympathize with her plight and her desperation to get her child back, it's best that she remain unaware that I've come here. Once I've documented my findings, I'll contact her. If there is a legal battle in the future, it's best to approach the matter with facts rather than raw emotion.

Hopefully the lawyer Gloria has engaged will contact the Quinns through the proper legal channels shortly.

For myself, I hope to see Seth tomorrow and gain some insight into the situation. It would be helpful to determine how much he knows about his parentage. As I have only recently become fully informed, I've not yet completely assimilated all the facts and their repercussions.

We will soon see if small towns are indeed a hotbed of information on their inhabitants. I intend to learn all I can learn about Professor Raymond Quinn before I'm done.

THREE

THE TYPICAL VENUE FOR SO-
cializing, information gathering, and mating rituals, small
town or big city, Sybill observed, was the local bar.

Whether it was decorated with brass and ferns or peanut
shells and tin ashtrays, whether the music was whiny country
or heart-reeling rock, it was the traditional spot for gathering
and exchanging information.

Shiney's Pub in St. Christopher's certainly fit the bill. The
decor here was dark wood, cheap chrome, and faded posters
of boats. The music was loud, she decided, unable to fully
identify the style booming out of the towering amps flanking
the small stage where four young men pounded away at guitars
and drums with more enthusiasm than talent.

A trio of men at the bar kept their eyes glued to the baseball
game on the small-screen TV bracketed to the wall behind the
bar. They seemed content to watch the silent ballet of pitcher
and batter while they nursed brown bottles of beer and ate
fistfuls of pretzels.

The dance floor was jammed. There were only four couples,

but the limited space caused several incidents of elbow rapping and hip bumping. No one seemed to mind.

The waitresses were decked out in foolish male-fantasy outfits—short black skirts, tiny, tight V-neck blouses, fishnet stockings, and stiletto heels.

Sybill felt instant sympathy.

She tucked herself into a wobbly table as far away from the amps as humanly possible. The smoke and noise didn't bother her, nor did the sticky floor or the jittery table. Her choice of seating afforded her the clearest view of the occupants.

She'd been desperate to escape her hotel room for a couple of hours. Now she was set to sit back, enjoy a glass of wine, and observe the natives.

The waitress who approached was a petite brunette with an enviable bustline and a cheery smile. "Hi. What can I get you?"

"A glass of Chardonnay and a side of ice."

"Coming right up." She set a black plastic bowl filled with pretzels on the table and picked her way back to the bar, taking orders as she went.

Sybill wondered if she'd just had her first encounter with Ethan's wife. Her information was that Grace Quinn worked at this bar. But there had been no wedding ring on the little brunette's finger, and Sybill assumed that a new bride would certainly wear one.

The other waitress? That one looked dangerous, she decided. Blond, built, and brooding. She was certainly attractive, in an obvious way. Still, nothing about her shouted newlywed either, particularly the way she leaned over an appreciative customer's table to give him the full benefit of her cleavage.

Sybill frowned and nibbled on a pretzel. If that was Grace Quinn, she would definitely be scratched from mother-figure status.

Something happened in the ball game, Sybill assumed, as

the three men began to shout, cheering on someone named Eddie.

Out of habit she took out her notebook and began to record observations. The backslapping and arm punching of male companions. The body language of the females, leaning in for intimacy. The hair flipping, the eye shifting, hand gesturing. And of course, the mating ritual of the contemporary couple through the dance.

That was how Phillip saw her when he came in. She was smiling to herself, her gaze roaming, her hand scribbling. She looked, he thought, very cool, very remote. She might have been behind a thin sheet of one-way glass.

She'd pulled her hair back so that it lay in a sleek tail on her neck and left her face unframed. Gold drops studded with single colored stones swung at her ears. He watched her put her pen down to shrug out of a suede jacket of pale yellow.

He had driven in on impulse, giving in to restlessness. Now he blessed that vaguely dissatisfied mood that had dogged him all evening. She was, he decided, exactly what he'd been looking for.

"Sybill, right?" He saw the quick surprise flicker in her eyes when she glanced up. And he saw that those eyes were as clear and pure as lake water.

"That's right." Recovering, she closed her notebook and smiled. "Phillip, of Boats by Quinn."

"You here alone?"

"Yes . . . unless you'd like to sit down and have a drink."

"I'd love to." He pulled out a chair, nodding toward her notebook. "Did I interrupt you?"

"Not really." She shifted her smile to the waitress when her wine was served.

"Hey, Phil, want a draft?"

"Marsha, you read my mind."

Marsha, Sybill thought. That eliminated the perky brunette. "It's unusual music."

"The music here consistently sucks." He flashed a smile, quick, charming, and amused. "It's a tradition."

"Here's to tradition, then." She lifted her glass, sipped, then with a little hmmm began transferring ice into the wine.

"How would you rate the wine?"

"Well, it's basic, elemental, primitive." She sipped again, smiled winningly. "It sucks."

"That's also a proud Shiney's tradition. He's got Sam Adams on draft. It's a better bet."

"I'll remember that." Lips curved, she tilted her head. "Since you know the local traditions, I take it you've lived here for some time."

"Yeah." His eyes narrowed as he studied her, as something pushed at the edges of his memory. "I know you."

Her heart bounded hard into her throat. Taking her time, she picked up her glass again. Her hand remained steady, her voice even and easy. "I don't think so."

"No, I do. I know that face. It didn't click before, when you were wearing sunglasses. Something about . . ." He reached out, put a hand under her chin and angled her head again. "That look right there."

His fingertips were just a bit rough, his touch very confident and firm. The gesture itself warned her that this was a man used to touching women. And she was a woman unused to being touched.

In defense, Sybill arched an eyebrow. "A woman with a cynical bent would suspect that's a line, and not a very original one."

"I don't use lines," he murmured, concentrating on her face. "Except originals. I'm good with images, and I've seen that one. Clear, intelligent eyes, slightly amused smile. Sybill . . ." His gaze skimmed over her face, then his lips curved slowly. "Griffin. *Doctor* Sybill Griffin. *Familiar Strangers.*"

She let out the breath that had clogged in her lungs. Her success was still very new, and having her face recognized continued to surprise her. And, in this case, relieve her. There was no connection between Dr. Griffin and Seth DeLauter.

"You are good," she said lightly. "So, did you read the book or just look at my picture on the dust jacket?"

"I read it. Fascinating stuff. In fact, I liked it enough to go out and buy your first one. Haven't read it yet though."

"I'm flattered."

"You're good. Thanks, Marsha," he added when she set his beer in front of him.

"Y'all just holler if you need anything." Marsha winked. "Holler loud. This band's breaking sound records tonight."

Which gave him an excuse to edge his chair closer and lean in. Her scent was subtle, he noted. A man had to get very close to catch its message. "Tell me, Dr. Griffin, what's a renowned urbanite doing in an unapologetically rural water town like St. Chris?"

"Research. Behavioral patterns and traditions," she said, lifting her glass in a half toast. "Of small towns and rural communities."

"Quite a change of pace for you."

"Sociology and cultural interest aren't, and shouldn't be, limited to cities."

"Taking notes?"

"A few. The local tavern," she began, more comfortable now. "The regulars. The trio at the bar, obsessed with the ritual of male-dominated sports to the exclusion of the noise and activities around them. They could be home, kicked back in their Barcaloungers, but they prefer the bonding experience of passive participation in the event. In this way they have companionship, partners with whom to share the interest, who will either argue or agree. It doesn't matter which. It's the pattern that matters."

He found he enjoyed the way her voice took on a lecturing tone that brought out brisk Yankee. "The O's are in a hot pennant race, and you're deep in Orioles' territory. Maybe it's the game.''

"The game is the vehicle. The pattern would remain fairly constant whether the vehicle was football or basketball.'' She shrugged. ''The typical male gains more enjoyment from sports if he has at least one like-minded male companion with him. You have only to observe commercials aimed primarily at the male consumer. Beer, for instance,'' she said, tapping a finger on his glass. ''It's quite often sold by showcasing a group of attractive men sharing some common experience. A man then buys that brand of beer because he's been programmed to believe that it will enhance his standing with his peer group.''

Because he was grinning, she lifted her eyebrows. ''You disagree?''

"Not at all. I'm in advertising, and that pretty much hit the nail.''

"Advertising?'' She ignored the little tug of guilt at the pretense. ''I wouldn't think there would be much call for that here.''

"I work in Baltimore. I'm back here on weekends for a while. A family thing. Long story.''

"I'd like to hear it.''

"Later.'' There was something, he thought, about those nearly translucent blue eyes framed by long, inky lashes that made it nearly impossible to look anywhere else. ''Tell me what else you see.''

"Well . . .'' It was a fine skill, she decided. A masterwork. The way he could look at a woman as if she were the most vital thing in the world at that one moment. It made her heart bump pleasantly. ''You see the other waitress?''

Phillip glanced over, watched the frivolous bow on the back of the woman's skirt swivel as she walked to the bar. ''Hard to miss her.''

"Yes. She fulfills certain primitive and typical male-fantasy requirements. But I'm referring to personality, not physicality."

"Okay." Phillip ran his tongue around his teeth. "What do you see?"

"She's efficient, but she's already calculating the time until closing. She knows how to size up the better tippers and play to them. She all but ignores the table of college students there. They won't add much to her bill. You'd see the same survival techniques from an experienced and cynical waitress in a New York bar."

"Linda Brewster," Phillip supplied. "Recently divorced, on the prowl for a new, improved husband. Her family owns the pizza place, so she's been waitressing off and on for years. Doesn't care for it. Do you want to dance?"

"What?" Then that's not Grace either, she thought and struggled to tune back in. "I'm sorry?"

"The band's slowed it down if they haven't turned it down. Would you like to dance?"

"All right." She let him take her hand to lead her through the tables to the dance floor, where they shoehorned themselves into the crowd.

"I think this is supposed to be a version of 'Angie,'" Phillip murmured.

"If Mick and the boys heard what they're doing to it, they'd shoot the entire band on sight."

"You like the Stones?"

"What's not to like?" Since they could do no more than sway, she tilted her head back to look at him. It wasn't a hardship to find his face so close to hers, or to be forced to press her body firmly to his. "Down-and-dirty rock and roll, no frills, no fuss. All sex."

"You like sex?"

She had to laugh. "What's not to like? And though I appreciate the thought, I don't intend to have any tonight."

"There's always tomorrow."

"There certainly is." She considered kissing him, letting him kiss her. As an experiment that would certainly include an aspect of enjoyment. Instead, she turned her head so cheeks brushed. He was entirely too attractive for an impulsive and uncalculated risk.

Better safe, she reminded herself, than stupid.

"Why don't I take you to dinner tomorrow?" Skillfully, he slid a hand up her spine, back down to her waist. "There's a nice place right in town. Terrific view of the Bay, best seafood on the Shore. We can have a conversation in normal tones, and you can tell me the story of your life."

His lips had brushed her ear, sending a shocking ripple of reaction down to her toes. She should have known, she thought, that anyone who looked like he did would be damn good at sexual maneuvers.

"I'll think about it," she murmured and, deciding to give as good as she got, skimmed her fingertips over the back of his neck. "And let you know."

When the song ended, and the next picked up on a blast of sound and speed, she eased away. "I have to go."

"What?" He leaned down so she could shout in his ear.

"I have to go. Thanks for the dance."

"I'll walk you out."

Back at the table, he pulled out some bills while she gathered her things. The first step outside into the cool and quiet air made her laugh. "Well, that was an experience. Thank you for adding to it."

"I wouldn't have missed it. It's not very late," he added, taking her hand.

"Late enough." She pulled out the keys to her car.

"Come by the boatyard tomorrow. I'll show you around."

"I might just do that. Good night, Phillip."

"Sybill." He didn't bother to resist, simply brought her hand to his lips. Over their joined fingers, his eyes locked with hers. "I'm glad you picked St. Chris."

"So am I."

She slipped into her car, relieved that she had to concentrate on the task of switching on the lights, releasing the brake, starting the engine. Driving wasn't second nature to a woman who had depended on public transportation or private car services most of her life.

She focused on reversing, on putting the car in drive to make the turn onto the road. And she firmly ignored the faint echo of pressure on her knuckles where his lips had touched.

But she didn't quite resist glancing in the rearview mirror and taking one last look at him before she drove away.

Phillip decided that going back into Shiney's would be absurdly anticlimactic. He thought about her as he drove home, the way her eyebrows arched when she made a point or enjoyed a comment. That subtle and intimate scent she wore that told a man that if he'd gotten close enough to catch a whiff, maybe, just maybe, he'd have a chance to get closer.

He told himself she was the perfect woman for him to invest some time in getting closer to. She was beautiful; she was smart; she was cultured and sophisticated.

And just sexy enough to make his hormones stand at attention.

He liked women, and missed having time for conversations with them. Not that he didn't enjoy talking with Anna and Grace. But let's face it, it wasn't quite the same as talking with a woman when you could also fantasize about taking her to bed.

And he'd been missing that particular area of male-female relationships just lately. He rarely had time to do more than stumble into his apartment after a ten- or twelve-hour workday. His once interesting and varied social calendar had taken some large hits since Seth had come to the family.

The week was dedicated to his accounts and consultations with the lawyer. The fight with the insurance company on payment of his father's death benefits was coming to a head.

The resolution of permanent guardianship of Seth would be decided within ninety days. The responsibility of dealing with the mountain of paperwork and phone calls that sprang from those actions was his. Details were his strong point.

Weekends were consumed by household duties, the business, and whatever had slipped through the cracks during the week.

When you added it all up, he mused, it didn't leave much time for cozy dinners with attractive women, much less the ritual of slipping between the sheets with those women.

Which explained his recent restlessness and moodiness, he supposed. When a man's sex life virtually vanished, he was bound to get a little edgy.

The house was dark but for the single beam of the porch light when he pulled into the drive. Barely midnight on Friday night, he thought with a sigh. How the mighty have fallen. There would have been a time when he and his brothers would have been out cruising, looking for action. Well, he and Cam would have dragged Ethan along, but once they'd hounded him into it, Ethan would have held up his end.

The Quinn boys hadn't spent many Friday nights snoozing.

These days, he thought as he climbed out of the Jeep, Cam would be upstairs cozied up to his wife and Ethan would be tucked into Grace's little house. Undoubtedly they both had smiles on their faces.

Lucky bastards.

Knowing he wouldn't be able to sleep, he skirted the house and walked to where the edge of the trees met the edge of the water.

The moon was a fat ball riding the night sky. It shed its soft white light over the dark water, wet eelgrass, and thick leaves.

Cicadas were singing in their high, monotonous voices, and deep in those thick woods, an owl called out in tireless two-toned notes.

Perhaps he preferred the sounds of the city, voices and traffic muffled through glass. But he never failed to find this spot appealing. Though he missed the city's pace, the theater and museums, the eclectic mix of food and people, he could appreciate the peace and the stability found right here day after day. Year after year.

Without it, he had no doubt he would have found his way back to the gutter. And died there.

"You always wanted more for yourself than that."

The chill washed through him, from gut to fingertips. Where he had been standing, staring out at the moonlight showering through the trees, he was now staring at his father. The father he'd buried six months before.

"I only had one beer," he heard himself say.

"You're not drunk, son." Ray stepped forward so that the moonlight shimmered over his dramatic mane of silver hair and into the brilliant blue eyes that were bright with humor. "You're going to want to breathe now, before you pass out."

Phillip let out his breath in a *whoosh*, but his ears continued to ring. "I'm going to sit down now." He did, slowly, like a creaky old man, easing himself down onto the grass. "I don't believe in ghosts," he said to the water, "or reincarnation, the afterlife, visitations, or any form of psychic phenomenon."

"You always were the most pragmatic of the lot. Nothing was real unless you could see it, touch it, smell it."

Ray sat beside him with a contented sigh and stretched out long legs clad in frayed jeans. He crossed his ankles, and on his feet were the well-worn Dock-Sides that Phillip himself had packed into a box for the Salvation Army nearly six months before.

"Well," Ray said cheerfully, "you're seeing me, aren't you?"

"No. I'm having an episode most likely resulting from sexual deprivation and overwork."

"I won't argue with you. It's too pretty a night."

"I haven't reached closure yet," Phillip said to himself. "I'm still angry over the way he died, and why, and all the unanswered questions. So I'm projecting."

"I figured you'd be the toughest nut of the three. Always had an answer for everything. I know you've got questions, too. And I know you've got anger. You're entitled. You've had to change your life and take on responsibilities that shouldn't have been yours. But you did it, and I'm grateful."

"I don't have time for therapy right now. There's no place on the schedule to fit sessions in."

Ray let out a hoot of laughter. "Boy, you're not drunk, and you're not crazy either. You're just stubborn. Why don't you use that flexible mind of yours, Phillip, and consider a possibility?"

Bracing himself, Phillip turned his head. It was his father's face, wide and lined with life and filled with humor. Those bright-blue eyes were dancing, the silver hair ruffling in the night air. "This is an impossibility."

"Some people said when your mother and I took you and your brothers in, that it was an impossibility we'd make a family, make a difference. They were wrong. If we'd listened to them, if we'd gone by logic, none of you would have been ours. But fate doesn't give a horse's ass about logic. It just is. And you were meant to be ours."

"Okay." Phillip shot out a hand and jerked it back in shock. "How could I do that? How could I touch you if you're a ghost?"

"Because you need to." Casually, Ray gave Phillip's shoulder a quick pat. "I'm here, for the next little while."

Phillip's throat filled even as his stomach tightened into knots. "Why?"

"I didn't finish. I left it up to you and your brothers. I'm sorry for that, Phillip."

It wasn't happening, of course, Phillip told himself. He was probably in the first stages of a minor breakdown. He could feel the air against his face, warm and moist. The cicadas were still shrilling, the owl still hooting.

If he was having an episode, he thought again, it seemed only right to play it out. "They're trying to say it was suicide," he said slowly. "The insurance company's fighting the claim."

"I hope you know that's bullshit. I was careless, distracted. I had an accident." There was an edge to Ray's voice now, an impatience and annoyance that Phillip recognized. "I wouldn't have taken the easy way. And I had the boy to think about."

"Is Seth your son?"

"I can tell you that he belongs to me."

Both his head and his heart ached as he turned to stare out at the water again. "Mom was still alive when he was conceived."

"I know that. I was never unfaithful to your mother."

"Then how—"

"You need to accept him, for himself. I know you care for him. I know you're doing your best by him. You have that last step to take. Acceptance. He needs you, all of you."

"Nothing's going to happen to him," Phillip said grimly. "We'll see to that."

"He'll change your life, if you let him."

Phillip let out a short laugh. "Believe me, he already has."

"In a way that will make your life better. Don't close yourself off to those possibilities. And don't worry too much about this little visit." Ray patted him companionably on the knee. "Talk to your brothers."

"Yeah, like I'm going to tell them I sat outside in the middle of the night and talked to . . ." He looked over, saw nothing but the moonlight on the trees.

"Nobody," he finished and wearily laid down on the grass to stare up at the moon. "God, I need a vacation."

Four

It wouldn't do to appear too anxious, Sybill reminded herself. Or to get there too early. It had to be casual. She had to be relaxed.

She decided not to take her car. It would look more like a careless visit if she walked down from the waterfront. And if she included the visit to the boatyard in an afternoon of shopping and wandering, it would appear more impulsive than calculated.

To calm herself, she roamed the waterfront. A pretty Indian-summer Saturday morning drew tourists. They poked and strolled along as she did, dropping into the little shops, pausing to watch boats sail or motor on the Bay. No one seemed to be in a particular hurry or have a specific destination.

That in itself, she mused, made an interesting contrast to the usual urban Saturday when even the tourists seemed to be in a rush to get from one place to the next.

It would be something to consider and analyze and perhaps theorize over in her book. And because she *did* find it interesting, she slipped her mini recorder out of her bag and murmured a few verbal notes and observations.

"Families appear to be relaxed rather than harried or desperately seeking the entertainment they've traveled to find. The natives seem to be friendly and patient. Life is slow to reflect the pace set by the people who make their living here."

The little shops weren't doing what she'd term a bustling business, yet the merchants didn't have that anxious and sly-eyed look prevalent among the vendors where the crowds were thick and the wallets tightly guarded.

She bought a few postcards for friends and associates in New York, then, more out of habit than need, selected a book on the history of the area. It would help her in her research, she imagined. She lingered over a pewter fairy with a teardrop crystal hanging from her elegant fingers. But she resisted it, firmly reminding herself that she could purchase any sort of foolishness she wanted in New York.

Crawford's appeared to be a popular spot, so she strolled in and treated herself to an ice cream cone. It gave her something to do with her hands as she walked the few blocks to Boats by Quinn.

She appreciated the value of props. Everyone used them in the continuing play of living, she thought. A glass at a cocktail party, a paperback book on the subway. Jewelry, she realized when she caught herself twisting her necklace around her nervous fingers.

She dropped the chain, and concentrated on enjoying her scoop of raspberry sherbet.

It didn't take long to walk to the outskirts of town. She calculated that the waterfront area ran for barely a mile from end to end.

The neighborhoods ran west from the water. Narrow streets with tidy houses and tiny lawns. Low fences designed as much for backyard gossiping, she mused, as for boundary lines. Trees were large and leafy, still holding the deep, dark green of summer. It would be, she thought, an attractive sight when they turned with autumn.

Kids played in yards or rode bikes along the sloping sidewalks. She saw a teenage boy lovingly waxing an old Chevy compact, singing in a loud, just-out-of-tune voice to whatever played through his headphones.

A long-legged mutt with floppy ears rushed a fence as she passed, barking in deep, rusty clips. Her heart did a quick dance when he planted his huge paws on the top of the fence. And she kept walking.

She didn't know much about dogs.

She spotted Phillip's Jeep in the pothole-filled parking lot beside the boatyard. An aging pickup truck kept it company. The doors and several of the windows of the building were wide open. Through them came the buzz of saws and the Southern rock beat of John Fogerty.

Okay, Sybill, she thought and took a deep breath as she carefully swallowed the last of her cone. Now or never.

She stepped inside and found herself momentarily distracted by the look of the place. It was huge, and dusty and bright as a spotlighted stage. The Quinns were hard at work, with Ethan and Cam fitting a long, bent plank into place on what she assumed was a hull in progress. Phillip stood at a big, dangerous-looking power saw, running lumber through it.

She didn't see Seth.

For a moment she simply watched and wondered if she should slip back out again. If her nephew wasn't there, it would be more sensible to postpone the visit until she was sure he was.

He might be away for the day with friends. Did he have any friends? Or he could be home. Did he consider it his home?

Before she could decide, the saw switched off, leaving only John Fogerty crooning about a brown-eyed, handsome man. Phillip stepped back, pushed up his safety goggles, turned. And saw her.

His smile of welcome came so quickly, so sincerely, that she had to clamp down on a hard tug of guilt. "I'm interrupting." She raised her voice to compete with the music.

"Thank God." Dusting his hands on his jeans, Phillip started toward her. "I've been stuck with looking at these guys all day. You're a big improvement."

"I decided to play tourist." She jiggled the shopping bag she carried. "And I thought I'd take you up on the offer of a tour."

"I was hoping you would."

"So . . ." Deliberately, she shifted her gaze to the hull. It was safer, she decided, than looking into those tawny eyes for any length of time. "That's a boat?"

"It's a hull. Or will be." He took her hand, drew her forward. "It's going to be a sport's fisher."

"Which is?"

"One of those fancy boats men like to go out on to act manly, fish for marlin, and drink beer."

"Hey, Sybill." Cam shot her a grin. "Want a job?"

She looked at the tools, the sharp edges, the heavy lumber. "I don't think so." It was easy to smile back, to look over at Ethan. "It looks like the three of you know what you're doing."

"We know what we're doing." Cam wiggled his thumb between himself and Ethan. "We keep Phillip around for entertainment."

"I'm not appreciated around here."

She laughed and began to circle the hull. She could understand the basic shape but not the process. "I assume this is upside down."

"Good eye." Phillip only grinned when she cocked an eyebrow. "After she's planked, we'll turn her and start on the decking."

"Are your parents boatbuilders?"

"No, my mother was a doctor, my father a college professor. But we grew up around boats."

She heard it in his voice, the affection, the not-quite-settled grief. And hated herself. She'd intended to ask him more about his parents in some detail, but couldn't. "I've never been on a boat."

"Ever?"

"I imagine there are several million people in the world who haven't."

"Want to?"

"Maybe. I've enjoyed watching the boats from my hotel window." As she studied it, the hull became a puzzle she needed to solve. "How do you know where to begin to build this? I assume you work from a design, blueprints or schematics or whatever you call it."

"Ethan's been doing the bulk of the design work. Cam fiddles with it. Seth draws it up."

"Seth." Her fingers tightened on the strap of her purse. Props, she thought again. "Didn't you say he was in middle school?"

"That's right. The kid's got a real talent for drawing. Check these out."

Now she heard pride and it flustered her. Struggling for composure, she followed him to a far wall, where drawings of boats were roughly framed in raw wood. They were good—very, very good. Clever sketches done with pencil and care and talent.

"He . . . A young boy drew these?"

"Yes. Pretty great, huh? This is the one we just finished." He tapped a hand on the glass. "And this one's what we're working on now."

"He's very talented," she murmured around the lump in her throat. "He has excellent perspective."

"Do you draw?"

"A little, now and then. Just a hobby." She had to turn away to settle herself. "It relaxes me, and it helps in my work." Determined to smile again, she tossed her hair over her shoulder and aimed a bright, easy one at Phillip. "So, where's the artist today?"

"Oh, he's—"

He broke off as two dogs raced into the building. Sybill took an instinctive step back as the smaller of the two made a beeline in her direction. She made some strangled sound of distress just as Phillip jabbed out a finger and issued a sharp command.

"Hold it, you idiot. No jumping. No jumping," he repeated, but Foolish's forward motion proved too much for all of them. He was already up, already had his paws planted just under Sybill's breasts. She staggered a bit, seeing only big, sharp teeth bared in what she took for fierceness rather than a sloppy doggie grin.

"Nice dog," she managed in a stutter. "Good dog."

"Stupid dog," Phillip corrected and hauled Foolish down by the collar. "No manners. Sit. Sorry," he said to Sybill when the dog obligingly plopped down and offered his paw. "He's Foolish."

"Well, he's enthusiastic."

"No, Foolish is his name—and his personality. He'll stay like that until you shake his paw."

"Oh. Hmm." Gingerly she took the paw with two fingers.

"He won't bite." Phillip angled his head, noting there was a good deal more distress than irritation in her eyes. "Sorry— are you afraid of dogs?"

"I . . . maybe a little—of large, strange dogs."

"He's strange, all right. The other one's Simon, and he's considerably more polite." Phillip scratched Simon's ears as the dog sat calmly studying Sybill. "He's Ethan's. The idiot belongs to Seth."

"I see." Seth had a dog, was all she could think as Foolish offered his paw yet again, eyeing her with what appeared abject adoration. "I don't know very much about dogs, I'm afraid."

"These are Chesapeake Bay retrievers—or Foolish mostly is. We're not sure what else he is. Seth, call off your dog before he slobbers all over the lady's shoes."

Sybill lifted her head quickly and saw the boy just inside the doorway. The sun was streaming at his back, and it cast his face into shadows. She saw only a tall, slightly built boy carrying a large brown bag and wearing a black-and-orange ball cap.

"He doesn't slobber much. Hey, Foolish!"

Instantly, both dogs scrambled to their feet and raced across the room. Seth waded through them, carrying the bag to a makeshift table fashioned from a sheet of plywood laid over two sawhorses.

"I don't know why I have to always go up for lunch and stuff," he complained.

"Because we're bigger than you," Cam told him and dived into the bag. "You get me the cold-cut sub loaded?"

"Yeah, yeah."

"Where's my change?"

Seth pulled a liter of Pepsi out of the bag, cracked the top and guzzled straight from the bottle. Then he grinned. "What change?"

"Look, you little thief, I've got at least two bucks coming back."

"Don't know what you're talking about. You must've forgotten to add on the carrying charges again."

Cam made a grab for him, and Seth danced agilely away, hooting with laughter.

"Brotherly love," Phillip said easily. "That's why I make

sure I only give the kid the right change. You never see a nickel back otherwise. Want some lunch?"

"No, I . . ." She couldn't take her eyes off Seth, knew she had to. He was talking with Ethan now, making wide, exaggerated gestures with his free hand while his dog took quick, playful leaps at his fingers. "I had something already. But you go ahead."

"A drink, then. Did you get my water, kid?"

"Yeah, fancy water. Waste of money. Man, Crawford's was packed."

Crawford's. With a sensation she couldn't quite define, Sybill realized they might have been in the store at the same time. Might have walked right by each other. She would have passed him on the street without a clue.

Seth glanced from Phillip to Sybill, studied her with mild interest. "You buying a boat?"

"No." He didn't recognize her, she thought. Of course he wouldn't. He'd been hardly more than a baby the only time they'd seen each other. There was no stunned familial awareness in his eyes, any more than there would have been in hers. But she knew. "I'm just looking around."

"That's cool." He went back to the bag and pulled out his own sandwich.

"Ah . . ." Talk to him, she ordered herself. Say something. Anything. "Phillip was just showing me your drawings. They're wonderful."

"They're okay." He jerked a shoulder, but she thought she saw a faint flush of pleasure on his cheeks. "I could do better, but they're always rushing me."

Casually—she hoped it was casually—she crossed to him. She could see him clearly now. His eyes were blue, but a deeper, darker blue than hers or her sister's. His hair was a darker blond than the little boy's in the picture she carried. He'd been nearly a towhead at four, and now his hair was a richer blond and very straight.

The mouth, she thought. Wasn't there some resemblance around the mouth and chin?

"Is that what you want to be?" She needed to keep him talking. "An artist?"

"Maybe, but that's mostly for kicks." He took a huge bite of his sandwich, then talked through it. "We're boatbuilders."

His hands were far from clean, she noted, and his face wasn't much better. She imagined such niceties as washing up before meals went by the wayside in a household of males. "Maybe you'll go into design work."

"Seth, this is Dr. Sybill Griffin." Phillip offered Sybill a plastic cup of bubbling water over ice. "She writes books."

"Like stories?"

"Not exactly," she told him. "Like observations. Right now I'm spending some time in the area, observing."

He wiped his mouth with a swipe from the back of his hand. The hand Foolish had enthusiastically licked, before and after, Sybill noted with an inward wince.

"You going to do a book about boats?" he asked her.

"No, about people. People who live in small towns, and right now people who live in small towns by the water. How do you like it—living here, I mean?"

"I like it okay. Living in the city sucks." He picked up the soft drink bottle, glugged again. "People who live there are nuts." He grinned. "Like Phil."

"You're a peasant, Seth. I worry about you."

With a snort, Seth bit into his sandwich again. "I'm going out on the dock. We got some ducks hanging out."

He bounced out, dogs trailing behind him.

"Seth's got very definite opinions," Phillip said dryly. "I guess the world's pretty black and white when you're ten."

"He doesn't care for the urban experience." Nerves, she noted, had been drowned out by sheer curiosity. "Has he spent time with you in Baltimore?"

"No. He lived there for a while with his mother." His tone had darkened, making Sybill raise an eyebrow. "Part of that long story I mentioned."

"I believe I mentioned I'd enjoy hearing it."

"Then have dinner with me tonight, and we'll exchange those life stories."

She looked toward the cargo doors. Seth had gone out through them, very much at home. She needed to spend more time with him. Observing. And, she decided, she needed to hear what the Quinns had to say about the situation. Why not start with Phillip?

"All right. I'd like that."

"I'll pick you up at seven."

She shook her head. He seemed perfectly safe, perfectly fine, but she knew better than to take chances. "No, I'll meet you there. Where's the restaurant?"

"I'll write it down for you. We can start the tour in my office."

IT WAS EASY ENOUGH, AND she had to admit it was interesting. The tour itself didn't take long. Other than the huge work area, there was little to the boatyard—just Phillip's closet-size office, a small bathroom, and a dark, dingy storeroom.

It was obvious even to the untrained eye that the work center of the operation was its heart and soul.

It was Ethan who patiently instructed her on smooth-lap planking, about waterlines and bow shapes. She thought he would have made an excellent teacher, with his clear, simple phrasing and willingness to answer what must have been very basic questions.

She watched, genuinely fascinated, as the men held timber in a box and pumped out steam until the plank bowed into the shape they desired. Cam demonstrated how the ends were rabbeted together to form the smooth joints.

Watching Cam with Seth, she was forced to admit there was a definite bond between them. If she had come across them knowing nothing, she would have assumed they were brothers, or perhaps father and son. It was all in the attitude, she decided.

Then again, they had an audience, she mused, and were likely on their best behavior.

She would see how they acted once they became used to her.

CAM LET OUT A LONG, LOW whistle when Sybill left the building. He wiggled his eyebrows meaningfully at Phillip. "Very nice, bro. Very nice, indeed."

Phillip flashed a grin, then lifted his bottle of water to his lips. "Can't complain."

"She going to be around long enough to, ah . . ."

"If there's a God."

Seth laid a plank down by the saw, let out a huff. "Shit, you mean you're going to start poking at her? Is that all you guys think about?"

"Other than pounding on you?" Phillip whipped off Seth's hat and bopped the boy over the head with it. "Sure, what else?"

"You guys are always getting married," Seth said in disgust and tried to grab his hat.

"I don't want to marry her, I just want to have a nice, civilized dinner with her."

"Then bounce on her," Seth finished.

"Christ. He gets that from you," Phillip accused Cam.

"He came that way." Cam wrapped an arm around Seth's neck. "Didn't you, brat?"

The panic didn't come now, as it used to whenever Seth was touched or held. Instead he wriggled and grinned. "At least I think of something besides girls all the time. You guys are really lame."

"Lame?" Phillip put Seth's hat on his own head to free his hands, then rubbed them together. "Let's toss this runt fish off the dock."

"Can you do that later?" Ethan asked while Seth shouted in wild and delighted objection. "Or do I have to build this damn boat by myself?"

"Later, then." Phillip leaned down until he and Seth were nose to nose. "And you won't know when, you won't know where, you won't know why."

"Man, I'm shaking now."

I SAW SETH TODAY.

At her laptop, Sybill gnawed her bottom lip, then deleted the first sentence she'd typed.

I made contact with the subject this afternoon.

Better, she decided. More objective. To approach this situation properly, it would be best if she thought of Seth as the subject.

There was no recognition on either side. This is, of course, as expected. He appears to be healthy. He's attractive, slimly built yet sturdy. Gloria was always thin, so I suspect he's inherited her basic body type. He's blond, as she is—or was when I last saw her.

He seemed to be comfortable with me. I'm aware that some children are shy around strangers. That doesn't appear to be the case here.

Though he was not at the boatyard when I arrived, he came in shortly after. He'd been sent to the store for lunch. From the ensuing complaints and conversation, I can assume he is often expected to run errands. This could be construed two ways. One that the Quinns take advantage of having a young boy available and use him accordingly. Or two, that they are instilling a sense of responsibility.

The truth likely resides in the middle.

He has a dog. I believe this to be a usual, even traditional occurrence for a child living in suburban or rural areas.

He also has a talent for drawing. I was somewhat taken by surprise by this. I have some talent for it myself, as does my mother. Gloria, however, never showed any skill or interest in art. This shared interest may be a way to develop a rapport with the boy. It will be necessary to have some time alone with him to assist me in choosing the correct course to take.

The subject is, in my opinion, comfortable with the Quinns. He seems to be content and secure. There is, however, a certain roughness, a mild crudeness in him. Several times during the hour or so I spent with him, I heard him swear. Once or twice he was rather absently corrected, otherwise his language was ignored.

He was not required to wash his hands before eating, nor did any of the Quinns correct him for speaking with his mouth full or for feeding the dogs bits of his lunch. His manners are by no means appalling, but they are far from strictly polite.

He mentioned preferring living here to the city. In fact, he was most disdainful of urban life. I have agreed to have dinner with Phillip Quinn tonight and will urge him to tell me the facts of how Seth came to be with the Quinns.

How those facts agree with, and differ from, the facts

I received from Gloria will help me assimilate the situation.

The next step will be to obtain an invitation to the Quinn house. I'm very interested to see where the boy is living, to see him and the Quinns on this stage. And to meet the women who are now a part of his foster family.

I hesitate to contact Social Services and identify myself until I have completed this personal study.

Sybill sat back, tapping her fingers on the desk as she skimmed over her notes. It was so little, really, she thought. And her own fault. She'd thought she was prepared for that first meeting, but she wasn't.

Seeing him had left her dry-mouthed and sad. The boy was her nephew, her family. Yet they were strangers. And wasn't that nearly as much her fault as it was Gloria's? Had she ever really tried to make a connection, to bring him into her life?

True, she had rarely known where he was, but had she ever gone out of her way to find him, or her sister?

The few times Gloria had contacted her over the years for money, always for money, she had asked about Seth. But hadn't she simply taken Gloria's word that the child was fine? Had she ever demanded to speak with him, to see him?

Hadn't it simply been easier for her to send money over the wire and forget about them again?

Easier, she admitted. Because the one time she had let him in, the one time she had let herself open her home and her heart, he'd been taken away. And she had suffered.

This time she would do something. She would do whatever was right, whatever was best. She wouldn't allow herself to become too emotionally involved, however. After all, he wasn't her child. If Gloria retained custody, he would still move out of her life again.

But she would make the effort, take the time, see that he

was situated well. Then she would get on with her life and her work.

Satisfied, she saved the document and shifted to another to continue her notes for her book. Before she could begin, the phone on her desk rang.

"Yes. Dr. Griffin."

"Sybill. It took me a great deal of time and trouble to track you down."

"Mother." On a long sigh Sybill closed her eyes. "Hello."

"Would you mind telling me what you're doing?"

"Not at all. I'm researching a new book. How are you? How's Father?"

"Please, don't insult my intelligence. I thought we'd agreed you would stay out of this sordid little affair."

"No." As it always did when faced with a family confrontation, Sybill's stomach pitched. "We agreed that you would prefer I stay out of it. I decided I prefer not to. I've seen Seth."

"I'm not interested in Gloria, or her son."

"I am. I'm sorry that upsets you."

"Can you expect it to do otherwise? Your sister has chosen her own life and is no longer a part of mine. I will not be dragged into this."

"I have no intention of dragging you into this." Resigned, Sybill reached into her purse and found the small cloisonné box she used to store aspirin. "No one knows who I am. And even if I'm connected to Dr. and Mrs. Walter Griffin, that hardly follows to Gloria and Seth DeLauter."

"It can be followed, if anyone becomes interested enough to pursue it. You can't accomplish anything by staying there and interfering in this situation, Sybill. I want you to leave. Go back to New York, or come here to Paris. Perhaps you'll listen to your father if not to me."

Sybill washed down the aspirin with water, then dug out antacids. "I'm going to see this through. I'm sorry."

There was a long silence ripe with temper and frustration. Sybill closed her eyes, left them closed, and waited.

"You were always a joy to me. I never expected this kind of betrayal. I very much regret that I spoke with you about this matter. I wouldn't have if I'd known you would react so outrageously."

"He's a ten-year-old boy, Mother. He's your grandson."

"He is nothing to me, or to you. If you continue this, Gloria will make you pay for what you see as kindness."

"I can handle Gloria."

There was a laugh now, short and brittle as glass. "So you always believed. And you were always wrong. Please don't contact me, or your father, about any of this. I'll expect to hear from you when you've come to your senses."

"Mother—" The dial tone made Sybill wince. Barbara Griffin was a master at having the last word. Very carefully, Sybill set the receiver on the hook. Very deliberately, she swallowed the antacid.

Then, very defiantly, she turned back to her screen and buried herself in work.

FIVE

SINCE SYBILL WAS ALWAYS
on time and nearly everyone else in the world, as far as she
was concerned, never was, she was surprised to find Phillip
already sitting at the table he'd reserved for dinner.

He rose, offered her a killer smile and a single yellow rose.
Both charmed her and made her suspicious.

"Thank you."

"My pleasure. Sincerely. You look wonderful."

She'd gone to some trouble in that area, but more for herself than for him. The call from her mother had left her miserably depressed and guilty. She'd tried to fight off both
emotions by taking a great deal of time and putting a great
deal of effort into her appearance.

The simple black dress with its square neck and long, snug
sleeves was one of her favorites. The single strand of pearls
was a legacy from her paternal grandmother and much loved.
She'd swept her hair up in a smooth twist and added sapphire
cabochon earrings that she'd bought in London years before.

She knew it was the sort of feminine armor that women
slipped into for confidence and power. She'd wanted both.

"Thank you again." She slid into the booth across from him and sniffed the rose. "And so do you."

"I know the wine list here," he told her. "Trust me?"

"On wine? Why not?"

"Good." He glanced toward the server. "We'll have a bottle of the number 103."

She laid the rose beside the leather-bound menu. "Which is?"

"A very nice Pouilly Fuisse. I remember from Shiney's that you like white. I think you'll find this a few very important steps up from what you had there."

"Almost anything would be."

He cocked his head, took her hand. "Something's wrong."

"No." Deliberately she curved her lips. "What could be wrong? It's just as advertised." She turned her head to look out the window beside her, where the Bay stretched, dark blue and excitingly choppy under a sky going rosy with sunset. "A lovely view, a pretty spot." She turned back. "An interesting companion for the evening."

No, he thought, watching her eyes. Something was just a little off. On impulse he slid over, cupped her chin in his hand, and laid his lips lightly on hers.

She didn't draw away, but allowed herself to experience. The kiss was easy, smooth, skilled. And very soothing. When he drew back, she raised an eyebrow. "And that was because?"

"You looked like you needed it."

She didn't sigh, but she wanted to. Instead, she put her hands in her lap. "Thank you once again."

"Any time. In fact . . ." His fingers tightened just a little on her face, and this time the kiss moved a bit deeper, lasted a bit longer.

Her lips parted under his before she realized that she'd meant it to happen. Her breath caught, released, and her pulse shivered as his teeth scraped lightly, as his tongue teased hers into a slow, seductive dance.

Her fingers were linked and gripped tight, her mind just beginning to blur when he eased away.

"And that was because?" she managed.

"I guess I needed it."

His lips brushed over hers once, then again, before she found the presence of mind to lay a hand on his chest. A hand, she realized, that wanted to ball into a fist on that soft shirt and hold him in place rather than nudge him away.

But she nudged him away. It was simply a matter of handling him, she reminded herself. Of staying in control.

"I think as appetizers go, that was very appealing. But we should order."

"Tell me what's wrong." He wanted to know, he realized. Wanted to help, wanted to smooth those shadows out of her incredibly clear eyes and make them smile.

He hadn't expected to develop a taste for her so quickly.

"It's nothing."

"Of course it is. And there can't be anything much more therapeutic than dumping on a relative stranger."

"You're right." She opened her menu. "But most relative strangers aren't particularly interested is someone else's minor problems."

"I'm interested in you."

She smiled as she shifted her gaze from the entrées to his face. "You're attracted to me. That's not always the same thing."

"I think I'm both."

He took her hand, held it as the wine was brought to the table, as the label was turned for his approval. He waited while a sample was poured into his glass, watching her in that steady, all-else-aside way she'd discovered he had. He lifted it, sipped, still looking at her.

"It's perfect. You'll like it," he murmured to her while their glasses were being filled.

"You're right," she told him after she sipped. "I like it very much."

"Shall I tell you tonight's specials," their waiter began in a cheerful voice. While he recited, they sat, hands linked, eyes locked.

Sybill decided she heard about every third word and didn't really give a damn. He had the most incredible eyes. Like old gold, like something she'd seen in a painting in Rome. "I'll have the mixed salad, with the vinaigrette, and the fish of the day, grilled."

He kept watching her, his lips curving slowly as he drew her hand across the table to kiss her palm. "The same. And take your time. I'm very attracted," he said to Sybill as the waiter rolled his eyes and walked away. "And I'm very interested. Talk to me."

"All right." What harm could it do? she decided. Since, sooner or later, they would have to deal with each other on a different sort of level, it might be helpful if they understood one another now. "I'm the good daughter." Amused at herself, she smiled a little. "Obedient, respectful, polite, academically skilled, professionally successful."

"It's a burden."

"Yes, it can be. Of course, I know better, intellectually, than to allow myself to be ruled by parental expectations at this stage of my life."

"But," Phillip said, giving her fingers a squeeze, "you are. We all are."

"Are you?"

He thought of sitting by the water in the moonlight and having a conversation with his dead father. "More than I might have believed. In my case, my parents didn't give me life. They gave me *the* life. This life. In yours," he considered, "since you're the good daughter, is there a bad daughter?"

"My sister has always been difficult. Certainly she's been a disappointment to my parents. And the more disappointed they've become in her, the more they expect from me."

"You're supposed to be perfect."

"Exactly, and I can't be." Wanted to be, tried to be, couldn't be. Which, of course, equaled failure. How could it be otherwise? she mused.

"Perfect is boring," Phillip commented. "And intimidating. Why try to be either? So what happened?" he asked when she only frowned.

"It's nothing, really. My mother is angry with me just now. If I give in and do what she wants . . . well, I can't. I just can't."

"So you feel guilty and sad and sorry."

"And afraid that nothing will ever be the same between us again."

"As bad as that?"

"It could be," Sybill murmured. "I'm grateful for all the opportunities they gave me, the structure, the education. We traveled quite a bit, so I saw a great deal of the world, of different cultures, while I was still a child. It's been invaluable in my work."

Opportunities, Phillip thought. Structure, education, and travel. Nowhere had she listed love, affection, fun. He wondered if she realized she'd described a school more than a family. "Where did you grow up?"

"Um. Here and there. New York, Boston, Chicago, Paris, Milan, London. My father lectured and held consultations. He's a psychiatrist. They live in Paris now. It was always my mother's favorite city."

"Long-distance guilt."

It made her laugh. "Yes." She sat back as their salads were served. Oddly enough, she did feel a little better. It seemed slightly less deceptive to have told him something about her-self. "And you grew up here."

"I came here when I was thirteen, when the Quinns became my parents."

"Became?"

"It's part of that long story." He lifted his wineglass, studying her over its rim. Normally if he brought up that pe-riod of his life with a woman, what he told was a carefully edited version. Not a lie, but a less-than-detailed account of his life before the Quinns.

Oddly enough, he was tempted to tell Sybill the whole, the ugly and unvarnished truth. He hesitated, then settled on some-thing between the two.

"I grew up in Baltimore, on the rough side. I got into trouble, pretty serious trouble. By the time I was thirteen, I was headed for worse. The Quinns gave me a chance to change that. They took me in, brought me to St. Chris. Became my family."

"They adopted you." She'd had that much information, from researching everything she could find on Raymond Quinn. But it didn't give her the why.

"Yeah. They already had Cam and Ethan, and they made room for one more. I didn't make it easy for them initially, but they stuck with me. I never knew either of them to back off from a problem."

He thought of his father, broken and dying in a hospital bed. Even then Ray's concerns had been for his sons, for Seth. For family.

"When I first saw you," Sybill began, "the three of you, I knew you were brothers. No real physical resemblance, but something less tangible. I'd say you're an example of how environment can offset heredity."

"More an example of what two generous and determined people can do for three lost boys."

She sipped her wine to soothe her throat before she spoke. "And Seth."

"Lost boy number four. We're trying to do for him what my parents would have done, what our father asked us to do. My mother died several years ago. It left the four of us floundering some. She was an incredible woman. We couldn't have appreciated her enough when we had her."

"I think you did." And moved by the sound of his voice, she smiled at him. "I'm sure she felt very loved."

"I hope so. After we lost her, Cam took off for Europe. Racing—boats, cars, whatever. He did pretty well at it. Ethan stayed. Bought his own house, but he's locked into the Bay. I moved back to Baltimore. Once an urbanite," he added with a quick smile.

"The Inner Harbor, Camden Yards."

"Exactly. I came down here off and on. Holidays, the occasional weekend. But it's not the same."

Curious, she tilted her head. "Would you want it to be?" She remembered her secret thrill when she'd gone off to college. To be on her own, not to have every movement and word weighed and judged. Freedom.

"No, but there were times, are times, I miss the way it was. Don't you ever think back to some perfect summer? You're sixteen, your driver's license is shiny and new in your wallet, and the world is all yours."

She laughed, but shook her head. She hadn't had a driver's license at sixteen. They'd been living in London that year, as she recalled. There had been a uniformed driver to take her where she'd been allowed to go, unless she managed to slip out and ride the Tube. That had been her small rebellion.

"Sixteen-year-old boys," she said, while their salad plates were removed, their entrées served, "are more emotionally attached to their cars than sixteen-year-old girls are."

"It's easier for that boy to get himself a girl if he has wheels."

"I doubt you had any trouble in that area, with or without a car."

"It's tough to neck in the backseat until you've got one."

"True enough. And now you're back here, and so are your brothers."

"Yeah. My father had Seth through complicated and not entirely clear circumstances. Seth's mother . . . well, you'll hear talk if you stay in the area for any length of time."

"Oh?" Sybill cut into her fish, hoping that she could swallow it.

"My father taught English lit at the university, the Eastern Shore campus of Maryland. A little less than a year ago a woman came to see him. It was a private meeting, so we don't have the details, but from all accounts it wasn't pleasant. She went to the dean and accused my father of sexual harassment."

Sybill's fork clattered onto her plate. As casually as she could, she lifted it again. "That must have been very difficult for him, for all of you."

"Difficult isn't quite the word for it. She claimed to have been a student here years back and said that at that time he had demanded sex for grades, intimidated her, had an affair with her."

No, she couldn't swallow, Sybill realized, gripping her fork until her fingers ached. "She had an affair with your father?"

"No, she said she did. My mother would still have been alive," he said half to himself. "In any case, there was no record of her ever attending the university. My father taught on that campus for more than twenty-five years, without a whisper of improper behavior. She took a shot at destroying his reputation. And it left a smear."

Of course there'd be no truth to it, Sybill thought wearily. It was Gloria's usual pattern. Accuse, damage, run. But she herself still had a part to play. "Why? Why would she do that?"

"Money."

"I don't understand."

"My father gave her money, a great deal of it. For Seth. She's Seth's mother."

"You're saying that she . . . she traded her son for money?" Not even Gloria could do something so appalling, she told herself. Surely, not even Gloria. "That's difficult to believe."

"Not all mothers are maternal." He jerked a shoulder. "He had a check for several thousand made out to Gloria De-Lauter—that's her name—and he went away for a few days, then came back with Seth."

Saying nothing, she picked up her water glass, cooled her throat. *He came and got Seth,* Gloria had sobbed to her. *They've got Seth. You have to help me.*

"A few months later," Phillip continued, "he drew almost all his savings out into a cashier's check. He was on his way back from Baltimore when he had an accident. He didn't make it."

"I'm so sorry." She murmured the words, recognizing their inadequacy.

"He hung on until Cam got in from Europe. He asked the three of us to keep Seth, to look out for him. We're doing everything we can to keep that promise. I can't say it wasn't rough for a while," he added, smiling a little now. "But it's never been dull. Moving back here, starting the boat business, not such a bad deal. Cam got a wife out of it," he added with a grin. "Anna is Seth's caseworker."

"Really? They couldn't have known each other very long."

"I guess when it hits, it hits. Time doesn't factor in."

She'd always believed it did, vitally. To be successful, marriage took planning and dedication and a strong, solid knowledge of one's partner, an assurance of compatibility, an assessment of personal goals.

Then again, that portion of the Quinn dynamics wasn't her concern.

"That's quite a story." How much was true? she wondered, sick at heart. How much was slanted? Was she supposed to believe that her sister had sold her own son?

Somewhere in the middle, she decided. The real truth could generally be found somewhere between two opposing stories.

Phillip didn't know, she was sure of that now. He had no clue what Gloria had been to Raymond Quinn. When that single fact was added to the mix, how did it change everything else?

"At this point it's working out. The kid's happy. Another couple of months and the permanent guardianship should be wrapped. And this big brother stuff has its advantages. Gives me somebody to boss around."

She needed to think. She had to put emotion aside and think. But she had to get through the evening first. "How does he feel about that?"

"It's a perfect setup. He can bitch to Cam or Ethan about me, to me about Cam or Ethan. He knows how to play it. Seth's incredibly smart. They did placement tests when my father enrolled him in school here. He's practically off the charts. His final report card for last year? Straight A's."

"Really?" She found herself smiling. "You're proud of him."

"Sure. And me. I'm the one who got roped into being homework monitor. Until recently I'd forgotten how much I hate fractions. Now that I've told you my long story, why don't you tell me what you think of St. Chris?"

"I'm just getting my bearings."

"Does that mean you'll be staying a while yet?"

"Yes. A while."

"You can't really judge a water town unless you spend some time on the water. Why don't you go sailing with me tomorrow?"

"Don't you have to get back to Baltimore?"

"Monday."

She hesitated, then reminded herself that this was exactly why she was here. If she was to find that real truth, she couldn't back away now. "I'd like that. I can't guarantee what kind of sailor I'll be."

"We'll find out. I'll pick you up. Ten, ten-thirty?"

"That'll be fine. All of you sail, I imagine."

"Right down to the dogs." He laughed at the expression on her face. "We won't bring them along."

"I'm not afraid of them. I'm just not used to them."

"You never had a puppy."

"No."

"Cat?"

"No."

"Goldfish?"

She laughed, shook her head. "No. We moved around quite a bit. Once I had a schoolmate in Boston whose dog had puppies. They were darling." Odd, she thought, to have remembered that now. She'd wanted one of those pups desperately.

It had been impossible, of course. Antique furniture, important guests, social obligations. Out of the question, her mother had said. And that had been the end of it.

"Now I move around quite a bit. It's not practical."

"Where do you like best?" he asked her.

"I'm flexible. Wherever I end up tends to suit me, until I'm somewhere else."

"So right now it's St. Chris."

"Apparently. It's interesting." She gazed out the window, where the rising moon glittered light onto the water. "The pace is slow, but it's not stagnant. The mood varies, as the weather varies. After only a few days, I'm able to separate the natives from the tourists. And the watermen from everyone else."

"How?"

"How?" Distracted, she looked back at him.

"How can you tell one from the other?"

"Just basic observation. I can look out of my window onto the waterfront. The tourists are couples, more likely families, occasionally a single. They stroll, or they shop. They rent a boat. They interact with each other, the ones in their group. They're out of their milieu. Most will have camera, map, maybe binoculars. Most of the natives have a purpose for being there. A job, an errand. They might stop and say hello to a neighbor. You can see them easing back on their way as they end the conversation."

"Why are you watching from the window?"

"I don't understand the question."

"Why aren't you down on the waterfront?"

"I have been. But you usually get a purer study when you, the observer, aren't part of the scene."

"I'd think you'd get more varied and more personal input if you were." He glanced up as the waiter arrived to top off their wine and offer them dessert.

"Just coffee," Sybill decided. "Decaf."

"The same." Phillip leaned forward. "In your book, the section on isolation as a survival technique, the example you used of having someone lying on the sidewalk. How people would look away, walk around. Some might hesitate before hurrying past."

"Noninvolvement. Disassociation."

"Exactly. But one person would eventually stop, try to help. Once one person broke the isolation, others would begin to stop, too."

"Once the isolation is breached, it becomes easier, even necessary for others to join. It's the first step that's the most difficult. I conducted that study in New York and London and Budapest, all with similar results. It follows the urban survival technique of avoiding eye contact on the street, of blocking the homeless out of our line of sight."

"What makes that first person who stops to help different from everyone else?"

"Their survival instincts aren't as well honed as their compassion. Or their impulse button is more easily pushed."

"Yeah, that. And they're involved. They're not just walking through, not just there. They're involved."

"And you think that because I observe, I'm not."

"I don't know. But I think that observing from a distance isn't nearly as rewarding as experiencing up close."

"Observing's what I do, and I find it rewarding."

He slid closer and kept his eyes on hers, ignoring the waiter who tidily served their coffee. "But you're a scientist. You experiment. Why don't you give experiencing a try? With me."

She looked down, watched his fingertip toy with hers. And felt the slow heat of response creep into her blood. "That's a very novel, if roundabout, way of suggesting that I sleep with you."

"Actually, that wasn't what I meant—though if the answer's yes, I'm all for it." He flashed her a grin as she shifted her gaze warily to his. "I was going to suggest that we take a walk on the waterfront when we've finished our coffee. But if you'd rather sleep with me, we can be in your hotel room in, oh, five minutes flat."

She didn't evade when his head lowered to hers, when his lips slid lazily into a lovely fit over hers. The taste of him was cool, with an underlying promise of heat. If she wanted it. And she did. It surprised her how much, just at that one moment, she wanted the flash and burn—the demand that would override the tension inside her, the worry, the doubts.

But she'd had a lifetime of training against self-indulgence, and now she laid a hand lightly on his chest to end the kiss, and the temptation.

"I think a walk would be pleasant."

"Then we'll walk."

HE WANTED MORE. PHILLIP told himself he should have known that a few tastes of her would stir up the need. But he hadn't expected that need to be quite so sharp, quite so edgy. Maybe part of it was sheer ego, he mused as he took her hand to walk with her along the quiet waterfront. Her response had been so cool and controlled. It made him wonder what it would be like to peel that intellect away, layer by layer, and find the woman beneath. To work his way down to pure emotion and instinct.

He nearly laughed at himself. Ego, indeed. For all he knew, that formal, slightly distant response was precisely all that Dr. Sybill Griffin intended to give him.

If so, that made her a challenge he was going to have a very difficult time resisting.

"I see why Shiney's is a popular spot." She slanted him a smiling look. "It's barely nine-thirty and the shops are closed, the boats are moored. A few people strolling along, but for the most part everything here is tucked in for the night."

"It's a little livelier during the summer. Not much, but a little. It's cooling off. Are you warm enough?"

"Mmm. Plenty. It's a lovely breeze." She stopped to look out at the swaying masts of boats. "Do you keep your boat here?"

"No, we have a dock at home. That's Ethan's skipjack."

"Where?"

"It's the only skipjack in St. Chris. There are only a couple of dozen left on the Bay. There." he gestured. "The single mast."

To her untrained eye, one sailboat looked very much the same as the next. Size varied, of course, and gloss, but essentially they were all boats. "What's a skipjack?"

"It evolved from the flat-bottomed bay-crabbing skiffs."
He drew her closer as he spoke. "They were enlarged, designed with a V-shaped hull. Had to be easily and inexpensively built."

"So they go out crabbing in them."

"No, mostly the watermen use motor-powered workboats for crabbing. The skipjack is for oysters. Back in the early 1800s they passed a law in Maryland that allowed only sail-powered vessels to dredge for oysters."

"Conservation?"

"Exactly. The skipjack came out of that, and it still survives. But there aren't many of them. There aren't many oysters either."

"Does your brother still use it?"

"Yeah. It's miserable, cold, hard, frustrating work."

"You sound like the voice of experience."

"I've put in some time on her." He stopped near the bow and slipped an arm around Sybill's waist. "Sailing out in February, with that wind cutting through you, bouncing on the high chop of a winter storm . . . all in all, I'd rather be in Baltimore."

She chuckled, studying the boat. It looked ancient and rough, like something out of an earlier time. "Without having set foot on it, I'm going to agree with you. So why were you bouncing on the high chop of a winter storm instead of in Baltimore?"

"Beats the hell out of me."

"I take it this isn't the boat you invited me out on tomorrow."

"No. That one's a tidy little pleasure sloop. Do you swim?"

She arched an eyebrow. "Is that a statement on your sailing abilities?"

"No, it's a suggestion. The water's cool, but not so cold you couldn't take a dip if you like."

"I didn't bring a bathing suit with me."

"And your point is?"

She laughed and started walking again. "I think a sail's enough for one day. I've got some work I want to finish up tonight. I enjoyed dinner."

"So did I. I'll walk you to your hotel."

"There's no need. It's just around the corner."

"Nonetheless."

She didn't argue. She had no intention of allowing him to walk her to her door, or to talk his way into her suite. All in all, she felt she was handling him, and a difficult, confusing situation, very well. An early night, she mused, would give her time to sort out her thoughts and feelings before she saw him again the next day.

And since the boat was docked at his home, the odds were good that she would see Seth again, too.

"I'll come down in the morning," she began as she stopped a few feet from the lobby entrance. "Ten or so?"

"Fine."

"Is there anything I should bring? Besides Dramamine?"

He shot her a grin. "I'll take care of it. Sleep well."

"You, too."

She prepared herself for the easy and expected good-night kiss. His lips were soft, undemanding. Pleased with both of them, she relaxed, started to back away.

Then his hand cupped the back of her neck firmly, his head changed angles, and for one staggering moment, the kiss went hot and wild and threatening. The hand she'd laid on his shoulder curled into a fist, gripping his jacket, hanging on for balance as her feet all but swept out from under her. Her mind went blank as her pulse leapt to roar in her spinning head.

Someone moaned, low and deep and long.

It lasted only seconds, but it was as shocking and burning as a brand. He saw the stunned arousal in her eyes when they

opened and stared into his. And he felt that basic need claw
to a new level inside him.

Not a cool, controlled, and distant response this time, he
decided. One layer down, he mused, and skimmed his thumb
along her jawline.

"I'll see you in the morning."

"Yes—good night." She recovered quickly and sent him
a smile before turning. But she pressed an unsteady hand to
her jittery stomach as she slipped into the lobby.

She'd miscalculated that one, she admitted, fighting to take
slow, even breaths as she walked to the elevator. He wasn't
as smooth, polished, and harmless as he appeared on the surface.

There was something much more primitive and much more
dangerous inside that attractive package than she'd realized.

And whatever it was, she found it entirely too compelling
for her own good.

SIX

I⊤ WAS LIKE RIDING A BIKE. Or sex, Phillip mused as he tacked, threading through the light traffic on the Bay toward an available slip on the waterfront. It had been a while since he'd done any solo sailing, but he hadn't forgotten how. If anything, he'd forgotten how much he enjoyed being out on the water on a breezy Sunday morning, with the sun warm and the water blue and the wicked screams of gulls echoing on the air.

He was going to have to start finding time for simple pleasures again. Since this was the first full day he'd taken off in more than two months, he intended to make the most of it.

He certainly intended to make the most of a few golden hours on the Bay with the intriguing Dr. Griffin.

He looked over at the hotel, idly trying to calculate which window might be hers. From what she'd told him, he knew it faced the water, giving her a view of the life that pulsed there and enough distance for her research.

Then he saw her, standing on a tiny balcony, her glossy, mink-colored hair sleeked back and haloed in the sunlight, her face aloof and unreadable from so far away.

Not so aloof close up, he thought, replaying their last sizzle of a kiss in his mind. No, there'd been nothing aloof in that long, throaty moan, nothing distant in that quick, hard tremble her body had made against his. That instinctive, involuntary signal of blood calling to blood.

Her eyes, that water-clear blue, hadn't been cool; nor had they been intriguingly remote when he'd lifted his mouth from hers and looked into them. Instead, they'd been just a little clouded, just a little confused. And all the more intriguing.

He hadn't quite been able to get her taste out of his system, not on the drive home, not through the night, not now, seeing her again. And knowing she stood and watched him.

What, he wondered, do you observe, Dr. Griffin? And what do you intend to do about it?

Phillip flashed her a quick smile, snapped her a salute to let her know he'd seen her. Then he shifted his attention away from her and maneuvered into dock.

His brows lifted in surprise as he saw Seth standing on dock waiting to secure the lines. "What're you doing here?"

Expertly, Seth looped the bow line over the post. "Playing errand boy again." There was a hint of disgust in the tone, but Seth had to work to put it there. "They sent me down from the boatyard. Donuts."

"Yeah?" Phillip stepped nimbly onto the dock. "Artery cloggers."

"Real people don't eat tree bark for breakfast," Seth sneered. "Just you."

"And I'll still be strong and good-looking when you're a wheezing old man."

"Maybe, but I'll have more fun."

Phillip tugged Seth's ball cap off, batted him lightly with it. "Depends, pal, on your definition of fun."

"I guess yours is poking at city girls."

"That's one of them. Another is hounding you over your

homework. You finish *Johnny Tremaine* for your book report?''

"Yeah, yeah, yeah." Seth rolled his eyes. "Man, don't you ever take a day off?"

"What, when my life is devoted to you?" He grinned at Seth's snort. "So, what'd you think of it?"

"It was okay." Then he jerked a shoulder, a purely Quinn movement. "It was pretty good."

"We'll put together some notes for your oral report later tonight."

"Sunday night's my favorite night of the week," Seth said. "It means you'll be gone for four days."

"Come on, you know you miss me."

"Shit."

"You count the hours until I come home."

Seth barely suppressed a giggle. "Like hell." Then he did giggle as Phillip snagged him around the waist for a tussle.

Sybill heard the bright, happy sound as she walked toward them. She saw the wide grin on Seth's face. Her heart did a long, slow roll in her chest. What was she doing here? she asked herself. What did she hope to accomplish?

And how could she walk away until she found out?

"Good morning."

Distracted by her voice, Phillip glanced over, dropping his guard just long enough for Seth's elbow to slip through and into his gut. He grunted, wrapped an arm around Seth's neck, and leaned down. "I'll have to beat you up later," he said in a stage whisper. "When there aren't any witnesses."

"You wish." Flushed with pleasure, Seth settled his cap securely on his head and feigned disinterest. "Some of us gotta work today."

"And some of us don't."

"I thought you were going with us," Sybill said to Seth. "Would you like to?"

"I'm just a slave around here." Seth looked longingly at

the boat, then shrugged. "We got a hull to build. Besides, Pretty Boy here will probably capsize her."

"Smart-ass." Phillip made a grab, but Seth danced laughingly out of reach.

"Hope she can swim!" he called out, then raced away.

When Phillip looked back at Sybill, she was gnawing her bottom lip. "I'm not going to capsize her."

"Well . . ." Sybill glanced toward the boat. It seemed awfully small and fragile. "I can swim, so I suppose it's all right."

"Christ, kid comes along and completely smears my rep. I've been sailing longer than the brat's been alive."

"Don't be angry with him."

"Huh?"

"Please, don't be angry with him. I'm sure he was just joking with you. He didn't mean to be disrespectful."

Phillip just stared at her. She'd actually gone pale, and her hand was nervously twisting the thin gold chain she wore around her neck. There was active and acute distress in her voice. "Sybill, I'm not mad at him. We were just fooling around. Relax." Baffled, he rubbed his knuckles lightly over her jaw. "Razzing each other is just our clever male way of showing affection."

"Oh." She wasn't certain whether to be embarrassed or relieved. "I guess that shows I didn't have any brothers."

"It would have been their job to make your life a living hell." He leaned down, touched her lips lightly with his. "It's traditional."

He stepped onto the boat, held out a hand. After the briefest of hesitations, she let him take hers.

"Welcome aboard."

The deck rocked under her feet. She did her best to ignore it. "Thank you. Do I have an assignment?"

"For now, sit, relax, and enjoy."

"I should be able to manage that."

At least she hoped so. She sat on one of the padded benches, gripping it tightly as he stepped out again to release the lines. It would be fine, she assured herself. It would be fun.

Hadn't she watched him sail into port, or dock, or whatever you would call it? He'd seemed very competent. Even a bit cocky, she decided, the way he'd scanned the hotel until he saw her standing out on her balcony.

There had been something foolishly romantic about that, she thought now. The way he had sailed across the sun-splashed water, searching for her, finding her. Then the quick smile and wave. If her pulse had bumped a little, it was an understandable and human response.

He made such a picture, after all. The faded jeans, the crisp T-shirt tucked into them as blindingly white as the sails, that gilded hair, and the warmly tanned, sleekly muscled arms. What woman wouldn't feel a bump at the prospect of spending a few hours alone with a man who looked like Phillip Quinn?

And kissed like Phillip Quinn.

Though she had promised herself she wouldn't dwell on that particular talent of his. He'd shown her just a little too much of that skill the night before.

Now with the sails lowered, he motored gently away from the dock. She found some security in the low rumble of the engine. Not that different from a car, really, she supposed. This vehicle just happened to drive over water.

Nor were they really alone. Her hands relaxed their death grip on the bench as she watched other boats skim and glide. She saw a boy who was surely no older than Seth, tucked into a tiny boat with a triangular red sail. If it was an activity considered safe for children, surely she could handle it.

"Hoisting sails."

She turned her head, smiled absently at Phillip. "What did you say?"

"Watch."

He moved gracefully over the deck, working the lines. Then suddenly the sails rose, snapped in the wind, filled with it. Her heartbeat skipped and scrambled, and her fingers tightened once more on the bench.

No, she'd been wrong, she saw that now. This was nothing at all like a car. It was primitive and beautiful and thrilling. The boat no longer seemed small, or fragile, but powerful, just a little dangerous. And breathtaking.

Very much like the man who captained her.

"It's lovely from down here." Though she kept her hands firmly locked on the bench, she smiled over at Phillip. "They always look pretty when I watch from the window. But it's lovely to see the sails from below."

"You're sitting," Phillip commented as he took the wheel. "And you're enjoying, but I don't think you're relaxing."

"Not yet. I might get there." She turned her face to the wind. It tugged and teased at her hair, trying to free it from the band. "Where are we going?"

"Nowhere in particular."

Her smile warmed and widened. "I rarely have a chance to go there."

She hadn't smiled at him just that way before, Phillip thought. Without thinking, without weighing. He doubted she realized how that easy smile transformed her coolly beautiful face into something softer, more approachable. Wanting to touch her, he held out a hand.

"Come on up here, check out the view."

Her smile faded. "Stand up?"

"Yeah. There's no chop today. It's a smooth ride."

"Stand up," she repeated, giving each word separate weight. "And walk over there. On the boat."

"Two steps." He couldn't stop the grin. "You don't want to just be a bystander, do you?"

"Actually, yes." Her eyes widened when he stepped away from the wheel. "No, don't." She stifled a scream when he laughed and snagged her hand. Before she could dig in, he'd pulled her to her feet. Off balance, she fell against him and held on in terror and defense.

"Couldn't have planned that one better," he murmured and holding her, stepped back to the wheel. "I like getting close enough to smell you. A man has to get almost right here . . ." He turned his head, nuzzled his lips on her throat.

"Stop." Thrills and fears raced through her. "Pay attention."

"Oh, believe me"—his teeth caught and nipped her earlobe—"I am."

"To the boat. Pay attention to the boat."

"Oh, yeah." But he kept one arm snug around her waist. "Look out over the bow, to port. The left," he explained. "That little swash there goes back into the marsh. You'll see herons and wild turkey."

"Where?"

"Sometimes you have to go in to find them. But you can catch sight of them now and then, the herons standing like a sculpture in the high grass or rising up from it, the turkeys bobbling their way out of the trees."

She wanted to see, she discovered. She hoped she would see.

"In another month, we'll have geese flying over. From their view this area wouldn't look much different from the Everglades."

Her heart was still jumping, but she inhaled slowly, exhaled deliberately. "Why?"

"The marshland. It's too far from the beaches for the developers to be very interested. It's largely undisturbed. Just one of the Bay's assets, one of the factors that makes it an estuary. A finer one for watermen than the fjords of Norway."

She inhaled again, exhaled. "Why?"

"The shallows, for one thing. A good estuary needs shallows so the sun can nourish aquatic plants, plankton. And the marshlands, for another. They add the tidal creeks, the coves. There.'' He brushed a kiss over the crown on her head. ''Now you're relaxing.''

With some surprise, she realized she wasn't simply relaxing. She'd already gotten there. ''So, you were appealing to the scientist.''

''Took your mind off your nerves.''

''Yes, it did.'' Odd, she thought, that he would know so quickly which switch to throw. ''I don't think I have my sea legs yet, but it is a pretty view. Still so green.'' She watched the passing of big, leafy trees, the deep pockets of shadows in the marsh. They sailed by markers topped with huge, scruffy nests. ''What birds build those?''

''Osprey. Now they're experts at those disassociation techniques. You can sail right by one when it's sitting on its nest, and it'll look right through you.''

''Survival instinct,'' she murmured. She'd like to see that, too. An osprey roosting on that rough circular nest, ignoring the humans.

''See those orange buoys? Crab pots. The workboat putting down that gut? He's going to check his pots, rebait. Over there, to starboard.'' He nudged her head to the right. ''The little outboard. Looks to me like they're hoping to catch some rockfish for Sunday dinner.''

''It's a busy place,'' she commented. ''I didn't realize there was so much going on.''

''On and under the water.''

He adjusted the sails and, heeling in, skimmed around a thick line of trees leaning out from shore. As they cleared the trees, a narrow dock came into view. Behind it was a sloping lawn, flower beds just starting to lose their summer brilliance. The house was simple, white with blue trim. A rocker sat on the wide covered porch, and bronze-toned mums speared out of an old crockery tub.

Sybill could hear the light, drifting notes of music floating through the open windows. Chopin, she realized after a moment.

"It's charming." She angled her head, shifting slightly to keep the house in view. "All it needs is a dog, a couple of kids tossing a ball, and a tire swing."

"We were too old for tire swings, but we always had the dog. That's our house," he told her, absently running his hand down her long, smooth ponytail.

"Yours?" She strained, wanting to see more. Where Seth lived, she thought, struck by dozens of conflicting emotions.

"We spent plenty of time tossing balls, or each other, in the backyard. We'll come back later and you can meet the rest of the family."

She closed her eyes and squashed the guilt. "I'd like that."

HE HAD A PLACE IN MIND. The quiet cove with its lapping water and dappled shade was a perfect spot for a romantic picnic. He dropped anchor where the eelgrass gleamed wetly, and the sky canopied in unbroken autumnal blue overhead.

"Obviously my research on this area was lacking."

"Oh?" Phillip opened a large cooler and retrieved a bottle of wine.

"It's full of surprises."

"Pleasant ones, I hope."

"Very pleasant ones." She smiled, raising a brow at the label on the wine he opened. "Very pleasant."

"You struck me as a woman who'd appreciate a fine dry Sancerre."

"You're very astute."

"Indeed I am." From a wicker hamper he took two wineglasses and poured. "To pleasant surprises," he said and tapped his glass to hers.

"Are there more?"

He took her hand, kissed her fingers. "We've barely started." Setting his glass aside, he unfolded a white cloth and spread it on the deck. "Your table's ready."

"Ah." Enjoying herself, she sat, shaded her eyes against the sun, and smiled up at him. "What's today's special?"

"Some rather nice paté to stir the appetite." To demonstrate, he opened a small container and a box of stoned wheat crackers. He spread one for her and held it to her lips.

"Mmm." She nodded after the first bite. "Very nice."

"To be followed by crab salad à la Quinn."

"Sounds intriguing. And did you make it with your own two hands?"

"I did." He grinned at her. "I'm a hell of a cook."

"The man cooks, has excellent taste in wine, appreciates ambience, and wears his Levi's very well." She bit into the paté again, relaxed now, the ground familiar and easily negotiated. "You appear to be quite a catch, Mr. Quinn."

"I am indeed, Dr. Griffin."

She laughed into her wine. "And how often have you brought some lucky woman to this spot for crab salad à la Quinn?"

"Actually, I haven't been here with a woman since the summer of my sophomore year in college. Then it was a fairly decent Chablis, chilled shrimp, and Marianne Teasdale."

"I suppose I should be flattered."

"I don't know. Marianne was pretty hot." He flashed that killer grin again. "But being callow and shortsighted, I threw her over for a pre-med student with a sexy lisp and big brown eyes."

"Lisps do weaken a man. Did Marianne recover?"

"Enough to marry a plumber from Princess Anne and bear him two children. But, of course, we know she secretly yearns for me."

Laughing, Sybill spread a cracker for him. "I like you."

"I like you, too." He caught her wrist, holding it as he nibbled at the cracker she held. "And you don't even lisp."

When his lips continued to nibble, at the tips of her fingers now, it wasn't quite as easy to breathe. "You're very smooth," she murmured.

"You're very lovely."

"Thank you. What I should say," she continued, and eased her hand out of his, "is that while you're very smooth, and very attractive, and I'm enjoying spending time with you, I don't intend to be seduced."

"You know what they say about intentions."

"I tend to hold to mine. And while I do enjoy your company, I also recognize your type." She smiled again and gestured with her glass. "A hundred years ago, the word 'rogue' would have come to mind."

He considered a moment. "That didn't sound like an insult."

"It wasn't meant to be. Rogues are invariably charming and very rarely serious."

"I have to object there. There are some issues that I'm very serious about."

"Let's try this." She peeked in the cooler and took out another container. "Have you ever been married?"

"No."

"Engaged?" she asked as she opened the lid and discovered a beautifully prepared crab salad.

"No."

"Have you ever lived with a woman for a consecutive period of six months or more?"

With a shrug, he took plates out of the hamper, passed her a pale-blue linen napkin. "No."

"So, we can theorize that one of the issues about which you are not serious is relationships."

"Or we can theorize that I have yet to meet the woman I want a serious relationship with."

"We could. However . . ." She narrowed her eyes at his face as he scooped salad onto the plates. "You're what, thirty?"

"One." He added a thick slice of French bread to each plate.

"Thirty-one. Typically, by the age of thirty a man in this culture would have experienced at least one serious, long-term, monogamous relationship."

"I wouldn't care to be typical. Olives?"

"Yes, thanks. Typical is not necessarily an unattractive trait. Nor is conformity. Everyone conforms. Even those who consider themselves the rebels of society conform to certain codes and standards."

Enjoying her, he tilted his head. "Is that so, Dr. Griffin?"

"Quite so. Gang members in the inner city have internal rules, codes, standards. Colors," she added, selecting an olive from her plate. "In that way they don't differ much from members of the city council."

"You had to be there," Phillip mumbled.

"Excuse me?"

"Nothing. What about serial killers?"

"They follow patterns." Enjoying herself, she tore a chunk off her slice of bread. "The FBI studies them, catalogs them, profiles them. Society wouldn't term them standards certainly, but in the strictest sense of the word, that's precisely what they are."

Damned if she didn't have a point, he decided. And found himself only more fascinated. "So you, the observer, size people up by noting what rules, codes, patterns they follow."

"More or less. People aren't so very difficult to understand, if you pay attention."

"What about those surprises?"

She smiled, appreciating the question as much as she appreciated that he would think to ask it. Most laymen she'd socialized with weren't really interested in her work. "They're factored in. There's always margin for error, and for adjustments. This is wonderful salad.'' She sampled another bite. ''And the surprise, a pleasant one, is that you would have gone to the trouble to prepare it.''

''Don't you find that people are usually willing to go to some trouble for someone they care for?'' When she only blinked at him, he tilted his head. ''Well, well, that threw you off.''

''You barely know me.'' She picked up her wine, a purely defensive gesture. ''There's a difference between being attracted to and caring for. The latter takes more time.''

''Some of us move fast.'' He enjoyed seeing her flustered. It would be, he decided, a rare event. Taking advantage of it, he slid closer. ''I do.''

''So I've already observed. However—''

''However. I like hearing you laugh. I like feeling you tremble just slightly when I kiss you. I like hearing your voice slide into that didactic tone when you expand on a theory.''

At the last comment she frowned. ''I'm not didactic.''

''Charmingly,'' he murmured, skimming his lips over her temple. ''And I like seeing your eyes in that moment when I start to confuse you. Therefore, I believe I've crossed over into the care-for stage. So let's try your earlier hypothesis out on you and see where that leaves us. Have you ever been married?''

His mouth was cruising just under her ear, making it very difficult to think clearly. ''No. Well, not really.''

He paused, leaned back, narrowed his eyes. ''No or not really?''

''It was an impulse, an error in judgment. It was less than six months. It didn't count.'' Her brain was fogged, she decided, trying to inch away for some breathing room. He only scooted her back.

''You were married?''

''Only technically. It didn't . . .'' She turned her head to make her point, and his mouth was there. Right there to meet hers, to urge her lips to part and warm and soften.

It was like sliding under a slow-moving wave, being taken down into silky, shimmering water. Everything inside her went fluid. A surprise, she would realize later, that she'd neglected to factor into this particular pattern.

"It didn't count," she managed as her head fell back, as his lips trailed smoothly down her throat.

"Okay."

If he'd taken her by surprise, she'd done exactly the same to him. At her sudden and utter surrender to the moment, his need churned to the surface, thrashing there. He had to touch her, to fill his hands with her, to mold those pretty curves through the thin, crisp cotton of her blouse.

He had to taste her, deeper now, while those little hums of shock and pleasure sounded in her throat. As he did, as he touched and as he tasted, her arms came around him, her hands sliding into his hair, her body turning to fit itself against him.

He felt her heart thud in time with his own.

Panic punched through pleasure when she felt him tug at the buttons of her blouse. "No." Her own fingers shook as she covered his. "It's too fast." She squeezed her eyes shut, struggling to find her control, her sense, her purpose. "I'm sorry. I don't go this fast. I can't."

It wasn't easy to check the urge to ignore the rules, to simply press her under him on the deck until she was pliant and willing again. He put his tense fingers under her chin and lifted her face to his. No, it wasn't easy, he thought again as he saw both desire and denial in her eyes. But it was necessary.

"Okay. No rush." He rubbed his thumb over her bottom lip. "Tell me about the one that didn't count."

Her thoughts had scattered to the edges of her mind. She couldn't begin to draw them together while he was looking at her with those tawny eyes. "What?"

"The husband."

"Oh." She looked away, concentrated on her breathing.

"What are you doing?"

"Relaxation technique."

Humor danced back and made him grin at her. "Does it work?"

"Eventually."

"Cool." He shifted until they were hip to hip and timed his breathing to hers. "So this guy you were technically married to . . ."

"It was in college, at Harvard. He was a chemistry major." Eyes shut, she ordered her toes to relax, then her arches, her ankles. "We were barely twenty and just lost our heads for a short time."

"Eloped."

"Yes. We didn't even live together, because we were in different dorms. So it wasn't really a marriage. It was weeks before we told our families, and then, naturally, there were several difficult scenes."

"Why?"

"Because . . ." She blinked her eyes open, found the sun dazzling. Something plopped in the water behind her, then there was only the lap of it, kissing the hull. "We weren't suited, we had no feasible plans. We were too young. The divorce was very quiet and quick and civilized."

"Did you love him?"

"I was twenty." Her relaxation level was reaching her shoulders. "Of course I thought I did. Love has little complexity at that age."

"So spoken from the advanced age of what twenty-seven, twenty-eight?"

"Twenty-nine and counting." She let out a last long breath. Satisfied and steady, she turned to look at him again. "I haven't thought of Rob in years. He was a very nice boy. I hope he's happy."

"And that's it for you?"

"It has to be."

He nodded, but found her story strangely sad. "Then I have to say, Dr. Griffin, that using your own scale, you don't take relationships seriously."

She opened her mouth to protest, then wisely, shut it again. Casually, she picked up the wine bottle and topped off both glasses. "You may be right. I'll have to give that some thought."

SEVEN

SETH DIDN'T MIND RUNNING
herd on Aubrey. She was kind of his niece now that Ethan
and Grace were married. Being an uncle made him feel adult
and responsible. Besides, all she really wanted to do was race
around the yard. Every time he threw a ball or a stick for one
of the dogs, she went into gales of laughter. A guy couldn't
help but get a kick out of it.

She was pretty cute, too, with her curly gold hair and her
big green eyes that looked amazed at everything he did.
Spending an hour or two on a Sunday entertaining her wasn't
a bad deal.

He hadn't forgotten where he had been a year ago. There'd
been no big backyard that fell off into the water, no woods to
explore, no dogs to wrestle with, no little girl who looked at
him like he was Fox Mulder, all the Power Rangers and Superman rolled into one.

Instead, there'd been grungy rooms three flights up from
the street. And those streets had been a dark carnival at night,
a place where everything had its price. Sex, drugs, weapons,
misery.

He'd learned that no matter what went on in those grungy rooms, he shouldn't go out after dark.

There'd been no one to care if he was clean or fed, if he was sick or scared. He'd never felt like a hero there, or even very much like a kid. He'd felt like a thing, and he'd learned quickly that things are often hunted.

Gloria had ridden all the rides in that carnival, again and again. She'd brought the freaks and the hustlers into those rooms, selling herself to whoever would pay the price of her next spin.

A year ago Seth hadn't believed his life would ever be any different. Then Ray came and took him to the house by the water. Ray showed him a different world and promised he would never have to go back to the old one.

Ray had died, but he had kept his promise all the same. Now Seth could stand in the big backyard with water lapping at its edges and throw balls and sticks for the dogs to chase while an angel-faced toddler laughed.

"Seth, let me! Let me!" Aubrey danced on her sturdy little legs, holding up both hands for the mangled ball.

"Okay, you throw it."

He grinned while she screwed up her face with concentration and effort. The ball bounced inches away from the toes of her bright-red sneakers. Simon snapped it up, making her squeal with delight, then politely offered it back.

"Oooh, good doggie." Aubrey batted the patient Simon on either side of his jaw. Angling for attention, Foolish nudged his way in, shoved her down on her butt. She rewarded him with a fierce hug. "Now you," she ordered Seth. "You do it."

Obliging her, Seth winged the ball. He laughed as the dogs raced after it, bumping their bodies like two football players rushing downfield. They crashed into the woods, sending a pair of birds squawking skyward.

At that moment, with Aubrey bouncing with giggles, the

dogs barking, the fresh September air on his cheeks, Seth was completely happy. A part of his mind focused on it, snatched at it to keep. The angle of the sun, the brilliance of light on the water, the creamy sound of Otis Redding drifting through the kitchen window, the bitchy complaints of the birds, and the rich salty scent of the bay.

He was home.

Then the putt of a motor caught his attention. When he turned he saw the family sloop angling in toward the dock. At the wheel, Phillip raised a hand in greeting. Even as Seth returned the wave, his gaze shifted to the woman standing beside Phillip. It felt as if something brushed over the nape of his neck, light and cagey as the legs of a spider. Absently he rubbed at it, shrugged his shoulders, then took Aubrey firmly by the hand.

"Remember, you have to stay in the middle of the dock."

She gazed up at him adoringly. "Okay. I will. Mama says never, never go by the water by myself."

"That's right." He stepped onto the dock with her and waited for Phillip to come alongside. It was the woman who, awkwardly, tossed him the bow line. Sybill something, he thought. For a moment, as she balanced herself, as their eyes met, he felt that sly tickle on the nape of his neck again.

Then the dogs were bounding onto the dock and Aubrey was laughing again.

"Hey, Angel Baby." Phillip helped Sybill step onto the dock, then winked down at Aubrey.

"Up," she demanded.

"You bet." He swung her onto his hip and planted a smacking kiss on her cheek. "When are you going to grow up and marry me?"

"Tomorrow!"

"That's what you always say. This is Sybill. Sybill, meet Aubrey, my best girl."

"She's pretty," Aubrey stated and flashed her dimples.

"Thank you. So are you." As the dogs bumped her legs, Sybill jolted and took a step back. Phillip shot out a hand to grab her arm before she backed her way off the dock and into the water.

"Steady there. Seth, call off the dogs. Sybill's a little uneasy around them."

"They won't hurt you," Seth said with a shake of his head that warned Sybill she'd just dropped several notches in his estimation. But he snagged both dogs by the collar, holding them back until she could ease by.

"Everybody inside?" Phillip asked Seth.

"Yeah, just hanging until dinner. Grace brought over a monster chocolate cake. Cam sweet-talked Anna into making lasagna."

"God bless him. My sister-in-law's lasagna is a work of art," he told Sybill.

"Speaking of art, I wanted to tell you again, Seth, how much I liked the sketches you've done for the boatyard. They're very good."

He shrugged his shoulders, then bent down to scoop up two sticks to toss and distract the dogs. "I just draw sometimes."

"Me, too." She knew it was foolish, but Sybill felt her cheeks go warm at the way Seth studied her, measured and judged. "It's something I like to do in my spare time," she went on. "I find it relaxing and satisfying."

"Yeah, I guess."

"Maybe you'll show me more of your work sometime."

"If you want." He pushed open the door to the kitchen and headed straight to the refrigerator. A telling sign, Sybill mused. He was at home here.

She took a quick scan of the room, filing impressions. There was a pot simmering on what seemed to be an ancient stove. The scent was impossibly aromatic. Several small clay pots lined the windowsill over the sink. Fresh herbs thrived in them.

The counters were clean, if a bit worn. A pile of papers was stacked on the end beneath a wall phone and anchored with a set of keys. A shallow bowl was centered on the table and filled with glossy red and green apples. A mug of coffee, half full, stood in front of a chair under which someone had kicked off shoes.

"Goddamn it! That ump ought to be shot in the head. That pitch was a mile high."

Sybill arched an eyebrow at the furious male voice from the next room. Phillip merely smiled and jiggled Aubrey on his hip. "Ball game. Cam's taking this year's pennant race personally."

"The game! I forgot." Seth slammed the refrigerator door and raced out of the kitchen. "What's the score, what inning is it, who's up?"

"Three to two, A's, bottom of the sixth, two outs, a man on second. Now sit down and shut up."

"Very personally," Phillip added, then set Aubrey down when she wiggled.

"Baseball often becomes a personal challenge between the audience and the opposing team. Especially," Sybill added with a sober nod, "during the September pennant race."

"You like baseball?"

"What's not to like?" she said and laughed. "It's a fascinating study of men, of teamwork, of battle. Speed, cunning, finesse, and always pitcher against batter. In the end it all comes down to style, endurance. And math."

"We're going to have to take in a game at Camden Yards," he decided. "I'd just love to hear your play-by-play technique. Can I get you anything?"

"No, I'm fine." More shouts, more cursing burst out of the living room. "But I think it might be dangerous to leave this room as long as your brother's team is down a run."

"You're perceptive." Phillip reached out to curve his hand over her cheek. "So, why don't we stay right here and—"

"Way to go, Cal!" Cam shouted from the living room. "That son of a bitch is amazing."

"Shit." Seth's voice was cocky and smug. "No stinking California outfielder's going to blow one by Ripken."

Phillip let out a sigh. "Or maybe we should head out back and take a walk for a few innings."

"Seth, I believe we've discussed acceptable word usage in this house."

"Anna," Phillip murmured. "Coming downstairs to lay down the law."

"Cameron, you're supposed to be an adult."

"It's baseball, sugar."

"If the pair of you don't watch your language, the TV goes off."

"She's very strict," Phillip informed Sybill. "We're all terrified of her."

"Really?" Sybill considered as she glanced toward the living room.

She heard another voice, lower, softer, then Aubrey's firm response. "No, Mama, please. I want Seth."

"She's okay, Grace. She can stay with me."

The easy, absent tone of Seth's voice had Sybill considering. "It's unusual, I'd think, for a boy Seth's age to be so patient with a toddler."

Phillip shrugged his shoulders and walked to the stove to start a pot of fresh coffee. "They hit it off right away. Aubrey adores him. That has to boost the kid's ego, and he's really good with her."

He turned, smiling as two women walked into the room. "Ah, the ones who got away. Sybill, these are the women my brothers stole from me. Anna, Grace, Dr. Sybill Griffin."

"He only wanted us to cook for him," Anna said with a laugh and held out a hand. "It's nice to meet you. I've read your books. I think they're brilliant."

Taken by surprise, both by the statement and the lush and

outrageous beauty of Anna Spinelli Quinn, Sybill nearly fumbled. "Thank you. I appreciate you tolerating a Sunday-evening intrusion."

"It's no intrusion. We're delighted."

And, Anna thought, incredibly curious. In the seven months she'd known Phillip, this was the first woman he'd brought home to Sunday dinner.

"Phillip, go watch baseball." She waved him toward the doorway with the back of her hand. "Grace and Sybill and I can get acquainted."

"She's bossy, too," Phillip warned Sybill. "Just yell if you need help, and I'll come rescue you." He gave her a hard, firm kiss on the mouth before she could think to evade it, then deserted her.

Anna gave a long, interested hum, then smiled brightly. "Let's have some wine."

Grace pulled out a chair. "Phillip said you were going to stay in St. Chris a while and write a book about it."

"Something like that." Sybill took a deep breath. They were just women, after all. A stunning dark-eyed brunette and a cool lovely blonde. There was no need to be nervous. "Actually, I plan to write about the culture and traditions and social landscapes of small towns and rural communities."

"We have both on the Shore."

"So I see. You and Ethan are recently married."

Grace's smile warmed, and her gaze shifted to the gold band on her finger. "Just last month."

"And you grew up here, together."

"I was born here. Ethan moved here when he was about twelve."

"Are you from the area, too?" she asked Anna, more comfortable in the role of interviewer.

"No, I'm from Pittsburgh. I moved to D.C., wandered down to Princess Anne. I work for Social Services, as a caseworker. That's one of the reasons I was so interested in your books.'' She set a glass of deep-red wine in front of Sybill.

''Oh, yes, you're Seth's caseworker. Phillip told me a little about the situation.''

''Mmm,'' was Anna's only comment as she turned to take a bib apron from a hook. ''Did you enjoy your sail?''

So, Sybill realized, discussing Seth with outsiders was off-limits. She ordered herself to accept that, for now. ''Yes, very much. More than I'd expected to. I can't believe I've gone so long without trying it.''

''I had my first sail a few months ago.'' Anna set a huge pot of water on the stove to boil. ''Grace has been sailing all her life.''

''Do you work here, in St. Christopher's?''

''Yes, I clean houses.''

''Including this one, thank the Lord,'' Anna put in. ''I was telling Grace she ought to start a company. Maids Are Us or something.'' When Grace laughed, Anna shook her head. ''I'm serious. It would be a terrific service, to the working woman in particular. You could even do commercial buildings. If you trained two or three people, word of mouth alone would get it going.''

''You think bigger than I do. I don't know how to run a business.''

''I bet you do. Your family's been running the crab house for generations.''

''Crab house?'' Sybill interrupted.

''Picking, packing, shipping.'' Grace lifted a hand. ''Odds are, if you've had crab while you've been here, it came to you via my father's company. But I've never been involved in the business end.''

''That doesn't mean you couldn't handle your own business.'' Anna took a chunk of mozzarella out of the refrigerator and began to grate it. ''A lot of people out there are more than willing to pay for good, reliable, and trustworthy domestic services. They don't want to spend what little free time they might have cleaning the house, cooking meals, separating laundry. Traditional roles are shifting—don't you agree, Sybill? Women can't spend every spare second of their time in the kitchen."

"Well, I would agree, but . . . well, here you are."

Anna stopped, blinked, then threw back her head and laughed. She looked, Sybill thought, like a woman who should be dancing around a campfire to the sound of violins rather than cozily grating cheese in a fragrant kitchen.

"You're right, absolutely." Still chuckling, Anna shook her head. "Here I am, while my man lounges in front of the TV, deaf and blind to anything but the game. And this is often the scene on Sundays around here. I don't mind. I love to cook."

"Really?"

Hearing the suspicion in Sybill's voice, Anna laughed again. "Really. I find it satisfying, but not when I have to rush in from work and toss something together. That's why we take turns around here. Mondays are leftovers from whatever I've cooked Sunday. Tuesdays we all suffer through whatever Cam cooks, because he's simply dreadful in the kitchen. Wednesdays we do takeout, Thursdays I cook, Fridays Phillip cooks, and Saturdays are up for grabs. It's a very workable system when it works."

"Anna's planning on having Seth take over as chef on Wednesdays within the year."

"At his age?"

Anna shook back her hair. "He'll be eleven in a couple of weeks. By the time I was his age, I could make a killer red sauce. The time and effort it takes to teach him and to convince him he's still a male if he knows how to make a meal will be worth it in the end. And," she added, sliding wide, flat noodles into the boiling water, "if I use the fact that he can outdo Cam in any area, he'll be an A student."

"They don't get along."

"They're wonderful together." Anna tilted her head as the living room exploded with shouts, cheers, stomping. "And Seth likes nothing more than to impress his big brother. Which means, of course, they argue and prod each other constantly." She smiled again. "I take it you don't have any brothers."

"No. No, I don't."

"Sisters?" Grace asked and wondered why Sybill's eyes went so cool.

"One."

"I always wanted a sister." Grace smiled over at Anna. "Now I've got one."

"Grace and I were both only children." Anna squeezed Grace's shoulder as she walked by to mix her cheeses. Something in that easy, intimate gesture stirred a tug of envy inside Sybill. "Since we fell in with the Quinns, we've been making up rapidly for coming from small families. Does your sister live in New York?"

"No." Sybill's stomach clenched reflexively. "We're not terribly close. Excuse me." She pushed away from the table. "Can I use the bathroom?"

"Sure. Down the hall, first door on the left." Anna waited until Sybill walked out, then pursed her lips at Grace. "I can't decide what I think about her."

"She seems a little uncomfortable."

Anna shrugged her shoulders. "Well, I guess we'll have to wait and see, won't we?"

In the little powder room off the hall, Sybill splashed water on her face. She was hot, nervous, and vaguely sick to her stomach. She didn't understand this family, she thought. They were loud, occasionally crude, pieced together from different origins. Yet they seemed happy, at ease with each other, and very affectionate.

As she patted her face dry, she met her own eyes in the mirror. Her family had never been loud or crude. Except for those ugly moments when Gloria had pushed the limits. Just now she couldn't honestly say for certain if they had ever been happy, ever been at ease with each other. And affection had never been a priority or something that was expressed in an overt manner.

It was simply that none of them were very emotional people, she told herself. She had always been more cerebral, out of inclination, she decided, and in defense against Gloria's baffling volatility. Life was calmer if one depended on the intellect. She knew that. Believed that absolutely.

But it was her emotions that were churning now. She felt like a liar, a spy, a sneak. Reminding herself that she was doing what she was doing for the welfare of a child helped. Telling herself that the child was her own nephew and she had every right to be there, to form opinions, soothed.

Objectivity, she told herself, pressing her fingertips against her temples to smother the nagging ache. That's what would get her through until she'd gathered all the facts, all the data, and formed her opinion.

She stepped out quietly and took the few steps down the hall toward the blaring noise of the ball game. She saw Seth sprawled on the floor at Cam's feet and shouting abuse at the set across the room. Cam was gesturing with his beer and arguing the last call with Phillip. Ethan simply watched the game, with Aubrey curled in his lap, dozing despite the noise.

The room itself was homey, slightly shabby, and appeared comfortable. A piano was angled out from the corner. A vase of zinnias and dozens of small-framed snapshots crowded its polished surface. A half empty bowl of potato chips sat at Seth's elbow. The rug was littered with crumbs, shoes, the Sunday paper, and a grubby, well-gnawed hunk of rope.

The light had faded, but no one had bothered to switch on a lamp.

She started to step back, but Phillip glanced over. Smiled. Held out a hand. She walked to him, let him draw her down to the arm of his chair. "Bottom of the ninth," he murmured. "We're up by one."

"Watch this reliever kick this guy's sorry ass." Seth kept his voice down, but it rang with glee. He didn't even flinch when Cam slapped him on the head with his own ball cap. "Oh, yeah! Struck him *out*!" He leaped up, did a victory boogie. "We are number one. Man, I'm starving." He raced off to the kitchen and soon could be heard begging for food.

"Winning ball games works up an appetite," Phillip decided, absently kissing Sybill's hand. "How's she doing in there?"

"She appeared to be on top of things."

"Let's go see if she made antipasto."

He pulled her into the kitchen, and within moments it was crowded with people. Aubrey rested her head on Ethan's shoulder and blinked like an owl. Seth stuffed his mouth with tidbits from an elaborate tray and did a play-by-play of the game.

Everyone seemed to be moving, talking, eating at the same time, Sybill thought. Phillip put another glass of wine in her hand before he was drafted to deal with the bread. Because she felt slightly less confused by him than by the others, Sybill stuck to his side as chaos reigned.

He cut thick slices of Italian bread, then doctored them with butter and garlic.

"Is it always like this?" she murmured to him.

"No." He picked up his own glass of wine, touched it lightly to hers. "Sometimes it's really loud and disorganized."

BY THE TIME HE DROVE HER back to her hotel, Sybill's head was ringing. There was so much to process. Sights, sounds, personalities, impressions.

She had survived complex state dinners with less confusion than a Sunday dinner with the Quinns.

She needed time, she decided, to analyze. Once she was able to write down her thoughts, her observations, she would align them, dissect them, and begin to draw her initial conclusions.

"Tired?"

She sighed once. "A little. It was quite a day. A fascinating one." Blew out a breath. "And a fattening one. I'm definitely going to make use of the hotel's health club in the morning. I enjoyed myself," she added as he parked near the lobby entrance. "Very much."

"Good. Then you'll be willing to do it again." He climbed out, skirted the hood, then took her hand as she stepped onto the curb.

"There's no need for you to take me up. I know the way."

"I'll take you up anyway."

"I'm not going to ask you to come in."

"I'm still going to walk you to your door, Sybill."

She let it go, crossing with him to the elevators, stepping inside with him when the doors opened. "So, you'll drive to Baltimore in the morning?" She pushed the button for her floor.

"Tonight. When things are fairly settled here, I drive back Sunday nights. There's rarely any traffic, and I can get an earlier start on Mondays."

"It can't be easy for you, the commute, the demands on your time, and the tug-of-war of responsibilities."

"A lot of things aren't easy. But they're worth working for." He caressed her hair. "I don't mind putting time and effort into something I enjoy."

"Well . . ." She cleared her throat and walked out of the elevator the minute the doors opened. "I appreciate the time and effort you put into today."

"I'll be back Thursday night. I want to see you."

She slipped her key card out of her purse. "I can't be sure right now what I'll be doing at the end of the week."

He simply framed her face with his hands, moved in and covered her mouth with his. The taste of her, he thought. He couldn't seem to get enough of the taste of her. "I want to see you," he murmured against her lips.

She'd always been so good at staying in control, at distancing herself from attempts at seduction, from resisting the persuasions of physical attractions. But with him, each time she could feel herself slipping a little farther, a little deeper.

"I'm not ready for this," she heard herself say.

"Neither am I." Still, he drew her closer, held her tighter and took the kiss toward desperation. "I want you. Maybe it's a good thing we both have a few days to think about what happens next."

She looked up at him, shaken, yearning, and just a little frightened of what was happening inside her. "Yes, I think it's a very good thing." She turned, had to use both hands to shove the key card into its slot. "Drive carefully." She stepped inside, closed the door quickly, then leaned back against it until she was certain her heart wasn't going to pump its way out of her chest.

It was insane, she thought, absolutely insane to get this involved this quickly. She was honest enough with herself, scientist enough not to skew the results with incorrect data, to admit that what was happening to her where Phillip Quinn was concerned had nothing whatsoever to do with Seth.

It should be stopped. She closed her eyes and felt the pressure of his mouth still vibrating on her lips. And she was afraid it couldn't be stopped.

EIGHT

I<small>T WAS PROBABLY A CHANCY</small>
step to take. Sybill wondered if it could possibly be illegal.
Loitering near St. Christopher's Middle School certainly made
her feel like some sort of criminal, no matter how firmly she
told herself she was doing nothing wrong.

She was simply walking on a public street in the middle of
the afternoon. It wasn't as though she was stalking Seth, or
planning to abduct him. She only wanted to talk to him, to
see him alone for a little while.

She'd waited until the middle of the week, watching from
a careful distance on Monday and Tuesday to gauge his routine, and the timing. Habitually, she now knew, the buses lum-
bered up to school several minutes before the doors opened
and children began pouring out.

Elementary first, then middle, then the high school students.

That alone was a lesson in the process of childhood, she
mused. The compact little bodies and fresh round faces of the
elementary children, then the more gangling, somewhat awkward forms of those who hovered around puberty. And last,

the astonishingly adult and more individual young people who strolled out of the high school.

It was a study in itself, she decided. From dangling shoe-laces and gap-toothed smiles to cowlicks and ball jackets to baggy jeans and shining falls of hair.

Children had never been a part of her life, or her interests. She'd grown up in a world of adults and had been expected to acclimate, to conform. There had been no big yellow school buses, no wild rebel yells when bursting out of the school doors into freedom, no lingering in the parking lot with some leather-jacketed bad boy.

So she observed all those things here like an audience at a play and found the mix of drama and comedy both amusing and informative.

When Seth hurried out, bumping bodies with the dark-haired boy she'd decided was his most usual companion, her pulse quickened. He whipped his ball cap out of his pocket and put it on his head the moment he was through the doors. A ritual, she thought, symbolizing the change of rules. The other boy fished in his pocket and pulled out a fistful of bub-blegum. In seconds it was wadded into his mouth.

The noise level rose, making it impossible for her to hear their conversation, but it appeared to be animated and included a great deal of elbow jabbing and shoulder punching.

Typical male affection pattern, she concluded.

They turned their backs on the buses and began to walk down the sidewalk. Moments later, a smaller boy raced up to them. He bounced, Sybill noted, and seemed to have a great deal to say for himself.

She waited a moment longer, then casually took a path that would intersect with theirs.

"Shit, man, that geography test was nothing. A bozo could've aced it." Seth shrugged to distribute the weight of his backpack.

The other boy blew an impressive candy-pink bubble,

popped it, then sucked it in. "I don't know what's the big damn deal about knowing all the states and capitals. It's not like I'm going to live in North Dakota."

"Seth, hello."

Sybill watched him stop, adjust his train of thought, and focus on her. "Oh, yeah, hi."

"I guess school's done for the day. You heading home?"

"The boatyard." There was that little dance on the nape of his neck again. It irritated him. "We got work."

"I'm going that way myself." She tried a smile on the other boys. "Hi, I'm Sybill."

"I'm Danny," the other boy told her. "That's Will."

"Nice to meet you."

"We had vegetable soup for lunch," Will informed everyone grandly. "And Lisa Harbough threw up *all over*. And Mr. Jim had to clean it up, and her mom came to get her, and we couldn't write our vocabulary words." He danced around Sybill as he relayed the information, then shot her an amazingly innocent, wonderfully bright smile that she was helpless to resist.

"I hope Lisa's feeling better soon."

"Once when I threw up I got to stay home and watch TV all day. Me and Danny live over there on Heron Lane. Where do you live?"

"I'm just visiting."

"My Uncle John and Aunt Margie moved to South Carolina and we got to visit them. They have two dogs and a baby named Mike. Do you have dogs and babies?"

"No . . . no, I don't."

"You can get them," he told her. "You can go right to the animal shelter and get a dog—that's what we did. And you can get married and make a baby so it lives in your stomach. There's nothing to it."

"Jeez, Will." Seth rolled his eyes, while Sybill only managed to blink.

"Well, I'm going to have dogs and babies when I grow up. As many as I want." He flashed that hundred-watt smile again, then raced away. " 'Bye."

"He's such a geek," Danny said with the shuddering disdain of older brother for younger. "See you, Seth." He bounded after Will, turned briefly to run backward and flipped a wave toward Sybill. " 'Bye."

"Will's not really a geek," Seth told Sybill. "He's just a kid, and he's got diarrhea of the mouth, but he's pretty cool."

"He's certainly friendly." She shifted her shoulder bag, smiled down at him. "Do you mind if I walk the rest of the way with you?"

"It's okay."

"I thought I heard you say something about a geography test."

"Yeah, we took one today. It was nothing."

"You like school?"

"It's there." He jerked his shoulder. "You gotta go."

"I always enjoyed it. Learning new things." She laughed lightly. "I suppose I was a geek."

Seth angled his head, narrowing his eyes as he studied her face. A looker, Phillip had called her, he remembered. He guessed she was. She had nice eyes, the light color a sharp contrast to the dark lashes. Her hair wasn't as dark as Anna's, nor light like Grace's. It was really shiny, he noted, and the way she pulled it back all smooth and stuff left her face right out there.

She might be cool to draw sometime.

"You don't look like a geek," Seth announced just as Sybill felt heat begin to rise into her cheeks under his long, intense study. "Anyway, that would be a nerd."

"Oh." She wasn't sure if she'd just qualified for nerd status and decided not to ask. "What do you like studying best?"

"I don't know. Mostly it's just a bunch of—stuff," he decided, quickly censoring his opinion. "I guess I like it better when we get to read about people instead of things."

"I've always liked to study people." She stopped and gestured toward a small two-story gray house with a trim front yard. "My theory would be that a young family lives there. Both husband and wife work outside the home and they have a preschooler, most likely a boy. Odds are that they've known each other a number of years and have been married less than seven."

"How come?"

"Well, it's the middle of the day and no one's home. No cars in the drive, and the house looks empty. But there's a tricycle there and several large toy trucks. The house isn't new, but it's well kept. Most young couples both work today in order to buy a home, have a family. They live in a small community. Younger people rarely settle in small towns unless one or both of them grew up there. So I'd theorize that this couple lived here, knew each other, eventually married. It's likely they had their first child within the first three years of marriage and the toys indicate he's three to five."

"That's pretty cool," Seth decided after a moment.

However foolish it was, she felt a surge of pride that she might have avoided nerddom after all. "But I'd want to know more, wouldn't you?"

She'd caught his interest. "Like what?"

"Why did they choose this particular house. What are their goals? What is the status of their relationship? Who handles the money, which indicates the disposition of power, and why? If you study people, you see the patterns."

"How come it matters?"

"I don't understand."

"Who cares?"

She considered. "Well, if you understand the patterns, the social picture on a large scale, you learn why people behave in certain manners."

"What if they don't fit?"

Bright boy, she thought on another, deeper wave of pride. "Everyone fits some pattern. You factor in background, genetics, education, social strata, religious and cultural roots."

"You get paid for that?"

"Yes, I suppose I do."

"Weird."

Now, she concluded, she had definitely been relegated to nerd status. "It can be interesting." She racked her brain to come up with an example that would salvage his opinion of her. "I did this experiment once in several cities. I arranged for a man to stand on the street and stare up at a building."

"Just stare at it?"

"That's right. He stood there and stared up, shading his eyes from the sun when he had to. Before long someone stopped beside him and stared up at the same building. Then another and another, until there was a crowd of people, all looking up at that building. It took much longer for anyone to actually ask what was going on, what were they looking at. No one really wanted to be the first to ask because that was an admission that you didn't see what you assumed everyone else was seeing. We want to conform, we want to fit in, we want to know and see and understand what the person beside us knows and sees and understands."

"I bet some of them thought someone was going to jump out of a window."

"Very likely. The average time an individual stood, looking, interrupting their schedule, was two minutes." She believed she'd caught his imagination again, and so she hurried on. "That's actually quite a long time to stare at a perfectly ordinary building."

"That's pretty cool. But it's still weird."

They were coming to the point where he would have to veer off to go to the boatyard. She thought quickly and in a rare move went with impulse. "What do you think would happen if you conducted the same experiment in St. Christopher's?''

"I don't know. The same thing?"

"I doubt it." She sent him a conspirator's smile. "Want to try it?"

"Maybe."

"We can head over to the waterfront now. Will your brother worry if you're a few minutes late? Should you go tell him you're with me?"

"Nah. Cam doesn't keep me on a leash. He cuts me some slack time."

She wasn't sure how she felt about the loose discipline in that area, but at the moment she was happy to take advantage of it. "Let's try it, then. I'll pay you in ice cream."

"You got a deal."

They turned away from the boatyard. "You can pick a spot," she began. "It's necessary to stand. People don't generally pay attention to someone who's sitting and looking. They often assume the person is simply daydreaming or resting."

"I get it."

"It's more effective if you look up at something. Is it okay if I videotape?"

He raised his eyebrows as she took a neat compact video recorder out of her bag. "Yeah, I guess. You carry that around all the time?"

"When I'm working, I do. And a notebook, and a micro audio tape recorder, backup batteries and tapes, extra pencils. My cell phone." She laughed at herself. "I like being prepared. And the day they make a computer small enough to fit in a purse, I'm going to be the first in line."

"Phil likes all that electronic stuff, too."

"The baggage of the urbanite. We're desperate not to waste a minute. Then, of course, we can't get away from anything because we're plugged in every second of the day."

"You could just turn everything off."

"Yes." Oddly she found the simplicity of his statement profound. "I suppose I could."

Pedestrian traffic was light on the waterfront. She saw a workboat unloading the day's catch and a family taking advantage of the balmy afternoon by splurging on ice cream sundaes at one of the little outdoor tables. Two old men, their faces nut brown and deeply seamed, sat on an iron bench with a checkerboard between them. Neither seemed inclined to make a move. A trio of women chatted in the doorway of one of the shops, but only one of them carried a bag.

"I'm going to stand over there." Seth pointed to his spot. "And look up at the hotel."

"Good choice." Sybill stayed where she was as he strolled off. Distance was necessary to keep the experiment pure. She lifted the camera, zoomed in as Seth moved away. He turned once, shot her a quick, cocky smile.

And when his face filled her view screen, emotions she hadn't been prepared for flooded her. He was so handsome, so bright. So happy. She struggled to pull herself back from a dangerous edge that she was afraid was despair.

She could walk away, she thought, pack up and leave, never see him again. He would never know who she was or what they were to each other. He would never miss whatever she could bring into his life. She was nothing to him.

She'd never really tried to be.

It was different now, she reminded herself. She was making it different now. Deliberately she ordered her fingers to relax, her neck, her arms. She was causing no harm by getting to know him, spending some time studying his situation.

She taped him as he settled on his spot, lifted his face. His profile was finer, more angled than Gloria's, Sybill decided. Perhaps his bone structure had come from his father.

His build wasn't Gloria's either, as she'd first assumed, but more like her own, and her mother's. He would be tall when he finished growing, mostly leg, and on the slim side.

His body language, she saw with a slight jolt, was typical Quinn. Already, he'd taken on some of the traits of his foster family. That hip-shot stance, hands tucked into pockets, head angled.

She fought back an annoying spurt of resentment and ordered herself to focus on the experiment.

It took just over a minute for the first person to stop beside Seth. She recognized the big woman with the gray-streaked hair who manned the counter at Crawford's. Everyone called her Mother. As expected, the woman shifted her gaze, tilted her face up to follow Seth's line of sight. But after a quick scan, she patted Seth on the shoulder.

"What're you looking at, boy?"

"Nothing."

He muttered it so that Sybill edged closer to try to pick up his voice on the tape.

"Well, hell, you stand there for long looking at nothing, people're going to think you're pixilated. Why aren't you down to the boatyard?"

"I'm going in a minute."

"Hey, Mother. Hi, Seth." A pretty young woman with dark hair stepped into the frame, glanced up at the hotel. "Something going on up there? I don't see anything."

"Nothing to see," Mother informed her. "Boy's just standing looking at nothing. How's your mama, Julie?"

"Oh, she's a little under the weather. She's got a sore throat and a little cough."

"Chicken soup, hot tea and honey."

"Grace brought some soup over this morning."

"You see she eats it. Hey, there, Jim."

"Afternoon." A short, stocky man in white rubber boots clumped over, gave Seth a friendly swat on the head. "What you staring at up there, boy?"

"Jeez, can't a guy just stand around?" Seth turned his face

to the camera, rolled his eyes for Sybill and made her chuckle.

"Stand here long, gulls'll light on you." Jim winked at him. "Cap'n's in for the day," he added, referring to Ethan. "He gets to the boatyard before you, he's gonna want to know why."

"I'm going, I'm going. Man." Shoulders rounded, head down, Seth stalked back to Sybill. "Nobody's falling for it."

"Because everyone knows you." She switched off the camera, lowered it. "It changes the pattern."

"You figured that would happen?"

"I theorized," she corrected, "that in a closely knit area where the subject was known, the pattern would be that an individual would stop. They would probably look first, then question. There's no risk, no loss of ego when questioning a familiar person, and a young one at that."

He frowned over toward where the trio continued to chat. "So, I still get paid."

"Absolutely, and you'll likely rate a section in my book."

"Cool. I'll take a cookie dough cone. I've got to get to the boatyard before Cam and Ethan hassle me."

"If they're going to be angry with you, I'll explain. It's my fault you're late."

"They won't be pissed or anything. Besides, I'll tell them it was, like, for science, right?" When he flashed that grin she had to resist an unexpected urge to hug him.

"That's exactly right." She risked laying a hand on his shoulder as they started toward Crawford's. She thought she felt him stiffen and casually let her hand drop away. "And we can always call them on my cell phone."

"Yeah? Way cool. Can I do it?"

"Sure, why not?"

• • •

TWENTY MINUTES LATER
Sybill was at her desk, fingers racing over her keyboard.

Though I spent less than an hour with him, I would conclude that the subject is extremely bright. Phillip informed me that he achieves high grades academically, which is admirable. It was satisfying to discover that he has a questioning mind. His manners are perhaps a bit rough, but not unpleasant. He appears to be considerably more outgoing socially than his mother or I were at his age. In that, I mean he seems quite natural with relative strangers without the polite formality that was stressed in my own upbringing. Part of this may be due to the influence of the Quinns. They are, as I have noted previously, informal, casual people.

I would also conclude from watching both the children and the adults with whom he interacted today, that he is generally well liked in this community and accepted as part of it. Naturally I cannot, at this early stage, conclude whether or not his best interest would be served by remaining here.

It's simply not possible to ignore Gloria's rights, nor have I attempted, as yet, to discover the boy's wishes as concern his mother.

I would prefer that he grow accustomed to me, feel comfortable around me, before he learns of our family connection.

I need more time to . . .

She broke off as the phone rang and, scanning her hastily typed notes, picked up the receiver.

"Dr. Griffin."

"Hello, Dr. Griffin. Why do I suspect I've interrupted your work?"

She recognized Phillip's voice, the amusement in it, and

with a flare of guilt lowered the top of her computer. "Because you're a perceptive man. But I can spare a few minutes. How are things in Baltimore?"

"Busy. How's this? The visual is a handsome young couple, beaming smiles as they carry their laughing toddler to a mid-size sedan. Caption: 'Myerstone Tires. Your family matters to us.' "

"Manipulative. The consumer is led to believe that if he or she buys another brand, the family doesn't matter to that other company."

"Yeah. It works. Of course, we're hitting the car mags with a different image. Screaming convertible in kick-ass red, long, winding road, sexy blonde at the wheel. 'Myerstone Tires. You can drive there, or you can BE there.' "

"Clever."

"The client likes it, and that takes a load off. How's life in St. Chris?"

"Quiet." She bit her lip. "I ran into Seth a bit ago. Actually, I drafted him to help me with an experiment. It went well."

"Oh, yeah? How much did you have to pay him?"

"An ice cream cone, double scoop."

"You got off cheap. The kid's an operator. How about dinner tomorrow night, a bottle of champagne to celebrate our mutual successes?"

"Speaking of operators."

"I've been thinking about you all week."

"Three days," she corrected and, picking up a pencil, began to doodle on her pad.

"And nights. With this account settled, I can get out a little earlier tomorrow. Why don't I pick you up at seven?"

"I'm not sure where we're going, Phillip."

"Neither am I. Do you need to be?"

She understood that neither of them was speaking of restaurants. "It's less confusing that way."

"Then we'll talk about it, and maybe we'll get past the confusion. Seven o'clock."

She glanced down, noticed that she'd unconsciously sketched his face on her notepad. A bad sign, she thought. A very dangerous sign. "All right." It was best to face complications head-on. "I'll see you tomorrow."

"Do me a favor?"

"If I can."

"Think of me tonight."

She doubted she had any choice in the matter. " 'Bye."

IN HIS OFFICE FOURTEEN STORIES above the streets of Baltimore, Phillip pushed back from his slick black desk, ignored the beep on his computer that signaled an interoffice e-mail and turned toward his wide window.

He loved his view of the city, the renovated buildings, the glimpses of the harbor, the hustle of cars and people below. But just now he didn't see any of it.

He literally couldn't get Sybill out of his mind. It was a new experience for him, this continual tug on his thoughts and concentration. It wasn't as if she was interfering with his routine, he reflected. He could work, eat, brainstorm, do his presentations as skillfully as he had before he'd met her.

But she was simply there, he decided. A tickle at the back of his mind through the day, that inched forward to the front when his energies weren't otherwise occupied.

He wasn't quite sure if he enjoyed having a woman demand so much of his attention, particularly a woman who was doing very little to encourage him.

Maybe he considered that light sheen of formality, that cautious distance she tried to maintain, a challenge. He thought he could live with that. It was just another of the entertaining and varied games men and women played.

But he worried that something was happening on a level he'd never explored. And if he was any judge, she was just as unsettled by it as he.

"It's just like you," Ray said from behind him.

"Oh, Jesus." Phillip didn't spin around, didn't goggle. He simply shut his eyes.

"Pretty fancy office you got here. Been a while since I got in." Ray prowled the room casually, pursing his lips at a black-framed canvas splashed with reds and blues. "Not bad," he decided. "Brain stimulator. I'd guess that's why you put it in your office, get the juices going."

"I refuse to believe that my dead father is standing in my office critiquing art."

"Well, that wasn't what I wanted to talk about anyway." But he paused by a metal sculpture in the corner. "But I like this piece, too. You always had high-class taste. Art, food, women." He grinned cheerfully as Phillip turned. "The woman you've got on your mind now, for instance. Very high-class."

"I need to take some time off."

"I'd agree with you there. You've been up to and over your head for months. She's an interesting woman, Phillip. There's more to her than you see, or than she knows. I hope when the times comes you'll listen to her, really listen to her."

"What are you talking about?" He held up a hand, palm out. "Why am I asking you what you're talking about when you're not here?"

"I'm hoping that the pair of you will stop analyzing the steps and stages and accept what is." Ray shrugged, slipped his hands into the pockets of his Orioles fielder's jacket. "But you have to go your own way. It's going to be hard. There's not much time left before it gets a lot harder. You'll stand between Seth and what hurts him. I know that. I want to tell you that you can trust her. When it's down to the sticking point, Phillip, you trust yourself, and you trust her.''

A new chill skidded down his spine. "What does Sybill have to do with Seth?''

"It's not for me to tell you that.'' He smiled again, but his eyes didn't match the curve of his lips. "You haven't talked to your brothers about me. You need to. You need to stop feeling you have to control all the buttons. You're good at it, God knows, but give a little.''

He drew in a deep breath, turned a slow circle. "Christ, your mother would've gotten a kick out of this place. You've done a hell of a job with your life so far.'' Now his eyes smiled. "I'm proud of you. I know you'll handle what comes next.''

"You did a hell of a job with my life,'' Phillip murmured. "You and Mom.''

"Damn right we did.'' Ray winked. "Keep it up.'' When the phone rang, Ray sighed. "Everything that happens needs to happen. It's what you do about it that makes the difference. Answer the phone, Phillip, and remember Seth needs you.''

Then there was nothing but the ringing of the phone and an empty office. With his gaze locked on where his father had been, Phillip reached for the phone.

"Phillip Quinn.''

As he listened, his eyes hardened. He grabbed a pen, and began to take notes on the detective's report on the most recent movements of Gloria DeLauter.

NINE

"SHE'S IN HAMPTON." PHIL-
lip kept his eyes on Seth as he relayed the information. He
watched Cam lay a hand on the boy's rigid shoulder, an unspoken sign of protection. "She was picked up by the police—
drunk and disorderly, possession."

"She's in jail." Seth's face was white as bone. "They can
keep her in jail."

"She's there now." How long she would stay there, Phillip
thought, was another matter. "She probably has enough
money to post bond."

"You mean she can pay them money and they'll let her
go?" Beneath Cam's hand, Seth began to tremble. "No matter
what?"

"I don't know. But for now we know exactly where she
is. I'm going down to talk to her."

"Don't! Don't go there."

"Seth, we've talked about this." Cam massaged the shaking shoulder as he turned Seth to face him. "The only way
we're going to fix this for good is to deal with her."

"I won't go back." It was said in a whisper, but a furious one. "I'll never go back."

"You won't go back." Ethan unhitched his tool belt, laid it on the workbench. "You can stay with Grace until Anna gets home." He looked at Phillip and Cam. "We'll go to Hampton."

"What if the cops say I have to? What if they come while you're gone and—"

"Seth." Phillip interrupted the rising desperation. He crouched, took Seth's arms firmly. "You have to trust us."

Seth stared back at him with Ray Quinn's eyes, and those eyes were glazed with tears and terror. For the first time, Phillip looked into them and felt no shadowy resentment, no doubts.

"You belong with us," he said quietly. "Nothing's going to change that."

On a long, shuddering breath Seth nodded. He had no choice, could do nothing but hope. And fear.

"We'll take my car," Phillip stated.

"GRACE AND ANNA WILL calm him down." Cam shifted restlessly in the passenger seat of Phillip's Jeep.

"It's hell being that scared." From the backseat, Ethan glanced at the speedometer and noted that Phillip was pushing eighty. "Not being able to do anything but wait and see."

"She's fucked herself," Phillip said flatly. "Getting arrested isn't going to help her custody case, if she tries to make one."

"She doesn't want the kid."

Phillip spared a brief glance at Cam. "No, she wants

money. She isn't going to bleed any out of us. But we're going to get some answers. We're going to end it.''

She'd lie, Phillip thought. He had no doubt that she would lie and wheedle and maneuver. But she was wrong, dead wrong, if she thought she could get past the three of them to Seth.

You'll handle what comes next, Ray had said.

Phillip's hands tightened on the wheel. He kept his eyes on the road. He'd handle it, all right. One way or the other.

WITH HER HEAD THROBBING, her stomach rolling, Sybill walked into the small county police station. Gloria had called her, weeping and desperate, begging her to send money for bail.

For bail, Sybill thought now, fighting off a shudder.

Gloria said it was a mistake, she reminded herself, a terrible misunderstanding. Of course, what else could it have been? She'd nearly wired the money. She still wasn't sure what had stopped her, what had pushed her to get into her car and drive.

To help, of course, she told herself. She only wanted to help.

"I'm here for Gloria DeLauter," she told the uniformed officer who sat behind a narrow, cluttered counter. "I'd like to see her, if possible."

"Your name?"

"Griffin. Dr. Sybill Griffin. I'm her sister. I'll post her bond, but I'd . . . I'd like to see her."

"Can I see some ID?"

"Oh, yes." She fumbled in her purse for her wallet. Her hands were damp and shaky, but the cop simply watched her with cool eyes until she offered identification.

"Why don't you have a seat?" he suggested, then scraped back his own chair and slipped into an adjoining room.

Her throat was dry and desperate for water. She wandered the small waiting area with its grouping of hard plastic chairs in industrial beige until she found a water fountain. But the water hit her tortured stomach like frigid balls of lead.

Had they put her in a cell? Oh, God, had they actually put her sister in a cell? Is that where she would have to see Gloria?

But under the sorrow, her mind was working coolly, pragmatically. How had Gloria known where to reach her? What was she doing so close to St. Christopher's? Why was she accused of having drugs?

That was why she hadn't wired the money, she admitted now. She wanted the answers first.

"Dr. Griffin."

She jolted, turned to the officer with her eyes wide as a doe's caught in headlights. "Yes. Can I see her now?"

"I'll need to take your purse. I'll give you a receipt."

"All right."

She handed it over to him, signed the log where he indicated, accepted the receipt for her belongings.

"This way."

He gestured toward a side door, then opened it into a narrow corridor. On the left was a small room furnished only with a single table and a few chairs. Gloria sat at one, her right wrist cuffed to a bolt.

Sybill's first thought was that they'd made a mistake. This wasn't her sister. They'd brought the wrong woman into the room. This one looked far too old, far too hard, with her bony body, the shoulders like points of wings, the contrast of breasts pressing against a tiny, snug sweater so hard that the nipples stood out in arrogant relief.

Her frizzed mass of straw-colored hair had a dark streak shooting up the center, deep lines dug in around her mouth, and the calculation in her eyes was as sharp as those shoulders.

Then those eyes filled, that mouth trembled.

"Syb." Her voice cracked as she held out an imploring hand. "Thank God you've come."

"Gloria." She stepped forward quickly, took that shaking hand in her own. "What happened?"

"I don't know. I don't understand any of it. I'm so scared." She laid her head on the table and began to weep in loud, racking sobs.

"Please." Instinctively Sybill sat and draped her arm around her sister as she looked over at the cop. "Can we be alone?"

"I'll be right outside." He looked back at Gloria. If he thought what a change this was from the screaming, cursing woman who'd been pulled in a few hours ago, his face revealed nothing.

He stepped out, shut the door, and left them alone.

"Let me get you some water."

Sybill rose, hurried over to the water jug in the corner, and filled a thin triangle of paper. She cupped her hands around her sister's, holding it steady.

"Did you pay the bail? Why can't we just go? I don't want to stay here."

"I'll take care of it. Tell me what happened."

"I said I don't know. I was with this guy. I was lonely." She sniffed, accepting the tissue that Sybill passed her. "We were just talking for a while. We were going to go out to lunch, then the cops came up. He ran away and they grabbed me. It all happened so fast."

She buried her face in her hands. "They found drugs in my purse. He must have put them there. I just wanted someone to talk to."

"All right, I'm sure we'll straighten it all out." Sybill wanted to believe, to accept, and she hated herself because she couldn't. Not quite. "What was his name?"

"John. John Barlow. He seemed so sweet, Sybill. So understanding. I was feeling really low. Because of Seth." She lowered her hands and her eyes were tragic. "I miss my little boy so much."

"Were you coming to St. Christopher's?"

Gloria lowered her gaze. "I thought, if I just had a chance to see him."

"Is that what the lawyer suggested?"

"The—oh . . ." The hesitation was brief, but it set off warning bells in Sybill's head. "No, but lawyers don't understand. They just keep asking for money."

"What's your lawyer's name? I'll call him. He may be able to help straighten this out."

"He's not from around here. Look, Sybill, I just want to get out of here. You can't believe how horrible it is. That cop out there?" She nodded toward the door. "He put his hands on me."

Sybill's stomach began to pitch again. "What do you mean?"

"You know what I mean." The first hint of annoyance sliced through. "He felt me up, and he said he'd be back later for more. He's going to rape me."

Sybill shut her eyes, pressed her fingers to them. When they were teenagers, Gloria had accused more than a dozen boys and men of molesting her, including her high school counselor and principal. Even their own father.

"Gloria, don't do this. I said I would help you."

"I'm telling you that bastard put his hands all over me. As soon as I'm out of here, I'm filing charges." She crumpled the paper cup, heaved it. "I don't give a damn if you believe me or not. I know what happened."

"All right, but let's deal with now. How did you know where to find me?"

"What?" A dark rage had been sliding over her brain, and she had to struggle to remember her role. "What do you mean?"

"I didn't tell you where I was going, where I would be. I

said I would contact you. How did you know to call me at the hotel in St. Christopher's?''

It had been a mistake, which Gloria had realized shortly after making the call. But she'd been drunk and furious. And damn it, she didn't have the cash on her to make bail. What she had left was safely tucked away. Until the Quinns added to it.

She wasn't thinking when she called Sybill, but she'd had time to think since. The way to play sister Sybill, she knew, was to tug on the guilt and responsibility strings.

"I know you.'' She offered a watery smile. "I knew that when I told you what happened with Seth, you'd help. I tried your apartment in New York.'' Which she had, more than a week ago. "And when your answering service said you were out of town, I explained how I was your sister and there was an emergency. They gave me the number of the hotel.''

"I see.'' It was plausible, Sybill decided, even logical. "I'll take care of the bail, Gloria, but there are conditions.''

"Yeah.'' She gave a short laugh. "That sounds familiar.''

"I need the name of your lawyer so I can contact him. I want to be brought up to date on the status of this situation with Seth. I want you to talk to me. We'll have dinner and you can explain to me about the Quinns. You can explain to me why they claim Ray Quinn gave you money for Seth.''

"The bastards are liars.''

"I've met them,'' she said calmly. "And their wives. I've seen Seth. It's very difficult for me to equate what you told me with what I've seen.''

"You can't put everything all neat and tidy into reports. Christ, you're just like the old man.'' She started to get up, snarled at the jerk of the cuff on her wrist. "The two eminent Dr. Griffins.''

"This has nothing to do with my father,'' Sybill said quietly. "And everything, I suspect, to do with yours.''

"Fuck this.'' Gloria twisted her lips into a vicious smile.

"And fuck you. The perfect daughter, the perfect student, the perfect goddamn robot. Just pay the fucking bail. I got money put by. You'll get it back. I'll get my kid back without your help, sister dear. My kid. You want to take the word of a bunch of strangers over your own flesh and blood, you go right ahead. You always hated me anyway."

"I don't hate you, Gloria. I never have." But she could, she realized, as the ache began in her head and heart. She was afraid she very easily could. "And I'm not taking anyone's word over yours. I'm just trying to understand."

Deliberately Gloria turned her face away so Sybill wouldn't see her smile of satisfaction. She'd found the right button to push after all, she decided. "I need to get out of here. I need to get cleaned up." She made certain her voice broke. "I can't talk about this anymore. I'm so tired."

"I'll go deal with the paperwork. I'm sure it won't take long."

As she rose, Gloria grabbed her hand again, pressed it to her cheek. "I'm sorry. I'm so sorry I said those things to you. I didn't mean them. I'm just upset and confused. I feel so alone."

"It's all right." Sybill pulled her hand free and walked to the door on legs that felt as brittle as glass.

Outside, she downed two aspirin and chased them with antacids as she waited for the bail to be processed. Physically, she thought, Gloria had changed. The once astonishingly pretty girl had hardened, toughened like dried leather. But emotionally, Sybill feared, she was exactly the same unhappy, manipulative, and disturbed child that had taken dark joy in disrupting their home.

She would insist that Gloria agree to therapy, she decided. And if drug abuse was part of the problem, she would see to it that Gloria went into rehab. Certainly the woman she'd just spoken with wasn't capable of taking custody of a young boy. She would explore the possibilities of what was best for him until Gloria was back on track.

She would need to see a lawyer, of course. First thing in the morning she would find a lawyer and discuss Gloria's rights and Seth's welfare.

She would have to face the Quinns.

The thought of that had her stomach clutching again. A confrontation was inevitable, unavoidable. Nothing left her feeling more miserable and vulnerable than angry words and hateful emotions.

But she would be prepared. She would take the time to think through what had to be said, anticipate their questions and demands so she would have the proper responses. She would, above all, remain calm and objective.

When she saw Phillip walk into the building, her mind went blank. Every ounce of color drained out of her face. She stood frozen when his gaze whipped to hers, when it narrowed and hardened.

"What are you doing here, Sybill?"

"I . . ." It wasn't panic that spurted through her but embarrassment. Shame. "I had business."

"Really?" He stepped closer, while his brothers stood back in speculative silence. He saw it in her face—guilt and more than a little fear. "What kind of business would that be?" When she didn't answer, he angled his head. "What's Gloria DeLauter to you, Dr. Griffin?"

She ordered herself to keep her gaze steady, her voice even. "She's my sister."

His fury was ice cold and deadly. He balled his hands into his pockets to keep from using them in a way that was unforgivable. "That's cozy, isn't it? You bitch," he said softly, but she flinched as if he had struck her. "You used me to get to Seth."

She shook her head, but she couldn't voice the denial. It was true, wasn't it? She had used him, had used all of them. "I only wanted to see him. He's my sister's son. I had to know he was being cared for."

"Then where the hell have you been for the last ten years?"

She opened her mouth, but swallowed the excuses and explanations as Gloria was led out.

"Let's get the hell out of here. You buy me a drink, Syb." Gloria hitched a cherry-red shoulder bag over her arm, aimed an invitational smile at Phillip. "We'll talk all you want. Hi, there, handsome." She shifted her weight, put a fist on her hip, and let the smile spread to the other men. "How's it going?"

Under other circumstances the contrasts between the women might have been laughable. Sybill stood pale and quiet, her glossy brown hair brushed smoothly back, her mouth unpainted, her eyes shadowed. She exuded simple elegance in a tailored gray blazer and slacks and a white silk blouse, while Gloria offered sharp bones and overblown curves poured into black jeans and a snug T-shirt that plunged between her breasts.

She'd taken the time to repair her makeup, and her lips were as slickly red as her handbag, her eyes darkly lined. She looked, Phillip decided, like precisely what she was: an aging whore looking for an angle.

She fished a cigarette out of a crumpled pack in her bag, then wiggled it between her fingers. "Got a light, big guy?"

"Gloria, this is Phillip Quinn." The formal introduction echoed hollowly in her ears. "His brothers, Cameron and Ethan."

"Well, well, well." Gloria's smile went sharp and ugly. "Ray Quinn's wicked trio. What the hell do you want?"

"Answers," Phillip said shortly. "Let's take this outside."

"I got nothing to say to you. You make one move I don't like, I'll start screaming." She jabbed with the unlit cigarette. "There's a houseful of cops in here. We'll see how you like spending some time in a cage."

"Gloria." Sybill put a restraining hand on her arm. "The

only way to straighten this out is to discuss it rationally.''

"They don't look like they want a rational discussion to me. They want to hurt me." She shifted tacks skillfully, throwing her arms around Sybill, clinging to her. "I'm afraid of them. Sybill, please help me."

"I'm trying to. Gloria, no one's going to hurt you. We'll find a place where we can all sit down and talk this through. I'll be right there with you."

"I'm going to be sick." She yanked back, wrapped her arms around her stomach, and dashed into the bathroom.

"Quite a performance," Phillip decided.

"She's upset." Sybill linked her hands together, twisted her fingers. "She's not in any shape to deal with this tonight."

He shifted his gaze back to Sybill's, and it was ripe with derision. "Do you want me to believe you bought that? Either you're incredibly gullible, or you think I am."

"She spent most of the afternoon in jail," Sybill snapped back. "Anyone would be upset. Can't we discuss all of this tomorrow? It's waited this long, surely it can wait one more day."

"We're here now," Cam put in. "We'll deal with it now. Are you going to go in there and bring her out, or am I?"

"Is that how you plan to resolve this? By bullying her. And me?"

"You don't want to get me started on how I plan to resolve this," Cam began, and shrugged off Ethan's calming hand. "After what she put Seth through, there's nothing we can do to her that she hasn't earned."

Sybill glanced uncomfortably behind her at the uniformed officer manning the desk. "I don't think any of us want to cause a scene in a police station."

"Fine." Phillip took her arm. "Let's just step outside and cause one."

She held her ground, partly out of fear, partly common

sense. "We'll meet tomorrow, at whatever time is convenient for you. I'll bring her to my hotel."

"You keep her out of St. Chris."

Sybill winced when Phillip's fingers tightened on her arm. "All right. Where do you suggest?"

"I'll tell you what I suggest," Cam began, but Phillip held up a hand.

"Princess Anne. You bring her into Anna's office at Social Services. Nine o'clock. That keeps everything official, doesn't it? Everything aboveboard."

"Yes." Relief trickled through her. "I can agree to that. I'll bring her. You have my word."

"I wouldn't give you two cents for your word, Sybill." Phillip leaned in slightly. "But if you don't bring her, we'll find her. Meanwhile, if either of you tries to get within a mile of Seth, you'll both be spending time in a cell." He dropped her arm and stepped back.

"We'll be there at nine," she said, resisting the urge to rub her aching arm. Then she turned and went into the bathroom to get her sister.

"Why the hell did you agree to that?" Cam demanded as he stalked outside behind Phillip. "We've got her, here and now."

"We'll get more out of her tomorrow."

"Bullshit."

"Phillip's right." As much as he detested it, Ethan accepted the change of plans. "We keep it in official surroundings. We keep our heads. It's better for Seth."

"Why? So his bitch of a mother and his lying auntie have more time to put their heads together? Christ, when I think Sybill was alone with Seth for a good hour today, I want to—"

"It's done," Phillip snapped. "He's fine. We're fine." With fury bubbling through his blood, he slammed into the

Jeep. "And there are five of us. They won't get their hands on Seth."

"He didn't recognize her," Ethan pointed out. "That's funny, isn't it? He didn't know who Sybill was."

"Neither did I," Phillip murmured and shoved the Jeep into gear. "But I do now."

SYBILL'S PRIORITY WAS TO get Gloria a hot meal, keep her calm, and question her carefully. The little Italian restaurant was only a few blocks from the police station, and after a hurried glance, Sybill decided it would fill the bill.

"My nerves are shot to hell." Gloria puffed greedily on a cigarette while Sybill maneuvered into a parking spot. "The nerve of those bastards, coming after me like that. You know what they'd have done if I'd been alone, don't you?"

Sybill only sighed and stepped out of the car. "You need to eat."

"Yeah, sure." Gloria sniffed at the decor the minute they stepped inside. It was bright and cheerful, with colorful Italian pottery, thick candles, striped tablecloths, and decorative bottles of herbed vinegars. "I'd rather have a steak than Wop food."

"Please." Forcing back irritation, she took Gloria's arm and requested a table for two.

"Smoking section," Gloria added, already pulling out another cigarette as they were led to the noisier bar area. "Gin and tonic, a double."

Sybill rubbed her temples. "Just mineral water. Thank you."

"Loosen up," Gloria suggested when the hostess left them alone. "You look like you could use a drink."

"I'm driving. I don't want one anyway." She shifted away

from the smoke Gloria blew toward her face. "We have to talk, seriously."

"Let me get some lubrication, will you?" Gloria smoked and scanned the men at the bar, toying with which one she'd pick up if she didn't have her deadly dull sister along.

Christ, Sybill was a bore. Always had been, she mused, drumming her fingers on the table and wanting her goddamn drink. But she was useful, and always had been. If you played her right, laid on plenty of tears, she came through.

She needed a hammer with the Quinns, and Sybill was the perfect choice. Upstanding, fucking respectable Dr. Griffin. "Gloria, you haven't even asked about Seth?"

"What about him?"

"I've seen him several times, spoken with him. I've seen where he's living, where he goes to school. I met some of his friends."

Gloria clicked into the tone of her sister's voice, adjusted her attitude. "How is he?" She worked up a shaky smile. "Did he ask about me?"

"He's fine. Really wonderful, actually. He's grown so much since I saw him."

Ate like a horse, Gloria remembered, and was always growing out of his clothes and shoes. Like she was made of fucking money or something.

"He didn't know who I was."

"What do you mean?" Gloria snatched up her drink the minute it was set on the table. "You didn't tell him?"

"No, I didn't." Sybill glanced up at the waitress. "We need a few more minutes before ordering."

"So you were poking around incognito." Gloria let out a long, hoarse laugh. "You surprise me, Syb."

"I thought it best that I observe the situation before changing the dynamics."

Gloria snorted. "Now that sounds just like you. Man, you don't change. 'Observe the situation before changing the dynamics,' " she repeated in her imitation of a snooty voice. "Christ. The situation is those sons of bitches have my kid. They threatened me, and God knows what they're doing to him. I want some dough to work on getting him back."

"I sent you money for the lawyer," Sybill reminded her.

Gloria clinked ice against her teeth as she drank. And the five thousand had come in handy, she thought now. How the hell could she have known how fast the money she'd bled out of Ray would slip away? She had expenses, didn't she? She'd wanted to have some fun for a change. Should have demanded twice as much from him, she decided.

Well, she'd get it out of those bastards he'd raised.

"You got the money I wired for your lawyer, didn't you, Gloria?"

Gloria took another deep drink. "Yeah, well, lawyers suck you dry, don't they? Hey!" She called out, signaling to the waitress and pointing at her empty glass. "Hit me again, will you?"

"If you drink like that and you don't eat, you're going to be sick again."

Like hell, Gloria sneered as she snatched up her menu. She didn't intend to stick her finger down her throat again. Once was more than enough. "Hey, they got steak Florentine. I can handle that. Remember when the old man took us off to Italy that summer? All those hot-looking dudes on motorbikes. Holy God, I had a hell of a time with that guy, what was his name. Carlo or Leo or whatever. I snuck him into the bedroom. You were too shy to stay and watch, so you slept in the parlor while we did the deed half the night."

She snatched up her fresh glass, lifted it in toast. "God bless the Italians."

"I'll have the linguini with pesto and the insalada mista."

"Give me the steak, bloody." Gloria held out the menu without looking at the waitress. "Skip the rabbit food. Been a while, hasn't it, Syb? What, four, five years?"

"Six," Sybill corrected. "It's been just over six since I came home to find you and Seth gone, along with a number of my personal possessions."

"Yeah, sorry about that. I was messed up. It's tough raising a kid on your own. Money's always tight."

"You never told me very much about his father."

"What's to tell? Old news." She shrugged it off and rattled the ice in her glass.

"All right, then, let's deal with current events. I need to know everything that happened. I need to understand it in order to help you and to know how to handle our meeting with the Quinns tomorrow."

The gin and tonic thudded onto the table. "What meeting?"

"We're going in to Social Services tomorrow morning to air out the problems, discuss the situation, and try to reach a solution."

"The hell I am. The only thing they want is to fuck me over."

"Keep your voice down," Sybill ordered sharply. "And listen to me. If you want to straighten yourself out, if you want your son back, this has to be done calmly and legally. Gloria, you need help, and I'm willing to help you. From what I can see, you're not in any shape to take Seth back right now."

"Whose side are you on?"

"His." It came out of her mouth before she realized that it was the absolute truth. "I'm on his side, and I hope that puts me on yours. We need to resolve what happened today."

"I told you I was set up."

"Fine. It still needs to be resolved. The courts aren't going to be very sympathetic to a woman who's facing charges of possession."

"Great, why don't you get on the witness stand and tell

them how worthless I am? That's what you think anyway. That's what all of you always thought.''

"Please, stop it." Lowering her voice to a murmur, Sybill leaned over the table. "I'm doing everything I know how to do. If you want to prove to me you want to make this work, you have to cooperate. You have to give something back, Gloria.''

"Nothing's ever been free with you."

"We're not talking about me. I'll pay your legal fees, I'll talk to Social Services, I'll work to make the Quinns understand your needs and your rights. I want you to agree to rehab.''

"For what?"

"You drink too much."

She sneered, deliberately gulping down more gin. "I've had a rough day."

"You had drugs in your possession."

"I said they weren't fucking mine."

"You've said that before," Sybill said, coolly now. "You get counseling, you get therapy, you get rehab. I'll arrange it, I'll foot the bill. I'll help you find a job, a place to stay."

"As long as it's your way." Gloria tossed back the rest of her drink. "Therapy. You and the old man used that to solve everything."

"Those are the conditions."

"So you're running the show. Jesus, order me another drink. I've gotta piss." She swung her purse over her shoulder and strode past the bar.

Sybill sat back and closed her eyes. She wasn't going to order Gloria another drink, not when her sister's words were already beginning to slur. That would be another bitter little battle, she imagined.

The aspirin she'd taken had failed miserably. Pain was drumming at both temples in a sick and consistent rhythm. Across her forehead was a squeezing band of iron. She wanted nothing quite so much as to stretch out on a soft bed in a dark room and sink into oblivion.

He despised her now. It made her ache with regret and shame to remember the contempt she'd seen in Phillip's eyes. Maybe she deserved it. At that moment she simply couldn't think clearly enough to be sure. But she was sorry for it.

More than that, she was furious with herself for letting him and his opinion of her come to matter so much in such a short time. She'd known him for only a matter of days and had never, never intended to allow his emotions or hers to become entangled.

A casual physical attraction, a few mutually enjoyable hours in each other's company. That was all it was supposed to be. How had it become more?

But she knew when he'd held her, when he'd sent her blood swimming with those long, intimate kisses, she'd wanted more. Now she, who had never considered herself particularly sexy or overly emotional, was a frustrated, pitiful wreck because one man had jiggled a lock he was no longer interested in opening.

There was nothing to be done about it, she reminded herself. Certainly, considering the circumstances, she and Phillip Quinn had never been meant to develop a personal relationship of any kind. If they managed to have one now, it would be because of the child. They would both be adult, coldly polite, and—in the end, she hoped—reasonable.

For Seth's sake.

She opened her eyes as the waitress served her salad and hated the pity she saw on a stranger's face.

"Can I get you anything else? More water?"

"No. I'm fine, thank you. You could take that," she added, indicating Gloria's empty glass.

Her stomach rebelled at the thought of food, but she ordered herself to pick up her fork. For five minutes she toyed with the salad, poking at it while her gaze drifted regularly toward the rear of the restaurant.

She must be ill again, Sybill thought wearily. Now she would have to go back, hold Gloria's head, listen to her whining, and mop up the mess. One more pattern.

Battling both resentment and the shame that trickled from it, she rose and walked back to the ladies' room.

"Gloria, are you all right?" There was no one at the sinks and no answer from any of the stalls. Resigned, Sybill began to nudge doors open. "Gloria?"

In the last stall she saw her own wallet lying open on the closed lid of the toilet. Stunned, she snatched it up, flipped through it. Her various identifications were there, and her credit cards.

But all her cash was gone, along with her sister.

TEN

W<small>ITH HER MIND JUMBLED</small>
with pain, her hands unsteady, and her system begging to shut
down for the night, Sybill keyed open her hotel door. If she
could just get to her migraine medication, to a dark room, to
oblivion, she would find a way to deal with tomorrow.

She would find a way to face the Quinns, alone, with the
shameful sting of failure.

They would believe she'd helped Gloria run away. How
could she blame them? She was already a liar and a sneak in
their eyes. In Seth's.

And, she admitted, in her own.

With slow deliberation, she turned the bolt, fixed the safety
lock, then leaned back against the door until she could will
her legs to move again.

When the light switched on, she stifled a yelp and covered
her eyes in defense.

"You're right about the view," Phillip said from her terrace doors. "It's spectacular."

She lowered her hand, forced her mind to engage. He'd
removed his jacket and tie, she noted, but otherwise he looked

151

just as he had when he'd confronted her at the police station. Polished, urbane, and bitterly angry.

"How did you get in?"

His smile was cold, turning his eyes a hard, chilly gold. The color of an icy winter sun. "You disappoint me, Sybill. I'd have thought your research on your subject would have included the fact that one of my formative skills was breaking and entering."

She stayed where she was, supported by the door. "You were a thief?"

"Among other things. But enough about me." He stepped forward to settle on the arm of the sofa, like a casual friend making himself comfortable for a chatty visit. "You fascinate me. Your notes are incredibly revealing, even to a layman."

"You read my notes?" Her gaze swung toward the desk and her laptop. She couldn't quite find outrage through the prickly blanket of pain enveloping her head, but she knew it must be there. "You had no right to come in here, uninvited. To break into my computer and read my work."

So calm, Phillip thought, and rose to help himself to a beer from her mini bar. What kind of woman was she? "As far as I'm concerned, Sybill, all bets are off. You lied to me, you used me. You had it all worked out, didn't you? When you waltzed into the boatyard last week, your agenda was set."

He couldn't stay calm. The longer she stood, staring at him with no expression on her face, the higher his temper spiked. "Infiltrate the enemy camp." He slammed the beer onto the table. The crack of glass on wood split through her head like an axe. "Observe and report, pass information to your sister. And if being with me helped you slide more smoothly behind the lines, you were willing to make the sacrifice. Would you have slept with me?"

"No." She pressed a hand to her head and nearly gave in to the need to slip to the floor and curl into a ball. "I never meant for things . . ."

"I think you're lying." He crossed to her, taking her arms and drawing her up to her toes. "I think you'd have done anything. Just one more object lesson, right? And with the added benefit of helping your bitch of a sister bleed us for more money. Seth doesn't mean any more to you than he does to her. Just a means to an end for both of you."

"No, that's not—I can't think." The pain was excruciating. If he hadn't been holding her up, she would have gone to her knees and begged. "I—we'll discuss it tomorrow. I'm not well."

"You and Gloria have that in common too. I'm not falling for it, Sybill."

Her breath began to hitch, her vision to blur. "I'm sorry. I can't stand it. I have to sit down. Please, I have to sit down."

He focused in, past his fury. Her cheeks were dead pale, her eyes glassy, her breath coming fast and uneven. If she was faking illness, he decided, Hollywood had missed a major star.

Muttering an oath, he pulled her to the sofa. She all but melted onto the cushions.

Too ill to be embarrassed, she closed her eyes. "My briefcase. My pills are in my briefcase."

He picked up the soft black leather case beside the desk, riffled through it and found the prescription bottle. "Imitrex?" He looked over at her. She had her head back, her eyes closed, and her hands fisted in her lap as if she could center the pain there and squeeze it to death. "Major migraine drugs."

"Yes. I get them now and again." She had to focus, she ordered herself, had to relax. But nothing she did eased her past the vicious pain. "I should have had them with me. If I'd had them with me it wouldn't have gone this far."

"Here." He handed her a pill and water he'd taken from the mini bar.

"Thank you." She nearly bobbled the water in her rush. "It takes a while, but it's better than the injection." She closed her eyes again and prayed he would just leave her alone.

"Have you eaten?"

"What? No. I'll be all right."

She looked fragile, terrifyingly so. Part of him thought she deserved to hurt, was tempted to leave her with her misery. But he picked up the phone and asked for room service.

"I don't want anything."

"Just be quiet." He ordered up soup and tea, then began to prowl the room.

How could he have misjudged her so completely? Pegging people quickly and accurately was one of his most finely honed skills. He'd seen an intelligent, interesting woman. A classy one, with humor and taste. But beneath the glossy surface, she was a liar, a cheat, and an opportunist.

He nearly laughed. He'd just described the boy he'd worked half his life to bury.

"In your notes you say you haven't seen Seth since he was about four. Why did you come here now?"

"I thought I could help."

"Who?"

The hope that the pain would begin to recede gave her the strength to open her eyes. "I don't know. I thought I could help him, and Gloria."

"You help one, you hurt the other. I read your notes, Sybill. Are you going to try to tell me you care about him? 'The subject appears healthy.' He's not a fucking subject, he's a child."

"It's necessary to be objective."

"It's necessary to be human."

It was a dart, sharp enough to strike her heart and make it ache as well. "I'm not very good with emotions. Reactions and behavioral patterns are more my forte than feelings. I'd hoped to be able to keep a certain distance from the situation, to analyze it, to determine what was best for all involved. I haven't been doing a good job of it."

"Why didn't you do anything before?" he demanded.

"Why didn't you do anything to analyze the situation when Seth was with your sister?"

"I didn't know where they were." Then she let out a breath and shook her head. It was no time for excuses, and the man staring at her with those cold eyes wouldn't accept them in any case. "I never seriously tried to find out. I sent her money now and again if she contacted me and asked for it. My connection with Gloria was usually unproductive and unpleasant."

"For Christ's sake, Sybill, we're talking about a little boy here, not your views on sibling rivalry."

"I was afraid to get attached," she snapped out. "The one time I did, she took him away. He was her child, not mine. There was nothing I could do about it. I asked her to let me help, but she wouldn't. She's been raising him all alone. My parents have disinherited her. My mother won't even acknowledge that she has a grandson. I know Gloria has problems, but it can't be easy for her."

He simply stared at her. "Are you serious?"

"She's had no one to depend on," Sybill began, then closed her eyes again as a knock sounded on the door. "I'm sorry, but I don't think I can eat."

"Yes, you can."

Phillip opened the door for the room service waiter, directed him to set the tray on the table in front of the sofa. He dispatched him quickly, with cash and a generous tip.

"Try the soup," he ordered. "You need something in your system or the medication's going to end up making you nauseous. My mother was a doctor, remember."

"All right." She spooned it up slowly, telling herself it was just more medicine. "Thank you. I'm sure you're not in the mood to be kind."

"It's harder for me to kick you when you're down. Eat up, Sybill, and we'll go a round or two."

She sighed. The leading edge of the headache was dulling.

She could handle it now, she thought. And him as well. "I hope you'll at least attempt to understand my point of view on this. Gloria called me a few weeks ago. She was desperate, terrified. She told me she'd lost Seth."

"Lost him?" Phillip let out a short, sarcastic laugh. "Oh, that's rich."

"I thought abduction at first, but I was able to get some of the details out of her. She explained that your family had him, had taken him from her. She was almost hysterical, so afraid she'd never get him back. She didn't have the money to pay her lawyer. She was fighting an entire family, an entire system all alone. I wired her the money for the lawyer, and I told her I'd help. That she should wait until I contacted her."

As her system began to settle again, she reached for one of the rolls in the basket beside her bowl and broke it open. "I decided to come and see the situation for myself. I know Gloria doesn't always tell the entire truth, that she can slant things to suit her position. But the fact remains that your family had Seth and she didn't."

"Thank God for that."

She stared at the bread in her hand, wondered if she could manage to put it in her mouth and chew. "I know you're providing him with a good home, but she's his mother, Phillip. She has a right to keep her own son."

He watched her face carefully, measured the tone of her voice. He didn't know whether to be furious or baffled by both. "You actually believe that, don't you?"

Color was seeping back into her cheeks. Her eyes had cleared and now met his steadily. "What do you mean?"

"You believe that my family took Seth, that we took advantage of some poor single mother down on her luck and snatched the kid, that she wants him back. That she even has a lawyer working on custody."

"You do have him," Sybill pointed out.

"That's right. And he's exactly where he belongs and is

going to stay. Let me give you some facts. She blackmailed my father, and she sold Seth to him.''

"I know you believe that, but—"

"I said *facts,* Sybill. Less than a year ago, Seth was living in a set of filthy rooms on the Block in Baltimore, and your sister was on the stroll."

"On the stroll?"

"God, where do you come from? She was hooking. This isn't a whore with a heart of gold here, this isn't a desperate, down-on-her-luck unwed mother doing anything she has to to survive and keep her child fed. She was keeping her habit fed."

She only shook her head, slowly, side to side, even as part of her mind accepted everything he said. "You can't know all this."

"Yes, I can know it. Because I live with Seth. I've talked with him, I've listened to him."

Her hands went icy. She lifted the pot of tea to warm them, poured some slowly into a cup. "He's just a boy. He could have misunderstood."

"Sure. I bet that's it. He just misunderstood when she brought a john up to the place, when she got so stoned she sprawled on the floor and he wondered if she was dead. He just misunderstood when she beat the hell out of him when she was feeling testy."

"She hit him." The cup rattled into the saucer. "She hit him?"

"She beat him. No controversial yet civilized spanking, Dr. Griffin. Fists, belts, the back of the hand. Have you ever had a fist in the face?" He held his up to hers. "Figure it out. Proportionately, this would be about right, comparing a grown woman's fist to, say, a five-, six-year-old boy. Put liquor and drugs into that fist and it comes faster and harder. I've been there."

He angled his fist away, studied it. "My mother preferred

smack—to the uninitiated that's heroin. If she missed her fix, you learned to stay far out of her way. I know just what it is to have a vicious, fucked-up female take her fists to me.'' His gaze whipped back to Sybill's. ''Your sister won't ever have the chance to use them on Seth again.''

''I—she needs to go into therapy. I never . . . He was fine when I saw him. If I'd known she was abusing him—''

''I haven't finished. He's a good-looking kid, isn't he? Some of Gloria's clients thought so.''

The color that had come back to her cheeks fell away. ''No.'' Shaking her head, she pushed away from him and staggered to her feet. ''No, I don't believe that. That's hideous. That's impossible.''

''She didn't do anything to stop it.'' He ignored the pale cheeks and fragility now and pushed. Hard. ''She didn't do a goddamn thing to protect him. Seth was on his own there. He fought them off or hid. Sooner or later, there would have been one he couldn't fight off or hide from.''

''That's not possible. She couldn't.''

''She could—especially if it earned her a few extra bucks. It took months with us before he could stand to be touched in even the most casual way. He has nightmares still. And if you say his mother's name, it makes you sick to see the fear that comes into his eyes. That's your situation, Dr. Griffin.''

''God. How can you expect me to accept all that? To believe she's capable of that?'' She pressed a hand to her heart. ''I grew up with her. I've known you less than a week, and you expect me to accept this horror story, this vileness as fact?''

''I think you believe it,'' he said after a moment. ''I think, under it all, you're smart enough, and let's say observant enough to know the truth.''

She was terrified. ''If it is the truth, why didn't the authorities do anything? Why wasn't he helped?''

''Sybill, have you lived on that smooth plateau so long that

you really don't know what life's like on the street? How
many Seths there are out there? The system works some of
the time, for the few and the lucky. It didn't work for me. It
didn't work for Seth. Ray and Stella Quinn worked for me.
And just under a year ago, my father paid your sister the first
installment on a ten-year-old boy. He brought Seth home, he
gave him a life, a decent one.''

''She said—she said he took Seth.''

''Yeah, he took him. Ten thousand the first time, a couple
of other payments of about the same. Then last March she
wrote him a letter demanding a lump-sum payment. A hundred
fifty thousand, cash, and she'd walk away.''

''A hundred and—'' Appalled, she broke off, struggled to
concentrate on verifiable facts. ''She wrote a letter?''

''I've read it. It was in the car with my father when he was
killed. He was on his way back from Baltimore. He'd cleaned
out most of his bank accounts. I'd have to guess she's gone
through a big chunk of it by now. She wrote us, demanding
more money, just a few months ago.''

She turned away, walked quickly to the terrace doors, and
flung them open. The need for air was urgent, and she gulped
it in like water. ''I'm supposed to accept that Gloria has done
all of this, and her primary motive is money?''

''You sent her money for her lawyer. What's his name?
Why hasn't our lawyer been contacted by him?''

She squeezed her eyes shut. It wouldn't help to feel betrayed, she reminded herself. ''She evaded the question when
I asked her. Obviously, she doesn't have a lawyer, and it's
doubtful she ever intended to consult one.''

''Well, you're slow''—the sarcasm rang clearly—''but you
do catch on.''

''I wanted to believe her. We were never close as children,
and that has to be as much my fault as hers. I'd hoped I could
help her, and Seth. I thought this was the way.''

''So, she played you.''

"I felt responsible. My mother is so unbending on this. She's angry that I came here. She has refused to acknowledge Gloria since she ran off at eighteen. Gloria claimed to have been molested by the counselor at our school. She was always claiming to have been molested. They had a terrible row, my mother and she, and Gloria was gone the next day. She'd taken some of my mother's jewelry, my father's coin collection, some cash. I didn't hear from her for nearly five years. Those five years were a relief.

"She hated me," Sybill said quietly and continued to stare out at the lights on the water. "Always, as long as I can remember. It didn't matter what I did, whether I fought with her or stepped back and let her have her way, she detested me. It was easier for me to keep my distance. I didn't hate her, I simply felt nothing. And when I brush everything else aside right now, it's exactly the same. I can't feel anything for her. It must be a flaw," she murmured. "Maybe it's genetic."

With a weak smile, she turned around again. "It might make an interesting study one day."

"You never had a clue, did you, of what she was doing?"

"No. So much for my renowned observational skills. I'm sorry, Phillip. I'm so terribly sorry for what I've done, and haven't done. I promise you I didn't come here to harm Seth. And I give you my word I'll do whatever I can to help. If I can go into Social Services in the morning, speak with Anna, your family. If you'll allow it, I'd like to see Seth, try to explain."

"We won't be taking him to Anna's office. We're not letting Gloria near him."

"She won't be there."

His eyes flickered. "I beg your pardon?"

"I don't know where she is." Defeated, she spread her hands. "I promised I'd bring her. I meant to."

"You just let her walk? Goddamn it."

"I didn't—not intentionally." She sank down onto the sofa

again. "I took her to a restaurant. I wanted to get her a meal, talk to her. She was agitated and drinking too much. I was annoyed with her. I told her we were going to straighten everything out, that we were going to have a meeting in the morning. I made ultimatums. I should have known better. She didn't like it, but I didn't see what she could do about it."

"What sort of ultimatums?"

"That she would get counseling, go into rehab. That she would get help, get herself straightened out before she tried to gain custody of Seth. She went to the ladies' room, and when she didn't come back out, I went in looking for her."

She lifted her hands, let them fall uselessly. "I found my wallet. She must have taken it out of my purse. She left me my credit cards," she added with a wry smile. "She'd know I would cancel them straight off. She only took the cash. It's not the first time she's stolen from me, but it always surprises me." She sighed, shrugged it off. "I drove around for nearly two hours, hoping I'd find her. But I didn't, and I don't know where she is. I don't know what she intends to do."

"She messed you over pretty good, didn't she?"

"I'm an adult. I can take care of myself, and I'm responsible for myself. But Seth . . . if even a part of what you've told me is true . . . he'll hate me. I understand that and I'll have to accept it. I'd like the chance to talk to him."

"That'll be up to him."

"Fair enough. I need to see the files, the paperwork." She linked her fingers together. "I realize you can require me to get a court order, but I'd like to avoid that. I'd process this better if I had it all in black and white."

"It's not as simple as black and white when you're dealing with people's lives and feelings."

"Maybe not. But I need facts, documentation, reports. Once I have them, if I'm persuaded that Seth's best interest is to remain with your family, through legal guardianship or adoption, I'll do whatever I can to help that happen."

She had to push now, she told herself. She had to push to make him give her another chance. Just one more chance. "I'm a psychologist, and I'm the birth mother's sister. I'd think my opinion would bear weight in court."

He studied her objectively. Details, he thought. He was the man who handled the details, after all. Those she was adding would only help settle everything the way he wanted it settled. "I imagine it would, and I'll discuss it with my family. But I don't think you get it, Sybill. She isn't going to fight for Seth. She's never intended to fight for him. She's just trying to use him to get more money. She's not going to get that, either, not another dime."

"So I'm superfluous."

"Maybe. I haven't decided." He rose, jingling the change in his pockets as he paced. "How are you feeling?"

"Better. Fine. Thank you. I'm sorry to have fallen apart like that, but the migraine was a full-blown one."

"You get them often?"

"A few times a year. I'm usually able to get to the medication at onset, so they're not too bad. When I left this evening I was distracted."

"Yeah, bailing your sister out of jail would be a distraction." He glanced back at her with mild curiosity. "How much did it take to spring her?"

"Bail was set at five thousand."

"Well, I'd say you can kiss that good-bye."

"Most likely. The money isn't important."

"What is?" He stopped, turned toward her. She looked exhausted and disconcertingly fragile still. An unfair advantage was still an advantage, he decided, and pressed. "What is important to you, Sybill?"

"Finishing what I've started. You may not need my help, but I don't intend to walk away until I've done what I can."

"If Seth doesn't want to see you or speak to you, he won't. That's bottom line. He's had enough."

She straightened her shoulders before they could slump. "Regardless of whether he agrees to see or speak with me, I intend to stay until the legalities are settled. You can't force me to leave, Phillip. You can make it difficult for me, uncomfortable, but you can't make me leave until I'm satisfied."

"Yeah, I can make it difficult for you. I can make it damn near impossible for you. And I'm considering just that." He leaned over, ignoring her instinctive jerk, and caught her chin firmly in his hand. "Would you have slept with me?"

"Under the circumstances, I believe that's moot."

"Not to me it isn't. Answer the question."

She kept her eyes level with his. That was a matter of pride, though she felt she had little of that or her dignity left intact. "Yes." When his eyes flared, she jerked her chin away. "But not because of Seth or Gloria. I would have slept with you because I wanted you. Because I was attracted to you and when I was around you for any length of time my priorities became blurred."

"Your priorities became blurred." He rocked back on his heels, dipped his hands into his pockets. "Jesus, you're a case. Why do I find that snotty attitude intriguing?"

"I don't have a snotty attitude. You asked a question, I answered it honestly. And, you'll note, in the past tense."

"Now I've got something else to consider. If I want to change that to present tense. Don't say it's moot, Sybill," he warned when she opened her mouth. "I'm bound to take that as a dare. If we end up in bed tonight, neither one of us is going to like ourselves in the morning."

"I don't like you very much right now."

"We're on the same curve there, honey." He jingled his change again, then shrugged. "We'll keep the meeting at Anna's office in the morning. As far as I'm concerned, you can see all the paperwork, including your sister's blackmail letters. As far as Seth goes, I don't make any promises. If you try to go around me and my family to get to him, you'll regret it.''

"Don't threaten me."

"I'm not. I'm giving you facts. It's your family who likes threats." His smile was sharp, dangerous, and without an ounce of humor. "The Quinns make promises, and they keep them."

"I'm not Gloria."

"No, but we still have to see just who you are. Nine o'clock," he added. "Oh, and Dr. Griffin, you may want to look over your own notes again. When you do it might be interesting, psychologically speaking, to ask yourself why you find it so much more rewarding to observe than to participate. Get some sleep," he suggested as he walked to the door. "You're going to want to be sharp tomorrow."

"Phillip." Going with the impulse of temper, she rose and waited for him to turn around, with the door open at his back. "Isn't it fortunate that circumstances changed before we made the mistake of sex?"

He angled his head, both impressed and amused that she'd dared such a dangerous parting shot. "Darling, I'm counting my blessings."

He closed the door with a quiet snap.

ELEVEN

SETH NEEDED TO BE TOLD.
There was only one way to do it, and that was straight out, as a family. Ethan and Grace would bring him home as soon as Aubrey was settled with the baby-sitter.

"We shouldn't have let her out of our sight." Cam paced the kitchen, hands jammed in his pockets, gray eyes hard as flint. "God knows where she took off to, and instead of having answers, instead of straightening her ass out, we've got nothing."

"That's not entirely true." Anna brewed coffee. It wouldn't help to settle nerves, she thought, but everyone would want it. "I'll have a police report for the file. You couldn't very well drag her out of the station house, Cameron, and force her to talk to you."

"It would've been a hell of a lot more satisfying than watching her walk."

"Momentarily, perhaps. But it remains in Seth's best interest, and ours, to handle everything in an official, by-the-book manner."

"How do you think Seth's going to feel about that?" He

whirled, and the leading edge of his temper whipped out at his wife and his brother. "Do you think he's going to feel it's in his best interest that we had Gloria and did nothing?"

"You did do something." Because she understood his frustration, Anna kept her voice calm. "You agreed to meet her in my office. If she doesn't keep the appointment, it's another strike against her."

"She won't be anywhere near Social Services tomorrow," Phillip began, "but Sybill will."

"And we're supposed to trust her?" Cam snapped out. "All she's done so far is lie."

"You didn't see her tonight," Phillip said evenly. "I did."

"Yeah, and we know what part of your anatomy you're looking with, bro."

"Stop it." Anna stepped quickly between them as two pairs of fists curled, two pairs of eyes flashed. "You're not going to beat each other brainless in this house." She slapped a hand on Cam's chest, then Phillip's, found them both immovable. "It's not going to help anyone if you rip pieces off each other. We need a united front. Seth needs it," she added, pushing harder when she heard the front door open. "Now, both of you sit down. Sit down!" She hissed it, the image of those ready fists swinging over her head, adding both urgency and authority to her voice.

With their gazes still heated and locked, both men dragged out chairs and sat. Anna had time for one relieved breath before Seth came in, trailed by two dogs with cheerfully swatting tails.

"Hey, what's up?" His cheerful grin vanished immediately. A lifetime of living with Gloria's wildly swinging moods had taught him to gauge atmosphere. The air in the kitchen was simmering with tension and temper.

He took a step back, then froze as Ethan came in behind him and laid a hand on his shoulder. "Coffee smells good," he said mildly, and the hand on Seth's shoulder remained, part restraint, part support.

"I'll get some cups." Grace hurried past them to the cupboard. She knew she'd be better off with her hands busy. "Seth, do you want a Coke?"

"What happened?" His lips felt stiff and his hands cold.

"It's going to take a little while to explain it all." Anna walked to him, put her hands on his cheeks. The first order of business, she determined, was to erase the fear that had come into his eyes. "But you don't have to worry."

"Did she ask for more money again? Is she coming here? Did they let her out of jail?"

"No. Come sit down. We'll explain everything." She shook her head at Cam before he could speak and locked her eyes with Phillip's as she guided Seth toward the table. He had more firsthand information, she decided. It was best that it come from him.

Where the hell was he supposed to start? Phillip dragged a hand through his hair. "Seth, do you know anything about your mother's family?"

"No. She used to tell me stuff. One day she'd say how her parents were rich, really rolling in it, but they died and some slick lawyer stole all the money. Another day she'd say how she was an orphan and she'd run away from this foster home because the father tried to rape her. Or how her mother was this movie star who gave her up for adoption so she wouldn't lose her career. She was always changing it."

His gaze shifted around the room as he spoke, trying to read faces. "Who cares?" he demanded, ignoring the soft drink Grace set in front of him. "Who the hell cares, anyway? There wasn't anybody or she'd've tapped them for money."

"There is somebody, and it seems she did tap them for money off and on." Phillip kept his voice quiet and calm, as a person would when soothing a frantic puppy. "We found out today that she has parents, and a sister."

"I don't have to go with them." Alarm rang in his head as he surged out of his chair. "I don't know them. I don't have to go with them."

"No, you don't." Phillip took Seth's arm. "But you need to know about them."

"I don't want to." His gaze flew to Cam's, pleaded. "I don't want to know. You said I could stay. You said nothing was going to change that."

It made Cam sick to see that desperation, but he pointed to the chair. "You are staying. Nothing is going to change that. Sit down. You never solve anything by running."

"Look around, Seth." Ethan's tone was soft, the voice of reason. "You've got five people here, standing with you."

He wanted to believe it. He didn't know how to explain that it was so much easier to believe in lies and threats than in promises. "What are they going to do? How did they find me?"

"Gloria called her sister a few weeks ago," Phillip began when Seth sat again. "You don't remember her sister?"

"I don't remember anybody," Seth muttered and hunched his shoulders.

"Well, it seems she spun a tale for the sister, told her that we'd stolen you from her."

"She's full of shit."

"Seth." Anna drilled him with a look that made him squirm.

"She conned the sister out of some money for a lawyer," Phillip continued. "Said she was broke and desperate, that we'd threatened her. She needed the money to get you back."

Seth wiped his mouth with the back of his hand. "She bought it? She must be an idiot."

"Maybe. Or maybe she's a soft touch. Either way, the sister didn't buy the whole package. She wanted to check things out for herself. So she came to St. Chris."

''She's here?'' Seth's head whipped up. ''I don't want to see her. I don't want to talk to her.''

''You already have. Sybill is Gloria's sister.''

Seth's dark-blue eyes widened, and the angry flush faded from his cheeks. ''She can't be. She's a doctor. She writes books.''

''Nonetheless, she is. When Cam and Ethan and I drove down to Hampton, we saw her.''

''You saw her? You saw Gloria?''

''Yeah, we saw her. Hold on.'' Phillip laid a hand over Seth's rigid one. ''Sybill was there, too. She was posting bail. So it all came out.''

''She's a liar.'' Seth's voice began to hitch. ''Just like Gloria. She's a damn liar.''

''Let me finish. We agreed to meet them both in the morning, in Anna's office. We have to get the facts, Seth,'' he added when the boy snatched his hands free. ''It's the only way we're going to fix this for good.''

''I'm not going.''

''You can decide that for yourself. We don't think Gloria's going to show. I saw Sybill just a little while ago. Gloria had given her the slip.''

''She's gone.'' Relief and hope struggled to beat back fear. ''She's gone again?''

''It looks that way. She took money out of Sybill's wallet and split.'' Phillip glanced over at Ethan, judged his brother's reaction to the news as angry resignation. ''Sybill will be in Anna's office in the morning. I think it would be better if you went in with us, talked to her there.''

''I don't have anything to say to her. I don't know her. I don't care about her. She should just go away and leave me alone.''

''She can't hurt you, Seth.''

''I hate her. She's probably just like Gloria, only she pretends to be different.''

Phillip thought of the fatigue, the guilt, the misery he'd seen on Sybill's face. But he said, "That's for you to decide, too. But you need to see her and hear what she has to say to do that. She said she'd only seen you once. Gloria came to New York and you stayed at Sybill's place for a little while. You were about four."

"I don't remember." His face went stony with stubbornness. "We stayed in a lot of places."

"Seth, I know it doesn't seem fair." Grace reached over to give the hands he had balled into fists on the table a quick, reassuring squeeze. "But your aunt may be able to help. We'll all be there with you."

Cam saw the refusal in Seth's eyes and leaned forward. "Quinns don't walk away from a fight." He paused until Seth's gaze shifted to his. "Until they win it."

It was pride and the fear of not living up to the name they'd given him that stiffened his shoulders. "I'll go, but nothing she says is going to mean dick to me." With eyes hot and brooding, he turned to Phillip. "Did you have sex with her?"

"Seth!" Anna's voice was sharp as a slap, but Phillip only raised a hand.

Maybe his first instinct was to tell the boy it was none of his business, but he knew how to think past the quick retort and study the whole. "No, I didn't."

Seth gave a stiff shrug. "That's something, then."

"You come first." Phillip saw the surprise flicker in Seth's eyes at the statement. "I made a promise that you would, so you do. Nothing and no one changes that."

Beneath the warm thrill, Seth felt a greasy tug of shame. "Sorry," he mumbled it and stared down at his own hands.

"Fine." Phillip sipped at the coffee that had gone cold in his cup. "We'll hear what she has to say in the morning, then she'll hear what we have to say. What you have to say. We'll go from there."

• • •

SHE DIDN'T KNOW WHAT SHE was going to say. She felt sick inside. The dregs of a migraine hangover fuzzed her brain, and her nerves were stretched to the breaking point at the prospect of facing the Quinns. And Seth.

They had to hate her. She doubted very much they could feel more contempt for her than she felt for herself. If what Phillip had told her was true—the drugs, the beatings, the men—she had by the sin of omission left her own nephew in hell.

There was nothing they could say to her that was worse than what she had said to herself during the endless, sleepless night. But she was sick with anticipation of what was to come as she pulled into the small parking lot attached to Social Services.

It was bound to become ugly, she thought, as she tilted her rearview mirror and carefully applied lipstick. Hard words, cold looks—and she was so pitifully vulnerable to both.

She could stand against them, she told herself. She could maintain that outward calm no matter what was happening to her insides. She'd learned that defense over the years. Remain aloof and detached, and survive.

She would survive this. And if she could somehow ease Seth's mind, whatever wounds she suffered would be worth it.

She stepped out of the car, a cool and composed woman in a elegantly simple silk suit the color of mourning. Her hair was swept up in a sleek twist, her makeup was subtle and flawless.

Her stomach was raw and burning.

She stepped inside the lobby. Already the waiting area contained a scattering of people. An infant whimpered restlessly in the arms of a woman whose eyes were glazed with fatigue. A man in a flannel shirt and jeans sat with his face grim and his fisted hands dangling between his knees. Two other women sat in a corner. Mother and daughter, Sybill deduced. The younger woman had her head cradled on the other's shoulder and wept silently out of eyes blackened by fists.

Sybill turned away.

"Dr. Griffin," she told the receptionist. "I have an appointment with Anna Spinelli."

"Yes, she's expecting you. Down this hall, second door on your left."

"Thank you." Sybill closed her hand around the strap of her purse and walked briskly to Anna's office.

Her heart plummeted to her stomach when she reached the doorway. They were all there, waiting. Anna sat behind the desk, looking professional in a navy blazer, her hair pinned up. She was scanning an open file.

Grace sat with her hand swallowed by Ethan's. Cam stood at the narrow window, scowling, while Phillip sat, flipping through a magazine.

Seth sat between them, staring down at the floor, his eyes curtained by his lashes, his mouth set, his shoulders hunched.

She gathered her courage, started to speak. But Phillip's eyes flicked up and found hers. The one long look warned her he hadn't softened overnight. She ignored her trembling pulse and angled her head in acknowledgment.

"You're prompt, Dr. Griffin," he said, and instantly all eyes were on her.

She felt scalded and pinned all at once, but she took the last step over the threshold into what she fully understood was Quinn turf. "Thank you for seeing me."

"Oh, we're looking forward to it." Cam's voice was dangerously soft. His hand, Sybill noted, had gone to Seth's shoulder in a gesture that was both possessive and protective.

"Ethan, would you close the door?" Anna folded her hands

on the open file. "Please sit down, Dr. Griffin."

It wouldn't be Sybill and Anna here. All the friendly female connection that came from cozy kitchens and simmering pots was gone.

Accepting that, Sybill took the vacant seat facing Anna's desk. She set her purse in her lap, clutched it with boneless fingers, and smoothly, casually, crossed her legs.

"Before we begin, I'd like to say something." She took a slow breath when Anna nodded in agreement. Sybill shifted and looked directly at Seth. He kept his eyes on the floor. "I didn't come here to hurt you, Seth, or to make you unhappy. I'm sorry that I seem to have done both. If living with the Quinns is what you want, what you need, then I want to help see that you stay with them."

Seth lifted his head now and stared at her with eyes that were stunningly adult and harsh. "I don't want your help."

"But you may need it," she murmured, then turned back to Anna. Sybill saw speculation there, and what she hoped was an open mind. "I don't know where Gloria is. I'm sorry. I gave my word I would bring her here this morning. It's been a very long time since I'd seen her, and I . . . I hadn't realized how much she'd . . . how unstable she is."

" 'Unstable.' " Cam snorted at the term. "That's a rich one."

"She contacted you," Anna began, shooting her husband one warning look.

"Yes, a few weeks ago. She was very upset, claimed that Seth had been stolen from her and that she needed money for her lawyer, who was going to fight a custody case. She was crying, nearly hysterical. She begged me to help her. I got as much information as I could. Who had Seth, and where he was living. I sent her five thousand dollars."

Sybill lifted her hands. "I realized yesterday when I spoke with her that there was no lawyer. Gloria has always been a clever actress. I'd forgotten that, or I chose to forget that."

"Were you aware that she had a drug problem?"

"No—again, not until yesterday. When I saw her, and spoke with her, it became clear that she's not capable at this time of handling the responsibility of a child."

"She doesn't want the responsibility of a child," Phillip commented.

"So you said," Sybill responded coolly. "You indicated that she wanted money. I'm aware that money is important to Gloria. I'm also aware that she's not stable. But it's difficult for me to believe, without proof, that she's done all that you claim."

"You want proof?" Cam stepped forward, fury all but visible in waves around him. "You got it, sugar. Show her the letters, Anna."

"Cam, sit down." Anna's order was firm before she turned back to Sybill. "Would you recognize your sister's handwriting?"

"I don't know. I suppose I might."

"I have a copy of the letter found in Raymond Quinn's car when he was killed, and one of the letters sent to us more recently."

She took them out of the file and passed them over the desk into Sybill's hands.

Words and phrases leaped out at her, burned into her mind. *Quinn, I'm tired of playing nickel and dime. You want the kid so bad, then it's time to pay for him. . . . A hundred and fifty grand's a pretty good bargain for a good-looking boy like Seth.*

Oh, God, was all Sybill could think. Dear God.

The letter to the Quinns after Ray's death was no better.

Ray and me had an agreement.

If you're set on keeping him . . . I'm going to need some money . . .

Sybill willed her hands to remain steady.

"She took this money?"

"Professor Quinn drew out cashier's checks to Gloria DeLauter, twice for ten thousand dollars, once for five." Anna spoke clearly and without emotion. "He brought Seth De-Lauter to St. Christopher's late last year. The letter you have is postmarked March tenth. The following day Professor Quinn arranged to cash out his bonds, some stock, and he drew large sums of cash out of his bank account. On March twelfth, he told Ethan he had business in Baltimore. On his return, he was killed in a single-car accident. There were just over forty dollars in his wallet. No other money was found."

"He promised I wouldn't have to go back," Seth said dully. "He was decent. He promised, and she knew he'd pay her."

"She asked for more. From you. From all of you."

"And miscalculated." Phillip leaned back, studying Sybill. Nothing showed, he noted, but her pallor. "She won't bleed us, Dr. Griffin. She can threaten all she wants, but she won't bleed us, and she won't get Seth."

"You also have a copy of the letter I wrote to Gloria DeLauter," Anna stated. "I informed her that Seth was under the protection of Social Services, that an investigation by this office was under way on charges of child abuse. If she comes into the county, she'll be served with a restraining order and a warrant."

"She was furious," Grace spoke up. "She called the house right after she got Anna's letter. She threatened and demanded. She said she wanted money or she'd take Seth. I told her she was wrong." Grace looked over, held Seth's gaze. "He's ours now."

She'd sold her son, was all Sybill could think. It was just as Phillip had said. All of it was just as he'd said. "You have temporary guardianship."

"It'll be permanent shortly," Phillip informed her. "We intend to see to that."

Sybill laid the papers back on Anna's desk. Inside she was

cold, brutally cold, but she linked her fingers lightly on top of her purse and spoke evenly to Seth. "Did she hit you?"

"What the hell do you care?"

"Answer the question, Seth," Phillip ordered. "Tell your aunt what life was like with her sister."

"Okay, fine." He bit the words off, but his sneer was wobbly around the edges. "Sure, she knocked me around when she felt like it. If I was lucky, she was too drunk or stoned for it to hurt much. I could usually get away, anyhow." He shrugged as if it didn't matter in the least. "Sometimes she got me by surprise. Maybe she hadn't been able to turn enough tricks to score. So she'd wake me up and pound on me a while. Or she'd cry all over me."

She wanted to turn away from that image, as she'd turned away from the desperate strangers in the waiting area. Instead she kept her gaze steady on Seth's face. "Why didn't you tell anyone, find someone to help you?"

"Like who?" Was she stupid, Seth thought? "The cops? She told me what the cops would do. I'd end up in juvie and some guy would use me like some of her johns wanted to. They could do whatever they wanted once I was inside. As long as I was out, I could get away."

"She lied to you," Anna said softly while Sybill tried to find words, any words. "The police would have helped."

"She knew?" Sybill managed. "About the men who tried to . . . touch you?"

"Sure, she thought it was funny. Hell, when she's stoned, she thinks most everything is funny. It's when she's drunk that she gets mean."

Could this monster the boy spoke of so casually be her sister? "How . . . Do you know why she decided to contact Professor Quinn?"

"No, I don't know anything about it. She got wired up one day, started talking about hitting a gold mine. She took off for a few days."

"She left you alone?" Why that should horrify her, after everything else she'd heard, Sybill couldn't say.

"Hey, I can take care of myself. When she came back, she was flying. Said I was finally going to be of some use. She had some money—real money, because she went out and scored a lot of dope without hooking. She stayed stoned and happy for days. Then Ray came. He said I could come with him. At first I thought he was like the guys she brought home. But he wasn't. I could tell. He looked sad and tired."

His voice had changed, she noted, softened. So, she thought, he grieves, too. Then she saw the ripe disgust come into his eyes.

"She came on to him," Seth said shortly, "and he got real upset. He didn't yell or anything, but he got real hard in the eyes. He made her leave. He had money with him, and he said if she wanted it, to leave. So she took it and went. He told me he had a house by the water, and a dog, and that I could live there if I wanted. And no one would mess with me."

"You went with him."

"He was old," Seth said with a shrug. "I figured I could get away from him if he tried anything. But you could trust Ray. He was decent. He said I'd never have to go back to the way things were. And I won't. No matter what, I won't go back. And I don't trust you." His eyes were adult again, his voice controlled and derisive. "Because you lied, you pretended to be decent. All you were doing was spying on us."

"You're right." She thought it the hardest thing she'd ever done, or would ever have to do, to meet those scornful eyes in a child's face and admit her own sins. "You have no reason to trust me. I didn't help you. I could have, all those years ago when she brought you to New York. I didn't want to see. It was easier not to. And when I came home one day and both of you were gone, I didn't do anything about that, either. I told myself it wasn't my concern, that you weren't my responsibility. That wasn't just wrong, it was cowardly."

He didn't want to believe her, didn't want to hear the regret and the apology in her voice. He balled his hands into fists on his knees. "It doesn't have anything to do with you now, either."

"She's my sister. I can't change that." Because it hurt to see the contempt in his eyes, she turned back to Anna. "What can I do to help? Can I make a statement to you? Talk to your lawyer? I'm a licensed psychologist, and Gloria's sister. I would assume that my opinion might carry some weight toward the guardianship."

"I'm sure it would," Anna murmured. "It won't be easy for you."

"I have no feelings for her. I'm not proud to say that, but it's the simple truth. I feel nothing toward her whatsoever, and the sense of responsibility I thought I should feel to her is over. As much as he may wish it otherwise, I'm Seth's aunt. I intend to help."

She rose and scanned the faces in the room while her stomach pitched and rolled. "I'm terribly sorry, for all of this. I realize an apology is useless. I have no excuse for what I did. Reasons, but no excuses. It's perfectly clear that Seth is where he belongs, where he's happy. If you'll give me a moment to gather my thoughts, I'll give you a statement."

She walked out, without hurry, and continued to the outside, where she could find air.

"Well, she went about it wrong, but she seems level right now." Cam got up, paced off some of his energy in the crowded office. "She sure doesn't shake easily."

"I wonder," Anna murmured. She, too, was a trained observer, and instinct told her there was a great deal more going on under that placid surface than any of them might guess. "Having her on our side will, without question, help. It might be best if you left the two of us alone so I can talk with her. Phillip, you'll want to call the lawyer, explain the situation, and see if he wants to depose her."

"Yeah, I'll take care of it." He frowned thoughtfully at the fingers drumming on his knee. "She had a picture of Seth in her Filofax."

"What?" Anna blinked at him.

"I went through her things before she got back to the hotel last night." He smiled a little, then shrugged as his sister-in-law closed her eyes. "Seemed like the thing to do at the time. She's got this snapshot of Seth when he was little, tucked in her Filofax."

"So what?" Seth demanded.

"So, it was the only picture I found anywhere. It's interesting." He lifted his hands, dropped them again. "On another path, it could be that Sybill knows something about Gloria's connection to Dad. Since we can't question Gloria, we ought to ask her."

"Seems to me," Ethan said slowly, "that whatever she knows would've come from Gloria. Be tough to believe it. I think she'd tell us what she knows," he continued, "but what she knows might not be fact."

"We don't know fact or fiction," Phillip pointed out, "until we ask her."

"Ask me what?" Steadier, determined now to finish it out, Sybill stepped back into the room and closed the door quietly at her back.

"The reason Gloria hit on our father." Phillip rose so their eyes were level. "The reason she knew he would pay to protect Seth."

"Seth said he was a decent man." Sybill's gaze roamed the faces of the men. "I think you're proof of that."

"Decent men don't have adulterous affairs with women half their age, then walk away from a child conceived from that affair." Bitterness coated Phillip's voice as he took another step toward Sybill. "And there's no way you're going to convince us that Ray slept with your sister behind our mother's back, then walked away from his son."

"What?" Without realizing it, Sybill shot a hand out to grip his arm, as much in shock as to keep her balance as she reeled from it. "Of course he didn't. You told me you didn't believe that Gloria and your father . . ."

"Others do."

"But that's—where did you get the idea that Seth was his son, his son by Gloria?"

"It's easy enough to hear it in town if you keep your ears open." Phillip narrowed his eyes at her face. "It's something your sister planted. She claimed he molested her, then she blackmails him, sells him her son." He looked back at Seth, into Ray Quinn's eyes. "I say it's a lie."

"Of course it's a lie. It's a horrible lie."

Desperate to do at least this one thing right and well, she went to Seth, crouched in front of him. She wanted badly to take his hand, but resisted her impulse when he leaned away from her.

"Ray Quinn wasn't your father, Seth. He was your grandfather. Gloria's his daughter."

His lips trembled, and those deep-blue eyes shimmered. "My grandfather?"

"Yes. I'm sorry she didn't tell you, so sorry you didn't know before he . . ." She shook her head, straightened. "I didn't realize there was confusion about this. I should have. I only learned about it myself a few weeks ago."

She took her seat again, prepared herself. "I'll tell you everything I know."

TWELVE

IT WAS EASIER NOW, ALMOST
like a lecture. Sybill was used to giving lectures on social
topics. All she had to do was divorce herself from the subject
and relay information in a clear and cohesive manner.

"Professor Quinn had a relationship with Barbara Harrow," she began. She put her back to the window so that she
could face all of them as she spoke. "They met at American
University in Washington. I don't have a great many of the
details, but what I do know indicates that he was teaching
there and she was a graduate student. Barbara Harrow is my
mother. Gloria's mother."

"My father," Phillip said. "Your mother."

"Yes. Nearly thirty-five years ago. I assume they were attracted to each other, physically at least. My mother . . ." She
cleared her throat. "My mother indicated that she believed he
had a great deal of potential, that he would rise up the ranks
in academia quickly. Status is an essential requirement to my
mother's contentment. However, she found herself disappointed in his . . . what she saw as his lack of ambition. He
was content to teach. Apparently he wasn't particularly inter-

181

ested in the social obligations that are necessary for advancement. And his politics were too liberal for her tastes."

"She wanted a rich, important husband." Cueing in quickly, Phillip raised his eyebrows. "And she discovered he wasn't going to be it."

"That's essentially true," Sybill agreed in a cool, steady voice. "Thirty-five years ago, the country was experiencing unrest, its own internal war between youth and establishment. Colleges were teeming with minds that questioned not only an unpopular war, but the status quo. Professor Quinn, it would seem, had a lot of questions."

"He believed in using the brain," Cam muttered. "And in taking a stand."

"According to my mother, he took stands." Sybill managed a small smile. "Often unpopular with the administration of the university. He and my mother disagreed, strongly, on basic principles and beliefs. At the end of the term, she went home to Boston, disillusioned, angry, and, she was to discover, pregnant."

"Bullshit. Sorry," Cam said shortly when Anna hissed at him. "But it's bullshit. There's no way he would have ignored responsibility for a kid. No way in hell."

"She never told him." Sybill folded her hands as all eyes swung back to her. "She was furious. Perhaps she was frightened as well, but she was furious to find herself pregnant by a man she'd decided was unsuitable. She considered terminating the pregnancy. She'd met my father, and they had clicked."

"He was suitable," Cam concluded.

"I believe they suited each other." Her voice chilled. They were her parents, damn it. She had to be left with something. "My mother was in a difficult and frightening position. She wasn't a child. She was nearly twenty-five, but an unwanted and unplanned pregnancy is a wrenching episode for a woman of any age. In a moment of weakness, or despair, she confessed all of it to my father. And he offered her marriage. He loved her," Sybill said quietly. "He must have loved her very much. They were married quickly and quietly. She never went back to Washington. She never looked back."

"Dad never knew he had a daughter?" Ethan covered Grace's hand with his.

"No, he couldn't have. Gloria was three, nearly four when I was born. I can't say what the relationship between her and my parents was like in those early years. I know that later on, she felt excluded. She was difficult and temperamental, demanding. Certainly she was wild. Certain standards of behavior were expected, and she refused to meet them."

It sounded so cold, Sybill thought now. So unyielding. "In any case, she left home when she was still a teenager. Later, I discovered that both of my parents, and myself, sent her money, independently of each other. She would contact one of us and plead, demand, threaten, whichever worked. I wasn't aware of any of this until Gloria called me last month, about Seth."

Sybill paused a moment until she could compose her thoughts. "Before I came here, I flew to Paris to see my parents. I felt they needed to know. Seth was their grandchild, and as far as I knew, he'd been taken away from Gloria and was living with strangers. When I told my mother what had happened, and she refused to become involved, to offer any assistance, I was stunned and angry. We argued." Sybill let out a short laugh. "She was surprised enough by that, I think, to tell me what I've just told you."

"Gloria had to know," Phillip pointed out. "She had to know Ray Quinn was her father or she'd never have come here."

"Yes, she knew. A couple of years ago, she went to my mother when my parents were staying in D.C. for a few months. I can assume it was an ugly scene. From what my mother told me, Gloria demanded a large sum of money or she'd go to the press, to the police, to whoever would listen and accuse my father of sexual abuse, my mother of collusion in it. None of that is true," Sybill said wearily. "Gloria always equated sex with power, and acceptance. She routinely accused men, particularly men in positions of authority, of molesting her.

"In this instance, my mother gave her several thousand dollars and the story I've just told you. She promised Gloria that it was the last penny she would ever see from her, the last word she would ever speak to her. My mother rarely, very rarely, goes back on a promise of any kind. Gloria would have known that."

"So she hit on Ray Quinn instead," Phillip concluded.

"I don't know when she decided to find him. It may have stewed in her mind for a time. Now she would consider this the reason she was never loved, never wanted, never accepted as she felt she deserved to be. I imagine she blamed your father for that. Someone else is always to blame when Gloria has difficulties."

"So she found him." Phillip rose from his chair to pace. "And, true to form, demanded money, made accusations, threatened. Only this time she used her own son as the hammer."

"Apparently. I'm sorry. I should have realized you weren't aware of all the facts. I suppose I assumed your father had told you more of it."

"He didn't have time." Cam's voice was cold and bitter.

"He told me he was waiting for some information," Ethan remembered. "That he'd explain everything once he found out."

"He must have tried contacting your mother." Phillip pinned Sybill with a look. "He would have wanted to speak with her, to know."

"I can't tell you that. I simply don't know."

"I know," Phillip said shortly. "He would have done what he felt was right. For Seth first, because he's a child. But he would have wanted to help Gloria. To do that, he needed to talk to her mother, find out what had happened. It would have mattered to him.''

''I can only tell you what I know or what's been told to me.'' Sybill lifted her hands, let them fall. ''My family has behaved badly.'' It was weak, she knew. ''All of us,'' she said to Seth. ''I apologize for myself, and for them. I don't expect you to . . .'' What? she wondered, and let it go. ''I'll do anything I can to help.''

''I want people to know.'' Seth's eyes swam when he lifted them to her face. ''I want people to know he was my grandfather. They're saying things about him, and it's wrong. I want people to know I'm a Quinn.''

Sybill could only nod. If this was all he asked of her, she would make certain she gave it. Drawing a breath, she looked at Anna. ''What can I do?''

''You've made a good start already.'' Anna glanced at her watch. She had other cases and another appointment scheduled in ten minutes. ''Are you willing to make the information you've given us official, and public?''

''Yes.''

''I have an idea how to start that ball rolling.''

The embarrassment factor couldn't be weighed, Sybill reminded herself. She could and would live with the whispers and the speculative looks that were bound to come her way once she followed through on Anna's suggestion.

SHE'D TYPED UP HER STATE-
ment herself, spending two hours in her room choosing the right words and phrasing. The information had to be clear, the details of her mother's actions, of Gloria's, even her own.

When it was proofed and printed out, she didn't hesitate. She took the pages down to the front desk, and calmly requested that they be faxed to Anna's office.

"I'll need the originals back," she told the clerk. "And I expect a reply by return fax."

"I'll take care of this for you." The young, fresh-faced clerk smiled professionally before she slipped into the office behind the desk.

Sybill closed her eyes briefly. No turning back now, she reminded herself. She folded her hands, composed her features, and waited.

It didn't take long. And there was no mistaking from the wide eyes of the clerk that at least part of the transmission had been scanned. "Do you want to wait for the reply, Dr. Griffin?"

"Yes, thank you." Sybill held out a hand for the papers, nearly smiling as the clerk jolted, then quickly passed them across the desk.

"Are you, ah, enjoying your stay?"

Can't wait to pass on what you read, can you? Sybill thought. Typical, and totally expected human behavior. "It's been an interesting experience so far."

"Well, excuse me a moment." The clerk dashed into the back room again.

Sybill was just releasing a sigh when her shoulders tensed. She knew Phillip was behind her before she turned to face him. "I sent the fax to Anna," she said stiffly. "I'm waiting for her reply. If she finds it satisfactory, I'll have time to go to the bank before it closes and have the document notarized. I gave my word."

"I'm not here as a guard dog, Sybill. I thought you could use a little moral support."

She all but sniffed. "I'm perfectly fine."

"No, you're not." To prove it to both of them, he rested a hand on the rigid cords in her neck. "But you put on a hell of a show."

"I prefer to do this alone."

"Well, you can't always get what you want. As the song

says." He glanced over with an easy smile, his hand still on Sybill's nape, as the clerk hurried out with an envelope. "Hi, there, Karen. How's it going?"

The clerk blushed clear to the hairline, her eyes darting from his face to Sybill's. "Fine. Um . . . here's your fax, Dr. Griffin."

"Thank you." Without flinching Sybill took the envelope and tucked it into her bag. "You'll bill my account for the service."

"Yes, of course."

"See you around, Karen." Smoothly, Phillip slid his hand from Sybill's neck to the small of her back to guide her across the lobby.

"She'll have told her six best friends by her next break," Sybill murmured.

"At the very least. The wonders of small towns. The Quinns will be the hot topic of discussion over a number of dinner tables tonight. By breakfast, the gossip mill will be in full swing."

"That amuses you," Sybill said tightly.

"It reassures me, Dr. Griffin. Traditions are meant to reassure. I spoke to our lawyer," he continued as they crossed the waterfront. Gulls swooped, dogging a workboat on its way to dock. "The notarized statement will help, but he'd like to take your deposition, early next week if you can manage it."

"I'll make an appointment." In front of the bank she stopped and turned toward him. He'd changed into casual clothes, and the wind off the water ruffled his hair. His eyes were concealed behind shaded lenses, but she wasn't certain she cared to see the expression in them. "It might look less as if I'm under house arrest if I go in alone."

He merely lifted his hands, palms out, and stepped back. She was a tough nut, he decided when she strode into the bank. But he had a feeling that, once cracked, there was something soft, even delectable inside.

He was surprised that someone as intelligent, as highly trained in the human condition as she was couldn't see her own distress, couldn't or wouldn't admit that there had been something lacking in her own upbringing that forced her to build walls.

He'd nearly been fooled, he mused, into believing she was cold and distant and untouched by the messier emotions. He couldn't be sure what it was that insisted he believe differently. Maybe it was nothing more than wishful thinking, but he was determined to find out for himself. And soon.

He knew that making her family secrets accessible and so informally public would be humiliating for her, and perhaps painful. But she'd agreed without condition and was following through without hesitation.

Standards, he thought. Integrity. She had them. And he believed that she had heart as well.

Sybill offered a thin smile as she came back out. "Well, that's the first time I've seen a notary's eyes nearly pop out of her head. I think that should—"

The rest of her babbling statement was lost as his mouth rushed to cover hers. She lifted a hand to his shoulder, but her fingers only curled into the soft material of his sweater.

"You looked like you needed it," he murmured, and skimmed a hand over her cheek.

"Regardless—"

"Hell, Sybill, we've already got them talking. Why not add to the mystery?"

Her emotions were rocking, making it difficult for her to hold on to any threads of composure. "I've no intention of standing here making a spectacle of myself. So if you'll—"

"Fine. Let's go somewhere else. I've got the boat."

"The boat? I can't go out on the boat. I'm not dressed for it. I have work." I need to think, she told herself, but he was already pulling her to the dock.

"A sail will do you good. You're starting on another headache. The fresh air should help."

"I don't have a headache." Only the nasty, simmering threat of one. "And I don't want to—" She nearly yelped, so stunned was she when he simply plucked her off her feet and set her down on the deck.

"Consider yourself shanghaied, doc." Quickly, competently, he freed the lines and leaped aboard. "I have a feeling you haven't had nearly enough of that kind of treatment in your short, sheltered life."

"You don't know anything about my life, or what I've had. If you start that engine, I'm going to—" She broke off, grinding her teeth as the motor putted to life. "Phillip, I want to go back to my hotel. Now."

"Hardly anybody ever says no to you, do they?" He said it cheerfully as he gave her a firm nudge onto the port bench. "Just sit back and enjoy the ride."

Since she didn't intend to leap overboard and swim back to shore in a silk suit and Italian shoes, she folded her arms. It was his way of paying her back, she supposed, by taking away her freedom of choice, asserting his will and his physical dominance.

Typical.

She turned her head to stare out over the light chop. She wasn't afraid of him, not physically. He had a tougher side than she'd originally thought, but he wouldn't hurt her. And because he cared for Seth, deeply, she'd come to believe, he needed her cooperation.

She refused to be thrilled when he hoisted the sails. The sound of the canvas opening itself to the wind, the sight of the sun beating against the rippling white, the sudden and smooth angling of the boat, meant nothing to her, she insisted.

She would simply tolerate this little game of his, give him no reaction. Undoubtedly, he would grow weary of her silence and inattention and take her back.

"Here." He tossed something, making her jump. She looked down and saw the sunglasses that had landed neatly in her lap. "Sun's fierce today, even if the temperature's cooling. Indian summer's around the corner."

He smiled to himself when she said nothing, only slid the sunglasses primly on her nose and continued to stare in the opposite direction.

"We need a good hard frost first," he continued conversationally. "When the leaves start to turn, the shoreline near the house is a picture. Golds and scarlets. You get that deep blue sky behind them, and the water mirror-bright, that spice of fall on the air, and you could start to believe there's no place else on the planet you'd ever want to be."

She kept her mouth firmly shut, tightened the fold of her arms across her breasts.

Phillip merely tucked his tongue in his cheek. "Even a couple of avowed urbanites like you and I can appreciate a fine fall day in the country. Seth's birthday's coming up."

Out of the corner of his eye he saw her head jerk around, her mouth tremble open. She shut it again, but this time when she turned away, her shoulders where hunched defensively.

Oh, she felt all right, Phillip mused. There were plenty of messy emotions stewing inside that cool package of hers.

"We thought we'd throw him a party, have some of his pals over to raise hell. You already know Grace bakes a hell of a chocolate cake. We've got his present taken care of. But just the other day I saw these art supplies in this shop in Baltimore. Not a kid's setup, a real one. Chalk, pencils, charcoal, brushes, watercolors, paper, palettes. It's a specialty shop a few blocks from my office. Somebody who knew something about art could breeze in there and pick out just the right things."

He'd intended to do so himself, but he saw now that his instincts to tell her about it had been true. She was facing him now, and though the sun flashed off her sunglasses, he could see from the angle of her head that he had her full attention.

"He wouldn't want anything from me."

"You're not giving him enough credit. Maybe you're not giving yourself enough either."

He trimmed the sails, caught the wind, and saw the instant she recognized the curve of trees along the shore. She got unsteadily to her feet. "Phillip, however you may feel about me right now, it can't help the situation for you to push me at Seth again so soon."

"I'm not taking you home." He scanned the yard as they passed. "Seth's at the boatyard with Cam and Ethan, in any case. You need a distraction, Sybill, not a confrontation. And for the record, I don't know how I feel about you at the moment."

"I've told you everything I know."

"Yeah, I think you've given me the facts. You haven't told me how you feel, how those facts affect you personally, emotionally."

"It isn't the issue."

"I'm making it an issue. We're tangled up here, Sybill, whether we like it or not. Seth's your nephew, and he's mine. My father and your mother had an affair. And we're about to."

"No," she said definitely, "we're not."

He turned his head long enough to shoot her a glittering look. "You know better than that. You're in my system, and I know when a woman's got me in hers."

"And we're both old enough to control our more basic urges."

He stared at her another moment, then laughed. "Hell we are. And it's not the sex that worries you. It's the intimacy."

He was hitting all the targets. It didn't anger her nearly as much as it frightened her. "You don't know me."

"I'm beginning to," he said quietly. "And I'm someone

else who finishes what I start. I'm coming about.'' His voice was mild now. "Watch the boom.''

She stepped out of the way, sat. She recognized the little cove where they had shared wine and paté. Only a week ago, she thought dully. Now so much had changed. Everything had changed.

She couldn't be here with him, couldn't risk it. The idea of handling him now was absurd. Still, she could do nothing but try.

Coolly, she eyed him. Casually, she smoothed her hand over the sophisticated twist the wind had disordered. Caustically, she smiled. "What, no wine this time? No music, no neat gourmet lunch?''

He dropped the sails, secured the boat. "You're scared.''

"You're arrogant. And you don't worry me.''

"Now you're lying." While the boat swayed gently underfoot, he stepped forward and took the sunglasses from her. "I worry you, quite a bit. You keep thinking you have me pegged, then I don't follow the script. I imagine most of the men you've let hover around your life have been fairly predictable. Easier for you.''

"Is this your definition of a distraction?'' she countered.

"It fits my definition of a confrontation.''

"You're right." He pulled his own sunglasses off, tossed them aside. "We'll analyze later.''

He moved quickly. She knew he was capable of lightning motion but hadn't expected him to snap from cynic to lover in the blink of an eye. His mouth was hot, hungry, and hard on hers. His hands gripped her arms, pressing her against him so that as the heat and the need poured out, she couldn't tell if it came from him or from herself.

He'd spoken no less than the truth when he told her she was in his system. Whether she was poison or salvation didn't seem to matter. She was in there and he couldn't stop the flow.

He jerked her back so that their lips parted, but their faces remained close. His eyes were as gold and powerful as the flare of the sun. "You tell me you don't want me, you don't want this. Tell me and mean it, and it stops here."

"I—"

"No." Impatient, suffering, he shook her until her gaze lifted to his again. "No, you look at me and say it."

She'd already lied, and the lies weighed on her like lead. She couldn't bear another. "This will only complicate things, make them more difficult."

Unmistakable triumph flashed into those tawny eyes. "Damn right it will," he muttered. "Just now, I don't give a damn. Kiss me back," he demanded. "And mean it."

She couldn't stop herself. This kind of raw, wicked need was new to her, and left her defenseless. Her mouth met his, just as hungry now, just as desperate. And the low, primal moan that escaped was an echo to the beat of desire between her legs.

She stopped thinking. Found herself swamped and spinning with sensations, emotions, yearnings. The kiss roughened, tee-tered toward pain as his teeth scraped and nipped. She clutched at her hair, gasping for air, shaking with shock as that skillful mouth streaked down her throat and sent wild chills over her skin.

For the first time in her life, she surrendered utterly to the physical. And craved the taking.

He pulled at her jacket, tugging the soft silk off her shoulders and tossing it heedlessly aside. He wanted flesh, the feel of it under his hands, the taste of it in his mouth. He yanked the slim ivory shell over her head and filled his hands with her trembling lace-covered breasts.

Her skin was warmer than the silk, and somehow smoother. With one impatient flick he opened her bra, then dragged it aside. And satisfied his need to taste.

The sun blinded her. Even with her eyes tightly shut, the strength of it pounded on her lids. She couldn't see, only feel.

That busy, almost brutal mouth devoured her, those rough and demanding hands doing as they pleased. The whimper in her throat was a scream in her head.

Now, now, now!

Fumbling, she dragged at his sweater, finding the muscle and scars and flesh beneath as he yanked her skirt down her hips. Her stockings ended with thin bands of stretchy lace high on her thighs. Another time he might have appreciated the mix of practicality and femininity. But now he was driven to possess, and he thrilled darkly at her stunned gasp when he ripped aside the thin triangle blocking him from her. Before she could draw the next breath, he plunged his fingers into her and shot her violently over the edge.

She cried out, shocked, staggered at that vicious slap of heat. It sliced through her without warning, sending her flying, flailing.

"Oh, God. Phillip." When her head dropped weakly on his shoulder, her body going from spring-taut to limp, he swept her off her feet and pressed her down on one of the narrow benches.

The blood was pounding in his head. His loins screamed for release. His heart hammered like a dull axe against his ribs.

His breath was ragged, his vision focused on her face like a laser as he freed himself. His fingers dug into her hips as he lifted and opened them. And he plunged. Hard and deep so that his long, long groan melted into hers.

She closed around him, a tight, hot glove. Moved under him, a trembling, eager woman. Breathed his name, a breathless, aching sigh.

He drove into her again, again, strong, steady strokes that she rose to meet. Her hair escaped its pins, flowed like rich mink. He buried his face in it, lost in her scent, in her heat, in the sheer, shimmering glory of a woman aroused beyond reason.

Her nails dug into his back, her cry muffled against his shoulder as she came. Her muscles clamped around him, owned him, destroyed him.

He was as limp as she, wrecked, struggling to fill his burning lungs with air. Beneath him, her body continued to quake, the aftershock of hard, satisfying sex.

When his vision cleared, he could see the three pieces of her pretty businesswoman's suit scattered along the deck. And one black high heel. It made him grin even as he shifted just enough to nip lightly at her shoulder.

"I usually try for more finesse," he said. Slyly, he skimmed a hand down to toy with the thin lace at the top of her stocking, experimenting with textures. "Oh, you're full of surprises, Dr. Griffin."

She was floating, somewhere just above reality. She couldn't seem to open her eyes, to move her hand. "What?"

At the dreamy, distant sound of her voice, he lifted his head to study her face. Her cheeks were flushed, her mouth swollen, her hair a tumbling mass. "As an objective observation, I have to conclude you've never been ravished before."

There was amusement in his tone, and just enough male arrogance to snap her back to earth. She opened her eyes now, and saw the sleepy smile of victory in his. "You're heavy," she said shortly.

"Okay." he shifted, sat up, but pulled her up and around until she straddled his lap. "You're still wearing your stockings, and one of your shoes." He grinned and began to knead the muscles of her tight little butt. "Christ, that's sexy."

"Stop it." The heat was pouring back, a combination of embarrassment and fresh desire. "Let me up."

"I haven't finished with you yet." He dipped his head, circled his tongue lazily around her nipple. "You're still soft and warm. Tasty," he added, flicking his tongue over her stiffened nipple, sucking lightly until her breathing thickened yet again. "I want more. So do you."

Her body arched back, beautifully fluid as he trailed his mouth up to the hammering pulse in her neck. Oh, yes, yes, she wanted more.

"But this time," he promised, "it'll take a little longer."

On a yielding moan, she lowered her mouth to his. "I guess there's time."

THE SUN WAS ANGLED LOW when he shifted her yet again. Her body felt golden and bruised, energized and exhausted. She'd had no idea she could claim such a sexual appetite, and now that she did, she hadn't a clue what she would do about it.

"We have to discuss . . ." She frowned at herself, draped an arm over her body. She was half naked and damp from him. And more confused than she'd ever been in her life. "We—this—can't continue."

"Not right this minute," he agreed. "Even I have my limitations."

"I didn't mean . . . This was just a diversion, as you said. Something we both apparently needed on a physical level. And now—"

"Shut up, Sybill." He said it mildly, but she caught the edge of annoyance. "It was a hell of a lot more than a diversion, and we'll discuss it to pieces later."

He scooped the hair out of his eyes, studied her. She was just beginning to feel awkward, he realized, uneasy with being naked, and with the situation. So he smiled. "Right now, we're a mess. So there's only one thing to do before we get dressed and head in."

"What?"

Still smiling, he pulled off her shoe, then scooped her up into his arms. "Just this," he said, and tossed her over the side.

She managed one scream before she hit. What surfaced was a furious woman with tangles of wet hair in her eyes. "You son of a bitch! You idiot!"

"I knew it." He stepped onto the gunwale and laughed like a loon. "I just knew you'd be gorgeous when you're angry."

He dived in to join her.

THIRTEEN

No one had ever treated her the way Phillip Quinn had treated her. Sybill couldn't decide what she thought of that, much less what to do about it.

He'd been rough, careless, demanding. He had, in his own words, ravished her—and more than once. Though she couldn't claim to have put up even what could remotely be termed a struggle, it had been a long way from a civilized seduction.

Never in her life had she slept with a man she'd known for such a short time. To do so was reckless, potentially dangerous, and certainly irresponsible. Even factoring in the overwhelming and unprecedented chemistry between them, it was foolish behavior.

Worse than foolish, she admitted, because she very much wanted to be reckless, with him, again.

She would have to consider the matter carefully, as soon as she could get her mind off her body and the incredible pleasure it had experienced under those fast, take-charge hands.

Now he was sailing her back to the waterfront at St. Christopher's, completely at ease with himself, and with her. She never would have guessed he'd just spent more than an hour engaged in wild, frantic sex.

If she hadn't been a party to it.

There was no doubt in her mind that what they'd done would further complicate an already horribly complicated situation. Both of them would have to be coldly sensible now, and carefully practical. She did her best to tidy her damp, tangled hair as the wind whipped at it.

Conversation, she decided, to bridge the gap between sex and sensibility.

"How did you get the scars?"

"Which ones?" He tossed the question over his shoulder, but he thought he knew. Most women wanted to know.

"On your chest. They look surgical."

"Mmm. Long story." This time he threw a smile back with the look. "I'll bore you with it tonight."

"Tonight?"

Oh, he just loved it when her brows buckled together, forming that little concentration line between them. "We have a date, remember?"

"But I . . . hmmm."

"I confuse the hell out of you, don't I?"

Annoyed, she slapped at the hair that insisted on blowing over her eyes. "And you enjoy that?"

"Darling, I can't begin to tell you how much. You keep trying to slip me into one of your slots, Sybill, and I'll keep sliding back out again. You figured on a fairly safe, one-dimensional urban professional who likes his wine aged and his women cultured. But that's only part of the picture."

As he entered the harbor, he dropped the sails, switched to motor. "First glance at you, I have to figure well-bred, well-educated, career-oriented city woman who likes her wine white and her men at a safe distance. But that's only part of the picture, too."

He cut the engine, let the boat bump gently at dock. Gave

her hair a friendly tug before he climbed out to secure the lines. "I think we'll both be well entertained while we uncover the rest of the canvas."

"A continuation of a physical relationship is—"

"Inevitable," he finished, and offered her a hand. "Let's not waste time or energy pretending otherwise. We can call it basic chemistry for now." He tugged her to him the minute her feet hit the dock, and proved his point with one, long fiery kiss. "It works for me."

"Your family won't approve."

"Family approval's important to you."

"Of course."

"I don't discount it either. Normally, this wouldn't be any of their business. In this case, it is." It bothered him, more than a little. "But it's my family, and my concern, not yours."

"This may sound hypocritical at this point, but I don't want to do anything else that will hurt or disturb Seth."

"Neither do I. But I'm not going to let a ten-year-old take charge of my personal life. Relax, Sybill." He skimmed his fingers over her jaw. "This isn't the Montagues and the Capulets."

"I'm hardly thinking of you as Romeo," she said, so dryly that he laughed and kissed her again.

"You might, darling, if I put my mind to it. But for now, let's just be who we are. You're tired." He rubbed his thumb gently under her eye. "You've got thin skin, Sybill, the shadows show. Go take a nap. We can make do with room service later."

"With—"

"I'll bring the wine," he said cheerfully and leaped back into the boat. "I've got a bottle of Chateau Olivier I've been wanting to sample," he shouted over the motor. "No need to dress up," he added with a wicked grin as he maneuvered the boat away from the dock and out of earshot.

She wasn't sure what she would have shouted at him if

she'd lost what was left of her control. Instead she stood on the dock in her wrinkled but elegant silk suit, her hair a damp mess and her dignity as shaky as her heart.

CAM RECOGNIZED THE SIGNS. A fast sail on a breezy afternoon might relax a man, loosen his muscles, clear his head. But he only knew one thing that put that lazy, satisfied gleam in a man's eyes.

He recognized that gleam in his brother's eyes when Phillip slid up to the dock to toss him the lines. You son of a bitch, was his first thought.

He caught the stern line, yanked it taut. "You son of a bitch."

Phillip only lifted his eyebrows. He'd been expecting that reaction, though not quite so quickly. He'd already ordered himself to hold on to his temper, to explain his position. "Always a friendly welcome at the Quinns'."

"I figured you were past the stage where you thought with your dick."

Not quite as calm as he'd planned to be, Phillip stepped off the boat and stood facing his brother. He recognized the signs, too. Cam was spoiling for a fight. "Actually, I tend to let my dick think for itself. Though we often agree."

"You're either crazy or stupid, or you just don't give a damn. A kid's life is in the balance here, his peace of mind, his trust."

"Nothing's going to happen to Seth. I'm doing everything I can to make sure of that."

"Oh, I get it. You fucked her for his sake."

Phillip's hands shot out, and before the bright fury fully registered he had them gripped on Cam's jacket. Now their faces were close, and both were warrior hard. "You were tearing up the sheets with Anna last spring. How much were you thinking about Seth when you had her under you?''

Cam's fist rammed up, under Phillip's guard. The blow rocked his head back but didn't loosen his hold. Instinct blanked out reason as he shoved Cam back and prepared to tear in.

He swore viciously when Ethan clamped an arm around his throat from behind.

"Cool off," Ethan ordered on more of a sigh than a snarl. "Both of you—or I'll toss you in until you do." He tightened his hold on Phillip's windpipe just enough to show he meant it and scowled at Cam. "Get ahold of yourself, damn it. Seth's had a rough day. You want to add to it?"

"No, I don't want to add to it," Cam said bitterly. "This one doesn't give a good damn, but I do."

"My relationship with Sybill and my concern for Seth are two separate matters."

"Like hell."

"Let go of me, Ethan." Because Phillip's tone was cool and deliberate, Ethan released him. "You know, Cam, I don't remember you being so interested in my sex life since we both had our sights set on Jenny Malone."

"We're not in high school anymore, pal."

"No, we're not. And you're not my keeper. Either of you," he added, shifting so that he could look at both of them. He would explain himself because it mattered. Because they mattered. "I've got feelings for her, and I'm going to take the time to figure out what they are. I've made a lot of changes in my life over the last few months, and I've gone along with what the two of you wanted. But goddamn it, I'm entitled to a personal life."

"I wouldn't argue with that, Phil." Ethan glanced toward the house, hoping Seth was busy with his homework or his drawings and not spying out the window. "I don't know how Seth's going to feel about this part of your personal life."

"There's something none of you are taking into consideration. Sybill is Seth's aunt."

"That's exactly what I am taking into consideration," Cam shot back. "She's Gloria's sister, and she came in here on a lie."

"She came in here believing a lie." It was an important distinction, Phillip thought. A vital distinction. "Did you read the statement she faxed to Anna?"

Cam hissed between his teeth, hooked his thumbs in his pockets. "Yeah, I saw it."

"What do you think it cost her to put that down in black and white, to know everybody in town would be talking about it, about her, within twenty-four hours?" Phillip waited a beat, noting that the muscle in Cam's jaw relaxed, fractionally. "How much more do you want her to pay?"

"I'm not thinking about her. I'm thinking about Seth."

"And she's the best defense we've got against Gloria DeLauter."

"You think she'll stand up to it?" Ethan wondered. "When push comes to shove?"

"Yeah, I do. He needs his family, all his family. That's what Dad would want. He told me . . ." Catching himself, Phillip frowned out over the dark water.

Cam pursed his lips, exchanged a look with Ethan, and nearly smiled. "Been feeling a little odd lately, Phillip?"

"I'm fine."

"Maybe you're stressed out some." Since he'd only gotten in one punch, Cam felt entitled to enjoy himself. "I thought I saw you talking to yourself a couple of times."

"I don't talk to myself."

"Maybe you think you're talking to somebody who isn't there." He did smile now, widely and wickedly. "Stress is a killer. Eats at the mind."

Ethan didn't quite swallow a chuckle, and Phillip glared at him. "You got something to say about the state of my mental health?"

"Well . . ." Ethan scratched at his chin, "you've been looking a little tense lately."

"For Christ's sake, I'm entitled to look a little tense." He threw out his arms as if to encompass the world that too often weighed on his shoulders. "I put in ten, twelve hours a day in Baltimore, then come down here and sweat like a goddamn galley slave in the boatyard. That's when I'm not frying my brains over the books and the bills or playing housewife at the grocery store or making sure Seth doesn't slide out of his homework."

"Always was bitchy," Cam mumbled.

"You want bitchy?" Phillip took one threatening step forward, but this time Cam grinned and spread his hands.

"Ethan'll just toss you off the dock. Me, I don't feel like a swim just now."

"First few times with me, I thought I was dreaming."

Confused, unsure if he wanted to punch Cam or just sit down for a while, Phillip looked back at Ethan. "What the hell are you talking about?"

"I thought we were discussing your mental health." Ethan's tone was mild, conversational now. "It was good to see him. Hard to know you'd have to let him go again, but it was worth it."

A chill danced up Phillip's spine, and he put his suddenly unsteady hands safely in his pockets. "Maybe we should be talking about your mental health."

"We figured when it was your turn, you'd head for the therapist's couch." Cam grinned again. "Or Aruba."

"I don't know what you're talking about."

"Yes, you do." Ethan spoke calmly, then settled down on the dock, legs dangling, to take out a cigar. "It's your turn. Looks like he took us in the same order he took us in."

"Symmetry," Cam decided, dropping down beside Ethan. "He'd have liked the symmetry of it. I talked to him the first time the day I met Anna." He thought back to it, the way he'd seen her cross the back lawn with that knockout face and that ugly suit. "I guess that's a kind of symmetry, too."

The chill was still dancing, tapping fast now, up and down Phillip's spine. "What do you mean, 'talked to him'?"

"Had a conversation." Cam plucked the cigar out of Ethan's mouth and helped himself to a puff. "Of course, I figured I'd cracked." He glanced up, smiled. "You figure you've cracked, Phil?"

"No. I've just been working too hard."

"Shit, drawing pictures, coming up with jingles. Big deal."

"Kiss ass." But with a sigh, he sat on the dock. "Are the two of you trying to tell me you've talked to Dad? The one who died in March? The one we buried a few miles from here?"

In an easy gesture Cam passed Phillip the cigar. "You trying to tell us you haven't?"

"I don't believe in that sort of thing."

"Doesn't much matter what you believe when it happens," Ethan pointed out and took back his cigar. "Last time I saw him was the night I asked Grace to marry me. He had a bag of peanuts."

"Christ Jesus," Phillip murmured.

"I could smell them, the same way I can smell this cigar smoke, the water, Cam's leather jacket."

"When people die, that's it. They don't come back." Phillip paused a moment, waiting until the cigar came back down the line to him. "Did you—touch him?"

Cam angled his head. "Did you?"

"He was solid. He couldn't be."

"It's either that," Ethan pointed out, "or we're all crazy."

"We barely had time to say good-bye, and no time to understand." Cam let out a breath. His grief had eased and softened. "He bought us each a little more time. That's what I think."

"He and Mom bought us all time when they made us Quinns." He couldn't think about it, Phillip decided. Not now, at any rate. "It must have ripped him when he found out he had a daughter he'd never known."

"He'd have wanted to help her, save her," Ethan murmured.

"He'd have seen it was too late for her. But not for Seth," Cam concluded. "So he'd have done whatever he could do to save Seth."

"His grandson." Phillip watched an egret soar, then slide silently into the dark. And he was no longer cold. "He'd have seen himself in the eyes, but he would've wanted answers. I've been thinking about that. The logical step would have been for him to try to locate Gloria's mother, have her confirm it."

"It would have taken time." Cam considered it. "She's married, she's living in Europe, and from what Sybill said, she wasn't interested in contacting him."

"And he ran out of time," Phillip concluded. "But now we know. And now, we make it stick."

SHE HADN'T MEANT TO SLEEP. Sybill indulged in a long, hot shower, then wrapped herself in a robe with the intention of adding to her notes. She ordered herself to drum up the courage to call her mother, to speak her mind and demand a written corroboration of her own notarized statement.

She did neither. Instead she fell face down on the bed, closed her eyes, and escaped.

The knocking at the door pulled her out of sleep into groggy. She stumbled out of bed, fumbled for the light switch. With her mind still fuzzy, she walked through the parlor and barely had the presence of mind to check the peephole.

She let out a self-directed annoyed sigh as she flipped off the locks.

Phillip took one look at her tousled hair, sleepy eyes, and

practical navy terry robe, and smiled. "Well, I did tell you not to dress up."

"I'm sorry. I fell asleep." Distracted, she pushed at her hair. She hated being mussed, particularly when he looked so fresh and alert. And gorgeous.

"If you're tired, I'll take a rain check."

"No, I . . . if I sleep any more now I'll end up wide awake at three A.M. I hate hotel rooms at three A.M." She stepped back to let him in. "I'll just get dressed."

"Stay comfortable," he suggested, and used his free hand to cup the nape of her neck and bring her forward for a casual kiss. "I've already seen you naked. And a very appealing sight it was."

It appeared, she decided, that her dignity was still just out of reach. "I'm not going to claim that was a mistake."

"Good." He set the wine he carried on her coffee table.

"But," she said, with what she considered admirable patience, "neither was it wise. We're both sensible people."

"Speak for yourself, doc. I stop feeling sensible every time I get a whiff of you. What *is* that you wear?"

She leaned back when he leaned in to sniff at her. "Phillip."

"Sybill." And he laughed. "How about if I attempt to be civilized and not cart you off to bed until you're a little more awake?"

"I appreciate your restraint," she said tightly.

"And so you should. Hungry?"

"What is this almost pathological need of yours to feed me?"

"You're the analyst," he told her with a shrug. "I've got the wine. You got some glasses?"

She might have sighed, but it wouldn't have been constructive. She did want to talk to him, to put their relationship on an even footing again. To ask his advice. And, she hoped, to enlist his help in persuading Seth to accept her friendship.

She took the two short, thick glasses the hotel provided, lifting her eyebrow when Phillip sneered at them. He had a damn sexy sneer.

"They're an insult to this very delightful wine," he said, as he opened the bottle with the stainless-steel corkscrew he'd brought with him. "But if they're the best you can offer we'll just have to make do."

"I forgot to pack my Waterford."

"Next time." He poured the pretty straw-colored wine into the glasses, handed her one. "To beginnings, middles, and endings. We seem to be at all three."

"Which means?"

"The charade's ended, the teamwork is established, and we've just become lovers. I'm happy with all three aspects of our very interesting relationship."

"Teamwork?" She picked the aspect that didn't shame her or make her nervous.

"Seth's a Quinn. With your help we'll make that legal and permanent, and soon."

She stared down into her wine. "It's important to you that he have your name."

"His grandfather's name," Phillip corrected. "And it can't be nearly as important to me as it is to Seth."

"Yes, you're right. I saw his face when I told him. He looked almost awed. Professor Quinn must have been an extraordinary man."

"My parents were special. They had the kind of marriage you rarely see. A true partnership, based on trust, respect, love, passion. It hasn't been easy wondering if my father broke that trust."

"You were afraid that he had cheated on your mother with Gloria, fathered a child with her." Sybill sat down. "It was hideous of her to plant that seed."

"It was also hell living with the seeds in me that I couldn't quite stomp out. Resentment for Seth. Was he my father's son?

His true son, while I was just one of the substitutes? I knew better," he added as he sat beside her. "In my heart. But it's one of those mind games that nag at you at three A.M."

If nothing else, she realized, she'd eased his mind on that one point. But it wasn't enough. "I'm going to ask my mother to corroborate my statement in writing. I don't know that she will. I doubt that she will," Sybill admitted. "But I'll ask, I'll try."

"Teamwork, see." He took her hand in his, nuzzling it, which had her turning her head to study him warily.

"Your jaw's bruised."

"Yeah." He grimaced, wiggled it. "Cam still has a damn sneaky left."

"He hit you?"

The absolute shock in her voice made him laugh. Obviously the good doctor didn't come from a world where fists flew. "I was going to hit him first, but he beat me to it. Which means I owe him one. I'd have paid him back then and there, but Ethan got me in a choke hold."

"Oh, God." Swamped with distress, she got to her feet. "This was about us. About what happened today on the boat. It should never have happened. I knew it would cause trouble between you and your family."

"Yes," he said evenly, "it was about us. And we worked it out. Sybill, my brothers and I have been pounding on each other as long as we've been brothers. It's a Quinn family tradition. Like my father's waffle recipe."

Distress continued to ripple through her. But confusion ran with it. Fists and waffles? she wondered, pulling a hand through her disordered hair. "You fight with them, physically?"

"Sure."

To try to compute it, she pressed her fingers to her temples. It didn't help a bit. "Why?"

He considered, smiled. "Because they're there?" he suggested.

"And your parents allowed this type of violent behavior."

"My mother was a pediatrician. She always stitched us up." He leaned forward to pour himself more wine. "I think I'd better explain the whole picture. You know that Cam, Ethan, and I are adopted."

"Yes. I did some research before I came . . ." She trailed off, glanced back at her laptop. "Well, you know that already."

"Yeah. And you know some of the facts, but not the meaning. You asked me about my scars. It doesn't start there," he mused. "Not really. Cam was the first. Ray caught him trying to steal my mother's car one morning."

"Her car? Steal her car?"

"Right out of the driveway. He was twelve. He'd run away from home and was planning on going to Mexico."

"At twelve he was stealing cars with plans to go to Mexico."

"That's right. The first of the Quinn bad boys." He lifted his glass to toast his absent sibling. "He'd been beaten, again, by his drunk father, and he'd figured it was time to run or die."

"Oh." She braced a hand on the arm of the sofa as she lowered herself again.

"He passed out, and my father carried him inside. My mother treated him."

"They didn't call the police?"

"No. Cam was terrified, and my mother recognized the signs of continual physical abuse. They made inquiries, arrangements, worked with the system and circumvented it. And they gave him a home."

"They just made him their son?"

"My mother said once that we were all hers already. We just hadn't found each other before. Then there was Ethan. His mother was a hooker in Baltimore, a junkie. She relieved boredom by knocking him around. And then she got the bright idea that she could supplement her income by selling her eight-year-old son to perverts.''

Sybill clutched her glass in both hands and rocked. She said nothing, could say nothing.

''He had a few years of that. One night one of her customers finished with Ethan, and with her, and got violent. Since his target was her and not her kid, she objected. Stabbed him. She ran, and when the cops got there they took Ethan to the hospital. My mother was doing guest rounds.''

''They took him, too,'' Sybill murmured.

''Yeah, that's the long and short of it.''

She raised her glass, sipped slowly, watched him over the rim. She didn't know the world he was describing. Logically, she knew it existed, but it had never touched hers. Until now. ''And you?''

''My mother worked the Block in Baltimore. Strip joints, turned tricks on the side. A little bait and switch now and then, some short cons.'' He shrugged. ''My father was long gone. He did some time in Jessup for armed robbery, and when he got out he didn't look us up.''

''Did she . . . did she beat you?''

''Now and then, until I got big enough, strong enough, that she worried I might hit back.'' His smile was thin and sharp. ''She was right to worry. We didn't care for each other much. But if I wanted a roof over my head, and I did, I needed her, and I had to pull my weight. I picked pockets, lifted locks. I was pretty good at it. Hell,'' he said with a faint stir of pride, ''I was damn good at it. Still, I stuck with small shit. The kind you turn into easy cash or drugs. If things were really tight, I sold myself.''

He saw her eyes widen in shock, flick away from his.

''Survival's not always pretty,'' he said shortly. ''Most of the time I had my freedom. I was tough, and I was mean, and I was smart. Maybe I got picked up once in a while and rattled through the system, but I always popped out again. Another few years of that life, and I'd have been in Jessup—or the morgue. Another few years of that life,'' he continued, watching her face, ''and Seth would have gone the same way.''

Struggling to absorb it, she stared into her wine. ''You see your situations as similar, but—''

''I recognized Gloria yesterday,'' he interrupted. ''A pretty woman gone brittle. Hard and sharp at the eyes, bitter at the mouth. She and my mother would have recognized each other, too.''

What could she say, how could she argue when she'd seen the same thing, felt the same? ''I didn't recognize her,'' she said quickly. ''For a moment I thought there was a mistake.''

''She recognized you. And she played the angles, pushed the buttons. She'd know how.'' He paused a moment. ''She'd know exactly how. So do I.''

She looked at him then, noted he was studying her coolly. ''Is that what you're doing? Pushing buttons, playing angles?''

Maybe it was, he thought. They would both have to figure that out before much longer. ''Right now I'm answering your question. Do you want the rest?''

''Yes.'' She didn't hesitate, for she'd discovered she very much wanted to hear it all.

''When I was thirteen, I thought I had it handled. I figured I was just fine. Until I found myself face down in the gutter, bleeding to death. Drive-by shooting. Wrong place, wrong time.''

''Shot?'' Her gaze whipped back to his. ''You were shot.''

''In the chest. Probably should have killed me. One of the doctors who made sure I didn't die knew Stella Quinn. She and Ray came to see me in the hospital. I figured them for weirdos, do-gooders, your basic assholes. But I played along with them. My mother was done with me, and I was going to end up solid in the system. I thought I'd use them until I was steady on my feet again. Then I'd take what I needed and cut out.''

Who was this boy he described to her? And how was she

to reconcile him with the man beside her? "You were going to rob them?"

"It's what I did. What I was. But they . . ." How to explain it? he wondered. The miracle of them. "They just wore that away. Until I fell in love with them. Until I'd have done anything, been anything, to make them proud of me. It wasn't the paramedics or the surgical team that saved my life. It was Ray and Stella Quinn."

"How old were you when they took you in?"

"Thirteen. But I wasn't a kid like Seth. I wasn't a victim like Cam and Ethan. I made my choices."

"You're wrong." For the first time, she reached out and, taking his face in her hands, she kissed him gently.

He lifted his hands to her wrists, had to concentrate on not squeezing her skin the way that soft kiss had squeezed his heart. "That's not the reaction I expected."

It wasn't the one she'd expected to have. But she found herself feeling pity for the boy he described to her and admiration for the man he'd made himself into. "What reaction do you usually get?"

"I've never told anyone outside the family." He managed a smile. "Bad for the image."

Touched, she rested her forehead against his. "You're right. It could have been Seth," she murmured. "What happened to you, it could have been Seth. Your father saved him from that. You and your family saved him, while mine's done nothing. And worse than nothing."

"You're doing something."

"I hope it's enough." When his mouth came to hers, she let herself slide into comfort.

FOURTEEN

PHILLIP UNLOCKED THE BOAT-
yard at seven A.M. The very fact that his brothers hadn't given
him grief about not working the day before, or about taking
a full Sunday off the previous week, had his guilt quota at
peak.

He expected he had a good hour, maybe a little more before
Cam showed up to continue work on the hull of the sport's
fisher. Ethan would put in a morning of crabbing, taking advantage of the fall season, before heading in to work that afternoon.

So he would have the place to himself, and the quiet and
solitude to deal with the paperwork he'd neglected the week
before.

Quiet didn't mean silence. His first act when entering his
cramped office was to hit the lights. The next was to switch
on the radio. Ten minutes later, he was nose-deep in accounts
and very much at home.

Well, they owed just about everybody, he concluded. Rent,
utilities, insurance premiums, the lumberyard, and the ever
popular MasterCard.

The government had demanded its share in the middle of September, and the bite had been just a little nasty. The next tax nibble wasn't far enough away to let him relax.

He juggled figures, toyed with them, stroked them, and decided red wasn't such a bad color. They'd made a tidy profit on their first job, the bulk of which had been poured back into the business. Once they turned the hull, they would get another draw from their current client. That would keep their heads above water.

But they weren't going to see a lot of the color black for a time yet.

Dutifully, he cut checks, updated the spreadsheet, reconciled figures, and tried not to mourn the fact that two and two stubbornly insisted on making four.

He heard the heavy door below open, then slam.

"Hiding up there again?" Cam called out.

"Yeah, having a real party."

"Some of us have real work to do."

Phillip looked at the figures dancing over his computer screen and laughed shortly. It wasn't real work to Cam, he knew, unless you had a tool in your hand.

"Best I can do," he muttered and shut the computer down. He stacked the outgoing bills on the corner of the desk, tucked the paychecks in his back pocket, then headed down.

Cam was strapping on a tool belt. He wore a ball cap backward to keep his hair out of his eyes, and it flowed beneath the down-sloped bill. Phillip watched him slide the wedding band off his finger and tuck it carefully into his front pocket.

Just as he would take it out after work, Phillip mused, and slip it back in place. Rings could catch on tools and cost a man a finger. But neither of his brothers left theirs at home. He wondered if there was some symbolism, or comfort, in having that statement of marriage on them, one way or the other, at all times.

Then he wondered why he was wondering and nudged the question, and the idea of it, aside.

Since Cam had reached the work area first, the radio wasn't tuned to the lazy blues Phillip would have chosen, but to loud, kiss-my-ass rock. Cam eyed him coolly as Phillip tugged on a tool belt of his own.

"Didn't expect to see you in so bright and early this morning. Figured you had a late night."

"Don't go there again."

"Just a comment." Anna had already chewed him out when he complained to her about Phillip's involvement with Sybill. He should be ashamed, he shouldn't interfere, he should have some compassion for his brother's feelings.

He'd rather take that brother's fist in the face any day than a hot verbal slap from his wife.

"You want to fool around with her, it's your business. She's a pleasure to look at. I'd say she's got a wide cold streak in her, though."

"You don't know her."

"And you do?" Cam lifted a hand when Phillip's eyes flashed. "Just trying to get a handle on it. It's going to matter to Seth."

"I know she's willing to do what she can so he's where he needs to be. Reading between the lines, I'd say she grew up in a repressive, restrictive atmosphere."

"A rich one."

"Yeah." Phillip strode to a pile of planks. "Yeah, private schools, chauffeurs, country clubs, servants."

"It's a little tough to feel sorry for her."

"I don't think she's looking for sympathy." He hefted a plank. "You said you wanted to get a handle on her. I'm telling you she had advantages. I don't know if she had any affection."

Cam shrugged and, deciding they'd get more accomplished working together, took the other end of the plank to fit it into place on the hull. "She doesn't strike me as deprived. She strikes me as cold."

"Restrained. Cautious." He remembered the way she reached out to him the night before. Still, it had been the first time she'd done so, the only time. He clamped down on the frustration of not being sure that Cam wasn't right. "Are you and Ethan the only ones entitled to a relationship with a woman that satisfies your hormones and your brain?"

"No." Cam lapped the ends. Deliberately he relaxed his shoulders. There was something in Phillip's voice that gave away that frustration, and something else. "No, we're not. I'll talk to Seth about her."

"I'll talk to him myself."

"All right."

"He matters to me, too."

"I know he does."

"He didn't." Phillip pulled out his hammer to nail the laps. "Not as much as he did to you. Not enough. It's different now."

"I know that, too." For the next few minutes they worked in tandem, without words. "You stood up for him anyway," Cam added when the plank was in place. "Even when he didn't matter enough."

"I did it for Dad."

"We all did it for Dad. Now we're doing it for Seth."

BY NOON, THE SKELETON OF the hull had taken on the flesh of wood. The smooth-lap construction was labor-intensive, tedious and exacting. But it was their trademark, a choice that offered extreme structural strength and required great skill by the boatbuilder.

No one would argue that Cam was the most skilled of the

three of them in woodworking. But Phillip thought he was holding his own.

Yeah, he thought, standing back to scan the exterior planking or skin of the hull. He was holding his own.

"You pick up any lunch?" Cam asked before he poured water from a jug into his mouth.

"No."

"Shit. I bet Grace packed Ethan one of those monster lunches of hers. Fried chicken, or thick slabs of honey-baked ham."

"You got a wife," Phillip pointed out.

Cam snorted, rolled his eyes. "Oh, yeah. I can just see me talking Anna into packing me a lunch every day. She'd smack me with her briefcase as she marched out the door to work. There are two of us," he considered. "We can take Ethan, especially if we catch him by surprise when he comes in."

"Let's go the easier route." Phillip dug into his pocket, pulled out a quarter. "Heads or tails?"

"Heads. Loser gets it, and buys it."

Phillip flipped the coin, caught it and slapped it onto the back of his hand. The eagle's beak seemed to sneer at him. "Damn it. What do you want?"

"Meatball sub, large chips, and six gallons of coffee."

"Fine, clog your arteries."

"Last I checked they don't stock any tofu at Crawford's. Don't know how you eat that crap. You're going to die anyway. Might as well go with a meatball sub."

"You go your way, I'll go mine." He reached in his pocket again for Cam's paycheck. "Here, don't spend it all in one place."

"Now I can retire to that little grass shack on Maui. You got Ethan's?"

"What there is of it."

"Yours?"

"I don't need it."

Cam narrowed his eyes as Phillip pulled on his jacket. "That's not the way it works."

"I'm in charge of the books, I say how it works."

"You put in your time, you take your share."

"I don't need it," Phillip said, with heat this time. "When I do, I'll take it." He stalked out, leaving Cam fuming.

"Stubborn son of a bitch," Cam muttered. "How am I supposed to rag on him when he pulls crap like that?"

He bitched plenty, Cam mused. He nagged his brothers to distraction over the pettiest detail. Then he handled the details, he thought as he capped the water jug. He'd back you into a corner, then he'd go to the wall for you.

It was enough to drive you nuts.

Now he was getting himself twisted up over a woman none of them knew they could trust if things got sticky. He, for one was going to keep a close eye on Sybill Griffin.

And not just for Seth's sake. Phillip might have the brains, but he was just as stupid as the next guy when it came to a pretty face.

"AND YOUNG KAREN LAW-son who's been working down at the hotel since she hooked up with the McKinney boy last year saw it written down, in black and white. She called her mama, and as Bitty Lawson's a good friend of mine and my longtime bridge partner—though she'll trump your ace if you don't watch her—she called me right up and let me know."

Nancy Claremont was in her element, and that element was gossip. As her husband owned a sizable chunk of St. Chris, meaning she did as well, and part of that chunk was the old barn those Quinn boys—a wild bunch if you asked her—rented for their boatyard—though God knew what else went on in there—she knew it was not only her right but her duty to pass on the succulent tidbit that had come her way the previous afternoon.

Of course, she'd used the most convenient method first. The telephone. But you didn't get the pleasure of face-to-face reaction over the phone. So she'd brought herself out, dressed in her brand-new pumpkin-colored pantsuit, fresh out of the J. C. Penney catalog.

There was no point in being the most well-off woman in St. Christopher's if you didn't flaunt it a bit. And the best place to flaunt, and to spread gossip, was Crawford's.

Second-best was the Stylerite Beauty Salon over on Market, and that, as she'd made an appointment for a cut, color, and curl, was her next stop.

Mother Crawford, a fixture in St. Chris for all of her sixty-two years, sat behind the counter in her smeared butcher apron, her tongue tucked firmly in her cheek.

She'd already heard the news—not much got by Mother, and nothing got by her for long—but she disposed herself to hear Nancy out.

"To think that child is Ray Quinn's grandson! And that writer lady with her snooty airs is the sister of that nasty girl who said all those terrible things. That boy's her nephew. Her own kin, but did she say one word about it? No, sir, she did not! Just hoity-toitying around, going off sailing with Phillip Quinn, and a lot more than sailing, if you ask me. The way young people carry on today without a snap of their fingers for morals."

She snapped her own, inches from Mother's face, and her eyes glittered with malicious delight.

Since Mother sensed that Nancy was about to veer off the subject at hand, she shrugged her wide shoulders. "Seems to me," she began, knowing the scatter of people in the store had their ears bent her way, "that there are a lot of people around this town who ought to be hanging their heads after what was being passed around about Ray. Whispering about him behind his back when he was living, and over his grave when he passed on, about him cheating on Stella, God rest her, and having truck with that DeLauter woman. Well, it wasn't true, was it?''

Her sharp eyes scanned the store, and indeed, a few heads did lower. Satisfied, she beamed her gaze hard into Nancy's glittering eyes. "Seems to me you were willing enough to believe bad about a good man like Ray Quinn.''

Sincerely insulted, Nancy puffed out her chest. "Why, I never believed a word of it, Mother.'' Discussing such matters, she thought to herself, wasn't the same as believing them. "Truth is, a blind man couldn't have missed the way that boy's got Ray's eyes. Had to be a blood relation. Why, I said to Silas just the other day, I said, 'Silas, I wonder if that boy could be a cousin or something to Ray?' "

She'd said no such thing, of course. But she might have, if she'd thought of it.

"Never thought about him being Ray's grandson, though. Why, to think Ray had a daughter all these years.''

Which, of course, proved he'd done something wrong in the first place, didn't it? She'd always suspected that Ray Quinn had been wild in his youth. Maybe even a hippie. And everyone knew what *that* meant.

Smoking marijuana, and having orgies and running around naked.

But that wasn't something she intended to bring up to Mother. That little morsel could wait until she was shampooed and tucked into the styling chair at the salon.

"And that she turned out wilder than those boys he and Stella brought home,'' she rattled on. "That girl over to the hotel must be just as—''

She broke off when the door jingled. Hoping for a fresh ear, she was thrilled to see Phillip Quinn walk in. Better than an addition to her audience, it was one of the actors on the very interesting stage.

Phillip only had to open the door to know what subject was under discussion. Or had been, until he stepped inside. Silence fell with a clang, and eyes darted toward him, then guiltily away.

Except for Nancy Claremont's and Mother's.

"Why, Phillip Quinn, I don't know as I've seen you since your family picnic on the Fourth of July." Nancy fluttered at him. Wild or not, he was a handsome man. Nancy considered flirting one of the best ways to loosen a man's tongue. "That was a fine day."

"Yes, it was." He walked up to the counter, knowing that stares were being bulleted at his back. "I need a couple of subs, Mother Crawford. A meatball and a turkey."

"We'll fix you up, Phil. Junior!" She shouted over at her son, who jolted at her tone despite being thirty-six and the father of three.

"Yes 'um."

"You going to ring up these people or just scratch your butt the rest of the afternoon?"

He colored, muttered under his breath, and turned his attention back to the cash register.

"You working down to the boatyard today, Phillip?"

"That's right, Mrs. Claremont."

He busied himself choosing a bag of chips for Cam, then wandered back to the dairy case to decide on yogurt for himself.

"That young boy usually comes in to pick up lunch, doesn't he?"

Phillip reached in, took out a carton at random. "He's in school today. It's Friday."

" 'Course it is." Nancy laughed, playfully patting the side of her head. "Don't know where my mind is. Fine-looking young boy. Ray musta been right proud."

"I don't doubt it."

"We've been hearing that he's got some blood relations close by."

"There's never been anything wrong with your hearing, Mrs. Claremont, that I recall. I'll need a couple of large coffees to go, Mother."

"We'll fix you up there, too. Nancy, you got more than enough news to blow around for the day. You keep trying to squeeze more out of this boy, you're going to miss your hair appointment."

"I don't know what you could be meaning." Nancy sniffed, shot Mother a furious look, then fluffed at her hair. "But I have to be going. The husband and I are going to the Kiwanis dinner-dance tonight, and I need to look my best."

She flounced out, making a beeline for the beauty shop.

Inside, Mother narrowed her eyes. "The rest of you got business, Junior'll ring you up. But this ain't no lounge. You want to stand around and gawk, go stand outside."

Phillip disguised a chuckle as a cough when several people decided they had business elsewhere.

"That Nancy Claremont's got less sense than a peahen," Mother proclaimed. "Bad enough she dresses herself up like a pumpkin from head to foot, but she don't even know how to be subtle."

Mother turned back to Phillip and grinned. "Now, I won't say I don't have as much got-to-know as the next, but by God, if you can't try to jiggle a little information out of a body without being so blessed obvious, you're not just rude, you're stupid with it. Can't abide bad manners or a soft brain."

Phillip leaned on the counter. "You know, Mother, I've been thinking maybe I'd change my name to Jean-Claude, then move to the wine country of France, the Loire valley, and buy myself a vineyard."

She tucked her tongue in her cheek again, eyes bright. She'd heard this tale, or one of its variations, for years. "Do tell."

"I'd watch my grapes ripen in the sun. I'd eat bread that was hot and fresh, and cheese that wasn't. It would be a fine, satisfying life. But I've got just one problem."

"What's that?"

"It won't be any good unless you come with me." He grabbed her hand, kissing it lavishly while she roared with laughter.

"Boy, you are a caution. Always were." She gasped for breath, wiped her eyes. Then she sighed. "Nancy, she's a fool, but she's not mean, not deep down. Ray and Stella, they were just people to her. They were a lot more than that to me."

"I know that, Mother."

"People got something new to talk about, they're going to gum it to death."

"I know that, too." He nodded. "So did Sybill."

Mother's eyebrows lifted and fell as she realized the implication. "The girl's got guts. Good for her. Seth, he can be proud he's got blood kin that brave. And he can be proud a man like Ray was his granddaddy." She paused to put the finishing touches on the subs. "I think Ray and Stella would've liked that girl."

"Do you?" Phillip murmured.

"Yep. I like her." Mother grinned again as she quickly wrapped the subs in white paper. "She's not hoity-toity like Nancy wants to think. Girl's just shy."

Phillip had reached over for the subs, and now his mouth fell open. "Shy? Sybill?"

"Sure is. Tries hard not to be, but it costs her some. Now you get that meatball back to your brother before it gets cold."

"WHY DO I HAVE TO CARE about a bunch of queer-os who lived two hundred years ago?"

Seth had his history book open, his mouth full of grape

Bubblicious, and a stubborn look in his eye. After a ten-hour day of manual labor, Phillip wasn't in the mood for one of Seth's periodic snits.

"The founding fathers of our country were not queer-os."

Seth snorted and jabbed a finger at the full-page drawing of the Continental Congress. "They're wearing dorky wigs and girly clothes. That says queer-o to me."

"It was the fashion." He knew the kid was yanking his chain, but he couldn't seem to stop his leg from jerking on cue. "And the use of the word 'queer-o' to describe anyone because of their fashion sense or their lifestyle demonstrates ignorance and intolerance."

Seth merely smiled. Sometimes he just liked making Phillip grind his teeth the way he was doing now. "A guy wears a curly wig and high heels, he deserves what he gets."

Phillip sighed. It was another reaction Seth enjoyed. He didn't really mind the history crap. He'd aced the last test, hadn't he? But it was just plain boring to have to pick out one of the queer-os and write some dopey biography.

"You know what these guys were?" Phillip demanded, then narrowed his eyes in warning when Seth opened his mouth. "Don't say it. I'll tell you what they were. Rebels, troublemakers, and tough guys."

"Tough guys? Get real."

"Meeting the way they did, drawing up papers, making speeches? They were giving England, and most especially King George, the finger." He caught a flash of amused interest in Seth's eyes. "It wasn't the tea tax, not really. That was just the platform, the excuse. They weren't going to take any shit from England anymore. That's what it came down to."

"Making speeches and writing papers isn't like fighting."

"They were making sure there was something to fight for. You have to give people an alternative. If you want them to toss out Brand X, you have to give them Brand Y, and make it better, stronger, tastier. What if I told you Bubblicious is a rip-off?'' Phillip asked, inspired as he snatched up the giant pack on Seth's desk.

"I like it okay." To prove it, Seth blew an enormous purple bubble.

"Yeah, but I'm telling you that it sucks and that the people who make it are creeps. You're not going to just toss it in the trash because I say so, right?"

"Damn straight."

"But if I gave you a new choice, if I told you about this Super Bubble Blow—"

"Super Bubble Blow? Man, you slay me."

"Shut up. SBB, it's better. It lasts longer, costs less. Chewing it'll make you and your friends, your family, your neighbors happier, stronger. SBB is the gum of the future, of *your* future. SBB is right!" Phillip added, putting a ring in his voice. "Bubblicious is wrong. With SBB you'll find personal and religious freedom, and no one will ever tell you that you can only have one piece."

"Cool." Phillip was weird all right, Seth thought with a grin, but he was fun. "Where do I sign up?"

With a half laugh, Phillip tossed the gum back on the desk. "You get the picture. These guys were the brains and the blood, and it was their job to get the people excited."

The brains and the blood, Seth thought. He liked it, and figured he could work it into his report. "Okay, maybe I'll pick Patrick Henry. He doesn't look as dorky as some of the other guys."

"Good. You can access information on him on the computer. When you hit the bibliography of books on him, print it out. The library in Baltimore's bound to have more of a selection than the one at school."

"Okay."

"And your composition for English is ready to turn in tomorrow?"

"Man, you never let up."

"Let's see what you've got."

"Jeez." Grumbling all the way, Seth dug into his binder and tugged out the single sheet.

It was titled "A Dog's Life" and described a typical day through the eyes of Foolish. Phillip felt his lips twitch as the canine narrator told of his delight in chasing rabbits, his irritation with bees, the thrill of hanging out with his good and wise friend Simon.

Christ, the kid was clever, he mused.

As Foolish ended his long, demanding day curled up on his bed, which he generously shared with his boy, Phillip handed the page back. "It's great. I guess we now know how you come by your storytelling talent naturally."

Seth's lashes lowered as he carefully slipped the composition back into place. "Ray was pretty smart and all, being a college professor."

"He was pretty smart. If he'd known about you, Seth, he'd have done something about it a lot sooner."

"Yeah, well . . ." Seth gave that Quinn shoulder jerk.

"I'm going to talk to the lawyer tomorrow. We may be able to speed things up a little, with Sybill's help."

Seth picked up his pencil to doodle on his blotter. Just shapes, circles, triangles, squares. "Maybe she'll change her mind."

"No, she won't."

"People do, all the time." He'd waited for weeks, ready to run if the Quinns had changed theirs. When they hadn't, he'd started to believe. But he was always ready to run.

"Some people keep their promises, no matter what. Ray did."

"She's not Ray. She came here to spy on me."

"She came to see if you were all right."

"Well, I am. So she can go."

"It's harder to stay," Phillip said quietly. "It takes more guts to stay. People are already talking about her. You know what that's like, when people look at you out of the corners of their eyes and whisper.''

"Yeah. They're just jerks."

"Maybe, but it still stings."

He knew it did, but he gripped his pencil more tightly, added pressure to his doodling. "You've just got a case on her."

"I might. She sure is a looker. But if I do have a case on her, that doesn't change the basic facts. Kid, you haven't had that many people give a good damn about you in your life."

He waited until Seth's eyes slid over to his, held. "It took me a while, maybe too long, to give a good damn myself. I did what Ray asked me to, because I loved him."

"But you didn't want to do it."

"No, I didn't want to do it. It was a pain in the ass. You were a pain in the ass. But that started to change, little by little. I still didn't want to do it, it was still a pain in the ass, but somewhere along the way I was doing it for you as much as for Ray."

"You thought maybe I was his kid, and that pissed you off."

So much, Phillip thought, for adults believing they kept their secrets and sins from children. "Yeah. That was one little angle I couldn't get rid of until yesterday. I couldn't accept the idea that he might have cheated on my mother, or that you might be his son."

"But you put my name on the sign anyway."

Phillip stared a moment, then let out a half laugh. Sometimes, he realized, you do what's right without really thinking about it, and it makes a difference. "It belonged there, just like you belong here. And Sybill already gave a good damn about you, and now we know why. When somebody cares, it's just plain stupid to push them away."

"You think I should see her and talk to her and stuff." He'd thought about it himself. "I don't know what to say."

"You saw her and talked to her before you knew. You could try it that way."

"Maybe."

"You know how Grace and Anna are all wired up about this birthday dinner of yours next week?"

"Yeah." He lowered his head a little more so the huge grin didn't show. He couldn't believe it, not really. A birthday dinner and he got to pick the food, then like a party with pals the next day. Not that he was going to call it a party, because that was really lame when you were turning eleven.

"What do you think of asking her if she'd like to come over for that? The family dinner deal."

The grin vanished. "I don't know. I guess. She probably wouldn't want to come anyway."

"Why don't I ask her? You could cop another present out of it."

"Yeah?" A smile came back, sly and slow. "She'd have to make it a good one, too."

"That's the spirit."

FIFTEEN

THE NINETY-MINUTE APPOINT-
ment with the Baltimore lawyer had left Sybill jittery and exhausted. She thought she'd been prepared for it; after all, she'd
had two and a half days to get ready, since she'd called first
thing Monday morning and had been squeezed into his schedule on Wednesday afternoon.

At least it was over, she told herself. Or this first stage of
it was over. It had been more difficult than she'd imagined to
tell a perfect stranger, professional or not, the secrets and flaws
of her family. And herself.

Now she had to cope with a cold, chilly rain, Baltimore
traffic, and her own less-than-stellar driving skills. Because she
wanted to put the traffic and the driving off as long as possible,
she left her car in the parking garage and faced the rain as a
pedestrian.

Fall had already pushed summer back a big step in the city,
she noted, shivering as she scooted across the street at the
crosswalk. The trees were starting to turn, little blushes of red
and gold edging the leaves. The temperature had plummeted

with the wet weather, and the wind lashed out, tugging at her umbrella as she approached the harbor.

She might have preferred a dry day, so she could have wandered, explored, appreciated the nicely rehabbed old buildings, the tidy waterfront, the historic boats moored there. But it had its appeal, even in a hard, frigid rain.

The water was stone-gray and choppy, its edges blurring into the sky so that it wasn't possible to tell where either ended. Most of the visitors and tourists had taken shelter indoors. Any who went by, went by in a hurry.

She felt alone and insignificant standing in the rain, looking at the water, wondering what the hell to do next.

With a sigh, she turned and studied the shops. She was going to a birthday party on Friday, she reminded herself. It was time she bought her nephew a present.

I⊤ TOOK HER MORE THAN AN hour, comparing, selecting, rejecting art supplies. Her focus was so narrowed, she didn't note the bright glee in the clerk's eyes as she began to pile up her choices. It had been more than six years since she'd bought Seth a gift, she thought. She was going to make up for that.

It had to be just the right pencils, the perfect collection of chalks. She examined watercolor brushes as if the wrong choice would mean the end of the world as she knew it. She tested the weight and thickness of drawing paper for twenty minutes, then agonized over a case for all the supplies.

In the end, she decided simplicity was the answer. A young boy would likely feel more comfortable with a plain walnut case. It would be durable, too. If he took care, it was something he would have for years.

And maybe, after enough of those years passed, he could look at it and think of her kindly.

"Your nephew's going to be thrilled," the clerk informed her, giddy as she rang up the purchases. "These are quality supplies."

"He's very talented." Distracted, Sybill began to nibble on her thumbnail, a habit she'd broken years before. "You'll pack everything carefully and box it?"

"Of course. Janice! Would you come over and give me a hand? Are you from the area?" she asked Sybill.

"No, no, I'm not. A friend recommended your store."

"We very much appreciate it. Janice, we need to pack and box these supplies."

"Do you gift-wrap?"

"Oh, I'm sorry, we don't. But there's a stationery store in this center. They have a lovely selection of gift wrap and ribbon and cards."

Oh, God, was all Sybill could think. What kind of paper did one choose for an eleven-year-old boy? Ribbon? Did boys want ribbons and bows?

"That comes to five hundred eighty-three dollars and sixty-nine cents." The clerk beamed at her. "How would you like to pay for that?"

"Five—" Sybill caught herself. Obviously, she decided, she'd lost her mind. Nearly six hundred dollars for a child's birthday? Oh, yes, she'd absolutely gone insane. "Do you take Visa?" she asked weakly.

"Absolutely." Still beaming, the clerk held out her hand for the gold card.

"I wonder if you could tell me . . ." She blew out a breath as she took out her Filofax and flipped to the Q's in the address book. "How to get to this address."

"Sure, it's practically around the corner."

It would be, Sybill thought. If Phillip had lived several blocks away, she might have resisted.

I<small>T WAS A MISTAKE, SHE</small>
warned herself as she struggled back into the rain, fighting
with two enormous shopping bags and an uncooperative umbrella. She had no business just dropping in on him.

He might not even be home. It was seven o'clock. He was
probably out to dinner. She would be better off going back to
her car and driving back to the Shore. The traffic was lighter
now, if the rain wasn't.

At least she should call first. But damn it, her cell phone
was in her purse, and she only had two hands. It was dark and
it was raining and she probably wouldn't find his building
anyway. If she didn't locate it within five minutes, she would
turn around and go back to the parking garage.

She found the tall, sleekly elegant building within three and
despite a case of nerves, stepped gratefully into the warm, dry
lobby.

It was quiet and classy, with ornamental trees in copper
pots, polished wood, a few deep-cushioned chairs in neutral
tones. The familiar elegance would have relieved her if she
hadn't felt like a wet rat invading a luxury liner.

She had to be crazy coming here like this. Hadn't she told
herself when she'd set out for Baltimore that day that she
wouldn't do this? She hadn't told him about the appointment
because she hadn't wanted him to know she would be in Baltimore. He'd only try to persuade her to spend time with him.

For heaven's sake, she'd just seen him on Sunday. There
was no sensible reason for this desperate urge to see him now.
She would go back to St. Christopher's right now, because she
had made a terrible mistake.

She cursed herself as she walked to the elevator, stepped
inside, and pushed the button for the sixteenth floor.

What was wrong with her? Why was she doing this?

Oh, God, what if he was home but he wasn't alone? The sheer mortification of that possibility struck her like a blow to the stomach. They'd never said anything about exclusivity. He had a perfect right to see other women. For all she knew, he had a platoon of women. Which only proved she'd lost all common sense by becoming involved with him in the first place.

She couldn't possibly drop in on him like this, unannounced, uninvited, unexpected. Everything she'd been taught about manners, protocol, acceptable social behavior ordered her to stab the down button and leave. Every ounce of pride demanded that she turn around before she was humiliated.

She had no idea what it was that overcame all of that and pushed her out of the elevator and to the door of 1605.

Don't do this, don't do this, don't do this. The order screamed in her head even as she watched her finger depress the buzzer beside his door.

Oh, God, oh, God, oh, God, what have I done? What will I say? How can I explain?

Please don't be home, was her last desperate thought seconds before the door opened.

"Sybill?" His eyes widened in surprise, his lips curved.

Lord help her, she began to babble. "I'm so sorry. I should have called. I don't mean to—I shouldn't have . . . I had to come into the city, and I was just . . ."

"Here, let me have those. You buy out the store?" He was pulling the wet bags out of her icy hands. "You're freezing. Come inside."

"I should have called. I was—"

"Don't be silly." He dumped the bags and began to peel her out of her dripping raincoat. "You should have let me know you were coming into Baltimore today. When did you get in?"

"I—about two-thirty. I had an appointment. I was just— it's raining," she blurted out, hating herself. "I'm not used to driving in traffic. Not really used to driving at all, actually, and I was a little nervous about it.''

She rambled on, while he studied her, his brows lifted. Her cheeks were flushed, but he didn't think it was from the cold. Her voice was skittish, and that was new. And interesting. She couldn't seem to figure out what to do with her hands.

Though the raincoat had protected her neat slate-gray suit, her shoes were soaked and her hair was dewed with rain.

"You're wired up, aren't you?" he murmured. He put his hands on her arms, rubbed up and down to warm them. "Relax."

"I should have called," she said for the third time. "It was rude, presumptuous—"

"No, it wasn't. A little risky, maybe. If you'd gotten here twenty minutes earlier, I wouldn't have been home yet." He drew her a little closer. "Sybill, relax."

"Okay." She closed her eyes.

Amusement flickered into his own as he watched her take slow deep breaths.

"Does that breathing stuff really work?" he asked with a chuckle.

The irritation in her voice was barely noticeable, but it was there. "Studies have proven that the flow of oxygen and mental focus relieves stress."

"I bet. I've done studies of my own. Let's try it my way." He brought his mouth to hers, rubbed gently, persuasively until hers softened, yielded, warmed. His tongue danced lightly over hers, teasing out a sigh. "Yeah, that works for me," he murmured, brushing his cheek over her damp hair. "Works just fine for me. How about you?"

"Oral stimulation is also a proven remedy for stress."

He chuckled. "I'm in danger of becoming crazy about you. How about some wine?"

She didn't care to analyze his definition of crazy just then. "I wouldn't mind one glass. I shouldn't, really. I'm driving."

Not tonight you're not, he thought, but only smiled. "Sit down. I'll be right back."

She went back to the concentrated breathing as he slipped into another room. After her nerves settled a bit, she studied the apartment.

A conversation pit in deep forest-green dominated the living area. In its center was a square coffee table. Riding over it was a large sailboat in what she recognized as Murano glass. A pair of green iron candlesticks held fat white candles.

At the far side of the room there was a small bar with a pair of black leather stools. Behind it was a vintage poster for Nuits-St.-Georges Burgundy, depicting an eighteenth-century French calvary officer sitting on a cask with a glass, a pipe, and a very satisfied smile.

The walls were white and splashed here and there with art. A framed print of a stylish poster for Tattinger champagne, with a elegant woman, surely that was Grace Kelly, in a sleek black evening gown behind a slim flute of bubbling wine, hung over a round glass table with curved steel legs. There was a Joan Miró print, an elegant reproduction of Alphonse Mucha's *Automne*.

Lamps were both sparely modern and elegantly Deco. The carpet was thick and pale gray, the uncurtained window wide and wet with rain.

She thought the room displayed masculine, eclectic, and witty taste. She was admiring a brown leather footstool in the shape of a barnyard pig when he returned with two glasses.

"I like your pig."

"He caught my eye. Why don't you tell me about what must have been a very interesting day?"

"I didn't even ask if you had plans." She noted he was dressed in a soft black sweatshirt and jeans and wasn't wearing any shoes. But that didn't mean—

"I do now." Taking her hand he led her across to the deep

cushioned U-shaped sofa. "You saw the lawyer this afternoon."

"You knew about that."

"He's a friend. He keeps me up to date." And, Phillip
admitted to himself, he'd been acutely disappointed when she
hadn't called him to let him know she was coming to the city.
"How'd it go?"

"Well, I think. He seems confident that the guardianship
will go through. I couldn't persuade my mother to make a
statement, though."

"She's angry with you."

Sybill took a quick swallow of wine. "Yes, she's angry,
and no doubt deeply regrets the momentary lapse that allowed
her to tell me what happened between her and your father."

He took her hand. "It's difficult for you. I'm sorry."

She looked down at their linked fingers. How easily he
touched, she thought absently. As if it was the most natural
thing in the world. "I'm a big girl. Since it's doubtful that this
little incident, however newsworthy it is in St. Christopher's,
will ripple across the Atlantic to Paris, she'll get over it."

"Will you?"

"Life moves on. Once the legalities are dealt with, there
won't be any motive for Gloria to make trouble for you and
your family. For Seth. She will, I imagine, continue to make
trouble for herself, but there's nothing I can do about that.
Nothing I want to do about it."

A cold streak, Phillip wondered, or a defense? "Even after
the legalities are dealt with, Seth will still be your nephew.
None of us would stop you from seeing him, or being part of
his life."

"I'm not a part of his life," she said flatly. "And as he
makes his life, it would only be distracting and unconstructive
for him to have reminders of his old life. It's a miracle that
what Gloria did to him hasn't scarred him more deeply. Whatever sense of security he has, it's due to your father, to you

and your family. He doesn't trust me, Phillip, and he has no reason to.''

"Trust has to be earned. You have to want to earn it."

She rose, walked to the dark window and looked out on the city lights that wavered behind the rain. "When you came to live with Ray and Stella Quinn, when they were helping you change your life, remake yourself, did you maintain contact with your mother, with your friends in Baltimore?''

"My mother was a part-time whore who resented every breath I took, and my friends were dealers, junkies, and thieves. I didn't want contact with them any more than they wanted it with me."

"Regardless." She turned back to face him. "You understand my point."

"I understand it, but I don't agree with it."

"I imagine Seth does."

He set his glass aside as he rose. "He wants you there on his birthday Friday."

"You want me there," she corrected. "And I very much appreciate you for persuading Seth to allow it."

"Sybill—"

"Speaking of which," she said quickly. "I found your art store." She gestured toward the bags he'd set by the door.

"That?" He stared at the bags. "*All* of that?"

Immediately she began to nibble on her thumbnail. "It's too much, isn't it? I knew it. I got caught up. I can take some of it back or just keep it for myself. I don't take enough time to draw anymore."

He'd walked over to examine the bags, the boxes inside. "*All* of this?" With a laugh, he straightened, shook his head. "He'll love it. He'll go nuts."

"I don't want him to think of it as a bribe, like I'm trying to buy his affection. I don't know what got into me. Once I started, I couldn't seem to stop."

"If I were you, I'd stop questioning my motives for doing

something nice, something impulsive, and just a bit over the top.'' Gently he tugged at her hand. ''And stop biting your nails.''

''I'm not biting my nails. I never . . .'' Insulted, she looked down at her hand, saw the ragged thumbnail. ''Oh, God, I'm biting my nails. I haven't done that since I was fifteen. Where's my nail file?''

Phillip edged closer to her as she grabbed her handbag and took out a small manicure set. ''Were you a nervous kid?''

''Hmm?''

''A nail-biter.''

''It was a bad habit, that's all.'' Smoothly, efficiently, she began to repair the damage.

''A nervous habit, wouldn't you say, Dr. Griffin?''

''Perhaps. But I broke it.''

''Not entirely. Nail biting,'' he murmured, moving toward her. ''Migraines.''

''Only occasionally.''

''Skipping meals,'' he continued. ''Don't bother to tell me you've eaten tonight. I know better. It seems to me that your breathing and concentrating isn't quite doing the job on stress. Let's try my way again.''

''I really have to go.'' She was already being drawn into his arms. ''Before it gets too late.''

''It's already too late.'' He brushed his lips over hers once, twice. ''You really have to stay. It's dark, it's cold, it's raining,'' he murmured, nibbling on, toying with her lips. ''And you're a terrible driver.''

''I'm just . . .'' The nail file slipped out of her fingers. ''Out of practice.''

''I want to take you to bed. I want to take you to my bed.'' The next kiss was deeper, longer, wetter. ''I want to slip you out of that lovely little suit, piece by piece, and see what's going on under it.''

''I don't know how you do this.'' Her breath was already

coming too fast, her body going too soft. "I can't keep my thoughts aligned when you're touching me."

"I like them scattered." He slid his hands under her trim jacket until his thumbs skimmed the sides of her breasts. "I like you scattered. And trembling. It makes me want to do all sorts of things to you when you tremble."

Quick flares of heat, sharp stabs of ice were already racing over her. "What sorts of . . . things?"

He made a low, delighted sound against the side of her throat. "I'll show you," he offered, and picked her up.

"I don't do this." She pushed back her hair, staring at him as he carried her into the bedroom.

"Do what?"

"Go to a man's apartment, let him carry me to bed. I don't do this."

"We'll just consider it a change in behavioral patterns then." He kissed her thoroughly before laying her down on the bed. "Caused by . . ." He paused to light a trio of candles on an iron stand in the corner. "Direct stimulation."

"That could work." The candlelight did wonders for an already impossibly handsome face. "It's just that you're so attractive."

He chuckled and slid onto the big bed to nip at her chin. "And you're so weak."

"Not usually. Actually, my sexual appetites are slightly below average, ordinarily."

"Is that so?" He lifted her just enough to slip the jacket away.

"Yes. I've found, for myself . . . oh . . . that while a sexual interlude can be pleasant . . ." Her breath caught as his fingers slowly released the buttons of her blouse.

"Pleasant?" he prompted.

"It rarely, if ever, has more than a momentary impact. Of course, that's due to my hormonal makeup."

"Of course." He lowered his mouth to the soft swell of

her breasts that rose temptingly above the cups of her bra. And licked.

"But—but—" She clenched her fists at her sides as his tongue swept under the fabric and shot off shock waves.

"You're trying to think."

"I'm trying to see if I can."

"How's it going?"

"Not very well."

"You were telling me about your hormonal makeup," he reminded her, watching her face as he tugged her skirt down over her hips.

"I was? Oh, well ... I had a point." Somewhere, she thought vaguely, a shiver going through her as he traced a fingertip over her midriff.

He saw with delight that she wore those sexy thigh-hugging stockings again, this time in sheer smoky-black. He imagined she'd considered that the black bra and panties were proper coordinates.

He thanked God for her practical mind.

"Sybill, I love what goes on under your clothes."

He moved his mouth to her belly, tasted heat and woman, felt her muscles quiver. She made a helpless little sound in her throat as her body shifted under him.

He could take her anywhere. The power of knowing that flooded him like wine. As he took her, slowly now, wanting them both to linger at each stage, he let himself sink.

He peeled those stockings down those lovely, long thighs, following the path with his mouth all the way to her toes. Her skin was creamy, smooth, fragrant. Perfect. And only more alluring when it quivered lightly under his.

He slipped fingertips and tongue beneath that silky fantasy snug over her hips in teasing strokes so that she arched, shuddered, and moaned. Heat was there. Centered just there. Wet, arousing heat.

And when the teasing drove them both mad, he stripped that

barrier aside and plunged into the hot taste of her. She cried out,
her body rising, her hands fisting in his hair as he spun her to
peak. When she was limp and gasping he took more.

And showed her more.

He could have anything. Everything. She was powerless to
deny him, to stem the tidal wave of sensations that swamped
her. The world had become him, only him. The flavor of his
skin in her mouth, the texture of his hair against her flesh or
in her hands, the movement of his muscle beneath her fingers.

Murmurs, his murmurs, echoed in her spinning head. The
sound of her own name, a whisper of pleasure. Her breath
sobbed out as she found his mouth with hers, poured everything she was into that hot flood of emotion.

Again, again, again. The urgent demand circled in her head,
as she clung and gave, gave, gave.

Now it was his hands that fisted, on either side of her head
as the shock of feeling slammed into him, flashing against
desire, melting into a need so urgent it was pain.

She opened for him, a breathless invitation. And filling her,
sinking inside her, he lifted his head and watched her face in
the golden shaft of candlelight.

Her eyes were on his, her lips parted as the breath trembled
through them. Something clicked, a lock opening, a connection made. He found his hands groping for hers, fingers twin-
ing together.

Slow, smooth, with each movement a fresh shock of pleasure. Soft, silky, a promise in the dark. He saw her eyes glaze,
felt the tension, the ripple, and closed his mouth over hers to
capture the gasp as she climaxed.

''Stay with me.'' He murmured it as his lips roamed her
face, as his body moved in hers. ''Stay with me.''

What choice did she have? She was defenseless against
what he brought to her, helpless to refuse what he demanded
in return.

The pressure built again, an internal demand that refused

to be denied. When she tumbled free, he gathered her close and fell with her.

"I WAS GOING TO COOK," HE said sometime later when she lay over him, limp and speechless. "But I think we'll order in. And eat in bed."

"All right." She kept her eyes closed, commanding herself to listen to the beat of his heart and pay no attention to the voice of her own.

"You can sleep in tomorrow." Idly he toyed with her hair. He wanted her there in the morning, badly wanted her there in the morning. It was something to think about later. "Maybe do some sight-seeing or shopping. If you hang around for most of the day, you can follow me home."

"All right." She simply didn't have the strength to assert herself. Besides, she told herself, it made sense. The Baltimore Beltway was confusing, unfamiliar ground. She would enjoy spending a few hours exploring the city. It was certainly foolish to drive all the way back tonight, in the rain, in the dark.

"You're awfully agreeable."

"You caught me in a weak moment. I'm hungry, and I don't want to face driving tonight. And I miss the city, any city."

"Ah, so it's not my irresistible charm and awesome sexual prowess."

She couldn't stop the smile. "No, but they don't hurt."

"I'll make you an egg-white omelette in the morning, and you'll be my slave."

She managed to laugh. "We'll see about that."

She was afraid she was entirely too close to a slavish condition now. The heart she was desperately trying to ignore continued to insist that she'd fallen in love with him.

That, she warned herself, would be a much bigger, more permanent mistake, than knocking on his door on a rainy evening.

SIXTEEN

W HEN A TWENTY-NINE-YEAR-
old woman changed her clothes three times before attending
an eleven-year-old boy's birthday party, she was in trouble.

Sybill lectured herself on this simple fact even as she
stripped off a white silk blouse—white silk, for Lord's sake,
what had she been thinking of—and exchanged it for a teal
turtleneck.

She was going to a simple, informal family dinner party,
she reminded herself, not a diplomatic reception. Which, she
admitted with a sigh, wouldn't have posed nearly as much of
a social or fashion dilemma. She knew exactly what to wear,
how to behave, and what was expected of her at a formal
reception, a state dinner, a gala, a charity ball.

It was a pathetic statement on her narrow social experience,
she concluded, that she knew neither how to dress nor how to
behave at her own nephew's birthday dinner.

She slipped a long chain of silver beads over her head, took
it off, cursed herself and put it on again. Underdressed, over-
dressed, what did it matter? She wouldn't fit in anyway. She
would pretend she did, the Quinns would pretend she did, and

everyone would be desperately relieved when she said her good-byes and went away.

Two hours, she told herself. She would only stay two hours. Surely she could survive that. Everyone would be polite, would avoid awkward or nasty scenes for Seth's sake.

She picked up her brush to smooth her hair back, then secured it with a clip at the nape of her neck before critically studying herself in the mirror. She looked confident, she decided. Pleasant, nonthreatening.

Except . . . maybe the color of the sweater was too vivid, too bold. Gray might be better, or brown.

Good God.

The ringing of the phone was such a welcome diversion, she all but leapt on it. "Yes, hello, Dr. Griffin."

"Syb, you're still there. I was afraid you'd taken off."

"Gloria." Her stomach plummeted to her unsteady knees. Very carefully she lowered herself to the side of the bed. "Where are you?"

"Oh, I'm around. Hey, I'm sorry I ditched you the other night. I was messed up."

Messed up, Sybill thought. It was a good term for certain conditions. From the rapid pace of Gloria's speech, she assumed her sister was messed up even now. "You stole money out of my wallet."

"I said I was messed up, didn't I? I panicked, you know, needed some cash. I'll pay you back. You talk to those Quinn bastards?"

"I had a meeting with the Quinn family, as I promised I would." Sybill uncurled the hand she'd bunched into a fist and spoke evenly. "I'd given them my word, Gloria, that both of us would meet them to discuss Seth."

"Well, I didn't give mine, did I? What'd they say? What're they going to do?"

"They say you were working as a prostitute, that you

abused Seth physically, that you allowed your clients to make sexual advances toward him.''

"Liars. Fucking liars. They just want to kick me around, that's all. They—''

"They said," Sybill went on, coolly now, "that you accused Professor Quinn of molesting you nearly a dozen years ago, intimated that Seth was his. That you blackmailed him, that you sold Seth to him. That he gave you more than a hundred and fifty thousand dollars.''

"All bullshit.''

"Not all, but part. Your part could be accurately described as bullshit. Professor Quinn didn't touch you, Gloria, not twelve years ago, not twelve months ago.''

"How do you know? How the hell do you know what—''

"Mother told me that Raymond Quinn was your father.''

There was silence for a moment, then only Gloria's quick breathing. "Then he owed me, didn't he? He *owed* me. Big-deal college professor with his boring little life. He owed me plenty. It was his fault. It was all his fault. All those years, he didn't give me dick. He took in scum from the street, but he didn't give me dick.''

"He didn't know you existed.''

"I told him, didn't I? I told him what he'd done, and who I was and what he was going to do about it. And what does he do? He just stares at me. He wants to talk to my mother. He's not going to give me a fucking dollar until he talks to my mother.''

"So you went to the dean and claimed he'd molested you.''

"Put the fear of God into him. Tight-assed son of a bitch.''

She'd been right, Sybill thought. Her instincts when she'd walked into that room at the police station had been right after all. It was a mistake. This woman was a stranger. "And when that didn't work, you used Seth.''

"Kid's got his eyes. Anybody can see that.'' There was a sucking noise, a hiss, as Gloria dragged on a cigarette.

"Changed his tune once he got a look at the kid."

"He gave you money for Seth."

"It wasn't enough. He owed me. Listen, Sybill . . ." Her voice shifted, whined and trembled. "You don't know what it's like. I've been raising that kid on my own since he was a baby and that prick Jerry DeLauter took off. Nobody was going to help me. Our dear mother wouldn't even accept a phone call from me, and that prissy freak she married and tried to pass off as my father wouldn't either. I could've dumped the kid, you know. I could've dumped him anytime. The money Social Services doles out for a kid is pitiful."

Sybill stared out through her terrace doors. "Does it always come back to money?"

"It's easy to look down when you've got plenty of it," Gloria snapped. "You never had to hustle, you never had to worry. Perfect daughter always had plenty of everything. Now it's my turn."

"I would have helped you, Gloria. I tried to years ago when you brought Seth to New York."

"Yeah, yeah, same old tune. Get a job, straighten up, get clean, get dry. Shit, I don't want to dance to that, get it? This is my life I'm living here, baby sister, not yours. You couldn't pay me to live yours. And that's my kid, not yours."

"What's today, Gloria?"

"What? What the hell are you talking about?"

"Today is September twenty-eighth. Does that mean anything to you?"

"What the hell's it supposed to mean? It's fucking Friday."

And your son's eleventh birthday, Sybill thought and straightened her shoulders, took her stand. "You won't get Seth back, Gloria, though we're both aware that that's not your goal."

"You can't—"

"Shut up. Let's stop playing games. I know you. I haven't wanted to, I've preferred to pretend otherwise, but I know you.

If you want help, I'm still willing to get you into a clinic, to pay the bill for rehab.''

"I don't need your goddamn help.''

"Fine, that's your choice. You won't get another penny out of the Quinns, you won't come near Seth again. I've given my deposition to their lawyer and a notarized statement to Seth's caseworker. I've told them everything, and if necessary, I'll testify in court that Seth's wishes and his best interest are served by his remaining, permanently, with the Quinns. I'll do everything I can to see that you don't use him anymore.''

"You bitch.'' The hiss was filled with anger, but under it was shock. "You think you can screw me this way? You think you can toss me off and side with those bastards against me? I'll ruin you.''

"You can certainly try, but you won't succeed. You made your deal, now it's done.''

"You're just like her, aren't you?'' Gloria spit the words out like bullets. "You're just like our ice cunt of a mother. Perfect society princess, and underneath you're nothing but bitch.''

Maybe I am, Sybill thought wearily, maybe I'm going to have to be. "You blackmailed Raymond Quinn, who'd done nothing to harm you. It worked. At least it worked well enough for you to be paid. It won't work with his sons, Gloria. And it won't work with me. Not anymore.''

"Won't it? Well, try this. I want a hundred thousand. A hundred thousand, or I'm going to the press. *National Enquirer, Hard Copy.* Let's see how fast your lousy books sell once I tell my story.''

"Sales will likely increase twenty percent,'' Sybill said mildly. "I won't be blackmailed, Gloria. You do what you like. And think about this. You're facing criminal charges in Maryland, and there's a restraining order against you to keep you away from Seth. The Quinns have evidence. I've seen it,'' she continued, thinking of the letters Gloria had written. "Fur-

ther criminal charges for extortion and child abuse may be
brought. I'd cut my losses if I were you."

She hung up on the spew of obscenities and, closing her
eyes, lowered her head between her knees. The nausea was a
greasy sea in her stomach, the sneaky edge of a migraine was
creeping closer. She couldn't stop the trembling. She'd held it
off during the phone call, but she couldn't stop it now.

She stayed just as she was until she could control her
breathing again, until the worst threat of sickness receded.
Then she rose, took one of her pills to ward off the migraine
and added blusher to her pale cheeks. She gathered her purse,
Seth's gifts, a jacket against the chill, and left.

THE DAY HAD BEEN END-
less. How was a guy supposed to sit through hours and hours
of school on his birthday? I mean, he was double ones now,
and everything. He was going to get pizza and french fries
and chocolate cake and ice cream and probably even presents.

He'd never actually had a birthday present before, Seth
mused. Not that he could remember, anyway. He'd probably
end up with clothes and shit, but it would still be a present.

If anybody ever showed up.

"What's taking them so long?" Seth demanded, again.

Determined to be patient, Anna continued to slice potatoes
for the homemade fries that Seth had requested as part of his
birthday menu. "They'll be along."

"It's almost six. How come I had to come home after
school instead of going to the boatyard?"

"Because," Anna said, and left it at that. "Stop poking
into everything, will you?" she added as Seth opened the refrigerator, again. Shut it, again. "You're going to be stuffing
your face soon enough."

"I'm starving."

"I'm making the fries right now, aren't I?"

"I thought Grace was going to make them."

Steely-eyed, Anna stared at him over her shoulder. "Are you suggesting that I can't make french fries?"

He was bored and restless enough to be pleased that he'd jabbed her ego. "Well, she makes really good ones."

"Oh." She turned completely around. "And I don't."

"You do okay. Anyway, we'll have the pizza." He nearly pulled it off, but snorted out a chuckle.

"Brat." Anna made a laughing dive at him. He danced away howling.

"That's the door, that's the door. I'll get it!" He raced off, leaving Anna grinning after him.

But the wicked laughter faded from his eyes when he yanked open the door and saw Sybill on the porch. "Oh. Hi."

Her heart sank, but she fixed on a polite smile. "Happy birthday."

"Yeah, thanks." Watching her cautiously, he opened the door.

"I appreciate you inviting me." At a loss, she held out both shopping bags. "Are you allowed to have your gifts?"

"Sure, I guess." Then his eyes widened. "All that?"

She nearly sighed. He sounded so much like Phillip had. "It all sort of goes together."

"Cool. Hey, it's Grace." Hampered by the bags, which he held now, he bumped past her onto the porch.

The joy in his voice, the quick, delighted smile on his face was such a marked contrast from the way he'd looked at her, Sybill's sinking heart cracked.

"Hey, Grace! Hey, Aubrey! I'll tell Anna you guys are here."

He darted inside again, leaving Sybill standing by the open door without a clue how to proceed. Grace got out of the car and smiled. "Sounds like he's excited."

"Yes, well . . ." She watched Grace set a bag on the hood

of the car, followed by a large clear-plastic cake holder. Then she reached in to unstrap a babbling Aubrey from her car seat. "Do you need a hand?"

"Actually, I could use two. Just a minute, baby. If you keep wriggling . . ." She tossed another smile over her shoulder as Sybill walked over. "She's been wired all day. Seth is Aubrey's favorite person."

"Seth! He's got a birthday. We baked a cake."

"We sure did." Grace hauled Aubrey out, then passed her to an astonished Sybill. "Would you mind? She wanted to wear that dress, but the run from here to the house is bound to be a disaster."

"Oh, well . . ." Sybill found herself staring down into a beaming, angelic face and holding a bouncing little body dressed in party-pink ruffles.

"We're having a party," Aubrey told her and put both her hands on Sybill's cheeks to ensure her full attention. "I'll have a party next time when I'm three. You can come."

"Thank you."

"You smell pretty. I do, too."

"You certainly do." Sybill's initial stiffness couldn't stand up under that cheerfully charming smile. Phillip's Jeep pulled in behind Grace's, and most of the stiffness returned as Cam slid out of the passenger seat and shot her a cool, unmistakably warning look.

Aubrey let out a shriek of greeting. "Hi! Hi!"

"Hi, there, beautiful." Cam walked over, kissed Aubrey lightly on her comically pursed lips, then aimed those flinty eyes at Sybill. "Hello, Dr. Griffin."

"Sybill." Well able to interpret the chilly exchange, Phillip strode over, laid a supporting hand on her shoulder, and leaned in for the kiss Aubrey was offering. "Hi, there, sweetie."

"I have a new dress."

"And you look stunning in it."

In the way of females, Aubrey deserted Sybill without a

glance and held out her arms to Phillip. He managed the transfer easily, settling her on his hip. "Been here long?" he asked Sybill.

"No, I just got here." She watched Cam carry three large cardboard boxes of pizza into the house. "Phillip, I don't want to cause any—"

"Let's go inside." He took her hand, pulling her along. "We've got to get this party going, don't we, Aub?"

"Seth gets presents. They're secrets." She whispered it and leaned in close. "What are they?"

"Uh-uh, I'm not telling." He set her down when they stepped into the house, gave her frilled bottom a friendly pat, and sent her off. She shouted for Seth and scrambled toward the kitchen. "She'll blab."

Determined to make it work, Sybill put her smile back in place. "I won't."

"Nope. You can just wait for it. I'm going to grab a fast shower before Cam beats me to it and uses all the hot water." He gave her a quick, absent kiss. "Anna'll get you a drink," he added as he headed upstairs.

"Great." On a huff of breath, Sybill steeled herself to deal with the Quinns alone.

The kitchen was pandemonium. Aubrey was squealing, Seth was talking a mile a minute. Potatoes were frying, with Grace manning the stove since Cam had Anna trapped against the refrigerator with a gleam of pure lust in his eyes.

"You know how I get when I see you in an apron."

"I know how you get when you see me breathe." And she hoped it would never change. Nonetheless, she narrowed her eyes at him. "Hands off, Quinn. I'm busy."

"You've been slaving over a hot stove. You really ought to take a shower. With me."

"I'm not going to—" She spotted the movement out of the corner of her eye. "There you are, Sybill." In a move that looked very practiced, and very effective to Sybill, Anna shifted and jammed her elbow into her husband's stomach. "What can I get you to drink?"

"Ah . . . the coffee smells wonderful, thank you."

"I'll take a beer." Cam snagged one out of the fridge. "And go clean up." He aimed that look at Sybill again, then strode out.

"Seth, stay out of those bags," Anna ordered as she pulled down a mug. "No gifts yet." She'd made the decision to keep him from opening Sybill's gifts until after dinner. She calculated that his aunt would make her excuses and run as quickly as she could manage it after the little ritual was complete.

"Man! Is it my birthday or what?"

"Yes, if you live through it. Why don't you take Aubrey into the other room? Entertain her for a while. We'll eat as soon as Ethan gets here."

"Well, where is he, anyway?" Grumbling, Seth stalked out with Aubrey on his heels and didn't catch the quick grin Grace and Anna exchanged.

"That goes for you dogs, too." Anna gave Foolish a nudge with her foot and pointed her finger. With canine sighs, both dogs clipped out of the kitchen.

"Peace." Anna closed her eyes to absorb it. "Momentary peace."

"Is there anything I can do to help?"

With a shake of her head, Anna passed over the mug of coffee. "I think we've got it under control. Ethan should be here any minute. In the big surprise." She walked to the window to look out through the gathering dark. "I hope you've brought an adolescent appetite," she added. "Tonight's menu consists of pepperoni-and-sausage pizza, peanut-oil fries, homemade hot fudge sundaes, and Grace's killer chocolate cake."

"We'll all be in the hospital," Sybill commented before she thought it through. Even as she winced, Anna was laughing.

"We who are about to die salute you. Uh-oh, there's Ethan." She'd lowered her voice to a stage whisper. At the stove, Grace dropped her slotted spoon with a clatter. "Did you burn yourself?"

"No, no." Chuckling weakly, Grace stepped back. "No, I'm, ah . . . I'm just going to run out and . . . help Ethan."

"All right but—hmmm," Anna finished when Grace hurried past her and out the door. "Jumpy," she muttered, then hit the outside lights. "It's not quite dark yet, but it will be by the time we finish this." She salvaged the last of the fries and switched off the stove. "Cam and Phillip better put a fire under it. Oh, God, it's cute! Can you see?"

Too curious to resist, Sybill joined her at the kitchen window. She saw Grace standing on the dock, caught in the last light of the day, and Ethan just stepping onto it. "It's a boat," she murmured. "A little sailboat."

"A ten-footer. They call it a pram." Anna's smile nearly split her face. "The three of them have been building it over at Ethan's old house—the one he rents out? The tenants let them use the shed over there so Seth wouldn't know about it."

"They built it for him?"

"Whenever they could steal an hour. Oh, he's going to love it. Well, what's this?"

"What?"

"That," Anna said and stared hard through the glass. She could see Grace talking, her hands locked together, Ethan staring at her. Then he lowered his head to hers. "I hope there's not any . . ." She trailed off as Ethan drew Grace close, buried his face in her hair and rocked. And her arms came up around him. "Oh, oh." Tears flooded Anna's eyes. "She must be—she's pregnant! She's just told him. I know it. Oh, look!" She gripped Sybill's shoulder when Ethan scooped a laughing Grace up into his arms. "Isn't that beautiful?"

The two of them were wrapped around each other, making

one silhouette in the last light of day. "Yes, yes, it is."

"Look at me." Laughing at herself, Anna yanked off a paper towel and blew her nose. "I'm a mess. This is going to get to me, I know it is. I'm going to want one." She blew again, sighed. "I was so sure I could wait a year or two. I'm never going to be able to wait that long now. Not for that. I can just see Cam when I—" She stopped herself. "Sorry," she said with a watery laugh.

"It's all right. It's lovely that you're so happy for them. That you're so happy for yourself. This is really a family occasion, especially now. Anna, I really should go."

"Don't be a coward," Anna said, pointing her finger. "You're here, and you're going to have to face this nightmare of indigestion and noise just like the rest of us."

"I simply think—" All she could do was close her mouth when the door burst open. Ethan was still carrying Grace and the pair of them wore huge smiles.

"Anna, we're having a baby." Ethan made the announcement with a catch in his voice.

"What, am I blind?" She brushed Ethan aside to kiss Grace first. "I've had my nose to the window. Oh, congratulations!" Then threw her arms around both of them. "I'm so happy."

"You have to be godmother." Ethan turned his face to kiss her. "We wouldn't have gotten this far without you."

"Oh, that does it." Anna burst into tears just as Phillip walked in.

"What's going on? Why's Anna crying? Jesus, Ethan, what happened to Grace?"

"I'm fine. I'm wonderful. I'm pregnant."

"No kidding?" He plucked her out of Ethan's arms to kiss her lavishly.

"What the hell is going on in here?" Cam demanded.

Still holding Grace, Phillip grinned at him. "We're having a baby."

"Oh, yeah?" He arched his eyebrow. "How does Ethan feel about the two of you?"

"Ha-ha," was Phillip's comment as he set Grace carefully on her feet.

"You feel all right?" Cam asked her.

"I feel terrific."

"You look terrific." Cam drew her into his arms, rubbed his chin over her head. And the tenderness with which he did both had Sybill blinking in surprise. "Nice going, bro," Cam murmured to Ethan.

"Thanks. Can I have my wife back now?"

"I'm nearly done." Cam held Grace at arm's length. "If he doesn't take good care of you and the little Quinn in there, I'll beat the hell out of him for you."

"Are we ever going to eat?" Seth demanded, then stopped at the kitchen doorway and stared. "Why're Anna and Grace crying?" He swept an accusing look around the room, including Sybill in the heat. "What happened?"

"We're happy." Grace sniffled and accepted the tissue that Sybill dug out of her purse. "I'm going to have a baby."

"Really? Wow. Wow. That's cool. That's way cool. Does Aub know?"

"No, Ethan and I will tell her, in a little while. But now I'm going to go get her because there's something you need to see. Outside."

"Outside." He started for the door, but Phillip stepped neatly in his path.

"Not yet."

"What is it? Come on, move. Jeez. Let me see what's out there."

"We should blindfold him," Phillip considered.

"We should gag him," was Cam's suggestion.

Ethan took care of matters by hauling Seth over his shoulder. When Grace brought Aubrey in, Ethan winked, shifted the wriggling Seth, and headed out the door.

"You're not throwing me in again!" Seth's voice rang with terrified delight and giggles. "Come on, guys, the water's really cold."

"Wimp," Cam sneered when Seth lifted his face from Ethan's back.

"If you try," Seth warned, eyes dancing with joy and challenge, "I'm taking at least one of you with me."

"Yeah, yeah, big talk." Phillip pushed Seth's face back down. "Ready?" he asked when everyone was assembled at the edge of the water. "Good. Do it, Ethan."

"Man, the water's *cold*!" Seth began, ready to scream when Ethan dropped him. But he was set on his feet and he was turned to face the pretty little wooden boat with sky-blue sails that rippled lightly in the evening wind. "What—where did that come from?"

"The sweat of our brows," Phillip said dryly while Seth gaped at the boat.

"Is it—who's buying it?"

"It's not for sale," Cam said simply.

"It . . . is it . . ." It couldn't be, he thought, while his heart thumped with nerves and hope and shock. But hope was paramount. In the past year he'd learned to hope. "Is it mine?"

"You're the only one with a birthday around here," Cam reminded him. "Don't you want a closer look?"

"It's mine?" He whispered it first, with such staggered delight and shock that Sybill felt her eyes sting. *"Mine?"* He exploded with it as he whirled around. This time the sheer joy on his face closed her throat. "To keep?"

"You're a good sailor," Ethan told him quietly. "She's a tight little boat. She's steady, but she moves."

"You built her for me." His gaze shot from Ethan's face to Phillip's to Cam's. "For me?"

"Nah, we built her for some other brat." Cam gave him a light swat on the side of the head. "What do you think? Go take a look."

"Yeah." His voice quavered as he turned. "Yeah, can I get in her? Can I sit in her?"

"For Christ's sake, she's yours, isn't she?" His voice rough with emotion, Cam grabbed Seth's hand and hauled him onto the dock.

"I think this is a guy thing," Anna murmured. "Let's give them a few minutes to pull themselves together."

"They love him so much." Sybill watched another moment as the four males made noises over a little wooden boat. "I don't think I realized it, really, until just now."

"He loves them, too." Grace pressed her cheek to Aubrey's.

AND IT WAS MORE, SYBILL thought later as she picked at the meal in the noisy kitchen. It had been that shock on Seth's face. The utter disbelief that someone loved him, could love him enough to understand his heart's desire. And understanding, make the effort to give it.

The pattern of his life, she thought wearily, had been broken, shifted, then reformed. And all before she'd really come into it. Now it was set, the way it was meant to be set.

She didn't belong here. She couldn't stay here. She couldn't bear it.

"I really should go," she said with a well-mannered smile. "I want to thank you for—"

"Seth hasn't opened your gift yet," Anna interrupted. "Why don't we let him rip, then we'll have some cake."

"Cake!" Aubrey whacked her palms on her high chair. "Blow the candles out and make a wish."

"Soon," Grace told her. "Seth, take Sybill into the living room so you can open your gift."

"Sure." He waited for Sybill to stand, then with a jerk of his shoulder started out.

"I got it in Baltimore," she began, miserably awkward, "so if it doesn't suit, if you don't like it, Phillip could exchange things for you."

"Okay." He pulled a box out of the first bag, sat Indian-style on the floor, and within seconds was tearing the paper it had taken her untold agonies to choose to shreds.

"You could have used newspaper," Phillip told her and, chuckling, nudged her into a chair.

"It's a box," Seth said, puzzled, and Sybill's heart sank at his disinterested tone.

"Yes, well . . . I kept the receipt. So you can take it back and get whatever you'd like."

"Yeah, okay." But he caught the hard beam in Phillip's eye and made an effort. "It's a nice box." But he wanted to roll his eyes. Then he idly flicked the brass hook, flipped the top. "Holy shit!"

"Christ, Seth." Cam muttered it, glancing over his shoulder as Anna walked in from the kitchen.

"Man, look at all this stuff! It's got, like, everything. Charcoals and pastels and pencils." Now he looked at Sybill with that staggered shock. "I get to have it all?"

"It goes together." Nervous, she twisted her silver beads around her finger. "You draw so well, I thought . . . You may want to experiment with other mediums. The other box has more supplies."

"More?"

"Watercolors and brushes, some paper. Ah . . ." She eased onto the floor as Seth gleefully ripped into the second box. "You may decide you like acrylics, or pen and ink, but I lean toward watercolors myself, so I thought you might like to try your hand at it."

"I don't know how to do it."

"Oh, well, it's a simple process, really." She leaned over to take one of the brushes and began to explain the basic technique. As she spoke, she forgot her nerves, smiled at him.

The light from the lamp slanted over her face, caught something, something in her eyes that jiggled at the corners of his memory.

"Did you have a picture on the wall? Flowers, white flowers in a blue vase?"

Her fingers tightened on the brush. "Yes, in my bedroom in New York. One of my watercolors. Not a very good one."

"And you had colored bottles on a table. Lots of them, different sizes and stuff."

"Perfume bottles." Her throat was closing again, so she was forced to clear it. "I used to collect them."

"You let me sleep in your bed with you." His eyes narrowed as he concentrated on the vague blips of memory. Soft smells, soft voice, colors and shapes. "You told me some story, about a frog."

The Frog Prince. Into her mind flashed the image of how a little boy had curled against her, the bedside lamp holding back the dark for both of them, his bright-blue eyes intense on her face as she'd calmed his fears with a tale of magic and happily ever after.

"You had—when you came to visit, you had bad dreams. You were just a little boy."

"I had a puppy. You bought me a puppy."

"Not a real one, just a stuffed toy." Her vision was blurring, her throat closing, her heart breaking. "You . . . you didn't have any toys with you. When I brought it home you asked me whose it was, and I told you it was yours. That's what you called it. Yours. She didn't take it when she—I have to go."

She shot to her feet. "I'm sorry. I have to go." And bolted out the door.

SEVENTEEN

S HE GOT TO HER CAR AND
yanked at the door handle before she realized she'd locked it.
Which was, she told herself frantically, a stupid, knee-jerk
urban habit that had no more place in this pretty rural neighborhood than she did.

The next thing she realized was that she'd run out of the
house without her purse, her jacket, her keys. And that she
would walk back to the hotel before she would go back inside
and face the Quinns again after her rude and emotional behavior.

She whirled when she heard footsteps behind her and
wasn't sure if she was relieved or embarrassed to see Phillip
coming toward her. She didn't know what she was, what *it*
was that was bubbling up inside her, burning and swelling her
heart and her throat. She only knew she had to escape it.

"I'm sorry. I know that was rude. I really have to go." In
the rush to get out, the words bumped and tumbled over each
other. "Would you mind getting my purse? I need my purse.
My keys. I'm sorry. I hope I didn't spoil—"

Whatever was bubbling in her throat was rising higher, choking her. "I have to go."

"You're shaking." He said it gently and reached for her, but she jerked back.

"It's cold. I forgot my jacket."

"It's not that cold, Sybill. Come here."

"No, I'm leaving. I have a headache. I—no, don't touch me."

Ignoring her words, he drew her firmly against him, wrapped his arms tight around her and held on. "It's all right, baby."

"No, it's not." She wanted to scream it. Was he blind? Was he stupid? "I shouldn't have come. Your brother hates me. Seth's afraid of me. You—your—I—"

Oh, it hurt. The pressure in her chest was agony, and it was spreading. "Let me go. I don't belong here."

"Yes, you do."

He'd seen it, that connection, when she and Seth had stared at each other. Her eyes such a clear blue, his so brilliant. He'd all but heard the click.

"No one hates you. No one's afraid of you. Let go, will you?" He pressed his mouth to her temple, would have sworn he felt the pain hissing there. "Why won't you let go?"

"I'm not going to cause a scene. If you'd just get my purse, I'll go."

She was holding herself rigid as marble, but the marble was cracking, he thought, and trembling with the pressure. If she didn't let go she would explode. So he would have to push. "He remembered you. He remembered that you cared."

Through the hideous pressure there was a stab, and the stab pierced her heart. "I can't stand it. I can't bear it." Her hands gripped his shoulders, fingers clenching and unclenching. "She took him away. She took him away. It broke my heart."

She was sobbing now, her arms tight around his neck. "I know. I know it did. That's the way," he murmured, and simply picked her up, sat on the grass, and cradled her against him. "It's about damn time."

He rocked her while tears that were hot and desperate flooded out of her and soaked his shirt. Cold? he thought as the firestorm of grief whipped through her. There was nothing cold in her but the fear of emotional pain.

He didn't tell her to stop, even when the sobs shook her so violently it seemed her bones might snap. He didn't offer promises of comfort or solutions. He knew the value of purging. So he simply stroked and rocked, cradling her while she wept out the pain.

When Anna stepped out on the porch, Phillip shook his head at her, stroking still. He continued to rock her as the door shut again and left them alone.

When she'd cried herself dry, her head felt swollen and hot, her throat and stomach raw. Weak and disoriented, she lay exhausted in his arms. "I'm sorry."

"Don't be. You needed that. I don't think I've ever known anyone who needed a crying jag more."

"It doesn't solve anything."

"You know better than that." He rose and, helping her up, pulled her toward his Jeep. "Get in."

"No, I need to—"

"Get in," he repeated with just a hint of impatience. "I'll go get your purse and your jacket." He lifted her into the passenger seat. "But you're not driving." His eyes met her tired, puffy ones. "And you're not going to be alone tonight."

She didn't have the energy to argue. She felt hollowed out and insubstantial. If he took her back to the hotel, she could sleep. She'd take a pill if she had to and escape. She didn't want to think. If she started to think she might feel again. If she felt again, if any part of that flood of feeling came back, she would drown in it.

Because his face looked grim and entirely too determined when he strode out of the house with her things, Sybill accepted her own cowardice and closed her eyes.

He didn't speak, simply climbed in beside her, leaned over to secure her seat belt, then started the car. He let the blessed silence hang throughout the drive. She didn't protest when he came into the lobby with her or when he opened her purse for her key card at her door.

He took her hand again and led her directly to the bedroom. "Get undressed," he ordered. As she stared at him with those swollen, red-rimmed eyes, he added, "I'm not going to jump you, for Christ's sake. What do you take me for?"

He didn't know where the flare of temper had come from. Maybe it was looking at her like this, seeing her so utterly wrecked and defenseless. Turning on his heel, he marched into the bathroom.

Seconds later, she heard the drum of water in the tub. He came out with a glass and aspirin. "Swallow. If you don't take care of yourself, someone else has to."

The water felt like glory on her abused throat, but before she could thank him, he'd pulled the glass out of her hand and set it aside. She swayed a little, and blinked when he tugged her sweater over her head.

"You're going to take a hot bath and relax."

She was too stupefied to argue as he continued to undress her like a doll. When he laid her clothes aside, she shivered a little but didn't speak. She only stared at him when he picked her up, carried her into the bathroom and deposited her in the tub.

The water was high, and a great deal hotter than she considered healthy. Before she could get her mind around the words to mention it, he flicked off the stream.

"Sit back, shut your eyes. Do it!" he said with such unexpected force that she obeyed. She kept them closed even when she heard the door click shut behind him.

She stayed there for twenty minutes, nearly nodding off twice. Only the vague fear of drowning kept her from sinking into sleep. And the niggling idea that he would come back in, pull her out, and dry her off himself was what made her climb shakily out of the tub.

Then again, maybe he'd gone. Maybe he'd finally gotten disgusted with her outburst and left her alone. Who could blame him?

But he was standing by the terrace doors in her bedroom when she stepped out, looking out at her view of the Bay. "Thank you." She knew it was awkward, for both of them, and struggled to make the effort when he turned and stared at her. "I'm sorry—"

"You apologize again, Sybill, you're going to piss me off." He walked toward her as he spoke, laid his hands on her shoulders. He cocked his eyebrows when she jumped. "Better," he decided, running his fingers over her shoulders and neck, "but not perfect. Lie down."

He sighed, pulled her toward the bed. "I'm not after sex. I do have some small level of restraint, and I can call on it when I'm faced with an emotionally and physically exhausted woman. On your stomach. Come on."

She slid onto the bed and couldn't quite muffle the moan when his fingers began to knead along her shoulder blades.

"You're a psychologist," he reminded her. "What happens to someone who represses their feelings on a regular basis?"

"Physically or emotionally?"

He laughed a little, straddled her, then got seriously down to work. "I'll tell you what happens, doc. They get headaches, heartburn, stomach pains. If and when the dam breaks, it all floods out so hard and so fast that they make themselves sick."

He tugged the robe off her shoulders and used the heels of his hands to press the muscles.

"You're angry with me."

"No, I'm not, Sybill. Not with you. Tell me about when Seth stayed with you."

"It was a long time ago."

"He was four," Phillip prompted and concentrated on the muscles that had just tensed. "You were in New York. Same place you have now?"

"Yes. Central Park West. It's a quiet neighborhood. Safe."

Exclusive, Phillip thought. No trendy East Village for Dr. Griffin. "Couple of bedrooms?"

"Yes. I use the second as my office."

He could almost see it. Tidy, organized, attractive. "I guess that's where Seth slept."

"No, Gloria took that room. We put Seth on the living room sofa. He was just a little boy."

"They just showed up on your doorstep one day."

"More or less. I hadn't seen her in years. I knew about Seth. She'd called me when the man she'd married left her. I sent her money off and on. I didn't want her to come. I never said she couldn't, but I didn't want her to come. She's so . . . disruptive, so difficult."

"But she did come."

"Yes. I came back from a lecture one afternoon and she was waiting outside the building. She was furious because the doorman wouldn't let her in, wouldn't let her go up to my apartment. Seth was crying, and she was screaming. It was just . . ." She sighed. "Typical, I suppose."

"But you let her in."

"I couldn't just send her away. All she had was this little boy and a backpack. She begged me to let them stay for a while. She said she'd been hitchhiking. That she was broke. She started crying, and Seth just crawled onto the couch and fell asleep. He must have been exhausted."

"How long did they stay?"

"A few weeks." Her mind began to drift between then and now, sliding back and forth in time. "I was going to help her get a job, but she said she needed to rest first. She said she'd been sick. Then she said a truck driver in Oklahoma had raped her. I knew she was lying, but . . ."

"She was your sister."

"No, no." She said it wearily. "If I'd been honest, I would have admitted that that had stopped mattering years before. But Seth was . . . He hardly spoke. I didn't know anything about children, but I got a book and it indicated he should have been much more verbal."

He nearly smiled. It was so easy to picture her selecting the proper book, studying it, trying to put everything in order.

"He was like this little ghost," she murmured. "This little shadow in the apartment. When Gloria would go out for any length of time and leave him with me, he'd creep out a little. And the first night she didn't come home until morning, he had a nightmare."

"And you let him sleep with you and told him a story."

"*The Frog Prince*. My nanny told it to me. She liked fairy tales. He was afraid of the dark. I used to be afraid of the dark." Her voice was thick and slow with fatigue. "I used to want to sleep in my parents' bed when I was afraid, but I wasn't allowed to. But . . . I didn't think it would hurt him, just for a little while."

"No." Now he could see her, a young girl with dark hair and light eyes, trembling in the dark. "It wouldn't have hurt."

"He used to like to look at my perfume bottles. He liked the colors and the shapes. I bought him crayons. He always liked to draw pictures."

"You got him a stuffed dog."

"He liked to watch the dogs being walked in the park. He was so sweet when I gave it to him. He carried it around everywhere. He slept with it."

"You fell in love with him."

"I loved him so much. I don't know how it happened. It was only a few weeks."

"Time doesn't always factor in." He skimmed her hair back so he could see her profile. The curve of her cheek, the angle of her brow. "It doesn't always play a part."

"It's supposed to, but it didn't. I didn't care that she took my things. I didn't care that she stole from me when she left. But she took him. She didn't even let me say good-bye to him. She took him, and she left his little dog because she knew it would hurt me. She knew I would think about him crying for it at night, and worry. So I had to stop. I had to stop thinking about it. I had to stop thinking about him."

"It's all right. That part's all over now." He stroked gently, nudging her closer to sleep. "She won't hurt Seth anymore. Or you."

"I was stupid."

"No, you weren't." He stroked her neck, her shoulders, felt her body rise and fall on a long, long sigh. "Go to sleep."

"Don't go."

"No, I'm not." He frowned at how fragile the nape of her neck looked under his fingers. "I'm not going anywhere."

And that was a problem, he realized as he smoothed his hands down her arms, over her back. He wanted to stay with her, to be with her. He wanted to watch her sleep just the way she was sleeping now, deep and still. He wanted to be the one who held her when she cried, for he doubted that she cried often, or that she had anyone to hold her when she did.

He wanted to watch those quiet lake eyes of hers go bright with laughter, that lovely, soft mouth curve with it. He could spend hours listening to the way her voice changed tones, from warm amusement to prim formality to earnestness.

He liked the way she looked in the morning, vaguely surprised to see him beside her. And at night, with pleasure and passion flickering over her face.

She hadn't a clue how revealing that face was, he thought, as he tugged down the covers, shifting her until he could spread them over her. Oh, it was subtle, like her scent. A man had to get close, very close, before he understood. But he'd gotten close, very close, without either of them realizing it.

And he'd seen the way she'd watched his family, with wistfulness, with yearning.

Always staying a step back, always the observer.

And he'd seen the way she'd watched Seth. With love, and with longing, and again from a distance.

So as not to intrude? To protect herself? He thought it was a combination of both. He wasn't quite sure exactly what went on in her heart, in her mind. But he was determined to find out.

"I think I might be in love with you, Sybill." He said it quietly as he stretched out beside her. "Damn if that doesn't complicate things for both of us."

SHE WOKE IN THE DARK, AND for a moment, just a flash, she was a child again and afraid of all those things that lurked in the shadows. She had to press her lips together, very hard, until it hurt. Because if she cried out one of the servants would hear and might tell her mother. Her mother would be annoyed. Her mother wouldn't like it that she'd cried about the dark again.

Then she remembered. She wasn't a child. There was nothing lurking in the shadows but more shadows. She was a grown woman who knew it was foolish to be afraid of the dark when there was so much else to fear.

Oh, she'd made a fool of herself, she thought, as more memories slipped through. A terrible fool of herself. Letting herself become upset that way. Worse, letting it show until she'd had no control, none whatsoever. Instead of maintaining her composure, she'd rushed out of the house like an idiot.

Inexcusable.

Then she'd cried all over Phillip. Wept like a baby right in the front yard as if she'd . . .

Phillip.

Mortification had her moaning aloud, covering her face with her hands. She sucked in a gasp when an arm came around her.

"Ssh."

She recognized his touch, his scent even before he drew her against him. Before his mouth brushed her temple, before his body fit comfortingly to hers.

"It's all right," he murmured.

"I—I thought you'd gone."

"I said I'd stay." He slitted his eyes open, scanned the dull red glow of the bedside alarm. "Three A.M. hotel time. Should have figured it."

"I didn't mean to wake you." As her eyes grew accustomed to the dark, she could make out the sweep of his cheekbone, the ridge of his nose, the shape of his mouth. Her fingers itched to touch.

"When I wake up in the middle of the night in bed with a beautiful woman, it's hard to mind."

She smiled, relieved that he wasn't going to press her about her earlier behavior. It could just be the two of them now. No yesterday to mourn over, no tomorrow to worry about.

"I imagine you've had a lot of practice."

"Some things you want to get just right."

His voice was so warm, his arm so strong, his body so firm. "When you wake up in the middle of the night in bed with a woman, and she wants to seduce you, do you mind?"

"Hardly ever."

"Well, if you wouldn't mind . . ." She shifted, slid her body over his, found his lips with her lips, his tongue with her tongue.

"I'll let you know as soon as I start to mind."

Her laugh was low and warm. Gratitude moved through her, for what he'd done for her, what he'd come to be to her. She wanted so badly to show him.

It was dark. She could be anything she wanted to be in the dark.

"Maybe I won't stop if you do."

"Threats?" He was every bit as surprised, and aroused, by the teasing purr of her voice as he was by the deliberate, circling trail of her fingertips down his body. "You don't scare me."

"I can." She began to follow the trail with her mouth. "I will."

"Give it your best shot. Jesus." His eyes all but crossed. "Bull's-eye."

She laughed again and lapped at him like a cat. When his body quivered, and his breathing grew thick and ragged, she scraped her nails slowly up his sides and down again.

What a wonder the male form was, she thought, dreamily exploring it. Hard, smooth, the planes and angles so perfectly fashioned to mate with woman. With her.

Silky here, then rough. Firm, then yielding. She could make him want and ache just as he made her want and ache. She could give, she could take just as he did and all the wonderful and wicked things people did in the dark, she could do.

He'd go mad if she continued. He'd die if she stopped. Her mouth was hot and restless, and everywhere. Those elegant fingers had the blood raging through his veins. As their flesh grew damp, her body slipped and slid over his, a pale silhouette in the dark.

She was any woman. The only woman. He craved her like life.

Dreamlike, she rose up over him, shrugging out of her robe, arching her back, shaking her hair back. What soared through her now was freedom. Power. Lust. Her eyes gleamed, catlike against the dark, bewitching him.

She lowered herself, taking him inside her slowly, dimly aware of what effort it cost him to allow her to set the pace. Her breath caught, released on a moaning sigh of pleasure.

Caught again, released again when his hands captured her breasts, squeezed, possessed.

She rocked, small movements, torturously slow, arousing herself with the power. And kept her eyes on his. He shuddered beneath her, his muscles bunched, his body tight between her thighs. Strong, she thought, he was so strong. Strong enough to let her take him as she chose.

She skimmed her hands over his chest, then lowered. Her hair curtained their faces as her mouth closed hard over his. A tangle of tongues and teeth and breath.

The orgasm rolled through her like a wave, growing, building, then sweeping her up and over. She reared back with it, body bowing, and rode it out.

Then she rode him.

He gripped her hips, his fingers digging in as she surged over him. All reckless speed and clashing light now, all heat and greed. His mind emptied, his lungs screamed, and his body climbed desperately toward release.

When he found it, it was brutal and brilliant.

She seemed to melt over him, her body as soft and hot and fluid as a pool of liquid wax. Her heart thudded hard against the frantic beat of his own. He couldn't speak, couldn't find the air to push the words free. But the ones that shimmered on his tongue were three that he'd been careful never to say to a woman.

Triumph still glowed inside her. She stretched, lazy and satisfied as a cat, then curled herself against him. "That," she said sleepily, "was exactly right."

"What?"

She chuckled softly and ended on a yawn. "I may not have scared you, but I fried your brain."

"No question." A sex-scrambled brain. Men who started thinking about love, much less bringing the word up when they were hot and naked and wrapped around a woman, just got themselves in trouble.

"First time I ever liked waking up at three A.M." Already half asleep, she pillowed her head on his shoulder. She shifted. "Cold," she muttered.

He reached down and tugged up the tangled sheets and blankets. She nipped an edge with her fingers, pulled them up to her chin.

For the second time in one night, Phillip lay awake, staring at the ceiling while she slept deep and still beside him.

EIGHTEEN

IT WAS BARELY LIGHT WHEN
Phillip crawled out of bed. He didn't bother to moan. What
good would it do? Just because he'd barely slept, his mind
was fogged with fatigue and worry, and he had an entire day
of backbreaking manual labor ahead of him was no reason to
complain.

The fact that there was no coffee was a damn good reason
to complain.

Sybill stirred as he started to dress. "You have to go to the
boatyard?"

"Yeah." He rolled his tongue over his teeth as he jerked
up his slacks. Christ, he didn't even have a toothbrush with
him.

"Do you want me to order up some breakfast? Coffee?"

Coffee. The word alone was like a siren's song in his blood.

But he grabbed his shirt. If she ordered coffee, he would
have to talk to her. He didn't think it was a smart move to
have a conversation when he was in such a foul mood. And
why was he in a foul mood? he asked himself. Because he
hadn't slept and she'd managed to sneak through his legendary

defenses while he wasn't looking and make him fall in love with her.

"I'll get some at home." His voice was clipped and edgy. "I have to go back and change anyway." Which was why he was up so damn early.

The sheets rustled as she sat up. He watched her out of the corner of his eye and reached for his socks. She looked tousled and tumbled and temptingly soft.

Yeah, she was sneaky all right. Hitting him over the head like that with her vulnerability, sobbing in his arms that way and looking so damned hurt and defenseless. Then waking up in the middle of the night and turning into some sort of a sex-fantasy goddess.

Now she was offering him coffee. She had a hell of a nerve.

"I appreciate you staying last night. It helped."

"I'm here to serve," he said shortly.

"I . . ." She gnawed on her bottom lip, alerted and confused by his tone. "It was a difficult day for both of us. I suppose I'd have been wiser to stay away. I was already a little off balance after Gloria's call, and then—"

His head shot up. "What? Gloria called you?"

"Yes." And now, Sybill thought, she'd only proven why that was information best kept to herself. He was upset. Everyone was going to be upset.

"She called you? Yesterday?" With his temper simmering, he picked up his shoe, examined it. "And you didn't think that it was worth mentioning before this?"

"I didn't see any point in it." Because her hands couldn't seem to keep still, she pushed at her hair, tugged at the sheet. "I wasn't going to mention it at all, actually."

"Weren't you? Maybe you forgot, momentarily, that Seth is my family's responsibility. That we have a right to know if your sister's going to cause more trouble. A need to know," he said, rising as his anger rapidly approached flash point. "So that we can protect him."

"She won't do anything to—"

"How the hell do you know?" He exploded with it, rounding on her so that she clutched the sheets in white-knuckled fingers. "How can you know? By *observing* from ten paces back. Goddamn it, Sybill, this isn't a fucking exercise. This is life. What the hell did she want?"

She wanted to shrink, as she always did from anger. She coated her heart and her voice with ice, as she always did to face it. "She wanted money, of course. She wanted me to demand it from you, to give her more myself. She shouted at me, too, and swore at me, just as you are. It appears that staying ten paces back has put me directly in the middle."

"I want to know if and when she contacts you again. What did you tell her?"

Sybill reached for her robe, and her hand was steady. "I told her that your family would not give her anything. And neither would I. That I had spoken with your lawyer. That I had added, and would continue to add, my weight and influence to see that Seth remains a permanent part of your family."

"That's something, then," he muttered, frowning at her as she pulled on her robe.

"It's the least I can do, isn't it?" Her tone was frigid, distant and final. "Excuse me." She strode into the bathroom, shut the door.

From where he stood, Phillip heard the deliberate click of the lock. "Well, fine, that's just fine." He snarled at the door, grabbed his jacket, then got the hell out before he made matters any worse than they already were.

T HEY DIDN'T GET ANY BET-ter when he arrived home to find less than half a cup of coffee left in the pot. When he discovered midway through his shower that Cam had obviously used most of the hot water, he decided that just made it all perfect.

Then he stepped into his room, a towel slung around his hips, and found Seth sitting on the side of his bed.

Definitely perfect.

"Hey." Seth eyed him steadily.

"You're up early."

"I thought I'd maybe go in with you for a couple of hours."

Phillip turned to pull underwear and jeans out of his dresser. "You aren't working today. You've got your friends coming over later for the party."

"That's not till this afternoon." Seth lifted a shoulder. "There's time."

"Suit yourself."

He'd expected Phillip to be steamed. He had a thing for Sybill, didn't he? Seth reminded himself. It had been tough to come in here, to wait, to know he'd have to say something.

So he said the single thing that was most on his mind. "I didn't mean to make her cry."

Shit, was all Phillip could think. He yanked on his Jockeys. He wasn't going to get out of this. "You didn't. She was just due for a cry, that's all."

"I guess she's pretty pissed off."

"No, she's not." Resigned to it now, Phillip pulled on his jeans. "Look, women are hard to understand under the best of circumstances. These circumstances pretty much suck."

"I guess." Maybe he wasn't so steamed after all. "I just sort of remembered some stuff." Seth stared at the scars on Phillip's chest because it was easier than looking into his eyes. And because, well, the scars were so cool. "Then she got so whacked out about it and everything."

"Some people don't know what to do with feelings." He sighed, sat on the bed beside Seth, and was bitterly ashamed of himself. He'd blasted Sybill right between the eyes because *he* hadn't known what to do with his feelings. "So they cry, or they yell, or they go off and sulk in a corner. She cares about you, but she doesn't know exactly what to do about it. Or what you want her to do about it."

"I don't know. She's . . . she's not like Gloria." His voice rose a pitch. "She's decent. Ray was decent, too, and I've got—they're like relatives, right? So I've got . . ."

Understanding came quickly and squeezed his heart. "You've got Ray's eyes." Phillip kept his voice matter-of-fact, knowing Seth would believe him if he said it right. "The color and the shape, but that something that was behind them, too. The something that was decent. You've got a sharp brain, just like Sybill. It thinks, it analyzes, it wonders. And under all that, it tries to do what's right. What's decent. You've got both of them in you." He nudged Seth's shoulder with his own. "Pretty cool, huh?"

"Yeah." The smile bloomed. "It's cool."

"Okay, scram, or we're never going to get out of here."

HE ARRIVED AT THE BOAT-yard nearly forty-five minutes behind Cam and expected to get grief for it. Cam was already at the shaper, rabbeting the next run of planks. Bruce Springsteen shouted from the radio about his glory days. In defense, Phillip turned the volume down. Instantly Cam's head came up.

"I can't hear it over the tool unless it's loud."

"None of us will be able to hear if you keep blasting our ears for hours every day."

"What? Did you say something?"

"Ha-ha."

"Well, we're cheerful, aren't we?" Cam reached over and switched off the power. "So, how's Sybill?"

"Don't start on me."

Cam angled his head while Seth shifted his gaze from man to man and anticipated the entertainment value of a Quinn battle. "I asked a simple question."

"She'll survive." Phillip snatched up a tool belt. "I realize you'd prefer to see her run out of town on a rail, but you'll have to make do with the fact that I gave her a verbal bashing this morning rather than a physical one."

"Why the hell did you do that?"

"Because she pissed me off!" Phillip shouted. "Because it all pisses me off. Especially you."

"Fine, you want to try for a physical bashing, I'm available. But I asked a goddamn simple question." Cam pulled the board off the shaper and heaved it toward the stack, where it landed with a clatter. "She already took a punch in the gut yesterday. Why the hell would you add to it this morning?"

"You're defending her?" Phillip stepped forward until they were nose to nose. "You're defending her, after all the shit you've handed me over her?"

"I've got eyes, don't I? I saw her face last night. What the hell do you take me for?" He jabbed a finger into Phillip's chest. "Anybody who'd kick a woman when she's that torn up ought to have his neck snapped."

"You son of a—" Phillip's fist was clenched and halfway through the swing before he stopped himself. He would have enjoyed a few bloody rounds, especially since Ethan wasn't there to break it up. But not when he was the one who deserved to be bloodied.

He unclenched his fist, spreading his fingers as he turned away to try to find some control. He saw Seth watching him with dark, interested eyes and snarled. "Don't you start."

"I didn't say a word."

"Look, I took care of her, okay?" He dragged a hand through his hair and aimed his rationalization at both of them. "I let her cry it out, patted her hand. I dumped her into a hot tub, tucked her into bed. I stayed with her. Maybe I got an hour's sleep out of the deal, so I'm feeling just a little testy right now.''

"Why'd you yell at her?" Seth wanted to know.

"Okay." He took a steadying breath, pressed his fingers to his tired eyes. "This morning she told me that Gloria had called her. Yesterday. Maybe I overreacted, but damn it, she should have told us."

"What did she want?" Seth's lips had gone white. Instinctively, Cam stepped over and laid a hand on his shoulder.

"Don't let her spook you, kid. You're beyond that now. What's the deal?" he demanded of Phillip.

"I didn't get details. I was too busy blasting Sybill for not telling me sooner. The gist of it was money." Phillip shifted his gaze to Seth, spoke directly to him. "She told Gloria to kiss ass. No money, no nothing, no how. She told her she'd been to the lawyer and was making sure you stayed just where you are."

"Your aunt's no pushover," Cam said easily, giving Seth's shoulder a quick squeeze. "She's got spine."

"Yeah." Seth straightened his own. "She's okay."

"Your brother over there," Cam continued, nodding toward Phillip. "He's an asshole, but the rest of us have sense enough to know that Sybill didn't bring up the phone call yesterday because it was a party. She didn't want anybody to get upset. A guy doesn't turn eleven every day."

"So I screwed up." Muttering to himself, Phillip grabbed a plank and prepared to beat out his frustrations with nail and wood. "I'll fix it."

SYBILL NEEDED TO DO SOME fixing of her own. It had taken her most of the day to work up both the courage and the plan. She pulled into the Quinn driveway just after four, and was relieved not to see Phillip's Jeep.

He'd be at the boatyard for another hour at least, she calculated. Seth would be with him. As it was Saturday night, they would most likely stop on the way home, pick up some takeout.

It was their pattern, and she knew her behavioral patterns, even if she didn't seem to be able to fully connect with the people who were doing the behaving.

Ten paces back, she thought, and was hurt all over again.

Annoyed, she ordered herself out of the car. She would do what she had come to do. It should take no more than fifteen minutes to apologize to Anna, for the apology to be accepted, at least outwardly. She would explain about the call from Gloria, in detail, so that it could be documented. Then she would leave.

She would be back at her hotel, buried in her work, long before Phillip arrived on the scene.

She knocked briskly on the door.

"It's open," came the response. "I'd rather kill myself than get up."

Warily, Sybill reached for the knob, hesitated, then opened the door. All she could do was stare.

The Quinn living room was usually cluttered, always appeared lived-in, but just now it appeared to have been lived in by a rampaging platoon of insane elves.

Paper plates, plastic cups, several of them dumped or spilled, littered the floor and the tables. Small plastic men were strewn everywhere as if a war had been waged, and the casualties were horrendous. Obviously fatal accidents had taken place with model cars and trucks. Shreds of wrapping paper were sprinkled over all like confetti on a particularly wild New Year's Eve.

Sprawled in a chair, surveying the damage, was Anna. Her hair was in her face, and her face was pale.

"Oh, great," she muttered, turning narrowed eyes to Sybill. "Now she shows up."

"I—I'm sorry?"

"Easy for you to say. I've just spent two and a half hours battling ten eleven-year-old boys. No—not boys," she corrected between her teeth. "Animals, beasts. Spawns of Satan. I just sent Grace home with orders to lie down. I'm afraid this experience might affect the baby. He could be born a mutant."

The children's party, Sybill remembered, her dazzled eyes scanning the room. She'd forgotten. "It's over?"

"It will never be over. I will wake up at night for the rest of my life, screaming, until they cart me off to a padded room. I have ice cream in my hair. There's some sort of . . . mass on the kitchen table. I'm afraid to go in there. I think it moved. Three boys managed to fall in the water and had to be dragged out and dried off. They'll probably catch pneumonia and we'll be sued. One of those creatures who disguised himself as a young boy ate approximately sixty-five pieces of cake, then got into my car—I don't know how he got by me, they're like lightning—and proceeded to throw up."

"Oh, dear." Sybill knew it wasn't a laughing matter. It shocked her to realize that her stomach muscles were quivering. "I'm so sorry. Can I help you, ah, clean up?"

"I'm not touching any of it. Those men—the one who claims to be my husband and his idiot brothers—they're going to do it. They're going to scrub and clean and wipe and shovel. They're going to do it all. They knew," she said in a vicious whisper. "They knew what a boy's birthday party would mean. How was I to know? But they did, and they hid themselves away down at that boatyard, using that lame excuse about contract deadlines. They left me and Grace alone with this, this unspeakable duty." She shut her eyes. "Oh, the horror."

Anna was silent for a moment, her eyes still closed. "Go ahead. You can laugh. I'm too weak to get up and belt you."

"You worked so hard to do this for Seth."

"He had the time of his life." Anna's lips curved as she opened her eyes. "And since I'm going to make Cam and his brothers clean it up, I'm feeling pretty good about it, all in all. How are you?"

"I'm fine. I came to apologize for last night."

"Apologize for what?"

The question threw her off rhythm. She was already running behind schedule, she thought, distracted by the chaos and Anna's rambling monologue. Sybill cleared her throat and began again. "For last night. It was rude of me to leave without thanking you for—"

"Sybill, I'm too tired to listen to nonsense. You weren't rude, you have nothing to apologize for, and you'll annoy me if you keep this up. You were upset, and you had a perfect right to be."

And that blew Sybill's carefully prepared speech all to hell. "I honestly don't understand why people in this family won't listen to, much less accept, a sincere apology for regrettable behavior."

"Boy, if that's the tone you use when you lecture," Anna observed with admiration, "your audience must sit at attention. But to answer your question, I suppose we don't because we so often indulge in what could be termed regrettable behavior ourselves. I'd ask you to sit down, but those are really lovely slacks and I have no idea what nasty surprises there are on any of the cushions."

"I don't intend to stay."

"You couldn't see your face," Anna said more gently. "When he looked up at you, when he told you what he remembered. But I could see it, Sybill. I could see it was a great deal more than duty or responsibility or a valiant attempt to do what was right that brought you here. It must have crushed you when she took him away all those years ago."

"I can't do this again." The burn of tears scalded the back of her eyes. "I just can't do this again."

"You don't have to," Anna murmured. "I just want you to know I understand. In my work I see so many damaged people. Battered women, abused children, men who are at the end of their ropes, the elderly we so blithely displace. I care, Sybill. I care about every one of them who come to me for help."

She sighed a little and spread her fingers. "But in order to help them, I have to hold part of myself back, be objective, realistic, practical. If I threw all my emotions into every one of my cases, I couldn't do my job. I'd burn out, burn up. I understand the need for a little distance."

"Yes." The painful tension drained out of Sybill's shoulders. "Of course you do."

"It was different with Seth," Anna went on. "Right from the first minute, everything about him pulled at me. I couldn't stop it. I tried, but I couldn't. I've thought about that, and I believe, sincerely, that my feelings for him were there, just there, even before I met him. We were meant to be a part of each other's lives. He was meant to be part of this family, and this family was meant to be mine."

Risking the consequences, Sybill eased down on the arm of the sofa. "I wanted to tell you . . . you're so good with him. You and Grace. You're so good for him. The relationship he has with his brothers is wonderful, and it's vital. That strong male influence is important for a boy. But the female, what you and Grace give him, is just as vital."

"You have something to give him, too. He's outside," Anna told her. "Drooling over his boat."

"I don't want to upset him. I really have to go."

"Running away last night was understandable and acceptable." Anna's gaze was direct, level and challenging. "Running now isn't."

"You must be very good at your job," Sybill said after a moment.

"I'm damn good at it. Go talk to him. If I manage to get out of this chair in this lifetime, I'll put some fresh coffee on."

It wasn't easy. But then Sybill supposed it wasn't meant to be. Crossing that lawn toward the boy who sat in the pretty little boat, so obviously dreaming of fast sails.

Foolish saw her first and, alerted, raced toward her, barking. She braced herself and put a hand out, hoping to ward him off. Foolish skimmed his head under it, turning the defensive gesture into a stroke.

His fur was so soft and warm, his eyes so adoring, his face so fittingly silly that she relaxed into a smile. "You really are foolish, aren't you?"

He sat, batting at her with his paw until she took it and shook. Satisfied, he raced back toward the boat, where Seth watched and waited.

"Hi." He stayed where he was, pulling on the line and making the small triangle of sail sway.

"Hello. Have you taken it out yet?"

"Nah. Anna wouldn't let me and any of the guys go out in her today." He jerked a shoulder. "Like we'd drown or something."

"But you had a good time at your party."

"It was cool. Anna's a little pissed—" He stopped and looked toward the house. She really hated it when he swore. "She's pretty steamed about Jake barfing in her car, so I figured I'd hang out here until she levels."

"That's probably very sensible."

Then silence fell, heavy, as they both looked out over the water and wondered what to say.

Sybill braced herself. "Seth, I didn't say good-bye to you last night. I shouldn't have left the way I did."

"It's okay." He shrugged again.

"I didn't think you remembered me. Or any of the time you stayed with me in New York."

"I thought I'd made it up." It was too hard to sit in the boat and look so far up. He climbed out, then sat on the dock to dangle his legs. "Sometimes I'd dream about some of it. Like the stuffed dog and stuff."

"Yours," she murmured.

"Yeah, that's pretty lame. She didn't talk about you or anything, so I thought I'd just made it up."

"Sometimes . . ." She took the risk and sat beside him. "Sometimes it was almost like that for me, too. I still have the dog."

"You kept it?"

"It was all I had left of you. You mattered to me. I know it may not seem like that now, but you did. I didn't want you to."

"Because I was hers?"

"Partly." She had to be honest, had to give him that, at least. "She was never kind, Seth. Something was twisted in her. It seemed that she could never be happy unless the people closest to her weren't. I didn't want her back in my life. I'd planned to give her a day or two, then arrange to have the two of you moved to a shelter. That way I would fulfill my family obligation and protect my own lifestyle."

"But you didn't."

"I made excuses at first. Just one more night. Then I admitted that I was letting her stay because I wanted to keep you there. If I found her a job, helped her get an apartment, worked with her to put her life back together, I could keep you close. I'd never had—you were the . . ."

She ordered herself to take one cleansing breath and just say it. "You loved me. You were the first person who ever did. I didn't want to lose that. And when I did, I pulled myself back, right back to where I'd been before you came. I was thinking much more of myself than of you. I'd like to make up for that, a little, by thinking of you now.''

He looked away from her, down at the feet he was kicking back and forth over the water. "Phil said how she called and you told her to kiss ass.''

"Not precisely in those words.''

"But that's what you meant, right?''

"I guess it was.'' She nearly smiled. "Yes.''

"You guys got the same mother, right, but, like, different fathers?''

"Yes, that's right.''

"Do you know who my father was?''

"I never met him, no.''

"No, I mean do you know who he was? She was always making up different guys and names and shit. And stuff,'' he corrected. "I just wondered, that's all.''

"I only know his name was Jeremy DeLauter. They weren't married long, and—''

"Married?'' His gaze flew back to hers. "She never got married. She was just BS-ing you.''

"No, I saw the marriage license. She had it with her when she came to New York. She thought I could help her track him down and sue him for child support.''

He considered a moment, absorbing the possibility. "Maybe. It doesn't matter. I figured she just took the name from some guy she lived with sometime. If he got hooked up with her, he must've been a loser.''

"I could arrange for a search. I'm sure we could locate him. It would take some time.''

"I don't want that.'' There wasn't any panic in his voice, just disinterest. "I was just wondering if you knew him, that's all. I got a family now.'' He lifted his arm as Foolish nosed into his armpit, and wrapped it around the dog's neck.

"Yes, you do.'' Aching a little, she started to rise. She hesitated, her eye drawn toward a flash of white. She saw the heron soar, gliding over the water just at the edge of the trees. Then it was gone, around the bend, leaving barely a ripple on the air.

A lovely thing, she thought. A lovely spot. A harbor for troubled souls, for young boys who only needed a chance to become men. Perhaps she couldn't thank Ray and Stella Quinn for what they'd done here, but she could show her gratitude by stepping aside now and letting their sons finish the job with Seth.

"Well, I should go."

"The art stuff you gave me, it's really great."

"I'm glad you like it. You have talent."

"I fooled around some with the charcoal last night."

She hesitated again. "Oh?"

"I'm not getting it right." He twisted his head to look up at her. "It's a lot different than a pencil. Maybe you could show me how to do it."

She stared hard over the water because she knew he wasn't asking. He was offering. Now, it seemed, she was being given a chance, and a choice. "Yes, I could show you."

"Now?"

"Yes." She concentrated on keeping her voice even. "I could show you now."

"Cool."

NINETEEN

So, he'd been a little hard on her, Phillip told himself. Maybe he felt that she should have told him immediately that Gloria had contacted her. Party or no party, she could have taken him aside and filled him in. But he shouldn't have jumped all over her and then walked out.

Still, in his own defense, he'd felt raw and annoyed and unsettled. He'd spent the first part of the night worried about her, and the second part worried about himself. Was he supposed to be happy that she'd wormed her way through his defenses? Was he supposed to jump for joy that in a matter of weeks she'd managed to drill a hole in the highly polished shield he'd maintained so expertly for over thirty years?

He didn't think so.

But he was willing to admit that he hadn't behaved well. He was even willing to offer a peace token in the form of vintage champagne and long-stemmed roses.

He'd packed the basket himself. Two bottles of Dom, well chilled, two crystal flutes—he wasn't about to insult that brilliant French monk with hotel glasses—the beluga he'd craftily hidden, for just such an occasion, inside an empty carton of plain low-fat yogurt, knowing that no one in his family would touch it.

He'd made the toast points himself and had selected both the blush-pink roses and the vase with care.

He thought she might be a tad resistant to the visit. It never hurt to pave the way with champagne and flowers. And since he intended to do a little worming himself, they couldn't hurt. He was going to loosen her up, he decided, talk to her, and more, get her talking. He wasn't leaving until he had a much clearer view on just who Sybill Griffin was.

He rapped cheerfully on her door. That was going to be his approach—casual cheer. He shot a quick, charming smile at the peephole when he heard footsteps, saw the vague, telltale shadow.

And he stood as those footsteps receded.

Okay. Maybe more than a tad resistant, he concluded, and knocked again. "Come on, Sybill. I know you're there. I want to talk to you."

Silence, he discovered, didn't have to be empty. It could be crowded with ice.

Okay, fine, he thought, scowling at the door. She wanted to do it the hard way.

He set the basket beside the door, then marched back down the hall to the fire stairs and started down. For what he had in mind it was wiser not to be seen leaving the lobby.

"Ticked her off good, didn't you?" Ray commented as he jogged down the steps beside his son.

"Christ almighty." Phillip glared into his father's face. "Next time why don't you just shoot me in the head? It'd be less embarrassing than to die of a heart attack at my age."

"Your heart's strong enough. So, she's not speaking to you."

"She'll talk to me," Phillip said grimly.

"Bribing with bubbly?" Ray jerked a thumb behind him.

"It works."

"The flowers are a good touch. I could usually get around your mother with flowers. Quicker if I groveled."

"I'm not groveling." On that he was firm. "It was just as much her fault."

"It's never just as much their fault," Ray said with a wink. "The sooner you accept that, the sooner you'll get makeup sex."

"Jesus, Dad." He could only rub a hand over his face. "I'm not going to talk to you about sex."

"Why not? Wouldn't be the first time." He sighed as they came to the ground level. "Seems to me your mother and I talked to you plenty, and talked to you straight, about sex. Gave you your first condoms, too."

"That was then," Phillip muttered. "I've got the hang of it now."

Ray let out a rippling, delighted laugh. "I bet you do. But then again, sex isn't the prime motive here. It's always a motive," he added. "We're men, we can't help it. Lady up there, she's got you worried, though, because it's not just about sex. It's about love."

"I'm not in love with her. Exactly. I'm just . . . involved."

"Love always was a tough one for you." Ray stepped out into the windy night, zipped up the frayed sideline jacket he wore over his jeans. "When it came to females, that is. Anytime things started to head toward serious, you'd start moving fast and loose in the opposite direction." He grinned at Phillip. "Looks to me like you're moving straight ahead this time."

"She's Seth's aunt." Annoyance pricked at the back of his neck as he walked around the building. "If she's going to be part of his life, our lives, I need to understand her."

"Seth's part of it. But you slapped her back this morning because you were scared."

Phillip planted his feet, legs spread, rolled his shoulders as he studied Ray's face. "Number one, I can't believe I'm standing here arguing with you. Number two, it occurs to me that you were a hell of a lot better at letting me run my own life when you were alive than you are as a dead man.''

Ray only smiled. ''Well, I've got what you might call a broader point of view now. I want you happy, Phil. I'm not going to move on until I'm sure the people who matter to me are happy. I'm ready to move on,'' he said quietly. ''To be with your mother.''

''Have you—did you . . . How is she?''

''She's waiting for me.'' The glow slipped over Ray's face and into his eyes. ''And she's never been what you could call the waiting type.''

''I miss her, so much.''

''I know. So do I. She'd be flattered, and annoyed, too, that under it all you've never been willing to settle for less than the kind of woman she was.''

Staggered, because it was true, and a secret that he'd kept carefully locked up, Phillip stared. ''It's not that, not altogether that.''

''Part of that, then.'' Ray nodded. ''You have to find your own, Phil. And make your own. You're getting there. You did a fine job with Seth today. So did she,'' he said, glancing up at the light shining through Sybill's bedroom window. ''You make a fine team, even when you're pulling in different directions. That's because you both care, more than you might understand.''

''Did you know he was your grandson?''

''No. Not at first.'' He sighed now. ''When Gloria found me she hit me with all of it at once. I never knew about her, and there she was, shouting, swearing, accusing, demanding. Couldn't calm her down or make sense of it. Next thing I knew she'd gone to the dean with that story about how I'd molested her. She's a troubled young woman.''

''She's a bitch.''

Ray only moved his shoulders. ''If I'd known about her

sooner . . . well, that's done. I couldn't save Gloria, but I could save Seth. One look at him and I knew. So I paid her. Maybe that was wrong, but the boy needed me. It took me weeks to track down Barbara. All I wanted from her was confirmation. I wrote to her, three times. Even called Paris, but she wouldn't speak to me. I was still working on that when I had the accident. Stupid,'' he admitted. ''I let Gloria upset me. I was angry with her, myself, everything, worried about Seth, about how the three of you would take it when I explained it all. Driving too fast, not paying attention. Well.''

''We would have stood with you.''

''I know that. I let myself forget it, and that was stupid, too. Stella was gone, the three of you had your own lives, and I let myself brood, and forget. You're standing with Seth now, and that's more important.''

''We're nearly there. With Sybill adding her voice, the permanent guardianship's a given.''

''She's adding more than her voice, and she'll add more yet. She's stronger than she gives herself credit for. Than anyone gives her credit for.''

In a swift change of mood, Ray clucked his tongue, shook his head. ''I guess you're going up there.''

''That's the plan.''

''Never quite lost that unfortunate skill. Maybe this time that's a good thing. That girl could use some surprises in her life.'' Ray winked again. ''Watch your step.''

''You're not going to come up, are you?''

''No.'' Ray slapped Phillip's shoulder and let out a hearty laugh. ''Some things a father just doesn't need to see.''

''Good. But since you're here, make it easier for me. Give me a boost up to that first balcony.''

''Sure. They can't arrest me, can they?''

Ray cupped his hands, giving Phillip's foot a helpful push, then stood back to watch him make the climb. He watched, and he smiled. "I'm going to miss you," he said quietly and faded into shadows.

IN THE PARLOR, SYBILL CON-
centrated fiercely on her work. She didn't give a damn if it had been petty, unreasonable behavior to ignore Phillip's knock. She'd had enough emotional upheaval for one weekend. And besides, he'd given up quickly enough, hadn't he?

She listened to the wind rattle against her windows, set her teeth, and pounded the keyboard.

The import of internal news appears to outweigh that of the external. While television, newspapers, and other information sources are as readily available in the small community as they are in large urban areas, the actions and involvements of one's neighbors take precedent when the population is limited.

Information is passed on, with varying degrees of accuracy, through word of mouth. Gossip is an accepted form of communication. The network is admirably quick and efficient.

Disattending—the pretense of not hearing a private conversation in a public place—is not as prevalent in the small community as in the large city. However, in transient areas such as hotels, disattending is still a consistent and acceptable behavioral pattern. I would conclude that the reason for this is the regular comings and goings of outsiders in this type of area. Overt attention is paid, however, in other areas such as

Her fingers froze, her mouth dropped open, as she watched Phillip slide her terrace door open and step inside.

"What—"

"The locks on these things are pathetic," he said. He walked to the front door, opened it, and picked up the basket and vase of flowers he'd left there. "I figured I could risk these. We don't get a lot of thievery around here. You might want to add that to your notes." He set the vase of roses on her desk.

"You climbed up the building?" She could only stare at him, amazed.

"The wind's a bitch, too." He opened the basket, took out the first bottle. "I could use a drink. How about you?"

"You climbed up the building?"

"We've already established that." He opened the wine with an expert and muffled pop.

"You can't . . ." She gestured wildly. "Just break in here, open champagne."

"I just did." He poured two glasses and discovered it didn't do his ego any harm to have her gaping at him. "I'm sorry about this morning, Sybill." Smiling, he offered her a glass of champagne. "I was feeling pretty rough, and I took it out on you."

"So you apologize by breaking into my room."

"I didn't break anything. Besides, you weren't going to open the door, and the flowers wanted to be in here. So did I. Truce?" he said and waited.

He'd climbed up the building. She still couldn't get over it. No one had ever committed such a bold and foolish act for her. She stared at him, into those golden angel eyes, and felt herself softening. "I have work."

He grinned because he saw the yielding. "I have beluga."

She tapped her fingers on the wrist rest of her keyboard. "Flowers, champagne, caviar. Do you usually come so well equipped when you break and enter?"

"Only when I want to apologize and throw myself on the mercy of a beautiful woman. Got any mercy to spare, Sybill?"

"I suppose I might. I wasn't keeping Gloria's phone call from you, Phillip."

"I know you weren't. Believe me, if I hadn't figured that out myself, Cam would have beaten it into my head this morning."

"Cam." She blinked in shock. "He doesn't like me."

"You're wrong. He was worried about you. Can I persuade you to take a break from work?"

"All right." She saved her file, shut down the machine. "I'm glad we're not angry with each other. It only complicates things. I saw Seth this afternoon."

"So I hear."

She accepted the wine, sipped. "Did you and your brothers clean up the house?"

He gave her a pained and pitiful look. "I don't want to talk about it. I'm going to have nightmares as it is." He took her hand, drew her over to the sofa. "Let's talk about something less frightening. Seth showed me the charcoal sketch of his boat that you helped him with."

"He's really good. He catches on so quickly. Really listens, pays attention. He's got a fine eye for detail and perspective."

"I saw the one you did of the house, too." Casually, Phillip leaned forward for the bottle and topped off her wine. "You're really good, too. I'm surprised you didn't pursue art as a profession."

"I had lessons as a girl. Art, music, dance. I took a few courses in college." Desperately relieved that they were no longer at odds, she settled back and enjoyed her wine. "It wasn't anything serious. I'd always known I'd go into psychology."

"Always?"

"More or less. The arts aren't for people like me."

"Why?"

The question confused her, put her on guard. "It wasn't practical. Did you say you had beluga in there?"

There, he thought, the first step back. He'd simply have to go around her. "Mmm-hmm." He took out the container and the toast points, refilled her glass. "What instrument do you play?"

"Piano."

"Yeah? Me, too." He shot her an easy smile. "We'll have to work up a duet. My parents loved music. All of us play something."

"It's important that a child learn to appreciate music."

"Sure, it's fun." He spread a toast point, offered it. "Sometimes the five of us would kill a Saturday night playing together."

"You all played together? That was nice. I always hated playing in front of anyone. It's so easy to make a mistake."

"So what if you did? Nobody's going to cut off your fingers for hitting a sour note."

"My mother would be mortified, and that would be worse than—" She caught herself, frowned into her wine, started to set it aside. He moved smoothly, adding more to her glass.

"My mother really loved to play the piano. That's why I picked it up at first. I wanted to share something with her specifically. I was so in love with her. We all were, but for me she was everything strong and right and kind about women. I wanted her to be proud of me. Whenever I saw that she was, whenever she told me she was, it was the most amazing feeling."

"Some people strive all their lives for their parents' approval and never come close to gaining their pride." There was something bitter and cold in her voice. She caught it herself and managed a weak laugh. "I'm drinking too much. It's going to my head."

Deliberately he filled her glass again. "You're among friends."

"Overindulging in alcohol—even lovely alcohol—is an abuse."

"Overindulging on a regular basis is an abuse," he corrected. "Ever been drunk, Sybill?"

"Of course not."

"You're due." He tapped his glass to hers. "Tell me about the first time you tasted champagne."

"I don't remember. We were often served watered wine at dinner when we were children. It was important that we learn to appreciate the proper wines, how they were served, what to serve them with, the correct glass for red, the correct glass for white. I could easily have coordinated a formal dinner party for twenty when I was twelve."

"Really?"

She laughed a little, let the wine froth in her head. "It's an important skill. Can you imagine the horror if one bungles the seating? Or serves an inferior wine with the main course? An evening in ruins, reputations in tatters. People expect a certain level of tedium at such affairs, but not a substandard Merlot."

"You attended a lot of formal dinner parties?"

"Yes, indeed. First, several smaller, what you might term 'practice' ones with intimates of my parents, so that I could be judged ready. When I was sixteen, my mother gave a large, important dinner for the French ambassador and his wife. That was my first official appearance. I was terrified."

"Not enough practice?"

"Oh, I had plenty of practice, hours of instruction on protocol. I was just so painfully shy."

"Were you?" he murmured, tucking her hair behind her ear. Score one for Mother Crawford, he thought.

"So silly. But any time I had to face people that way, my stomach would seize up and my heart would pound so hard. I lived in terror that I would spill something, say something I shouldn't, or have nothing to say at all."

"Did you tell your parents?"

"Tell them what?"

"That you were afraid?"

"Oh." She waved her hand at that, as if it were the most absurd of questions, then picked up the bottle to pour more champagne. "What would be the point? I had to do what was expected of me."

"Why? What would happen if you didn't? Would they beat you, lock you in a closet?"

"Of course not. They weren't monsters. They'd be disappointed, they'd disapprove. It was horrible when they looked at you that way—tight-lipped, cold-eyed—as if you were defective. It was easier just to get through it, and after a while, you learned how to deal with it."

"Observe rather than participate," he said quietly.

"I've made a good career out of it. Maybe I didn't fulfill my obligations by making an important marriage and giving a lifetime of those beastly dinner parties and raising a pair of well-behaved, properly bred children," she said with rising heat. "But I made good use of my education and a good career, which I'm certainly more suited for than the other. I'm out of wine."

"Let's slow down a little—"

"Why?" She laughed and plucked out the second bottle herself. "We're among friends. I'm getting drunk, and I think I like it."

What the hell, Phillip thought and took the bottle from her to open it. He'd wanted to dig under that proper and polished surface of hers. Now that he was there, there was no point in backing off.

"But you were married once," he reminded her.

"I told you it didn't count. It was *not* an important marriage. It was an impulse, a small and failed attempt at rebellion. I make a poor rebel. Mmm." She swallowed champagne, gestured with her glass. "I was supposed to marry one of the sons of my father's associate from Britain."

"Which one?"

"Oh, either. They were both quite acceptable. Distant relations of the queen. My mother was quite determined to have her daughter associated by marriage with royalty. It would have been a triumph. Of course I was only fourteen, so she had plenty of time to work out the plan, the timing. I believe she'd decided I could become engaged, formally, to one or the other when I was eighteen. Marriage at twenty, first child at twenty-two. She had it all worked out.''

''But you didn't cooperate.''

''I didn't get the chance. I might very well have cooperated. I found it very difficult to oppose her.'' She brooded over that for a moment, then washed it away with more champagne. ''But Gloria seduced them both, at the same time, in the front parlor while my parents were attending the opera. I believe it was Vivaldi. Anyway . . .'' She waved her hand again, drank again. ''They came home, found this situation. There was quite a scene. I snuck downstairs and watched part of it. They were naked—not my parents.''

''Naturally.''

''High on something, too. There was a lot of shouting, threatening, pleading—this from the Oxford twins. Did I mention they were twins?''

''No, you didn't.''

''Identical. Blond, pale, lantern-jawed. Gloria didn't give two damns about them, of course. She did it, knowing they'd be caught, because my mother had chosen them for me. She hated me. Gloria, not my mother.'' Her brow knit. ''My mother didn't hate me.''

''What happened?''

''The twins were sent home in disgrace and Gloria was punished. Which led, inevitably, to her striking back by accusing my father's friend of seducing her, which led to another miserable scene and her finally running off. It was certainly less disruptive with her gone, but it gave my parents more time to concentrate on forging me. I used to wonder why they saw me more as creation than child. Why they couldn't love me. But then . . .'' She settled back again. ''I'm not very lovable. No one's ever loved me.''

Aching for her, the woman and the child, he set his glass aside and framed her face gently with his hands. ''You're wrong.''

''No, I'm not.'' Her smile was soaked in wine. ''I'm a professional. I know these things. My parents never loved me, certainly Gloria didn't. The husband, who didn't count, didn't love me. There wasn't even one of those kindly, good-hearted servants you read about in books, who held me against her soft, generous bosom and loved me. No one even bothered to pretend enough to use the words. You, on the other hand, are very lovable.'' She ran her free hand up his chest. ''I've never had sex when I've been drunk. What do you suppose it's like?''

''Sybill.'' He caught her hand before she could distract him. ''They underestimated and undervalued you. You shouldn't do the same to yourself.''

''Phillip.'' She leaned forward, managed to nip his bottom lip between her teeth. ''My life's been a predictable bore. Until you. The first time you kissed me, my mind just clicked off. No one ever did that to me before. And when you touch me . . .'' Slowly she brought their joined hand to her breast. ''My skin gets hot and my heart pounds, and my insides get loose and liquid. You climbed up the building.'' Her mouth roamed over his jaw. ''You brought me roses. You wanted me, didn't you?''

''Yes, I wanted you, but not just—''

''Take me.'' She let her head fall back so she could look into those wonderful eyes. ''I've never said that to a man before. Imagine that. Take me, Phillip.'' And the words were part plea, part promise. ''Just take me.''

The empty glass slipped out of her fingers as she wrapped her arms around him. Helpless to resist, he lowered her to the sofa. And took.

. . .

THE DULL ACHE BEHIND HER eyes, the more lively one dancing inside her temples, was no more than she deserved, Sybill decided as she tried to drown both of them under the hot spray of the shower.

She would never, as God was her witness, overindulge in any form of alcohol again.

She only wished the aftermath of drink had resulted in memory loss as well, as a hangover. But she remembered, much too clearly, the way she'd prattled on about herself. The things she'd told Phillip. Humiliating, private things, things she rarely even told herself.

Now she had to face him. She had to face him and the fact that in one short weekend she had wept in his arms, then had given him both her body and her most carefully guarded secrets.

And she had to face the fact that she was hopelessly, and dangerously, in love with him.

Which was totally irrational, of course. The very fact that she believed she could have developed such strong feelings for him in such a short amount of time and association was precisely why those emotions were hopeless. And dangerous.

Obviously she wasn't thinking clearly. This barrage of feelings that had tumbled into her so quickly made it all but impossible to maintain an objective distance and analyze.

Once Seth was settled, once all the details were arranged, she would have to find that distance again. The simplest and most logical method was to begin with geographical distance and go back to New York.

Undoubtedly she would come to her senses once she'd picked up the threads of her own life again and slipped back into a comfortable, familiar routine.

However miserably dull that seemed just now.

She took the time to brush her wet hair back from her face, to carefully cream her skin, adjust the lapels of her robe. If she couldn't quite take full advantage of her breathing techniques to compose herself, it was hardly any wonder, what with the drag of the hangover.

But she stepped out of the bathroom with her features calmly arranged, then walked into the parlor, where Phillip was just pouring coffee from the room service tray.

"I thought you could use this."

"Yes, thank you." She carefully censored her gaze to avoid the empty champagne bottle and the scatter of clothing that she'd been too drunk to pick up the night before.

"Did you take any aspirin?"

"Yes. I'll be fine." She said it stiffly, accepted the cup of coffee and sat with the desperate care of an invalid. She knew she was pale, hollow-eyed. She'd gotten a good look at herself in the steamy mirror.

And she got a good look at Phillip now. He wasn't pale at all, she noted, nor was he hollow-eyed.

A lesser woman would despise him for it.

As she sipped her coffee and studied him, her muddled mind began to clear. How many times, she wondered, had he refilled her glass the night before? How many times had he refilled his own? It seemed to her there was a wide discrepancy between the two.

Resentment began to stir as she watched him generously heap jam on a piece of toast. Even the thought of food had her shaky stomach lurching.

"Hungry?" she said sweetly.

"Starving." He took the lid off a plate of scrambled eggs. "You should try to eat a little."

She'd rather die. "Sleep well?"

"Yeah."

"And aren't we bright-eyed and chipper this morning?"

He caught the tone, slanted her a cautious look. He'd

wanted to take it slow, give her some time to recover before they discussed anything. But it appeared that she was recovering rapidly.

"You had a little more to drink than I did," he began.

"You got me drunk. It was deliberate. You charmed your way in here and started pouring champagne into me."

"I hardly held your nose and poured it down your throat."

"You used an apology as an excuse." Her hands began to shake, so she slammed the coffee onto the table. "You must have known I'd be angry with you, and you thought you'd just ease your way into my bed with Dom Perignon."

"The sex was your idea," he reminded her, insulted. "I wanted to talk to you. And the fact is, I got more out of you after you were buzzed than I ever would have otherwise. So I loosened you up." And damn if he was going to feel guilty over it. "And you let me in."

"Loosened me up," she whispered, getting slowly to her feet.

"I wanted to know who you are. I have a right to know."

"You—you did plan it. You planned to come in here, to charm me into drinking just a little too much so you could pry into my personal life."

"I care about you." He moved toward her, but she slapped his hand away.

"Don't. I'm not stupid enough to fall for that again."

"I do care about you. And now I know more, and understand more about you. What's wrong with that, Sybill?"

"You tricked me."

"Maybe I did." He took her arms, keeping a firm grip when she tried to pull back. "Just hold on. You had a privileged, structured childhood. I didn't. You had advantages, servants, culture. I didn't. Do you think less of me because until I was twelve I ran the streets?"

"No. But this has nothing to do with that."

"No one loved me either," he continued. "Not until I was

twelve. So I know what it's like on both sides. Do you expect me to think less of you because you survived the cold?"

"I'm not going to discuss it."

"That's not going to work anymore. Here's emotion for you, Sybill." He brought his mouth down on hers, dragging her into the kiss, into the swirl. "Maybe I don't know what to do about it yet either. But it's there. You've seen my scars. They're right out there. Now I've seen yours."

He was doing it again, making her weaken and want. She could rest her head on his shoulder, have his arms come around to hold her. She only had to ask. And couldn't.

"There's no need to feel sorry for me."

"Oh, baby." Gently this time, he touched his lips to hers. "Yes, there is. And I admire what you managed to become despite it all."

"I was drinking too much," she said quickly. "I made my parents sound cold and unfeeling."

"Did either of them ever tell you they loved you?"

She opened her mouth, then sighed. "We simply weren't a demonstrative family. Not every family is like yours. Not every family shows their feelings and touches and . . ." She trailed off, hearing the trace of panicked defense in her own voice. For what, she wondered wearily. For whom?

"No, neither of them ever said that to me. Or to Gloria, as far as I know. And any decent therapist would conclude that their children reacted to this restrictive, overly formal, and demanding atmosphere by choosing different extremes. Gloria chose wild behavior as a bid for attention. I conformed in a bid for approval. She equated sex with affection and power and fantasized about being desired and forced by men in authority, including her legal and her biological fathers. I avoided intimacy in sex out of fear of failure and selected a field of study where I could safely observe behavior without risk of emotional involvement. Is that clear enough?"

"The operative word, I'd say, is 'chose.' She chose to hurt, you chose not to be hurt."

"That's accurate."

"But you haven't been able to keep it up. You risked being hurt with Seth. And you're risking being hurt with me." He touched her cheek. "I don't want to hurt you, Sybill."

It was very likely too late to prevent that, she thought, but she gave in enough to rest her head on his shoulder. She didn't have to ask for his arms to come around her. "Let's just see what happens next," she decided.

TWENTY

Fear, Sybill wrote, *is a common human emotion. And being human, it is as complex and difficult to analyze as love and hate, greed, passion. Emotions, and their causes and effects, are not my particular field of study. Behavior is both learned and instinctive and very often contains no true emotional root. Behavior is much more simple, if no more basic, than emotion.*

    I'm afraid.

    I'm alone in this hotel, a grown woman, educated, intelligent, sensible, and capable. Yet I'm afraid to pick up the phone on the desk and call my own mother.

    A few days ago, I wouldn't have termed it fear, but reluctance, perhaps avoidance. A few days ago I would have argued, and argued well, that contact with her over the issue of Seth would only cause disruption in the order of things and produce no constructive results. Therefore, contact would be useless.

    A few days ago, I could have rationalized that my feelings for Seth stemmed from a sense of moral and familial obligation.

A few days ago, I could, and did, refuse to acknowledge my envy of the Quinns with their noisy and unstructured and undisciplined interactive behavior. I would have admitted that their behavior and their unorthodox relationship were interesting, but never would I have admitted that I had a yearning to somehow slip into that pattern and become part of it.

Of course, I can't. I accept that.

A few days ago, I attempted to refute the depth and the meaning of my feelings for Phillip. Love, I told myself, does not come so quickly or so intensely. This is attraction, desire, even lust, but not love. It's easier to refute than to face. I'm afraid of love, of what it demands, what it asks, what it takes. And I'm more afraid, much more, of not being loved in return.

Still, I can accept this. I understand perfectly the limitations of my relationship with Phillip. We are both adults who have made our own patterns and our own choices. He has his needs and his life, as I do mine. I can be grateful that our paths crossed. I've learned a great deal in the short time I've known him. A great deal I've learned has been about myself.

I don't believe I'll be quite the same as I was.

I don't want to be. But in order to change, truly, to grow, there are actions that must be taken.

It helps to write this out, even though the order and sense are faulty.

Phillip called just now from Baltimore. I thought he sounded tired, yet excited. He had a meeting with his attorney about his father's life insurance claim. For months now, the insurance company has refused to settle. They instigated an investigation into Professor Quinn's death and held off paying the claim over the suspicion of suicide. Financially, of course, it put a strain on the Quinns with Seth to provide for and a new business to run, but they have doggedly pursued legal action over this issue.

I don't think I realized until today how vital it is to them to win this battle. Not for the money, as I originally assumed, but to clear any shadow on their father's name. I don't believe suicide is always an act of cowardice. I once considered it myself. Had the proper note written, the necessary pills in my hand. But I was only sixteen and understandably foolish. Naturally I tore the letter up, disposed of the pills, and put the matter aside.

Suicide would have been rude. Inconvenient for my family.

Doesn't that sound bitter? I had no idea I'd harbored all this anger.

But the Quinns, I've learned, considered the taking of one's own life selfish, cowardly. They have refused all along to accept or to allow others to believe that this man they love so much was capable of such a singular selfish act. Now, it appears, they will win this battle.

The insurance company has offered to settle. Phillip believes my deposition may have swayed them toward this response. He may be right. Of course, the Quinns are, perhaps genetically, ill-suited to settlements. All or nothing, is precisely how Phillip put it to me. He believes, as does his attorney, that they will have all very shortly.

I'm happy for them. Though I never had the privilege of meeting Raymond and Stella Quinn, I feel I know them through my association with their family. Professor Quinn deserves to rest in peace. Just as Seth deserves to take the Quinn name and to have the security of a family who will love and care for him.

I can do something to ensure that all of that happens. I will have to make this call. I will have to take a stand. Oh, my hands shake just at the possibility. I'm such a

*coward. No, Seth would call me a wimp. That's some-
how worse.*

*She terrifies me. There it is in black and white. My
own mother terrifies me. She never raised a hand to me,
rarely raised her voice, yet she shoved me into a mold
of her own making. I barely struggled.*

My father? He was too busy being important to notice.

Oh, yes, I see a great deal of anger here.

*I can call her, I can use the very status that she in-
sisted I achieve to gain what I want from her. I'm a
respected scientist, in some small way a public figure. If
I tell her I'll use that, if I make her believe I will, unless
she provides a written statement to the Quinns' attorney,
detailing the circumstances of Gloria's birth, admitting
that Professor Quinn attempted several times to contact
her for verification of Gloria's paternity, she will despise
me. But she will do it.*

*I only have to pick up the phone to do for Seth what
I failed to do years ago. I can give him a home, a family,
and the knowledge that he has nothing to fear.*

"SON OF A BITCH." PHILLIP
wiped sweat off his forehead with the back of his hand. Blood
from a nasty but shallow scrape smeared over his skin. He
grinned like an idiot at the hull he and his brothers had just
turned. "That's a big bastard."

"It's a beautiful bastard." Cam rolled his aching shoulders.
The turning of the hull meant more than progress. It meant
success. Boats by Quinn was doing it again, and they were
doing it right.

"She's got a fine line." Ethan ran a calloused hand over
the planking. "A pretty shape to her."

"When I start thinking a hull looks sexy," Cam decided.

"I'm going home to my wife. Well, we can score her waterline and get back to work, or we can just admire her for a while."

"You score her waterline," Phillip suggested. "I'm going up and running the paperwork for the draw. It's time to hit your old racing pal up for some cash. We can use it."

"You cut the paychecks?" Ethan asked him.

"Yeah."

"Yours?"

"I don't—"

"Need it," Cam finished. "Cut one anyway, goddamn it. Buy your sexy lady some bauble with it. Blow it on some overpriced wine or lay it on the throw of the dice. But cut your check this week." He studied the hull again. "It means something this week."

"Maybe it does," Phillip agreed.

"The insurance company's going to fold their hand," Cam added. "We're going to win there."

"People are already changing their tune." Ethan rubbed a layer of sawdust off the planking. "The ones who wanted to whistle lies under their breath. We've already won there. You worked the hardest to make sure we did," he said to Phillip.

"I'm just the detail man. Either one of you tried to have more than a five-minute conversation with a lawyer . . . well, you'd nod off from boredom, Ethan, and Cam would end up punching him. I won by default."

"Maybe." Cam grinned at him. "But you skated out of a lot of the real work by talking on the phone, writing letters, zinging off faxes. It just comes down to you being secretary. Without the great legs and ass."

"Not only is that sexist, but I do have great legs and a terrific ass."

"Oh, yeah? Let's see 'em." He moved fast, diving and taking Phillip down onto that reputedly terrific ass.

Foolish scrambled up from his nap by the lumber and raced over to join in.

"Christ! Are you crazy!" Laughter prevented Phillip from rolling free. "Get off me, you moron."

"Give me a hand here, Ethan." Cam grinned, swearing as Foolish lapped eagerly at his face. Phillip struggled half-heartedly when Cam sat on him. "Come on," he urged when Ethan merely shook his head. "When's the last time you pantsed somebody?"

"Been a while." Ethan considered as Phillip began to struggle in earnest. "Maybe the last time was Junior Crawford at his bachelor party."

"Well, that's ten years ago, anyway." Cam grunted as Phillip nearly succeeded in bucking him off. "Come on, he's put on some muscle the last few months. And he's feisty."

"Maybe for old time's sake." Getting into the spirit, Ethan evaded a couple of well-aimed kicks and got a firm hold on the waistband of Phillip's jeans.

"Excuse me," was the best Sybill could manage when she walked in on air blue with curses and the sight of Phillip being held down on the beaten-wood floor while his brothers . . . well, she couldn't quite tell what they were trying to do.

"Hey." Cam avoided a fist to the jaw, barely, and grinned hugely at her. "Want to give us a hand? We're just trying to get his pants off. He was bragging about his legs."

"I . . . hmmm."

"Let him up now, Cam. You're embarrassing her."

"Hell, Ethan, she's seen his legs before." But without Ethan lending his weight, it was either let go or get bloody. It seemed simpler, if less fun, to let go. "We'll finish up later."

"My brothers forgot they're out of high school." Phillip got to his feet, brushing off his jeans and his dignity. "They were feeling a little rambunctious because we turned the hull."

"Oh." She shifted her attention to the boat, and her eyes widened. "You've made so much progress."

"It's got a ways to go yet." Ethan studied it himself, visualizing it complete. "Deck, cabin, bridge, belowdecks. Man wants a damn hotel suite in there."

"As long as he's paying for it." Phillip crossed to Sybill, ran a hand down her hair. "Sorry I got in too late to see you last night."

"That's all right. I know you've been busy with work and the lawyer." She shifted her purse from hand to hand. "Actually I have something that may help. With the lawyer, with both situations. Well . . ."

She reached into her purse and took out a manila envelope. "It's a statement from my mother. Two copies, both notarized. I had her overnight them. I didn't want to say anything until they'd arrived, and I'd read them to see . . . I think they'll be useful."

"What's the deal?" Cam demanded as Phillip quickly skimmed the neatly typed two-page statement.

"It confirms that Gloria was Dad's biological daughter. That he was unaware of it and that he attempted to contact Barbara Griffin several times during a period from last December to this March. There's a letter from Dad written to her in January, telling her about Seth, his agreement with Gloria to take custody."

"I read your father's letter," Sybill told him. "Perhaps I shouldn't have, but I did. If he was angry with my mother, it didn't show in the words. He just wanted her to tell him if it was true. He was going to help Seth anyway, but he wanted to be able to give him his birthright. A man who worried that much about a child would hardly have taken his own life. He had too much to give, and was too ready to give it. I'm so sorry."

" 'He just needs a chance, and a choice,' " Ethan read when Phillip passed the letters to him, then cleared his throat. " 'I couldn't give one to Gloria, if she's mine, and she won't take it now. But I'll see that Seth has both. Whether he's mine by blood or not, he's mine nonetheless now.' It sounds like him. Seth should read this."

"Why did she agree to this now, Sybill?" Phillip asked her.

"I convinced her that it was best for all concerned."

"No." He caught her chin in his hand, lifted her face to his. "There's more. I know there is."

"I promised her that her name, and the details, would be kept as private as possible." She made a restless little movement, then let out a breath. "And I threatened to write a book telling the entire story if she didn't do this."

"You blackmailed her," Phillip said with stunned admiration.

"I gave her a choice. She chose this one."

"It was hard for you."

"It was necessary."

Now he put both of his hands on her face, gently. "It was hard, and brave, and brilliant."

"Logical," she began, then shut her eyes. "And yes, hard. She and my father are very angry. They may not forgive me. They're capable of not forgiving."

"They don't deserve you."

"The point is Seth deserves you, so . . ." She trailed off as he closed his mouth over hers.

"Okay, move aside." Cam elbowed Phillip away and took Sybill by the shoulders. "You did good," he said, then kissed her with a firmness that made her blink.

"Oh," was all she managed.

"Your turn," Cam stated, then gave her a gentle nudge toward Ethan.

"My parents would have been proud of you." He kissed her in turn, then patted her shoulders when her eyes filled.

"Oh, no, don't let her do that." Instantly, Cam took her arm and pulled her back to Phillip. "No crying in here, no crying allowed in the boatyard."

"Cam gets jittery when women cry."

"I'm not crying."

"They always say that," Cam muttered, "but they never mean it. Outside. Anybody who cries has to do it outside. It's a new rule."

Chuckling, Phillip pulled Sybill toward the door. "Come on. I want a minute alone with you anyway."

"I'm not crying. I just never expected your brothers to . . . it's not usual for me to be—" She stopped herself. "It's very nice to be shown you're appreciated and liked."

"I appreciate you." He drew her close. "I like you."

"And it's very nice." She indulged in the luxury of both. "I've already spoken with your attorney and with Anna. I didn't want to fax the papers from the hotel as I did give my word the contents would be kept private. But both of them agree that this last document should move everything along. Anna believes that your petition for permanent guardianship will go through as early as next week."

"That soon?"

"There's nothing in the way of it. You and your brothers are Professor Quinn's legal sons. Seth is his grandchild. His mother agreed, in writing, to transfer custody. Reneging on that might stall the decree, but no one believes at this point that it would change it. Seth is eleven, and at his age his desires would be taken into account. Anna's going to push for a hearing early next week."

"It seems strange, it all coming together like this. All at once."

"Yes." She looked up as a flock of geese swept overhead. Seasons change, she thought. "I thought I would walk down to the school. I'd like to talk to him, tell him some of this myself."

"I think that's a good idea. You timed it well."

"I'm good at schedules."

"How about scheduling a family meal tonight at the Quinns, to celebrate?"

"Yes, all right. I'll walk him back here."

"Great. Hold on a minute." He went back inside, returning moments later with a very energetic Foolish on a red leash. "He could use a walk, too."

"Oh, well, I . . ."

"He knows the way. All you have to do is hold on to this end." Amused, Phillip stuck the leash in her hand, then watched her eyes go wide as Foolish made his dash. "Tell him to heel," Phillip shouted as Sybill trotted after the dog. "He won't, but it'll sound like you know what you're doing."

"This is not funny." She muttered it as she jogged awkwardly after Foolish. "Slow down. Heel! God."

He not only slowed, but stopped, burying his nose in a hedge with such determination she was terrified he would race through it and take her with him. But he only lifted his leg and looked immensely pleased with himself.

By her count, he lifted his leg eight times before they turned the corner down from the school and she caught sight of the buses. "What kind of a bladder do you have?" she demanded, looking hopefully for Seth while she struggled to cling to the leash and prevent Foolish from rocketing toward the crowd of children pouring out of the building. "No. Sit. Stay. You might bite someone."

Foolish slanted her a look that seemed to say, Please, get serious. But he sat, smacking her heels rhythmically with his tail. "He'll be along in a minute," she began, then let out a yelp as Foolish leaped up and raced forward. He'd spotted Seth first and was running on love.

"No, no, no, no," Sybill panted uselessly just as Seth caught sight of them. He let out a yelp himself, of pure joy, and dashed toward the dog as if they'd been cruelly separated for years.

"Hey! Hi!" Seth laughed as Foolish made one adoring leap and bathed his face. "How's it going, boy? Good dog. You're a good dog." Belatedly, he looked over at Sybill. "Hey."

"Hey, yourself. Here." She shoved the leash into his hand. 'Not that he pays any attention to it."

"We've kind of had trouble with leash training."

"No kidding." But she managed a smile now to include Seth and Danny and Will when they hurried up behind him. 'I thought I'd walk back to the boatyard with you. I wanted o talk to you."

"Sure, that's cool."

She stepped determinedly out of Foolish's path, then quickly back again as a bright-red sports car screamed up to he curb and stopped with a wild squeal of brakes. Before she could snarl at the driver that he was in a school zone, she saw Gloria in the passenger seat.

Sybill's movement was fast and instinctive. She put Seth protectively behind her.

"Well, well, well," Gloria drawled and eyed them both out of the window.

"Go get your brothers," Sybill ordered Seth. "Go right now."

But he couldn't move. He could only stand and stare while he fear settled in his stomach like balls of ice. "I won't go with her. I won't go. I won't."

"No, you won't." She took his hand firmly in hers. 'Danny, Will, run to the boatyard right now. Tell the Quinns we need them. Hurry. Go straight there."

She heard the smack of running sneakers on the sidewalk but didn't look. She kept her eyes trained on her sister as Gloria slipped out of the car.

"Hey, kid. Miss me?"

"What do you want, Gloria?"

"Everything I can get." She fisted a hand on the hip of her lipstick-red jeans and winked at Seth. "Wanna go for a ide, kiddo? We can do some catching up."

"I'm not going anywhere with you." He wished he had un. He had a place in the woods, a place he'd picked out and fixed up. A hiding place. But it was too far away. Then he felt Sybill's hand, warm and strong on his. "I'm not ever going with you again."

"You'll do what the hell I tell you." Fury flashed in her eyes as she started forward. For the first time in his life, Foolish bared his teeth and growled a vicious threat. "Call off that fucking dog."

"No," Sybill said it simply, quietly, and felt a surge of love for Foolish. "I'd keep my distance, Gloria. He'll bite." She scanned the car, the leather-jacketed man behind its wheel beating a rhythm on the dash to the blasting radio. "It looks like you landed on your feet."

"Yeah, Pete's okay. We're heading out to California. He's got connections. I need cash."

"You're not going to get it here."

Gloria pulled out a cigarette, smiling at Sybill as she lit it. "Look, I don't want the kid, but I'm going to take him unless I get a stake. The Quinns'll pay to get him back. Everybody's happy, no harm done. If you mess with me on this, Syb, I'm going to tell Pete to get out of the car."

Foolish shifted from growling to snarling. Sharp canine teeth bared. Sybill raised a brow. "Go ahead. Tell him."

"I want what's due me, goddamn it."

"You've had more than your due all your life."

"Bullshit! It was you who got everything. The perfect daughter. I hate your fucking guts. I've hated you all my life." She grabbed Sybill by the front of her jacket and all but spit in her face. "I wish you were dead."

"I know that. Now take your hands off me."

"You think you can make me?" With a laugh, Gloria shoved Sybill back a step. "You never had the guts before, did you? You'll take it, and you'll take it, and you'll give me what I want, just like always. Shut that dog up!" she shouted at Seth as Foolish strained at the leash and snapped wildly. "Shut him up and get in the goddamn car before I—"

Sybill didn't see her own hand come up, didn't realize the order had gone from her brain to her arm. But she felt her muscles tighten, her rage erupt, and then Gloria was sprawled on the ground gaping at her.

"You get in the goddamn car," she said evenly, not even looking at the Jeep that screeched up to the curb. Not blinking when Foolish dragged himself and Seth closer and growled low in his throat at the woman on the ground. "You go to California, or you go to hell, but you stay away from this boy, and you stay away from me. Keep out of this," she snapped at Phillip as he and his brothers burst out of the Jeep.

"Get in the car and go, Gloria, or I'll pay you back right now for everything you ever did to Seth. Everything you ever did to me. Get up and go, or when the cops get here to take you in for jumping bail, when we add charges of child abuse and extortion, there won't be much left of you to put in a cell."

When Gloria didn't move, Sybill reached down and, with a strength born of fury, hauled her to her feet. "Get in the car and go, and don't ever try to get near this boy again. You won't get through me, Gloria. I swear to you."

"I don't want the damn kid. I just want some money."

"Cut your losses. I'm not going to bother holding that dog or the Quinns back after another thirty seconds. Want to take all of us on?"

"Gloria, are you coming or not?" The driver flicked his cigarette out the car window. "I don't have all day to hang around this bumfuck town."

"Yeah, I'm coming." She tossed her head. "You're welcome to him. All he ever did was slow me down and get in my way. I'm going to score big in L.A. I don't need anything from you."

"Good," Sybill murmured as Gloria climbed back in the car. "Because you'll never get anything from me again."

"You knocked her down." Seth wasn't shaking, nor was

he pale now. As the sports car shrieked away, the look he sent Sybill was filled with gratitude, and with awe. "You knocked her down."

"I guess I did. Are you all right?"

"She never even looked at me, really. Foolish was going to bite her."

"He's a wonderful dog." When he leaped on her now, she pressed her face into the warmth of his neck. "He's a fabulous dog."

"But you knocked her down. Sybill knocked her right on her butt," he shouted as Phillip and his brothers walked over.

"So I saw." Phillip put a hand to her cheek. "Nice going, champ. How do you feel?"

"I feel . . . fine," she realized. No cramping, no chills, no sick headache. "I feel just fine." Then she blinked as Seth threw his arms around her.

"You were great. She's never coming back. You scared the shit out of her."

The bubbly little laugh that rose into her throat caught her by surprise. Leaning down, she buried her face in Seth's hair. "Everything's just the way it's supposed to be now."

"Let's go home." Phillip slid his arm around her shoulders. "Let's all go home."

"HE'S GOING TO BE TELLING that story for days," Phillip decided. "Weeks."

"He's already embellishing on it." Amazingly serene, Sybill walked with Phillip by the water's edge while the heroic Foolish romped in the yard behind them with Simon. "The way he tells it now, I beat Gloria to a pulp and Foolish lapped up the blood."

"You don't sound all that displeased by it."

"I never knocked anyone down before in my life. Never

stood my ground that way. I wish I could say I did it all for Seth, but I think part of it was for me, too. She won't come back, Phillip. She lost. She is lost.''

"I don't think Seth will ever be afraid of her again."

"He's home. This is a good place." She turned in a circle to take in the trim house, the woods going deep with twilight, the last sparkle of the sun on the water. "I'll miss it when I'm back in New York."

"New York? You're not going for a while yet."

"Actually, I'm planning on going back right after the hearing next week." It was something she'd made up her mind on. She needed to resume her own life. Staying longer would accomplish nothing but adding to the emotional mess.

"Wait. Why?"

"I have work."

"You're working here." Where did the panic come from? he wondered. Who pushed the button?

"I have meetings with my publisher that I've put off. I need to get back. I can't live in a hotel forever, and Seth's settled now."

"He needs you around. He—"

"I'll visit. And I'm hoping he'll be allowed to come see me occasionally." She'd worked it all out in her head, and now she turned to smile at him. "I promised to take him to a Yankees game next spring."

It was as if it were already done, he realized, struggling against that panic. As if she were already gone. "You've talked to him about it."

"Yes, I thought I should let him know."

"And this is how you let me know?" he shot back. "It's been nice, pal, see you around?"

"I'm not sure I'm following."

"Nothing. Nothing to follow." He walked away. He wanted his own life back, too, didn't he? Here was his chance.

End of complications. All he had to do was wish her well and wave good-bye. ''That's what I want. It's always been what I wanted.''

''Excuse me?''

''I'm not looking for anything else. Neither one of us was.'' He whirled back to her, temper glinting in his eyes. ''Right?''

''I'm not sure what you mean.''

''You've got your life, I've got mine. We just followed the current, and here we are. Time to get out of the water.''

No, she decided, she wasn't following him. ''All right.''

''Well, then.'' Assuring himself that he was fine with it, he was calm. He was even pleased. He started back toward her.

The last of the sun shimmered over her hair, into those impossibly clear eyes, shadowed the hollow of her throat above the collar of her blouse. ''No.'' He heard himself say it, and his mouth went dry.

''No?''

''A minute, just one minute.'' He walked away again, this time to the edge of the water. He stood there, staring down like a man contemplating diving in well over his head. ''What's wrong with Baltimore?''

''Baltimore? Nothing.''

''It's got museums, good restaurants, character, theater.''

''It's a very nice city,'' Sybill said cautiously.

''Why can't you work there? If you have to go into New York for a meeting, you can hop the shuttle or the train. Hell, you can drive it in under four hours.''

''I'm sure that's true. If you're suggesting I relocate to Baltimore—''

''It's perfect. You'd still be living in the city, but you'd be able to see Seth whenever you wanted.''

And you, she thought, yearning toward the picture. But she shook her head. It would kill her to go on this way. And she knew it would spoil the happiness she'd had, the new self she'd discovered. ''It's just not practical, Phillip.''

"Of course it's practical." He turned around, strode back to her. "It's perfectly practical. What's impractical is going back to New York, putting up that distance again. It's not going to work, Sybill. It's just not going to work."

"There's no point in discussing it now."

"Do you think this is easy for me?" he exploded. "I *have* to stay here. I have commitments, responsibilities, to say nothing of roots. I've got no choice. Why can't you bend?"

"I don't understand."

"I have to spell it out? Damn it." He took her by the shoulders, gave her a quick, impatient shake. "Don't you get it? I love you. You can't expect me to let you walk away. You have to stay. The hell with your life and my life. Your family, my family. I want *our* life. I want *our* family."

She stared at him, the blood ringing in her ears. "What? What?"

"You heard what I said."

"You said . . . you said you loved me. Do you mean it?"

"No, I'm lying."

"I . . . I've already knocked one person down today. I can do it again." Just then, she thought she could do anything. Anything at all. It didn't matter if there was fury in his eyes, if his fingers were digging into her arms. If he looked fit to kill. She could handle this. She could handle him. She could handle anything.

"If you meant it," she said, her voice admirably cool. "I'd like you to say it again. I've never heard it before."

"I love you." Calming, he touched his lips to her brow. "I want you." To each temple. "I need you to stay with me." Then her mouth. "Give me more time to show you what we'll be like together."

"I know what we'll be like together. I want what we'll be like together." She let out a shuddering breath, resisted the urge to close her eyes. She needed to see his face, to remember it exactly as it was at this moment, with the sun sinking, the sky going peach and rose, and a flock of birds winging overhead. "I love you. I was afraid to tell you. I don't know why. I don't think I'm afraid of anything now. Are you going to ask me to marry you?"

"I was about to muddle my way through that part." On impulse, he pulled out the simple white band holding back her hair and tossed it over her shoulders where the dogs gave loud and delighted chase. "I want your hair in my hands," he murmured, threading his fingers through the thick, rich brown. "All my life I said I would never do this because there would never be a woman who would make me need to or want to. I was wrong. I found one. I found mine. Marry me, Sybill."

"All my life I said I would never do this because there would never be a man who'd need me or want me, or matter enough to make me want. I was wrong. I found you. Marry me, Phillip, and soon."

"How does next Saturday strike you?"

"Oh." Emotion flooded her heart, poured into it, out of it, warm and smooth and real. "Yes!" She leaped, throwing her arms around him.

He spun her in a circle, and for a moment, just for a flash, he thought he saw two figures standing on the dock. The man with silver hair and brilliantly blue eyes, the woman with freckles dancing over her face and wild red hair blowing in the evening breeze. Their hands were linked. They were there, then they were gone.

"This one counts," he murmured, holding her hard and close. "This one counts for both of us."

Can't get enough of Nora Roberts?
Try the #1 *New York Times* bestselling
In Death series, by Nora Roberts
writing as J. D. Robb.

Turn the page to see where it all began . . .

NAKED IN DEATH

SHE WOKE IN THE DARK. Through the slats on the window shades, the first murky hint of dawn slipped, slanting shadowy bars over the bed. It was like waking in a cell.

For a moment she simply lay there, shuddering, imprisoned, while the dream faded. After ten years on the force, Eve still had dreams.

Six hours before, she'd killed a man, had watched death creep into his eyes. It wasn't the first time she'd exercised maximum force, or dreamed. She'd learned to accept the action and the consequences.

But it was the child that haunted her. The child she hadn't been in time to save. The child whose screams had echoed in the dreams with her own.

All the blood, Eve thought, scrubbing sweat from her face with her hands. Such a small little girl to have had so much blood in her. And she knew it was vital that she push it aside.

Standard departmental procedure meant that she would spend the morning in Testing. Any officer whose discharge of weapon resulted in termination of life was required to undergo emotional and psychiatric clearance before resuming duty. Eve considered the tests a mild pain in the ass.

She would beat them, as she'd beaten them before.

When she rose, the overheads went automatically to low setting, lighting her way into the bath. She winced once at her reflection. Her eyes were swollen from lack of sleep, her skin nearly as pale as the corpses she'd delegated to the ME.

Rather than dwell on it, she stepped into the shower, yawning.

"Give me one oh one degrees, full force," she said and shifted so that the shower spray hit her straight in the face.

She let it steam, lathered listlessly while she played through the events of the night before. She wasn't due in Testing until nine, and would use the next three hours to settle and let the dream fade away completely.

Small doubts and little regrets were often detected and could mean a second and more intense round with the machines and the owl-eyed technicians who ran them.

Eve didn't intend to be off the streets longer than twenty-four hours.

After pulling on a robe, she walked into the kitchen and programmed her AutoChef for coffee, black; toast, light. Through her window she could hear the heavy hum of air traffic carrying early commuters to offices, late ones home. She'd chosen the apartment years before because it was in a heavy ground and air pattern, and she liked the noise and crowds. On another yawn, she glanced out the window, followed the rattling journey of an aging airbus hauling laborers not fortunate enough to work in the city or by home 'links.

She brought the *New York Times* up on her monitor and scanned the headlines while the faux caffeine bolstered her system. The AutoChef had burned her toast again, but she ate it anyway, with a vague thought of springing for a replacement unit.

She was frowning over an article on a mass recall of droid cocker spaniels when her telelink blipped. Eve shifted to communications and watched her commanding officer flash onto the screen.

"Commander."

"Lieutenant." He gave her a brisk nod, noted the still-wet hair and sleepy eyes. "Incident at Twenty-seven West Broadway, eighteenth floor. You're primary."

Eve lifted a brow. "I'm on Testing. Subject terminated at twenty-two thirty-five."

"We have override," he said, without inflection. "Pick up your shield and weapon on the way to the incident. Code Five, Lieutenant."

"Yes, sir." His face flashed off even as she pushed back from the screen. Code Five meant she would report directly to her commander, and there would be no unsealed interdepartmental reports and no cooperation with the press.

In essence, it meant she was on her own.

B ROADWAY WAS NOISY AND crowded, a party that rowdy guests never left. Street, pedestrian, and sky traffic were miserable, choking the air with bodies and vehicles. In her old days in uniform she remembered it as a hot spot for wrecks and crushed tourists who were too busy gaping at the show to get out of the way.

Even at this hour steam was rising from the stationary and portable food stands that offered everything from rice noodles to soy dogs for the teeming crowds. She had to swerve to avoid an eager merchant on his smoking Glida-Grill, and took his flipped middle finger as a matter of course.

Eve double-parked and, skirting a man who smelled worse than his bottle of brew, stepped onto the sidewalk. She scanned the building first, fifty floors of gleaming metal that knifed into the sky from a hilt of concrete. She was propositioned twice before she reached the door.

Since this five-block area of West Broadway was affectionately termed Prostitute's Walk, she wasn't surprised. She flashed her badge for the uniform guarding the entrance.

"Lieutenant Dallas."

"Yes, sir." He skimmed his official CompuSeal over the door to keep out the curious, then led the way to the bank of elevators. "Eighteenth floor," he said when the doors swished shut behind them.

"Fill me in, Officer." Eve switched on her recorder and waited.

"I wasn't first on the scene, Lieutenant. Whatever happened upstairs is being kept upstairs. There's a badge inside waiting for you. We have a homicide, and a Code Five in number eighteen-oh-three."

"Who called it in?"

"I don't have that information."

He stayed where he was when the elevator opened. Eve stepped out and was alone in a narrow hallway. Security cameras tilted down at her, and her feet were almost soundless on the worn nap of the carpet as she approached 1803. Ignoring the hand plate, she announced herself, holding her badge up to eye level for the peep cam until the door opened.

"Dallas."

"Feeney." She smiled, pleased to see a familiar face. Ryan Feeney was an old friend and former partner who'd traded the street for a desk and a top-level position in the Electronics Detection Division. "So, they're sending computer pluckers these days."

"They wanted brass, and the best." His lips curved in his wide, rumpled face, but his eyes remained sober. He was a small, stubby man with small, stubby hands and rust-colored hair. "You look beat."

"Rough night."

"So I heard." He offered her one of the sugared nuts from the bag he habitually carried, studying her, and measuring if she was up to what was waiting in the bedroom beyond.

She was young for her rank, barely thirty, with wide brown eyes that had never had a chance to be naive. Her doe-brown hair was cropped short, for convenience rather than style, but suited her triangular face with its razor-edge cheekbones and slight dent in the chin.

She was tall, rangy, with a tendency to look thin, but Feeney knew there were solid muscles beneath the leather jacket. But Eve had more—there was also a brain, and a heart.

"This one's going to be touchy, Dallas."

"I picked that up already. Who's the victim?"

"Sharon DeBlass, granddaughter of Senator DeBlass."

Neither meant anything to her. "Politics isn't my forte, Feeney."

"The gentleman from Virginia, extreme right, old money. The granddaughter took a sharp left a few years back, moved to New York and became a licensed companion."

"She was a hooker." Dallas glanced around the apartment. It was furnished in obsessive modern—glass and thin chrome, signed holograms on the walls, recessed bar in bold red. The wide mood screen behind the bar bled with mixing and merging shapes and colors in cool pastels.

Neat as a virgin, Eve mused, and cold as a whore. "No surprise, given her choice of real estate."

"Politics makes it delicate. Victim was twenty-four, Caucasian female. She bought it in bed."

Eve only lifted a brow. "Seems poetic, since she'd been bought there. How'd she die?"

"That's the next problem. I want you to see for yourself."

As they crossed the room, each took out a slim container, sprayed their hands front and back to seal in oils and fingerprints. At the doorway, Eve sprayed the bottom of her boots to slicken them so that she would pick up no fibers, stray hairs, or skin.

Eve was already wary. Under normal circumstances there would have been two other investigators on a homicide scene, with recorders for sound and pictures. Forensics would have been waiting with their usual snarly impatience to sweep the scene.

The fact that only Feeney had been assigned with her meant that there were a lot of eggshells to be walked over.

"Security cameras in the lobby, elevator, and hallways," Eve commented.

"I've already tagged the discs." Feeney opened the bedroom door and let her enter first.

It wasn't pretty. Death rarely was a peaceful, religious experience to Eve's mind. It was the nasty end, indifferent to saint and sinner. But this was shocking, like a stage deliberately set to offend.

The bed was huge, slicked with what appeared to be genuine satin sheets the color of ripe peaches. Small, soft-focused spotlights were trained on its center where the naked woman was cupped in the gentle dip of the floating mattress.

The mattress moved with obscenely graceful undulations to the rhythm of programmed music slipping through the headboard.

She was beautiful still, a cameo face with a tumbling waterfall of flaming red hair, emerald eyes that stared glassily at the mirrored ceiling, long, milk-white limbs that called to mind visions of *Swan Lake* as the motion of the bed gently rocked them.

They weren't artistically arranged now, but spread lewdly so that the dead woman formed a final X dead-center of the bed.

There was a hole in her forehead, one in her chest, another horribly gaping between the open thighs. Blood had splattered on the glossy sheets, pooled, dripped, and stained.

There were splashes of it on the lacquered walls, like lethal paintings scrawled by an evil child.

So much blood was a rare thing, and she had seen much too much of it the night before to take the scene as calmly as she would have preferred.

She had to swallow once, hard, and force herself to block out the image of a small child.

"You got the scene on record?"

"Yep."

"Then turn that damn thing off." She let out a breath after Feeney located the controls that silenced the music. The bed flowed to stillness. "The wounds," Eve murmured, stepping closer to examine them. "Too neat for a knife. Too messy for a laser." A flash came to her—old training films, old videos, old viciousness.

"Christ, Feeney, these look like bullet wounds."

Feeney reached into his pocket and drew out a sealed bag. "Whoever did it left a souvenir." He passed the bag to Eve. "An antique like this has to go for eight, ten thousand for a legal collection, twice that on the black market."

Fascinated, Eve turned the sealed revolver over in her hand. "It's heavy," she said half to herself. "Bulky."

"Thirty-eight caliber," he told her. "First one I've seen outside of a museum. This one's a Smith and Wesson, Model Ten, blue steel." He looked at it with some affection. "Real classic piece, used to be standard police issue up until the latter part of the twentieth. They stopped making them in about twenty-two, twenty-three, when the gun ban was passed."

"You're the history buff," Which explained why he was with her. "Looks new." She sniffed through the bag, caught the scent of oil and burning. "Somebody took good care of this. Steel fired into flesh," she mused as she passed the bag back to Feeney. "Ugly way to die, and the first I've seen it in my ten years with the department."

"Second for me. About fifteen years ago, Lower East Side, party got out of hand. Guy shot five people with a twenty-two before he realized it wasn't a toy. Hell of a mess."

"Fun and games," Eve murmured. "We'll scan the collectors, see how many we can locate who own one like this. Somebody might have reported a robbery."

"Might have."

"It's more likely it came through the black market." Eve glanced back at the body. "If she's been in the business for a few years, she'd have discs, records of her clients, her trick books." She frowned. "With Code Five, I'll have to do the door-to-door myself. Not a simple sex crime," she said with a sigh. "Whoever did it set it up. The antique weapon, the wounds themselves, almost ruler-straight down the body, the lights, the pose. Who called it in, Feeney?"

"The killer." He waited until her eyes came back to him. "From right here. Called the station. See how the bedside unit's aimed at her face? That's what came in. Video, no audio."

"He's into showmanship." Eve let out a breath. "Clever bastard, arrogant, cocky. He had sex with her first. I'd bet my badge on it. Then he gets up and does it." She lifted her arm, aiming, lowering it as she counted off, "One, two, three."

"That's cold," murmured Feeney.

"He's cold. He smooths down the sheets after. See how neat they are? He arranges her, spreads her open so nobody can have any doubts as to how she made her living. He does it carefully, practically measuring, so that she's perfectly aligned. Center of the bed, arms and legs equally apart. Doesn't turn off the bed 'cause it's part of the show. He leaves the gun because he wants us to know right away he's no ordinary man. He's got an ego. He doesn't want to waste time letting the body be discovered eventually. He wants it now. That instant gratification."

"She was licensed for men and women," Feeney pointed out, but Eve shook her head.

"It's not a woman. A woman wouldn't have left her looking both beautiful and obscene. No, I don't think it's a woman. Let's see what we can find. Have you gone into her computer yet?"

"No. It's your case, Dallas. I'm only authorized to assist."

"See if you can access her client files." Eve went to the dresser and began to carefully search drawers.

Expensive taste, Eve reflected. There were several items of real silk, the kind no simulation could match. The bottle of scent on the dresser was exclusive, and smelled, after a quick sniff, like expensive sex.

The contents of the drawers were meticulously ordered, lingerie folded precisely, sweaters arranged according to color and material. The closet was the same.

Obviously the victim had a love affair with clothes and a taste for the best and took scrupulous care of what she owned.

And she'd died naked.

"Kept good records," Feeney called out. "It's all here. Her client list, appointments—including her required monthly health exam and her weekly trip to the beauty salon. She used the Trident Clinic for the first and Paradise for the second."

"Both top-of-the-line. I've got a friend who saved for a year so she could have one day for the works at Paradise. Takes all kinds."

"My wife's sister went for it for her twenty-fifth anniversary. Cost damn near as much as my kid's wedding. Hello, we've got her personal address book."

"Good. Copy all of it, will you, Feeney?" At his low whistle, she looked over her shoulder, glimpsed the small gold-edged palm computer in his hand. "What?"

"We've got a lot of high-powered names in here. Politics, entertainment, money, money, money. Interesting, our girl has Roarke's private number."

"Roarke who?"

"Just Roarke, as far as I know. Big money there. Kind of guy that touches shit and turns it into gold bricks. You've got to start reading more than the sports page, Dallas."

"Hey, I read the headlines. Did you hear about the cocker spaniel recall?"

"Roarke's always big news," Feeney said patiently. "He's got one of the finest art collections in the world. Arts and antiques," he continued, noting when Eve clicked in and turned to him. "He's a licensed gun collector. Rumor is he knows how to use them."

"I'll pay him a visit."

"You'll be lucky to get within a mile of him."

"I'm feeling lucky." Eve crossed over to the body to slip her hands under the sheets.

"The man's got powerful friends, Dallas. You can't afford to so much as whisper he's linked to this until you've got something solid."

"Feeney, you know it's a mistake to tell me that." But even as she started to smile, her fingers brushed against something between cold flesh and bloody sheets. "There's something under her." Carefully, Eve lifted the shoulder, eased her fingers over.

"Paper," she murmured. "Sealed." With her protected thumb, she wiped at a smear of blood until she could read the protected sheet.

ONE OF SIX

"It looks hand-printed," she said to Feeney and held it out. "Out boy's more than clever, more than arrogant. And he isn't finished."

Welcome to Nora Roberts's captivating saga about the lives and loves of a family on the windswept shores of the Chesapeake Bay.

Cameron, Ethan, Phillip, and Seth are four brothers bound by the love of the extraordinary couple who raised them. Now, Seth Quinn is finally home. . . .

After a harrowing boyhood with his drug-addicted mother, Seth was taken in by the Quinn family and grew up with three older brothers who watched over him with love. Now a grown man returning from Europe as a successful painter, Seth is settling down on Maryland's Eastern Shore, surrounded once again by Cam, Ethan, and Phil, their wives and children, and all the blessed chaos of the extended Quinn clan.

Still, a lot has changed in St. Christopher's since he's been gone—and the most intriguing change of all is the presence of Dru Whitcomb Banks. A city girl who has opened a florist shop in their seaside town, she craves independence and the challenge of establishing herself without the influence of her wealthy connections. In Seth, she sees another kind of challenge—one that she can't resist.

"Roberts . . . delivers . . . luscious prose."
                                        —*The Boston Globe*

*Don't miss the other books
in the Chesapeake Bay Saga*
SEA SWEPT
RISING TIDES
INNER HARBOR

*Turn the page for a complete list of titles by
Nora Roberts and J. D. Robb from Berkley. . . .*

Nora Roberts

Series

Irish Born Trilogy
BORN IN FIRE
BORN IN ICE
BORN IN SHAME

Dream Trilogy
DARING TO DREAM
HOLDING THE DREAM
FINDING THE DREAM

Chesapeake Bay Saga
SEA SWEPT
RISING TIDES
INNER HARBOR
CHESAPEAKE BLUE

Gallaghers of Ardmore Trilogy
JEWELS OF THE SUN
TEARS OF THE MOON
HEART OF THE SEA

Three Sisters Island Trilogy
DANCE UPON THE AIR
HEAVEN AND EARTH
FACE THE FIRE

Key Trilogy
KEY OF LIGHT
KEY OF KNOWLEDGE
KEY OF VALOR

In the Garden Trilogy
BLUE DAHLIA
BLACK ROSE
RED LILY

Circle Trilogy
MORRIGAN'S CROSS
DANCE OF THE GODS
VALLEY OF SILENCE

Sign of Seven Trilogy
BLOOD BROTHERS
THE HOLLOW
THE PAGAN STONE

Bride Quartet
VISION IN WHITE
BED OF ROSES
SAVOR THE MOMENT
HAPPY EVER AFTER

The Inn BoonsBoro Trilogy
THE NEXT ALWAYS
THE LAST BOYFRIEND
THE PERFECT HOPE

The Cousins O'Dwyer Trilogy
DARK WITCH
SHADOW SPELL
BLOOD MAGICK

The Guardians Trilogy
STARS OF FORTUNE
BAY OF SIGHS
ISLAND OF GLASS

eBooks by Nora Roberts

Cordina's Royal Family
AFFAIRE ROYALE
COMMAND PERFORMANCE
THE PLAYBOY PRINCE
CORDINA'S CROWN JEWEL

The Donovan Legacy
CAPTIVATED
ENTRANCED
CHARMED
ENCHANTED

The O'Hurleys
THE LAST HONEST WOMAN
DANCE TO THE PIPER
SKIN DEEP
WITHOUT A TRACE

Night Tales
NIGHT SHIFT
NIGHT SHADOW
NIGHTSHADE
NIGHT SMOKE
NIGHT SHIELD

The MacGregors
PLAYING THE ODDS
TEMPTING FATE
ALL THE POSSIBILITIES
ONE MAN'S ART
FOR NOW, FOREVER
REBELLION/IN FROM THE COLD
THE MACGREGOR BRIDES
THE WINNING HAND
THE MACGREGOR GROOMS
THE PERFECT NEIGHBOR

The Calhouns
COURTING CATHERINE
A MAN FOR AMANDA
FOR THE LOVE OF LILAH
SUZANNA'S SURRENDER
MEGAN'S MATE

Irish Legacy
IRISH THOROUGHBRED
IRISH ROSE
IRISH REBEL

LOVING JACK
BEST LAID PLANS
LAWLESS

BLITHE IMAGES
SONG OF THE WEST
SEARCH FOR LOVE
ISLAND OF FLOWERS
THE HEART'S VICTORY
FROM THIS DAY
HER MOTHER'S KEEPER
ONCE MORE WITH FEELING
REFLECTIONS
DANCE OF DREAMS
UNTAMED
THIS MAGIC MOMENT
ENDINGS AND BEGINNINGS
STORM WARNING
SULLIVAN'S WOMAN
FIRST IMPRESSIONS
A MATTER OF CHOICE

LESS OF A STRANGER
THE LAW IS A LADY
RULES OF THE GAME
OPPOSITES ATTRACT
THE RIGHT PATH
PARTNERS
BOUNDARY LINES
DUAL IMAGE
TEMPTATION
LOCAL HERO
THE NAME OF THE GAME
GABRIEL'S ANGEL
THE WELCOMING
TIME WAS
TIMES CHANGE
SUMMER LOVE
HOLIDAY WISHES

Nora Roberts & J. D. Robb

REMEMBER WHEN

J. D. Robb

NAKED IN DEATH
GLORY IN DEATH
IMMORTAL IN DEATH
RAPTURE IN DEATH
CEREMONY IN DEATH
VENGEANCE IN DEATH
HOLIDAY IN DEATH
CONSPIRACY IN DEATH
LOYALTY IN DEATH
WITNESS IN DEATH
JUDGMENT IN DEATH
BETRAYAL IN DEATH
SEDUCTION IN DEATH
REUNION IN DEATH
PURITY IN DEATH
PORTRAIT IN DEATH
IMITATION IN DEATH
DIVIDED IN DEATH
VISIONS IN DEATH
SURVIVOR IN DEATH
ORIGIN IN DEATH
MEMORY IN DEATH
BORN IN DEATH
INNOCENT IN DEATH
CREATION IN DEATH
STRANGERS IN DEATH
SALVATION IN DEATH
PROMISES IN DEATH
KINDRED IN DEATH
FANTASY IN DEATH
INDULGENCE IN DEATH
TREACHERY IN DEATH
NEW YORK TO DALLAS
CELEBRITY IN DEATH
DELUSION IN DEATH
CALCULATED IN DEATH
THANKLESS IN DEATH
CONCEALED IN DEATH
FESTIVE IN DEATH
OBSESSION IN DEATH
DEVOTED IN DEATH
BROTHERHOOD IN DEATH
APPRENTICE IN DEATH

Anthologies

FROM THE HEART
A LITTLE MAGIC
A LITTLE FATE

MOON SHADOWS
(with Jill Gregory, Ruth Ryan Langan, and Marianne Willman)

The Once Upon Series
(with Jill Gregory, Ruth Ryan Langan, and Marianne Willman)

ONCE UPON A CASTLE   ONCE UPON A ROSE
ONCE UPON A STAR   ONCE UPON A KISS
ONCE UPON A DREAM   ONCE UPON A MIDNIGHT

SILENT NIGHT
(with Susan Plunkett, Dee Holmes, and Claire Cross)

OUT OF THIS WORLD
(with Laurell K. Hamilton, Susan Krinard, and Maggie Shayne)

BUMP IN THE NIGHT
(with Mary Blayney, Ruth Ryan Langan, and Mary Kay McComas)

DEAD OF NIGHT
(with Mary Blayney, Ruth Ryan Langan, and Mary Kay McComas)

THREE IN DEATH

SUITE 606
(with Mary Blayney, Ruth Ryan Langan, and Mary Kay McComas)

IN DEATH

THE LOST
(with Patricia Gaffney, Mary Blayney, and Ruth Ryan Langan)

THE OTHER SIDE
(with Mary Blayney, Patricia Gaffney, Ruth Ryan Langan, and Mary Kay McComas)

TIME OF DEATH

THE UNQUIET
(with Mary Blayney, Patricia Gaffney, Ruth Ryan Langan, and Mary Kay McComas)

MIRROR, MIRROR
(with Mary Blayney, Elaine Fox, Mary Kay McComas, and R. C. Ryan)

DOWN THE RABBIT HOLE
(with Mary Blayney, Elaine Fox, Mary Kay McComas, and R. C. Ryan)

Also available . . .

THE OFFICIAL NORA ROBERTS COMPANION
(edited by Denise Little and Laura Hayden)

NORA ROBERTS

CHESAPEAKE BLUE

JOVE
New York

A JOVE BOOK
Published by Berkley
An imprint of Penguin Random House LLC
penguinrandomhouse.com

Copyright © 2002 by Nora Roberts
Excerpt from *Naked in Death* by J. D. Robb copyright © 1995 by Nora Roberts
Penguin Random House supports copyright. Copyright fuels creativity, encourages
diverse voices, promotes free speech, and creates a vibrant culture. Thank you for buying
an authorized edition of this book and for complying with copyright laws by not
reproducing, scanning, or distributing any part of it in any form without permission.
You are supporting writers and allowing Penguin Random House to continue to
publish books for every reader.

A JOVE BOOK, BERKLEY, and the BERKLEY & B colophon
are registered trademarks of Penguin Random House LLC.

ISBN: 9780515136265

G. P. Putnam's Sons hardcover edition / December 2002
Jove international edition / June 2003
Jove mass-market edition / February 2004

Printed in the United States of America
19 21 23 25 26 24 22 20 18

Cover design and photo composition by Rita Frangie

TO EVERY READER WHO EVER ASKED

*When are you going to
tell Seth's story?*

There is a destiny that makes us brothers;
None goes his way alone:
All that we send into the lives of others
Comes back into our own.

EDWIN MARKHAM

Art is the accomplice of love.

RÉMY DE GOURMONT

ONE

H<small>E WAS COMING</small> home.

Maryland's Eastern Shore was a world of marshes and mudflats, of wide fields with row crops straight as soldiers. It was flatland rivers with sharp shoulders, and secret tidal creeks where the heron fed.

It was blue crab and the Bay, and the watermen who harvested them.

No matter where he'd lived, in the first miserable decade of his life, or in the last few years as he approached the end of his third decade, only the Shore had ever meant home.

There were countless aspects, countless memories of that home, and every one was as bright and brilliant in his mind as the sun that sparkled off the water of the Chesapeake.

As he drove across the bridge, his artist's eye wanted to capture that moment—the rich blue water and the boats that skimmed its surface, the quick white waves and the swoop of greedy gulls. The way the land skimmed its edge, and spilled back with its browns and greens. All the thickening leaves of the gum and oak trees, with those flashes of color that were flowers basking in the warmth of spring.

He wanted to remember this moment just as he remembered the first time he'd crossed the Bay to the Eastern Shore, a surly, frightened boy beside a man who'd promised him a life.

HE'D sat in the passenger seat of the car, with the man he hardly knew at the wheel. He had the clothes on his back, and a few meager possessions in a paper sack.

His stomach had been tight with nerves, but he'd fixed what he thought was a bored look on his face and had stared out the window.

If he was with the old guy, he wasn't with *her*. That was as good a deal as he could get.

Besides, the old guy was pretty cool.

He didn't stink of booze or of the mints some of the assholes Gloria brought up to the dump they were living in used to cover it up. And the couple of times they'd been together, the old guy, Ray, had bought him a burger or pizza.

And he'd talked to him.

Adults, in his experience, didn't talk to kids. At them, around them, over them. But not to them.

Ray did. Listened, too. And when he'd asked, straight out, if he—just a kid—wanted to live with him, he hadn't felt that strangling fear or hot panic. He'd felt like maybe, just maybe, he was catching a break.

Away from her. That was the best part. The longer they drove, the farther away from her.

If things got sticky, he could run. The guy was really old. Big, he was sure as shit big, but old. All that white hair, and that wide, wrinkled face.

He took quick, sidelong glances at it, began to draw the face in his mind.

His eyes were really blue, and that was kind of weird because so were his own.

He had a big voice, too, but when he talked it wasn't like yelling. It was kind of calm, even a little tired, maybe.

He sure looked tired now.

"Almost home," Ray said as they approached the bridge. "Hungry?"

"I dunno. Yeah, I guess."

"My experience, boys are always hungry. Raised three bottomless pits."

There was cheer in the big voice, but it was forced. The child might have been barely ten, but he knew the tone of falsehood.

Far enough away now, he thought. If he had to run. So he'd put the cards on the table and see what the fuck was what.

"How come you're taking me to your place?"

"Because you need a place."

"Get real. People don't do shit like that."

"Some do. Stella and I, my wife, we did shit like that."

"You tell her you're bringing me around?"

Ray smiled, but there was a sadness in it. "In my way. She died some time back. You'd've liked her. And she'd have taken one look at you and rolled up her sleeves."

He didn't know what to say about that. "What am I supposed to do when we get where we're going?"

"Live," Ray told him. "Be a boy. Go to school, get in trouble. I'll teach you to sail."

"On a boat?"

Now Ray laughed, a big booming sound that filled the car and for reasons the boy couldn't understand, untied the nerves in his belly. "Yeah, on a boat. Got a brainless puppy—I always get the brainless ones—I'm trying to housebreak. You can help me with that. You're gonna have chores, we'll figure that out. We'll lay down the rules, and you'll follow them. Don't think because I'm an old man I'm a pushover."

"You gave her money."

Ray glanced away from the road briefly and looked into eyes the same color as his own. "That's right. That's what she understands, from what I can see. She never understood you, did she, boy?"

Something was gathering inside him, a storm he didn't recognize as hope. "If you get pissed off at me, or tired of having me around, or just change your mind, you'll send me back. I won't go back."

They were over the bridge now, and Ray pulled the car to the shoulder of the road, shifted his bulk in the seat so they were face-to-face. "I'll get pissed off at you, and at my age I'm bound to get tired from time to time. But I'm making you a promise here and now, I'm giving you my word. I won't send you back."

"If she—"

"I won't let her take you back," Ray said, anticipating him. "No matter what I have to do. You're mine now. You're my family now. And you'll stay with me as long as that's what you want. A Quinn makes a promise," he added, and held out a hand, "he keeps it."

Seth looked at the offered hand, and his own sprang damp. "I don't like being touched."

Ray nodded. "Okay. But you've still got my word on it." He pulled back onto the road again, gave the boy one last glance. "Almost home," he said again.

Within months, Ray Quinn had died, but he'd kept his

word. He'd kept it through the three men he'd made his sons. Those men had given the scrawny, suspicious and scarred young boy a life.

They had given him a home, and made him a man.

Cameron, the edgy, quick-tempered gypsy; Ethan, the patient, steady waterman; Phillip, the elegant, sharp-minded executive. They had stood for him, fought for him. They had saved him.

His brothers.

THE gilded light of the late-afternoon sun sheened the marsh grass, the mudflats, the flat fields of row crops. With the windows down he caught the scent of water as he by-passed the little town of St. Christopher.

He'd considered swinging into town, heading first to the old brick boatyard. Boats by Quinn still custom made wooden boats, and in the eighteen years since the enter-prise had started—on a dream, on guile, on sweat—it had earned its reputation for quality and craftsmanship.

They were probably there, even now. Cam cursing as he finished up some fancywork in a cabin. Ethan quietly lap-ping boards. Phil, up in the office conjuring up some snazzy ad campaign.

He could go by Crawford's, pick up a six-pack. Maybe they'd have a cold one, or more likely Cam would toss him a hammer and tell him to get his ass back to work.

He'd enjoy that, but it wasn't what was drawing him now. It wasn't what was pulling him down the narrow country road where the marsh still crept out of the shadows and the trees with their gnarled trunks spread leaves glossy with May.

Of all the places he'd seen—the great domes and spires

of Florence, the florid beauty of Paris, the stunning green hills of Ireland—nothing ever caught at his throat, filled up his heart, like the old white house with its soft and faded blue trim that sat on a bumpy lawn that slid back into quiet water.

He pulled in the drive, behind the old white 'Vette that had been Ray and Stella Quinn's. The car looked as pristine as the day it had rolled off the showroom floor. Cam's doing, he thought. Cam would say it was a matter of showing proper respect for an exceptional machine. But it was all about Ray and Stella, all about family. All about love.

The lilac in the front yard was smothered with blooms. That was a matter of love, too, he reflected. He'd given Anna the little bush for Mother's Day when he was twelve.

She'd cried, he remembered. Big, beautiful brown eyes flooded with tears, laughing and swiping at them the whole time he and Cam planted it for her.

She was Cam's wife, and so that made Anna his sister. But inside, he thought now, where it counted, she was his mother.

The Quinns knew all about what was inside.

He got out of the car, into the lovely stillness. He was no longer a scrawny boy with oversized feet and a suspicious eye.

He'd grown into those feet. He was six-one with a wiry build. One that could go gawky if he neglected it. His hair had darkened and was more a bronzed brown than the sandy mop of his youth. He tended to neglect that as well and, running a hand through it now, winced as he recalled his intention to have it trimmed before leaving Rome.

The guys were going to rag on him about the little pony-tail, which meant he'd have to keep it for a while, out of principle.

He shrugged and, dipping his hands into the pockets of his worn jeans, began to walk, scanning the surroundings. Anna's flowers, the rockers on the front porch, the woods that haunted the side of the house and where he'd run wild as a boy.

The old dock swaying over the water, and the white sailing sloop moored to it.

He stood looking out, his face, hollow-cheeked and tanned, turned toward the water.

His lips, firm and full, began to curve. The weight he hadn't realized was hanging from his heart began to lift.

At the sound of a rustle in the woods, he turned, enough of the wary boy still in the man to make the move swift and defensive. Out of the trees shot a black bullet.

"Witless!" His voice had both the ring of authority and easy humor. The combination had the dog skidding to a halt, all flopping ears and lolling tongue as it studied the man.

"Come on, it hasn't been that long." He crouched, held out a hand. "Remember me?"

Witless grinned the dopey grin that had named him, instantly flopped down and rolled to expose his belly for a rub.

"There you go. That's the way."

There had always been a dog for this house. Always a boat at the dock, a rocker on the porch and a dog in the yard.

"Yeah, you remember me." As he stroked Witless, he looked over to the far end of the yard where Anna had planted a hydrangea over the grave of his own dog. The loyal and much-loved Foolish.

"I'm Seth," he murmured. "I've been away too long."

He caught the sound of an engine, the sassy squeal of

tires from a turn taken just a hair faster than the law allowed. Even as he straightened, the dog leaped up, streaked away toward the front of the house.

Wanting to savor the moment, Seth followed more slowly. He listened to the car door slam, then to the lift and lilt of her voice as she spoke to the dog.

Then he just looked at her, Anna Spinelli Quinn, with the curling mass of dark hair windblown from the drive, her arms full of the bags she'd hefted out of the car.

His grin spread as she tried to ward off the desperate affection from the dog.

"How many times do we have to go over this one, simple rule?" she demanded. "You do not jump on people, especially me. Especially me when I'm wearing a suit."

"Great suit," Seth called out. "Better legs."

Her head whipped up, those deep brown eyes widened and showed him the shock, the pleasure, the welcome all in one glance.

"Oh my God!" Heedless of the contents, she tossed the bags through the open car door. And ran.

He caught her, lifted her six inches off the ground and spun her around before setting her on her feet again. Still he didn't let go. Instead, he just buried his face in her hair.

"Hi."

"Seth. Seth." She clung, ignoring the dog that leaped and yipped and did his best to shove his muzzle between them. "I can't believe it. You're here."

"Don't cry."

"Just a little. I have to look at you." She had his face framed in her hands as she eased back. So handsome, she thought. So grown-up. "Look at all this," she murmured and brushed a hand at his hair.

"I meant to get some of it whacked off."

"I like it." Tears still trickled even as she grinned. "Very bohemian. You look wonderful. Absolutely wonderful."

"You're the most beautiful woman in the world."

"Oh boy." She sniffled, shook her head. "That's no way to get me to stop all this." She swiped at tears. "When did you get here? I thought you were in Rome."

"I was. I wanted to be here."

"If you'd called, we would've met you."

"I wanted to surprise you." He walked to the car to pull the bags out for her. "Cam at the boatyard?"

"Should be. Here, I'll get those. You need to get your things."

"I'll get them later. Where's Kevin and Jake?"

She started up the walk with him, glanced at her watch as she thought about her sons. "What day is this? My mind's still spinning."

"Thursday."

"Ah, Kevin has rehearsal, school play, and Jake's got softball practice. Kevin's got his driver's license, God help us, and is scooping up his brother on his way home." She unlocked the front door. "They should be along in an hour, then peace will no longer lie across the land."

It was the same, Seth thought. It didn't matter what color the walls were painted or if the old sofa had been replaced, if a new lamp stood on the table. It was the same because it *felt* the same.

The dog snaked around his legs and made a beeline for the kitchen.

"I want you to sit down." She nodded to the kitchen table, under which Witless was sprawled, happily gnawing on a hunk of rope. "And tell me everything. You want some wine?"

"Sure, after I help you put this stuff away." When her

eyebrows shot up, he paused with a gallon of milk in his hand. "What?"

"I was just remembering the way everyone, including you, disappeared whenever it was time to put groceries away."

"Because you always said we put things in the wrong place."

"You always did, on purpose so I'd kick you out of the kitchen."

"You copped to that, huh?"

"I cop to everything when it comes to my guys. Nothing gets by me, pal. Did something happen in Rome?"

"No." He continued to unpack the bags. He knew where everything went, where everything had always gone in Anna's kitchen. "I'm not in trouble, Anna."

But you are troubled, she thought, and let it go for now. "I'm going to open a nice Italian white. We'll have a glass and you can tell me all the wonderful things you've been doing. It seems like years since we've talked face-to-face."

He shut the refrigerator and turned to her. "I'm sorry I didn't get home for Christmas."

"Honey, we understood. You had a showing in January. We're all so proud of you, Seth. Cam must've bought a hundred copies of the issue of the *Smithsonian* magazine when they did the article on you. The young American artist who's seduced Europe."

He shrugged a shoulder, such an innately Quinn gesture, she grinned. "So sit," she ordered.

"I'll sit, but I'd rather you caught me up. How the hell is everyone? What're they doing? You first."

"All right." She finished opening the bottle, got out two glasses. "I'm doing more administrative work these days than casework. Social work involves a lot of paperwork, but it's not as satisfying. Between that and having two teenagers in the house, there's no time to be bored. The boat business is thriving."

She sat, passed Seth his glass. "Aubrey's working there."

"No kidding?" The thought of her, the girl who was more sister to him than any blood kin, made him smile. "How's she doing?"

"Terrific. She's beautiful, smart, stubborn and, according to Cam, a genius with wood. I think Grace was a little disappointed when Aubrey didn't want to pursue dancing, but it's hard to argue when you see your child so happy. And Grace and Ethan's Emily followed in her mother's toe shoes."

"She still heading to New York end of August?"

"A chance to dance with the American Ballet Company doesn't come along every day. She's grabbing it, and she swears she'll be principal before she's twenty. Deke's his father's son—quiet, clever and happiest when he's out on the water. Sweetie, do you want a snack?"

"No." He reached out, laid a hand over hers. "Keep going."

"Okay, then. Phillip remains the business's marketing and promotion guru. I don't think any of us, including Phil, ever thought he'd leave the ad firm in Baltimore, give up urban living and dig down in Saint Chris. But it's been, what, fourteen years, so I don't suppose we can call it a whim. Of course he and Sybill keep the apartment in New York. She's working on a new book."

"Yeah, I talked to her." He rubbed the dog's head with his foot. "Something about the evolution of community in cyberspace. She's something. How are the kids?"

"Insane, as any self-respecting teenager should be. Bram was madly in love with a girl named Cloe last week.

That could be over by now. Fiona's interests are torn between boys and shopping. But, well, she's fourteen, so that's natural."

"Fourteen. Jesus. She hadn't had her tenth birthday when I left for Europe. Even seeing them on and off over the last few years, it doesn't seem . . . it doesn't seem possible that Kevin's driving, and Aub's building boats. Bram's sniffing after girls. I remember—" He cut himself off, shook his head.

"What?"

"I remember when Grace was pregnant with Emily. It was the first time I was around someone who was having a baby—well, someone who wanted to. It seems like five minutes ago, and now Emily's going to New York. How can eighteen years go by, Anna, and you not look any older?"

"Oh, I've missed you." She laughed and squeezed his hand.

"I've missed you, too. All of you."

"We'll fix that. We'll round everybody up and have a big, noisy Quinn welcome-home on Sunday. How does that sound?"

"About as perfect as it gets."

The dog yipped, then scrambled out from under the table to run toward the front door.

"Cameron," Anna said. "Go on out and meet him."

He walked through the house, as he had so often. Opened the screen door, as he had so often. And looked at the man standing on the front lawn, playing tug-of-war with the dog over a hunk of rope.

He was still tall, still built like a sprinter. There were glints of silver in his hair now. He had the sleeves of his work shirt rolled up to the elbows, and his jeans were white at the stress points. He wore sunglasses and badly beaten Nikes.

At fifty, Cameron Quinn still looked like a badass.

In lieu of greeting, Seth let the screen door slam behind him. Cameron glanced over, and the only sign of surprise was his fingers sliding off the rope.

A thousand words passed between them without a sound. A million feelings, and countless memories. Saying nothing, Seth came down the steps as Cameron crossed the lawn. Then they stood, face-to-face.

"I hope that piece of shit in the driveway's a rental," Cameron began.

"Yeah, it is. Best I could do on short notice. Figured I'd turn it in tomorrow, then use the 'Vette for a while."

Cameron's smile was sharp as a blade. "In your dreams, pal. In your wildest dreams."

"No point in it sitting there going to waste."

"Less of one to let some half-assed painter with delusions of grandeur behind its classic wheel."

"Hey, you're the one who taught me to drive."

"Tried to. A ninety-year-old woman with a broken arm could handle a five-speed better than you." He jerked his head toward Seth's rental. "That embarrassment in my driveway doesn't inspire the confidence in me that you've improved in that area."

Smug now, Seth rocked back on his heels. "Test-drove a Maserati a couple of months ago."

Cam's eyebrows winged up. "Get out of here."

"Had her up to a hundred and ten. Scared the living shit out of me."

Cam laughed, gave Seth an affectionate punch on the

arm. Then he sighed. "Son of a bitch. Son of a bitch," he said again as he dragged Seth into a fierce hug. "Why the hell didn't you let us know you were coming home?"

"It was sort of spur-of-the-moment," Seth began. "I wanted to be here. I just needed to be here."

"Okay. Anna burning up the phone lines letting everybody know we're serving fatted calf?"

"Probably. She said we'd have the calf on Sunday."

"That'll work. You settled in yet?"

"No. I got stuff in the car."

"Don't call that butt-ugly thing a car. Let's get your gear."

"Cam." Seth reached out, touched Cam's arm. "I want to come home. Not just for a few days or a couple weeks. I want to stay. Can I stay?"

Cam drew off his sunglasses, and his eyes, smoke-gray, met Seth's. "What the hell's the matter with you that you think you have to ask? You trying to piss me off?"

"I never had to try, nobody does with you. Anyway, I'll pull my weight."

"You always pulled your weight. And we missed seeing your ugly face around here."

And that, Seth thought as they walked to the car, was all the welcome he needed from Cameron Quinn.

THEY'D kept his room. It had changed over the years, different paint for the walls, a new rug for the floor. But the bed was the same one he'd slept in, dreamed in, waked in.

The same bed he'd sneaked Foolish into when he'd been a child.

And the one he'd sneaked Alice Albert into when he'd thought he was a man.

He figured Cam knew about Foolish, and had often wondered if he'd known about Alice.

He tossed his suitcases carelessly on the bed and laid his battered paint kit—one Sybill had given him for his eleventh birthday—on the worktable Ethan had built.

He'd need to find studio space, he thought. Eventually. As long as the weather held, he could work outdoors. He preferred that anyway. But he'd need somewhere to store his canvases, his equipment. Maybe there was room in the old barn of a boatyard, but that wouldn't suit on a permanent basis.

And he meant to make this permanent.

He'd had enough of traveling for now, enough of living among strangers to last him a lifetime.

He'd needed to go, to stand on his own. He'd needed to learn. And God, he'd needed to paint.

So he'd studied in Florence, and worked in Paris. He'd wandered the hills of Ireland and Scotland and had stood on the cliffs in Cornwall.

He'd lived cheap and rough most of the time. When there'd been a choice between buying a meal or paint, he'd gone hungry.

He'd been hungry before. It had done him good, he hoped, to remember what it was like not to have someone making sure you were fed and safe and warm.

It was the Quinn in him, he supposed, that made him hell-bent to beat his own path.

He laid out his sketch pad, put away his charcoal, his pencils. He would spend time getting back to basics with his work before he picked up a brush again.

The walls of his room held some of his early drawings. Cam had taught him how to make the frames on an old miter box at the boatyard. Seth took one from the wall to study it. It showed promise, he thought, in the rough, undisciplined lines.

But more, much more, it showed the promise of a life.

He'd caught them well enough, he decided. Cam, with his thumbs tucked in his pockets, stance confrontational. Then Phillip, slick, edging toward an elegance that nearly disguised the street smarts. Ethan, patient, steady as a redwood in his work clothes.

He'd drawn himself with them. Seth at ten, he thought. Thin, narrow shoulders and big feet, with a lift to his chin to mask something more painful than fear.

Something that was hope.

A life moment, Seth thought now, captured with a graphite pencil. Drawing it, he'd begun to believe, in-the-gut believe, that he was one of them.

A Quinn.

"You mess with one Quinn," he murmured as he hung the drawing on the wall again, "you mess with them all."

He turned, glanced at the suitcases and wondered if he could sweet-talk Anna into unpacking for him.

Not a chance.

"Hey."

He looked toward the doorway and brightened when he saw Kevin. If he had to fiddle with clothes, as least he'd have company. "Hey, Kev."

"So, you really hanging this time? For good?"

"Looks like."

"Cool." Kevin sauntered in, plopped on the bed and propped his feet on one of the suitcases. "Mom's really jazzed about it. Around here, if Mom's happy, everybody's happy. She could be soft enough to let me use her car this weekend."

"Glad I can help." He shoved Kevin's feet off the suitcase, then unzipped it.

He had the look of his mother, Seth thought. Dark, curling hair, big Italian eyes. Seth imagined the girls were already tumbling for him like bowling pins.

"How's the play?"

"It rocks. Totally rocks. *West Side Story*. I'm Tony. When you're a Jet, man."

"You stay a Jet." Seth dumped shirts haphazardly in a drawer. "You get killed, right?"

"Yeah." Kevin clutched his heart, shuddered with his face filled with pain and rapture. Then slumped. "It's great, and before I do the death thing, we've got this kick-ass fight scene. Show's next week. You're gonna come, right?"

"Front row center, pal."

"Check out Lisa Maxdon, she plays Maria. Total babe. We've got a couple of love scenes together. We've been doing a lot of practicing," he added and winked.

"Anything for art."

"Yeah." Kevin scooted up a little. "Okay, so tell me about all the Euro chicks. Pretty hot, huh?"

"The only way to get burned. There was this girl in Rome. Anna-Theresa."

"A two-named girl." Kevin shook his fingers as if he'd gotten them too close to a flame. "Two-named girls are way sexy."

"Tell me. She worked in this little trattoria. And the way she served pasta al pomodoro was just amazing."

"So? Did you score?"

Seth sent Kevin a pitying look. "Please, who're you talking to here?" He dumped jeans in another drawer. "She had hair all the way down to her ass, and a very fine ass it was.

Eyes like melted chocolate and a mouth that wouldn't quit."

"Did you draw her naked?"

"I did about a dozen figure studies. She was a natural. Totally relaxed, completely uninhibited."

"Man, you're killing me."

"And she had the most amazing . . ." Seth paused, his hands up to chest level to demonstrate. "Personality," he said, dropping his hands. "Hi, Anna."

"Discussing art?" she said dryly. "It's so nice of you to share some of your cultural experiences with Kevin."

"Um. Well." The killing smile she was aiming in his direction had always made Seth's tongue wither. Instead of trying to use it, he fell back on an innocent grin.

"But tonight's session on art and culture is now over. Kevin, I believe you have homework."

"Right. I'll get right to it." Seeing his history assignment as an escape hatch, Kevin bolted.

Anna stepped into the room. "Do you think," she asked Seth pleasantly, "that the young woman in question would appreciate being whittled down to a pair of breasts?"

"Ah . . . I also mentioned her eyes. They were nearly as fabulous as yours."

Anna took a shirt out of the open drawer, folded it neatly. "Do you think that's going to work with me?"

"No. Begging might. Please don't hurt me. I just got home."

She took out another shirt, folded it. "Kevin's sixteen, and I'm perfectly aware his major interest at this time is naked breasts and his fervent desire to get his hands on as many as possible."

Seth winced. "Jeez, Anna."

"I am also aware," she continued without breaking stride,

"that this predilection—while hopefully becoming more civilized and controlled—remains deep-seated in the male species throughout its natural life."

"Hey, you want to see some of my landscape sketches from Tuscany?"

"I am surrounded by you." Sighing a little, she took out yet another shirt. "Outnumbered, and have been since I walked into this house. That doesn't mean I can't knock every one of your stupid heads together when necessary. Understood?"

"Yes, ma'am."

"Good. Show me your landscapes."

LATER, when the house was quiet and the moon rode over the water, she found Cam on the back porch. She stepped out, and into him.

He wrapped an arm around her, rubbing her shoulder against the night's chill. "Settle everyone down?"

"That's what I do. Chilly tonight." She glanced up at the sky, at the ice points of stars. "I hope it stays clear for Sunday." Then she simply turned her face into his chest. "Oh, Cam."

"I know." He stroked a hand over her hair, rubbed his cheek against it.

"To see him sitting at the kitchen table. Watching him wrestling with Jake and that idiot dog. Even hearing him talking about naked women with Kevin—"

"What naked women?"

She laughed, shook back her hair as she looked at him. "No one you know. It's so good to have him home."

"I told you he'd come back. Quinns always come back to the roost."

"I guess you're right." She kissed him, one long, warm meeting of lips. "Why don't we go upstairs?" She slid her hands down, gave his butt a suggestive squeeze. "And I'll settle you down, too."

TWO

"RISE AND SHINE, pal. This ain't no flophouse."
The voice, and the gleeful sadism behind it, had
Seth groaning. He flopped onto his stomach, dragged the
pillow over his head. "Go away. Go far, far away."

"If you think you're going to spend your days around
here sleeping till the crack of noon, think again." With relish, Cam yanked the pillow away. "Up."

Seth opened one eye, rolled it until he focused on the
bedside clock. It wasn't yet seven. He turned his face back
into the mattress and mumbled a rude suggestion in Italian.

"If you think I've lived with Spinelli all these years and
don't know that means 'kiss my ass,' you're stupid as well
as lazy."

To solve the problem, Cam ripped the sheets away,
snagged Seth's ankles and dragged him to the floor.

"Shit. *Shit!*" Naked, his elbow singing where it had
cracked the table, Seth glared up at his persecutor. "What

the hell's with you? This is my room, my bed, and I'm trying to sleep in it."

"Put some clothes on. I've got something for you to do out back."

"Goddamn it, you could give a guy twenty-four hours before you start on him."

"Kid, I started on you when you were ten, and I'm not close to being finished. I've got work, so let's get moving."

"Cam." Anna strode to the doorway, hands on hips. "I told you to wake him up, not knock him down."

"Jesus." Mortified, Seth tore the sheet out of Cam's hands and clutched it around his waist. "Jesus, Anna, I'm naked here."

"Then get dressed," she suggested, and walked away.

"Out back," Cam told him as he strode from the room. "Five minutes."

"Yeah, yeah, yeah."

Some things never changed, Seth thought as he yanked on jeans. He could be sixty living in this house, and Cam would still roust him out of bed like he was twelve.

He snagged what was left of a University of Maryland sweatshirt and dragged it over his head as he stalked from the room.

If there wasn't coffee, hot and fresh, somebody was going to get their ass seriously kicked.

"Mom! I can't find my shoes!"

Seth glanced toward Jake's room as he headed for the stairs.

"They're down here," Anna called back. "In the middle of my kitchen floor, where they don't belong."

"Not *those* shoes. Jeez, Mom. The *other* shoes."

"Try looking up your butt," came the carefully modulated suggestion from Kevin's room. "Your head's already up there."

"No problem finding your butt," was the hissed response. "Since you wear it right on your shoulders."

Such familiar family dynamics would have made Seth smile—if it hadn't been shy of seven A.M. If his elbow hadn't been throbbing like a bitch. If he had had a hit of caffeine.

"Neither one of you could find your butts with your own hands," he grumbled as he sulked down the steps.

"What the hell's up with Cam?" he demanded of Anna when he stalked into the kitchen. "Is there any coffee? Why does everybody wake up yelling around here?"

"Cam needs to see you outside. Yes, there's a half pot left, and everyone wakes up yelling because it's how we like to greet the day." She poured coffee into a thick white mug. "You're on your own for breakfast. I have an early meeting. Don't pout, Seth. I'll bring home ice cream."

The day began to look marginally brighter. "Rocky Road?"

"Rocky Road. Jake! Get these shoes out of my kitchen before I feed them to the dog. Go outside, Seth, or you'll spoil Cam's sunny mood."

"Yeah, he looked real chipper when he yanked me out of bed." Stewing over it, Seth walked out the kitchen door.

There they were, almost as Seth had drawn them so many years before. Cam, thumbs in pockets, Phillip, slicked up in a suit, Ethan, with a faded gimme cap over his windblown hair.

Seth swallowed coffee, and the heart that had lodged in his throat. "This is what you dragged me out of bed for?"

"Same smart mouth." Phillip caught him in a hug. His

eyes, nearly the same tawny gold as his hair, skimmed over Seth's ragged shirt and jeans. "Christ, kid, didn't I teach you anything?" With a shake of his head, he fingered the dull-gray sleeve. "Italy was obviously wasted on you."

"They're just clothes, Phil. You put them on so you don't get cold or arrested."

With a pained wince, Phillip stepped back. "Where did I go wrong?"

"Looks okay to me. Still a little scrawny. What's this?" Ethan tugged on Seth's hair. "Long as a girl's."

"He had it in a pretty little ponytail last night," Cam told him. "He looked real sweet."

"Up yours," Seth said, laughing.

"We'll get you a nice pink ribbon," Ethan said with a chuckle and grabbed Seth in a bear hug.

Phillip nipped the mug out of Seth's hand, took a sip. "We figured we'd come by and get a look at you before Sunday."

"It's good to see you. Really good to see you." Seth flicked a glance at Cam. "You could've said everyone was here instead of dumping me out of bed."

"More fun that way. Well." Cam rocked back on his heels.

"Well," Phillip agreed, and set the mug on the porch rail.

"Well." Ethan gave Seth's hair another tug. Then got an iron grip on his arm.

"What?"

Cam only grinned and locked a hold on his other arm. Seth didn't need the gleam in their eyes to understand.

"Come on. You're kidding, right?"

"It's got to be done." Before Seth could begin to struggle, Phillip scooped his legs out from under him. "It's not like you've got to worry about getting that snazzy outfit wet."

"Cut it out." Seth bucked, tried to kick as he was carried off the porch. "I mean it. That water's fucking cold."

"Probably sink like a stone," Ethan said mildly as they muscled Seth toward the dock. "Looks like living in Europe turned him into a wimp."

"Wimp, my ass." He fought against their hold, fought not to laugh. "Takes three of you to take me out. Bunch of feeble old men," he snarled. With grips, he thought, like steel.

That had Phillip's brow quirking. "How far do you think we can throw him?"

"Let's find out. One," Cam announced as they stood swinging him between them on the dock.

"I'll kill you." Swearing, laughing, Seth wiggled like a fish.

"Two," Phillip said with a grin. "Better save your breath, kid."

"Three. Welcome home, Seth," Ethan said as the three of them hurled him in the air.

He was right. The water was freezing. It stole the breath he hadn't bothered to save, chilled him right down to the bone. When he surfaced, spitting it out, shoving at his hair, he heard his brothers howling with delight, saw them ranged together on the dock with the early sun showering down and the old white house behind them.

I'm Seth Quinn, he thought. And I'm home.

THE early-morning dip went a long way toward purging any jet lag. Since he was up, Seth decided he might as well get things done. He drove back to Baltimore, turned in the rental, and after some wheeling and dealing at a dealership, drove toward the Shore the proud owner of a muscular Jaguar convertible in saber silver.

He knew it shouted: Officer, may I have a speeding ticket please! But he couldn't resist.

Selling his art was a two-edged sword. It sliced at his heart each time he parted with a painting. But he was selling very well and might as well reap some of the benefits.

His brothers, he thought smugly, were going to be green when they got a load of his new ride.

He cut back on his speed as he cruised into St. Chris. The little water town with its busy docks and quiet streets was another painting to him, one he'd re-created countless times, from countless angles.

Market Street with its shops and restaurants ran parallel to the dock, where crab pickers still set up tables on weekends to perform for the tourists. Watermen like Ethan would bring the day's catch there.

The town spread back with its old Victorian houses, its saltboxes and clapboards shaded by leafy trees. Lawns would be tidy. Neat, quaint, historic drew in the tourists, who would browse in the shops, eat in the restaurants, cozy up in one of the B and B's for a relaxing weekend at the Shore.

Locals learned to live with them, just as they learned to live with the gales that blew in from the Atlantic, and the droughts that sizzled their soybean fields. As they learned to live with the capricious Bay and her dwindling bounty.

He passed Crawford's and thought of sloppy submarine sandwiches, dripping ice cream cones and town gossip.

He'd ridden his bike on these streets, racing with Danny and Will McLean. He'd cruised with them in the secondhand Chevy he and Cam had fixed up the summer he turned sixteen.

And he'd sat—man and boy—at one of the umbrella tables while the town bustled by, trying to capture what it was about this single spot on the planet that shone so bright for him.

He wasn't sure he ever had, or ever would.

He eased into a parking space so he could walk down to the dock. He wanted to study the light, the shadows, the colors and shapes, and was already wishing he'd thought to bring a sketch pad.

It amazed him, constantly, how much beauty there was in the world. How it changed and it shifted even as he watched. The way the sun struck the water at one exact instant, how it spread or winked away behind a cloud.

Or there, he thought, the curve of that little girl's cheek when she lifted her face to look at a gull. The way her laugh shaped her mouth, or the way her fingers threaded through her mother's in absolute trust.

There was power in that.

He stood watching a white boat heel to in blue water, its sails snap full as they caught the wind.

He wanted to be out on the water again, he realized. Be part of it. Maybe he'd shanghai Aubrey for a few hours. He'd make a couple more stops, then swing by the boatyard and see if he could steal her.

Scanning the street, he started back for his car. A sign painted on a storefront caught his attention. *Bud and Bloom,* he read. Flower shop. That was new. He strolled closer, noting the festive pots hanging on either side of the glass.

The window itself was filled with plants and what he thought of as whatnots. Clever ones, though, Seth thought, finding himself amused by the spotted black-and-white cow with pansies flowing over its back.

In the lower right-hand corner of the window, written in the same ornate script, was: *Drusilla Whitcomb Banks, Proprietor.*

It wasn't a name he recognized, and since the painted script informed him the shop had been established in September of the previous year, he imagined some fussy widow, on the elderly side. White hair, he decided, starched dress with a prim floral print to go with sensible shoes and the half-glasses she wore on a gold chain around her neck.

She and her husband had come to St. Chris for long weekends, and when he'd died, she'd had too much money and time on her hands. So she'd moved here and opened her little flower shop so that she could be somewhere they'd been carefree together while doing something she'd secretly longed to do for years.

The story line made him like Mrs. Whitcomb Banks and her snobby cat—she'd *have* to have a cat—named Ernestine.

He decided to make her, and the many women in his life, happy. With flowers on his mind, Seth opened the door to the musical tinkle of bells.

The proprietor, he thought, had an artistic eye. It wasn't just the flowers—they were, after all, just the paint. She had daubed, splashed and streamed her paints very well. Flows of colors, a mix of shapes, a contrast of textures covered the canvas of her shop. It was tidy, just as he'd expected, but not regimented or formal.

He knew enough of flowers from the years of living with Anna to recognize how cleverly she'd paired hot-pink gerbera with rich blue delphiniums, snowy-white lilies with the elegance of red roses. Mixed in with those sweeps of color were the fans and spikes and tongues of green.

And the whimsy again, he noted, charmed. Cast-iron pigs, flute-playing frogs, wicked-faced gargoyles.

There were pots and vases, ribbons and lace, shallow dishes of herbs and thriving houseplants. He got the impression of cannily arranged clutter in a limited and well-used space.

Over it all were the fairy-tale notes of "Afternoon of a Faun."

Nice going, Mrs. Whitcomb Banks, he decided and prepared to spend lavishly.

The woman who stepped out of the rear door behind the long service counter wasn't Seth's image of the talented widow, but she sure as hell belonged in a fanciful garden.

He gave his widow extra points for hiring help who brought faeries and spellbound princesses to a man's mind.

"May I help you?"

"Oh yeah." Seth crossed to the counter and just looked at her.

Long, slim and tidy as a rose, he thought. Her hair was true black, cut close to follow the lovely shape of her head while leaving the elegant stem of her neck exposed. It was a look, he thought, that took considerable female guts and self-confidence.

It left her face completely unframed so that the delicate ivory of her skin formed a perfect oval canvas. The gods had been in a fine mood the day they'd created her, and had drawn her a pair of long, almond-shaped eyes of moss green, then added a nimbus of amber around her pupils.

Her nose was small and straight, her mouth wide to go

with the eyes, and very full. She'd tinted it a deep, seductive rose.

Her chin had the faintest cleft, as if her maker had given it a light finger brush of approval.

He would paint that face; there was no question about it. And the rest of her as well. He saw her lying on a bed of red rose petals, those faerie eyes glowing with sleepy power, those lips slightly curved, as if she'd just wakened from dreaming of a lover.

Her smile didn't waver as he studied her, but the dark wings of her eyebrows lifted. "And just what can I help you with?"

The voice was good, he mused. Strong and smooth. Not a local, he decided.

"We can start with flowers," he told her. "It's a great shop."

"Thanks. What sort of flowers did you have in mind today?"

"We'll get to that." He leaned on the counter. In St. Chris, there was always time for a little conversation. "Have you worked here long?"

"From the beginning. If you're thinking ahead to Mother's Day, I have some lovely—"

"No, I've got Mother's Day handled. You're not from around here. The accent," he explained when those brows lifted again. "Not Shore. A little north, maybe."

"Very good. D.C."

"So, the name of the shop. Bud and Bloom. Is that from Whistler?"

Surprise, and speculation, flickered over her face. "As a matter of fact, it is. You're the first to tag it."

"One of my brothers is big on stuff like that. I can't re-

CHESAPEAKE BLUE ⁓ 31

member the quote exactly. Something about perfect in its
bud as in its bloom."

"'The masterpiece should appear as the flower to the
painter—perfect in its bud as in its bloom.'"

"Yeah, that's it. I probably recognized it because that's
what I do. I paint."

"Really?" She reminded herself to be patient, to relax
into the rhythm. Part of the package in the little town was
slow, winding conversations with strangers. She'd already
sized him up. His face was vaguely familiar, and his eyes,
a very striking blue, were frank and direct in their interest.
She wouldn't stoop to flirtation, certainly not to make a
sale, but she could be friendly.

She'd come to St. Chris to be friendly.

Because she imagined he painted houses, she sorted
through her mind for an arrangement that would suit his
budget. "Do you work locally?"

"I do now. I've been away. Do you work here alone?"
He glanced around, calculating the amount of work that
went into maintaining the garden she'd created. "Does the
proprietor come in?"

"I work alone, for now. And I am the proprietor."

He looked back at her and began to laugh. "Boy, I
wasn't even close. Nice to meet you, Drusilla Whitcomb
Banks." He held out a hand. "I'm Seth Quinn."

Seth Quinn. She laid her hand in his automatically and
did her own rapid readjustment. Not a face she'd seen
around town, she realized, but one she'd seen in a magazine. No housepainter, despite the old jeans and faded
shirt, but an artist. The local boy who'd become the toast of
Europe.

"I admire your work," she told him.

"Thanks. I admire yours. And I'm probably keeping you from it. I'm going to make it worth your while. I've got some ladies to impress. You can help me out."

"Ladies? Plural?"

"Yeah. Three, no four," he corrected, thinking of Aubrey.

"It's a wonder you have time to paint, Mr. Quinn."

"Seth. I manage."

"I bet you do." Certain types of men always managed. "Cut flowers, arrangements or plants?"

"Ah . . . cut flowers, in a nice box. More romantic, right? Let me think." He calculated route and time, and decided he'd drop by to see Sybill first. "Number one is sophisticated, chic, intellectual and practical-minded, with a soft-gooey center. Roses, I guess."

"If you want to be predictable."

He looked back at Dru. "Let's be unpredictable."

"Just a moment. I have something in the back you should like."

Something out here I like, he thought as she turned toward the rear door. He gave his heart a little pat.

Phillip, Seth thought as he wandered the shop, would approve of the classic, clean lines of that ripening, peach-colored suit she wore. Ethan, he imagined, would wonder how to give her a hand with all the work that must go into running the place. And Cam . . . well, Cam would take one long look at her and grin.

Seth supposed he had bits of all three of them inside him.

She came back carrying an armload of streamlined and exotic flowers with waxy blooms the color of eggplant.

"Calla lilies," she told him. "Elegant, simple, classy and in this color spectacular."

"You nailed her."

She set them in a cone-shaped holding vase. "Next?"

"Warm, old-fashioned in the best possible way." Just thinking of Grace made him smile. "Simple in the same way. Sweet but not sappy, and with a spine of steel."

"Tulips," she said and walked to a clear-fronted, refrigerated cabinet. "In this rather tender pink. A quiet flower that's sturdier than it looks," she added as she brought them over for him to see.

"Bingo. You're good."

"Yes, I am." She was enjoying herself now—not just for the sale, but for the game of it. This was the reason she'd opened the shop. "Number three?"

Aubrey, he thought. How to describe Aubrey. "Young, fresh, fun. Tough and unstintingly loyal."

"Hold on." With the image in mind, Dru breezed into the back again. And came out with a clutch of sunflowers with faces as wide as a dessert plate.

"Jesus, they're perfect. You're in the right business, Drusilla."

It was, she thought, the finest of compliments. "No point in being in the wrong one. And since you're about to break my record for single walk-in sales, it's Dru."

"Nice."

"And the fourth lucky woman?"

"Bold, beautiful, smart and sexy. With a heart like . . ." Anna's heart, he thought. "With a heart beyond description. The most amazing woman I've ever known."

"And apparently you know quite a few. One minute." Again, she went into the back. He was admiring the sunflowers when Dru came back with Asiatic lilies in triumphant scarlet.

"Oh man. They're so Anna." He reached out to touch one of the vivid red petals. "So completely Anna. You've just made me a hero."

"Happy to oblige. I'll box them, and tie ribbons on each that coordinate with the color of the flowers inside. Can you keep them straight?"

"I think I can handle it."

"Cards are included. You can pick what you like from the rack on the counter."

"I won't need cards." He watched her fit water-filled nipples on the end of the stems. No wedding ring, he noted. He'd have painted her regardless, but if she'd been married it would have put an end to the rest of his plans.

"What flower are you?"

She flicked him a glance as she arranged the first flowers in a tissue-lined white box. "All of them. I like variety." She tied a deep purple ribbon around the first box. "As it appears you do."

"I kind of hate to shatter the illusion that I've got a harem going here. Sisters," he said, gesturing toward the flowers. "Though the sunflowers are niece, cousin, sister. The exact relationship's a little murky."

"Um-hm."

"My brothers' wives," he explained. "And one of my brothers' oldest daughter. I figured I should clear that up since I'm going to paint you."

"Are you?" She tied the second box with pink ribbon edged with white lace. "Are you really?"

He took out his credit card, laid it on the counter while she went to work on the sunflowers. "You're thinking I'm just looking to get you naked, and I wouldn't have any objection to that."

She drew gold ribbon from its loop. "Why would you?"

"Exactly. But why don't we start with your face? It's a good face. I really like the shape of your head."

For the first time, her fingers fumbled a bit. With a half laugh, she stopped and really looked at him again. "The shape of my head?"

"Sure. You like it, too, or you wouldn't wear your hair that way. Makes a powerful statement with a minimum of fuss."

She tied off the bow. "You're clever at defining a woman with a few pithy phrases."

"I like women."

"I figured that out." As she finished up the red lilies, a pair of customers came in and began to browse.

A good thing, Dru thought. It was time to move the artistic Mr. Quinn along.

"I'm flattered you admire the shape of my head." She picked up his credit card to ring up the sale. "And that someone of your talent and reputation would like to paint me. But the business keeps me very busy, and without a great deal of free time. What free time I do have, I'm extremely selfish with."

She gave him his total, slid the sales slip over for his signature.

"You close at six daily and don't open on Sundays."

She should've been annoyed, she thought, but instead she was intrigued. "You don't miss much, do you?"

"Every detail matters." After signing the receipt, he plucked out one of her gift cards, turned it over to the blank back.

He drew a quick study of her face as the blossom of a long-stemmed flower, then added the phone number at home before he signed it. "In case you change your mind," he said, offering it.

She studied the card, found her lips quirking. "I could probably sell this on eBay for a tidy little sum."

"You've got too much class for that." He piled up the boxes, hefted them. "Thanks for the flowers."

"You're welcome." She came around the counter to open the door for him. "I hope your . . . sisters enjoy them."

"They will." He shot her a last look over his shoulder. "I'll be back."

"I'll be here." Tucking the sketch into her pocket, she closed the door.

IT had been great to see Sybill, to spend an hour alone with her. And to see the pleasure she got from arranging the flowers in a tall, clear vase.

They were perfect for her, he concluded, just as the house she and Phillip had bought and furnished, the massive old Victorian with all the stylized details, was perfect for her.

She'd changed her hairstyle over the years, but now it was back to the way he liked it best, swinging sleek nearly to her shoulders with all that richness of color of a pricey mink coat.

She hadn't bothered with lipstick for the day of working at home, and wore a simple and crisp white shirt with pegged black trousers, what he supposed she thought of as casual wear.

She was the mother of two active children, as well as being a trained sociologist and successful author. And looked, Seth thought, utterly serene.

He had reason to know that that serenity had been hard-won.

She'd grown up in the same household as his mother. Half sisters who were like opposite sides of a coin.

Since even the thought of Gloria DeLauter clenched his stomach muscles, Seth pushed it aside and concentrated on Sybill.

"When you, Phil and the kids came over to Rome a few months ago, I didn't think the next time I'd see you would be here."

"I wanted you to come back." She poured them each a glass of iced tea. "Totally selfish of me, but I wanted you back. Sometimes in the middle of whatever was going on, I'd stop and think: Something's missing. What's missing? Then, oh yes, Seth. Seth's missing. Silly."

"Sweet." He gave her hand a squeeze before picking up the glass she set down for him. "Thanks."

"Tell me everything," she demanded.

They talked of his work and hers. Of the children. Of what had changed and what had stayed the same.

When he got up to leave, she wrapped her arms around him and held on just a minute longer. "Thanks for the flowers. They're wonderful."

"Nice new shop on Market. The woman who owns it seems to know her stuff." He walked with Sybill, hand in hand, toward the door. "Have you been in there?"

"Once or twice." Because she knew him, very well, Sybill smiled. "She's very lovely, isn't she?"

"Who's that?" But when Sybill merely tipped her head, he grinned. "Caught me. Yeah, she's got some face. What do you know about her?"

"Nothing, really. She moved here late last summer, I think, and had the store open by fall. I believe she's from the D.C. area. It seems to me my parents know some Whitcombs, and some Bankses from around there. Might be relatives." She shrugged. "I can't say for certain, and my parents and I don't . . . communicate very often these days."

He touched her cheek. "I'm sorry."

"Don't be. They have two spectacular grandchildren whom they largely ignore." As they've ignored you, she thought. "It's their loss."

"Your mother's never forgiven you for standing up for me."

"Her loss." Sybill spoke very precisely as she caught his face in her hands. "My gain. And I didn't stand alone. No one ever does in this family."

She was right about that, Seth thought as he drove toward the boatyard. No Quinn stood alone.

But he wasn't sure he could stand pulling them into the trouble he was very much afraid was going to find him, even back home.

THREE

ONCE DRU HAD rung up the next sale and was alone in the shop again, she took the sketch out of her pocket.

Seth Quinn. Seth Quinn wanted to paint her. It was fascinating. And as intriguing, she admitted, as the artist himself. A woman could be intrigued without being actively interested.

Which she wasn't.

She had no desire to pose, to be scrutinized, to be immortalized. Even by such talented hands. But she was curious, about the concept of it, just as she was curious about Seth Quinn.

The article she'd read had included some details on his personal life. She knew he'd come to the Eastern Shore as a child, taken in by Ray Quinn before Ray died in a single-car accident. Some of the story was a little nebulous. There'd been no mention of parents, and Seth had been very closed-mouthed in the interview in that area. The facts given were that Ray Quinn had been his grandfather, and on his death, Seth had been raised by Quinn's three adopted sons. And their wives as they had come along.

Sisters, he'd said, thinking of the flowers he'd bought. Perhaps they had been for the women he considered his sisters.

It hardly mattered to her.

She'd been more interested in what the article had said about his work, and how his family had encouraged his early talent. How they had supported his desire to study in Europe.

It was a fortunate child, in Dru's opinion, who had a family who loved him enough to let him go—to let him discover, to fail or succeed on his own. And, she thought, who apparently welcomed him back just as unselfishly.

Still, it was difficult to imagine the man the Italians had dubbed *il maestro giovane*—the young master—settling down in St. Christopher to paint seascapes.

Just as she assumed it was difficult for many of her acquaintances to imagine Drusilla Whitcomb Banks, young socialite, contentedly selling flowers in a small waterfront shop.

It didn't matter to her what people thought or what they said—any more than she supposed such things mattered to Seth Quinn. She'd come here to get away from the demands and expectations, the sticky grip of family, and the unrelenting upheaval of being used as the fraying rope in the endless game of tug-of-war her parents played.

She'd come to St. Chris for peace, the peace that she'd yearned for most of her life.

She was finding it.

Though her mother would be thrilled—perhaps, stubbornly, *because* her mother would be thrilled at the prospect of her precious daughter capturing the interest of Seth Quinn—Dru had no intention of cultivating that interest. Neither the artistic interest, nor the more elemental and frankly sexual interest she'd seen in his eyes when he'd looked at her.

Or, if she was being honest, the frankly sexual interest she'd felt for him.

The Quinns were, by all reports, a large, complex and unwieldy family. God knew she'd had her fill of family.

A pity, she admitted, tapping the card on her palm before dropping it into a drawer. The young master was attractive, amusing and appealing. And any man who took the time to buy flowers for his sisters, and wanted to make sure each purchase suited the individual style of the recipient, earned major points.

"Too bad for both of us," she murmured, and shut the drawer with a final little snap.

H E was thinking of Dru as she was thinking of him, and pondering just what angles, just what tones would work best on a portrait. He liked the idea of a three-quarter view of her face, with her head turned to the left, but her eyes looking back, out of the canvas.

That would suit the contrast of her cool attitude and sexy chic.

He never doubted she'd consent to pose. He had an entire arsenal of weapons to battle a model's reluctance. All he had to do was decide which one would work best on Drusilla.

Tapping his fingers on the wheel to the outlaw beat of Aerosmith that blasted out of his stereo, Seth considered her.

There was money in her background, he decided. Seth recognized designer cut and good fabric even if he was more interested in the form beneath the fashion. Then there was the cadence of her voice. It said high-class private school to him.

She'd tagged James McNeill Whistler for the name of her shop. Which meant, he thought, she'd had a very tony education, or someone pounding poetry and literature into her head as Phil had done with him.

Probably both.

She was comfortable with her looks and didn't fluster when a man made it clear she attracted him.

She wasn't married, and instinct told him she wasn't attached. A woman like Dru didn't relocate to tag along after a boyfriend or lover. She'd moved from Washington, started a business and run it solo because that's just the way she wanted it.

Then he remembered just how far off the mark he'd been regarding the fictional Widow Whitcomb Banks, and decided to hedge his bets by doing a little research before approaching her again.

Seth pulled into the parking lot of the old brick barn the Quinns had bought from Nancy Claremont when the woman's tight-fisted, tight-assed husband had keeled over dead of a heart attack while arguing with Cy Crawford over the price of a meatball sub.

Initially they'd rented the massive building, one that had been a tobacco warehouse in the 1700s, a packinghouse in the 1800s and a glorified storage shed for much of the 1900s.

Then it had been a boatyard, transformed and outfitted by the brothers Quinn. For the last eight years, it had belonged to them.

Seth looked up at the roof as he climbed out of the car. He'd helped reshingle that roof, he remembered, and had nearly broken his neck doing it.

He'd smeared the hot fifty-fifty mix on seams, and burned his fingers. He'd learned to lap boards in the bottomless well of Ethan's patience. He'd sweated like a pig along with Cam repairing the dock. And had escaped by whatever means presented themselves every time Phil had tried to shoehorn him into learning to keep the books.

He walked to the front, stood with his hands on his hips studying the weathered sign. BOATS BY QUINN. And noted that another name had been added to the four that had been there since the beginning.

Aubrey Quinn.

Even as he grinned, she shoved out of the front door.

She had a tool belt slung at her hips and an Orioles fielder's cap low over her forehead. Her hair, the color of burnt honey, was pulled through the back loop to swing at her back.

Her scarred and stained work boots looked like a doll's. She had such little feet.

And a very big voice, he thought when she let out a roaring whoop as she charged him.

She leaped, boosted herself with a bounce of her hands off his shoulders and wrapped her legs around his waist. The bill of her cap rapped him in the forehead when she pressed her mouth to his in a long, smacking kiss.

"My Seth." With a loud hooting laugh, she chained her arms around his neck. "Don't go away again. Damn it, don't you dare go away again."

"I can't. Too much happens around here when I'm gone. Tip back," he ordered, and dipped her away far enough to study her face.

At two, she'd been a tiny princess to him. At twenty, she was an athletic, appealing handful.

"Jeez, you got pretty," he said.

"Yeah? You too."

"Why aren't you in college?"

"Don't start." She rolled her bright green eyes and hopped down. "I did two years, and I'd've been happier on a chain gang. This is what I want to do." She jerked a thumb toward the sign. "My name's up there to prove it."

"You always could wrap Ethan around your finger."

"Maybe. But I didn't have to. Dad got it, and after some initial fretting, so did Mom. I was never the student you were, Seth, and you were never the boatbuilder I am."

"Shit. I leave you alone for a few years, and you get delusions of grandeur. If you're going to insult me, I'm not going to give you your present."

"Where is it? What is it?" She attacked by poking her fingers in his ribs where she knew him to be the most vulnerable. "Gimme."

"Cut it out. Okay, okay. Man, you don't change."

"Why mess with perfection? Hand over the loot and nobody gets hurt."

"It's in the car." He pointed toward the lot and had the satisfaction of seeing her mouth drop open.

"A Jag? Oh baby." She darted over the stubble of lawn to the lot to run her fingers reverently over the shining silver hood. "Cam's going to cry when he sees this. He's just going to break down and cry. Let me have the keys so I can test her out."

"Sure, when we're slurping on Sno Kones in hell."

"Don't be mean. You can come with me. We'll buzz up to Crawford's and get some . . ." She trailed off as he got the long white box out of the trunk. She blinked at the box, blinked at him before her eyes went soft and dewy.

"You bought me flowers. You got me a girl present. Oh, let me see! What kind are they?" She pulled a work knife out of her belt, sliced the ribbon, then yanked up the lid. "Sunflowers. Look how happy they are."

"Reminded me of you."

"I really love you." She stared hard at the flowers. "I've been so mad at you for leaving." When her voice broke, he gave her an awkward pat on the shoulder. "I'm not going to cry," she muttered and sucked it in. "What am I, a sissy?"

"Never."

"Okay, well, anyway, you're back." She turned to hug him again. "I really love the flowers."

"Good." He slapped a hand on the one that was trying to sneak into his pocket. "You're not getting the keys. I've got to take off anyway. I've got flowers for Grace. I want to swing by and see her on my way home."

"She's not there. This is her afternoon for running errands, then she'll pick Deke up from school and drop him off for his piano lesson and so on and so on. I don't know how she does it all. I'll take them to her," Aubrey added. "Flowers will take some of the sting out of missing you today."

"Tell her I'll try to get by tomorrow, otherwise I'll see her Sunday." He carted the box from his trunk to the snappy little blue pickup.

Aubrey laid her flowers in the cab with her mother's. "You've got some time now. Let's go get Cam and show off your car. I tell you, he's going to break down and sob like a baby. I can't wait."

"You've got a mean streak, Aub." Seth slung his arm

around her shoulders. "I like that about you. Now, tell me what you know about the flower lady. Drusilla."

"Aha." Aubrey leered up at him as they walked toward the building. "So that's the way the garden grows."

"Might."

"Tell you what. Meet me at Shiney's after dinner. Say about eight. Buy me a drink and I'll spill everything I know."

"You're underage."

"Yeah, like I've never sipped a beer before," she retorted. "A soft drink, Daddy. And remember, I'll be legal in less than six months."

"Until then, when I'm buying, you drink Coke." He tipped down the bill of her cap, then dragged open the door to the noise of power tools.

CAM didn't break down and weep, Seth thought later, but he had drooled a little. Nearly genuflected. Right before, Seth mused as he parked in front of Shiney's Pub, Cam—being bigger and meaner than Aubrey—snagged the keys and peeled off to take it for a spin.

Then, of course, they spent a very satisfying hour standing around admiring the engine.

Seth glanced at the pickup beside his car. One thing about Aubrey, she was always prompt.

He opened the door to Shiney's and felt yet one more homecoming. Another constant of St. Chris, he thought. Shiney's Pub would always look as if it needed to be hosed down, the waitresses would always be leggy, and it would offer the very worst live bands to be found in the entire state of Maryland.

While the lead singer massacred Barenaked Ladies,

Seth scanned the tables and bar for a little blonde in a fielder's cap.

His eyes actually passed over her, then arrowed back.

She was indeed at the bar, urbane and curvy in unrelieved black, her burnt-honey hair spiraling down her back as she carried on a heated conversation with a guy who looked like Joe College.

Mouth grim, body poised for a confrontation, Seth headed over to show College Boy just what happened when a guy hit on his sister.

"You're full of it." Aubrey's voice snapped like a whip and had Seth's mouth moving into a snarl. "You are so absolutely full of it. The pitching rotation is solid, the infield's got good gloves. The bats are coming around. By the All-Star Game, the Birds will be playing better than five-hundred ball."

"They won't see five hundred all season," her opponent shot back. "And they're going to be digging another level down in the basement by the All-Star Game."

"Bet." Aubrey dug a twenty out of her pocket, slapped it on the bar.

And Seth sighed. She might've looked like a tasty morsel, but nobody nibbled on his Aubrey.

"Seth." Spotting him, Aubrey reached out, hooked his arm and yanked him to the bar. "Sam Jacoby," she said with a nod toward the man sitting beside her. "Thinks because he plays a little softball he knows something about the Bigs."

"Heard a lot about you." Sam held out a hand. "From this sentimental slob here who thinks the Orioles have a shot at climbing their pitiful way up to mediocre this season."

Seth shook hands. "If you want to commit suicide, Sam, get a gun. It's got to be less painful than inciting this one to peel every inch of skin slowly off your body with a putty knife."

"I like to live dangerously," he said and slid off the stool. "Take a seat. I was holding it for you. Gotta split. See you around, Aub."

"You're going to owe me twenty bucks in July," she called out, then shifted her attention to Seth. "Sam's a nice enough guy, except for the fatal flaw that encourages him to root for the Mariners."

"I thought he was hitting on you."

"Sam?" Aubrey gazed back toward the tables with a smug and female look in her eye that made Seth want to squirm. "Sure he was. I'm holding him in reserve. I'm sort of seeing Will McLean right now."

"Will?" Seth nearly choked. "Will McLean?" The idea of Aubrey and one of his boyhood pals together—that way—had Seth signaling the bartender. "I really need a beer. Rolling Rock."

"Not that we get to see each other that often." Knowing she was turning the screw, Aubrey continued gleefully. "He's an intern at Saint Chris General. Rotations at the hospital are a bitch. But when we do manage the time, it's worth it."

"Shut up. He's too old for you."

"I've always gone for older men." Deliberately, she pinched his cheek. "Cutie pie. Plus there's only, like, five years' difference. Still, if you want to talk about my love life—"

"I don't." Seth reached for the bottle the bartender set in front of him, drank deep. "I really don't."

"Okay, enough about me then, let's talk about you. How many languages did you score in when you were plundering Europe?"

"Now you sound like Kevin." And it wasn't nearly as comfortable a topic to explore with Aubrey. "I wasn't on a sexual marathon. I was working."

"Some chicks really fall for the artistic type. Maybe your flower lady's one of them, and you'll get lucky."

"Obviously you've been hanging around with my brothers too much. Turned you into a gutter brain. Just tell me what you know about her?"

"Okay." She grabbed a bowl of pretzels off the bar and began to munch. "So, she first showed up about a year ago. Spent a week hanging around. Checking out retail space," she said with a nod. "I got that from Doug Motts. Remember Dougie—roly-poly little kid? Couple years behind you in school."

"Vaguely."

"Anyway, he lost the baby fat. He's working at Shore Realtors now. According to Doug, she knew just what she was looking for, and told them to contact her in D.C. when and if anything that came close opened up. Now, Doug . . ." She pointed toward her empty glass when the bartender swung by. "He'd pretty much just started at the Realtor's and was hoping to hook this one. So he poked around some, trying to dig up information on his prospective client. She'd told him she'd visited Saint Chris a couple times when she was a kid, so that gave Doug his starting point."

"Ma Crawford," Seth said with a laugh.

"You got it. What Ma Crawford doesn't know ain't worth knowing. And the woman's got a memory like a herd of elephants. She recalled the Whitcomb Bankses. Name like that, who wouldn't? But they stuck out more because she remembered Mrs. WB from when *she* was a girl visiting here with her family. Her really seriously kick-your-butt-to-Tuesday rich family. Whitcomb Technologies. As in we make everything. As in Fortune Five Hundred. As in Senator James P. Whitcomb, the gentleman from Maryland."

"Ah. *Those* Whitcombs."

"You bet. The senator, who would be the flower lady's grandfather, had an affection for the Eastern Shore. And his daughter, the current Mrs. WB, married Proctor Banks—what kind of name is Proctor, anyway?—of Banks and Shelby Communication. We're talking mega family dough with this combo. Like a fricking empire."

"And young, nubile and extremely wealthy Drusilla rents a storefront in Saint Chris and sells flowers."

"Buys a building in Saint Chris," Aubrey corrected. "She bought the place, prime retail space for our little kingdom. A few months after Doug had the good fortune to be manning the desk at Shore Realtors when she walked in, that place went on the market. Previous owners live in PA, rented it to various merchants who had their ups and downs there. Remember the New Age shop—rocks, crystals, ritual candles and meditation tapes?"

"Yeah. Guy who ran it had a tattoo of a dragon on the back of his right hand."

"That place lasted longer than anybody figured it would, but when the lease came up for renewal last year, it went bye-bye. Doug, smelling commission, gives the young WB a call to tell her a rental just opened up on Market, and she makes him salivate when she asks if the owners are interested in selling. When they were, and a deal was struck, he sang the 'Hallelujah Chorus.' Then she makes him the happiest man in Saint Chris when she tells him to find her a house, too. She comes down, takes a look at the three he shows her, takes a liking to this ramshackle old Victorian on Oyster Inlet. Prime real estate again," Aubrey added. "No flies on flower lady."

"That old blue house?" Seth asked. "Looked like a half-eaten gingerbread house? She bought *that*?"

"Lock and stock." Aubrey nodded as she crunched pretzels. "Guy bought it about three years ago, snazzed it up, wanted to turn it."

"Nothing much around there but marsh grass and thickets." But it rose over a curve of the flatland river, he remembered. That tobacco-colored water that could gleam like amber when the sun beamed through the oak and gum trees.

"Your girl likes her privacy," Aubrey told him. "Keeps to herself. Courteous and helpful to her customers, polite, even friendly, but carefully so. She blows cool."

"She's new here." God knew he understood what it was like to find yourself in a place, one that had just exactly what you wanted, and not be sure if you'd find your slot.

"She's an outlander." Aubrey jerked a shoulder in a typical Quinn shrug. "She'll be new here for the next twenty years."

"She could probably use a friend."

"Looking to make new friends, Seth? Somebody to go chicken necking with?"

He gestured for another beer, then leaned in until his nose bumped hers. "Maybe. Is that what you and Will do in your spare time?"

"We skip the chicken, and just neck. But I'll take you out in the pram if you've got a hankering. I'll captain. It's been so long since you manned a sail, you'd probably capsize her."

"Like hell. We'll go out tomorrow."

"That's a date. And speaking of dates, your new friend just came in."

"Who?" But he knew, even before he swiveled around on the stool. Before he scanned the evening crowd and spotted her.

She looked sublimely out of place among the watermen with their wind-scored faces and scarred hands and the university students with their trendy shoes and baggy shirts.

Her suit was still crisp and perfect, her face an oval of alabaster in the dull light.

She had to know heads turned as she walked in, he thought. Women always knew. But she moved with purpose and easy grace around the stained tables and rickety chairs.

"Classy" was Aubrey's one-word summation.

"Oh yeah." Seth dug out money for the drinks, tossed it on the bar. "I'm ditching you, kid."

Aubrey widened her eyes in exaggerated shock. "Color me amazed."

"Tomorrow," he said, then leaned down to give her a quick kiss before strolling off to intercept Dru.

She stopped by a table and began speaking to a waitress. Seth's attention was so focused on Dru it took him a moment to recognize the other woman.

Terri Hardgrove. Blond, sulky and built. They'd dated for a couple of memorable months during his junior year of high school. It had not ended well, Seth recalled and nearly detoured just to avoid the confrontation.

Instead he tried an easy smile and kept going until he caught some of their conversation.

"I'm not going to take the place after all," Terri said as she balanced her tray on the shelf of one hip. "J.J. and me worked things out."

"J.J." Dru angled her head. "That would be the lowlife,

lying scum you never wanted to see again even if he was gasping his last, dying breath?"

"Well." Terri shifted her feet, fluttered her lashes. "We hadn't worked things out when I said that. And I thought, you know, screw him, I'll just get me a place of my own and get back in the game. It was just that I saw your For Rent sign when I was so mad at him and all. But we worked things out."

"So you said. Congratulations. It might've been helpful if you'd come by this afternoon as we'd agreed and let me know."

"I'm really sorry, but that's when . . ."

"You were working things out," Dru finished.

"Hey, Terri."

She squealed. It came flooding back to Seth that she'd always been a squealer. Apparently, she hadn't grown out of it.

"Seth! Seth Quinn! Just look at you."

"How's it going?"

"It's going just fine. I heard you were back, but now here you are. Big as life and twice as handsome, and famous, too. It's sure been some while since Saint Chris High."

"Some time," he agreed and looked at Dru.

"Y'all know each other?" Terri asked.

"We've met," Dru said. "I'll leave you to catch up on old times. I hope you and J.J. are very happy."

"You and J.J. Wyatt?"

Terri preened. "That's right. We're practically engaged."

"We'll catch up later. You can tell me all about it." He took off, leaving Terri pouting at his back as he caught up with Dru.

"J.J. Wyatt," Seth began as he stepped beside Dru. "Offensive tackle on the Saint Chris High Sharks. Went on to crush as many heads as he could manage at the local university before even his bulldog skill on the football field couldn't keep him from flunking out."

"Thank you for that fascinating slice of local history."

"You're pissed. Why don't I buy you a drink and you can tell me all about it?"

"I don't want a drink, thank you, and I'm getting out of here before my eardrums are permanently damaged by that amazingly loud and untalented band's horrendous version of 'Jack and Diane.' "

He decided it was a point in her favor that she could recognize the mangled song, and pulled open the door for her.

"The flowers were a hit."

"I'm glad to hear it." She took her keys out of a streamlined, buff-colored purse.

He started to suggest they go somewhere else for a drink, but could see by the irritated line between her eyebrows that she'd just shut him down.

"So, you've got a space to rent?"

"Apparently." She moved, dismissively, to the driver's side of a black Mercedes SUV.

Seth got his hand on the handle before she did, then just leaned companionably against the door. "Where?"

"Above the shop."

"And you want to rent it?"

"It's empty. It seems like a waste of space. I can't drive my car unless I'm inside of it," she pointed out.

"Above the shop," he repeated, and brought the building back into his mind. Two stories, yeah, that was right. "Bank of three windows, front and back," he said aloud. "Should be good light. How big is it?"

"Nine hundred square feet, including a small galley-style kitchen."

"Big enough. Let's take a look."

"Excuse me?"

"Show me the space. I might be interested."

She gave the keys in her hand an impatient jiggle. "You want me to show you the apartment now?"

"You don't want to waste space, why waste time?" He opened her car door. "I'll follow you back. It won't take long," he said with that slow, easy grin. "I make up my mind pretty quick."

FOUR

S HE MADE UP her mind quickly as well, Dru thought as she backed out of the pub's lot. And she had Seth Quinn pegged.

A confident man, and a talented one. Each aspect probably fed into the other. The fact that his rough edges managed to have a sheen of polish was intriguing, something she was certain he knew very well.

And used very well.

He was attractive. The lean, lanky build that looked as though it had been designed to wear those worn-out jeans. All that burnished blond hair, straight as a pin and never quite styled. The hollowed cheeks, the vivid blue eyes. Not just vivid in color, she thought now. In intensity. The way he looked at you, as if he saw something no one else could see. Something you couldn't see yourself.

It managed to be flattering, jolting and just a bit off-putting all at once.

It made you wonder about him. And if you were wondering about a man, you were thinking about him.

Women, she concluded, were like paints on a palette to him. He could dab into any one of them at his whim. The way he'd been snuggled up with the blonde in the bar—a little play she'd noted the instant she herself had walked in—was a case in point.

Then there'd been the way he'd smiled at the waitress, the terminally foolish Terri. Wide, warm and friendly, with just a hint of intimacy. Very potent, that smile, Dru mused, but it wasn't going to work on her.

Men who bounced from woman to woman because they could were entirely too ordinary for her tastes.

Yet here she was, she admitted, driving back to the shop to show him the second-floor apartment when what she really wanted to do was go home to her lovely, quiet house.

It was the sensible thing to do, of course. There was no point in the space staying empty. But it galled that he'd assumed she'd take the time and trouble simply because he wanted her to.

There was no problem finding a parking space now. It was barely nine on a cool spring evening, but the waterfront was all but deserted. A few boats moored, swaying in the current, a scatter of people, most likely tourists, strolling under the light of a quarter moon.

Oh, how she loved the waterfront. She'd nearly howled with glee when she'd been able to snag the building for her shop, knowing she'd be able to step outside any time of the day and see the water, the crabbers, the tourists. To feel that moist air on her skin.

Even more, to feel part of it all, on her own merits, her own terms.

It would have been smarter, more sensible again, to have taken the room above for her own living quarters. But she'd made the conscious and deliberate decision not to live where she worked. Which, Dru admitted as she swung away from Market to drive to the rear of her building, had been a handy excuse to find a place out of the town bustle, someplace on the water again. An indulgent space all her own.

The house in Georgetown had never felt all her own.

She killed the lights, the engine, then gathered her purse. Seth was there, opening her door, before she could do it for herself.

"It's pretty dark. Watch your step." He took her arm, started to steer her to the wooden staircase that led to the second level.

"I can see fine, thanks." She eased away from him, then opened her bag for the keys. "There's parking," she began. "And a private entrance, as you see."

"Yeah, I see fine, too. Listen." Halfway up the stairs, he laid a hand on her arm to stop her. "Just listen," he said again and looked out over the houses that lined the road behind them. "It's great, isn't it?"

She couldn't stop the smile. She understood him perfectly. And it was great, that silence.

"It won't be this quiet in a few weeks." He scanned the dark, the houses, the lawns. And again she thought he saw what others didn't. "Starting with Memorial Day the tourists and the summer people pour in. Nights get longer, warmer, and people hang out. That can be great, too, all that noise. Holiday noise. The kind you hear when you've got an ice cream cone in your hand and no time clock ticking away in your head."

He turned, aimed those strong blue eyes at her. She could have sworn she felt a jolt from them that was elementally physical.

"You like ice cream cones?" he asked her.

"There'd be something wrong with me if I didn't." She moved quickly up the rest of the steps.

"Nothing wrong with you," he murmured, and stood with his thumbs tucked in his front pockets while she unlocked the door.

She flicked a switch on the wall to turn on the lights, then deliberately left the door open at his back when he stepped in.

She saw immediately she needn't have bothered. He wasn't giving her a thought now.

He crossed to the front windows first, stood there looking out in that hip-shot stance that managed to be both relaxed and attentive. And sexy, she decided.

He wore a pair of ragged jeans with more style than a great many men managed to achieve in a five-thousand-dollar suit.

There were paint flecks on his shoes.

She blinked, tuning back in to the moment when he began to mutter.

"Excuse me?"

"What? Oh, just calculating the light—sun, angles. Stuff." He crossed back to the rear windows, stood as he had at the front. Muttered as he had at the front.

Talked to himself, Dru noted. Well, it wasn't so odd, really. She held entire conversations with herself in her head.

"The kitchen—" Dru began.

"Doesn't matter." Frowning, he stared up at the ceiling,

his gaze so intense and focused she found herself staring up with him.

After a few seconds of standing there, silent, staring up, she felt ridiculous. "Is there a problem with the ceiling? I was assured the roof was sound, and I know it doesn't leak."

"Uh-huh. Any objection to skylights—put in at my expense?"

"I . . . well, I don't know. I suppose—"

"It would work."

He wandered the room again, placing his canvases, his paints, his easel, a worktable for sketching, shelves for supplies and equipment. Have to put in a sofa, or a bed, he thought. Better a bed in case he worked late enough to just flop down for the night.

"It's a good space," he said at length. "With the skylights, it'll work. I'll take it."

She reminded herself that she hadn't actually agreed to the skylights. But then again, she couldn't find any reason to object to them. "That was quick, as advertised. Don't you want to see the kitchen, the bathroom?"

"They got everything kitchens and bathrooms are supposed to have?"

"Yes. No tub, just a shower stall."

"I'm not planning on taking too many bubble baths." He moved back to the front windows again. "Prime view."

"Yes, it's very nice. Not that it's any of my business, but I assume you have any number of places you can stay while you're here. Why do you need an apartment?"

"I don't want to live here, I want to work here. I need studio space." He turned back. "I'm bunking at Cam and Anna's, and that suits me. I'll get a place of my own eventually, but not until I find exactly what I want. Because I'm not visiting Saint Chris. I'm back for good."

"I see. Well, studio space then. Which explains the skylights."

"I'm a better bet than Terri," he said because he felt her hesitation. "No loud parties or shouting matches, which she's famous for. And I'm handy."

"Are you?"

"Hauling, lifting, basic maintenance. I won't come crying to you every time the faucet drips."

"Points for you," she murmured.

"How many do I need? I really want the space. I need to get back to work. What do you say to a six-month lease?"

"Six months. I'd planned on a full year at a time."

"Six months gives us both an early out if it's not jelling."

She pursed her lips in consideration. "There is that."

"How much are you asking?"

She gave him the monthly rate she'd settled on. "I'll want first and last month's rent when you sign the lease. And another month's rent as security deposit."

"Ouch. Very strict."

Now she smiled. "Terri annoyed me. You get to pay the price."

"Won't be the first time she's cost me. I'll have it for you tomorrow. I've got a family thing on Sunday, and I have to order the skylights, but I'd like to start moving things in right away."

"That's fine." She liked the idea of him painting over her shop, of knowing the building that was hers was fulfilling its potential. "Congratulations," she said and offered a hand. "You've got yourself a studio."

"Thanks." He took her hand, held it. Ringless, he thought again. Long, faerie fingers and unpainted nails. "Given any thought to posing for me?"

"No."

His grin flashed at her flat, precise answer. "I'll talk you into it."

"I'm not easily swayed. Let's clear this all up before we start on what should be a mutually satisfying business relationship."

"Okay, let's. You have a strong, beautiful face. As an artist, as a man, I'm drawn to the qualities of strength and beauty. The artist wants to translate them. The man wants to enjoy them. So, I'd like to paint you, and I'd like to spend time with you."

Despite the breeze that danced through the open door, she felt entirely too alone with him. Alone, and boxed in by the way he held her hand, held her gaze.

"I'm sure you've had your quota of women to translate and enjoy. Such as the buxom blonde in black you were cozied up with at the bar."

"Who . . . ?"

Humor exploded on his face. It was, Dru thought, like light bursting through shadows.

"Buxom Blonde in Black," he repeated, seeing it as a title. "Jesus, she'll *love* that. There'll be no living with her. That was Aubrey. Aubrey Quinn. My brother Ethan's oldest daughter."

"I see." And it made her feel like an idiot. "It didn't seem to be a particularly avuncular relationship."

"I don't feel like her uncle. It's more a big-brother thing. She was two when I came to Saint Chris. We fell for each other. Aubrey's the first person I ever loved, absolutely.

She's got strength and beauty, too, and I've certainly trans-
lated and enjoyed them. But not in quite the same way I'd
like to do with yours."

"Then you're going to be disappointed. Even if I were
interested, I don't have the time to pose, and I don't have
the inclination to be enjoyed. You're very attractive, Seth,
and if I were going to be shallow—"

"Yeah." Another brilliant, flashing grin. "Let's be shallow."

"Sorry." But he'd teased a smile out of her again. "I gave
it up. If I were going to be, *I* might enjoy *you*. But as it
stands, we're going to settle for the practical."

"We can start there. Now, since you asked me a question
earlier, I get to ask you one."

"All right, what?"

He saw by the way her face turned closed-in and wary
that she was braced for something personal she wouldn't
care to answer. So he shifted gears. "Do you like steamed
crabs?"

She stared at him for nearly ten seconds and gave him
the pleasure of watching her face relax. "Yes, I like
steamed crabs."

"Good. We'll have some on our first date. I'll be by in
the morning to sign the lease," he added as he walked to
the open door.

"The morning's fine."

He looked down as she leaned over to lock the door behind them. Her neck was long, elegant. The contrast between it and the severe cut of the dark hair was sharp and
dramatic. Without thinking, he skimmed a finger along the
curve, just to sample the texture.

She froze, so that for one instant they made a portrait of

themselves. The woman in the rich-colored suit, slightly bent toward a closed door, and the man in rough clothes with a fingertip at the nape of her neck.

She straightened with a quick jerk of movement, and Seth let his hand drop away. "Sorry, irritating habit of mine."

"Do you have many?"

"Yeah, afraid so. That one wasn't anything personal. You've got a really nice line back there." He stuck his hands in his pockets so it wouldn't become personal. Not yet.

"I'm an expert on lines, nice or otherwise." She breezed by him and down the steps.

"Hey." He jogged after her. "I've got better lines than that one."

"I'll just bet you do."

"I'll try some out on you. But in the meantime . . ." He opened her car door. "Is there any storage space?"

"Utility room. There." She gestured toward a door under the steps. "Furnace and water heater, that sort of thing. And some storage."

"If I need to, can I stick some stuff in there until I get the space worked out? I've got some things coming in from Rome. They'll probably be here Monday."

"I don't have a problem with that. The key's inside the shop. Remind me to give it to you tomorrow."

"Appreciate it." He closed the door for her when she'd climbed in, then he knocked on the window. "You know," he said when she rolled down the window, "I like spending time with a smart, self-confident woman who knows what she wants and goes out and gets it. Like you got this place. Very sexy, that kind of direction and dedication."

He waited a beat. "That was a line."

She kept her eyes on his as she rolled the glass up between their faces again.

And she didn't let herself chuckle until she'd driven away.

THE best thing about Sundays, in Dru's opinion, was waking up slowly, then clinging to that half-dream state while the sunlight shivered through the trees, slid through the windows and danced on her closed lids.

Sundays were knowing absolutely nothing had to be done, and countless things could be.

She'd make coffee and toast a bagel in her own kitchen, then have her breakfast in the little dining room while she leafed through catalogues for business.

She'd putter around the garden she'd planted—with her own hands, thank you—while listening to music.

There was no charity luncheon, no community drive, no obligatory family dinner or tennis match at the club cluttering up her Sundays now.

There was no marital spat between her parents to referee, and no hurt feelings and sorrowful looks because each felt she'd taken the side of the other.

All there was, was Sunday and her lazy enjoyment of it.

In all the months she'd lived here, she'd never once taken that for granted. Nor had she lost a drop of the flood of pleasure it gave her to stand and look out her own windows.

She did so now, opening the window to the cool morning. From there she could admire her own private curve of the river. There were no houses to get in the way and make her think of people when she only wanted to be.

There was the speckled leaves of the liverwort she'd

planted under the shade of oaks, its buds a cheery pink. And lily of the valley, with its bells already dancing. And there, the marsh grass and rushes with the little clearing she'd made for the golden-yellow iris that liked their feet wet.

She could hear the birds, the breeze, the occasional plop of a fish or a frog.

Forgetting breakfast, she wandered through the house to the front door so she could stand on the veranda and just look. She wore the boxers and tank she'd slept in, and there was no one to comment on the senator's granddaughter's dishabille. No reporter or photographer looking for a squib for the society page.

There was only lovely, lovely peace.

She picked up her watering can and carried it inside to fill while she started the coffee.

Seth Quinn had been right about one thing, she thought. She was a woman who knew what she wanted and went out and got it. Perhaps it had taken her some time to realize what that thing was, but when she had, she'd done what needed to be done.

She'd wanted to run a business where she could feel creative and happy. And she'd been determined to be successful, in her own right. She'd toyed with the idea of a small nursery or gardening service.

But she wasn't fully confident in her skills there. Her gardening ventures had been largely confined to her little courtyard in Georgetown, and potted plants. And while she'd been very proud of her efforts there and delighted with the results, it hardly qualified her as an expert.

But she knew flowers.

She'd wanted a small town, where the pace was easy and the demands few. And she'd wanted the water. She'd always been pulled to the water.

She loved the look of St. Christopher, the cheerful tidiness of it, and the ever changing tones and moods of the Bay. She liked listening to the clang from the channel markers, and the throaty call of a foghorn when the mists rolled in.

She'd grown accustomed to and nearly comfortable with the casual friendliness of the locals. And the good-heartedness that had sent Ethan Quinn over to check on her during a storm the previous winter.

No, she'd never live in the city again.

Her parents would have to continue to adjust to the distance she'd put between them. Geographically and emotionally. In the end, she was certain it was best for everyone involved.

And just now, however selfish it might be, she was more concerned with what was best for Drusilla.

She turned off the tap and, after sampling the coffee, carried it and the watering can outside to tend to her pots.

Eventually, she thought, she would add a greenhouse so that she could experiment with growing her own flowers to sell. But she'd have to be convinced she could add the structure without spoiling the fanciful lines of her home.

She loved its peaks and foolishly ornate gingerbread trim. Most would consider it a kind of folly, with its fancywork and deep blue color out here among the thickets and marsh. But to her it was a statement.

Home could be exactly where you needed, exactly what you needed it to be, if you wanted it enough.

She set her coffee down on a table and drenched a jardiniere bursting with verbena and heliotrope.

At a rustle, she looked over. And watched a heron rise like a king over the high grass, over the brown water.

"I'm happy," she said out loud. "I'm happier than I've ever been in my life."

She decided to forgo the bagel and catalogues and changed into gardening clothes instead.

For an hour she worked on the sunny side of the house where she was determined to establish a combination of shrubbery and flower bed. The bloodred blooms of the rhododendrons she'd planted the week before would be a strong contrast to the blue of the house once they burst free. She'd spent every evening for a month over the winter planning her flowers. She wanted to keep it simple and a little wild, like a mad cottage garden with columbine and delphiniums and sweet-faced wallflowers all tumbled together.

There were all kinds of art, she thought smugly as she planted fragrant stock. She imagined Seth would approve of her choices of tone and texture here.

Not that it mattered, of course. The garden was to please herself. But it was satisfying to think an artist might find her efforts creative.

He certainly hadn't had much to say for himself the day before, she remembered. He'd whipped in just after she opened the doors, handed over the agreed amount, looped his signature on the lease, snatched up the keys, then bolted.

No flirtation, no persuasive smile.

Which was all for the best, she reminded herself. She didn't want flirtations and persuasions right at the moment.

Still, it would have been nice, on some level, to imagine holding the option for them in reserve.

He'd probably had a Saturday-morning date with one of the women who'd pined for him while he'd been gone. He looked like the type women might pine for. All that scruffy hair, the lanky build.

And the hands. How could you not notice his hands—wide of palm, long of finger. With a rough elegance to them that made a woman—some women, she corrected—fantasize about being stroked by them.

Dru sat back on her heels with a sigh because she knew she'd given just that scenario more than one passing thought. *Only because it's the first man you've been attracted to in . . . God, who knew how long?*

She hadn't so much as had a date in nearly a year.

Her choice, she reminded herself. And she wasn't going to change her mind and end up with Seth Quinn and steamed crabs.

She would just go on as she was, making her home, running her business while he went about his and painted over her head every day.

She'd get used to him being up there, then she'd stop noticing he was up there. When the lease was up, they'd see if . . .

"Damn it. The key to the utility room."

She'd forgotten to give it to him. Well, he'd forgotten to remind her to give it to him.

Not my problem, she thought and yanked at a stray weed. *He's the one who wanted to use the storage, and if he hadn't been in such a hurry to go, she would've remembered to give him the key.*

She planted cranesbill, added some larkspur. Then, cursing, pushed to her feet.

It would nag at her all day. She'd obsess, she admitted as she stalked around the house. She'd worry and wonder about whatever it was he had coming in from Rome the next day. Easier by far to take the duplicate she had here at home, drive over to Anna Quinn's and drop it off.

It wouldn't take more than twenty minutes, and she could go by the nursery while she was out.

She left her gardening gloves and tools in a basket on the veranda.

SETH grabbed the line Ethan tossed him and secured the wooden boat to the dock. The kids leaped out first. Emily with her long dancer's body and sunflower hair, and Deke, gangly as a puppy at fourteen.

Seth caught Deke in a headlock and looked at Emily. "You weren't supposed to grow up while I was gone."

"Couldn't help it." She laid her cheek on his, rubbed it there. "Welcome home."

"When do we eat?" Deke wanted to know.

"Guy's got a tapeworm." Aubrey leaped nimbly onto the dock. "He ate damn near half a loaf of French bread five minutes ago."

"I'm a growing boy," he said with a chuckle. "I'm going to charm Anna out of something."

"He actually thinks he's charming," Emily said with a shake of her head. "It's a mystery."

The Chesapeake Bay retriever Ethan called Nigel landed in the water with a happy splash, then bounded up onshore to run after Deke.

"Give me a hand with this, Em, since the jerk's off and running." Aubrey grabbed one end of the cooler Ethan had set on the dock. "Mom may water up," she said to Seth under her breath. "She's really anxious to see you."

Seth stepped to the boat, held out his hand and closed it around Grace's. If Aubrey had been the first person he'd loved, Grace had been the first woman he'd both loved *and* trusted.

Her arms slid around him as she stepped on the dock, and her cheek rubbed his with that same female sweetness as Emily's had. "There now," she said quietly, on a laughing sigh. "There now, that feels just exactly right. Now everything's where it belongs."

She leaned back, smiled up at him. "Thank you for the tulips. They're beautiful. I'm sorry I wasn't home."

"So was I. I figured I'd trade them for some of your homemade fries. You still make the best."

"Come to dinner tomorrow. I'll fix some for you."

"With sloppy joes?"

She laughed again, reached back with one hand to take Ethan's. "Well, that hasn't changed, has it? With sloppy joes. Deke will be thrilled."

"And chocolate cake?"

"Guy expects a lot for a bunch of flowers," Ethan commented.

"At least I didn't swipe them from Anna's garden, then try to blame it on innocent deer and bunny rabbits."

Ethan winced, sent a wary look toward the house to make certain Anna wasn't within hearing distance. "Let's not bring that up again. Damn near twenty years ago, and she'd still scalp me for it."

"I heard you got them from the very pretty florist on Market Street." Grace tucked her arm around Seth's waist as they walked toward the house. "And that you've rented the place above the shop for a studio."

"Word travels."

"Fast and wide," Grace agreed. "Why don't you tell me all about it?"

"Nothing to tell, yet. But I'm working on it."

* * *

SHE was running behind now, and it was her own fault. There was no reason, no *sane* reason she'd felt compelled to shower, to change out of her grubby gardening clothes. Certainly no reason, she thought, irritated with herself, to have spent time on her precious Sunday fussing with makeup.

Now it was past noon.

Didn't matter, she told herself. It was a lovely day for a drive. She'd spend two minutes on Seth Quinn and the key, then indulge herself at the nursery.

Of course now she'd have to change *back* into her gardening clothes, but that was neither here nor there. She'd plant, then make fresh lemonade and sit and bask in the glow of a job well done.

Feel the air! Brisk with spring, moist from the water. The fields on either side of the road were tilled and planted, and already running green in the rows. She could smell the sharp edge of fertilizer, the richer tones of earth that meant spring in the country.

She made the turn, caught the glint of the sun off the mudflats before the trees took over with their deep shadows.

The old white house was perfect for its setting. Edged by woods, with water hemming its back, and the tidy, flower-decked lawn skirting its front. She'd admired it before, the way it sat there, so cozy and comfortable with its front porch rockers and faded blue shutters.

While she felt the whimsy and the privacy of her own home suited her perfectly, she could admire the character of the Quinn place. It gave a sense of order without regimentation. The kind of home, she reflected, where feet were allowed to prop on coffee tables.

No one would have dreamed to rest a heel on her mother's Louis XIV. Not even her father.

The number of cars in the drive made her frown. A white Corvette—vintage, she assumed—a sturdy SUV of some sort that appeared to have some hard miles on it. A snappy little convertible, a dented, disreputable-looking hatchback that had to be twenty years old, a manly pickup truck and a sleek and muscular Jaguar.

She hesitated, then mentally assigned the vehicles. The SUV was the family car. The 'Vette was undoubtedly former race-car driver Cameron Quinn's—as would be the truck as work vehicle, giving Anna the convertible and the old hand-me-down to the oldest boy, who must be old enough to drive.

The Jag was Seth's. She'd noticed it, with some admiration, the night before. And if she hadn't, she'd heard all about his recent acquisition from chatting customers in her shop.

She nosed up behind it.

Two minutes, she reminded herself, and grabbed her purse as she turned off the engine.

Instantly, she heard the blast of music. The teenagers, she figured as she started toward the front door, her steps unconsciously timed to the beat of Matchbox 20.

She admired the pots and tubs of flowers on the porch. Anna, she knew, had a clever hand for mixing flowers. She knocked briskly, then bumped it up to a pound before she sighed.

No one was going to hear her over the music, even if she used a battering ram.

Resigned, she stepped off the porch and started toward the side of the house. She heard more than music now. There were shouts, squeals and what she could only describe as maniacal laughter.

The kids must be having a party. She'd just go back, pass off the key to one of Anna's boys and be on her way.

The dog came first, a cannonball of black fur with a lolling tongue. He had a bark like a machine gun, and though she was very fond of dogs, Dru stopped on a dime.

"Hi there. Ah, nice dog."

He seemed to take that as an invitation to race two wild circles around her, then press his nose to her crotch.

"Okay." She put a firm hand under his jaw, lifted it. "That's just a little too friendly." She gave him a quick rub, then a nudge, and managed one more step before the boy streaked screaming around the side of the house. Though he held a large plastic weapon in his hand, he was in full retreat.

He managed to veer around her. "Better run," he puffed out, an instant before she saw a flash of movement out of the corner of her eye.

An instant before she was shot dead in the heart, by a stream of cold water.

The shock was so great that her mouth dropped open but she couldn't manage a sound. Just behind her the boy murmured, "Uh-oh."

And deserted the field.

Seth, the water rifle in his hand, his hair dripping from the previous attack, took one look at Dru. "Oh, shit."

Helpless, Dru looked down. Her crisp red shirt and navy pants were soaked. The splatter had managed to reach her face, making the time she'd spent fiddling with it a complete waste.

She lifted her gaze, one that turned from stunned to searing when she noted that Seth looked very much like a man struggling not to laugh.

"Are you *crazy*?"

"Sorry. Really." He swallowed hard, knowing the laugh fighting to burst out of his throat would damn him. "Sorry," he managed as he walked to her. "I was after Jake—little bastard nailed me. You got caught in the cross fire." He tried a charming smile, dug a bandanna out of the back pocket of his jeans. "Which proves there are no innocent bystanders in war."

"Which proves," she said between her teeth, "that some men are idiots who can't be trusted with a child's toy."

"Hey, hey, this is a Super Soaker 5000." He lifted the water gun but, catching the gleam in her eyes, hastily lowered it again. "Anyway, I'm really sorry. How about a beer?"

"You can take your beer and your Super Soaker 5000 and—"

"Seth!" Anna rushed around the house, then let out a huge sigh. "You moron."

"Jake," he said under his breath and vowed revenge. "Anna, we were just—"

"Quiet." She jabbed a finger at him, then draped an arm around Dru's shoulder. "I apologize for the idiot children. You poor thing. We'll get you inside and into some dry clothes."

"No, really, I'll just—"

"I insist," Anna interrupted, herding her toward the front of the house. "What a greeting. I'd say things aren't usually so crazy around here, but I'd be lying."

Keeping a firm hand on Dru—Anna knew when someone was poised for escape—she guided her into the house and up the stairs.

"It's a little crazier today as the whole gang's here. A welcome-home for Seth. The guys are about to boil up some crabs. You'll stay."

"I couldn't intrude." Her temper was rapidly sliding toward embarrassment. "I just stopped by to drop off the utility-room key for Seth. I really should—"

"Have some dry clothes, some food, some wine," Anna said warmly. "Kevin's jeans ought to work." She pulled a blue cotton shirt out of her own closet. "I'll just see if I can find a pair in the black hole of his room."

"It's just a little water. You should be down with your family. I should go."

"Honey, you're soaked and you're shivering. Now get out of those wet things. We'll toss them in the dryer while we eat. I'll just be a minute."

With this, she strode out and left Dru alone in the bedroom.

The woman hadn't seemed so . . . formidable, Dru decided, on her visits to the flower shop. She wondered if anyone ever won an argument with her.

But the truth was, she was chilled. Giving up, she stripped off the wet shirt, gave a little sigh and took off the equally wet bra. She was just buttoning up when Anna came back in.

"Success." She offered Dru a pair of Levi's. "Shirt okay?"

"Yes, it's fine. Thank you."

"Just bring your wet things down to the kitchen when you're ready." She started out again, then turned back. "And, Dru? Welcome to bedlam."

Close enough, Dru thought. She could hear the shouts and laughter, the blast of music through the open window.

It seemed to her half of St. Christopher must be partying in the Quinns' backyard.

But when she snuck a peek out, she realized the noise was generated by the Quinns all by themselves. There were teenagers of varying sizes and sexes running around, and two, no three dogs. Make that four, she noted as an enormous retriever bounded out of the water and raced over the lawn to shake drops on as many people as possible.

The young boy Seth had been chasing was doing precisely the same thing. Obviously, Seth had managed to catch up with him.

Boats were tied to the dock—which explained, she supposed, why the number of cars in the drive didn't match the number of picnickers.

The Quinns sailed.

They were also loud, wet and messy. The scene below was nothing like any of her parents' outdoor social events or family gatherings. The music would have been classical, and muted. The conversations would have been calm and ordered. And the tables would have been meticulously set with some sort of clever theme.

Her mother was brilliant with themes, and dictated her precise wishes to the caterer, who knew how to deliver.

She wasn't certain she knew how to socialize, even briefly, in the middle of this sort of chaos. But she could hardly do otherwise without being rude.

She changed into the Levi's. The boy—Kevin, she thought Anna had said—was tall. She had to roll up the legs a couple of times into frayed cuffs.

She glanced in the pretty wood-framed mirror over the bureau and, sighing, took a tissue to deal with the mascara smudges under her eyes caused by her unexpected shower.

She gathered the rest of her wet things and started downstairs.

There was a piano in the living room. It looked ancient and well used. The red lilies she'd sold Seth stood in a cut-crystal vase atop it, and spilled their fragrance into the air.

The sofa appeared new, the rug old. It was, Dru thought, very much a family room, with cheerful colors, cozy cushions, a few stray dog hairs and the female touches of the flowers and candles. Snapshots were scattered here and there, all in different frames. There had been no attempt at coordination, and that was the charm of it, she decided.

There were paintings—waterscapes, cityscapes, still lifes—that she was certain were Seth's. But it was a lovely little pencil sketch that drew her over.

It was the rambling white house, flanked by woods, trimmed by water. It said, with absolute simplicity: This is home. And it touched a chord in her that made her yearn.

Stepping closer, she studied the careful signature in the bottom corner. Such a careful signature, she recognized it as a child's even before she read the date printed beneath.

He'd drawn it when he was a child, she realized. Just a little boy making a picture of his home—and already recognizing its value, already talented and insightful enough to translate that value, that warmth and stability with his pencil.

Helplessly, her heart softened toward him. He might be an idiot with an oversized water pistol, but he was a good man. If art reflected the artist, he was a very special man.

She followed the sound of voices back into the kitchen. This, she recognized immediately, was another family center, one captained by a female who took cooking seriously. The long counters were a pristine white making a bright, happy contrast to the candy-apple-red trim. They were covered with platters and bowls of food.

Seth stood with his arm around Anna's shoulders. Their heads were close together, and though she continued to unwrap a bowl, there was a unity in their stance.

Love. Dru could feel the flow of it from across the room, the simple, strong, steady flow of it. The din might have continued from outside, people might have winged in and out the back door, but the two of them made a little island of affection.

She'd always been attracted to that kind of connection, and found herself smiling at them before the woman—that would be Grace—backed out of the enormous refrigerator with yet another platter in hand.

"Oh, Dru. Here, let me take those."

Grace set the bowl aside; Anna and Seth turned. And Dru's smile dimmed into politeness.

Her heart might have softened toward the artist, but she wasn't about to let the idiot off the hook too easily.

"Thanks. They're only damp really. The shirt got the worst of it."

"I got the worst of it." Seth tipped his head toward Anna before he stepped forward. "Sorry. Really. I don't know how I mistook you for a thirteen-year-old boy."

The stare she aimed at him could have frozen a pond at ten paces. "Why don't we just say I was in the wrong place at the wrong time and leave it at that."

"No, this is the right place." He took her hand, lifted it to his lips in what she imagined he thought of as a charming gesture. And damn it, it was. "And it's always the right time."

"Gack," was Jake's opinion as he swung through the

back door. "Crabs are going in," he told Seth. "Dad says for you to get your ass out there."

"Jake!"

Jake sent his mother an innocent look. "I'm just the messenger. We're *starving*."

"Here." Anna stuffed a deviled egg in his mouth. "Now carry this outside. Then come back, without slamming the door, and apologize to Dru."

Jake made mumbling noises around the egg and carried the platter outside.

"It really wasn't his fault," Dru began.

"If this wasn't, something else was. Something always is. Can I get you some wine?"

"Yes, thanks." Obviously, she wasn't going to be able to escape. And the fact was, she was curious about the family that lived in a young artist's pencil sketch. "Ah, is there something I can do to help?"

"Grab whatever, take it out. We'll be feeding the masses shortly."

Anna lifted her eyebrows as Seth grabbed a platter, then pushed the door open for Dru and her bowl of coleslaw. Then Anna wiggled those eyebrows at Grace. "They look cute together."

"They do," Grace agreed. "I like her." She wandered to the door to spy out with Anna. "She's always a little cool at first, then she warms up—or relaxes, I guess. She's awfully pretty, isn't she? And so . . . polished."

"Money usually puts a gleam on you. She's a bit stiff yet, but if this group can't loosen her up, nothing can. Seth's very attracted."

"So I noticed." Grace turned her head toward Anna. "I guess we'd better find out more about her."

"My thoughts exactly." She went back to fetch the wine.

* * *

THE Quinn brothers were impressive examples of the species individually. As a group, Dru decided, they were staggering. They might not have shared blood, but they were so obviously fraternal—tall, lanky, handsome and most of all male.

The quartet around the huge steaming pot simply exuded manhood like other men might a distinctive aftershave. She didn't doubt for a moment that they knew it.

They were what they were, she thought, and were pretty damned pleased about it.

As a woman she found that sort of innate self-satisfaction attractive. She respected confidence and a good, healthy ego. When she wandered around to the brick pit where they steamed the crabs to deliver, at Anna's request, a foursome of cold beer, she caught the end of a conversation.

"Asshole thinks he's Horatio fucking Hornblower." From Cam.

"More like Captain fucking Queed." Muttered by Ethan.

"He can be anybody he wants, as long as his money's green." Delivered with a shrug by Phillip. "We've built boats for assholes before, and will again."

"One fuckhead's the same as—" Seth broke off when he spotted Dru.

"Gentlemen." She never batted an eyelash. "Cold beer for hot work."

"Thanks." Phillip took them from her. "Heard you've already cooled off once today."

"Unexpectedly." Relieved of the bottles, she lifted her wineglass to her lips, sipped. "But I prefer this method to the Super Soaker 5000." Ignoring Seth, she looked at

Ethan. "Did you catch them?" she asked, gesturing to the pot.

"Deke and I, yeah." He grinned when Seth cleared his throat. "We took him along for ballast," he told Dru. "Got blisters on his city hands."

"Couple days in the boatyard might toughen him up," Cam speculated. "Always was puny though."

"You're just trying to insult me so I'll come in and do the hot fifty-fifty work." Seth tipped back his beer. "Keep dreaming."

"Puny," Phillip said, "but smart. Always was smart."

"I wonder if I could come in sometime, take a look around at your work."

Cam tilted his head toward Dru. "Like boats, do you?"

"Yes, I do."

"Why don't we go for a sail," Seth asked her.

She spared him a glance that was on the edge of withering. "Keep dreaming," she suggested and strolled away.

"Classy," was Phillip's opinion.

"She's a nice girl," Ethan said as he checked the pot.

"Hot," Cam commented. "Very, very hot."

"You want to cool off, I'll be happy to stick the Super Soaker 5000 up your ass," Seth told him.

"Got a bead on her?" Cam shook his head as if in pity. "She looks out of your league to me, kid."

"Yeah." Seth gulped more beer. "I'm a big fan of inter-league play."

Phillip watched Seth wander off, then chuckled. "Our boy's going to be spending a hell of a lot of money on flowers for the next little while."

"That particular bloom's got some long stems on her," Cam remarked.

"Got careful eyes." Ethan gave the traditional Quinn

shoulder jerk when Cam frowned at him. "Watches every-thing, including Seth, but it's all one step back, you know. Not because she's shy—the girl isn't shy. She's careful."

"She comes from big money and politics." Phillip con-sidered his beer. "Bound to make you careful."

"Saint Chris is a funny place for her to end up, isn't it?" To Cam's mind, family forged you—the family you were born to or the family you made. He wondered how Dru's had forged her.

SHE'D intended to stay no more than an hour. A polite hour while her clothes dried. But somehow she was drawn into a conversation with Emily about New York. And one with Anna about gardening. Then there were the mutual acquaintances with Sybill and Phillip from D.C.

The food was wonderful. When she complimented the potato salad, Grace offered her the recipe. Dru wasn't quite sure how to announce that she didn't cook.

There were arguments—over baseball, clothes, video games. It didn't take her long to realize it was just another kind of interaction.

Dogs sidled up to the table and were ordered firmly away—usually after someone snuck food into a canine mouth. The breeze blew in cool over the water while as many as six conversations went on at the same time.

She kept up. Early training had honed her ability to have something to say to everyone and anyone in social situa-tions. She could comment about boats and baseball, food and music, art and travel even when the talk of them and more leaped and swirled around her.

She nursed a second glass of wine and stayed far longer than she'd intended. Not just because she couldn't find a polite way to leave. Because she liked them. She was amused by and envious of the intimacy of the family. Despite their numbers and the obvious differences—could sisters be less alike than the sharp-tongued, sports-loving Aubrey and Emily, the waiflike ballerina?—they were all so firmly interlinked.

Like individual pieces of one big, bold puzzle, Dru decided. The puzzle of family always fascinated her. Certainly her own continued to remain a mystery to her.

However colorful and cheerful they seemed on the surface, Dru imagined the Quinn puzzle had its share of shadows and complications.

Families always did.

As did men, she thought, turning her head deliberately to meet Seth's dead-on stare. She was perfectly aware that he'd watched her almost continuously since they'd sat down to eat. Oh, he was good at the conversation juggling, too; she'd give him that. And from time to time he'd tune his attention fully on someone else. But his gaze, that straight-on and vivid blue gaze, would always swing back to her.

She could feel it, a kind of heat along her skin.

She refused to let it intrigue her. And she certainly wasn't going to let it fluster her.

"The afternoon light's good here." His eyes still on Dru, he scooped up a forkful of pasta salad. "Maybe we'll do some outdoor work. You got anything with a long, full skirt? Strapless or sleeveless to show off your shoulders. Good strong shoulders," he added with another scoop of pasta. "They go with the face."

"That's lucky for me, isn't it?" She dismissed him with a slight wave of her hand and turned to Sybill. "I enjoyed your last documentary very much, the studies and examples of blended family dynamics. I suppose you based some of your findings on your own experiences."

"Hard to get away from it. I could study this bunch for the next couple of decades and never run out of material."

"We're all Mom's guinea pigs," Fiona stated as she handily picked out another crab. "Better watch out. You hang out around here, Seth'll have you naked on a canvas and Mom'll have you analyzed in a book."

"Oh, I don't know." Aubrey gestured with her drink. "Annie Crawford hung around here for months, and Seth never did paint her—naked or otherwise. I don't think Sybill ever wrote about her either, unless I missed the one about societal placement of brainless bimbos."

"She wasn't brainless," Seth put in.

"She called you Sethie. As in, 'Oh, Sethie, you're a regular Michael Dee Angelo.' "

"Want me to start trotting out some of the guys you hung with a few years back? Matt Fisher, for instance?"

"I was young and shallow."

"Yeah, you're old and deep now. Anyway"—he shifted that direct gaze to Dru again—"you got a long, flowy thing? Little top?"

"No."

"We'll get something."

Dru sipped the last of her wine, tilted her head slightly to indicate interest. "Has anyone ever declined to be painted by you?"

"No, not really."

"Let me be the first."

"He'll do it anyway," Cam told her. "Kid's got a head like a brick."

"And that comes from the most flexible, most reasonable, most accommodating of men," Anna declared as she rose. "Anybody got room for dessert?"

They did, though Dru didn't see how. She declined offers of cakes, pies, but lost the battle of wills over a double fudge brownie that she nibbled on before changing back into her own clothes.

She folded the borrowed shirt and jeans, set them on the bed, took one last look around the cozy bedroom, then started down.

Dru stopped short in the kitchen doorway when she spotted Anna and Cam in front of the sink in an embrace a great deal more torrid than she expected from parents of teenagers.

"Let's go upstairs and lock the door," Dru heard him say—and wasn't sure where to look when she noted Cam's hands slide around possessively to squeeze his wife's butt. "No one will miss us."

"That's what you said after dinner last Thanksgiving." There was both warmth and fun in her voice when Anna linked her arms around Cam's neck. "You were wrong."

"Phil was just jealous because he didn't think of it first."

"Later, Quinn. If you behave, I might just let you . . . Oh, Dru."

From the easy grins on their faces, Dru concluded she was the only one of the trio who was the least bit embarrassed. "I'm sorry. I wanted to thank you for the hospitality. I really enjoyed the afternoon."

"Good. Then you'll come again. Cam, let Seth know Dru's leaving, will you?" And damned if she didn't give his butt a squeeze before easing out of his arms.

"Don't bother. You have a wonderful family, a beautiful home. I appreciate your letting me share them today."

"I'm glad you dropped by," Anna said, giving Cam a silent signal as she laid an arm over Dru's shoulder to walk her to the front door.

"The key." Shaking her head, Dru dug into her purse. "I completely forgot the reason I came by in the first place. Would you give this to Seth? He can store whatever he needs to in there for the time being. We'll work out the details later."

Anna heard the kitchen door slam. "You might as well give it to him yourself. Come back," she said, then gave Dru a quick, casual kiss on the cheek.

"Taking off?" A little winded, Seth hurried up to catch Dru on the front porch. "Why don't you stay? Aubrey's getting a softball game together."

"I have to get home. The key." She held it out while he only stood looking at her. "Utility room? Storage?"

"Yeah, yeah." He took it, stuffed it in his pocket. "Listen, it's early, but if you want to split, we can go somewhere. A drive or something."

"I have things to do." She walked toward her car.

"We'll have to try for less of a crowd on our second date."

She paused, looked back at him over her shoulder. "We haven't had a first date yet."

"Sure we did. Steamed crabs, just as predicted. You get to pick the menu and venue for date number two."

Jiggling the car keys in her hand, she turned to face him. "I came by to give you the key, got blasted with a water gun and had a crab feast with your large, extended family. That doesn't make this a date."

"This will."

He had a smooth move—so smooth she never saw it coming. Maybe if she had, she'd have evaded. Or maybe not. But that wasn't the issue as his hands were cupped on her shoulders and his mouth was warm and firm on hers.

He lifted her, just slightly. He tilted his head, just a little. So his lips rubbed hers—a seductive tease—and his hands cruised down her body to add an unexpected punch of heat.

She felt the breeze flutter against her cheeks, and heard the blast of music as someone turned the stereo up to scream again. And when the hard line of him pressed against her, she realized she'd been the one to move in.

The long, liquid tugs deep in her belly warned her, but still she shot her fingers through that thick, sun-streaked hair and let his hands roam.

He'd meant to *suggest* with a kiss, to tease a smile or a frown out of her so he could have the pleasure of watching either expression move over her face.

He'd only intended to skim the surface, perhaps to show them both hints of what could lie beneath. But when she'd leaned into him, locked around him, he sank.

Women were a dazzling array of colors for him. Mother, sister, lover, friend. But he'd never had another woman strike him with such brilliance. He wanted to steep in it, in her until they were both drenched.

"Let me come home with you, Drusilla." He skimmed his lips over her cheek, down to her throat, back up and along the finger-brush indentation in her chin, and to her mouth. "Let me lie down with you. Be with you. Let me touch you."

She shook her head. She didn't like speed, she reminded herself. A smart woman never turned a corner until she'd looked at the map for the entire route—and even then, she went forward only with caution.

"I'm not impulsive, Seth. I'm not rash." She put her hands on his shoulders to nudge him away, but her gaze was direct. "I don't share myself with a man just because there's heat."

"Okay." He pressed his lips to her forehead before he stepped back. "Stay. We'll play some ball, maybe go for a sail. We'll keep it simple today."

With some men, the suggestion would have been just another ploy to persuade her into bed. But she didn't sense that with him. He meant what he said, she decided. "I might actually like you after a while."

"Counting on it."

"But I can't stay. I left a number of things undone to come by, and I've stayed much longer than I intended."

"Didn't you ever ditch school?"

"No."

He braced a hand on the car door before she could open it, and his face was sincerely shocked. "Not once?"

"Afraid not."

"A rule player," he considered. "Sexy."

She had to laugh. "If I said I'd skipped school once a week, you'd have called me a rebel and said *that* was sexy."

"Got me. How about dinner tomorrow night?"

"No." She waved him away from the car door. "I need to think about this. I don't want to be interested in you."

"Which means you are."

She slid behind the wheel. "Which means I don't want to be. I'll let you know if I change my mind. Go back to your family. You're lucky to have them," she said, then closed the car door.

He watched her back out, then drive away. His blood was still warm from the kiss, and his mind too full of her and the possibilities for him to take notice of the car that eased from the shoulder of the road by the trees, then followed after Dru's.

FIVE

~⌢~

SHE KNEW HE'D moved in. Now and again when Dru went into the back room of the shop, she could hear music through the vents. It didn't surprise her that he played it loud, or that his choices varied from head-banging rock to mellow blues and into passionate opera.

Nothing about Seth Quinn surprised her.

He came and went during the first week of his lease without any rhyme or reason she could see. Occasionally he breezed in and out of the shop, to ask if she needed any-thing, to let her know he'd be starting on the skylights, to tell her he'd moved some things into the storage space and made a copy of the key.

He was always friendly, never seemed particularly rushed. And never once attempted to follow up on the steamy afternoon kiss.

It irked her, for a number of reasons. First, she'd been set to deflect any follow-up, at least for the time being. She had no intention of Seth, or any man, taking her availability for granted.

That was simply principle.

And, of course, it was expected that he *would* follow up. A man didn't ask to take you to bed one day, then treat you like a casual neighbor the next.

So perhaps he had surprised her after all. Which only irritated her more.

Just as well, she told herself as she worked on the small tabletop arrangements she sold to one of the waterfront's upscale restaurants. She was settling into St. Chris, into her business, into the kind of life she'd always wanted— without knowing she wanted it. A relationship, whether it was an affair, a romance or just no-strings sex, would change the balance.

And she was so enjoying the balance.

The only person who needed anything from her, demanded anything from her, expected anything from her these days was herself. That, in itself, was like a gift from God.

Pleased with the combination of narcissus and sprekelia, she loaded the arrangements into refrigeration. Her parttime delivery man would pick them up, along with the iris and tulips and showy white lilies ordered by a couple of the local B and B's.

She heard Seth arrive—the sound of the car door slamming, the crunch of footsteps over gravel, then the quick slap of them up the back steps.

Moments later came the music. Rock today, she noted with a glance at the overhead vent. Which probably meant he'd be up on the roof shortly, working on the skylights.

She went back into the shop, picked up the plant she'd

earmarked, then headed out the back and up the steps. A polite knock wouldn't do, not with the music blaring, so she used the side of her fist to pound.

"Yeah, yeah, it's open. Since when do you guys knock?"

He turned, in the act of strapping on a tool belt, as she opened the door. "Hey." His smile came quick and easy. "I thought you were one of my brothers, but you're a lot better-looking."

"I heard you come in." She would not be a cliché, she promised herself. She would *not* entertain ridiculous fantasies because she'd come upon a long, lanky male wearing a tool belt. "I thought you might like these."

"What? Wait." Amused at himself, he walked into the tiny kitchen where he'd set a tabletop stereo and turned down the volume. "Sorry."

His hammer bounced against his hip. He was wearing jeans that were equal parts holes and denim. His T-shirt was faded gray and splotched with paint and what was probably some sort of engine grease. He hadn't shaved.

She was not, absolutely not, attracted to rough, untidy men.

Usually.

"I brought you a plant." Her tone was sharper, more impatient than she intended. Her own words came back to haunt her. No, she didn't want to be interested in Seth Quinn.

"Yeah?" Despite her tone, he looked very pleased as he crossed over and took the pot from her. "Thanks," he said as he studied the green leaves and little white blossoms.

"It's a shamrock," she told him. "Quinn. It seemed to fit."

"Guess it does." Then those blue eyes lifted, locked on hers. "I appreciate it."

"Don't let it dry out." She glanced up. Two skylights were already installed. And he was right, she mused, they made all the difference. "You've been busy."

"Hmm. Traded some time at the boatyard for some labor here. Cam's going to give me a hand today, so we should finish up."

"Well then." She glanced around. After all, she reminded herself, she owned the place. She could take some interest in what went on there.

He had canvases stacked against two of the walls. An easel with a blank canvas was already set up in front of the windows. She wasn't sure how he'd managed to muscle the enormous worktable up the stairs and through the rather narrow door, but it was plopped in the center of the room and already covered with the detritus of the artist: brushes, paints, a mason jar of turpentine, rags, pencils, chalks.

There were a couple of stools, an old wooden chair, an even older table topped by a particularly ugly lamp.

Shelves, again wood, held more painting supplies.

He'd hung nothing on the walls, she noted. There was nothing but space, tools and light.

"You seem to be settling in. I'll let you get back to it." But one of the propped canvases drew her. It was a wash of purple over green. A riot of wild foxglove under pearly light pulled her in so that she could almost feel the brush of leaves and petals on her skin.

"A roadside in Ireland," he said. "County Clare. I spent a few weeks there once. Everywhere you look it's a painting. You can never really translate it on canvas."

"I think you have. It's wonderful. Simple and strong. I've never seen foxglove growing wild on a roadside in Ireland. But now I feel I have. Isn't that the point?"

He stared at her a moment. The morning sun speared through the skylight and streamed over her, accented the line of jaw and cheek. "Just stand there. Just stand right there," he repeated as he swung to his worktable. "Ten minutes. Okay, I lied. Twenty tops."

"Excuse me?"

"Just stand there. Damn it, where's my—ah." He scooped up a hunk of charcoal, then dragged his easel around. "No, don't look at me. Look over there. Wait."

He moved quickly, snatching up the painting of foxgloves, pulling out a nail from his pouch, then pounding it into the wall. "Just look at the painting."

"I don't have time to—"

"At the painting." This time his voice snapped, so full of authority and impatience, she obeyed before she thought it through. "I'll pay you for the time."

"I don't want your money."

"In trade." He was already stroking the charcoal over the canvas. "You've got that house by the river. You probably need things done off and on."

"I can take care of—"

"Uh-huh, uh-huh. Tilt your chin up a little, to the right. Jesus, Jesus, this light. Relax your jaw. Be pissed off later, just let me get this."

Who the hell was he? she wondered. He stood there, legs apart, body set like a man poised to fight. He had a tool belt slung at his hips and was sketching in charcoal as if his life depended on it.

His eyes were narrowed, so intense, so *focused*, that her heart jumped a little each time they whipped up and over her face.

On the stereo AC/DC was on the highway to hell. Through the open window came the cry of gulls as they swooped over the bay. Not entirely sure why she'd allowed herself to be ordered around, she stood and studied the foxgloves.

She began to see it gracing her bedroom wall.

"How much do you want for it?"

His eyebrows remained knit. "I'll let you know when I've finished it."

"No, the painting I'm staring at while I'm trying not to be annoyed with you. I'd like to buy it. You have an agent, I imagine. Should I contact him or her?"

He only grunted, not the least interested in business at the moment, and continued to work. "Don't move your head, just your eyes. And look at me. That's some face, all right."

"Yes, and I'm certainly all aflutter by your interest in it, but I have to go down and open for the day."

"Couple more minutes."

"Would you like to hear my opinion of people who can't take no for an answer?"

"Not right now." Keep her occupied, keep her talking, he thought quickly. Oh Jesus, it was perfect—the light, the face, that cool stare out of mossy green eyes. "I hear you've got old Mr. Gimball doing deliveries for you. How's that working out?"

"Perfectly fine, and as he's going to be pulling up in back very shortly—"

"He'll wait. Mr. Gimball used to teach history when I was in middle school. He seemed ancient then, as creaky as the dead presidents he lectured about. Once some of us found this big snake skin. We brought it in and curled it up on Mr. G's desk chair before third period."

"I'm sure you thought that was hysterically funny."

"Are you kidding? I was eleven. I nearly cracked a rib

laughing. Didn't you ever pull stunts like that on teachers in your private school for girls?"

"No, and why do you assume I went to a private school for girls?"

"Oh, sugar, it's all over you." He stepped back, nodded at the canvas. "Yeah, and it looks good on you." He reached forward, softened a line of charcoal with his thumb before he looked over at her. "You want to call this a sitting or our second date?"

"Neither." It took every ounce of will, but she didn't cross over to look at what he'd drawn.

"Second date," he decided, as he tossed the charcoal aside, absently picked up a rag to clean it off his hands. "After all, you brought me flowers."

"A plant," she corrected.

"Semantics. You really want the painting?"

"That would depend on how much really wanting it jacks up the price."

"You're pretty cynical."

"Cynicism is underrated. Why don't you give me your representative's name? Then we'll see."

He loved the way that short, sleek hair followed the shape of her head. He wanted to do more than sketch it. He needed to paint it.

And to touch it. To run his hands over that silky, dense black until he'd know its texture in his sleep.

"Let's do a friendly trade instead. Pose for me, and it's yours."

"I believe I just did."

"No. I want you in oil." And in watercolors. In pastels.
In bed.

He'd spent a great deal of time thinking about her over the last few days. Enough time to have concluded that a woman like her—with her looks, her background—would be used to men in active pursuit.

So he'd slowed things down, deliberately, and had waited for her to take the next step. To his way of thinking, she had. In the form of a houseplant.

He wanted her personally as much as he wanted her professionally. It didn't matter which came first, as long as he got both.

She shifted her gaze to the painting again. It was always a pleasure, and a bit of a shock, when he saw desire in someone's eyes when they looked at his work. Seeing it in Dru's he knew he'd scored, professionally.

"I have a business to run," she began.

"I'll work around your schedule. Give me an hour in the mornings before you open when you can manage it. Four hours on Sundays."

She frowned. It didn't seem like so very much, when he put it like that. And oh, the painting was gorgeous. "For how long?"

"I don't know yet." He felt a little ripple of irritation. "It's art, not accounting."

"Here?"

"To start, anyway."

She debated, argued with herself. Wished she'd never seen the damn painting. Then because it was a foolish woman who made any agreement without looking at all the terms, she walked to the easel, around the canvas. And studied her own face.

She'd expected something rough and, well, sketchy, as he'd taken no more than fifteen minutes to produce it. Instead, it was detailed and stunning—the angles, the shadows, the curves.

She looked very cool, she decided. A bit aloof and so

very, very serious. Cynical? she thought and gave in to the smile that tugged at her mouth.

"I don't look particularly friendly," she said.

"You weren't feeling particularly friendly."

"Can't argue with that. Or with the fact that you have an amazing gift." She sighed. "I don't have a dress with a long, full skirt and a sleeveless top."

And he grinned. "We'll improvise."

"I'll give you an hour tomorrow. Seven-thirty to eight-thirty."

"Ouch. Okay." He walked over, took the painting from the wall, held it out to her.

"You're trusting."

"Trust is underrated."

When her hands were full, he took her arms. He gave her that slight lift again, brought her to her toes. And the door swung open.

"Nope," Seth muttered as Cam strode in. "They never knock."

"Hi, Dru. Kiss the girl on your own time, kid. I don't smell any coffee." Obviously at home, he went toward the kitchen, then spotted the canvas. His face lit with pure delight. "Easiest fifty I ever made. I bet Phil Seth here would talk you into posing before the week was up."

"Oh, really?"

"No offense. Rembrandt here wants to paint something, he finds a way. He'd be a fool to pass up the chance to do that," he added, and the look on his face when he studied the canvas again was so filled with pride, she softened. "He's a pain in the ass half the time, but he's no fool."

"I'm aware of the pain-in-the-ass factor. I'll reserve judgment on whether or not he's a fool until I get to know him better. Seven-thirty," she said to Seth on her way out. "That's A.M."

Cam said nothing, just laid a beat with an open hand on his heart.

"Kiss ass."

"So, are you going to paint her, or poke at her?" Cam hooted out a laugh at Seth's vicious snarl. "What goes around comes around, kid. You spent a lot of time being disgusted at the idea of us poking at girls—as you put it— not so long ago."

"Since it is more than fifteen years that's not so long ago in your mind, it proves you're really getting old. Sure you should go up on the roof? Might have a spell up there and fall off."

"I can still kick your ass, kid."

"Sure. With Ethan and Phil holding me down, you might have a shot at taking me." He laughed when Cam caught him in a headlock. "Oh man, now I'm scared."

But they both remembered a time he would have been, when a skinny, smart-mouthed young boy would have frozen with terror at a touch, rough or gentle.

Knowing it, remembering it, Seth nearly blurted out the trouble he was keeping so tightly locked in the far corner of his mind.

No, he'd handled it, he told himself. And would handle it again, if and when.

H E was a man of his word. When the last of the skylights was in place, he followed Cam to the boatyard to put in a few hours.

Once, he'd thought he'd make his living here, working

side by side with his brothers building wooden sailing vessels. The fact was, some of his best memories were tucked inside the old brick building, flavored with his sweat, a little blood and the thrill of learning to be a part of something.

It had changed over the years. Refined, as Phillip would say. The walls were no longer bare and patched drywall, but painted a simple, workingman's white.

They'd fashioned a sort of entryway that opened to the stairs leading to Phillip's office and the second-story loft. It separated, in theory, the main work area.

Lining the walls were rough-framed sketches of various boats built by Quinn over the years. They depicted the progress of the business, and the growth of the artist.

He knew, because Aubrey had told him, that an art collector had come in two years before and offered his brothers a quarter million for the fifty sketches currently on display.

They'd turned him down flat, but had offered to build him a boat based on any sketch he liked.

It had never been about money, he thought now, though there had been some lean times during those first couple years. It had always been about the unit. And a promise made to Ray Quinn.

The work area itself hadn't changed very much. It was still a big, echoing, brightly lit space. There were pulleys and winches hanging from the ceiling. Saws, benches, stacks of lumber, the smell of freshly sawn wood, linseed oil, sweat, coffee, the boom of rock and roll, the buzz of power saws, the lingering scent of onions from someone's lunchtime sub.

It was all as familiar to him as his own face.

Yes, once he'd thought he'd spend his life working there, listening to Phillip bitch about unpaid invoices, watching Ethan's patient hands lapping wood, sweating with Cam as they turned a hull.

But art had consumed it. The love of it had taken him away from boyhood ambitions. And had, for a time, taken him from his family.

He was a man now, he reminded himself. A man who would stand on his own ground, fight his own battles and be what it was he was meant to be.

Nothing, no one, was going to stop him.

"You plan on standing there with your thumb up your ass much longer?" Cam asked him. "Or are we going to get some work out of you this afternoon?"

Seth shook himself back to the present. "Doesn't look like you need me," he pointed out.

He spotted Aubrey working on the deck planking of a skiff, her electric screwdriver whirling. She wore an Orioles fielder's cap with her long tail of hair pulled through the back. Ethan was at the lathe, turning a mast with his faithful dog sprawled at his feet.

"Hull of that skiff needs to be caulked and filled."

Grunt work, Seth thought and sighed. "And what are you going to be doing?"

"Basking in the glory of my little empire."

The basking included detailing the bulkhead for the cockpit, the sort of carpentry Cam turned into an art.

Seth did the grunt work; it was hardly the first time. He knew how to plank, he thought, a bit resentfully as Aubrey's drill continued its bump and grind over his head.

"Hey." She bent down to talk to him. "Will's got the night off. We're going to get some pizza, catch a flick after. You want in?"

It was tempting. He wanted to connect with Will again, not only because they'd been friends, but because he wanted to check out any guy who was sniffing around Aubrey.

He weighed that against spending the evening as a fifth wheel.

"Village Pizza?"

"Still the best in Saint Chris."

"Maybe I'll swing in," Seth decided. "Say hi to Will. I'll pass on the flick. I've got to get started early tomorrow."

"I thought you artistic types called your own hours."

Seth worked oakum into a seam of beveled planking on the hull. "Subject's calling these."

"What subject?" She sat back on her heels, then suddenly understood when she noted the expression on his face. "Ooooh, fancy flower lady's going to pose for the famous artist. I got more juice on her."

"I'm not interested in gossip." He managed to hold firm on that for nearly ten seconds. "What kind of juice?"

"Juicy juice, sweetheart. I got it from Jamie Styles, who got it from her cousin who was a Senate page a few years ago. Dru and a certain high-level White House aide were a very hot item back then."

"How hot?"

"Hot enough to burn up the society columns in the *Post* for nearly a year. And to warrant what Jamie's cousin describes as an engagement ring with a diamond the size of a doorknob. Then the diamond disappears, hot goes cold, and the high-level aide starts burning up the newsprint with a blonde."

"She was engaged?"

"Yeah. Briefly, according to my source. It came out that the blonde was a factor *before* the broken engagement. If you get my drift."

"He was cheating on Dru with the bimbo?"

"It so happens that this blonde was—is—a hotshot lawyer, assistant White House counsel or something."

"Must've been tough on Dru, having all that personal business splashed around in the press."

"She strikes me as someone who'd stand up to it pretty well. She's nobody's doormat. And I bet you a month's pay she busted that cheating bastard's balls before she stuffed the ring down his throat."

"You would," Seth said with approval and pride. "Right before you mopped the floor with his lying tongue. But Dru doesn't come off as the violent type. More like she froze him to death with one chilly look and a few icy words."

Aubrey snorted. "A lot you know about women. Still waters, pal of mine. They not only run deep, you bet your ass they can run hot, too."

MAYBE, Seth thought as he dropped his filthy, aching body back behind the wheel of his car. But he'd lay money Dru had sliced the guy in two without spilling a single drop of blood.

He knew what it was to have little personal details of your life—embarrassing, intimate details—nibbled on by the press.

It could be she'd come here to get away from all that. He knew just how she felt.

He glanced at the time as he pulled out. He could use that pizza Aubrey had mentioned, and it seemed a waste of effort to drive all the way home to shower off the day's work, then head right back into town.

So he'd just swing by and clean up at the studio. He'd brought over some towels and soap. He even remembered to toss a spare pair of jeans and a shirt into the closet.

He might just find Dru still at the shop and talk her into a friendly pizza. Which would, he thought, pleased with the idea, constitute date number three.

She'd get that cool, I-am-not-amused expression on her face when he called it that, he thought. And that quick light in her eyes that gave her humor away.

He was crazy about that contrast.

He could spend hours—days—contemplating the varieties of shadow and light in her.

But her car was gone from the little lot behind her building. He considered calling her, persuading her to come back into town, before he remembered he didn't have a phone.

He'd have to take care of that, he mused. But since he couldn't call from there, he'd clean up, buzz over to Village Pizza and call her from a pay phone.

Somebody was bound to have her number.

Better, he decided as he started up the steps, he'd get a pizza to go and stop by her house on the way home. With a bottle of Merlot.

What kind of woman would turn a guy away when he had pizza and wine?

Satisfied with the plan, he stepped inside, and felt something skid under his foot. Frowning, he reached down and picked up the folded note that had been slipped under his door.

His stomach pitched as the bottom fell out of his world.

Ten thousand should hold me. I'll be in touch.

Seth simply sat on the floor just inside the studio door and crumpled the paper into a tiny, mean ball.

Gloria DeLauter was back. He hadn't expected her to find or follow him so quickly. He hadn't been prepared, he admitted, to find her nipping at his heels barely two weeks after he'd left Rome.

He'd wanted time to think, to decide. He flipped the little wad of paper across the room. Well, ten thousand would buy him time, if he wanted to piss the money away.

He'd done it before.

When it came to his mother, there was no price he wouldn't pay to be free of her. And more, to keep his family free of her.

It was, of course, exactly what she counted on.

SIX

~

H E WAS SITTING on the dock, pole fishing with a smear of Anna's Brie for bait. The sun was summer-hot on his back, with an August weight to it that drenched the skin and set the brain to dreaming.

He wore nothing but cut-off jeans and a pair of wire-rim sunglasses.

He liked looking through them at the way the light beat down from a hazy blue sky and smacked the water. And he thought, idly, that he might just set the pole aside in a bit and slide right in to cool off.

The water lapped lazily against the hull of the little pram with blue sails tied to the dock. A jay was bitching in the trees, and when a stingy little breeze passed by, it carried a hint of roses from a bush that had lived there longer than he.

The house was quiet. The lawn leading to it was lush and freshly mown. He could smell that, too. Newly cut grass, roses, lazy water. Summer smells.

It didn't strike him as odd, though it was still spring.

Something had to be done, and he wished to God he knew what, to keep that house quiet, the air summer-peaceful. And his family safe.

He heard the yip of a dog, then the scrambling of canine feet on the dock. Seth didn't look up, even when the cold nose nudged at his cheek. He simply lifted an arm so the dog could wriggle against his side.

It was always comforting, somehow, to have a dog at your side when your thoughts were heavy.

But that wasn't enough for the dog, whose tail pounded a drumbeat on the dock as its tongue slathered over Seth's cheek.

"Okay, okay, cool it. Thinking here," he began, then felt his heart jump into his throat as he shifted to nudge the dog down.

Not Cam's dog, but his own. Foolish, who'd died in Seth's arms five years before. Speechless, Seth stared as those familiar doggie eyes seemed to laugh into his at the world's best joke.

"Wait a minute, wait a minute." Joy and shock tangled inside him as he grabbed the dog's muzzle. Warm fur, cold nose, wet tongue. "What the hell is this?"

Foolish gave another cheerful bark then flopped adoringly across Seth's lap.

"There you are, you stupid idiot," Seth murmured, as unspeakable love gushed inside him. "There you are, you idiot. Christ, oh Christ, I've missed you." He bobbled the pole, let go of it as he grabbed for his dog.

A hand reached out, snagged the pole before it dropped into the water.

"Wouldn't want to waste that fancy cheese." The woman who sat beside him, legs dangling over the dock, took charge of the pole. "We figured Foolish would cheer you up. Nothing like a dog, is there? For companionship, love, comfort and pure entertainment. Nothing biting today?"

"No, not . . ."

The words slipped back down his throat as he looked at her. He knew that face; he'd seen it in pictures. Long and thin, scattershot freckles over the nose and cheeks. She had a shapeless khaki hat over messy red curls that were streaked with silver. And her dark green eyes were unmistakable.

"You're Stella. Stella Quinn." Stella Quinn, he thought as he tried to make sense of it, who'd been dead more than twenty years.

"You turned out handsome, didn't you? Always thought you would." She gave the stubby ponytail a friendly tug. "Need a haircut, boy."

"I guess I'm dreaming."

"I guess you are," she said easily, but her hand moved from his hair to his cheek and gave it a rub before she tipped down his dark glasses. "You've got Ray's eyes. I fell for his eyes first, you know."

"I always wanted to meet you." You got your wishes in dreams, Seth decided.

"Well, here we are." With a chuckle, she tapped his sunglasses back in place. "Never too late, is it? Never cared much for fishing myself. Like the water—to look at, to swim in. Still, fishing's good for thinking, or not thinking at all. If you're going to brood, might as well have a line in the water. You never know what you'll pull up."

"I never dreamed about you before. Not like this."

The fact was, he'd never dreamed with this kind of clarity. He could feel the warm fur under his hand, and the steady beat of heart as Foolish panted in the heat.

He felt the strength of the sun on his bare back, and could hear, in the distance, the putt and purr of a workboat. The jay never stopped its piercing song.

"We figured it was time I got to play Grandma." She gave Seth an affectionate pat on the knee. "I missed that while I was here. Getting to fuss and coo over the babies when they came, spoiling you and the others. Dying's damn inconvenient, let me tell you."

When he simply stared at her, she let out a long, clear laugh. "It's natural enough to be a little spooked. It's not every day you sit around talking to a ghost."

"I don't believe in ghosts."

"Hard to blame you." She looked out over the water, and something in her face spoke of absolute contentment. "I'd've baked cookies for you, though I was never much of a cook. But you can't have everything, so you take what you can get. You're Ray's grandson, so that makes you mine."

His head was reeling, but he didn't feel dizzy. His pulse was galloping, but he didn't feel fear. "He was good to me. I only had him for a little while, but he was . . ."

"Decent." She nodded as she said it. "That's what you told Cam when he asked you. Ray was decent, you said, and you sure as hell hadn't had much decent up till then, poor little guy."

"He changed everything for me."

"He gave you a chance to change everything. You've done a pretty good job of it, so far. Can't choose where you come from, Seth. My boys and you know that better than anyone. But you can choose where you end up, and how you get there."

"Ray took me in, and it killed him."

"You say something like that and mean it, you're not as

smart as everyone thinks. Ray'd be disappointed to hear you say it."

"He wouldn't have been on that road if it hadn't been for me."

"How do you know that?" She poked him again. "If not that road that day, another road another day. Damn fool always drove too fast. Things happen, and that's that. They happen a different way, we'd sit around complaining about it just the same. Waste a lot of living on the ifs and ors, if you ask me."

"But—"

"But hell. George Bailey learned his lesson, didn't he?"

Baffled, fascinated, Seth shifted. "Who?"

Stella rolled her eyes toward heaven. "*It's a Wonderful Life.* Jimmy Stewart as George Bailey. Decides it would be better for everyone if he'd never been born, so an angel shows him the way things would've worked out if he hadn't."

"And you're going to show me?"

"Do I look like an angel to you?" she asked, amused.

"No. But I'm not thinking it'd be better if I'd never been born either."

"Change one thing, change everything. That's the lesson. What if Ray hadn't brought you here, if he hadn't run into that damn telephone pole? Maybe Cam and Anna wouldn't have met. Then Kevin and Jake wouldn't have been born. You wishing them away?"

"No, Jesus, of course not. But if Gloria—"

"Ah." With a satisfied nod, Stella lifted a finger. "There's the nub, isn't it? No point in saying 'if Gloria,' or 'but Gloria.' Gloria DeLauter is reality."

"She's back."

Her face softened, her voice gentled. "Yes, honey, I know. And it weighs on you."

"I won't let her touch their lives again. I won't let her fuck up my family. She only wants money. It's all she's ever wanted."

"You think?" Stella sighed. "Well, if you do, I suppose you'll give it to her. Again."

"What else can I do?"

"You'll figure it out." She handed him the pole.

He woke sitting on the side of the bed, his hand loosely fisted as if it held a fishing pole.

And when he opened those fingers, they shook a little. When he drew one careful breath, he'd have sworn he smelled the faint drift of summer grass.

Weird, he thought and raked his fingers through his hair. Very weird dream. And he could swear he felt the lingering warmth from his dog stretched across his lap.

THE first ten years of his life had been a prison of fear, abuse and neglect. It had made him stronger than most ten-year-old boys. And a great deal more wary.

Ray Quinn's pre-Stella affair with a woman named Barbara Harrow had been brief. He'd put it so completely behind him that his three adopted sons had been totally unaware of it. Just as Ray had been unaware of the product of that affair.

Gloria DeLauter.

But Gloria had known about Ray, and had tracked him down. In her usual style she'd used extortion and blackmail to bleed Ray for money. And had, in essence, sold her son to her father. But Ray had died suddenly, before he found the way to tell his sons, and his grandchild, of the connection.

To the Quinn brothers, Seth had simply been another of Ray Quinn's strays. They'd been bound to him by no more than a promise to a dying man. But that had been enough.

They'd changed their lives for him. They'd given him a home, stood up for him, shown him what it was to be part of a family. And they'd fought to keep him.

Anna had been his caseworker. Grace his first surrogate mother. And Sybill, Gloria's half sister, had brought back the only soft memories of his childhood.

He knew how much they'd sacrificed to give him a life. A life as decent as Ray Quinn. By the time Gloria had stepped back into the picture, hoping to bleed them for more money, he'd been one of them.

One of the brothers Quinn.

This wasn't the first time Gloria had approached him for money. He'd had three years to forget her, to feel safe after his new family had circled around him. Then she'd slithered back to St. Chris and had extorted money from a fourteen-year-old boy.

He'd never told them of it.

A few hundred that first time, he remembered. It was all he could manage without his family finding out—and had satisfied her. For a little while.

He'd paid her off each time she'd come back, until he'd fled to Europe. His time there hadn't been only to work and to study, but to escape.

She couldn't hurt his family if he wasn't with them, and she couldn't follow him across the Atlantic.

Or so he'd thought.

His success as an artist, the resulting publicity, had given Gloria big ideas. And bigger demands.

He wondered now if it had been a mistake to come home, as much as he'd needed to. He knew it was a mistake to continue to pay her. But the money meant nothing. His family meant everything.

He imagined Ray had felt the same.

In the clear light of day, he knew the sensible thing, the *sane* thing would be to tell her to get lost, to ignore her. To call her bluff.

But then he'd get one of her notes, or come face-to-face with her, and he'd clutch. He found himself strangled between his helpless childhood and the desperate need to shield the people he loved.

So he paid, with a great deal more than money.

He knew how she worked. She wouldn't pop up on his doorstep right away. She'd let him stew and worry and wonder, until ten thousand seemed like a bargain for a little peace of mind. She wouldn't be staying in St. Chris, wouldn't risk being seen and recognized by his brothers or sisters. But she'd be close.

However dramatic, however paranoid it was, he'd swear he could all but feel her—the hate and the greed—breathing down his neck.

He wasn't running again. She wouldn't make him deprive himself of home and family a second time. He would, as he had before, lose himself in his work and live his life. Until she came.

He'd wheedled a second morning session out of Dru. From the sitting the previous week he knew she expected him to be prepared when she arrived, precisely at seven-thirty, and for him to be ready to start. And to stop exactly sixty minutes later.

And to ensure he did, she'd brought a kitchen timer with her.

The woman had no tolerance for artistic temperament. That was all right with Seth. In his opinion, he didn't have an artistic temperament.

He was using pastels, just a basic study for now. It was an extension of the charcoal sketch. A way for him to learn her face, her moods, her body language before he roped her into the more intense portraits he'd already planned in his mind.

When he looked at her, he felt all the models he'd used throughout his career had been simply precursors to Drusilla.

She knocked. He'd told her it wasn't necessary, but she kept that formal distance between them. That, he thought as he walked to the door, would have to be breached.

There could be no formality, and no distance, between them if he was to paint her as he needed to paint her.

"Right on time. Big surprise. Want coffee?"

He'd had his hair cut. It was still long enough to lay over the collar of the torn T-shirt that seemed to be his uniform, but the ponytail was gone. It surprised her that she missed it. She'd always felt that sort of thing was an affectation on a man.

He'd shaved, too, and could almost be deemed tidy if you ignored the holes in the knees of his jeans and the paint splatters on his shoes.

"No, thanks. I've had a cup already this morning."

"One?" He closed the door behind her. "I can barely form a simple declarative sentence on one hit of coffee. How do you do it?"

"Willpower."

"Got a lot of that, do you?"

"As a matter of fact."

To his amusement, she set the timer on his workbench,

set at sixty. Then went directly to the stool he'd set out for her, slid onto it.

She noticed the change immediately.

He'd bought a bed.

The frame was old—a simple black iron head—and the footboard showed some dings. The mattress was bare and still had the tags.

"Moving in after all?"

He glanced over. "No. But it's better than the floor if I end up working late and bunking here. Plus it's a good prop."

Her brow lifted. "Oh, really?"

"Are you usually so preoccupied with sex, or is it just around me?" It made him laugh when her mouth dropped open. "A prop," he continued as he moved to his easel, "like that chair over there, those old bottles." He gestured toward the bottles stacked in a corner. "The urn and this cracked blue bowl I've got in the kitchen. I pick up things as they catch my eye."

He studied his pastels, and his mouth curved. "Including women."

She relaxed her shoulders. He'd notice if they were stiff, and it would make her feel even more foolish. "That's quite a speech for one 'oh, really.' "

"Sugar, you pack a lot of punch into an 'oh, really.' Do you remember the pose?"

"Yes." Obediently she propped her foot on the rung of the stool, laced her hands around her knee, then looked over her left shoulder as if someone had just spoken to her.

"That's perfect. You're really good at this."

"I sat like this for an hour just a few days ago."

"An hour," he repeated as he began to work. "Before the wild debauchery of the weekend."

"I'm so used to wild debauchery it doesn't have a particular impact on my life."

It was his turn. "Oh, really?"

He mimicked her tone so perfectly, she broke the pose to look toward him, laughing. He always managed to make her laugh. "I minored in WD in college."

"Oh, if only." His fingers hurried to capture the bright, beautiful laughter. "I know your type, baby. You walk around being beautiful, smart, sexy and unapproachable so we guys just suffer and dream."

It was, obviously, the wrong thing to say as the humor on her face died instantly—like flipping a switch. "You don't know anything about me, or my type."

"I didn't say that to hurt your feelings. I'm sorry."

She shrugged. "I don't know you well enough for you to hurt my feelings. I know you just well enough to have you annoy me."

"Then I'm sorry for that. I was joking. I like hearing you laugh. I like seeing it."

"Unapproachable." She heard herself mutter it before she could bite down on the urge. Just as her head jerked around before she could pull back the temper. "Did you think I was so damned unapproachable when you grabbed me and kissed me?"

"I'd say the act speaks for itself. Look. A lot of times when a guy sees a woman—a beautiful one he's attracted to—he gets clumsy. It's easier to figure she's out of reach than to analyze his own clumsiness. Women . . ."

If furious was what he was going to get out of her, then he'd capture fury in pastels. "They're a mystery to us. We want them. We can't help it. That doesn't mean you don't scare the hell out of us, one way or the other, more than half the time."

She would have sniffed if he wouldn't have made such a predictable response. "Do you honestly expect me to believe you're afraid of women?"

"Well, I had some advantage, with all those sisters." He was working now, but she'd forgotten he was working. Sometimes, that was only better. So he continued to talk while she frowned at him. "But the first girl I was ever serious about? It took me two weeks to get up the nerve to call her on the phone. Your kind doesn't know what my kind go through."

"How old were you?"

"Fifteen. Marilyn Pomeroy, a giddy little brunette."

"And how long were you serious about Marilyn?"

"About as long as it took me to work up the nerve to call her. Two weeks, give or take. What can I say? Men are no damn good."

Her lips twitched and curved. "That goes without saying. I was serious about a boy when I was fifteen. Wilson Bufferton Lawrence. The Fourth. Buff to his friends."

"Jesus, where do you guys come up with these names? What do you do with somebody named Buff? Play polo or squash?"

He'd leveled her temper, she realized. It was something else he was good at. Since he didn't appear to mind her being mad, it often seemed a waste of time to *be* mad.

"Tennis, actually. On what you'd call our first official date, we played tennis at the club. I beat him in straight sets, and that was the end of our tender romance."

"You'd have to expect someone who answers to Buff to be an asshole."

"I was crushed, then I was mad. I liked being mad better."

"Me too. What became of Buff?"

"Hmmm. As I was informed by my mother over the weekend, he's going to be married for the second time this fall. His first marriage lasted slightly longer than our long-ago tennis match."

"Better luck next time."

"Naturally," she said, very soberly, "he's in finance, as is expected of a fourth-generation Lawrence, and the happy couple is house hunting for their little fifty-room love nest as we speak."

"It's nice to know you're not still bitter."

"I was reminded, a total of five times, I believe, that I've yet to afford my parents the pleasure of spending lavish amounts of money on a wedding that would show the Lawrences, among others, a thing or two."

"So . . . you and your mother had a nice visit on Mother's Day." Though her expression now all but radiated irritation, he kept working. "Careful, you could spill blood with that sneer."

She took a deep breath, angled her head properly again. "My visits with my mother can rarely be defined as 'nice.' I suspect you spent this past Sunday going to see each one of your mothers—sisters."

"It's hard to pin down just what they are. Yeah, I spent some time with each of them. Took them their presents. And since each one of them cried, I figure they were a big hit."

"What did you get them?"

"I did small family portraits. Anna and Cam and the boys, and so on, for each one."

"That's nice. That's lovely," she said softly. "I got my mother a Baccarat vase and a dozen red roses. She was very pleased."

He set down his pastels, dusted his hands on his jeans as he crossed to her. And took her face in his hands. "Then why do you look so sad?"

"I'm not sad."

In response, he simply pressed his lips to her forehead, keeping them there as he felt her tense, then relax.

She couldn't remember ever having a conversation like this with anyone before. And she couldn't fathom why it seemed perfectly natural to have it with him. "It would be difficult for you to understand a conflicted family when yours is so united."

"We have plenty of conflicts," he corrected.

"No. Not at the core, you don't. I need to get downstairs."

"I still have some time left," he said, holding her in place when she started to slide off the stool.

"You've stopped working."

"I still have some time left," he repeated, and gestured to her timer. "If there's one thing I know about, it's family conflict, and what it does to you inside. I spent the first third of my life in a constant state of conflict."

"You're speaking of before you came to live with your grandfather? I've read stories about you, but you don't discuss that aspect," she said when his head came up.

"Yeah." He waited for the constriction in his chest to ease. "Before. When I lived with my biological mother."

"I see."

"No, sugar, you don't. She was a whore and a drunk and a junkie, and she made the first few years of my life a nightmare."

"I'm sorry." He was right, she supposed, it was something she couldn't see clearly. But she touched his hand, then took his hand, in an instinctive gesture of comfort. "It must have been horrible for you. Still, it's obvious she's nothing to you."

"That's what you got out of one statement from me and a handful of articles?"

"No. That's what I got after eating crab and potato salad with you and your family. Now you look sad," she murmured, and shook her head. "I don't know why we're talking about these things."

He wasn't sure why he'd brought up Gloria himself. Maybe it was as simple as speaking out loud to chase away ghosts. Or as complex as needing Dru to know who he was, all the way through.

"That's what people do, people who are interested in each other. They talk about who they are and where they've come from."

"I told you—"

"Yeah, you don't want to be interested. But you are." He traced a finger over her hair, from the short, spiky bangs to the tender nape. "And since we've been dating for several weeks—"

"We haven't dated at all."

He leaned down and caught her up in a kiss as hot as it was brief. "See?" Before she could comment, his mouth took hers again. Softer now, slower, deeper, with those wonderful hands skimming over her face, along her throat and shoulders.

Every muscle in her body went loose. Every vow she'd made about men and relationships crumbled.

When he eased back, she took a careful breath. And changed her line in the sand. "I may end up sleeping with you, but I'm not dating you."

"So, I'm good enough to have sex with, but I don't get a candlelit dinner? I feel so cheap."

Damn it. *Damn* it. She liked him. "Dating's a circular, often tortuous route to sex. I choose to skip it. But I said I might sleep with you, not that I would."

"Maybe we should play tennis first."

"Okay. You're funny. That's appealing. I admire your work, and I like your family. All completely superfluous to a physical relationship, but a nice bonus all in all. I'll think about it."

Saved by the bell, she thought when the timer buzzed. She got off the stool, then wandered to the easel. She saw her face a half dozen times. Different angles, different expressions. "I don't understand this."

"What?" He joined her at the easel. *"Bella donna,"* he murmured, and surprised a shiver out of her.

"I thought you were doing a study of me sitting on the stool. You started it, but you've got all these other sketches scattered around it."

"You weren't in the mood to pose today. You had things on your mind. They showed. So I worked with them. It gives me some insight, and some ideas about what I want in a more formal portrait."

He watched her brow knit. "You said I could have four hours on Sunday," he reminded her. "I'd like to work outside, weather permitting. I've been by your house. It's terrific. Any objection to working there?"

"At my house?"

"It's a great spot. You know that or you wouldn't be there. You're too particular to settle. Besides, it'll be simpler for you. Ten o'clock okay?"

"I suppose."

"Oh, and about the foxgloves? How many more sittings can I get if I frame it for you?"

"I don't—"

"If you bring it back to me, I'll frame it, then you can decide what it's worth in trade. Fair enough?"

"It's down in the shop. I was going to take it to a framer this week."

"I'll stop down and get it before I leave today." He walked his fingers up her arm. "I guess there's no point in asking you to have dinner with me tonight."

"None at all."

"I could just stop by your place later for some quick, cheap sex."

"That's awfully tempting, but I don't think so." She strolled to the door, then glanced back at him. "If and when we go there, Seth, I can promise it won't be cheap. And it won't be quick."

When the door closed, he rubbed his belly that had tightened at that last provocative look she'd sent him.

He glanced back at the canvas. She was, he decided, quite a number of women rolled up in one fascinating package. Every single one of them appealed to him.

"SOMETHING'S troubling him." Anna boxed Cam into the bathroom—one place almost guaranteed to provide space for an uninterrupted conversation in her personal madhouse. She paced the confined area and talked to his silhouette on the shower curtain.

"He's okay. He's just getting his rhythm back."

"He's not sleeping well. I can tell. And I swear I heard him talking to himself the other night."

"You do plenty of solo babbling when you're pissed off," Cam mumbled.

"What did you say?"

"Nothing. Just talking to myself."

With an expression between smug and grim—because she'd heard him perfectly—Anna flushed the toilet. Then smiled in cool satisfaction as he cursed at the sudden blast of hot water. "Goddamn it, why do you *do* that?"

"Because it irritates you and gets your attention. Now about Seth—"

"He's painting," Cam said in exasperation. "He's working at the boatyard, he's catching up with the family. Give him some time, Anna."

"Have you noticed what he's not doing? He's not going out with his friends. He's not dating Dru, or anyone else. Though it's clear from the way he looks at her there isn't going to *be* anyone else for the time being."

Or ever, she concluded.

"He's downstairs playing video games with Jake," she continued. "On a Friday night. Aubrey told me he's only hung out with her once since he got back home. How many weekends did you hang around the house when you were his age?"

"This is Saint Chris, not Monte Carlo. All right, all right," he said quickly, before she flushed on him again. The woman could be vicious. He loved that about her. "So he's preoccupied, I'm not blind. I got pretty preoccupied myself when I got tangled up with you."

"If I thought it was infatuation, or interest or just healthy lust where Dru's considered, I wouldn't be worried. And I am worried. I can't put my finger on it, but when I'm worried about one of my men, there's a reason."

"Fine. So go hound him."

"No. I want you to go hound him."

"Me?" Cam whisked back the curtain enough to stare at her. "Why me?"

"Because. Mmm, you sure are cute when you're wet and annoyed."

"That's not going to work."

"Maybe I should come in there and wash your back," she said and began to unbutton her blouse.

"Okay, that's going to work."

SEVEN

C AM JOGGED DOWNSTAIRS. There was nothing like a spin in the shower with Anna to brighten his mood. He poked a head in the den where his youngest son and Seth were waged in deadly, bloody battle. There were curses, grunts, shouts.

Some of them were from the animation on-screen.

As usual, Cam found himself drawn into the war. Axes swung, blood flew, swords clashed. And he lost track of reality until Jake let out a triumphant cry.

"I kicked your ass."

"Shit, you got lucky."

Jake pumped his joystick in the air. "I *rule*, baby. Bow to the king of Mortal Kombat."

"In your dreams. Let's go again."

"Bow to the king," Jake repeated joyously. "Worship me, lesser mortal."

"I'll worship you."

Seth made his grab. Cam watched them wrestle for a

moment. More grunts, impossible threats, a young boy's dopey giggles. Seth and Jake, he thought, weren't so different in age than he and Seth.

But Jake had an innocence Seth had never been allowed. Jake had never had to question who he was, or if the hands reaching for him meant him harm.

Thank God for it.

Cam leaned lazily against the doorjamb and yelled, "Come on, Anna, they're just fooling around."

At the mention of her name, Seth and Jake rolled apart and shot twin looks of panic and guilt toward the doorway.

"Got you," Cam barked with amusement.

"That was cold, Dad."

"That's how to win a battle without a single blow. You." He pointed at Seth. "Let's go."

"Where ya going?" Jake demanded, scrambling up. "Can I go?"

"Have you cleaned your room, done your homework, found the cure for cancer and changed the oil in my car?"

"Come on, Dad," Jake whined.

"Seth, grab some beer and head outside. I'll be right along."

"Sure. Later, kid"—Seth tapped a fist in his palm—"I'm taking you out."

"You couldn't take me out if you brought me flowers and a box of chocolate."

"Good one," Cam commented as Seth snorted out a laugh and left the room.

"I've been saving it," Jake told him. "How come I can't go with you guys?"

"I need to talk to Seth."

"Are you mad at him?"

"Do I look mad at him?"

"No," Jake said after a careful study of his father's face. "But you can be sneaky about that stuff."

"I just need to talk to him."

Jake jerked a shoulder, but Cam saw the disappointment in his eyes—Anna's Italian eyes—before he plopped back on the floor and reached for his joystick.

Cam squatted. "Jake." He caught the scent of bubble gum and youthful sweat. There were grass stains on the knees of Jake's jeans. His shoes were untied.

It struck him unexpectedly, as it often did, that staggering slap of emotion that was love and pride and puzzlement rolled into one strong fist against his heart.

"Jake," he said again and ran his hand over his son's hair. "I love you."

"Jeez." Jake hunched his shoulders and, with his chin tucked, shifted his gaze up to meet his father's. "I know, and stuff."

"I love you," Cam repeated. "But when I get back, there's going to be a bloody coup, and a new king in Quinn-land. And believe what I'm saying, you will bow to me."

"You wish."

Cam rose, pleased with the cocky expression on Jake's face. "Your days of rule are numbered. Start praying, pal."

"I'll pray that you don't slobber on me when you're begging for mercy."

He had to admit, Cam decided as he walked toward the back door, he'd raised a bunch of wiseasses. It did a man proud.

"What's up?" Seth asked, tossing Cam a beer as he swung out the back door.

"Gonna take a little sail."

"Now?" Automatically, Seth looked up at the sky. "It'll be dark in an hour."

"Afraid of the dark, Mary?" Cam sauntered to the dock, stepped nimbly into the day sailer. He set the beer aside while Seth cast off.

As he had countless times in the past, Seth lifted the oar to push away from the dock. He hoisted the main, and the sound of the canvas rising was sweet as music. Cam manned the rudder, finessing the wind so they glided, smooth and nearly silent, away from shore.

The sun was low, its beams striking the water, sheening the marsh grass, dying in the narrow channels where the shadows went deep and the water went dark and secret.

They motored through, maneuvering between markers, down the river, through the sound. And into the Bay. Balanced to the sway, Seth hoisted the jib, trimmed the sails.

And Cam caught the wind.

They flew in the wooden boat with its bright work glinting and its sails white as dove's wings. There was salt in the air, and the thrilling roll, that rise and fall of waves as deeply blue as the sky.

The speed, the freedom, the absolute joy of skating over the water while the sun went soft toward twilight drained every worry, every doubt, every sorrow from Seth's heart.

"Coming about," Cam called out, setting to tack to steal more wind, steal more speed.

For the next fifteen minutes, they barely spoke.

When they slowed, Cam stretched out his legs and popped the top on his beer. "So, what's going on with you?"

"Going on?"

"Anna's radar tells her something's up with you, and she nagged me into finding out what it is."

Seth bought some time by opening his own beer, taking

the first cold sip. "I've just been back a couple weeks, so I've got a lot on my mind, that's all. Figuring things out, settling in, that kind of thing. She doesn't have to worry."

"I'm supposed to go back and tell her she doesn't have to worry? Oh yeah, that'll go down real smooth." He took another drink. "Look, we don't have to go through all that you-know-you-can-talk-to-me-about-anything crap, do we? Going that route's only going to make us both feel like morons."

"No." But it worked a smile out of Seth. "Just tell her I'm thinking about what happens next. I've got to get a place of my own sooner or later. My rep's bugging me about putting together another showing, and I'm not sure what direction I want to take there. I haven't even finished putting the studio together yet."

"Uh-huh." Cam glanced toward shore, and the pretty old house tucked back on the banks of the river.

When Seth followed the look, he shifted in the bow. He'd been so wrapped up in the sail, he hadn't noticed the direction.

"Sexy flower queen's not home yet," Cam commented. "Maybe she's got a date."

"She doesn't date."

"Is that why you haven't moved on her yet?"

"Who says I haven't?"

Cam only laughed, sipped beer. "If you had, kid, you'd look a hell of a lot more relaxed."

Got me there, Seth thought, but shrugged.

"In fact, I can drop you off here. You can try the 'I was just in the neighborhood so can I come in and get you naked' gambit."

"That one ever work for you?"

"Ah." Cam let out a long, wistful sigh, stared up at the

sky as if into deep, dreamy memories. "The stories I could tell. The way I figure it, the more a guy gets sex, the more he thinks about it. And the less a guy gets sex, the more he thinks about it. But at least when he's getting it, he sleeps better."

Seth patted his pockets. "Got a pen? I want to write that one down."

"She's a very tasty morsel."

Amusement fled. "She's not a fucking snack."

"Okay." Having nailed the answer he wanted, Cam nodded. "I wondered if you were really tangled up about her."

Seth hissed out a breath, looked back toward the fanciful blue house tucked among the trees until it was out of sight. "I don't know what I am. I've got to get my life settled, and until I do, I don't have time for . . . tangles. But I look at her and . . ." He shrugged. "I can't figure it out. I like being around her. Not that she's easy. Half the time it's like dealing with a porcupine. One in a tiara."

"Women without spines are fine for a one-nighter, or a good time. But when you're looking for the long haul . . ."

Shock and panic erupted on Seth's face. "I didn't say that. I just said I liked being around her."

"And you got puppy eyes when you said it."

"Bullshit." And the fact that he could feel the heat of a flush working up his neck mortified him. He could only hope the light was too dim for Cam to spot it.

"Another minute, you'd've whimpered. You going to trim that jib, or just let her reef?"

Muttering to himself, Seth adjusted the lines. "Look, I want to paint her, I want to spend some time with her. And I want to get her into bed. I can manage all three on my own, thanks."

"If you do, maybe you'll start sleeping better."

"Dru doesn't have anything to do with how I'm sleeping. Or not much anyway."

Cam came about again and headed toward home. Twilight was falling. "So are you going to tell me what's keeping you up at night, or do I have to pry that out of you, too? You don't tell me, Anna's going to make both of our lives hell until you spill it."

He thought of Gloria, and the words crammed in his throat. If he let the first one out, the rest wouldn't just spill. It would be an avalanche. All he could see was his family buried under it.

He could tell Cam anything. Anything but that.

But maybe it was time to unload something else. "I had this really weird dream."

"Are we going back to sex?" Cam asked. "Because if we are we should've brought more beer along."

"I dreamed about Stella."

The wicked humor on Cam's face drained, leaving it naked and vulnerable. "Mom? You dreamed about Mom?"

"I know it's weird. I never even met her."

"What was she . . ." It was strange how grief could hide inside you. Like a virus, lying low for months, even years, only to spring out and leave you weak and helpless again. "What were you doing?"

"Sitting on the dock in back of the house. It was summer. Hot, sweaty, close. I was fishing, just a pole and a line and some of Anna's Brie."

"You'd better've been dreaming," Cam managed. "Or you're a dead man."

"See, that's the thing. The line's in the water, but I *knew* I'd copped the cheese for bait. And I could smell roses, feel the heat of the sun. Then Foolish plops down next to me. I know he's gone—I mean in the dream I know—so I'm pretty damn surprised to see him. Next thing I know Stella's sitting on the dock beside me."

"How did she look?"

It didn't seem like an odd question while they were gliding along on quiet water in the dimming light. It seemed perfectly rational. "She looked terrific. She had on this old khaki hat, no brim. The kind you just yank down over your head, and her hair was falling all out of it."

"Jesus." Cam remembered the old hat, and the way she'd stuffed her unmanageable hair under it. Did they have a picture of her in that ugly cap? He couldn't recall.

"I don't want to mess you up with this."

Cam only shook his head. "What happened in the dream?"

"Not a whole lot. We just sat there and talked. About you guys, and Ray and . . ."

"What?"

"How they figured it was time she got to play Grandma, since she'd missed out on that before. It wasn't what we said so much as how real it seemed. Even when I woke up sitting on the side of the bed, it seemed real. I don't know how to explain it."

"No, I get you." Hadn't he had a number of conversations with his father, after Ray had died? And hadn't his brothers both had similar experiences?

But it had been so long now. Longer yet since they'd lost their mother. And none of them had ever had that wrenching chance to talk to her again. Even in dreams.

"I always wanted to meet her," Seth continued. "It feels like I have."

"How long ago was this?"

"Last week, I guess. And before you start, I didn't say anything at the time because I figured you might freak. You gotta admit, it's a little spooky."

You ain't seen nothing yet, Cam thought. But that was one of the aspects of being a Quinn Seth would have to find out on his own.

"If you dream about her again, ask her if she remembers the zucchini bread."

"The what?"

"Just ask her," Cam said as they drifted home.

WHEN they got home, dinner was cooking. And Dan McLean was standing by the stove, holding a beer and leaning in for Anna to feed him a spoonful of red sauce.

"What the hell's he doing here?" Cam demanded, and fixed a scowl on his face because Dan would expect it.

"Mooching. That's terrific, Miz Q. Nobody makes it like you. It makes having to see his face again easier," he added, and nodded toward Seth.

"Weren't you mooching here two weeks ago?" Cam asked him.

"Nah. I mooched at Ethan's two weeks ago. I like to spread myself around."

"More of you to spread around than there was last time I saw you." Seth hooked his thumbs in his pockets and took a long look at his childhood friend. Dan had filled out in a way that indicated solid gym time.

"Can't men just say, 'Hi, it's good to see you again'?" Anna wondered.

"Hi," Seth echoed. "It's good to see you again."

They moved together in the one-armed hold that constitutes a male hug.

Cam sniffed at the simmering pots. "Christ, I'm tearing up. This is so touching."

"Why don't you set the table," Anna suggested to Cam. "Before you make a sentimental fool of yourself."

"Let the moocher set it. He knows where everything is. I've got to go dethrone and execute our youngest child."

"Make sure you do it within twenty minutes. We're eating in twenty-one."

"I'll set the table, Miz Q."

"No, get out of my kitchen. Take your beer and manly ways outside. I don't know why I couldn't have had just one girl. I don't know why that was too much to ask."

"Next time this one comes over to eat our food, make him put on a dress," Cam called over his shoulder as he headed for the den and his son's date with destiny.

"Cam loves me like a brother," Dan said and, at home, opened the refrigerator to get Seth a beer. "Let us go and sit outside like men, scratching and telling sexual lies."

They sat on the steps. Each took a pull from his beer. "Aub says you're digging in this time. Got yourself a studio over the florist."

"That's right. Aub says? My information is your little brother's after her."

"When he gets the chance. I see more of her than I see of Will. They've got him doing so many double shifts at the hospital he calls out 'stat!' and other sexy medical terms in his sleep."

"You guys still bunking together?"

"Yeah, for now. Mostly I've got the apartment to myself. He lives and breathes the hospital. Will McLean, M.D. Ain't that some shit?"

"He really got off dissecting frogs in biology. You wimped out."

Even from this distance, the thought made Dan grimace. "It was, and continues to be, a disgusting rite of passage. No frog's ever caused me harm. Now that you're back, it screws my plans to visit you in Italy, have the two of us sit at some sidewalk cafe—"

"Trattoria."

"Whatever, and ogle sexy women. Figured we'd catch a lot of action, with you being all artistic and me being so damn handsome."

"What happened to that teacher you were seeing? Shelly?"

"Shelby. Yeah, well, that's another thing that put my little fantasy in the dust." Dan dug in his pocket, pulled out a jeweler's box and flipped the top with his thumb.

"Holy hell, McLean," Seth managed as he blinked at the diamond ring.

"Got big plans tomorrow night. Dinner, candlelight, music, get down on one knee. The whole package." Dan blew out a shaky breath. "I'm scared shitless."

"You're getting married?"

"Man, I hope so, because I love her to pieces. You think she'll go for this?"

"How do I know?"

"You're the artist," Dan said and shoved the ring under Seth's nose. "How's it look to you?"

It looked like a fancy gold band with a diamond in the center. But friendship demanded more than that. "It looks great. Elegant, classic."

"Yeah, yeah." Obviously pleased, Dan studied it again. "That's her, man. That's Shelby. Okay." Breathing out, he put the box back in his pocket. "Okay then. She really wants to meet you. She's into that art crap. That's how I hit on her the first time. Aubrey dragged me to this art show at the university because Will was tied up. And there's Shelby standing in front of this painting that looked like maybe a chimp had done. I mean, what is with that shit that's just streaks and splatters of paint? It's a scam, if you ask me."

"I'm sure Pollock died in shame."

"Yeah, right, whatever. Anyhow, I went up to her and pulled that 'what does it say to you?' kind of line. And you know what she says?"

Enjoying seeing his friend so besotted, Seth leaned back against the step. "What did she say?"

"She said the five-year-olds in her kindergarten class do better work with fingerpaints. Man oh man, it was love. So that's when I pulled out the big guns and told her I had this friend who was an artist, but he painted real pictures. Then I drop your name and she nearly fainted. I guess that's when it really hit me you'd become a BFD."

"You still have that sketch I did of you and Will hanging over your toilet?"

"It's in a place of honor. So, how about you meet Shelby and me some night next week? For a drink, maybe something to eat."

"I can do that, but she may fall for me and leave you brokenhearted."

"Yeah, that'll happen. But just in case, she's got this friend—"

"No." The horror of it had Seth throwing up a blocking hand. "No fix-ups. You'll just have to take your chances on your girl falling under the spell of my fatal charm."

* * *

AFTER the meal, and the noise, Seth let Dan drag him off for a night at Shiney's. It turned into a marathon of reminiscence and bad music.

They'd left the porch and living room lamp on for him, so he made it all the way upstairs before he tripped over the dog sprawled across the bathroom doorway.

He cursed under his breath, limped off to his room and stripped down to the skin where he stood. His ears were still ringing from the last horrendous set when he flopped facedown on the bed.

It was good to be home, was his last thought, and he fell dreamlessly into sleep.

"MOM?" In the office of the boatyard, Phillip sat heavily in his chair. "He dreamed about Mom?"

"Maybe it was a dream, maybe it wasn't."

Ethan rubbed his chin. "He said she was wearing that old cap?"

"That's right."

"She wore it often enough," Phillip pointed out. "He's probably seen a picture of her wearing it."

"She's not wearing it in any of the pictures we've got sitting around our place." Cam had looked. "I'm not saying he hasn't seen a picture, and I'm not saying it wasn't just a dream. But it's odd. She used to come down and sit on the dock with us like that. She didn't care much for fishing, but if one of us was sitting out there brooding over something, she'd come out and sit until we started talking about whatever it was we had in our craw."

"She was good at it," Ethan agreed. "Good at getting down to the meat of it."

"It doesn't mean this is anything like what happened with us after Dad died."

"You didn't want to believe that either," Ethan pointed out as he hunted up a bottle of water from Phillip's office refrigerator.

"I know this. Something's bothering the kid and he doesn't want to talk about it. Not to me anyway." It stung a little, Cam admitted. "If anybody can get it out of him, it's Mom. Even in a dream. In the meantime, I guess we just watch him. I'm going down before he figures out we're up here talking about him."

Cam started out, then stopped and turned back. "I told him if he dreams about her again to ask her about the zucchini bread."

Both his brothers looked blank. Ethan remembered first and laughed so hard he had to sit on the edge of the desk.

"Christ." Phillip eased back in his chair. "I'd forgotten all about that."

"We'll see if she remembers," Cam said, then started down into the din of the work area. He'd gotten to the last step when the outer door opened, spilling in sunshine just ahead of Dru.

"Well, hello, gorgeous. Looking for my idiot brother?"

"Which idiot brother?"

His grin was pure appreciation. "You catch on. Seth's earning his keep."

"Actually, I wasn't—" But Cam already had her hand and was leading her along.

Legs spread, his back to her, Seth stood on the decking of the boat, stripped to the waist. His back and arms showed considerably more muscle than might be expected from a man who wielded a paintbrush for a living. He guzzled from a bottle of water like a man who hadn't had a drink in a week.

Her own mouth went dry watching him.

Shallow, Dru told herself. Shallow, shallow, shallow, to be interested in a man simply because he looked hot and hard and handsome. She appreciated intellect and strength of character and personality and . . . a really excellent butt, she admitted.

Sue her.

She managed to avoid licking her lips before he turned. He reached up to swipe at his brow with his forearm, then spotted her.

Now, in addition to the long male body clad only in jeans and work boots, her senses were assaulted by the lethal power of his smile.

She saw his mouth move—it was, like his butt, excellent. But the words he spoke were drowned out by the music.

Willing to assist, Cam walked over and turned the stereo down to merely loud.

"Hey!" Aubrey's head popped up from under the deck. "What gives?"

"We've got company."

Dru watched, with some interest, as Seth ran a hand over Aubrey's shoulder as he jumped down from the deck. "We're on for tomorrow, right?" he asked her as he walked over, pulling a bandanna out of his pocket to wipe his hands and face.

"Yes." Dru noted that Aubrey continued to watch, with considerable interest of her own. "I didn't mean to interrupt your work. I was running some errands while Mr. G watches the shop, and I thought I'd come in and have a look at the operation here."

"I'll show you around."

"You're busy." And your blond companion is watching me like your guard dog, Dru decided. "In any case, I'm told it's probably you I want to see," she said to Cam.

Cam gestured at Seth. "I told you that's what all the pretty ladies say. What can I do for you?"

"I want to buy a boat."

"Is that so?" Cam draped an arm around her shoulders and turned to lead her toward the stairs. "Well, sugar, you've come to the right place."

"Hey!" Seth called out. "I can talk about boats."

"Junior partner. We try to humor him. So, what kind of boat are you interested in?"

"Sloop. Eighteen feet. Arc bottom, cedar hull. Probably a spoon bow, though I'd be flexible if the designer has another idea. I want something with good balance, reliable stability, but when I want to move, I want to move."

She turned to study the gallery of sketches and told herself she'd admire the art of them later. For now, she wanted to make her point.

"This hull, this bow," she said, gesturing to two sketches. "I want something dependable, quick to the wind, and I want a boat that lasts."

She obviously knew her boats. "A custom job like that's going to cost you."

"I don't expect it comes free, but I don't discuss terms with you, do I? I believe that's your brother Phillip's area—and if there are any other specific design details, that would be Ethan's."

"Done your homework."

"I like to know who I'm dealing with, and I prefer dealing with the best. That, by all accounts, is Quinn Brothers. How soon can you work up a design?"

Man, oh man, Cam thought, you're going to drive the kid crazy. And it's going to be fun to watch. "Let's go upstairs and we'll figure it out."

IT was Ethan who walked her down and out thirty minutes later. The lady, he'd discovered, knew port from starboard, had very specific ideas about what she wanted, and held her own against a group of men who'd never had their rough edges quite smoothed off.

"We'll have a draft of the design drawn up by the end of next week," he told her. "Sooner if we can browbeat Seth into doing most of it."

"Oh?" She sent what she hoped was a casual glance toward the work area. "Does he do some of the designing?"

"When we can pin him down. Always had a knack. Pretty obvious he draws better than the three of us put together, and then some."

She followed his gaze and looked at the gallery of boats. "It's a wonderful collection, and retrospective, I suppose. You can see his artistic progress very clearly."

"This one here." He tapped his finger against the sketch of a skipjack. "He did this drawing when he was ten."

"Ten?" Fascinated, she moved closer, studying it now as a student might study the early works of a master in a museum. "I can't imagine what it would be like to be born with that kind of gift. It would be a burden for some, wouldn't it?"

In his way, Ethan took his time considering, following the lines of his old skipjack as seen through the eyes and talent of a child. "I guess it would. Not for Seth. It's a joy for him, and what you'd call a channel. Always has been. Well."

He was never long on conversation, so offered her a quiet smile and his hand. "It's going to be a pleasure doing business with you."

"Likewise. Thanks for making time for me today."

"We always got time."

He showed her out, then wandered into the driving beat of Sugar Ray and power sanders. He was halfway to the lathe when Seth shut off his tool.

"Dru up with the guys?"

"Nope. She went on."

"Went on? Well, damn it, you could've said something." He vaulted down from the boat and sprinted for the door.

Aubrey frowned after him. "He's half stuck on her already."

"Seems like." Ethan tilted his head at the look on her face. "Problem?"

"I don't know." She shrugged. "I don't know. She's just not what I pictured for him, that's all. She's all kind of stiff and fancy, with a high snoot factor, if you ask me."

"She's alone," Ethan corrected. "Not everybody's as easy with people as you are, Aubrey. Besides the fact, it's what Seth pictures that matters."

"Yeah." But she was far from sold on Drusilla.

EIGHT

∽

SINCE HE HADN'T told her what to wear for the sitting, Dru settled on the simple, with blue cotton pants and a white camp shirt. She watered her gardens, changed her earrings twice, then made a fresh pot of coffee.

Maybe the hoops had been a better choice, she thought, fingering the little lapis balls dangling from her ear. Men liked women in hoop earrings. Probably had some strange sultry gypsy fetish.

And what the hell did she care?

She wasn't sure she wanted him to make another move on her. One move, after all, invariably led to another, and she wasn't interested in the chessboard of relationships just now.

Or hadn't been.

Jonah had certainly checkmated her, she thought, and enjoyed the little flash of anger. The problem had been she'd believed she was in control of the board there, that all the game pieces were in correct positions.

She'd been completely oblivious to the fact that he'd been playing on another board simultaneously.

His disloyalty and deception had damaged her heart and her pride. While her heart had healed, perhaps too easily, she admitted, her pride remained bruised.

She would never be made a fool of again.

If she was going to develop a relationship with Seth—and the jury was still out on that one—it would be on her terms.

She'd proven to herself that she was more than an ornament for a man's arm, a notch in his bedpost or a rung in the ladder of his career advancement.

Jonah had miscalculated on that score.

More important, she'd proven that she could stand on her own and make a very contented life.

Which didn't mean, she admitted, that she didn't miss a certain amount of companionship, or sexual heat, or the heady challenge of the mating dance with an interesting, attractive man.

She heard his tires crunch on her gravel drive. One step at a time, she told herself, and waited for him to knock.

All right, she thought, so she did feel a rush of heat the minute she opened the door and looked at him. It only proved that she was human, and she was healthy.

"Good morning," she said, as manners had her stepping back to let him inside.

"Morning. I love this place. I just realized that if you hadn't snapped it up before I got back home, I would have."

"Lucky for me."

"I'll say." He scanned the living area as he wandered. Strong colors, good fabrics, he mused. It could've used a little more clutter for his taste, but it suited her with its good, carefully selected pieces, the fresh flowers and the tidy air of it all.

"You said you wanted to work outside."

"Yeah. Oh, hey, your painting." He shifted the package wrapped in brown paper under his arm and handed it to her. "I'll hang it for you if you've picked your spot."

"That was quick." And because she couldn't resist, she sat on the sofa and ripped off the wrapping.

He'd chosen thin strips of wood stained a dull gold that complemented the rich tones of the flowers and foliage so that the frame was as simple and strong as the painting.

"It's perfect. Thank you. It's a wonderful start to my Seth Quinn collection."

"Planning on a collection?"

She ran a finger over the top of the frame as she looked up at him. "Maybe. And I'd take you up on hanging it for me because I'm dying to see how it looks, but I don't have the proper hanger."

"Like this?" He dug the one he'd brought with him out of his pocket.

"Like that." She angled her head, considered. "You're very handy, aren't you?"

"Damn near indispensable. Got a hammer, and a tape measure, or should I get mine out of my car?"

"I happen to have a hammer and other assorted household tools." She rose, went into the kitchen and came back with a hammer so new it gleamed.

"Where do you want it?"

"Upstairs. My bedroom." She turned to lead the way. "What's in the bag?"

"Stuff. The guy who rehabbed this place knew what he

was doing." Seth examined the satin finish on the banister as they climbed to the second floor. "I wonder how he could stand to let it go."

"He likes the work itself—and the profit. Once he's finished, he's bored and wants to move on. Or so he told me when I asked just that."

"How many bedrooms? Three?"

"Four, though one's quite small, more suited to a home office or a little library."

"Third floor?"

"A finished attic, which has potential for a small apartment. Or," she said with a glance at him, "an artist's garret."

She turned into a room, and Seth saw immediately she'd selected what suited her best here as well. The windows gave her a view of the river, a sweep of trees and shady garden. The window trim was just fussy enough to be charming, and she'd chosen to drape filmy white gauze in a kind of long swag around them in lieu of formal curtains. It diffused the sunlight and still left the view and the craftsmanship of the trim.

She'd gone for cerulean blue on the walls, scattered a couple of floral rugs on the pine floor, and had stuck with antiques for the furnishings.

The bed was tidily made, as he'd expected, and covered with a white quilt with intricate interlocking rings and rosebuds that seemed to have been crafted specifically for the sleigh bed.

"Great piece." He leaned down to get a closer look at the workmanship of the quilt. "Heirloom?"

"No. I found it at an arts-and-crafts fair in Pennsylvania last year. I thought the wall between these windows. It'll be good light without direct sun."

"Good choice." He held the painting up. "And it'll be

like another window, so you'll have flowers during the winter."

Her thoughts, Dru admitted, exactly.

"About here?"

She stepped back, checked the position from several different angles—resisting, only because it was a bit too suggestive, lying down on the bed to see how it would look to her when she woke in the mornings.

"That's perfect."

He reached behind the painting, scraped a vague mark on the wall with his thumbnail, then set it aside to measure.

It was odd, she thought, having a man in her bedroom again. And far from unpleasant to watch him with his tools and his painting, his rough clothes and his beautiful hands.

Far from unpleasant, she admitted, to imagine those beautiful hands on her skin.

"See what you think about what's in the bag," he said without looking around.

She picked it up, opened it. And her eyebrows lifted high as she took out the long, filmy skirt—purple pansies rioting against a cool blue background—and the thin-strapped, narrow top in that same shade of blue.

"You're a determined man, aren't you?"

"It'll look good on you, and it's the look I'm after."

"And you get what you're after."

He glanced back now, his expression both relaxed and cocky. "So far. You got any of those . . ." He made a circle with his finger in the air. "Hoop ear things. They'd work with that."

I should've known, Dru thought, but only said, "Hmm."

She laid the skirt and top on the bed, then stepped back as he fixed the painting on its hook. "Left bottom needs to come up a little—too much. There. That's perfect. Painted, framed and hung by Quinn. Not a bad deal on my side."

"It looks good from my end, too," he said, staring at her.

When he took a step toward her, she considered taking one toward him. Before the phone rang.

"Excuse me." For the best, she assured herself as she picked up the bedside phone. "Hello."

"Hello, princess."

"Dad." Pleasure, distress and, shamefully, a thread of annoyance knotted inside her. "Why aren't you on the seventh green by this time on a Sunday morning?"

"I've got some difficult news." Proctor let out a long sigh. "Sweetheart, your mother and I are getting divorced."

"I see." The pulse in her temple began to throb. "I need you to wait just a minute." She pushed the hold button, turned to Seth. "I'm sorry, I need to take this. There's coffee in the kitchen. I shouldn't be long."

"Okay." Her face had gone blank on him. It was very still and very empty. "I'll grab a cup before I go out to set up. Take your time."

She waited until she heard him start down the steps, then sat on the side of the bed and reconnected with her father. "I'm sorry, Dad. What happened?" And bit her tongue before she could finish the question with: this time.

"I'm afraid your mother and I haven't been getting along for quite a while. I've tried to shield you from our problems. I have no doubt we'd have taken this step years ago if it hadn't been for you. But, well, these things happen, princess."

"I'm very sorry." She knew her job well and finished with, "Is there anything I can do to help?"

"Ah well. I'm sure I'd feel better if I could explain things to you, so I'm sure you're not upset by all this. It's too complicated to discuss on the phone. Why don't you come up this afternoon? We'll have lunch, just you and me. Nothing would brighten my day more than spending it with my little girl."

"I'm sorry. I've got a commitment today."

"Surely, under the circumstances, this is more important."

Her temple throbbed, and guilt began to roil in her stomach. "I can't break this engagement. In fact, I was just about to—"

"All right. That's all right," he said in a voice that managed to be both long-suffering and brisk. "I'd hoped you'd have some time for me. Thirty years. Thirty, and it comes down to this."

Dru rubbed at the tension banding the back of her neck. "I'm sorry, Dad."

She lost track of the times she echoed that phrase during the rest of the conversation. But she knew when she hung up she was exhausted from repeating it.

No sooner had she set the phone down, than it rang again.

Thirty years, Dru thought, might account for the sixth sense her parents had in regard to each other. Resigned, she picked up the phone.

"Hello, Mom."

HE'D spread a red blanket on the grass near the bank of the river where there were both beams of sunlight and dappled shade. He added a wicker picnic basket, propping an open bottle of wine and a stemmed glass against it. A slim book with a ragged white cover lay beside it.

She'd changed into the clothes he'd brought, put on the

hoop earrings as he'd requested. And had used the time to steady herself.

His table was up, his sketch pad on it. At the foot was a portable stereo, but instead of the driving rock, it was Mozart. And that surprised her.

"Sorry I held you up," she said as she stepped off the porch.

"No problem." One look at her face had him crossing to her. He put his arms around her and, ignoring her flinch, held her gently.

A part of her wanted to burrow straight into that unquestioning offer of comfort. "Do I look that bad?"

"You look that sad." He brushed his lips over her hair. "You want to do this some other time?"

"No. It's nothing, really. Just habitual family insanity."

"I'm good at that." He tipped her head back with his fingers. "An expert on family insanity."

"Not this kind." She eased back. "My parents are getting divorced."

"Oh baby." He touched her cheek. "I'm sorry."

"No, no, no." To his bafflement, she laughed and pressed the heels of her hands to her temples. "You don't get it. They whack the *D* word around like a Ping-Pong ball. Every couple of years I get the call. 'Dru, I have difficult news.' Or 'Dru, I'm not sure how to tell you.' Once, when I was sixteen, they actually separated for nearly two months. Being careful to time it during my summer break so my mother could flee to Europe with me for a week, then my father could drag me off with him to Bar Harbor to sail."

"Sounds more like you've been the Ping-Pong ball."

"Yes, it does. They wear me out, which is why I ran away before . . . before I started to despise them. And still,

I wish to God they'd just go through with it. That sounds cold and selfish and horrible."

"No, it doesn't. Not when you've got tears in your eyes."

"They love me too much," she said quietly. "Or not enough. I've never been able to figure it out. I don't suppose they have either. I can't be with them, standing in as their crutch or their referee the rest of my life."

"Have you told them?"

"Tried. They don't hear." She rubbed her arms as if smoothing ruffled feathers. "And I have absolutely no business dumping my mess in your lap."

"Why not? We're practically going steady."

She let out a half laugh. "You're awfully good at that."

"I'm good at so many things. Which one is this?"

"At listening, for one." She leaned forward, kissed his cheek. "I've never been particularly good at asking anyone to listen. I don't seem to have to with you. And for two"— she kissed his other cheek—"you're good at making me laugh, even when I'm annoyed."

"I'll listen some more—and make you laugh—if you kiss me again. And aim for here this time," he added, tapping a finger to his lips.

"Thanks, but that's about it. Let's put it away. There's nothing I can do about them." She eased away from him. "I assume you want me on the blanket."

"Why don't we toss this for today and go for a sail? It always clears my head."

"No, you're already set up, and it'll take my mind off things. But thanks, really, Seth."

Satisfied that the sadness on her face had lifted, he nodded. "Okay. If you decide you want to stop after all, just say so. First, lose the shoes."

She stepped out of the canvas slides. "A barefoot picnic."

"There you go. Lie down on the blanket."

She'd assumed she'd be sitting on it, skirts spread as she read the book. But she stepped onto the blanket. "Face up or down?"

"On your back. Scoot down a little more," he suggested as he walked around her. "Let's have the right arm over your head. Bend your elbow, relax the hand."

"I feel silly. I didn't feel silly in the studio."

"Don't think about it. Bring your left knee up." She did, and when the skirt came with it, smoothed it back down over her legs.

"Oh, come on." He knelt down and had her eyes going to slits when he pulled up the hem of the skirt so it exposed her left leg to mid-thigh.

"Aren't you supposed to say something about how you're not hitting on me, but that this is all for the sake of art?"

"It is for the sake of art." The back of his fingers skimmed her thigh as he fussed with the lie of the material. "But I'm hitting on you, too." He slid the strap of her top off her shoulder, studied the result, nodded.

"Relax. Start with your toes." He rubbed a hand over her bare foot. "And work your way up." Watching her, he ran his hand up her calf, over her knee. "Turn your head toward me."

She did, and glanced over the paint supplies he'd set up by his easel. "Aren't those watercolors? I thought you said you wanted oil."

"This one's for watercolors. I've got something else in mind for oils."

"So you keep saying. Just how many times do you think you can persuade me to do this?"

"As many as it takes. You're having a quiet afternoon by the water," he told her as he began sketching lightly on the paper. "A little sleepy from wine and reading."

"Am I alone?"

"For the moment. You're just daydreaming now. Go wherever you want."

"If it were warmer, I'd slide into the river."

"It's as warm as you want it to be. Close your eyes, Dru. Dream a little."

She did as he asked. The music, soft, romantic, was a caress on the air.

"What do you think of when you paint?" she asked him.

"Think?" At the question his mind went completely blank. "I don't know. Ah . . . shape, I guess. Light, shadow. Jeez. Mood. I don't have an answer."

"You just answered the question I didn't ask. It's instinct. Your talent is instinctive. It has to be, really, as you were so clever at drawing so young."

"What did you want to do when you were a kid?" Her body was a long, slim flow to him. Shape.

"Lots of things. A ballerina, a movie star, an explorer. A missionary."

"Wow, a missionary. Really?" The sun slid through the leaves and lay softly on her skin. Light and shadow.

"It was a brief ambition, but a profound one. What I didn't think I'd be was a businesswoman. Surprise."

"But you like it."

"I love it. I love being able to take what I once assumed was a personal passion and a small talent for flowers and do something with it." Her mind began to drift, like the river that flowed beside her. "I've never been able to talk to anyone the way I seem to be able to talk to you."

"No kidding?" She looked like a faerie queen—the exotic shape of her eyes, the sexy pixie cap of dark hair. The utter female confidence of the pose. A faerie queen drowsing alone in her private glade. Mood.

"Why do you think that is?" he wondered.

"I haven't a clue." And with a sigh, she fell asleep.

THE music had changed. A woman with a voice like heartbreak was singing about love. Still half dreaming, Dru shifted. "Who is that singing?" she murmured.

"Darcy Gallagher. Some pipes there. I caught a show she did with her two brothers a couple years ago in County Waterford. Little place called Ardmore. It was amazing."

"Mmm. I think I've heard—" She broke off when she opened her eyes and found Seth sitting beside the blanket with a sketchbook instead of standing behind the table. "What're you doing?"

"Waiting for you to wake up."

"I fell asleep." Embarrassed, she rose on one elbow. "I'm sorry. How long was I out?"

"Dunno. Don't have a watch." He set the book aside. "No need to be sorry. You gave me just what I was after."

Trying to clear her head, she looked over at the table. The watercolor paper was, frustratingly, out of her line of sight. "You finished?"

"No, but I got a hell of a start. Watch or no watch, my stomach's telling me it's lunchtime." He flipped the lid on a cooler.

"You brought a real picnic."

"Hamper was for art, cooler's for practicality. We've got bread, cheese, grapes, some of this pâté Phil swears by." He pulled out plates as he spoke. "And though I had to debase myself and beg, some of Anna's pasta salad. And this terrific wine I discovered in Venice. It's called Dreams. Seemed to fit."

"You're trying to make this a date," she said warily.

"Too late." He poured the first glass, handed it to her. "It already is a date. I wanted to ask why you took off so fast yesterday, when you came by the boatyard."

"I'd finished my business." She chose a chilled grape, bit through its tart skin. "And I had to get back to work."

"So you want a boat?"

"Yes, I do. I like to sail."

"Come sailing with me. That way you can check out how seaworthy a boat by Quinn is."

"I'll think about it." She sampled the pâté, made a sexy little sound of pleasure. "Your brother Phillip has excellent taste. They're very different, your brothers. Yet they hang together like a single unit."

"That's family."

"Is it? No, not always, not even usually, at least in my experience. Yours is unique, in a number of ways. Why aren't you scarred?"

He looked up from scooping out pasta salad. "Sorry?"

"There's been enough information dribbled through the stories I've read about you, and what I've heard just living in Saint Chris, to tell me you had a very hard childhood. You told me so yourself. How do you get through that without being damaged?"

The press articles had barely skimmed the surface, Seth thought. They knew nothing of the young boy who had hidden from or fought off more than once the slick, groping hands of the drunks or druggies Gloria had brought home.

They didn't know about the beatings or the blackmail, or the fear that remained a hard kernel lodged in his heart.

"They saved me." He said it with a simple honesty that made her throat burn. "It's not an exaggeration to say that they saved my life. Ray Quinn, then Cam and Ethan and Phil. They turned their world around for me, and because of it, turned mine around with it. Anna and Grace and Sybill, Aubrey, too. They made a home for me, and nothing that happened before matters nearly as much as everything that came after."

Unspeakably moved, she leaned forward and touched her lips to his. "That's for three. For making me like you. You're a good man. I don't know just what to do with you."

"You could start by trusting me."

"No." She eased back again, broke off a small hunk of bread. "Nothing starts with trust. Trust develops. And with me, that can take considerable time."

"I can probably guarantee I'm nothing like the guy you were engaged to." When her body went rigid, he shrugged. "I'm not the only one who gets written about or talked about."

And when she'd touched on a personal area, she reminded herself, he hadn't frozen up. "No, you're nothing like Jonah. We never had a picnic with his sister's pasta salad."

"Dinner at Jean-Louis at the Watergate or whatever tony French place is currently in fashion. Openings at the Kennedy Center. Clever cocktail parties inside the Beltway, and the occasional Sunday afternoon brunch with copacetic friends." He waited a beat. "How'd I do?"

"Close enough." Dead on target.

"You're way outside the Beltway now. His loss."

"He seems to be bearing up."

"Did you love him?"

She opened her mouth, then found herself answering with complete honesty. "I don't know anymore. I certainly believed I did or I'd never have planned to marry him. He was attractive, brilliant, had a deadly sarcasm that often posed for witty—and sometimes was. And, as it turned out, the fidelity of an alley cat. Better I found that out before we were married than after. But I learned something valuable about myself due to the experience. No one cheats on me without serious consequences."

"Bruised his balls, did you?"

"Oh, worse." She nibbled delicately on pâté. "He left his cashmere coat, among other items, at my place. While I was coldly packing up his things, I took it back out of the packing box, cut off the sleeves, the collar, the buttons. And since that was so satisfying, I put, one by one, all his Melissa Etheridge CDs in the microwave. She's a wonderful artist, but I can't listen to her today without feeling destructive urges. Then I put his Ferragamo loafers in the washing machine. These acts were hard on my appliances, but good for my soul. Since I was on a roll, I started to flush my three-carat, square-cut Russian white diamond engagement ring down the toilet, but sanity prevailed."

"What did you do with it?"

"I put it in an envelope, wrote 'For His Sins' on the front, then dropped it into the collection box at a little church in Georgetown. Overdramatic, but again, satisfying."

This time Seth leaned over, touched his lips to hers. "Nice job, champ."

"Yes, I thought so." She brought her knees up, sipped her wine while she looked out over the water. "A number of my acquaintances think I left D.C. and moved here because of Jonah. They're wrong. I've loved it here since that first time we came with my grandfather. When I knew I had to make the break, start fresh, I tried to imagine myself living in different places, even different countries. But I always came back here in my head. It wasn't impulsive, though again, a lot of people think so. I planned it for years. That's how I do things, plan them out. Step by step."

She paused, rested her chin on her knees as she studied him. "Obviously, I've missed a step somewhere with you or I wouldn't be sitting here on the grass drinking wine on a Sunday afternoon and telling you things I had no intention of talking about."

She lifted her head again, sipped wine. "You listen. That's a gift. And a weapon."

"I'm not going to hurt you."

"Healthy people don't step toward a relationship with the intention of hurting each other. Still, they do. Maybe it'll be me who ends up hurting you."

"Let's see." He cupped a hand at the back of her neck, rubbing lightly as he bent down to lay his lips on hers. "No," he said after a moment. "No bruises yet."

Then shifting, he framed her face with his hands to lift it until their lips met again.

Very soft, suddenly deep and wrenchingly gentle, his mouth moved on hers. With silky glides he teased her tongue into a dance as his fingers trailed down the line of her throat, over the curve of her shoulders.

She tasted of the wine that spilled unnoticed when her hand went limp on the glass. He found the quick catch and release of her breath when she drew him closer as arousing as a moan.

He laid her back on the blanket, sliding down with her as her arms linked around his neck.

She wanted his weight. She wanted his hands. She wanted his mouth to go on and on taking from hers. She felt the brush of his fingers on her collarbone, and shivered. They skimmed over the thin material of her top, then slipped down to dance over her breast.

He murmured her name before he grazed his teeth over her jaw. And his hand, so beautifully formed, so rough from work, molded her.

Heat flashed through her, urging her to give and to take. Instead, she pressed a hand to his shoulder. "Wait. Seth."

His mouth came back to hers, hungrier now, and with the dangerous flavor of urgency. "Let me touch you. I have to touch you."

"Wait."

He bit off an oath, rested his forehead on hers while his blood raged. He could feel her body vibrating under his, and knew she was just as needy. "Okay. Okay," he managed. "Why?"

"I'm not ready."

"Oh, sugar. Any more ready, you'd be past me."

"Wanting you isn't the same as being ready." But she was afraid he was right. "I didn't intend for this to happen, not like this. I'm not going to make love with a man who appears to be involved with someone else."

"Involved with who? Jesus, Dru, I just got back home, and I haven't looked at another woman since the first time I saw you."

"You've been involved with this one long before you saw me." He looked so blank, so disheveled, so frustrated she wanted to giggle. But she stayed firm. "Aubrey."

"What about Aubrey?" It took him several jolting seconds to understand her meaning. "*Aubrey?* Me and . . .

Christ on a crutch, are you kidding?" He'd have laughed if the idea hadn't left him so shocked. "Where do you get that?"

"I'm not blind." Irritated, she shoved at him. "Move, will you?"

"I'm not involved with . . ." He couldn't even say it, but he sat back. "It's not like that. Jesus, Dru, she's my sister."

"No, she isn't."

"Niece."

"Nor is she that. And maybe you are oblivious to what's between you—though you don't strike me as a dolt—but I doubt very much she is."

"I don't think about her that way."

"Maybe you haven't, on a conscious level."

"At all." The very idea had panic dancing in his throat. "None of the levels. Neither does she."

Dru smoothed down her skirt. "Are you certain?"

"Yeah." But the seed had been planted. "Yes. And if you've got some insane notion that me being with you is somehow cheating on Aubrey, you can forget it."

"What I think," Dru said calmly, "is that I'm not going to have an affair with a man who I suspect is attracted to someone else. Maybe you should work this out with Aubrey before anything goes any further between us. But for now I think we'd better call it a day. Do you mind if I take a look at the painting?"

"Yes." He snapped it out. "I mind. You can see it when it's finished."

"All right." Well, well, she mused, artistic temperament rears its head. "I'll just pack up the food for you. I assume you want at least one more sitting," she said as she began to pack the cooler. "I should be able to give you some time next Sunday."

He stood, stared down at her. "You're a case. Some ass-hole cheats on you so that means we're all cheats?"

"No." She understood his temper, and since it seemed a reasonable conclusion for him to make, she didn't lose hers. "Not at all. In fact, I think you're as honest as they come. I couldn't consider being with you if I thought otherwise. But as I said, I'm not ready to take this step with you, and I have reservations over your feelings toward someone else—and hers toward you."

She looked up then. "I've been the clichéd victim of the other woman, Seth. I won't do that to anyone else."

"Sounds like instead of you asking me about scars, I should've asked you."

She rose now, nodded. "Yes, maybe you should have. Since you're going to sulk, I'll leave you to it."

He caught her arm before she could breeze by, whipped her around so fast she felt fear burst like a bomb in her throat. "You keep taking those steps one at a time, sugar. It might take you longer to fall on your face, but you'll fall just as hard."

"Let me go now."

He released her, turned his back on her to pack up his gear. More shaken than she wanted to admit, Dru made herself walk slowly into the house.

It was, she admitted, still a retreat.

NINE

WOMEN. SETH TOSSED the cooler into the trunk of the car, heaved the hamper in behind it. Just when you thought you understood them, they turned into aliens. And those aliens had the power to change a normal, reasonable man into a blithering idiot.

There was nothing a man could do to keep up with them.

He tossed in the blanket, kicked the tire, then yanked the blanket back out again. He stared over at her house and gave it a satisfactory snarl.

His mutters were a combination of curses, pithy remarks and considerable blithering as he stomped back for his folding table and watercolor paper.

And there she was, sleeping on the red blanket in the dappled sunlight. All long limbs and color, with the face of a sleeping faerie queen.

"I ought to know who I'm attracted to," he told her as he carefully lifted the painting-in-progress and carried it to the car. "One guy turns out to be a putz, and damns us all?"

He laid the paper on the blanket, scowled at it. "Well, that's your problem, sister."

Sister, he thought and felt an uneasy jittering in his gut. Why the hell had she put that in his head about Aubrey? It was off, that's all. It was way, way off.

It had to be.

He loved Aubrey. Of course he did. But he'd never thought about . . . Had he?

"You see, you *see*?" He jabbed a finger at the painting. "That's what your kind does to us. You confuse everything until we start questioning our own brains. Well, it's not going to work with me."

Because it was more comfortable, he switched back to temper as he finished loading his car. He had nearly made the turn for home when he swung the car around, punched the gas.

"We'll just settle this thing." He spoke aloud and nodded at the painting. "Once and for all. And we'll see who's the idiot."

He pulled up in the drive at Aubrey's house, leaped out of the car and strode to the door with his outrage and temper still leading the way. He didn't knock. No one would have expected him to.

The living room, like the rest of the house, was picture-pretty, cluttered just enough to be comfortable, and ruthlessly clean. Grace had a knack for such things.

Once she'd made her living as a single parent cleaning other people's homes. Now she ran her own business, a cleaning service with more than twenty employees who handled homes and businesses on the Shore.

Her own home was one of her best advertisements—and at the moment it was also entirely too quiet.

"Aubrey?" he shouted up the stairs. "Anyone home?"

"Seth?" Grace hurried in from the kitchen. In her bare feet and cropped pants, her hair pulled carelessly back from her face, she looked entirely too young to have a daughter some wrong-headed woman thought he was attracted to.

Jesus, he'd *baby-sat* for Aubrey.

"Come on back," she told him with a quick kiss. "Ethan and Deke are out back fixing the lawn mower. I was just making some lemonade."

"I just dropped by to see Aubrey about . . ." Oh no, he thought, he couldn't go there with Grace. "Is she around?"

"She plays softball Sunday afternoons."

"Right." Seth jammed his hands in his pockets and scowled. "Right."

"Honey, is something wrong? Did you and Aubrey have a fight?"

"No. No, I just need to . . . talk to her about something."

"She should be back in an hour or so. Emily, too. Em's off with her boyfriend. Why don't you go on out with Ethan and Deke, stay for dinner? We're cooking out later."

"Thanks, but . . . I've got some things . . ." It felt weird, too weird, looking at Grace's face, seeing Aubrey in it and thinking what he was thinking. "I gotta go."

"But—" She was talking to his back as he rushed out the door. Anna was right, Grace thought with a sigh. Something was troubling their boy.

IT was the bottom of the sixth, with two on, two out when Seth arrived at the park. Aubrey's team, the Blue Crabs, was down by a run to their longtime nemesis, the Rockfish.

Spectators munched on hot dogs, slurped cold drinks

from paper cups and hurled the expected insults or encouragements at the players. June was coming on with her usual hot breath and moist hands, making spring a fond memory. Sun poured onto the field and drenched it in heat and humidity.

Steam from the concession stand pumped out as Seth passed it to clamber up the stands.

He spotted Junior Crawford, a billed cap shielding his bald head and wrinkled gnome face, with a boy of no more than three perched on his bony knee.

"Hey there, Seth." Junior scooted his skinny ass over an inch in invitation. "How come you ain't down there on the field?"

"Came back too late for the draft." He scanned the field first and noted Aubrey was on deck as the current batter took ball three. Then he winked at the little boy. "Who's this guy?"

"This here's Bart." Junior gave the boy a bounce. "My great-grandson."

"Great-grandson?"

"Yup, got us eight grands now, and this one." Junior's attention swung back to the field at the crack of the bat. "Gone foul," he muttered. "Straighten out that bat, Jed Wilson!" he shouted. "Chrissake."

"Jed Wilson? Is that Mrs. Wilson's grandson?"

"The same. Affable enough boy, right enough, but can't bat worth shit."

"Worth shit," Bart said happily.

"Now, boy." Chuckling, Junior wagged his finger at Bart. "You know you're gonna get me in the doghouse again if you go saying that in front of your mama."

"Worth shit! Pappy!" Bart bubbled out a laugh, then

poked his mangled hot dog toward Seth. "Bite?"

"Sure." Grateful for the distraction, Seth leaned down and pretended to take a huge bite.

When ball four was called, the crowd erupted, and Junior let out a whoop. "Walked him. By God. You're in for it now, you stinking Rockfish."

"Stinking Rockfish," Bart echoed joyfully.

"We're gonna see some action now, goddamn it! Now we'll see what's what."

The Blue Crab fans began to croon "Aub-*rey*! Aub-*rey*!" as she swaggered to the plate.

"Knock one out, Aub! That girl can do it," Junior said with such wild enthusiasm Seth wondered he didn't have a stroke on the spot. "You watch!" He stabbed Seth with the razor point of his elbow. "You just watch her slam that bastard."

"Slam that bastard!" Bart shouted, waving his mushed hot dog and dripping mustard.

For both their sakes, Seth nipped the boy from Junior's knee and set him on his own.

She was a pleasure to watch, Seth thought. No question about it. That compact, athletic build. The undeniable femaleness of it despite—maybe because of—the mannish baseball jersey.

But that didn't mean he thought about her . . . that way.

She scuffed at the plate. There was a short exchange with the catcher Seth imagined was derisive on both sides. She took a couple of testing swings. Wiggled her butt.

Jesus, why was he looking at her butt?

And took a hard cut at the first pitch.

The crowd surged to their feet on a roar. Aubrey shot toward first like a bullet banged from its gun.

Then the crowd deflated, and she jogged back to the plate as the ball curved foul.

The crowd began to chant her name again as she picked up the bat and went through the same routine. Two swings, wiggle the bat, wiggle the butt and set for the pitch.

She took it, checking her swing. And when the ump called strike two, she rounded on him. Seth could see her lips move, could hear the bite of her words in his head.

Strike, my ass. Any more outside, that pitch would have been in Virginia. Just how big a strike zone you want to give this guy?

Don't refer to the dubious sexual practices of his mother, Seth warned her mentally. Don't go there and get tossed.

Whether she'd learned some control in the last couple years or his warning got through, Aubrey skinned the ump with one baleful look, then stepped back in the batter's box.

The chant rose again, feet began to stomp on wood until the bleachers vibrated. In Seth's lap, little Bart squeezed what was left of the dog and bun to pulp and shouted, "Slam the bastard."

And she did.

Seth knew the minute the ball met her bat that it was gone. So, obviously, did Aubrey because she held her position—shoulders front, hips cocked, front leg poised like a dancer—as she watched the ball sail high and long.

The crowd was on their feet, an eruption of sound as she tossed her bat aside and jogged around the bases.

"Goddamn fricking grand slam." Junior sounded as if he was about to weep. "That girl is a fricking peach."

"Fricking peach," Bart agreed and leaned over from Seth's arms to plant a sloppy kiss on Junior's cheek.

* * *

THE Rockfish went scoreless in the seventh, shut down on a strikeout, and a spiffy double play started by Aubrey at short. Seth wandered down toward the dugout as the fans began to drift toward home. He saw Aubrey standing, glugging Gatorade straight from the jug.

"Nice game, Slugger."

"Hey." She tossed the jug to one of her teammates and sauntered over to Seth. "I didn't know you were here."

"Came in bottom of the sixth, just in time to see you kick Rockfish ass."

"Fast ball. Low and away. He should've known better. I thought you were painting the flower girl today."

"Yeah, well, we had a sitting."

She cocked a brow, then rubbed at her nose as Seth stared at her. "What? So, I've got dirt on my face."

"No, it's not that. Listen, I need to talk to you."

"Okay, talk."

"No, not here." He hunched his shoulders. They were surrounded, he thought. Players, spectators, kids. Dozens of familiar faces. People who knew both of them. My God, did other people think he and Aubrey . . . ?

"It's, ah, you know. Private."

"Look, if something's wrong—"

"I didn't say anything was wrong."

She huffed out a breath. "Your face does. I rode in with Joe and Alice. Let me tell them I'm catching a lift home with you."

"Good. Great. I'll meet you at the car."

He shifted the blanket and painting to the backseat. Leaned on the hood. Paced around the car. When Aubrey walked toward him, a mitt in her hand, a bat over her shoulder, he tried to look at her the way he would if he'd never met her before.

But it just wouldn't work.

"You're starting to get me worried, Seth," she said.

"Don't. Here, let me put those in the trunk. I've got my stuff in the back."

She shrugged, passed off her ball gear, then peered into the backseat. "Wow." Transfixed, she yanked open the door for a better look at the watercolor. "No wonder you've been so hot to paint her. This is wonderful. Jeez, Seth, I never get used to it."

"It's not finished."

"I can see that," she said dryly. "It's sexy, but it's soft. And intimate." She glanced up at him, those pretty green eyes meeting his.

He tried to gauge if he felt any sort of a sexual jolt, the way he did when Dru's darker ones leveled on his face.

It was almost too embarrassing to think about.

"Is that what you're after?"

"What?" Appalled, he gaped at her. "Is what what I'm after?"

"You know, soft, sexy, intimate."

"Ah . . ."

"With the painting," she finished, feeling totally confused.

"The painting." The terror in his belly churned into faint nausea. "Yeah, that's it."

Now her face registered mild surprise when he opened the car door for her. "We in a hurry?"

"Just because you hit grand slams doesn't mean a guy shouldn't open the door for you." He bit the words off as he rounded the car, slammed in the other side. "If Will doesn't treat you with some respect, you ought to ditch him."

"Hold on, hold on. Will treats me just fine. What are you in such a lather about?"

"I don't want to talk about it yet." He pulled out, started to drive.

She let him have silence. She knew him well enough to understand that when he had something in his craw, he went quiet. Went inside Seth to a place even she wasn't permitted.

When he was ready, he'd talk.

He pulled into the lot of the boatyard, sat tapping his hands on the steering wheel for a moment. "Let's walk around to the dock, okay?"

"Sure."

But when he got out, she continued to sit until he came around and wrenched the door open. "What're you doing?"

"Merely waiting for you to treat me with the proper respect." She fluttered her lashes and slid out of the car. Then, laughing at him, pulled a pack of Juicy Fruit from her back pocket, offered it.

"No, thanks."

"What's up, Seth?" she asked as she unwrapped a stick of gum.

"I need to ask you for a favor."

She folded the gum into her mouth. "What do you need?"

He stepped onto the dock, stared out at the water, and at the osprey resting on a post before he turned back to her. "I need to kiss you."

She lifted her palms. "That's it? God, I was wondering if you had six months to live or something. Okay. Jeez, Seth, you've kissed me hundreds of times. What's the big deal?"

"No." He crossed his arms over his chest, then ran his

hands over his hips and finally stuck them in his pockets. "I mean, I need to *kiss* you."

"Huh?" Shock registered on her face.

"I need to settle something, so I need to kiss you. Like a regular guy would."

"Seth." She patted his arm. "This is weird. Did you get hit on the head or something?"

"I know it's weird," he shot back. "Do you think I don't know it's weird? Imagine how I feel bringing it up in the first place."

"How come you brought it up in the first place?"

He stalked down the dock, back again. "Dru has this idea that I—that we—Christ. That I'm attracted to you in a guy way. And possibly vice versa. Probably."

Aubrey blinked twice, slow as an owl. "She thinks I've got the hots for you?"

"Oh, Jesus, Aub."

"She thinks there's something like that between you and me, so she gave you the boot."

"More or less," he muttered.

"So you want to plant one on me because of her?"

"Yes. No. I fucking don't know." Could it be any worse? he wondered. Could he be more embarrassed, more itchy, more stupid?

"She put this damn idea in my head. I can't work it back out again. What if she's right?"

"What if she's right?" There was a laugh burbling in her throat, but she managed to swallow it. "What if you've got some suppressed fantasy going about us? Get real, Seth."

"Look, look." Impassioned in a way that made her blink again, he took her by the shoulders. "It's not going to kill you to kiss me."

"Okay, okay. Go ahead."

"Okay." He blew out a breath, started to lower his head, then straightened again. "I can't remember my moves. Give me a minute."

He stepped back, turned away and tried to clear his head. "Let's try this." He turned back, laid his hands on her hips to draw her against him. Seconds passed. "You could put your arms around me or something."

"Oh, sorry." She reached up, threaded her fingers together behind his head. "How's this?"

"Fine. That's fine. Come up a little," he suggested, so she rose on her toes. He bent his head. His mouth was a breath from hers when she snorted out a laugh.

"Oh Christ."

"Sorry. Sorry." The fit of giggles forced her to move back and hold her stomach. He stood, scowling, until she controlled herself. "I balked, that's all. Here we go." She started to put her arms around him again. "Shit, wait." Conscientiously, she took the gum out of her mouth, folded it into the old wrapper in her pocket. "If we're going to do this, let's do it right. Right?"

"If you can control the pig snorts."

"Free lesson, sport: When you're about to tangle tongues with a woman, you don't mention pork or swine."

She put her arms around him again, took a good strong hold this time and moved in herself before either of them could think about it.

They stayed locked, the breeze off the water fluttering over them. There was a hum as a car drove by on the road behind them, and the sudden desperate barking of a dog as it chased along behind the fence until the car disappeared.

Their lips separated, their eyes met. The silence between them held for several long seconds.

Then they began to laugh.

Still holding each other, they rocked in a kind of whooping hilarity that would have put either one of them on the ground without the support. He lowered his forehead to hers on a relieved breath.

"So." She gave his butt a friendly pinch. "You want me, don't you?"

"Shut up, Aubrey."

He gave her, his sister, a fierce hug before he eased back. "Thanks."

"No problem. Anyway, you're good at it."

"You too." He rubbed his knuckles over her cheek. "And we're never going to do that again."

"That's a deal."

He started to swing an arm around her shoulders, then stopped as an appalling thought struck. "You're not going to tell anybody about this, right? Like your mom, or Will. Anybody."

"Are you kidding?" Even the idea of it had her shuddering. "You either. Promise." She spat into her palm, held it out.

Seth grimaced down at her hand. "I should never have taught you that one." But resigned, and respectful of the pledge, he spat into his own, then solemnly shook hands.

HE was too restless to go home. And, he admitted, he needed a little more time before he faced his family with the kiss incident still fresh in his mind.

He had half a mind to go back to Dru's and let her know

just how off the mark, how insulting, how *wrong* she'd been.

But the other half of his mind, the smarter half, warned him he wasn't in the mood to have a rational conversation with her yet.

She'd made him doubt himself, and it stung. He'd worked hard to reach and maintain his level of confidence, in himself, in his work, in his family. No woman was allowed to shake it.

So they'd just move back a step before things went any further. He'd paint her because he couldn't do otherwise. But that would be all.

He didn't need to be involved with a woman who was that complicated, that unpredictable and that damn opinionated.

It was time to slow down, to concentrate on work and family. To solve his own problems before he took on anyone else's.

He parked at his studio, carted his equipment and the painting up the steps. He used his new cell phone to call home and let Anna know he wouldn't be back for dinner.

He turned on music, then set up to work on the watercolor from memory.

As with sailing, worries, annoyances, problems faded away when he painted. As a child, he'd escaped into drawing. Sometimes it had been as dramatic as survival, others as simple as warding off boredom. It had always been a pleasure for him, a quiet and personal one or a soaring celebration.

In his late teens he'd harbored tremendous guilt and doubt because he'd never suffered for his art, never felt the drama of emotional conflict over it.

When he'd confessed all that to Cam, his brother had

stared at him. "What, are you stupid?" Cam had demanded.

It had been exactly the right response to snap Seth out of a self-involved funk.

There were times when a painting pulled away from him and he was left baffled and frustrated by the image in his mind that refused to be put on canvas.

But there were times when it flew for him, beyond any height he'd imagined he could achieve.

When the light dimmed through the windows and he was forced to hit the overheads, he stepped back from the canvas, stared at what he'd done. And realized this was one of the times it had flown.

There was a vibrancy to the colors—the green of the grass and leaves, the sunstruck amber of the water, the shock of red from the blanket and the milky white of her skin against it. The garden of flowers on her skirt was bold, a contrast to the delicate way the filmy material draped high on her thigh.

There was the curve of her shoulder, the angle of her arm, the square edge of the blanket. And the way the diffused fingers of light fell over the dreamy expression on her face.

He couldn't explain how he'd done it. Any more than he'd been able to tell Dru what he thought about when painting. The technical aspects of the work were just that. Technicalities. Necessary, essential, but as unconsciously accomplished when he worked as breathing.

But how it was that a painting would sometimes draw out the heart of the artist, the core of the subject and allow it to breathe, he couldn't say.

Nor did he question it. He simply picked up his brush and went back to work.

And later when, still fully dressed, he tumbled into bed,

he dropped straight into sleep with the image of Drusilla sleeping beside him.

"WHAT are you calling it?" Stella asked him.

They were standing in front of the painting, studying it in the glare of his studio lights. "I don't know. I haven't thought about it."

"*Beauty Sleeps,*" Stella suggested. "That's what I'd call it."

She was wearing an oversized chambray shirt and baggy jeans with flat canvas shoes that looked as though they'd walked a lot of miles. And when she tucked her arm through Seth's he could smell hints of lemon from her shampoo and soap.

"We're proud of you, Seth. Not for the talent so much. That's God-given. But for being true to it. Being true to what you have and what you are, that's what makes the difference."

She stepped back and looked around. "Wouldn't hurt you to clean up this place some. Being an artist doesn't mean you have to be a slob."

"I'll take care of it in the morning."

She sent him a wry look. "Now where have I heard that one before? That one there." Stella jerked her head toward the painting. "She's neat as a pin. Maybe too neat—which sure as hell isn't your problem. Worries about letting anything shift out of place. Untidiness confuses her, especially when it comes to her own emotions. You've got to figure they're pretty messy where you're concerned already."

He lifted a shoulder in a way that made Stella smile. "I'm putting the brakes on there. She's too much damn work."

"Uh-huh." She twinkled at him. "You keep telling yourself that, boy."

He wanted to leave that area alone. He didn't mind messy emotions, but his own were in such a state he couldn't be sure he'd ever manage to tidy them up again.

"Cam said I should ask you about the zucchini bread."

"He did, did he? Maybe he thinks I've forgotten. Well, you can tell him I may be dead, but I've still got my wits. I wasn't much of a cook. Ray handled that end for the most part. But now and again I stuck my oar in. One day in the fall I got a yen for zucchini bread. We'd planted the stuff, and Christ knows we had more than we could eat in six years. Especially since Ethan wouldn't touch a morsel. So I got out the cookbook and tried my hand at baking some zucchini bread. Four loaves, from scratch, and I set them on a rack to cool. I was damn proud of that bread, too."

She paused a moment, tipped her head up as if looking at the memory. "About a half hour later, I walked back into the kitchen. Instead of four loaves, there were just three. My first thought was, well, those boys have been in here and helped themselves. Felt pretty smug about that one. Until I looked out the kitchen window. What do you think I saw?"

"I've got no clue." But he was sure he was going to enjoy it.

"I'll tell you what I saw," she said with a jut of her chin. "My boys, and my loving husband, out there in the yard using the zucchini bread I'd made from scratch as a goddamn football. Whooping and hollering and tossing that thing around like it was the Super Bowl. I was out that door like a shot, gonna skin the lot of them. About that time, Phil heaved that loaf high and hard, and Ethan loped over to receive. And Cam—he always was quick as a snake—he streaked over the grass, leaped up to intercept. Misjudged, though. The loaf caught him right about here."

She tapped just over her eyebrow. "Knocked him flat on his ass, too. Damn thing was hard as a brick."

She laughed, rocking back and forth on her heels as if her humor had weight. "Ethan snapped up the bread, stepped right over Cam as he sat there with his eyes rolling back in his head, and made the touchdown. By the time I got out to Cam to check him out and give them a piece of my mind, he'd shaken it off and the four of them were howling like loons. They called it the Bread Bowl. Last time I ever baked bread, I'll tell you that. I miss those days. I sure do miss them."

"I wish I'd had time with you. I wish I'd had time with you and Ray."

She moved to him, brushed at the stray tendrils of hair that had fallen over his forehead. The gesture was so tender it made his heart ache.

"Is it okay if I call you Grandma?"

"Of course it is. Sweet boy," Stella murmured. "She couldn't cut that sweet heart out of you, no matter how hard she tried. She couldn't understand it either, that's why hurting you's always been so easy for her."

They weren't talking about Dru now, he thought. But about Gloria. "I don't want to think about her. She can't hurt me anymore."

"Can't she? Trouble's coming. Trouble always does. You be strong, you be smart, and you be true. You hear me? You're not alone, Seth. You'll never be alone."

"Don't go."

"You're not alone," she repeated.

But when he woke with the early sunlight just sliding through his windows, it seemed he was.

Worse, he saw the folded note under the door. He forced himself to get up, to walk over and pick it up.

Lucy's Diner, next to the By-Way Hotel on Route 13.
Eleven o'clock tonight.
Make sure it's in cash.

Trouble's coming. Seth thought he heard the echo of a voice. *Trouble always does.*

TEN

AUBREY STEWED ABOUT it, picked it apart and put it together again. And the more she fumed and fiddled, the madder she got. Temper made it very clear in her mind that Drusilla Whitcomb Banks needed a come-to-Jesus talk, and Aubrey Quinn was just the one to give it to her.

Since she and Seth had made a pact, she couldn't vent to her mother, her father. She couldn't go by Sybill's and ask for some sort of psychological evaluation of the thing. And she couldn't go to Anna just to spew out her annoyance and resentment.

So it built, layer by layer, until she'd worked up quite a head of steam by the time she left the boatyard at five o'clock.

She practiced what she intended to say as she drove into town. The cool, the controlled, the keen-edged slice of words that would cut Little Miss Perfect down to size.

No one got away with making Seth unhappy.

Mess with one Quinn, she thought as she scooted her pickup into a space at the curb, mess with them all.

In her work boots, dirty T-shirt and well-sprung jeans, she marched into Bud and Bloom.

Yeah, she was perfect, all right, Aubrey thought, and bit down on her ire while Dru wrapped a bunch of daisies for Carla Wiggins. Just perfect in her pink silk blouse and wood-nymph hair. The slacks were stone gray and fluid. Probably silk, too, Aubrey thought, annoyed with herself for admiring the classy, casual look.

Dru's gaze shifted up and over as the door opened. What might have been polite warmth chilled into caution when Aubrey glared at her.

At least that was something.

Carla, bouncy and glowing, turned. "Hi, Aubrey. That was some game yesterday. Everybody's talking about your home run. Bases loaded," she said to Dru. "Aub knocked those Rockfish out of the water."

"Really?" Dru had heard the same, a half dozen times, already that day. "Congratulations."

"I swing to score."

"I about had a heart attack when that ball flew." Carla patted her tidy little breasts to demonstrate. "Jed's still flying. He got walked," she said to Dru, "to load the bases before Aubrey came to bat. Anyway, I'm cooking dinner for his parents tonight—talk about the wedding plans some more—and there I was running around straightening the place up—I took a half day off work—and it hit me I didn't have any flowers for a centerpiece. It's going to be spaghetti and meatballs. That's Jed's favorite. Just fun and cheerful, you know. So Dru said daisies would be nice in that red vase I've got. What do you think?"

Aubrey looked at the flowers, moved her shoulder.

"They're pretty. Friendly, I guess. Kind of simple and sweet."

"That's it. That's just exactly right." Carla fussed with her fine blond hair. "I don't know why I get so nervous. I've known Jed's folks all my life. It's just different now that we're getting married in December. I told Dru my colors are going to be midnight blue and silver. I didn't want to go with the red and green, you know, but wanted to keep it Christmassy and festive. Do you really think those colors will work?" Carla chewed on her lip as she looked back at Dru. "For the flowers and all."

"Beautifully." The warmth came back into Dru's face. "Festive, as you say, and romantic, too. I'm going to put some ideas together, then you and your mother and I will go over everything. Don't worry about a thing."

"Oh, I can't help it. I'll drive everyone crazy before December. I've got to run." She scooped up the flowers. "They'll be coming along in an hour."

"Have a nice evening," Dru said.

"Thanks. See you later, Aubrey."

"Yeah. Hi to Jed."

The door closed behind Carla, and as the bells on it stopped ringing, the cheer that had filled the shop faded.

"I don't think you're in the market for flowers." Dru folded her hands. "What can I do for you?"

"You can stop screwing with Seth's brain and putting me in the role of the other woman."

"Actually, I was worried that was my role, and I didn't care for it."

All the cool, controlled, keen-edged words Aubrey had practiced flew out of her head. "What the hell's wrong with you? Do you think Seth would be poking at you if he were interested in someone else?"

" 'Poking at'?"

Aubrey hunched her shoulders. "Family phrase," she muttered. "What do you take him for? He'd never move on you if he was moving on someone else. He's not like that, and if you don't already know it, you're just stupid."

"Calling me stupid is going to end this conversation before it gets started."

"So is punching you in the nose."

Dru lifted her chin—Aubrey gave her points for it, and for the derisive tone. "Is that how you solve your disagreements?"

"Sometimes. It's quick." Aubrey showed her teeth. "And I owe it to you for the 'buxom blonde in black' remark."

Dru winced, but she kept her voice even. "A stupid comment doesn't make me stupid. But it was uncalled for and ill advised. I apologize for it. I suppose you've never had something pop out of your mouth that you've instantly regretted."

"All the time," Aubrey said, cheerful now. "Apology accepted. But that doesn't cover the bases regarding Seth. You messed with his head and you made him unhappy. That's worth a hell of a lot more than a punch in the nose, from where I stand."

"It wasn't my intention to do either." And she felt a flare of guilt. She'd had no trouble making him mad, but she'd never meant to make him unhappy. Still, she'd done what she thought right for everyone.

"I won't be a game piece to a man, even if he doesn't realize that's what he's making me. I've seen the two of you together. I saw the way you looked at me yesterday when I came into the boatyard. I'm standing here right now with you jumping down my throat because of what you are to each other."

"You want to know what we are to each other?" Riled up

again, Aubrey leaned on the counter. "We're family. And if you don't know family loves each other and sticks up for each other and worries when one of them looks to be getting in deep where he doesn't belong, then I'm sorry for you. And if the way I look at you makes you unhappy, too bad. I'm going to keep right on looking at you, because I'm not sure you're good for him."

"Neither am I," Dru said calmly and stopped Aubrey in her tracks. "There we have a point of agreement."

"I just don't get you," Aubrey admitted. "But I get Seth. He already cares about you. I've known him . . . I don't remember ever not knowing him, and I can see it when he's gone soft on someone. You hurt him yesterday, and I can't stand to see him hurting."

Dru looked down, saw that her hands were gripping the counter. Deliberately, she relaxed them. "Let me ask you something. If you found yourself getting involved with a man—at a point in your life where it's really the last thing you want, but it's happening anyway—and you see that man has a relationship with another woman—a really attractive, vibrant, interesting woman—that you can't define—all you can see is that it's special and it's intimate and beyond your scope—how would you feel?"

Aubrey opened her mouth, shut it again. She had to take another moment before she answered. "I don't know. Damn it. Damn it, Dru, I love him. I love him so much that when he was in Europe it was like a piece of me was missing. But it's not sexual or romantic or anything like that. He's my best friend. He's my brother. He's my Seth."

"I never had a best friend, or a brother. My family doesn't have the . . . vitality of yours. Maybe that's why it's hard for me to understand."

"You'd have gotten a clue if you'd seen the two of us cracking up after kissing yesterday." Aubrey's lips twitched. "That's Seth for you. You planted that seed and so he worries over it, picks at it. 'Gee, am I screwing around with her, am I messing up people I care about? How can I fix it?' So he tracks me down and gives me the big picture, tells me he needs to kiss me—a real guy-girl smackeroo—so we can make sure there's nothing going on in that direction."

"Oh God." Dru closed her eyes. "And he didn't see that was insulting to you?"

"Nope." Surprised, and rather pleased Dru had seen that angle, Aubrey leaned more companionably on the counter. "I didn't let it bother me that way because he was so stupid about the whole thing, so worried and flustered. So we had our little experiment. He gets major points in the lip-lock department. He knows how to kiss."

"Yes, he does."

"There was relief all around because the earth did not move. It didn't even tremble. Then we laughed ourselves silly, and we're fine. I wasn't going to tell you that part," Aubrey added. "I thought letting it hang would make you suffer more. But since you said I was attractive and vibrant and interesting, I'm cutting you a break."

"Thanks. And I'm sorry. It was beginning to . . ." Dru trailed off, shook her head. "Never mind."

"We've come this far, don't hold back now."

She started to shake her head again, then realized that was one of her flaws. She held back. "All right. What's happening between Seth and me was beginning to worry me a little. I had someone I cared about, very much, cheat on me. I started to see myself as that woman, with some sympathy for her position. I didn't want to have any sympathy for her. I prefer despising her."

"Well, sure." Nothing could have been clearer to Aubrey's way of thinking. "You can relax. The field's all yours. Are we square on that?"

"Yes. Yes, we are. I appreciate your coming in to talk to me, and not punching me."

"Punching you would've pissed off Seth, not to mention my parents, so it's just as well. I guess I'd better get going."

"Aubrey." It was always a terrifying thing for Dru to go with impulse. "I don't make friends easily. It's not one of my skills. I'm terrific at making acquaintances, at social small talk and casual conversation. But I don't have many friends."

She took a long breath. "I'm going to close a little early today. It'll take me a few minutes to close out and lock up. Are you in a hurry, or would you like to go have a drink?"

Seth was a goner, Aubrey realized. He'd never hold out against those hints of vulnerability and need hiding under the polish. "Got any good wine at your place?"

"Yes." Dru's lips curved. "I do."

"I'll swing by home, grab a shower. Meet you there."

FROM his studio window, Seth watched Aubrey stride back out to her truck. He'd seen her stride in nearly a half hour before. And though he hadn't been able to see her face, he'd read her body language clearly.

She'd been ready to brawl.

He hadn't gone down. Until he'd seen Gloria, and locked that entire business back in his mental vault, he was keeping a distance from his family.

But he'd listened for the sounds of shouts or breaking

glass. If it had come to that, he'd have run down to pull them apart.

But it hadn't come to that, he noted as Aubrey jumped nimbly into the cab of her truck and zipped off without any indication of temper.

One less worry, he supposed, as he walked into the kitchen to look at the clock on the stove. A little more than five hours left to obsess, he thought. Then he'd meet Gloria, give her the cash he'd withdrawn from his account.

And get back to his life.

DRU had barely walked through the door when Aubrey pulled into the drive. It gave her no time to fuss with the crackers and cheese she'd planned to set out, or to wash the fat purple grapes she'd picked up on the way home.

However casual the invitation, she was accustomed to entertaining a certain way. That certain way wasn't having her guest walk in, push a brown bag into her hand, then look around and whistle.

"Cool. Front page, *House & Garden*." She sent Dru a cheeky grin. "That wasn't really a dig. Man, my mother would love this. She's been itching to get a look at the inside. You got a cleaning service?" Aubrey asked and smoothed a finger over a tabletop. No dust.

"No. It's just me, and I don't—"

"Ought to. Working woman and blah, blah. Mom can give you the whole pitch. Big place." Aubrey began to wander without invitation as Dru stood holding the bag. "I want a big one when I get out on my own. Rattle around a bit, you know? Change from living with what feels like a million people sometimes. Then I'll be lonely and miss them and spend half my time at the house anyway."

She looked up. "High ceilings," she commented. "Must cost you some to heat this place in the winter."

"Would you like to see the bills?" Dru said dryly and made her laugh.

"Maybe later. I'd rather have wine. Oh, those are cookies in the bag. Mom baked some yesterday. Double chocolate chip. Awesome. Kitchen this way?"

"Yes." Dru sighed, then followed, decided to try to go with the flow.

"Nancy Neat, aren't you?" Aubrey said after one glance, then opened the back door. "Man, this is great! It's like your own little island. Do you ever get spooked out here all alone, city girl?"

"No. I thought I might," Dru said as she set the bag on the counter and got out a bottle of Pinot Grigio. "But I don't. I like listening to the water, and the birds and the wind. I like being here. I don't want the city. And I realized the first morning I woke up here, in the quiet, with the sun coming in the windows, I never did. Other people wanted it for me."

She poured the wine. "Do you want to sit out on the patio?"

"That'd be good. I'll bring the cookies."

So they had tart white wine and fat-filled cookies while the sun slid slowly down behind the trees.

"Oh." Aubrey swallowed a mouthful. "I should tell you, Seth and I made a pact not to tell anybody about the big experiment."

"The . . . oh."

"I don't figure you count, since it was your idea. Sort of. But since I spilled it, I've either got to kill you, or you have to swear not to tell anybody."

"Does this oath involve my blood in any way?"

"I usually do it with spit."

Dru thought about it for about two seconds. "I'd rather not involve any bodily fluids. Is my word good enough?"

"Yeah." Aubrey picked up another cookie. "People like you keep their word."

"People like me?"

"Yeah. Breeding," she said with a broad wave of a hand. "You're a fucking purebred."

"I'll assume that's a compliment of some sort."

"Sure. You've got this 'I'm much too cultured and well-bred to make an issue of it' air. You always look perfect. I admire that even when I hate it. It's not like you're all fussy and girly and stuff. You just always look good."

Aubrey stopped, mouth full. Then swallowed fast. "Oh hey, listen, I'm not coming on to you or anything. I like guys."

"Oh, I see. Then I suppose there's no point in us having a big experiment of our own." After two long beats, Dru's laughter burst out. She had to lean back, hold her sides as they ached from the force of it. "Your face. Priceless. It's the first time I've ever seen you speechless."

"That was good." Nodding approval, Aubrey picked up her wine. "That was damn good. I might just like you after all. So, are you going to talk Seth out of the watercolor portrait when he's finished?"

"I don't know." Would he finish it? she wondered. Or was he too angry with her to *see* her as he had? No, he'd finish it, she decided. The artist would have no choice.

"If it were me, I'd wheedle it out of him."

"I think I'd feel strange having a painting of myself hanging on the wall. Besides, I haven't seen it. He was too angry to let me."

"Yeah, he gets all tight-assed when he's mad. Okay,

here's a tip." Watching Dru, Aubrey rested her elbows on the table. "You don't want to cry. What you want to do is bravely battle back tears. You know, so your eyes get all shiny and wet and your lip quivers a little. Hold on."

She leaned back again, closed her eyes, took a couple of deep breaths. Then she opened them again, stared at Dru with a kind of wide-eyed, pitiful expression as tears swam into her eyes.

"My God," Dru murmured in admiration. "That's really good. In fact, it's brilliant."

"Tell me." Aubrey sniffled. "You can let one spill over if you have to, but that's it." A single tear dripped down her cheek. Then she giggled. "You start to flood, and he's all about patting your head and stuffing a paint rag or what-ever in your hand before he goes into full retreat. Then you've lost him. But you give him the shimmery-eyes, quivery-lip deal, and he'll do anything. It *destroys* him."

"How did you learn to do that?"

"Hey, I work with guys." Aubrey swiped the single tear off her cheek. "You develop your weapons. You can bite the tip of your tongue to get started if you have to. Me, I can turn it on and off. Speaking of guys, why don't you tell me about that creep you were engaged to, then we can trash him."

"Jonah? Assistant communications director. West Wing staff, a man with the president's ear. Brilliant mind, smooth style, gorgeous face and a body made for Armani."

"This isn't making me hate him. Get to the dirt."

"It's not far under the surface. Washington social circles—my grandfather remains a strong force in Wash-ington, and my family is influential. Socially active. We met at a cocktail party, and things moved from there. Smoothly and at a reasonable pace. We enjoyed each other, and we liked each other. Had interests and people and philosophies in common. Then, I thought we loved each other."

It was never anger she felt when she thought of that. But sadness.

"Maybe we did. We became lovers—"

"How was he? In the sack?"

Dru hesitated, then poured more wine. She didn't discuss this sort of thing. Then again, she realized, she'd never had anyone who made her feel able to discuss this sort of thing.

Aubrey made it seem easy.

"What the hell. He was good. I thought we were good—but then again, lovers fall into the same category as friends with me. I don't make them easily."

"That'd make it hurt more when it gets messed up," Aubrey offered.

"Yeah, I guess it does. But I thought Jonah and I were good together, in bed and out of it. I was ready when he asked me to marry him. We'd been moving in that direction, and I was prepared. I'd thought it through."

Curious now, Aubrey tilted her head. "If you had to think it through, maybe you weren't in love with him."

"Maybe not." Dru looked away, watched the fluttering flight of a butterfly, listened to the quiet hum of a boat motor as someone cruised by on the river. "But I need to think things through. The bigger the step, the longer and more carefully I think. I wasn't sure I wanted to be married. My parents' marriage—well, it's not like your parents' marriage. But I felt, with Jonah, it would be different. We never quarreled."

"Never?" Pure shock covered Aubrey's face. "You never had a good shouting fight?"

"No." She smiled a little now as she realized how dull that would seem to anyone named Quinn. "When we disagreed, we discussed."

"Oh yeah, that's how we handle things in my family. We discuss our disagreements. We just do it at the top of our lungs. So you and this guy were good in bed, you didn't fight and you had a lot in common. What happened?"

"We got engaged, we had a round of parties and began making plans for a wedding set for the following summer. July because that was most convenient for our schedules. He was busy with work, and I was busy letting my mother drag me around to bridal shows. We house-hunted—Jonah and me, my mother and me, my father and me."

"That's a lot of hunting."

"You have no idea. Then one night, we were at his apartment. We went to bed. While we were making love, I kept feeling something scrape at the small of my back. Eventually I had to stop. It was funny, really, I made a joke out of it. Then we turned on the lights and I went over the sheets. And came up with another woman's earring."

"Oh." Aubrey's face filled with sympathy. "Ouch."

"I even recognized it. I'd seen her wearing them at some event or other. I'd admired them, commented on them. Which is probably why she made sure to leave it there, where I'd find it at the worst possible moment."

"Bitch."

"Oh yes." Dru lifted her glass in a half toast. "Oh yes indeed. But she loved him, and that was a discreet and surefire way to get me out of the picture."

"No excuses." Aubrey wagged a finger. "She was trespassing on another woman's man, even if the man wasn't worth jack shit. She was as sneaky as he was, and just as guilty."

"You're right. No excuses. They deserve each other."

"Damn straight. So, did you tie his dick in a knot? What?"

Dru let out a long sigh. "God, I wish I could be you. I wish I could, even for one single day. No, I got up, and I got dressed, while he started making excuses. He loved me. This other thing was just physical, it didn't mean anything."

"Christ." Disgust was ripe in her voice. "Can't they ever come up with something original?"

"Not in my experience." The instant, unqualified sympathy and support eased some of the rawness she still carried over it all. "He had needs, sexual needs that I was just too restrained to meet. He'd just wanted to get it out of his system before settling down. Basically, he said that if I'd been hotter, more responsive or creative in bed, he wouldn't have had to look elsewhere for that kind of satisfaction."

"And yet he lives," Aubrey murmured. "You let him turn the thing around on you instead of cutting off his balls and hanging them on his ears."

"I wasn't a complete doormat," Dru objected, and told her about the systematic destruction of Jonah's prized possessions.

"Nuked his CDs. That's a good one. I feel better now. Just as a suggestion, instead of cutting up his cashmere coat? I'd have filled the pockets with, oh, I don't know, say a nice mixture of raw eggs, motor oil, a little flour to thicken it up, maybe a hint of garlic. All easily accessed household items. Then, I'd've folded it up really neat, with the pockets to the inside. Wouldn't he have been surprised when he pulled it out of the box?"

"I'll keep that in mind, should the occasion ever come up again."

"Okay. But I really like the CDs, and the bit with the

shoes. If the guy was anything like Phil about his shoes, that one really hurt. What do you say we take a walk, work off some of these cookies? Then we can order some Chinese."

It wasn't, Dru realized, so hard to make a friend after all. "That sounds terrific."

THE diner was lit like a runway, and business wasn't exactly booming. Seth sat on the sun-faded red vinyl of the booth in the very back. Gloria wasn't there. She would be late.

She always came late. It was, he knew, just another way for her to show she had the upper hand.

He ordered coffee, knowing he wouldn't drink it. But he needed the prop. The ten thousand in cash was in an old canvas bag on the seat beside him.

There was a man with shoulders wide as Montana sitting on a stool at the counter. His neck was red from the sun, and his hair shaved so sharp and close it looked as if it could slice bread. He was wearing jeans, and the tin of tobacco he must have carried habitually in his pocket had worn a white circle in the fading denim.

He ate apple pie à la mode with the concentration of a surgeon performing a tricky operation.

The Waylon Jennings tune crooning out of a corner juke suited him right down to the ground.

Behind the counter, the waitress wore candy pink with her name stitched in white over the right breast. She picked up a pot of coffee from the warmer, breezed up to the pie eater, and stood, hip cocked, as she topped off his cup.

Seth's fingers itched for his sketch pad.

Instead he drew in his head to pass the time. The counter

scene—done in bright, primary colors. And the couple midway down the line of booths who looked as if they'd been traveling all day and were now worn to nubs. They ate without conversation. But at one point the woman passed the man the salt, and he gave her hand a quick squeeze.

He'd call it *Roadside*, he thought. Or maybe *Off Route 13*. It relaxed him considerably to pull it all together in his mind.

Then Gloria walked in, and the painting faded away.

She'd gone beyond thin. He could see the sharp bones pressing against the skin at the sides of her throat, the whip-edge blades of her hips jutting against the tight red pants. She wore open-toed, backless heels that flipped and clicked against her feet and the aged linoleum.

Her hair was bleached a blond that was nearly white, cut short and spiky, and only accented how thin her face had become. The lines had dug deep around her mouth, around her eyes. The makeup she'd applied couldn't hide them.

He imagined that upset and infuriated her when she looked in the mirror.

She hadn't yet hit fifty, he calculated, but looked as though she'd been dragged face first over it some time before.

She slid in across from him. He caught a drift of her perfume—something strong and floral. It either hid the smell of whiskey, or she'd held off on her drinking before the meeting.

"Your hair was longer last time," she said, then shifted to flash her teeth at the waitress. "What kind of pie you got tonight?"

"Apple, cherry, lemon meringue."

"I'll have a slice of cherry, with vanilla ice cream. How about you, Seth honey?"

Her voice, just her voice, set his teeth on edge. "No."

"Suit yourself. You got any chocolate sauce?" she asked the waitress.

"Sure. You want that, too?"

"You just dump it over the ice cream. I'll have coffee, too. Well now." She leaned back, slung one arm over the back of the booth. Skinny as she was, he noted, the skin there was starting to sag. "I figured you'd stay over in Europe, keep playing with the Italians. Guess you got homesick. And how are all the happy Quinns these days? How's my dear sister, Sybill?"

Seth lifted the bag from the seat beside him, watched her focus in on it as he laid it on the tabletop. But when she reached out, he closed his fist around it.

"You take it, and you go. You make a move toward anyone in my family, you'll pay. You'll pay a hell of a lot more than what's in this bag."

"That's a hell of a way to talk to your mother."

His tone never changed. "You're not my mother. You never were."

"Carried you around inside me for nine months, didn't I? I brought you into the world. You owe me."

He unzipped the bag, tilted it so she could see the contents. The satisfaction on her face dragged at his belly. "There's your payment. You stay away from me and mine."

"You and yours, you and yours. Like you got something with those assholes I give two shits about. Think you're a big shot now, don't you? Think you're something special. You're nothing."

Her voice rose enough to have the man at the counter take notice and the waitress give them a wary look. Seth rose, took ten dollars out of his wallet and tossed it on the table.

"Maybe I am, but I'm still better than you."

Her hand curled into a claw, but she fisted it, laid it on the table as he walked out. She snatched the bag, tucked it against her hip on the seat.

Down payment, she mused. Enough to tide her over for a few weeks while she worked out the rest.

She wasn't done with Seth. Not by a long shot.

ELEVEN

~

H E BURROWED IN his studio. He used painting as an escape, an excuse, and as a channel for his frustration.

He knew his family was worried about him. He'd barely seen them, or anyone else for that matter, for three days. He hadn't been able to go back to them after leaving Gloria.

He wouldn't take any part of her into their homes, their lives. She was the monkey on his back, and he'd do whatever it took to stop her from leaping onto theirs.

Money was a small price to pay to get rid of her. She'd be back. She always came back. But if ten thousand bought a space of peace, it was a bargain.

So, he'd work through his anger until he found that peace.

He'd hauled the big canvas up from storage, and he'd painted what he felt. The messy mix of emotions and images took shape and color and, as they did, emptied out of him.

He ate when he was hungry, slept when his vision blurred. And painted as if his life depended on it.

That's what Dru thought as she stood in the doorway. It was a battle between life and death, between sanity and despair waged with a brush.

He had one in his hand, stabbed at the canvas, sliced at it. Another was clamped between his teeth like a weapon in reserve. Music boomed, a violent guitar riff that was like a battle cry. Paint was splattered on his shirt, his jeans, his shoes. Her floor.

A kind of blood loss, she thought and gripped the vase she carried.

He hadn't heard her knock over the blasting music, but looking at him now, she realized he wouldn't have heard her if the room had been silent and she'd screamed his name.

He wasn't in the room. He was in the painting.

She told herself to back up and close the door, that she was trespassing on his privacy and his work. But she couldn't.

To see him like this was compelling, intimate, oddly erotic. He seduced her with a passion that wasn't simply beyond anything she understood, but was as distant from her world as the moon.

So she watched as he switched one brush for the other, as he swiped and swirled at the paint, then whipped at the canvas. Bold, almost vicious strokes, then delicate ones that seemed to hold a kind of contained fury.

Despite the breeze spilling in through the windows, she could see the dark line of sweat riding up the center back of his shirt, the damp gleam on the flesh of his arms and throat.

This was labor, she thought, and not all for love.

He'd told her he'd never suffered for art, but he'd been wrong, Dru realized. Anything that consumed so utterly came with pain.

When he stepped back from the canvas, she thought he stared at it as if it had appeared out of thin air. The hand that held the brush fell to his side. He took the one he'd clamped between his teeth, set it aside. Then rubbed, almost absently, at the muscles of his right arm, flexed his fingers.

She started to ease back now, but he turned, peered at her like a man coming out of a trance. He appeared to be exhausted, a little shell-shocked and painfully vulnerable.

Since she'd missed her chance to leave unnoticed, she did the only thing she could think of. She walked in, crossed over to his stereo and turned the music down.

"I'm sorry. You didn't hear me knock." She didn't look at the painting. She was almost afraid to. So she looked at him. "I've interrupted your work."

"No." He shoved away the stray strands of hair that fell over his forehead. "I think it's finished."

He hoped to Christ it was, because he didn't have any more to give it. It had, finally, blessedly, emptied him.

He shifted to his workbench to clean his brushes. "What do you think?" he asked with a nod of his head toward the canvas.

It was a storm at sea. Brutal, savage, and somehow alive. The colors were dark and fearful—blues, greens, blacks, vicious yellows that combined like painful bruises.

She could hear the wind screaming, feel the terror of the man who fought a desperate battle to keep his boat from being swallowed by towering walls of waves.

The water lashed, lightning speared out of the turbulent sky. She saw faces—just ghostly hints of them—in the feral clouds that spewed a sharp and angry rain. More, she realized as she was drawn to it, more faces in the sea.

They seemed hungry to her.

The single boat, the single man, were alone in the primal war.

And in the distance, there was land, and light. There, that small piece of the sky was clear and steady blue. There was home.

He was fighting his way home.

"It's powerful," she managed. "And it's painful. You don't show his face, so I wonder, would I see despair or determination, excitement or fear? And that's the point, isn't it? You don't show his face so we look and we see what we'd feel if we were the one fighting our demons alone."

"Don't you wonder if he'll win?"

"I know he will because he has to get home. They're waiting for him." She looked over at him. He was still caught up in the painting, and rubbing his right hand with his left.

"Are you all right?"

"What?" He glanced at her, then down at his hands. "Oh. Yeah. They cramp sometimes when I've been at it too long."

"How long have you been working on this?"

"I don't know. What day is it?"

"That long. Then I imagine you want to get home and get some rest." She picked up the vase of flowers she'd set beside his stereo. "I put this together before I closed tonight." She held it out. "A peace offering."

It was a mix of blooms and shapes in a squat blue vase. "Thanks. It's nice."

"I don't know whether to be disappointed or relieved

that you haven't been up here the last few days stewing over our disagreement."

He gave the flowers a quick sniff. Something in the bouquet smelled a little like vanilla. "Is that what we had?"

"Well, we weren't in agreement. I was wrong. I very rarely am."

"Is that so?"

"Very rarely," she acknowledged. "So it's always a shock when I am, and when I am, I like to admit it, apologize and move on as quickly as possible."

"Okay. Why don't you tell me which portion of the disagreement you were wrong about?"

"About you and Aubrey. Not only wrong about the aspect of your relationship, but wrong to make an issue out of something that's your personal business."

"Huh. So you were wrong twice."

"No. That equals one mistake with two parts. I was wrong once. And I am sorry."

He set the flowers down, then rolled his shoulders to try to ease some of the stiffness. "How do you know you were wrong?"

Well, she thought, if she'd expected him to let it go with an apology, she should have known better. "She stopped by the shop the other day and explained things to me very clearly. Then we had some wine and Chinese at my place."

"Back up. I explained things to you, and you kick me out—"

"I never—"

"Metaphorically. Aub explains things to you, and everything's peachy?"

"Peachy?" She chuckled, shrugged. "Yes."

"You just took her word for it, then ate spring rolls?"

"That's right." It pleased her to think of it. The entire evening with Aubrey pleased her. "Since she wasn't trying to get me into bed, she didn't have any incentive, that I could see, to lie about it. And if she had been interested in you in a romantic or sexual way, she'd have no motive for clearing the path where I was concerned. Which means I was wrong, and I apologize."

"I don't know why," he said after a moment. "I can't put my finger on it, but that pisses me off again. I want a beer. Do you want a beer?"

"Does that mean you accept my apology?"

"I'm thinking about it," he called back from the kitchen. "Go back to that 'clearing the path' part. I think that might turn the tide."

She accepted the bottle he handed her when he came back in. "I don't know you, not very well," she said.

"Sugar, I'm an open book."

"No, you're not. And neither am I. But it seems I'd like to get to know you better."

"How about pizza?"

"Excuse me?"

"How about we order some pizza because I'm starving. And I'd like to spend some time with you. You hungry?"

"Well, I—"

"Good. Where the hell's that phone?" He shoved at things on his workbench, rattled items on his shelves, then finally dug the phone out from under a pillow on the bed. "Speed dial," he told her after he pushed some buttons. "I keep all vital numbers— Hi, it's Seth Quinn. Yeah, I'm good. How about you? You bet. I want a large, loaded."

"No," Dru said and had him frowning over at her.

"Hold it a minute," he said into the phone. "No, what?"

"No toppings."

"No toppings?" He gaped at her. "*None?* What are you, sick?"

"No toppings," she repeated, primly now. "If I want a salad, I have a salad. If I want meat, I have meat. If I want pizza, I have pizza."

"Man." He huffed out a breath, rubbed his chin in a way she'd seen Ethan do. "Okay, make that half totally boring and half loaded. Yeah, you got it. At my place over the flower shop. Thanks."

He disconnected, then tossed the phone back on the bed. "Won't take long. Look, I need to clean up." He dug into a packing box and came out with what might have been fresh jeans. "I'm going to grab a shower. Just, you know, hang. I'll be right back."

"Can I look at some of your other paintings?"

"Sure." He waved a hand as he carried his beer into the little bathroom. "Go ahead."

And just like that, she realized, they were back on even ground. Or as even as it ever had been. Just hang, he'd said, as if they were friends.

Wasn't it a wonder that she felt they were. Friends. Whatever else happened, or didn't happen between them, they were friends.

Still, she waited until the door was shut and she heard the shower running before she moved over to the painting propped on the easel by the front windows.

The breath caught in her throat. She supposed it was a typical reaction for someone seeing themselves as a painting. That moment of surprise and wonder, the simple fascination with self, as seen through another's eyes.

She wouldn't see herself this way, she realized. Not as romantic and relaxed and sexy all at once. Made bold by the colors, made dreamy by the light, and sexy by the pose with her leg bare and the bright skirt carelessly draped.

Made, somehow, powerful even at rest.

He'd finished it. Surely it was finished, because it was perfect. Perfectly beautiful.

He'd made her beautiful, she thought. Desirable, she supposed, and still aloof because it was so clear she was alone—that she wished to be alone.

She'd told him she didn't know him well. Now more than ever she understood how true that was. And how could anyone really know him? How could anyone understand a man who had so much inside him, who was capable of creating something so lovely and dreamy in one painting, and something so passionate and fierce in another?

Yet with every step she took with him, she wanted to know more.

She wandered to the stacks of canvases, sat on the floor, set her beer aside and began to learn.

Sun-washed scenes of Florence with red-tiled roofs, golden buildings, crooked, cobbled streets. Another exploding with color and movement—Venice, she realized—all a blur with the crowds.

An empty road winding through luminous green fields. A nude, her eyes dark and slumberous, her hair in untamed splendor around her face and shoulders, and the glory of Rome through the window at her back.

A field of sunflowers baking in the heat that was almost palpable—and the laughing face of a young girl running through them trailing a red balloon behind her.

She saw joy and romance, sorrow and whimsy, desire and despair.

He saw, she corrected. He saw everything.

When he came back in, she was sitting on the floor, a painting in her lap. The beer sat untouched beside her.

He crossed over, picked up the bottle. "How about wine instead?"

"It doesn't matter." She couldn't take her attention away from the painting.

It was another watercolor, one he'd done from memory on a rainy day in Italy. He'd been homesick and restless.

So he'd painted the marsh he'd explored as a boy with its tangle of gum and oak trees, with its wigeongrass and cattails, with its luminous light trapped in dawn.

"That spot's not far from the house," he told her. "You can follow that path back to it." He supposed that's what he'd been doing in his head when he'd painted it. Following the path back.

"Will you sell it to me?"

"You keep coming up here, I'm not going to need an agent." He crouched down beside her. "Why this one?"

"I want to walk there, through that mist. Watch it rise over the water while the sun comes up. It makes me feel . . ."

She trailed off as she tipped her face up to look at him.

He hadn't put on a shirt, and there were still a few stray beads of water gleaming on his chest. His jeans rode low, and he hadn't fastened the top button.

She imagined sliding her finger there, just over that line of denim. Just under it.

"Feel what?" he prompted.

Needy, she thought. Itchy. Brainless.

"Um." With some effort, she shifted to admire the painting again. "A little lonely, I suppose. But not in a sad way. Because it's beautiful there, and the path means you're only alone if you want to be."

He leaned in, closer to the painting. She smelled the shower on him—soap and water—and her stomach muscles tightened even as those in her thighs went loose. "Where would you put it?"

If this was desire, Dru realized, if this was lust, she'd never felt its like before.

"Ah, in my office at home. So when I'm tired of working on the books, I can look at it. And take a quiet walk."

She eased away from him, propped the painting up again. "So, can I buy it?"

"Probably." He straightened as she did, and their bodies brushed. From the glint in his eye she decided he was perfectly aware of her reaction to him. "Did you see your portrait?"

"Yes." It gave her an excuse to put a little distance between them when she walked to it. "It's lovely."

"But you don't want to buy it?"

"It's not for me. What will you call it?"

"Beauty Sleeps," he said, then frowned as the dream he'd forgotten came back to him. "Zucchini football," he muttered.

"Excuse me?"

"Nothing. Just a weird flash. Pizza," he said at the brisk knock on the door.

He snatched his wallet off the workbench and, still shirtless and barefoot, went to the door. "Hey, Mike, how's it going?"

"Hanging loose."

The skinny, pimply-faced teenager handed Seth the pizza box. Then his gaze shifted, and he caught sight of Dru. The way his Adam's apple bobbed, the way surprise, interest and envy sped over his young, bumpy face, warned Dru there would be fresh fruit on the grapevine, and it would have her and Seth clustered together.

"Um, hi. Um. Grandma sent you a bunch of napkins and stuff." He shoved the paper bag into Seth's hands as well.

"Great. Tell her thanks. Here you go, Mike. Keep the change."

"Yeah. Well. Um. See you."

"Looks like Mike's got a little crush on you," Seth commented as he booted the door closed.

"I'd say Mike's double-timing it back to Village Pizza so he can spread the word that the artist and the florist are having hot pizza and hot sex."

"I hope he's right. If we're going to make the first part come true, we'd better dig into this." He dropped the box on the bed. "You need a plate?"

Her heart had given a little lurch, but she nodded. "Yes, I need a plate."

"Now, now, don't get twitchy. I'll get you a glass of very nice Chianti instead of the beer."

"I can drink the beer."

"You could," he commented as he headed into the kitchen again. "But you'd rather have the wine. I'll drink the beer. And, sugar, if you don't like people talking about you, you shouldn't live in a tight-knit little community."

"I don't mind people talking about me so much." Not the way they did here, she thought, that was different, so much less bitchy than the way they gossiped in Washington. "I just don't care for them talking about me doing something before I have a chance to do it."

"Would that be the pizza or the sex?" he asked as he came back with paper plates.

"I haven't decided." She pushed through the clothes in his packing box until she found a denim work shirt. "Put this on."

"Yes 'm. Can you handle sitting on the bed to eat if I promise not to jump you?"

She sat and, using one of the white plastic forks Mike's grandmother had put into the bag, worked a slice free. She plopped it on her plate, then using the same method, lifted a piece of his half.

"You know, we've been dating for a while now—"

"We are not dating. This is not a date. This is a pizza."

"Right. Anyway." He sat down, cross-legged, his shirt carelessly unbuttoned.

It was worse, she realized than no shirt at all.

"We haven't asked some of the essential questions to make sure this relationship has a chance."

"Such as?"

"Vacation weekend. The mountains or the shore?"

"Mountains. We live at the shore."

"Agreed." He bit into the pizza. "Favorite guitar player. Eric Clapton or Chet Atkins?"

"Chet who?"

He actually went pale. "Oh God." With a wince, he rubbed his heart. "Let's skip that one. It's too painful. Scariest movie ever—classic category, *Psycho* or *Jaws*?"

"Neither. *The Exorcist.*"

"Good one. Who would you trust, with your life, against the forces of evil? Superman or Batman?"

"Buffy—the vampire slayer."

"Get out." He swigged beer. "Superman. It *has* to be Superman."

"One whiff of kryptonite and he's down for the count. Besides"—she polished off her slice and went for another—"Buffy has a much more interesting wardrobe."

He shook his head in disgust. "Let's move on. Shower or bath?"

"It would depend on—"

"No, no, no." He snagged more pizza. "No depends. Pick."

"Bath." She licked sauce off her finger. "Long, hot and full of bubbles."

"Just as I suspected. Dog or cat."

"Cat."

He set the slice down. "That is just so wrong."

"I work all day. Cats are self-reliant, and they don't chew your shoes."

He shook his head in deep regret. "This might be the end of things between us. Can this relationship be saved? Quick. French fries or caviar?"

"Really, that's ridiculous. French fries, of course."

"Do you mean it?" As if hope had sprung giddily into his heart, he grabbed her hand in a tight grip. "You're not just saying that to string me along so you can have your way with me?"

"Caviar is fine on occasion, but it's hardly an essential element of life."

"Thank God." He gave her hand a loud kiss, then went back to eating. "Other than a woeful ignorance of music and poor judgment over pets, you did really well. I'll sleep with you."

"I don't know what to say. I'm so touched. Tell me about the woman in the painting—the brunette sitting in front of the window in Rome."

"Bella? Want some more wine?"

She lifted that eyebrow in the way that stirred his blood. "Are you stalling?"

"Yeah, but do you want some more wine anyway?"

"All right."

He got up to get the bottle, topped off Dru's glass before sitting down again. "You want to know if I slept with her?"

"Amazing. I'm transparent as glass to you." She took another bite of pizza. "You could tell me it's none of my business."

"I could. Or I could lie to you. She's a tour guide. I'd see her now and then when I was out and around. We got to know each other. I liked her. I painted her, and I slept with her. We enjoyed each other. It never got any deeper or more complicated than that. I don't sleep with every woman who models for me. And I don't paint every woman I sleep with."

"I wondered. And I wondered if you'd lie to me. That's a habit of mine, assuming someone will give the handy lie instead of the more complicated truth. You're not the kind of man I'm used to."

"Drusilla—" He broke off with a muttered oath when his cell phone rang.

"Go ahead. I'll put this away for you."

She eased from the bed, gathered the pizza box, the plates, while he flipped on the phone. "Yeah? No, I'm okay. I was distracted. Anna, I'm fine. I finished the painting I was working on. As I matter of fact I'm not starving myself to death. I just had pizza with Dru. Uh-huh. Sure. I'll be home tomorrow. Absolutely. I love you, too."

He hung up as Dru came back in. "Anna."

"Yes, I heard." She picked up the phone, set it on a nearby table. "Do you know you have beer, wine, a month's supply of soft drinks and now leftover pizza as the total contents of your refrigerator?"

"There used to be half a meatball sub, but I ate it."

"Oh, well then." She walked to the door. Locked it. The sound of that turning lock might have echoed in her head, but it wasn't going to stop her.

She crossed to him.

"The last time I went to bed with a man it was a humiliating experience for me. That's been nearly two years ago now. I haven't particularly missed sex. It's very possible, on some level, I'm using you to take back something I feel someone else took from me."

Since he was still sitting cross-legged on the bed, she slid onto his lap, hooked her legs around his hips, her arms around his neck. "Do you mind?"

"I can't say I do." He ran his hands up her back. "But here's the thing. You may get more than you bargained for."

"Calculated risk," she murmured and brought her mouth to his.

TWELVE

H IS HANDS GLIDED over her skin, and nerves sparked under it. She wanted this, wanted him. The decision to come to his bed had been her own. But she knew the pounding of her heart was as much from panic as from desire.

And so, she realized as those wonderful hands rubbed up and down her back, did he.

"Relax." He whispered it as his lips trailed over her cheek. "It's not brain surgery."

"I don't think I want to relax." Those nerves were a separate kind of thrill, running fast along the tingle of needs. "I don't think I can."

"Okay." And still he stroked, easy hands, easy lips. "Then just be sure."

"I'm sure. I am sure." She eased back. She wanted to see his face. "I never seem to do anything unless I am." She brushed at the strands of hair that fell over his forehead. "It's just . . . been a while."

How could she tell him she'd lost her confidence in this area? If she told him, she'd never be sure that whatever happened between them now was as much her doing as his.

"So we'll take it slow."

She steadied herself. Intimacy, she'd always believed, took courage as well as desire. She'd taken the step. She'd locked the door. She'd come to his bed. Now she'd take another.

"Maybe." Watching him, she unbuttoned her shirt, saw his gaze drift down. Saw the blue of his eyes deepen as she parted the cotton, let it fall off her shoulders. "Maybe not."

He trailed his fingertips along the swell of her breasts, the soft flesh above the fancy white lace of her bra.

"You know one of the really great things about women?" he said conversationally as his fingers danced down over lace and back again. "Not just that they have breasts—which can't be over-appreciated—but all the cool things they put them in."

It made her laugh even as her skin began to shiver. "Like lingerie, do you?"

"Oh yeah." He toyed with the right strap, then nudged it off her shoulder. "On women, that is. I used to swipe Anna's Victoria's Secret catalogues so I could . . . Well." He nudged the left strap. "Probably shouldn't get into that at such a moment. You wearing panty things that match this?"

A quickening of power began to throb under the nerves. "I guess you'll just have to find out for yourself."

"I just bet you are." He leaned in to rub his lips over her shoulder. "You're a coordinated sort of woman. You know what other part—anatomically speaking—I really like about you?"

His lips were gliding along her throat now, rousing and soothing at the same time. "I hesitate to ask."

"This right here." His fingers stroked the nape of her neck. "Drives me crazy. I'll warn you I'm going to have to bite it in just a little while, so don't be alarmed."

"I appreciate you . . . mmmm." His teeth scraped along her jaw, closing lightly over her chin before they nipped at her bottom lip.

"You were starting to relax," he whispered when her breath caught. "Can't have that."

This time his mouth took hers, hot, hard, in a proprietary kiss that was almost a branding. The leap from playful to possessive was so fast, so high she could do nothing but cling while he ravaged.

Steady, she thought as her mind reeled. Had she believed she'd needed to be steady and sure? Oh no, this breathless race was better. So much better.

Her legs tightened around his waist, her body strained. On a jolt of need she answered the demand of the kiss with demands of her own.

No, this wasn't just want, she realized. This was craving.

She shoved at his shirt, pushing it off his shoulders so that her fingers could dig into flesh, could mold muscle.

Her scent was everywhere, as if she'd bathed in wildflowers. The delicacy of it, the silky texture of that fragrant skin misted his mind. The quiet, throaty moans she made when he touched, when he tasted, sprinted through his blood.

The light was changing, softening toward evening. He wanted to see that gentle sunlight glow over her, watch it catch in the green and gold of her eyes.

Her breath trembled out, and she arched back when he

feasted on the long line of her throat. Flowed back, as if boneless, when his tongue slid toward her breast.

Struggling not to rush, he lifted his head to look down at her. "Flexible, aren't you?"

"I take"—she shuddered, bowed—"yoga. Twice a week."

"Mother of God," was all he could manage as the long, lean length of her stretched back with her legs still locked around his waist.

Almost reverently now, his hands moved over her, exploring the slope of shoulder, curve of breast, the line of torso. He flipped open the button at her waist and eased the zipper down. Slowly.

"I was right." He tortured them both by slipping his fingers just under the elastic of white lace panties. "Coordinated. In more ways than one."

Tucking his hands under her hips, he lifted them. And nuzzled at her belly. He felt the muscles quiver under his lips, then jerk when he pressed his mouth to the lace between the V of cotton.

The thrill coiled inside her, tight as a fist, then spread, fingers of pleasure that stroked toward an aching. When her legs trembled, he nudged them down, then drew the trim, tailored slacks away.

"I need to work my way up to the nape of your neck." His lips and fingers played over her legs. "It may take a while."

"That's okay." Her breath caught, then released on a sigh. "Take your time."

He didn't rush. As the aches built she fisted her hands in the sheets to stop herself from begging. She wanted to comb her fingers through his hair, to run them over his body, but was afraid if she released her anchor, even for an instant, she would fly out of this pool of swirling pleasures.

She wanted to drown in it.

He nipped lightly at her thigh and had her turning her face into the mattress, choking back a moan. His tongue slipped and slid along the edge of lace, turned moan into sob. Then stroked under it so sob became quick, gasping cries.

Her need was his need, and still his hands were easy as he rolled the lace down, as he brushed his palm over the heat. Watching her rise up, seeing her eyes go shocked, go blind as he urged her up, was glorious.

When she went limp, he moved up her body with lazy kisses. He wanted her to tremble, to call out his name, to clamp around him as if life depended on it.

And she would, he promised himself as he suckled her breast through the lace. Before they were done, she would.

Her heart was thudding under his mouth, and its beat kicked higher when he pulled the lace away and took flesh.

Her fingers tangled in his hair, pressed him closer, then streaked down his back.

"Let me." Her voice was thick and dreamy as she tugged at his jeans. "Let me."

The music was a low, pumping, primal beat, as urgent as her pulse. She rolled as she dragged denim away, pressed her body along the length of his. Found his mouth in a desperate kiss.

She needed, needed to fill herself with him, and took her lips on a wild journey over his face, his throat, his chest.

God, so hard, so lean, so male.

She wanted, wanted him to fill her, to know that shock, that wonder of being invaded, of being joined. But when she would have straddled him, have taken him into her, he reared up.

"Not yet." And flipped her over on her stomach.

"I want—"

"So do I. Christ, so do I."

When he closed his teeth over the nape of her neck, the erotic shock had her crying out. Her hands closed over the iron rungs of the headboard, but there was no anchor this time.

She went wild.

She bucked under him, felt herself hurtling toward something like madness. "God. Oh God. Now."

His hand shot under her, and those clever fingers plunged into her, into the heat and the wet. She came on a violent leap that left her helpless and shuddering.

When her hands unclasped the rungs, he pushed her to her back. "Now," he said, and crushed his mouth to hers, swallowing her scream as he drove into her.

She closed around him, arched to him. A fast rise and fall, flesh pounding damply against flesh. Each time her breath would catch, his blood beat.

So he watched her as the last glints of sunlight glowed on her face, caught in the green and gold of her eyes as they hazed with tears.

She lifted a hand to his cheek, and there was a kind of wonder in her voice when she said, "Seth."

The beauty of it all but drowned him.

He watched her still as everything inside them shattered.

THE next best thing to making love, in Seth's opinion, was floating along on the warm river of satisfaction after making love. There was something incredibly soft and lovely about a woman's body after completion that made it the perfect resting place.

They'd lost sunset and were drifting toward dusk. Somewhere along the way, he realized, his last CD had finished playing. Now there was only the sound of wind rising up and Drusilla's breathing.

Rain was coming. He could smell it—could sense the storm dancing on the air.

He'd have to shut the windows. Eventually.

He lifted a hand to stroke it along the side of her breast. "I guess you're relaxed now," he murmured. "Whether you like it or not."

"I guess I am."

He certainly was, she thought. That was a good sign. Wasn't it? She hated herself for being stupid. Hated knowing that now that her mind was clearing again, the doubts were creeping in.

She could hardly ask if it had been good for him without sounding like a ridiculous cliché.

But it didn't stop her from wanting to know.

"Thirsty?" he asked her.

"A bit."

"Hmm." He nuzzled in. "I'll get us something, when I can move again."

She combed her fingers through his hair. He had such soft hair, so straight, so full of lights. "Ah . . . you're all right?"

"Uh-huh. Rain's coming in."

She glanced toward the windows. "No, it isn't."

"I mean rain's coming." He turned his head to look out at the sky. "Storm's blowing in. Your car windows up?"

Why the hell was he asking about her car windows when she'd just had a life-altering experience? "Yes."

"Good."

She stared at the ceiling. "I should go, before it rains."

"Uh-uh." He wrapped her close, then rolled over with her. "You should stay, and we'll listen to the rain when we make love again."

"Again?"

"Mmm. Did you know you have this little dimple right at the base of your spine?" He skimmed his finger there as he opened his eyes, and saw her face. "Something wrong?"

"I don't know. Is there?"

He caught her head in his hands, and considered. "I know that face. You're mildly peeved and working toward seriously pissed. What's wrong? Was I too rough?"

"No."

"Not rough enough, what? Hey." He gave her head a little shake. "Tell me what's wrong, Dru."

"Nothing. Nothing. You're an incredible lover. I've never been with anyone as thorough or exciting."

"Then what is it?" he demanded as she pulled away and sat up.

"I said it's nothing." She could hear the testiness of her own voice. God, she thought, she'd whine in a minute. The first threatening rumble of thunder seemed the perfect accent to her mood. "You might say *something* about me. Even the standard, 'Oh baby, that was amazing.' "

"Oh baby, that was amazing." He might have laughed, but he saw the glint in her eye wasn't just temper. "Hold on." He had to move fast to grab her before she could scoot off the bed. And to avoid a tussle, just rolled on top of her again to keep her in place. "Just what happened between you and that guy you were engaged to?"

"That's hardly relevant now."

"It is when you've just plopped him down in bed with us."

She opened her mouth, prepared to strike out with a sharp, damning reply. And sighed instead. "You're right. You're absolutely right. And I'm absolutely stupid. Let me up. I can't carry on any sort of conversation this way."

He eased back so she could shift. And said nothing when she tugged the sheet up over her breasts, though he recognized the gesture as a lifting of the shield.

She tried to gather her thoughts as thunder rolled again and lightning shuddered through the dark. "He cheated on me, and as he claimed to love me, his reason was the fact that I was unimaginative in bed."

"Were you taking yoga back then?" When she merely stared, coolly, Seth shook his head. "Sugar, if you bought that line, you are stupid."

"I was going to *marry* him. We'd ordered the invitations. I'd had my first fitting for the wedding dress. Then I find out he's been romping between the sheets—ones I bought, for your information—with a *lawyer*."

Wind blew in a gust through the windows, and lightning slashed behind it. But he didn't look away from her. He didn't rush over to shut the windows against the oncoming rain.

"And he expected me to understand his reasoning," she went on. "He expected me to go through with the wedding because it was just sex, which was something I wasn't particularly skilled at."

Prick, Seth thought. The kind of prick that gave regular guys a bad name. "And do you figure a guy who'd go shopping for wedding invitations with one woman and sneak around with another is worth one minute of your time?"

"Hardly, or I wouldn't have walked out on him, causing myself and my family considerable embarrassment. I'm not thinking of him. I'm thinking of me."

She was wrong about that, but he let it go. "Do you want me to tell you what it was like being with you? It was magic." He leaned forward to touch his lips to hers. "Magic."

When he took her hand, she looked down at the way they joined. Then sighing, looked toward the windows. "It's raining," she said softly.

"Stay with me awhile." He brought their joined hands to his lips. "We'll listen to it."

I T was still raining when she rose. The soft, steady patter after the storm turned the room into a cozy nest, one she wished she could wallow in.

"Stay the night. I'll even run out early and hunt up something decent for breakfast."

"I can't." It seemed so intimate, so romantic to talk to him in the dark that her first reaction was disappointment when he turned on the light. The second was shock as she realized she was in full view of the windows. "For heaven sake." She scrambled with her underwear toward the bathroom.

"Yeah, like there's anyone out there at this time of night, in the rain." Unconcerned with modesty, he got up and, comfortably naked, followed her. He managed to stop the door from slamming in his face. "Look at it this way, you'll only have to walk downstairs to go to work in the morning."

"I don't have any clothes. Any fresh clothes," she added

when he gestured to the shirt still in a heap on the bedroom floor. "Only a man could suggest I go to work in the morning wearing the same thing I wore yesterday. Would you mind getting that shirt for me?"

He obliged her, but that didn't mean he couldn't stall. "Bring extra clothes tomorrow. I'll pick up some supplies. We'll have dinner. I can cook," he claimed when she lifted an eyebrow. "Adequately. Or we could hang at your place, and you could fix dinner."

"I don't cook, even adequately."

"We can go out, then come back here. Or your place," he added, easing his arms around her. "I don't care where. A planned date, instead of our usual impromptu."

"This wasn't a date." She wiggled away to button her shirt. "This was sex."

"Excuse me. We had food, alcoholic beverages, conversation and sex. That, baby, is a date."

She could feel her lips quiver into a smile. "Damn. You got me."

"Exactly." He caught her around the waist again when she moved by him, drew her back against him. "Have dinner with me, go to bed with me, wake up with me."

"All right, but we'll have to eat after eight. I have a yoga class tomorrow."

"You're just saying that to torment me. But since we're on the subject, can you actually hook your heel behind your head?"

She laughed and pulled away. "I've got to go. It's after midnight. I'll come back here around eight. I'll risk your cooking."

"Great. Hey, do you want me to frame the watercolor for you?"

She beamed at him. "I can have it?"

"That depends. I'm willing to trade a painting for a painting."

"You've already finished the one of me."

"I want another."

She put on her shoes. "You've done two."

"One day, when I'm a dead, famous artist whose work is studied, and the prices of which are ridiculously jacked up, they'll call this my Drusilla period."

"Interesting. If that's what you want as payment, I'll pose again."

"Sunday."

"Yes, fine. Do you know what you're looking for with this one? What you want me to wear?"

"I know exactly what I'm looking for." He walked over, laid his hands on her shoulders and kissed her. "And you'll be wearing rose petals."

"I beg your pardon?"

"Red rose petals. Seeing as you're a florist, you should be able to get me a supply."

"If you think I'm going to pose wearing nothing but . . . No."

"You want the watercolor?"

"Not enough to be blackmailed."

She turned away, but he only caught her hand, spun her back. "You admire my work enough to want to own it."

"I admire your work very much, but you're not painting me naked."

"Okay, I'll wear clothes, but you're wearing rose petals. Ssh." He tapped a finger on her lips before she could speak again. "Obviously I'm not having you pose nude so I can get you into bed because I've already gotten you into bed. And for the record, I don't use art that way. I've had this image in my head since the first time I saw you. I have to paint it."

He took her hands. "I need to paint it. But I'll make you a deal."

"What's the deal?"

"I won't show it to anyone. When it's finished, you'll decide what to do with it."

He recognized the look on her face—one of mulling and consideration.

And knew he had her.

"I decide?"

"I'll trust you to be honest about it. You have to trust me to paint what I see, what I feel. Deal?"

"Red rose petals." She angled her head. "I'm going to order a lot of them."

SETH walked whistling into the boatyard the next morning. He carried a box of doughnuts, fresh from the bakery.

Cam was already at work, drilling turnbuckles into a hull.

"She's a beauty," Seth called out as he strolled up to the prettily proportioned yawl. "You guys must've busted tail to get her this close to finished so soon."

"Yeah. She's done except for a little brightwork, some details in the cabin. Client wants to pick her up Sunday."

"Sorry I didn't give you a hand the last couple days."

"We managed."

There wasn't a sting in the tone, but there was the implication of one. "Where's everybody?"

"Phil's upstairs. Ethan and Aubrey are checking crab pots this morning. I've got Kevin coming in after school. Another week or so he'll be sprung, put in more time."

"Sprung? School'll be over already? What the hell day is it?"

"You'd keep up better if you checked in at home once in a while."

"I've been busy, Cam."

"Yeah." Cam set another turnbuckle. "So I hear."

"What're you pissed off about?" Seth tossed the bakery box onto the deck. "I'm here, aren't I?"

"You sashay in and sashay out as the mood strikes you. Decide to come swaggering in today because you finally got lucky last night?"

"What's it to you?"

"What's it to me?" Cam set the drill aside, vaulted down to the floor—a quick blur of aggravated male. "You want to know what it is to me, you asshole? It's a hell of a lot to me when you up and disappear for the best part of a week. You go around with some damn black cloud over your head, then hole up in your studio. It's a hell of a lot to me when I have to watch Anna worrying because you can't be bothered to tell us what the fuck's going on. You think you can just walk back in here feeling fine because you finally got Dru's skirt over her head?"

Guilt, which had begun to shimmer, exploded into a red flash of fury. Seth moved before he thought, shoving Cam back against the hull. "Don't talk about her like that. She's not some easy lay I used to scratch an itch. Don't you ever talk about her like that."

Cam knocked Seth back a full step. They were squared off now, nose to nose. Boxers who didn't give a damn about the bell. "You don't treat your family like this. Like a goddamn convenience."

Temper was a vicious dog that snapped at both their throats.

"You want to go a round with me?" Cam invited as fists bunched.

"Hold it, hold it. Jesus Christ, hold it!" Phillip all but leaped between them, pushed them apart. "What the hell's going on here? I could hear the two of you all the way upstairs."

"Kid thinks he can take me," Cam replied hotly. "I'm about to let him try."

"Hell you are. You two want to pound on each other, you take it outside. As a matter of fact, Seth, you go. Cool off." Phillip pointed toward the cargo doors and the dock beyond them. "You've been scarce enough around here lately, another few minutes isn't going to matter."

"This is between me and Cam."

"This is a place of business," Phillip corrected. "Our business, so that brings me into it. Keep it up, and the first one to take a punch at you may be me. I've had enough aggravation from you."

"What the hell are you talking about?"

"I'm talking about keeping promises, remembering your responsibilities. I'm talking about having a client who expects a completed design, which you agreed to do. Where the hell is it, Seth?"

He opened his mouth, closed it. Drusilla's sloop. He'd forgotten it. Just, he remembered, as he'd forgotten he'd told Anna he'd pick up the mulch she wanted for a new flower bed. And the ride he'd promised Bram in his new car.

As his anger turned inward, he stalked out of the cargo doors.

"Pissant," Cam grumbled. "Needs a kick in the ass."

"Why don't you get off his back?"

Baffled, still steaming, Cam rounded on Phillip. "Well,

fuck you. You're the one who just finished stomping on him."

"I've been as worried and annoyed as you have," he shot back. "But that's enough. He's old enough to come and go as he pleases. When you were his age, you were racing around Europe and getting your hand up as many skirts as you could manage."

"I never broke my word."

"No." Calmer now, Phillip looked out to where Seth stood on the end of the dock. "And from the look of him, he didn't intend to break his either. How long are you going to let him stand out there feeling like shit?"

"A week or two ought to be enough."

At Phillip's steady stare, Cam hissed out a breath, and felt most of the temper expel with it. "Damn it. I must be getting old. I hate that. I'll go deal with it."

Seth heard the footsteps on the dock. He turned. Braced. "Go ahead and take a shot. But you only get the first one free."

"Kid, I'll only need one."

"Christ, I'm sorry," Seth blurted out. "I'm sorry I let you down. I'll do whatever grunt work you need. I'll get the design finished today. I'll make it up to you."

"Oh hell." This time Cam raked his fingers through his hair. Who felt like shit now? he asked himself. "You didn't let me down. You worried me, you pissed me off, but you didn't let me down. Nobody expects you to give all your time to this place. Or to be at home every spare minute. Damn it, first Anna's nagging at me because you're home too much and she doesn't think it's good for you. Then she's ragging because you're not home at all. How the hell did I get caught in the middle?"

"Just lucky, I guess. I had some things I had to take care

of. That's all. And I was working. I got caught up in it and forgot the rest. The family's not a convenience for me, Cam. You can't believe that. It's a miracle. If it wasn't for you—"

"Stop right there. This isn't about old business, it's about now."

"I wouldn't have a now without you."

"You wouldn't have one without Ray. None of us would. Leave it at that." He jammed his hands in his pockets, looked out over the water.

Jesus, he thought. It didn't matter how old a kid got. They were still yours.

"So, you're serious about the sexy florist?"

Unconsciously Seth mirrored Cam's stance, and now they looked over the water together. "It appears that way."

"Maybe now that you've scratched that itch we'll get some work out of you."

"I seem to have some energy to spare this morning," Seth replied.

"Yeah, it always worked that way for me, too. What kind of doughnuts did you pick up?"

They were okay, Seth thought. Somehow, no matter what went on, they came back to being okay. "Variety pack. I got dibs on the Bavarian cream."

"I'm a jelly man myself. Let's go before Phil finds them."

They started back in together, then Seth stopped short. "Zucchini football."

Color drained out of Cam's cheeks. "What the hell did you say?"

"The Bread Bowl. The zucchini bread. She baked bread and you guys used it as a football. She told me."

"When?" Shaken, Cam gripped Seth's shoulders. "When did you see her?"

"I don't know. I don't. I dreamed it. Felt like I dreamed it," he murmured. His stomach jittered, but it wasn't unease he felt. It was, he realized, a kind of joy.

He'd spoken with Stella, he thought. He had a grandmother who'd shared a story with him.

"That's right, isn't it?" That joy leaped out in his voice, filled his face. "And you—you tried to intercept a pass and got hit above the eye. Knocked you down, nearly out. That's right, isn't it?"

"Yeah." Cam had to steady himself. It was a good memory. There were so many good ones. "She came running out the back door, shouting at us just as I was making the jump. I turned, and bam. Fucking galaxy of stars. That bread was like a goddamn brick. She was a hell of a doctor, but she never could cook worth a damn."

"Yeah, she told me."

"So, she bent down, looked at my pupils or whatever, held up fingers for me to count. Said it was just as well I got beaned. Saved her the trouble. Then we all started laughing—me and Dad, Phil and Ethan. Bunch of lunatics. Mom stood there, staring at us, with her hands on her hips. I can still see it. See her."

He let out a long breath. "Then she went back in and got another loaf so we could keep playing. She tell you that part?"

"No." Seth laid a hand on Cam's shoulder as they turned toward the cargo doors. "I guess she wanted you to tell me."

THIRTEEN

W HEN THE DOUGHNUTS were devoured, and
Seth was hunkered down in a corner refining Ethan's
basic design for Dru's sloop, Dru stepped outside her shop
to snip off any faded blossoms in the whiskey barrel tub of
verbena and heliotrope beside the front door.

The night's storm had cooled the air, swept away the
dragging humidity and left the morning fresh and bell-
clear.

The Bay was rich blue, still kicking a bit from the turbulence of the night. Boats were already rolling over it. The
watermen in their workboats, the vacationers in their
rented skiffs or motorboats shared the waters. The summer
people who moored their boats and stole time to use them
were out early. Why waste a minute of a perfect day? Dru
mused.

In a few months, she'd be able to spend a pretty morning
working on rigging, washing down the deck, polishing the

brightwork of her own boat. Owning a boat meant a great deal more than casting off, hoisting sails and riding the wind. It meant pouring time, money, energy into maintenance. But that, she thought, was part of the pleasure. Or would be for her.

She liked to work. It had been one of the many small self-realizations that had come to her over the years. She liked working, producing and the satisfaction of standing back and seeing what she'd managed to do on her own.

She enjoyed the *business* end of running a business. The bookkeeping, the supplies, filling orders, calculating profit. It suited her sense of order just as the nature of her business suited her love of beauty for the sake of beauty.

The boat, when it was finished, would be her personal reward for making it all come together.

And Seth . . . She wasn't entirely sure what Seth was. The night she'd spent with him had been glorious. But like a boat, a relationship with him would never be all smooth sailing, and there was bound to be maintenance.

Just where would they be, she wondered, if the wind that had carried them to this point stalled on them? What would they do if they ran into a serious storm, or ran aground, or simply—as so many did—found the excitement draining from the ride?

And she wished she could do no more than enjoy the moment without looking ahead for problems.

He intrigued her and challenged her. He aroused her and amused her. He stirred up feelings in her no one had—not even, she was forced to admit, the man she'd nearly married.

She was drawn to his solid sense of self, his honesty and his ease. And she was fascinated by the hints of the turbulence and passions she saw bubbling just under the surface of that ease.

He was, she believed, the most compelling man she'd ever met. He made her happy. Now they were lovers, and she was already looking for the trouble ahead.

Because if you didn't look ahead, she reminded herself, you rammed straight into those problems and sank.

She carried the little shears back inside, into the storeroom, where she put it on its place on the shelf. She wished she could talk to someone, another woman, about the thrill and anxiety running so fast inside her. She wanted to be able to sit down with a friend and have a silly conversation where she could ramble on about everything she was feeling.

About how her heart started to flop around when he smiled at her. How it raced when he touched her. How scary and wonderful it was to be with someone who liked and accepted her for who she needed to be.

She wanted to tell someone that she was falling in love.

None of the women in her previous social circle would understand. Not the way she *needed* to be understood. They would be interested, certainly, even supportive. But she couldn't imagine telling any of them how he'd bitten the nape of her neck, then have them groan and sigh in envy.

And *that's* what she wanted.

She couldn't call her mother and tell her she'd had the most incredible sex of her life with a man she was stumbling into love with.

It just wasn't the kind of conversation either of them would be comfortable having.

Though her instincts told her there was nothing she

could say to shock Aubrey, and she was dead certain she'd get the exact reaction she was looking for from her new friend, Aubrey's connection to Seth made that possibility just a bit too sticky.

So she was on her own, Dru supposed. Which was exactly where she'd wanted to be in the first place. But now that she had something to share, now that she felt her life shifting under her feet, there was no one to reach out to.

It was her own doing, she admitted. She could either live with it, or begin to change it. Opening up meant more than taking a lover. It meant more than dipping a toe into the waters of a new friendship.

It meant work. So she'd work.

The bells on the front door jingled, signaling her first customer of the day. Dru squared her shoulders. She'd proven she could remake her life once. She could do it again.

Prepared to be more than the polite and efficient florist, she stepped out of the storeroom with a warm smile.

"Good morning. How can I help you?"

"Oh, I'm not sure. I'm just going to look around."

"Help yourself. It's a gorgeous day, isn't it?" Dru walked over to prop open the front door. "Too gorgeous to be closed in. Are you visiting Saint Chris?"

"That's right," Gloria said. "Taking a nice little vacation."

"You picked a perfect time." Dru ignored a frisson of unease at the way she was being studied. "Are you here with your family?"

"No, just me." Gloria flicked fingers over the petals of an arrangement, and kept her eyes on Dru. "Sometimes a girl just has to get away on her own. You know?"

"Yes, I do." She didn't look like the type to spend time

or money on flowers, Dru thought. She looked . . . hard, edgy—and cheap. Her shorts were too tight, too brief, and her top too snug. When she caught what she thought was a whiff of whiskey along with the woman's florid perfume, she wondered if she was about to be robbed.

Then she dismissed the thought. Nobody robbed florists, certainly not in St. Chris. And if the woman had any sort of weapon it would have to be very, very tiny to be concealed under that outfit.

And to judge someone because she didn't care for the style of her dress wasn't the way to begin the new phase of becoming more personable with her customers.

"If you're looking for something to cheer up your hotel room while you're here, I have carnations on special this week. They have a nice fragrance and they're very low maintenance."

"That might work. You know, you look familiar, and you don't sound like a local. Maybe I've met you before. Do you spend much time in D.C.?"

Dru relaxed again. "I grew up there."

"That's got to be it. The minute I saw you, I thought . . . Wait a minute! You're Katherine's daughter. Prucilla—no, no, Drusilla."

Dru tried to imagine her mother having any sort of acquaintance with the thin, badly dressed woman who smelled of cheap perfume and whiskey. Then cursed herself for being a snob.

"That's right."

"Well, I'll be damned." Gloria planted her hands on her hips, made her smile large and friendly. She'd done her research. "What the hell are you doing down here?"

"I live here now. So you know my mother?"

"Sure, sure. I worked on several committees with Kathy.

Haven't run into her in a while. I guess it's been three or four years. Last time, I think it was a fund-raiser for literacy. Book and author dinner at the Shoreham."

The event had been written up in the *Washington Post,* with enough detail in the archives Gloria had looked up on-line to make her claim smooth. "How is she, and your father?"

No, Dru thought, she wasn't a snob. She was simply a good judge of character. But she spoke evenly. "They're both very well, thank you. I'm sorry, I didn't get your name."

"It's Glo. Glo Harrow," she said, using her mother's maiden name. "Hell of a small world, huh? Seems to me the last time I talked to Kath, you were engaged. She was over the moon about that. Guess it didn't work out."

"No, it didn't."

"Well, men are like buses. Another one always comes along. You know, my mother's friendly with your grandfather." And that was true enough, though "acquainted" would have been more accurate. "The senator, he just keeps trucking along. A regular institution."

"He's an amazing man." Dru spoke coolly now.

"Gotta admire him. A man his age still active the way he is. Then you figure with the family money, he never had to work a day in his life, much less dedicate himself to politics. Tough arena, even for a young man, the way people like to sling mud these days."

"People have always slung mud. My family's never believed that financial advantage means letting someone else do the work."

"Gotta admire that, like I said."

When a man walked in, Dru bit down on her rising irritation and turned toward him. "Good morning."

"Hi. Hey, don't mind me, just finish what you're doing. I'm not in a rush."

"Would you like to look around some more, Ms. Harrow?"

"No." She'd spent more than enough time on this visit. "Why don't I take a dozen of those . . . what was on special?"

"Carnations." Dru gestured to the holding vase where she'd arranged samples in every color. "Would you like any specific color or combination?"

"No, no, just mix them up."

Gloria read the sign under the display and calculated it was a cheap enough price to pay for the up-close look. She took out cash, laid it on the counter.

Now that the contact had been made, Gloria wanted to be gone. She didn't care for the way the guy who'd come in was watching her and trying to pretend he wasn't watching her.

"I hope you enjoy them."

"I already am. Give my best to your mom when you talk to her," Gloria added as she started out.

"Oh, I will." Dru turned to her new customer. Some of the temper that had begun to simmer leaked out on her face.

"Bad time?"

"No, of course not." She readjusted her thoughts. "How can I help you?"

"First, I'm Will. Will McLean." He offered a hand.

"Oh, you're Aubrey's friend." Seriously cute, Aubrey had said. And with perfect accuracy, Dru decided as they shook hands. "It's nice to meet you."

"You, too. I just got off shift, figured on swinging by to see Aub—maybe catch up with Seth, before I go home and crash in a dark room for a few hours. Those flowers Seth got my girl a few weeks back were a really big hit. Can't let him get an edge on me. What've you got that'll knock her out, and make up for me working doubles most of the week?"

"How's your budget?"

"Just got paid." He patted his back pocket. "Sky's the limit."

"In that case, wait right here." She paused, reconsidered. The morning jolt wasn't going to spoil her plans for a more open Drusilla. "Better yet, come on back. If you like what I have in mind, you can sit down, get off your feet for a few minutes while I put them together for you."

"I look that bad?"

"You look exhausted." She gestured him back. "Go ahead, have a seat," she told him while she went to a re-frigerated unit. "Delivered fresh this morning," she said as she took out a single long-stemmed rose in cotton-candy pink. "A dozen of these are guaranteed to knock her out."

He sniffed it when she held it out. "Smells great. Maybe I should make it two dozen. I've had to cancel two dates in the last ten days."

"Two dozen will put her in a coma."

"Perfect. Can you put them in one of those fancy boxes?"

"Absolutely." She moved to the work counter. "You and your brother are becoming my best customers. He bought me out of yellow roses about a week ago."

"He got himself engaged."

"Yes, I know. He was floating along about six inches above ground. You and your brother and Seth have been friends a long time."

"Since we were kids," Will concurred. "I can't believe

he's been back a month and I haven't been able to catch up with him. Dan says Seth's been pretty tied up himself between his work, the boatyard and you. Whoops." The crooked smile flashed as he rubbed his eyes. "Sorry. Tongue gets loose when I'm brain-dead."

"That's all right. I don't imagine it's a secret Seth and I are . . ." What? "Seeing each other," she decided.

Will did his best to stifle a yawn. "Well, if we ever get our schedules aligned, maybe the six of us can do something."

"I'd like that." Dru laid the roses and baby's breath in the tissue-lined box. "I'd like that a lot."

"Good. Ah, can I ask you something? That woman who was in here before? Was she hassling you?"

"Why do you ask?"

"I don't know, just a feeling. Plus there was something about her. I think I know her from somewhere. Can't put my finger on it, but it doesn't feel right. Do you know what I mean?"

"I know exactly what you mean." She glanced over at him. He was a friend of Aubrey's, of Seth's. The new, more open Dru was going to consider him a friend as well.

"She claimed to know my mother, but she didn't." No one, Dru thought, absolutely no one referred to her mother as Kathy. It was Katherine, and on rare occasions, Kate. But never Kathy, never Kath. "I don't know what she was after, but I'm glad you came in when you did."

"You want me to stick around awhile, in case she comes back?"

"No, but thanks. She doesn't worry me."

"You called her Harrow?" Will shook his head. "Doesn't ring any bells. But I know her from somewhere. When I come up with it, I'll let you know."

"I appreciate it."

* * *

IT was a mistake to call her mother. Dru realized it immediately. But she hadn't been able to get the morning customer out of her mind. The only way to check out the story was to ask.

Her mother had breezily told her she knew no one named Glo Harrow, though she did know a Laura Harrow, and a former Barbara Harrow. Dru was lulled by her mother's cheerful mood, and the news that she and Dru's father were reconciled.

For the moment, at least.

But the conversation had soon shot down its usual paths. Why didn't she come home for the weekend—better, for the summer? Why didn't they all go spend a few days at the family enclave in North Hampton?

Reasons were brushed aside, excuses ignored, until when they hung up, Dru had no doubt her mother was just as irritated and unhappy as she herself was.

It reminded her to leave bad enough alone.

But she discovered even that was too little, too late, when her mother walked into the shop ten minutes before closing.

"Sweetheart!" Katherine threw out her arms as she rushed to the counter, then wrapped them like ropes around Dru. "I'm so happy to see you. Just so happy."

"Mom." Dru patted Katherine's back and hated herself for the desire to pull away. "What are you doing here?"

"As soon as we hung up, I realized I just couldn't wait to see you. I miss my baby. Just let me look at you." Katherine eased back, stroked a hand over Dru's hair. "When are you going to grow this back? You have such beautiful hair, and here you go around with it chopped off like a boy. You're so thin! You're losing weight."

"I'm not losing weight."

"I worry about you not eating properly. If you'd hire some household staff—"

"Mom, I don't want household staff. I'm eating very well. I haven't lost an ounce since I saw you last month. You look wonderful."

It was invariably true. She wore a beautifully cut pink jacket over pearl gray trousers, both perfectly draped over a figure she maintained with scrupulous diet and exercise.

"Oh, I feel like a hag these days." Katherine waved a hand in dismissal.

Dru softened. "No, you don't, because you have very keen vision and any number of mirrors."

"You're so sweet."

"Did you drive down alone?"

"Henry," she said, referring to her chauffeur. "I told him to take half an hour, walk around a bit. It's a charming little town, really, for a holiday."

"Yes, it is." Dru kept her voice pleasant. "Those of us who live here are very grateful tourists find it as charming as we do."

"But what do you find to do? Oh, don't get angry. Don't get angry." Katherine waved a hand again as she wandered to the front window. "You're so far away from the city. Everything it offers, everything you're used to. Darling, you could live *anywhere*. Though God knows, I'd go mad if you moved away any farther than you have. But seeing you bury yourself here just hurts my heart."

"I'm not buried. And Saint Christopher isn't the end of the earth. If I wanted whatever the city had to offer, I could be there in an hour's drive."

"I'm not speaking geographically, Dru, but culturally, socially. This area's very picturesque, but you've cut yourself off from your life, your family, your friends. My goodness, darling, when's the last time you had a date with an eligible man?"

"Actually, I had one just last night."

"Really?" Katherine arched her brow much as Dru herself was prone to do. "What did you do?"

She didn't bother to bite her tongue. "We had pizza, and sex."

Katherine's mouth opened into a shocked *O*. "Well, my God, Drusilla."

"But that's hardly the issue. I wasn't satisfied with my life, so I changed it. Now I am satisfied. I wish you could be happy for me."

"This is all Jonah's fault. I could just strangle him."

"No, he's only one minor pebble in the bowl. I don't want to go over and over this again with you, Mom. I'm sorry we don't understand each other."

"I only want the best for you. You're my whole life."

Dru's head began to throb. "I don't want to be your whole life. I shouldn't be your whole life. Dad—"

"Well, of course, your father. God knows why I put up with the man half the time. But we do have twenty-eight years invested in each other."

"Is that what your marriage is? An investment?"

"How in the world did we get off on such a topic? This isn't at all why I came down."

"Do you love him?" Dru demanded, and watched her mother blink.

"Of course I do. What a question. And however we disagree, we both have one perfect point of agreement. You are the most precious thing in our lives. Now." She leaned over, kissed Dru on both cheeks. "I have a wonderful surprise for you." She gripped Dru's hand. "We'll run over to your little house right now so you can get your passport, pack a few essentials. No need for much, we'll take care of the wardrobe when we get there."

"Get where?"

"Paris. It's all arranged. I had this wonderful brainstorm after we talked this morning. I called your father, and he'll be joining us in a day or so. The plane's waiting for us at the airport. We'll spend some time in Aunt Michelle's flat in Paris, shop—oh, and we'll throw a little dinner party. Then we'll drive south and spend a week at the villa. Get out of the heat and crowds."

"Mom—"

"Then I think you and I should run off and have a nice girls' weekend. We never spend any real time together any-more. There's this marvelous spa not far from—"

"Mom. I can't go with you."

"Oh, don't be silly. It's all set. You don't have to worry about a single detail."

"I can't go. I have a business to run."

"Really, Dru. Surely you can close down for a few weeks, or ask someone to take care of it. You can't let this hobby of yours deprive you of every bit of fun."

"It's not a hobby. It deprives me of nothing. And I can't blithely close down so I can trot around France."

"Won't."

"All right, won't."

Tears sprang into Katherine's eyes. "Don't you see how much I need to do this for you? You're my baby, my sweet baby. I worry myself sick thinking about you down here alone."

"I'm not alone. I'm almost twenty-seven years old. I need to make my life. You and Dad need to make yours. Please don't cry."

"I don't know what I've done wrong." Katherine opened her purse, pulled out a tissue. "Why you won't take a little bit of your time to be with me. I feel so abandoned."

"I haven't abandoned you. Please—" When the bells jingled, Dru looked over. "Seth," she said with desperate relief.

"I thought I'd come by before you . . ." He trailed off when he saw the woman sniffling into a tissue. "Sorry. Ah . . . I'll come back."

"No. No." She had to force herself not to leap in front of the door to block his path of retreat. She knew nothing would dry her mother up as quickly as social introductions. "I'm glad you stopped in. I'd like you to meet my mother. Katherine Whitcomb Banks, Seth Quinn."

"Nice to meet you."

"And you." Katherine gave him a watery smile as she offered a hand. "You'll have to forgive me. I've been missing my daughter, and it's made me overly emotional." Now as she dabbed at her eyes, they began to sharpen. "Seth Quinn. The artist?"

"Yes," Dru confirmed, brightly now. "We've admired Seth's work, haven't we, Mom?"

"Very much. Very much. My brother and his wife were in Rome last year and fell in love with your painting of the Spanish Steps. I was very envious of their find. And you grew up here, didn't you?"

"Yes, ma'am. My family's here."

"It's so important to remember family," Katherine said with a sorrowful look at Dru. "How long will you be in the area?"

"I live here."

"Oh, but I thought you lived in Europe."

"I was staying in Europe for a while. I live here. This is home."

"I see. Will you be having a showing in D.C., or Balti-more?"

"Eventually."

"You must be sure to let me know when. I'd love to see more of your work. I'd be delighted to have you to dinner when it's convenient for you. Do you have a card, so I can send you an invitation?"

"A card?" He grinned, quick and bright. He couldn't help it. "No, sorry. But you can let Dru know. She knows how to get ahold of me."

"I see." And now she was beginning to. "We'll do it very soon."

"Mom's leaving for Paris," Dru said quickly. "When you get back," she told her mother, and nudged her toward the door, "we'll see about getting together."

"Bon voyage." Seth lifted a hand in farewell.

"Thank you, but I'm not sure I'll be—"

"Mom. Go to Paris." Dru gave her a firm kiss on the cheek. "Enjoy yourself. Have a wonderful, romantic holi-day with Dad. Buy out Chanel. Send me a postcard."

"I don't know. I'll think about it. It was lovely to meet you, Seth. I hope to see you again, very soon."

"That'd be great. Have a good trip."

He waited, tapping his fingers on his thighs as Dru walked her mother out. More like goose-stepped her out, he corrected. He saw, through the window, her loading Katherine into a cream-colored Mercedes sedan, with uni-formed driver.

It reminded him of a small point he'd forgotten. Dru's family was loaded. Easy enough to forget it, he mused. She didn't live rich. She lived normal.

When she came back in, she locked the door, then leaned back against it. "I'm sorry."

"For what?"

"For using you to wheedle out of a very uncomfortable situation."

"What are friends for?" He moved to her, tapped her chin with his finger. "Do you want to tell me why she was crying and you looked so miserable?"

"She wanted me to go to Paris. Just like that," Dru added, lifting her hands, then letting them drop. "She'd made all the arrangements without asking me, then drove down here expecting me to leap with joy, rush out and pack a bag and go."

"I guess some people would have."

"Some people don't have a business to run," she snapped. "Some people haven't already been to Paris more times then they can count anyway. And *some* people don't like to have their lives neatly arranged for them as if they were still eight years old."

"Sugar." Because he could feel her vibrating with anger and frustration, he rubbed his hands down her arms. "I didn't say you should have, but that some people would have. Got you wound up, didn't she?"

"She nearly always does. And I know she doesn't actually mean to. She really thinks she's doing it for me. They both do, and that makes it worse. She makes assumptions she shouldn't make, makes decisions for me she no longer has the right to make, then I hurt her feelings when I don't go along."

"If it makes you feel any better, I got reamed by Cam this morning because I haven't been around and forgot to do some stuff I said I'd do."

Dru angled her head. "Did he cry?"

"He might've gotten a little misty. Okay, no," he said, relieved when her mouth curved. "But we were on the verge of punching each other when Phil broke it up."

"Well, I can hardly hit my mother. Did you work it out with your brother?"

"Yeah, we're okay. I need to go by and grovel to Anna for a while, but I thought I'd drop off the boat design." He nodded toward the large folder he'd set on the counter.

"Oh." She pressed her fingers to her temples. "Can I look at it later? I need to close up or I'll be late for my class."

"Yoga. Oh yeah. You shouldn't miss that. We still on for tonight?"

"Do you want to be on for tonight?"

"I've been thinking about you all day. About being with you."

It warmed her. "I suppose I might have given you a passing thought. Though I've been pretty busy in here today."

"So I hear. Will came by the boatyard and nearly gave Aub a heart attack with that forest of roses."

"Did she like them?"

"She got gooey—and it's not easy to make Aubrey gooey. Will, on the other hand, looked dead on his feet. I figure he's got to be seriously stuck on her to come by here, buy flowers, give them to her when he looked like he hadn't slept for a week."

"I liked him, and his brother. You're lucky to have friends that go back to childhood."

"Don't you?"

"Not really. In any case," she went on to avoid the subject, "I had yet another odd visit just before he came in. Some woman," she continued as she cashed out, locked up her cash from the day. "She claimed to know my mother, but once she started talking, I knew she didn't. Not only from what she said, but how she looked. That sounds like snobbery, but it's just logic."

"How did she look?"

"Hard, cheap and not like anyone who's ever worked on a charity committee with my mother. She was pumping me, feeling me out." Dru shrugged. "Not that unusual when you come from an influential family."

There was ice in the pit of his stomach. "What did she say? What did she do?"

"Nothing much. I think she was laying groundwork for something, but then Will came in. She bought some carnations and left. Funny, he said he thought he recognized her from somewhere."

And now a sickness coated his throat. "She tell you her name?"

"Mmm? Yes." Dru took a last glance around, gathered her purse and keys. "Harrow, Glo Harrow. I've really got to get moving."

She stopped short, surprised when his hand clamped down on her arm. "Seth?"

"If she comes in again, I want you to call me."

"Why? She's just some woman hoping to con me out of some money, or an introduction to my grandfather. Believe me, I've handled that sort of thing all my life."

"I want you to promise me. I mean it. If she comes in, you go in the back, pick up the phone and call me."

She started to tell him she didn't need protection, but there was a fire, an urgency in his voice that had her nodding instead. "All right. I promise."

FOURTEEN

H E HAD TO wait until morning, until Dru slipped downstairs to prepare her daily orders. He'd barely slept. Though he'd struggled to lock the turmoil aside, he'd lain awake most of the night.

Even the pleasure of having Dru curled beside him had been tainted.

But he had to be sure.

Though his gut told him Gloria had tromped on yet another part of his life, he knocked on the McLean brothers' apartment door. He had to be sure.

Dressed for work, an enormous cup of coffee in his hand, Dan answered. "Hey, what's up? You just caught me. I've got an early meeting."

"I need to talk to Will."

"Good luck. He's the dead man in the bedroom down the hall. Want coffee? He'll probably pull his resurrection act by noon."

"This can't wait."

"Hey, Seth, really, the guy's wasted." Since Seth was already walking through the debris of the living room, Dan went after him. "No, that's mine." Resigned, Dan jerked a thumb toward a second door. There was a sign tacked to it that advised:

Take two aspirin and go far, far away.

Seth didn't bother to knock, but pushed the door open into the dark. Through the light that spilled in from the hallway, Seth could see blackout drapes were pulled tight over the window. The room itself was barely closet-sized and mostly bed.

Will lay on it, faceup, his arms flung out to the sides as if he'd fallen backward in that position and hadn't moved since. He wore Marvin the Martian boxer shorts and one sock.

He snored.

"Let me get my camera," Dan mumbled. "Listen, Seth, this is his first chance for eight straight in two weeks. He wanted to make up time with Aubrey, so he didn't get in until after two. He was barely conscious when he came in the door."

"It's important."

"Well, shit." Dan walked over to the window. "He'll probably be speaking in tongues." And ruthlessly whipped the drapes back.

The bright morning sun flashed over the bed. Will didn't twitch. Seth leaned over the bed, shook Will by the shoulder. "Wake up."

"Glumph missitop."

"Told ya." Dan moved to the bed. "Here's how it works."

He put his mouth close to Will's ear and shouted, "Code blue! Code blue! Dr. McLean, report to Exam Room Three. Stat!"

"Whazit?" Will sprang into a sitting position as if the top half of his body had been shot from a bow. "Where's the crash cart? Where's . . ." Some part of his brain cleared as he blinked into Seth's face. "Aw fuck." He started to flop back, but Seth grabbed his arm.

"I have to talk to you."

"You bleeding internally?"

"No."

"You will be if you don't get the hell out of here and let me sleep." He grabbed a pillow from behind him, put it over his face to block out the light. "Don't see a guy in years, then you can't get rid of him. Go away, and take the moron who used to be my brother with you."

"You were in Dru's shop yesterday."

"I'm gonna cry in a minute."

"Will." Seth yanked the pillow away. "The woman who was in there when you came in. You said you thought you recognized her."

"Right now I wouldn't recognize my own mother. In fact, who the hell are you and what are you doing in my bedroom? I'm calling the cops."

"Tell me what she looked like."

"If I tell you, will you go away?"

"Yeah. Please."

"Christ, let me think." Yawning hugely, Will scrubbed his hands over his face. He sniffed. Sniffed again. "Coffee." His eyes began to track until they landed on Dan's cup. "I want that coffee."

"This is mine, jerkwad."

"Give me that goddamn coffee or I'm telling Mom you think that yellow dress makes her ass look fat. Your life won't be worth living."

"Give him the damn coffee," Seth snapped.

Dan handed it over.

Will slurped, gulped. Seth waited for him to just dunk his head in the oversized cup and lap with his tongue. "Okay, what was the question?"

Seth fisted a hand at his side, imagined his rage inside it. Trapped and controlled. "The woman you saw in Dru's shop."

"Yeah, right." Will yawned again, tried to concentrate. "Something about her weirded me out. Dressed like she should've been working a corner in Baltimore. Not that I'd know anything about that," he added with a cherubic smile. "Bleached, bony, blond. What my dad would call shopworn. Diagnosis from a quick visual would be serious alcohol abuse, along with some recreational chemicals. Bad tone to her skin. Liver damage, probably."

"How old?" Seth demanded.

"Running toward fifty, but hard years. Could've been younger. Serious smoker's rasp, too. She leaves her body to science, we ain't getting much out of it."

"Yeah." Seth sat heavily on the side of the bed.

"Like I told Dru, there was something familiar about her. Couldn't place it. Maybe it was just the type. Hard, edgy, sort of, I dunno, predatory. What? Did she come back and hassle Dru? I'd've hung around if I'd thought . . ."

Then his jaw dropped as the picture fell into place. "Oh shit. Jesus Christ on a crutch. Gloria DeLauter."

Seth pressed the heels of his hands to his forehead. "Fuck me."

"Wait a minute, wait a minute." Dan held up both hands.

"You're saying Gloria DeLauter was in Dru's flower shop? Yesterday? That can't be. She's gone, she's been gone for years."

"It was her," Will stated. "It didn't click until just now. We only saw her that one time," he said to Dan, "but it's a pretty strong memory. Her yelling and trying to get Seth in that car. Sybill knocking her down, Foolish snarling like he was going to take a chunk out of her. She's changed, but not that much."

"No." Seth dropped his hands. "Not that much."

"What the hell's she doing back here?" Will demanded. "You're not a kid now. She can't try to drag you off so she can squeeze your brothers for ransom or some shit. She can't be looking for a sloppy mother-son reunion, so what's the point?"

"Will's a little slow," Dan commented, "especially when it comes to the dark side. Money would be the point, right, Seth? Our pal here's a successful artist, climbing up the shiny ladder of fame and fortune. Whatever hole she's been in, she'd have heard about it. Now she's back wanting her cut of the profits."

"That covers most of it," Seth grumbled.

"I still don't get it." Will shoved at his hair. "You don't owe her a damn thing. She's got nothing on you."

"I've been paying her for years."

"Aw hell, Seth."

"She just kept popping up. I gave her money so she'd go away again. Stupid, but I couldn't see what else to do to keep her from hassling my family. They'd gotten the business off the ground, and the kids were coming along. I didn't want her making trouble for them."

"They don't know?" Will asked.

"No, I never told anybody." He'd put it inside, in the

place he tried to keep locked away from what his life had become. "She tracked me down in Rome a few months ago. That's when I figured there wasn't any point in me being three thousand miles away. I wanted to come home. She hit me up again about a week ago. Usually she backs off for longer. A year or two. I thought I'd bought some time. But if she went into Dru's shop, it wasn't because she wanted to buy some fucking daisies."

"What do you want us to do?" Dan asked him.

"Nothing you can do. Just keep a lid on this until I figure it out. Meanwhile, I'll wait. See what she does next."

BUT he couldn't just wait. He spent hours driving to hotels, motels, B and B's trying to find her, without a clue what he'd do if and when he did.

He started the search with more fury than plan, thinking only that he needed to confront her, to drive her off by whatever means necessary. But as he drove to and from hotels, he began to cool off. He began to think as she thought. Coldly.

If she thought Dru mattered to him, she would be used. Tool, weapon, victim. Very likely all three. If and when he found her, he would need to take care to paint his relationship with Dru as a casual one. Even a callous one.

If there was one thing Gloria understood, even respected, it was using someone else. Using anyone else for your own purposes.

As long as she thought he was using Dru for sex and studio space, Dru would be safe.

Then at least one person he cared about wouldn't be smeared with Gloria's brush.

He was forty miles outside of St. Christopher before he found an answer.

The motel boasted a pool, cable TV and family suites. The desk clerk was young and perky enough to make Seth decide she'd been hired as summer help.

He leaned on the counter, spoke in a friendly manner. "Hi. How's it going?"

"Just fine, thanks. Will you be checking in?"

"No, I'm here to see a friend. Gloria DeLauter?"

"DeLauter. One moment, please." She caught her bottom lip between her teeth as she began to tap her keyboard. "Um, could you spell the last name?"

"Sure."

When he had, she tapped again, then looked up apologetically. "I'm sorry. There's no DeLauter registered."

"Huh. Oh, you know what, she might've registered under Harrow. That's the name she uses for business."

"Gloria Harrow?" She went back to the keyboard, then frowned. "I'm afraid Miss Harrow checked out."

"She checked out?" Seth straightened, did everything he could to keep his tone mild. "When?"

"Just this morning. I checked her out myself."

"That's weird. Blond? Thin? About this tall." He held up a hand to estimate.

"Yes, that's right."

"Well, hell, I must've messed up the dates. Thanks." He started out, then turned back casually. "She didn't mention heading down to Saint Christopher, did she?"

"No. Seems to me she headed out the other way. Gosh, I hope nothing's wrong."

"Just a mix-up," he said and let himself feel a cautious trickle of relief. "Thanks for your help."

* * *

HE told himself she was gone. She'd taken the ten thousand and split. She'd checked out Dru, and that was worrying, but Seth imagined Gloria had, once she'd met her, dismissed the idea of him and Dru having any sort of serious relationship she could exploit.

The fact was, he was far from sure where he stood with Dru himself.

She wasn't the type who wore her heart on her sleeve, he thought. Or anywhere else he could get a good look at it. And wasn't part of his fascination with her the very fact that she was so contained?

At least it had been; interest and attraction had melded into something a great deal stronger.

Now he wanted more.

One way he used to see into people was by painting them.

He knew she was far from sold on the idea of posing for him again—particularly in the way he had in mind. But he set up his studio on Sunday morning as if she were in enthusiastic agreement.

"Why won't you just take money for the painting?"

"I don't want money." He arranged the sheets on the bed, ones he'd borrowed from Phil after a raid on his brother's linen closet.

The material was soft, would drape fluidly. And their color, the palest honeysuckle, would be perfect against the bold red of the rose petals and the delicate white of Dru's skin.

He wanted that mix of tones and moods—warm, hot, cool—because she was all of them.

"That's the point of selling your work, isn't it?" She

clutched her robe closed at the throat and cast uneasy glances at the bed. "To make money?"

"I don't paint for money. That's a handy by-product, and I leave it to my rep."

"I'm not a model."

"I don't want a model either." Dissatisfied, he shoved, dragged, pushed, until he'd changed the angle and position of the bed. "Professionals can give you a terrific study. But I find using regular people gives me more. Besides, I can't use anyone but you for this work."

"Why?"

"Because it's you."

She hissed between her teeth as he opened the first bag of petals. "What does that *mean*?"

"I see you." He tossed petals on the sheets in seemingly random patterns. "Just relax and leave it to me."

"I can't possibly relax when I'm lying naked on a bed strewn with rose petals and you're staring at me."

"Sure you can." He added more petals, stepped back, considered.

"We made love on that bed a few hours ago."

"Exactly." Now he looked at her, smiled. "It'd help if you thought about that when I'm working."

"Oh, did you have sex with me to put me in the right mood?"

"No, I had sex with you because I can't seem to get enough of you. But the mood's another handy by-product."

"Let me tell you where you can put your handy by-product."

He only laughed, then grabbed her before she could stride into the bathroom. "I'm crazy about you."

"Stop it." She seethed as he nibbled on her earlobe. "I mean it, Seth."

"Absolutely crazy. You're so beautiful. Don't be shy."

"You can't get me to strip with flattery or cajolery."

"Cajolery. Very cool word. How about appealing to your appreciation of art? Just try." He skimmed his lips down to hers. "Give me one hour. If you're still uncomfortable, we'll rethink this. The human body's natural."

"So's cotton underwear."

"It sure is, the way you wear it."

And of course, he made her laugh. "One hour?" She eased back. "And I get the painting?"

"Deal. Now is this music okay with you, or do you want me to put on something to strip by."

"Oh, you're very funny."

"Let's just take this off." He untied the robe, eased it gently from her shoulders. "I love looking at you. I love the shape of you." He spoke softly, easing her toward the bed. "The way your skin looks in the light. I want to show you how you look to me."

"How is seducing me supposed to help me relax?"

"Lie down. Don't think about anything yet. I want you turned on your side, facing me. Your arm like this." He lifted it, draped it low over her breasts.

She did her best to ignore the sensation along her skin where his fingertips, his knuckles brushed. "I feel . . . exposed."

"Revealed," he corrected. "It's different. Slide this knee up. Keep this arm angled down. Palm up, open. Good. Comfortable?"

"I can't believe I'm doing this. This is not me."

"Yes, it is." He reached into the bag, scattered petals over her, letting some drift into her open palm before he placed some more deliberately on her hair, on the slope of her breasts, over her arm, along the line of hip and leg.

"Try to hold that for me." He stepped back, ran his gaze over her in a way that made her skin flush.

"Seth."

"Just try not to move too much. I need your body first. I'm not too worried about the head and face just yet. Talk to me." He retreated behind the canvas.

"About what? How ridiculous I feel?"

"Why don't we go for a sail this evening? We'll bum dinner off of Anna and go out after."

"I can't think about dinner, and I certainly don't want to think about your sister-in-law when I'm . . . People are going to see this, see *me*. Naked."

"People are going to see a painting of a striking woman."

"My mother," Dru said in sudden horror.

"How is she? She and your father still back together?"

"As far as I know. They went to Paris, but they're not happy with me."

"Hard to make everybody happy all the time." He sketched the curve of her shoulder, the stem of her neck, the slender line of torso. "When's the last time you were in Paris?"

"About three years ago. My aunt's wedding. She lives there now—outside of Paris, actually, but they keep a flat in the city."

So he talked to her of Paris, satisfied when he saw the tension draining out of her body. Then he began to paint.

The contrast of the red against white skin, the glint of light, the delicacy of the sheets with their deeper shadows in the soft folds. He wanted the elegance of her open hand and the strong muscles in her calf.

She shifted slightly, but he said nothing to correct her pose. The conversation he carried on to keep her relaxed was in a different part of his mind. The rest was steeped in the image he created with paint and brush.

Here was his faerie queen again, but now she was awake. Now she was aware.

She stopped thinking about the pose, her modesty. It was an incredible thrill to watch him work. An exhilaration. Did he realize, she wondered, how the intensity came over him? The way his eyes changed, took on a certain fierceness of effort that was in direct opposition to the casual flow of his words.

Did he see himself? Surely he must. He had to know the fluidity and focus that were so much a part of his technique. The sexuality of it. And the beauty, the power, that made the subject he took along with him feel beautiful, feel powerful.

She forgot the time limit they'd set. Whatever fantasy he'd created in his mind, she'd become too much a part of it to break the spell.

Did the subject always fall in love with the artist? she wondered. Was it just the nature of things for her to feel this outrageous intimacy with him, and this stupefying need for him?

How had he become the first man, the only man, she wanted to give to? To give anything he asked. It was frightening to know it, to understand that love could mean giving up so much of self.

What would be left of her if she yielded to it?

When his gaze moved over her, as if absorbing what she was, she shivered.

"Are you cold?" His voice was impatient. Then, as if he turned a knob, he spoke more easily. "Sorry, are you cold?"

"No. Yes. Maybe a bit. A little stiff."

He frowned, then glanced down at his wrist for the watch he'd once again forgotten to put on. "Probably hit the hour."

"At least." She worked up a smile.

"You need a break. You want some water? Juice? Did I buy juice?"

"Water's fine. Can I sit up now?"

"Sure, sure." He wasn't looking at her now in any case, but at the work.

"And can I see what you've done so far?"

"Uh-huh." He set down his brush, picked up a rag. And never took his eyes off the canvas.

Dru slipped out of bed, picked up the robe and, wrapping herself into it, walked to him.

The bed was the center of the canvas, with much of the outer space still white and unpainted. She was the center of the bed.

He'd yet to paint her face, so she was only a body—long limbs adorned with rose petals. Her arm covered her breasts, but it wasn't a gesture of modesty. One of flirtation, she thought. Of invitation. Of knowledge.

Only a fraction done, she realized, and already brilliant. Did she ever look and see light and shadow playing so beautifully?

He'd chosen the bed well. The slim iron bars offered simplicity and a timelessness. The delicate tone of the sheets warmed her skin and was yet another contrast to all the rich, bold strokes.

"It's beautiful."

"It will be," he agreed. "This is a good start."

"You knew I wouldn't stop you once I'd seen what you'd done."

"If you'd looked and hadn't seen what I wanted you to see, I'd have failed. Drusilla."

She studied him. Her pulse scrambled when she saw that same narrowed intensity on his face, the strength of focus, of purpose. The need that vibrated around him when he worked.

But now, it was for her.

"I've never wanted anyone like this," she managed. "I don't know what it means."

"I don't give a damn." He pulled her against him, captured her mouth.

He was already yanking off her robe as he dragged her toward the bed.

A part of her—that had been born and bred in luxury, in grace—was shocked at the treatment. Shocked more by her response to it. And the part that responded triumphed.

She tore at his shirt even as they tumbled onto sheets strewn with rose petals.

"Touch me. Oh, touch me." She clawed her way over him. "The way I imagine you touching me when you're painting me."

His hands streaked over her, rough and needy, stroking the flames that had simmered as she'd lain naked for him. It energized her, sparked in her blood until she felt herself become a quivering mass of raw need tangled with reckless greed.

Her mouth warred with his in a frantic battle to give.

He was lost in her, trapped in the maze of emotions she'd wound through him. Steeped in the flood of sensations she aroused by every caress, every taste, every word.

Hunger for more stumbled against a rocky ledge of love.

When he drew her close, held—held tight—he fell over.

Some change, some tenderness eked through the urgency. It swamped her, and she went pliant against him.

Now mouths met, a long, sumptuous kiss. Now hands brushed skin delicately. The air thickened, filled with the scents of roses, of paint, of turpentine, all stirred by the breeze off the water.

She rose over him, and looked down at love.

Her throat ached. Her heart swelled. Unbearably moved, she lowered her lips to his until her throat ached from the sweetness.

This, she knew, was more than pleasure, beyond desire and need. This, if only she could let it, was everything.

If it was consuming, then she would be consumed. And she took him inside her, gave herself over to the everything.

Slow and silky, deep and intent, they moved together. Trembled as they climbed, sighed as they floated. It seemed to her colors, the rich bold tones he'd used in the painting, spread inside her.

He lifted to her, finding her mouth with his again as his arms enfolded her. Wrapped tight, they surrendered.

For a time they didn't speak. She kept her head on his shoulder, looked at the light through the window.

He'd opened a window, she realized. One she'd been so certain needed to remain shut. Now the light, the air was streaming through.

How could she ever close it again?

"I've never made love on rose petals before," she said quietly. "I liked it."

"Me too."

She plucked one from his back. "But now look what we've done." She held it out to him. "The artist is going to be very annoyed with us."

"He should be, but he's not. Besides"—joy, pure joy, was running inside him in long, loose strides—"the artist is very inventive."

"I can verify that."

"Give me another hour."

She leaned back to stare at him. "You're going to paint again? Now?"

"Trust me. It's important, really important. Just—here." She was still gaping at him when he shifted her and gave her a light shove back onto the bed. "Do you remember the pose, or do you need me to set you?"

"Do I . . . oh, for heaven sake." More than a little miffed, she rolled to her side, flopped her arm over her breasts.

"Okay, I'll set you." Cheerful, energized, he moved her, redistributed rose petals, stepped back, then forward again to make more adjustments.

"It's okay to pout now, but turn your head toward me."

"I'm not pouting. I'm entirely too mature to pout."

"Whatever." He grabbed his jeans, tugged them on. "I need the angle of your head . . . chin up. Whoa, not that far, sugar. That's better," he said, grabbing the brush he needed. "Tilt your head, just a . . . Ah, yeah, that's it. You're amazing, you're perfect. You're the best."

"You're full of shit."

"Now, that's mature." He went to work. "And a little crude coming from you."

"I can be crude when the occasion calls for it." As far as she was concerned, having a man more interested in his work than in holding her when she'd just fallen in love was the perfect occasion.

"Okay, shut up. Just look at me now, listen to the music."

"Fine. I've nothing to say to you anyway."

Maybe not, he thought, but her face had a great deal to say. And he wanted it all. He painted the arrogant angle of it, the strong chin with that lovely shadow in the center, the sculpted cheekbones, the gorgeous shape of her eyes, eyebrows, the straight patrician line of her nose.

But for the rest, for her mouth, for the look *in* her eyes, he needed something more.

"Don't move," he ordered as he came back to the bed. "I want you to think about how much I want you."

"I beg your pardon?"

"Think about how powerful you are, the way you look. As if you're just waking up and you see me looking at you. Craving you. You've got all the power here."

"Is that so?"

"I'm desperate for you." He leaned down, his lips a whisper from hers. "You know it. All you have to do is crook a finger. All you have to do is smile." He laid his lips on hers, took the kiss slow and deep, gave her a taste of his yearning. "And I'm a slave."

He backed up, his eyes on hers as he eased around the canvas. "It's you, Drusilla. You."

Her lips curved, a kind of knowing. In her eyes an invitation shimmered that was both luminous and languid.

He saw everything he wanted in that one moment, the awareness, the confidence, the desire and the promise.

"Don't change."

He saw nothing but her, felt nothing but her to the point where he was almost unaware of his own hand moving. Of mixing the paint, dabbing it, stroking it, all but breathing it onto the paper so that her face bloomed for him.

He caught what he could, knew he would see that light on her face forever. It would be there when he needed to complete the work.

It would be there, in his mind and heart, whenever he was alone. Whenever he was lonely.

"I can do it," he said, and laid aside his brush. "When I do, it'll be the most important thing I've ever done. Do you know why?"

She couldn't speak now, could barely breathe over the tumult of her heart. She could only shake her head.

"Because this is what you are to me. What I knew, somehow, you'd be to me from the first moment. Drusilla." He stepped toward the bed. "I love you."

Her breath shuddered out. "I know." She pressed a hand to her heart, in wonder that it didn't simply burst free in one mad leap of joy. "I know. I'm terrified. Oh God, Seth, I'm terrified, because I love you, too."

She sprang up, scattering rose petals, and leaped into his arms.

FIFTEEN

⁓

HURRICANE ANNA SWEPT through the house and had her men ducking for cover. She blew through the living room, snatching socks, shoes, ball caps, empty glasses. Those who didn't move fast enough to evacuate were forced to catch hurled items, or get beaned.

By the time she reached the kitchen, the survivors had made themselves scarce. Even the dog had gone into hiding.

From what he hoped was a safe distance, Seth cleared his throat. "Um, Anna, it's just dinner."

She rounded on him. He figured he outweighed her by a good forty pounds, and still his belly contracted in something like fear at the kill lights in her dark eyes. "Just dinner?" she repeated. "And I suppose you think food just makes itself?"

"No. But whatever we were having is fine. Is great," he amended. "Dru's not fussy or anything."

"Oh, Dru's not fussy or anything," Anna tossed back as

she yanked open cupboards, pulled out ingredients, slammed them shut again. "So it's just fine to give me an hour's notice that we're having company for dinner."

"It's not company, exactly. I thought we'd just grab something, then—"

"Oh, you thought you'd just grab something." She walked toward him with the slow, deliberate steps that struck terror into the very center of his heart. "Maybe we'll just order pizza and have her pick it up on the way."

Cam, hoping her skewering Seth like a bug would keep her attention diverted, tried to sidle in to sneak a beer out of the fridge. He should've known better.

"And you." She bared her teeth at Cam. "You think you can march into my kitchen in your dirty shoes? Don't you even think about plopping your butt down in the living room, sucking on that beer. You're not king around here."

He had the beer, and whipped it behind his back just in case she got any ideas. "Hey, I'm an innocent bystander."

"There are no innocents in this house. Stay!" she ordered when Seth tried to slip out of the room. "I'm not finished with you."

"Okay, okay. Look, what's the big deal? Somebody's always dropping by for dinner. Kevin had that freak friend of his over just the other night."

"He's not a freak," Kevin called out from the safety of the living room.

"Hey, he had a nose ring and kept quoting Dylan Thomas."

"Oh, Marcus. He's a freak. I thought you meant Jerry."

"See?" Seth lifted his hands. "We've got so many people in and out of here we can't even keep them straight."

"This is different." Since Anna had just pulled a large

chef's knife out of the block, and Cam, the coward, had deserted the field, Seth decided not to argue.

"Okay. I'm sorry. I'll help."

"Damn right you will. Red potatoes." She stabbed the knife toward the pantry. "Scrub."

"Yes 'm."

"Quinn!"

"What?" Voice aggrieved, Cam eased back into the doorway but kept the beer out of sight. "I didn't do anything."

"Exactly. Shower. Do *not* throw your towel on the floor. Shave."

"Shave?" He rubbed a hand over his chin and looked harassed. "It's not morning."

"Shave," she repeated and began to mince garlic with such violent enthusiasm, Seth tucked his fingers safely in his pockets, just in case.

"Jesus Christ." Cam curled his lip at Seth and stalked away.

"Jake! Pick up your crap on the floor of the den. Kevin! Run the vacuum."

"Why do you want them to hate me?" Seth pleaded.

Anna's only answer was a steely look. "When you've scrubbed those potatoes, I want them cut into chunks. About this size," she said, holding up her thumb and forefinger. "When you finish that, put out the guest soap and towels in the downstairs bath. The first one I catch using the guest soaps or leaving handprints on the towels gets their fingers chopped off," she called out.

She dumped ingredients into a bowl and whisked.

"It's not all my crap on the den floor, I want you to know." Jake stomped in, shot Seth a sneer. "Lots of other people throw crap around this place, too."

"What do you think you're doing?" Anna demanded as Jake pulled open the refrigerator.

"I was just going to get a—"

"No, you're not. I want you to set the table—"

"It's Kev's night to set and clear. I'm on dish duty."

"Tonight you set and wash."

"How come I have to set and wash? I didn't invite some dopey girl to dinner."

"Because I said so. Set the table in the dining room. Use the good dishes."

"How come we're eating in there? It's not Thanksgiving."

"And the linen napkins," she added. "The ones with roses on them. Six place settings. Wash your hands first."

"Jeez. She's just a girl. You'd think the Queen of England or somebody was coming over."

He stalked to the sink, ran water while he curled his lip, exactly as his father had done. "I'm *never* bringing a girl over here."

"I'll remind you of that in a couple of years." Because the idea of her little boy bringing a girl home to dinner made her eyes sting, Anna sniffed and poured marinade over chicken breasts.

"I'll think twice about it myself," Seth muttered under his breath.

"I beg your pardon?"

He winced. "Nothing. It's just, well hell, Anna, I've brought girls over before. Dru even ate here before and you didn't go into a fit over it."

"That's different. She dropped by unexpectedly, and you barely knew her."

"Yeah, but—"

"And you may have brought girls here before, but you

never invited the woman you're in love with to dinner before. Men don't understand anything. They understand nothing at all, and I don't know why I've been plagued by a herd of them."

"Don't cry. Oh man. Oh God. Please, don't do that."

"I'll cry if I want to. You just try to stop me."

"Nice going," Jake muttered and fled to the dining room.

"I'll make the chicken." Desperate, Seth abandoned his potatoes and rushed over to stroke Anna's hair. "You just tell me what you want me to do with it. And the rest of it, too. And I'll do the dishes after, and . . ." He stepped back. "I never said I was in love with Dru."

"What, now I'm blind and stupid?" She grabbed the olive oil and Dijon to mix up her special sauce for the potatoes. "Get me the damn Worcestershire sauce."

Instead, he took her hands, then ran his up her arms. "I barely finished telling her. How come you know this stuff?"

"Because, you stupid idiot, I love you. Get away from me. I'm busy."

He laid his cheek on hers, and sighed.

"Damn it." She threw her arms around him. "I want you to be happy. I want you to be so happy."

"I am." He pressed his face into her hair. "A little spooked along with it."

"It's not real if you're not a little spooked." She held tight another moment, then let go. "Now get out of here. Guest soaps, towels. Toilet seats down. And find a pair of jeans that doesn't have holes."

"I'm not sure I have any. And thanks, Anna."

"You're welcome. But you're still doing the dishes."

From the dining room came Jake's enthusiastic *woo-hoo*.

* * *

" I appreciate your letting me impose this way. Again."

Anna chose a dark blue vase for the cheerful black-eyed Susans Dru had brought her. "We're happy to have you. It's no trouble at all."

"I can't imagine a last-minute dinner guest, after you've worked all day, is no trouble at all."

"Oh, it's just chicken. Nothing fussy." Anna smiled thinly as Jake rolled his eyes dramatically behind Dru's back. "Is there something you want, Jake?"

"Just wondering when we're going to eat."

"You'll be the first to know." She set the flowers on the kitchen table. "Go tell Seth to come open this lovely wine Dru brought for us. We'll have a glass before dinner."

"People could starve around here," Jake complained—in a whisper—as he trooped out of the kitchen.

"Is there anything I can do to help?" Dru asked. The kitchen smelled fantastic. Something, she assumed it was the chicken, was simmering in a covered skillet.

"We're under control, thanks." With a deft hand, Anna lifted the lid on the skillet, shook it lightly by the handle, poked with a kitchen fork, then set the lid back. "Do you cook?"

"Not like this. I've gotten very adept at boiling pasta, nuking up jarred sauce and mixing it together."

"Oh. My heart," Anna said, and laughed. "Raw clay. I love molding raw clay. One of these days I'll show you how to make a nice, basic red sauce, and see where we can go from there. Seth." Anna beamed at him when he came in. "Open the wine, will you? Pour Dru a glass. You can take her out and show her how my perennials are coming along while I finish putting dinner together."

"I'm glad to help," Dru protested. "I may not cook, but I follow instructions well."

"Next time. Just go out with Seth, enjoy your wine. We'll be ready in ten minutes."

Anna shooed them out, then, delighted with herself, rubbed her hands together before diving into the rest of the preparations.

In fifteen minutes, they were seated in the rarely used dining room, a half dozen tea lights flickering. The dog, Dru noted, had been banished.

"These are beautiful dishes," Dru commented.

"I love them. Cam and I bought them in Italy, on our honeymoon."

"If you break one," Jake put in as he attacked his chicken, "you get shackled in the basement so the rats can eat your ears."

"Jake!" With a baffled laugh, Anna passed the potatoes to her left. "What a thing to say. We don't even have a basement."

"That's what Dad said you'd do, even if you had to dig a basement. Right, Dad?"

"I don't know what you're talking about. Eat some asparagus."

"Do I have to?"

"If I have to, you have to."

"Neither of you have to." Anna prayed for patience.

"Cool, more for me." Kevin reached enthusiastically for the platter before he caught his mother's warning look. "What? I like it."

"Then ask for it, Mr. Smooth, instead of diving across the table. We don't let them out of the kennel very often," Cam told Dru.

"I always wanted brothers."

"What for?" Jake asked her. "They mostly just pound on you."

"Well, you do look pretty well battered," she considered. "I always thought it would be fun to have someone to talk to—and to pound on. Someone to take some of the heat when my parents were annoyed or irritated. When you're an only child, there's no one to diffuse the focus, if you know what I mean. And no one to eat the asparagus when you don't want it."

"Yeah, but Kev swiped half the good Halloween candy last year."

"Jeez, get over it."

Jake eyed his brother. "I never forget. All data is stored in my memory banks. And one day, candy pig, you will pay."

"You're such a geek."

"Thesbo."

"That's Jake's latest insult." Seth gestured with his wineglass. "A play on thespian, since Kev's into that."

"Rhymes with lesbo," Jake explained helpfully while Anna stifled a groan. "It's a slick way of calling him a girl."

"Clever. I enjoyed your school play last month," she said to Kevin. "I thought it was wonderfully done. Are you thinking of going on to study theater in college?"

"Yeah. I really like it. Plays are cool, but I like movies even better. The guys and I have made some really awesome videos. The last one we did, *Slashed*, was the best. It's about this one-armed psycho killer who stalks these hunters through the woods. Carves them up, one by one, in revenge because one of them shot off his arm in this freak hunting accident. It has flashbacks and everything. Want to see it?"

"Sure."

"I didn't know you went to Kevin's play."

Dru shifted her attention to Seth. "I like to keep up with community events. And I love little theater."

"We could've gone together."

She picked up her wine, smiled at him over it in a way that made Anna's heart swell. "Like a date?"

"Dru has a philosophical objection to dating," Seth said, with his eyes on hers. "Why is that?"

"Because it often involves men who don't interest me. But primarily I haven't had time for that sort of socializing since I moved here. Starting up, then running the shop have been priorities."

"What made you decide to be a florist?" Anna asked her.

"I had to ask myself what I could do—then out of that, what I'd enjoy the most. I enjoyed flowers. I took some courses, and discovered I had a talent with them."

"It takes a lot of courage to start a business, and to come to a new place to do it."

"I'd have withered if I'd stayed in Washington. That sounds dramatic. I needed a new place. My own place. Everything I considered doing, everywhere I considered going, kept circling back around to Saint Christopher and a flower shop. A flower shop puts you right in the deep end of the pool."

"How is that?" Cam wondered.

"You become instantly intimate with the community. When you sell flowers, you know who's having a birthday, an anniversary. You know who's died, who's had a baby. Who's in love, or making up from a fight, who got a promotion, who's ill. And in a small town, like this one, you invariably get details along with it."

She thought for a moment, then spoke in a lazy Shore

accent. "Old Mrs. Wilcox died—would've been eighty-nine come September. Came home from the market and had a stroke right there in the kitchen while she was putting away her canned goods. Too bad she didn't make things up with her sister before it was too late. They haven't spoke word one to each other in twelve years."

"That's good." Amused, Cam propped his chin on his hand. More than looks and brains, he thought. There was warmth and humor in there, too. Once you tickled it out of her.

Seth was toast.

"And I thought it was just pushing posies," he added.

"Oh, it's a great deal more than that. When a man comes in, frantic because he just remembered his wedding anniversary, it's my job not to simply put the right flowers into his hands, but to remain discreet."

"Like a priest," Cam put in and made her laugh.

"Not so far from that. You'd be amazed at the confessions I hear. It's all in a day's work."

"You love it," Anna murmured.

"I do. I really do. I love the business itself, and I love being part of something. In Washington . . ." She caught herself, a bit amazed at how easily she'd rambled. "Things were different," she said at length. "This is what I was looking for."

H E followed her home, where they sat on her porch steps in the warm summer night, watching fireflies dance in the dark.

"You had a good time?"

"I had a wonderful time. The dinner, getting to know your family a little better. The sail."

"Good." He brought her hand to his lips. "Because Anna's going to pass the word, and you'll be expected to repeat the performance at Grace's, and at Sybill's."

"Oh." She hadn't thought of that. "I'll need to reciprocate. I'll need to have everyone over for . . ."

She'd have to have it catered, of course. And she'd have to determine how best to keep a number of teenagers entertained.

"I'm out of my league," she admitted. "The kind of dinner party I'm used to hosting isn't what's called for here."

"You want to have everyone over?" The idea delighted him. "We'll get a grill and cook out. We'll toss on some steaks and corn on the cob. Keep it simple."

We, she thought. Somehow they'd slid from individuals into *we*. She wasn't quite sure how she felt about it.

"I've been meaning to ask you something." He leaned back on the step so he could study her profile. "What's it like to grow up filthy rich?"

That eyebrow winged, the way he loved. "We preferred the term 'lavishly wealthy' to 'filthy rich.' And obviously, it has its points."

"I bet. We sort of established why the lavishly wealthy society chick is running a flower shop on the waterfront, but how come she doesn't have household help, or a staff of employees?"

"I have Mr. G, who's worked out perfectly. He's flexible, dependable, and he knows and loves flowers. And I plan on hiring someone else, to work part-time in the shop. I needed to make certain there'd be enough business to justify it first. I'm going to start looking very soon."

"But you do the books."

"I like doing the books."

"And the ordering, and the inventory, whatever."

"I like—"

"Yeah, got that. Don't get defensive." It amused him when her shoulders stiffened. "You like manning the rudder. Nothing wrong with that."

"Speaking of rudders, I like the sloop design. I like it very much. I'm going to contact Phillip and have him draw up the contract."

"Good, but you're evading the subject. How come you don't have a housekeeper?"

"If this is a plug for Grace's service, Aubrey's already nagging me about it. I'm going to talk to her."

"It wasn't, but that's a good idea." He ran his fingers down her leg, an unconscious gesture of intimacy. "Spread the wealth, and free up your time. A twofer."

"You're awfully interested in wealth all of a sudden."

"In you," he corrected. "Sybill's the only person I know, really know, who came from money. And I get the drift that her family's pretty small potatoes compared to yours. Your mother comes down to see you, driven by a uniformed chauffeur. Snazzy stuff. You don't even have somebody coming in to scrub the john. So I ask myself how come that is. Does she *like* scrubbing johns?"

"It was a childhood dream of mine," she said dryly.

"Anytime you want to fulfill the dream in the studio bathroom, feel free."

"That's very generous of you."

"Well, I love you. I do what I can."

She nearly sighed. He loved her. And he wanted to understand her. "Money," she began, "great amounts of money solve a lot of problems. And create others. But one way or the other, rich or poor, if you stub your toe, your toe hurts. It can also insulate you, so that you don't meet or develop friendships with people outside that charmed circle.

You gain a great deal, you miss a great deal. Certainly you miss a great deal when your parents feel so strongly about shielding you from a variety of things out of that circle."

She turned to look at him now. "That's not 'poor little rich girl' talk. It's just fact. I had a privileged upbringing. I never wanted for a single material thing, and will never have to. I had an exceptional education, was allowed to travel extensively. And if I'd stayed in that charmed circle, I think I'd have died by inches."

She shook her head. "There's that drama again."

"I don't think it's dramatic. There are all kinds of hunger. If you don't get fed, you starve."

"Then I guess we could say I needed a different menu. In the Washington house, my mother runs a staff of sixteen. It's a beautiful home, perfectly presented. This is the first place I've had alone. When I moved to my own place in Georgetown, they—despite my telling them I didn't want or need live-in help—hired a housekeeper for me as a housewarming gift. So, I was stuck."

"You could have refused."

Dru only shook her head. "Not as easy as you think, and it would have created more conflict when I'd just gone through the battle of moving out on my own. In any case, it wasn't the housekeeper's fault. She was a perfectly nice, absolutely efficient and completely pleasant woman. But I didn't want her there. I kept her because my parents were frantic enough at the idea of me no longer living at home, and kept on me about how worried they were about me, how much better they felt knowing I had someone reliable living with me. And I was just tired of the hammering."

"Nobody pushes buttons better than family."

"Not in my experience," she agreed. "It seems ridiculous to complain about having someone who'll cook, clean, run errands and so on. But you give up your privacy in ex-change for the convenience and leisure. You are never, never alone. And no matter how pleasant, how loyal, how discreet a household staff may be, they know things about you. They know when you've had an argument with your parents, or your lover. They know what you eat, or don't eat. When you sleep, or don't sleep. They know if you've had sex, or haven't had sex. Every mood, every move, and if they're with you long enough, every thought you have is shared with them.

"I won't have that here." She let out a breath. "Besides, I like taking care of myself. Seeing to my own details. I like knowing I'm good at it. But I'm not sure how good I'll be at putting together a dinner party for the Quinn horde."

"If it makes you feel any better, Anna was a maniac for the hour before you got there tonight."

"Really?" The idea warmed her. "It does make me feel better. She always seems so completely in charge."

"She is. She scares us boneless."

"You worship her. Every one of you. It's fascinating. This is very new territory for me, Seth."

"For me, too."

"No." She turned her head. "It's not. Family gatherings, whether they're casual or traditional, impromptu or planned, are very old territory for you. You don't need a map. You're very lucky to have them."

"I know it." He thought of where he'd come from. He thought of Gloria. "I know it."

"Yes, it shows. You're all so *full* of each other. They made room for me because you asked them to. You care for me, so they'll care for me. It won't be like that with my family. If and when you meet them, you'll be very care-fully questioned, studied, analyzed and judged."

"So, they're looking out for you."

"No, not so much for me as themselves. The family name—names," she corrected. "The position. Discreet inquiries will be made as to your financial stability, to ensure you're not after my money. While my mother will be, initially, thrilled that I'm involved with someone with your panache in art circles—"

"Panache. You do use those cool words."

"It's shallow."

"Oh, give her a break." He ruffled her hair as he might have a ten-year-old boy's. "I'm not going to be insulted because someone's impressed with my reputation as an artist."

"You may be insulted when your background is quietly and thoroughly investigated, when the credit line on Boats by Quinn is checked."

The idea of the background check had his blood chilling. "Well, for Christ's sake."

"You need to know. This is standard operating procedure in my family. Jonah passed with high marks, and his political connections were a bonus. Which is why no one was particularly pleased with me for calling off the wedding. I'm sorry. I know I'm spoiling the mood of the evening, but I realized with the way things seem to be moving between us you needed to know this sooner rather than later."

"Okay. Tell me this sooner rather than later." He took her hand, toyed with her fingers. "If they don't like what they find, do things stop moving between us?"

"I pulled myself away from there, from them, because I couldn't live that way." And curled her fingers into his. "I make up my own mind, and heart."

"Then let's not worry about it." He drew her into his arms. "I love you. I don't care what anyone else thinks."

* * *

HE wanted it to be just that simple.

He'd learned that love was the single most powerful force. It could overcome and overset greed, pettiness, hate, envy. It changed lives.

God knew it had changed his.

He believed in the untapped power of love, whether it showed itself in passion or selflessness, in fury or in tenderness.

But love was rarely simple. It was its facets, its complexities that made it such a strong force.

So, loving Dru, he faced the fact that he would have to tell her everything. He wasn't born at the age of ten. She had a right to know where he'd come from, and how. He had to find the way to tell her of his childhood. Of Gloria.

Eventually.

He told himself he deserved the time to just be with her, to enjoy the freshness of their feelings for each other. He made excuses.

He wanted her to get to know and become more comfortable with his family. He needed to finish the painting. He wanted to put his time and effort into building her boat, so that when it was done it would somehow belong to both of them.

There was no time limit, after all. No need to rush everything. Days passed into weeks and Gloria made no contact. It was easy to convince himself she'd gone again. Maybe this time she'd stay gone.

He bargained with himself. He wouldn't think about any of it until after the July Fourth celebrations. Every year, the Quinns held a huge come-one, come-all picnic. Family, friends, neighbors gathered at the house, as they had since Ray and Stella's day, to eat, drink, gossip, swim in the cool water of the inlet and watch the fireworks.

But before the beer and crab, they were due for champagne and caviar. With obvious reluctance, and after considerable nagging by both her parents, Dru had agreed to attend one of the Washington galas with Seth as her escort.

"Shit, look at you." Cam stood in the bedroom doorway and whistled at Seth in his tux. "All slicked up in your monkey suit."

"You only wish you could look this good." Seth shot his cuffs. "I get the feeling I'm going to be the artist on display at this little soiree. I nearly bought a cape and beret instead of a tux. But I restrained myself."

He began to fuss with the tie. "This rig was Phil's pick. Classic, according to him, but not dated."

"He oughta know. Stop messing with that. Jesus." Cam straightened from the doorjamb and crossed over to fuss with Seth's tie himself. "You've got more nerves than a virgin on prom night."

"Yeah, maybe. I'll be swimming in a lot of blue blood this evening. I don't want to drown in it."

Cam's eyes shifted up, met his. "Money don't mean jack. You're as good as any of them and better than most. Quinns don't take second place to anyone."

"I want to marry her, Cam."

There was a little clutch in his belly. The trip from boy to man, he thought, never took as long as you thought it should. "Yeah, I got that."

"When you marry someone you take on their family, their baggage, the whole shot."

"That's right."

"I deal with hers, she has to deal with mine. I get through tonight in one piece, she makes it though the insanity around here on the Fourth, then . . . I have to tell her about before. About Gloria, a lot more than I have. I have to tell her about . . . all of it."

"If you're thinking she'll run, then she's not the one for you. And knowing women, and I do, she's not the running type."

"I'm not thinking she'll run. I don't know what she'll do. What I'll do. But I have to lay it out for her and give her the chance to decide where she wants to go from there. I've put it off too long already."

"It's history. But it's your history so you have to tell her. Then put it away again." Cam stepped back. "Real slick." He gave Seth's biceps a squeeze, knowing it would ease the trouble on his face. "Oooh, you've been lifting."

"Cram it."

Seth was laughing when he left the house, grinning when he opened his car door. And the panic slammed into his throat like a fist when he saw the note on the front seat.

Tomorrow night, ten o'clock.
Miller's Bar, St. Michael's.
We'll talk.

She'd come here, he thought as he balled the paper in his hand. To his home. Within feet of his family.

Yeah, they'd talk. Damn right they'd talk.

SIXTEEN

⟊⟊⟊

H E R E M E M B E R E D TO tell her she looked
beautiful. She did, in the stoplight-red dress that
skimmed down her body and left her back bare but for a
crisscross of skinny, glittering straps.

He remembered to smile, to make conversation on the
drive to Washington. He ordered himself to relax. He
would deal with Gloria as he always dealt with her.

He told himself she could take nothing from him but
money.

And he knew it was a lie.

Wasn't that what Stella had intimated in the dream? he
thought now. It wasn't just money Gloria wanted. She
wanted to gouge at his heart until every bit of happiness
bled out of it.

She hated him for being whole. On some level, he'd always known that.

"I appreciate your going to all this trouble tonight."

He glanced over, brushed a hand over hers. "Come on.

It's not every day I get to mix with the movers and shakers at some spiffy party. Very swank," he added.

"I'd rather be at home, sitting on the porch swing."

"You don't have a porch swing."

"I keep meaning to buy one. I'd like to be sitting on my imaginary porch swing, having a nice glass of wine while the sun sets." And so, she thought, would he.

Whatever he said, something was wrong. She knew his face so well now—well enough that she could close her eyes and paint it, feature by feature, in her mind. There was definitely trouble lurking behind his eyes.

"Two hours," she said. "We'll stay two hours, then we're gone."

"This is your deal, Dru. We'll stay as long as you like."

"I wouldn't be going at all if I could've avoided it. My parents double-teamed me on this one. I wonder if we ever really get beyond the point where a parent can emotionally blackmail us into doing something we don't want to do."

Her words made him think of Gloria, and dread curled in his stomach. "It's just a party, sugar."

"Oh, if only. A party's where you go to have fun, to relax and enjoy the company of people you have something in common with. I don't have anything in common with these people anymore. Maybe I never did. My mother wants to show you off, and I'm going to let her because she wore me down."

"Well, you've got to admit, I look terrific tonight."

"Can't argue with that. And you're trying to cheer me up. So thanks. I'll promise to do the same on the way home when you're glazed and incoherent from being interrogated."

"Does it matter to you, what they think of me?"

"Of course." Amused with herself, she took out her lipstick and missed the way his jaw tightened. "I want all those people who gave me that sticky sympathy over my breakup with Jonah, all the ones who brought it up to my face hoping I'd say or do something they could dine out on the following evening, to take one look at you. I want them to think, Well, well, Dru certainly landed on her feet, didn't she? She bagged herself *il maestro giovane.*"

Tension settled on the back of his neck, too weighty to be shrugged off. "So, I'm a status symbol now," he said, and tried to keep it light.

She freshened her lipstick, capped the tube. "Better than a Harry Winston diamond necklace. It's mean, it's petty, it's pitifully female. But I don't care. It's a revelation to realize I've just that much of my mother in me that I want to show you off, too."

"There's no escaping where we come from. No matter how far we run."

"Now that's depressing. If I believed that, I'd jump off a cliff. Believe me, I am *not* going to end up chairing committees and giving ladies' teas on Wednesday afternoons."

Something in the quality of his silence had her reaching over to touch his arm. "Two hours, Seth. Maximum."

"It'll be fine," he told her.

S E T H got his first real taste of Dru's previous life minutes after they entered the ballroom.

Groups of people mixed and mingled to the muted background music of a twelve-piece orchestra. The decor was a patriotic red, white and blue echoed in flowers, table linens, balloons and bunting.

A huge ice sculpture of the American flag had been carved as if it were waving in a breeze.

There was a great deal of white on the female guests as well, which took its form in diamonds and pearls. Dress was conservative, traditional and very, very rich.

Part political rally, he supposed. Part social event, part gossip mill.

He'd do it in acrylics, he thought. All sharp colors and shapes with bright crystal light.

"Drusilla." Katherine swept up, resplendent in military blue. "Don't you look lovely? But I thought we said you'd wear the white Valentino." She kissed Dru's cheek and, with an indulgent *tsk-tsk,* brushed her fingers over Dru's hair.

"And Seth." She held out a hand to him. "How wonderful to see you again. I was afraid you must be stuck in traffic. I was so hoping you and Dru would come stay with us for the weekend so you wouldn't have that terrible drive."

It was the first he'd heard of it, but he rose to the occasion. "I appreciate the invitation, but I couldn't get away. I hope you'll forgive me and save me a dance. That way I'll be able to say I danced with the two most beautiful women in the room."

"Aren't you charming?" She pinked up prettily. "And you can be certain I'll do just that. Come now, I must introduce you. So many people are looking forward to meeting you."

Before she could turn, Drusilla's father strode up. He was a striking man with silver-streaked black hair and hooded eyes of dense brown. "There's my princess." He caught Dru in a fierce and possessive embrace. "You're so late, you had me worried."

"We're not late."

"For heaven's sake, let the girl breathe," Katherine demanded, and tugged at Proctor's arm.

In an instant, Seth had the image of Witless trying to wedge his way in between Anna and anyone who tried to hug her when he was nearby.

"Proctor, this is Drusilla's escort, Seth Quinn."

"Good to meet you. Finally." Proctor took Seth's hand in a firm grip. Those dark eyes focused on Seth's face. Studied.

"It's good to meet you." Just when Seth began to wonder if he was about to be challenged to Indian-wrestle, Proctor released his hand.

"It's a pity you couldn't make time to come down for the weekend."

"Yes, I'm sorry about that."

"Dad, it's not Seth's fault. I told you—both of you—that I couldn't manage it. If I—"

"Dru's shop is terrific, isn't it?" Seth interrupted, his tone cheerful as he took champagne from a tray offered by a waiter, passed flutes to Katherine, to Dru, to Proctor before taking one for himself. "I'm sure the business aspects are complicated and challenging, but I'm speaking aesthetically. The use of space and light, the evolving blend of color and texture. One artist's eye admiring another," he said easily. "You must be incredibly proud of her."

"Of course we are." Proctor's smile was sharp, lethally so. *She's my girl*, it said as clearly as Katherine's tugging had done. "Drusilla is our most cherished treasure."

"How could she be anything but?" Seth replied.

"There's Granddad, Seth." Dru reached down, gripped Seth's hand. "I really should introduce you."

"Sure." He shot a beaming smile at her parents. "Excuse us a minute."

"You're very good at this," Dru told him.

"The tact and diplomacy department. Probably get that from Phil. You might've mentioned the weekend invite."

"Yes, I'm sorry. I should have. I thought I was saving us both, and instead I put you in the hot seat."

They were stopped a half dozen times on the way to the table where Senator Whitcomb was holding court. Each time, Dru exchanged a light kiss or handshake, made introductions, then eased away.

"You're good at it, too," Seth commented.

"Bred in the bone. Hello, Granddad." She bent down to kiss the handsome, solidly built man.

He had a rough and cagey look about him, Seth thought. Like a boxer who dominated in the ring as much with wit as with muscle. His hair was a dense pewter, and his eyes the same brilliant green as his granddaughter's.

He got to his feet to catch her face in two big hands. His smile was magnetic. "Here's my best girl."

"You say that to all your granddaughters."

"And I mean it, every time. Where's that painter your mother's been burning my ears about? This one here." Keeping one hand on Dru's shoulder, he sized Seth up. "Well, you don't look like an idiot, boy."

"I try not to be."

"Granddad."

"Quiet. You got sense enough to be making time with this pretty thing?"

Seth grinned. "Yes, sir."

"Senator Whitcomb, Seth Quinn. Don't embarrass me, Granddad."

"It's an old man's privilege to embarrass his grand-daughters. I like your work well enough," he said to Seth.

"Thank you, Senator. I like yours well enough, too."

Whitcomb's lips pursed for a moment, then curved up. "Seems to have a backbone. We'll see about this. My sources tell me you're making a decent living off your painting."

"Quiet," Seth told Dru when she opened her mouth. "I'm lucky to be able to make a living doing something I love. As your record indicates you're a strong patron of the arts, you obviously understand and appreciate art for art's sake. Financial rewards are secondary."

"Build boats, too, don't you?"

"Yes, sir. When I can. My brothers are the finest designers and builders of wooden sailing vessels in the East. If you visit Saint Chris again, you should come by and see for yourself."

"I might just do that. Your grandfather was a teacher. Is that right?"

"Yes," Seth said evenly. "He was."

"The most honorable of professions. I met him once at a political rally at the college. He was an interesting and exceptional man. Adopted three sons, didn't he?"

"Yes, sir."

"But you come from his daughter."

"In a manner of speaking. I wasn't fortunate enough to have my grandfather for the whole of my life, as Dru's been fortunate enough to have you. But his impact on me, his import to me, is every bit as deep. I hope he'd be half as proud of me as I am of him."

Dru laid a hand on Seth's arm, felt the tension. "If you've finished prying for the moment, I'd like to dance. Seth?"

"Sure. Excuse me, Senator."

"I'm sorry." Dru turned into Seth's arms on the dance floor. "I'm so sorry."

"Don't be."

"I am. It's his nature to demand answers, however personal."

"He didn't seem to want to roast me over an open fire, like your father."

"No. He's not as possessive, and he's more open to letting me make my own decisions, trust my own instincts."

"I liked him." That, Seth thought, was part of the problem. He'd seen a shrewd and intelligent man who loved his grandchild, and expected the best for her. Who obviously concluded that she'd expect the best for herself.

And the best was unlikely to be a stray with a father he'd never met and a mother with a fondness for blackmail.

"He's usually more subtle than that," she said. "And more reasonable. The situation with Jonah infuriated him. Now, I suppose, he'll be overprotective where I'm concerned for a while. Why don't we just go?"

"Running away doesn't work. Believe me, I've tried it."

"You're right, and that's very annoying."

She eased back when the music stopped, and saw Jonah over his shoulder. "If it's not one thing," she said quietly, "it's two more. How's your tact and diplomacy holding up?"

"So far, so good."

"Lend me some," she said, then let her lips curve into a cool and aloof smile.

"Hello, Jonah. And Angela, isn't it?"

"Dru." Jonah started to lean in, as if to kiss her cheek. He stopped short at the warning that flickered in her eyes, but his transition to a polite handshake was silky smooth. "You look wonderful, as always. Jonah Stuben," he said to Seth and offered a hand.

"Quinn, Seth Quinn."

"Yes, the artist. I've heard of you. My fiancée, Angela Downey."

"Congratulations." Well aware dozens of eyes were on her, Dru kept her expression bland. "And best wishes," she said to Angela.

"Thank you." Angela kept her hand tucked tight through Jonah's arm. "I saw two of your paintings at a showing of contemporary artists at the Smithsonian last year. One seemed a very personal study in oil, with an old white house, shady trees, people gathered around a big picnic table, and dogs in the yard. It was lovely, and so serene."

"Thanks." *Home*, Seth thought. One he'd done from memory and his rep had shipped back for the gallery.

"And how's your little business, Dru?" Jonah asked her. "And life in the slow lane?"

"Both are very rewarding. I'm enjoying living and working among people who don't slide into pretense every morning along with their wing tips."

"Really?" Jonah's smile went edgy. "I got the impression from your parents that you were moving back shortly."

"You're mistaken. And so are they. Seth, I'd love a little fresh air."

"Fine. Oh, Jonah, I want to thank you for being such a complete asshole." Seth smiled cheerfully at Angela. "I hope you're very happy together."

"That was neither tactful nor diplomatic," Dru admonished.

"I guess I get the calling an asshole an asshole from Cam. The restraint for not busting his balls for calling your shop 'your little business' is probably Ethan's influence. Want to go out on the terrace?"

"Yes. But . . . give me a minute, will you? I'd like to go out alone, settle down. Then we can make the rest of the rounds and get the hell out of here."

"Sounds good to me."

He watched her go, but before he could find someplace to hide, Katherine swooped down on him.

Outside, Dru took two steadying breaths, then a sip from the champagne she'd taken before stepping onto the terrace.

This town, she thought, looking out at the lights and the landmarks, smothered her. Was it any wonder she'd bolted to a place where the air was clear?

She wanted to sit on her porch, to feel that quiet satisfaction after a long day's work. She wanted to know Seth was beside her, or would be.

How strange it was that she could see that image so clearly, could see it spinning on, day after day. Year after year. And she could barely make out the shape and texture of the life she'd led before. All she knew was the weight of it at moments like this.

"Drusilla?"

She glanced over her shoulder, managed to suppress the sigh—and the oath—when Angela stepped up to her. "Let's not pretend we have something to say to each other, Angela. We played for the crowd."

"I have something to say to you. Something I've wanted to say for a long time. I owe you an apology."

Dru lifted an eyebrow. "For?"

"This isn't easy for me. I was jealous of you. I resented you for having what I wanted. And I used that to justify sleeping with the man you were going to marry. I loved him, I wanted him, so I took what was available."

"And now you have him." Dru lifted a hand, palm up. "Problem solved."

"I didn't like being the other woman. Sneaking around, taking whatever scraps he had left over. I convinced myself it was your fault, that was the only way I could live with it. All I had to do was get you out of the way and Jonah and I could be together."

"You did do it on purpose." Dru turned, leaned back against the railing. "I wondered."

"Yes, I did it on purpose. It was impulse, and one I've regretted even though . . . well, even though. You didn't deserve to find out that way. You hadn't done anything. You were the injured party, and I played a large role in hurting you. I'm very sorry for it."

"Are you apologizing because your conscience is bothering you, Angela, or because it'll tidy up the path before you marry Jonah?"

"Both."

Honesty at least, Dru thought, she could respect. "All right, you're absolved. Go forth and sin no more. He wouldn't have had the guts to apologize, to come to me this way, face-to-face, and admit he was wrong. Why are you with someone like that?"

"I love him," Angela said simply. "Strong points, weak points, the whole package."

"Yes, I think you do. Good luck. Sincerely."

"Thank you." She started back in, then stopped. "Jonah's never looked at me the way I saw Seth Quinn look at you. I don't think he ever will. Some of us settle for what we can get."

And some of us, Dru realized, get more than we ever knew we wanted.

* * *

HE was worn out when they got back to Dru's. From the drive, from the tension, from the thoughts circling like vultures in his mind.

"I owe you big."

He turned his head, stared at her blankly. "What?"

"I owe you for tolerating everything. My grandfather's interrogation, my ex-fiancé's smugness, my mother's prancing you around for over an hour like you were a prize stallion at a horse show, for all the questions, the intimations, the speculations. You had to run the gauntlet."

"Yeah, well." He jerked his shoulders, shoved open the car door. "You warned me."

"My father was rude, several times."

"Not especially. He just doesn't like me." Hands in his pockets, Seth walked with her toward the front door. "I get the impression he's not going to like any guy, particularly, who touches his princess."

"I'm not a princess."

"Oh, sugar, when your family's got themselves a couple of business and political empires, you're a princess. You just don't want to live in an ivory tower."

"I'm not what they assume I am. I don't want what they persist in believing I want. I'm never going to please them in the way they continually expect. This is my life now. Will you stay?"

"Tonight?"

"To start."

He stepped inside with her. He didn't know what to do with the despair, with the sudden, urgent fear that he was going to lose everything he'd tried so hard to hold on to.

He pulled her close, as if to prove he could hold on to

this. And could hear the mocking laughter rising in his brain.

"I need . . ." He pressed his face into the curve of her neck. "Goddamn it. I need—"

"What?" Trying to soothe, she stroked her hands over his back. "What do you need?"

Too much, he thought. More, he was sure, than fate would ever let him have. But for now, for tonight, all needs could be one.

"You." He spun her around, shoved her back against the door in a move as sharp and shocking as a whiplash. His mouth cut off her gasp of surprise in a kiss that burned toward the savage.

"I need you." He stared down into her wide, stunned eyes. "I'm not going to treat you like a princess tonight." He dragged her dress up to the waist, and his hand, rough and intimate, pressed between her legs. "You're not going to want me to."

"Seth." She gripped his shoulders, too dazed to push him away.

"Tell me to stop." He stabbed his fingers into her, drove up her hard and fast.

Panic, excitement, burst inside her with the darkest of pleasures. "No." She let herself fly, vowed to take him with her. "No, we won't stop."

"I'll take what I need." He snapped one of the thin jeweled straps so the material slithered down to cling to the tip of her breast. "You may not be ready for what I need tonight."

"I'm not fragile." Her breath clogged in her throat. "I'm not weak." Though she shuddered, her gaze stayed on his. "You might not be ready for what I need tonight."

"We're about to find out." He whipped her around,

pressed her against the door and fixed his teeth on the nape of her neck.

She cried out, her hands fisting against the door as his raced over her.

They had loved urgently, with great tenderness, even with laughter. But she'd never known the kind of desperation he showed her now. A desperation that was ruthless, reckless and rough. She hadn't known she could revel in it, could feel that same whippy violence herself. Or that she could rejoice in the snapping of her own control.

He assaulted her senses, and left her writhing on the wreckage.

He yanked the second strap, broke the elegant jeweled length in half so the dress slid down into a red puddle on the floor.

She wore a strapless bra and a garter of champagne lace, sheer, sheer hose and high silver heels. When he turned her, looked at her, his fingers dug into her shoulders.

She was quivering now, her skin flushed and damp. And that power, that knowledge were in her eyes. "Take me to bed."

"No." He molded her breasts. "I'm going to take you here."

Then his hands were on her hips, lifting her up, bringing her to him. He ravaged her mouth while he took his hands on an impatient journey over lace and flesh and silk. While his blood pounded, he ran the same hot trail with his mouth.

He wanted to eat her alive, to feed on her until this grinding hunger was finally sated. He wanted to lose his mind so he could think of nothing but this driving primal need.

The delicacy of her skin only made him mad to possess it. Her fresh female scent only stirred feral appetites.

When she exploded against him, he knew only a bright and burning triumph.

She dragged at his jacket, her fingers fumbling in her rush, her choked cries muffled against his mouth. Dizzy, desperate, she yanked at his tie.

"Please." She no longer cared that she was reduced to begging. "Please. Hurry."

He was still half dressed when he pulled her to the floor. And she was arching up in demand when he drove himself into her.

Her nails raked over his shirt, under it to dig into flesh gone hot and damp. Racing with him now, she met him thrust for frantic thrust.

Their breath in rags, their hearts slamming to the same primal beat, they surrendered to the frenzy.

Rider and ridden, they plunged off the edge together.

She lay spent, and used, and blissful on the bare, polished floor with the light from her prized Tiffany lamp spreading jewels in the air. As the pounding of blood in her ears faded, she could hear the night sounds coming through her open windows.

The water, the lazy call of an owl, the song of insects.

The heat still pumped from him, and spread through her like a drug. She rubbed her foot indolently against his ankle.

"Seth?"

"Hmm."

"I never thought I'd hear myself say this, but I'm so very glad we went to that tedious, irritating party tonight. In fact, if they put you in this kind of mood, I think we should go to one at least once a week."

He turned his head, saw the bright pool of red on the floor. "I'll pay to have your dress fixed."

"Okay, but it might be awkward to explain the damage to a tailor."

He came from violence, he thought. He knew how to control it, channel it. He recognized the difference between passions and punishments. He knew sex could be mean, just as he knew what had just happened between them was a world away from what he'd known and seen during the first years of his life.

And still . . .

"There's a lot you don't know about me, Dru."

"I imagine there's a lot we don't know about each other yet. We've both been with other people, Seth. We're not children. But I know I've never felt like this about anyone else. And for the first time in my life, I don't seem to need to plan every detail, to know every option. That's . . . liberating for me. I like discovering who you are, who I am. Who we are together."

She stroked her fingers through his hair. "Who we will be together. For me, it's a wonderful part of being in love. The discovery," she said as he lifted his head to look down at her. "The knowing there's time to discover more."

He was afraid time was the problem, and that it was running out.

"You know what I'd like you to do now?" she asked him.

"What would you like me to do now?"

"Carry me up to bed." She hooked her arms around his neck. "Here's something you didn't know about me. I've always, secretly, of course, fantasized about having some strong, gorgeous man carry me up the stairs. It goes against my sense of intellect, but there you are."

"A secret romantic fantasy." Determined to have this one night of peace, he laid his lips lightly on hers. "Very interesting. Let's see if I can fulfill that for you."

He rose, then glanced down at himself. "I'm going to lose the shirt first. It's a pretty silly image, some guy wearing nothing but a tuxedo shirt, carrying a naked woman upstairs."

"Good idea."

He dealt with the studs, the cuff links, then tossed the shirt over by her dress. He reached down for her; she reached up for him.

"How's it going so far?"

"Perfectly," she said, nuzzling his neck as he carried her toward the stairs. "Tell me something I don't know about you."

It broke his stride, but he shifted her and continued up the stairs. "I've been dreaming about my grandfather's wife. I never met her. She died before I came to Saint Chris."

"Really? What kind of dreams?"

"Very detailed, very clear dreams where we have long conversations. I used to listen to the guys talk about her and wish I'd gotten a chance to know her."

"I think that's lovely, and loving."

"The thing is, I don't think they're dreams. I think I'm having these conversations with her."

"You think that when you're dreaming?"

"No." He laid Dru on the bed, stretched out beside her, then drew her against his side. "I think that right now."

"Oh."

"That got you."

"I'm thinking." She shifted until her head rested comfortably in the nook of his neck. "You think they're some sort of visitation? That you're communicating with her spirit?"

"Something like that."

"What do you talk about?"

He hesitated, and evaded. "Family. Just family stuff. She told me things I didn't know, stuff that happened when my brothers were kids. Stuff that turned out to be true."

"Really?" She snuggled against him. "Then I suppose you'd better listen to her."

"THAT'S a smart woman you've got there," Stella commented.

They walked through the moist, heavy night air near the verge of Dru's river. The lamp in the living room window sent pretty colored light against the glass.

"She's got a strong, complicated brain. Everything about her's on the strong and complicated side."

"Strong's sexy," Stella said. "Don't you think she looks to you for the same? Strength of mind, of character, of heart? All the rest is just glands—not that there's anything wrong with glands. Makes the world go round."

"I fell for her so fast. One minute I'm standing up, the next I'm flat on the ground. I never thought it would be the same for her. But it is. Somehow."

"What're you going to do about it?"

"I don't know." He picked up a stone, skipped it out over the ink-black river. "You take somebody on, for the long haul, you take up their baggage, too. My baggage is damn heavy, Grandma. I have a feeling it's about to get a lot heavier."

"You've handcuffed yourself to that baggage, Seth. You've got the key, you always have. Don't you think it's time to use it and pitch that load overboard?"

"She'll never go away and stay away."

"Probably not. What you do about it is what makes the

size of the load. Too damn stubborn to share it. Just like your grandfather."

"Really?" The idea simply warmed his heart. "Do you think I take after him in some ways?"

"You got his eyes." She reached up, touched his hair. "But you know that already. And his stubborn streak. Always figured he could handle things himself. Irritating. Had a calm way about him—until he blew. You're the same. And you've made the same damn mistakes he made with Gloria. You're letting her use your love for your family, and for Dru, as a weapon."

"It's just money, Grandma."

"Hell it is. You know what you have to do, Seth. Now go on and do it. Though being a man, you'll find a way to screw it up some first."

His jaw set. "I'm not dragging Dru through this."

"Hell. That girl doesn't want a martyr." She planted her hands on her hips and scowled at him. "Stubborn to the point of stupid. Just like your grandfather," she muttered.

And was gone.

SEVENTEEN

THE BAR WAS a dive, the sort of place where drinking was a serious, mostly solitary occupation. The blue curtain of smoke, thick enough to part with your hands, turned it all into a poorly produced black-and-white movie scene. The lights were dim, encouraging patrons to mind their own, with the added benefit of hiding the stains when someone decided to mind his neighbor's.

It smelled of last year's cigarettes and last week's beer.

The recreation and socializing area consisted of a stingy strip of space along the side where a pool table had been jammed. A bunch of guys were playing a round of eight ball while a few more stood around sucking beers, the expressions of bored disgust on their faces showing the world what badasses they were.

The air-conditioning unit was framed in a window with a sheet of splintered plywood, and did little more than stir the stink and make noise.

Seth took a seat at the end of the bar and, playing it safe, ordered a Bud in the bottle.

He supposed it was fitting she'd dragged him out to a place like this. She'd dragged him into them often enough when he was a kid—or if she'd had transportation, he'd slept in the car while she'd gone in.

Gloria might have been raised in a solid upper-class environment, but all the benefits and advantages of that upbringing had been wasted on a spirit that continually sought, and found, the lowest level.

He'd stopped wondering what it was inside her that drove her to hate, to despise anything decent. What compelled her to use anyone who'd ever had reason to care for her until she'd sucked them dry or destroyed them.

Her addictions—men, drugs, liquor—didn't cause it. They were only one more form of her absolute self-indulgence.

But it was fitting it would be here, he thought, as he sat and listened to the sharp smack of balls, the rattling whine of the failing AC, and smelled the smells that pulled him back into the nightmare of his childhood.

She'd have come in to pick up a john, he remembered, if she needed cash. Or if she'd had money, to drink herself drunk—unless booze hadn't been her drug of choice for that night. Then she'd have come in to score.

If the john was the target, she'd take him back to whatever hole they were living in. Sex noises and wild laughter in the next room. If it was drink or drugs, and they put her in a good mood, there would've been a stop at some all-night place. He'd have eaten that night.

If the mood had turned nasty, there would have been fists instead of food.

Or so it had been until he'd been big enough, fast enough, mean enough to avoid the punches.

"You gonna drink that beer?" the bartender demanded, "or just look at it all night?"

Seth shifted his gaze, and the cold warning on his face had the bartender easing back a step. Keeping his eyes level, Seth pulled a ten out of his pocket, dropped it on the bar by his untouched beer.

"Problem?" His voice was a soft threat.

The bartender shrugged and got busy elsewhere.

When she walked in, a couple of the pool players looked over, checked her out. Seth imagined Gloria considered their leering smirks a flattering assessment.

She wore denim cutoffs that hugged her bony hips and frayed at the hem just below crotch level. The snug top was hot pink, left several inches of midriff bare. She'd had her belly button pierced and added a tattoo of a dragonfly beside the gold bar. Her nails, fingers and toes were coated in a glitter polish that looked black in the ugly light.

She slid onto a stool, then sent the pool players one long, hot look.

It only took one look at her eyes for Seth to realize at least a portion of the money he'd given her had gone up her nose.

"G and T," she told the bartender. "Easy on the T."

She took out a cigarette, flicked on a silver lighter, then blew a slow stream of smoke at the ceiling. She crossed her legs, and her foot jiggled in triple time.

"Hot enough for you?" she said and laughed.

"You've got five minutes."

"What's your hurry?" She sucked in more smoke, tapped her glittery nails in a rapid tattoo on the bar. "Drink your beer and relax."

"I don't drink with people I don't like. What do you want, Gloria?"

"I want this gin and tonic." She picked up the glass the bartender set in front of her. Drank long and deep. "Maybe a little action." She sent the pool players another look, licked her lips in a way that curdled Seth's stomach. "And just lately I've been thinking I need a nice little place at the beach. Daytona maybe."

She took another drink, left lipstick smeared on the rim. "You, now, you don't want a place of your own, do you? Still living in that same house, crowded in with those kids and dogs. You're in a rut."

"Stay away from my family."

"Or what?" She sent him a smile as glittery and black as her nails. "You'll tell your big brothers on me? You think the Quinns worry me? They've all gone soft and stupid, the way people do when they hang around some dead-ass town their whole fucking, useless lives, breeding noisy kids and sitting around the TV every night like a bunch of goddamn zombies. Only smart thing they did was take you in so they could get the old man's money—just like that asshole married my spineless sister for hers."

She tossed back the rest of her drink, rapped it hard twice on the bar to signal for another. Her body was in constant motion—the jiggling foot, the tapping fingers, the swivel of her head on her neck. "The old man was my blood, not theirs. That money should've been mine."

"You bled him for plenty before he died. But it's never enough, is it?"

"Fucking A." She fired up another cigarette. "You got yourself some smarts, after all these years. Hooked yourself up with a live one, didn't you? Drusilla Whitcomb Banks. Woo-hoo." Gloria threw back her head, let out a hoot. "Fancy stuff. Rich stuff. Bagging her's the only smart thing you ever did. Set yourself up for life."

She snatched the glass the minute the bartender set it down. "'Course you've been doing pretty well for yourself drawing pictures. Better than I realized." She crunched down on ice. "Can't figure why people'd piss away all that money on something to hang on the wall. Takes all kinds."

He laid a hand on her wrist, slowly closed his fingers around it in a grip mean enough to make her jolt. "Understand this: You go near my family or Dru, you go around anyone who matters to me, and you'll find out exactly what I'm capable of. It'll be a hell of a lot worse on you than Sybill knocking you on your ass the way she did years ago."

She leaned her face into his. "You threatening me? *Son?*"

"I'm promising you."

Through the drugs and alcohol, she caught some hint of that promise. And eased back, as the bartender had done. "That your bottom line?" She picked up her drink with her free hand, and her thin, used face went cagey. "You want me to steer clear of your nearest and dearest?"

"That's my bottom line."

"Here's mine." She jerked her hand free, reached for her cigarette. "We've been playing nickel and dime long enough, you and me. You're raking in the dough with your pictures, and you're screwing your way into a big, fat pile of it. I want my cut. One-time deal, lump-sum payment, and I'm gone. That's what you want, right? You want me gone."

"How much?"

Satisfied, she took another deep drag, let the smoke

stream into his face. He'd always been the easiest of marks. "One million."

He didn't even blink. "You want a million dollars."

"I've done my homework, sweetie pie. You get big bucks when the suckers plunk it down for your paintings. You pulled in a pile over there in Europe. Who knows how long you can run that con? Add to that the fancy piece you're busy banging."

She shifted on the stool, recrossed her legs. The mix of drugs and alcohol raging through her system made her feel powerful. Made her feel *alive*.

"She's rolling in it. Lots of money there. Old money, too. The kind of money that doesn't like scandal. Mess things up for you if it got out in the press that the senator's purebred granddaughter was spreading her legs for a mongrel. One that was ripped from his mother's arms when she came to the father she'd never known for help. I can play it all kinds of ways," she added. "You and the Quinns won't come out clean in any of them. And the dirt'll stick to your girlfriend, too. She won't hang around once the shit starts to fly."

She signaled for a third drink, shifted again. "She'll dump you, and fast, and maybe people won't be so willing to shell out for your pictures once they hear my side of things. Oh, I bought him his first little paint kit. Sniff, sniff."

She threw back her head and laughed, the sound so full of malice and glee, the pool players stopped smacking balls to look over. "Press'll lap it up. Fact is, I could sell the story, make a nice little bundle. But I'm giving you a chance to buy it first. You can consider it an investment. You pay me, and I'm out of your life once and for all. You don't, and someone else will."

His face was blank, had stayed blank throughout her rant. He wouldn't give her even his disgust. "Your story's bullshit."

"Sure it is." She laughed and gulped gin. "People can't get enough bullshit, not when it's piling up on somebody else. I'll give you a week to come up with it—cash. But I want a down payment. We'll just call it good-faith money. Ten thousand. You bring it here, tomorrow night. Ten o'clock. You don't show, then I start making some calls."

He got to his feet. "Spend another ten on nose candy, Gloria, you'll be dead in the back room of some dump like this long before you can enjoy any part of that million."

"Just let me worry about me. Pay for the drinks."

He simply turned his back on her and walked toward the door.

H E couldn't go home, not when he intended to sit in the dark and get quietly and thoroughly drunk.

He knew better. He knew it was an escape, self-pity, a one-way trip. Steady, deliberate drinking was a crutch, an illusion, a trapdoor.

He didn't give a damn. So he poured another shot of Jameson and studied its deep amber glow in the single light he'd turned on in his studio.

His brothers had given him his first taste of whiskey on his twenty-first birthday. Just the four of them, Seth remembered, sitting around the kitchen table with the kids and the women gone.

It was one of those solid, rich-toned memories that he knew would never leave him. The sharp scent of the cigar smoke after Ethan had passed them around. The sting of the whiskey on his tongue, down his throat, mellowing out as it reached his belly. The sound of his brothers' voices, their laughter, and the absolute certainty he'd felt of his own belonging.

He hadn't cared much for the taste of the whiskey. Still didn't. But it was what a man reached for when his single intention was oblivion.

He'd long since stopped questioning what Gloria De-Lauter was, and how she became. Part of her was inside him, and he accepted that as he would a birthmark. He didn't believe in the sins of the father—or mother. He didn't believe in tainted blood. Each one of his brothers had come from some sort of horror, and they were the best men he knew.

Whatever there was of Gloria inside him had been drowned out by the decency and pride and compassion given to him by the Quinns.

Maybe that alone was part of the reason she hated him— hated all of them. It didn't matter why. She was part of his life, and he had to deal with her.

One way or the other.

He sat drinking by that single light in a room filled with his paintings and the tools of the work he loved. He'd already made his decision, and he would live with it. But for tonight, he'd cloud his future with Irish whiskey and the throb of the mournful blues he'd chosen as his drinking music.

When his cell phone rang he ignored it. Picked up the bottle, poured another shot.

DRU hung up and paced her living room. She'd tried Seth's number half a dozen times, had worn a path on the floor over the last two hours. Since Aubrey had called, looking for him.

He wasn't with Aubrey, as he'd told Dru he would be that evening. Nor was he with Dru—as he'd told Aubrey and his family he would be.

So where the hell was he?

He'd been off. *Something* had been off, she decided, since the night before. Even before the party, she thought now. Before the drive. There'd been some kind of repressed violence in him—viciously repressed, she realized. It had, eventually, taken its form in rough sex.

And even then, after they'd exhausted each other, she'd sensed an underlying turbulence. She'd let it go, Dru admitted. It wasn't in her nature to pry. She resented the way her parents questioned and picked apart her every mood. Moods, she liked to think, were often private matters.

Now he'd lied to her. That, she felt strongly, was not his nature.

If something was wrong, she needed to help. Wasn't that part of the duty of love?

She checked her watch, barely stopped herself from wringing her hands. It was after midnight. What if he was hurt? What if he'd been in an accident?

And what if he'd simply wanted an evening to himself?

"If he did, he should have said so," she mumbled and marched to the door.

There was one place she imagined he could be. She wasn't going to rest until she checked.

On the drive into town she lectured herself. Her relationship with Seth didn't mean he had to account to her for every minute of his time. They both had lives, interests, obligations of their own. She certainly wasn't the sort of woman who couldn't be content and productive with her own company.

But that didn't give him the right to lie to her about his plans for the evening. If he'd just answer his goddamn phone, she wouldn't be driving into town in the middle of the night to look for him like some clichéd, nagging sitcom wife.

And she was going to ream him inside out for making her feel like one.

She'd worked up a good head of steam by the time she turned toward the rear lot and saw his car parked. The insult of it nearly had her driving right past and back home again. He couldn't have told her, and everyone else, that he'd wanted to work? He couldn't just pick up the phone and . . .

She slammed on the brakes.

What if he couldn't get to the phone? What if he was unable to answer because he was unconscious, or ill?

She whipped the car into the lot, leaped out and charged up the stairs.

The image of him lying helpless on the floor was so strong that when she burst in, saw him sitting on the bed pouring liquor from a bottle into a short glass, it didn't register.

"You're all right." The relief came first, made her knees weak. "Oh, Seth, God! I was so worried."

"What for?" He set the bottle down, studied her out of bleary eyes as he drank.

"Nobody knew where . . ." Realization came next, made her blood boil. "You're drunk."

"Working on it. Got a ways to go yet. What're you doing here?"

"Aubrey called looking for you hours ago. Your stories got crossed. Since you didn't answer your phone, I was foolish enough to worry about you."

He was still much too sober. Sober enough to consider her mood could make it easier on both of them. "If you came running in here hoping to catch me in bed with another woman, I'm sorry to disappoint you."

"It never occurred to me that you would cheat." Nearly as baffled as she was angry, she walked toward the bed, noted the level of whiskey in the bottle. "Then again, it never crossed my mind that you'd need to lie to me either. Or that you'd sit here alone drinking yourself drunk."

"Told you there's a lot you don't know about me, sugar." He jerked a thumb at the bottle. "Want one? Glasses in the kitchen."

"No, thank you. Is there a reason you're worrying your family and having a drinking marathon?"

"I'm a big boy, Dru, and I don't need you crawling up my ass because I want a couple drinks. This is more my style than a couple polite belts of champagne at some boring political gala. You can't deal with it, it's not my problem."

It stung, and had her chin lifting. "I was obliged to go. You weren't. That choice was yours. You want to drown yourself in a whiskey bottle, that's certainly your choice as well. But I won't be lied to. I won't be made a fool of."

He gave a careless shrug and, riding on the whiskey, decided he knew what was best for her. A few more jabs to the pride, he thought, and she'd be gone.

"You know the problem with women? You sleep with them a few times, you tell them what they want to hear. You show them a good time. Right away, they start crowding you. Take a little breather, and they're all over you like lice on a monkey. Jesus, I knew I should never've gone to that deal with you last night. Told myself it'd give you ideas."

"Ideas?" she repeated. She felt her throat fill and burn. *"Ideas?"*

"Can't just let things be, can you?" He shook his head, poured another drink. "Always got to be looking ahead. What's the deal for tomorrow, what's going to happen next week? You're plotting out a future, sugar, and that's just not what I'm about. You're a hell of a lot of fun to be with once you loosen up, but we'd better quit while we're ahead."

"You—you're dumping me?"

"Aw now, don't put it like that, sweetheart. We just need to throttle back some."

Grief rolled up, and numbed her. "All this, all this was just for, what, for sex and art? I don't believe that. I don't."

"Let's not make a big thing out of it." He reached for the bottle again. Poured whiskey onto whiskey. Anything to keep from looking at her, at the tears swimming in her eyes.

"I trusted you, with my body and my heart. I never asked you for anything. You always gave it before I could. I don't deserve to be treated this way, discarded this way, only because I fell in love with you."

He looked at her then, and the combination of pride and sadness on her face destroyed him. "Dru—"

"I love you." She said it calmly, while she could still be calm. "But that's my problem. I'll leave you alone with yours, and your bottle."

"Goddamn it. Goddamn it, don't go," he said when she spun toward the door. "Dru, don't walk out. Please don't." He shoved the glass onto the table, dropped his head in his hands. "I can't do this. I can't let her steal this from me, too."

"You think I'm going to stand here and cry in front of you? Even *speak* to you when you're drunk and insulting?"

"I'm sorry. Christ, I'm sorry."

"You are that. You're very sorry." The hand that gripped the doorknob trembled, and a tear spilled over. The combination infuriated her. "I don't want your pathetic guilty male conscience because you hurt me enough to bring on a few tears. What I really want right now is for you to go straight to hell."

"Please don't walk out the door. I don't think I could stand it." Everything inside him—grief, guilt, loathing and love—clamped his throat like strangling hands. "I thought I should shove you out before you got pulled under. I can't do it. I can't *stand* it. I don't know if it's selfish or if it's right, but I can't let you go. For God's sake, don't walk on me."

She stared at him, at the naked misery on his face. Her heart, already cracked, split in two. "Seth, please tell me what's wrong. Tell me what's hurting you."

"I shouldn't have said those things to you. It was stupid."

"Tell me why you said them. Tell me why you're sitting here alone, drinking yourself sick."

"I was sick before I bought the bottle. I don't know where to start." He raked his hands through his hair. "The beginning, I guess." He pressed his fingers to his lids. "I got about halfway drunk. I'm going to need some coffee."

"I'll make it."

"Dru." He lifted his hands again, then just let them fall. "Everything I said to you since you walked in the door was a lie."

She took a deep breath. For now, she thought, she would tuck the anger and hurt away, and listen. "All right. I'll make you coffee, then you can tell me the truth."

* * *

"IT goes back a long time," he began. "Back before my grandfather. Before Ray Quinn married Stella. Before he met her. Dru, I'm sorry I hurt you."

"Just tell me. We'll deal with that later."

He drank coffee. "Ray met this woman, and they got involved. They had an affair," he corrected. "They were both young and single, so why not? Anyway, he wasn't the type she was looking for. You know, a teacher, one who leaned toward the left while she leaned right. She came from a family like yours. What I mean is—"

"I know what you mean. She had a certain social position, and certain social aspirations."

"Yeah." He let out a breath, drank more coffee. "Thanks. She broke it off, left. She was pregnant, and not too pleased about it from the way I've heard it. She met another guy, one she clicked with. So she decided to go through with the pregnancy, and she married him."

"She never told your grandfather about the child."

"No, she never told him. Little ways down the road, she had a second daughter. She had Sybill."

"Sybill, but . . . oh." Dru let it sift in her mind until it fell into place. "I see. Ray Quinn's daughter, Sybill's half sister. Your mother."

"That cuts through it. She—Gloria. Her name's Gloria. She's not like Sybill. Gloria hated her. I think she must've been born hating everyone. Whatever she had growing up, it never seemed to be enough."

He was pale, and looked so drawn and ill, Dru had to bank down on the urge to simply gather him close and comfort. "For some, nothing is ever enough."

"Yeah. She took off with some guy at some point, got

knocked up. That would be me. Turns out he married her. That's not important. I've never met him. He doesn't come into this."

"Your father—"

"Sperm donor," Seth corrected. "I don't know what happened between them. I don't lose sleep over it. When Gloria ran out of money, she went back home, took me with her. I don't remember any of that. They didn't kill the fatted calf for her. Gloria's got an affection for the bottle, and various chemical enhancements. I think she came and went for a few years. I know when Sybill had a place of her own in New York, she dumped me there. I don't remember much about it. Didn't remember Sybill at all when I first met her again. I was a couple years old. Sybill gave me this stuffed dog. I called it Yours. You know, when I asked whose it was she said . . ."

"Yours," Dru finished, and touched, brushed a hand over his hair. "She was kind to you."

"She was great. Like I said, I don't remember much, except feeling safe when I was with her. She took us in, bought us food, clothes, took care of me when Gloria didn't show up for a few days. And Gloria paid her back by stealing everything she could fence when Sybill was out, and taking off with me."

"You didn't have a choice. Children don't."

"I'm not taking on responsibility for it. I'm just saying. I don't know why she didn't leave me and head out on her own. I can only figure it was because Sybill and I had made a connection, because we . . ."

"Because you'd started to love each other." Dru took his hand, let his fingers grip tight on hers. "And she resented you both, so she couldn't have that."

He closed his eyes a moment. "It helps that you get it."

"You didn't think I would."

"I don't know what I thought. She fucks me up; that's the only excuse I've got."

"Save the excuses. Tell me the rest."

He set the coffee aside. It wasn't doing anything for his headache or queasy stomach but making him more awake and aware of them. "We lived a lot of different places, for short amounts of time. She had a lot of men. I knew about sex before I could write my own name. She'd get drunk or high, so I was on my own a lot. She ran low on money, couldn't get high, she'd take it out on me."

"She hit you."

"Jesus, Dru. However perceptive you are, you don't know that kind of world. Why should you? Why should anybody?" He pulled himself in. "She'd beat the shit out of me if she felt like it. I'd go hungry if she didn't feel like feeding me. And if she paid for drugs with sex, I'd hear them going at it in the next room. There wasn't much I hadn't seen by the time I was six."

It sickened her. It made her want to weep. But if Seth needed anything from her now, it was strength. "Why didn't Social Services do something to help you?"

He just looked at her for a moment, as if she'd spoken in a language he didn't recognize. "We didn't hang around in places where concerned adults call the authorities on junkie mothers and their abused kids. She was mean, but she's never been stupid. I thought about running away, started to save up for it. A nickel here, a quarter there. When I was old enough, she dumped me in school—gave her more time to cruise. I loved it. I loved school. Never admitted it, couldn't be so uncool, but I loved it."

"None of your teachers realized what was going on?"

"It never occurred to me to tell anybody." He shrugged.

"It was life, that's all. And under it, I was just so fucking scared of her. Then . . . I guess I was about seven the first time. One of the men she brought back with her . . ."

He shook his head, pushed to his feet. Even after all the years between, the memories could slick his skin with sweat. "Some of them had a taste for young boys."

Her heart simply stopped, then jolted again to pound in her throat. "No. No."

"I always got away. I was fast, and I was mean. I found places to hide. But I knew what it meant when one of them tried to put his hands on me. I knew what it meant. It was a long time before I could stand anyone touching me. I couldn't stand being touched. I can't get through this if you cry."

She willed back the tears that threatened to overflow. But she rose, crossed to him. Without a word she wrapped her arms around him.

"Poor baby," she crooned, rocking him. "Poor little boy."

Undone, he pressed his face to her shoulder. The smell of her hair, of her skin was so clean. "I didn't want you to know about this."

"Did you think I would love you less?"

"I just didn't want you to know."

"I do know, and I'm so awed by who you are. You think this is beyond my scope, because of my background. But you're wrong." She held tight. "You're wrong. She never broke you, Seth."

"She might have, but for the Quinns. I have to finish." He drew himself away. "Let me finish it."

"Come sit down."

He went with her, sat on the side of the bed again. "During one of her scenes with her mother, Gloria found out about Ray. It gave her someone else to hate, someone else to blame for all the injustices she liked to think were aimed at her. He was teaching at the university here when she found him. This was after Stella had died, after my brothers were adults and had moved out of the house. Cam was in Europe, Phil in Baltimore and Ethan had his own place in Saint Chris. She blackmailed Ray."

"For what? He didn't even know she existed."

"Didn't matter to her. She demanded money; he paid. She wanted more, went to the dean and spun some lie about sexual harassment. Tried to pass me off as Ray's kid. It didn't fly, but it started planting seeds here and there. He made a deal with her. He wanted to get me away from her. He wanted to take care of me."

"He was a good man. Every time I've heard his name mentioned by anyone in Saint Chris, it's with affection and respect."

"He was the best," Seth agreed. "She knew he was a good man. That's the kind of thing she despises, and needs to use. So she sold me to him."

"Well, that was a mistake," Dru said mildly. "And the first decent thing she ever did for you."

"Yeah." He let out a long breath. "You get it. I didn't know who he was. All I knew was that this big old man treated me . . . decent, and I wanted to stay in that house on the water. When he made promises, he kept them, and he never hurt me. He made me toe the line, but, hell, you wanted to when it was Ray's line. He had a puppy, and I never had to go hungry. Most of all, I was away from her, for the first time away from her. I was never going back. He said I'd never have to, and I believed him. But she came back."

"Realized her mistake."

"Realized she'd sold off cheap. She wanted more money or she was taking me. He gave her more, kept giving it. One day, he had an accident on the way back from paying her. It was bad. They called Cam back from Europe. I still remember the first time I saw him, the first time I saw the three of them together, standing around Ray's hospital bed. Ray made them promise to take care of me, to keep me with them. He didn't tell them about Gloria or the connection. Maybe he wasn't thinking about that. He was dying, and he knew it, and he just wanted to make sure I was safe. He trusted them to take care of me."

"He knew his sons," Dru said aloud.

"He knew them—better than I did. When he died, I figured they'd ship me off, or I'd have to run off. I never figured they'd keep me around. They didn't know me, so what did they care? But they kept their promise to Ray. They changed their lives around for him, and for me. They made a home—pretty wild one at first with Cam running it."

For the first time since he'd begun, some of the misery lifted. Humor slid into his voice. "He was always blowing something up in the microwave or flooding the kitchen. Guy didn't have a clue. I pushed at them, gave them—Cam mostly—as much grief as I could dish out. And I could dish out plenty. I kept waiting for them to kick me out, or smack me senseless. But they stuck with me. They stood up for me, and when Gloria tried to hose them like she'd done with Ray, they fought for me. Even before we found out I was Ray's grandson, they'd made me one of them."

"They love you, Seth. Anyone can see it's as much for your sake as it is for their father's."

"I know it. There's nothing I wouldn't do for them. Including paying off Gloria, the way I've been doing on and off since I was fourteen."

"She didn't stay away."

"No. She's back now. That's where I was tonight, meeting her to discuss her latest terms. She came into your shop. Guess she wanted to get a close-up look at you while she was figuring her angles on this one."

"The woman." Dru stiffened, rubbed suddenly chilled arms. "Harrow, she said. Glo Harrow."

"It's DeLauter. I think Harrow's a family name. She knows about your family. The money, the connections, the political implications. She's added that to the mix. She'll do her best to hurt you, the way she'll do whatever she can to hurt my family if I don't give her what she's after."

"It's just another form of blackmail. I know something about this kind of blackmail, the kind that uses your feelings to squeeze you dry. She's using your love as a weapon."

A chill danced over his skin at the phrase, and he heard the echo of Stella's voice in his mind. "What did you say?"

"I said she's using your love as a weapon, and you're handing it to her. It has to stop. You have to tell your family. Now."

"Jesus, Dru, I haven't figured out if telling them's the right thing to do. Much less telling them at two in the morning."

"You know very well it's the right thing, the only thing to do. Do you think what time it is matters to them?"

She crossed to the workbench where he'd tossed his phone. "I'd say Anna would be the one to call first, and she can contact the others." She held out the phone. "Do you want to call her and tell her we're on our way, or shall I?"

"You're awful damn bossy all of a sudden."

"Because you need to be bossed just at the moment. Do

you think I'm going to stand by and let her do this to you? Do you think any of us will?"

"The point is, she's the monkey on my back. I don't want her taking swipes at you, my family. I need to protect you from that."

"Protect me? You're lucky I don't knock you senseless with this phone. Your solution was to let me go. Do you think I want some self-sacrificing white knight?"

He nearly smiled. "Would that be the same thing as a martyr?"

"Close enough."

He held out his hand. "Don't hit me. Just give me the phone."

EIGHTEEN

⌒

THE KITCHEN HAD always been the place for family meetings. Discussions, small celebrations were held there; decisions and plans were made there. Punishments were meted out and praise was given most often at the old kitchen table no one had ever considered replacing.

It was there they gathered now, with coffee on the stove and the lights bright enough to push away the dark. It seemed to Dru there were too many of them to fit in that limited space. But they made room for one another. They made room for her.

They had all come without hesitation, dragging themselves and their sleeping kids out of bed. They had to be alarmed, but no one peppered Seth with questions. She could feel the tension quivering in the sluggish, middle-of-the-night air.

The younger ones were shuffled upstairs and back to any available bed, with Emily in charge. Dru imagined there was quite a bit of whispered speculation going on up there by anyone who'd managed to stay awake.

"I'm sorry about this," Seth began.

"You drag us all out of bed at two in the morning, you've got a reason." Phillip closed his hand over Sybill's. "You kill somebody? Because if we've got to dispose of a body this time of night, we'd better get started."

Grateful for the attempt to lighten the mood, Seth shook his head. "Not this time. Might be easier all around if I had."

"Spit it out, Seth," Cam told him. "The sooner you tell us what's wrong, the sooner we can do something about it."

"I met with Gloria tonight."

There was silence, one long beat. Seth looked at Sybill, understanding she'd be the most upset. "I'm sorry. I was going to try to find a way not to tell you, but there isn't one."

"Why wouldn't you tell us?" There was strain in Sybill's voice, and her hand tightened visibly on Phillip's. "If she's in the area and bothering you, we need to know."

"It's not the first time."

"It's going to be the last." Fury snapped into Cam's voice. "What the hell is this, Seth? She's been back around before and you didn't mention it?"

"I didn't see the point in getting everyone worked up— the way you're going to be worked up now."

"Fuck that. When? When did she start coming back around you?"

"Cam—"

"If you're going to tell me to calm down," he said to Anna, "you're wasting your breath. I asked you a question, Seth."

"Since I was about fourteen."

"Son of a bitch." Cam shoved back from the table. Across from him, Dru jumped. She'd never seen that kind of rage, the kind with a ready violence that threatened to smash everything in its path.

"She's been coming around you all this time, for years, and you don't say a goddamn word?"

"No point yelling at him yet." Ethan leaned on the table, and though his voice was calm, there was something in his eyes that warned Dru his manner of fury would be every bit as lethal as his brother's. "She get money from you?"

Seth started to speak, then just shrugged.

"Now you can yell at him," Ethan muttered.

"You paid her? You've been paying her?" Shock vibrated as Cam stared at Seth. "What the hell's the *matter* with you? We'd've booted her greedy ass to Nebraska if you'd said one goddamn word about it. We took all the legal steps to keep her away from you. Why the hell did you let her bleed you?"

"I'd've done anything to keep her from touching any one of you. It was just money. For Christ's sake, what do I care about that as long as she went away again?"

"But she didn't stay away," Anna said quietly. Quietly because her own temper was simmering under the surface. If it boiled over, it would make Cam's seem like a little boy's tantrum. "Did she?"

"No, but—"

"You should've trusted us. You had to know we'd be there for you."

"Oh God, Anna, I knew that."

"This isn't the way to show it," Cam snapped.

"I gave her money." Seth held out his hands. "Just money. It was all I knew how to do, to protect you. I needed to do *something*, anything I could to pay you back."

"Pay us back? For what?"

"You *saved* me." Emotions swelled in Seth's voice and the almost desperate flood of them silenced the room. "You gave me everything I've ever had that was decent, that was clean, that was fucking *normal*. You changed your lives for me, and you did it when I was nothing to you. You made me family. Goddamn it. Goddamn it, Cam, you made me."

It took a moment before he could speak, but when he did Cam's voice was rough, and it was final. "I don't want to hear that kind of crap from you. I don't want to hear about fucking checks and fucking balances."

"That's not what he meant." Struggling with tears, Grace spoke softly. "Sit down now. Sit down now, Cam, and don't slap at him that way. He's right."

"What the hell does that mean?" But Cam dropped back in his chair. "Just what the hell does that mean?"

"He never lets me say it," Seth managed. "None of them ever let me—"

"Hush now," Grace said. "They did save you, and they started it when you were nothing more than a promise to their father, because they loved him. Then they did it for you, because they loved you. All of us loved you. If you weren't grateful for what they did, for what they've never stopped doing, there'd be something wrong with you."

"I wanted to—"

"Wait." Grace only had to lift a finger to stop him. "Love doesn't require payment. Cam's right about that. There are no checks and balances here."

"I needed to give something back. But that wasn't all. She said things about Aubrey." He stared at Grace as the color ran out of her face.

Aubrey, who'd been silently weeping, found her voice. "What? She used me?"

"Just things like wasn't she pretty, and wouldn't it be a shame if anything happened to her. Or her little sister, or her cousins. Christ, I was terrified. I was fucking fourteen. I was scared to death if I said anything to anybody she'd find a way to hurt Aubrey, or one of the kids."

"Of course you were," Anna said. "She counted on that."

"And when she said I owed her for all the trouble I'd caused her, how she needed a few hundred for traveling money, I figured it was the best way to get rid of her. Jesus, Grace was pregnant with Deke, and Kevin and Bram were just babies. I just wanted her gone and away from them."

"She knew that." Sybill let out a sigh, rose to go to the coffeepot. "She knew how much your family mattered to you, so that's what she used. She was always good at finding just the right button to push. She pushed mine often enough when I was a lot older than fourteen." She laid a hand on his shoulder, squeezed as she topped off mugs. "Ray was a grown man, but he paid her."

"She'd go away, months at a time," Seth continued. "Even years. But she came back. I had money. My share from the boatyard, what you gave me from Ray, then from some paintings. She hit me twice when I was in college, then came back for a third. I'd figured out she wasn't going anywhere, not for long. I knew it was stupid to keep paying her. I had the chance to go to Europe to study, to work. I took it. Wasn't any point in her coming around here if I was gone."

"Seth." Anna waited until he looked at her. "Did you go to Europe to get away from her? To get her away from us?"

The look he sent her was so fierce, so full of love it made Dru's throat hurt. "I wanted to go. I needed to find out what I could do with my work, on my own. That was just another door you opened up for me. But in the back of my mind . . . Well, it weighed in, that's all."

"Okay." Ethan turned his mug in slow circles. "You did what you thought you had to do then. What about now?"

"About four months ago, she showed up on my doorstep in Rome. She had some guy with her she was stringing along. She'd heard about me—read stuff—and figured the pot was a whole lot richer now. She said she'd go to the press, to the galleries, and give them the whole story. Her story," he amended. "The way she'd twisted it around. Dragging Ray's name through the dirt again. I paid her off, and I came home. I wanted to come home. But it turns out I brought her back with me."

"You never brought her anywhere," Phillip corrected. "Get that through your thick head."

"Okay, she came back. Only this time the money didn't send her off again. She's been staying around, somewhere. She came into Dru's shop."

"Did she threaten you?" Temper fired into Cam's face again. "Did she try to hurt you?"

"No." Dru shook her head. "She knows Seth and I are involved. So she's added me to the mix, using me as another weapon to hurt him. I don't know her, but from everything I've heard, everything I'm hearing, she wants that as much as she wants money. To hurt him. To hurt all of you. I don't agree with what Seth did, but I understand why he did it."

Her gaze traveled around the table, from face to face. "I shouldn't be sitting here at this table while you talk about this. This is family business, and as personal as it gets. But no one questioned my being here."

"You're Seth's," Phillip said simply.

"You can't know how special you are. All of you. This . . . unit. Whether Seth's trying to protect that unit was right or wrong, smart or stupid doesn't much matter at this point. The point is he loved you all too much to do otherwise—and she knew it. Now it has to stop."

"There's a woman with brains," Cam said. "Did you pay her tonight, kid?"

"No, she set new terms. She'll go to the press, tell her story. Blah blah." He shrugged, and realized a great deal of the weight on his shoulders had already lifted. "But she's got a new spin, pulling Dru into it. Senator's granddaughter in sex scandal. It's bull, but if she does it, it's going to pull everybody in. Reporters hounding her at the flower shop, hounding all of you, turning her family upside down. All of us, too."

"Screw her," Aubrey said, very clearly.

"Another girl with brains." Cam winked at Aubrey. "How much she want this time?"

"A million."

Cam choked on the coffee he'd just sipped. "A million—a million fucking dollars?"

"She won't get a penny." Face grim, Anna patted Cam on the back. "Not a penny this time, or ever again. Is that right, Seth?"

"I knew when I sat with her in that dive she had me meet her in, that I had to cut it off. She'll have to do whatever she's going to do."

"We won't be sitting on our hands," Phillip promised. "When are you supposed to meet her again?"

"Tomorrow night, with a ten-thousand-dollar down payment."

"Where?"

"This redneck bar in Saint Michael's."

"Phil's thinking." Cam grinned a wide, wide grin. "I love when that happens."

"Yeah, I'm thinking."

"Why don't I start some breakfast." Grace got to her feet. "And you can tell us all what you're thinking."

DRU listened to the ideas, the arguments and, incredibly from her point of view, the laughter and casual insults as a plan took shape.

Bacon sizzled, eggs were scrambled and coffee was brewed. She wondered if the lack of sleep had made her dull-witted, or if it was just impossible for an outsider to keep up with the dynamics.

When she started to get up, to help set the table, Anna laid a hand on her shoulder, rubbed. "Just sit, honey. You look exhausted."

"I'm all right. It's just I don't think I really understand. I suppose Gloria hasn't committed an actual crime, but it just seems as if you should talk to the police or a lawyer instead of trying to deal with it all yourselves."

Conversation snapped off. For a few seconds there was no sound but the gurgle of the coffeepot and the snap of frying meat.

"Well now," Ethan said in his thoughtful way, "that would be one option. Except you have to figure the cops would just tell Seth how he was a moron to give her money in the first place. Seems we've already covered that part here."

"She *blackmailed* him."

"In a manner of speaking," Ethan agreed. "They're not going to arrest her for it, are they?"

"No, but—"

"And I guess a lawyer might write a whole bunch of papers and letters and what-all about it. Maybe we could sue her or something. You can sue anybody for any damn thing, it seems to me. Maybe it goes to court. Then it gets ugly and it drags out."

"It isn't enough to stop the extortion," Dru insisted. "She should pay for what she's done. You work in the system," she said to Anna.

"I do. And I believe in it. I also know its flaws. As much as I want this woman to pay for every moment of pain and worry and unhappiness she's brought Seth, I know she won't. We can only deal with now."

"We deal with our own." Cam spoke in a tone of flat finality. "Family stands up. That's all there is."

Dru leaned toward him. "And you're thinking I won't stand up."

Cam leaned right back. "Dru, you're as pretty as they come, but you're not sitting at this table for decoration. You'll stand up. Quinn men don't fall for a woman unless she's got a spine."

She kept her eyes on his. "Is that a compliment?"

He grinned at her. "That was two compliments."

She eased back, nodded. "All right. So you handle it your way. The Quinn way," she added. "But I think it might be helpful to find out if, considering her lifestyle and habits, she has any outstanding warrants. A call to my grandfather ought to get us that information before tomorrow night. It wouldn't hurt for her to realize we play hard, too."

"I like her," Cam said to Seth.

"Me too." But Seth took Dru's hand. "I don't want to drag your family into this."

"Not wanting to drag yours into it or me into it is why we're sitting here at four in the morning." She took the platter of eggs Aubrey passed, scooped some onto her plate. "Your bright idea was to get drunk and dump me. How'd that work out for you?"

He took the platter, tried a smile. "Better than expected."

"No thanks to you. I wouldn't advise you going down that path again. Pass the salt."

While his family looked on, he reached over, took her face in his hands and kissed her. Hard and long. "Dru," he said. "I love you."

"Good. I love you, too." She took his wrist, squeezed lightly. "Now pass the salt."

HE didn't think he would sleep, but he dropped off like a stone for four hours. When he woke in his old room, disoriented and soft-brained, his first clear thought was that she wasn't beside him.

He stumbled out of the room and downstairs to find Cam alone in the kitchen. "Where's Dru?"

"She went into work, about an hour ago. Borrowed your car."

"She went in? Jesus." Seth rubbed his hands over his face, tried to get his brain to engage after too much whiskey, too much coffee, too little sleep. "Why didn't she just close for the day? She couldn't have gotten very much sleep."

"She looked like she handled it a lot better than you did, pal."

"Yeah, well, she didn't down half a bottle of Jameson first."

"You play, you pay."

"Yeah." He opened a cupboard to search for the kitchen aspirin. "Tell me."

Cam poured a glass of water, handed it to Seth. "Down those, then let's take a walk."

"I need to clean up, get into town. Maybe I can give Dru a hand in the shop. Something."

"She'll hold for a few minutes." Cam opened the kitchen door. "Let's take it outside."

"If you're planning on kicking my ass, it won't take much this morning."

"Thought about it. But I think it's been kicked enough for now."

"Look, I know I fucked up—"

"Just shut up." Cam gave Seth a shove out the door. "I've got some things to say."

He headed for the dock, as Seth had expected. The sun was strong and hot. It was barely nine in the morning, and already the air had a mean, threatening weight that promised to gain more muscle before it was done.

"You pissed me off," Cam began. "I'm mostly over it. But I want something made clear—and I'm speaking for Ethan and Phil. Get that?"

"Yeah, I get it."

"We didn't give up a goddamn thing for you. Shut up, Seth," he snapped out when Seth opened his mouth. "Just shut the hell up and listen." He let out a breath. "Ha. Looks like I'm still pissed off after all. Grace has some points, and I'm not going to argue about them. But none of us gave up jack."

"You wanted to race—"

"And I raced," Cam snapped out. "I told you to shut up. Now shut the fuck up until I'm done. You were ten years old, and we did what we were supposed to do. Nobody wants a fucking obligation from you, nobody wants payment from you, and it's a goddamn insult for you to think otherwise."

"It's not like that."

Cam stepped closer. "Do you want me to tie your tongue in a knot or are you going to shut up?"

Because he *felt* ten again, Seth shrugged.

"Things changed for you the way they were supposed to change. Things changed for us, too. Ever stop to think that if I hadn't been stuck with some smart-assed, skinny, pain-in-the-ass kid I might not have met Anna? I might have had to live my whole life without her—and without Kevin and Jake. Phil and Sybill, same deal. They found each other because you were in the middle. I figure Ethan and Grace might be getting around to dating just about now, almost twenty years after the fact, if you being part of things hadn't nudged them along."

He waited a beat. "So, how much do we owe you for our wives and children? For pulling us back home, for giving us a reason to start the business?"

"I'm sorry."

Pure frustration had Cam dragging at his own hair. "I don't want you to be sorry, for sweet Christ's sake! I want you to wake up."

"I'm awake. I don't feel much like George Bailey, but I'm awake. *It's a Wonderful Life*," Seth added. "Grandma—Stella told me I ought to think about it."

"Yeah. She loved old movies. I should've figured if anybody could put a chip in that rock head of yours, it would be Mom."

"I guess I didn't listen to her either. I think she's pissed off at me, too. I should've told you right along."

"You didn't, and that's done. So we start with now. We'll deal with her tonight."

"I'm looking forward to it." Seth turned with a slow smile. "I never thought I'd say it, but I'm looking forward to meeting her tonight. It's been a long time coming. So . . . you want to kick my ass, or slap me around?"

"Get a grip on yourself. Just wanted to clear the air." Cam slung a friendly arm around Seth's shoulder. Then shoved him into the water. "I don't know why," Cam said when Seth surfaced, "but doing that always makes me feel better."

"Glad I could help," Seth sputtered and let himself sink.

"YOU'RE staying here. That's the end of it."

"And when did we come to the point where you dictate where I go and what I do? Play it back for me, I must have missed it the first time around."

"I'm not going to argue about this."

"Oh yes," Dru said, almost sweetly, "you are."

"She's not getting near you again. That's number one. The place I'm meeting her is a dive, and you don't belong there. That's two."

"Oh, I see. Now you decide where I belong. That's a tune I've been hearing all my life. I don't care for it."

"Dru." Seth paused, then paced to the back door of the family kitchen, back again. "This is hard enough without me going in there worrying about some asshole hassling you. The place is one step up from a pit."

"I don't know why you think I can't handle assholes. I've been handling you, haven't I?"

"That's real funny, and I'll bust into hilarity over it later.

I want this done and over. I want it behind me. Behind us. Please." He changed tack, laid his hand gently on her shoulder. "Stay here and let me do what I have to do."

It was turmoil in his eyes now rather than temper. And she responded to it. "Well, since you ask so nicely."

His shoulders relaxed as he laid his forehead on hers. "Okay, good. Maybe you should stretch out for a little while. You didn't get much sleep last night."

"Don't push it, Seth."

"Right. I should go."

"You know who you are." She turned her head to brush her lips over his. "And so do I. She doesn't. She never could."

SHE let him go, and stood on the front porch with the other Quinn women as the two cars drove away.

Anna lowered the hand she'd lifted in a wave. "There go our strong, brave men, off to battle. And we womenfolk stay behind, tucked up safe."

"Put on the aprons," Aubrey mumbled. "Make potato salad for tomorrow's picnic."

Dru glanced around, saw the same look in her companions' eyes she knew was in her own. "I don't think so."

"So." Sybill rolled her shoulders, glanced at her watch. "How much lead time do we give them?"

"Fifteen minutes ought to be about right," Anna decided.

Grace nodded. "We'll take my van."

SETH sat at the bar, brooding into his untouched beer. He figured the dread in the pit of his stomach was natural.

She'd always put it there. The venue, he supposed, was the perfect place for this showdown with her, with his early childhood, with his own ghosts and demons.

He intended to walk out of it when he was finished, and leave all of that misery behind, just another smear on the dirty air.

He needed to feel clean again, complete again. He wondered if Ray would have understood this nasty tug-of-war between fury and grief.

He liked to think so. Just as he liked to think some part of Ray was sitting beside him in the bar.

But when she walked in, there was only the two of them. The drinkers, the pool players, the bartender, even that nebulous connection with the man who'd been his grandfather faded away.

It was just Seth, and his mother.

She relaxed onto a stool, crossed her legs and sent the bartender a wink.

"You look a little rough around the edges," she said to Seth. "Tough night?"

"You look the same. You know, I've been sitting here thinking. You had a pretty good deal growing up."

"Shit." She snagged the gin and tonic the bartender put in front of her. "Lot you know about it."

"Big house, plenty of money, good education."

"Fuck that." She drank deep. "Bunch of jerks and assholes."

"You hated them."

"My mother's a cold fish, stepfather's pussy-whipped. And there's Sybill, the perfect daughter. I couldn't wait to get the hell out and live."

"I don't know about your parents. They don't have anything to do with me either. But Sybill never hurt you. She took you in, took both of us in when you landed on her doorstep, broke and with nowhere else to go."

"So she could lord it over me. Goddamn superior bitch."

"Is that why you stole from her when we were in New York? Cleaned her out and took off after she'd given you a place to stay?"

"I take what I need. That's how you get ahead in life. Had to support you, didn't I?"

"Let's not bullshit. You never gave a damn about me. The only reason you didn't take off without me, dump me on Sybill, was because you knew she cared about me. So you took me away, you stole her things because you hated her. You stole so you could buy drugs."

"Oh yeah, she'd've loved it if I'd left you behind. She could've gone around feeling righteous, telling everybody how worthless I was. Fuck her. Whatever I took out of her place, I was entitled to. Gotta look out for number one in this life. Never could teach you that."

"You taught me plenty." When Gloria rattled the ice in her glass, he signaled the bartender for another drink. "Ray didn't even know about you, but you hated him. When he found out, when he tried to help you, you only hated him more."

"He owed me. Bastard doesn't keep his dick zipped, knocks up some idiot coed, he oughta pay."

"And he paid you. He didn't know Barbara was pregnant with you, he never knew you existed. But when you told him, he paid you. And it wasn't enough. You tried to ruin him with lies. Then you used his decency against him and sold me to him like I was a puppy you were tired of."

"Fucking A I was tired of you. Kept you around for ten

years, cramping my style. Old man Quinn owed me for giving him a grandson. And it all worked out pretty well for you, didn't it?"

"I guess I owe you for that one." He lifted his beer in a toast, sipped. "But it worked out pretty well for you, at least when he was alive. You just kept hitting him up for more money, using me as the bait."

"Hey, he could've tossed you back anytime. You were nothing to him, just like I was nothing."

"Yeah, some people are just stupid, weak, natural marks, believing a promise made to a ten-year-old boy needs to be kept. The same type who think that same kid deserves a shot at a decent life, a home, a family. He'd have given you the same, if you'd wanted it."

"You think I wanted to be stuck in some backwater bum-fuck town, paying homage to an old man who picks up strays?" She gulped her gin. "That's your scene, not mine. And you got it, so what're you bitching about? And if you want to keep it, you'll pay. Just like you've always paid. You got the down payment?"

"How much you figure you've gotten from me over the years, Gloria? Between what you bled out of Ray, what you've been bleeding out of me? Must be a couple hundred thousand, at least. Of course, you never got anything out of my brothers. You tried—the usual lies, threats, intimidation—but they didn't bleed so easy. You do better with old men and kids."

She smirked. "They'd've paid if I'd wanted them to pay. I had better things to do. Bigger fish to fry. You wanna fry your own fish now, keep that fancy art career you've got going from getting screwed up, wanna keep sticking it to the senator's granddaughter, you pay for it."

"So you said. Let me get the terms clear. I pay you, one million dollars starting with the ten-thousand-dollar down payment tonight—"

"In cash."

"Right, in cash, or you'll go to the press, to Dru's family, and spin another web of lies about how you were used and abused by the Quinns, starting with Ray. You'll smear them and me and Dru along with it. The poor, desperate woman, girl really, struggling to raise a child on her own, begging for help only to be forced to give up the child."

"Has a nice ring. Lifetime Movie of the Week."

"No mention in there of the tricks you turned while that child was in the next room—or the men you let touch him. No mention of the drugs, the booze, the beatings."

"Bring out the violins." She leaned in, very close. "You were a pain in the ass. You're lucky I kept you around as long as I did." And lowered her voice. "You're lucky I didn't sell you to one of my johns. Some would've paid top dollar."

"You would have, sooner or later."

She shrugged. "Had to get something out of you, didn't I?"

"You've been tapping me for money since I was fourteen. I've paid you to protect my family, myself. Mostly I've paid you because the peace of mind was worth a hell of a lot more than the money. I've let you blackmail me."

"I want what's due me." She snatched the third drink. "I'm making you a deal here. One lump-sum payment and you keep your nice, boring life. Screw with me, and you'll lose it all."

"A million dollars or you'll do whatever you can to hurt my family, ruin my career and destroy my relationship with Dru."

"In a nutshell. Pay up."

He nudged his beer aside, met her eyes. "Not now, not ever again."

She grabbed his shirt in her fist, yanked his face close to hers. "You don't want to fuck with me."

"Oh yeah, I do. I have." He reached in his pocket, pulled out a mini recorder. "Everything we've said is on here. Might be a problem in court, if I decide to go to the cops."

When she grabbed for it, he cuffed her wrist with his hand. "Speaking of cops, they'll be interested to know you jumped bail down in Fort Worth. Solicitation and possession. You go public and some hard-ass skip tracer is going to be really happy to scoop you up and haul you back to Texas."

"You son of a bitch."

"Truer words," he said mildly. "But you go right ahead and try to sell your version of things. I figure anybody who wants to write a story about all this will be really interested in this informal interview."

"I want my money." She shrieked it, tossed what was left in her glass in his face.

The quartet playing pool looked over. The biggest of them tapped his cue against his palm as he sized Seth up.

She leaped off the stool, and fury had her practically in tears. "He stole my money."

The four men started forward. Seth rose from the stool.

And his brothers walked in, ranged themselves beside him.

"That seems to even things up." Cam tucked his thumbs in his front pockets and gave Gloria a fierce grimace. "Been a while."

"You bastards. You're all fucking bastards. I want what's mine."

"We've got nothing of yours." Ethan spoke quietly. "We never did."

"I take anything from her?" Seth asked the bartender.

"Nope." He continued to wipe the bar. "You want trouble, take it outside."

Phillip scanned the faces of the four men. "You want trouble?"

The big man tapped his cue twice more. "Bob says he didn't take nothing, he didn't take nothing. None of my never mind."

"How about you, Gloria? You want trouble?" Phillip asked her.

Before she could speak, the door opened. The women came in.

"Goddamn it," Cam muttered under his breath. "Should've figured it."

Dru walked directly to Seth, slid her hand into his. "Hello again, Gloria. It's funny, my mother doesn't remember you at all. She isn't the least bit interested in you. But my grandfather is." She took a piece of paper out of her pocket. "This is the number to his office on the Hill. He'll be happy to speak to you if you'd like to call him."

Gloria slapped the paper from Dru's fingers, then retreated quickly when Seth stepped forward.

"I'll make you sorry for this." She shoved through them, pausing briefly to snarl at Sybill.

"You shouldn't have come back, Gloria," Sybill told her. "You should've cut your losses."

"Bitch. I'll make you sorry. I'll make you all sorry." With one last bitter glance, she shoved through the door.

"You were supposed to stay home," Seth told her.

"No, I wasn't." Dru touched his cheek.

NINETEEN

~

T HE HOUSE AND the yard were crowded with people. Crabs were steaming, and a half dozen picnic tables were loaded with food.

The Quinns' annual Fourth of July celebration was well under way.

Seth pulled a beer from the keg, grabbed some shade, and took a break from the conversations to sketch.

His world, he thought. Friends, family, slow Shore voices and squealing kids. The smells of spiced crabs, of beer, of talcum powder and grass. Of the water.

A couple of kids were out in a Sunfish with a bright yellow sail. Ethan's dog was splashing in the shallows with Aubrey—old times.

He heard Anna's laugh and the cheerful clink of horseshoes.

Independence Day, he thought. He would remember this one for the rest of his life.

"We've been doing this here since before you were born," Stella said from beside him.

The pencil squirted out of Seth's fingers. No dream this time, he thought in a kind of breathless wonder. He was sitting in the warm, dappled shade, surrounded by people and noise.

And talking to a ghost.

"I wasn't sure you were speaking to me."

"Nearly made a mess of it, and that ticked me off. But you figured things out in the end."

She was wearing the old khaki hat, a red shirt and baggy blue shorts. Without any real thought, Seth picked up the pencil, turned the page in his book and began to draw her as she looked, sitting contentedly in the shade.

"Part of me was always scared of her, no matter what. But that's gone now."

"Good. Stay that way, because she'll always cause trouble. My God, look at Crawford. How'd he get so old? Time just goes by, no matter what the hell you do. Some things you let go. Some things are worth repeating. Like this party, year after year after year."

He continued to sketch, but his throat had tightened. "You're not coming back again, are you?"

"No, honey. I'm not coming back again."

She touched him, and he would never forget the sensation of her hand on his knee. "Time to look forward, Seth. You don't want to ever forget what's behind you, but you've got to look ahead. Look at my boys." She let out a long sigh as she gazed over at Cam, and Ethan, and Phillip. "All grown up, with families of their own. I'm glad I told them that I loved them, that I was proud of them, while I was still breathing."

She smiled now, patted Seth's knee. "Glad I got a chance to tell you I love you. And I'm proud of you."

"Grandma—"

"Make a good life for yourself or I'm going to be ticked off at you again. Here comes your girl," she said, and was gone.

His heart wrenched in his chest. And Dru sat down beside him. "Want company?" she asked.

"As long as it's you."

"So many people." She leaned back on her elbows. "It makes me think Saint Chris must look like a ghost town right now."

"Just about everyone swings by, at least for a while. It whittles down by nightfall, and the rest of us stay here and watch the fireworks."

Some things you let go, he remembered. Some are worth repeating.

"I love you, Drusilla. Just thought that was worth repeating."

She angled her head, studied the odd little smile on his face. "You can repeat it whenever you like. And if you come home with me afterward, we can make our own fireworks."

"That's a date."

She sat up again, examined his drawing. "That's wonderful. Such a strong face—and a friendly one." She glanced around for the model. "Where is she? I don't remember seeing her."

"She's not here anymore." He took a last look at the sketch, then gently closed the book. "Wanna go for a swim?"

"It's hot enough, but I didn't think to bring a suit."

"Really?" Grinning, he stood up, pulled her to her feet. "But you can swim, right?"

"Of course I can swim." As soon as the words were out, she recognized the gleam in his eye. "Don't even think about it."

"Too late." He scooped her up.

"Don't—" She wiggled, shoved, then began to panic as he jogged toward the dock. "This isn't funny."

"It will be. Don't forget to hold your breath."

He ran straight down the dock and off the end.

"IT'S a Quinn thing," Anna said as she handed Dru a dry shirt. "I can't explain it. They're always doing that."

"I lost a shoe."

"They'll probably find it."

Dru sat on the bed. "Men are so strange."

"We just have to remember that in some areas, they're really just five years old. These sandals ought to fit you well enough." She offered them.

"Thanks. Oh, they're fabulous."

"I love shoes. I lust for shoes."

"With me it's earrings. I have no power against them."

"I like you very much."

Dru stopped admiring the sandals and looked up. "Thank you. I like you very much, too."

"It's a bonus. I would have made room for any woman Seth loved. All of us would. So you're a very nice bonus. I wanted to tell you."

"I . . . I don't have experience with families like yours."

"Who does?" With a laugh, Anna sat on the bed beside her.

"Mine isn't generous. I'm going to try to talk to my parents again. Seeing what Seth's been through, what he faced down last night, made me realize I have to try. But whatever understanding we reach, we'll never be like yours. They won't welcome him the way you're welcoming me."

"Don't be so sure." She wrapped an arm around Dru's shoulders. "He has a way of winning people over."

"Certainly worked with me. I love him." She pressed a hand to her stomach. "It's terrifying how much."

"I know the feeling. It'll be dark soon." Anna gave Dru a quick squeeze. "Let's go get a glass of wine and get a good spot to watch the show."

When she stepped outside, Seth met her with one very soggy canvas slide and a sheepish grin. "Found it."

She snatched it, set it beside the back door where she'd put its mate. "You're a baboon."

"Mrs. Monroe brought homemade peach ice cream." He brought his hand out, with a double-scoop cone in it, from behind his back.

"Hmm." She sniffed, but she took the cone.

"Want to sit on the grass with me and watch fireworks?"

She took a long lick. "Maybe."

"Gonna let me kiss you when nobody's looking?"

"Maybe."

"Gonna share that ice cream?"

"Absolutely not."

WHILE Seth was trying to cadge his share of a peach ice cream cone, and excited children were bouncing in anticipation of that first explosion of light and color in the night sky, Gloria DeLauter pulled into the parking lot of Boats by Quinn.

She jerked to a halt and sat stewing in the messy juices of her fury laced with a pint of gin.

They'd pay. All of them would pay. Bastards. Thought they could scare her off, gang up on her the way they had and go back to their stupid house and laugh about it.

They'd see who laughed when she was finished with them.

They *owed* her. She beat the heel of her hand on the steering wheel as rage choked her.

She was going to make that son of a bitch she'd given birth to sorry. She'd make all of them sorry.

She shoved out of the car, stumbling as the gin spun in her head. She weaved her way to the trunk. *God!* She loved being high. People who went through life sober and straight were the assholes. World was fucking full of assholes, she thought as she stabbed her key at the trunk lock.

You need to get into a program, Gloria.

That's what they told her. Her worthless mother, her spineless stepfather, her tight-assed sister. The sainted sucker Ray Quinn had tried that with her, too.

It was all bullshit.

On the fourth try, she managed to get the key in the lock. She lifted the trunk, then hooted with delight as she dragged out the two cans of gasoline.

"We're gonna have some motherfucking fireworks, all right."

She stumbled again, stepped right out of one of her shoes but was too drunk to notice. Limping now, she carted the cans to the door, then straightened up, caught her breath.

It took her a while to uncap the first can, and as she fought with it she cursed the gawky kid at the gas station who'd filled them for her.

Just another asshole in a world of assholes.

But her good humor returned when she splashed gasoline on the doors and the sharp, dangerous smell of it stung the air.

"Stick your wood boats up your ass. Fucking Quinns."

She splashed it on the brick, on glass, on the pretty barberry bushes Anna had planted along the foundation. When one can was empty, she started on the second.

It was a thrill to heave it, still half full, through the front window. She danced in the dark to the sound of breaking glass.

Then she hobbled back to the trunk and retrieved the two bottles she'd filled with gas earlier and plugged with rags. "Molotov cocktail." She giggled, swayed. "I got a double for you bastards."

She fumbled out her lighter and flicked. And was smiling when she set the flame to the rag.

It caught faster than she'd expected, burned the tips of her fingers. On a little shriek, she heaved it toward the window, shattered it on brick.

"Shit!" Flames leaped along the bushes, ate down to the ground and crept toward the doors. But she wanted more.

She edged closer and, with the heat soaking her face, lit the second rag. Her aim was better this time, and she heard the boom of glass and flame as the bottle crashed on the floor inside the building.

"Kiss my ass!" She screamed it and gave herself the pleasure of watching the fire sprint before she ran to her car.

THE rocket exploded across the sky in a fountain of gold against black. With Dru nestled between his legs, his arms around her waist, Seth felt almost stupidly content.

"I really missed this when I was overseas," he told her.

"Sitting in the backyard on the Fourth of July and watching the sky go crazy." He turned his lips to the nape of her neck. "Do I still get the fireworks later?"

"Probably. In fact, if you play your cards right, I might let you . . ."

She trailed off, glancing over as Seth did at the sound of raised voices. He was on his feet, pulling Dru to hers even as Cam raced toward them.

"Boatyard's on fire."

THE fire department was already fighting the blaze. The doors and windows were gone, and the brick around them blackened. Seth stood, hands fisted, as water pumped through the openings and smoke billowed out.

He thought of the work inside that old brick barn. The sweat and the blood that went into it, the sheer determination and family pride.

Then he bent down and picked up the high-heeled backless shoe at his feet. "It's hers. Stay with Anna and the rest," he told Dru, and went to his brothers.

"COUPLE of kids heard the explosion and saw the car drive away." Cam rubbed his hands over eyes that stung from smoke. "Not much doubt it was arson since she left the gas cans behind. They got the make and model of her car, and a description. She won't get far."

"She'll see this as payback," Seth said. "Fuck with me, I'll fuck with you more."

"Yeah, well, she's got a surprise coming. This time she's going to jail."

"She messed us up real good first."

"We're insured." Cam stared at the blackened brick, the trampled bushes, the stream of smoke still belching out of the broken door.

The pain in his heart was a physical stab. "We put this place together once, we can do it again. And if you're planning on taking any guilt trips—"

"No." Seth shook his head. "That's done." He held out his hand as Aubrey walked to them.

"We're okay." She squeezed his fingers. "That's what counts." But the tears on her cheeks weren't all from smoke.

"Hell of a mess," Phillip said as he walked up. His face was smeared with soot, his clothes filthy with it. "But it's out. Those kids who called nine-one-one saved our asses. Fire department responded in minutes."

"You got their names?" Cam asked him.

"Yeah." He let out a breath. "Ethan's over talking with the fire marshal. He'll let us know when we're clear to go in. It's gonna be a while with the arson investigation on top of it."

"Which one of us is going to talk the women into taking the kids home?"

Phillip stuck his hand in his pocket, pulled out a coin. "Flip you for it. Heads it's your headache, tails it's mine."

"Deal. But I flip. Your fingers are a little too sticky to suit me."

"You saying I'd cheat?"

"Over this? Damn right."

"That's cold," Phillip complained, but handed over the coin.

"Damn it." Cam hissed through his teeth when he flipped heads.

"Don't even think about saying two out of three."

Scowling, Cam tossed Phillip the coin, then stalked over to argue with the women.

"Well." Phillip folded his arms and studied the building. "We could say screw it, move to Tahiti and open a tiki bar. Spend our days fishing until we're brown as monkeys and our nights having jungle sex with our women."

"Nah. Live on an island, you end up drinking rum. Never had a taste for it."

Phillip slapped a hand on Seth's shoulder. "Then I guess we stick. Want to break it to Ethan?" He nodded toward his brother as Ethan crossed the muddy lawn.

"He'll be okay. He doesn't like rum either." But the optimism Seth was fighting to hold on to wavered when he saw Ethan's face.

"They picked her up." Ethan swiped a forearm over his sweaty brow. "Sitting in a bar not five miles out of town. You all right with that?" he asked Seth.

"I'm fine with that."

"Okay then. Maybe you ought to go talk your girl into going on home. It's going to be a long night here."

IT was a long night, and a long day after. It would be, Seth thought, some long weeks before Boats by Quinn was back in full operation.

He'd tromped through the wreckage and the stink of the building, mourned with his brothers and Aubrey the loss of the pretty, half-built hull of a skiff that was now no more than scraps of blackened teak.

He grieved over the sketches he'd drawn from childhood on, which were nothing but ashes. He could, and would, reproduce them. But he couldn't replace them, nor the joy each one had given him.

When there was no more to do, he went home, cleaned up and slept until he could do more.

It was nearly dusk the next evening when he drove to Dru's. He was tired down to the bone, but as clearheaded as he'd been in his life. He hauled the porch swing he'd bought out of the bed of the truck he'd borrowed from Cam, got his tools.

When she stepped out, he was drilling in the first hook.

"You said you wanted one. This seemed like the place for it."

"It's the perfect place." She walked over, touched his shoulder. "Talk to me."

"I will. That's why I'm here. Sorry I didn't get in touch today."

"I know you've been busy. Half the town's been in and out of my shop, just like half the town was there at the fire last night."

"We got more help than we could handle. Fire didn't spread to the second level."

She knew. Word spread every bit as quickly as flame. But she let him talk.

"Main level's a wreck. Between the fire, the smoke, the water, we'll have to gut it. Lost most of the tools, toasted a hull. Insurance adjuster was out today. We'll be okay."

"Yes, you'll be okay."

He stepped over to drill for the second hook. "They arrested Gloria. Kids made her car, and the kid who sold her the gas ID'd her. Plus she left her fingerprints all over the gas can she dumped outside the building. When they picked her up for questioning, she was still wearing one shoe. Losing shoes seems to be going around."

"I'm so sorry, Seth."

"Me too. I'm not taking it on," he added. "I know it's not

my fault. All she managed to do was mess up a building. She didn't hurt us. She can't. We've built something she can't touch."

He looped the chain, hooked a link. Tugged to test it. "Not that she'll stop trying."

He walked around, looped the other chain. "She'll go to jail." He spoke conversationally, and she wondered if he thought she couldn't see the fatigue on his face. "But she won't change. She won't change because she can't see herself. And when she gets out, it's a pretty sure bet she'll come back this way, sooner or later, make another play for money. She's in my life, and I can deal with that."

He gave the swing a little nudge, sent it swaying. "It's a lot to ask someone else to take on."

"Yes, it is. I plan on having a long heart-to-heart with my parents. But I don't think it'll change anything. They're overly possessive, discontent people who will, most likely, continue to use me as a weapon against each other, or an excuse not to face their own marriage on its own terms. They're in my life, and I can deal with that."

She paused, tilted her head. "It's a lot to ask someone else to take on."

"Guess it is. Want to try this out?"

"I do."

They sat, swung gently as dusk thickened and the water lapped the shore. "Does it work for you?" he asked her.

"It certainly does. This is exactly where I would've hung it."

"Dru?"

"Hmmm?"

"Are you going to marry me?"

Her lips tipped up at the corners. "That's my plan."

"It's a good plan." He took her hand, lifted it to his lips. "Are you going to have children with me?"

Her eyes stung, but she kept them closed and continued to swing gently. "Yes. That's the second stage of the plan. You know how I feel about stages."

He turned her hand over, kissed her palm. "Grow old with me, here, in the house by the water."

She opened her eyes now, let the first tear spill down her cheek. "You knew that would make me cry."

"But just a little. Here." He drew a ring out of his pocket, a simple gold band with a small round ruby. "It's pretty plain, but it was Stella's—it was my grandmother's." Slipped it on her finger. "The guys thought she'd like me to have it."

"Oh-oh."

"What?"

Her fingers tightened on his as she pulled his hand to her cheek. "It may not be just a little after all. It's the most beautiful thing you could have given me."

He laid his lips on hers, drawing her in as she wrapped her arms around him. "Somebody really smart told me you've got to look ahead. You can't forget what's behind you, but you got to move forward. It starts now. For us, it starts now."

"Right now."

She laid her head on his shoulder, held his hand tight in hers. They rocked on the swing in the heavy night air while the water turned dark with night, and the fireflies began to dance.

Can't get enough of Nora Roberts?
Try the #1 *New York Times* bestselling
In Death series, by Nora Roberts
writing as J. D. Robb.

Turn the page to see where it all began . . .

NAKED IN DEATH

S HE WOKE IN the dark. Through the slats on the window shades, the first murky hint of dawn slipped, slanting shadowy bars over the bed. It was like waking in a cell.

For a moment she simply lay there, shuddering, imprisoned, while the dream faded. After ten years on the force, Eve still had dreams.

Six hours before, she'd killed a man, had watched death creep into his eyes. It wasn't the first time she'd exercised maximum force, or dreamed. She'd learned to accept the action and the consequences.

But it was the child that haunted her. The child she hadn't been in time to save. The child whose screams had echoed in the dreams with her own.

All the blood, Eve thought, scrubbing sweat from her face with her hands. Such a small little girl to have had so much blood in her. And she knew it was vital that she push it aside.

Standard departmental procedure meant that she would spend the morning in Testing. Any officer whose discharge of weapon resulted in termination of life was required to undergo emotional and psychiatric clearance before resuming duty. Eve considered the tests a mild pain in the ass.

She would beat them, as she'd beaten them before.

When she rose, the overheads went automatically to low setting, lighting her way into the bath. She winced once at her reflection. Her eyes were swollen from lack of sleep, her skin nearly as pale as the corpses she'd delegated to the ME.

Rather than dwell on it, she stepped into the shower, yawning.

"Give me one oh one degrees, full force," she said and shifted so that the shower spray hit her straight in the face.

She let it steam, lathered listlessly while she played through the events of the night before. She wasn't due in Testing until nine, and would use the next three hours to settle and let the dream fade away completely.

Small doubts and little regrets were often detected and could mean a second and more intense round with the machines and the owl-eyed technicians who ran them.

Eve didn't intend to be off the streets longer than twenty-four hours.

After pulling on a robe, she walked into the kitchen and programmed her AutoChef for coffee, black; toast, light. Through her window she could hear the heavy hum of air traffic carrying early commuters to offices, late ones home. She'd chosen the apartment years before because it was in a heavy ground and air pattern, and she liked the noise and crowds. On another yawn, she glanced out the window, followed the rattling journey of an aging airbus hauling laborers not fortunate enough to work in the city or by home 'links.

She brought the *New York Times* up on her monitor and scanned the headlines while the faux caffeine bolstered her system. The AutoChef had burned her toast again, but she ate it anyway, with a vague thought of springing for a replacement unit.

She was frowning over an article on a mass recall of droid cocker spaniels when her telelink blipped. Eve shifted to communications and watched her commanding officer flash onto the screen.

"Commander."

"Lieutenant." He gave her a brisk nod, noted the still wet hair and sleepy eyes. "Incident at Twenty-seven West Broadway, eighteenth floor. You're primary."

Eve lifted a brow. "I'm on Testing. Subject terminated at twenty-two thirty-five."

"We have override," he said, without inflection. "Pick up your shield and weapon on the way to the incident. Code Five, Lieutenant."

"Yes, sir." His face flashed off even as she pushed back from the screen. Code Five meant she would report directly to her commander, and there would be no unsealed interdepartmental reports and no cooperation with the press.

In essence, it meant she was on her own.

BROADWAY was noisy and crowded, a party that rowdy guests never left. Street, pedestrian, and sky traffic were miserable, choking the air with bodies and vehicles.

In her old days in uniform she remembered it as a hot spot for wrecks and crushed tourists who were too busy gaping at the show to get out of the way.

Even at this hour steam was rising from the stationary and portable food stands that offered everything from rice noodles to soy dogs for the teeming crowds. She had to swerve to avoid an eager merchant on his smoking Glida-Grill, and took his flipped middle finger as a matter of course.

Eve double-parked and, skirting a man who smelled worse than his bottle of brew, stepped onto the sidewalk. She scanned the building first, fifty floors of gleaming metal that knifed into the sky from a hilt of concrete. She was propositioned twice before she reached the door.

Since this five-block area of West Broadway was affectionately termed Prostitute's Walk, she wasn't surprised. She flashed her badge for the uniform guarding the entrance.

"Lieutenant Dallas."

"Yes, sir." He skimmed his official CompuSeal over the door to keep out the curious, then led the way to the bank of elevators. "Eighteenth floor," he said when the doors swished shut behind them.

"Fill me in, Officer." Eve switched on her recorder and waited.

"I wasn't first on the scene, Lieutenant. Whatever happened upstairs is being kept upstairs. There's a badge inside waiting for you. We have a homicide, and a Code Five in number eighteen-oh-three."

"Who called it in?"

"I don't have that information."

He stayed where he was when the elevator opened. Eve stepped out and was alone in a narrow hallway. Security cameras tilted down at her, and her feet were almost soundless on the worn nap of the carpet as she approached 1803. Ignoring the hand plate, she announced herself, holding her badge up to eye level for the peep cam until the door opened.

"Dallas."

"Feeney." She smiled, pleased to see a familiar face. Ryan Feeney was an old friend and former partner who'd traded the street for a desk and a top-level position in the Electronics Detection Division. "So, they're sending computer pluckers these days."

"They wanted brass, and the best." His lips curved in his wide, rumpled face, but his eyes remained sober. He was a small, stubby man with small, stubby hands and rust-colored hair. "You look beat."

"Rough night."

"So I heard." He offered her one of the sugared nuts from the bag he habitually carried, studying her, and measuring if she was up to what was waiting in the bedroom beyond.

She was young for her rank, barely thirty, with wide brown eyes that had never had a chance to be naive. Her doe-brown hair was cropped short, for convenience rather than style, but suited her triangular face with its razor-edge cheekbones and slight dent in the chin.

She was tall, rangy, with a tendency to look thin, but Feeney knew there were solid muscles beneath the leather jacket. But Eve had more—there was also a brain, and a heart.

"This one's going to be touchy, Dallas."

"I picked that up already. Who's the victim?"

"Sharon DeBlass, granddaughter of Senator DeBlass."

Neither meant anything to her. "Politics isn't my forte, Feeney."

"The gentleman from Virginia, extreme right, old money. The granddaughter took a sharp left a few years back, moved to New York and became a licensed companion."

"She was a hooker." Dallas glanced around the apartment. It was furnished in obsessive modern—glass and thin chrome, signed holograms on the walls, recessed bar in bold red. The wide mood screen behind the bar bled with mixing and merging shapes and colors in cool pastels.

Neat as a virgin, Eve mused, and cold as a whore. "No surprise, given her choice of real estate."

"Politics makes it delicate. Victim was twenty-four, Caucasian female. She bought it in bed."

Eve only lifted a brow. "Seems poetic, since she'd been bought there. How'd she die?"

"That's the next problem. I want you to see for yourself."

As they crossed the room, each took out a slim container, sprayed their hands front and back to seal in oils and fingerprints. At the doorway, Eve sprayed the bottom of her boots to slicken them so that she would pick up no fibers, stray hairs, or skin.

Eve was already wary. Under normal circumstances there would have been two other investigators on a homicide scene, with recorders for sound and pictures. Forensics would have been waiting with their usual snarly impatience to sweep the scene.

The fact that only Feeney had been assigned with her meant that there were a lot of eggshells to be walked over.

"Security cameras in the lobby, elevator, and hallways," Eve commented.

"I've already tagged the discs." Feeney opened the bedroom door and let her enter first.

It wasn't pretty. Death rarely was a peaceful, religious experience to Eve's mind. It was the nasty end, indifferent to saint and sinner. But this was shocking, like a stage deliberately set to offend.

The bed was huge, slicked with what appeared to be genuine satin sheets the color of ripe peaches. Small, soft focused spotlights were trained on its center where the naked woman was cupped in the gentle dip of the floating mattress.

The mattress moved with obscenely graceful undulations to the rhythm of programmed music slipping through the headboard.

She was beautiful still, a cameo face with a tumbling waterfall of flaming red hair, emerald eyes that stared glassily at the mirrored ceiling, long, milk-white limbs that called to mind visions of *Swan Lake* as the motion of the bed gently rocked them.

They weren't artistically arranged now, but spread lewdly so that the dead woman formed a final X deadcenter of the bed.

There was a hole in her forehead, one in her chest, another horribly gaping between the open thighs. Blood had splattered on the glossy sheets, pooled, dripped, and stained.

There were splashes of it on the lacquered walls, like lethal paintings scrawled by an evil child.

So much blood was a rare thing, and she had seen much too much of it the night before to take the scene as calmly as she would have preferred.

She had to swallow once, hard, and force herself to block out the image of a small child.

"You got the scene on record?"

"Yep."

"Then turn that damn thing off." She let out a breath after Feeney located the controls that silenced the music. The bed flowed to stillness. "The wounds," Eve murmured, stepping closer to examine them. "Too neat for a knife. Too messy for a laser." A flash came to her—old training films, old videos, old viciousness.

"Christ, Feeney, these look like bullet wounds."

Feeney reached into his pocket and drew out a sealed bag. "Whoever did it left a souvenir." He passed the bag to Eve. "An antique like this has to go for eight, ten thousand for a legal collection, twice that on the black market."

Fascinated, Eve turned the sealed revolver over in her hand. "It's heavy," she said half to herself. "Bulky."

"Thirty-eight caliber," he told her. "First one I've seen outside of a museum. This one's a Smith and Wesson, Model Ten, blue steel." He looked at it with some affection. "Real classic piece, used to be standard police issue up until the latter part of the twentieth. They stopped making them in about twenty-two, twenty-three, when the gun ban was passed."

"You're the history buff." Which explained why he was with her. "Looks new." She sniffed through the bag, caught the scent of oil and burning. "Somebody took good care of this. Steel fired into flesh," she mused as she passed the bag back to Feeney. "Ugly way to die, and the first I've seen it in my ten years with the department."

"Second for me. About fifteen years ago, Lower East Side, party got out of hand. Guy shot five people with a twenty-two before he realized it wasn't a toy. Hell of a mess."

"Fun and games," Eve murmured. "We'll scan the collectors, see how many we can locate who own one like this. Somebody might have reported a robbery."

"Might have."

"It's more likely it came through the black market." Eve glanced back at the body. "If she's been in the business for a few years, she'd have discs, records of her clients, her trick books." She frowned. "With Code Five, I'll have to do the door-to-door myself. Not a simple sex crime," she said with a sigh. "Whoever did it set it up. The antique weapon, the wounds themselves, almost ruler straight down the body, the lights, the pose. Who called it in, Feeney?"

"The killer." He waited until her eyes came back to him. "From right here. Called the station. See how the bedside unit's aimed at her face? That's what came in. Video, no audio."

"He's into showmanship." Eve let out a breath. "Clever bastard, arrogant, cocky. He had sex with her first. I'd bet my badge on it. Then he gets up and does it." She lifted her arm, aiming, lowering it as she counted off, "One, two, three."

"That's cold," murmured Feeney.

"He's cold. He smooths down the sheets after. See how neat they are? He arranges her, spreads her open so nobody can have any doubts as to how she made her living. He does it carefully, practically measuring, so that she's perfectly aligned. Center of the bed, arms and legs equally apart. Doesn't turn off the bed 'cause it's part of the show. He leaves the gun because he wants us to know right away he's no ordinary man. He's got an ego. He doesn't want to waste time letting the body be discovered eventually. He wants it now. That instant gratification."

"She was licensed for men and women," Feeny pointed out, but Eve shook her head.

"It's not a woman. A woman wouldn't have left her looking both beautiful and obscene. No, I don't think it's a woman. Let's see what we can find. Have you gone into her computer yet?"

"No. It's your case, Dallas. I'm only authorized to assist."

"See if you can access her client files." Eve went to the dresser and began to carefully search drawers.

Expensive taste, Eve reflected. There were several items of real silk, the kind no simulation could match. The bottle of scent on the dresser was exclusive, and smelled, after a quick sniff, like expensive sex.

The contents of the drawers were meticulously ordered, lingerie folded precisely, sweaters arranged according to color and material. The closet was the same.

Obviously the victim had a love affair with clothes and a taste for the best and took scrupulous care of what she owned.

And she'd died naked.

"Kept good records," Feeney called out. "It's all here. Her client list, appointments—including her required monthly health exam and her weekly trip to the beauty salon. She used the Trident Clinic for the first and Paradise for the second."

"Both top of the line. I've got a friend who saved for a year so she could have one day for the works at Paradise. Takes all kinds."

"My wife's sister went for it for her twenty-fifth anniversary. Cost damn near as much as my kid's wedding. Hello, we've got her personal address book."

"Good. Copy all of it, will you, Feeney?" At his low whistle, she looked over her shoulder, glimpsed the small gold-edged palm computer in his hand. "What?"

"We've got a lot of high-powered names in here. Politics, entertainment, money, money, money. Interesting, our girl has Roarke's private number."

"Roarke who?"

"Just Roarke, as far as I know. Big money there. Kind of guy that touches shit and turns it into gold bricks. You've got to start reading more than the sports page, Dallas."

"Hey, I read the headlines. Did you hear about the cocker spaniel recall?"

"Roarke's always big news," Feeney said patiently. "He's got one of the finest art collections in the world. Arts and antiques," he continued, noting when Eve clicked in and turned to him. "He's a licensed gun collector. Rumor is he knows how to use them."

"I'll pay him a visit."

"You'll be lucky to get within a mile of him."

"I'm feeling lucky." Eve crossed over to the body to slip her hands under the sheets.

"The man's got powerful friends, Dallas. You can't afford to so much as whisper he's linked to this until you've got something solid."

"Feeney, you know it's a mistake to tell me that." But even as she started to smile, her fingers brushed against something between cold flesh and bloody sheets. "There's something under her." Carefully, Eve lifted the shoulder, eased her fingers over.

"Paper," she murmured. "Sealed." With her protected thumb, she wiped at a smear of blood until she could read the protected sheet.

ONE OF SIX

"It looks hand-printed," she said to Feeney and held it out. "Our boy's more than clever, more than arrogant. And he isn't finished."

**Welcome to Nora Roberts's captivating saga
about the lives and loves of a family on the
windswept shores of the Chesapeake Bay.**

Cameron, Ethan, Phillip, and Seth are four brothers bound by
the love of the extraordinary couple who raised them. Now
grown and living on their own, the oldest Quinns must return
home to honor their father's last request. . . .

Ethan Quinn is a quiet man whose heart runs as deep as
the waters he loves. And now, with his father gone, Ethan
is determined to make the family boat-building business a
success. But amid his achievements lie the most important
challenges of his life.

There's a young boy who needs him, and a woman and child
he loves but never believed he could have. To shape his life
around them, Ethan must face his own dark past and accept
not only who he is but what he hopes to become.

"A warm, satisfying romance with a dash of mystery that will
keep readers engrossed."   —*Library Journal*

---

*Don't miss the other books
in the Chesapeake Bay Saga*

SEA SWEPT
INNER HARBOR
CHESAPEAKE BLUE

*Turn the page for a complete list of titles by
Nora Roberts and J. D. Robb from Berkley. . . .*

Series

Irish Born Trilogy
BORN IN FIRE
BORN IN ICE
BORN IN SHAME

Dream Trilogy
DARING TO DREAM
HOLDING THE DREAM
FINDING THE DREAM

Chesapeake Bay Saga
SEA SWEPT
RISING TIDES
INNER HARBOR
CHESAPEAKE BLUE

Gallaghers of Ardmore Trilogy
JEWELS OF THE SUN
TEARS OF THE MOON
HEART OF THE SEA

Three Sisters Island Trilogy
DANCE UPON THE AIR
HEAVEN AND EARTH
FACE THE FIRE

Key Trilogy
KEY OF LIGHT
KEY OF KNOWLEDGE
KEY OF VALOR

In the Garden Trilogy
BLUE DAHLIA
BLACK ROSE
RED LILY

Circle Trilogy
MORRIGAN'S CROSS
DANCE OF THE GODS
VALLEY OF SILENCE

Sign of Seven Trilogy
BLOOD BROTHERS
THE HOLLOW
THE PAGAN STONE

Bride Quartet
VISION IN WHITE
BED OF ROSES
SAVOR THE MOMENT
HAPPY EVER AFTER

The Inn BoonsBoro Trilogy
THE NEXT ALWAYS
THE LAST BOYFRIEND
THE PERFECT HOPE

The Cousins O'Dwyer Trilogy
DARK WITCH
SHADOW SPELL
BLOOD MAGICK

The Guardians Trilogy
STARS OF FORTUNE
BAY OF SIGHS
ISLAND OF GLASS

Ebooks by Nora Roberts

Nora Roberts & J. D. Robb

Anthologies

FROM THE HEART
A LITTLE MAGIC
A LITTLE FATE

MOON SHADOWS
(with Jill Gregory, Ruth Ryan Langan, and Marianne Willman)

The Once Upon Series
(with Jill Gregory, Ruth Ryan Langan, and Marianne Willman)

ONCE UPON A CASTLE	ONCE UPON A ROSE
ONCE UPON A STAR	ONCE UPON A KISS
ONCE UPON A DREAM	ONCE UPON A MIDNIGHT

SILENT NIGHT
(with Susan Plunkett, Dee Holmes, and Claire Cross)

OUT OF THIS WORLD
(with Laurell K. Hamilton, Susan Krinard, and Maggie Shayne)

BUMP IN THE NIGHT
(with Mary Blayney, Ruth Ryan Langan, and Mary Kay McComas)

DEAD OF NIGHT
(with Mary Blayney, Ruth Ryan Langan, and Mary Kay McComas)

THREE IN DEATH

SUITE 606
(with Mary Blayney, Ruth Ryan Langan, and Mary Kay McComas)

IN DEATH

THE LOST
(with Patricia Gaffney, Mary Blayney, and Ruth Ryan Langan)

THE OTHER SIDE
(with Mary Blayney, Patricia Gaffney, Ruth Ryan Langan, and Mary Kay McComas)

TIME OF DEATH

THE UNQUIET
(with Mary Blayney, Patricia Gaffney, Ruth Ryan Langan, and Mary Kay McComas)

MIRROR, MIRROR
(with Mary Blayney, Elaine Fox, Mary Kay McComas, and R. C. Ryan)

DOWN THE RABBIT HOLE
(with Mary Blayney, Elaine Fox, Mary Kay McComas, and R. C. Ryan)

Also available . . .

THE OFFICIAL NORA ROBERTS COMPANION
(edited by Denise Little and Laura Hayden)

RISING TIDES

NORA ROBERTS

JOVE
New York

A JOVE BOOK
Published by Berkley
An imprint of Penguin Random House LLC
penguinrandomhouse.com

ISBN: 9780515123173

Jove mass-market edition / August 1998
Berkley trade paperback edition / June 2013

Printed in the United States of America
42 44 46 48 50 49 47 45 43

For the witty and delightful Christine Dorsey
Yes, Chris, I mean you.

PROLOGUE

Ethan climbed out of his dreams and rolled out of bed. It was still dark, but he habitually started his day before night yielded to dawn. It suited him, the quiet, the simple routine, the hard work that would follow.

He'd never forgotten to be grateful that he'd been able to make this choice and have this life. Though the people responsible for giving him both the choice and the life were dead, for Ethan, the pretty house on the water still echoed with their voices. He would often find himself glancing up from his lone breakfast in the kitchen expecting to see his mother shuffle in, yawning, her red hair a wild tangle from sleep, her eyes half blind with it.

And though she'd been gone nearly seven years, there was a comfort in that homey morning image.

It was more painful to think of the man who had become his father. Raymond Quinn's death was still too fresh after a mere three months for there to be comfort. And the circumstances surrounding it were both ugly and unex-

1

plained. His death had come in a single-car accident in broad daylight on a dry road, on a March day that had only hinted of spring. The car was traveling fast, with its driver unable—or unwilling—to control it on a curve. Tests had proven that there had been no physical reason for Ray to crash into the telephone pole.

But there was evidence of an emotional reason, and that lay heavy on Ethan's heart.

Ethan thought of it as he readied himself for the day— giving his hair, still damp from the shower, a cursory swipe with his comb, which did nothing to tame the thick waves of sun-bleached brown. He shaved in the foggy mirror, his quiet blue eyes sober as he scraped lather and a night's worth of beard from a tanned, bony face that held secrets he rarely chose to share.

There was a scar that rode along the left of his jaw-line—courtesy of his oldest brother and patiently stitched up by his mother. It had been fortunate, Ethan thought as he rubbed a thumb absently over the faded line, that their mother had been a doctor. One of her three sons was usually in need of first aid.

Ray and Stella had taken them in, three half-grown boys, all wild, all damaged, all strangers. And had made them a family.

Then months before his death, Ray had taken in another.

Seth DeLauter belonged to them now. Ethan never questioned it. Others did, he knew. There was talk buzzing through the little town of St. Christopher's that Seth was not just another of Ray Quinn's strays but his illegitimate son. A child conceived with another woman while his wife was still alive. A younger woman.

Ethan could ignore the talk, but it was impossible to ignore the fact that ten-year-old Seth looked at you with Ray Quinn's eyes.

There were shadows in those eyes that Ethan also recognized. The wounded recognized the wounded. He knew that Seth's life, before Ray had taken him on, had been a nightmare. He'd lived through one himself.

The kid was safe now, Ethan thought as he pulled on baggy cotton pants and a faded work shirt. He was a Quinn now, even if the legalities hadn't been completely worked out. They had Phillip to deal with that. Ethan figured his detail-mad brother would handle that end of things with the lawyer. And he knew that Cameron, the eldest of the Quinn boys, had managed to form a tenuous bond with Seth.

Fumbled his way to it, Ethan thought with a half smile. It had been like watching two angry tomcats spit and claw. Now that Cam had married the pretty social worker, things might just settle down some.

Ethan preferred a settled life.

They had battles yet, with the insurance company refusing to honor Ray's policy because there was suspicion of suicide. Ethan's stomach clutched, and he took a moment to will himself relaxed again. His father would never have killed himself. The Mighty Quinn had always faced his problems and had taught his sons to do the same.

But it was a cloud over the family that refused to blow away. There were others, too. The sudden appearance in St. Christopher's of Seth's mother and her accusations of sexual molestation, made to the dean of the college where Ray had taught English literature. That hadn't held— there'd been too many lies, too many shifts in her story. But there was no denying that his father had been shaken. There was no denying that shortly after Gloria DeLauter had left St. Chris again, Ray had gone away, too.

And he'd returned with the boy.

Then there was the letter found in the car after Ray's accident. An obvious blackmail threat from the DeLauter woman. There was the fact that Ray had given her money, a great deal of money.

Now she had disappeared again. Ethan wanted her to

stay gone, but he knew the talk wouldn't stop until all the answers were clear.

Nothing he could do about it, Ethan reminded himself. He stepped out into the hall, gave a quick knock on the door opposite his. Seth's groan was followed by a sleepy mutter, then an annoyed curse. Ethan kept going, heading downstairs. He had no doubt that Seth would bitch again about getting up so early. But with Cam and Anna in Italy on their honeymoon, and Phillip in Baltimore until the weekend, it was Ethan's job to get the boy up, to get him headed over to a friend's house to stay until it was time to leave for school.

Crabbing season was in full swing, and a waterman's day started before the sun. So until Cam and Anna returned, so did Seth's.

The house was silent and dark, but he moved through it easily. He had a house of his own now, but part of the deal in gaining guardianship of Seth had been for the three brothers to live under the same roof and share the responsibilities.

Ethan didn't mind responsibilities, but he missed his little house, his privacy and the ease of what had been his life.

He flicked on the lights in the kitchen. It had been Seth's turn to clean it up after dinner the evening before, and Ethan noted that he'd done a half-assed job. Ignoring the cluttered and sticky surface of the table, he moved directly to the stove.

Simon, his dog, stretched lazily out of his curl. His tail thumped on the floor. Ethan set the coffee to brew, greeting the retriever with an absent scratch on the head.

The dream was coming back to him now, the one he'd been caught in just before waking. He and his father, out on the workboat checking crab pots. Just the two of them. The sun had been blinding bright and hot, the water mirror-clear and still. It had been so vivid, he thought now, even the smells of water and fish and sweat.

His father's voice, so well remembered, had carried over the sounds of engine and gulls.

"I knew you'd look after Seth, the three of you."

"You didn't have to die to test that out." There was resentment in Ethan's tone, an underlying anger he hadn't allowed himself to admit while awake.

"It wasn't what I had in mind, either," Ray said lightly, culling crabs from the pot under the float that Ethan had gaffed. His thick orange fisherman's gloves glowed in the sun. "You can trust me on that. You got some good steamers here and plenty of sooks."

Ethan glanced at the wire pot full of crabs, automatically noting size and number. But it wasn't the catch that mattered, not here, not now. "You want me to trust you, but you don't explain."

Ray glanced back, tipping up the bright-red cap he wore over his dramatic silver mane. The wind tugged at his hair, teased the caricature of John Steinbeck gracing his loose T-shirt into rippling over his broad chest. The great American writer held a sign claiming he would work for food, but he didn't look too happy about it.

In contrast, Ray Quinn glowed with health and energy, ruddy cheeks where deep creases only seemed to celebrate a full and contented mood of a vigorous man in his sixties with years yet to live.

"You've got to find your own way, your own answers." Ray smiled at Ethan out of brilliantly blue eyes, and Ethan could see the creases deepen around them. "It means more that way. I'm proud of you."

Ethan felt his throat burn, his heart squeeze. Routinely he rebaited the pot, then watched the orange floats bob on the water. "For what?"

"For being. Just for being Ethan."

"I should've come around more. I shouldn't have left you alone so much."

"That's a crock." Now Ray's voice was both irritated and impatient. "I wasn't some old invalid. It's going to piss me off if you think that way, blame yourself for not looking after me, for Christ's sake. Same way you wanted to blame Cam for going off to live in Europe—and even Phillip for going off to Baltimore. Healthy birds leave the nest. Your mother and I raised healthy birds.''

Before Ethan could speak, Ray raised a hand. It was such a typical gesture, the professor making a point and refusing interruption, that Ethan had to smile. ''You missed them. That's why you wanted to be mad at them. They left, you stayed, and you missed having them around. Well, you've got them back now, don't you?''

''Looks that way.''

''And you've got yourself a pretty sister-in-law, the beginnings of a boatbuilding business, and this . . .'' Ray gestured to take in the water, the bobbing floats, the tall, glossily wet eelgrass on the verge where a lone egret stood like a marble pillar. ''And inside you, you've got something Seth needs. Patience. Maybe too much of it in some areas.''

''What's that supposed to mean?''

Ray sighed gustily. ''There's something you don't have, Ethan, that you need. You've been waiting around and making excuses to yourself and doing not a damn thing to get it. You don't make a move soon, you're going to lose it again.''

''What?'' Ethan shrugged and maneuvered the boat to the next float. ''I've got everything I need, and what I want.''

''Don't ask yourself what, ask yourself who.'' Ray clucked his tongue, then gave his son a quick shoulder shake. ''Wake up, Ethan.''

And he had awakened, with the odd sensation of that big, familiar hand on his shoulder.

But, he thought as he brooded over his first cup of coffee, he still didn't have the answers.

ONE

"GOT US SOME NICE peelers here, cap'n." Jim Bodine culled crabs from the pot, tossing the marketable catch in the tank. He didn't mind the snapping claws—and had the scars on his thick hands to prove it. He wore the traditional gloves of his profession, but as any waterman could tell you, they wore out quick. And if there was a hole in them, by God, a crab would find it.

He worked steadily, his legs braced wide for balance on the rocking boat, his dark eyes squinting in a face weathered with age and sun and living. He might have been taken for fifty or eighty, and Jim didn't much care which end you stuck him in.

He always called Ethan Cap'n, and rarely said more than one declarative sentence at a time.

Ethan altered course toward the next pot, his right hand nudging the steering stick that most waterman used rather than a wheel. At the same time, he operated the throttle and gear levels with his left. There were constant small

7

adjustments to be made with every foot of progress up the line of traps.

The Chesapeake Bay could be generous when she chose, but she liked to be tricky and make you work for her bounty.

Ethan knew the Bay as well as he knew himself. Often he thought he knew it better—the fickle moods and movements of the continent's largest estuary. For two hundred miles it flowed from north to south, yet it measured only four miles across where it brushed by Annapolis and thirty at the mouth of the Potomac River. St. Christopher's sat snug on Maryland's southern Eastern Shore, depending on its generosity, cursing it for its caprices.

Ethan's waters, his home waters, were edged with marshland, strung with flatland rivers with sharp shoulders that shimmered through thickets of gum and oak.

It was a world of tidal creeks and sudden shallows, where wild celery and widgeongrass rooted.

It had become his world, with its changing seasons, sudden storms, and always, always, the sounds and scents of the water.

Timing it, he grabbed his gaffing pole and in a practiced motion as smooth as a dance hooked the pot line and drew it into the pot puller.

In seconds, the pot rose out of the water, streaming with weed and pieces of old bait and crowded with crabs.

He saw the bright-red pincers of the full-grown females, or sooks, and the scowling eyes of the jimmies.

"Right smart of crabs," was all Jim had to say as he went to work, heaving the pot aboard as if it weighed ounces rather than pounds.

The water was rough today, and Ethan could smell a storm coming in. He worked the controls with his knees when he needed his hands for other tasks. And eyed the clouds beginning to boil together in the far western sky.

Time enough, he judged, to move down the line of traps in the gut of the bay and see how many more crabs had crawled into the pots. He knew Jim was hurting some for cash—and he needed all he could come by himself to keep afloat the fledgling boatbuilding business he and his brothers had started.

Time enough, he thought again, as Jim rebaited a pot with thawing fish parts and tossed it overboard. In leapfrog fashion, Ethan gaffed the next buoy.

Ethan's sleek Chesapeake Bay retriever, Simon, stood, front paws on the gunwale, tongue lolling. Like his master, he was rarely happier than when out on the water.

They worked in tandem, and in near silence, communicating with grunts, shrugs, and the occasional oath. The work was a comfort, since the crabs were plentiful. There were years when they weren't, years when it seemed the winter had killed them off or the waters would never warm up enough to tempt them to swim.

In those years, the watermen suffered. Unless they had another source of income. Ethan intended to have one, building boats.

The first boat by Quinn was nearly finished. And a little beauty it was, Ethan thought. Cameron had a second client on the line—some rich guy from Cam's racing days—so they would start another before long. Ethan never doubted that his brother would reel the money in.

They'd do it, he told himself, however doubtful and full of complaints Phillip was.

He glanced up at the sun, gauged the time—and the clouds sailing slowly, steadily eastward.

"We'll take them in, Jim."

They'd been eight hours on the water, a short day. But Jim didn't complain. He knew it wasn't so much the oncoming storm that had Ethan piloting the boat back up the gut. "Boy's home from school by now," he said.

"Yeah." And though Seth was self-sufficient enough to stay home alone for a time in the afternoon, Ethan didn't like to tempt fate. A boy of ten, and with Seth's temperament, was a magnet for trouble.

When Cam returned from Europe in a couple of weeks, they would juggle Seth between them. But for now the boy was Ethan's responsibility.

The water in the Bay kicked, turning gunmetal gray now to mirror the sky, but neither men nor dog worried about the rocky ride as the boat crept up the steep fronts of the waves, then slid back down into the troughs. Simon stood at the bow now, head lifted, his ears blowing back in the wind, grinning his doggie grin. Ethan had built the workboat himself, and he knew she would do. As confident as the dog, Jim moved to the protection of the awning and, cupping his hands, lit a cigarette.

The waterfront of St. Chris was alive with tourists. The early days of June lured them out of the city, tempted them to drive from the suburbs of D.C. and Baltimore. He imagined they thought of the little town of St. Christopher's as quaint, with its narrow streets and clapboard houses and tiny shops. They liked to watch the crab pickers' fingers fly, and eat the flaky crab cakes or tell their friends they'd had a bowl of she-crab soup. They stayed in the bed-and-breakfasts—St. Chris was the proud home of no less than four—and they spent their money in the restaurants and gift shops.

Ethan didn't mind them. During the times when the Bay was stingy, tourism kept the town alive. And he thought there would come a time when some of those same tourists might decide that having a hand-built wooden sailboat was their heart's desire.

The wind picked up as Ethan moored at the dock. Jim jumped nimbly out to secure lines, his short legs and squat body giving him the look of a leaping frog wearing white rubber boots and a grease-smeared gimme cap.

At Ethan's careless hand signal, Simon plopped his butt down and stayed in the boat while the men worked to unload the day's catch and the wind made the boat's sun-faded green awning dance. Ethan watched Pete Monroe walk toward them, his iron-gray hair crushed under a battered billed hat, his stocky body outfitted in baggy khakis and a red checked shirt.

"Good catch today, Ethan."

Ethan smiled. He liked Mr. Monroe well enough, though the man had a bone-deep stingy streak. He ran Monroe's Crab House with a tightly closed fist. But, as far as Ethan could tell, every man's son who ran a picking plant complained about profits.

Ethan pushed his own cap back, scratched the nape of his neck where sweat and damp hair tickled. "Good enough."

"You're in early today."

"Storm's coming."

Monroe nodded. Already his crab pickers who had been working under the shade of striped awnings were preparing to move inside. Rain would drive the tourists inside as well, he knew, to drink coffee or eat ice cream sundaes. Since he was half owner of the Bayside Eats, he didn't mind.

"Looks like you got about seventy bushels there."

Ethan let his smile widen. Some might have said there was a hint of the pirate in the look. Ethan wouldn't have been insulted, but he'd have been surprised. "Closer to ninety, I'd say." He knew the market price, to the penny, but understood they would, as always, negotiate. He took out his negotiating cigar, lit it, and got to work.

The first fat drops of rain began to fall as he motored toward home. He figured he'd gotten a fair price for his crabs—his eighty-seven bushels of crabs. If the rest of the summer was as good, he was going to consider dropping another hundred pots next year, maybe hiring on a part-time crew.

Oystering on the Bay wasn't what it had been, not since parasites had killed off so many. That made the winters hard. A few good crabbing seasons were what he needed to dump the lion's share of the profits into the new business—and to help pay the lawyer's fee. His mouth tightened at that thought as he rode out the swells toward home.

They shouldn't need a damn lawyer. They shouldn't have to pay some slick-suited talker to clear their father's good name. It wouldn't stop the whispers around town anyway. Those would only stop when people found something juicier to chew on than Ray Quinn's life and death.

And the boy, Ethan mused, staring out over the water that trembled under the steady pelting of rain. There were some who liked to whisper about the boy who looked back at them with Ray Quinn's dark-blue eyes.

He didn't mind for himself. As far as Ethan was concerned people could wag their tongues about him until they fell out of their flapping mouths. But he minded, deeply, that anyone would speak a dark word about the man he'd loved with every beat of his heart.

So he would work his fingers numb to pay the lawyer. And he would do whatever it took to guard the child.

Thunder shook the sky, booming off the water like cannon fire. The light went dim as dusk, and those dark clouds burst wide to pour out solid sheets of rain. Still he didn't hurry as he docked at his home pier. A little more wet, to his mind, wouldn't kill him.

As if in agreement with the sentiment, Simon leaped out to swim to shore while Ethan secured the lines. He gathered up his lunch pail, and with his waterman's boots thwacking wetly against the dock, headed for home.

He removed the boots on the back porch. His mother had scalded his skin often enough in his youth about tracking mud for the habit to stick to the man. Still, he didn't think anything of letting the wet dog nose in the door ahead of him.

Until he saw the gleaming floor and counters.

Shit, was all he could think as he studied the pawprints and heard Simon's happy bark of greeting. There was a squeal, more barking, then laughter.

"You're soaking wet!" The female voice was low and smooth and amused. It was also very firm and made Ethan wince with guilt. "Out, Simon! Out you go. You just dry off on the front porch."

There was another squeal, baby giggles, and the accompanying laughter of a young boy. The gang's all here, Ethan thought, rubbing rain from his hair. The minute he heard footsteps heading in his direction, he made a beeline for the broom closet and a mop.

He didn't often move fast, but he could when he had to.

"Oh, Ethan." Grace Monroe stood with her hands on her narrow hips, looking from him to the pawprints on her just-waxed floor.

"I'll get it. Sorry." He could see that the mop was still damp and decided it was best not to look at her directly. "Wasn't thinking," he muttered, filling a bucket at the sink. "Didn't know you were coming by today."

"Oh, so you let wet dogs run through the house and dirty up the floors when I'm not coming by?"

He jerked a shoulder. "Floor was dirty when I left this morning, didn't figure a little wet would hurt it any." Then he relaxed a little. It always seemed to take him a few minutes to relax around Grace these days. "But if I'd known you were here to skin me over it, I'd have left him on the porch."

He was grinning when he turned, and she let out a sigh.

"Oh, give me the mop. I'll do it."

"Nope. My dog, my mess. I heard Aubrey."

Absently Grace leaned on the doorjamb. She was tired, but that wasn't unusual. She had put in eight hours that day, too. And she would put in another four at Shiney's Pub that night serving drinks.

Some nights when she crawled into bed she would have sworn she heard her feet crying.

"Seth's minding her for me. I had to switch my days. Mrs. Lynley called this morning and asked if I'd shift doing her house till tomorrow because her mother-in-law called her from D.C. and invited herself down to dinner.

Mrs. Lynley claims her mother-in-law is a woman who looks at a speck of dust like it's a sin against God and man. I didn't think you'd mind if I did y'all today instead of tomorrow.''

"You fit us in whenever you can manage it, Grace, and we're grateful.''

He was watching her from under his lashes as he mopped. He'd always thought she was a pretty thing. Like a palomino—all gold and long-legged. She chopped her hair off short as a boy's, but he liked the way it sat on her head, like a shiny cap with fringes.

She was as thin as one of those million-dollar models, but he knew Grace's long, lean form wasn't for fashion. She'd been a gangling, skinny kid, as he recalled. She'd have been about seven or eight when he'd first come to St. Chris and the Quinns. He supposed she was twenty-couple now—and "skinny" wasn't exactly the word for her anymore.

She was like a willow slip, he thought, very nearly flushing.

She smiled at him, and her mermaid-green eyes warmed, faint dimples flirting in her cheeks. For reasons she couldn't name, she found it entertaining to see such a healthy male specimen wielding a mop.

"Did you have a good day, Ethan?"

"Good enough.'' He did a thorough job with the floor. He was a thorough man. Then he went to the sink again to rinse bucket and mop. "Sold a mess of crabs to your daddy.''

At the mention of her father, Grace's smile dimmed a little. There was distance between them, had been since she'd become pregnant with Aubrey and had married Jack Casey, the man her father had called ''that no-account grease monkey from upstate.''

Her father had turned out to be right about Jack. The man had left her high and dry a month before Aubrey was born. And he'd taken her savings, her car, and most of her self-respect with him.

But she'd gotten through it, Grace reminded herself. And she was doing just fine. She would keep right on doing fine, on her own, without a single penny from her family—if she had to work herself to death to do it.

She heard Aubrey laugh again, a long, rolling gut laugh, and her resentment vanished. She had everything that mattered. It was all tied up in a bright-eyed, curly-headed little angel just in the next room.

"I'll make you up some dinner before I go."

Ethan turned back, took another look at her. She was getting some sun, and it looked good on her. Warmed her skin. She had a long face that went with the long body—though the chin tended to be stubborn. A man could take a glance and he would see a long, cool blonde—a pretty body, a face that made you want to look just a little longer.

And if you did, you'd see shadows under the big green eyes and weariness around the soft mouth.

"You don't have to do that, Grace. You ought to go on home and relax a while. You're on at Shiney's tonight, aren't you?"

"I've got time—and I promised Seth sloppy joes. It won't take me long." She shifted as Ethan continued to stare at her. She'd long ago accepted that those long, thoughtful looks from him would stir her blood. Just another of life's little problems, she supposed. "What?" she demanded, and rubbed a hand over her cheek as if expecting to find a smudge.

"Nothing. Well, if you're going to cook, you ought to hang around and help us eat it."

"I'd like that." She relaxed again and moved forward to take the bucket and mop from him and put them away herself. "Aubrey loves being here with you and Seth. Why don't you go on in with them? I've got some laundry to finish up, then I'll start dinner."

"I'll give you a hand."

"No, you won't." It was another point of pride for her. They paid her, she did the work. All the work. "Go on in the front room—and be sure to ask Seth about the math test he got back today."

"How'd he do?"

"Another A." She winked and shooed Ethan away. Seth had such a sharp brain, she thought as she headed into the laundry room, off the kitchen. If she'd had a better head for figures, for practical matters when she'd been younger, she wouldn't have dreamed her way through school.

She'd have learned a skill, a real one, not just serving drinks and tending house or picking crabs. She'd have had a career to fall back on when she found herself alone and pregnant, with all her hopes of running off to New York to be a dancer dashed like glass on brick.

It had been a silly dream anyway, she told herself, unloading the dryer and shifting the wet clothes from the washer into it. Pie in the sky, her mama would say. But the fact was, growing up, there had only been two things she'd wanted. The dance, and Ethan Quinn.

She'd never gotten either.

She sighed a little, holding the warm, smooth sheet she took from the basket to her cheek. Ethan's sheet—she'd taken it off his bed that day. She'd been able to smell him on it then, and maybe, for just a minute or two, she'd let herself dream a little of what it might have been like if he'd wanted her, if she had slept with him on those sheets, in his house.

But dreaming didn't get the work done, or pay the rent, or buy the things her little girl needed.

Briskly she began to fold the sheets, laying them neatly on the rumbling dryer. There was no shame in earning her keep by cleaning houses or serving drinks. She was good at both, in any case. She was useful, and she was needed. That was good enough.

She certainly hadn't been useful or needed by the man

she was married to so briefly. If they'd loved each other, really loved each other, it would have been different. For her it had been a desperate need to belong to someone, to be wanted and desired as a woman. For Jack . . . Grace shook her head. She honestly didn't know what she had been for Jack.

An attraction, she supposed, that had resulted in conception. She knew he believed he'd done the honorable thing by taking her to the courthouse and standing with her in front of the justice of the peace on that chilly fall day and exchanging vows.

He had never mistreated her. He had never gotten mean drunk and knocked her around the way she knew some men did wives they didn't want. He didn't go sniffing after other women—at least not that she knew about. But she'd seen, as Aubrey grew inside her and her belly rounded, she'd seen the look of panic come into his eyes.

Then one day he was simply gone without a word.

The worst of it was, Grace thought now, she'd been relieved.

If Jack had done anything for her, it was to force her to grow up, to take charge. And what he'd given her was worth more than the stars.

She put the folded laundry in a basket, hitched the basket on her hip, and walked into the front room.

There was her treasure, her curly blond hair bouncing, her pretty, rosy-cheeked face alight with joy as she sat on Ethan's lap and babbled at him.

At two, Aubrey Monroe resembled a Botticelli angel, all rose and gilt, with bright-green eyes and dimples denting her cheeks. Little kitten teeth and long-fingered hands. Though he could decipher only half her chatter, Ethan nodded soberly.

"And what did Foolish do then?" he asked as he figured out she was telling him some story about Seth's puppy.

"Licked my face." Her eyes laughing, she took both

hands and ran them up over her cheeks. "All over." Grinning, she cupped her hands on Ethan's face and fell into
a game she liked to play with him. "Ouch!" She giggled,
rubbed his face again. "Beard."

Obliging, he skimmed his knuckles over her smooth
cheek, then jerked his hand back. "Ouch. You've got one,
too."

"No! You."

"No." He pulled her close and planted noisy kisses on
her cheeks while she wriggled in delight. "You."

Screaming with laughter now, she wiggled away and
dived for the boy sprawled on the floor. "Seth beard."
She covered his cheek with sloppy kisses. Manhood demanded that he wince.

"Jeez, Aub, give me a break." To distract her, he
picked up one of her toy cars and ran it lightly down her
arm. "You're a racetrack."

Her eyes beamed with the thrill of a new game. Snatching the car, she ran it, not quite so gently, over any part
of Seth she could reach.

Ethan only grinned. "You started it, pal," he told Seth
when Aubrey walked over Seth's thigh to reach his other
shoulder.

"It's better than getting slobbered on," Seth claimed,
but his arm came up to keep Aubrey from tumbling to the
floor.

For a few moments, Grace simply stood and watched.
The man, relaxed in the big wing chair and grinning down
at the children. The children themselves, their heads
close—one delicate and covered with gold curls, the other
with a shaggy mop shades and shades deeper.

The little lost boy, she thought, and her heart went out
to him as it had from the first day she'd seen him. He'd
found his way home.

Her precious girl. When Aubrey had been only a fluttering in her womb, Grace had promised to cherish, to
protect, and to enjoy her. She would always have a home.

And the man who had once been a lost boy, who had slipped into her girlish dreams years before and had never really slipped out again. He had made a home.

The rain drummed on the roof, the television was a low, unimportant murmur. Dogs slept on the front porch, and the moist wind blew through the screen door.

And she yearned where she knew she had no business yearning—to set down the basket of laundry, to go over and climb into Ethan's lap. To be welcomed there, even expected there. To close her eyes, for just a little while, and be part of it all.

Instead she retreated, finding herself unable to step into that quiet, lazy ease. She went back to the kitchen, where the overhead lights were bright and just a little hard. There, she set the basket on the table and began to gather what she needed to make dinner.

When Ethan came in a few moments later to hunt up a beer, she had meat browning, potatoes frying in peanut oil, and a salad under way.

"Smells great." He stood awkwardly for a minute. He wasn't used to having someone cook for him—not for years—and then not a woman. His father had been at home in the kitchen, but his mother . . . They'd always joked that whenever she cooked, they needed all her medical skills to survive the meal.

"It'll be ready in half an hour or so. I hope you don't mind eating early. I've got to get Aubrey home and bathed and then change for work."

"I never mind eating, especially when I'm not doing the cooking. And the fact is, I want to get to the boatyard for a couple hours tonight."

"Oh." She looked back, blowing at her bangs. "You should have told me. I'd have hurried things up."

"This pace works for me." He took a pull from the bottle. "You want a drink or something?"

"No, I'm fine. I was going to use that salad dressing

Phillip made up. It looks so much prettier than the store-bought.''

The rain was letting up, petering out into slow, drizzling drops with watery sunlight struggling to break through. Grace glanced toward the window. She was always hoping to see a rainbow. ''Anna's flowers are doing well,'' she commented. ''The rain's good for them.''

''Saves me from dragging out the hose. She'd have my head if they died on her while she's gone.''

''Wouldn't blame her. She worked so hard getting them planted before the wedding.'' Grace worked quickly, competently as she spoke. Draining crisp potatoes, adding more to the sizzling oil. ''It was such a beautiful wedding,'' she went on as she mixed sauce for the meat in a bowl.

''Came off all right. We got lucky with the weather.''

''Oh, it couldn't have rained that day. It would have been a sin.'' She could see it all again, so clearly. The green of the grass in the backyard, the sparkling of water. The flowers Anna had planted glowing with color—and the ones she'd bought spilling out of pots and bowls alongside the white runner that the bride had walked down to meet her groom.

A white dress billowing, the thin veil only accentuating the dark, deliriously happy eyes. Chairs had been filled with friends and family. Anna's grandparents had both wept. And Cam—rough-and-tumble Cameron Quinn—had looked at his bride as if he'd just been given the keys to heaven.

A backyard wedding, Grace thought now. Sweet, simple, romantic. Perfect.

''She's the most beautiful woman I've ever seen.'' Grace said it with a sigh that was only lightly touched with envy. ''So dark and exotic.''

''She suits Cam.''

''They looked like movie stars, all polished and glossy.'' She smiled to herself as she stirred spicy sauce into the meat. "When you and Phillip played that waltz for their first dance, it was the most romantic thing I've ever seen." She sighed again as she finished putting the salad together. "And now they're in Rome. I can hardly imagine it."

"They called yesterday morning to catch me before I left. They said they're having a good time."

She laughed at that, a rippling, smoky sound that seemed to cruise along his skin. "Honeymooning in Rome? It would be hard not to." She started to scoop out more potatoes and swore lightly as oil popped and splattered on the side of her hand. "Damn." Even as she was lifting the slight burn to her mouth to soothe it, Ethan leaped forward and grabbed her hand.

"Did it get you?" He saw the pinkening skin and pulled her to the sink. "Run some cold water on it."

"It's nothing. It's just a little burn. Happens all the time."

"It wouldn't if you were more careful." His brows were knitted, his hand gripping her fingers firmly to keep her hand under the stream of water. "Does it hurt?"

"No." She couldn't feel anything but his hand on her fingers and her own heart thundering in her chest. Knowing she'd make a fool of herself any moment, she tried to pull free. "It's nothing, Ethan. Don't fuss."

"You need some salve on it." He started to reach up into the cupboard to find some, and his head lifted. His eyes met hers. He stood there, the water running, both of their hands trapped under the chilly fall of it.

He tried never to stand quite so close to her, not so close that he could see those little gold dust flecks in her eyes. Because he would start to think about them, to wonder about them. Then he'd have to remind himself that this was Grace, the girl he'd watched grow up. The woman who was Aubrey's mother. A neighbor who considered him a trusted friend.

"You need to take better care of yourself." His voice

was rough as the words worked their way through a throat that had gone dust-dry. She smelled of lemons.

"I'm fine." She was dying, somewhere between giddy pleasure and utter despair. He was holding her hand as if it were as fragile as spun glass. And he was frowning at her as if she were slightly less sensible than her two-year-old daughter. "The potatoes are going to burn, Ethan."

"Oh. Well." Mortified because he'd been thinking—just for a second—that her mouth might taste as soft as it looked, he jerked back, fumbling now for the tube of salve. His heart was jumping, and he hated the sensation. He preferred things calm and easy. "Put some of this on it anyway." He laid it on the counter and backed up. "I'll . . . get the kids washed up for dinner."

He scooped up the laundry basket on his way and was gone.

With deliberate movements, Grace shut the water off, then turned and rescued her fries. Satisfied with the progress of the meal, she picked up the salve and smoothed a little on the reddened splotch on her hand before tidily replacing the tube in the cupboard.

Then she leaned on the sink, looked out the window.

But she couldn't find a rainbow in the sky.

TWO

THERE WAS NOTHING like a Saturday—unless it was the Saturday leading up to the last week of school and into summer vacation. That, of course, was all the Saturdays of your life rolled into one big shiny ball.

Saturday meant spending the day out on the workboat with Ethan and Jim instead of in a classroom. It meant hard work and hot sun and cold drinks. Man stuff. With his eyes shaded under the bill of his Orioles cap and the really cool sunglasses he'd bought on a trip to the mall, Seth shot out the gaff to drag in the next marker buoy. His young muscles bunched under his *X-Files* T-shirt, which assured him that the truth was out there.

He watched Jim work—tilt the pot and unhook the oyster-can-lid stopper to the bait box on the bottom of the pot. Shake out the old bait, Seth noted and see the seagulls dive and scream like maniacs. Cool. Now get a good solid hold on that pot, turn it over, and shake it like crazy so the crabs in the upstairs section fall out into the washtub waiting for them. Seth figured he could do all that—if he really wanted to. He wasn't afraid of a bunch of stupid crabs just because they looked like big mutant bugs from Venus and had claws that tended to snap and pinch.

Instead, his job was to rebait the pot with a couple handfuls of disgusting fish parts, do the stopper, check to make sure there were no snags in the line. Eyeball the distance between markers and if everything looked good, toss the pot overboard. Splash!

Then he got to toss out the gaff for the next buoy.

He knew how to tell the sooks from the jimmies now. Jim said the girl crabs painted their fingernails because their pincers were red. It was wild the way the patterns on the underbellies looked like sex parts. Anybody could see that the guy crabs had this long T shape there that looked just like a dick.

Jim had shown him a couple of crabs mating, too—he called them doublers—and that was just too much. The guy crab just climbed aboard the girl, tucked her under him, and swam around like that for days.

Seth figured they had to like it.

Ethan had said the crabs were married, and when Seth had snickered, he lifted a brow. Seth had found himself intrigued enough to go to the school library and read up on crabs. And he thought he understood, sort of, what Ethan meant. The guy protected the girl by keeping her under him because she could only mate when she was in her last molt and her shell was soft, so she was vulnerable. Even after they'd done it, he kept carrying her like that until her shell was hard again. And she was only going to mate once, so it was like getting married.

He thought of how Cam and Miss Spinelli—Anna, he reminded himself, he got to call her Anna now—had gotten married. Lots of the women got all leaky, and the guys laughed and joked. Everybody made such a big deal out of it with flowers and music and tons of food. He didn't get it. It seemed to him getting married just meant you got to have sex whenever you wanted and nobody got snotty about it.

But it had been cool. He'd never been to anything like it. Even though Cam had dragged him out to the mall and made him try on suits, it was mostly okay.

Maybe sometimes he worried about how it was going to change things, just when he was getting used to the way things were. There was going to be a woman in the house now. He liked Anna okay. She'd played square with him even though she was a social worker. But she was still a female.

Like his mother.

Seth clamped down on that thought. If he thought about his mother, if he thought about the life he'd had with her—the men, the drugs, the dirty little rooms—it would spoil the day.

He hadn't had enough sunny days in his ten years to risk ruining one.

"You taking a nap there, Seth?"

Ethan's mild voice snapped Seth back to the moment. He blinked, saw the sun glinting off the water, the orange floats bobbing. "Just thinking," Seth muttered and quickly pulled in another buoy.

"Me, I don't do much thinking." Jim set the trap on the gunwale and began culling crabs. His leathered face creased in grins. "Gives you brain fever."

"Shit," Seth said, leaning over to study the catch. "That one's starting to molt."

Jim grunted, held up a crab with a shell cracking along the back. "This buster'll be somebody's soft-shell sandwich by tomorrow." He winked at Seth as he tossed the crab into the tank. "Maybe mine."

Foolish, who was still young enough to deserve the name, sniffed at the trap, inciting a quick and ugly crab riot. As claws snapped, the pup leaped back with a yelp.

"That there dog." Jim shook with laughter. "He don't have to worry about no brain fever."

• • •

Even when they'd taken the day's catch to the waterfront, emptied the tank, and dropped Jim off, the day wasn't over. Ethan stepped back from the controls. "We've got to go into the boatyard. You want to take her in?"

Though Seth's eyes were shielded by the dark sunglasses, Ethan imagined that their expression matched the boy's dropped jaw. It only amused him when Seth jerked a shoulder as if such things were an everyday occurrence.

"Sure. No problem." With sweaty palms, Seth took the helm.

Ethan stood by, hands casually tucked in his back pockets, eyes alert. There was plenty of water traffic. A pretty weekend afternoon drew the recreational sailors to the Bay. But they didn't have far to go, and the kid had to learn sometime. You couldn't live in St. Chris and not know how to pilot a workboat.

"A little to starboard," he told Seth. "See that skiff there? Sunday sailor, and he's going to cut right across your bow if you keep this heading."

Seth narrowed his eyes, studied the boat and the people on deck. He snorted. "That's because he's paying more attention to that girl in the bikini than to the wind."

"Well, she looks fine in the bikini."

"I don't see what's the big deal about breasts."

To his credit, Ethan didn't laugh out loud, but nodded soberly. "I guess part of that's because we don't have them."

"I sure don't want any."

"Give it a couple of years," Ethan murmured under the cover of the engine noise. And the thought of that made him wince. What the hell were they going to do when the kid hit puberty? Somebody was going to have to talk to him about . . . things. He knew Seth already had too much sexual knowledge, but it was all the dark and sticky sort. The same sort he himself had known about at much too early an age.

One of them was going to have to explain how things should be, could be—and before too much more time passed.

He hoped to hell it wasn't going to have to be him.

He caught sight of the boatyard, the old brick building, the spanking new dock he and his brothers had built. Pride rippled through him. Maybe it didn't look like much with its pitted bricks and patched roof, but they were making something out of it. The windows were dusty, but they were new and unbroken.

"Cut back on the throttle. Take her in slow." Absently Ethan put a hand over Seth's on the controls. He felt the boy stiffen, then relax. He still had a problem with being touched unexpectedly, Ethan noted. But it was passing. "That's the way, just a bit more to starboard."

When the boat bumped gently against the pilings, Ethan jumped onto the pier to secure lines. "Nice job." At his nod, Simon, all but quivering with anticipation, leaped overboard. Yipping frantically, Foolish clambered onto the gunwale, hesitated, then followed.

"Hand me up the cooler, Seth."

Grunting only a little, Seth hefted it. "Maybe I could pilot the boat sometime when we're crabbing."

"Maybe." Ethan waited for the boy to scramble safely onto the pier before heading to the rear cargo doors of the building.

They were already open wide and the soul-stirring sound of Ray Charles flowed out through them. Ethan set the cooler down just inside the doors and put his hands on his hips.

The hull was finished. Cam had put in dog's hours to get that much done before he left for his honeymoon. They'd planked it, rabbeting the edges so that they would lap, yet remain smooth at the seams.

The two of them had completed the steam-bent framing, using pencil lines as guides and "walking" each frame carefully into place with slow, steady pressure. The hull was solid. There would be no splits in a Quinn boat's planking.

The design was primarily Ethan's with a few adjustments here and there of Cam's. The hull was an arc-bottom, expensive to construct but with the virtues of stability and speed. Ethan knew his client.

He'd designed the shape of the bow with this in mind and had decided on a cruiser bow, attractive and, again, good for speed, buoyant. The stern was a counterdesign of moderate length, providing an overhang that would make the boat's length greater than her waterline length.

It was a sleek, appealing look. Ethan understood that his client was every bit as concerned with appearance as he was with basic seaworthiness.

He'd used Seth for grunt labor when it was time to coat the interior with the fifty-fifty mix of hot linseed oil and turpentine. It was sweaty work, guaranteed to cause a few burns despite caution and gloves. Still, the boy had held up fine.

From where he stood, Ethan could study the sheerline, the outline at the top edge of the hull. He'd gone with a flattened sheerline to ensure a roomier, drier craft with good headroom below. His client liked to take friends and family out for a sail.

The man had insisted on teak, though Ethan had told him pine or cedar would have done the job well enough for hull planking. The man had money to spend on his hobby, Ethan thought now—and money to spend on status. But he had to admit, the teak looked wonderful.

His brother Phillip was working on the decking. Stripped to the waist in defense against the heat and humidity, his dark bronze hair protected by a black cap without team name or emblem and worn bill to the back, he was screwing the deck planks into place. Every few seconds, the hard, high-pitched buzz of the electric driver competed with Ray Charles's creamy tenor.

"How's it going?" Ethan called over the din.

Phillip's head came up. His martyred-angel's face was damp with sweat, his golden-brown eyes annoyed. He'd just been reminding himself that he was an advertising executive, for God's sake, not a carpenter.

"It's hotter than a summer in hell in here and it's only June. We've got to get some fans in here. You got anything cold, or at least wet, in that cooler? I ran out of liquids an hour ago."

"Turn on the tap in the john and you get water," Ethan said mildly as he bent to take a cold soft drink from the cooler. "It's a new technology."

"Christ knows what's in that tap water." Phillip caught the can Ethan tossed him and grimaced at the label. "At least they tell you what chemicals they load in here."

"Sorry, we drank all the Evian. You know how Jim is about his designer water. Can't get enough of it."

"Screw you," Phillip said, but without heat. He glugged the chilly Pepsi, then raised a brow when Ethan came up to inspect his work.

"Nice job."

"Gee, thanks, boss. Can I have a raise?"

"Sure, double what you're getting now. Seth's the math whiz. What's zip times zip, Seth?"

"Double zip," Seth said with a quick grin. His fingers itched to try out the electric screwdriver. So far, nobody would let him touch it or any of the other power tools.

"Well, now I can afford that cruise to Tahiti."

"Why don't you grab a shower—unless you object to washing with tap water, too. I can take over here."

It was tempting. Phillip was grimy, sweaty, and miserably hot. He would cheerfully have killed three strangers for one cold glass of Pouilly-Fuisse. But he knew Ethan had been up since before dawn and had already put in what any normal person would consider a full day.

"I can handle a couple more hours."

"Fine." It was exactly the response Ethan had expected. Phillip tended to bitch, but he never let you down. "I think we can get this deck knocked out before we call it a day."

"Can I—"

"No," Ethan and Phillip said together, anticipating Seth's question.

"Why the hell not?" he demanded. "I'm not stupid. I won't shoot anybody with a stupid screw or anything."

"Because we like to play with it." Phillip smiled. "And we're bigger than you. Here." He reached into his back pocket, pulled out his wallet and found a five. "Go on down to Crawford's and get me some bottled water. If you don't whine about it, you can get some ice cream with the change."

Seth didn't whine, but he did mutter about being used like a slave as he called his dog and headed out.

"We ought to show him how to use the tools when we have more time," Ethan commented. "He's got good hands."

"Yeah, but I wanted him out. I didn't have the chance to tell you last night. The detective tracked Gloria DeLauter as far as Nags Head."

"She's heading south, then." He lifted his gaze to Phillip's. "He pin her yet?"

"No, she moves around a lot, and she's using cash. A lot of cash." His mouth tightened. "She's got plenty to toss around since Dad paid her a bundle for Seth."

"Doesn't look like she's interested in coming back here."

"I'd say she's got as much interest in that kid as a rabid alley cat has in a dead kitten." His own mother had been the same, Phillip remembered, when she'd been around at all. He had never met Gloria DeLauter, but he knew her. Despised her.

"If we don't find her," Phillip added, rolling the cold

can over his forehead, "we're never going to get to the truth about Dad, or Seth."

Ethan nodded. He knew Phillip was on a mission here, and knew he was most likely right. But he wondered, much too often for comfort, what they would do when they had the truth.

ETHAN'S PLANS AFTER A fourteen-hour workday were to take an endless shower and drink a cold beer. He did both, simultaneously. They'd gotten take-out subs for dinner, and he had his on the back porch alone, in the soft quiet of early twilight. Inside, Seth and Phillip were arguing over which video to watch first. Arnold Schwarzenegger was doing battle with Kevin Costner.

Ethan had already placed his bets on Arnold.

They had an unspoken agreement that Phillip would take responsibility for Seth on Saturday nights. It gave Ethan a choice for the evening. He could go in and join them, as he sometimes did for these movie fests. He could go up and settle in with a book, as he often preferred to do. He could go out, as he rarely did.

Before his father had died so suddenly and life had changed for all of them, Ethan had lived in his own little house, with his own quiet routine. He still missed it, though he tried not to resent the young couple who were now renting it from him. They loved the coziness of it and told him so often. The small rooms with their tall windows, the little covered porch, the shady privacy of the trees that sheltered it, and the gentle lap of water against shore.

He loved it, too. With Cam married and Anna moving in, he might have been able to slip out again. But the rental money was needed now. And, more important, he'd given his word. He would live here until all the legal battles were waged and won and Seth was permanently theirs.

He rocked, listening to the night birds begin to call. And must have dozed because the dream came, and came clearly.

"You always were more of a loner than the others," Ray commented. He sat on the porch rail, turned slightly so he could look out to the water if he chose. His hair was shiny as a silver coin in the half light, blowing free in the steady breeze. "Always liked to go off by yourself to think your thoughts and work out your troubles."

"I knew I could always come to you or Mom. I just liked to have a handle on things first."

"How about now?" Ray shifted to face Ethan directly.

"I don't know. Maybe I haven't gotten a good handle on it yet. Seth's settling in. He's easier with us. The first few weeks, I kept expecting him to rabbit off. Losing you hurt him almost as much as it did us. Maybe just as much, because he'd just started to believe things were okay for him."

"It was bad, the way he had to live before I brought him here. Still, it wasn't as bad as what you'd faced, Ethan, and you got through."

"Almost didn't." Ethan took out one of his cigars, took his time lighting it. "Sometimes it still comes back on me. Pain and shame. And the sweaty fear of knowing what's going to happen." He shrugged it off. "Seth's a little younger than I was. I think he's already shed some of it. As long as he doesn't have to deal with his mother again."

"He'll have to deal with her eventually, but he won't be alone. That's the difference. You'll all stand by him. You always stood by each other." Ray smiled, his big, wide face creasing everywhere at once. "What are you doing sitting out here alone on a Saturday night, Ethan? I swear, boy, you worry me."

"Had a long day."

"When I was your age, I put in long days and longer nights. You just turned thirty, for Christ's sake. Porch sitting on a warm Saturday night in June is for old men. Go on, take a drive. See where you end up.'' He winked. "I bet we both know where that's likely to be.''

The sudden blare of automatic gunfire and screams made Ethan jerk in his chair. He blinked and stared hard at the porch rail. There was no one there. Of course there was no one there, he told himself with a quick shake. He'd nodded off for a minute, that was all, and the movie action in the living room had wakened him.

But when he glanced down, he saw the glowing cigar in his hand. Baffled, he simply stared at it. Had he actually taken it out of his pocket and lit it in his sleep? That was ridiculous, absurd. He must have done it before he'd drifted off, the habit so automatic that his mind just didn't register the moves.

Still, why had he fallen asleep when he didn't feel the least bit tired? In fact, he felt restless and edgy and too alert.

He rose, rubbing the back of his neck, stretching his legs on a pacing journey up and down the porch. He should just go in and settle down with the movie, some popcorn, and another beer. Even as he reached for the screen door, he swore.

He wasn't in the mood for Saturday night at the movies. He would just take a drive and see where he ended up.

GRACE'S FEET WERE NUMB all the way to the ankles. The cursed high heels that were part of her cocktail waitress uniform were killers. It wasn't so bad on a weekday evening when you had time now and then to step out of them or even sit for a few minutes. But Shiney's Pub always hopped on Saturday night—and so did she.

She carted her tray of empty glasses and full ashtrays to the bar, efficiently unloading as she called out her order to the bartender. "Two house whites, two drafts, a gin and tonic, and a club soda with lime."

She had to pitch her voice over the crowd noise and what was loosely called music from the three-piece band Shiney had hired. The music was always lousy at the pub, because Shiney wouldn't shell out the money for decent musicians.

But no one seemed to care.

The stingy dance floor was bumper to bumper with dancers, and the band took this as a sign to boost the volume.

Grace's head was ringing like steel bells, and her back was beginning to throb in time with the bass.

Her order complete, she carried the tray through the narrow spaces between tables and hoped that the group of young tourists in trendy clothes would be decent tippers.

She served them with a smile, nodded at the signal to run a tab, and followed the hail to the next table.

Her break was still ten minutes away. It might as well have been ten years.

"Hey, there, Gracie."

"How's it going, Curtis, Bobbie." She'd gone to school with them in the dim, distant past. Now they worked for her father, packing seafood. "Usual?"

"Yeah, a couple of drafts." Curtis gave Grace his usual—a quick pat on her bow-clad butt. She'd learned not to worry about it. From him it was a harmless enough gesture, even a show of affectionate support. Some of the outlanders who dropped in had hands a great deal less harmless. "How's that pretty girl of yours?"

Grace smiled, understanding that this was one of the reasons she tolerated his pats. He always asked about Aubrey. "Getting prettier every day." She saw another hand pop up from a nearby table. "I'll get you those beers in just a minute."

She was carting a tray full of mugs, bowls of beer nuts, and glasses when Ethan walked in. She nearly bobbled it.

He never came into the pub on Saturday night. Sometimes he dropped in for a quiet beer midweek, but never when the place was crowded and noisy.

He should have looked the same as every second man in the place. His jeans were faded but clean, a plain white T-shirt tucked into them, his work boots ancient and scuffed. But he didn't look the same as other men—and never had to Grace.

Maybe it was the lean and rangy body that moved as easily as a dancer through the narrow spaces. Innate grace, she mused, the kind that can't be taught, and still so blatantly male. He always looked as though he was walking the deck of a ship.

It could have been his face, so bony and rugged and somewhere just at the edges of handsome. Or the eyes, always so clear and thoughtful, so serious that it seemed to take them a few seconds to catch up whenever his mouth curved.

She served her drinks, pocketed money, took more orders. And watched out of the corner of her eye as he squeezed into a standing spot at the bar directly beside the order station.

She forgot all about her much-desired break.

"Three drafts, bottle of Mich, Stoli rocks." Absently, she brushed at her bangs and smiled. "Hi, Ethan."

"Busy tonight."

"Summer Saturday. Do you want a table?"

"No, this is fine."

The bartender was busy with another order, which gave her some breathing room. "Steve's got his hands full, but he'll work his way down here."

"I'm not in any hurry." As a rule, he tried not to think about how she looked in the butt-skimming skirt, those endless legs in black fishnet, the narrow feet in skinny heels. But tonight he was in a mood, and so he let himself think.

Just at that moment, he could have explained to Seth

just what the big deal was about breasts. Grace's were small and high, and a soft portion of the curve showed over the low-cut bodice of her blouse.

Suddenly, he desperately wanted a beer.

"You get a chance to sit down at all?"

She didn't answer for a moment. Her mind had gone glass-blank at the way those quiet, thoughtful eyes had skimmed over her. "I, ah . . . yes, it's nearly time for my break." Her hands felt clumsy as she gathered up her order. "I like to go outside, get away from the noise." Struggling to act normally, she rolled her eyes toward the band and was rewarded with Ethan's slow grin.

"Do they ever get worse than this?"

"Oh, yeah, these guys are a real step up." She was nearly relaxed again as she lifted the tray and headed off to serve.

He watched her, while he sipped the beer Steve had pulled for him. Watched the way her legs moved, the way the foolish and incredibly sexy bow swayed with her hips. And the way she bent her knees, balancing the tray, lifting drinks from it onto a table.

He watched, eyes narrowing, as Curtis once again gave her a friendly pat.

His eyes narrowed further when a stranger in a faded Jim Morrison T-shirt grabbed her hand, tugging her closer. He saw Grace flash a smile, give a shake of her head. Ethan was already pushing away from the bar, not entirely sure what he intended to do, when the man released her.

When Grace came back to set down her tray, it was Ethan who grabbed her hand. "Take your break."

"What? I—" To her shock he was pulling her steadily through the room. "Ethan, I really need to—"

"Take your break," he said again and shoved the door open.

The air outside was clean and fresh, the night warm and breezy. The minute the door closed behind them, the noise shut down to a muffled echoing roar and the stink of smoke, sweat, and beer became a memory.

"I don't think you should be working here."

She gaped at him. The statement itself was odd enough, but to hear him deliver it in a tone that was obviously annoyed was baffling. "Excuse me?"

"You heard me, Grace." He shoved his hands in his pockets because he didn't know what to do with them. Left free, they might have grabbed her again. "It's not right."

"It's not right?" she repeated, at sea.

"You're a mother, for God's sake. What are you doing serving drinks, wearing that outfit, getting hit on? That guy in there practically had his face down your blouse."

"Oh, he did not." Torn between amusement and exasperation, she shook her head. "For heaven's sake, Ethan, he was just being typical. And harmless."

"Curtis had his hand on your ass."

Amusement was veering toward annoyance. "I know where his hand was, and if it worried me, I'd have knocked it off."

Ethan took a breath. He'd started this, wisely or not, and he was going to finish it. "You shouldn't be working half naked in some bar or knocking anybody's hand off your ass. You should be home with Aubrey."

Her eyes went from mildly irritated to blazing fury. "Oh, is that right, is that your considered opinion? Well, thank you so much for sharing it with me. And for your information, if I wasn't working—and I'm damn well not half naked—I wouldn't have a home."

"You've got a job," he said stubbornly. "Cleaning houses."

"That's right. I clean houses, I serve drinks, and now and then I pick crabs. That's how amazingly skilled and versatile I am. I also pay rent, insurance, medical bills, utilities, and a baby-sitter. I buy food, I buy clothes, gas. I take care of myself and my daughter. I don't need you coming around here telling me it's not right."

"I'm just saying—"

"I hear what you're saying." Her heels were throbbing, and every ache in her overtaxed body was making itself known. Worse, much worse, was the hard prick of embarrassment that he would look down on her for what she did to survive. "I serve cocktails and let men look at my legs. Maybe they'll tip better if they like them. And if they tip better I can buy my little girl something that makes her smile. So they can look all they damn well please. And I wish to God I had the kind of body that filled out this stupid outfit, because then I'd earn more."

He had to pause before speaking, to gather his thoughts. Her face was flushed with anger, but her eyes were so tired it broke his heart. "You're selling yourself short, Grace," he said quietly.

"I know exactly how much I'm worth, Ethan." Her chin angled. "Right down to the last penny. Now, my break's over."

She spun on her miserably throbbing heels and stalked back into the noise and the smoke-clogged air.

THREE

"NEED BUNNY, TOO."

"Okay, baby, we'll get your bunny." It was, Grace thought, always an expedition. They were only going as far as the sandbox in the backyard, but Aubrey never failed to demand that all her stuffed pals accompany her.

Grace had solved this logistical problem with an enormous shopping bag. Inside it were a bear, two dogs, a fish, and a very tattered cat. The bunny joined them. Though Grace's eyes were gritty from lack of sleep, she grinned broadly as Aubrey tried to heft the bag herself.

"I'll carry them, honey."

"No, me."

It was, Grace thought, Aubrey's favorite phrase. Her baby liked to do things herself, even when it would be simpler to let someone else do the job. Wonder where she gets that from, Grace mused and laughed at both of them.

"Okay, let's get the crew outside." She opened the screen door—it squeaked badly, reminding her that she needed to oil the hinges—and waited while Aubrey dragged the bag over the threshold and onto the tiny back porch.

Grace had livened up the porch by painting it a soft blue and adding clay pots filled with pink and white geraniums. In her mind, the little rental house was temporary, but she didn't want it to *feel* temporary. She wanted it to feel like home. At least until she saved enough money for a down payment on a place of their own.

Inside, the room sizes were on the stingy side, but she'd solved that—and helped her bank balance—by keeping furniture to a minimum. Most of what she had were yard sale bargains, but she'd painted, refinished, re-covered, and turned each piece into her own.

It was vital to Grace to have her own.

The house had ancient plumbing, a roof that leaked water after a hard rain, and windows that leaked air. But it had two bedrooms, which had been essential. She'd wanted her daughter to have a room of her own, a bright, cheerful room. She had seen to that, papering the walls herself, painting the trim, adding fussy curtains.

It was already breaking her heart knowing that it was about time to dismantle Aubrey's crib and replace it with a youth bed.

"Be careful on the steps," Grace warned, and Aubrey started down, both tiny tennis shoes planting themselves firmly on each of the steps on the descent. The minute she hit bottom, she began to run, dragging her bag behind her and squealing in anticipation.

She loved the sandbox. It made Grace proud to watch Aubrey make her traditional beeline for it. Grace had built it herself, using scrap lumber that she meticulously sanded smooth and painted a bright Crayola red. In it were the pails and shovels and big plastic cars, but she knew Aubrey would touch none of them until she'd set out her pets.

One day, Grace promised herself, Aubrey would have a real puppy, and a playroom so that she could have friends visit and spend long, rainy afternoons.

Grace crouched down as Aubrey placed her toys carefully in the white sand. "You sit right in here and play while I mow the lawn. Promise?"

"Okay." Aubrey beamed up at her, dimples winking. "You play."

"In a little while." She stroked Aubrey's curls. She could never get enough of touching this miracle that had come from her. Before rising, she looked around, mother's eyes scanning for any danger.

The yard was fenced, and she had installed a childproof lock on the gate herself. Aubrey tended to be curious. A flowering vine rambled along the fence that bordered her house and the Cutters' and would have it buried in bloom by summer's end.

No one was stirring next door, she noted. Too early on a Sunday morning for her neighbors to be doing more than lazing about and thinking of breakfast. Julie Cutter, the eldest daughter of the house, was her much-treasured baby-sitter.

She noted that Julie's mother, Irene, had spent some time in her garden the day before. Not a single weed dared show its head in Irene Cutter's flowers or in her vegetable patch.

With some embarrassment, Grace glanced toward the rear of her yard, where she and Aubrey had planted some tomatoes and beans and carrots. Plenty of weeds there, she thought with a sigh. She'd have to deal with that after cutting the lawn. God only knew why she'd thought she would have time to tend a garden. But it had been such fun to dig the dirt and plant the seeds with her little girl.

Just as it would be such fun to step into the sandbox and build castles and make up games. No, you don't, Grace ordered herself and rose. The lawn was nearly ankle-high. It might have been rented grass, but it was hers now, and her responsibility. No one was going to say that Grace Monroe couldn't tend her own.

She kept the ancient secondhand lawn mower under an

equally ancient drop cloth. As usual, she checked the gas level first, casting another glance over her shoulder to be certain Aubrey was still tucked in the sandbox. Gripping the starter cord with both hands, she yanked. And got a wheezing cough in response.

"Come on, don't mess with me this morning." She'd lost count of the times she'd fiddled and repaired and banged on the old machine. Rolling her protesting shoulders, she yanked again, then a third time, before letting the cord snap back and pressing her fingers to her eyes. "Wouldn't you just know it."

"Giving you trouble?"

Her head jerked around. After their argument the night before, Ethan was the last person Grace expected to see standing in her backyard. It didn't please her, particularly since she'd told herself she could and would stay mad at him. Worse, she knew how she looked—old gray shorts and a T-shirt that had seen too many washings, not a stitch of makeup and her hair uncombed.

Damn it, she'd dressed for yard work, not for company.

"I can handle it." She yanked again, her foot, clad in a sneaker with a hole in the toe, planted on the side of the machine. It nearly caught, very nearly.

"Let it rest a minute. You're just going to flood it."

This time the cord snapped back with a dangerous hiss. "I know how to start my own lawn mower."

"I imagine you do, when you're not mad." He walked over as he spoke, all lean and easy male in faded jeans and a work shirt rolled up to his elbows.

He had come around back when she didn't answer her door. And he knew he'd stood watching her a little longer than was strictly polite. She had such a pretty way of moving.

He had decided sometime during the restless night that he had better find a way to make amends. And he'd spent a good part of his morning trying to figure how to do so. Then he'd seen her, all those long, slim limbs the sun was turning pale gold, the sunny hair, the narrow hands. And he'd just wanted to watch for a bit.

"I'm not mad," she said in an impatient hiss that proved her statement a lie. He only looked into her eyes.

"Listen, Grace—"

"Eeee-than!" With a shriek of pure pleasure, Aubrey scrambled out of the sandbox and ran to him—full-out, arms extended, face lit up with joy.

He caught her, swung her up and around. "Hey, there, Aubrey."

"Come play."

"Well, I'm—"

"Kiss."

She puckered her little lips with such energy that he had to laugh and give them a friendly peck.

"Okay!" She wiggled down and ran back to her sandbox.

"Look, Grace, I'm sorry if I was out of line last night."

The fact that her heart had melted when he held her daughter only made her more determined to stand firm. "If?"

He shifted his feet, clearly uncomfortable. "I just meant that—"

His explanation was interrupted as Aubrey raced back with her beloved stuffed dogs. "Kiss," she stated, very firmly, and held them up to Ethan. He obliged, waiting until she raced away again.

"What I meant was—"

"I think you said what you meant, Ethan."

She was going to be stubborn, he thought with an inward sigh. Well, she always had been. "I didn't say it very well. I get tangled up with words most of the time. I hate to see you working so hard." He paused, patient, when Aubrey came back, demanding a kiss for her bear. "I worry about you some, that's all."

Grace angled her head. "Why?"

"Why?" The question threw him. He bent to kiss the

stuffed bunny that Aubrey batted against his leg. "Well, I . . . because."

"Because I'm a woman?" she suggested. "Because I'm a single parent? Because my father considers that I smeared the family name by not only having to get married but getting myself divorced?"

"No." He took a step closer to her, absently kissing the cat that Aubrey held up to him. "Because I've known you more than half my life, and that makes you part of it. And because maybe you're too stubborn or too proud to see when somebody just wants to see things go a little easier for you."

She started to tell him she appreciated that, felt herself begin to soften. Then he ruined it.

"And because I didn't like seeing men paw at you."

"Paw at me?" Her back went up; her chin went out. "Men were not pawing at me, Ethan. And if they do, I know what to do about it."

"Don't get all riled up again." He scratched his chin, struggled not to sigh. He didn't see the point in arguing with a woman—you could never win. "I came over here to tell you I was sorry, and so maybe I could—"

"Kiss!" Aubrey demanded and began to climb up his leg.

Instinctively, Ethan pulled her up into his arms and kissed her cheek. "I was going to say—"

"No, kiss Mama." Bouncing in his arms, Aubrey pushed at his lips to make them pucker. "Kiss Mama."

"Aubrey!" Mortified, Grace reached for her daughter, only to have Aubrey cling to Ethan's shirt like a small golden burr. "Leave Ethan be now."

Changing tactics, Aubrey laid her head on Ethan's shoulder and smiled sweetly—one arm clinging like a vine around his neck as Grace tugged at her. "Kiss Mama," she crooned and batted her eyes at Ethan.

If Grace had laughed instead of looking so embarrassed—and just a little nervous—Ethan thought he could have brushed his lips over her brow and settled the matter. But her cheeks had gone pink—it was so endearing. She wouldn't meet his eyes, and her breath was unsteady.

He watched her bite her bottom lip and decided he might as well settle the matter another way entirely.

He laid a hand on Grace's shoulder with Aubrey caught between them. "This'll be easier," he murmured and touched his lips lightly to hers.

It wasn't easier. It rocked her heart. It could barely be considered a kiss, was over almost before it began. It was nothing more than a quiet brush of lips, an instant of taste and texture. And a whiff of promise that made her long, desperately, impossibly.

In all the years he'd known her, he had never touched his mouth to hers. Now, with just this fleeting sampling, he wondered why he'd waited so long. And worried that the wondering would change everything.

Aubrey clapped her hands in glee, but he barely heard it. Grace's eyes were on his now, that misty, swimming green, and their faces were close. Close enough that he only had to ease forward a fraction if he wanted to taste again. To linger this time, he thought, as her lips parted on a trembling breath.

"No, me!" Aubrey planted her small, soft mouth on her mother's cheek, then Ethan's. "Come play."

Grace jerked back like a puppet whose strings had been rudely yanked. The silky pink cloud that had begun to fog her brain evaporated. "Soon, honey." Moving quickly now, she plucked Aubrey out of Ethan's arms and set her on her feet. "Go on and build me a castle for us to live in." She gave Aubrey a gentle pat on the rump and sent her off at a run.

Then she cleared her throat. "You're awfully good to her, Ethan. I appreciate it."

He decided the best place for his hands, under the circumstances, was his pockets. He wasn't sure what to do about the itchy feeling in them. "She's a sweetheart." Deliberately, he turned to watch Aubrey in her red sandbox.

"And a handful." She needed to get her feet back under her, Grace told herself, and to do what needed to be done next. "Why don't we just forget last night, Ethan? I'm sure you meant it all for the best. Reality's just not always what we'd choose or what we'd like it to be."

He turned back slowly, and those quiet eyes of his focused on her face. "What do you want it to be, Grace?"

"What I want is for Aubrey to have a home, and a family. I think I'm pretty close to that."

He shook his head. "No, what do you want for Grace?"

"Besides her?" She looked over at her daughter and smiled. "I don't even remember anymore. Right now I want my lawn mowed and my vegetables weeded. I appreciate you coming by like this." She turned away and prepared to give the starter cord another yank. "I'll be by the house tomorrow."

She went very still when his hand closed over hers.

"I'll cut the grass."

"I can do it."

She couldn't even start the damn lawn mower, he thought, but was wise enough not to mention it. "I didn't say you couldn't. I said I'd do it."

She couldn't turn around, couldn't risk what it would do to her system to be that close again, face to face. "You have chores of your own."

"Grace, are we going to stand here all day arguing over who's going to cut this grass? I could have it done twice over by the time we finish, and you could be saving your string beans from being choked out by those weeds."

"I was going to get to them." Her voice was thin. They were both bent over, all but spooned together. The flash of sheer animal lust that streaked through the familiar yearning for him staggered her.

"Get to them now." He murmured it, willing her to move. If she didn't, and very quickly, he might not be able to hold himself back from putting his hands on her. And putting them on her in places they had no business being.

"All right." She shifted away, moving sideways while her heart knocked at her ribs in short rabbit punches. "I appreciate it. Thanks." She bit her lip hard because she was going to babble. Determined to be normal, she turned and smiled a little. "It's probably the carburetor again. I've got some tools."

Saying nothing, Ethan grabbed the cord with one hand and yanked it hard, twice. The engine caught with a dyspeptic roar. "It ought to do," he said mildly when he saw her mouth thin in frustration.

"Yeah, it ought to." Struggling not to be annoyed, she strode quickly to her vegetable patch.

And bent over, Ethan thought as he began to cut the first swath. Bent over in those thin cotton shorts in a way that forced him to take several long, careful breaths.

She didn't have a clue, he decided, what it had done to his usually well-disciplined hormones to have her trim little butt snugged back against him. What it did to the usually moderate temperature of his blood to have all that long, bare leg brushing against his.

She might be a mother—a fact that he reminded himself of often to keep dark and dangerous thoughts at bay—but as far as he was concerned, she was nearly as innocent and unaware as she'd been at fourteen.

When he'd first begun to have those dark and dangerous thoughts about her.

He'd stopped himself from acting on them. For God's sake, she'd just been a kid. And a man with his past had no right to touch anyone so unspoiled. Instead, he'd been her friend and had found contentment in that. He'd thought he could continue to be her friend, and only her friend. But just lately those thoughts had been striking him more often and with more force. They were becoming very tricky to control.

They both had enough complications in their lives, he reminded himself. He was just going to mow her lawn,

maybe help her pull some weeds. If there was time he'd
offer to take them into town for some ice cream cones.
Aubrey was partial to strawberry.

Then he had to go down to the boatyard and get to
work. And since it was his turn to cook, he had to figure
out that little nuisance.

But mother or not, he thought, as Grace leaned over to
tug out a stubborn dandelion, she had a pair of amazing
legs.

GRACE KNEW SHE
shouldn't have let herself be persuaded to go into town,
even for a quick ice cream cone. It meant adjusting her
day's schedule, changing into something less disreputable
than her gardening clothes, and spending more time in
Ethan's company when she was feeling a bit too aware of
her needs.

But Aubrey loved these small trips and treats, so it was
impossible to say no.

It was only a mile into St. Chris, but they went from
quiet neighborhood to busy waterfront. The gift and souvenir shops would stay open seven days a week now to
take advantage of the summer tourist season. Couples and
families strolled by with shopping bags filled with memories to take home.

The sky was brilliantly blue, and the Bay reflected it,
inviting boats to cruise along its surface. A couple of Sunday sailors had tangled the lines of their little Sunfish, letting the sails flop. But they appeared to be having the time
of their lives despite that small mishap.

Grace could smell fish frying, candy melting, the co-
conut sweetness of sunblock, and always, always, the
moist fragrance of the water.

She'd grown up on this waterfront, watching boats, sailing them. She ran free along the docks, in and out of the

shops. She learned to pick crabs at her mother's knee, gaining the speed and skill needed to separate out the meat, that precious commodity that would be packaged and shipped all over the world.

Work hadn't been a stranger, but she'd always been free. Her family had lived well, if not luxuriously. Her father didn't believe in spoiling his women with too much pampering. Still, he'd been kind and loving even though set in his ways. And he'd never made her feel that he was disappointed that he had only a daughter instead of sons to carry his name.

In the end, she'd disappointed him anyway.

Grace swung Aubrey up on her hip and nuzzled her.

"Busy today," she commented.

"Seems to get more crowded every summer." But Ethan shrugged it off. They needed the summer crowds to survive the winters. "I heard Bingham's going to expand the restaurant, fancy it up, too, to bring more people in year-round."

"Well, he's got that chef from up north now, and got himself reviewed in the *Washington Post* magazine." She jiggled Aubrey on her hip. "The Egret Rest is the only linen-tablecloth restaurant around here. Spiffing it up should be good for the town. We always went there for dinner on special occasions."

She set Aubrey down, trying not to remember that she hadn't seen the inside of the restaurant in over three years. She held Aubrey's hand and let her daughter tug her relentlessly toward Crawford's.

This was another standard of St. Chris. Crawford's was for ice cream and cold drinks and take-out submarine sandwiches. Since it was noon, the shop was doing a brisk business. Grace ordered herself not to spoil things by mentioning that they should be eating sandwiches instead of ice cream.

"Hey, there, Grace, Ethan. Hello, pretty Aubrey." Liz Crawford beamed at them even as she skillfully built a cold-cut sub. She'd gone to school with Ethan and had dated him for a short, careless time that they both remembered with fondness.

Now she was the sturdy, freckle-faced mother of two, married to Junior Crawford, as he was known to distinguish him from his father, Senior.

Junior, skinny as a scarecrow, whistled between his teeth as he rang up sales, and sent them a quick salute.

"Busy day," Ethan said, dodging an elbow from a customer at the counter.

"Tell me." Liz rolled her eyes, deftly wrapped the sub in white paper and handed it, along with three others, over the counter. "Y'all want a sub?"

"Ice cream," Aubrey said definitely. "Berry."

"Well, you go on down and tell Mother Crawford what you have in mind. Oh, Ethan, Seth was in here shortly ago with Danny and Will. I swear, those kids grow like weeds in high summer. Loaded up on subs and soda pop. Said they were working down to your boatyard."

He felt a faint flicker of guilt, knowing that Phillip was not only working but riding herd on three young boys. "I'll be heading down there myself soon."

"Ethan, if you don't have time for this . . ." Grace began.

"I've got time to eat an ice cream cone with a pretty girl." So saying, he lifted Aubrey up and let her press her nose to the glass-fronted counter that held the buckets of hand-dipped choices.

Liz took the next order, and spared a wiggling-eyebrow glance toward her husband that spoke volumes. Ethan Quinn and Grace Monroe, it stated clearly. Well, well. What do you think of that?

They took their cones outside, where the breeze was warm off the water, and wandered away from the crowds to find one of the small iron benches the city fathers had campaigned for. Armed with a fistful of napkins, Grace set Aubrey on her lap.

"I remember when you'd come here and know the name of every face you'd see," Grace murmured. "Mother Crawford would be behind the counter, reading a paperback novel." She felt a wet drip from Aubrey's ice cream plop on her leg below the hem of her shorts and wiped it up. "Eat around the edges, honey, before it melts away."

"You'd always get strawberry ice cream, too."

"Hmm?"

"As I recall," Ethan said, surprised that the image was so clear in his mind, "you had a preference for strawberry. And grape Nehi."

"I guess I did." Grace's sunglasses slipped down her nose as she bent to mop up more drips. "Everything was simple if you had yourself a strawberry cone and a grape Nehi."

"Some things stay simple." Because her hands were full, Ethan nudged Grace's glasses back up—and thought he caught a flicker of something in her eyes behind the shaded lenses. "Some don't."

He looked out to the water as he applied himself to his own cone. A better idea, he decided, than watching Grace take those long, slow licks from hers. "We used to come down here on Sundays now and then," he remembered. "All of us piling into the car and riding into town for ice cream or a sub or just to see what was up. Mom and Dad liked to sit under one of the umbrella tables at the diner and drink lemonade."

"I still miss them," she said quietly. "I know you do. That winter I caught pneumonia—I remember my mother and yours. It seemed every time I woke up, one or the other of them was right there. Dr. Quinn was the kindest woman I ever knew. My mama—"

She broke off, shook her head.

"What?"

"I don't want to make you sad."

"You won't. Finish it."

"My mother goes to the cemetery every year in the spring and puts flowers on your mother's grave. I go with her. I didn't realize until the first time we went how much my mother loved her."

"I wondered who put them there. It's nice knowing. What's being said . . . what some people are saying about my father would have got her Irish up. She'd have scalded more than a few tongues by now."

"That's not your way, Ethan. You have to tend to that business your own way."

"They would both want us to do what's best for Seth. That would come first."

"You are doing what's best for him. Every time I see him he looks lighter. There was such a heaviness over him when he first came here. Professor Quinn was working his way through that, but he had such troubles of his own. You know how troubled he was, Ethan."

"Yeah." And the guilt weighed like a stone, dead center in his heart. "I know."

"Now I have made you sad." She shifted toward him so that their knees bumped. "Whatever troubled him, it was never you. You were one strong, steady light in his life. Anyone could see that."

"If I'd asked more questions . . ." he began.

"It's not your way," she said again and, forgetting her hand was sticky, touched it to his cheek. "You knew he would talk to you when he was ready, when he could."

"Then it was too late."

"No, it never is." Her fingers skimmed lightly over his cheek. "There's always a chance. I don't think I could get from one day to the next if I didn't believe there's always a chance. Don't worry," she said softly.

He felt something move inside him as he reached up to cover her hand with his. Something shifting and opening. Then Aubrey let out a wild squeal of joy.

"Grandpa!"

Grace's hand jerked, then dropped like a stone. All

the warmth that had flowed out of her chilled. Her shoulders went straight and stiff as she turned forward again and watched her father walk toward them.

"There's my dollbaby. Come see Grandpa."

Grace let her daughter go, watched her race and be caught. Her father didn't wince or shy away from the sticky hands or smeared lips. He laughed and hugged and smacked his lips when kissed lavishly.

"Mmm, strawberry. Gimme more." He made munching noises on Aubrey's neck until she screamed with delight. Then he hitched her easily on his hip and crossed the slight distance to his daughter. And no longer smiled. "Grace, Ethan. Taking a Sunday stroll?"

Grace's throat was dry, and her eyes burned. "Ethan offered to buy us some ice cream."

"Well, that's nice."

"You're wearing some of it now," Ethan commented, hoping to ease some of the rippling tension that moved in the air.

Pete glanced down to his shirt, where Aubrey had transferred some of her favored strawberries. "Clothes wash. Don't often see you around the waterfront on a Sunday, Ethan, since you started building that boat."

"Taking an hour before I get started on it today. Hull's finished, deck's nearly."

"Good, that's good." He nodded, meaning it, then shifted his gaze to Grace. "Your mother's in the diner. She'll want to see her granddaughter."

"All right. I—"

"I'll take her over," he interrupted. "You can go on home when you're ready to, and your mother'll bring her on by your place in an hour or two."

She'd have preferred he slap her than speak to her in that polite and distant tone. But she nodded, as Aubrey was already babbling about Grandma.

"Bye! Bye, Mama. Bye, Ethan," Aubrey called over Pete's shoulder and blew noisy kisses.

"I'm sorry, Grace." Knowing it was inadequate, Ethan took her hand and found it stiff and cold.

"It doesn't matter. It can't matter. And he loves Aubrey. Just dotes on her. That's what counts."

"It's not fair to you. Your father's a good man, Grace, but he hasn't been fair to you."

"I let him down." She rose, quickly wiping her hands on the napkins she'd balled up. "And that's that."

"It's nothing more than his pride butting up against yours."

"Maybe. But my pride's important to me." She tossed the napkins into a trash container and told herself that was the end of it. "I've got to get back home, Ethan. There's a million things I should be doing, and if I've got a couple hours free, I'd better do them."

He didn't push, but was surprised how strongly he wanted to. He hated being nudged and nagged to talk about private matters himself. "I'll drive you home."

"No, I'd like to walk. Really like to walk. Thanks for the help." She managed a smile that looked almost natural. "And the ice cream. I'll be by the house tomorrow. Make sure you tell Seth his laundry goes in the hamper, not on the floor."

She walked away, her long legs eating up the ground. She made certain she was well away before she allowed her steps to slow. Before she rubbed a hand over the heart that ached no matter how firmly she ordered it not to.

There were only two men in her life she had ever really loved. It seemed neither of them could want her as she needed them to want her.

FOUR

ETHAN DIDN'T MIND MU-
sic when he worked. The fact was, his taste in music was
both broad and eclectic—another gift of the Quinns. The
house had often been filled with it. His mother had played
a fine piano with as much enthusiasm for the works of
Chopin as for those of Scott Joplin. His father's musical
talent had been the violin, and it was that instrument Ethan
had gravitated to. He enjoyed the varying moods of it, and
its portability.

Still, he found music a waste of sound whenever he
was concentrating on a job, as he usually didn't hear it
after ten minutes anyway. Silence suited him best during
those times, but Seth liked the radio in the boatyard up,
and up loud. So to keep peace, Ethan simply tuned out the
head-punching rock and roll.

The hull of the boat had been caulked and filled, a
labor-intensive and time-consuming task. Seth had been a
lot of help there, Ethan admitted, giving him an extra pair
of hands and feet when he needed them. Though Christ

knew the boy could complain about the job as much as
Phillip did.

Ethan tuned that out as well—to stay sane.

He hoped to finish leveling off the decking before Phillip arrived for the weekend, planing first on one diagonal,
then across the next at a right angle.

With any luck, he could get some solid work done that
week and the next on the cabin and cockpit.

Seth bitched about being on sanding detail, but he did
a decent job of it. Ethan only had to tell him to go back
and hit portions of the hull planking again a couple of
times. He didn't mind the boy's questions, either. Though
he had a million of them once he started.

"What's that piece over there for?"

"The bulkhead for the cockpit."

"Why'd you cut it out already?"

"Because we want to get rid of all the dust before we
varnish and seal."

"What's all this other shit?"

Ethan paused in his own work, looking down from his
position to where Seth frowned at a stack of precut lumber.
"You got the sides and cabin ends, the toerail and drop-
boards."

"It seems like an awful lot of pieces for one stupid
boat."

"There's going to be a lot more."

"How come this guy doesn't just buy a boat that's already built?"

"Good thing for us he isn't." The client's deep pockets,
Ethan mused, were giving Boats by Quinn its foundation.
"Because he liked the other boat I built for him—and so
he can tell all his big-shot friends he had a boat designed
and hand-built for him."

Seth changed his sandpaper and applied himself again.
He didn't mind the work, really. And he liked the smells
of wood and varnish and that linseed oil, too. But he just
didn't get it. "It's taking forever to put it together."

"Been at it less than three months. Lots of people spend a year—even longer—to build a wooden boat."

Seth's jaw dropped. "A year! Jesus, Ethan."

The loud, and very normal whine, made Ethan's mouth twitch. "Relax, this isn't going to take us that long. Once Cam gets back and can put in full days on it, we'll move along. And once school's out, you can pick up a lot of the grunt work."

"School is out."

"Hmm?"

"Today was it." Now Seth grinned, wide and bright. "Freedom. It's a done deal."

"Today?" Pausing in his work, Ethan frowned. "I thought you had a couple days yet."

"Nope."

He'd lost track of things somewhere, Ethan supposed. And it wasn't Seth's style—not yet, anyway—to volunteer information. "Did you get a report card?"

"Yeah—I passed."

"Let's see how." Ethan set his tools down, brushed his hands on his jeans. "Where is it?"

Seth shrugged his shoulders and kept sanding. "It's in my backpack over there. No big deal."

"Let's see it," Ethan repeated.

Seth did what Ethan considered his usual dance. Rolling his eyes, shrugging his shoulders, adding a long-suffering sigh. Oddly enough, he didn't end with an oath, as he was prone to. He walked over to where he'd dumped his backpack and riffled through it.

Ethan leaned down over the port side to take the paper Seth held up. Noting the mutinous expression on Seth's face, he expected the news would be grim. His stomach did a quick clench and roll. The required lecture, Ethan thought with an inner sigh, was going to be damned uncomfortable for both of them.

Ethan studied the thin, computer-generated sheet, pushing back his cap to scratch his head. "*All* A's?"

Seth jerked a shoulder again, stuffed his hands in his pockets. "Yeah, so?"

"I've never seen a report card with all A's before. Even Phillip used to have some B's, and maybe a C tossed in."

Embarrassment, and the fear of being called Egghead or something equally hideous rose swiftly. "It's no big deal." He held up a hand for the report card, but Ethan shook his head.

"The hell it's not." But he saw Seth's scowl and thought he understood it. It was always hard to be different from the pack. "You got a good brain and you ought to be proud of it."

"It's just there. It's not like knowing how to pilot a boat or anything."

"You got a good brain and you use it, you'll figure out how to do most anything." Ethan folded the paper carefully and tucked it in his pocket. Damn if he wasn't going to show it off some. "Seems to me we ought to go get a pizza or something."

Puzzled, Seth narrowed his eyes. "You packed those lame sandwiches for dinner."

"Not good enough now. The first time a Quinn gets straight A's ought to rate at least a pizza." He saw Seth's mouth open and shut, watched the staggered delight leap into his eyes before he lowered them.

"Sure, that'd be cool."

"Can you hold off another hour?"

"No problem."

Seth grabbed his sandpaper and began to work furiously. And blindly. His eyes were dazzled, his heart in his throat. It happened whenever one of them referred to him as a Quinn. He knew his name was DeLauter still. He had to put it at the top of every stupid paper he did for school, didn't he? But hearing Ethan call him a Quinn made that little beam of hope that Ray had first ignited in him months before shine just a little brighter.

He was going to stay. He was going to be one of them. He was never going back into hell again.

It made it worth being called down to Moorefield's office that day. The vice principal had reeled him in an hour before freedom. It had made his stomach jitter, as it always did. But she'd sat him down and told him she was proud of his progress.

Man, how mortifying.

Okay, so maybe he hadn't punched anybody in the face in the last couple months. And he'd been handing in his stupid homework assignments every dumb day because somebody was always nagging him about them. Phillip was the worst nag in that particular area. It was like the guy was a homework cop or something, Seth thought now. And yeah, he'd been raising his hand in class now and then, just for the hell of it.

But to have Moorefield single him out that way had been so . . . *bleech*, he decided. He'd almost wished she'd hauled his butt in to give him another dose of In-School Suspension.

But if a bunch of dopey A's made a guy like Ethan happy, it was okay.

Ethan was absolutely cool in Seth's estimation. He worked outside all day, and his hands had scars and really thick calluses. Seth figured you could practically pound nails into Ethan's hands without him even feeling it, they were so hard and tough. He owned two boats—that he'd built himself—and he knew everything about the Bay and sailing. And didn't make a big deal about it.

A couple of months back Seth had watched *High Noon* on TV, even though it had been in lame black and white and there hadn't even been any blood or explosions. He'd thought then that Ethan was just like that Gary Cooper guy. He didn't say a lot, so you mostly listened when he did. And he just did what needed to be done without a lot of show.

Ethan would have faced down the bad guys, too. Because it was right. Seth had mulled it over for a while and had decided that's what a hero was. Somebody who just did what was right.

ETHAN WOULD HAVE BEEN stunned and mortally embarrassed, if he'd been able to read Seth's thoughts. But the boy was an expert at keeping them to himself. On that level, he and Ethan were as close as twins.

It might have crossed Ethan's mind that Village Pizza was only a short block from Shiney's Pub, where Grace would be starting her shift, but he didn't mention it.

Couldn't take the boy into a bar anyway, Ethan mused as they headed into the bright lights and noise of the local restaurant. And Seth was bound to complain, loudly, if Ethan asked him to wait in the car for just a couple minutes while he poked his head in. Likely Grace would complain, too, if she caught on that he was checking on her.

It was best to let it go and concentrate on the matters at hand. He tucked his hands into his back pockets and studied the menu posted on the wall behind the counter. "What do you want on it?"

"You can forget the mushrooms. They're gross."

"We're of a mind there," Ethan murmured.

"Pepperoni and hot sausage." Seth sneered, but he spoiled it by bouncing a little in his sneakers. "If you can handle it."

"I can take it if you can. Hey, Justin," he said with a smile of greeting for the boy behind the counter. "We'll take a large, pepperoni and hot sausage, and a couple of jumbo Pepsis."

"You got it. Here or to go?"

Ethan scanned the dozen tables and booths offered and noted that he wasn't the only one who'd thought to celebrate the last day of school with pizza. "Go nab that last booth back there, Seth. We'll take it here, Justin."

"Have a seat. We'll bring the drinks out."

Seth had dumped his backpack on the bench and was tapping his hands on the table in time to the blast of Hootie and the Blowfish from the juke. "I'm going to go kick some video ass," he told Ethan. When Ethan reached back for his wallet, Seth shook his head. "I got money."

"Not tonight you don't," Ethan said mildly and pulled out some bills. "It's your party. Get some change."

"Cool." Seth snagged the bills and raced off to get quarters.

As Ethan slid into the booth, he wondered why so many people thought a couple hours in a noisy room was high entertainment. A huddle of kids was already trying to kick some video ass at the trio of machines along the back wall; the juke had switched to Clint Black—and that country boy was wailing. The toddler in the booth behind him was having a full-blown tantrum, and a group of teenage girls were giggling at a decibel level that would have made Simon's ears bleed.

What a way to spend a pretty summer night.

Then he saw Liz Crawford and Junior with their two little girls at a nearby booth. One of the girls—that must be Stacy, Ethan thought—was talking quickly, making wide gestures, while the rest of the family howled with laughter.

They made a unit, he mused, their own little island in the midst of the jittery lights and noise. He supposed that's what family was, an island. Knowing you could go there made all the difference.

Still the tug of envy surprised him, made him shift uncomfortably on the hard seat of the booth and scowl into space. He'd made his mind up about having a family years before, and he didn't care for this sharp pull of longing.

"Why, Ethan, you look fierce."

He glanced up as the drinks were set on the table in

front of him, straight into the flirtatious eyes of Linda Brewster.

She was a looker, no question about it. The tight black jeans and scoop-necked black T-shirt hugged her well-developed body like a coat of fresh paint on a classic Chevy. After her divorce was final—one week ago Monday—she'd treated herself to a manicure and a new hairdo. Her coral-tipped nails skimmed through her newly bobbed, streaky blond hair as she smiled down at Ethan.

She'd had her eye on him for a time now—after all, she had separated from that useless Tom Brewster more than a year before and a woman had to look to the future. Ethan Quinn would be hot in bed, she decided. She had instincts about these things. Those big hands of his would be mighty thorough, she was sure. And attentive. Oh, yes.

She liked his looks, too. Just a little tough and weathered. And that slow, sexy smile of his . . . when you managed to drag one out of him, just made her want to lick her lips in anticipation.

He had that quiet way about him. Linda knew what they said about still waters. And she was just dying to see just how deep Ethan Quinn's ran.

Ethan was well aware where her eye had wandered, and he was keeping his peeled as well. For running room. Women like Linda scared the hell out of him.

"Hi, Linda. Didn't know you were working here." Or he'd have avoided Village Pizza like the plague.

"Just helping my father out for a couple of weeks." She was flat broke, and her father—the owner of Village Pizza—had told her he'd be damned if she was going to sponge off him and her mother. She should get her sassy butt to work. "Haven't seen you around lately."

"I've been around." He wished she'd move along. Her perfume gave him the jitters.

"I heard you and your brothers rented that old barn of Claremont's and are building boats. I've been meaning to come down and take a look."

"Not much to see." Where the hell was Seth when he needed him? Ethan wondered a little desperately. How long could those damn quarters last?

"I'd like to see it anyway." She skimmed those slick-tipped nails down his arm, gave a low purr as she felt the ridge of muscle. "I can slip out of here for a while. Why don't you run me down there and show me what's what?"

His mind blanked for a moment. He was only human. And she was running her tongue over her top lip in a way designed to draw a man's eyes and tickle his glands. Not that he was interested, not a bit, but it had been a long time since he'd had a woman moaning under him. And he had a feeling Linda would be a champion moaner.

"Copped top score." Seth plopped into the booth, flushed with victory, and grabbed his Pepsi. He slurped some up. "Man, what's keeping that pizza? I'm starved."

Ethan felt his blood start to run again and nearly sighed with relief. "It'll be along."

"Well." Despite annoyance at the interruption, Linda smiled brilliantly at Seth. "This must be the new addition. What's your name, honey? I can't quite recollect."

"I'm Seth." And he sized her up quickly. Bimbo, was his first and last thought. He'd seen plenty of them in his short life. "Who're you?"

"I'm Linda, an old friend of Ethan's. My daddy owns the place."

"Cool, so maybe you could tell them to put a fire under that pizza before we die of old age here."

"Seth." The word and Ethan's quiet look were all it took for the boy to close his mouth. "Your daddy still makes the best pizza on the Shore," Ethan said with an easier smile. "You be sure to tell him."

"I will. And you give me a call, Ethan." She wiggled her left hand. "I'm a free woman these days." She wandered away, hips swinging like a well-oiled metronome.

"She smells like the place at the mall where they sell all that girl stuff." Seth wrinkled his nose. He hadn't liked her because he'd seen just a shadow of his mother in her eyes. "She just wants to get in your pants."

"Shut up, Seth."

"It's true," Seth said with a shrug, but happily let the subject drop when Linda came back bearing pizza.

"Y'all enjoy, now," she told them, leaning over the table just a little farther than necessary in case Ethan had missed the view the first time around.

Seth snagged a piece and bit in, knowing it was going to scorch the roof of his mouth. The flavors exploded, making the burn more than worth it. "Grace makes pizza from scratch," he said around a mouthful. "It's even better than this."

Ethan only grunted. The thought of Grace after he'd entertained—however unwillingly—a brief and sweaty fantasy about Linda Brewster made him twitchy.

"Yeah. We ought to see if she'd make it for us one of the days she comes to clean and stuff. She comes tomorrow, right?"

"Yeah." Ethan took a piece, annoyed that most of his appetite had deserted him. "I suppose."

"Maybe she'd make one up before she goes."

"You're having pizza tonight."

"So?" Seth polished off the first piece with the speed and precision of a jackal. "You could, like, compare. Grace ought to open a diner or something so she wouldn't have to work all those different jobs. She's always working. She wants to buy a house."

"She does?"

"Yeah." Seth licked the side of his hand where sauce dripped. "Just a little one, but it has to have a yard so Aubrey can run around and have a dog and stuff."

"She tell you all that?"

"Sure. I asked how come she was busting her butt cleaning all those houses and working down at the pub, and she said that was mostly why. And if she doesn't make enough, she and Aubrey won't have a place of their own by the time Aub starts kindergarten. I guess even a little house costs big bucks, right?''

"It costs," Ethan said quietly. He remembered how satisfied, how proud he'd been when he'd bought his own place on the water. What it had meant to him to know he'd succeeded at what he did. "It takes time to save up."

"Grace wants to have the house by the time Aubrey starts school. After that, she says how she has to start saving for college." He snorted and decided he could force down a third piece. "Hell, Aubrey's just a baby, it's a million years till college. Told her that, too," he added, because it pleased him for people to know he and Grace had *conversations*. "She just laughed and said five minutes ago Aubrey had gotten her first tooth. I didn't get it."

"She meant kids grow up fast." Since it didn't look as though his appetite would be coming back, Ethan closed the top on the pizza and took out bills to pay for it. "Let's take this back to the boatyard. Since you don't have school in the morning, we can put in a couple more hours."

HE PUT IN MORE THAN A couple. Once he got started, he couldn't seem to stop. It cleared his mind, kept it from wandering, wondering, worrying.

The boat was definite, a tangible task with a foreseeable end. He knew what he was doing here, just as he knew what he was doing out on the Bay. There weren't so many shadow areas of maybes or what ifs.

Ethan continued to work even when Seth curled up on a drop cloth and fell asleep. The sound of tools running didn't appear to disturb him—though Ethan wondered how anyone could sleep with the best part of a large sausage-and-pepperoni pizza in his stomach.

He started work on the ends and corner posts for the cabin and cockpit coaming while the night wind blew lazily through the open cargo doors. He'd turned the radio off so that now the only music was the water, the gentle notes of it sliding against the shore.

He worked slowly, carefully, though he was well able to visualize the completed project. Cam, he decided, would handle most of the interior work. He was the most skilled of the three of them at finish carpentry. Phillip could handle the rough-ins; he was better at sheer manual labor than he liked to admit.

If they could keep up the pace, Ethan calculated that they could have the boat trimmed and under sail in another two months. He would leave figuring the profits and percentages to Phillip. The money would feed the lawyers, the boatyard, and their own bellies.

Why hadn't Grace ever told him she wanted to buy a house?

Ethan frowned thoughtfully as he chose a galvanized bolt. Wasn't that a pretty big step to be discussing with a ten-year-old boy? Then again, he admitted, Seth had asked. He himself had only told her she shouldn't be working herself so hard—he hadn't asked why she insisted on it.

She ought to make things up with her father, he thought again. If the two of them would just bend that stiff-necked Monroe pride for five minutes, they could come to terms. She'd gotten pregnant—and there was no doubt in Ethan's mind that Jack Casey had taken advantage of a young, naive girl and should be shot for it—but that was over and done.

His family had never held grudges, small or large. They'd fought, certainly—and he and his brothers had often fought physically. But when it was done, it was over.

It was true enough that he'd harbored some seeds of resentment because Cam had raced off to Europe and Phillip had moved to Baltimore. It had happened so fast after their mother died, and he'd still been raw. Everything had changed before he could blink, and he'd stewed over that.

But even with that, he would never have turned his back

on either of them if they'd needed him. And he knew they wouldn't have turned their backs on him.

It seemed to him the most foolish and wasteful thing imaginable that Grace wouldn't ask for help, and her father wouldn't offer it.

He glanced at the big round clock nailed to the wall over the front doors. Phillip's idea, Ethan remembered with a half grin. He'd figured they'd need to know how much time they were putting in, but as far as Ethan knew, Phillip was the only one who bothered to mark down the time.

It was nearly one, which meant Grace would be finishing up at the pub in about an hour. It wouldn't hurt to load Seth in the truck and do a quick swing by Shiney's. Just to . . . check on things.

Even as he started to rise, he heard the boy whimper in his sleep.

Pizza's finally getting to him, Ethan thought with a shake of the head. But he supposed childhood wouldn't be complete without its quota of bellyaches. He climbed down, rolling his shoulders to work out the kinks as he approached the sleeping boy.

He crouched beside Seth, laid a hand on his shoulders, and gave a gentle shake.

And the boy came up swinging.

The bunched fist caught Ethan squarely on the mouth and knocked his head back. The shock, more than the quick and bright pain, had him swearing. He blocked the next blow, then took Seth's arm firmly. "Hold it."

"Get your hands off me." Wild, desperate, and still caught in the sticky grip of the dream, Seth flailed at the air. "Get your fucking hands off me."

Understanding came quickly. It was the look in Seth's eyes—stark terror and vicious fury. He'd once felt both himself, along with a shuddering helplessness. He let go, lifted both of his hands palms out. "You were dreaming." He said it quietly, without inflection, and listened to Seth's ragged breathing echo on the air. "You fell asleep."

Seth kept his fists bunched. He didn't remember falling asleep. He remembered curling up, listening to Ethan work. And the next thing he knew, he was back in one of those dark rooms, where the smells were sour and too human and the noises from the next room were too loud and too animal.

And one of the faceless men who used his mother's bed had crept out and put hands on him again.

But it was Ethan who was watching him, patiently, with too much knowledge in his serious eyes. Seth's stomach twisted not only at what had been, but that Ethan should now know.

Because he couldn't think of words or excuses, Seth simply closed his eyes.

It was that which tilted the scales for Ethan. The surrender to helplessness, the slide into shame. He'd left this wound alone, but now it seemed he would need to treat it after all.

"You don't have to be afraid of what was."

"I'm not afraid of anything." Seth's eyes snapped open. The anger in them was adult and bitter, but his voice jerked like the child he was. "I'm not afraid of some stupid dream."

"You don't have to be ashamed of it, either."

Because he was, hideously, Seth sprang to his feet. His fists were bunched again, ready. "I'm not ashamed of anything. And you don't know a damn thing about it."

"I know every damn thing about it." Because he did, he hated to speak of it. But despite the defiant stance, the boy was trembling, and Ethan knew just how alone he felt. Speaking of it was the only thing left for him to do. The right thing to do.

"I know what dreams did to me, how I had them for a long time after that part of things was over for me." And still had them now and again, he thought, but there was no need to tell the boy he might have to face a lifetime of flashing back and overcoming. "I know what it does to your guts."

"Bullshit." The tears were burning the backs of Seth's eyes, humiliating him all the more. "Nothing's wrong with me. I got the hell out, didn't I? I got away from her, didn't I? I'm not going back either, no matter what."

"No, you're not going back," Ethan agreed. No matter what.

"I don't care what you or anybody thinks about what went on back then. And you're not tricking me into saying things about it by pretending you know."

"You don't have to say anything about it," Ethan told him. "And I don't have to pretend." He picked up the cap Seth's blow had knocked off his head, ran it absently through his hands before putting it back on. But the casual gesture did nothing to ease the tight, slick ball of tension in his gut.

"My mother was a whore—my biological mother. And she was a junkie with a taste for heroin." He kept his gaze on Seth's and his voice matter-of-fact. "I was younger than you when she sold me the first time, to a man who liked young boys."

Seth's breathing quickened as he took a step back. *No,* was all he could think. Ethan Quinn was everything strong and solid and . . . normal. "You're lying."

"People mostly lie to brag, or to get out of some stupid thing they've done. I don't see the point in either—and less in lying about this."

Ethan took his cap off again because it suddenly felt too tight on his head. Once, twice, he raked his hand through his hair as if to ease the weight. "She sold me to men to pay for her habit. The first time, I fought. It didn't stop it, but I fought. The second time, I fought, and a few times more after that. Then I didn't bother fighting because it just made it worse."

Ethan's gaze stayed level on the boy's. In the harsh overhead lights Seth's eyes were dark, and not as calm as they had been when Ethan had begun to speak. Seth's chest hurt until he remembered to breathe again. "How'd you stand it?"

"I stopped caring." Ethan shrugged his shoulders. "I stopped *being*, if you know what I mean. There wasn't anybody I could go to for help—or I didn't know there was. She moved around a lot to keep the social workers off her tail."

Seth's lips felt dry and tight. He rubbed the back of his hand over them violently. "You never knew where you're going to wake up in the morning."

"Yeah, you never knew." But all the places looked the same. They all smelled the same.

"But you got away. You got out."

"Yeah, I got out. One night after her john had finished with both of us, there was . . . some trouble." Screams, blood, curses. Pain. "I don't remember everything exactly, but the cops came. I must have been in a pretty bad way because they took me to the hospital and figured things out quick enough. I ended up in the system, might have stayed there. But the doctor who treated me was Stella Quinn."

"They took you."

"They took me." And saying that, just that, soothed the sickness in Ethan's gut. "They didn't just change my life, they saved it. I had the dreams for a long time after, the sweaty ones where you wake up trying to breathe, sure you're back in it. And even when you realize you're not, you're cold for a while."

Seth knuckled the tears away, but he didn't feel ashamed of them now. "I always got away. Sometimes they put their hands on me, but I got away. None of them ever . . ."

"Good for you."

"I still wanted to kill them, and her. I wanted to."

"I know."

"I didn't want to tell anybody. I think Ray knew, and

Cam sort of knows. I didn't want anybody to think I . . . to look at me and think . . ." He couldn't express it, the shame of having anyone look at him and see what had happened, and what could have happened, in those dark, smelly rooms. "Why did you tell me?"

"Because you need to know it doesn't make you less of a man." Ethan waited, knowing that Seth would decide whether he accepted the truth of that.

What Seth saw was a man, tall, strong, self-possessed, with big, callused hands and quiet eyes. One of the weights that hung on his heart lifted. "I guess I do." And he smiled a little. "Your mouth's bleeding."

Ethan dabbed at it with the back of his hand and knew they'd crossed a thin and shaky line. "You got a good right jab. I never saw it coming." He held out a hand, testing, and ruffled Seth's sleep-tumbled hair. The boy's smile stayed in place. "Let's clean up," Ethan said, "and go home."

FIVE

GRACE HAD A MORNING
full of chores. The first load of laundry went in at seven-
fifteen while the coffee was brewing and her eyes were
still mostly shut. She watered her porch plants and the little
pots of herbs on her kitchen windowsill, and yawned
hugely.

As the coffee began to scent the air and give her hope,
she washed the glasses and bowls Julie had used the night
before while baby-sitting. She closed the open bag of potato chips, tucked it into its place in the cupboard, then
wiped the crumbs from the counter where Julie had had
her snack while talking on the phone.

Julie Cutter wasn't known for her neatness, but she
loved Aubrey.

At precisely seven-thirty—and after half a cup of coffee—Aubrey woke.

Reliable as the sunrise, Grace thought, heading out of
the tiny galley kitchen toward the bedroom off the living
room. Rain or shine, weekday or weekend, Aubrey's in-

ternal clock buzzed away at seven-thirty every morning.

Grace could have left her in the crib and finished her coffee, but she looked forward to this moment every day. Aubrey stood at the side of the crib, her sunbeam curls tangled from sleep, her cheeks still flushed with it. Grace could still remember the first time she'd come in and seen Aubrey standing, her wobbly legs rocking, her face glowing with success and surprise.

Now Aubrey's legs seemed so sturdy. She lifted one, then the other, in a kind of joyful march. She laughed out loud when Grace came into the room. "Mama, Mama, hi, my mama."

"Hello, my baby." Grace leaned over the side for the first nuzzle and sighed. She knew how lucky she was. There couldn't have been a child on the planet with a sunnier nature than her little girl. "How's my Aubrey?"

"Up! Out!"

"You bet. Gotta pee?"

"Gotta pee," Aubrey agreed and giggled when Grace lifted her out of the crib.

The toilet training was coming along, Grace decided, checking Aubrey's overnight diaper as they headed into the bathroom. It had its hits and its misses.

Aubrey hit it this time, and Grace launched into the lavish praise over bodily functions that only a parent with a toddler could understand. Teeth and hair were brushed in the closet-size bathroom Grace had brightened up with mint-green walls and awning-striped curtains.

Then the breakfast routine began. Aubrey wanted cold cereal with bananas but no milk. She plopped her hand over the bowl when Grace started to pour it on, shaking her head vigorously. "No, Mama, no. Cup. Please."

"Okay, milk in a cup." Grace filled one, set it on the high-chair tray beside the bowl. "Eat up, now. We've got lots to do today."

"Do what?"

"Let's see." Grace made herself a piece of toast while

she went through the projected day. "We have to finish the laundry, then we promised Mrs. West we'd wash her windows today."

A three-hour job, Grace estimated.

"Then we have to go to the market."

Aubrey gasped in pleasure. "Miss Lucy."

"Yes, you'll see Miss Lucy." Lucy Wilson was one of Aubrey's favorite people. The supermarket cashier always had a smile—and a lollipop—for Aubrey. "After we put the groceries away, we're going to the Quinns'."

"Seth!" Milk dribbled out of her grin.

"Well, honey, I don't know for certain that he'll be there today. He may be out on the boat with Ethan, or over at his friends' house."

"Seth," Aubrey said again, very definitely, and her mouth puckered up into a stubborn pout.

"We'll see." Grace mopped up the spills.

"Ethan."

"Maybe."

"Doggies."

"Foolish, for sure." She kissed the top of Aubrey's head and gave herself the luxury of a second cup of coffee.

AT EIGHT-FIFTEEN GRACE was armed with a stack of newspapers and a spray bottle that contained a mix of vinegar and ammonia. Aubrey was entertaining herself on the grass with her Mattel See 'n Say. Every few seconds a cow mooed or a pig oinked. And Aubrey never failed to echo the sound.

By the time Aubrey had switched her affections to her building blocks, Grace had finished cleaning and polishing the outside of the windows on the front and side of the cottage and was right on schedule. She would have stayed on schedule if Mrs. West hadn't come out with tall glasses of iced tea and a desire to chat.

"I don't know how to thank you for seeing to this for me, Grace." Mrs. West, the grandmother of many, had brought Aubrey her drink in a bright plastic cup with ducks on the side.

"I'm happy to do it, Mrs. West."

"Just can't do like I used to, with my arthritis. And I do like my windows to shine." She smiled, deepening the wrinkles on her weather-scored face. "And you do make them shine. My granddaughter, Layla, said how she'd wash them for me. But I tell you the truth and shame the devil, Grace, that girl's a scatterbrain. She'd like as not start the job and end up sleeping in the vegetable patch. Don't know what's to become of that girl."

Grace laughed and scrubbed at the next window. "She's only fifteen. Her mind's on boys and clothes and music."

"Tell me." Mrs. West nodded so vigorously that her second chin wobbled with the movement. "Why, at her age I could pick a crab clean faster than you could blink. Earned my keep, and kept my mind on my work till the work was done." She winked. "Then I thought about boys."

She let out a hearty laugh before smiling at Aubrey. "That's one pretty little lamb you got yourself there, Gracie."

"The light of my life."

"Good as gold, too. Why, my Carly's youngest boy, Luke? He's not still for two minutes running and spends every waking hour looking for trouble. Just last week I caught him climbing up my parlor curtains like a house cat." Still, the memory made her chuckle. "He's a terror, that Luke is."

"Aubrey has her moments, too."

"Can't believe it. Not with that angel face. You're going to have to beat the boys off with a stick to keep them from sniffing around that sweetheart one of these days.

Pretty as a picture. Already seen her holding hands with one.''

Grace bobbled her spray bottle and looked around quickly to make certain her little girl hadn't grown up while she wasn't looking. "Aubrey?"

Mrs. West laughed again. "Walking on the waterfront with that Quinn boy—the new one."

"Oh, Seth." The sense of relief was so ridiculous, Grace set the bottle down and picked up her glass to drink. "Aubrey's got a crush on him."

"Good-looking boy. My young Matt goes to school with him—told me how Seth came to sock that little bully Robert a few weeks back. Couldn't help but feel it was about time somebody did. How they doing over at the Quinns?"

The question was her main purpose for coming out, but Mrs. West believed in leading up to matters.

"Just fine."

Mrs. West rolled her eyes. This pump needed more priming. "That girl Cam up and married sure is a beauty. She'll have to have quick hands, too, to keep that one in line. Always was wild."

"I think Anna can handle him."

"Went off to some foreign place to honeymoon, didn't they?"

"Rome. Seth showed me a postcard they sent. It's beautiful."

"Always puts me in mind of that movie with Audrey Hepburn and Gregory Peck—where she's a princess. Don't make movies like that anymore."

"*Roman Holiday*." Grace smiled wistfully. She had a weakness for the classic and romantic.

"That's the one." Grace looked a bit like Audrey Hepburn, Mrs. West mused. Coloring was wrong, of course, with Grace being blond as a Viking, but she had the big eyes and the cool, pretty face. Lord knew, she was skinny enough.

"Never been anyplace foreign." Which included, in
Mrs. West's mind, two-thirds of the United States. "They
coming back soon?"

"A couple days."

"Hmm. Well, that house needs a woman, no question.
Can't imagine what it's like over there, four males in one
house. Must smell like a gym sock half the time. Don't
know a man on this earth who can manage to pee and hit
the toilet with the whole stream."

Grace laughed and went back to her windows. "They
aren't so bad. The fact is, Cam was keeping the house
pretty well before they hired me to take over. But the only
one of them who remembers to empty the pockets before
tossing his pants at the hamper is Phillip."

"If that's the worst of it, it's not bad. I expect Cam's
wife'll take over the house once they get back."

Grace's hand tightened on her wad of newspaper as her
heart did a quick hitch. "I . . . She works full-time in Princess Anne."

"Most likely she'll take over," Mrs. West said again.
"A woman likes her house kept her way. Best thing for
the boy, I expect, having a woman there full-time. Don't
know what Ray was thinking of this time around, I swear.
A good-hearted man he was, but once Stella passed . . .
shifted his moorings, I'd say. A man his age taking on a
boy thataway. No matter what was what. Not that I believe
one word of the nasty gossip you hear now and then.
Nancy Claremont is the worst, flapping her lips every
chance she gets."

Mrs. West waited a beat, hoping that Grace would flap
hers. But Grace was frowning intently at the window.

"You know if that insurance inspector's coming around
again?"

"No," Grace said quietly, "I don't. I hope not."

"Don't see how it makes a matter where the boy came
from as far as the insurance company goes. Even if Ray
did suicide himself—and I'm not saying it's so—they

can't prove it, can they? Because . . .'' She paused dramatically, as she did whenever she made the argument. "They weren't there!''

She said the last on a note of triumph, just as she had when she'd made the same statement to Nancy.

"Professor Quinn wouldn't have killed himself,'' Grace murmured.

" 'Course not.'' But it did make for such interesting talk. "But the boy—'' She broke off, her ears pricking up. "There goes my telephone. You just let yourself in when you want to do the inside, Grace,'' she said as she hurried off.

Grace said nothing, kept working steadily. But her mind was whirling. It shamed her that she couldn't concentrate on Professor Quinn. She could think only of herself and of what might happen.

Would Anna come back from Rome and want to take over the house? Would Grace lose her job there and the extra money that went with it? Worse—much worse— would she lose those opportunities to see Ethan once or twice a week? To share a meal now and then?

She'd gotten used to—even dependent on—being a part of his life, even a peripheral part, she realized. And as pathetic as it was, she loved folding his clothes, smoothing the sheets on his bed. She even allowed herself to believe that he would think of her when he found one of her little notes around the house. Or slipped between freshly laundered sheets at night.

Was she going to lose that, too—and lose the pleasure of seeing him coming in from his boat or scooping Aubrey up when she demanded a kiss, or glancing over at her and giving her that slow smile?

Was all of that going to be only pictures she tucked away in her mind now?

Her days would go on and on, without even that to look forward to. And her nights would go on and on, alone.

She squeezed her eyes tight, struggling with despair.

Then opened them again when Aubrey tugged at the hem of her shorts.

"Mama. Miss Lucy?"

"Soon, honey." Because she needed to, Grace lifted Aubrey into her arms for a fierce hug.

IT WAS NEARLY ONE BY the time Grace finished putting away the groceries and fixing Aubrey's lunch. She was only half an hour behind, and she thought she could make that up without too much trouble. It just meant moving a little quicker and keeping her mind on her work. No more projecting, she ordered herself as she strapped Aubrey into the car seat. No more foolishness.

"Seth, Seth, Seth," Aubrey chanted, bouncing madly.

"We'll see." Grace climbed behind the wheel, put the key in the ignition, and turned it. The response was a wheeze and a thump. "Oh, no, you don't. No, you don't. I don't have time for this." A little panicked, she turned the key again, pumped the gas pedal, and sighed with relief when the engine caught. "That's more like it," she muttered as she backed out of the short driveway. "Here we go, Aubrey."

"Here we go!"

Five minutes later, midway between her house and the Quinns', the old sedan coughed again, shuddered, then belched out steam from under the hood.

"Dammit!"

"Dammit!" Aubrey echoed joyfully.

Grace only pressed the heels of her hands to her eyes. It was the radiator, she was sure of it. Last month it had been the fan belt, and before that, the brake pads. Resigned, she eased to the side of the road and got out to open the hood.

Smoke billowed, made her cough and step away. Resolutely, she swallowed back the knot of despair in her throat. Maybe it wouldn't be anything major. It could just be some belt again. And if it wasn't—she sighed hugely— she would have to decide if it was better to pump more money into this wreck or to worry her beleaguered budget into buying another wreck.

Either way, there was nothing to be done about it now.

She opened the passenger-side door and unbuckled Aubrey. "The car's sick again, honey."

"Awww."

"Yeah, so we're going to leave it right here."

"Alone?"

Aubrey's concern over inanimate objects made Grace smile again. "Not for long. I'm going to call the car man to come take care of it."

"Make it feel all better."

"I hope so. Now we're going to walk to Seth's house."

"Okay!" Delighted by the change of routine, Aubrey set out at a scramble.

A quarter of a mile later, Grace was carrying her.

But it was a pretty day, she reminded herself. And walking gave her a chance to look and really see. Honeysuckle was tangling along the fence that bordered a tidy field of soybeans, and the scent was lovely. She picked off a blossom for Aubrey.

By the time they skirted the marsh that edged Quinn land, her arms were aching. They stopped to study a turtle sunning on the side of the road, to let Aubrey giggle over the way its head retreated into its shell when she reached out to touch.

"Can you walk for a while now, baby?"

"Tired." With her eyes pleading, Aubrey lifted her arms. "Up!"

"Okay, up you come. Nearly there." It was past nap time, Grace thought. Aubrey wanted her nap directly after lunch every day. She would sleep for two hours, almost to the minute, then wake up ready to roll.

Aubrey's head was already a snoozing weight on Grace's shoulder when she climbed the porch and slipped into the house.

Once she had her daughter tucked onto the couch, she hurried upstairs to strip beds, gather and sort laundry. With the first load in, she made a quick call to the mechanic who did his best to keep her ailing car alive.

She rushed upstairs again, remaking the beds with fresh sheets. To save herself steps, she kept cleaning supplies on each floor. Grace tackled the bathroom first, scrubbing and rinsing in a flurry until chrome and tile sparkled.

It would be, she realized, her last full hit on the Quinn place before Cam and Anna returned. But she'd already decided, sometime during the mile walk from her broken-down car, to carve out a couple of hours for a quick polish the day they were expected home.

She had pride in her work, didn't she? And certainly another woman would notice the tidiness, the clean corners, the few extra touches she tried to add. A professional woman like Anna, a woman with a demanding career, would see, wouldn't she, that Grace was needed here?

She raced downstairs again to check on Aubrey, to drag wet clothes out of the washer into a basket and put the second load in.

She would make sure there were fresh flowers in the master bedroom when the newlyweds returned. And she'd put out the good fingertip towels. She would leave a note for Phillip to pick up some fruit so she could arrange it prettily in the bowl on the kitchen table.

She'd make time to paste-wax the hardwood floors and wash and iron the curtains.

She hung clothes on the line quickly, without any of her usual enjoyment in the task. Still, the simple routine began to calm her. Everything would be all right, somehow.

She caught herself swaying and shook her head to clear it. Fatigue had come quickly, like a punch to the jaw. If she had bothered to calculate the time she'd been on her feet and moving that day, she would have counted seven hours, on a short five hours' sleep the night before. What she did calculate was that she had another twelve to go. And she needed a break.

Ten minutes, she promised herself, and as she sometimes did on long days, stretched out right in the grass by the clothes that waved on the line. A ten-minute nap would recharge her system and still give her time to scrub down the kitchen before Aubrey woke up.

ETHAN DROVE HOME from the waterfront. He'd cut his day on the water short, letting Jim and his son take the workboat out again to check the pots in the Pocomoke. Seth was off with Danny and Will, and Ethan figured on grabbing himself a quick, if delayed, lunch, then spending the next several hours at the boatyard. He wanted to finish the cockpit, maybe get the roof of the cabin started. The more he managed to do, the less time it would be before Cam could get into the finish and fancy work.

He slowed down when he saw Grace's car on the side of the road, then pulled over quickly. He only shook his head when he looked under the open hood. Damn thing was held together with spit and prayers, he decided. She shouldn't be driving something so unreliable. Just what if, he thought sourly, the goddamn thing had decided to break down when she'd been coming home from the pub in the middle of the night?

He took a closer look and hissed through his teeth. The radiator was a dead loss, and if she was entertaining the idea of replacing it, he'd just have to talk her out of it.

He would find her a decent secondhand car. Fix it up for her—or ask Cam, who knew engines like Midas knew gold, to tune it up. He wasn't having her driving around in a wreck like this, and with the baby, too.

He caught himself, took a couple steps back. It wasn't any of his business. The hell it wasn't, he thought, with an uncharacteristic flash of temper. She was a friend, wasn't she? He had a right to help out a friend, especially one who needed some looking after.

And God knew—whether or not Grace did—that she needed some looking after. He got back in his truck and drove home with a scowl on his face.

He'd nearly slammed the screen door before he saw Aubrey curled up on the couch. The scowl didn't have a chance. He eased the door shut and walked quietly over to her. Her hand was bunched into a fist on the cushion. Unable to resist, he took it gently and marveled at those tiny, perfect fingers. She had a bow around one of her curls, a little ribbon of blue lace that he imagined Grace had tied on that morning. It was lopsided now, and only sweeter for it.

He couldn't help hoping that she woke before he had to head out again.

But now, he needed to find Aubrey's mother and discuss reliable transportation.

He cocked his head, decided it was too quiet for her to be upstairs doing whatever it was she did up there. He walked into the kitchen and noted that the signs of a hurried breakfast were still in evidence. She hadn't gotten to that yet. But the washing machine was humming, and he caught a glimpse of clothes flapping in the breeze on the line outside.

The minute he stepped to the door he saw her. And hit full panic. He didn't know what he thought, only that she was lying on the grass. Terrible images of illness and injury crowded into his head as he rushed outside. He was barely one full stride away from her when he realized she wasn't unconscious. She was sleeping.

Curled up much as her daughter was inside. One fist bunched near her cheek, her breathing slow and deep and even. He gave in to his weakened knees and sat down beside her, waited for his heartbeat to return to something approaching normal.

He sat, listening to the clothes flap on the line, to the water lick the eelgrass, and to the birds chatter while he wondered what the hell he was going to do with her.

In the end, he simply sighed, rose, then bending down gathered her up into his arms.

She stirred in them, snuggled, made his blood run a little too fast for comfort. "Ethan," she murmured, turning her face into the curve of his neck and inciting the bright fantasy of rolling over that sun-warmed grass with her.

"Ethan," she said again, skimming her fingers along his shoulder. And making him hard as iron. Then again, "Ethan," only this time in a squeak of shock as she jerked her head up and stared at him.

Her eyes were dazed with sleep and bright with surprise. Her mouth made a soft O that was gloriously tempting. Then color flooded her cheeks.

"What? What is it?" she managed over a stomach-churning combination of arousal and embarrassment.

"You're going to take a nap, you ought to have as much sense as Aubrey and take it inside out of the sun." He knew his voice was rough. He couldn't do anything about it. Desire had him by the throat with gleefully nipping claws.

"I was just—"

"Scared ten years off me when I saw you lying there. I thought you'd fainted or something."

"I only stretched out for a minute. Aubrey was sleeping, so—Aubrey! I need to check on Aubrey."

"I just did. She's fine. You'd have shown more sense if you'd stretched out on the couch with her."

"I don't come here to sleep."

"You were sleeping."

"Just for a minute."

"You need more than a minute."

"No, I don't. It's just that things got complicated today, and my brain got tired."

It almost amused him. He stopped in the kitchen, still holding her, and looked into her eyes. "Your brain got tired?"

"Yeah." It nearly shut off entirely now. "I needed to rest my mind a minute, that's all. Put me down, Ethan."

He wasn't ready to, not quite yet. "I saw your car about a mile down the road from here."

"I called Dave and told him. He's going to get to it as soon as he can."

"You walked from there to here, carting Aubrey?"

"No, my chauffeur drove us in. Put me down, Ethan." Before she exploded.

"Well, you can give your chauffeur the rest of the day off. I'll drive you home when Aubrey wakes up."

"I can get myself home. I've barely started on the house. Now I need to get back to it."

"You're not walking two and a half miles."

"I'll call Julie. She'll run down and pick us up. You must have work to do yourself. I'm . . . behind schedule," she said, desperately now. "I can't catch up if you don't put me down."

He considered her. "There's not much to you."

The shimmer of need wavered into annoyance. "If you're going to tell me I'm skinny—"

"I wouldn't say skinny. You've got fine bones, that's all." And smooth, soft flesh to cover them. He set her on her feet before he forgot he intended to look after her. "You don't have to worry with the house today."

"I do. I need to do my job." Her nerves were a jittery mess. The way he was looking at her made her want to take one flying leap back into his arms and also made her want to hightail it out the back door like a rabbit. She'd never experienced such a dramatic tug-of-war on her system, and could only stand her ground. "I can do it quicker if you aren't underfoot."

"I'll get out of your way as soon as you call Julie and see if she'll come by and get you." He reached up and brushed some dandelion fluff out of her hair.

"Okay." She turned, punched in numbers on the kitchen phone. Maybe it would be best, she thought wildly as the phone started to ring, if Anna didn't want her around after she got home. It seemed she couldn't be with Ethan for ten minutes anymore without getting jumpy. If it kept up, she was bound to do something to embarrass them both.

SIX

ETHAN DIDN'T MIND PUT-
ting in long hours on the boat at night. Especially when
he could work alone. It hadn't taken much persuasion for
him to agree to let Seth camp out with the other boys in
their backyard. It gave Ethan an evening alone—a rarity
now—and time to work without having to tune in to questions and comments.

Not that the boy wasn't entertaining, Ethan mused. The
fact was, he was firmly attached to Seth. Accepting Seth
into his life had been natural because Ray had asked it of
him. But the affection, the appreciation, and the loyalty
had grown and solidified until it simply was.

But that didn't mean the kid couldn't wear down his
energies.

Ethan kept it to handwork tonight. Even if you *felt*
awake and alert at midnight, the odds were you'd be a bit
sluggish, and he didn't want to risk losing a finger to the
power tools. In any case, it was soothing to work in the

quiet, to hand-sand edges and planes until you felt them
go smooth.

They would be ready to seal the hull before the week
was out, and he could start Seth on sanding the rubrails.
If Cam dived right in on dealing with belowdecks, and if
Seth didn't bitch too much about working with putty and
caulk and varnish over the next week or two, they'd do
well enough.

He checked his watch, saw that time was getting away
from him, and began to put away his tools. He swept up,
since Seth wasn't there to wield the broom.

By quarter after one, he was parked outside of the pub.
He didn't intend to go inside anymore than he intended to
let Grace walk the mile and a half home when she clocked
out. So he settled back, switched on his dome light, and
passed the time reading his dog-eared copy of *Cannery
Row*.

INSIDE, IT WAS LAST CALL.
The only thing that would have made Grace happier would
have been if Dave had told her that all she needed to get
her car up and running was some used chewing gum and
a rubber band.

Instead he'd told her it would cost the equivalent of
three years' worth of both, and then she'd be lucky if the
old bucket ran another five thousand miles.

It was something she would have to worry about later;
at the moment, she had her hands full dealing with an
overly insistent customer who was stopping off in St. Chris
on his way down to Savannah and was sure Grace would
like to be his form of entertainment for the night.

"I got me a hotel room." He winked at her when she
stooped to serve his final drink of the night. "And it's got
a big bed and twenty-four-hour room service. We could
have us a hell of a party, honey pie."

"I don't do a lot of partying, but thanks."

He grabbed her hand, pulled it just enough to throw off her balance so she had to grip his shoulder or tumble into his lap. "Then now's your chance." He had dark eyes, and he aimed them leeringly at her breasts. "I got a real fondness for long-legged blondes. Always treat them special."

He was tiresome, Grace thought as he breathed one more beer into her face. But she had handled worse. "I appreciate that, but I'm going to finish up my shift and go home."

"Your place is fine with me."

"Mister—"

"Bob. You just call me Bob, baby."

She had to yank to get free. "Mister, I'm just not interested."

Of course she was, he thought, sending her a smile he knew was dazzling. He'd paid two grand to get his teeth bonded, hadn't he? "The hard-to-get routine always turns me on."

Grace decided he wasn't worth even a single disgusted sigh. "We're closing in fifteen; you're going to need to settle your tab."

"Okay, okay, don't get bitchy." He smiled widely and pulled out a money clip thick with bills. He always salted it with a couple of twenties on the outside, then filled it with singles. "You figure what I owe, then we'll . . . negotiate your tip."

Sometimes, Grace decided, it was best to keep your mouth firmly shut. What wanted to come out was vicious enough to get her fired. So she walked away and took her empties to the bar.

"He giving you trouble, Grace?"

She smiled weakly at Steve. It was just the two of them working now. The other waitress had clocked out at midnight, claiming a migraine. Since she'd been pale as a ghost, Grace had shooed her out and agreed to cover.

"He's just another of those gifts to womankind. Nothing to worry about."

"If he's not gone by closing, I'll wait until you're locked in your car and headed home."

She made a noncommittal humming noise. She hadn't mentioned her lack of transportation because she knew Steve would insist on driving her home. He lived twenty minutes away, in the opposite direction. And had a pregnant wife waiting for him.

She cashed out tables, cleared them, and noted with relief that her problem customer finally rose to leave. He paid his $18.83 bar bill with cash, leaving $20 on the table. Though he'd managed to monopolize most of her time and attention for the past three hours, Grace was too tired to be annoyed at the pitiful tip.

It didn't take long for the pub to empty. The crowd had been mostly college students, out for a couple of beers and conversation on a weekday night. By her calculations they'd turned about ten tables no more than twice since her shift had started at seven. Her tips for the evening weren't going to make much of a dent in the new car she would have to buy.

It was so quiet, they both jumped like rabbits when the phone rang. Even while Grace laughed at their reaction, the blood drained out of Steve's face. "Mollie," was all he said as he leaped on the phone. He answered it with a stuttering, "Is it time?"

Grace stepped forward, wondering if she was strong enough to catch him if he keeled over. When he began nodding rapidly, she felt her smile spread wide.

"Okay. You—you call the doctor, right? Everything's ready to go. How far apart . . . Oh, God, oh, God, I'm on my way. Don't move. Don't do anything. Don't worry."

He dropped the phone off the hook, then froze. "She's—Mollie—my wife—"

"Yes, I know who Mollie is—we went to school together from kindergarten on." Grace laughed. Then because he looked so dear, and so terrified, she cupped his face in her hands and kissed him. "Go. But you drive careful. Babies take their time coming. They'll wait for you."

"We're having a baby," he said slowly, as if testing each word. "Me and Mollie."

"I know. And it's just wonderful. You tell her I'm going to come see her, and the baby. Of course, if you just stand there like somebody glued your feet to the floor, I guess she'll have to drive herself to the hospital."

"God! I have to go." He knocked over a chair on his way to the door. "Keys, where are the keys?"

"Your car keys are in your pocket. Bar keys are behind the bar. I'll lock up, Daddy."

He stopped, tossed one huge, electrifying grin over his shoulder. "Wow!" And was gone.

Grace was still chuckling as she picked up the chair and replaced it upside down on the table.

She thought of the night when she had gone into labor with Aubrey. Oh, she'd been so afraid, so excited. She had indeed driven herself to the hospital. There'd been no husband there to panic with her. There'd been no one to sit with her, to tell her to breathe, to hold her hand.

When the pain and aloneness had been at its worst, she weakened and let the nurse call her mother. Of course her mother came, and stayed with her, and saw Aubrey into the world. They cried together, and laughed together, and it had made it all right again.

Her father hadn't come. Not then, not later. Her mother had made excuses, tried to smooth it over, but Grace had understood she was not to be forgiven. Others had come, Julie and her parents, friends and neighbors.

Ethan and Professor Quinn.

They'd brought her flowers, pink and white daisies and rosebuds. She had pressed one of each in Aubrey's baby book.

It made her smile to remember, so when the door behind her opened, she turned with a chuckle. "Steve, if you don't get going, she'll . . ." Grace trailed off, experiencing more annoyance than fear when she saw the man step inside. "We're closed," she said firmly.

"I know, honey pie. I figured you'd find a way to hang back and wait for me."

"I'm not waiting for you." Why the hell hadn't she locked the door behind Steve? "I said we're closed. You'll have to leave."

"You want to play it that way, fine." He sauntered over, leaned on the bar. He'd been working out regularly for months now and knew the stance showed off his well-toned muscles. "Why don't you fix us both a drink? And we'll talk about that tip."

Her patience dried up. "You already gave me a tip, now I'll give you one. If you're not out that door in ten seconds, I'm calling the cops. Instead of spending the night on your big hotel bed, you'll spend it in a cell."

"I got something else in mind." He grabbed her, shoved her back against the bar, and ground himself against her. "See? You had it in mind, too. I saw the way you've been eyeing me. I've been waiting all night for some action."

She couldn't get her knee up to ram it against what he was so proudly pushing against her. She couldn't get her hands free to shove or scratch. Panic started as a tickle in her throat, then spread like a hot flood when he shot a hand under her skirt.

She was preparing to bite, scream, and spit when he was suddenly airborne. All she could do was stay pressed against the bar and stare at Ethan.

"You all right?"

He said it so quietly that her head bobbed up and down in automatic response. But his eyes weren't quiet. There was rage in them, so primal and primitive that she shuddered.

"Go on out and wait in the truck."

"I—he—" Then she squealed. It would embarrass her to remember it later, but it was the only sound that came out of her tight throat when the man rushed at Ethan like a battering ram, head lowered, fists clenched.

She watched, staggered as Ethan simply pivoted, jabbed once, twice, and flicked the man off like a fly. Then he bent, grabbed the man by the shirtfront, and hauled him up on his rubbery legs.

"You don't want to be here." His voice was steel with dangerously sharp edges. "Because if I see you here after the next two minutes, I'm going to kill you. And unless you got family or close personal friends, nobody's going to give a damn."

He tossed him away, with what seemed to Grace no more than a twist of the wrist, and the man crashed into a table. Then Ethan turned his back as if the guy didn't exist. But none of the stony fury had faded from his face when he looked at Grace.

"I told you to go wait in the truck."

"I have to— I need to—" She pressed a hand between her breasts and pushed up as if to shove the words clear. Neither of them looked as the man scrambled up and stumbled out the door. "I have to lock up. Shiney—"

"Shiney can go to hell." Since it didn't appear that she was going to move, Ethan grabbed her hand and hauled her to the door. "He ought to be horsewhipped for letting a lone woman lock up this place at night."

"Steve—he—"

"I saw that sonofabitch go flying out of here like a bomb was ticking." Ethan intended to have a nice long talk with Steve as well. Soon, he promised himself grimly as he pushed Grace into the truck.

"Mollie—she called. She's in labor. I told him to go."

"You would. Damn idiot woman."

The statement, delivered with such bubbling fury, stopped the trembling that had just begun, cut off the babbling gratitude she'd been about to express. He'd saved her, was all she'd been able to think, like a knight in a fairy tale. But the thin, romantic mist that had been shimmering over her still-reeling brain evaporated.

"I'm certainly not an idiot."

"You sure as hell are." He whipped the truck out of the lot, spitting gravel and knocking Grace back against her seat. His rare but formidable temper was in full swing, and there was no stopping it until it had blown itself out.

"That man was the idiot," she shot back. "I was just doing my job."

"Doing your job damn near got you raped. The son of a bitch had his hand under your skirt."

She could still feel it, the way it had groped at her. Nausea bubbled up to her throat and was ruthlessly swallowed down. "I'm aware of that. Things like that don't happen at Shiney's."

"It just did happen at Shiney's."

"It doesn't draw that kind of clientele usually. He wasn't local. He was—"

"He was there." Ethan swung into her drive, hit the brakes, then shut the engine off with a hard flick of the wrist. "And so were you. Mopping up some bar in the middle of the goddamn night, by yourself. And what were you going to do when you were done? Walk almost two damn miles?"

"I could have gotten a ride, except—"

"Except you're too stiff-necked to ask for one," he finished. "You'd rather limp home in those mile-high heels than ask a favor."

She had sneakers in her bag, but decided it wouldn't help to mention it. Her bag, she remembered, which was back at the unlocked pub. Now she would have to go back first thing in the morning, get her things, and lock up before the boss checked.

"Well, thank you very much for your opinion of my failings, and the lecture. And the damn ride home." She shoved at the door, only to have Ethan grab her arm and yank her back.

"Where the hell do you think you're going?"

"I'm going home. I'm going to soak my stiff-neck and my idiot-brain and go to bed."

"I haven't finished."

"*I've* finished." She jerked free and jumped out. If it hadn't been for the blasted heels, she might have made it. But he was out the opposite door and blocking her way before she'd taken three strides. "I have nothing more to say." Her voice was cold and dismissive. Her chin was high.

"Good. You can just listen. If you won't quit at the pub—which is just what you should do—you're going to take some basic precautions. Reliable transportation comes first."

"Don't you tell me what I have to do."

"Shut up."

She did, but only because she was stunned speechless. She'd never, in all the years she'd known him, seen Ethan like this. In the moonlight she could see that the fury in his eyes hadn't dimmed a bit. His face was like stone, the shadows flittering over it making it seem harsh, even dangerous.

"We'll see that you get a car you can trust," he continued, in that same edgy tone. "And you won't be closing on your own again. When you finish your shift, I want somebody walking you out to your car and waiting until you lock it and drive off."

"That's just ridiculous."

He stepped forward. Though he didn't touch her, didn't lift a hand, she backed up a pace. Her heart began to pound too fast and too loud in her head.

"What's ridiculous is you thinking you can handle every damn thing by yourself. And I'm tired of it."

She sputtered, hating herself. "*You're* tired of it?"

"Yeah, and it's going to stop. I can't do much about

your working yourself half to death, but I can do something about the rest. You don't make arrangements at the pub to see you're safe, I will. You're going to stop asking for trouble."

"Asking for it?" Outrage gushed through her in such a boiling wave, she was surprised that the top of her head didn't simply blow off. "I wasn't *asking* for anything. That bastard wouldn't take no for an answer, no matter how many times I said it."

"That's just what I'm talking about."

"You don't know what you're talking about," she said in a furious whisper. "I handled him, and I would have kept handling him if—"

"How?" There was red around the edges of his vision. He could still see the way she'd been pressed up against the bar, her eyes wide and frightened. Her face had been ghost-pale, her eyes huge and sheened like glass. If he hadn't come in . . .

And because the thought of what could have been scraped raw at the center of his brain, his already slippery control shattered.

"Just how?" he demanded, in one quick move yanking her hard against him. "Go ahead, show me."

She twisted, shoved. And her pulse began to race. "Stop it."

"You think telling him to stop once he's got your scent's going to make a difference?" Lemons and fear. "Once he feels the way you fit?" Subtle curves and long lines. "He knew there was no one to stop him, that he could do anything he wanted."

Everything inside her was in a mindless rush—her heart, her blood, her head. "I wouldn't—I would have stopped him."

"Stop me."

He meant it. A part of him wanted desperately for her to stop him, to do or say something that would hold the wildness in check. But his mouth was on hers, rough and needy, swallowing her gasps, inciting more and reveling in her fast, hard trembles.

When she moaned, when her lips yielded, parted, answered his, he lost his mind.

He dragged her onto the grass, rolled with her, atop her. The thick bolt he'd kept locked on his desires exploded open, and what poured out was reckless greed and primal lust. He ravaged her mouth with the single-minded hunger of a starving wolf.

Swamped with needs so long buried, she arched against him, straining center to center, core to core. Her system stuttered with shocked pleasure, then roared into full raging life. Pumping heat, strangled moans, quivering delights.

This was not the Ethan she knew, or the one she'd dreamed would finally touch her. There was no gentleness, no care, but she gave herself to him, thrilled at the sensation of being swept away.

She wrapped long limbs around him to bind him closer, let her fingers dive into his hair, grip there. And shivered with the dark delight of knowing he was stronger.

He feasted on her mouth, her throat, while he tugged at the low, snug bodice. He was desperate for flesh, the feel of it, the taste of it. Her flesh, her flavor.

Her breast was small and firm, the skin smooth as satin against his wide, hard palm. Her heart jackhammered under it.

She whimpered, stunned at the sensation of that rough hand cupping her, kneading her, churning an echoing tug between her legs, where muscles had gone liquid and lax.

And sighed his name.

She might have shot him. The sound of her voice, the hitch of her breath, the shivers on her skin, slapped him back cold and hard.

He rolled away, onto his back, and struggled to find his breath, his sanity. His decency. They were in her front yard, for God's sake. Her baby was sleeping inside the house. He'd nearly, very nearly done worse than the man in the pub. He'd very nearly betrayed trust, friendship, and vulnerability.

This beast inside of him was precisely the reason he'd sworn never to touch her. Now by loosing it, he'd broken his vow and ruined everything.

"I'm sorry." A pitiful phrase, he thought, but he didn't have any other words. "God, Grace, I'm sorry."

Her blood was still flowing hot, and that wonderful, terrifying need aroused to screaming. She shifted, reached out to touch his face. "Ethan—"

"There's no excuse," he said quickly, sitting up so she wasn't touching him—tempting him. "I lost my temper and I stopped thinking straight."

"Lost your temper." She stayed where she was, sprawled on the grass that now seemed too cold, her face lifted to the moon that now shone too bright. "So you were just mad," she said dully.

"I was mad, but that's no excuse for hurting you."

"You didn't hurt me." She could still feel his hands on her, the rough, insistent press of them. But the sensation then, the sensation now, wasn't one of pain.

He thought he could handle it now—looking at her, touching her. She would need it, he imagined. He couldn't have lived with himself if she was afraid of him. "The last thing I want to do is hurt you." As gentle as a doting parent, he tidied her clothes. When she didn't cringe, he stroked a hand over her tousled hair. "I only want what's best for you."

She didn't cringe, but she did, suddenly and sharply, slap his hand aside. "Don't treat me like a child. A few minutes ago you were treating me like a woman easy enough."

There'd been nothing easy about it, he thought grimly. "And I was wrong."

"Then we were both wrong." She sat up, brushing briskly at her clothes. "It wasn't one-sided, Ethan. You know that. I didn't try to make you stop because I didn't want you to stop. That was your idea."

He was baffled, and abruptly nervous. "For Christ's sake, Grace, we were rolling around in your front yard."

"That's not what stopped you."

With a quiet sigh, she brought her knees up, wrapped her arms around them. The gesture, so purely innocent, contrasted sharply with the tiny skirt and fishnet stockings and made his stomach muscles tie themselves into hot, slippery knots again.

"You'd have stopped anyway, wherever it happened. Maybe because you remembered it was me, but it's harder for me to think that you don't want me now. So you're going to have to tell me you don't if you want things to go back to the way they were before."

"They belong back where they were before."

"That's not an answer, Ethan. I'm sorry to press you about it, but I think I deserve one." It was hard, brutal, for her to ask, but the taste of him still lingered on her lips. "If you don't think about me that way, and this was just temper pushing you to teach me a lesson, then you have to say so, straight out."

"It was temper."

Accepting the fresh bruise to her heart, she nodded. "Well, then, it worked."

"That doesn't make it right. What I just did makes me too close to that bastard in the bar tonight."

"I didn't want him to touch me." She drew in a long breath, held it, let it out slowly. But he didn't speak. Didn't speak, she thought, but moved back. He might not have shifted an inch, but he'd moved away from her in the way that counted most.

"I'm grateful to you for being there tonight." She started to rise, but he was on his feet ahead of her, offering a hand. She took it, determined not to embarrass either of them any further. "I was afraid, and I don't know if I could have handled it on my own. You're a good friend,

Ethan, and I appreciate you wanting to help."

He slid his hands into his pockets, where they would be safe. "I talked to Dave about another car. He's got a line on a couple decent used ones."

Since screaming would accomplish nothing, she had to laugh. "You don't waste any time. All right, I'll talk to him about it tomorrow." She glanced toward the house where the front porch light gleamed. "Do you want to come in? I could put some ice on your knuckles."

"He had a jaw like a pillow. They're fine. You need to get to bed."

"Yeah." Alone, she thought, to toss and turn. And wish. "I'm going to come by on Saturday for a couple hours. Just to spruce things up before Cam and Anna get home."

"That'd be nice. We'd appreciate it."

"Well, good night." She turned, walked across the grass toward the house.

He waited. He told himself he just wanted to see her safely inside before he left. But he knew it was a lie, that it was cowardice. He'd needed the distance before he could finish answering her question.

"Grace?"

She closed her eyes briefly. All she wanted now was to get inside, crawl into bed, and indulge in a good, long cry. She hadn't let herself have a serious jag in years. But she turned back, made her lips curve. "Yes?"

"I think about you that way." He saw, even with the distance, the way her eyes widened, darkened, the way her pretty smile slid away so that she only stared. "I don't want to. I tell myself not to. But I think about you that way. Now go on inside," he told her gently.

"Ethan—"

"Go on. It's late."

She managed to turn the knob, to step inside, shut the

door behind her. But she turned quickly to the window to watch him get back in his truck and drive away.

It was late, she thought with a shiver that she recognized as hope. But maybe it wasn't too late.

SEVEN

"I APPRECIATE YOU HELP-
ing me out, Mama."

"Helping you out?" Carol Monroe tsk-tsked the
thought away as she knelt to tie the laces on Aubrey's pink
sneaker. "Taking this cube of sugar home with me for the
afternoon is pure pleasure." She gave Aubrey a chuck under the chin. "We're going to have us a time, aren't we,
honey?"

Aubrey grinned, knowing her ground. "Toys! We got
toys, Gramma. Dollbabies."

"You bet we do. And I might just have a surprise for
you when we get there."

Aubrey's eyes grew huge and bright. She sucked in her
breath to let out a sharp squeal of delight as she jumped
down from the chair to race through the house in her own
version of a victory dance.

"Oh, Mama, not another doll. You spoil her."

"Can't," Carol said firmly, giving her knee a push to

help herself straighten. "Besides, it's my privilege as a granny."

Since Aubrey was occupied running and shouting, Carol took a moment to study her daughter. Not sleeping enough, as usual, she decided, noting the shadows smudged under Grace's eyes. Not eating enough to feed a bird either, though she'd brought over Grace's favorite homemade peanut butter cookies to try to put some flesh on her girl's delicate bones.

A child not yet twenty-three ought to paint her face a little, put some curl in her hair, and go out kicking up her heels a night or two instead of working herself into the ground.

Since Carol had said as much a dozen times or more and had been ignored on the subject a dozen times or more, she tried a different tack. "You got to quit that night work, Gracie. It doesn't agree with you."

"I'm fine."

"Good hard work's necessary for living, and admirable, but a person's got to mix in some pleasure and fun or they dry right up."

Because she was weary of hearing the same song, however the notes might vary, Grace turned and scrubbed at her already spotless kitchen counter. "I like working at the pub. It gives me a chance to see people, talk to them." Even if it was just to ask them if they'd like another round. "The pay's good."

"If you're low on cash—"

"I'm fine." Grace set her teeth. She'd have suffered the torments of hell before she would admit that her budget was strained to breaking—and that solving her transportation problems was going to mean robbing Peter to pay Paul for the next several months. "The extra money comes in handy, and I'm good at waitressing."

"I know you are. You could work down at the cafe, have day hours."

Patiently, Grace rinsed out her dishcloth and hung it

over the divider of the double sink to dry. "Mama, you know that isn't possible. Daddy doesn't want me working for him."

"He never said that. Besides, you help out with picking crabs when we're shorthanded."

"I help you out," Grace specified as she turned. "And I'm happy to do it when I can. But we both know I can't work at the cafe."

Her daughter was as stubborn as two mules pulling in opposite directions, Carol thought. It was what made her her father's daughter. "You know you could soften him up if you tried."

"I don't want to soften him up. He made it plain how he feels about me. Let it be, Mama," she murmured when she saw her mother preparing to protest. "I don't want to argue with you, and I don't want to put you in the position ever again of having to defend one of us against the other. It's not right."

Carol threw up her hands. She loved them both, husband and daughter. But she'd be damned if she could understand them. "No one can talk to either of you once you get that look on your face. Don't know why I waste breath trying."

Grace smiled. "Me, either." Grace stepped close, bent down and kissed her mother's cheek. Carol was six inches shorter than Grace's five feet eight. "Thanks, Mama."

Carol softened, as she always did, and combed a hand through her short, curly hair. It had once been as blond by nature as her daughter's and granddaughter's. But nature being what it was, she now gave it a quiet boost with Miss Clairol.

Her cheeks were round and rosy, her skin surprisingly smooth, given her love of the sun. But then, she didn't neglect it. There wasn't a single night she climbed into bed without carefully applying a layer of Oil of Olay.

Being female wasn't just an act of fate, in Carol Monroe's mind. It was a duty. She prided herself that though she was coming uncomfortably close to her forty-fifth birthday, she still managed to resemble the china doll her husband had once called her.

They'd been courting then, and he'd taken some trouble to be poetic.

He usually forgot such things these days.

But he was a good man, she thought. A good provider, a faithful husband, and a fair man in business. His problem, she knew, was a soft heart too easily bruised. Grace had bruised it badly simply by not being the perfect daughter he'd expected her to be.

These thoughts came and went as she helped Grace gather up what Aubrey would need for an afternoon visit. Seemed to her children needed so much more these days. Time was, she would stick Grace on her hip, toss a few diapers into a bag, and off they'd go.

Now her baby was grown, with a baby of her own. Grace was a good mother, Carol thought, smiling a bit as Aubrey and Grace selected just which stuffed animal should have the privilege of a visit to Grandma's. The fact was, Carol had to admit, Grace was better at the job than she had been herself. The girl listened, weighed, considered. And maybe that was best. She herself had simply done, decided, demanded. Grace was so biddable as a child, she'd never thought twice about what unspoken needs had lived inside her.

And the guilt stayed with her because she had known of Grace's dream to study dance. Instead of taking it seriously, Carol passed it off as childish nonsense. She hadn't helped her baby there, hadn't encouraged, hadn't believed.

The ballet lessons had simply been a natural activity for a girl child as far as Carol had been concerned. If she'd had a son, she'd have seen to it that he played in the Little League. It was . . . just the way things were done, she thought now. Girls had tutus and boys had ball gloves. Why did it have to be more complicated than that?

But Grace had been more complicated, Carol admitted. And she hadn't seen it. Or hadn't wanted to see.

When Grace came to her at eighteen and told her she had her summer job money saved, that she wanted to go to New York to study dance, and begged for help with the expenses, she'd told her not to be foolish.

Young girls just out of high school didn't go haring off to New York City, of all places on God's Earth, on their own. Dreams of ballerinas were supposed to slide into dreams of brides and wedding gowns.

But Grace had been dead set on following her dream and had gone to her father and asked that the money they'd put aside for her college fund be used to pay tuition to a dance school in New York.

Pete had refused, of course. Maybe he'd been a little harsh about it, but he'd meant it for the best. He was just being sensible, just looking out for his little girl. And Carol had agreed wholeheartedly. At the time.

But then Carol watched as her daughter had worked tirelessly, saved every penny, month after month. She'd been bound and determined to go, and seeing it, Carol had tried to nudge her husband into letting her.

He hadn't budged, and neither had Grace.

She was barely nineteen when that slick-talking Jack Casey came around. And that was that.

She couldn't regret it, not when Aubrey had come from it. But she could regret that the pregnancy, the hasty marriage and hastier divorce, had driven a thicker wedge between father and daughter.

But what was couldn't be changed, she told herself and took Aubrey's hand to lead her to the car. "You're sure this car Dave has for you runs all right?"

"Dave says it does."

"Well, he ought to know." He was a good mechanic, Carol thought, even if he had been the one to hire Jack Casey. "You know you could borrow mine for a while— give yourself more chance to shop around."

"This one will be fine." She hadn't even laid eyes on the secondhand sedan Dave had picked out for her. "We're going to do the paperwork on Monday, then I'll have wheels again."

After securing Aubrey in the car seat, Grace slipped in while her mother took the wheel.

"Go, go, go! Go, fast, Gramma," Aubrey demanded. Carol flushed when Grace cocked a brow.

"You've been speeding again, haven't you?"

"I know these roads like the back of my hand, and I haven't had a single ticket in my life."

"Because the cops can't catch you." With a laugh, Grace strapped herself in.

"When do the newlyweds get home?" Not only did Carol want to know, she preferred to have the conversation veer away from her notoriously heavy foot.

"I think they're due in about eight tonight. I just want to give the house a buff, maybe put something on for dinner in case they're hungry when they get here."

"I imagine Cam's wife'll appreciate it. What a beautiful bride she was. I've never seen lovelier. Where she managed to get that dress when the boy gave her so little time to plan a wedding, I don't know."

"Seth said she went to D.C. for it, and the veil was her grandmother's."

"That's fine. I have my wedding veil put aside. I always imagined how pretty it would look on you on your wedding day." She stopped, and could cheerfully have bitten her tongue.

"It would have looked a little out of place in the county courthouse."

Carol sighed as she pulled into the Quinns' driveway. "Well, you'll wear it next time."

"I'll never get married again. I'm not good at it." While her mother gaped at the statement, Grace climbed quickly out of the car, then leaned in the window and kissed Aubrey soundly. "You be a good girl, you hear?

And don't let Grandma feed you too much candy."

"Gramma has chocolate."

"Don't I know it! Bye, baby. Bye, Mama. Thanks."

"Grace . . ." What could she say? "You, ah, you just call when you're done here and I'll come by and pick you up."

"We'll see. Don't let her run you ragged," Grace added and hurried up the steps.

She knew she'd timed it well. Everyone would be at the boatyard working. She was determined not to feel awkward about what had happened the night before last. But she did—she felt miserably awkward and she wanted time to settle before she had to face Ethan again.

This was a home that always felt warm and welcoming. Caring for it soothed her. Because she knew that a large part of her motivation for working on it that afternoon was self-serving, she put more effort into the job. The results would be the same, wouldn't they, she thought guiltily as she ran the old buffer over the hardwood floors to make the wax gleam. Anna would come home to a spotless house, with the scents of fresh flowers, polish, and pot-pourri perfuming the air.

A woman shouldn't have to come home from her honeymoon to dust and clutter. And God knew the Quinn men generated plenty of both.

She was needed here, damn it. All she was doing was proving it.

She spent extra time in the master bedroom, fussing with the flowers she'd begged off Irene, then changing the position of the vase half a dozen times before she cursed herself. Anna would put them where she wanted them to be anyway, she reminded herself. And would probably change everything else while she was at it. More than likely, she would want new everything, Grace decided as she pressed the curtains she'd washed until not the tiniest wrinkle showed in the thin summer sheers.

Anna was city-bred and probably wouldn't care for the

worn furniture and country touches. Before you knew it, she'd have things decked out in leather and glass, and all Dr. Quinn's pretty things would be packed up in some box in the attic and replaced with pieces of sculpture nobody could understand.

Her jaw tightened as she rehung the curtains, gave them a quick fluff.

Cover the lovely old floors with some fancy wall-to-wall carpet and paint the walls some hot color that made the eyes sting. Resentment bubbled as she marched into the bathroom to put a bunch of early rosebuds in a shallow bowl.

Anybody with any sense could see the place only needed a little care, a bit more color here and there. If she had any say in it . . .

She stopped herself, realizing that her fists were clenched, and her face, reflected in the mirror over the sink, was bright with fury. "Oh, Grace, what is *wrong* with you?" She shook her head, nearly laughed at herself. "In the first place you don't have any say, and in the second you don't know that she's going to change a single thing."

It was just that she could, Grace admitted. And once you changed one thing, nothing was quite the same again.

Isn't that what had happened between her and Ethan? Something had changed, and now she was both afraid and hopeful that things wouldn't be quite the same.

He thought of her, she mused and sighed at her own reflection. And what did he think? She wasn't a beauty, and she'd never filled out enough to be sexy. Now and then, she knew, she caught a man's eye, but she never held it.

She wasn't smart or particularly clever, had neither stimulating conversation nor flirtatious ways. Jack had once told her she had stability. And he'd convinced them both, for a while, that that was what he wanted. But stability wasn't the sort of trait that attracted a man.

Maybe if her cheekbones were higher or her dimples

deeper. Or if her lashes were thicker and darker. Maybe if that flirty curl hadn't skipped a generation and left her hair straight as a pin.

What did Ethan think when he looked at her? She wished she had the courage to ask him.

She looked—and saw the ordinary.

When she had danced she hadn't felt ordinary. She'd felt beautiful and special and deserving of her name. Dreamily, she dipped into a plié, settling crotch on heels, then lifting again. She'd have sworn her body sighed in pleasure. Indulging herself, she flowed into an old, well-remembered movement, ending on a slow pirouette.

"Ethan!" She squeaked it out, color flooding her cheeks when she saw him in the doorway.

"I didn't mean to startle you, but I didn't want to interrupt."

"Oh, well." Mortified, she snatched up her cleaning rag, twisted it in her hands. "I was just . . . finishing up in here."

"You always were a pretty dancer." He'd promised himself he would put things back the way they'd been between them, so he smiled at her as he would a friend. "You always dance around the bathroom after you clean it?"

"Doesn't everyone?" She did her best to answer his smile, but the heat continued to sting her cheeks. "I thought I'd be done before y'all got back. I guess the floors took longer than I figured on."

"They look nice. Foolish already had a slide. Surprised you didn't hear it."

"I was daydreaming. I thought I'd—" Then she managed to clear her brain and get a good look at him. He was filthy, covered with sweat and grime and God knew what. "You're not thinking of taking a shower in here?"

Ethan lifted a brow. "It crossed my mind."

"No, you can't."

He shifted back because she'd taken a step forward. He

had a good idea just how he smelled at the moment. That was reason enough to keep his distance, but worse, she looked so fresh and pretty. He'd taken a solemn vow not to touch her again, and he meant to keep it.

"Why?"

"Because I don't have time to clean it up again after you, or the bath downstairs, either. I still have to fry the chicken. I thought I'd make that and a bowl of potato salad so you wouldn't have to worry about heating anything up when Cam and Anna get home. I have to deal with the kitchen after, so I just don't have time, Ethan."

"I've been known to mop up a bathroom after I've used one."

"It's not the same. You just can't use it."

Flustered, he took off his cap, dragged a hand through his hair. "Well, then, that's a problem because we've got three men here who need to scrape off a few layers of dirt."

"There's a bay right outside your door."

"But—"

"Here." She opened the cabinet under the sink for a fresh bar of soap. Damned if she'd have them use the pretty guest soaps she set out in a dish. "I'll get you towels and some fresh clothes."

"But—"

"Go on now, Ethan, and tell the others what I said." She shoved the soap into his hand. "You're already scattering dust everywhere."

He scowled at the soap, then at her. "You'd think the Royal Family was dropping by for a visit. Damn it, Grace, I'm not stripping down to my skin and jumping off the dock."

"Oh, like you've never done it before."

"Not with a female around."

"I've seen naked men a time or two, and I'm going to be too busy to take Polaroids of you and your brothers.

Ethan, I've just spent the best part of my day getting this house to shine. You're not spreading your dirt around.''

Disgusted, because in his experience arguing with a woman's made-up mind was as painful and fruitless as banging your head against a brick wall, he shoved the soap in his pocket. ''I'll get the damn towels.''

''No, you won't. Your hands are filthy. I'll bring them out.''

Muttering to himself, he went downstairs. Phillip's reaction to the bathing arrangements was a shrug. Seth's was pure glee. He darted outside, calling for the dogs to follow, and sent shoes, socks, shirt, scattering as he raced for the dock.

''He'll probably never want to take a regular bath again,'' Phillip commented. He sat on the dock to remove his shoes.

Ethan remained standing. He wasn't taking off a blessed thing until Grace delivered the towels and clothes and was back in the house. ''What are you doing?'' he demanded when Phillip pulled his sweat-stained T-shirt over his head.

''I'm taking off my shirt.''

''Well, put it back on. Grace is coming out.''

Phillip glanced up, saw that his brother was perfectly serious, and laughed. ''Get a grip, Ethan. Even the sight of my amazing and manly chest isn't likely to send her over the edge.''

To prove it, he rose and shot Grace a grin as she crossed the lawn. ''I heard something about fried chicken,'' he called out.

''I'm about to get to it.'' When she reached the dock, she set the towels and clean clothes in neat piles. Then she straightened, smiling out to where Seth and the dogs splashed. She imagined they'd scared every bird and fish away for two miles. ''This arrangement suits them just fine.''

''Why don't you take a dip with us?'' Phillip suggested

and swore he heard Ethan's jaw crack. "You can scrub my back."

She laughed and picked up the clothes that had already been discarded. "It's been a while since I've gone skinny-dipping, and as appealing as it sounds, I've got too much to do to play right now. You give me the rest of your clothes, I'll get them washed before I go."

"Appreciate it." But when Phillip reached for his belt buckle, Ethan jabbed an elbow into his ribs.

"You can wash them later if you're set on it. Go in the house."

"He's shy." Phillip wiggled his brows. "I'm not."

Grace only laughed again, but she headed back to the house to give them privacy.

"You shouldn't tease her that way," Ethan muttered.

"I've been teasing her that way for years." Phillip peeled himself out of his work-stained jeans, delighted to be rid of them.

"Now it's different."

"Why?" Phillip started to slip out of his silk boxers, then caught the look in Ethan's eye. "Oh. Well, well. Why didn't you say so?"

"I got nothing to say." Because Grace was in the house now and he couldn't imagine her pressing her nose to the window, he pulled off his shirt.

"It's her voice that always got me."

"Huh?"

"That throaty sound," Phillip continued, pleased to be able to rile Ethan about something. "Low and smooth and sexy."

Gritting his teeth, Ethan pried off his work boots. "Maybe you shouldn't listen so hard."

"What can I do? Can I help it if I have perfect hearing? Perfect eyesight, too," he added, judging the distance between them. "And as far as I can see, there's nothing wrong with the rest of her either. Her mouth's particularly attractive. Full, shapely, unpainted. Looks tasty to me."

Ethan took two slow breaths as he tugged off his jeans. "Are you trying to irritate me?"

"I'm giving it my best shot."

Ethan stood, gauged his man. "You want to go in head-first, or feetfirst?"

Pleased, Phillip grinned. "I was going to ask you the same thing."

Both waited a beat, then charged, grappled. And with Seth's rousing cheers ringing, wrestled each other into the water.

Oh, my, Grace thought with her nose pressed up against the window. *Oh, my.* If she'd ever seen two more impressive examples of the male form, she couldn't say when. She'd only intended to sneak a quick glance. Really. Just one innocent little peek. But then Ethan had peeled off his shirt and . . .

Well, damn it, she wasn't a saint. And what harm did it do to anyone just to look?

He was just so beautiful, inside and out. And God, if she could get her hands on him again for just five minutes, she thought she could die a happy woman. Maybe she could, since he wasn't indifferent—the way she'd always assumed he was.

There'd been nothing indifferent in the way his mouth had crushed down on hers, or the way his hands had rushed over her.

Stop, she ordered herself and stepped back from the window. The only thing she was going to accomplish this way was to get herself all worked up. She knew how to channel her more intimate needs, and that was to work until they passed away again.

But if her mind wasn't completely on her chicken, who could blame her?

• • •

She had the potatoes cooling for the salad and the chicken frying when Phillip came back in. Gone was the image of the sweaty laborer. In its place was the smooth, the gilded, the casually sophisticated. He winked at her. "Smells like heaven in here."

"I made extra so you can have it for lunch tomorrow. You just put those clothes in the laundry room, and I'll see to them in a minute."

"I don't know what we'd do without you around here."

She bit her lip and hoped everyone felt the same. "Is Ethan still in the water?"

"No, he and Seth are doing something to the boat." Phillip went to the refrigerator and took out a bottle of wine. "Where's Aubrey today?"

"With my mother. In fact she just called and wants to keep her a little longer. I guess one of these days I'm going to have to give in and let her stay overnight." She glanced down blankly at the glass of cool golden wine he offered her. "Oh, thanks." What she knew about wine wouldn't fill a thimble, but she sipped because it was expected. Then her brows lifted. "This isn't anything like what they serve down at the pub."

"I wouldn't think so." He considered what they called the house white down at Shiney's one shaky step up from horse piss. "How are things going there?"

"Fine." She gave serious attention to her chicken, wondering if Ethan had mentioned the incident. Unlikely, she decided when Phillip didn't press. She relaxed again and let Phillip entertain her while she worked.

He was always full of stories, she mused. Of easy, even careless conversation. She knew he was smart and successful and had slipped into city living like a duck in water. But he never made her feel inadequate or silly. And in a cozy way, he made her feel just a little more feminine than she had before he'd come into the room.

That was why Grace's eyes were laughing and her

mouth prettily curved when Ethan came in. Phillip sat, sipping wine while she put the finishing touches on the meal.

"Oh, you're making that up."

"I swear." Phillip held up a hand in oath and grinned as Ethan came in. "The client wants the goose to be the spokesperson, so we're writing dialogue. Goose Creek Jeans, fine feathers for everyday living."

"That's the silliest thing I ever heard."

"Hey." Phillip toasted her. "Watch them sell. I've got a few phone calls to make." He rose, deliberately rounding the table to kiss her and make Ethan seethe. "Thanks for feeding us, darling."

He strolled out, whistling.

"Can you imagine, making a living writing words for a goose." Amused, Grace shook her head as she tucked the bowl of potato salad into the refrigerator. "Everything's done, so you can eat when you're hungry. Your clothes are in the dryer. You don't want to leave them sitting in there after it's done or they'll be wrinkled."

She moved around, tidying the kitchen as she spoke. "I'd wait and fold them for you, but I'm running a bit behind."

"I'll drive you home."

"I'd appreciate it. I'm dealing with the car on Monday, but until then . . ." She lifted her shoulders and saw with one last glance that she had nothing left to do. Still, she eyed every nook and corner as she walked through the house to the front door.

"How are you getting to work?" Ethan demanded when they were in his truck.

"Julie's taking me. Shiney's taking me home himself." She cleared her throat. "When I explained what happened the other night he was upset. Not mad at me, but really upset it had happened. He was set to skin Steve, but under the circumstances—they had a boy, by the way. Eight and a half pounds. They're calling him Jeremy."

"I heard," was Ethan's only comment

Now she drew a bolstering breath. "About what happened, Ethan, I mean afterward—"

"I've got something to say about that." He'd worked it out carefully, word by word. "I shouldn't have been mad at you. You were scared and I spent more time yelling at you than making sure you were all right."

"I knew you weren't really mad at me. It was just—"

"I've got to finish this," he said, but waited until he'd turned into her driveway. "I had no business touching you that way. I'd promised myself I never would."

"I wanted you to."

Though the quiet words caused his stomach to clench, he shook his head. "It's not going to happen again. I've got reasons, Grace, good ones. You don't know, and you wouldn't understand."

"I can't understand if you don't tell me what they are."

He wasn't going to tell her what he'd done, or what had been done to him. And what he was afraid still lurked inside him ready to spring out if he didn't keep that cage locked. "They're my reasons." He shifted to look at her because it was only right to say what he had to say facing her. "I could have hurt you, and I nearly did. That's not going to happen again."

"I'm not afraid of you." She reached out to touch, to stroke his cheek, but he grabbed her hand and held her off.

"You're never going to have to be. You matter to me." He gave her hand a quick squeeze, then released it. "You always have."

"I'm not a child anymore, and I won't break if you touch me. I want you to touch me."

Full, shapely, unpainted lips. Phillip's words echoed in his head. And now Ethan knew, God help him, exactly how tasty they were. "I know you think you do, and that's why we're going to try to forget that the other night happened."

"I'm not going to forget it," she murmured, and the way she looked at him, her eyes soft and full of need, made his head swim.

"It's not going to happen again. So you stay clear of me for a while." Desperation tinged his voice as he leaned across and shoved open her door. "I mean it, Grace, you just stay clear of me for a while. I've got enough to worry about."

"All right, Ethan." She wouldn't beg. "If that's what you want."

"That's exactly what I want."

This time he didn't wait until she was in the house but backed out of the drive the minute she closed the truck's door.

For the first time in more years than he could count, he thought seriously about getting blind drunk.

EIGHT

S<small>ETH KEPT WATCH FOR</small>
them. His excuse for being in the front yard as the shadows
grew long was the dogs. Not that it was an excuse, exactly,
he thought. He was trying to teach Foolish not just to chase
the battered, well-chewed tennis ball but to bring it back
the way Simon did. The trouble was that Foolish would
race back to you with the ball, then expect you to play
tug-of-war for it.

Not that Seth minded. He had a supply of balls and
sticks and an old hunk of rope that Ethan had given him.
He could toss and tug as long as the dogs were willing to
run. Which was, as far as he could tell, just about forever.

But while he played with the dogs, he kept his ears
tuned for the sound of an approaching car.

He knew they were on their way home because Cam
had called from the plane. Which was just about the cool-
est thing Seth could think of. He couldn't wait to tell
Danny and Will how he'd talked to Cam while Cam had
been flying over the Atlantic Ocean.

He'd already looked up Italy in the atlas and found Rome. Had traced his finger back and forth, back and forth across that wide ocean from Rome to the Chesapeake Bay, to the little smudge on Maryland's Eastern Shore that was St. Christopher's.

For a little while he'd been afraid they wouldn't come back. He imagined Cam calling and saying they'd decided to stay over there so he could race again.

He knew Cam had lived all over the place, racing boats and cars and motorcycles. Ray had told him all about it, and there was a thick scrapbook in the den that was filled with all kinds of newspaper and magazine pictures and articles about how many races Cam had won. And how many women he'd fooled around with.

And he knew that Cam had won this big-deal race in his hydrofoil—which Seth wished he could ride in just once—right before Ray had run into the telephone pole and died.

Phillip had finally tracked him down in Monte Carlo. Seth had found that place in the atlas, too, and it didn't look all that much bigger than St. Chris. But they had a palace there and fancy casinos and even a prince.

Cam had come home in time to see Ray die. Seth knew he hadn't planned to stay very long. But he had stayed. After they'd had sort of a fight, he'd told Seth he wasn't going anywhere. That they were stuck with each other and he was staying put.

Still, that was before he'd gotten married and everything, before he'd gone back to Italy. Before Seth had started to worry that both Cam and Anna would forget about him and the promises they'd made.

But they hadn't. They were coming back.

He didn't want them to know he was waiting for them or that he was excited that they would be home any minute. But he was. He couldn't understand why he was all pumped up about it. They'd only been gone a couple of weeks, and Cam was a pain in the ass most of the time anyway.

And once Anna was living there, everybody would say how he had to watch his language because there was a woman in the house.

A part of him worried that Anna would change things. Even though she was his caseworker, she might get tired of having a kid around. She had the power to send him away. More power now, he thought, because she was doing it with Cam all the time.

He reminded himself that she'd played it straight with him, from the minute she'd pulled him out of class and sat down with him in the school cafeteria to talk.

But working on a case and living in the same house with that case was different, wasn't it?

And maybe, just maybe, she'd played straight with him, she'd been nice to him, because she'd liked having Cam poke at her. She'd wanted to get married to him. Now that she was, she wouldn't have to be nice anymore. She could even write in one of her reports that he'd be better off somewhere else.

Well, he was going to watch, and he was going to see. He could still run if things got sticky. Though the idea of running made his stomach hurt in a way it had never done before.

He wanted to be here. He wanted to run in the yard, throwing sticks to the dogs. To crawl out of bed when it was still dark and eat breakfast with Ethan and go out on the water crabbing. To work in the boatyard or go down to Danny's and Will's.

To eat real food whenever he was hungry and sleep in a bed that didn't smell like somebody else's sweat.

Ray had promised him all of that, and though Seth had never trusted anyone, he'd trusted Ray. Maybe Ray had been his father, maybe he hadn't. But Seth knew he'd paid Gloria a lot of money. He thought of her as Gloria now and not as his mother. It helped to add more distance.

Now Ray was dead, but he'd made each of his sons promise to keep Seth in the house by the water. Seth figured they probably hadn't liked the idea, but they'd promised anyway. He'd discovered that the Quinns kept their word. It was a new and wonderful concept to him, a promise kept.

If they broke it now, he knew it would hurt more than anything had hurt him before.

So he waited, and when he heard the car—the not-quite-tamed roar of the Corvette—his stomach jittered with excitement and nerves.

Simon woofed twice in greeting, but Foolish set up a din of wild, half-terrified barking. When the sleek white car pulled into the drive, both dogs raced toward it, tails waving like flags. Seth stuck hands that had gone sweaty into his pockets and strolled over casually.

"Hi!" Anna shot him a brilliant smile.

Seth could see why Cam had gone for her, all right. He himself had sketched her face a number of times in secret. He liked to draw above all else. His fledgling artist's eye appreciated the sheer beauty of that face—the dark, almond-shaped eyes, the clear, pale-gold skin, the full mouth, and the exotic hint of cheekbones. Her hair was windblown, a dark, curling mass. Her wedding ring set glinted, diamonds and gold, as she stepped out of the car.

And caught him unprepared in a laughing, bone-crushing hug. "What a terrific welcome party!"

Though the embrace had surprised him into wanting to linger there, he wiggled free. "I was just out fooling with the dogs." He looked over at Cam, shrugged. "Hey."

"Hey, kid." Lean and dark, and just a little dangerous to the eye, Cam unfolded his length from the low-riding car. His grin was quicker than Ethan's, sharper than Phillip's. "Just in time to help me unload."

"Yeah, sure." Seth glanced up, noted the small mountain of luggage strapped to the roof of the car. "You didn't take all that crap with you."

"We picked up some Italian crap while we were there."

"I couldn't stop myself," Anna said with a laugh. "We had to buy another suitcase."

"Two," Cam corrected.

"One's just a tote—it doesn't count."

"Okay." Cam popped the trunk, pulled out a generous dark-green suitcase. "You carry the one that doesn't count."

"Putting your bride to work already?" Phillip crossed to the car, waded through the dogs. "I'll take that, Anna," he said and kissed her with an enthusiasm that had Seth rolling his eyes at Cam.

"Turn her loose, Phil," Ethan said mildly. "I'd hate for Cam to have to kill you before he even gets in the house. Welcome home," he added and smiled when Anna turned to give him as enthusiastic a kiss as Phillip had given her.

"It's good to be home."

THE TOTE, IT TURNED OUT, contained gifts, which Anna immediately began to dispense, along with stories of each one. Seth only stared down at the bright-blue-and-white soccer shirt she'd given him. No one had ever gone on a trip and brought him back a present. The fact was, if he thought about it, he could count the gifts he'd been given—something for nothing—on the fingers of one hand.

"Soccer's big over in Europe," Anna told him. "They call it football, but it's not like our football." She dug deeper, then pulled out an oversized book with a glossy cover. "And I thought you might like this. It's not as good as seeing the paintings. It really grabs you by the throat to see them in person, but you'll get the idea."

The book was filled with paintings, glorious colors and shapes that dazzled his eyes. An art book. She'd remembered that he liked to draw and had thought of him.

"It's cool." He muttered it because he couldn't trust his voice.

"She wanted to buy everyone shoes," Cam commented. "I had to stop her."

"So I only bought myself a half a dozen pair."

"I thought it was four."

She smiled. "Six. I snuck two by you. Phillip, I stumbled across Maglis. I could have wept."

"Armani?"

She sighed lustily. "Oh, yeah."

"Now I'm going to cry."

"You can sob over fashion later," Cam told them. "I'm starving."

"Grace was here." Seth wanted to try on his shirt right away but thought it would be too lame. "She cleaned everything—made us wash up in the Bay—and she fried chicken."

"Grace made fried chicken?"

"And potato salad."

"There's no place like home," Cam murmured and headed for the kitchen. Seth waited a few seconds, then followed.

"I guess I could eat another piece," he said casually.

"Get in line." Cam pulled the platter and bowl out of the fridge.

"Don't they give you stuff to eat on the plane?"

"That was then, this is now." Cam heaped a plate with food, then leaned back against the counter. The kid looked tanned and healthy, he noted. The eyes were still wary, but his face had lost that rabbit-about-to-run look. He wondered if it would surprise Seth as much as it had himself to know he'd missed the smart-mouthed brat. "So, how's it been going?"

"Okay. School's done, and I've been helping Ethan out on the boat a lot. Pays me slave's wages there and at the boatyard."

"Anna's going to want to know what you got on your report card."

"A's," Seth muttered around a mouthful of drumstick, and Cam choked.

"All?"

"Yeah—so what?"

"She's going to love that. Want to make more points with her?"

Seth jerked a shoulder again, narrowing his eyes as he considered what he would be asked to do to please the woman of the house. "Maybe."

"Put the soccer shirt on. It took her damn near half an hour to pick out the right one. Major points if you wear it the same night she gives it to you."

"Yeah?" As easy as that? Seth thought and relaxed into a grin. "I guess I can give her a thrill."

"HE REALLY LIKED HIS shirt," Anna said as she meticulously tucked away the contents of one suitcase. "And the book. I'm so glad we thought of the book."

"Yeah, he liked them." Cam figured the next day, even next year, was soon enough to unpack. Besides, he liked stretching out on the bed and watching her—watching his wife, he thought with an odd little thrill—fuss around the room.

"He didn't freeze up when I hugged him. That's a good sign. And his interaction with Ethan and Phillip is easier, more natural, than it was even a couple of weeks ago. He was anxious to see you again. He's feeling a little threatened by me. I change the dynamics around here just at the point where he was getting used to how things worked. So he's waiting, and he's watching for what'll happen next. But that's good. It means he considers this his home. I'm the intruder."

"Miz Spinelli?"

She turned her head, arched a brow. "That's Mrs. Quinn to you, buster."

"Why don't you turn off the social worker until Monday?"

"Can't." She slipped one of her new shoes out of its bag and nearly cooed at it in delight. "The social worker is very pleased with the status of this particular case. And Mrs. Quinn, the brand-new sister-in-law, is determined to win Seth's trust, and maybe even his affection."

She slipped the shoe back into the bag and wondered how long she should wait before asking Cam to customize their closet. She knew just what she had in mind, and he was good with his hands. Considering, she studied him. Very, very good with his hands.

"I suppose I could finish unpacking tomorrow."

He smiled slowly. "I suppose you could."

"I feel guilty about it. Grace has this place so spotless."

"Why don't you come over here. We'll work on that guilt."

"Why don't I?" She tossed the shoe over her shoulder and, with a laugh, jumped him.

"SHE'S COMING ALONG."

Cam studied the boat. It was barely seven in the morning, but his internal clock was still set to Rome. Since he'd awakened early, he hadn't seen the point in letting his brothers sleep the day away.

So the Quinns stood, under the hard, bright lights of the boatyard, contemplating the job at hand. Seth mimicked their stance—hands in pockets, legs spread and braced, face sober.

It would be the first time the four of them had worked on the boat together. He was wildly thrilled.

"I figured you could start belowdecks," Ethan began.

"Phillip estimates four hundred hours to finish the cabin."

Cam snorted. "I can do it in less."

"Doing it right," Phillip put in, "is more important than doing it fast."

"I can do it fast *and* right. The client'll have this baby under sail and the galley stocked with champagne and caviar in less than four hundred hours."

Ethan nodded. Since Cam had come through with another client, who wanted a sport fishing boat, he dearly hoped that was true. "Then let's get to work."

And work kept his mind off things his mind had no business being on. The brain had to be focused to use the lathe—if you were fond of your hands. Ethan turned the wood slowly, carefully, forming the mast. Ear protectors turned the hum of the motor and the hot rock blasting from the radio into a muffled echo.

He imagined there was conversation going on behind him, too. And the occasional ripe curse. He could smell the sweet scent of wood, the sting of epoxy, the stench of tar used to coat bolts.

Years ago, the three of them had built his workboat. She wasn't fancy, and he couldn't claim she had a pretty face, but she was sound and she was game. They'd built his skipjack as well because he'd been determined to dredge oysters in the traditional craft. Now the oysters were nearly gone, and his boat joined the other handful in the Bay, pulling in extra money during the summer by giving tours.

He rented it to Jim's brother during tourist season, because it helped them both and was the practical thing to do. But it bothered him some to see the fine old vessel used that way. Just as it bothered him some to know other people lived and slept in the house that was his.

But when push came to shove, money mattered. Seth's laugh snuck through his ear protectors and reminded him why it mattered now more than ever.

When his hands cramped from the work, he turned off

the lathe to give them a rest. Noise filled his ears when he took off the protectors.

He could hear the pounding of Cam's hammer echoing from belowdecks. Seth was coating the centerboard with Rust-Oleum so the steel plate gleamed with wet. Phillip had the nastier job of soaking the inside of the centerboard case with creosote. It was good old-growth red cedar, which should discourage any marine borers, but they'd decided not to take chances.

A boat by Quinn was built to last.

He felt a stir of pride watching them and could almost imagine his father standing beside him, big hands fisted on his hips, a wide grin on his face.

"It makes a picture," Ray said. "The kind your mother and I loved to study. We had plenty of them put aside, to take out and look over again once you all grew up and went off your own ways. We never really had the chance because she left first."

"I still miss her."

"I know you do. She was the glue that kept us all together. But she did a good job of it, Ethan. You're still stuck."

"I guess I'd have died without her, without you. Without them."

"No." Ray laid a hand on Ethan's shoulder, shook his head. "You were always strong, heart and mind. You came out the other side of hell as much because of what's inside you as what we did. You should remember that more often. Just look at Seth. He handles things differently than you did, but he's got a lot of the same qualities inside him. He cares, deeper than he wants to. He thinks deeper than he lets on. And his wants go deeper than he'll admit even to himself."

"I see you in him." It was the first time Ethan had allowed himself to say it, even to himself. "I don't know how to feel about it."

"Funny, I see each one of you in him. The eye of the

beholder, Ethan.'' Then he gave Ethan a quick slap on the back. "That's a damn fine boat coming along there. Your mother would have gotten a kick out of this.''

"Quinns build to last,'' Ethan murmured.

"Who're you talking to?" Seth demanded.

Ethan blinked, felt his head go light, filled with thoughts thin as strands of cotton. "What?" He pushed a hand up his forehead, into his hair, knocking his cap back. "What?"

"Man, you look weird." Seth cocked his head, fascinated. "How come you're standing here talking to yourself?"

"I was . . ." Asleep on my feet? he wondered. "Thinking," he said. "Just thinking out loud." Suddenly the noise and smells seemed to roar into his dizzy brain. "I need some air," he muttered and hurried out through the cargo doors.

"Weird," Seth said again. He started to say something to Phillip, then was distracted as Anna came through the front door carrying an enormous hamper.

"Anybody interested in lunch?"

"Yeah!" Always interested, Seth made a beeline. "Did you bring the chicken?"

"What's left of it," she told him. "And ham sandwiches thick as bricks. There's a cooler of iced tea in the car. Why don't you go haul it in?"

"My hero," Phillip said, wiping his hands on his jeans before relieving her of the hamper. "Hey, Cam! There's a gorgeous woman out here with food."

The hammering stopped instantly. Seconds later, Cam's head popped up through the cabin roof. "My woman. I get first dibs on the food."

"There's plenty to go around. Grace isn't the only one who can put meals together for a bunch of hungry men. Though her fried chicken's a gift from the gods."

"She's got a way with it." Phillip agreed. He set the hamper down on a makeshift table fashioned of a sheet of plywood laid over two sawhorses. "She cooked for Ethan regularly when you two were away." He dug out a ham sandwich. "I get the feeling something's happening there."

"Happening where?" Cam wanted to know as he jumped down to explore the hamper.

"With Ethan and Grace."

"No shit?"

"Mmm." The first bite made Phillip close his eyes in pleasure. He might have preferred French cuisine served on fine china, but he could appreciate a well-built sandwich balanced on a paper plate. "My deathless observation skills have homed in on certain signs. He watches her when she's not looking. She watches him when he's not looking. And I got some interesting gossip from Marsha Tuttle. She works down at the pub with Grace," he explained to Anna. "Shiney's adding a security system and has a new policy that none of the waitresses are to close up alone."

"Did something happen?" Anna asked.

"Yeah." He looked over to be certain Seth hadn't come back in. "A few nights ago some bastard came in after closing. Grace was alone. He put his hands on her and, according to Marsha, would have done more. But it just so happened Ethan was outside. Interesting coincidence if you ask me, when we're talking of our early-to-bed, early-to-rise brother. Anyway, he put some dents in the guy." He took another healthy bite.

Cam thought of slender, fine-boned Grace. Thought of Anna. "I hope they were nice deep dents."

"I think we can assume the guy didn't walk off whistling. Of course, in typical Ethan style, he doesn't mention it, so I have to hear it from Marsha over the fresh produce at the market Friday night."

"Was Grace hurt?" Anna knew all too well what it was to be trapped, to be helpless, to be faced with what a certain kind of man would do to a woman. Or a child.

"No. Must have shaken her up, but she's like Ethan there. Never mentioned it. But there were several long, silent looks between them yesterday. And after Ethan ran her home, he came back sizzling." Remembering, Phillip chuckled to himself. "Which for Ethan is saying something. Got himself a couple of beers and went out in the sloop for an hour."

"Grace and Ethan." Cam considered it. "They'd fit." He saw Seth come in and decided to give the topic a rest. "Where is Ethan, anyway?"

"He went outside." With a grunt, Seth set the cooler down and nodded toward the cargo doors. "He said he needed some air, and I guess he did. He was standing there talking to himself." Thrilled with the bounty, Seth dived into the hamper. "He was, like, carrying on a conversation with someone who wasn't there. He looked weird."

The back of Cam's neck prickled. Still, he moved casually, dumping food on a plate. "I could use some air myself. I'll just take him a sandwich."

He saw Ethan standing out on the end of the pier, staring out at the water. The shore of St. Chris with all its pretty houses and yards was on either side, but Ethan looked straight out, over the light chop to the horizon.

"Anna brought some food out."

Ethan folded up his thoughts and glanced down at the plate. "Nice of her. You hit lucky with her, Cam."

"Don't I know it." What he was about to do made him a little nervous. But, after all, he was a man who lived for risks. "I still remember the first day I saw her. I was pissed off at the world. Dad was hardly buried, and everything I wanted seemed to be somewhere else. The kid had given me plenty of grief that morning, and it occurred to me that the next part of my life wasn't going to be racing, it wasn't going to be Europe. It was going to be right here."

"You gave up the most. Coming back here."

"It seemed like it at the time. Then Anna Spinelli

walked across the yard while I was fixing the back steps. She gave me my second jolt of the day."

Since the food was there, and Cam seemed inclined to talk, Ethan took the plate and sat on the edge of the dock. An egret flew by, silent as a ghost. "A face like hers is bound to give a man a jolt."

"Yeah. And I was already feeling a little edgy. Not an hour before, I'd had this conversation with Dad. He was sitting in the back porch rocker."

Ethan nodded. "He always liked sitting there."

"I don't mean I remembered him sitting there. I mean I saw him there. Just like I'm seeing you now."

Slowly, Ethan turned his head, looked into Cam's eyes. "You saw him, sitting in the rocker on the porch."

"Talked to him, too. He talked to me." Cam shrugged, gazed out over the water. "So, I figure I'm hallucinating. It's the stress, the worry, maybe the anger. I've got things to say to him, questions I want answered, so my mind puts him there. Only that's not what it was."

Ethan stepped carefully onto boggy ground. "What do you figure it was?"

"He was there, that first time and the others."

"Other times?"

"Yeah, the last was the morning before the wedding. He said it would be the last because I'd figured out what I needed to figure out for now." Cam rubbed his hands over his face. "I had to let him go again. It was a little easier. I didn't get all the questions answered, but I guess the ones that mattered most were."

He sighed, feeling better, and helped himself to one of the chips on Ethan's plate. "Now you'll either tell me I'm crazy or that you know what I'm talking about."

Thoughtfully, Ethan tore one of the sandwiches in half, handed a share to Cam. "When you follow the water, you get to know there's more to things than you can see or touch. Mermaids and serpents." He smiled a little. "Sailors know about them, whether they've ever seen them or not. I don't think you're crazy.''

''Are you going to tell me the rest?''

''I've had some dreams. I thought they were dreams,'' he corrected himself, ''but lately I've had a couple when I was awake. I guess I have questions, too, but I have a hard time pushing somebody into answers. It's good to hear his voice, to see his face. We didn't have enough time to really say good-bye before he died.''

''Maybe that's part of it. It's not all of it.''

''No. But I don't know what he wants me to do that I'm not doing.''

''I imagine he'll stick around until you figure it out.'' Cam bit into the sandwich and felt amazingly content. ''So, what does he think of the boat?''

''He thinks it's a damn fine boat.''

''He's right.''

Ethan studied his sandwich. ''Are we going to tell Phil about this?''

''Nope. But I can't wait until it happens to him. What do you bet he'll think about heading to some fancy shrink? He'll want one with lots of initials after his name and an office on the right side of town.''

''Her name,'' Ethan corrected and began to smile. ''He'll want a good-looking female if he's going to lie down on a couch. It's a pretty day,'' he added, suddenly appreciating the warm breeze and the flash of sun.

''You've got another ten minutes to enjoy it,'' Cam told him. ''Then your ass goes back to work.''

''Yeah. Your wife makes a damn good sandwich.'' He angled his head. ''How do you think she'd do at sanding wood?''

Cam considered, liked the image. ''Let's go talk her into letting us find out.''

NINE

ANNA WAS THRILLED TO have the afternoon off. She loved her job, had both affection and respect for the people she worked with. She believed absolutely in the function and the goals of social work. And she had the satisfaction of knowing she made a difference.

She helped people. The young single mother with nowhere to turn, the unwanted child, the displaced elderly person. Inside her burned a deep and bright desire to help them find their way. She knew what it was to be lost, to be desperate, and what one person who offered a hand, who refused to snatch that hand back even when it was slapped or snapped at, could change.

And because she had been determined to help Seth DeLauter, she'd found Cam. A new life, a new home. New beginnings.

Sometimes, she thought, rewards came back to you a hundredfold.

Everything she'd ever wanted—even when she hadn't

known she wanted it—was tied up in that lovely old house on the water. A white house with blue trim. Rockers on the porch, flowers in the yard. She remembered the first day she'd seen it. She'd traveled along this same road, with the radio blaring. Of course, the top had been up then, so the wind wouldn't tug her hair free of its pins.

That had been a business call, and Anna had been determined to be all business.

The house had charmed her, the simplicity of it, the stability. Then she walked around the pretty two-story house by the water and saw an angry, uncooperative, and sexy man repairing the back porch steps.

Nothing had been quite the same for her since.

Thank God.

It was her house now, she thought with a smug grin as she drove fast along the road flanked by wide, flat fields. Her house in the country, with the garden she'd imagined . . . and the angry, uncooperative, sexy man? He was hers, too, and so much more than she'd ever imagined.

She drove along that long, straight road with Warren Zevon howling about werewolves in London. But this time, she didn't care if the wind tugged at her once tidily pinned hair. She was going home, so the top was down and her mood was light.

She had work to do, but the reports she needed to complete could be done on her laptop at home. While her red sauce simmered on the stove, she decided. They'd have linguini—to remind Cam of their honeymoon.

Not that this particular event seemed to be over, even if they were back on the Shore rather than in Rome. She wondered if this wild and wicked passion they had for each other would ever ease.

And hoped not.

Laughing at herself, she zipped into the drive. And nearly rammed her pretty little convertible into the rear of a dull gray sedan with a rusted bumper. Once her heart had bumped back down into its proper place, she puzzled over it.

It certainly wasn't Cam's kind of car, she decided. He might like to tinker with engines, but he preferred the fast and the sleek body to go around them. This aged and sturdy body looked anything but fast.

Phillip? She let out a snort. The fastidious Phillip Quinn wouldn't have placed his Italian-loafer-shod foot on the worn floorboard of such a vehicle.

Ethan, then. But she found herself frowning. Pickups and Jeeps were Ethan's style, not compact sedans that had fenders still painted with gray primer.

They were being robbed, she thought with a jolt that turned her heartbeat into a jackhammer. In broad daylight. No one ever thought to lock the doors around here, and the house was sheltered from its neighbors by trees and the marsh.

Someone was inside, picking through their things, right now. Eyes narrowed, she slammed out of the car. They weren't getting away with it. It was her house now, damn it, and her things, and if any half-baked burglar thought he could . . .

She trailed off as she looked into the sedan and saw the big pink rabbit. And the car seat. A house burglar with a toddler in tow?

Grace, she realized with a sigh. It was one of Grace Monroe's cleaning days.

City girl, she chided herself. Put the city instincts away. You're in another place now. Feeling monumentally foolish, she returned to her own car and hefted her briefcase and the bag of fresh produce she'd picked up on the way home.

As she stepped onto the porch, she heard the monotonous hum of the vacuum, underscored by the bright tinkle of a commercial on TV. Good domestic sounds, Anna thought. And she was more than delighted that she wasn't the one running the vacuum.

Grace nearly dropped the wand when Anna came through the door. Obviously flustered, she stepped back, tripping the foot switch to turn the machine off. "I'm sorry. I thought I'd be finished before anyone got home."

"I'm early." Though her arms were full, Anna crouched in front of the chair where Aubrey sat manically scribbling purple crayon on a picture of an elephant in her coloring book. "That's beautiful."

"It's a phant."

"It's a terrific phant. Prettiest phant I've seen all day." Because Aubrey's nose just seemed to demand it, Anna gave it a quick kiss.

"I'm nearly done." Nerves danced down Grace's spine. Anna looked so professional in her business suit. The fact that her hair was tumbling out of its pins only made her seem . . . professionally sexy, Grace decided. "I finished upstairs, and in the kitchen. I didn't know . . . I wasn't sure what you'd like, but I made up a casserole—scalloped potatoes and ham. It's in the freezer."

"Sounds great. I'm cooking tonight." Anna rose and jiggled her bag cheerfully. She nearly stepped out of her shoes but then stopped herself. It didn't seem right to start cluttering things up when Grace was still in the middle of cleaning.

She'd wait until later.

"But I won't get off early tomorrow," she continued. "So it'll come in handy."

"Well, I . . ." Grace knew she was a little sweaty, a little grimy, and she felt miserably outclassed by Anna's crisp blouse and tailored suit. And oh, those shoes, she thought, doing her best not to make her survey obvious. They were so pretty, so classic, and the leather looked soft enough to sleep on.

Her toes curled in shame inside her frayed white sneakers. "The laundry's nearly done, too. There's a load of towels in the dryer. I didn't know where you wanted me to put your things, so I folded everything and left it on the bed in your room.''

"I appreciate it. Catching up after a couple of weeks away takes forever." Anna caught herself before she squirmed. She'd never had a housekeeper in her life, and she wasn't quite sure of the proper procedure. "I should put these away. You want something cold to drink?"

"No, thanks. No. I should finish up and get out of your way."

Curious, Anna thought. Grace had never seemed cool or nervous before. Though they didn't know each other well, Anna had felt they were friendly. One way or the other, she decided, they had to come to terms. "I'd really like to talk to you if you have the time."

"Oh." Grace ran her hand up and down the metal wand of the vacuum. "Sure. Aubrey, I'm going in the kitchen with Mrs. Quinn."

"Me, too!" Aubrey scrambled up and raced ahead. By the time her mother caught up, she was sprawled on the floor, intently creating a purple giraffe.

"That's her color this week," Grace commented. Automatically she went to the refrigerator and took out the pitcher of lemonade she'd made. "She tends to settle on one until she wears the crayon down to a nub, then she picks another."

Her hand froze on the glass she'd been about to take from a cupboard. "I'm sorry," she said stiffly. "I wasn't thinking."

Anna set her bag down. "About what?"

"Making myself at home in your kitchen."

Aha, Anna thought, there was the problem. Two women, one house. They were both a little uneasy about the situation. She took a plump tomato from the bag, examined it, then set it on the counter. Next year she was going to try to grow her own.

"You know what I liked about this house from the first time I stepped into the kitchen? It's the kind of place where

it's easy to make yourself at home. I wouldn't want that
to change.''

She continued to unload her bag, setting carefully chosen vegetables on the counter.

Grace had to bite her tongue to keep from mentioning
that Ethan didn't care for mushrooms when Anna set a bag
of them beside the peppers.

''It's your home now,'' Grace said slowly. ''You'll
want to tend to it your own way.''

''That's true. And I am thinking of making some
changes. Would you mind pouring that lemonade? It looks
wonderful.''

Here it comes, Grace thought. Changes. She poured two
glasses, then took the plastic cup from the counter to fill
for Aubrey. ''Here, honey, now don't spill.''

''Aren't you going to ask me what changes?'' Anna
wondered.

''It's not my place.''

''When did we get to have places?'' Anna demanded
with just enough annoyance to put Grace's back up.

''I work for you—for the time being, anyway.''

''If you're about to tell me you're quitting you're really
going to spoil my day. I don't care how much progress
women have made, if I'm alone in this house with four
men, I'll end up doing ninety percent of the housework.
Maybe not at first,'' she continued, pacing now, ''but
that's just how it'll end up. It won't matter that I have a
full-time job on top of it, either. Cam hates housework,
and he'll do anything he can to get out of it. Ethan's neat
enough, but he has a habit of making himself scarce. And
Seth, well, he's ten, so that says it all. Phillip only lives
here on weekends, and he'll make the argument that he
didn't make the mess in the first place.''

She whirled back. ''Are you telling me you're quitting?''

It was the first time Grace had seen Anna under full
steam, and she was both impressed and baffled. ''I thought

you just said you were going to make some changes and you were going to let me go.''

"I'm thinking about getting some new pillows and having the sofa re-covered," Anna said impatiently, "not losing the person I already realize I'm going to depend on for my sanity around here. Do you think I didn't know who made sure I didn't come home to a houseful of dishes and laundry and dust? Do I look like an idiot to you?''

"No, I . . ." The beginnings of a smile flirted at Grace's mouth. "I worked my tail off so you'd notice."

"Okay." Anna let out a breath. "Why don't we sit down and start over?''

"That'd be good. I'm sorry."

"For?"

"For all the nasty things I let myself think about you over the last few days.'' She smiled fully as she sat down. "I forgot how much I liked you."

"I'm outnumbered around here, Grace. I could sure use another woman. I don't know exactly how these things are done, and since I'm the outsider here—"

"You're not an outsider." Grace all but gaped in shock. "You're Cam's wife."

"And you've been a part of his life, of all their lives, a great deal longer." She turned her hands palms up, smiled. "Let's get this one thing out of the way so we can forget it. Whatever you've been doing around here works just fine for me. I appreciate knowing you're doing it so I can concentrate on my marriage, on Seth, and on my job. Are we clear there?''

"Yeah."

"And since my instincts tell me you're a kind, understanding person, I'm going to confess that I need you a lot more than you need me. And throw myself on your mercy.''

The quick, easy laugh made shallow dimples flicker in Grace's cheeks. "I don't think there's anything you couldn't do."

"Maybe not, but I swear to God I don't want to be Wonder Woman. Don't leave me alone with all these men."

Grace nibbled on her lip for a moment. "If you're going to have the living room sofa redone, you'll need new curtains."

"I was thinking priscillas."

They beamed at each other, in perfect accord.

"Mama! Gotta pee!"

"Oh." Grace sprang up and scooped a frantically dancing Aubrey into her arms. "We'll be right back."

Anna had a good chuckle, then rose, stripped off her jacket, and prepared to start her sauce. This kind of cooking—the familiar, the dependable—relaxed her. And since she had no doubt that it would earn her points with the Quinn men when they got home, she intended to enjoy herself.

It pleased her as well that she'd cemented a basis of friendship with Grace. She wanted that benefit of small towns and country living—the neighbors. One of the reasons she'd been restless during her time in D.C. was the lack of connection with the people who lived and worked around her. When she'd moved to Princess Anne she'd found something of the old-neighborhood ease she'd grown up with in her grandparents' well-established section of Pittsburgh.

And now, she thought, she had the opportunity to become good friends with a woman she admired and believed she would enjoy.

When Grace and Aubrey came back into the room, she smiled. "You hear stories about toilet training being a nightmare for everyone involved."

"There are hits and misses." Grace gave Aubrey a quick squeeze before setting her down. "Aubrey's such a good girl, aren't you, sweetie?"

"I didn't wet my pants. I get a nickel for the piggy bank."

When Anna roared with laughter, Grace winced good-naturedly. "And bribery works."

"I'm all for it."

"I should finish up."

"Are you in a hurry?"

"Not really." Cautious, Grace glanced at the kitchen clock. By her judgment, Ethan shouldn't be back for at least an hour.

"Maybe you could keep me company while I put this sauce together."

"I suppose I could." It had been . . . she couldn't remember how long it had been since she'd just sat in the kitchen with another woman. The simplicity of it nearly made her sigh. "There's a show that Aubrey likes to watch that's just coming on. Is it all right if I settle her down with it? I can do the rest of the vacuuming when it's over."

"Great." Anna slid her tomatoes into the pot to let them simmer and soften.

"I've never made spaghetti sauce from scratch," Grace said when she came back in. "I mean, all the way from fresh tomatoes."

"Takes more time, but it's worth it. Grace, I hope you don't mind, but I heard what happened the other night at the bar where you work."

Surprise made Grace blink and forget to memorize the ingredients Anna had set out. "Ethan told you?"

"No. You have to pull on Ethan's tongue to get him to tell anything." Anna wiped her hands on the bib apron she'd put on. "I don't want to pry, but I have some experience with sexual assault. I want you to know you can talk to me if you need to."

"It wasn't as bad as it could have been. If Ethan hadn't been there . . ." She trailed off, discovered that thinking about it still made her cold inside. "Well, he was. I should have been more careful."

Anna had a quick flash of a dark road, the bite of gravel

against her back as she was shoved to the ground. "It's a mistake to blame yourself."

"Oh, I don't—not that way. I didn't deserve what he tried to do. I didn't encourage him. The fact is, I made it clear I wasn't interested in him or his hotel bed. But I should have locked up after Steve left. I wasn't thinking, and that was careless."

"I'm glad you weren't hurt."

"I could have been. I can't afford to be careless." She glanced to the doorway where the bright music and Aubrey's brighter laughter came through. "I've got too much at stake."

"Single parenting's hard. I see the problems that can come out of it all the time. You're brilliant at it."

Now it wasn't surprise, but shock. No one had ever called her brilliant at anything. "I just . . . do."

"Yes." Anna smiled. "My mother died when I was eleven, but before that she was a single parent. When I look back and remember, I see that she was brilliant at it too. She just did. I hope I'm half as good at 'just doing' as both of you when I have a child."

"Are you and Cam planning on it?"

"I'm good at planning," Anna said with a laugh. "I want to give just being married a little time, but yes, I want children." She looked out the window to where the flowers she'd planted were blooming. "This is a wonderful place to raise kids. You knew Ray and Stella Quinn?"

"Oh, yes. They were wonderful people. I still miss them."

"I wish I'd known them."

"They'd have liked you."

"Do you think?"

"They'd have liked you for yourself," Grace told her. "And they'd have loved what you've done for the family. You helped bring them back together. I think they got a little lost for a while—after Dr. Quinn died. Maybe they all had to go their own way, just like they had to come back.''

"Ethan stayed.''

"He's rooted here—in the water, like eelgrass. But he drifted, too. And spent too much time alone. His house is around the bend that the river takes away from the waterfront.''

"I've never seen it.''

"It's tucked away,'' Grace murmured. "He likes his privacy. Sometimes on a quiet night if I went walking, when I was carrying Aubrey, I could hear him play his music. Just catch the notes on the air if the wind was right. It sounded lonely. Lovely and lonely.''

Eyes that were dazzled by love saw some things with perfect clarity. "How long have you been in love with him?''

"Seems like all my life,'' Grace murmured, then caught herself. "I didn't mean to say that.''

"Too late. You haven't told him?''

"No.'' At even the thought of it, Grace's heart clutched in panic. "I shouldn't be talking about this. He'd hate it. It'd embarrass him.''

"Well, he's not here, is he?'' Amused and delighted, Anna beamed. "I think it's terrific.''

"It's not. It's awful. It's just awful.'' Horrified, she pressed a hand to her mouth to hold back a sudden and unexpected rush of tears. "I ruined it. Ruined everything, and now he doesn't even want to be around me.''

"Oh, Grace.'' Flooded with sympathy, Anna abandoned her chopping to wrap her arms tight around Grace's stiff form, then nudged her toward a chair. "I can't believe that.''

"It's true. He told me to stay away.'' Her voice hitched, mortifying her. "I'm sorry. I don't know what's got into me. I never cry.''

"Then it's time you broke tradition.'' Anna tore off a

couple of sheets of paper towels and offered them. "Go ahead, you'll feel better."

"I feel so stupid." With the dam broken, Grace sobbed into the paper towels.

"There's nothing to feel stupid about."

"There is, there is. I made it so we can't even be friends anymore."

"How did you do that?" Anna asked gently.

"I was pushing myself at him. I guess I thought—after the night he kissed me . . ."

"He kissed you?" Anna repeated, and immediately began to feel better.

"He was mad." Grace pressed her face into the towel, breathing deep until she could regain some control. "It was after what happened at the pub. I've never seen him like that. I've known him most of my life and never knew he could be like that. I'd have been scared if I hadn't known him—the way he tossed that man aside like he was a bag of feathers. And he had this look in his eyes that made them hard and different, and . . ." She sighed and admitted the worst. "Exciting. Oh, it's horrible to think that."

"Are you kidding?" Anna reached over and squeezed her hand. "I wasn't even there and I'm excited."

With a watery laugh, Grace mopped at her face. "I don't know what came over me, but he was yelling at me. It got my back up, and we had a fight when he took me home. He was saying that I should quit my job and talking to me like I'd lost every working brain cell in my head."

"Typical male reaction."

"That's right." Abruptly angry all over again, Grace nodded. "It was just typical, and I never would have expected that from him. Then we were rolling around on the grass."

"You were?" Absolutely delighted, Anna grinned.

"He was kissing me, and I was kissing him back, and

it was wonderful. All my life I'd wondered how it would be, and then there it was and it was better than anything I'd ever imagined. Then he stopped and said he was sorry.''

Anna closed her eyes. "Oh, Ethan, you idiot."

"He told me to go inside, but just before I did he said he thought about me. That he didn't want to, but he did. So I hoped that things would start to change."

"I'd say they'd changed already."

"Yes, but not the way I'd hoped. The day you and Cam came back, I was here when he got home. And it seemed like, maybe . . . but he took me back to my house. He told me he'd thought it through and he wasn't going to touch me again and I was to steer clear of him for a while." She let out a long breath. "So I am."

Anna waited a moment, then shook her head. "Oh, Grace, you idiot." When Grace frowned, Anna leaned across the table. "Obviously the man wants you and it scares the hell out of him. You have the power here. Why aren't you using it?"

"The power? What power?"

"The power to get what you want if what you want is Ethan Quinn. You just need to get him alone and seduce him."

Grace snorted. "Seduce him? Me seduce Ethan? I couldn't do that."

"Why couldn't you?"

"Because I . . ." There had to be a simple and logical reason. "I don't know. I don't think I'd be good at it."

"I bet you'd be great at it. And I'm going to help you."

"You are?"

"Absolutely." Anna rose to fuss with her sauce and to think. "When's your next night off?"

"Tomorrow."

"Good, that's just enough time. I'd keep Aubrey for you overnight, but that might make it too obvious, and we'd better be subtle. Is there someone you'd trust with her?''

''My mother's been wanting to take her overnight, but I couldn't—''

''Perfect. You might feel inhibited with the baby in the house. I'll figure out how to get him over there.''

She turned around, studied Grace. Cool, classic looks, she mused. Big, sad eyes. The man was already a goner. ''You'll want to wear something simple but feminine.'' Considering, she tapped a fingertip against her teeth. ''Pastel would be best, a fragile color, soft green or pink.''

Because her head was starting to spin, Grace put a hand to it. ''You're going too fast.''

''Well, someone has to. At this rate, you and Ethan will still be circling each other when you're sixty. No jewelry,'' she added. ''Just the bare minimum of makeup. Wear your usual scent, too. He's used to it, it'll say something to him.''

''Anna, it doesn't matter what I wear if he doesn't want to be there.''

''Of course it matters.'' As a woman who had a long-term love affair with clothes, she was very nearly shocked at the suggestion. ''Men don't think they notice what a woman wears—unless it's next to nothing. But they do, subconsciously. And it helps click the mood or the image.''

Lips pursed, she added fresh basil to the sauce and got out a skillet for sautéing onions and garlic. ''I'm going to try to get him over there close to sunset. You should light some candles, put on music. The Quinns like their music.''

''What would I say to him?''

''I can only take you so far here, Grace,'' Anna said dryly. ''And I'm betting you'll figure it out when the time comes.''

She was far from convinced of that. While new scents began to romance the air, Grace worried her lip. ''It feels like I'd be tricking him.''

"And your point would be?"

Grace chuckled. And gave up. "I have a pink dress. I bought it for Steve's wedding a couple years ago."

Anna glanced over her shoulder. "How does it look on you?"

"Well . . ." Grace's lips curved slowly. "Steve's best man hit on me before they cut the cake."

"Sounds like a deal."

"I still don't—" Grace stopped as her mother's ear caught the tinkling music from the living room. "That's the end of Aubrey's show. I have to finish up in there."

She rose quickly, panicked at the thought of Ethan coming home before she was gone. Surely everything she felt must show on her face. "Anna, I appreciate what you're trying to do, but I just don't think it's going to work. Ethan knows his own mind."

"Then it won't hurt him to come around to your house and see you in a pink dress, will it?"

Grace blew out a breath. "Does Cam ever win an argument with you?"

"On the rare occasion, but never when I'm at my best."

Grace edged toward the door, knowing that Aubrey's sit-and-behave time was nearly up. "I'm glad you came home early today."

Anna tapped her wooden spoon on the lip of her pot. "Me, too."

TEN

THE FOLLOWING DAY AS sunset approached, Grace wasn't certain she was glad at all. Her nerves were stretched so tight she could feel them straining and bubbling under her skin. Her stomach continually jumped in quick little rabbit hops. And her head was beginning to throb in a sharp, insistent rhythm.

It would be just perfect, she thought in disgust, if Anna managed to get Ethan over, and she simply pitched forward, ill and babbling, at his feet.

That would be seductive.

She should never have agreed to this foolishness, she told herself as she paced through her little house yet again. Anna had thought so quickly, made up her mind so fast and put everything in motion so smoothly, that she'd been swept along before she could calculate the pitfalls.

What in the world would she *say* to him if he came? Which he probably wouldn't, she thought, caught between relief and despair. He probably wouldn't even come and then she'd have sent her baby away for the night for nothing.

It was too quiet. There was nothing but the early-evening breeze rustling through the trees for company. If Aubrey had been there—where she belonged—they'd have been reading her bedtime story now. She would have been all scrubbed and powdered and curled up under Grace's arm in the rocker. Snuggly and sleepy.

When she heard her own sigh, Grace pressed her lips tightly together and marched to the small stereo system on the yellow pine shelves in the living room. She selected CDs from her collection—an indulgence that she refused to feel guilty over—and let the house fill with the weeping and romantic notes of Mozart.

She walked to the window to watch the sun drop lower in the sky. The light was going soft, slipping away shade by shade. In the ornamental plum that graced the Cutters' front yard a lone whippoorwill began to sing to the twilight. She wished she could laugh at herself, silly Grace Monroe standing by the window in her pink dress waiting for a star to wish on.

But she lowered her forehead to the glass, closed her eyes, and reminded herself that she was too old for wishes.

ANNA THOUGHT SHE would have done very well in the espionage game. She had kept her plans locked tight behind closed lips—no matter how desperately she'd wanted to spill out everything to Cam.

She had to remind herself that he was, after all, a man. And he was Ethan's brother, which was another strike against him. This was a woman thing. She thought she was very subtle about keeping her eye on Ethan as well. He wasn't going to escape somewhere directly after dinner, as was his habit, nor would he have a clue that his sister-in-law was keeping him on a short rein.

The ice cream idea had been a brainstorm. She'd picked up a gallon on the way home and now had all three of her men, as she liked to think of them, settled on the back porch downing bowls of Rocky Road.

Timing and execution, she told herself, and rubbed her hands together before she stepped out on the porch. "It's going to be a warm night. It's hard to believe it's nearly July already."

She wandered to the porch rail to lean over and scan her flower beds. Coming right along, she thought with a sense of righteous satisfaction. "I thought we could have a backyard picnic on the Fourth."

"They have fireworks on the waterfront," Ethan put in. "Every year, half hour after sunset. You can see them from right here on the porch."

"Really? That would be perfect. Wouldn't it be fun, Seth? You could have your friends over and we'd cook burgers and dogs."

"That'd be cool." He was already down to scraping his bowl and calculating how to finesse seconds.

"Have to dig out the horseshoes," Cam decided. "Do we still have them, Ethan?"

"Yeah, they're around."

"And music." Anna shifted just enough to rub her husband's knee. "The three of you could play. You don't play together nearly often enough to suit me. I'll have to make a list. You'll have to tell me who we should invite—and the food. Food." She thought she feigned flustered irritation very well as she pushed away from the porch rail. "How could I have forgotten? I promised Grace to trade her my recipe for tortellini for hers for fried chicken."

She dashed inside to retrieve the index card that she'd neatly written the recipe on—something she'd never done before in her life—then dashed back out again. All apologetic smiles.

"Ethan, would you run this over to her?"

He stared at the little white card. If he hadn't been sitting down, his hands would have jumped into his pockets. "What?"

"I promised I'd get her this today and it completely slipped my mind. I'd run it over myself, but I still have a report to finish. I'm just dying to try out that fried chicken," she went on quickly, pushing the recipe card into his hand, then all but dragging him to his feet.

"It's kind of late."

"Oh, it's not even nine o'clock." Don't give him time to think, she warned herself. Don't give him a chance to pick out the flaws. She pulled him into the house, used smiles and fluttering lashes to move him along. "I really appreciate it. I'm so scatterbrained these days. I feel like I'm chasing my own tail half the time. Tell her I'm sorry I didn't get it to her sooner and to be sure to let me know how it turns out once she tries it. Thanks so much, Ethan," she added, rising up to give him a quick, affectionate peck on the cheek. "I love having brothers."

"Well . . ." He was baffled, closing in on miserable, but the way she said that, the way she smiled when she did, left him helpless. "I'll be right back."

I don't think so, Anna thought with a wisely controlled chuckle as she cheerily waved him off. The second his truck was out of sight, she dusted her palms together. Mission accomplished.

"Just what the hell was that?" Cam demanded, making her jolt with surprise.

"I don't know what you mean." She would have sailed past him and into the house, but he stepped out, blocked her path.

"Oh, yeah, you know what I mean." Intrigued, he angled his head. She was trying to look innocent, he decided, but couldn't pull it off. Too much pure glee in her eyes. "Exchanging recipes, Anna?"

"So what?" She lifted a shoulder. "I'm a very good cook."

"No argument there, but you're not the recipe-emergency type, and if you'd been so hell-bent on giving one to Grace, you'd have picked up the phone. Which is something you didn't give Ethan a chance to point out, since you were so busy batting your lashes at him and cooing like some empty-headed twit."

"Twit?"

"Which you're not," he continued, slowly backing her up until she was trapped against the porch rail. "At all. Shrewd, savvy, sharp." He laid his hands on either side of her hips to cage her. "That's what you are."

It was, she supposed, a fine compliment. "Thank you, Cameron. Now I really should get to that report."

"Uh-uh. Why'd you con Ethan into going over to Grace's?"

She shook back her hair, aimed a bland look dead into his eyes. "I'd think a shrewd, savvy, sharp guy like you ought to be able to figure that out."

His brows drew together. "You're trying to get something going between them."

"Something *is* going between them, but your brother is slower than a lame turtle."

"He's slower than a lame turtle with bifocals, but that's Ethan. Don't you think they should muddle through this on their own?"

"All they need is five minutes alone, and that's all I did—work it out so they'd have a few minutes alone. Besides"—she slipped her arms up and around his neck—"we deliriously happy women want everyone else to be deliriously happy, too."

He cocked a brow. "Do you think I'm going to fall for that?"

She smiled, then leaned over to nip his bottom lip. "Yeah."

"You're right," he murmured and let her convince him.

• • •

ETHAN SAT IN HIS TRUCK for a full five minutes. Recipes? That was the dumbest damn thing he'd ever heard of. He'd always thought Anna was a sensible woman, but here she was, sending him off to deliver recipes, for Christ's sake.

And he wasn't ready to see Grace just yet. Not that his mind wasn't made up about her, but . . . even a rational man had certain weaknesses.

Still, he didn't see how he was going to get out of it, as he was already here. He'd make it quick. She was probably putting the baby to bed, so he'd just get it done and get out of her way.

Like a man condemned, he dragged himself out of the truck and to her front door. Through the screen he could see the flickering lights of candles. He shifted his feet and noticed that music was playing, something with weeping strings and soaring piano.

He'd never felt more ridiculous in his life than he did standing there on Grace's front porch holding a recipe for a pasta dish while music slid around the warm summer night.

He knocked on the wood frame, not too loudly, as he worried about waking Aubrey. He gave serious thought to sticking the card in the door and hightailing it, but he knew that would be cowardice, plain and simple.

And Anna would want to know why he hadn't brought her the instructions for Grace's fried chicken.

When he saw her he wished to God Almighty he'd taken the coward's way.

She walked out from the kitchen, at the back of the house. It was a tiny place, had always made Ethan think of a dollhouse, so she didn't have far to travel. To him it seemed he watched her walk through that music, that light for hours.

She wore pale, fragile pink that skimmed down to her

ankles, with a row of tiny pearl buttons from the hollow of her throat to the hem that flowed around her bare feet. He had rarely seen her in a dress, but now he was too thunderstruck by the sight of her to question why she was wearing it.

All he could think was she looked like a rose, long and slim and just ready to bloom. And his tongue tangled up in his mouth.

"Ethan." Her hand trembled lightly as she reached down, opened the screen. Maybe she hadn't needed a star to wish on after all. For here he was, standing close and watching her.

"I was . . ." Her scent, familiar as his own, seemed to wrap around his brain. "Anna sent you—she asked me to bring this by."

Mystified, Grace took the card he held out. At the sight of the recipe she had to bite the inside of her cheek to keep from laughing. Her nerves backed off just enough that her eyes smiled when she lifted them to his. "That was nice of her."

"You got hers?"

"Her what?"

"The one she wants. The chicken thing."

"Oh, yes. Back in the kitchen. Come on in while I get it." What chicken thing? she wondered, nearly giddy from suppressed laughter that she knew would come out well on the hysterical side. "The, um, casserole, right?"

"No." She had such a tiny waist, he thought. Such narrow feet. "Fried."

"Oh, that's right. I'm so scatterbrained lately."

"It's going around," he mumbled. He decided it was safer to look anywhere but at her. He noted the pair of fat white candles burning on the counter. "You blow a fuse?"

"Excuse me?"

"What's wrong with your lights?"

"Nothing." She could feel the heat rise into her cheeks.

She didn't have a recipe for fried chicken written down anywhere. Why would she? You just did the same as you always did when it came time to make it. "I like candlelight sometimes. It goes with the music."

He only grunted, wishing she would hurry up so he could get the hell away. "You already put Aubrey to bed?"

"She's spending the night with my mother."

His eyes, which had been steadfastly studying her ceiling, shot down and met hers. "She's not here?"

"No. It's her first overnight. I've already called over there twice." She smiled a little, and her fingers reached up to fiddle with the top button of her dress in a way that made Ethan's mouth water. "I know she's only a few miles away, and as safe as she'd be in her own crib, but I couldn't help it. The house feels so different without her here."

"Dangerous" was the word he'd have used. The pretty little dollhouse was suddenly as deadly as a minefield. There wasn't any little girl innocently sleeping in the next room. They were alone, with music sobbing and candles flickering.

And Grace was wearing a pale-pink dress that just begged to have those little white buttons undone, one by one by one.

The tips of his fingers began to itch.

"I'm glad you stopped by." Holding tight to her courage, she took a step forward and tried to remember that she had the power. "I was feeling a little blue."

He took a step back. More than his fingertips was itching now. "I said I'd be back directly."

"You could stay for . . . coffee or whatever?"

Coffee? If his system got any more wired than it was at that moment, it would have jumped right through his skin to dance the hornpipe. "I don't think . . ."

"Ethan, I can't steer clear of you the way you asked me. St. Chris is too small, and our lives are too tangled up together." She could feel the pulse in her throat pounding against her skin in hard, insistent little knocks. "And I don't want to. I don't want to steer clear of you, Ethan."

"I said I had my reasons." And he could think of what they were if she'd just stop looking at him with those big green eyes. "I'm just watching out for you, Grace."

"I don't need you to watch out for me. We're all grown up, both of us. We're alone, both of us." She stepped closer. She could smell his after-work shower on him, but under it, as always, was the scent of the Bay. "I don't want to be alone tonight."

He edged back. If he hadn't known her better, he'd have sworn she was stalking him. "I've made up my mind on this." But damn it, it wasn't his mind working overtime, it was his loins. "Just stay back, Grace."

"It seems like I've been staying back forever. I want to move forward, Ethan, whatever that means. I'm tired of staying back or standing still. If you don't want me, I'll live with that. But if you do . . ." She moved closer, lifted a hand to lay it on his heart. And discovered that his heart was pounding. "If you do, then why won't you take me?"

He backed hard into the counter. "Stop it. You don't know what you're doing here."

"Of course I know what I'm doing." She snapped it out, suddenly furious with the pair of them. "I'm just not doing a good job of it, since you'd rather climb up my kitchen wall than lay a finger on me. What do you think I'd do, shatter into a million pieces? I'm a grown woman, Ethan. I've been married, I've had a child. I know what I'm asking you, and I know what I want."

"I know you're a grown woman. I've got eyes."

"Then use them, and look at me."

How could he do otherwise? Why had he ever believed he could? There, standing in shadow and light, was everything he yearned for. "I'm looking at you, Grace." With my back to the wall, he thought. And my heart in my throat.

"Here's a woman who wants you, Ethan. One who needs you." She saw his eyes change at that, sharpen, darken, focus. On an unsteady breath, she stepped back. "Maybe I'm what you want. What you need."

He was afraid she was, and that telling himself he could and would do without had been an exercise in futility. She was so lovely, all rose and gold in the candlelight, her eyes so clear and honest. "I know you are," he said at length. "But that wasn't supposed to change anything."

"Do you have to think all the time?"

"It's getting hard to," he murmured. "Right at the moment."

"Then don't. Let's both stop thinking." Even as the blood pounded in her brain, she kept her gaze locked on his. And lifted her hands, trembling hands, to the top button of her dress.

He watched her unfasten it, staggered at how that single, simple gesture, that tiny inch of exposed skin, could electrify him. He felt his lungs clog, his blood sizzle, and his needs, all the long-denied needs, beg for release.

"Stop, Grace." He said it gently. "Don't do that."

Her hands fell back to her sides in defeat, and she shut her eyes.

"Let me do it."

Her eyes blinked open, stared stunned at his sober gaze as he stepped to her. She took in one shaky breath and held it.

"I've always wanted to," he murmured and slipped the next tiny button free.

"Oh." The breath she held came out in a hitch and a sob. "Ethan."

"You're so pretty." She was already trembling. He lowered his head to brush a kiss over her lips and soothe. "So soft. I've got rough hands." Watching her, he skimmed his knuckles down her cheek, over her throat. "But I won't hurt you."

"I know. I know you won't."

"You're shaking." He undid another button, then another.

"I can't help it."

"I don't mind." Patiently he eased the buttons free to her waist. "I guess I knew, deep down, if I walked in here tonight, I wouldn't be able to walk away again."

"I've been wishing you'd walk in here. I've been wishing it a long time."

"So have I." The buttons were so tiny, his fingers so big. Her skin, where the dress parted, where the edge of his thumb slid up, was so soft and warm. "You tell me if I do something you don't like. Or if I don't do something you want."

The sound she made was part moan, part laugh. "I'm not going to be able to talk in a minute. I can't get my breath. But I wish you'd kiss me."

"I was getting to it." He nibbled gently, teasingly, because he hadn't taken his time the first time he'd tasted her. Now he would linger, sample, find a rhythm that suited them both. When her sigh filled his mouth, it was sweet. He loosened more buttons and let the long, deepening kiss spin out.

Touched her nowhere else, not yet. Only mouth against mouth with flavors mixed. When she swayed, he lifted his head, looked into her eyes. Clouded now, heavy and aware.

"I want to see you." Slowly, inch by inch, he slipped the dress from her shoulders. They were sun-kissed, strong, gracefully curved. He'd always thought she had the prettiest shoulders, and now he indulged himself by tasting them.

The hum in her throat told him she was both surprised and pleased by the attention. He had a great deal more to give her.

She'd never been touched this way, as if she were something rare and precious. What that touch stirred in her was so new and warm. Her skin seemed to soften and sensitize under the brush of his lips, the blood beneath to go thick and lazy. She only sighed as her dress slid down to pool at her feet.

When he eased back again, she could only stare up at him in wonder. Her lashes fluttered, her pulse skipped when he stroked his fingers lightly over the swell of her breast above her simple cotton bra. She had to bite her lip to hold back the groan when he flicked open the hook, when he gently cupped her breast in his palms.

"Do you want me to stop?"

"Oh, God." Her head fell back, and this time the groan escaped. His workingman's thumbs were skimming slowly, rhythmically over her nipples. "No."

"Hold on to me, Grace." He spoke quietly, and when her hands came to his shoulders and gripped, he brought his mouth to hers again, drawing more this time, asking more until she went limp.

Then he lifted her into his arms. He waited until her eyes opened again. "I'm taking you, Grace."

"Thank God, Ethan."

He had to smile when she pressed her face into the curve of his shoulder. "I'll protect you."

For a moment as he carried her off, she thought of dragons and black knights. Then the more practical meaning got through. "I—take the Pill. It's all right. I haven't been with anybody since Jack."

He'd known that in his heart, but hearing it only added to his steadily rising need.

She'd lighted candles in the bedroom as well. Slim tapers there that lanced up out of tiny white shells. The white of her iron headboard glowed in the soft light. White daisies sprang out of a clear glass vase on the small table beside the bed.

She thought he would lay her down, but instead he sat,

cradling her, holding her, drugging her with those slow, endless kisses until her pulse beat thickly, grew sluggish. Then his hands began to move.

Everywhere he touched a small fire fanned into flame.

Callused hands, slipping, sliding over her skin. Long, rough-edged fingers stroking, pressing. There, oh, yes, just there.

The day-long stubble of beard rubbed the sensitive curve of her breasts as his tongue circled, then flicked. And always, always, his mouth coming back to hers for one more, just one more endless, mind-reeling kiss.

She tugged at his shirt, hoping to give back some of the pleasure, some of the magic. Found the scars and the muscle and the man. His torso was lean, his shoulders broad, the flesh warm under her seeking fingers. The breeze whispered through the open window, the call of the whippoorwill chasing after it. And the sound no longer seemed so lonely.

He eased her back, settled her head on the pillow, then bent to pull off his boots. Pale-gold candlelight swayed against shadows the color of smoke. Both shades shimmered over her. He watched as her hand snuck up to cover her breast, and he paused long enough to take it and kiss the knuckles.

"I wish you wouldn't," he murmured. "You're such a pleasure to look at."

She hadn't thought she'd feel shy, knew it was foolish, but she had to order herself to let her hand fall onto the bed. When he slipped out of his jeans she had to struggle with her breathing all over again. No fairy-tale knight had ever been built more magnificently or borne scars more heroically.

Desperate with love, she held out her arms in welcome.

He slipped into them, careful not to press his full weight onto her. She was fragile, he reminded himself, so slim and so much more innocent than she believed.

As the rising moon slanted its first light through the window, he began to show her.

Sighs and murmurs, long, slow caresses, quiet sips and tastes. His hands aroused, devastated, but never hurried. Hers explored, admired, and forgot to hesitate. He found where she was most sensitive, the underside of her breast, the back of her knee, the sweet, shallow, seductive valley between her thigh and her center.

So focused on her was he that his own rising need took him by surprise, flashing once, hard and strong and dragging out his moan when he took her breast into his mouth.

She arched, shuddering at the edgier demand.

And the rhythm changed.

With his breath growing ragged, he lifted his head, his eyes intent on her face. His hand slid between her thighs, pressed there against the heat. Found her already wet.

"I want to see you go over." He played his fingers over her, in her, as her breath quickened. Pleasure, panic, excitement all raced over her face. He watched her climb, closer, closer, with her breath tearing, then releasing on a strangled cry as she peaked.

She tried to shake her head to clear it, but the delicious dizziness continued to spin. The familiar room revolved, hazed, so that only his face was clear, was real. She felt drunk and dazed and unspeakably aroused.

This, finally this, was love as she'd dreamed it would be.

Her skin quivered as he slid slowly up her body, his mouth laying a warm, damp trail.

"Please." It wasn't enough. Even this wasn't enough. She craved the mating, the union, the final intimacy. "Ethan." She opened for him, arched. "Now."

His hands cupped her face, his lips covered her lips. "Now," he murmured against them and filled her.

Their long, groaning sighs blended, that first endless shudder of pleasure as he buried himself inside her rocked them both. When they began to move, they moved together, smoothly, silkily as if they'd only been waiting.

Desire was fluid, its current steady. They rode it, thrilling to the pace, to the deep, resonant pleasure of each long, slow stroke. Grace swirled close to the edge, felt the orgasm build, slide through her system like velvet ribbon so that she rose up, farther up, wallowed in the glow, then floated down into weightless wonder.

He pressed his face into her hair, and let himself follow.

HE WAS SO QUIET IT worried her. He held her, but he would have known she'd need him to. Still he didn't speak, and the longer the silence stretched the more she feared what he would say when he broke it.

So she broke it first.

"Don't tell me you're sorry. I don't think I could stand it if you told me you were sorry."

"I wasn't going to. I promised myself I'd never touch you like this, but I'm not sorry I did."

She rested her head on his shoulder, just under his chin. "Will you touch me like this again?"

"Right this minute?"

Because she caught the lazy amusement in his voice, she relaxed and smiled. "I know better than to rush you on anything." She lifted her head because it was vital that she know. "Will you, Ethan? Will you be with me again?"

He traced a finger through her hair. "I don't see talking either one of us out of it after tonight."

"If you started to, I'd have to try to seduce you again."

"Yeah?" A smile crept over his face. "Then maybe I should start talking."

Thrilled, she rolled over him and hugged hard. "I'd be better at it the next time, too, because I wouldn't be so damned nervous."

"Nerves didn't seem to get in your way. I nearly swallowed my tongue when you walked to the door in that pink dress.'' He started to nuzzle her hair, stopped, narrowed his eyes. ''What were you doing wearing a dress to sit around at home?''

''I don't know . . . I just was.'' She turned her head, ran kisses along his throat.

''Hold on.'' Knowing just how quickly she could distract him, he took her shoulders and lifted her up. ''A pretty dress, candlelight . . . it's almost like you were expecting me to come along.''

''I'm always hoping you will,'' she said and tried to kiss him again.

''Sending me off with a recipe, for Christ's sake.'' In a smooth and easy move he plopped her on her butt beside him, then sat up. ''You and Anna got your heads together on this, didn't you? Set me up.''

''What a ridiculous thing to say.'' She tried for indignant, but could only manage guilty. ''I don't know where you get these ideas.''

''You never could lie worth spit.'' Firmly, he took her chin in one hand, holding it until her eyes shifted to his. ''It took me a while to figure it, but I've got it now, don't I?''

''She was only trying to help. She knew I was upset about the way things were between us. You've got a right to be mad, but don't take it out on her. She was only—''

''Did I say I was mad?'' he interrupted.

''No, but . . .'' She trailed off, drew in a careful breath. ''You're not mad?''

''I'm grateful.'' His grin was slow and wicked. ''But maybe you ought to try to seduce me again. Just in case.''

ELEVEN

In the dark, while an owl still hooted, Ethan shifted, easing out from under the arm Grace had wrapped around his chest. In response she snuggled closer. The gesture made him smile.

"Are you getting up?" she asked in a voice that was muffled against his shoulder.

"I've got to. It's after five already." He could smell rain on the air, hear it coming in the rising wind. "I'm going to get a shower. You go back to sleep."

She made a sound that he took for assent and burrowed into the pillow.

He moved lightly through the dark, though he had to check himself a couple of times on the way to the bathroom. He didn't know her house as well as his own. He waited until he was inside before turning on the light so the backwash of it wouldn't spill into the hall and disturb her.

The room was scaled to match the rest of the house, so small he could have stood in the center and touched each side wall with his hands. The tiles were white, the walls above them papered in a thin candy stripe. He knew she'd hung the paper herself. She rented from Stuart Claremont, and the man wasn't known for his generosity or his sense of decor.

He had to grin at the orange-billed rubber duck nested on the side of the tub. One sniff at the soap made him realize why Grace always smelled faintly of lemons. While he appreciated the fragrance on her, he hoped sincerely that Jim wouldn't notice the citrus scent on him.

He ducked his head under what he thought of as a piss-trickle of spray. She needed a new showerhead, he decided, and as he rubbed a hand over his face, noted that he needed a shave. Both would have to wait.

But it was likely that now that things had changed between them, she would let him take care of a few things around the house for her. She'd always been so blessed stubborn about accepting help. It seemed to him that even a proud woman like Grace would be less stiff about taking help from a lover than a friend.

That's what they were now, Ethan reflected. No matter how many promises he'd made to himself. It wouldn't end with one night. Neither one of them was built that way, and it had as much to do with heart as it did with loins. They'd taken the step and that step involved commitment.

That's what worried him most.

He would never be able to marry her, have children with her. She would want more children. She was too fine a mother, had too much love to give not to want them. Aubrey deserved brothers or sisters.

There wasn't any point in thinking about it, he reminded himself. Things were the way things were. And right now he had a right, and a need to live in the moment. They would love each other as much as they could for as long as they could. That would be enough.

It took him barely five minutes to discover that Grace's hot water heater was as small as the rest of the house. Even the miserly trickle of water turned cool, then cold, before he'd managed to rinse away all the lather.

"Cheap bastard," he muttered, thinking of Claremont. He switched off the spray and wrapped one of the bright-pink towels around his waist. He intended to go back and dress in the dark, but when he opened the door, he could see the light from the kitchen and hear Grace's still sleep-husky voice singing about finding love, just in the nick of time.

While the first drops of rain pattered against the windows, he stepped into the scent of bacon frying and coffee brewing. And the sight of Grace wrapped in a short cotton robe the color of spring leaves. His heart gave such a hard bounce of joy he was surprised it didn't simply leap out of his throat and land quivering in her hands.

He moved quick and quiet, so that when he wrapped his arms around her, pressed his lips to the top of her head, she jolted in surprise.

"I told you to go back to sleep."

She leaned back against him, closing her eyes and absorbing the lovely thrill of a kitchen embrace. "I wanted to fix you breakfast."

"You don't have to do things like that." He turned her around. "I don't expect things like that. You need your rest."

"I wanted to do it." His hair was dripping, his chest gleaming with wet. The sparkling gush of lust both delighted and shocked her. "Today's special."

"I appreciate it." He bent, intending to give her one soft morning kiss. But it deepened, lengthened until she was on her toes straining against him.

He had to pull himself back, block off the rushing need to tug off the robe and take her. "The bacon's going to burn," he murmured, and this time pressed his lips to her forehead. "I'd better get dressed."

She turned the bacon briskly to give him time to cross

the room. Anna had been right, she thought, about having power. "Ethan?"

"Yeah?"

"I've got an awful lot of need for you stored up." She glanced over her shoulder, and her smile was smug. "I hope you don't mind."

The blood danced gleefully out of his head. She wasn't just flirting, she was challenging. He had a feeling she knew she'd already won. The only safe answer he could think of was a grunt before he retreated to the bedroom.

He wanted her. Grace did a quick dance and spin. They'd made love three times, three beautiful, glorious times during the night, had slept wrapped around each other. And he still wanted her.

It was the most beautiful morning of her life.

IT RAINED ALL DAY. THE water was rough as the tongue of a shrew and just as likely to lash. Ethan fought to keep the boat on course and was glad he hadn't let the boy come with them. He and Jim had worked in worse, but he imagined Seth would have spent a good portion of the day hung over the rail.

But foul weather couldn't spoil his mood. He whistled even as rain slapped his face and the boat pitched under him like a rodeo bronc.

Jim eyed him sideways a few times. He'd worked with Ethan long enough to know the boy was the friendly, good-natured sort. But a whistling fool he wasn't. He smiled to himself as he hauled up another pot. Looked like the boy did something more energetic than reading in bed last night, if you asked him.

About time, too—if you asked him. By his reckoning Ethan Quinn was round about thirty years of age. A man should oughta be settled down with a wife and kids by that time of life. A waterman was better off going home to a hot meal and a warm bed. A good woman helped you through, gave you direction, cheered you up when the Bay got stingy. As God knew it could.

He wondered who this particular woman might be. Not that he stuck his nose in other people's business. He minded his own and expected his neighbors to do the same. But a man had a right to a little curiosity about things.

He pondered on how to bring the subject around when an under-the-limit she-crab found a tiny hole in his glove and snapped before he could toss her back.

"Little bitch," he said with a wince but without much heat.

"She get you?"

"Yeah." Jim watched her splash back into the waves. "I'll be back for you before the season's over."

"Looks like you need new gloves there, Jim."

"The wife's picking me up some today." He shoved the thawing alewives they used for bait into the trap. "Sure helps matters to know you got a woman to do for you some."

"Uh-huh." Ethan shoved the steering stick with one hand, picked up the gaff with the other, and timed the chop and the distance.

"A man spends the day working on the water, it's a comfort to know his woman's waiting for him."

A little surprised that they were having a conversation, Ethan nodded. "I suppose. We'll just finish up this line, Jim, then head in."

Jim culled the next pot, let the silence settle between them. A few gulls were having what Jim thought of as a pissing match overhead, screaming and diving and threatening each other over loose fish parts.

"You know, me and Bess, we'll be married thirty years come next spring."

"Is that so?"

"Steadies a man, a woman does. You wait too long to

marry up, though, you get set in your ways."

"I guess."

"You'd be around thirty now, wouldn't you, Cap'n?"

"That's right."

"Don't want to get set in your ways."

"I'll keep that in mind," Ethan told him and shot out the gaff.

Jim merely sighed and gave up.

WHEN ETHAN WANDERED into the boatyard, Cam was at the skill saw and three young boys were sanding the hull. Or pretending to.

"You hire a new crew?" Ethan asked as Simon trotted over to investigate.

Cam glanced to where Seth chattered away with Danny and Will Miller. "It keeps them out of my hair. You give up on crabs today?"

"Pulled in enough." He pulled out a cigar and lit it while he gazed thoughtfully out the open cargo doors. "Rain's coming down pretty hard."

"Tell me about it." Cam sent an accusing scowl toward the streaming windows. "That's why those three were in my hair. The little one'll talk your ears blue. And if you don't have the others doing something to keep them busy, they make trouble out of thin air."

"Well." Ethan puffed out smoke, watched the kids send Simon into ecstasy with rough rubs and scratches. "At the rate they're going, they'll have that hull sanded down in ten or twenty years."

"That's something we have to talk about."

"Hiring on those kids for the next two decades?"

"No, work." It was as good a time as any to take a break. Cam stooped and pumped iced tea out of the cooler. "I got a call from Tod Bardette this morning."

"The friend of yours who wants the fishing boat?"

"That's right. Now, Bardette and I go back a ways. He knows what I can do."

"He offer you another race?"

He had, Cam mused, cutting the dust in his throat with the sweet tea. Turning it down had stung, but the sting had eased more quickly this time around. "I made a promise here. I'm not breaking it."

Ethan tucked a hand in his back pocket and looked toward the boat. This place, this business, had been his dream, not Cam's, not Phillip's. "I didn't mean it that way. I guess I know what you put away to pull this off."

"We needed it."

"Yeah, but you're the only one who's given up anything to make it happen. I haven't bothered to thank you for it, and I'm sorry for that."

Every bit as uncomfortable as his brother, Cam stared at the boat. "I'm not exactly suffering here. The business is going to help us get permanent guardianship of Seth—and it's satisfying on its own account. Of course, Phil's bitching about our cash flow every time you turn around."

"That's his strength."

"Bitching?"

Ethan grinned around the cigar clamped in his teeth. "Yeah, and cash flows. You and me, we could never pull this off without him nagging us about the details."

"We may have more for him to nag about. That's what I started to tell you. Bardette has a friend who's interested in a custom catboat. He wants fast and he wants pretty, fitted out and sailing by March."

Ethan frowned and worked timetables in his head. "It's going to take us another seven or eight weeks to finish this one, and that puts us into end of August, beginning of September."

Calculating, he leaned back against the workbench, his eyes narrowed against the smoke. "Then we got the sport's fisher. I can't see us finishing her off before January, and that's pushing. That doesn't give us enough time to deliver.''

''No, not the way things are. I can give it full-time and after crab season's over, I imagine you'll put in more hours here.''

''Oystering isn't what it was, but—''

''You'll have to decide if you can juggle more time off the water, Ethan, and in here.'' He knew what he was asking. Ethan didn't just live on the water, he lived for it. ''Phil's going to have to make some hard decisions before much longer, too. We're not going to have the cash to hire on laborers for a while yet.'' He blew out a breath. ''Unless we count a couple of kids. This friend of Bardette's isn't ready to commit. He's going to come down and take a look at the place, and us, and what we've got here. I figure we make sure Phillip's around to sweet-talk him into a contract and a deposit.''

Ethan hadn't expected it to happen so soon, to have one dream grow and steal from the other. He thought of the chill winter months spent dredging, the rise and fall of the skipjack over hard chop, the long, often frustrating search for oyster, for rockfish, for a living.

A nightmare for some, he supposed. But hope and glory for him.

He took the time to look around the building. The boat, nearly finished, waiting for willing and able hands under the hard overhead lights. Seth's drawings were framed on the wall and spoke of dreams and sweat. Tools, still shiny under a coating of dust, stood silent, waiting.

Boats by Quinn, he mused. If you wanted to grab ahold of one thing, you had to let go of another.

''I'm not the only one who can captain the workboat or the skipjack.'' He saw both the question and the understanding in Cam's eyes and jerked a shoulder. ''It's just juggling time where it needs to be spent most.''

''Yeah.''

''I guess I could work up a design for a cat.''

"And have Seth do the drawing," Cam added and laughed when Ethan grimaced. "We all have our strengths, pal. Art isn't yours."

"I'll think about it," Ethan decided. "And we'll see what happens next."

"Good enough. So . . ." Cam drained his cup. "How'd the recipe exchange go?"

Ethan ran his tongue around the inside of his cheek. "I'm going to have a talk with your wife about that."

"Be my guest." Smiling, Cam plucked the cigar from Ethan's fingers and took a trio of careless puffs. "You sure look . . . relaxed today, Ethan."

"I'm relaxed enough," he said evenly. "And I'd think you might have seen fit to mention to me that Anna had some plot to improve my sex life for me."

"I might have, if I'd known about it. Then again, since your sex life needed some improvement, I might not." On impulse, Cam grabbed Ethan in a headlock. "Because I love you, man." He only laughed when the elbow plowed into his stomach. "See? It even improved your reflexes."

Ethan shifted, angled his weight, and reversed their positions. "You're right," he said and rubbed his knuckles hard on the top of Cam's head for good measure.

SINCE IT WAS HIS NIGHT to cook, Ethan added an egg to a bowl of ground beef. He didn't mind cooking. It was just one of those things you did to get through. He'd harbored a small, selfish, and purely chauvinistic hope that Anna would take over the kitchen duties as woman of the house.

She'd squashed that hope like a bug.

Of course, having her around did spread out the chore. But the worst of it, as far as he was concerned, was figuring out the menu. It was different from cooking for himself. He'd learned quickly enough that when you cooked for a family, everybody was a critic.

"What is that?" Seth demanded when Ethan shook oatmeal into the mix.

"Meat loaf."

"Looks like crap to me. Why can't we have pizza?"

"Because we're having meat loaf."

Seth made a gagging sound as Ethan dumped some tomato soup into the mix. "Gross. I'd rather eat dirt."

"There's plenty of it outside."

Seth shifted from foot to foot, rose up on his toes to get a closer look at the bowl. The rain was driving him crazy. There was nothing to *do*. He was starving to death, he had six million mosquito bites, and there was nothing but kid crud and news on TV.

When he listed this litany of complaints, Ethan merely shrugged. "Go bug Cam."

Cam had told him to go bug Ethan. Seth knew from hard experience that it took much longer to bug Ethan than Cam.

"How come you put all that crap in there if it's called meat loaf?"

"So it doesn't taste like crap when you eat it."

"I bet it does."

For a kid who only months before hadn't known where his next meal was coming from, Ethan thought darkly, Seth had gotten mighty particular. Instead of saying so, he aimed a single, sharp dart. "Cam's cooking tomorrow."

"Oh, man. Poison." Seth rolled his eyes dramatically, grabbed his throat, and staggered around the room. Ethan might have been mildly amused if the dogs hadn't gotten into the act by scrambling in and barking wildly.

By the time Anna walked in, Ethan had the meat loaf in the oven and was dumping aspirin into his palm.

"Hi. Miserable day. Traffic was filthy." She raised an eyebrow as Ethan downed the pills. "Headache, huh? All-day rain can sure give you one."

"This one's named Seth."

"Oh." Concerned, she poured herself a glass of wine and prepared to listen. "There's bound to be periods of stress and difficulties. He has a tremendous amount to overcome, and his belligerence is a defense."

"Did nothing but complain for the last hour. My ears are still ringing. Doesn't want meat loaf," Ethan muttered and snagged a beer from the fridge. " 'Why can't we have pizza?' He ought to be grateful somebody's putting food in his belly. Instead he's saying it looks like crap and will likely taste worse. Then he gets the dogs all fired up so I can't even work in peace for five damn minutes. And . . ."

He trailed off, steely-eyed, when he saw her grinning. "Easy for you to be amused by it."

"I am, I'm sorry. But I'm even more pleased. Oh, Ethan, it's so wonderfully normal. He's behaving just like an annoying ten year old after a rainy day. A couple of months ago he'd have spent that time sulking in his room instead of giving you a headache. It's such tremendous progress."

"He's progressing into being a pain in the ass."

"Yes." She felt tears of delight sting her eyes. "Isn't it marvelous? He must have been really annoying if it was enough to try your unflappable patience. At this rate he'll be a terror by Christmas."

"And that's a good thing?"

"Yes. Ethan, I've worked with children who haven't faced nearly the miseries Seth has, and it can take them so much longer to adjust, even with counseling. You and Cam and Phillip have done wonders for Seth."

Cooling off, Ethan sipped his beer. "You had a hand in it."

"Yes, I did, which makes me as happy on a professional level as I am on a personal one. And to prove it, I'll give you a hand with dinner." So saying, she shrugged out of her jacket and began to roll up her sleeves. "What did you have in mind to go with the meat loaf?"

He'd planned on sticking some potatoes in the micro-wave because they didn't require any fussing, and maybe digging some frozen peas out. But . . .

"I thought maybe some of those cheese noodles you make would go nice as a side dish."

"The alfredo? Cholesterol city, added to meat loaf, but what the hell. I'll fix them. Why don't you sit down until the headache passes?"

It already had, but it seemed smarter not to mention it.

He sat, prepared to enjoy his beer—and fix his sister-in-law's wagon. "Oh, Grace said I should thank you for the recipe. She'll let you know how it turns out for her."

"Oh?" Turning to hide her satisfied smile, Anna reached for an apron.

"Yeah, I got the fried chicken makings for you—stuck it in the cookbook." He hid his own smile with his beer when her head swiveled.

"You . . . oh, well . . ."

"I'd have given it to you last night, but it was late when I got back, and you were in bed. I ran into Jim when I left Grace's."

"Jim?" Puzzled annoyance showed clearly on her face.

"Went on over to his place to help him tune up this outboard that's been giving him trouble."

"You were at Jim's last night?"

"Stayed later than I meant to, but there was a ball game on. The O's were playing out in California."

She could have cheerfully smashed him over the head with his own beer bottle. "You spent last night working on an engine and watching a ball game?"

"Yeah." He sent her an innocent look. "Like I said, I got in kinda late, but it was a hell of a game."

She huffed out a breath, yanked open the refrigerator to get out cheese and milk. "Men," she muttered. "All of them idiots."

"What's that?"

"Nothing. Well, I hope you had a fine time watching

your baseball game.'' While Grace was home alone, miserable.

"I can't remember enjoying myself more. Went into extra innings.'' He was grinning now, just couldn't help it. She looked so flustered and furious and was trying desperately to hide it.

"Well, hot damn.'' Fuming, she shifted to get the fettuccine out of the cupboard and saw his face. She turned slowly, holding the package of pasta. "You didn't go over to Jim's to watch a ball game last night.''

"Didn't I?'' He lifted a brow, glanced thoughtfully at his beer, then sipped. "You know, come to think of it, you're right. That was some other time.''

"You were with Grace.''

"Was I?''

"Oh, Ethan.'' With clenched teeth she slammed the jar down. "You're making me crazy! Where were you last night?''

"You know, I don't believe anyone's asked me that since my mother died.''

"I'm not trying to pry—''

"You're not?''

"All right, all right, I am trying to pry and you make it impossible to be subtle about it.''

He leaned back in his chair, studying her. He'd liked her, almost from the first—even when she made him uneasy. Wasn't it funny, he mused, to realize that sometime over the last few weeks, he had come to love her. Which mean that teasing her was, well, required.

"You're not asking me if I spent the night in Grace's bed, are you?''

"No. No, of course not.'' She snatched up the pasta, then set it down again. "Not exactly.''

"Were the candles her idea, or yours?''

Anna decided it was a good time to get out a skillet. She just might need a weapon. "Did they work?''

"Yours, I imagine; probably the dress, too. Grace's

mind doesn't work that way. She's not what you'd call . . . sneaky.''

Anna hummed and prepared to make her cheese sauce.

"And it was sneaky, underhanded, meddling, to send me over there that way."

"I know it. But I'd do it again." More skillfully next time, she promised herself. "You can be annoyed with me all you want, Ethan, but I've never seen anyone more in need of some meddling."

"You're a pro at it. I mean, being a social worker, you make a living meddling in people's lives."

"I help people who need it," she said, firing up the skillet. "God knows you did." She yelped when his hand dropped on her shoulder. She half expected him to give her a quick shake, so when he kissed her cheek she could only blink at him.

"I appreciate it."

"You do?"

"Not that I'd care to have you do it again, but this once, I appreciate it."

"She makes you happy." Everything inside Anna softened. "I can see it."

"We'll see how long I can make her happy."

"Ethan—"

"Let it stand." He kissed her again, as much in warning as affection. "We'll take it a day at a time for a while."

"All right." But her smile bloomed. "Grace is working at the pub tonight, isn't she?"

"Yeah. And just so you don't have to bite your tongue in half to keep from asking, I'm thinking of going by for a while after dinner."

"Good." More than satisfied, Anna got to work. "Then we'll eat soon."

TWELVE

IT WAS LIKE WALKING WIDE awake into a dream, Grace thought, where you couldn't be sure what was going to happen next, but you just knew it would be wonderful. It was living inside a familiar world that had been polished into a constant state of anticipation and excitement.

Days and nights were still filled with work, responsibilities, small joys and petty annoyances. But for now, with this full rush of love, the joys seemed huge, the annoyances minute.

Everything she'd ever read about love was true, she discovered. The sun shined brighter, the air smelled fresher. Flowers were more colorful, the songs of birds more musical. Every cliché became her reality.

There were stolen moments—an embrace outside the pub during her break that left her jittery and delighted and unable to sleep long after she went home. A slow, intense look filled with awareness if she managed to linger long enough at the Quinn house to see him. It seemed she was in a constant state of yearning, only more acute now that she knew what could be.

What would be.

She wanted to touch and be touched, to take that long, slow ride into pleasure and passion again. Side by side with the yearning was the endless frustration that life constantly intruded on dreams.

There was never enough time to be alone, to simply be.

She often wondered if Ethan felt the same edgy need dogging his heels throughout his day. She thought it must be something inside her, some long-hidden sexual greed— and she didn't know whether to be delighted by it or mortified.

She only knew that she wanted him constantly, and that with every day that want passed into another night alone, that want increased. She wondered if he would be shocked, worried that he would be.

She needn't have.

He only hoped he'd timed it right, and that his excuses to Jim for taking in the catch before checking all the pots weren't as ridiculously transparent as they'd seemed. He wasn't going to let guilt eat at him either, Ethan promised himself as he secured his boat at his home dock.

He would work a couple extra hours that evening in the boatyard to make up for leaving Cam on his own that afternoon. If he didn't have one hour alone with Grace, if he didn't release some of this pressure that was building up, he'd go crazy. Then he'd be no good to anyone.

And if she'd already finished up at the house and left, well, he'd just have to hunt her down, that's all. He had enough control left not to scare her, or shock her, but he just couldn't get through another day without her.

His grin began to spread when he came through the back door and saw that the morning untidiness had yet to be cleared away. The washer was rumbling in the laundry room. She hadn't finished. He started into the living room, looking for signs of her.

The cushions were all smoothed and plumped, the furniture dust-free and shining. And as the floor above his head gave a quiet creak, he glanced up.

At that moment, he thought Fate was the most beautiful woman he'd ever known. Grace was in his bedroom, and what could be more perfect? It would be much easier to lure her into a daytime bed without jolting her sensibilities if she was already close by one.

He started up the stairs, delighted when he heard her humming.

Then his system suffered a sizzling lightning bolt of lust when he saw she wasn't just close by his bed, she was all but in it. She leaned over, smoothing and tucking fresh sheets, her long legs showcased in ragged cutoffs.

His blood raced, a roar of speed that left him breathless, that turned the low ache he'd learned to live with into a sharp and gnawing pain. He could see himself springing forward, dragging her onto the bed, pulling and tearing at her clothes until he could hammer himself inside her.

And because he could, because he wanted to, he made himself stand where he was until he was certain his control was firmly in place.

"Grace?"

She straightened, whirled, pressed a hand to her heart. "Oh. I . . . oh." She couldn't speak, could barely think coherently. What would *he* think, she wondered giddily, if he knew she'd been fantasizing about rolling naked and sweaty over those crisp clean sheets with him?

Her cheeks had gone pink, charming him. "Didn't mean to sneak up on you."

"That's all right." She let out a long breath, but it did nothing to calm her racing heart. "I didn't expect anyone to . . . what are you doing home so early in the day?" Quickly she clasped her hands together because they wanted to grab at him. "Are you sick?"

"No."

"It's not even three o'clock."

"I know." He stepped into the room, saw her press her lips together, moisten them. Take it slow, he reminded himself, don't spook her. "Aubrey's not with you?"

"No, Julie's minding her. Julie got a new kitten and Aubrey wanted to stay, so . . ." He smelled of the water, salt, and sun. It made her light-headed.

"Then we've got some time." He came a little closer. "I wanted to see you alone."

"You did?"

"I've been wanting to see you alone since we made love that night." He lifted his hand, gently encircled the nape of her neck. "I've been wanting you," he said quietly and lowered his mouth to hers.

So soft, so tender, her heart seemed to turn one long, loose somersault in her chest. Her knees went weak. They trembled even as she threw her arms around him, as she answered that tentative kiss with a flash of heat. His fingers dug into her skin, his mouth bruised hers. For one wild and wicked moment, she thought he would take her where they stood, fast and frantic and free.

Then his hands gentled, smoothed over her. His lips softened, cruising over hers now. "Come to bed with me," he murmured. "Come to bed with me," even as he lowered her, covered her.

She arched against him, wanting and willing, impatient with the clothes that separated her flesh from his. It seemed like years since she had last touched him, had last felt those hard planes, those iron muscles. Moaning his name, she tugged up his shirt, let her hands possess, and possessing, they aroused.

His breath came raggedly, burning his throat. Her movements under him urged him to hurry, hurry, but he was afraid he would bruise her if he didn't take time, didn't take care. So he fought to slow the pace, to taste rather than devour, to caress rather than demand.

But where as she had once seduced him, she now destroyed him.

He tugged off her shirt, found her naked beneath it. She saw his eyes flash, turn to a burning blue that all but scorched her skin. He was careful, so careful not to bruise, not to frighten. Slow, to slow the pace even while the brutal desire to take, take more, take swiftly, swarmed into him.

Then his mouth was on her, sucking her in with a desperate hunger that threatened to consume them both. She threw her arm back, reached, but there was nothing to hold on to except empty air. He dragged her up, his mouth streaking down her torso, teeth scraping, until, gasping for air, she folded herself around him.

He couldn't wait, knew it would kill him to wait. The only thought in his head was now, it had to be now, and even that was wrapped in the rusty edges of primal need. He tugged at her shorts, cursing, then plunged his fingers inside her.

She bucked, cried out, came. He watched her eyes go opaque, her head fall back so that the long line of her throat was there for him to feast on. Battling the violent urge to drive himself into her, he continued to taste until the sharp void was filled.

Then he freed himself from his jeans and slipped into her. She cried out again, her muscles clamping tight around him.

And he lost his mind.

Speed and heat and force. More. He shoved her knees up and stroked deeper, harder, darkly thrilled when her nails bit into his shoulders. He plunged inside her, quivering with raw, blind greed.

Sensations swamped her, scraped at her, stripped her into one shuddering mass of need. She thought she might die from it. When the next orgasm slammed into her, a hard, hot fist, she thought she had.

And went limp, her hands sliding from Ethan's damp shoulders, the silver flash of energy draining to leave her exhausted. She heard his long, low groan, felt his body plunge, then stiffen. When he collapsed on her, panting, her lips curved in a smile of pure female satisfaction.

The sunlight dazzled her eyes as she stroked her hands down and over his hips. "Ethan." She turned her head to kiss his hair. "No, not yet," she murmured when he started to shift. "Not yet."

He'd been rough with her, and he cursed himself for allowing the knot on his control to slip. "Are you all right?"

"Mmmmmm. I could lie here all day, just like this."

"I didn't take the time I meant to."

"We don't have as much as most people."

"No." He lifted his head. "You wouldn't even tell me if I'd hurt you." So he looked for himself, carefully studying her face. And he saw in it the sleepy satisfaction of a woman well, if hurriedly, loved. "I guess I didn't."

"It was exciting. It was wonderful knowing you wanted me so much." Lazily, she twirled a lock of his sun-tipped hair around her finger and hugged the gorgeously wicked sensation of being naked in bed with him in the middle of the day. "I'd been worried that I wanted you more than you could ever want me."

"You couldn't." To prove it, he kissed her long and slow and deep. "This isn't the way I want it for you. Cramming minutes alone between chores. And using those minutes to jump into bed because it's all we've got."

"I've never made love in the middle of the day before." She smiled. "I liked it."

On a long breath, he lowered his brow to hers. If it had been possible, he would have spent the rest of the day right there, inside her. "We're going to have to figure out a way to find a little more time now and again."

"I've got tomorrow night off. You could come by for dinner . . . and stay."

"I ought to take you out somewhere."

"There's nowhere I want to go. I'd like it if we could

have dinner in." Then her smile spread. "I'll make you some tortellini. I just got this new recipe."

When he laughed, she threw her arms around him and chalked up another of the happiest moments of her life. "Oh, I love you, Ethan." She was so giddy with it that it took her a moment to realize he was no longer laughing, had gone very still. Her wildly bounding heart slowed, and chilled.

"Maybe you don't want me to say that, but I can't help feeling it. I don't expect you to say it back, or feel obligated to—"

His fingers pressed lightly against her lips to silence her. "Give me a minute, Grace," he said quietly. His system had flooded, rising tides of joys, hopes, fears. He couldn't think past them, not clearly. But he knew her, knew that what he said now, and how he said it, would be vitally important.

"I've had feelings for you for so long," he began, "I can't remember when I didn't have them. I've spent just as long telling myself I shouldn't have them, so all of this is taking me some time to get used to."

When he shifted this time, she didn't try to stop him. She nodded, avoided his eyes and reached for her clothes. "It's enough that you want me, maybe even need me a little. It's enough for now, Ethan. This is all so new for both of us."

"They're strong feelings, Grace. You matter to me more than any woman ever has."

She looked at him now. If he said it, she knew he meant it. Hope began to beat in her heart again. "If you had feelings for me, strong feelings, why didn't you ever let me know?"

"First you weren't old enough," He pushed his hand through his hair, knowing that that was an evasion, an excuse, and not the core of it. He couldn't tell her the core of it. "And I wasn't real comfortable having the kind of thoughts and feelings for you I was having when you were still in high school.''

She could have leaped up on the bed and danced. ''Since I was in high school? All this time?''

''Yeah, all this time. Then you were in love with somebody else, so I didn't have any right to feel anything but friendship.''

She let out a careful breath, because it would be a confession that shamed her. ''I was never in love with anybody else. It was always you.''

''Jack—''

''I never loved him, and everything that went wrong between us was more my fault than his. I let him be the first man to touch me because I never thought you would. And about the time I realized how foolish that was, I was pregnant.''

''You can't say it was your fault.''

''Yes, I can.'' To keep her hands busy, she began to tidy the bed. ''I knew he wasn't in love with me, but I married him because I was afraid not to. And for a while I was ashamed, angry and ashamed.'' She lifted a pillow, tucked it into its case. ''Until one night when I was lying in bed thinking my life was over, and I felt this fluttering inside me.''

She closed her eyes, pressed the pillow against her. ''I felt Aubrey, and it was so . . . so huge, that little flutter, that I wasn't ashamed or angry anymore. Jack gave me that.'' She opened her eyes again and carefully laid the pillow on the bed. ''I'm grateful to him, and I don't blame him for leaving. He never felt that flutter. Aubrey was never real to him.''

''He was a coward, and worse, for leaving you weeks before the baby was born.''

''Maybe, but I was a coward, and worse, for being with him, for marrying him when I never had a fraction of the feeling for him that I did for you.''

''You're the bravest woman I know, Grace.''

"It's easy to be brave when you have a child depending on you. I guess what I'm trying to tell you is that if I made a mistake, it was in going so long without letting you know I loved you. Whatever feelings you have for me, Ethan, are more than I ever thought you would have. And that's enough."

"I've been in love with you for the best part of ten years, and it's still not enough."

She'd picked up the second pillow, and now it slipped out of her hands. When tears swam into her eyes, she closed them, squeezed tight. "I thought I could live without ever hearing you say that. Now I need to hear you say it again so I can get my breath back."

"I love you, Grace."

Her lips curved, her eyes opened. "You sound so serious, almost sad when you say it." Wanting to see him smile again, she held out a hand. "Maybe you should practice."

His fingers had just touched hers when the screen door slammed downstairs. Feet pounded on the stairs. Even as they jerked apart, Seth raced down the hall. He skidded to a halt at the door to his room, then stood, stared.

He glanced at the bed, the sheets not quite smoothed out, the pillow on the floor. Then his gaze shifted, and filled with a bitter fury that was much too adult in his young face.

"You bastard." There was loathing in the tone as he snapped at Ethan, then disgust as his eyes locked on Grace. "I thought you were different."

"Seth." She took a step forward, but he turned on his heel and ran. "Oh, God, Ethan." When she started to rush after the boy, Ethan took her arm.

"No, I'll go after him. I know what he's feeling. Don't worry." He gave her arm a squeeze before walking out. Still, she followed him to the steps, worried sick. She'd never seen such dark hate in the eyes of a child.

"Damn it, Seth, I told you to hurry up." Cam slammed

in the front door just as Ethan hit the bottom of the steps. Cam glanced up, saw Grace, and felt a grin tug at his mouth. "Oops."

"I don't have time for lame jokes," Ethan shot back. "Seth just took off."

"What? Why?" It struck him even before the word was out. "Oh, shit. He must have gone out the back."

"I'm going after him." He shook his head before Cam could protest. "It's me he's pissed off at right now. It's me he figures let him down. I have to fix it." He glanced up to where Grace sat on the steps. "Look after her," he murmured to Cam and headed for the back door.

Ethan knew Seth would have headed into the woods, and he had to trust that the boy wouldn't run too far into the marsh. He was a survivor, Ethan thought. But relief shimmered through him when he heard the rustle of brush and old leaves.

It was simple enough to spot where Seth had veered off the path. Ethan pushed through tangled vines, the prickle of briars, and followed. The leaves on the trees that arched overhead blocked the glare and the worst of the sun's heat. But the humidity was immense.

Sweat ran down Ethan's back, dripped into his eyes, as he patiently walked, and waited. He was well aware that Seth was evading him, keeping a few yards ahead. Finally he sat on a fallen log, deciding it would be easier to let the boy come to him.

It took ten long minutes, with gnats swarming in clouds and mosquitoes sniffing for blood, but finally Seth emerged from a thicket and faced him.

"I'm not going back with you." He all but spat it out. "If you try to make me, I'll just run again."

"I'm not going to make you do anything." From his seat on the log, Ethan studied him. Seth's face was filthy, streaked with dirt and sweat, flushed with heat and fury. His legs and arms were thoroughly scratched from pushing through briars.

They were going to sting like fury, Ethan knew, when Seth cooled off enough to notice.

"You want to sit down and talk this out?" he asked mildly.

"I don't believe anything you say. You're a liar. You're both fucking liars. You gonna try to tell me you weren't screwing each other?"

"No, that's not what we were doing."

Seth flew at him so fast, Ethan was thrown off guard enough to take the first fist solidly in the jaw. He would think later, much later, that the kid threw a fine punch. But at the moment it took all his concentration to wrestle Seth to the ground.

"I'll kill you! You bastard, I'll kill you as soon as I get a chance." He wiggled and struggled and fought and waited for the rain of blows.

"Just hold on." Frustrated as the slick, sweaty arms kept sliding out of his grip, Ethan gave Seth a quick shake. "You're not getting anywhere this way. I'm bigger than you are, and I'll just pin you down till you run out of steam."

"Take your hands off me." Seth set his teeth and snarled. "Son of a whore."

It was a blow harder, and more sharply aimed, than the fist had been. Ethan caught his breath and nodded slowly. "Yeah, that's what I am. That's why you and I know each other. You can run when I let you up, Seth. You can spill filth all over me. That's what people expect from sons of whores. I'm going to figure you want better for yourself than that."

Ethan eased back, sat on his heels and wiped the blood off his mouth. "That's the second damn time you've punched me in the face. You try it again, and I'm going to wallop your ass so you don't sit for a month."

"I hate your fucking guts."

"Fine. But you're going to have to hate them for the right reasons."

"All you wanted was to get between her legs, and she spread them for you."

"Watch it." In a lightning move, Ethan grabbed Seth by the shirt and hauled him up to his knees. "Don't you talk about her that way. You had sense enough to recognize right off what kind of person Grace was. That's why you trusted her, why you cared about her."

"I don't give a shit about her," Seth claimed and had to swallow hard before the hot tears poured out.

"If you didn't, you wouldn't be so mad at both of us. And wouldn't be feeling like we let you down."

He let Seth go, then rubbed his hands over his face. He knew how miserably inept he could be at explaining emotions. Especially his own. "I'm going to talk to you straight." He dropped his hands. "You're right about what went on before you came home, you're just wrong about what it meant."

Seth's lips quivered into a snarl. "I know what fucking means."

"Yeah, the way you know it it's ugly sounds in the next room, fast gropes in the dark, sour smells, money changing hands."

"Just because you didn't pay her doesn't—"

"Be quiet," Ethan said patiently. "I used to think that's all it was, or the only kind there was. Hard and heartless, sometimes mean. All you want from the other is what you can get for yourself. So that makes it selfish, too. You get some release, pull your pants up and walk away. It's not always wrong. If it doesn't matter to either one of you, if it gets you through the night, it's not always wrong. But it's not the only way, and it sure as hell isn't the best way."

He remembered now thinking that he hoped someone else would explain such things to the boy when the time came. But it appeared that the time was now and he was in charge.

He couldn't say it all with a grin and a wink as Cam

might, or smooth and fancy as Phillip surely would. He could only speak from the heart and hope it was right.

"Sex can be the same as eating. Just filling a hunger. Sometimes you pay for a meal, sometimes you trade something, and if it's fair you're giving as much as you're taking."

"Sex is just sex. They just pretty it up to sell books and movies."

"Do you figure that's all there is between Anna and Cam?"

Seth moved his shoulders, but he was thinking.

"They've got something that matters, and lasts, that lives get built on. It's not what you've grown up with, or what I spent the first part of my life with—that's why I can tell you straight."

Ethan pressed his fingers to his eyes and ignored the swarm of bugs and the sweat. "It's different when you care, when the other person isn't just a face or a body that's convenient and willing. I've had that. Most people do along the way. It's different when it's just that one person who matters, who makes it right. When it isn't all hunger pushing at you. When you want, more than anything, to give back more than you take. I never had with anyone what I have with Grace."

Seth shrugged and looked away, but not before Ethan saw the misery on his face. "I know you've got feelings for her, and that they're real and strong and important. Maybe part of you wanted her to be perfect, not to have the needs other women do. I think a bigger part of you wanted to protect her, to make sure nobody hurt her. So I'm telling you what I just finished finally telling her. I love her. I've never loved anybody else."

Seth stared off into the marsh. He hurt all over, but the worst of it was shame. "Does she love you back?"

"Yeah, she does. Damned if I can figure out why."

Seth thought he knew why. Ethan was strong, and he didn't put on a big show. He did what had to be done.

What was right. "I was going to take care of her when I got older. I guess you think that's pretty lame."

"No." He suddenly, urgently, wanted to pull the boy against him, but he knew the timing was wrong. "No, I think that's pretty great. It makes me proud of you."

Seth's gaze flicked up, then quickly away again. "I kind of, you know, love her. Sort of. Not like I want to see her naked or anything," he added quickly. "Just—"

"I get it." Ethan clamped down on the tip of his tongue to stifle the chuckle. The quick surge of amused relief tasted finer than an icy beer on a hot day. "Kind of like she was a sister, like you wanted the best for her."

"Yeah." And Seth sighed. "Yeah, I guess that's it."

Thoughtfully, Ethan sucked air between his teeth. "It's got to be tough for a guy to walk in and see that his sister's been with some guy."

"I hurt her. I wanted to."

"Yeah, you did. You'll have to apologize if you want to put things right with her."

"She'll think I'm stupid. She won't want to talk to me."

"She wanted to come after you herself. By this time, I'd say she's pacing around the backyard, worried sick."

Seth sucked in a breath that was too close to a sob to suit either of them. "I razzed Cam until he brought me home for my ball glove. And when I . . . I saw you in there, it made me think of how I would come back to wherever Gloria was living, and she'd be doing it with some guy."

Where sex was a business, Ethan thought, both ugly and mean. "It's hard to put those things aside, or let yourself believe there's a different way." Since he was still working on it himself, Ethan spoke carefully. "That making love, when you care, when it matters, when things are right, it's clean."

Seth sniffled, wiped at his eyes. "Gnats," he muttered.

"Yeah, they're a bitch out here."

"You should've slugged me, for saying that shit."

"You're right," Ethan decided after a moment. "I'll slug you next time. Now, let's go home."

He rose, brushed off his pants, then held out a hand. Seth stared up at him, saw kindness, patience, compassion. Qualities in a man he might have sneered at once because he'd found so little of them in anyone who had touched his life.

He put his hand in Ethan's and, without realizing it, left it there as they walked down the path. "How come you didn't hit me back even once?"

Little boy, Ethan thought, you've had too many hands raised against you in your short life. "Maybe I was afraid you could take me."

Seth snorted, blinking furiously at tears that still wanted to come. "Shit."

"Well, you're small," Ethan said, taking the cap from Seth's back pocket and snugging it down on Seth's head. "But you're a wiry little bastard."

Seth had to take long breaths as they came close to where the sunlight struck the edge of the woods, slanting white light.

He saw Grace, as Ethan had predicted, in the yard, hugging her arms as if she were chilled. She dropped them, took a quick step forward, then stopped.

Ethan felt Seth's hand flex in his and gave it a quick encouraging squeeze. "It'd go a long way to making things up to her," Ethan murmured, "if you were to run up and hug her. Grace is big on hugs."

It was what he'd wanted to do, what he was afraid to risk. He looked up at Ethan, jerked a shoulder, cleared his throat. "I guess I could, if it'd make her feel better."

Ethan stood back, watched the boy race across the lawn, watched Grace's face light with a smile as she threw open her arms to take him in.

THIRTEEN

IF YOU WERE GOING TO have to work over a long holiday weekend, Phillip figured, it might as well be at something fun. He loved his job. What was advertising, anyway, but a knowledge of people and of which buttons to push to nudge them into opening their wallets?

It was, he often thought, an accepted, creative, even expected twist on picking those wallets. For a man who had spent the first half of his life as a thief, it was the perfect career.

On this day before the celebration of America's independence, he put his skills to use in the boatyard, schmoozing a potential client. He much preferred it to manual labor.

"You'll forgive the surroundings." Phillip waved a well-manicured hand, encompassing the enormous space, the exposed rafters and hanging lights, the yet-to-be-painted walls and scarred floors. "My brothers and I believe in putting our efforts into the product and keeping our overhead minimal. Those are benefits that we pass along to our clients.''

At which time, Phillip thought, they had exactly one—with another in the box and this one nibbling at the line.

''Hmmm.'' Jonathan Kraft rubbed his chin. He was in his mid-thirties and fortunate enough to be a fourth-generation member of the pharmaceutical Krafts. Since his great-grandfather's humble beginnings as a storefront pharmacist in Boston, his family had built and expanded an empire on buffered aspirin and analgesics. It allowed Jonathan to indulge in his great love of sailing.

He was tall, fit, tanned. His hair was mink-brown and perfectly styled to showcase his square-jawed, handsome face. He wore buff-colored chinos, a navy cotton shirt, and well-broken-in Top-Siders. His watch was a Rolex, his belt hand-tooled Italian leather.

He looked exactly like what he was: a privileged, wealthy man with a love of the outdoors.

''You've only been in business a few months.''

''Officially,'' Phillip said with a flashing smile. His hair was a rich, deep bronze, styled to make the most of a face that the angels had gifted with an extra kiss of pure male beauty. He wore fashionably faded Levi's, a green cotton shirt, and olive-drab Supergas. His eyes were shrewd, his smile charming.

He looked exactly like what he'd made himself into: a sophisticated urbanite with an affection for fashion and the sea.

''We've built or worked on teams that built a number of boats over the years.'' Smoothly, he guided Jonathan toward the framed sketches hanging on the wall. Seth's artwork was displayed rustically, as Phillip felt suited the ambience of a traditional boatyard.

''My brother Ethan's skipjack. One of the handful that still goes under sail every winter to dredge for oysters in the Chesapeake. She's had over ten years in service.''

''She's a beauty.'' Jonathan's face turned dreamy, as

Phillip had suspected it would. However a man chose to pick wallets, he had to gauge his marks. "I'd like to see her."

"I'm sure we can arrange that."

He let Jonathan linger before nudging him gently along. "Now, you may recognize this one." He indicated the drawing of a sleek racing skiff. "The Circe. My brother Cameron was involved with both her design and her construction."

"And she beat my *Lorilee* to the finish line two years running." Jonathan grimaced good-naturedly. "Of course, Cam was leading the team."

"He knows his boats." Phillip heard the buzz of a drill from where Cameron worked belowdecks. He intended to bring Cam into this shortly.

"The sloop currently under construction is primarily Ethan's design, though Cam added some points. We're dedicated to serving the client's needs and wishes." He led Jonathan over to where Seth continued his hull sanding. Ethan stood on deck, attaching the rubrails. "He wanted speed, stability, and some luxuries."

Phillip knew the hull was a brilliant show of smooth lap construction—he'd put in plenty of sweaty hours on it himself. "She's built for show as well as function. Teak from stem to stern, at the client's direction," he added, knocking his knuckles cheerfully against the hull.

Phillip wiggled his brows at Ethan. Recognizing the signal, Ethan bit back a sigh. He knew he was going to hate this part, but Phillip had pointed out that it was good business to bring the potential client into the fold.

"The joints are wedged and married, without glue." Ethan rolled his shoulders, feeling as though he were giving an oral school report. He'd always hated them. "We figured if the old-time boat builders could make a joint last a century or so without glue, so could we. And I've seen too many glued joints fail."

"Hmmm," Jonathan said again, and Ethan took a breath.

"The hull's caulked in the traditional way—stranded cotton. Planking's tight, wood to wood on the inside. We rolled two strands of cotton in most of the seams. Hardly needed the mallet. Then we payed them with standard seam components."

Jonathan hummed again. He had only a vague idea what Ethan was talking about. He sailed boats—boats that he'd bought fresh and clean and finished. But he liked the sound of it.

"She appears to be a fine, tight boat. A pretty pleasure craft. I'll be looking for speed and efficiency as well as aesthetics."

"We'll see that you get it." Phillip smiled broadly, waving a finger at Ethan behind Jonathan's head. It was time to pull out the next round.

Ethan headed belowdecks, where Cam was fitting out the framing for an under-the-bunk cabinet. "Your turn up there," he muttered.

"Phil got him on the string?"

"Couldn't tell by me. I gave my little speech, and the guy just nodded and made noises. You ask me, he didn't know what the hell I was talking about."

"Of course he doesn't. Jonathan hires people to worry about maintaining his boats. He's never scraped a hull or replanked a deck in his life." Cam rose from his crouch, worked the stiffness out of his knees. "He's the kind of guy who drives a Maserati without knowing dick about engines. But he'd have been impressed with your salty waterman's drawl and rugged good looks."

As Ethan gave a snorting laugh, Cam elbowed past him. "I'll go give him my push."

He climbed topside and managed to look credibly surprised to see Jonathan onboard, studying the gunwales. "Hey, Kraft, how's it going?"

"Fast and far." With genuine pleasure, Jonathan shook

Cam's hand. "I was surprised when you didn't show at the San Diego regatta this summer."

"Got myself married."

"So I hear. Congratulations. And now you're building boats instead of racing them."

"I wouldn't count me out of racing entirely. I'm toying with building myself a cat over the winter if business slacks off any."

"Keeping busy?"

"Word gets out," Cam said easily. "A boat by Quinn means quality. Smart people want the best—when they can afford it." He grinned, fast and slick. "Can you afford it?"

"I'm thinking of a cat myself. Your brother must have mentioned it."

"Yeah, he ran it by me. You want light, fast, and tight. Ethan and I have been modifying a design for what I had in mind for me."

"That's bullshit," Seth murmured, only loud enough for Phillip to hear.

"Sure." Phillip winked at him. "But it's Class A bullshit." He leaned a little closer to Seth as Cam and Jonathan launched into the lure of racing a catboat. "Cam knows that while the guy likes him fine, he's competitive. Never beat Cam in a head-to-head race. So . . ."

"So he'd pay buckets of money to have Cam build him a boat that not even Cam could beat."

"There you go." Proud, Phillip gave Seth a light punch on the shoulder. "You got a quick brain there. Keep using it, and you won't be spending all your time sanding hulls. Now, kid, watch the master."

He straightened, beamed up. "I'd be happy to show you the drawings, Jonathan. Why don't we go into my office? I'll dig them out for you."

"Wouldn't mind taking a look." Jonathan climbed down. "The problem is, I need this boat seaworthy by

March first. I'll need time to test her, work out the kinks, break her in before the summer races."

"March first." Phillip pursed his lips, then he shook his head. "That might be a problem. Quality comes first here. It takes time to build a champion. I'll look over our schedule," he added, dropping an arm over Jonathan's shoulder as they walked. "We'll see what we can work out—but the contract's already in place, and the work sheets tell me May is the soonest we can deliver the top-quality product you expect and deserve."

"That's not going to give me much time to get the feel of her," Jonathan complained.

"Believe me, Jonathan, a boat by Quinn is going to feel fine. Just fine," he added, glancing back at his brothers with a quick and wolfish grin before he nudged Jonathan inside the office.

"He'll buy us till May," Cam decided, and Ethan nodded.

"Or he'll make it April and skin the poor bastard for a bonus."

"Either way." Cam clamped a hand on Ethan's shoulder. "We're going to have ourselves another contract by end of day."

Below, Seth snorted. "Shit, he'll wrap it up by lunch-time. The guy's toast."

Cam tucked his tongue in his cheek. "Two o'clock, soonest."

"Noon," Seth said, peering up at him.

"Two bucks?"

"Sure. I can use the money."

"YOU KNOW," CAM SAID as he dug out his wallet, "before you came along to ruin my life, I'd just won a bundle in Monte Carlo."

Seth sneered cheerfully. "This ain't Monte Carlo."

"You're telling me." He passed the bills over, then

winced when he saw his wife come into the building. "Cool it. Social worker heading in. She's not going to approve of minors gambling."

"Hey, I won," Seth pointed out, but he stuffed the bills in his pocket. "You bring any food?" he asked Anna.

"Oh, no, I didn't. Sorry." Distracted, she dragged a hand through her hair. There was a sick ball in the pit of her stomach that she did her best to ignore. She smiled, a curve of lips that didn't quite manage to reach her eyes. "Didn't you all pack lunch?"

"Yeah, but you usually bring something better."

"This time I've been pretty tied up putting food together for the picnic tomorrow." She ran a hand over his head, then left it lying on his shoulder. She needed the contact. "I just . . . thought I'd take a break and see how things were going around here."

"Phil just nailed this rich guy for a ton of money."

"Good, that's good," she said absently. "Then we should celebrate. Why don't I spring for ice cream? You think you can handle picking up some hot fudge sundaes at Crawford's?"

"Yeah." His face split into a grin. "I can handle it."

She dragged money out of her purse, hoping he didn't notice that her hands weren't quite steady. "No nuts on mine, remember?"

"Sure. I got it. I'm gone." He raced out, and she watched him, heartsick.

"What is it, Anna?" Cam put his hands on her shoulders, turned her to face him. "What happened?"

"Give me a minute. I broke records getting here, and I need some time to settle." She blew out a breath, drew one in, and felt marginally steadier. "Go get your brothers, Cam."

"Okay." But he lingered, rubbing his hands over her shoulders. It was rare for her to look so shaken. "Whatever it is, we'll fix it."

He walked to the cargo doors, where Ethan and Phil stood outside arguing over baseball. "Something's up," he said briefly. "Anna's here. She sent Seth off. She's upset."

She was standing by a workbench, with one of Seth's drawing books open, when they came in. It made her eyes sting to see her own face, carefully, skillfully sketched by the young boy's hand.

He'd been more than a case file, almost from the start. And now he was hers, as much as Ethan and Phillip were hers. Family. She couldn't stand to think that anything or anyone would hurt her family.

But she was steadier when she turned, scanned the quiet and concerned faces of the men who'd become essential to her life. "This came in today's mail." Her hand no longer trembled as she reached into her purse and pulled out the letter.

"It's addressed to 'The Quinns.' Just 'The Quinns,'" she repeated. "From Gloria DeLauter. I opened it. I thought it best, and well, my name's Quinn now, too."

She offered it to Cam. Saying nothing, he took out the single sheet of lined paper and passed the envelope to Phillip.

"She mailed it from Virginia Beach," Phillip murmured. "We lost her in North Carolina. She's sticking with the beaches, but coming north."

"What does she want?" Ethan stuffed hands that had curled into fists into his pockets. A low, simmering rage was already pumping through his blood.

"What you'd expect," Cam answered shortly. "Money. 'Dear Quinns,'" Cam read. "'I heard how Ray died. It's too bad. You might not know that Ray and me had an agreement. I think you'll want to make good on it since you're keeping Seth. I guess he's pretty settled in there in that nice house. I miss him. You don't know what a sacrifice it was for me to give him up to Ray, but I wanted what was best for my only son.'"

"You ought to have your violin," Phillip muttered to Ethan.

" 'I knew Ray would be good to him,' " Cam continued. " 'He did right by the three of you, and Seth's got
his blood.' "

He stopped reading for a moment. There it was, in black
and white. "Truth or lie?" He looked up at his brothers.

"That's to deal with later." Ethan felt the ache begin
around his heart and move in to squeeze. But he shook his
head. "Read the rest."

"Okay. 'Ray knew how much it hurt me to part with
the boy, so he helped me out. But now that he's gone, I'm
starting to worry that it might not be the best place for
Seth there with you. I'm willing to be convinced. If you're
set on keeping him, you'll keep up Ray's promise of helping me out. I'm going to need some money, like a sign
that you've got good intentions. Five thousand. You can
send it to me, care of General Delivery here in Virginia
Beach. I'll give you two weeks, figuring the mail's kind
of unreliable. If I don't hear back, I'll know you don't
really want the kid. I'll come get him. He must be missing
me something awful. Be sure to tell him his mom loves
him, and might be seeing him real soon.' "

"Bitch," was Phillip's first comment. "She's testing us
out, trying her hand at a little more blackmail to see if
we'll fall for it the way Dad did."

"You can't." Anna put a hand on Cam's arm, felt the
quiver of rage. "You have to let the system work. You
have to trust me to see that she doesn't do this. In court—"

"Anna." Cam shoved the letter into the hand Ethan had
held out. "We're not going to put that boy through a court
case. Not if there's another way."

"You don't mean to pay her. Cam—"

"I don't mean for her to have one fucking cent." He
prowled away, struggling to fight off fury. "She thinks
she's got us by the balls, but she's wrong. We're not one
lone old man." He whirled back, eyes blazing. "Let's see
her try to get through us to lay hands on Seth."

"She was pretty careful how she worded things," Ethan

commented as he scanned the letter again. "Doesn't make it less of a threat, but she's not stupid."

"She's greedy," Phillip put in. "If she's already angling for more after what Dad paid her, she's testing the depth of the well."

"She sees you as her source now," Anna agreed. "And there's no predicting what she'll do if she knows that source isn't easily tapped." Pausing, she pressed her fingers to her temples, ordered herself to think. "If she comes back into the county and attempts to make contact with Seth, I can have her detained, legally barred—at least temporarily—from direct contact with him. You have guardianship. And Seth is old enough to speak for himself. The question is, will he?"

She lifted her hands, frustrated, let them fall. "He's told me very little about his life before he came here. I'll need specifics in order to block any custody attempt on her part."

"He doesn't want her. And she doesn't want him." Ethan resisted, barely, crumpling the letter into a ball and heaving it. "Unless he's worth the price of another fix. She let her johns try for him."

Anna shifted to face him, kept her eyes calm and direct on his. "Did Seth tell you that? Did he tell you there had been sexual abuse and she'd been a party to it?"

"He told me enough." Ethan's mouth went hard and grim. "And it's up to him if he wants to tell anybody else and see it put in some goddamn county report."

"Ethan." Anna laid a hand on his rigid arm. "I love him, too. I only want to help him."

"I know." He stepped back because the anger was too fierce and too likely to spew on everyone. "I'm sorry, but there are times the system makes it worse. Makes you feel like you're being swallowed up." He struggled to block out the echo of pain. "He's going to know he's got us, with or without any system, to stand with him."

"The lawyer needs to know she made contact." Phillip

took the letter from Ethan, folded it, and tucked it back into the envelope. "And we have to decide how we're going to handle it. My first impulse is to go down to Virginia Beach, dig her out of her hole, and tell her in a way she'd understand just what's going to happen to her if she comes within fifty miles of Seth."

"Threatening her won't help . . ." Anna began.

"But it would feel damn good." Cam bared his teeth. "Let me do it."

"On the other hand," Phillip continued, "I think it might be very effective—and look very good if it ever comes to a legal battle—if our pal Gloria got an official letter from Seth's caseworker. Outlining the status, the options, and the conclusions reached. Contacting or attempting to contact a birth mother who may be rethinking giving up custody of her child—a child who's in your files—would come within the parameters of your job, wouldn't it, Anna?"

She mulled it over, knowing it was a fine line and expert balance would be required to walk it. "I can't threaten her. But . . . I may be able to make her stop and think. But the big question is, do we tell Seth?"

"He's afraid of her," Cam murmured. "Damn it, the kid's just starting to relax, to believe he's safe. Why do we have to tell him she's poking her finger back into his life?"

"Because he's got a right to know." Ethan spoke quietly. His temper had leveled off, and he was able to think clearly again. "He's got a right to know what he might have to fight. If you know what's after you, you've got a better chance. And because," he added, "the letter was addressed to the Quinns. He's one of us."

"I'd rather burn it," Phillip muttered. "But you're right."

"We'll all tell him," Cam agreed.

"I'd like to do the talking."

Both Cam and Phillip stared at Ethan. "You would?"

"He might take it easier from me." He looked over as Seth came through the door. "So let's find out."

"Mother Crawford put on extra hot fudge. Man, she just poured it on. There's about a million tourists up on the waterfront, and . . ."

His excited chatter trailed off. His eyes went from gleeful to wary. Inside his chest, his heart began to drum. He recognized trouble, bad trouble. It had its own smell. "What's the deal?"

Anna took the large bag from him and turned to set the plastic-topped dishes of ice cream out. "Why don't you sit down, Seth?"

"I don't need to sit down." It was easier to get a head start running if you were already on your feet.

"There was a letter came today." It was best, Ethan knew, if hard news was delivered fast and clean. "From your mother."

"She's here?" The fear was back, sharp as a scalpel. Seth took one quick step in retreat, going stiff as a board when Cam laid a hand on his shoulder.

"No, she's not here. But we are. You remember that."

Seth shuddered once, then planted his feet. "What the hell did she want? Why's she sending letters? I don't want to see it."

"Then you don't have to," Anna assured him. "Why don't you let Ethan explain, then we'll talk about what we're going to do."

"She knows Ray's dead," Ethan began. "I gotta figure she's known right along, but she's taken her time getting to it."

"He gave her money." Seth swallowed hard to gulp down the fear. Quinns weren't afraid, he told himself. They weren't afraid of anything. "She took off. She doesn't care that he's dead."

"I don't suppose she does, but she's hoping for more money. That's what the letter's about."

"She wants me to pay her?" Fresh and bright fear exploded in Seth's brain. "I don't have any money. What's she writing to me for money for?"

"She wasn't writing to you."

Seth took a ragged breath and concentrated on Ethan's face. The eyes were clear and patient, the mouth firm and serious. Ethan knew, was all he could think. Ethan knew what it was like. He knew about the rooms, the smells, the fat hands in the dark.

"She wants you to pay her." Part of him wanted to beg them to do it. To pay her whatever she wanted. He would swear in blood that he would do anything they asked of him for the rest of his life to honor the debt.

But he couldn't. Not with Ethan watching him, and waiting. And knowing.

"If you do, she'll just come back for more. She'll keep coming back." Seth rubbed the back of a sweaty hand over his mouth. "As long as she knows where I am she'll keep coming back. I have to go someplace else, someplace where she can't find me."

"You're not going anywhere." Ethan crouched so they were closer to eye level. "And she's not going to get any more money. She's not going to win."

Slowly, mechanically, Seth shook his head back and forth. "You don't know her."

"I know pieces of her. She's smart enough to know we're set on keeping you with us. That we love you enough to pay." He saw the flash of emotion in Seth's eyes before the boy lowered them. "And we would pay if that would end it, if that would ease things. But it won't end or ease it. It's like you said. She'd just come back."

"What are you going to do?"

"It's what we're going to do now. All of us," he said and waited for Seth's gaze to settle on his face again. "We'll go on as we've been going on, mostly. Phil will talk to the lawyer so we got that end covered."

"You tell him I'm not going back with her," Seth said

furiously, shooting a desperate look at Phillip. "No matter what, I'm not going back."

"I'll tell him."

"Anna's going to write her a letter," Ethan continued.

"What kind of letter?"

"A smart one," Ethan said with the hint of a smile. "With all those fifty-dollar words and that official-sounding stuff. She'll be doing it as your caseworker, to let Gloria know we've got the system and the law behind us. It might give her pause to think."

"She hates social workers," Seth put in.

"Good." For the first time in more than an hour, Anna smiled and meant it. "People who hate something are usually afraid of it, too."

"One thing that would help, Seth, if you can do it—"

He turned back to Ethan. "What do I have to do?"

"If you could talk to Anna, tell her how things were before—as close to exact as you can manage."

"I don't want to talk about it. It's over. I'm not going back."

"I know." Gently, Ethan put his hands on Seth's trembling shoulders. "And I know talking about it can be almost like being there again. It took me a long time to be able to tell my mother—to tell Stella. To say it all out loud, even though she already knew most of it. It started to get better after that. And it helped her and Ray get the legal crap handled."

Seth thought of *High Noon,* of heroes. Of Ethan. "It's the right thing to do?"

"Yeah, it's the right thing."

"Will you come with me?"

"Sure." Ethan rose, held out a hand. "We'll go home and talk it through."

FOURTEEN

"READY? MAMA? TIME to go?"

"Almost, Aubrey." Grace put the finishing touches on her potato salad, sprinkling paprika on to give it zest and color.

Aubrey had been asking her the same question since seven-thirty that morning. Grace decided the only reason she hadn't run out of patience with her daughter was because she felt just as anxious and eager as a two year old herself.

"*Maaamaaa.*"

At the deep frustration in Aubrey's voice, Grace had to swallow a chuckle. "Let me see." Grace tucked the clear wrap tidily around the bowl before she turned and studied her little girl. "You look pretty."

"I have a bow." In a purely female gesture, Aubrey lifted a hand and patted the ribbon Grace had threaded through her curls.

"A pink bow."

"Pink." With a smile, Aubrey beamed up at her mother. "Pretty Mama."

"Thanks, baby." She hoped Ethan thought so. How would he look at her? she wondered. How should they behave? There would be so many people there, and no one—well, besides the Quinns—no one knew they were in love.

In love, she thought with a long, dreamy sigh. It was such a marvelous place to be. She blinked when little arms wrapped around her legs and squeezed.

"Mama! Ready?"

Laughing, Grace hauled her up for a big hug and kiss. "All right. Let's go."

No GENERAL IN THE hours before a decisive battle ever ordered his troops into action with more authority and determination than Anna Spinelli Quinn.

"Seth, you set those folding chairs up under the shade trees over there. Isn't Phillip back with the extra ice yet? He's been gone twenty minutes. Cam! You and Ethan are putting those picnic tables too close together."

"Minute ago," Cam said under his breath, "they were too far apart." But he walked backward, hauling the table another foot.

"That's good. That's fine." Armed with bright red, white, and blue striped cloths, Anna hurried across the lawn. "Now you can move the umbrella tables, nearer the water, I think."

Cam narrowed his eyes. "You said you wanted them over by the trees."

"I changed my mind." She scanned the yard as she spread the tablecloths.

Cam opened his mouth to protest, but caught Ethan's warning shake of the head in time. His brother was right, he decided. Arguing wasn't going to change a thing.

Anna had been on a tear all morning, and when he said as much to Ethan as they moved out of earshot, it was with the irritation of the baffled.

"We're talking about a practical-minded, organized woman here," Cam added. "I don't know what's gotten into her. It's just a damn picnic."

"I guess women get that way over things like this," was Ethan's opinion. He remembered the way Grace had refused to let him take a shower in his own bathroom just because Cam and Anna were coming home. Who knew what went on in a female mind?

"She wasn't this bad over the wedding reception."

"I expect she had her mind on other things then."

"Yeah." Cam grunted as he picked up one of the round umbrella tables—again—and began to cart it toward the sun-dazzled water. "Phil's the smart one. He got the hell out of the house."

"He's always had a knack for it," Ethan agreed.

He didn't mind moving tables, or setting up chairs, or any of the dozens of chores—small and large—that Anna came up with. It helped keep his mind off weightier matters.

If he let himself think too much, he started to get a picture of Gloria DeLauter in his head. Because he'd never seen her, the image his brain conjured up was a tall, fleshy woman with tangled straw-colored hair, hard eyes smeared with sooty makeup, a mouth lax from too many trips to the bottle, too many matings with the needle.

The eyes were blue, like his own. The mouth, despite its slick coat of lipstick, shaped like his own. And he knew it wasn't Seth's mother's face he was seeing. It was his own mother's.

The picture wasn't dim and fuzzy as it had become over time. It was sharp and clear as yesterday.

It still had the power to ice his blood, to churn a sick animal fear in his stomach that was kin to shame.

It still made him want to strike out with bruised and bloodied fists.

He turned slowly as he heard the squeal of joy. And saw Aubrey racing over the lawn, her eyes bright as sunbeams. And saw Grace, standing by the porch steps, her smile warm and just a little shy.

You've got no right, the nasty little voice in his head hissed. *No right to touch something so fine and bright.*

But, oh, he had a need, one that swamped him like a storm surge and left him floundering. When Aubrey launched herself at him, his arms reached down, swung her up and around as she shrieked in delight.

He wanted her to be his. With a bone-deep longing, he wanted this perfect, this innocent, this laughing child to belong to him.

Grace's knees wobbled as she walked to them. The picture they made flashed into her mind, into her heart, where she knew it would imprint itself. The lanky man with big hands and a serious smile and the golden-bright child with a pink bow in her hair.

The sun poured over them as full and rich as the love that poured from her heart.

"She's been ready to come over since she opened her eyes this morning," Grace began. "I thought we could come a little early and I'd give Anna a hand." He was watching her so intently, so quietly, her nerves did a rapid dance under her skin. "There's not much left to do, but—"

She broke off because his arm had snaked out, wrapped around her fast and hard to pull her against him. She had time to draw in one startled breath before his mouth came down on hers. Rough and needy, it shot bolts of heat into her blood, sent her startled brain into a dizzying spin. Dimly she heard Aubrey's happy squeal.

"Kiss, Mama!"

Oh, yes, Grace thought, sprinting to catch up to this frantic pace he'd set. Please. Kiss me, kiss me, kiss me.

She thought she heard some sound from him, a sigh perhaps, that came from someplace too deep inside to make a sound. His lips softened. The hand that had clutched the back of her shirt like a man gripping his own life opened, stroked. This gentler, sweeter emotion that shimmered from him was no calmer than that first whip of greed; it only gilded the edges of the yearning he'd stirred.

She could smell him, heat and man. She could smell her daughter, powder and child. Her arms circled them both, instinctively making them a unit, holding there when the kiss ended and she could press her face into his shoulder.

He'd never kissed her in front of anyone. She knew Cam had only been a few feet away when Ethan had taken hold of her. And Seth would have seen . . . and Anna.

What did it mean?

"Kiss me!" Aubrey demanded, patting her hand against Ethan's cheek and puckering up.

He obliged her, then nuzzled at her neck where it would tickle and make her laugh. Then he turned his head and brushed his lips over Grace's hair. "I didn't mean to grab you that way."

"I was hoping you did," she murmured. "It made me feel you've been thinking about me. Wanting me."

"I've been thinking about you, Grace. I've been wanting you."

Because Aubrey was wiggling, he set her down and let her run off toward Seth and the dogs. "I meant I didn't mean to be rough with you."

"You weren't. I'm not fragile, Ethan."

"Yes, you are." When he saw Aubrey fall on Foolish so they could wrestle in the grass, he looked back at Grace, into her eyes. "Delicate," he said softly, "like the white china with pink roses we only use on Thanksgiving."

It made her heart flutter pleasantly that he would think so, even if she knew better. "Ethan—"

"I was always afraid I'd pick it up wrong, break it in half from being clumsy. I never really got used to it."

He skimmed his thumb lightly across her cheekbone, where the skin was warm and soft and silky. Then he dropped his hand to his side. "We'd better pitch in before Anna drives Cam over the edge."

GRACE'S STOMACH CON-tinued to flutter with nervous delight even when she went about the chore of carting food from the kitchen out to the picnic table. She would catch herself stopping, a bowl or platter in hand, to watch Ethan drive the horseshoe stakes into the ground.

Look how his muscles ripple under his shirt. He's so strong. Look at the way he shows Seth how to hold the hammer. He's so patient. He's wearing the jeans I washed just the other day. The cuffs have gone white and they're starting to fray. There was sixty-three cents in the right front pocket.

See how Aubrey climbs up on his back. She knows she'll be welcome. Yes, he reaches back, gives her a little hitch to secure her there, then goes back to work. He doesn't mind when she steals his cap and tries to put it on her own head. His hair's gotten long, and the ends glint in the sun when he shakes it back out of his eyes.

I hope he keeps forgetting to go to the barber for a while yet.

I wish I could touch it, right now. Make those thick, sun-bleached ends curl around my finger.

"It's a nice picture," Anna murmured from behind her and made Grace jolt. With a quiet laugh, Anna set down the enormous bowl of pasta salad. "I do the same thing with Cam sometimes. Just stand and watch him. The Quinns are very watchable men."

"I think I'm just going to take a quick glance, then I

can't stop looking.'' She grinned when Ethan rose, Aubrey still clinging to his back, and turned slow circles as if trying to find her.

"He has a wonderful, natural way with children," Anna commented. "He'll make a wonderful father."

Grace felt heat rise up into her cheeks. She'd been thinking the same thing. It was hard to believe that only a few weeks before she'd told her own mother she would never marry again. And now she was thinking, and wondering. And waiting.

It had been easy to put all thoughts of marriage aside when she hadn't believed she could ever have a life with Ethan. She made a poor job of marriage before because her heart had belonged to someone other than her husband. That was her fault, and she accepted the responsibility for the failure.

But she could make marriage shine with Ethan, couldn't she? They could build a home and a family and a future based on love and trust and honesty.

He wouldn't move quickly, she mused. It wasn't his way. But he loved her. She understood Ethan well enough to know that marriage would be the next step.

She was already poised to take it.

THE SMELL OF BURGERS smoking on the grill, the yeasty tang of beer pumped from a cold keg. The sounds of children laughing and adult voices lifted in bright conversation or lowered in juicy gossip. The low roar of a boat zipping over the water, with the thrilled shouts of its teenage occupants, the metallic clang of a horseshoe striking home.

There were scents and sounds and sights. There was the snappy red, white, and blue of the cloths covering the tables that were crowded with bowls and plates and platters and casseroles.

Mrs. Cutter's cherry pie. The Wilsons' shrimp salad. What was left of the bushel of corn the Crawfords had brought along. Jell-O molds and fruit salad, fried chicken and early vine tomatoes. People were spread out and gathered. On chairs, on the lawn, down at the dock, and on the porch.

Several men stood with hands on hips, watching the horseshoe match, their faces sober in the way men had when they kibitzed a sporting event. Babies napped in carriers or willing arms while others wailed for attention. The young splashed and swam in the cool water, and the old fanned themselves in the shade.

The sky was clear, the heat immense.

Grace watched Foolish nosing along the ground in search of dropped food. He'd found plenty, and she imagined he'd be sick as a—well, a dog—before the day was over.

She hoped it was never over.

She waded into the water, gripping Aubrey firmly despite the colorful floats wrapped around her arms. She dipped her daughter down, laughing when Aubrey's little legs began to kick with delight.

"In, in, in!" Aubrey demanded.

"Honey, I didn't bring my bathing suit." But she eased out a little more, until the water lapped at her knees, so she could let Aubrey splash.

"Grace! Grace! Watch this!"

Obliging, Grace squinted against the sun and watched Seth take a running leap off the dock, tucking knees, wrapping arms, and hitting the water like a bomb so that it shot it up in a glittering fountain. And all over her.

"Cannonball," he announced proudly when he surfaced. Then he grinned. "Gee, you got all wet."

"Seth, take me." Straining, Aubrey held out her arms. "Take me."

"Can't, Aub. Got bombs to blow." When he swam off to join the other boys, Aubrey began to sniffle.

"He'll come back and play later," Grace assured her.

"Now!"

"Soon." To ward off what Grace knew could turn into a fine temper, she tossed Aubrey up, catching her as she hit the water. She let her paddle and splash, then let her go, biting her lip as Aubrey reveled in the freedom.

"Swimming, Mama."

"I see that, baby. You're a good swimmer. But you stay close."

As Grace expected, the sun and water and excitement combined to tire the child out. When Aubrey blinked and widened her eyes as she did when she fought sleep, Grace drew her in. "Let's get a drink, Aubrey."

"Swimming."

"We'll swim some more. I'm thirsty." Grace lifted her, braced for the minor battle that was bound to come.

"What you got there, Grace, a mermaid?"

Mother and daughter looked up onto the wet slope and saw Ethan.

"She sure is pretty," he said, smiling into Aubrey's mutinous face. "Can I have her?"

"I don't know. Maybe." She leaned close to Aubrey's ear. "He thinks you're a mermaid."

Aubrey's lip trembled, but she'd nearly forgotten why she'd wanted to cry. "Like Ariel?"

"Yes, like Ariel in the movie." She started to climb out, then Ethan's hand was there, clasping hers firmly. And when she gained her balance, he plucked Aubrey out of her arms.

"Swimming," she told him, rather pitifully, then buried her face in the curve of his throat.

"I saw you swimming." She was cool and wet and curled against him. He reached out, took Grace's hand again and pulled her to level ground. This time, his fingers twined with hers and held. "Looks like I've got two mermaids now."

"She's tired," Grace said quietly. "It makes her cross

sometimes. She's wet,'' she added and started to take Aubrey from him.

''She's fine.'' He released her hand only because he wanted to skim his over Grace's damp and shining hair. ''You're wet, too.'' Then he slipped an arm around her shoulders. ''Let's walk in the sun for a while.''

''All right.''

''Maybe around the front of the house,'' he suggested, smiling a little as Aubrey's breath fluttered against his skin, evening out into sleep. ''Where there aren't so many people.''

With surprise and a low surge of pleasure, Carol Monroe watched Ethan take her daughter and granddaughter walking. With a woman's eyes she saw more than a neighbor and friend strolling with a neighbor and friend. Impulsively, she tugged on her husband's arm, distracting him from his absorption in the current round of horseshoes.

''Hold on, Carol. Junior and I are playing the winners of this round.''

''Look, Pete. Look at that. Grace is with Ethan.''

Vaguely annoyed, he flicked a glance around, shrugged. ''So what?''

''*With* him, Pete, you knothead.'' It was said with exasperation and affection. ''Like a boyfriend.''

''Boyfriend?'' He snorted, started to dismiss it—Christ knew, Carol had the screwiest ideas from time to time. Like when she was all het up to take a cruise down to the Bahamas. As if he couldn't take a sail any damn time of the day or night right in his own backyard. But then he caught—something—in the way Ethan leaned his body toward Grace, the way she tilted her head up.

It made Pete shift his feet, scowl, look away. ''Boyfriend,'' he muttered, and didn't know how the hell he was supposed to feel about that. He didn't poke his nose in his daughter's life, he reminded himself. She'd already gone her own way.

He scowled hard into the sun because he remembered

what it had been like to have his little girl rest her head on his shoulder the way Aubrey was doing right then and there with Ethan Quinn.

When they were little like that, he thought, they trusted you and looked up to you and believed what you told them even if you told them thunder was just angels clapping.

When they got older they started to tug away. And to want things that didn't make a damn bit of sense. Like money to live in New York City, and your blessing to marry some sneaky bastard who wasn't half good enough for them.

They stopped thinking you were the man with the answers, and they broke your damn heart. So you had to put it back together as best you could, with a lock on it so it couldn't happen again.

"Ethan's just what Grace needs," Carol was saying in a low voice—just in case any of the fuddy-duddies, who thought tossing a horseshoe at an iron peg was an exciting way to spend the day, had sharp ears. "That's a steady man, and he's got gentleness in him. He's a man she could lean on."

"Won't."

"What?"

"She won't lean on nobody. She's too proud for her own good, and always has been."

Carol merely sighed. If it was true, Grace had gotten every stubborn ounce of that pride from her father. "You've never even tried to meet her halfway."

"Don't you start on me, Carol. I've got nothing to say." He shifted away from her, ignoring the guilt because he knew the gesture would hurt her. "I want a beer," he muttered and stalked away.

Phillip Quinn and some of the others were gathered around the keg. Pete noted with an amused snort that Phillip was flirting with the Barrow girl, Celia. He couldn't blame the boy—she was built like a Playboy pinup and not afraid to show it off. It wasn't something a man stopped noticing even if he was old enough to be her father.

"Want me to pull you one, Mr. Monroe?"

" 'Preciate it." Pete nodded toward the celebrants in the backyard. "Got you a crowd here, today, Phil. Fine spread, too. I remember how your folks'd throw a picnic most every summer. It's nice you're keeping up the tradition."

"Anna thought of it," Phillip told him, handing Pete a foaming beer in a tall plastic cup.

"Women do, more'n men, I suppose. If I don't get the chance, you tell her I appreciate the invite. I gotta get back to the waterfront in an hour or so, set up for the display."

"You always put on a good one. Best fireworks on the Shore."

"Tradition," Pete said again. It was a word that mattered.

CAROL MONROE HADN'T been the only one to notice the way Ethan and Grace had walked off together. Speculation and sly grins started to spread over the potato salad and steamed crabs.

Mother Crawford wagged her fork at her good friend Lucy Wilson. "You ask me, Grace is going to have to put her foot down if she wants Ethan Quinn to come up to snuff before that baby's old enough for college. Never seen a man moved so slow."

"He's thoughtful," Lucy said loyally.

"Not saying different. Just saying slow. Seen them moony-eyed over each other since before that boy got his own workboat. Has to be nearly ten years passed. Stella and I—bless her soul—had a conversation over it a time or two."

Lucy sighed over her fruit salad, and not just because

she was watching her calories. "Stella knew her boys inside and out."

"That she did. I said to her one day, 'Stella, your Ethan's got cow's eyes for the young Monroe girl.' " And she laughed, said how he had himself a hard case of puppy love, but that sometimes it was the best way to start the real thing. Never could figure why Ethan didn't step forward a bit before Grace got herself tangled up with that Jack Casey. Never did like him much."

"He wasn't a bad sort, just weak. Look there, Mother," Lucy said, lowering her voice like a conspirator. She nodded toward Ethan and Grace, as they walked back around the side of the house, hands linked, the baby sleeping on his shoulder.

"Nothing weak about that one." Mother wiggled her brows and leered at her friend. "And slow can be a fine thing in bed, can't it, Lucy?"

Lucy hooted. "It can, Mother. That it can."

Blissfully unaware of the speculation buzzing about a quiet walk around the house on a hot summer afternoon, Grace stopped to pour some iced tea. Before she'd half filled the first glass, her mother was bustling over, beaming smiles.

"Oh, let me hold that precious girl. Nothing so soothing as sitting with a sleeping baby." She'd slipped Aubrey out of Ethan's arms while she talked, her voice low and quick. "It'll give me a fine excuse to sit in the shade a while and be quiet. I swear, Nancy Claremont's been talking both my ears off. You young people should be off enjoying yourself."

"I was going to lay her down," Grace began, but her mother just waved it away.

"No need, no need. I don't get nearly enough chances to hold her when she's still. Go on and finish your walk. Ought to get out of the sun, though. It's brutal."

"It's a good idea," Ethan mused as Carol hurried off,

cooing to the sleeping Aubrey. "A little shade and a little quiet wouldn't hurt."

"Well . . . all right, but I've only got another hour or so before I have to leave."

He'd been tugging her gently toward the trees, thinking that he could find a sheltered spot, a private spot, and kiss her again. He stopped at the verge and frowned at her. "Leave for what?"

"For work. I'm on at the pub tonight."

"It's your night off."

"It was—that is, it usually is, but I'm putting on some more hours."

"You work too many hours already."

She smiled, distracted—then relieved when the shade she walked into cut the intense heat in half. "It's just a few more. Shiney was good about helping me out so I can make up what I had to pay for the car. Oh, this is nice." She closed her eyes, breathed deep of the moist, cool air. "Anna said you and your brothers were going to play later. I'll be sorry to miss that."

"Grace, I told you if money was a problem, I'd help you out."

She opened her eyes again. "I don't need you to help me out, Ethan. I know how to work."

"Yeah, you know how. It's damn near all you do." He paced away from her, paced back as if trying to shake off what was biting at his gut. "I hate you working down there."

Her spine stiffened—she could feel it go hard and straight, vertebra by vertebra. "I don't want to fight with you about that again. It's a good job, honest work."

"I'm not fighting with you, I'm saying it." He stalked toward her, the swirling temper in his eyes surprising enough that she backed up against a tree.

"I've heard you say it before," she said evenly. "And it doesn't change the facts. I work there, and I'm going to go on working there."

"You need looking after." It scraped him raw that he couldn't be the one to do it.

"I don't."

Hell she didn't. There were already tired smudges under those changeable green eyes, and now she was telling him she'd be carting trays until two in the morning. "Did you pay Dave for the car yet?"

"Half." It was humiliating. "He was good enough to give me until next month to pay him the rest."

"You won't pay him." That, at least, was something he could do. Would do, by Christ. "I will."

She forgot about humiliation. Her chin came up, sharp and fast as a bullet. "You will not."

Another time he would have persuaded, cajoled. Or simply done the deed on the quiet. But something was bubbling up in him—something that had been there, simmering, since he'd turned that morning and seen her. It wouldn't let him think, only feel and act. With his eyes on hers he slipped a hand up, over her throat.

"Be quiet."

"I'm not a child, Ethan. You can't—"

"I'm not thinking about you like a child." Her eyes were bright and sharp. They were heating the something that was inside him to a boil. "I stopped being able to do that, and I can't go back to it. Do what I want this time."

She didn't know when her breath had started to back up or her skin to shiver. Dimly she felt the rough bark of the tree bite into her hands as she pressed them against it. She didn't think he was talking about her accepting a few hundred dollars for a car any longer.

"Ethan—"

His other hand was on her breast. He hadn't meant to put it there, but it covered her and his fingers began to flex and knead. Her shirt was still damp, just a little damp. He could feel her skin go hot under it. "Do what I want this time," he repeated.

Her eyes were huge. He was falling into them, drowning in them. Her heart was pounding against his hand, as if he held it beating in his palm. His mouth crushed down on hers with a violent greed that he was for once helpless to stem. He heard her shocked cry muffled against his assaulting mouth. And it only thrilled him darkly.

The heat swarmed from him, stunning her. His teeth nipped roughly into her lip, making her gasp, opening herself to the swift and skillful invasion of his tongue.

Sensations flew too quickly to separate one from the other, but all were dark and keen and compelling. His hands were everywhere, tugging up her shirt, claiming her breasts, scraping those deliciously rough palms over her. She felt him quiver, gripped his shoulders to balance them both.

Then he was yanking at her shorts.

No! Part of her mind drew back in shock, all but screamed it. He couldn't mean to take her, here, like this, only yards away from where people sat and children played. But another part of her simply moaned in shocked excitement and whispered yes.

Here. Now. Like this. Exactly like this.

When he drove into her, her scream would have carried some of both, but it was swallowed by his mouth, lost in his ragged breaths.

He thrust hard, fast, deep, his body surging into hers, his hands biting into her tight, round bottom as he plunged. His mind was wiped clean of everything but this one desperate need. When she came, exploding over him, around him, in him, his thrill was dark and primal and coated his skin with sweat.

His own climax had claws, hot-tipped, razor-sharp, that ripped through him brutally, so that his vision went red.

Even when it cleared he continued to shudder, to pant. Gradually he became aware of what was. He heard the wild drumming of a woodpecker deeper in the woods, the tinkle of laughter from beyond the trees. And Grace's sobbing breaths.

He felt the breezing cooling his skin. And her trembles.

"Oh, God. Goddamn it." His curse was quiet, vicious.

"Ethan?" She hadn't known, would never have believed anyone could have such a need inside them. For her. "Ethan," she said again and would have lifted her weak arms around him if he hadn't stepped back.

"I'm sorry. I—" There weren't words. Nothing he could say would be right, would be enough. He bent, slipped her shorts back up, fastened them. With the same deliberate care, he straightened her shirt. "I can't offer you an excuse for that. There isn't any."

"I don't want an excuse. I don't ever need one for what we do together, Ethan."

He stared at the ground while a sick pounding began in his head. "I didn't give you a choice." He knew what it was not to have a choice.

"I've already made my choice. I love you."

He looked at her then, everything that lived inside of him swirling into his eyes. Her mouth was swollen where he'd ravished it. Her eyes were enormous. Her body would carry bruises from his hands. "You deserve better."

"I like to think I deserve you. You made me feel . . . desired. That's not even the word." She pressed a hand to her still speeding heart. "Craved," she realized. "Craved. And now I'm sorry . . ." Her gaze flicked away from his. "I'm sorry for any woman who's never known what it is to be craved."

"I scared you."

"For a minute." Mortified, she blew out a breath. "Damn it, Ethan, do I have to tell you that I liked it? I felt helpless and overpowered and it was so exciting. You lost control, and you have this incredibly unshakable control most of the time. I liked knowing that something I did, or something I am, snapped it."

He pulled his hand through his hair. "You confuse me, Grace."

"I don't mean to. But I don't think that's such a bad thing, either."

He let out a sigh, then stepped forward just enough that he could smooth her tousled hair into place. "Maybe the trouble is we've been thinking we know each other so well. But we don't have all the pieces." He picked up her hand, studied it with that thoughtful frown she loved. Then he kissed her fingers in a way that made her lashes flutter.

"I don't ever want to hurt you. In any way." But he had, and he would.

He kept his hand in hers as he walked her back toward the sunlight. He would have to tell her about those pieces of himself soon. So she would understand why he couldn't give her more.

FIFTEEN

"So, I DON'T KNOW IF I'm going to go out with him anymore because he's getting way too possessive, you know? I don't want to hurt his feelings, but you gotta live, right?"

Julie Cutter crunched into the shiny green apple she'd plucked out of the fruit bowl in Grace's kitchen. She felt every bit as much at home there as she did next door. Comfortable, she hitched herself up to sit on the counter while Grace folded laundry on the table.

"Plus," Julie went on, gesturing with her apple, "I met this incredibly cute guy. He works at the computer store at the mall? He wears these little metal-frame glasses and has the sweetest smile." She grinned, lighting up her pretty heart-shaped face. "I asked him for his phone number, and he blushed."

"You asked him for his phone number?" Grace was listening with only half an ear. She loved it when Julie came over just to visit. She was always so full of fun and talk and energy. But today it was hard to concentrate. Her mind was so full of what had happened between her and Ethan in those shady woods. What had leapt out of him to devour her—and why it had left him so distant afterward?

"Sure." Julie cocked her head, her brown eyes full of humor. "Didn't you ever ask a guy out? Come on, Grace, we're at the dawn of the next millennium here. Most of them really like it when the woman takes the initiative. Anyway . . ." She shook back her long fall of straight-as-a-pin brown hair. "Jeff did—the sexy computer nerd? He got all flustered at first, but then he gave it to me, and when I called him I could tell he was happy about it. So we're going out Saturday, but I have to break up with Don first."

"Poor Don," Grace murmured, and glanced over absently as Aubrey knocked over the block tower she'd been building, then applauded its destruction.

"Oh, he'll get over it." Julie shrugged. "It's not like he's in love with me or anything. He's just used to having a chick."

Grace had to smile. A few months earlier, Julie had been wild about Don, rushing over to tell Grace every detail of their dates. Or, Grace suspected, at least an edited version of their dates. "You told me Don was the one."

"He was." Julie laughed. "For a while. I'm not ready for the *only* one yet."

Grace went to the refrigerator to pour the three of them a drink. At Julie's age—nineteen—she'd been pregnant, married, and worried about paying bills. She was only three years older than Julie, but it might as well have been three hundred. "You're right to look around, to be sure." She handed Julie a glass, held her gaze for a moment. "To be careful."

"I'm careful, Grace," Julie assured her, touched. "I'd like to be married one day. Especially if it means having a baby as beautiful as Aubrey. But I want to finish college, then see some of the world. Do . . . things," she added, gesturing widely. "I don't want to find myself tied down, changing diapers and working at some dead-end job because I let some guy talk me into . . .''

She trailed off, suddenly and sincerely appalled at herself. Eyes huge and apologetic, she slid off the counter. ''God, I'm sorry. I can be so thick sometimes. I didn't mean that you—''

''It's all right.'' She gave Julie's arm a quick squeeze. ''That's exactly what I did, exactly what I let happen to me. I'm glad you're smarter.''

''I'm a moron,'' Julie murmured, very close to tears. ''I'm an insensitive clod. I'm hateful.''

''No, you're not.'' Grace gave a light laugh and picked up a pair of Aubrey's rompers from the basket. ''You didn't hurt my feelings. I'd hate to think we weren't friends enough for you to be able to say what you think.''

''You're one of my best friends. And I've got a big mouth.''

''Well, you do.'' Grace chuckled at Julie's wince. ''But I like it.''

''I love you and Aubrey, Grace.''

''I know you do. Now stop worrying about it, and tell me where you're going with Jeff the cute computer guy?''

''Safe date. Movies and pizza.'' Julie let out a soft sigh of relief. She'd have . . . shaved her head and dyed it purple, she decided, before she'd do anything to hurt Grace. Hoping to make up, just a little, for her insensitivity, she beamed a smile.

''You know, I'd be happy to keep Aubrey on your next night off if you and Ethan want to go out.''

Grace had finished folding the rompers and started on socks. She stopped, staring, with a tiny white sock trimmed in yellow in each hand. ''What?''

''You know—catch a movie, go to a restaurant, whatever.'' She wiggled her brows on the ''whatever,'' then fought to bite back a grin at Grace's expression. ''You're not going to stand there and tell me you're not seeing Ethan Quinn.''

"Well, he's . . . I'm . . ." She looked helplessly down at Aubrey.

"If it was supposed to be a secret, he should be parking his truck somewhere other than your driveway on the nights he sleeps over."

"Oh, God."

"What's the problem? It's not like you're having this illicit affair—like Mr. Wiggins has been having with Mrs. Lowen on Monday afternoons at the motel on Route 13." At Grace's strangled sound, Julie just shrugged. "My friend Robin's working there and taking night classes at the college, and she says how he checks in every Thursday morning at ten-thirty while she waits in her car. Anyway—"

"What must your mother think?" Grace whispered.

"Mom? About Mr. Wiggins? Well—"

"No, no." Grace didn't want to think about the portly Mr. Wiggins's weekly motel romp. "About . . ."

"Oh, you and Ethan. I think she said something about 'high time.' Mom's not an idiot. He's such a *hunk*," Julie said with feeling. "I mean, the way he fills out a T-shirt is awesome. And that smile. It takes, like, ten minutes for it to finish moving over his face, and by then, man, you are *drooling*. Robin and I went down to the waterfront every day for a month last summer just to watch him off-load his catch."

"You did?" Grace said weakly.

"We both built a real case on him." She reached into the white stoneware cookie jar and found two oatmeal raisins. "I flirted with him, big time, whenever I got the chance."

"You . . . flirted with Ethan."

"Mmm." She nodded, swallowing cookie. "Really put some effort into it, too. Mostly I think it embarrassed him, but I got a couple of great smiles out of him." She smiled sunnily when Grace kept staring. "Oh, I'm way over it now, so don't worry."

"Good." Grace picked up the drink she'd neglected and drank deeply. "That's good."

"Still, he's got a terrific butt."

"Oh, Julie." Grace bit her lip to keep from giggling and sent a meaningful look toward her daughter.

"She's not listening. So, anyway, how'd I get started on this? Oh, yeah, I'll keep Aubrey for you if you want to go out."

"I, well, thanks." She was trying to decide if she wanted to get well off the subject of Ethan Quinn, or linger on it, when she heard a knock and saw him standing at her front door.

"Like magic," Julie murmured, and romance bloomed in her heart. "You know, why don't I take Aubrey over to see Mom for a while? I'll just keep her and feed her dinner."

"But I don't have to leave for work for nearly an hour yet."

Julie rolled her eyes. "So make good use of the time, pal." Then she scooped Aubrey up. "Want to come to my house, Aubrey? See my kitty cat?"

"Oooh, kitty. Bye, Mama."

"Oh, but—" They were already sailing out of her back door, with Aubrey calling for the kitty and waving madly. She looked at Ethan again, staring at his face through the screen, then lifted her hands.

He decided to take it as an invitation and stepped inside. "Was that Julie who ran off with Aubrey?"

"Yes. She's going to let Aubrey play with her kitten and have dinner over there."

"It's nice you have someone like Julie to look after her."

"I'd be lost without Julie." Puzzled, Grace angled her head. He was standing awkwardly, a hand tucked behind his back. "Is something wrong? Did you hurt your hand?"

"No." What an idiot he was, Ethan thought, offering her the flowers he had held behind him. "I thought you might like some." He wanted, desperately, to find ways to make up to her for the way he'd treated her in the woods.

"You brought me flowers."

"I stole some here and there. You may not want to mention it to Anna. I got the tiger lilies off the side of the road. They're blooming thick this year."

He'd picked her flowers. Not store-bought flowers but ones he'd stopped and selected and plucked with his own hands. On a long, trembling sigh, she buried her face in them. "They're beautiful."

"They made me think of you. Almost everything does." And when she lifted her head, when he saw that her eyes were stunned and soft, he wished he had more words, better ones, smoother ones. "I know you only have the one night off now. I'd like to take you to dinner if you don't have any plans."

"To dinner?"

"There's a place Anna and Cam like up in Princess Anne. Suit-and-tie place, but they claim the food's worth it. Would you like to?"

She realized she was nodding her head like a fool and made herself stop. "I'd like that."

"I'll come by for you. About six-thirty?"

There went her head, bobbing again like a spring robin drunk on worms. "Fine. That'd be fine."

"I can't stay now because they're expecting me at the boatyard."

"That's all right." She wondered if her eyes were as huge as they felt. She could have devoured him with them. "Thanks for the flowers. They're lovely."

"You're welcome." And with his eyes open, he leaned over, laid his lips on hers very gently, very softly. He watched her lashes flutter, watched the green of her irises go misty under those tiny flecks of gold. "I'll see you tomorrow night, then."

Her muscles had turned to putty. "Tomorrow," she

managed and breathed out a long, long sigh as he walked away and out her front door.

He'd brought her flowers. She clasped the stems in both hands, held them out and waltzed through the house with them. Beautiful, fragrant, soft-petaled flowers. And if some of those petals drifted to the floor as she danced, it only made the scene more romantic.

They made her feel like a princess, like a woman. She sniffed them lavishly as she circled back into the kitchen for a vase. Like a bride.

She stopped abruptly, staring at them. *Like a bride.*

Her head went light, her skin hot, her hands trembly. When she realized she was holding her breath, she let it out with a whoosh, but it caught and stumbled as she tried to pull air in again.

He'd brought her flowers, she thought again. He'd asked her to dinner. Slowly, she pressed a hand to her heart, found that it was pumping light and fast, very fast.

He was going to ask her to marry him. *To marry him.*

"Oh, my. Oh." Her legs wanted to fold, so she sat down, right on the floor of the kitchen with the flowers cradled in her arms like a child. Flowers, tender kisses, a romantic dinner for two. He was courting her.

No, no. She was jumping to conclusions. He would never move that quickly to the next step. She shook her head, picked herself up, and found an old wide-mouthed bottle for a vase. He was just being sweet. He was just being considerate. He was just being Ethan.

She turned on the faucet and filled the bottle. Just being Ethan, she thought again, and found her breath gone a second time.

Being Ethan, he would think and he would do things in a certain manner. Struggling for calm, for logic, she began to arrange the precious flowers, stem by stem.

They'd known each other for . . . she could hardly remember not knowing him. Now they were lovers. They were in love. Being Ethan, he would consider marriage the next step. Honorable, traditional. Right. He would believe it right.

She understood that but had expected it to be months yet before he drifted in that direction. Yet why would he wait, she asked herself, when they'd already waited for years?

But ... She had promised herself she would never marry again. She made that vow as she signed her name on the divorce papers. She couldn't fail so miserably at something ever again, or risk putting Aubrey through the misery and trauma. She'd made the decision that she would raise Aubrey alone, raise her well, raise her with love. That she herself would provide, would build the home, tend it, where her daughter could grow up happy and safe.

But that was before she had let herself believe Ethan would ever want them, would ever love her the way she loved him. Because it had always been Ethan. Always Ethan, she thought, closing her eyes. In her heart, in her dreams. Did she dare break her promise, one she had made so solemnly? Could she risk being a wife again, pinning her hopes and her heart on another man?

Oh, yes. Yes, she could risk anything if the man was Ethan. It was so right, so perfect, she thought, laughing to herself as her head and heart went light with joy. It was the happy-ever-after that she'd stopped letting herself yearn for.

How would he ask? She pressed her fingers to her lips, and those lips trembled and curved. Quietly, she thought, with his eyes so serious, so intent on hers. He would take her hand, in that careful way of his. They'd be outside with moonlight and breezes, with the scents of night all around them and the musical lap of water close by.

Simply, she thought, without poetry or fuss. He would look down at her, saying nothing for a long moment, then he would speak, without hurry.

I love you, Grace. I always will. Will you marry me?

Yes, yes, yes! She spun herself in giddy circles. She would be his bride, his wife, his partner, his lover. Now. Forever. She could give her child to him knowing, without hesitation, that he would love and cherish, would protect and tend. She would have more children with him.

Oh, God—Ethan's child growing inside her. Overwhelmed by the image, she pressed her hands to her stomach. And this time, this time, the life that fluttered inside her would be wanted and welcomed by both who'd made it.

They would make a life together, a wonderfully, thrillingly simple life.

She couldn't wait to begin it.

Tomorrow night, she remembered, and in a sudden panic, pushed at her hair. Dropped her hands to look at them in utter despair. Oh, she was a mess. She needed to look beautiful.

What would she wear?

She caught herself laughing, the laughter full of joy and nerves. For once she forgot work and schedules and responsibility and raced to her closet.

ANNA DIDN'T NOTICE the stolen flowers until the next day. Then she noticed them with a shout.

"Seth! Seth, you come out here right now." She had her hands on her hips, her sassy straw hat askew, her eyes snapping and dangerous.

"Yeah?" He came out, munching on a handful of pretzels, though dinner was simmering on the stove.

"Have you been messing with my flowers?" she demanded.

He slid a glance down to the mixed bed of annuals and perennials. And snorted. "What would I be messing with stupid flowers for?"

She tapped her foot. "That's what I'm asking you."

"I never touched them. Hey, you don't even want us to pull up weeds."

"That's because you don't know the difference between a weed and a daisy," she snapped. "Well, somebody's been in my flower beds."

"Wasn't me." He shrugged, then rolled his eyes in glee as she stormed past him into the house.

Somebody, Seth thought, was in for it big time.

"Cameron!" She stomped upstairs and into the bathroom where he was washing up from work. He glanced over, lifting a brow as water dripped from his face into the sink. She scowled for a moment, then shook her head. "Never mind," she muttered, slamming the door.

Cam would no more fiddle with her gardens than Seth, she decided. And if he was picking flowers for anyone, it damn well better be his loving wife, or she'd just murder him and be done with it.

Her eyes narrowed on the door to Ethan's room. And she made a low, threatening sound in her throat.

She did stop to knock, though it was only three staccato raps before she simply pushed open the door.

"Christ, Anna." Mortified, Ethan snatched up the slacks that lay on his bed and held them in front of him. He was wearing nothing but his briefs and a pained expression.

"Just save the modesty, I'm not interested. Have you been into my flowers?"

"Into your flowers?" Oh, he'd known this was coming. The woman had eyes like a cat when it came to her posies. But he hadn't expected the moment to come when he was half naked. Half, hell, he thought and clutched the slacks more firmly.

"Somebody's snapped off more than a dozen blooms. Snapped them right off." She advanced on him, her eyes scanning the room for evidence.

"Oh, well . . ."

"Problem?" Cam leaned on the doorjamb, tongue in his cheek. It was an amusing sight after a hard day's work, he decided. His well-riled wife stalking around his all-but-bare-assed brother.

"Somebody's been in my garden and they stole my flowers."

"No kidding? Want me to call the cops?"

"Oh, shut up." She whirled back to Ethan, who took a cautious and cowardly step in retreat. She looked fit to murder. "Well?"

"Well, I . . ." He'd intended to confess, throw himself on her mercy. But the woman glaring at him out of dark, furious eyes looked several quarts low on mercy. "Rabbits," he said slowly. "Probably."

"Rabbits?"

"Yeah." He shifted uncomfortably, wishing to Christ he'd at least gotten his pants on before she burst in. "Rabbits can be a problem with gardens. They just hop up and help themselves."

"Rabbits," she said again.

"Could be deer," he added, just a little desperately. "They'd graze over and eat every damn thing down to stubs." Counting on pity, he shot a look at Cam. "Right?"

Cam weighed the situation, knew Anna was city girl enough to buy it. Oh, Ethan would owe him for this, he decided and smiled. "Oh, yeah, deer and rabbits, big problem." Which having two dogs running tame pretty much eliminated, he mused.

"Why didn't anybody tell me!" She whipped off her hat, rapped it against her thigh. "What do we do about it? How do we make them stop?"

"Couple ways." Guilt stung, just a little, but Ethan rationalized that deer and rabbits *could* be a problem, so she should take precautions anyway. "Dried blood."

"Dried *blood*? Whose?"

"You can buy it at the garden store, and you just dump it around. It'll keep them away."

"Dried blood." Her lips pursed as she made a mental note to buy some.

"Or urine."

"Dried urine?"

"No." Ethan cleared his throat. "You just go out and . . . you know, around so they smell it and know there's a meat eater in the vicinity."

"I see." She nodded, satisfied, then whirled on her husband. "Well, get out there then and pee on my marigolds."

"Could use a beer first," Cam said and winked at his brother. "Don't worry, darling, we'll take care of it."

"All right." Calmer, she huffed out a breath. "Sorry, Ethan."

"Yeah, well, hmmm." He waited until she'd hurried out, then lowered himself to the edge of the bed. He slanted a look at Cam, who continued to lean against the door. "That wife of yours has a streak of mean in her."

"Yeah. I love it. Why'd you steal her flowers?"

"I just needed a few of them," Ethan muttered and pulled on his pants. "What the hell are they out there for if you get your head cut off for picking them?"

"Rabbits? And deer?" Cam began to hoot with laughter.

"They're garden pests right enough."

"Pretty brave rabbits who hop between two dogs and right up to the house to select a few flowers. If they got that far, they'd mow the whole garden down to the ground."

"She doesn't have to know that. For a while. I appreciate you backing me up. I thought she was going to punch me."

"She might have. Since I saved your pretty face, I figure you owe me."

"Nothing comes free," Ethan grumbled and stalked to the closet for a shirt.

"You got that right. Seth needs a haircut, and he's already outgrown his last pair of shoes."

Ethan turned, shirt dangling from his fingertips. "You want me to take him to the mall?"

"Right again."

"I'd rather have the punch in the face."

"Too late." Cam hooked a thumb in his front pocket and grinned. "So, why'd you need the flowers?"

"Just thought Grace would like them." Muttering, Ethan shrugged into his shirt.

"Ethan Quinn stealing flowers, going out—voluntarily—to a jacket-and-tie restaurant." Cam's grin widened, his eyebrows wiggled. "Serious business."

"It's a usual thing for a man to take a woman out to dinner, bring her flowers now and then."

"Not for you it isn't." Cam straightened, patted his flat belly. "Well, I guess I'll go choke down that beer so I can be a hero."

"Man's got no privacy around here," Ethan complained when Cam sauntered away. "Women come right on into your bedroom, don't even have the courtesy to leave when they see you don't have your pants on."

Scowling, he dragged one of his two ties out of the closet. "People ready to skin you alive over a few flowers. And the next thing you know, you're at the goddamn mall fighting crowds and buying shoes."

He wrestled the tie under his collar and began to deal with the knot. "Never had to worry when I was in my own place. I could walk around buck ass naked if I wanted to." He hissed at the tie that refused to cooperate. "I hate these fuckers."

"That's because you're happier tying a sheepshank."

"Who the hell wouldn't be?"

Then he stopped, his fingers freezing on the tie. His gaze stayed on the mirror, where he could see his father behind him.

"You're just a little nervous, that's all," Ray said with a smile and a wink. "Hot date."

Taking a careful breath, Ethan turned. Ray stood at the foot of the bed, his bright-blue eyes merry, the way Ethan remembered they would sparkle when he was particularly tickled about something.

He was wearing a squash-yellow T-shirt that sported a boat under full sail, faded jeans, and scuffed sandals. His hair was long, past his collar, and shining silver. Ethan could see the sun glint on it.

He looked exactly like what he was—had been. A robust and handsome man who appreciated comfortable clothes and a good laugh.

"I'm not dreaming," Ethan murmured.

"It was easier for you to think so at first. Hello, Ethan."

"Dad."

"I remember the first time you called me that. Took you a while to come to it. You'd been with us almost a year. Christ, you were a spooky kid, Ethan. Quiet as a shadow, deep as a lake. One evening when I was grading papers, you knocked on the door. You just stood there for a minute, thinking. God, it was a marvel to watch your mind work. Then you said, 'Dad, the phone's for you.' " Ray's smile went bright as sunlight. "You slipped right out again, or you'd have seen me make a fool of myself. Sniffled like a baby and had to tell whoever the hell it was on the phone I was having an allergy attack."

"I never knew why you wanted me."

"You needed us. We needed you. You *were* ours, Ethan, even before we found each other. Fate takes its own sweet time, but it always finds a way. You were so . . . fragile," Ray said after a moment, and Ethan blinked in surprise. "Stella and I were worried we'd do something wrong and break you."

"I wasn't fragile."

"Oh, Ethan, you were. Your heart was delicate as glass and waiting to be shattered. Your body was tough. We never worried about you and Cam pounding on each other those first months. Thought it did both of you good.''

Ethan's lips twitched. ''He usually started the pounding.''

''But you never were one to back off once your blood was up. Took some doing to get it up,'' he added. ''Still does. We watched you watch and settle and think and consider.''

''You gave me . . . time. Time to watch and settle, to think and consider. Everything I've got that's decent came from the two of you.''

''No, Ethan, we just gave you love. And that time, and the place.''

He wandered over to the window, to look out on the water and the boats that swayed gently at the dock. He watched an egret sail across a sky hazed with heat and plumped by clouds.

''You were meant to be ours. Meant to be here. Took to the water like you'd been born in it. Cam, he always just wanted to go fast, and Phillip preferred to sit back and enjoy the ride. But you . . .''

He turned back again, his gaze thoughtful. ''You studied every inch of the boat, every wave, every turn of a river. You'd practice tying knots for hours, and nobody had to nag you into swabbing the decks.''

''It came easy for me, right from the start. You wanted me to get a college degree.''

''For me.'' Ray shook his head. ''For me, Ethan. Fathers are human, after all, and I went through a time when I thought my sons needed to love schooling as much as I did. But you did what was right for you. You made me proud of you. I should have told you that more often.''

''You always let me know it.''

''Words count, though. Who would know that better than a man who spent his life trying to teach the young the love of them?'' He sighed now. ''Words count, Ethan, and I know some of them come hard for you. But I want you to remember that. You and Grace have a lot to say to each other yet.''

''I don't want to hurt her.''

''You will,'' Ray said quietly. ''By trying not to. I wish you could see yourself as I do. As she does.'' He shook his head again. ''Well, fate takes its time. Think of the boy, Ethan, think of Seth—and what pieces of yourself you see there.''

''His mother—'' Ethan began.

''Think of the boy for now,'' Ray said simply, and he was gone.

SIXTEEN

THERE WASN'T A HINT OF rain on the breezy summer air. The sky was a hot, staggering blue, an unbroken bowl that held a faint haze and fragile clouds. A single bird sang manically, as if mad to complete the song before the long day was over.

She was as nervous as a teenager on prom night. The thought of that made Grace laugh. No teenager had ever dreamed of nerves like these.

She fussed with her hair, wishing she had long, glossy curls like Anna's—exotic, Gypsy-like. Sexy.

But she didn't, she reminded herself firmly. And never would. At least the short, simple crop showed off the pretty gold drop earrings Julie had loaned her.

Julie had been so sweet and excited about what she'd termed the Big Date. She'd launched straight into a what-to-wear-and-what-to-wear-with-it routine—and naturally had deemed the contents of Grace's closet a total loss.

Of course, letting Julie drag her off to the mall had been sheer foolishness. Not that Julie had to yank very hard,

Grace admitted. It had been so long since she'd shopped simply for the simple pleasure of shopping. For the couple of hours they'd spent swarming through the shops, she'd felt so young and carefree. As if nothing was really more important than finding the right outfit.

Still, she'd had no business buying a new dress, even if she did get it on sale. But she couldn't seem to talk herself out of it. Just this one little indulgence, this one little luxury. She so desperately wanted something new and fresh for this special night.

She'd yearned for the sexy, sophisticated black with its shoestring straps and snug skirt. Or the boldly sensuous red with the daringly plunging neckline. But they hadn't suited her, as she'd known they wouldn't.

It had been no surprise that the simple powder-blue linen had been discounted. It had looked so plain, so ordinary, hanging on the rack. But Julie had pressed it on her, and Julie had an eye for such things.

She'd been right, of course, Grace thought now. It was simple, almost virginal, with its unadorned bodice and graceful lines. But it looked pretty on, with the color cool against her skin, and the skirt floating around her legs.

Grace traced a finger over the square neckline, faintly amazed that the bra Julie had nagged her into buying actually did gift her with a hint of cleavage. A miracle indeed, Grace thought with a little laugh.

Concentrating, she leaned close to the mirror. She'd done everything Julie had instructed with the borrowed makeup. And her eyes did look bigger and deeper, she decided. She'd done her best to blot away the signs of fatigue and thought she had succeeded. Maybe she hadn't managed more than a wink of sleep the night before, but she didn't feel in the least tired.

She felt energized.

She reached out, and her hand hovered over the samples of perfumes they'd been given at the cosmetics counter. Then she remembered that Anna had told her to wear her

own scent for Ethan before. That it would say something
to him.

Choosing that instead, she closed her eyes and dabbed
it on. With her eyes closed, imagining that his lips might
brush here, brush there, linger and taste where her pulse
beat that fragrance into life.

Still dreaming, she picked up a little ivory evening
bag—another loan—and checked its contents. She hadn't
carried such a small purse since ... well, before Aubrey
was born, she thought. It was so odd to look inside and
see none of the dozens of mother things she was used to
carrying. Only women things now, she mused. The little
compact she'd splurged on, a tube of lipstick she rarely
thought to use, her house key, a few carefully folded bills,
and a tissue that wasn't thin and ragged from wiping a
sticky face.

It made her feel feminine just to look at it, to slip her
feet into impractical heeled sandals—oh, she'd be scrambling to pay off her charge card when the bill came—to
turn in front of the mirror and watch her skirt follow the
movement.

When she heard his truck pull up outside, she dashed
across the room. Made herself stop. No, she wasn't going
to race to the door like an eager puppy. She would wait
right here until he knocked. And give her heart a chance
to beat normally again.

When he did knock, it was still thundering in her ears.
But she stepped out, smiled at him through the screen, and
moved toward the door.

He remembered watching her walk to the door like this
before, on the night they'd made love the first time. She'd
looked so lovely, so lonely with the candlelight flickering
around her.

But tonight she looked ... he didn't think he had words
for it. Everything about her seemed to glow—skin, hair,
eyes. It made him feel awkward, humble, reverent. He

wanted to kiss her to be certain she was real, and yet was afraid to touch.

He stepped back as she opened the screen, then took the hand she held out carefully. "You look different."

No, it wasn't poetry. And it made her smile. "I wanted to." She pulled the door closed behind her and let him lead her to his truck.

He wished immediately that he'd borrowed the 'Vette.

"The truck doesn't suit that dress," he said as she climbed in.

"It suits me." She swept her skirts in to be certain they didn't catch in the door. "I may look different, Ethan, but I'm still the same."

She settled back and prepared for the most beautiful evening of her life.

THE SUN WAS STILL UP and bright when they arrived in Princess Anne. The restaurant he'd chosen was in one of the old, refurbished houses where the ceilings were high and the windows tall and narrow. Candles yet to be lighted stood on tables draped in white linen, and the waiters wore jackets and formal black ties. Conversations from other diners were muted, as in church. She could hear her heels click on the polished floor as they were led to their table.

She wanted to remember every detail. The way the little table sat snug by the window, the painting of the Bay that hung on the wall behind Ethan. The friendly twinkle in the waiter's eyes when he offered them menus and asked if they'd like a cocktail.

But most of all she wanted to remember Ethan. The quiet smile in his eyes when he looked across the table at her, the way his fingertips continued to brush hers on the white linen.

"Would you like to have some wine?" he asked her.

Wine, candles, flowers. "Yes, that would be nice."

He opened the wine list, studied it thoughtfully. He knew she preferred white, and one or two of the types were familiar. Phillip always kept a couple of bottles chilling. Though God knew why any reasonable man would pay that much money on a regular basis for a drink.

Grateful that the selections were numbered and he wouldn't have to attempt to pronounce any French, he gave the waiter the order, privately pleased when he saw his choice met with approval.

"Hungry?"

"A little." She wondered if she'd be able to swallow a crumb around the delight in her throat. "It's just so nice to be here like this, with you."

"I should've taken you out before."

"This is perfect. There hasn't been much time for this."

"We can juggle some time." And it wasn't so bad, he discovered, wearing a tie, eating in a place surrounded by other people. Not when he got to look at her across the table. "You look rested, Grace."

"Rested?" The laugh bubbled out, making him smile uncertainly. Then her fingers squeezed his affectionately. "Oh, Ethan. I do love you."

THE SUN DIPPED LOWER, and the candles were lighted as they sipped wine and enjoyed a perfectly prepared meal served with flair. He told her about the progress of the boat, and of the new contract Phillip had finessed.

"That's wonderful. It's hard to believe you only started the business this spring."

"I'd thought about it for a long time," he told her. "Had a lot of the details worked out in my head."

He would have, of course, she thought. Thinking things through was innate with Ethan. "Even so, you're making

it work. Really making it work. I've thought about coming
by dozens of times.''

''Why haven't you?''

''Before . . . If I saw you too often or in too many different places, it worried me.'' She loved being able to tell
him, to watch his eyes change when she did. ''I was sure
you'd be able to see the way I felt about you—how I
wanted to touch you, and have you touch me.''

The blood hummed in his fingertips as they grazed hers.
And his eyes did change, just as she'd wanted, deepening
as they stared into hers. ''I'd talked myself out of you,''
he said carefully.

''I'm glad it didn't stick.''

''So am I.'' He brought her fingers over, touched his
lips to them. ''Maybe you'll come by the boatyard one of
these days, and I'll look at you . . . and I'll see.''

She angled her head. ''Maybe I will.''

''You could drop in some hot afternoon and . . .'' His
thumb cruised lazily over her knuckles. ''Bring fried
chicken.''

Her laugh was quick and easy. ''I should've figured
that's what really attracted you to me.''

''Yeah, it tipped the scales. A pretty face, sea-goddess
eyes, long legs, a warm laugh—they don't mean much to
a man. But you add a nice batch of southern fried chicken,
and you've got something.''

Delightfully flattered, she shook her head. ''And here I
was thinking I wouldn't get any poetry out of you.''

His gaze skimmed over her face, and for the first time
in his life he wished he had a talent for composing odes.
''Do you want poetry, Grace?''

''I want you, Ethan. Just the way you are.'' With a long,
contented sigh, she looked around the restaurant. ''And
you add an evening like this now and then . . .'' She shifted
her gaze back to him and grinned. ''And you've got something.''

"Sounds like a deal, since I like being out with you, like this. I like being anywhere with you."

She curled her fingers into his. "A long time ago. It seems like a long time, I used to dream about romance. The way I hoped it would be one day. This is better, Ethan. Real turned out to be better than the dream."

"I want you to be happy."

"If I was any happier, I'd have to be two people for it all to fit." Her eyes sparkled with the laugh as she leaned toward him. "And then you'd have to figure out what to do with two of me."

"One's all I need. Do you want to take a walk?"

Her heart soared. Would it be now? "Yes. I think a walk would be perfect."

The sun was nearly gone as they strolled along the pretty streets, casting shadows lovely and deep. In a sky dazzled by hot color, the moon was starting its rise. It wouldn't be full, Grace noted, but it didn't matter. Her heart was.

When he turned her into his arms just at the edge of the splash of light from a streetlamp, she melted into the long, slow kiss.

Different, Ethan thought again as he let himself take the kiss just a shade deeper. She felt softer, warmer, yielding against him, though he could feel faint tremors rippling through her.

"I love you, Grace." He said it to soothe both of them.

Her heart bounded straight into her throat, making her voice shaky. Stars were blinking to life overhead, brilliantly white points of light. "I love you, Ethan." She closed her eyes, held her breath in anticipation of the words.

"We'd better start back."

She blinked her eyes open. "Oh. Yes." Let out her breath. "Yes, you're right."

Foolish of her, she decided as they walked back to his truck. A man as careful and thorough as Ethan wouldn't propose to her on a street corner in Princess Anne. He would wait until they got back, until Julie had gone home and Aubrey had been checked on.

He'd wait until they were alone, private, in familiar surroundings. Of course, that was it. So she beamed a smile at him as he started the engine. "It was a wonderful dinner, Ethan."

THERE WAS MOONLIGHT, just as she'd imagined. It slanted through the window and slipped gently over Aubrey in her crib. Her baby dreamed happy dreams, she thought. And how much happier they would all be in the morning when they'd taken the next step toward becoming a family.

Aubrey already loved him, Grace thought as she stroked her daughter's hair. Just a short time ago, she had resolved to raise her child alone, to make certain that she was enough. All that was changing now. Ethan would be a father to her daughter, a loving parent who would watch over her.

One day they'd tuck Aubrey in together. One day they would stand over a crib watching another child sleep. With Ethan she could share the joy of a simple moment like that—that quiet moment in the moonwashed dark when you looked in and saw your child asleep and safe.

There was so much he could give them, she thought. And that she could give to him.

A man like Ethan, she knew, would feel that first flutter of life in his heart just as she would feel it in her womb. They could share that, and a lifetime of simple moments.

She moved quietly into the living room and saw Ethan standing, gazing through the screen door. She had an instant of panic. He wasn't going? He couldn't be leaving. Not now. Not before . . .

"Do you want some coffee?" she said it quickly, her voice rising before she could control it.

"No, thanks." He turned. "She sleeping all right?"

"Oh, yes, she's fine."

"She looks so much like you."

"Do you think?"

"Especially when she smiles. Grace . . ."

He watched her eyes fix on his, glow in the low light of the lamp. For a moment it seemed to him that nothing had come before, nothing would come after. It could be the three of them, there together on quiet nights just like this, in the little dollhouse. It could be his future. He wanted to believe it could be his life.

"I'd like to stay. I'd like to be with you tonight, if you want."

"I want. Of course I want." She thought she understood. He needed to show her love first. More than willing, she held out a hand. "Come to bed, Ethan."

He took care to be tender, to stroke her gently to peak. Holding her there, holding until her body bowed up, a trembling bridge of sensations. To make her float and sigh. He watched the moonlight dapple her skin, followed its shifting shadows with his fingertips, with his lips. Pleasured her.

Love surrounded her. It cradled her. It rocked her with a rhythm as gentle as a quiet sea. Gliding on it, she offered it back to him, a shimmering reflection.

His tenderness moved her to tears. She knew now that his needs could be ripe and raw and reckless. And that thrilled her. Yet this part of him, this compassionate, sensitive, and most generous part of him touched her heart at the core. She fell fathoms deeper into that wide well of love.

When he slipped into her, when they were joined, his mouth moved over hers to capture each sigh. She glided up, trembled on that silk-covered peak, holding, holding until he was trembling with her and they could catch each other on the slow tumble down.

After, he shifted her so that she curled into the curve of his arm. And stroked her. Her eyes grew heavy. Now, she thought as she began to drift. He would ask her now while they were both still glowing.

Waiting, she slid into sleep.

HE WAS TEN, AND THE last beating she'd given him had left his back a maze of purpling bruises and scarlet pain. She never hit him in the face. She'd learned quickly that most clients didn't care to see black eyes and bloody lips on the merchandise.

She'd stopped using her fists, mostly. She found a belt or a hairbrush more effective. She liked the thin, circular brushes that were all hard bristles. The first time she'd used one on him, the shock and pain had been so unspeakable that he'd fought back and it had been her lip that had been bloody. She'd used her fists then until he'd found escape in unconsciousness.

He was no match for her, and he knew it. She was a big woman and strong with it. When she was drunk, she was stronger yet and more ruthless. It didn't help to plead, it didn't help to cry, so he'd stopped doing both. And the beatings weren't as bad as the other. Nothing was.

She'd gotten twenty dollars for him the first time she'd sold him. He knew because she told him, and promised to give him two dollars for himself if he didn't make a fuss about it. He hadn't known what she was talking about. Not then. He hadn't known, not until she left him in the dark bedroom with the man.

Even then he didn't know, didn't understand. When those big, damp hands were on him, the fear was so blinding bright, the shame so dark, the terror so loud, as loud as his screams.

He'd screamed until nothing could crawl through his throat but a guttural whimper. Even the pain of being raped couldn't push more out of him.

She even gave him the two dollars. He burned it, there in the dirty sink in the horrible bathroom that stank of his own vomit, he watched the money curl up black. And his hate for her was just as black.

He promised himself, staring at his own hollow eyes in the spotty mirror, that if she ever whored him again, he would kill her.

"Ethan." Her heart tripping in her throat, Grace scrambled onto her knees to shake his shoulders. The skin under her hands was like ice. His body was rigid as stone, but trembling. It made her think wildly of earthquakes, volcanos. Boiling violence under a hard layer of rock.

The sounds he made had wakened her. They'd made her dream of an animal caught in a trap.

His eyes flew open. She could see only the glint of them in the dark, but they looked blind and wild. For a moment she was afraid that the boiling violence she sensed would break through and batter her.

"You were having a dream." She said it firmly, certain that that was what was needed to put Ethan back into those staring eyes. "It's all right now. It was a dream."

He could hear his breath rasping. More than a dream, he knew. It had been the cold-sweated flashback he hadn't had in years. But the result was the same. Nausea curled sickly in his stomach, his head pounded and swam with the pathetic echo of a young boy's scream. He shuddered once, violently, under the gentle hands on his shoulders.

"I'm okay."

But his voice was rough, and she knew he lied. "I'll get you some water."

"No, I'm okay." Not even water would settle on his jumping stomach. "Go back to sleep."

"Ethan, you're shaking."

He would stop it. He could stop it. It would only take

a little time and concentration. He saw that her eyes were huge, more than a little frightened. He was both sick and furious that he had brought even the memory of that horror to her bed.

Dear God, had he let himself believe, for even an instant, that it could be different for him? For them?

He forced himself to smile. "Just spooked me, that's all. Sorry I woke you."

Reassured because she saw a shadow of the man she loved come back into his eyes, she stroked his hair. "It must have been awful. Scared both of us."

"Must've been. Don't remember." The next lie, he thought, abominably weary. "Come on, lie back down. Everything's all right now."

She snuggled up beside him, hoping to comfort, and laid a hand over his heart. It was still racing. "Just close your eyes," she murmured as she would have to Aubrey. "Close your eyes and rest now. Hold on to me, Ethan. Dream of me."

Praying for peace, he did both.

W HEN SHE WOKE TO find him gone, Grace tried to tell herself that the weight of her disappointment was out of proportion. He hadn't wanted to disturb her so early, so he hadn't said good-bye.

Now that the sun was up, he would already be out on the water.

She rose, slipped on a robe, and padded in to make coffee and to grab those few minutes of alone time before Aubrey roused.

Then she sighed and stepped out on her little back porch. She knew her disappointment didn't stem from finding him up and gone when she woke. She'd been sure, so sure he was going to ask her to marry him. All the signs had been there, the scene set, the moment perfect. But the words hadn't come.

She'd all but written the script, she thought with a grimace, and he hadn't followed it. This morning was supposed to begin the next phase of their lives. She'd imagined running over to Julie's and sharing the joy of it, of calling Anna and babbling, begging for wedding advice.

Of telling her mother.

Of explaining it all to Aubrey.

Instead, it was a quiet morning.

After a beautiful night, she scolded herself. A lovely night. She had no business complaining about it. Annoyed with herself, she went back inside to pour the first cup of freshly brewed coffee.

Then she began to chuckle. What had she been thinking of? This was Ethan Quinn she was dealing with. Wasn't this the same man who'd waited—by his own admission—nearly a decade to so much as kiss her? At the rate he took things, it could be another one before he brought up the subject of marriage.

The only reason they'd moved from that first kiss to where they stood now was because she . . . well, she'd thrown herself at him, Grace admitted. Plain and simple. And she wouldn't have had the guts to do that if Anna hadn't shoved her along.

Flowers, she thought, turning so that she could smile at them, bright and pretty on her kitchen counter. Candlelight dinner, moonlit walks, and long, tender lovemaking. Yes, he was courting her—and would likely continue to do so until she went mad waiting for him to take the next step.

But that was Ethan, she admitted, and just one of the things she adored about him.

She sipped coffee, bit her lip. Why did he have to take the step? Why shouldn't she be the one to move things along? Julie had told her men liked it when a woman took the initiative. And hadn't Ethan liked it when she finally worked up the courage to ask him to make love with her?

She could do some courting herself, couldn't she? And she could move it along at a faster pace. God knew she was an expert at getting things done on schedule.

It would only take the courage to ask him. She blew out a breath. She'd have to find that, but she would dig inside herself until she did.

TEMPERATURES SOARED, and the humidity thickened in a syrupy morass that Cam not so cheerfully dubbed "fumidity." He worked below-decks, trimming out the cabin until the heat sent him top-side desperate for fluids and one stingy breeze.

Though he rarely complained about the working conditions, Ethan was—like Cam—stripped to the waist. Sweat poured as he patiently varnished.

"That's going to take a week to dry, it's so goddamn damp."

"Decent storm might blow some of it out."

"Then I wish to Christ we'd have one." Cam grabbed up the jug and glugged water straight from the lip.

"Close weather makes some people edgy."

"I'm not edgy, I'm hot. Where's the kid?"

"Sent him for some ice."

"Good idea. I could take a bath in it. There's no fucking air down there."

Ethan nodded. Varnishing was a miserable enough job in this weather, but working below in the little cabin where even the big fans couldn't reach was probably kin to working in hell. "Want to switch off for a while?"

"I can do my own goddamn job."

Ethan merely lifted a sweaty shoulder. "Suit yourself."

Cam gritted his teeth, then hissed. "Okay, I am edgy. The heat's frying my brain, and I keep wondering if that alley cat's gotten Anna's letter yet."

"Ought to. It went out Tuesday as soon as the post office broke the holiday. It's Friday now."

"I know what day it is, Ethan." Disgusted, Cam swiped sweat off his face and scowled at his brother. "Aren't you worried a damn bit about it?"

"It won't make any difference if I am or not. She'll do what she's going to do." His gaze flicked up to Cam's and was hard as a bunched fist. "Then we'll handle it."

Cam paced the deck, caught a whiff of air from the fans, paced back. "I never could understand how you can stay so calm when things go to hell."

"Practice," Ethan murmured and kept on varnishing.

Cam rolled his aching shoulders, drummed his fingers on his thigh. He had to think of something else or he'd go crazy. "How'd the big date go the other night?"

"Well enough."

"Jesus, Ethan, do I have to get the pliers?"

A smile moved over Ethan's mouth. "Had a nice dinner. Drank some of that Pouilly Fuisse Phil's so wild about. Tastes fine enough, but I don't see what the big fuss is about."

"So, you get laid?"

Ethan flicked up another glance, took in Cam's wide grin, and decided to take the question in the spirit it was asked. "Yeah—did you?"

Entertained, if no cooler, Cam threw back his head and laughed. "Damn, she's the best thing that ever happened to you. I don't just mean the sex, though that's got to be part of what's perked you up around here lately. The woman fits you like the proverbial glove."

Ethan paused, scratched his belly where sweat dribbled and itched. "Why?"

"Because she's rock-steady, pretty as a picture, patient as Job, and she's got enough humor about life to tickle out yours. I guess we'll be sprucing up the yard for another wedding before long."

Ethan's fingers tightened on his brush. "I'm not going to marry her, Cam."

It was the tone as much as the statement that made Cam's eyes narrow. Quiet despair. "I guess I could be reading you wrong," Cam said slowly. "I figured, the way things were moving, you were serious about her."

"I am serious, about Grace. About a lot of things." He dipped his brush again, watched the clean gold varnish drip. "Marriage isn't something I'm looking for."

Ordinarily Cam would have let a subject such as this drop. He'd have walked away from it with a shrug. Your business, brother. But he knew Ethan too well, had loved him too long to walk away from the pain. He crouched by the rail so their faces were closer.

"I wasn't looking for it either," he murmured. "Scared the hell out me. But when the woman comes into your life, *the* woman, it's scarier to let her go."

"I know what I'm doing."

The dug-in-at-the-heels look didn't stop Cam. "You always figure you do. I hope you're right this time. I sure as hell hope this isn't some shit that goes back to that ghost-eyed kid Mom and Dad brought home one day. The one who used to wake up screaming at night."

"Don't go there, Cam."

"Don't you go there, either. Mom and Dad did better by us than that."

"It has nothing to do with them."

"It all has everything to do with them. Listen—" He broke off with a mild oath as Seth came running in.

"Hey, this shit's already melting."

Cam straightened, scowled over at Seth out of habit rather than heat. "Didn't I tell you to find an alternate word for 'shit'?"

"You say it," Seth pointed out, shifting the bag of ice.

"That's beside the point."

Knowing the routine, Seth dumped the ice into the cooler. "Why?"

"Because Anna's going to have my ass if you keep it up. And if she has mine, pal, I'll have yours."

"Oh, now I'm scared."

"You oughta be."

They continued to bicker, Ethan continued the varnish. Tuning them out, concentrating on the job at hand, he locked his unhappiness away.

SEVENTEEN

I T WAS GOING TO BE PER-
fect. It was so obviously right, Grace wondered that she
hadn't thought of it before. A sunset sail on calm seas with
skies going pink and gold in the west was a custom-made
backdrop for both of them. The Bay was part of their lives,
what it offered and what it took.

She knew it was more than a place where Ethan
worked. It was a place he loved.

It had been easy to arrange. All she'd had to do was
ask. He looked surprised, then he smiled. "I'd forgotten
you love to sail," he said.

She was touched when he'd simply expected that Aubrey would come with them. There would be other times,
she thought. A lifetime for the three of them. But this
warm and breezy evening would be for the two of them
only.

Giddy laughter continued to rise up in her as she imagined his reaction when she asked him to marry her. She
could see it so clearly, the way he would stop, stare at her

with surprise in those wonderful blue eyes. She would smile, hold out her hand to him as they glided along with soft wind and dark water. And she would tell him everything that was in her heart.

I love you so much, Ethan. I always have and always will. Will you marry me? I want us to be a family. I want to live my life with you. To give you children. To make you happy. Haven't we waited long enough?

Then, she knew, that would be the moment his smile would begin. That slow, beautiful smile that moved degree by degree over the planes and shadows of his face, into his eyes. He would probably say something about how he'd intended to ask her. That he'd been getting to it.

They would both laugh, and they would hold each other as the sun dropped red beyond the shore. And their lives together would really begin.

"Where are you sailing off to, Grace?"

She blinked, saw Ethan smiling back at her from the wheel. "Daydreaming," she told him, chuckling at herself. "Sunset's the best time for daydreams. It's so peaceful."

She rose, nestled herself under his arm. "I'm so glad you can take a few hours off so we can do this."

"We're going to have the boat trimmed out within the month." He nuzzled his face in her hair. "Couple weeks ahead of schedule."

"You've all worked so hard."

"It's going to be worth it. The owner was here today."

"Oh?" This was part of it, too, she mused. The easy talk about their days. "What did he say?"

"Hardly shut up, so it's hard to know what he said half the time. Spouted off the latest this and that he'd read in his boating magazines, asked enough questions to make your head ring."

"But did he like it?"

"I figure he was pleased with her, since he grinned like a kid on Christmas morning the whole afternoon. After he left, Cam wanted to bet me that he would run her aground first time out on the Bay.''

"Did you take the bet?"

"Hell, no. He likely will. But you haven't really sailed the Bay until you've run aground.''

Ethan wouldn't, she mused, watching his big, competent hands on the wheel. He sailed clean.

"I remember when you and your family were building this sloop.'' She trailed her fingers over the wheel. "I was helping out at the waterfront the first time y'all took her out. Professor Quinn was at the wheel and you were working the lines. You waved at me.'' Chuckling, she angled her head to look up at him. "I was thrilled that you noticed me.''

"I was always noticing you."

She leaned up and kissed his chin. "But you were careful not to let me notice you noticing.'' On impulse she gave his jaw a teasing nip. "Until lately.''

"I guess I lost my knack for it.'' He turned his head until his mouth found hers. "Just lately.''

"Good.'' With a quiet laugh, she laid her head on his shoulder. "Because I like noticing you notice me.''

They weren't alone on the Bay, but he stayed well clear of the zipping motorboats out for a summer-evening cruise. A flock of gulls frantically swooped and swirled around the stern of a skiff where a young girl tossed out bread. Her laugh carried, high and bright, to mix with the greedy calls of the birds.

The breeze rose up, filling the sails and whisking away the wet heat of the day. The few clouds drifting in the west were going pink around the edges.

Almost time.

Odd, she realized, she wasn't a bit nervous. A little giddy perhaps, because her head felt so light, her heart so free. Hope, so long buried, was golden bright once freed.

She wondered if he would slip into one of the narrow channels where the shade would be thick and the water the color of tobacco. He could thread past the bobbing buoy markers to a quiet place, one without even the gulls for company.

He was so content with her beside him, Ethan let the wind choose the course. He should make adjustments, he thought. The sails would reef before long if he didn't. But he didn't want to let her go—not quite yet.

She smelled of her lemon soap, and her hair was soft against his cheek. This could be their lives, he thought. Quiet moments, evening sails. Standing together. Building little dreams into big ones.

"She's having the time of her life," Grace murmured.

"Hmmm?"

"The little girl there, feeding the gulls." She nodded in the direction of the skiff, smiling as she imagined Aubrey, a few years from now, laughing and calling to the gulls from the stern of Ethan's boat. "Uh-oh, here comes her little brother to demand his share." She laughed, charmed by the children. "They're nice together," she murmured, watching as the two of them heaved bread high into the air for eager beaks to snatch. "Company for each other. There're more lonely times for an only child."

Ethan closed his eyes a moment as his own half-formed daydream shattered. She would want more children. Deserve them. Life wasn't all pretty sails on the Bay.

"I need to trim the sails," he told her. "Do you want to take the wheel?"

"I'll trim them." She grinned at him as she ducked under his arm to move to port. "I haven't forgotten how to handle lines, Cap'n."

No, he thought, she hadn't forgotten. She was a good sailor, as at home on deck as she was in her own kitchen. She ran the rigging with the same skill that she showed when she served drinks to a crowd at the pub.

"There's not much you can't do, Grace."

"What?" She glanced up, then laughed. "It's not hard to know how to use the wind when you grow up with it."

"You're a natural sailor," he corrected. "A wonderful mother, a fine cook. You know how to make people easy around you."

Her pulse went from calm to frantic. Would he ask her now, after all, before she had the chance to ask him? "Those are all things I enjoy," she said, watching him watch her. "Making a home here in St. Chris contents me. You do the same, Ethan, because it contents you."

"I've got a need for this place," he said softly. "It's what saved me," he added, but he'd turned away and she didn't hear.

Grace waited another moment, willing him to speak, to tell her, to ask her. Then with a shake of her head, she crossed the deck again.

The sun was sinking, coming close, so close to that long nightly kiss of the shore. The water was calm, little wavelets waltzing against the hull. The sails were full and white.

The moment, she thought with a leap of heart, was now.

"Ethan, I love you so much."

He lifted an arm to bring her against his side. "I love you, Grace."

"I've always loved you. I always will."

He looked down at her then, and she saw the emotion come into his eyes, deepening the blue. She lifted a hand to his cheek, held it there as she drew in the next breath.

"Will you marry me?" She saw the surprise, as she'd expected, but she didn't notice the way his body went stiff as she rushed on. "I want us to be a family. I want to live my life with you. To give you children. To make you happy. Haven't we waited long enough?"

And she waited now, but she didn't see the slow smile slip across his face, into his eyes. He only continued to stare at her, with something she thought might be horror. Bony wings of panic fluttered in her stomach.

"I know you might have planned to do this differently, Ethan, and me asking you is a surprise. But I want us to be together, really together."

Why didn't he say something? her mind screamed. Anything. Why did he just stare at her as if she'd slapped him?

"I don't need courting." Her voice hitched and she stopped to try to steady it. "Not that I don't love things like flowers and candlelight dinners, but all I really need is for you to be there. I want to be your wife."

Afraid he would shatter if he looked into those hurt and baffled eyes another instant, he turned away. His hands white-knuckled on the wheel. "We have to come about."

"What?" She jerked back, staring at his set face, at the muscle that worked in his jaw. Her heart was still pounding, but no longer in anticipation. Now it was with dread. "You have nothing to say to me except that we have to come about?"

"No, I've things to say to you, Grace." His voice was as controlled as his heart was wild. "We have to go back so I can."

She wanted to shout at him to say them now, right now. But she nodded. "All right, Ethan. Come about."

THE SUN WAS GONE when they docked. Crickets and peepers sent up their nightly chorus, filling the air with shrill, too-bright music. Overhead a few stars blinked through the haze and a three-quarter moon shimmered.

The air had cooled quickly, but she knew that wasn't the reason she was cold. So cold.

He secured the lines himself, silently. Just as he'd sailed home, silently. He stepped back into the boat, sat across from her. The moon was still low, just riding the tops of the trees, but the early stars sprinkled down enough light for her to see his face.

There was no joy in it.

"I can't marry you, Grace." He spoke the words carefully, knowing they would hurt. "I'm sorry. I can't give you what you want."

She gripped her hands together tightly. She didn't know whether they wanted to ball into fists and pound or hang limp and shaking like an old woman's. "Then you lied when you said you loved me?"

It might be kinder to tell her so, he thought, then shook his head. No, it would only be cowardly. She deserved the truth. All of the truth. "I didn't lie. I do love you."

There were degrees of love. She wasn't fool enough to think differently. "But not the way you need to love a woman you'd marry."

"I couldn't love any woman more than I love you. But I'm—"

She held up a hand. Something had just occurred to her. If it was his reason for turning her away, she didn't think she could ever forgive him. "Is it because of Aubrey? Because I had a child with another man?"

He moved fast so rarely, it took her by surprise when he snatched her hand out of the air and squeezed it hard enough to rub bone against bone. "I love her, Grace. I'd be proud for her to think of me as her father. You have to know that."

"I don't have to know anything. You say you love me, and you love her, but you won't have us. You're hurting me, Ethan."

"I'm sorry. I'm sorry." He released her hand as if it had burned his palm. "I know I'm hurting you. I knew I would. I had no business letting things come to this."

"But you did," she said evenly. "You had to know I'd feel this way, that I'd expect you would feel the same."

"Yeah, I knew. I should have been honest with you. I've got no excuse for it." *Except I needed you. I needed you, Grace.* "Marriage isn't something I'm looking for."

"Oh, don't treat me like a fool, Ethan." She sighed now, too battered to be angry. "People like us don't have relationships, we don't have affairs. We get married and raise families. We're simple and basic, and as amusing as that might be to some, that's just who we are.''

He stared down at his hands. She was right, of course. Or would have been. But she didn't know he wasn't simple or basic. "It's not you, Grace."

"No?" Hurt and humiliation tangled inside her. She imagined Jack Casey would have said the same thing, if he'd taken the time to say anything before he left her. "If it's not me, who is it? I'm the only one here."

"It's me. I can't raise a family because of what I come from."

"What you come from? You come from St. Christopher's on the southern Eastern Shore. You come from Raymond and Stella Quinn."

"No." He lifted his gaze. "I come from the stinking slums of D.C. and Baltimore and too many other places to count. I come from a whore who sold herself, and me, for a bottle or a fix. You don't know what I come from. Or what I've been."

"I know you came from a terrible place, Ethan." She spoke gently now, wanting to soothe the brutal pain in his eyes. "I know your mother—your biological mother—was a prostitute."

"She was a whore," Ethan corrected. " 'Prostitute' is too clean a word."

"All right." Cautious now, for she saw more than pain, she nodded slowly. There was fury as well, just as brutal. "You lived through what no child should ever have to live through before you came here. Before the Quinns gave you hope and love and a home. And you became theirs. You became Ethan Quinn."

"It doesn't change the blood."

"I don't know what you mean."

"How the hell would you?" He shot it at her like a bullet, hot and dangerously sharp. How would she know? he thought furiously. She'd grown up knowing her parents, and their parents, never once having to question what they had passed on to her, what she'd taken from them.

But she would, before he was done, she'd know. And that would end it. "She was a big woman. I get my hands from her. My feet, the length of my arms."

He looked down at those arms now, at those hands that had bunched into fists without his being aware of it. "I don't know where I get the rest from because I don't think she knew who my father was any more than I did. Just another john she had bad luck with. She didn't get rid of me because she'd already had three abortions and was afraid to risk another. That's what she told me."

"That was cruel of her."

"Jesus Christ." Unable to sit any longer, he rose, leaped onto the dock to pace.

Grace followed more slowly. He was right about one thing, she realized. She didn't know this man, the one who moved in fast, jerky steps with his fists clenched as if he would use them viciously on anything that moved into his path.

So she stayed out of it.

"She was a monster. A fucking monster. She beat me senseless for the hell of it as often as when she figured she had a reason."

"Oh, Ethan." Helpless to do otherwise, she reached out for him.

"Don't touch me now." He wasn't sure what he might do if he put his hands on her just then. And it frightened him. "Don't touch me now," he repeated.

She let her empty arms fall to her sides, battled back the tears that wanted to come.

"She had to take me to the hospital once," he continued. "I guess she was afraid I was going to die on her. That's when we moved from D.C. to Baltimore. The doctor asked too many questions about how I fell down the steps and gave myself a concussion and a couple cracked ribs. I used to wonder why she didn't just leave me behind. But then, she got some welfare money because of me and had a live-in punching bag, so I guess that was reason enough. Until I was eight.''

He stopped pacing and stood still, stood facing her. There was so much rage inside him he could all but feel it searing his pores. And the bitter rise of it stung his throat. ''That was when she figured I'd better start earning my keep. She'd been in the life long enough to know where to go to find men who didn't much care for women. Men who would pay for children.''

She couldn't speak, even when she pressed a hand to her throat as if to push words, any words, out. She could only stand there, her face bone-white in the light of the rising moon and her eyes huge and horrified.

''The first time, you fight. You fight like your life depends on it, and part of you doesn't believe it's really going to happen. It just can't happen. Doesn't matter that you know what sex is because you've been around the ugly edge of it all your life. You don't know what this is, can't believe it's possible. Until it's happening. Until you can't stop it from happening.''

''Oh, Ethan. Oh, God. Oh, God.'' She began to weep, for him, for the little boy, for a world where such horrors could exist.

''She made twenty dollars, gave me two. And made a whore of me.''

''No,'' Grace said, helpless and sobbing. ''No.''

''I burned the money, but that didn't change anything. She gave me a couple of weeks, then she sold me again. You fight the second time, too. Harder even than the first, because now you know, and now you believe. And you keep fighting, every time, over and over through the same nightmare until you just give up. You take the money and you hide it because one day you'll have enough. Then you'll kill her and get out. God knows you want to kill her maybe even more than you want to get out.''

She closed her eyes. ''Did you?''

He heard the raspiness in her voice, took it for disgust

rather than the sick fury it was. A fury for him, underscored with a vicious hope that he had. Oh, that he had.

"No. After a while it's just your life. That's all. Nothing more, nothing less. You just live it."

He turned away now to stare toward the house, where
the lights glowed in the windows. Where music—Cam on
guitar—carried by the breeze played a pretty tune.

"I lived it until I was twelve and one of the men she'd
sold me to went a little crazy. He knocked me around
pretty hard, but that wasn't so unusual. But he was flying
on something and he went after her. They tore the place
apart, made enough trouble that a couple neighbors who'd
made it their business to mind their own got riled enough
to beat on the door.

"He had his hands around her throat," Ethan remembered. "And I was sprawled on the floor, looking up,
watching her eyes bulge, and I was thinking, Maybe he'll
do it. Maybe he'll do it for me. She got her hand on a
knife, and she jammed it into him. She jammed it into his
back just as the people beating on the door busted it in.
People were shouting and screaming. She pulled the son
of a bitch's wallet out of his pocket while he was bleeding
on the floor. And she ran. She never even looked at me."

He shrugged, turned back. "Somebody called the cops
and they got me to a hospital. I'm not clear on it, but that's
where I ended up. Doctors and cops and social workers,"
he said quietly. "Asking questions, writing things down.
I guess they went looking for her, but they never found
her."

He lapsed into silence so that there was only the lap of
water, the call of insects, the echoing notes of a guitar. But
she said nothing, knowing he wasn't finished. Not yet finished.

"Stella Quinn was at some medical conference in Baltimore, and she was doing guest rounds. She stopped by
my bed. I guess she'd looked at my chart, I don't remember. I just remember her being there, putting her hands on

the bed guard and looking down at me. She had kind eyes, not soft but kind. She talked to me. I didn't pay any attention to what she said, just her voice. She kept coming back. Sometimes Ray would be with her. One day she told me I could come home with them if I wanted.''

He fell silent again, as if that was the end. But all Grace could think was that the moment when the Quinns had offered him a home had been the beginning.

''Ethan, my heart breaks for you. And I know now that as much as I loved and admired the Quinns all these years, it wasn't enough. They saved you.''

''They saved me,'' he agreed. ''And after I decided to live, I did everything I could to be something that honored that, and them.''

''You are, and always have been, the most honorable man I know.'' She went to him, wrapped her arms around him, and held tight despite the fact that his arms didn't enfold her in return. ''Let me help,'' she murmured. ''Let me be with you. Ethan.'' She lifted her face, pressed her mouth to his. ''Let me love you.''

He shuddered, broke. His arms came round her now, fiercely. His mouth took the comfort she offered. He swayed there, holding on to her, a lifeline in a thrashing sea. ''I can't do this, Grace. It's not right for you.''

''You're right for me.'' She clung when he would have eased her away. ''Nothing you've said changes what I feel. Nothing could. I only love you more for it.''

''Listen to me.'' His hands were steady, but they were firm as they gripped her shoulders and pushed her back. ''I can't give you what you need, what you want, what you should have. Marriage, children, family.''

''I don't—''

''Don't tell me you don't need them. I know you do.''

She drew in air, let it out slowly. ''I need them with you. I need a life with you.''

''I can't marry you. I can't give you children. I promised myself I'd never risk passing on to a child whatever pieces of her are in me.''

"There's nothing of her in you."

"There is.'' His fingers tightened briefly. "You saw it that day in the woods when I took you against a tree like an animal. You saw it when I yelled at you over working in a bar. And I've seen it too many times to count when someone pushes me the wrong way once too often. Holding it back doesn't mean it's not there. I can't take vows with you or make a child with you. I love you too much to let you believe it's ever going to happen.''

"She scarred more than your body," Grace murmured. "It's your heart she really abused. I can help you heal it the rest of the way.''

He gave her a quick, gentle shake. "You're not listening to me. You're not hearing me. If you can't accept the way things have to be between us, I'll understand. I'll never blame you for stepping back and looking for what you want with someone else. The best thing for you is for me to let you go. And that's what I'm doing.''

"Letting me go?''

"I want you to go home.'' He released her and stepped back. Felt as if he'd entered a huge, dark void. "Once you think this all through, you'll see it my way. Then you can decide if we should go on seeing each other the way we have been or if you want me to leave you be.''

"I want—''

"No," he interrupted. "You don't know what you want right now. You need time, and so do I. I'd rather you went on. I don't want you here right now, Grace.''

She lifted a hand to her temple. "You don't want me here?''

"Not now.'' He set his jaw when he saw the hurt swim into her eyes. For her own good, he reminded himself. "Go home and leave me be for a while.''

She took a step back, then another. Then turned and ran. Around the house rather than through it. She couldn't bear having anyone see her with tears on her cheeks and this awful tearing pain in her heart. He wouldn't have her, was all she could think. He wouldn't let her be what he needed.

"Hey, Grace! Hey." Seth abandoned his pursuit of the lightning bugs that flickered and flashed through the dark and raced after her. "I've got about a million of these suckers." He started to hold up a jar.

Then he saw the tears, heard them in her ragged breathing as she fumbled with the door handle on her car. "What's wrong? Why are you crying? Did you get hurt?"

She sobbed out a breath, pressed a hand to her heart. Oh, yes, oh, yes, I'm hurt. "It's nothing. I have to go home. I can't—I can't stay."

She tore open the car door, stumbled inside.

Seth's eyes went from puzzled to grim as he watched her drive away. Hot with fury, he stormed around the side of the house, slapping the bright jar on the edge of the porch. He saw the shadow on the dock and strode toward it with fists clenched for battle.

"You bastard. You son of a bitch." He waited until Ethan turned, then rammed his fist as hard as he could into his gut. "You made her cry."

"I know I did." The fresh and physical pain jolted through him, and joined the rest. "This isn't your business, Seth. Go on in the house."

"Fuck you. You hurt her. Go on, try to hurt me. It won't be so easy." Teeth bared, Seth swung again, and again, until Ethan picked him up by collar and seat and held him dangling over the end of the dock.

"Cool off, you hear, or I'll toss you in." He added a hard, threatening shake, but his heart wasn't in it. "You think I wanted to hurt her? You think I got any pleasure out of it?"

"Then why did you?" Seth shouted, struggling like a baited fish.

"There wasn't any choice." Suddenly abominably

weary, Ethan dropped Seth to his feet on the dock. "Leave me alone," he murmured and sat on the edge. Giving in, he put his head in his hands, pressed his fingers to his eyes. "Just leave me alone."

Seth shifted his feet. It wasn't just Grace who was hurt. He hadn't really understood that a grown man could be, not this way. But Ethan was. Tentatively, he stepped forward. He stuck his hands in his pockets, pulled them out. Shuffled. Sighed. Then sat.

"Women," Seth said in a level and considering voice, "make a man want to shoot himself in the head and be done with it." It was something he'd heard Phillip say to Cam, and he thought it might be appropriate. He was rewarded when Ethan let out a short laugh, even if it wasn't a happy one.

"Yeah, I guess they can." Ethan draped an arm around Seth's shoulders, pulled the boy close to his side. And took a little comfort.

EIGHTEEN

ANNA WEIGHED HER PRI-
orities—and took the day off. She couldn't be sure what
time Grace would be by to tend the house, and she couldn't
risk missing her.

She didn't give a good damn what Ethan said—or
didn't say. There was a crisis.

If she'd believed they'd simply had a spat or misunderstanding, she would have been sympathetic or amused,
whichever was most called for. It wasn't a misunderstanding that had put misery into Ethan's eyes. Oh, he had a
way of hiding it, she mused as she slowly and ruthlessly
tugged out weeds that threatened her begonias in the front-
yard bed. And he hid his more personal feelings very well.
It just so happened she was a professional at filtering
through to emotion.

Too bad for him that he'd inherited a social worker for
a sister-in-law.

She'd poked at Seth a bit. There was no doubt in her
mind the boy knew something. But she'd run straight into

unwavering male loyalty. All she got out of him was a Quinn shrug and a zipped lip.

She could have wheedled it out nonetheless. But she hadn't had the heart to put a chip in that lovely bond. Seth could keep his loyalty to Ethan.

Anna would work on Grace.

She was positive they hadn't seen each other for days. It was pathetically easy to keep tabs on Ethan. He was out on the water every morning, in the boatyard every afternoon and through the evening. He poked at his dinner, then retreated to his room. Where she'd seen the light slanting under his door well into the night on several occasions.

Brooding, she thought with an impatient shake of her head. And if he wasn't brooding, he was looking for a fight.

She had broken up what would certainly have been bloodshed over the weekend when she walked in on the three brothers going nose to nose in the boatyard, Seth looking on with avid interest.

Whatever had caused it remained a mystery as she'd bounced straight off that same united male wall. Shrugs and snarls were all she got for her trouble.

Well, it was going to stop, she decided, and attacked some chickweed with enthusiasm. Women knew how to share and discuss. And if she had to bang Grace Monroe over the head with her garden spade, Grace was damn well going to share and discuss.

It was with pleasure that she heard Grace's car pull in. Anna tipped back her hat, rose, and offered a welcoming smile. "Hi, there."

"Hello, Anna. I thought you'd be at work."

"Took a mental health day." Oh, yes, misery here as well, she mused. And not quite as well coated as Ethan's. "You didn't bring Aubrey with you."

"No. My mother wanted her today." Grace ran a hand up and down the strap of the oversized bag over her shoulder. "Well, I'll get started and let you get back to your gardening."

"I was just looking for an excuse to take a break. Why don't we sit down on the porch a minute?"

"I really should get the first load of laundry in."

"Grace." Anna laid a gentle hand on her arm. "Sit down. Talk to me. I count you as one of my friends. I hope you count me as one of yours."

"I do." Grace's voice wavered. She had to take three breaths to steady it. "I do, Anna."

"Then let's sit down. Tell me what's happened to make you and Ethan so unhappy."

"I don't know if I can." But she was tired, bone-tired, so she sat down on the steps. "I guess I made a mess of everything."

"How?"

She'd cried herself dry, Grace thought. Not that it had helped. Maybe it would help to talk things over with another woman, one she was beginning to feel close to. "I let myself assume," she began. "I let myself plan. He picked me flowers," she said with a helpless lift of her hands.

"Picked you flowers?" Anna's eyes narrowed fractionally. Rabbits, my butt, she thought, but filed it away for later retribution.

"And he took me to dinner. Candles and wine. I thought he was going to ask me to marry him. Ethan does things stage by stage, and I thought he was leading up to proposing."

"Of course you did. You're in love with each other. He's devoted to Aubrey and she adores him. You're both nesters. Why wouldn't you think it?"

Grace stared for a moment, then let out a long breath. "I can't tell you what it means to hear you say that. I felt like such a fool."

"Well, stop. You're not a fool. I'm not, and I certainly thought it."

"We were both wrong. He didn't ask me. But he loved me that night, Anna. So tenderly. I never believed anyone would feel so much for me. He had a nightmare later."

"A nightmare."

"Yes." And she understood it now. "It was bad, very bad, but he pretended it wasn't. He told me not to worry and brushed it off. So I didn't think any more about it. Then." Thoughtfully, she rubbed a faint bruise on her thigh that she'd given herself bumping into a table at Shiney's.

"The next day I decided if I sat around waiting for Ethan to do the asking, I'd have gray hair on my wedding day. Ethan doesn't exactly rush through life."

"No, he doesn't. He gets things done in his own time, and gets them done well. But he could sure use a poke now and then."

"He does, doesn't he?" She couldn't stop the warm, wistful smile. "Sometimes he just thinks things to death. And I thought this was going to be one of those times, so I made up my mind to do the asking myself."

"You asked Ethan to marry you?" Anna chuckled, leaned back on the steps. "Atta girl, Grace."

"I had it all worked out. Everything I wanted to say and how to say it. I thought, on the water where he's most content, so I asked him to take me out for an evening sail. It was so lovely, with the sun setting and the sails bright and full of wind. And I asked him."

Anna slipped a hand over Grace's. "I gather he turned you down. But—"

"It was more than that. If you'd seen his face . . . He went so cold. He said he'd explain things to me when we got back. And he did. I don't feel right telling you, Anna, because it's Ethan's business. But he said he can't marry me, won't marry me or anyone. Ever."

Anna didn't speak for a moment. She was Seth's case-worker, which meant she'd had full access to the files on the three men who would stand as his guardians. She knew their pasts nearly as well as they did. "Is it because of what happened to him as a child?"

Grace's gaze flickered, then she stared straight ahead. "He told you?"

"No, but I know about it, most of it. It's part of my job."

"You know . . . what his mother—that woman—did to him, let other people do to him? He was only a little boy."

"I know that she forced him to have sex with clients for several years before she abandoned him. There are still copies of the medical reports in his file. I know that he was raped and beaten before Stella Quinn found him in the hospital. And I know what that kind of trauma, that kind of consistent abuse can do. Ethan could very well have become an abuser himself. It's a miserably common cycle."

"But he didn't."

"No, he became a thoughtful, considerate man with nearly unflappable control. The scars are there, under it. It's likely that his relationship with you has brought some of them closer to the surface."

"He won't let me help. Anna, he's got it into his head that he can't risk having children because he's got her blood in him. Bad blood that he would pass on. He won't marry because marriage means family to him."

"He's wrong, and he has the best example of how wrong in his own mirror. He not only has her blood but he spent the first twelve years—the most impressionable years—with her in an environment that could warp any young mind. Instead, he's Ethan Quinn. Why should his children—children that come from the two of you—be any less than he is?"

"I wish I had thought to say that," Grace murmured. "I was so shocked and sad and shaken." She closed her eyes. "I don't think it would have mattered if I had. He wasn't going to listen. Not to me," she said slowly. "He doesn't think I'm strong enough to live with what he's lived with.''

"He's wrong."

"Yes, he's wrong. But his mind's made up. He won't want me now. He says the choice is mine, but I know him. If I say I can accept this and we go on as we are, it'll eat at him until he pulls away."

"Can you accept it?"

"I've asked myself that, thought about that for days now. I love him enough to want to, maybe to settle for it, at least for a while. But it would eat at me, too." She shook her head. "No, I can't accept it. I can't accept only one part of him. And I won't ask Aubrey to accept anything less than a father."

"Good for you. Now, what are you going to do about it?"

"I don't know that there's anything I can do. Not when we both need different things."

Anna let out a huff of breath. "Grace, you're the only one who can decide. But let me tell you, Cam and I didn't just float to the altar on gossamer wings. We wanted different things—or thought we did. And to find out what we wanted together, we hurt each other, we got in each other's faces and we dealt with it."

"It's hard to get in Ethan's face about anything."

"But it's not impossible."

"No, it's not impossible, but . . . He wasn't honest with me, Anna. Underneath it all, I can't forget that. He let me spin my daydreams, all the time knowing he was going to cut the threads of them and let me fall. He's sorry for it, I know, but still . . .''

"You're angry."

"Yes, I guess I am. I had another man do that to me. My father,'' she added, coolly now. "I wanted to be a dancer, and he knew I was pinning my hopes on it. I can't say he ever encouraged me, but he let me go on taking lessons and wishing. And when I needed him to stand up and help me try for that dream . . . he cut the threads. I forgave him for it, or tried to, but things were never the same. Then I got pregnant and married Jack. I guess you could say that cut his threads, and he's never forgiven me.''

"Have you tried to resolve things there?"

"No, I haven't. He gave me a choice, too, just like Ethan did. Or what they seem to think of as a choice. Do this their way. Accept it, or do without them. So I'll do without.''

"I understand that. But while it may buffer your pride, what does it do to your heart?"

"When people break your heart, pride's all you've got left.''

And pride, Anna thought, could turn cold and bitter without heart. "Let me talk to Ethan."

"I'll talk to him, as soon as I can work out what needs to be said." She blew out a breath. "I feel better," she realized. "It helps to say it all out loud. And there was no one else I could say it to.''

"I care about both of you."

"I know. We'll be all right." She gave Anna's hand a squeeze before she rose. "You helped me stop feeling weepy. I hate feeling weepy. Now I'm going to work off some of this mad I didn't realize was in there." She managed to smile. "You're going to have a damn clean house when I'm done. I clean like a maniac when I'm working off a mad.''

Don't work it all off, Anna thought, as Grace went inside. Save some of it for that idiot Ethan.

IT TOOK TWO AND A HALF hours for Grace to scrub, rinse, dust, and polish her way through the second floor. She had a bad moment in Ethan's room, where the scent of him, of the sea, clung to the air, and the small, careless pieces of his daily life were scattered about.

But she drew herself in, calling on the same core of steel that had gotten her through a divorce and a painful family rift.

Work helped, as it always had. Good, strenuous manual labor kept both her hands and her mind busy. Life went on. She knew it firsthand. And you got through from one day to the next.

She had her child. She had her pride. And she still had dreams—though she'd come to the point that she preferred to think of them as plans.

She could live without Ethan. Not as fully perhaps, not as joyfully, certainly. But she could live and be productive and find contentment in the path she forged for herself and her daughter.

She was finished with tears and self-pity.

She started on the main floor with the same single-minded fervor. Furniture was polished until it gleamed. Glass was scrubbed until it sparkled. She hung out wash, swept porches, and battled dirt as if it were an enemy threatening to take over the earth.

By the time she got to the kitchen her back ached, but it was a small and satisfying pain. Her skin wore a light coat of sweat, her hands were pruny from wash water, and she felt as accomplished as a corporate president after a major business coup.

She checked the clock, measured time. She wanted to be finished and gone before Ethan came in from work. Despite the purging wrought by labor, there was a small, simmering ember of anger still burning in her heart. She knew herself well enough to understand that it would take very little to fan it to full flame.

If she fought with him, if she said even a portion of the things that had careened through her head over the last few days, they would never be able to be civil again, much less friends.

She wouldn't force the Quinns to take sides. And she wouldn't risk putting her precious and vital relationship with Seth at risk because two adults in his life couldn't mind their tempers.

"I won't lose my job over it, either," she muttered as she went to work on the countertops. "Just because he can't see what he's throwing out of his life."

She hissed out a breath, scooped her fingers through her hair, which the heat and her exertion had dampened at the temples. And calmed herself by giving the drip pans on the ancient range a good scouring.

When the phone rang, she snatched it up without thinking. "Hello?"

"Anna Quinn?"

Grace glanced out the window, saw Anna puttering happily among the back garden. "No, I'll—"

"I got something to say to you, bitch."

Grace stopped, two steps from the screen door. "What?"

"This is Gloria DeLauter. Who the hell do you think you are, threatening me?"

"I'm not—"

"I got rights. Do you hear me? I got fucking rights. The old man made a deal with me, and if you and your bastard husband and his bastard brothers don't live up to it, you're the ones who'll be sorry."

The voice wasn't just hard and harsh, Grace realized. It was manic, the words shooting out so fast that one ran into the back of the other. This was Seth's mother, she thought as more abuse rang in her ear. The woman who'd hurt him, who frightened him. Who'd taken money for him.

Sold him.

She wasn't aware that she had twisted the phone cord around her hand, that it was so tightly wrapped it bit into the flesh. Struggling for calm, she took a deep breath. "Miss DeLauter, you're making a mistake."

"You're the one who made the goddamn mistake, sending me that fucking letter instead of the money you owe me. You fucking *owe* me. You think I'm scared 'cause you're some asshole social worker. I don't give a shit if you're the goddamn Queen of goddamn England. The old man's dead, and if you want things to stay like they are you're going to deal with me. You think you can hold me off with words on paper? You're not going to stop me if I decide to come back and take that boy."

"You're wrong," Grace heard herself say, but her voice sounded far away, echoing in her head.

"He's my flesh and blood and I got a right to take what's mine."

"Try it." Rage tore through her like a storm surge. "You'll never put your hands on him again."

"I can do what I like with what's mine."

"He's not yours. You sold him. Now he's ours, and you're never going to get near him."

"He'll do what the hell I tell him to do. He knows he'll pay for it otherwise."

"You make one move toward him, I'll take you apart myself. Nothing you've done to him, however monstrous, is close to what I'll do to you. When I'm finished, they'll barely have enough left to scrape up and toss in a cell. That's just where you'll go for child abuse, neglect, assault, prostitution, and whatever it is they call a mother who sells her child to men for sex."

"What kind of lies has that brat been telling? I never laid a finger on him."

"Shut up. You shut the hell up." She'd lost track, mixed Seth's mother and Ethan's into one woman. One monster. "I know what you did to him, and there isn't a cage dark enough to lock you in to suit me. But I'll find one, and I'll shove you in it myself if you come near him again."

"I just want money." There was a wheedle in the voice now, both sly and a little scared. "Just some money to help me through. You've got plenty."

"I don't have anything for you but contempt. You stay away from here, and you stay away from that child, or you'll be the one who pays."

"You better think again. You just better think again." There was a muffled sound, then the clink of ice against glass. "You're no better than me. I'm not afraid of you."

"You should be afraid. You should be terrified."

"I'm . . . I'm not finished with this. I'm not done."

The click of the disconnect was loud. "Maybe not," Grace said in a soft and dangerous voice. "But neither am I."

"Gloria DeLauter," Anna murmured. She stood just on the other side of the screen door, where she'd been for the last two minutes.

"I don't think she's human. If she'd been here, if she'd been in this room, I'd have had my hands around her throat. I'd have choked her like an animal." She began to shake now, fury and reaction crashing against each other inside her. "I'd have killed her. Or tried."

"I know how it feels. It's hard to think about someone like her as a person and not a thing." Anna pushed the door open, her eyes on Grace. She would never have expected to see that white-hot rage in such a mild-tempered woman. "I see it all too often in my work, but I never get used to it."

"She was foul." Grace shuddered. "She thought I was you when I answered the phone. I tried to tell her at first, but she wouldn't listen. She just shouted and threatened and swore. I couldn't let her get away with it. I couldn't stand it. I'm sorry."

"It's all right. From the end of the conversation I could hear, I'd say you handled it. You want to sit down?"

"No, I can't. I can't sit." She shut her eyes, but still only saw that blinding red haze. "Anna, she said she'd come back and get Seth if you didn't give her money."

"That's not going to happen." Anna moved to the refrigerator, pulled out a bottle of wine. "I'm going to pour you a glass of this. You're going to drink it, slowly, while I get my notebook. Then I want you to try to tell me what she said, as close as possible to exactly what she said. Can you do that?''

''I can. I can remember.''

''Good.'' Anna glanced at the clock. ''We're going to want to document everything. If she does come back, we're going to be ready.''

''Anna.'' Grace stared down into the wine Anna had given her. ''He can't be hurt anymore. He shouldn't have to be afraid anymore.''

''I know it. We'll make sure he's not. I'll only be a minute.''

ANNA   TOOK   HER through the conversation twice. As she went through it the second time, Grace found herself unable to sit. She rose, leaving her glass of wine half full, and got a broom.

''The way she said things was every bit as vile as what she said,'' she told Anna as she began to sweep. ''She must use that same tone on Seth. I don't know how anyone can speak to a child that way.'' Then she shook her head. ''But she doesn't think of him as a child. He's a thing to her.''

''If you were called on to testify, you'd be able to swear under oath that she demanded money.''

''More than once,'' Grace agreed. ''Will it come to that, Anna? Will you have to take Seth into court?''

''I don't know. If it heads in that direction, we should be able to add extortion to the list of charges you reeled off. You must have scared her,'' she added with a small, satisfied smile. ''You'd have scared me.''

''Things just come flying out of my mouth when I get worked up.''

''I know what you mean. There are things I'd like to

say to her, but in my position, I can't. Or I shouldn't," she said with a long sigh. "I'll type this up for Seth's file, then I suppose I'll have to compose another letter to her."

"Why?" Grace's fingers tightened on the handle of the broom. "Why do you have to have any contact with her?"

"Cam and his brothers need to know, Grace. They need to know exactly what Gloria DeLauter and Seth were to Ray."

"It's not what some people are saying." Grace's eyes flashed as she yanked a dustpan out of the broom closet. She couldn't seem to sweep away the simmering anger inside her. "Professor Quinn wouldn't have cheated on his wife. He was devoted to her."

"They need to have all the facts, and so does Seth."

"I'll give you a fact. Professor Quinn had taste. He wouldn't have looked twice at a woman like Gloria DeLauter—unless it was with pity, or disgust."

"Cam certainly feels the same way. But another thing people say is that when they look at Seth they see Ray Quinn's eyes."

"Well, there's another explanation for it, that's all." Her own eyes were hot as she shoved the broom and dustpan away, yanked out a bucket and a mop.

"Perhaps. But it may have to be faced and dealt with that the Quinns hit a rocky patch in their marriage, as people often do. Extramarital affairs are distressingly common."

"I don't give a damn about all the statistics you hear on television or read in magazines about how three out of five men—or whatever it is—cheat on their wives." Grace dumped cleanser in the bucket, dropped it into the sink, and turned the water on full blast. "The Quinns loved each other, and they liked each other. And they had an admiration for each other. You couldn't be around them and not see it. They were tied only tighter together because of their sons. When you saw the five of them together, you were seeing family. Just the way the five of you are family.''

Touched, Anna smiled. ''Well, we're working on it.''

''You just haven't had as many years as the Quinns did.'' Grace hauled the bucket out of the sink. ''They were a unit.''

Units, Anna thought, often broke down. ''If something had happened between Ray and Gloria, would Stella have forgiven him?''

Grace thrust the mop into the bucket and gave Anna a cool, decisive look. ''Would you forgive Cam?''

''I don't know,'' Anna said after a moment. ''It would be hard to because I'd have killed him. But I might, eventually, put flowers on his grave.''

''Exactly.'' Satisfied, Grace nodded. ''That kind of betrayal doesn't swallow down easily. And it follows that if the Quinns had that kind of tension between them, their sons would have known it. Children aren't fools, no matter how many adults might think so.''

''No, they're not,'' Anna murmured. ''Whatever the truth is, they need to find it. I'm going to type up my notes,'' she said as she rose. ''Will you take a look at them, see if there's anything you want to add or change before they go into the file?''

''All right. I've still got some wash to hang out, then I'll be . . .''

They heard it at the same time, the wildly happy barking of dogs. Grace's reaction was pure distress. She'd lost track of the time, and Ethan was home.

Going on instinct, Anna slipped her notebook into a kitchen drawer. ''I want to talk to Cam about this before we tell Seth about the phone call.''

''Yes, that's best. I . . .''

''You can go out the back, Grace,'' Anna said quietly. ''Nobody could blame you for not wanting another emotional hit today.''

''I have wash to hang out.''

"You've done more than enough for one afternoon."

Grace straightened her shoulders. "I finish what I start." She turned into the laundry room and the lid of the washer clanged as she tossed it up. "Which is more than can be said of some people."

Anna lifted a brow. Ethan was in for a surprise, she decided. And wasn't it handy that she was around to see him get it?

NINETEEN

W<small>HEN HE SAW HER CAR</small> in the driveway, Ethan had to force himself not to rush into the house just for a look at her. A quick glimpse, just one. He could take all of her into his mind with just one look.

He hadn't known it was possible to miss a woman—to miss anything—the way he was missing Grace.

The way, he thought, that left him empty and achy and edgy every hour of every day until he was desperate to fill the void. Until he laid awake at night listening to the air breathe.

Until he thought he was losing his mind.

The control he'd kept in place for so many years where she was concerned seemed constantly shaky these days. The walls of that control had already been breached, were tumbled at his feet so that he could swear he was choking on their dust.

He supposed once a man let it go, it was hard to build it back up again.

But he'd left the choice in her hands, he reminded himself. Since she hadn't made a move in his direction in days, he was afraid he knew which choice she'd made.

He couldn't blame her for it.

She would find someone else—someone she could make a life with. The thought burned in his gut as he loitered by his truck, but he refused to let it pass. She deserved to have what she wanted out of life. That was marriage and children and a pretty home. A father for Aubrey, a man who would appreciate both of them for the treasures they were.

Another man.

Another man who would slip his arms around her waist, rub his mouth over hers. Hear her breath quicken, feel her bones go soft.

Some faceless son of a bitch who wasn't good enough for her would turn to her in the night, sink inside her. And smile every goddamn morning because he knew he could do it again.

Christ, Ethan thought, it was making him crazy.

Foolish bumped into his legs, a ratty tennis ball clamped hopefully in his mouth, his tail wagging persuasively. In a habitual move, Ethan tugged the ball free and tossed it. Foolish bounded after it, yapping furiously when Simon darted like a bullet from the left and intercepted.

Ethan only sighed when Simon pranced back, sat, and waited for the game to continue.

It was as good an excuse as any to stay outside, Ethan decided. He would fool with the dogs, go fiddle with his boat, stay out of Grace's way. If she had wanted to see him, she could have found him.

The dogs worked him around the side yard, and taking pity on the slower, less skilled Foolish, Ethan found a stick to toss along with the ball. It lightened his mood a little to watch them bash into each other, wrestle, fetch, and retrieve.

You could depend on a dog, he thought, giving the ball a higher, harder toss that sent Simon bounding in pursuit.

They never asked for more than you could give them.

He didn't see Grace until he was well around the house. Then he simply stood.

No, one look, one quick glimpse, wasn't enough. Would never be enough.

The sheet she lifted to the line flapped wetly in the breeze as she pegged it. The sun was on her hair. As he watched, she bent to the basket, took out a pillowcase, gave it a quick snap, then clipped it beside the sheet.

Love flooded into him, swamped him, left him weak and needy. Small details hammered him—the curve of her cheek in profile. Had he ever noticed how elegant her profile was? The way her hair sat on her head, feathered at the back of her neck. Was she letting it grow? The way the trim cuff of her shorts skimmed her thigh. She had such long, smooth thighs.

Foolish rapped his head against Ethan's leg and snapped him back.

Abruptly nervous, he wiped his hands on his work pants, shifted his feet. It was probably best, he decided, if he just slipped back around the front, went into the house and upstairs. He took the first step back, then pulled up short when she turned. She gave him a long look, one he couldn't read, then bent to take out another pillowcase.

"Hello, Ethan."

"Grace." He tucked his hands in his pockets. It wasn't often he heard her voice quite so cool.

"It's foolish to go all the way back around to the front of the house just to avoid me."

"I was . . . going to check something on the boat."

"That's fine. You can do that after I talk to you."

"I wasn't sure you'd want to talk to me." He approached her cautiously. Her tone of voice took the blistering heat right out of the day.

"I tried to talk to you the other night, but you weren't inclined to listen." She reached into the basket, apparently unperturbed that she was now hanging his underwear.

"Then I needed a little time to myself, to settle everything in my head."

"And have you?"

"Oh, I think so. First, I should tell you that what you told me about what you went through before you came here shocked me, and it hurt me, and I have nothing but pity for that little boy and rage about what happened to him." She glanced at him as she secured the next clothespin. "You don't want to hear that. You don't want to think that I have feelings about it, that it touched me."

"No," he said evenly. "No, I didn't want it to touch you."

"Because I'm so fragile. Because I'm so delicate of nature."

His brows drew together. "Partly. And—"

"So you hoarded that nasty little seed all for yourself," she went on, calmly working her way down the clothesline. "Even though there's nothing in or of my life that you don't know. It's the way it should be, in your opinion, that I'm an open book and you're a closed one."

"No, it wasn't that. Exactly."

"What could it have been exactly?" she wondered, but he didn't think it was a question and wisely formed no answer. "I've been thinking about that, Ethan. I've been thinking about a number of things. Why don't we go back a ways first? You like to do things in neat, logical steps. And since you like things to be done your way, we'll just be neat and logical."

The dogs, sensing trouble, retreated to the water. Ethan found himself envying them.

"You told me you've loved me for years. Years," she said with such quick fury that he nearly stumbled back. "But you don't do anything about it. You don't once, not once, come up to me and ask me if I'd like to spend some time with you. One word from you, one look from you, would have thrilled me. But oh, no, not Ethan Quinn, not with his broody mind and incredible control. You just kept your distance and let me pine over you."

"I didn't know you had those kind of feelings for me."

"Then you're blind as well as stupid," she snapped.

His brows drew together. "Stupid?"

"That's what I said." Seeing the outrage cross his face was balm to her battered ego. "I would never have looked twice at Jack Casey if you'd given me anything to hope for. But I needed someone to want me, and it sure as hell didn't appear it was ever going to be you."

"Now just a damn minute. I'm not to blame for you marrying Jack."

"No, I take the blame. I take the responsibility, and I don't regret it because it gave me Aubrey. But I blame you, Ethan." And those gold-flecked green eyes blazed with it. "I blame you for being too pigheaded to take what you wanted. And you haven't changed a damn bit."

"You were too young—"

She used both hands, and all the force of her temper went into the shove. "Oh, shut up. You had your say. Now I'm having mine."

IN THE KITCHEN, SETH'S eyes went hot. He made a dash for the door, only to be brought up short by Anna, who was eavesdropping as hard as she could.

"No, you don't."

"He yelled at her."

"She's yelling, too."

"He's fighting with her. I'm going to stop him."

Anna cocked her head. "Does she look like she needs any help?"

His mouth set, Seth glared through the screen. Then reconsidered when he saw Grace shove Ethan back a full step. "I guess not."

"She can handle him." Amused, she gave Seth a scrubbing pat on the top of the head. "How come you don't leap to my defense when Cam and I argue?"

"Because he's afraid of you."

Anna rolled her tongue into her cheek, enjoying the idea. "Oh, really?"

"Half afraid, anyway," Seth said with a grin. "He never knows what you'll do. And besides, you guys like to argue."

"Observant little brat, aren't you?"

He shrugged, cheerful now. "I see what I see."

"And know what you know." Laughing, she edged closer to the door with him, hoping for a better view.

"LET'S MOVE TO THE next step, Ethan." Grace shoved the empty basket out of her way with her foot. "Fast-forward a few years. Think you can keep up?"

He took a long breath because he didn't want to yell at her again. "You're pissing me off, Grace."

"Good. I mean to, and I hate to fail at something I'm working on."

He wasn't sure which emotion came out on top, annoyance or bafflement. "What's gotten into you?"

"Oh, I don't know, Ethan. Let's see—could it be the fact that you think I'm some brainless, helpless female? Yes, you know . . ." She jabbed her index finger into his chest like a drill into wood. "I bet that's just what's gotten into me."

"I don't think you're brainless."

"Oh, just helpless, then." Even as he opened his mouth she was rolling over him. "Do you think a helpless woman can do what I've been doing the last few years? Do you think—what was it you called me once—delicate, like your mama's good china. I'm not china!" she exploded.

"I'm good solid stoneware, the kind you can drop and it rattles around on the floor. It doesn't shatter. You have to *work* to break good stoneware, Ethan, and I'm not broken yet."

She punched a finger into his chest again, darkly pleased when his eyes flashed a warning. "I wasn't so helpless when I got you into my bed, was I? Which is just where I wanted you."

"You didn't get me anywhere."

"Hell, I didn't. And *you're* brainless if you think differently. I reeled you in like a goddamn rockfish."

It gave her pleasure, oh, such vivid pleasure, to see both fury and frustration race over his face. "If you think a statement like that flatters either of us—"

"I'm not trying to flatter you. I'm telling you straight out, I wanted you and I went after you. If I'd left the matter up to you, we'd have been pinching each other's butts in a nursing home."

"Jesus, Grace."

"Just be quiet." There was no stopping now, whatever the consequences, not with this roaring sea crashing in her head. "You just think about that, Ethan Quinn. You give that some good long thought and don't you *dare* call me fragile again."

He gave her a slow nod. "It's not the word that's coming to mind at the moment."

"Good. I haven't needed you or anyone to help me build a decent life for my baby. I used muscle, and I used guts to do what needed to be done, so don't you tell me I'm china."

"You wouldn't have had to do it all alone if you weren't too damn proud to settle things with your father."

The truth of that put a hitch in her step. But she balled her fists and rushed on. "We're talking about you and me. You say you love me, Ethan, but you don't for one minute understand me."

"I'm starting to agree with that," he muttered.

"You've got some ego-ridden male idea in your head that I need to be taken care of, protected, coddled—when what I need is to be needed and respected and loved. And you'd know that if you paid attention. You ask yourself this, Ethan, who seduced whom? Who said 'I love you' first. Who proposed marriage? Are you so nearsighted you can't see I've had to take every step first with you?"

"You make it sound like you've been leading me by the nose, Grace. I don't care for that."

"I couldn't lead you by the nose if I jabbed a fish hook in it. You go exactly where you want to go, Ethan, but you can be so infuriatingly slow. I love that about you, and I admire it, and now I understand it more. You had a terrible period in your life when you had no control, now you take care not to lose it. But you can slip from control into stubbornness in one short step, and that's just what you've done."

"I'm not being stubborn. I'm being right."

"Right? It's right for two people to love each other and not build a life out of it? It's right to pay all your life for what someone else did to you when you were too young to defend yourself against it? Is it right for you to say you can't and won't marry me because you're . . . stained and you made some ridiculous promise to yourself never to have a family of your own?"

It sounded off when she said it like that. It sounded . . . stupid. "It's the way it is."

"Because you say so."

"I told you how it is, Grace. I gave you the choice."

Her jaw hurt from clenching it. "People like to say they've given somebody a choice when what they're really saying is 'do this my way.' I don't like your way, Ethan. Your way only takes into account what was and doesn't add what is, or what could be. You think I don't know what you expected? You'd take your stand and sweet, delicate Grace would just fall in line."

"I didn't expect you to fall in line."

"Then crawl off, wounded, and pine after you for the rest of my life. You're getting neither. I'll give you a choice this time, Ethan. You straighten yourself out, you go on and think things through for the next eon or two, then you let me know what conclusions you've come to. Because my stand is this. It's marriage or it's nothing. I'll be damned if I'll spend the rest of my life pining over you. I can live without you." She tossed back her head. "Let's see if you're man enough to live without me."

She whirled around and stalked off, leaving him fuming.

"UPSTAIRS," ANNA HISSED at Seth. "He's coming inside. Now it's my turn."

"Are you going to yell at him, too?"

"Maybe."

"I want to watch."

"Not this time." She all but shoved him out of the room. "Upstairs. I mean it."

"Hell." He stomped to the stairs, waited a moment, then slipped back down the hallway.

Anna was pouring herself a homey cup of coffee when Ethan slammed the back door. Part of her wanted to go over and give him a big, sympathetic hug. He looked so miserably unhappy and confused. But the way she figured it, there were times when it was best all around to kick a good man when he was down.

"Want some?"

He flicked a glance at her and kept walking. "No, thanks."

"Hold it." She smiled sweetly when he stopped, when she all but saw the jittery waves of impatience shimmering around him. "I need to talk to you for a minute."

"I'm about talked out for the day."

"That's all right." Deliberately she pulled a chair out

from the table. "You sit down and I'll talk."

Women, Ethan decided as he dropped into the chair, were the bane of his existence. "I guess I'll take the coffee, then."

"All right." She poured him a mug, brought him a spoon so he could dump his customary heaps of sugar into it. She sat, folded her hands neatly, and continued to smile.

"You stupid jerk."

"Oh, Jesus." He rubbed his hands over his face, left them there. "Not another one."

"I'm going to make it easy on you at first. I'll ask a question, you answer. Are you in love with Grace?"

"Yes, but—"

"No qualifications." Anna cut him off. "The answer is yes. Is Grace in love with you?"

"Hard to say just now." He shifted his hand to nurse the point on his chest where she'd all but bored a hole in him.

"The answer is yes," Anna said coolly. "Are you both single, otherwise unattached adults?"

He could feel himself sinking into a sulk, and detested it. "Yeah—so?"

"Just laying the groundwork, gathering the facts. Grace has a child, correct?"

"You know damn well—"

"Correct." Anna lifted her cup, took a sip of coffee. "Do you have feelings of affection for Aubrey?"

"Of course I do. I love her. Who wouldn't?"

"And does she have feelings of affection for you?"

"Sure. What—"

"Wonderful. We've established the emotions of the parties involved. Now let's move on to stability. You have a profession, and a new business. You appear to be a man with skill, who's willing to work and has the capability of earning a good living. Have you incurred any large, outstanding debts you believe you'll have difficulty meeting?"

"For God's sake!"

"No offense intended," she said brightly. "I'm simply approaching this matter the way I assume you would, calmly, patiently, step by tedious step."

He narrowed his eyes at her. "Seems to me people are having major problems with how I do things lately."

"I love the way you do things." She reached across the table and gave his tense hand an affectionate squeeze. "I love you, Ethan. It's wonderful for me to have a big brother at this stage of my life."

He shifted in his chair. He was touched by the obvious sincerity in her eyes, but he had a feeling she was tenderizing him in preparation for the roasting to come. "I don't know what's going on around here."

"I think you'll figure it out. So, we'll say you're financially sound. Grace, as we know, is well capable of earning a living. You own your own home, and a one-third share in this one. Shelter certainly isn't an issue. So, we'll move on. Do you believe in the institution of marriage?"

He knew a trick question when he heard one. "It works for some people. Doesn't work for others."

"No, no, do you believe in the institution itself? Yes or no."

"Yes, but—"

"Then why the hell aren't you down on one knee with a ring in your big, clumsy hand, begging the woman you love to give your fat head another chance?"

"I'm a patient man," Ethan said slowly, "but I'm getting tired of insults."

"Don't you dare get out of that chair," she warned when he started to scrape it back. "I swear I'll belt you. God knows I want to."

"That's another thing that's going around." He subsided only because it seemed easier to get it all over with at once. "Go ahead then, say what you have to say."

"You think I don't understand. You think I can't relate

to what's eating you up inside. You're wrong. I was raped when I was ten years old."

Shock jolted his heart, pain squeezed his soul. "Jesus, Anna! Jesus, I'm sorry. I didn't know."

"Now you do. Does it change me, Ethan? Aren't I the same person I was thirty seconds ago?" She reached for his hand again, held it this time. "I know what it is to be helpless and terrified and want to die. And I know what it is to make something of your life, despite that. And I know what it is to have that horror in you always. No matter how much you've learned, no matter how much you've come to accept it and know it was never, ever your fault."

"It's not the same."

"It's never the same, not for any two people. We have something more in common as well. I never knew who my father was. Was he a good man or a bad one? Tall or short? Did he love my mother, or did he use her? I don't know what parts of him were passed to me."

"But you knew your mother."

"Yes, and she was wonderful. Beautiful. And yours wasn't. She beat you, physically and emotionally. She made you a victim. Why are you letting her keep you one? Why are you letting her win even now?"

"It's me now, Anna. There has to be something twisted, something sour inside a person to make them the way she was. I came from that."

"Sins of the fathers, Ethan?"

"I'm not taking on her sins, I'm talking about heredity. You can pass on the color of your eyes, your build. Weak hearts, alcoholism, longevity. Those things can run in families."

"You've given this a lot of thought."

"Yeah, I have. I had to make a decision, and I made it."

"So you decided you could never marry or have children."

"It wouldn't be fair."

"Well, then, you'd better talk to Seth before too long."

"Seth?"

"Someone has to tell him he's never going to be able to have a wife and children. It's best if he knows that early, so he can try to protect himself from becoming emotionally involved with a woman."

For a trio of heartbeats he could only gape at her. "What the hell are you talking about?"

"Heredity. We can't be sure what bad traits Gloria DeLauter passed down to him. God knows she's got something twisted inside her, just as you said. A whore, a drunk, a junkie, from all accounts."

"There's nothing wrong with that boy."

"What difference does that make?" She met Ethan's furious stare blandly. "He shouldn't be allowed to take chances."

"You can't mix him in with me this way."

"I don't see why. You both come from similar situations. In fact, there are far too many cases that come through social services nationally that slip into parallel categories. I wonder if we can pass a law to prevent children of abusers from marrying and having children of their own. Think of the risks we'd avoid."

"Why don't you just geld them?" he said viciously.

"That's an interesting concept." She leaned forward. "Since you're so determined not to pass on any unhealthy genes, Ethan, have you considered a vasectomy?"

The instinctive and purely male cringe nearly made her laugh. "That's enough, Anna."

"Is that what you would recommend to Seth?"

"I said that's enough."

"Oh, it's more than enough," she agreed. "But answer this last question. Do you think that bright, troubled child should be denied a full and normal life as an adult because he had the bad luck to be conceived by a heartless, perhaps even evil woman?"

"No." His breath shuddered out. "No, that's not what I think."

"No buts this time? No qualifications? Then I'll tell you that in my professional opinion, I couldn't agree with you more. He deserves everything he can grab, everything he can make, and everything we can give him to show him that he's his own person and not the damaged product of one vile woman. And neither are you, Ethan, anything but your own man. Stupid, maybe," she said with a smile as she rose. "But admirable, honorable, and incredibly kind."

She went to him, put an arm around his shoulders. When he sighed, turned his face to press it against her midriff, tears stung her eyes.

"I don't know what to do."

"Yes, you do," she murmured. "Being you, you'll have to think about it for a while. But do yourself a favor this time, and think fast."

"I guess I'll go down to the boatyard and work until I get it clear in my head."

Because she was feeling suddenly maternal toward him, she bent and kissed the top of his head. "Do you want me to pack you some food?"

"No." He gave her a squeeze before he rose. When he saw that her eyes were damp, he patted her shoulder. "Don't cry. Cam'll have my head if he finds out I made you cry."

"I won't."

"Well, then." He started out, hesitated, then turned back briefly to study her as she stood in the kitchen, her lashes wet, her hair tangled from being out in the breeze. "Anna, my mother—my real mother," he added, because Stella Quinn was in his mind all that was real—"would have loved you."

Hell, Anna thought as he walked away, she was going to cry after all.

Ethan kept going, particularly when he heard Anna's

sniffle. He needed to be alone, to clear out his head and let the thoughts gather again.

"Hey."

With his hand on the door, he looked over his shoulder and saw Seth on the stairs—where the boy had dashed like a skillful rabbit seconds before Ethan had started out of the kitchen.

"Hey what?"

Seth started down, slowly. He'd heard everything, every word. Even when his stomach had begun to pitch, he had stayed and listened. As he studied Ethan now, owlishly, he thought he understood. And he felt safe.

"Where you going?"

"Back to the boatyard. I got some things I want to finish up." Ethan let the door ease closed again. There was something in the boy's eyes, he thought. "You okay?"

"Yeah. Can I go out on the workboat with you tomorrow?"

"If you want."

"If I went with you, we'd finish sooner and be able to work on the boat with Cam. When Phil comes down on the weekend, we can all work on her together."

"That's how it goes," Ethan said, puzzled.

"Yeah. That's how it goes." All of them, Seth thought with a flash of pure joy, together. "It's hard work because it's hot as a bitch in heat."

Ethan bit back a chuckle. "Watch the mouth. Anna's in the kitchen."

Seth shrugged, but aimed a wary glance behind him. "She's cool."

"Yeah." Ethan's smile spread. "She's cool. Don't stay up half the night drawing or bugging your eyes out at the TV if you're working with me in the morning."

"Yeah, yeah." Seth waited until Ethan was outside, then snatched up the bag sitting beside the chair. "Hey!"

"Christ, boy, are you going to let me out of here before tomorrow?"

"Grace forgot her purse." Seth pushed it into Ethan's hand and kept his face bland and innocent. "I guess she had something on her mind when she left."

"I guess." Brows knit, Ethan stared down at it. Damn thing weighed ten pounds if it weighed an ounce, he thought.

"You ought to take it over to her. Women go nuts if they don't have their purses. See you."

He raced back inside, pounded up the stairs and straight to the first window that faced the front of the house. From there he could watch Ethan scratch his head, shove the purse under his arm like a football, and walk slowly to the truck.

His brothers sure could be weird, he thought. Then he grinned to himself. His brothers. Letting out a whoop, he raced down the steps to head for the kitchen and nag Anna for something to eat.

TWENTY

GRACE INTENDED TO
cool off and calm down before she stopped by her parents'
house to pick up Aubrey. When she was this emotionally
churned up, there was no hiding it from anyone, much less
from a mother or a very perceptive child.

The last thing she wanted was questions. The last thing
she felt capable of giving was explanations.

She'd said what needed to be said and done what
needed to be done. And she refused to feel sorry for it. If
it meant losing a long-standing friendship, one that she had
always treasured, it couldn't be helped. Somehow she and
Ethan would manage to be adult enough to be polite when
in public and not to drag anyone else into their battles.

It certainly wouldn't be an easy or happy situation, but
it could work. The same arrangement had worked for three
years with her father, hadn't it?

She drove around for twenty minutes, until her fingers
were no longed gripping the wheel like a vise and the
reflection of her face in the rearview mirror was no longer

capable of frightening children and small dogs.

She assured herself that she was now perfectly under control. So under control that she thought she'd take Aubrey out to McDonald's for a treat. And on her very next evening off, she was taking them both to Oxford for the Firemen's Carnival. She certainly wasn't going to stay around the house moping.

She didn't slam the door of her car, which she felt was an excellent sign of her now placid mood. Nor did she stomp up the steps of her parents' tidy Colonial. She even paused for a moment to admire the pale-purple petunias spilling out of a hanging planter near the picture window.

It was just bad luck and bad timing that her gaze shifted a few inches past the blooms and that she spotted her father through that picture window, lounging in his recliner like a king on his throne.

Temper geysered and blasted her through the door like a sharp-edged pebble from a well-aimed slingshot.

"I have a few things to say to you." She let the door slam at her back and marched up to where Pete rested his feet. "I've been saving them up."

He goggled at her for the five seconds it took for him to arrange his face. "If you want to speak to me, you'll do it in a civilized tone of voice."

"I'm through being civilized. I've had civilized up to here." She made a sharp slashing motion with her hand.

"Grace! Grace!" Cheeks flushed, eyes huge, Carol hustled in from the kitchen with Aubrey on her hip. "What's gotten into you? You'll upset the baby."

"Take Aubrey back to the kitchen, Mama. And it won't traumatize her for life to hear her mother raise her voice."

As if to prove arguments were inevitable, Aubrey threw back her head and sent up a wail. Grace stifled the urge to grab her, run out of the house with her, and smother her face with kisses until the tears stopped. Instead she stood firm. "Aubrey, stop that now. I'm not mad at you.

You go on in the kitchen with Grandma and have some juice.''

"Juice!" Aubrey sobbed it, at the top of her lungs, straining away from Carol with her arms held out to Grace and fat tears trembling on her cheeks.

"Carol, take the child in the kitchen and calm her down.'' Pete clamped down the exact urge as Grace's and waved a hand at his wife impatiently.

"Child hasn't shed a tear all day,'' he muttered, with an accusing look at Grace.

"Well, she's shedding them now,'' Grace snapped back, adding layers of guilt onto frustration as Aubrey's sobs echoed back from the kitchen. "And she'll forget them five minutes after they're dry. That's the beauty of being two. You get older, you don't forget tears as easily. You made me cry plenty of them.''

"You don't get through parenthood without causing some tears.''

"But some people can get through it without ever knowing the child they raised. You never looked at me and saw what I was.''

Pete wished he was standing. He wished he had shoes on his feet. A man was at a distinct disadvantage when he was kicked back in a recliner without his damn shoes on. "I don't know what you're talking about.''

"Or maybe you did—maybe I'm wrong about that. You looked, you saw, and you put it aside because it didn't fit in with what you wanted. You knew,'' she continued in a low voice that nonetheless snapped with fury. "You knew I wanted to be a dancer. You knew I dreamed of it, and you let me go right on. Oh, taking the lessons was fine with you. Maybe you grumbled about the cost of them from time to time, but you paid for them.''

"And a pretty penny it came to over all those years.''

"For what, Daddy?''

He blinked. No one had called him Daddy in nearly

three years and it pinched at his heart. "Because you were set on having them."

"What was the point if you were never going to believe in me, never going to let go enough or stand by enough to let me try to take the next step?"

"This is old business, Grace. You were too young to go to New York, and it was just foolishness."

"I was young, but not too young. And if it was foolishness, it was my foolishness. I'll never know if I was good enough. I'll never know if I could have made that dream real, because when I asked you to help me reach for it, you told me I was too old for nonsense. Too old for nonsense," she repeated, "but too young to be trusted."

"I did trust you." He jerked his chair up. "And look what happened."

"Yes, look what happened. I got myself pregnant. Isn't that how you put it at the time? Like it was something I managed all by myself just to annoy you."

"Jack Casey was no damn good. I knew it the first time I laid eyes on him."

"So you said, over and over again until he took on the gleam of forbidden fruit and I couldn't resist sampling it."

Now Pete's eyes flashed and he rose out of the chair. "You're blaming me for getting yourself in trouble?"

"No, I'm to blame if there has to be blame. And I won't make excuses. But I'll tell you this—he wasn't nearly as bad as you made him out to be."

"Left you high and dry, didn't he?"

"So did you, Daddy."

His hand shot up, shocking both of them. It didn't connect, and it trembled as he lowered it. He'd never done more than paddle her bottom when she was a toddler, and even then he'd suffered more than she had because of it.

"If you'd hit me," she said, struggling to keep her voice low and even, "it would be the first real feeling you've shown me since I came to you and Mama and told you I was pregnant. I knew you'd be angry and hurt and disappointed. I was so scared. But as bad as I thought it would be, it was worse. Because you didn't stand by me. The second time, Daddy, and the most important of all, and you weren't there for me.''

"A man's daughter comes in and tells him she's pregnant, that she's gone on and been with a man he took trouble to warn her away from, it takes him time to deal with it.''

"You were ashamed of me, and you were angry thinking of what the neighbors were going to say. And instead of looking at me and seeing that I was scared, all you saw was that I'd made a mistake you were going to have to live with.''

She turned away until she was sure, absolutely sure, there wouldn't be tears. "Aubrey is not a mistake. She's a gift.''

"I couldn't love her any more than I do.''

"Or me any less.''

"That's not true.'' He began to feel sick inside and more than a little scared himself. "That's just not true.''

"You stepped back when I married Jack. Stepped back from me.''

"You did some stepping back yourself.''

"Maybe.'' She turned around again. "I tried to make it once without you, putting my money away for New York. I couldn't do it on my own. I was going to make my marriage work without any help. But I couldn't do that, either. All I had left was the baby inside me, and I wasn't going to fail there, too. You never even came to the hospital when I had her.''

"I did.'' Groping, he picked up a magazine from the table, rolled it into a tube. "I went up and looked at her through the glass. She looked just like you did. Long legs and long fingers and nothing but yellow fuzz on her head. I went and looked in your room. You were asleep. I couldn't go in. I didn't know what to say to you.''

He unrolled the magazine, frowned at the fresh-faced

model on the cover, then dropped it back on the table. "I guess it made me mad all over again. You'd had a baby, and you didn't have a husband, and I didn't know what to do about it. I've got strong beliefs about that kind of thing. It's hard to bend."

"I didn't need you to bend very much."

"I kept waiting for you to give me the chance to. I thought when that son of a bitch ran out on you, you'd figure out you needed some help and come home."

"So you could have told me how right you were about everything."

Something flickered in his eyes that might have been sorrow. "I guess I deserve that, I guess that's what I would've done." He sat down again. "And damn it, I was right."

She gave a half laugh, weary around the edges. "Funny how the men I love are always so damn right where I'm concerned. Am I what you'd call a delicate woman, Daddy?"

For the first time in too long to remember she saw his eyes laugh. "Hell, girl, about as delicate as a steel rod."

"That's something, anyway."

"I always wished you had a little more give in you. Instead of coming once, just once, and asking for help, you're out there cleaning other people's houses, working until all hours in a bar."

"Not you, too," she murmured and moved to the window.

"Half the time if I see you down on the waterfront you've got shadows under your eyes. 'Course, the way your mother's jabbering, that'll change before long."

She glanced over her shoulder. "Change?"

"Ethan Quinn's not a man who'll let his wife wear herself to the bone working two jobs. That's the kind of man you should have been looking at all along. Honest, dependable."

She laughed again, pushed a hand through her hair.

"Mama's mistaken. I won't be marrying Ethan."

Pete started to speak again, closed his mouth. He was smart enough to learn by his mistakes. If he'd pushed her toward one man by pointing out his flaws, he might also push her away from another by listing his virtues.

"Well, you know your mother." He let it go at that. Trying to fit the words in his head, he plucked at the knee of his khakis. "I was afraid to let you go to New York," he blurted out, then shifted when she turned from the window to stare at him. "I was afraid you wouldn't come back. I was afraid, too, that you'd get yourself hurt up there. Hell, Gracie, you were only eighteen, and so damn green. I knew you were good at dancing. Everybody said so, and you always looked pretty to me. I figured if you got yourself up there and didn't get your head bashed in by some mugger, you'd find you wanted to stay. I knew you couldn't manage it unless I gave you the money to start you out, so I didn't. I thought you'd either stop wanting to go so damn bad, or if you didn't, it'd take you a year or two to put by enough."

When she said nothing, he sighed and leaned back. "A man works hard all his life building something, and while he's doing it he thinks that someday he'll pass it on to his child. My daddy passed the business on to me, and I always figured I'd pass it on to my son. Had a daughter instead, and that was fine. I never wanted to change that. But you never wanted what I was planning on giving you. Oh, you'd work. You were always a good worker, but anybody could see you were only doing a job. It wasn't going to be a life. Not your life."

"I didn't know you felt that way."

"Didn't matter how I felt. It wasn't for you, that's all. I started to think that you'd get married one day and maybe your husband would come into the business. That way I'd still be passing it on to you, and to your children."

"Then I married Jack, and you didn't get your dream, either."

His hands rested on his knees, and he lifted his fingers, let them fall. "Maybe Aubrey'll have an interest in it. I'm not planning on retiring anytime soon."

"Maybe she will."

"She's a good girl," he said, still looking down at his hands. "Happy. You . . . you're a fine mother, Grace. You're doing a better job than most under hard circumstance. You've made a good life for both of you, and done it on your own."

Her heart trembled and ached. "Thank you. Thank you for that."

"Ah . . . your mother would like it if you'd stay for dinner." Finally he looked up, and the eyes that met hers weren't cool, weren't distant. In them was both plea and apology. "I'd like it, too."

"So would I." Then she simply walked over, climbed into his lap and buried her face in his shoulder. "Oh, Daddy. I missed you."

"I missed you, Gracie." He began to rock and to weep. "I missed you, too."

ETHAN SAT ON THE TOP step of Grace's front porch and put her purse down beside him. He had to admit he'd been tempted several times to open it and poke inside to see just what a woman carted around with her that was so damned heavy and so indispensable.

But so far he'd managed to resist.

Now he wondered where she could be. He'd driven by her house nearly two hours earlier before going to the boatyard. Since her car wasn't in the drive, he didn't stop. Odds were, her door was unlocked and he could have set her purse inside the living room. But that wouldn't have accomplished anything.

He'd done some hard thinking while he worked. Some

of that thinking centered on how long it was going to take her to cool off from snarling mad to mildly irritated.

He figured he could deal with mildly irritated.

He decided it was probably best that she wasn't home quite yet. It gave them both more time to settle down.

"Got it all figured out yet?"

Ethan sighed. He'd smelled his father before he heard him, before he saw him sitting comfortably on the steps, feet crossed at the ankles. It was the salted peanuts in the bag Ray had in his lap. He had always had a fondness for salted peanuts.

"Not exactly. I can't seem to think it through so it gets clear."

"Sometimes you have to go with the gut instead of the head. You've got good instincts, Ethan."

"Following instinct's what got me into this. If I hadn't touched her in the first place . . ."

"If you hadn't touched her in the first place, you'd have denied both of you something a lot of people look for all their lives and never find." Ray rattled into the bag and pulled out a handful of nuts. "Why regret something that rare and that precious?"

"I hurt her. I knew I would."

"That's where you went wrong. Not in taking love when it was offered but in not trusting it for the long haul. You disappoint me, Ethan."

It was a slap. The kind that both knew would sting the most. Because it did, Ethan stared hard at the thirsty little pansies going leggy beside the steps. "I tried to do what I thought was right."

"For whom? For a woman who wanted to share your life, wherever that would take you? For the children you may or may not have. You're on dangerous ground when you second-guess God."

Annoyed, Ethan slanted a narrow look at his father's face. "Is there?"

"Is there what?"

"Is there a God? I figure you ought to know, seeing as you've been dead the last few months."

Ray threw back his big head, let out his wonderful rolling laugh. "Ethan, I've always appreciated your understated wit, and I wish I could discuss the mysteries of the universe with you, but time's passing."

Munching on nuts, he studied Ethan's face, and as he did, Ray's wickedly amused grin softened, warmed. "Watching you grow into a man was one of the greatest pleasures of my life. You've got a heart as big as your Bay. I hope you'll trust it. I want you to be happy. There'll be trouble coming for all of you."

"Seth?"

"He'll need his family. All his family," Ray added in a murmur, then shook his head. "There's too much misery in the short time we spend living, Ethan, to turn away happiness. You remember to value your joys." Then his eyes twinkled. "I'd brace myself, son. Your thinking time's over."

Ethan heard Grace's car, glanced toward the road. He knew without looking that his father was no longer beside him.

When Grace saw Ethan sitting on her front porch steps she wanted to lay her head on the steering wheel. She wasn't sure her heart could handle yet another trip through an emotional wringer.

Instead, she climbed out of the car and went around to unstrap the sleeping Aubrey from her car seat. With Aubrey's head heavy on her shoulder, she walked to the house and watched Ethan unfold his long legs and rise.

"I'm not willing to go through another round with you, Ethan."

"I brought your purse by. You left it at the house."

Startled, she frowned when he held it out to her. It showed just how jumbled her mind had been that she hadn't even realized she'd been without it. "Thank you."

"I need to talk to you, Grace."

"I'm sorry. I have to put Aubrey to bed."

"I'll wait."

"I said I'm not willing to talk about this again."

"I said I need to talk to you. I'll wait."

"Then you can just wait until I'm good and ready," she told him and sailed into the house.

It appeared she hadn't quite gotten down to mildly irritated, he decided. But he sat again. And he waited.

SHE TOOK HER TIME, stripping Aubrey down to her training pants, covering her with a soft sheet, tidying the bedroom. She went into the kitchen and poured herself a glass of lemonade she didn't want. But she drank every drop of it.

She could see him through the screen door, sitting on the steps. For a moment, she considered simply going to the door, closing it, and tossing the bolt to make her point. But she discovered she didn't have quite enough mad left to be that petty.

She opened the screen, let it close quietly.

"Is she down for the night?"

"Yes, she's had a long day. So have I. I hope this won't take long."

"I guess it doesn't have to. I want to tell you I'm sorry for hurting you, for making you unhappy." Since she didn't come down and join him on the steps, he stood and turned to her. "I went about it wrong, and I wasn't honest with you. I should have been."

"I don't doubt you're sorry, Ethan." She walked to the rail, leaned out, looked over her little patch of yard. "I don't know if we can be friends the way we were before. I know it's hard to be at odds with someone you care about. I made up with my father tonight."

"Did you?" He stepped forward, then stopped because she'd shifted away. Just a little, just enough to tell him he no longer had the right to touch. "I'm glad."

"I suppose I have you to thank for it. If I hadn't been so mad at you, I wouldn't have let myself be mad at him and get everything out. I'm grateful for that, and I appreciate your apology. Now I'm tired, so—"

"You said a lot of things to me today." She wasn't going to brush him off until he'd finished.

"Yes, I did." She shifted again, met his gaze straight on.

"Some of it was right, but not all. Not acting on how I felt about you before . . . it's the way it had to be."

"Because you say so."

"Because you couldn't have been more than fourteen when I started loving you, and wanting you. I was close to eight years older. I was a man when you were still a girl. It would have been wrong to touch you then. Maybe I waited too long." He stopped, shook his head. "I did wait too long. But I'd had time to think it through and I'd promised myself I wouldn't get you tangled up with me. You were the only one who I wanted enough that it mattered. Part of it was for me because I knew if I ever had you I wouldn't want to let you go."

"And you'd already decided that you would."

"I'd decided that I was going to live my life pretty much alone. I was managing that well enough until recently."

"You see it as a noble sacrifice. I see it as ignorance." She lifted her hands, knowing she was heating up again. "I guess we'd better leave it at that."

"You know damn well that if we were to get married you'd want more children."

"Yes, I would. And while I'll never agree with your reasoning for not making them together, there are other ways to make a family. You of all people should know. We could have adopted children."

He stared at her. "You . . . I figured you'd want to get pregnant."

"You figured right. I would want it because I would treasure your child living inside me, and knowing you were there with us. But that doesn't mean I couldn't find another way. What if I couldn't have children, Ethan? What if we were in love and planning to be married, and we found out I couldn't have babies? Would you stop loving me because of it? Would you tell me you couldn't marry me?"

"No, of course not. That's—"

"That's not love," she finished. "But it's not a matter of can't. It's a matter of won't. And I could have tried to understand your feelings if you hadn't kept them from me. If you hadn't turned me away when all I wanted was to help you. And I won't compromise on everything. I won't be with a man who doesn't respect my feelings and who won't share his problems with me. I won't be with a man who doesn't love me enough to stay. To make a promise to me to grow old with me and to be a father to my child. And I won't spend my life having an affair with you and then having to explain to my daughter why you didn't love and respect me enough to marry me."

She stepped toward the door.

"Don't." He shut his eyes, fought down panic. "Don't turn away from me, Grace."

"I'm not doing the turning away. Don't you see, Ethan? You've been doing the turning away all along."

"I've ended up right back where I started. Looking at you. Needing you. I'm never going to be able to stop now. I made so many promises to myself about you. I keep breaking them. I let her put her hands on this, too," he said slowly. "I let her put her mark on what we have. I want to clear that mark away, if you give me the chance."

He lifted his shoulders. "I've been doing some thinking."

She nearly smiled. "Well, there's news."

"Do you want to hear what I'm thinking now?" Following instinct, listening to his heart, he started up the stairs. "I'm thinking it's always been you, Grace, and only you. It's always going to be you, and only you. I can't help it if I want to take care of you. It doesn't mean I think you're weak. It's only because you're precious to me."

"Ethan." He would make her give in. She knew it. "Don't."

"And I'm thinking I'm not going to be able to give you the chance to live without me after all."

He took her hands, holding them when she tried to tug them free. And keeping his eyes on hers, he drew her out and down the steps to catch the last gilded light of the setting sun.

"I'll never let you down," he told her. "I'll never stop needing you to stand beside me. You make me happy, Grace. I haven't valued that enough, but I will from now on. I love you."

He touched his lips to her brow when she trembled. "The sun's setting. You said that was the best time for daydreams. Maybe it's the best time to pick the dream you want to hold on to. I want to hold on to this one. I need you to look at me," he said softly and lifted her face to his. "Will you marry me?"

Joy and hope blossomed within her. "Ethan—"

"Don't answer yet." But he'd seen the answer, and overcome with gratitude, he brought her hands to his lips. "Will you give Aubrey to me, let me give her my name? Let me be her father?"

Tears began to swim in her eyes. She willed them back. She wanted to see him clearly as he stood watching her with his face so serious, lit by the last quiet light of the day. "You know—"

"Not yet," he murmured and this time touched his lips to hers. "There's one more. Will you have my children, Grace?"

He saw the tears she'd been struggling to hold back spill over and wondered that he could ever have thought to deny them both that joy, that right, that promise.

"Make a life with me, one that comes from love, one that I can watch grow in you. Only a fool would believe that what comes from what we have together would be anything but beautiful."

She framed his face with her hands, took that picture into her heart. "Before I answer, I need to know that this is what you want, not just for me but for yourself."

"I want a family. I want to build what my parents built, and I need to build it with you."

Her lips curved slowly. "I'll marry you, Ethan. I'll give you my daughter. I'll make children with you. And we'll take care of each other."

He drew her close, just to hold, while the sun slipped away and the light shimmered into evening. Her heart beat quick and light against his. Her single quiet sigh echoed seconds before the whippoorwill began to sing in the plum tree next door.

"I was afraid you weren't going to be able to forgive me."

"So was I."

"Then I figured, hell, she loves me too much. I can get around her." The laugh rumbled out as he nuzzled her throat. "You're not the only one who can reel somebody in like a damn rockfish."

"Took you long enough to bait the hook."

"If you take your time about things, you end up with the best at the end of the day." He buried his face in her hair, wanting the scent and the texture. "Now, I've got the best. Good, solid stoneware."

Laughing, she leaned back so she could see his eyes. The humor there, she thought, was aimed at both of them. "You're a smart man, Ethan."

"Few hours ago you said I was stupid."

"You were." She pressed a noisy kiss on his cheek. "Now you're smart."

"I missed you, Grace."

She closed her eyes and held tight, thinking it was a

day for forgiveness. And hope. And beginnings. "I missed you, Ethan." She sighed, then gave the air a puzzled sniff. "Peanuts," she said and snuggled against him. "That's funny. I could swear I smell peanuts."

"I'll explain it to you." He tilted her head up for one soft kiss. "In a little while."

Can't get enough of Nora Roberts?
Try the #1 *New York Times* bestselling
In Death series, by Nora Roberts
writing as J. D. Robb.

Turn the page to see where it all began . . .

NAKED IN DEATH

SHE WOKE IN THE DARK.
Through the slats on the window shades, the first murky
hint of dawn slipped, slanting shadowy bars over the bed. It
was like waking in a cell.

For a moment she simply lay there, shuddering, imprisoned, while the dream faded. After ten years on the force,
Eve still had dreams.

Six hours before, she'd killed a man, had watched death
creep into his eyes. It wasn't the first time she'd exercised
maximum force, or dreamed. She'd learned to accept the
action and the consequences.

But it was the child that haunted her. The child she
hadn't been in time to save. The child whose screams had
echoed in the dreams with her own.

All the blood, Eve thought, scrubbing sweat from her face
with her hands. Such a small little girl to have had so much
blood in her. And she knew it was vital that she push it aside.

Standard departmental procedure meant that she would spend the morning in Testing. Any officer whose discharge of weapon resulted in termination of life was required to undergo emotional and psychiatric clearance before resuming duty. Eve considered the tests a mild pain in the ass.

She would beat them, as she'd beaten them before.

When she rose, the overheads went automatically to low setting, lighting her way into the bath. She winced once at her reflection. Her eyes were swollen from lack of sleep, her skin nearly as pale as the corpses she'd delegated to the ME.

Rather than dwell on it, she stepped into the shower, yawning.

"Give me one oh one degrees, full force," she said and shifted so that the shower spray hit her straight in the face.

She let it steam, lathered listlessly while she played through the events of the night before. She wasn't due in Testing until nine, and would use the next three hours to settle and let the dream fade away completely.

Small doubts and little regrets were often detected and could mean a second and more intense round with the machines and the owl-eyed technicians who ran them.

Eve didn't intend to be off the streets longer than twenty-four hours.

After pulling on a robe, she walked into the kitchen and programmed her AutoChef for coffee, black; toast, light. Through her window she could hear the heavy hum of air traffic carrying early commuters to offices, late ones home. She'd chosen the apartment years before because it was in a heavy ground and air pattern, and she liked the noise and crowds. On another yawn, she glanced out the window, followed the rattling journey of an aging airbus hauling laborers not fortunate enough to work in the city or by home 'links.

She brought the *New York Times* up on her monitor and scanned the headlines while the faux caffeine bolstered her system. The AutoChef had burned her toast again, but she ate it anyway, with a vague thought of springing for a replacement unit.

She was frowning over an article on a mass recall of droid cocker spaniels when her telelink blipped. Eve shifted to communications and watched her commanding officer flash onto the screen.

"Commander."

"Lieutenant." He gave her a brisk nod, noted the still-wet hair and sleepy eyes. "Incident at Twenty-seven West Broadway, eighteenth floor. You're primary."

Eve lifted a brow. "I'm on Testing. Subject terminated at twenty-two thirty-five."

"We have override," he said, without inflection. "Pick up your shield and weapon on the way to the incident. Code Five, Lieutenant."

"Yes, sir." His face flashed off even as she pushed back from the screen. Code Five meant she would report directly to her commander, and there would be no unsealed interdepartmental reports and no cooperation with the press.

In essence, it meant she was on her own.

BROADWAY WAS NOISY and crowded, a party that rowdy guests never left. Street, pedestrian, and sky traffic were miserable, choking the air with bodies and vehicles. In her old days in uniform she remembered it as a hot spot for wrecks and crushed tourists who were too busy gaping at the show to get out of the way.

Even at this hour steam was rising from the stationary and portable food stands that offered everything from rice noodles to soy dogs for the teeming crowds. She had to swerve to avoid an eager merchant on his smoking Glida-Grill, and took his flipped middle finger as a matter of course.

Eve double-parked and, skirting a man who smelled worse than his bottle of brew, stepped onto the sidewalk. She scanned the building first, fifty floors of gleaming metal that knifed into the sky from a hilt of concrete. She was propositioned twice before she reached the door.

Since this five-block area of West Broadway was affectionately termed Prostitute's Walk, she wasn't surprised. She flashed her badge for the uniform guarding the entrance.

"Lieutenant Dallas."

"Yes, sir." He skimmed his official CompuSeal over the door to keep out the curious, then led the way to the bank of elevators. "Eighteenth floor," he said when the doors swished shut behind them.

"Fill me in, Officer." Eve switched on her recorder and waited.

"I wasn't first on the scene, Lieutenant. Whatever happened upstairs is being kept upstairs. There's a badge inside waiting for you. We have a homicide, and a Code Five in number eighteen-oh-three."

"Who called it in?"

"I don't have that information."

He stayed where he was when the elevator opened. Eve stepped out and was alone in a narrow hallway. Security cameras tilted down at her, and her feet were almost soundless on the worn nap of the carpet as she approached 1803. Ignoring the hand plate, she announced herself, holding her badge up to eye level for the peep cam until the door opened.

"Dallas."

"Feeney." She smiled, pleased to see a familiar face. Ryan Feeney was an old friend and former partner who'd traded the street for a desk and a top-level position in the Electronics Detection Division. "So, they're sending computer pluckers these days."

"They wanted brass, and the best." His lips curved in his wide, rumpled face, but his eyes remained sober. He was a small, stubby man with small, stubby hands and rust-colored hair. "You look beat."

"Rough night."

"So I heard." He offered her one of the sugared nuts from the bag he habitually carried, studying her, and measuring if she was up to what was waiting in the bedroom beyond.

She was young for her rank, barely thirty, with wide brown eyes that had never had a chance to be naive. Her doe-brown hair was cropped short, for convenience rather than style, but suited her triangular face with its razor-edge cheekbones and slight dent in the chin.

She was tall, rangy, with a tendency to look thin, but Feeney knew there were solid muscles beneath the leather jacket. But Eve had more—there was also a brain, and a heart.

"This one's going to be touchy, Dallas."

"I picked that up already. Who's the victim?"

"Sharon DeBlass, granddaughter of Senator DeBlass."

Neither meant anything to her. "Politics isn't my forte, Feeney."

"The gentleman from Virginia, extreme right, old money. The granddaughter took a sharp left a few years back, moved to New York and became a licensed companion."

"She was a hooker." Dallas glanced around the apartment. It was furnished in obsessive modern—glass and thin chrome, signed holograms on the walls, recessed bar in bold red. The wide mood screen behind the bar bled with mixing and merging shapes and colors in cool pastels.

Neat as a virgin, Eve mused, and cold as a whore. "No surprise, given her choice of real estate."

"Politics makes it delicate. Victim was twenty-four, Caucasian female. She bought it in bed."

Eve only lifted a brow. "Seems poetic, since she'd been bought there. How'd she die?"

"That's the next problem. I want you to see for yourself."

As they crossed the room, each took out a slim container, sprayed their hands front and back to seal in oils and fingerprints. At the doorway, Eve sprayed the bottom of her boots to slicken them so that she would pick up no fibers, stray hairs, or skin.

Eve was already wary. Under normal circumstances there would have been two other investigators on a homicide scene, with recorders for sound and pictures. Forensics would have been waiting with their usual snarly impatience to sweep the scene.

The fact that only Feeney had been assigned with her meant that there were a lot of eggshells to be walked over.

"Security cameras in the lobby, elevator, and hallways," Eve commented.

"I've already tagged the discs." Feeney opened the bedroom door and let her enter first.

It wasn't pretty. Death rarely was a peaceful, religious experience to Eve's mind. It was the nasty end, indifferent to saint and sinner. But this was shocking, like a stage deliberately set to offend.

The bed was huge, slicked with what appeared to be genuine satin sheets the color of ripe peaches. Small, soft-focused spotlights were trained on its center where the naked woman was cupped in the gentle dip of the floating mattress.

The mattress moved with obscenely graceful undulations to the rhythm of programmed music slipping through the headboard.

She was beautiful still, a cameo face with a tumbling waterfall of flaming red hair, emerald eyes that stared glassily at the mirrored ceiling, long, milk-white limbs that called to mind visions of *Swan Lake* as the motion of the bed gently rocked them.

They weren't artistically arranged now, but spread lewdly so that the dead woman formed a final X dead-center of the bed.

There was a hole in her forehead, one in her chest, another horribly gaping between the open thighs. Blood had splattered on the glossy sheets, pooled, dripped, and stained.

There were splashes of it on the lacquered walls, like lethal paintings scrawled by an evil child.

So much blood was a rare thing, and she had seen much too much of it the night before to take the scene as calmly as she would have preferred.

She had to swallow once, hard, and force herself to block out the image of a small child.

"You got the scene on record?"

"Yep."

"Then turn that damn thing off." She let out a breath after Feeney located the controls that silenced the music. The bed flowed to stillness. "The wounds," Eve murmured, stepping closer to examine them. "Too neat for a knife. Too messy for a laser." A flash came to her—old training films, old videos, old viciousness.

"Christ, Feeney, these look like bullet wounds."

Feeney reached into his pocket and drew out a sealed bag. "Whoever did it left a souvenir." He passed the bag to Eve. "An antique like this has to go for eight, ten thousand for a legal collection, twice that on the black market."

Fascinated, Eve turned the sealed revolver over in her hand. "It's heavy," she said half to herself. "Bulky."

"Thirty-eight caliber," he told her. "First one I've seen outside of a museum. This one's a Smith and Wesson, Model Ten, blue steel." He looked at it with some affection. "Real classic piece, used to be standard police issue until the latter part of the twentieth. They stopped making them in about twenty-two, twenty-three, when the gun ban was passed."

"You're the history buff." Which explained why he was with her. "Looks new." She sniffed through the bag, caught the scent of oil and burning. "Somebody took good care of this. Steel fired into flesh," she mused as she passed the bag back to Feeney. "Ugly way to die, and the first I've seen it in my ten years with the department."

"Second for me. About fifteen years ago, Lower East Side, party got out of hand. Guy shot five people with a twenty-two before he realized it wasn't a toy. Hell of a mess."

"Fun and games," Eve murmured. "We'll scan the collectors, see how many we can locate who own one like this. Somebody might have reported a robbery."

"Might have."

"It's more likely it came through the black market." Eve glanced back at the body. "If she's been in the business for a few years, she'd have discs, records of her clients, her trick books." She frowned. "With Code Five, I'll have to do the door-to-door myself. Not a simple sex crime," she said with a sigh. "Whoever did it set it up. The antique weapon, the wounds themselves, almost ruler-straight down the body, the lights, the pose. Who called it in, Feeney?"

"The killer." He waited until her eyes came back to him. "From right here. Called the station. See how the bedside unit's aimed at her face? That's what came in. Video, no audio."

"He's into showmanship." Eve let out a breath. "Clever bastard, arrogant, cocky. He had sex with her first. I'd bet my badge on it. Then he gets up and does it." She lifted her arm, aiming, lowering it as she counted off, "One, two, three."

"That's cold," murmured Feeney.

"He's cold. He smooths down the sheets after. See how neat they are? He arranges her, spreads her open so nobody can have any doubts as to how she made her living. He does it carefully, practically measuring, so that she's perfectly aligned. Center of the bed, arms and legs equally apart. Doesn't turn off the bed 'cause it's part of the show. He leaves the gun because he wants us to know right away he's no ordinary man. He's got an ego. He doesn't want to waste time letting the body be discovered eventually. He wants it now. That instant gratification."

"She was licensed for men and women," Feeney pointed out, but Eve shook her head.

"It's not a woman. A woman wouldn't have left her looking both beautiful and obscene. No, I don't think it's a woman. Let's see what we can find. Have you gone into her computer yet?"

"No. It's your case, Dallas. I'm only authorized to assist."

"See if you can access her client files." Eve went to the dresser and began to carefully search drawers.

Expensive taste, Eve reflected. There were several items of real silk, the kind no simulation could match. The bottle of scent on the dresser was exclusive, and smelled, after a quick sniff, like expensive sex.

The contents of the drawers were meticulously ordered, lingerie folded precisely, sweaters arranged according to color and material. The closet was the same.

Obviously the victim had a love affair with clothes and a taste for the best and took scrupulous care of what she owned.

And she'd died naked.

"Kept good records," Feeney called out. "It's all here. Her client list, appointments—including her required monthly health exam and her weekly trip to the beauty salon. She used the Trident Clinic for the first and Paradise for the second."

"Both top-of-the-line. I've got a friend who saved for a year so she could have one day for the works at Paradise. Takes all kinds."

"My wife's sister went for it for her twenty-fifth anniversary. Cost damn near as much as my kid's wedding. Hello, we've got her personal address book."

"Good. Copy all of it, will you, Feeney?" At his low whistle, she looked over her shoulder, glimpsed the small gold-edged palm computer in his hand. "What?"

"We've got a lot of high-powered names in here. Politics, entertainment, money, money, money. Interesting, our girl has Roarke's private number."

"Roarke who?"

"Just Roarke, as far as I know. Big money there. Kind of guy that touches shit and turns it into gold bricks. You've got to start reading more than the sports page, Dallas."

"Hey, I read the headlines. Did you hear about the cocker spaniel recall?"

"Roarke's always big news," Feeney said patiently. "He's got one of the finest art collections in the world. Arts and antiques," he continued, noting when Eve clicked in and turned to him. "He's a licensed gun collector. Rumor is he knows how to use them."

"I'll pay him a visit."

"You'll be lucky to get within a mile of him."

"I'm feeling lucky." Eve crossed over to the body to slip her hands under the sheets.

"The man's got powerful friends, Dallas. You can't afford to so much as whisper he's linked to this until you've got something solid."

"Feeney, you know it's a mistake to tell me that." But even as she started to smile, her fingers brushed against something between cold flesh and bloody sheets. "There's something under her." Carefully, Eve lifted the shoulder, eased her fingers over.

"Paper," she murmured. "Sealed." With her protected thumb, she wiped at a smear of blood until she could read the protected sheet.

ONE OF SIX

"It looks hand-printed," she said to Feeney and held it out. "Our boy's more than clever, more than arrogant. And he isn't finished."